Martin
& Hannah

Martin & Hannah

A Novel

Catherine Clément

TRANSLATED BY
JULIA SHIREK SMITH

 Prometheus Books

59 John Glenn Drive
Amherst, New York 14228-2197

Published 2001 by Prometheus Books

Inquiries should be addressed to
Prometheus Books
59 John Glenn Drive
Amherst, New York 14228–2197
VOICE: 716–691–0133, ext. 207
FAX: 716–564–2711
WWW.PROMETHEUSBOOKS.COM

05 04 03 02 01   5 4 3 2 1

Library of Congress Cataloging-in-Publication Data

Clément, Catherine, 1939–
    [Martin et Hannah. English]
    Martin and Hannah / Catherine Clément ; translated by Julia Shirek Smith.
        p. cm.
    ISBN 1–57392–906–9 (alk. paper)
    1. Arendt, Hannah—Fiction. 2. Heidegger, Martin, 1889–1976—Fiction.
I. Smith, Julia Shirek. II. Title.

PQ2663.L38 M3713 2001
843'.914—dc21   00–045918

Printed in the United States of America on acid-free paper

For Anne Schuchman

Acknowledgments

I wish to thank Diana Arndt, Cécile Backès, Jean-Marie Clément, Jean-Étienne Cohen-Séat, Eglal Errera, François Fédier, Sandra Gaugger, Julia Kristeva, Nathalie Loiseau, Sylvain Sankalé, Daniel Schlosser, Philippe Sollers, and—it goes without saying—A. L.

Freiburg im Breisgau
Federal Republic of Germany

August 15, 1975

"God in Heaven!"

The elderly lady was struggling with her umbrella. A gusty shower slapped her wrinkled cheeks, lashed at her skirts, ravaged the snapdragons in the garden. She pressed a finger to the buzzer at the front gate.

No stirring in the house at the end of the path. A second try went unanswered. Annoyed, the elderly lady banged on the wooden slats and shouted a name: "Elfriede! Elfriede! I'm here."

Dragging footsteps. The bolt drawn. Out stepped another old woman, sheltered by the porch. "It's you," Elfriede said, not moving. "I wasn't expecting you so early, Hannah."

"Quite a tornado, I must say! And in the middle of August!"

"A summer storm," Elfriede pronounced, not leaving her spot. Her eyes swept over the flooded garden and its ruined flowers, then over the old woman with the hooked nose, muddy shoes, and bags under the eyes, who looked more than ever like a stubborn goat.

"Are you aware it's raining, Elfriede?" Hannah's tone was sharp this time.

Hannah Arendt, the arrogant Jewess, the American, Elfriede said to herself. *Shall I warn her? No. No, it's her turn to suffer.* "Don't budge. I'm coming."

And she only had to get an umbrella, open it with deliberate slowness, and walk across the garden. Hannah was fuming.

"You're soaked clear through," Elfriede said. "Come on now. Oh! Excuse me." Their frames unruly, the umbrellas collided. Hannah lowered hers, muttering.

"It was an accident," Elfriede sighed.

"Walk ahead of me," said Hannah. "I'll follow you."

"As usual," Elfriede muttered.

Buffeted by the wind, they scurried up the path together.

Elfriede Heidegger, the German, the lawful wife, Hannah thought to herself. *She who guards the door and leaves me outside. This time will I get to see him without a fuss?*

"Here we are," said the lady of the house. "Hang your raincoat on one of the pegs and take off your shoes. You'll see some slippers—"

"Ah, yes, I know. Where is he?"

"Do you want to see him right away?"

"But . . . Yes, of course," she replied, surprised. Hannah thought, *She's suggesting it on her own! Is he unwell? No, she would have used that to keep me out. No. There's something else.* Then, out of the blue she asked Elfriede, "Is the bottle ready?"

"What bottle?"

"The one he promised me to celebrate my Danish prize! You know, the Sonning Award. A nice bottle of wine. In the letter he wrote in July, he—"

"I'm not up on things," Elfriede snapped. "I don't have to show you, you know the way."

"But you're not going to be with us?"

"Not this time," said Elfriede.

Hannah's heart started to pound. When was the last time she'd seen him one-on-one? At least twenty years ago, or more? Not since . . . not since 1950, to be exact. Twenty-five years.

Whenever she crossed the Atlantic and returned to Germany, Hannah paid Martin Heidegger a visit. On these occasions, Madame would stand guard. Never far away, always ready to burst in. Keeping track of how long they talked. Every time, Martin gave in.

Once, only once, Martin had braved the wifely prohibition. In 1950, in Freiburg, it was Martin and Hannah, just the two of them. It was after Hannah's exile, after the extermination, after the birth of Israel, after the war. After Martin had been found guilty of Nazism, ruined. And twenty-five years later, Martin and Hannah were going to see each other tête-à-tête!

Yes, ever since Madame had learned of Hannah and Martin's adulterous affair, Madame had been on sentry duty. Camp Heidegger's chief guard never let down her surveillance. Entrenched, Martin was a prisoner in his own house.

"Go on, dear, go in," said Elfriede, her arms crossed. "No, not in the office. That way, by the window. In the dining room."

Hannah and Martin

Hannah closed the door gently.

He was seated before the casement window, a blanket over his lap, the usual black cap on his head.

"Hello, Martin, it's me! Weather you wouldn't send a dog out in! How are you?"

He didn't turn around, he didn't get up; he, always so courteous, almost stiff in his formality. Hannah didn't finish her sentence; hesitantly, she approached him. Was he asleep? No, he cleared his throat.

"I'm here, Martin." Her words resonated in the room. "Behind you. Very close to you."

No reply. The old lady went around the chair. "Martin," she whispered. "It's me."

He gazed at her, the unsteady look of an old man. His eyes were dull. "So tired," he mumbled. "Ears gone."

"You, who've gotten after me so often for my loud voice!" She spoke with a forced heartiness. "You can't have become deaf in just one year, Martin. Did you get my letter? I wrote I'd be visiting today."

He waved the question aside and started to cough.

"You have a cold," she realized. "Elfriede didn't tell me you were ill."

The coughing fit turned into wheezing. Mouth open, Martin stared into space, looking anxious.

"Take slow breaths," she said, placing her hand on the old man's chest. "Like that. Good, Martin."

Little by little, he caught his breath. Then he moved his tongue over his dry lips, closed his eyes, and said nothing.

"Still that recurring asthma," Hannah said. "Don't worry, I won't light up. Do you feel better?"

The old man rested his head on the back of the chair and did not answer. Hannah sat down across from him. Martin's face was quite expressionless.

"Come now," she whispered. "Don't act like a baby. The crisis is past. We're going to be able to have a heart-to-heart talk at last."

Not a quiver, not a twitch. Martin was made of stone.

"Look at me, at least! You haven't fallen into one of your depressions, I hope? Martin, open your eyes!"

Only the hands showed signs of life, stroking the woolen lap robe.

Hannah said to herself, *So this is why his wife left me alone with him. The bitch.* Holding his hands tightly, she said aloud, "Martin, don't give way to despair again. Your work is not finished! You are the greatest philosopher of the twentieth century. What reason do you have for sinking into this horrible abyss? Pull yourself out! In the old days you wrote such beautiful letters about my hands. Don't you still feel their warmth? Smile at me!"

Nothing. Tears in her eyes, Hannah released his hands.

The brilliant mind, the romantic heart that only she knew, they had flown away! The genius whom she had loved all her life, was he really just an old man with his head bowed? Not a single glimmer of intelligence. To what region of Being had Martin fled?

No, she was not going to abandon him to his silence. Noiselessly Hannah checked the door to see if Elfriede was listening. Then she came and sat down opposite Martin again, took a handkerchief from her purse and blew her nose vigorously.

"Martin, listen," she said, turning to the familiar form of address. "I haven't call you '*du*' for a very long time. We haven't talked one-on-one since . . . since our last night together. I don't know if we'll see each other again. If you hear me, raise one finger, I beg of you."

The hands with the age spots gripped the lap robe.

"This may be our last time!" Hannah shouted. "You have to know that I've never stopped loving you! Do you under-stand, Martin? Ever since 1924, in Marburg . . ." Hannah clenched her fists and waited.

"When you became a Nazi," she began, suddenly lowering her voice, "I thought I was over you. I stood firm until the end of the war. Then, there I was, coming back to you, and now I'm back again."

He had stirred. Imperceptibly, but he had stirred.

"You are here," she whispered. "I know it. Now I have to find out, Martin. Did you think about me in those years? Tell me, did you end up forgetting me?"

The old man's head fell forward.

"So, that's it," she said. "We are very much alike. I haven't succeeded in erasing you from my life. Me, the German Jew. That's how it is, I can't help loving you. It's the same with you. Am I right?"

A little sigh.

"I'm sixty-nine and you're even older. Don't abandon me," she begged. "Try . . . I've always helped you. Tell me I'm not mistaken. Tell me I'm still the one passion of your life. Martin! Say it!"

A hand came up, robotlike, then dropped again.

Ah! I'm ridiculous. Talking to an apathetic old man about

love. It doesn't make sense. No sense at all. He's unreachable. Well, I'm leaving. She stood up, hesitant. Then she leaned over and shyly placed her lips on the black cap. And she felt trembling fingers grasp hers. "Thank you," she said.

Their hands were still intertwined when the door opened.

"So, you've seen for yourself?" Elfriede asked. "Now, leave him be."

Not answering, Hannah kissed the old man's temple. He turned around abruptly, in his eyes the lightning flash of old. A sudden thunderstorm, soon over. He coughed. His cap slid down. His wife hurried to him.

"You're tiring him," said Elfriede, readjusting the cap. "Go on out, Hannah."

Once the women had left the room, the old man blinked and furtively rubbed his palm.

⟨∞⟩

Door shut, finally. Women gone. Free!

Love you always . . . Love you still . . . Love me, Me-I, Me-I . . . Tell me. Effort! Try! Say it! Tired, exhausted. Great love? Nazi, Nazism. Me-I, her forgotten? Silence! Depression, abyss? No, no, not at all. Apathetic, yes. Speech lost. Result, kiss, rub, fingers, touching, pleasure. Pretty good! A try, to see. Want to, a look, lightning, too hard . . . Failed! Can't!

The two, the women, together. Without him. Armored, attacks, arrows. No target. Then? No ground gained. Roots, diving in, past, sighs . . . distress. War, peace? Frontier, wasteland. Where to go?

Sleep. Not here. Like death. Die? Oh no, come on. Wait. Watch. Hold on.

"There you have it," Elfriede said. "You had to see for yourself. Martin isn't what he once was. You wouldn't have believed me anyway!"

"That's true," Hannah replied with a shudder. "What is wrong with him?"

"He's grown deaf. He has a cold, he's worn out. He hardly says a thing. Just disconnected words. He's quite old, you know."

"And depressed," added the elderly lady, sighing.

"Martin, depressed? Only once in his life has he been depressed, in 1946, when he was . . . well, when he was unfairly accused."

"Denazification. That's what it was called. And I know he is often depressed."

"That's not so! He is just old."

"Once again, you are in error," Hannah's tone was chilly. "You have been wrong over and over. About him, about me, about us, and about Hitler."

"I beg of you, Hannah, not today . . . I'm getting old, too. Let's not stand here in the draft. This hallway is freezing. Do you like coffee as much as ever?"

Hannah thought, *He is lost. If Elfriede is acting so conciliatory, it's because Martin is about to die.*

"We're going to the kitchen," ordered the wife, and she steered Hannah in the right direction. "You have to dry off, Hannah, and warm yourself."

Elfriede pulled out a chair, fetched the coffee pot, put on the kettle, set out cups, milk, and sugar, every motion as careful and deliberate as ever. "Yes, he's gone downhill in recent months," she said. "The doctor thought he'd had a mild stroke, but apparently it wasn't that. I'm the only one whose voice he responds to. Imagine, after so many years of marriage—"

"Ah, marriage, of course," Hannah sighed.

"No sarcasm, please, Hannah! These days, any little thing exhausts him. I know he's not going to be able to fall asleep tonight, because you were here."

"Really?" said Hannah, her heart joyful.

"I'm sure of it. He's very fond of you. But what a pity, Hannah!"

Never had they talked so calmly. Never had the two long-time enemies drunk coffee together in the kitchen. With her forget-me-not-blue eyes Elfriede was staring at Hannah. Wrinkled, bent, white-haired, her enemy was as beautiful as ever.

Slumped in her chair, Hannah said, "You talk of pity. I won't allow that. What an insult to Martin! Him, pitiful? He is too great—"

"Spare me. I'm no philosopher. I am not attached to words the way you are. I have great pity for him and I'm not ashamed of it. *I* am thinking only of my poor Martin. Seeing him in such a state—"

"The greatest mind of his era cannot fall apart," declared Hannah firmly. "He is still here, I sense it."

"No, he is no longer here. But he is still my husband, Professor Heidegger. Whether he loved you or didn't, that's not important. You will never be associated with his name. His work will stand. As for his private life. . . . People won't remember you, Hannah Arendt. Do you take milk?"

"Never," said Hannah, trembling with rage.

"And you still smoke as much?"

Hannah did not answer. War, until the last breath.

Elfriede

*W*ar it is, thought Elfriede.

Hannah had opened the hostilities in 1950, on the day the two women met for the first time.

Three years after Martin's humiliation.

Dismissed from the university, deprived of his livelihood, the illustrious Professor Heidegger's was in disgrace because of his appointment as Nazi rector of Freiburg in 1933. A post he resigned ten months later. Not even a year!

Because of one little year, he was punished following the Allied victory. The sentence was lifted in 1949. And in 1950, Madame Arendt sailed from America and barged into their marriage. One little year to resume her love life.

For it was obvious: Hannah loved Martin, as only Jewesses know how to love, with an ardor and determination . . . there were really no words to describe it. At eighteen, had she had any qualms about taking as her lover a family man seventeen years her senior? No! Unscrupulous Hannah had seduced him. And when she came back to Germany with her American fame and her prestige as a martyr, did Madame Arendt hesitate before summoning Martin? Not much. Martin was an inno-cent. He had always buckled under to Hannah. He even demanded that his wife make friends with his onetime mistress!

Oh, she knew how to depart, that Hannah. But above all, she knew how to return. She moved back and forth through the world, her one fixed point the Heidegger household. If

only she had stayed in her native Germany once and for all.
. . . No! Appearing, disappearing. Exited to France, escaped to
Spain, emigrated to the United States, beyond Martin's reach.
And all of a sudden, guess who's here? The eternal lover.

Nothing ever stopped her. Hannah had married twice.
She was a Zionist. At the war's end, Hannah wrote an article
attacking Martin, alleging that he was a dyed-in-the-wool
Nazi, as though all Germans hadn't supported Hitler's ideas.
And then, the Jewess brazenly returned to Freiburg.

Could he refuse to see her? He was too frightened! Poor
Martin. With the smug generosity of the victorious, Hannah
had got it into her head that she would save him. It was an
unstoppable move. The brilliant Madame Arendt made herself at home in the Heidegger household.

Well, actually, she had been there ever since her forcible
entry in 1924. But that was something Martin didn't confess
to his wife until twenty-five years after the act.

Martin had never been like other husbands. Fragile, he
remained fragile. He needed stability, an orderly life, silence,
pure air, calm. Elfriede had crafted him an indestructible nest.
Yes, well protected, he was able to think, construct the edifice
of his work. Beneath the authoritative stance of the great
philosopher, who could imagine his panic attacks, his terrors,
his fear of the world? His wife. Nobody else.

When Elfriede first met Martin, he was struggling to
recover from his years in the seminary. Whatever made him
enter the clerical life, for which he was completely unsuited?
Elfriede, a Lutheran, found it hard to form a picture of what
had led him down that path. In Martin's birthplace, the
Swabian market town of Messkirch, Catholics loyal to Rome
were persecuted by the Old Catholics. The latter did not
accept the doctrine of papal infallibility and preached a

German national Catholicism. They were modernists, rich and powerful, the elite of the city of Messkirch. Martin's father was a simple cooper, sacristan of the Messkirch church, a Roman Catholic, a poor man with no prospects. If Martin wanted an education, he had no choice: the little seminary at Konstanz, on the recommendation of the Messkirch priest.

But Martin was the dreamy sort, something his family noticed very early. He had gone into the seminary with the best of intentions, but he could not endure the discipline. The rigors, as he put it. The kneeling, the rituals. Catholicism demanded the impossible, and Martin suffered from breathing problems brought on by heart trouble or asthma—the diagnosis was never specific. The dignitaries of the church finally decided that young Heidegger did not have the robust health demanded by the priesthood. None of them suspected that the seminarian who could not breathe was a passionate thinker.

Idiots! Luther was right. Elfriede didn't care for Catholic priests, their phony chastity, their celibacy, the falseness of which was so apparent. Once released from his commitment to the priesthood, Martin took up theology at the university, where Elfriede was studying economics. In the gloomy library, she had noticed him. A puny young man with a serious face, as reserved as he could be.

Martin kept his head down much of the time, but when he raised it, his eyes could shine with a dark brightness. On a June afternoon, Elfriede was the object of one of his luminous looks, no sooner come than gone. When Martin stopped looking at Elfriede, the leaves of the linden trees lost their soft, tender glow. Ever after, she would be willing to give her life to see that light again in the eyes of the man she loved.

He wasn't especially well built; he wasn't blond or particularly good looking. He was so puny it would have been easy to make fun of him. Martin was so different, with his huge head and its defensive little mustache, his receding chin, his penetrating eyes. At times radiant, at others melancholy, he could be lovingly impish, he could appear cheerful or desperate. Sometimes he suffered from fits of choking. Martin was an uneasy soul in a square little body, his thought still unclear and his breathing threatened, a man yet to be born, calling silently for her help.

Elfriede had declared herself ready and willing. For him, she agreed to a Catholic marriage, promising that their children would be baptized. She, a Lutheran! She had said yes.

Then her work as queen bee began. To the soccer he had taken up in childhood, Martin added skiing, hiking, fresh air, space, the silence of the snows. His body filled out, he became imposing. He had been a *Privatdozent* at Freiburg, then he received promotion at the university. Elfriede gave him two sons, and she had a little place built for him up at a thousand meters, a simple clapboard cabin where he could think. Martin loved that rustic house with no running water, no electricity, deep in the forest. Martin's retreat, to fill him with inspiration.

The couple and their children lived in perfect harmony, and Martin worked. Then Hannah had come to upset their tidy, ordered life.

Back then, young Fraülein Arendt wore her hair loose; she had an oval face and melancholy eyes, dark like Martin's. Pretty girl, she must admit; Martin had some excuse. But today! Hannah was unrecognizable. Teeth going every which way. And that hair—brambles!

Elfriede smoothed her bun with a few brisk pats and smiled. "Do you ever think back to when you were eighteen, Hannah?"

Offended, Hannah replied, "What about you? I just can't picture you young."

"You haven't answered my question."

"I don't see what me at eighteen has to do with anything," she retorted. "Unless you're feeling the need to make me suffer. But we're both in the same boat, Elfriede."

"I'm older than you," Elfriede said, loud and clear.

"Nobody could tell!" said Hannah with a snort of laughter. "Always so nicely got up in your little flowered aprons. Well, I have to admit I've aged a lot. Are you happy now?"

"No. I asked you a question."

"Oh, what was it?" said Hannah.

"About the year you turned eighteen."

"Eighteen. . . . Let me see . . . I was in Marburg. A-ha! You're thinking about our affair. But really, Martin confessed the whole thing in 1950!"

"No!" shouted Elfriede. "Not the details."

"You want details!" Hannah was flabbergasted.

"No," she replied, embarrassed. "But . . ."

"But what? Say what you mean!"

"Martin didn't remember anything about the beginning."

"The beginning of what?" Hannah asked.

"Well, of the two of you, of course!"

"I see. You want to know who seduced whom, I imagine. Such an old story, Elfriede . . ."

Hannah

W ho had started it? The betrayed spouse's question.

Elfriede was the marrying kind. She had married Martin, a matter that did not brook discussion. There arose in Hannah a momentary longing for a household filled with children and headed by a unique man she could have loved for a lifetime. But she had loved two unique men and there had been no children. Useless regrets.

Was it she or was it Martin who had initiated things in 1924?

Hannah admired Professor Heidegger even before she'd seen him. His name was making the rounds in German universities as if it were the password to some secret society. A new philosopher had been born! A vibrant being in a loden coat, the hope of thinking, the heir to the prestigious past of German philosophy. Breaking with the dull droning of university lecturers, Heidegger dared to pose the fundamental questions in their pure and original form, questions buried under centuries of neglect. He dared to lift the boulders to rediscover the Greek source, dared to ponder the light of Being, its appearance, the distress over its loss, the constraints of time.

He had not published anything significant, but he was expected to usher in the dawn of a new world. According to students, there was nothing of the classical in his way of teaching: at the beginning they had trouble understanding him but were soon carried away by an intellectual excitement they had never before experienced. What was more, the official philosophers looked down on him. A good sign. These were bad times, for Germany could not get over its 1918 defeat, and the Weimar Republic struggled to keep poverty and bitterness in check. The budding genius was lifting the lid that had smothered thought.

Hearing all that over and over, Hannah had begun to picture a sort of Greek divinity, a slightly mad, aging Dionysus, as drunk on philosophy as was the god on his holy wine. At eighteen, she took a decisive step. She would depart her native Prussia and leave her mother for the first time. Young Fraülein Arendt, the philosophy student, would go to Marburg and study with Professor Heidegger.

She was surprised when he turned out to be so young. Well, he wasn't really that young. Thirty-five, maybe more, getting on to forty. Small, rather swarthy, olive complexion, wavy hair, a Gypsy. Yet he appeared to have his life in order. His shirts were pressed, his movements unhurried, his legs muscular under the long socks. For Professor Heidegger did not wear the frock coat customary at the university. Professor Heidegger sported knickerbockers and a brown jacket with edelweiss embroidered on the lapels. He would have had the ridiculous demeanor of a poetic peasant, had it not been for the dark glow of the eyes and the fleeting smile in midsentence.

The professor was so scholarly, so knowledgeable that his lectures would leave his audience perplexed. That was the first impression anyway, very hard on the uninitiated. Then the ear would grow accustomed to the mysteries of the lost texts and the audience would begin to grope its way toward an unfamiliar kingdom. To ideas, the professor brought a new force; to words, he restored vigor. How did this magician manage to recapture the true spirit of the most everyday speech? A sorcerer of genius, the professor knew how to find the energy and sparkle of the German language, cleansing it of its heavy layer of gangue. He would painstakingly strip words of their dead roots, which he would replant, and the roots would come back to life.

For example, while other German philosophers rattled on about decadence, Professor Heidegger did no more than divide up the word: "de-cadence." Then, lo and behold, a positive rhythm appeared, the good cadence that had gone astray. De-cadence was a loss of the proper tempo, which had been forgotten and was now recalled. To avoid de-cadence, don't get out of step. It was so bright and clear, so simple! Marveling, Hannah would repeat to herself the word "de-cadence," counting her steps as she walked.

Transported by his own magnetism, the professor would often be carried away. The invisible hazel wand that guided his sorcery would begin to vibrate and his words soared, enthusiastic, poetic, wild. He seemed to be awakening to thought, and at such moments his listeners either abandoned themselves to his words or were lost. Hannah abandoned herself.

Later, Martin was to tell her he had noticed her from the first. But at no time had Hannah felt his eyes rest on her. After all, everyone knew the professor did not see his students when he was lecturing. His gaze he kept to himself, or he might look at the sky beyond the casement window. Sometimes, yes, there would be a fleeting, penetrating flash that she attributed to the working of his mind. The flash would pass over her and fade away. It was impossible to catch the professor's eye: might as well stare straight at the sun and burn one's cornea, become blind. Or stupid. Hannah was content to listen and take notes.

And since she wasn't bold enough to ask for the meeting every student was supposed to have with the teacher, the professor himself invited her to his office, his manner stiff and formal.

It seems she was wearing a stylish hat that day; Martin had always made much of the matter of the hat. There wasn't anything special about it, just a small felt hat, close-fitting. The height of fashion. Anyway, the professor first noticed Hannah's cloche, then Hannah's raincoat. Then he had smiled at her, the smile of a man elated. And he, who so rarely glanced at anyone, never took his eyes off her. Oddly enough, Hannah retained no memory of that first conversation in the professor's office at the University of Marburg.

It was the beginning of beginnings. The immediate of Being. The Greeks would have said their meeting was wrought by the Gods. The lightning that struck was a bolt brandished by Zeus, guardian of human destiny. At eighteen, how could Hannah have resisted? She hadn't even tried. Martin was irresistible.

Heidegger, married? Did that matter to those of heroic stature? At the time, Hannah had no trouble convincing herself that their love did not obey human concerns. The everyday order of things was for the ordinary wife, she who kept the genius under lock and key, a prisoner in a humdrum world.

In Hannah's eyes, Martin's marriage stood as a tragic mistake, responsible for the disaster that befell him at the war's end. Martin's Nazism was Elfriede.

Elfriede had made her political choice long before Martin did. She became a card-carrying member of the National Socialist Party in 1920, when Adolf Hitler was only a terrorist agitator. Elfriede was a Nazi, a genuine Nazi. Elfriede had read

Mein Kampf. Elfriede was well aware of Hitler's hatred toward Jews. Elfriede had sensed the Führer's passion and rage, she had wanted it to be there. She was Prussian, picky, nationalistic, racist. Poor Martin.

That was the lawful wife. Jealous, irascible, always present. Guilty of the crime of exerting influence on a weakened god. Guilty of small-mindedness. Anti-Semitic, that went without saying.

And Hannah was supposed to supply her with details? Recount their secret rendezvous, their first embrace, their rapture? Tell her about Martin's body, its power, its joy when he was deep inside her? Discuss their pleasure?

Cigarette. Since crossing the threshold of the Heidegger house, Hannah had not smoked. But now, faced with this exacting wife who demanded an accounting, it was unavoidable. Her hands shook with impatience and under the table her feet tapped to the irregular rhythm of her racing heart. De-cadent, that old heart. Get its proper cadence back. Lighter, flame, smoke, release.

Through the coils of smoke, Hannah saw the forget-me-not eyes blaze with anger.

"Such an old story! How dare you say something like that?" Elfriede exclaimed. "Do you think I didn't see you kissing his hair a few minutes ago? You'll manage to harass him until the very end! He's not the one who sought you out, it was your doing! His life was complete. Teaching, family, and his books. You must have pursued him!"

"Pursued, that's the word," said Hannah sarcastically. "I gave him the eye, I waited for him outside the lecture hall, I raised my skirts and whispered dirty words. Come on, stop dreaming!"

"I'm sure you took the initiative," said Elfriede, obstinate.

"Oh, yes! Let's talk about that. I agreed to a meeting after class. The university required it. I said, 'Good evening, Herr Professor.' Then I kept quiet."

"That makes it worse!" shouted Elfriede. "And Martin, what did he do?"

"I can't remember. I think he continued the day's lecture for my benefit."

"And then you invited him to your room," whispered Elfriede. "And he knocked at your door."

"That's not the way it happened at all." Hannah smiled. "Don't look for the beginnings of love, Elfriede. They're not to be found."

"You people!" grumbled Elfriede. "You've always been good at stealing our men."

"Who do you mean by 'you people'?"

"You—" Elfriede stopped.

Hannah was waiting to pounce on her reply: "Go on!"

"Students," Elfriede supplied the word in a low voice.

"That's better," said Hannah. Unperturbed, she put out the cigarette. Elfriede was breathing hard. Hannah watched her closely.

"The town girls," continued Elfriede, looking grim. "Those little hussies. I used to see them hovering around him. And he, poor fellow, didn't notice anything! Martin was faithful. How did you get his attention? You tracked him down!"

"Tracked him down," Hannah repeated serenely. "It's hunters who do that. Or the police. They track down game, man or beast. That doesn't make for love, Elfriede. I know, because I've been tracked down."

"Don't hide behind the persecution of the Jews!" shouted Elfriede. "Ever since I've known you, you haven't stopped. You spend seven years as an exile in fair France, where they finally put you in a concentration camp, you cross into Spain, and then you board a ship in Lisbon. Enough of your travels! You know what I want to talk about, Hannah. Your impudence. You fear nothing."

"So I guess that's why I fled. When I chose to leave my country, I must have had no fear of what was to come."

"Oh, stop it!" yelled Elfriede, shaking.

Hannah closed her eyes.

Hannah
Berlin, 1933

She Flees Germany

It is evening. Mother and daughter each carry a suitcase. They left Berlin by taxi, and they have arrived at the inn on the edge of the woods. This is the meeting point for those who have decided to escape from the Nazis, a handful of travelers every week. Seated before bowls of soup with quenelles, the two women wait. Martha Arendt-Beerwald and Hannah Arendt, her daughter, names on the list of the organization arranging their journey. It is high time for them to depart.

It has already been a month since Arendt, Hannah, student, was interrogated for over a week by the police. Her mother was next; they questioned her for several hours.

She was unlucky, Martha. She had gone to spend a few days with her only daughter, something she did often. And then, disaster. Now she has to flee without delay, cannot even return to Königsberg where her husband, Hannah's stepfather, is expecting her.

This was bound to happen. For nearly a year, Hannah has been hiding suspects at her place in Berlin, most of them Communists. Whenever she visited, Martha would help the best she could. Hannah takes after her: In her youth Martha was an active revolutionary—like mother, like daughter.

Hannah has been accused of carrying documents for the German Zionist Organization, which means to inform the world about the new regime, Hitler's Third Reich. No sooner had he been chosen by the people than the German chancellor issued his first anti-Jewish decrees. Others will follow. No one wants to believe the Führer is going to carry out his plans to the letter.

Fortunately, the policeman interrogating Hannah was new to the political unit that dealt with opponents to the new regime. And he was a decent fellow, too. He had no hatred for Jews; the situation bothered him. He was not at all eager to scrutinize the famous documents. How was he supposed to handle this girl with the gentle eyes? So young, and a dangerous opponent? Hard to believe.

The first day, the policeman bought her cigarettes with his own money. The coffee wasn't strong enough for Hannah; he brewed more. He advised her not to waste money on a lawyer; he'd be able to clear things up and she'd go free! He even told her that Jews should hang on to their money because they were going to need it. In his own way, the policeman resisted the regime. They became friends.

He kept Hannah one short week. He may have been a bit taken with her.

Other agents of the political unit searched Hannah's quarters in vain. Martha didn't make any slips. Now, they have to flee.

Before leaving her apartment, Hannah burned anything that could incriminate her. Then she had one last delightful party with her friends, so festive she is still a bit hungover.

Strange to think that was just yesterday . . . Hannah stares at the little round dumplings in the soup, big familiar eyes.

Their only luggage is the two suitcases. They know only that they will be heading for the "Green Front," the escape route.

Hannah reviews the arrangements step-by-step. The actual crossing point is Karlsbad on the Czech border. Once they are through the Hartz Forest, Karlsbad is not far. Apparently it will be easy. They will go into a friendly house through the front entrance, which is in Germany. They will be invited for dinner and they will leave through the back door and be in Czechoslovakia. The border between the Third Reich and freedom runs right through the house. Those smuggling them across are Germans hostile to the Nazis. It seems so easy.

Hannah's young husband fled several months ago. Conspicuous because he was a journalist, he didn't wait to be arrested. Hannah is to join him later, in Paris. If all goes well.

Martha is shivering. It is cold. And she is not young.

"I promise you'll get back to Königsberg, Mutti," says her daughter, stroking her mother's hand. "Don't cry."

Tears well up in Martha's eyes.

Hannah, silent, is thinking of her German intellectual friends. Of those devotees of thinking who see in Hitler Germany's hope. Of Benno von Wiese, briefly her lover. "It's a historic moment," he said when Hitler became chancellor of the Reich. Hannah thinks of Martin, her only love, who has not spoken up against the anti-Jewish laws. Professor Heidegger says nothing; the professor becomes a supporter. Destroyed, her illusion. Written off, Martin.

"Never again," she mutters fiercely.

Since they're attacking the Jews, from now on she will defend herself as a Jew. This is something new for Hannah: She will concern herself with nothing but the Jewish question, at the grassroots, in the organization. Hannah will devote herself to practical action. She's through with intellectuals. They are treacherous.

The moment has arrived. They finish their soup and rise. It is dark. They must grab their suitcases and leave.

The crossing had gone without a hitch. In Prague, the Arendt ladies found help before going on to Geneva. There Hannah arranged for her mother's return to Königsberg and her husband. Then Hannah boarded the train for Paris, the haven of choice for German refugees. This was in 1933, five years before France, too, betrayed them.

⟨⟩

Hannah opened her eyes. "Let me finish, Elfriede." she lit her second cigarette. "You don't know me very well. You think I'm not afraid of anything. Ah, well! I was afraid of Martin before I knew him. I didn't track him down, you'd better accept that."

"You had your eyes closed"—Elfriede was hinting at something—"you were thinking about him."

"If I told you what I was lost in . . ." Hannah's voice was a whisper. "It's very odd. For some time the past has been coming back with no warning. Events in no real order. Old age gives rise to such phenomena, it seems."

Elfriede's looked concerned. "They say that at the moment of death, your whole life passes in front of you instantaneously," she said in hushed tones.

"Wait a minute, my dear. I am not dead!"

"No, but the same thing happens to me sometimes. Little snapshots. I hate it. You become disoriented." Elfriede said

"That's because you're no longer going by clock time. It's an entirely different rhythm. It's not unpleasant."

Elfriede was becoming less agitated. Hannah took advantage of the moment to inhale the smoke, and she coughed.

"You shouldn't be smoking." Elfriede sounded grumpy.

"You aren't allowed to, since your heart attack, are you? But you don't know obedience. Now stop!"

"You have to die of something. Could you please pour me a little more coffee. By the way, Elfriede, did you know it takes two to make love?"

Elfriede

*T*hat *stony contempt of hers*, thought Elfriede with a sudden flash of hatred. Not only had the woman stolen Martin, she had entered into competition with him. . . . A philosopher, this old lady with the wild hair? Certainly not! A student of Martin's, nothing more. Madame Arendt had achieved fame on her master's coattails. And if it weren't for the defeat of 1945 . . .

The word "defeat" had been banished from the German vocabulary. The conquered Germans were supposed to use the word "occupation." In 1945, the Allies won their victory. The world Elfriede had believed in was collapsing. The one emerging nearly engulfed Martin in the ruins. A bad end to the conflict had long been foreseen, but not bombs falling on Germany, not Berlin laid waste, or Dresden razed, or rubble and hunger. Nothingness, inertia.

The Heideggers had not been struck by bullets, their house had not been bombed, their sons hadn't been killed on the Eastern Front, in Russia. The family was unhurt, but the shock waves wounded Martin's honor, mortally. Denazification committee, summons, tribunal. Testimony, arguments. Verdict. Deprived of retirement and teaching, on grounds of Nazism. The Heidegger name had fallen from grace.

Elfriede wasn't sure when she went wrong. She had joined the National Socialist Party after reading the straightforward manifesto of Adolf Hitler, the unknown who wanted to regenerate Germany. In 1920, no one would have bet a pfennig on him. At a time when Germany was floundering in the swamps of democracy, Elfriede put her hope in a spiritual renewal, a reenergized fatherland. Where was her error? When should she have comprehended? The moment the head of the Nazi party won election in 1933, Germans closed ranks behind him in a show of democracy. Hitler had become chancellor quite legally. Elfriede was proud to have been ahead of the German people. Where was the flaw she had not perceived?

At all events, none of that was Martin's concern. Martin's only concern was thinking. But Elfriede loved order. For Martin's sake, for the sake of Germany and Europe, she had believed . . .

Better not think about it. Not while gazing across the table at Hannah, whose hook nose had grown longer with age. Elfriede asked herself what had been the worst with Madame Arendt.

In 1924, Elfriede had no inkling of the adulterous affair, so it caused her no suffering. In 1945, from her safe haven in far-away America, Hannah sought public revenge through an article condemning Martin. Again, if only she had stopped at that point! But with Hannah worse was always sure to come. Less than four years later she repented and saw Martin again. It was then, in 1950, that Elfriede learned of their past as lovers.

Hannah came back several times, to see Martin. Elfriede had insisted on being at their meetings. She censored letters from Hannah. She fought, and it took her two years to win. In 1952, Martin gave in. For twelve long years, Hannah was nowhere about. But she was persistent, the Jewess. One day she was back in Freiburg for yet another visit.

And that wasn't the worst. When Elfriede thought about it, the worst was knowing that his trashy Jewish mistress lent Martin credibility. Her husband's greatest protector was the famous Madame Arendt, crowned with fame and the Sonning Prize, which Denmark had just awarded her for contributions to Europe. Europe! Under Hitler, it had almost come into existence. Yes, at Martin's request there was a nice bottle of Rhine wine to celebrate Madame Arendt's prize. But Elfriede did not intend to drink with the enemy.

And Martin acted so humble, so noble . . .

From time to time, the Nazi past would be stirred up, and intrigues against Heidegger would begin anew. Thus, Elfriede knew only too well what lay behind the worst: the undeniable fact that ever since the defeat, Martin needed Hannah. As long as she lived, Hannah would defend Martin's work tooth and nail, out of passion.

Since 1967 Hannah had been visiting her old love at regular intervals. And while the two philosophers exchanged immortal words, Elfriede was left with nothing but shouts, scenes, surveillance. Elfriede made coffee and kept house.

Who else could have looked after things? Hannah? She was totally incompetent, poor thing. Hannah was just an intellectual. And besides, she smoked.

Martin and Hannah together, long ago, the pair of them. Two, it took two to make love. Martin and Hannah in bed, two naked bodies.

Pleased at striking home, Hannah took a drag on her cigarette. Elfriede, very pale, pursed her lips.

"Pull yourself together," said Hannah.

"Me? I'm quite together!" objected Elfriede. "It's just that you're so crude—"

"Because I don't mince words? You don't love all by yourself in a corner!"

"Maybe not," said Elfriede. "But a respectable woman does not seduce a married man."

"A married man does not commit adultery! Try all you want, Elfriede, but you can't escape the obvious. If Martin loved me, it was of his own free will."

"He loathed short hair," muttered Elfriede. "And girls who smoked."

"I was quite proper. My parents brought me up well!"

"Were you a virgin?"

"My God. So narrow-minded. No, I wasn't a virgin. I suppose Martin told you that to console you. But what does it matter?"

"It matters whether he was your first!" shouted Elfriede.

"He had a wife, I'd had a lover. We were equal, my dear."

"Equals, a man and a woman! You're dreaming!"

"You and I don't agree on that subject," said Hannah, the cigarette dangling out of the corner of her mouth. "My ideas are rather advanced, and besides, I smoke."

"You're smoking because you're not yourself." Elfriede's voice was scathing. "Your hair is a real mess."

"A mess?" said Hannah, plunging her fingers into the mop on her head. "It might be. With that storm—"

"I've known you to look quite smart. When you first returned to Germany, you were nicely turned out. Just look at that unbuttoned blouse, that wrinkled collar—"

"Dammit, Elfriede, what game are you playing? I'm beyond the age for lessons in grooming."

"Yes, but appearance counts," she retorted. "Especially when we get old. If we want to avoid becoming decrepit, we must—"

"We must, we must . . . What can we do against a body that's going? Besides, I'm traveling. Picture yourself getting off the plane in New York and arriving at my apartment; you'd be pretty wild looking, too."

Was she as rumpled as Elfriede said? Agitated, Hannah stubbed out her cigarette, buttoned up her blouse, smoothed her eyebrows.

Elfriede watched Hannah's hands flutter about. "No point in trying to straighten yourself up," she said. "You've changed, Hannah. You've let yourself go since your husband died. Obviously, a woman alone, with no children—"

"Excuse me?"

"I said that you are a widow, and childless. It's so sad."

"You're not going to throw your children up to me again!"

"They're the children Martin gave me. And you, he didn't give you—"

"Stop! You're becoming vulgar."

"But really, why didn't you have children?"

Hannah lit a third cigarette and inhaled ostentatiously.

Hannah

No babies, no children, Elfriede's battle cry. Barren Hannah with the empty breasts. And, her opposite, the German wife with the fruitful womb. Elfriede had given her country two healthy sons.

So predictable: her husband, her children. Her fortune, her *oeuvre*, defended by the huntress, the lioness. The lion was lost in his dreams, but the lioness guarded the territory, saw to meat for the cubs, and scanned the horizon for danger.

The great Arendt had nothing that equaled this animal achievement. Her philosophical work? For the Heideggers, of no value. Her political contributions? Incomprehensible. Her renown? A nuisance. No credits for her; she'd failed the exam.

Whenever she left the pleasant, cozy house in Freiburg, she would feel a bit down at the thought of returning to her hectic life in New York, her office, her typewriter, the morning cups of coffee. Never really awake without that bitter brew, the black drug that brought back the world. No lucidity without the day's upper. No life without coffee.

Coffee, coffee, no children. Two husbands, a divorce, friends and books. Taxi, plane, train, car, activities, trips, leaving, returning. A hectic life, round and round in a grinder like coffee beans. Out of control, disconnected, exhausting. No child.

There had been a time when crisscrossing the world was mentally stimulating. Back home after an overseas flight, once in line at the passenger check-in Hannah would stop thinking about the children she'd never had. In America it was easier not to be a mother, and Hannah had become American.

Celebrity. Hannah was a personality, invited everywhere. This year alone, speech in Boston at the opening ceremonies for the Bicentennial, lecture in Cologne, not to mention her courses at the New School for Social Research in New York. The year before, 1974, smack in the middle of her lecture series in Aberdeen, heart attack. Humiliation of the hospital stay, tests, quiet, diuretics, digitalis, and what else? Several months of idleness. Later, Hannah had received the Sonning Prize, in Copenhagen. Tired, she was tired. No child to help her.

And they were always asking her opinion. On the Watergate scandal, on Nixon's probable resignation, on the U.S. Supreme Court, on student strikes, on the end of the Vietnam War. Just when Hannah wanted only to reread the German mystics, Kant, the Greek philosophers, and be done with human affairs, with all the noise and fuss.

Recently she had received a letter from a young man who wanted to meet her before she passed away; after all, he wrote, she was getting on in years. That had made her feel strangely like a living monument, an altar on which people had better sacrifice before it was no more. How should she answer him? Yes, it wouldn't be long before she'd passed away.

Her friends were growing old. No children at her bedside to witness her last breath. And Heinrich Blücher, her second husband, was dead.

On one of her journeys, as she flew high above the clouds between Germany and New York, the sun was setting on the bright horizon and Hannah thought of old Sarah, to whom the Eternal had brought tidings of an infant when she was a hundred. Abraham's wife had laughed in the face of the heraldic angel, a hearty toothless laugh. But already Isaac grew in the barren womb, and the centenarian's withered breasts were filled with milk. And Isaac was born. Perhaps a nice loud laugh there in the wild blue yonder might be enough to conceive a baby at age sixty-nine—

Suddenly, as luck would have it, they entered a zone of turbulence. The flight attendant checked seat belts, Hannah put out her cigarette and cursed the bouncing that made her sick. Later the airship descended, and she was once again on terra firma, where there was neither man nor god to impregnate her.

Hannah's remarkable laugh, so adored by her friends, had given way to a sort of nostalgia, neither sad nor cheerful. A laugh poised between life and the acceptance of death, a laugh that did not ring out. Thinking was somewhat the better for it. The time was past for the peals of laughter of the Thracian peasant girl encountering the ancient Greek philosopher, that simpleton who knew nothing of the real world. Hannah would smile, and no more.

Finished, the time of a day-to-day life shared with her husband. Since Heinrich's death, her life was divided into before and after.

Before, there was her dear husband, her revolutionary, who had borne arms and fought with the Communist group Spartacus. Heinrich, her other unique love, pursued by the Nazis. The wonderful mate with whom she'd sailed from Lisbon and shared exile in America. From 1943 to 1970, such a long time . . .

Unpredictable Heinrich, disorganized, bubbling over with ideas, muddled, but steadfast.

Before, Hannah had shared independence with him. With

Heinrich, there were no obligations, no sanctions. No commitment, a love that was free. Together, on one's own with the other.

And then came the after. Elfriede had struck where it hurt: Hannah's husband was dead and Hannah was alone. Widowed? No? Alone. Heinrich had not given his wife children.

Over the course of their interminable quarrels, whenever Elfriede approached the shores of motherhood, Hannah would gun her down, her ammunition the misfortunes of war. The flight to France, the hard life of the German refugees.

Generally, the mention of Hannah's internment in France, at the Gurs concentration camp, was enough to silence Madame Heidegger. Why didn't Hannah have children? Because of Hitler. Checkmate, Elfriede, no goal scored.

Once again, it was time to start shooting.

"Do I have to remind you that in my childbearing years I had to run for my life?" Hannah's tone was sharp.

"You've been droning on about that forever, but it's not so! Instead of spending four years with a married man, you could have had children with a good husband! You had plenty of time, Hannah. Besides, you married Günther Stern in 1929, and then what? Nothing! No pregnancies!"

"You'd be wise not to bring up my first husband," Hannah said. "He thoroughly despises you."

"Stern? You know I've never met him!"

"You do have a short memory, Elfriede. You so admired his bulging muscles that you invited him to join the Nazi Party, and when he told you he was Jewish, you turned your back on him. It was at Todtnauberg, when Stern was a student. You were entertaining at Professor Heidegger's famous cabin. I've told you this a dozen times."

"A dozen times, I've told you it's all a story!" shouted Elfriede. "The incident didn't happen. I should think I would remember!"

"*He* remembers it quite well. He still talks about it."

"Impossible. He's lying to please you since you like to think I'm an anti-Semite, Hannah! It's not true. The truth is that you envy me my children. You're dying of jealousy."

"Oh, really?" said Hannah, blowing out smoke.

Elfriede struck her blow: "The fact is, you will die without ever having been a mother."

"And if I'd had a child of Martin's without telling you?"

"Without telling *him*? You would have done that? No. You would have shouted it from the rooftops. I know you, Hannah. You aren't a very good liar."

"You're right about that," said Hannah, smiling. "But I could have—"

She broke off. In another part of the house, something had just smashed. Or someone.

"That noise—" Elfriede's expression changed. "Did you hear it, Hannah?"

"Martin!" exclaimed the other old lady. "The study, quick!"

"No. You stay here. I'll go."

Hannah sat down heavily. Alone in the kitchen, she rotated the coffee cup in her hands and waited. Off in the other room, the wife would be picking up the broken vase— or Martin, maybe.

In the other room, maybe Martin was having a bad dream.

Martin
Messkirch, Swabia, 1899

The Owl

It is Sunday. Before daybreak. Standing in the hall, the boy holds the candle steady. His mother strikes the match, brings it close, touches it to the wick. A second for the wax to melt, and the candle catches. Two flames fuse into one, fragile and valiant.

"The same as usual, Martin," says the mother. "Protect it and keep going."

Down the hall walks the boy, sleepy guardian of the light. The mother opens the door. Outside, day is dawning. The flame glows in the residue of night. A few stars twinkle still. The sky hesitates between gray and pink. When it turns blue, the stars will fade.

In the loft, the owl swallows its prey. Tonight the boy will dislodge from a hidden corner the ball the beak dropped there, a round sticky mass of cracked bones and hair, the only sign of the owl's presence. Once in winter the boy saw two enormous circles, the staring eyes of the owl. Since then, the bird of night has been invisible.

A gust of wind! The flame wobbles. Wide awake now, the boy tightens his grip. The flame recovers. It lives, it melts.

Just as every Sunday, while he walks the distance between his house and the church, the boy lifts his fingers and pushes wax to the top so the candle will last for the mass. He burns his fingertips. Wax runs down his hand. Translucent, the drips fade and harden. Atop the white stem, the flame endures. The church bell will soon ring.

It is light. The stars are gone. Appeased by daylight, the candle flame does not glow as before. The portal is not far. Three steps, two, one . . .

"That's fine, Martin," says the priest. "You are a good choir boy. You've looked after the flame, it has held steady. You'll do the same."

The child takes a deep breath. He is no longer in charge of the candle. Just then, above his head, the clapper of the great bell starts to sway. From one side of the bronze, then the other, loud explosions of harmony, so near that the child trembles under the bursts of sound that come and go, louder and louder, raising him high, pulling him, exhausting him. . . . He cannot take any more. He covers his ears and runs as fast as his legs will carry him. He heads for the altar and turns on to the little bridge. A bridge?

A metal structure painted celadon green, the bridge spans a rising river nearly at flood stage. The storm is so violent the little bridge creaks. Terrified, the boy clings to the iron bars and leans over. It is dark and the water is rising, a muddy abyss where there is nothing. The cables strain in the fierce winds, the bridge sways, the child teeters. Don't fall! Hold on!

And it's all right! Two phosphorescent circles emerge from the waves and do not move. Fixed, luminous, lifesaving. The bridge stands. Because of the owl's eyes, the bridge holds. And now the dawn proffers the orange glow of the coming sun. The river lights up, aflame. Light, at last. And a gravely voice

rises out of the abyss: "The German, at odds with himself . . .
spirit torn apart . . . scattered . . . in his will and therefore
powerless in . . . losing the strength to affirm . . . life . . .
dream of a right in the stars . . . floundering on earth . . . of a
new Reich, of a new life!"

The voice of an owl swallowing its prey. Drawn in, the boy
steps over the guardrail and jumps . . .

Ground up in the belly of the river, he burns. A terrible
beak is pecking his brain to bits, digesting his thought, regur-
gitating it as pap. Don't give in! Hold on! No snorkel, but the
boy dives deep. He swims toward one shore, hesitates, floun-
ders, swims toward the other. Which one should he choose?
Which one is the real shore of life?

Inexplicably, there is land under his feet. The boy takes a
deep breath. Saved. So badly burned that his skin is coming
off in ribbons. In the distance, the metal bridge collapses with
a huge roar.

⟨⟩

Martin groans in his sleep.

Stars . . . Burned! No right. At odds with himself. Torn in two.
Powerless! Floundering . . . Don't give in! Hold on!

He awakens, he cries out, he wants to get up . . .
"Elfriede!"

"Here I am," she says. "It's nothing, Martin. A book fell on
the floor while you were asleep." She plants a kiss on his forehead. "I'm in the kitchen with Hannah. Call me if you need
anything."

Elfriede

Elfriede turned the knob and shut the door, careful not to let it squeak.

Nothing was more precious than Martin's sleep. When he slept, sometimes his features would relax and take on a little of their old assurance; his forehead would lose the anxious wrinkles; he might even smile in his dreams.

But at other times, his face would grow tense, distorted by fear. During the first week of life, a newborn often writhes in pain, the source a mystery to the mother. So it was with Martin's nightmares. What terrors tormented him? What images? Who was attacking him? He himself, or the other, the loathsome Führer?

Elfriede wished she could put him on her lap and place him against her stomach, as she had done with her babies. Although Martin was willing to be kissed, unfortunately he was too heavy to rock. He would probably go back to sleep, but Elfriede had no control over his dreams. She would have to return, reassure him.

As usual. The daily routine. A lifetime spent calming Martin. Where had they gone, the little flashes of impishness that would make his eyes narrow, the sudden enthusiasms that would make him so lively, the moments of impulsiveness? Now Elfriede's only reward was the satisfied sigh of the new-born with a full stomach. Martin was gradually retreating to the earliest stage of life.

Uneasy, Elfriede started toward the kitchen, where the enemy awaited her. Don't rush. Let Hannah sit and worry. Let it sink in that she had no say in the events of Martin's life. Martin's sleep was off-limits.

Don't let her see Martin in his dotage. Their old age was no one else's business.

What would the intruder say? "Is he all right?" Or maybe, "Is he alive?" Elfriede would say nothing. "Answer me! Quick, tell me!" Silence, revenge.

She turned the corner of the hallway, that awkward spot where she often bumped herself. The kitchen door was open. Hannah sat motionless, dreaming over her coffee cup.

Hannah
Königsberg, East Prussia, January 1916

Her First Test

The hospital. Martha holds her little daughter by the hand; she's leading her through the halls to the venereal disease department. The child has a fever and a bad sore throat. Last night she had another nosebleed. What will the doctor do? Poke into her nose a stick with a cotton swab, to cauterize? That hurts, burns. Or shove in her mouth a steel cone with a screw across it, to see down to her tonsils? That pushes hard and feels cold.

"What does it mean, venereal diseases?" the little girl asks.

The mother stiffens. She has decided never to lie. Hannah is ten years old.

"They are diseases people can die of," says the mother. "One of them killed your papa."

"Am I sick like Papa?"

"He died because he wasn't treated in time, darling. If you have his illness, they will treat you and you won't die."

"Is that why I have nosebleeds?"

"No, you caught cold. It's not at all like Papa's illness. Don't worry."

Hannah walks faster and escapes from her mother. She

grits her teeth; she won't cry. *Venereal disease*, she had better remember those words. Martha catches up with her. They're here.

"Hello, Frau Arendt," says the doctor. "Well, here's our little Hannah. What big eyes you have."

"But I've got these nasty braces on my teeth," retorts Hannah, opening her mouth wide. "I guess they'll come off someday."

"Of course! Meanwhile, be a nice girl and roll up your sleeve and give me your arm. I'm going to fasten this rubber tube tight—"

"Oh, no!" cries Hannah, spying the syringe.

"You won't feel a thing," he assures her. "I'm going to squeeze tighter. Make a fist, Hannah. You can do better than that."

Hannah shuts her eyes. Tiny ants run through her fingers. Tears sting her eyes; she must not cry. Ever.

"That's it," the doctor says. "Open your fist and sit still. You can look if you want. I'm almost done."

The needle has been stuck into a green bulge at the crook of the elbow and a black liquid is rising in the syringe.

"What's that?" asks Hannah.

"Your blood. I'm not taking much. You have five liters left. Keep still."

It hurts when the sharp needle is withdrawn. The child utters a little peep.

"Finished!" says the doctor. "See, it wasn't so bad. A bandage, now. . . . There we go. Bend your arm and hold it up. Go sit on that stool and be a good girl."

Her fingers tight on the compress, the child obeys. They hear nothing more from her.

Martha sighs. "Are you sure the test is reliable?" she asks in a low voice.

"Oh, perfectly. We are quite satisfied with the technique developed by Doctor Wassermann. A great advance. We'll have the results in a few days."

"And if—"

"It's most unlikely, Frau Arendt. Don't worry unnecessarily. We'll have to repeat the test every six months. But I'm optimistic; the child probably has nothing wrong."

"Probably," Martha whispers. "When we conceived Hannah, my husband thought he'd been cured. And then—"

"You ought to be tested, too," the doctor interrupts. "Another time, if you like. Were you aware of his illness before your marriage?"

"Yes. He told me he'd had syphilis and that he was over it."

"A-ha," says the doctor. "Tomorrow morning?"

Martha nods.

Syphilis, Hannah says to herself. *I have to remember that word, too.*

"Hannah. Sit still!" the doctor shouts at her. "Keep that arm bent. Perfect. In five minutes, it'll all be forgotten."

"What time tomorrow?" Martha asks.

"Let's see. I'll expect you at 9 A.M.," says the doctor, jotting down the appointment. "Goodbye, Frau Arendt. Goodbye, child. What a beautiful little girl!"

They are in the corridor. Martha is deathly pale. "It didn't hurt too much, did it, darling?"

"A little," Hannah sighs, seeking pity.

"We'll stop by the bakery," says Martha.

Hannah trots along, something on her mind. "Syphilis, that's the name of Papa's sickness?"

"Yes, darling. I promise I'll explain how you can keep from catching it."

"But, if I have it already, did Papa give it to me?"

"Papa did not give it to you!" exclaims the horrified mother. "I shall tell you about it!"

"Now!" Hannah stamps her foot.

"Hannah, don't you start in." Martha's tone is threatening. "If you get upset, you'll have a nosebleed."

The girl calms down. There's nothing worse than blood streaming from her nose.

Hannah

How old was she when her mother did what she had promised and explained? Fourteen? Thirteen? Thereabouts.

In the meantime, Hannah often heard the word "syphilis." Syphilis was a shameful illness. Fathers often contracted it, mothers rarely. When a man caught it, he wouldn't tell anyone, for he was ashamed. But people guessed because of his children: stunted creatures with nasty pimples and crooked spines, weak in the head—sometimes they'd be referred to as "mental defectives."

All the tests came back negative. Hannah had not inherited her father's syphilis, but the doctor did recommend that she have additional tests before marriage.

When Hannah began to menstruate, her enlightened mother had a frank talk with her. Hannah found it hard to comprehend that love could be fatal, or babies ruined.

"Alas," said her mother, "it's a fact of life. Yes, love between a man and a woman can transmit diseases. They are called 'venereal.' "

"As in Venus?" Hannah said.

As in Venus. But only syphilis could kill. It was responsible for millions of deaths in Europe.

"Women, too?"

Women, too.

Martha described the first chancre that would appear on the partner's penis, a dangerous sore because it went away quickly without treatment. It would be wise to choose her partners carefully when the time came.

"When?"

"You're too young."

So Hannah learned you had to keep a close eye on love, and she asked questions about her father.

He himself never knew from whom he had caught the disease. Paul Arendt was the fine son of a broad-minded Jewish family, and as a young man his life had followed the typical pattern: women before marriage, to learn how to satisfy a future wife. Paul had been infected. One encounter was enough. He was not to blame. Nobody was to blame.

But he had died an early death, a slow and horrible death. Hannah developed no nasty pimples, but before marriage she ought to be tested, according to the doctor.

The time came. Not of marriage, no, but the time of the body, without a ring on her finger. As a challenge, to see what it was like.

Her first was a kid of whom she had no reason to be wary. Even though . . . He was also sleeping with her best friend, but with Anne Mendelssohn, no danger. All the same, Hannah had looked, furtively, before she spread her legs. The kid was quick, the pleasure lacking. Later, with other lovers, Hannah managed to check for a chancre—you never know.

No children . . . The danger lurked in the shadows. Absurd, irrational.

Her first time with Martin, the danger flew away. She didn't check, she didn't think of it. Martin was slow, the pleasure intense. Then, as he would on every occasion, at 7 P.M. he left her and went home.

Never to wake up beside Martin when night was over. Never to see him greet a new day. "It's time, my love," he'd whisper when the hour had arrived. The period allotted to their love was ending, night was beginning, and he'd put on his clothes without a word. Their passion was to be clandestine or not at all. The question of a baby hadn't crossed Hannah's mind.

Later, the question just stopped coming up.

As an act of defiance, Hannah married Günther Stern, a boy her own age, and Jewish to boot. That was after Martin and because of him. Before her marriage, she had been tested, just in case. Nothing. Amazing, but there was nothing.

Günther and Hannah worked for a living; they were in no hurry to have a baby. Four years later, Hitler was chancellor of Germany.

Hannah left her country for Paris; she met Heinrich; miraculously, they survived and they sailed for America. At the end of the war, Hannah was already divorced and remarried, but she had reached forty. The question did not come up.

For her, it had been a simple matter. Motherhood was not to be her destiny. She would be an intellectual, with no room for a baby in her very busy life, and there was no remorse or regret.

She heard Elfriede's footsteps. The enemy was back.

Hannah stared at her, not saying a word. The other woman lowered her head. Serene, hiding a funny little smile.

So, he wasn't dead.

Elfriede waited for the question. Hannah played with her cup, silent. Elfriede was annoyed. She sat down. "It was nothing," she said, with a sigh. "A window not closed properly, a gust of wind, and a book fell."

"Martin?"

"The crash must have awakened him, and he was trying to stand up, poor thing! But I got there in time. I think he's even gone back to sleep."

"That's probably the best thing for him," Hannah said, her tone neutral.

"He sleeps a lot, you know. Far too much. I'm worried, Hannah. He's really not doing well."

"Are you sure he's not depressed? That's so often been a problem for him."

"I don't know. This time, it's not the same. He's aged overnight. I'm afraid, Hannah."

Elfriede had stopped waging war. Hannah, to her surprise, found the enemy's distress touching. She spoke gently: "When the time comes, you won't be able to keep him from dying. And it's so hard. When it happened with Blücher . . . It's a painful time. The important thing is that he not suffer."

"I know," said Elfriede. "He may slip away peacefully. That would be good. I think of it every morning. But I'm afraid."

"Fine! You're afraid, so be it. It's certainly not the first time! You have to fight the feeling. Haven't you experienced fear before?"

"Oh, yes! When my sons were prisoners in the Soviet

Union. And when the conquerors arrived. A dull fear that wouldn't let go. This isn't the same thing."

"But real fear, Elfriede, terror?"

"The air raids?"

"Air raids, you get used to them. What I'm talking about is terror. That's something I've experienced. Not you."

"You're going to bring up the Gurs camp again." Elfriede sighed. "You're going to carry on about the refugee ship that took you to America. You'll repeat the stories I know by heart. You'll wait for me to bow my head, and you'll gloat."

A ray of sun struck the copper utensils on the kitchen wall. In Hannah's head echoed the strains of a song from her childhood: "*S'brent briderlekh, s'brent! / Oy, undzer orem Shtetl brent!*"

"Wrong," said Hannah, barely audible. "You don't know where it came from, that kind of fear. I first felt it in 1914, when the Cossacks besieged my native city. You've heard of the Cossacks! But if you knew . . . that cry!"

"I have never seen Cossacks," Elfriede admitted. "Nor heard their cry."

"It wasn't theirs, Elfriede. It was the city crying out: 'The Cossacks are coming!' Even in the nice part of Königsberg, where we lived, the sounds of fear assaulted us from afar. The Cossacks, the Cossacks are coming. I remember an old Yiddish song that goes: 'It's burning, brothers, it's burning! / Oy, our poor Jewish village, it's burning!' "

Images of terror came flooding back, vivid pictures of a village in flames under an orangey sky. Weeping women in scarves raised their arms to the Eternal; a line of men formed a pathetic bucket brigade; in the distance a Cossack and his horse galloped toward the bright blue horizon. Fear was orange; violence, sky blue.

"Fear of the pogrom," she went on. "An intense, savage fear."

"Your life hasn't been easy," Elfriede conceded, embarrassed. "But you haven't had children to worry about. *You* have been free. You haven't experienced waiting for news of two sons in the war; I couldn't sleep, and I had to shield Martin. Later, we did without everything. I had to take a teaching job to make ends meet. Martin had no source of income—"

"His punishment," interrupted Hannah.

"And what did the Cossacks do in 1914?" Elfriede asked, uncomfortable.

"Their job," said Hannah. "Burning, raping, pillaging."

Suddenly, a sharp image. A man in a glass booth.

Hannah
Jerusalem, 1961

Immanuel Kant Comes Up

Hannah's back hurts.

It's endless, Israel's trial of the greatest Nazi war criminal. Testimony, questions, testimony, questions, fine points of law, on and on. The Israeli prosecutor takes a fiendish delight in harassing the few surviving witnesses to the extermination: "Why didn't you protest? Why didn't you fight back?" Tears in their eyes, they bow their heads, guilty. Why this question except to contrast the heroism of Israel with the capitulation of European Jewry? It's stupid, it's cruel. Furious, Hannah takes her notes, all the while wondering what she'll say in her report for the *New Yorker*.

To be here for this historic event, she canceled her classes, changed her plans, made quick travel arrangements. Hannah was not there for the famous Nuremberg trials at the end of the war, but now she's made a date with herself: she will be present for the judging of Adolf Eichmann, the Nazi organizer of one-way journeys to the death camps.

Seated in the press section, Hannah finds the day-to-day proceedings weighing heavy on her. The trial of the century is bogged down in judicial routine: no grandeur, no thought.

There's nobody who thinks Adolf Eichmann will not be sentenced to death. He knows it. The entire world knows it.

In his glass booth, the accused is eager to defend himself. He is completely truthful, not at all remorseful. Suddenly, Hannah sits up straight. Eichmann is speaking of Kant, Immanuel Kant. The man in charge of exterminating the Jews is waxing philosophical!

She cannot believe her ears.

Eichmann claims that in organizing the trains to the gas chambers he was merely following the philosophy of Kant. For, indeed, wasn't Kant the first to enunciate a moral law and the categorical imperative? And wasn't that what he, Eichmann, practiced? He went by the categorical imperative. "You must because you must." "You have to because you have to." Obey, unconditionally. Obey, without exception. And, most important, without feeling.

For, according to Kant, the moral law must ignore indignation, resentment, hate, and even pity. The moral law recognizes no feeling beyond a cold respect for obedience.

And that is what Immanuel Kant said. And despite the compassion Eichmann felt for his dear Jews, he was obliged to obey. For Eichmann is a kindhearted man. Witnessing a mass execution, he had almost passed out when the shots were fired. But the categorical imperative must not take human feelings into account.

The full force of Eichmann's words strikes Hannah. This frighteningly ordinary little man, see what he's done with German philosophy! Kant's ideas instrumental in the massacre of the Jews, my God!

The man is lying. He hasn't read Kant. The moral law is not a law of obedience but of morality. It calls for dealing with others as an end in itself, never as a means to an end. The law forbids transforming a human being into a number, a thing to be burned and disposed of like an old shoe, once gold fillings and long hair have been salvaged.

Hannah listens, on edge. No, Eichmann isn't lying. Yes, he has actually read *Critique of Practical Reason*. The criminal's sincerity overwhelms. He followed Kant's dictates in good faith so as to better organize the death trains. Good student that he was, he followed the lessons of German professors. Treason starts in the university.

In her report on the trial, Hannah will endeavor to explain the origins of this abominable obedience. Of this German misapprehension that leaves no room for repentance: "You must because you have to."

Kant's law is inherent in humanity. But Eichmann is outside humanity. He knows nothing of it.

"What are you thinking about, Hannah?"

She was startled. Elfriede's voice brought her back to the present. "An old memory," she said.

"But not a pleasant one, judging by your expression. The Cossacks, again?"

"Pretty close. Something worse."

"Your hardships are in the past, Hannah. You get prizes, you travel, you publish books. What don't you have?"

"My companion," Hannah whispered.

Elfriede stood up and pressed her face to the window. It was still raining. She spoke without turning around: "You're lucky to be an intellectual."

"You can't be serious," said Hannah.

"No responsibilities, no constraints, coming and going when you feel like it!" Elfriede exclaimed. "I've never had that freedom!"

"Wait a minute! You are actually telling me that I have the good fortune to be free because my husband is dead! What is it you want? To bury Martin once and for all?"

"Oh, Hannah, how can you—"

"I'm listening to you, my dear, that's how I can. My dear Blücher is dead, and you're implying I enjoy being fancy free! What do you take me for? A woman with no heart?"

"Knowing you, I imagined that . . ." Elfriede hesitated. "I assumed that your work was enough for you . . . I don't know, myself. I thought you were helped by philosophy."

"Well, you're wrong. You don't know my life, Elfriede"

"Nor you mine!" she blurted, whirling around. "Keeping house every day, always cooking, cleaning, making beds. Besides that, Martin's books, Martin's sleep, Martin's anxieties. You don't know what it's like, day after day!"

"Every day is worth living," said Hannah. "Even in grief. I love life."

"Because you've lived with more than one man! Think about it. One man, with all his torments!"

"You're the lucky one." Hannah smiled. "Just one man, but his name is Heidegger."

"Don't you believe it! You've never learned what marriage really is, Hannah. The sacrament . . ."

Elfriede tottered and grabbed the back of her chair.

Elfriede
Freiburg im Breisgau, March 1917

Her Wedding Day

The chapel is nearly empty. A few worshippers are sitting on the benches, chance spectators at a wartime wedding. The officiating priest has warned the engaged couple: under the circumstances, no organ, no music.

Elfriede doesn't have a long dress. She wears a light-colored coat and a plain hat with no bridal veil. Her fiancé is dressed in a dark loden suit with horn buttons, his most becoming outfit. He's a bit shaky. He runs a hand through his thick hair.

The day before, the priest called in Fräulein Elfriede Petri. He reminded her of the debt Martin Heidegger owed the church that supported him during his years as a seminarian. He did not fail to mention the moral force of Martin's father, the cooper faithful to the Roman Catholicism of Swabia. He dwelt on Martin's poverty, on the persecution of true Catholics by the "Old Catholics," those rich renegades, fanatical supporters of modernity. Dwelt on the deep faith of *Privatdozent* Heidegger, the young theologian destined for a brilliant career. Dwelt on his future as a German philosopher rooted in the noblest of traditions. The priest, citing the duties of the loving fiancée, made her promise to baptize their children as Catholics.

Martin is so fragile . . . Elfriede promised. What's Catholicism compared to the strength of an enduring love? Nothing. Not even for a Lutheran. The priest, in a white chasuble, prepares to administer the sacrament. She thinks of the consummation of the marriage and is a little frightened.

Elfriede stands tall. Short Martin raises himself to his full height and coughs, a sign of emotion. She slides her gloved hand down Martin's sleeve, touches his fingers lightly, then lets go. The priest's words she barely hears. Outside, there is a war on. The army, the front, the boom of cannons. Martin's "yes" is lost in space, but Elfriede's rings out, loud and clear. The sacrament of the Apostolic Roman Catholic Church unites them before God and man. They are man and wife for better or for worse.

They turn to each other awkwardly. Martin kisses the bride on the lips. Elfriede shudders with happiness.

Martin's parents didn't come; Elfriede's refused to come. There will be no feast, no celebration. There were no horses, no carriages. Just a few white hyacinths in Elfriede's hands. Now it is time to walk by the row of benches and appear before the eyes of the world. They must leave the confines of the chapel. Martin crooks his arm in a gesture so natural that Elfriede trembles.

She is proud of marrying Martin with such meager ceremony while her country is at war. Proud of being here alone, on his arm, proud of being his support, his help. She will bring him good fortune in spite of himself. He will be great. In the university courtyard, the cold sky is clear, and Martin's eyes are filled with tears.

Elfriede's heart beats to the rhythm of verses he wrote her

after a walk on the island of Reichenau: "bedazzled cargo / in the gray desert / of a great simplicity."

They have to go down the stone steps.

"Bedazzled," one step. "Cargo," two steps. "In the gray desert," two steps, a pause. The last step leads to the parvis, "Of a great simplicity."

That will be their life. The weather is not gray. A sharp blue outlines a simple future. They have arrived.

She snuggles in his arms and he closes them around her.

Elfriede

When the war ended badly in 1918, Germany paid a heavy price for its surrender, agreeing to a shameful peace settlement. The empire was succeeded by the republic, and with it came unprecedented crisis. In the name of liberties, German civilization deteriorated amid the corruption of urban life. The winners of the First World War showed no mercy. The Hapsburg Empire had been destroyed, and there was almost nothing left of Austria. Humiliated, the Germanic world was near collapse.

In Russia, the Reds terrorized their people and threatened Europe. America grew richer and richer, with money the only thing that counted. Clear thinking was nowhere in evidence.

Martin had been fortunate enough to escape combat.

Elfriede's happiness lay in her family. A son was born, then another, and they were not baptized. Hardly a pressing issue: what mattered was rebuilding the country.

Elfriede was careful not to bring up the baptism question. Anyway, a promise given in the name of Martin's past no longer made much sense to her. The past, still the past, damned clay sticking to the feet of the German colossus, keeping him from moving on. When there were so many people suffering, so many women in the streets complaining of hunger, so many mouths to feed, so much to pay out in war reparations!

One momentous evening, Martin announced to his wife

that he had freed her from her promise with a letter to the priest who had married them. On his own, he had broken their ties to the Catholic Church.

Well, almost on his own. A word here, a phrase there. Elfriede had limited herself to repeating, low-key, that Martin's philosophical genius required un-con-di-tion-al freedom. She would emphasize each syllable. You understand, Martin, without conditions. What was a marriage with conditions? Was it free? No. Martin had understood. With his usual sincerity, he informed his mentor when the moment came.

For a time Martin's thinking developed in obscurity. First, he cast off the heavy burden of the Roman faith of his childhood; then he felt a violent, vengeful hatred toward it. In the end, he fought God publicly. Before Martin, Nietzsche had written: "God is dead," and Martin picked up the torch of Nietzsche, that great German. The death of God opened up a new world.

To exist, thinking has no need of God. God is dead, the world can be born.

And Martin dedicated his life to that birth. Martin thought out the future. And for Elfriede, the present consisted of letting Martin think and helping the unfortunate of the times.

Raised Lutheran, Elfriede was still Lutheran in spirit. Hardened, keenly aware of Germany's deterioration, of the cesspool of Berlin where the waste of the German Republic rotted. That garbage had to be set ablaze and reduced to ashes, and Germans had to return to the true values that Martin embodied to perfection: pure snow, sports, nature, health, fresh air, love of mountain peaks, and important thinking.

With all her heart, Elfriede hoped for a blast of wind that

would sweep away the miasmas of democracy. Cleared out, the Berlin transvestites, the prostitutes, the bankers, the artists. Germany, cleansed of Jews. To topple decadence, a fierce and mighty wind was needed.

Using his own scholarly vocabulary, Martin spoke of "call," "absolute." And Elfriede dreamed of the day when she could lead her husband to the pinnacles of being sorely lacking in her country.

In 1933 that day came.

Long before Martin, Elfriede had seen the potential beneath the rough exterior of the little Austrian who made Germany his fatherland. Elfriede had struggled alone until the Führer came to power. Then, after some quiet reflection, Martin outdistanced his wife. Henceforth, he would take the lead.

Now there were two Nazis in the family: a responsible couple. The Heideggers naively followed the torch blazing out of the darkness. How could they have guessed that beneath the heroic posture lay a monster? Impossible to know.

In 1924 could she have guessed that Martin was deceiving her with Hannah Arendt? No, not that either.

Whenever Elfriede thought about it, she could hardly breathe.

"Y ou're about to fall!" Hannah boomed. "Can you hear me? Why, you're passing out!" She hurried over to Elfriede. "Lean on me. Sit down. Are you all right?"

"Thank you," said Elfriede, lightheaded.

"Should I call a doctor?"

"Don't bother. Just one of my dizzy spells. I have them."

"Whatever you say." The enemy deserved a break. What had Elfriede been talking about before the episode? Oh yes, the nature of marriage. And if Hannah hadn't been there to steady her, what would have happened? The wife would have gone crashing to the floor. A broken hip, and Martin off in his corner, asleep. A fine mess!

Elfriede was holding her temples and making a face. She drank a glass of water; a little color came into her cheeks.

"To think that you two are living all alone here," Hannah said. "What would happen if . . ."

"That's marriage. Growing old together."

"Yes, it's awful."

"Obviously, you don't know what you're talking about," Elfriede muttered.

"Excuse me? But you're not the only one who holds the key to . . . Let's see, how did you put it? Something like, 'what marriage really is.' My dear husband and I had our idea of what marriage was, if you can believe it!"

"Until death do you part," Elfriede said. "That's the holy sacrament of Christians."

Hannah was stunned into silence.

Elfriede blushed. "I didn't mean it like that." She was embarrassed. "I was quite fond of Herr Blücher."

"You only met him once!"

"Once was enough to see that your husband was calm and composed. He was very good for you."

"Drop it," Hannah snapped. "We loved each other, that's all there is to say."

"You probably did. All the same, you kept coming back to look up—"

"My former love," she interrupted. "That's what bothers you. For you, real marriage requires exclusiveness. If you want to see a love from the past, then you aren't really married, are you? But Blücher wasn't petty. He loved me enough to encourage me to see Martin again."

"Rubbish! I don't believe you."

"And not just see him, but come to his rescue," Hannah elaborated. "For you can be sure that, without him, I wouldn't have helped Martin with such . . ."

Elfriede turned around, on the alert. Hannah had not finished her sentence. "Why did you stop?" the wife asked. "Say it. With such *passion*."

The passion of Martin and Hannah, only too familiar to Elfriede. Back in 1950 Martin had proclaimed it, loud and clear. There were two realities, marriage and the other thing.

Surprised, Hannah looked at the enemy, who had spoken sadly and without hate. A frown on her face, Elfriede was deep in thought, pursuing her straight and narrow path. Then, sudden enlightenment: "But it's not you he loves, Hannah. It's an idea."

"An idea! Do you even know what an idea is? You . . . Really, I can't . . ." Hannah was at a loss for words. Then she resumed, with more assurance: "So, I'm an idea. Would you like to know how Martin and I found each other again in 1950?"

"No!" Elfriede was emphatic. "I know already!"

Hannah

It happened in August 1950. Hannah had agreed to her first visit back to the country that had driven her out. Her mission important, her motives could not be attacked: She was a member of the Commission on Jewish Cultural Reconstruction. But to go back, to set foot on the soil she had left when Hitler arrived—the idea was unbearable. Painful? Exciting?

Meticulously weighing the pros and cons, Hannah got ready to see Germany again. On the one hand, the nation of death; on the other, the German language. On the one hand, ruins; on the other, a sharing. For returning to her land would give her something irreplaceable: Hannah would be able to speak her mother tongue. She wouldn't have to worry about the German accent that interfered with her English. Speaking like everyone else and with everyone else would revive for her the best of Germany.

The itinerary of Frau Arendt's official mission required a stay in Freiburg.

But in Freiburg, Germany, there was Martin. Her onetime lover, a Nazi.

When Martin expressed himself, German became almost otherworldly. No one had crowned the queen of languages better than Martin Heidegger, the poet of philosophy. Without Martin, she would have to resign herself to hearing only the everyday speech of war-ravaged Germany. Without him, something would be missing from her refound Germany. Just his way of speaking, that is. Nothing else, of course.

Wipe out Martin's Nazi past? Impossible.

Hannah stopped in Paris, which she found unwelcoming. The Paris where she had once lived was now an untidy city with peevish inhabitants always in a rush. She visited Karl Jaspers, her old professor, an expatriate in Basel. Spared by choosing neutrality, Switzerland was irritating in its well-regulated, tidy way of life. Despite its war wounds, only Britain had escaped moral disaster. As for Germany, it was rebuilding on gigantic piles of rubble. Everywhere, en masse, displaced persons had lost their identity. Martin included, probably.

No sooner had she crossed the border into Germany than Hannah sent Martin a letter, unsigned. Since she would be staying over in Freiburg, as required by her work, she gave her address at the hotel—and left the rest to God.

Hannah arrived in Freiburg with no illusions.

And what happened? She arrived at her hotel, and the desk clerk handed her a message. A gentleman had just left it. As a matter of fact, the messenger was still there. At the end of the hall, Frau Arendt. Do you see him?

Martin.

The shock of recognition was immediate, physical. Quicker than the mind, more vivid than the war, it dazzled them both, Martin and Hannah. Martin's temples were silvery, his hairline receding, and she . . . Good heavens, Hannah had no memory of how she looked that night. Which of the two had said, "Come to me"?

Martin's wife was away, so he took Hannah to his house. And that was the place.

Only later did the words come, the tears, the explanations, Martin's shame. Hannah's role in the tragedy. The misfortune of their separation, the horror of the monstrous events. His face haggard, Martin uttered the word, "tragedy!"

Hannah said to herself, *Martin has realized his mistake.*

She was wrong. For Martin was not thinking of the tragedy of Nazism, not he. That hadn't even crossed his mind. For Martin, the tragedy was their breakup. His cowardice in love, his silence. Hannah's role in Martin's tragedy was simply that of a mortal woman abandoned by her god.

In face of his blindness, Hannah was speechless. Clarify for him? He didn't understand anything. Martin was still a big baby, as naive as ever. With such a critical spirit when it came to human affairs, how could he have taken such a tumble? How could he have fallen in with the agenda of the times, neglected his own rhythm, abandoned Being? Nothing was more contrary to his thinking. The philosopher had done himself a grave wrong.

A single misstep on the edge of the precipice. One small deviation, and the evil was done. Evil? It was not part of Martin's thinking. At the most he allowed that a notion of Being-At-Fault was a property of the thinking human.

Say to him: "Look at yourself, Martin! You wore the swastika on your lapel. You gave the Nazi salute, said the words, sang the hymns! And you say you loved me? How did you dare?" Yes, ask the questions, try, come on . . .

The words did not leave her mouth. Martin hadn't the slightest idea of any wrongdoing. Why did she want him to be something he wasn't?

A word came to her. *Escapade*. Martin had had a Nazi *escapade*. That was the way to put it.

She still loved him.

Sweet, loving words followed upon the lover's repentance. As in the old days, Martin called her my life, my Orient, my Greece.

Back in the time of their clandestine love, Martin would rhapsodize about his ideal Greece, describing it as only he could. The cradle of our origins, he'd say. Birthplace of philosophy. Under the cool gray light of olive trees, the spirit of Greece rose amid the Doric columns, and the spirit of Greece was Hannah, he said.

Hannah was the lost homeland. Hannah was the sea, the Orient of the dawn and Martin was the West of the setting sun, where sun and Being met. In that place of his dreams, Martin had no more to say. Body and soul, he would be lost in Hannah.

And strangely enough, over the years nothing had been lost by the wayside. Not Martin's words, nor his body, nor his Greece.

In a sense, Elfriede was not totally wrong. Martin did love an idea, an idea with two faces, like the androgyne with four legs, four arms, and two heads described by Aristophanes in Plato's *Symposium*. One half seeking its complement in the other, two sexes, one within the other. In Martin's mind, the image of two bodies immersed in the waters of the sea at sunset.

Martin swore her to secrecy: She would never reveal this 1950 rendezvous that had been as momentous as their first. They would share a universe no one else could enter.

After she left the next morning, Hannah found Martin's unopened letter in her pocket. She read it. Professor Heidegger was issuing Frau Arendt a rather formal invitation to spend the evening under his roof—his wife, away on business, would not be present.

If she had read that coldly worded invitation earlier, Frau Arendt just might not have replied. But, reading on, Hannah came to the gist of the letter.

In passing, as if it were a trifle, Martin wrote that he had confessed to his wife their four-year-long passion. Their 1924–1928 relationship, to be exact. A major step, but that wasn't all. Martin had informed his lawful spouse that Hannah was the passion of his life.

Not "had been," but "is." For it was spelled out in black and white, and signed, 'Martin Heidegger': "Elfriede knows that you are the passion of my life."

Martin and Hannah, in the here and now.

Hannah kept it, the letter that had preceded their reunion.

They had planned to meet again the next day. Elfriede came home, and Elfriede made her first scene.

Martin stood up to her. He went to see Hannah at the hotel. Elfriede was furious. Hannah left Freiburg and continued her mission. There was no third tête-à-tête for Hannah and Martin.

Their bodies had been separated, but their letters resumed, Freiburg– New York, New York–Freiburg, back and forth in a steady stream. Martin and Hannah were no longer apart. For two lovely years, Martin held firm in spite of wifely threats.

Thanks to endless invective, Elfriede finally carried the day. Beginning in 1952, a long silence between Hannah and Martin. Twelve years! An eternity!

In 1966, the year Hannah turned sixty, Martin wrote her a letter mostly about himself, but about Elfriede, too. So what, it was a letter. The next year, Hannah returned to Freiburg.

During the twelve-year parenthesis they had simply grown old. Martin no longer had the strength to insist on meetings away from home, away from his wife.

With a bit of trickery, Hannah got around Elfriede and feigned peace. She fabricated a story she forced herself to believe. Thus it was agreed between wife and mistress that the twelve years of silence were the result of Martin's injured pride: He couldn't take his former student's fame and the publication of her books. With that decided, the matter was not brought up again. At their age, jealous scenes were hardly appropriate.

Elfriede made her pouting obvious, but Martin could see Hannah, once in a while. Elfriede was not pleasant, but Hannah visited Martin, once in a while. Hate smoldered under the ashes, but now there were ashes in their hair. The two women had sealed their nonaggression pact with a decision to use first names.

"Hello, Hannah. How are you?"

"Quite well, thank you, Elfriede."

An armed politeness. Full quivers.

Hannah's 1974 visit had turned into a fiasco. Already somewhat feeble, Martin couldn't stand up to Elfriede. As usual, Martin and Hannah had met under surveillance, and poor Martin was silent. Yes, last year's visit would remain a bad memory.

And 1975! Even worse. A futile tête-à-tête with him, a long face-to-face with the enemy. Pitiful ending, unworthy of an impossible love.

For a long time now Elfriede had known about the passion of Martin and Hannah. All of it, except for the secret of 1950, the two bodies made one. Had the time come to tell the wife that secret? No, not while Martin was still alive. No.

Hannah had a flash of fantasy: He was going to die right here, right now, and she would shout in Elfriede's face how Martin had enjoyed Hannah's body. Hannah shuddering under Martin's hand. Martin atop Hannah, his penetration, his pleasure. And hers, such as no other man had given her.

Yes, Hannah was an idea of Martin's after all. An idea made flesh.

Across from her, the elderly wife with the ethereal hair was not giving an inch. Never had Elfriede searched Hannah's face with such a clear and steady gaze.

Put on an act. As if there were nothing wrong.

"So you're claiming Martin loves me because I represent an idea?" Hannah spoke up, with a forced laugh. "That's funny! But what idea, dear? Philosophy? Martin doesn't love me when I publish my books. But let's not go over that again. You know all about those years of silence to make me expiate my sin of pride."

"I didn't say it was about philosophy," Elfriede replied.

"Then what was it about? Do I seem like an abstraction?"

"Maybe. You're the stranger. The nomad. The woman Martin doesn't see every day. It's all so easy for you!"

"Oh, yes, the great happiness of being driven from one's native land," Hannah said, and she sighed. "What joy, to be stateless!"

"Right you are!" shouted Elfriede, lifting her head. "How lucky you were not to have a country! You didn't have to suffer its misfortunes! You didn't go through its defeat, its miseries!"

The enemy needed to be enlightened. Hannah armed herself for a battle of words: "To be stateless," she explained, "means to have nothing of one's own, only a flimsy roof over one's head. It means never knowing whether one has to abandon the house or not. It means wandering."

"That's it, the idea that makes him love you."

"The idea of wandering?" Hannah was surprised. "But Martin is such a homebody."

"Exactly! Don't you understand? You're transient. You've passed through his life here and there, you haven't lasted. He didn't watch you grow old and when you came back after the war, it had happened."

"But I was only forty!" Hannah burst out without thinking.

"Fortunately! Forty, that's not young. Luckily, it was too late. Otherwise, God knows what you might have done."

⌘

On that night in 1950, under the roof of his own house Martin had slept with his head on Hannah's breasts. About 3 A.M. he had awakened, rubbing his eyes like a child. Then he had stroked his chin, rough with white stubble from the day before. He had looked at himself in the mirror, putting on an impish face. Martin and Hannah, what a clever trick they were playing on life!

⌘

Hannah smiled.

"You have a weird look on your face, Hannah," Elfriede said suspiciously. "What are you thinking about?"

Hannah lied: "About you, Elfriede, About German women. Why are you so wrapped up in domesticity? You studied economics, you could have worked—"

"That's just what I did at home," Elfriede interrupted, annoyed.

"Ah, the good old German tradition! *Kinder, Küche, Kirche!*"

"Well, religion, you know . . ." Elfriede answered, making a face.

"Too bad. At least, if you'd had religion, you wouldn't have gone over to the wrong camp. It's true! In Hitler, you chose a human god. We Jews say that only the Eternal is God. But you were idolatrous, you deified a man. When I think of how the Jews went to the gas chamber singing the 'Schema Israel' . . ."

"I don't see the connection."

"Of course you don't. People about to die were praying to God. The idea of God. You, you adored a pair of twinkling eyes, a shrill voice, a uniform . . ."

"Adored! No, that's going too far. I simply believed."

"The Jews have done that, too. They believed in the Golden Calf. They, too, received harsh punishment. Thousands massacred by order of Moses. While those who sang in the face of death didn't believe, they prayed. There's a difference."

"You're saying they didn't believe in God?"

Hannah folded her hands and did not reply.

Elfriede had a moment of triumph. "So, the lady philosopher is silent."

Hannah spoke, discouraged: "How do I explain to you the difference between belief and prayer? I'm certainly not going to work up a lecture! I'm not talking about the traditional prayers that are recited, but about words spoken in the face of danger, whether one believes in God or not. Aren't you familiar with such prayers, which are spontaneous and pour out in a flood?"

Elfriede wasn't listening. Martin once wrote that silence is an essential response to a question. Be quiet and let Frau Arendt hold forth. But Elfriede did break in: "Just a minute, Hannah. I'm going to go see whether everything's all right." Escape the stream of words and get back to Martin.

He was asleep. Elfriede stroked the black cap and the sparse hair, once so dark. At her touch, Martin began snoring.

Martin
Todtnauberg, Black Forest, 1929

Compline

It is Sunday. Martin is in the cabin, awaiting his visitor. He has come here alone so he can write. The last rays of the sun gild the wainscoting. Soon the day will fade. Martin does not light the kerosene lamps; outside, the May sky still glows. The visitor pushes open the door. She is here.

He takes her hand, has her sit down in the half-light. She expresses herself timidly, but she thinks clearly. She is Jewish.

Martin leans over her as he talks. Then he brushes her lips. She pulls back, outraged. No, she's rebuffing him this time. "I understand," Martin says. "I've gone too far. Forgive me."

The visitor breathes more slowly, calms down, but her eyes are misty. Martin resumes the conversation where she left off the day before, talking of the philosophy of Plato. Hands folded on his lap, he is speaking quietly so as not to frighten her. When he warms to his subject, he stands up, stares out at the night, paces, sits down again. She does not stir. He finally lights the lamp. Reassured, the woman shows a more cheerful face.

Bread, butter, and pâté have been set out. The sandwiches do not interfere with their conversation. Relaxed, the young woman begins a lively commentary on the myth in the last book of Plato's *Republic*, and between mouthfuls, takes up the *Theaetetus*. Martin gazes at her pensively as she bites into the crust, crumbs on her lips, doughy bread on her tongue.

An hour goes by. The visitor says it is time to leave. Martin looks for a way to detain her. Why not walk down to the nearby Beuron Monastery? And listen to the office of the night, the "compline"?

She consents, relieved; that way, they'll be out of the cabin. Martin suggests going on foot. They'll walk at a brisk pace, it's not far. Fine with her. Deliberately, he goes on ahead. She is puffing a little in the dark. Martin is in a jolly mood, he teases her. "Come on, you have to walk faster!" She groans. He's trembling with joy.

The abbey church looms above the monastery buildings. They have arrived. As he pushes open the portal, Martin hears the hooting of the owl, "Hoo, hoo." His old friend.

They enter, sit on the bench, wait for the creaking of the wood that punctuates the monks' entrance. The polyphonic chant issues from the motionless forms of the monks and rises to the vaulted ceiling. A deep, rich harmony fills the abbey and brings tears to Martin's eyes.

His vision blurred, he can't see the monks in their stalls, the altar, the golden-winged statues. He sees only one luminous point, the red lamp of the consecration. A fixed point from which Martin departs into his world of dreams. He can't help it, his lungs fill to bursting, and he lets out an immense sigh, an exhalation that is a word: "Hannah."

The woman turns to him, dumbfounded. "I thought you detested the Catholic religion," she whispers.

"But . . . Yes," Martin replies. "What did I say?"

"You said, 'Amen,' and you let out a big sigh."

God be praised. The young woman didn't hear right.

Because she is not named Hannah. Hannah never came to Todtnauberg.

This one is Elisabeth, Elisabeth Blochmann, Lisi to her friends. She might have been a passable replacement for Hannah, but . . . It's not going to be.

"We'll talk about it later," he whispers to the woman beside him.

Martin focuses on the red lamp, its flame strong. There's nothing to restrain him. This isn't a church any more, it's a barn, and there are bales of hay. Drunk with desire, Martin rushes at the girl, pushes her to the ground, and makes love to her then and there. Her name is Hannah, he wants that to be her name. And she has her eyes closed. In and out to the rhythm of the monks' chant, he penetrates deep, right where she is. He swoons.

From the vaulted ceiling, a crash of thunder. When Martin recovers, the church is in ruins. The war has been fought. The red lamp lies broken on the tile floor. Lisi has disappeared, he is alone, ashes and smoke all around. He awakens.

⟨⟩

Unbelievable. Sex, in a dream? Amazing! Swelling, looming, entering, withdrawing, spurting. Come out of it still alive. Get old someday. Nothing any more. No . . . Survive. Dream of the lamp.

"Well?" said Hannah. "How is he?"

"Fine. Sleeping so soundly that he's snoring."

"That's excusable."

"Sometimes he has dreams. I hear him talking in his sleep."

Hannah was interested: "What does he dream about?"

"As if he tells me!"

"Maybe he doesn't know," said Hannah. "As long as he doesn't have nightmares that would wake the dead."

"Martin has only one nightmare." Elfriede was sure of that. "He dreams he's failing an exam."

"Well, as far as I know he never failed an exam."

"Of course he's never had a failure," replied Elfriede. "It's only in dreams that Martin fails. Part of getting old."

"He *has* aged," Hannah said, after a pause.

"So, you've noticed it! If only he would open his eyes! That's what really scares me. He doesn't want to see."

But he looked at me, Hannah said to herself. Aloud she said, "I think it's more that he doesn't want to talk. He is immersed in silence, which he loves."

"And me?"

There she goes again!

"But he loves you, too," Hannah conceded. "Silently."

"I guess so."

"After all, Elfriede, you're somewhat responsible for his being able to slip into silence. Didn't you try to protect him from the clamor of the world?"

"Yes. With all my strength."

"Of which you had no lack," said Hannah, derisively. "You *are* strong. For you have succeeded only too well in creating silence around him."

Elfriede felt shaky. Once, only once, she had failed.

Elfriede
Todtnauberg, Black Forest, July 1925
Her Failure at the Cabin

Summer in Todtnauberg, and the meadow is lush. The kids flop down in the grass, kick their legs in the air, tumble down the gentle slope, scuffle. Both boys shout with joy. Their mother pricks up her ears: Martin is working, there must be no noise. She opens the window and tells them to be quiet.

"But, Mommy, we're playing . . ."

"Quietly." She enunciates the word without raising her voice.

"What?" says the older brother. "We can't hear you."

"I said, 'Quietly,' " she shouts, losing patience.

The boys stop making noise. Elfriede can breathe. Not for long.

Martin's footsteps echo across the floor. She holds her breath . . . Too late. Martin wears his martyrish look.

"They didn't do it on purpose." Her tone is pleading.

Martin waves his arms in disbelief. He paces like a caged beast; then he puts on his dejected face.

"They are just children," she says.

"Can't you invent some game to keep them occupied?"

"Yes," she answers and rushes off to the meadow.

Behind the open window, the father can see the discussions from afar.

Elfriede is negotiating. Count daisy petals until you reach a hundred. No, says the younger brother, I can't go that high. Then how about picking flowers? We did that this morning, says the older brother. Why not make a cabin out of tree branches? Yes!

The kids scamper away, exultant.

The father stares hard at them before returning to his study. He shuts the door behind him.

How long will he take it? Elfriede is in a terrible state. Just yesterday, the boys were playing hide and seek. One looked for the other, who was crouched between the branches of a tall fir. Silently. The game would have continued peacefully if the clever little rascal hadn't slid down from the treetop. The younger boy called out in his high-pitched voice. "There you are! I win!"

Just then, Martin's footsteps on the floorboards. Instant punishment. When the children make noise, the father complains that he can't write. Nothing bothers him more.

Today they'll have to keep quiet. At any cost.

On the other side of the meadow, the boys gather branches, tie them together with string, cover them with a layer of shiny fir boughs. This takes time and attention. Not a peep from them the rest of the afternoon.

Now Elfriede has a chance to pump water for the evening meal. It's heavy, the pump handle, but she has no choice. Martin wants rustic living at high altitude, a trough, a pump, no modern devices. Wearily Elfriede tucks stray locks into her bun and glances at her watch: half an hour before sunset, dinner, and Martin's break. The kerosene lamp in his study is already lit. Later, after they eat, at half past eight it's family time at the chalet.

There are only three rooms: Martin's study, the dining

room, and the bedroom, where the children sleep. The adults, too. Family time is nighttime, when they all fall asleep together.

As the sun disappears behind the peaks, Elfriede dashes off to find the children, leads them back, keeps them quiet. Hush, Papa's working, silence, silence. They return to the house on tiptoe. Their father emerges from his study, uncommunicative.

"Do you know what? The boys built themselves a cabin," says Elfriede, pleased.

"That's nice," says the father mechanically. "A cabin, good idea. What are they going to use it for?"

"We'll work in it like you," says the older son. "It's our very own cabin. We're going to write. All by ourselves, away from everybody."

Martin's eyes light up.

That very evening, he decides. He's going to rent a room from a peasant, down in the plain, and shut himself up there, alone. Far from his young sons, far from his wife. Far from Todtnauberg. He'll be back the first of August.

Elfriede takes in this pronouncement without batting an eye. Martin has embarked on a major project which, as he told her earlier, involves the idea of time. She does not begrudge him his own time for doing his philosophy. She will stay with the children, who'll be able to yell as loud as they want.

When Martin announces his decision, Elfriede senses she has both gained and lost. Lost, the battle of silence. But she has gained a feeling of pride: She is helping her husband as he develops his thinking. Happy to see her so confident, Martin has given her a kiss and has told her the title of the work in progress: *Being and Time*.

While arranging the pillows for their last night at the cabin, Elfriede has a not very admirable sense of relief. Martin will be able to dream alone, but she will be free—well, almost free. In the high country he is leaving behind.

Elfriede

Twenty-five years later, Martin confessed his four years of deceitful adultery, from 1924 to 1928. The period of writing *Being and Time*.

When he told her, she remembered his withdrawing to the plain. It wasn't just the noise of the children he had been fleeing. Suddenly, Elfriede realized that her husband's loneliness was the loneliness of separated lovers. Inexpiable suffering.

She imagined their secret meetings. The letters he had been able to send without fear of discovery. The obscene fantasies he had indulged in whenever he felt like it, alone in his bed. Alone! No, after Martin's confession Elfriede knew he'd never been alone with himself. Hannah, the lady of the impossible love, had slipped in between him and himself. Absent from Martin's bed, the phantom woman had earned her official title, passion of his life.

So much for that. Today, there was no longer anyone in Martin, just emptiness. Even Hannah would not find him when she looked into his eyes, even Hannah would no longer be regaled with his words.

Hannah would soon run out of steam. Without a partner, the lady philosopher wouldn't have a dialogue, the lover wouldn't have her bliss. Elfriede and Hannah would be evenly matched, powerless against the terrifying silence.

Silence of a new kind, and Elfriede had discovered it only

lately. It was . . . closed in. Without hostility, but without meaning. Walled up in an inaccessible enclosure.

Until recently, Elfriede had always detected what was behind Martin's various silences, the color of each of them. Could a stranger have noted the differences? Hannah had not gone through life with Martin. She didn't know the gamut.

The solemn silence of thinking, that one no threat. The sad twilight silence, disturbing. The sharp silence of anxiety, uncontrollable. And the most trying, the one that had led him to leave the cabin. The silence of the beloved's absence.

What would the beloved do when confronted with the latest in the line of Martin's silences, the most ancient silence of all, that preceding death?

The beloved would be totally helpless. Tonight Hannah would leave. Instinctively, Elfriede knew there would be no more visits. For their last interview, she had rendered up to her rival a Martin behind a wall.

When she thought of Hannah departing empty-handed, Elfriede felt a satisfaction mixed with vexation. Fine, Hannah would leave, but what next? What if Martin didn't recover his speech? And what if her only reward at the end of a long mar-riage was this slow, final slipping away? Nothing else? Not a gesture, not a word?

"Y es, I really succeeded in protecting the great philosopher," Elfriede said. "Now, he's silent all the time! And I have to put up with it! Awful living like—"

"Maybe he doesn't perceive time the way we do, Elfriede. Maybe Martin is happy in the place where he's taken refuge. A place without hours, minutes, seconds. He is safe from time."

"Enough lecturing! Time, I've gone through it with him."

"But just experiencing it wasn't enough for Martin. He pondered time. And it was the subject of his most enduring work, the book with the magnificent title, *Being and Time*."

Elfriede's reaction was violent: "Don't mention that book! Please!"

I've really touched a nerve, thought Hannah. *Why is she so upset?* She lit a cigarette and spoke in a firm tone: "Elfriede, I owe it to you to tell you something. If it hadn't been for me, Martin never would have written *Being and Time*. Don't look at me like that! I know what you're going to say: When Martin started his project, I'd already left. But we were corresponding."

"I'm not surprised," Elfriede said stiffly. "And so?"

"It's because I wasn't there that Martin could write his book," Hannah said in a low voice. "Because we were apart. Martin was enduring a trial by time, on account of me. You, you were there. I wasn't. And so *I* was his inspiration. What do you have to say to that?"

"Just one thing," was the icy reply. "When Martin's mother died, he put the book in the casket, right over her heart. *Being and Time* departed with her, in death. The book was born from the passing of his mother."

Silence. *She's speechless,* Elfriede said to herself.

Finally the old lady said, "I didn't know that. But still . . ."

"Now what?"

"Nothing," said Hannah, her mind filled with words read long ago.

Hannah

W ords of Martin's from a 1925 letter. As if they were being whispered in her ear.

A steady correspondence had begun at the close of the academic year, after Hannah's departure from Marburg, a cautionary move. Less frequent, their meetings grew more intense. Never had Martin written more or better.

The letter in question dated from the period he had rented a room in a peasant dwelling so he could work in peace, without his family. He was turning out *Being and Time* with an enthusiasm for philosophy he would not have known without her, his secret young love. And that was what he had to tell her.

A love song, no mistaking. She, absent, was behind his first real book. Opened out at each step, closed up at each word, over and over the beloved would appear between the columns of the Greek temple only to be immediately veiled in shadow. So ephemeral that she was there no longer, not before, not now, not even forthwith, the absent one was a calyx open to the light. On the horizon of Being, time showed itself and quivered. Fugitive, thus present, Hannah was for Martin Greece unadorned.

Hannah had read those words so often and so avidly that they were transformed into speech. Hannah could hear Martin's words loud and clear on the horizon of Being.

When they were still together, after making love Martin

and Hannah would listen to Beethoven with the lamp off. Their intertwined fingers, their wordless mouths were suffused with a shadowy light. Curled up between Martin's outstretched legs, Hannah would try to move and he would squeeze her tighter, to rein in that impatient body. Music did not like restlessness, music could not endure reality. The body was not to interfere. Paralyzed, the young woman would let her mind go blank.

Then the scratchy sound announcing the record's end. Martin would relax his grip and lean over to force Hannah's lips open, insert his tongue into her mouth and breathe in the now-finished melody.

The music was already in the past. The interlude was over. Hannah would uncurl her legs and Martin would let her go. What remained was an echo of memory—that is, almost nothing. There were the words of the letter, of course; but they served only awkwardly to recreate a moment.

Why try to explain? The trace of Being was sealed within her. Break the seal? Too late. The power to unseal was no longer hers. Nor Martin's. A subtle presence, Martin's book, had passed into her. No one could do anything about it, not she, not he.

Yes, Martin could place the book on his mother's body, over her heart. Mere printed pages, neatly bound. No conflict between that and the gift of thinking. His lover had been infused with the spirit of the work; his mother had been given the material object, as was her due.

The dead woman and the absent woman were those destined to receive Martin's thinking.

Elfriede knew nothing of that letter to Hannah. Nor did she suspect Martin's duplicity. For there were two Martins. Heidegger, immersed in life, who spent his time as a family man; Martin, immersed in love, who left time behind so he could think. At 7 P.M. Martin turned back into Heidegger.

The lady lockkeeper had done her work, opening the sluicegates. Because of Hannah the waters poured out, foaming. She alone had made it possible for him to escape human concerns; thus the philosophy of Heidegger was born. Thanks to the ideal young woman who had surrendered to him and had adored him.

Not that he had asked her leave. But whether Martin intended it or not, fugitive Hannah would always be the secret door to what he called "Being-there."

The other door was Elfriede's. But it was only the door to worldly Care, in which Hannah had no part. The other door, guarded, was that of the house. The waters of thinking receded, grew slack. And then Martin was in danger. What had he become without Hannah? A Nazi.

"Well, Hannah, for once you don't have an answer." A little triumph for Elfriede. "You didn't influence him at all. Just remember that now!"

"Remember. Yes, I'll remember."

"And besides, you've got me to thinking. Once Martin said the idea of the connection between Being and time had come to him while he was skiing. So you can see how much he was thinking about you!"

"From the snow," said Hannah in a neutral tone. "It's always possible."

&c;

Hannah had never seen Martin ski. Sometimes, out her window in Marburg, she'd spotted him returning from the slopes, his skis on his back, color in his face. He used to say that sliding over the white surface was liberating. For then he would merge with the air, becoming weightless, incorporeal.

"That must be where it came from, don't you think?" said Elfriede. "Martin was so elated when he skied that—"

"That time made way for Being." Hannah had finished the sentence for her. "Skiing, flying over the snow, our interrupted love, for me it's all connected."

"You just won't drop it! We didn't have a part in Martin's work, not you, not I. A real philosopher does his thinking independently. And that doesn't describe you, Hannah."

"News to me," said Hannah, surprised. "So I didn't think on my own?"

"Insist, defend yourself! The fact is that you tried to compare yourself with Martin. One never shakes off a master of his quality! Martin was an innovator. You weren't."

"But I like the world the way it is! Martin rejects it and *I* accept it. I live in it!"

"Brilliant discovery. Who is the great philosopher? You, or him? I know I'm right. You'll end up having struggled in vain. After all, we're just women."

Weary, Hannah said nothing.

"There's something else," Elfriede mused. "Martin's time, I'm the one who gave it to him."

"You'll have to explain that," said Hannah.

"Before we were married, Martin had no schedule. He'd work willy-nilly, half the night."

"Night," Hannah said dreamily. "My, oh my—"

"Yes! It wasn't sensible. It was very hard to get him back to days! To reestablish a sleep routine, to insist on regular mealtimes. I set up daily working hours for him. I kept the children from crying, I provided him seclusion. Martin needed peace and quiet."

"You didn't *give* him his time. Time is just there. Nobody has the power to hand it out. You've never really thought about the meaning of your husband's work, have you? The time you're talking about, he calls 'Being-in-the-world.' "

Elfriede frowned.

"Being-in-the-world," Hannah repeated sententiously. "Being-in-the-world with Others. It is not the time of Being, but of worry. What he calls 'Care.' "

Seemingly detached, Elfriede smoothed out a fold in the tablecloth.

Hannah went on: "In everyday life, no one is himself. The 'they' reigns. Thus man lives, keeps busy, is, and is no one. And the time we're talking about, man loses."

Elfriede's hand moved back and forth patiently, straightening the tablecloth.

Hannah concluded: "So there you have the significance of everyday time, according to Martin."

"Have you finished your lecture?"

"No."

"What *I* know about the philosophy of Heidegger is that if I hadn't taken on Care as my responsibility, he wouldn't have had time to ponder Care. I don't mind that his family was Martin's 'they.' That he lived a solitary life with us. You're not telling me anything new."

"But I'm not through, Elfriede. There's still disclosedness, the clearing, the house of Being."

"You're reciting. You're quoting sentences. Being-in-the-world! Ask yourself what made up Martin's world. His true home."

"You and your children," Hannah admitted reluctantly.

"Now, why do you think he gave you up? Because he was afraid of my jealousy? Certainly not. I hadn't suspected a thing. He could have set up other meetings, continued the adultery without complications. So, he had another reason for breaking off. He left you to get back his orderly routine, his time. And very likely, his Care. But his Care, that was me."

Elfriede was expressing herself as if everything had suddenly become clear; she seemed to be discovering her life as she spoke. She was not crowing, she was not accusing.

She was speaking the truth. And it was horrible to hear.

"But we were lovers," said Hannah, perturbed. "If he had such a great need for order, why did I come into his life?"

"That business!" shouted Elfriede, her face flushed. "Apparently he succumbed to temptation. You were elegant, you came from the city, and I was a woman in an apron, braids pinned on my head. You wore a hat out of a fashion magazine, I remember. You had a look about you!"

"You've never told me any of that—"

"They used to call you 'the girl in green.' Because of your emerald velvet dress."

"That old dress I bought in Berlin! It really was becoming."

"Too becoming. That's why I always left you out when we had students over."

"What's happening here? These belated admissions—"

"I told you, I'm afraid. The time for quarreling is over, Hannah. Explain it to me. The two of you. What was it really about?"

Elfriede's look was easier to read than ever; she was desperate for answers. Hannah looked into those unclouded eyes and saw a yearning for truth. A taut, delicate thread.

Hannah sighed, and then she spoke: "I'll try to explain. If you were giver of time, then imagine what *I* was for Martin, if you can. The opposite, Elfriede. The moment, inconsistency, imperfection."

"Imperfection!" Elfriede sounded bitter. "So I was too perfect!"

"Yes, indeed. Martin desired the irregular. The hurried, secret rendezvous. The immediate that does not last. Real lovers have no other choice."

"And the thought of adultery didn't bother you?"

"No."

"I don't believe it! You can't love a married man without thinking about the one who waits for him at night. I had to be there, somewhere, between you."

"I'll tell you how it was," said Hannah gently. "When we were together, the outside world. . . . It's hard to explain. We're weren't living in time. And besides, we weren't actually living. We were within the moment."

"In married life, the moment exists, too!" shouted Elfriede.

"But when morning came, you were always there. Doing without was our dowry. Deprivation, always. For him, our love was a dent in time. For you, Elfriede, to love is to go along with time in its duration. But our love meant urgency, abandon, surprise. A lamp, wet spots on a wrinkled sheet—"

"Oh, stop it!"

"It's cruel, but you couldn't exist between us. There was no one between us, only a flash of Being. Love is like the unbounded sky one sees from a plane. No horizon, no land. How can I put it? Ah, let's see . . . It the same feeling when I swim."

"When you swim? In water?"

"And what *would* I swim in?" Hannah found that funny. "In the ocean, mostly. I get set, I arch my back, and I dive in. And there I am, cleaving the water and time, both at once. I stay bobbing up and down, calm, carried along. I give in. To what? The question doesn't arise. Martin would call it the clearing."

"But when you're swimming, you're alone, so I don't see what you're getting at."

"I mean that together Martin and I were that water. We no longer belonged to the earth. When I swim, I don't feel weight. Well, with me and Martin, it was like that. Weightlessness."

The forget-me-not-blue eyes filled with tears. "And I was at home, waiting!"

"I'm trying to understand what purposes we served, Elfriede. Don't be angry. You were his hearth and home, and I was his escape. After all, the child has to leave his mother before he can go back to her. You were his anchor. I, his adventure. You see how simple it is—"

Elfriede turned her head slowly to the right, to the left, to the right again.

"Why are you shaking your head?" Hannah asked.

"I'm not saying 'no.' " She sounded grouchy. "The back of my neck hurts."

"Poor Elfriede," said Hannah.

"Poor Elfriede, poor Elfriede." Her tone is mocking, nasal. "The good sheep dog guarding the house. Martin robbed me! The two of you robbed me. That time was mine. Really, you didn't think of me?"

"Well, I didn't, at any rate." Hannah was wise enough to put it that way. "We never talked about you. The idea of leaving you never occurred to him. I didn't ask for anything, just to be with him, however briefly."

"With no future?"

"Nothing."

"He told me that being with you had been like a dream. When he confessed, he told me it was long over, that you would never again have any kind of exclusive relationship. That he would never . . . well . . . that he wasn't with you any more except in spirit."

"He was speaking the truth," Hannah lied. "Calm yourself."

"Yes," said Elfriede, sighing. "In the long run, by taking care of him, I have been the guarantor of his philosophy."

The wife had recovered her patrimony.

Hannah said to herself: *The wound was that deep, that bloody! Elfriede only wants her place, like that of Martha in the Bible. In the kitchen. And it's up to me to keep mine.* Aloud, she said. "And as for me, he wanted me absent, outside of time."

"That's no life."

"No," said Hannah. "The 'they' of the world ended up carrying him away. Our rendezvous couldn't go on. I fled."

Hannah
Heidelberg, Baden Württemberg, 1929

She Waits at the Railroad Station

She sits on their favorite bench and waits. When the 4:30 from Marburg arrives, Martin will step off the train. They haven't seen each other in a week.

A few months ago, Martin wrote and asked her never to return to Marburg, even for a day, because of his wife. They will meet in other places, he'll decide when. The letter came as no surprise to Hannah. Their meetings will be all the more thrilling.

Hannah has promised herself she won't look at her watch.

In his latest letter, he asked her to be the essence of waiting: unique and ready to receive him, the faraway, longed-for homeland that makes the journey worthwhile.

The sky is gray for June. At one end of the platform a mother is keeping her brood in line. Now and then the children's voices break through Hannah's thoughts. She is focusing on her hands. It is 4:15.

What kind of rendezvous will it be? Hannah doesn't know Martin's schedule. An hour, ten minutes? An interval for a kiss or for going to bed? She tries not to think in terms of numbers, without success. Two hours, or nothing? Hannah shivers and pulls up her collar. She is a young lady meeting someone on the platform. Who? Her father, her lover, a girl-friend? Travelers wonder as they pass by her bench; then their thoughts turn elsewhere. Forgetfulness rules on the platform. The young lady waits.

It's 4:20. The artery in her neck begins to pulse. In antic-ipation, her excitement grows by leaps and bounds. She thinks to herself, *Welcome, desire. You are early for the meeting, indeed. Just a little while, and Martin will be here.* As he hoped, Hannah is all waiting. Nothing else matters.

The ear picks up the distant rumble of a train entering the station. Hannah jumps to her feet. He's coming! The loco-motive belches forth steam, and the passengers detrain in a white mist. Martin must be at the rear of the train. Hannah searches the faces of the passengers, who walk by without seeing her. Hats, mustaches, coats, indifferent glances, little veils, suitcases, where is he?

The train starts up again. Martin was not on it. The next train from Marburg will arrive in an hour.

Hannah goes back to her bench. Automatically she glances at her watch. She has time for coffee. Maybe a sandwich.

Once she's seated at a table, she stares at the hand Martin has not yet caressed. She takes out a notebook, a pen. She writes, "When I observe my hand—unfamiliar thing that is part of me—no longer do I have a country."

The railway platform is a no-man's-land.

Will he come? No harm in writing a poem while she waits. "No more here, no more now." The pen lingers over that line. How slowly the time is passing. Hannah hunches over, ter-ribly sad.

The hot coffee revives her. She sits up and writes on: "No longer subject to the how."

From what region of Being have these rebellious words sprung? Are they unexpected? Hannah rereads her poem: "When I observe my hand—unfamiliar thing that is part of me— / no longer do I have a country. / No more here, no more now. / No longer subject to a how."

Not subject to a how? Sacrilege! Hannah's hand has no authority to write against submission! On orders of Martin, Hannah knows she must submit to the how, and wait.

She carefully crosses out the last line.

A surge of anger takes her by surprise. Her hand claws the paper furiously, and she adds a new line: "Never again will a sign appear."

Martin will not appear.

Hannah tears a sheet out of the notebook. She's writing her breakup letter. Her hand obeys, is once more part of her. Hannah is regaining her freedom.

The last sentences are the hardest.

"I love you as I did from the first, you know that, and I have always known it."

That's not a proper conclusion. She hesitates, and her hand carries her along: "And God willing, I'll love you more after I'm dead." She signs her name.

Madness! But it's done.

Hannah finishes her coffee, pays, and leaves. Never again will she wait for Martin on the platform. Or anywhere else.

Leaving the station that day, Hannah picked up a cluster of flowers fallen from a chestnut tree. She spread out the sepals and stroked the fleshy pistil before tossing the cluster of blooms into the gutter. Then she went to see her lover, whom she had taken up with after Martin suggested she needed someone to fill her lonely hours.

⟨∽⟩

Hannah sighed. "I fled. And that's why we broke up, Elfriede. I wanted to live."

Elfriede gave her credit. "That was the right thing to do."

"But," Hannah went on, "I didn't vanish from his life. I suppose you understood that, much as you didn't want to?"

"My God, when he told me he wanted to see you again! When he explained he was confessing to make your reunion less complicated . . . He wept over it! After so many years, you and he! Hannah, it was awful!"

"You've led a sheltered life," Hannah said with a smile. "You're quite the child, Elfriede. So he was unfaithful? Is that the end of the world?"

"Infidelity, that would be nothing " said Elfriede. "But you are the passion of his life. He told me! My home was collapsing—"

"No, no." A sigh from Hannah. "It was just that your home contained a hidden door. He opened it for you that day."

"And there you were, on the other side of that door. Waiting for him."

"Was I waiting for him?" Hannah mused. "Martin's not a man that you can wait for easily. He's there. Or not there. Suddenly he looms up. No, I wasn't waiting for anything."

"Wait a minute! You summoned him in writing, I know that."

"I just let him know I was coming. That's different. I did no more than give him my address. I wanted to hear his explanation of the bad period."

"So, it's just what I said. A summons."

"Put yourself in my place. Had I really loved a Nazi? Me, A Jew. I wanted to know."

"That's not what happened," said Elfriede. "You knew, but you decided to forget. You wanted something else, Hannah. To be with him from time to time, just the two of you."

"I live in New York! With the Atlantic between us, you weren't in any danger."

"Yes, I was! You had come back into his life. You existed. He was writing you. He talked to me about you, about your travels. He'd wait for your visits. He needed you! And where did I fit in?"

"He doesn't need me; he needs both of us together," said Hannah. "He even ordered us to reconcile, and he, smack in the middle, was lording it over us like a sultan."

The two women looked at each other hesitantly before they burst out laughing.

"Martin and his two women. That's something we won't soon forget!" Hannah exclaimed. "An enduring memory. Ah, yes, when he had us join our hands in his! What a performance."

Elfriede
Freiburg im Breisgau, August 1950

Warm Hands

The three of them are in the Freiburg house. Elfriede by the door. Hannah at the window, her back turned. Martin paces back and forth between them, hands folded. The women have just come from the next room, where he left them alone long enough to get acquainted and exchange the kiss he insisted on.

"Well, did you give each other a kiss, as I wanted you to?" he asks.

"We did," says Hannah.

"But that hasn't changed anything," Elfriede is quick to point out.

Martin sighs heavily. "Is it so hard for you to come together?" he says.

Hannah turns around. Elfriede looks daggers at her. Neither woman will lower her eyes.

"But I'm not asking the impossible," Martin says. "I'm being open and honest here. Why turn that down? Be friends."

"Yes, but how?" says Hannah, her tone ironic. "Since she doesn't want to be."

"Elfriede," sighs Martin. "I beg of you. Do it for me."

Silence.

"I took you as my wife," he says. "Don't forget that."

"And her?" shouts Elfriede.

"That has nothing to do with our marriage. Nothing at all. And besides, she has a husband now. Come here, please."

Elfriede lowers her head. She's well acquainted with Martin's orders, gentle but dreadful. She's going to have to do what's she told. She joins her husband in the middle of the room.

"Come, Hannah," says Martin. "Don't be afraid. I'm here."

Hannah leaves her place at the casement and marches over to them.

"Give me your hand," he says. "You, too, Elfriede."

And Martin imprisons two hands in his.

Elfriede trembles. Hannah's hand, Martin on the verge of tears, his joyful smile, the affection that hovers over both women without favoring either.

Standing between Elfriede and Hannah, Martin is radiant with the sharing of his love.

The warmth of his hands heats the joined fingers. Surprised at her emotion, Elfriede feels the vise of jealousy loosen its grip. Hannah's free hand relaxes and strokes at random, timidly—his hand, her hand, all three. Good feeling, togetherness, a group embrace.

Elfriede lifts her head and meets Hannah's eyes. Bright, misty, almost gentle. Elfriede smiles at her through tears. Time stops. The two have come together.

Elfriede remembered exactly how she had felt that day. Hannah was smiling. Not a blink even, just that look of pure mockery. "Say what you want, Hannah, but you *were* touched."

"You think so?"

"Yes, during the one little moment that made him happy. I was touching your fingers; they were freezing, and so were mine. Then, you know as well as I do what happened. Our harmony didn't last long, but we did experience it. You can't deny that!"

"Martin is overly sentimental, you know," said Hannah, unimpressed. "Every little trifle arouses his feelings. The scene was touching, and so was Martin, with his dream. It's all right to let Martin dream once in a while."

Silence crept in, total silence. The teakettle was off, the rain had stopped, the brightness of afternoon entered and cast small squares of light on the kitchen wall. Time loosened its reins and the two women looked at each other wordlessly. Martin's dream was present in that neat and tidy room, between the wife and the mistress.

Hannah broke into the wondrous moment to continue in the same vein: "And it's quite all right to share once in a while. Don't you agree?"

"Yes," Elfriede answered, barely audible. "Once in a while." Then she grew silent, thoughtful. Martin was not good at sharing. Solitary hiker, solitary skier, on his own in philosophy, double-dealing in love. With men, maybe he was able to swap stories. But share, no! Being-with made him uncomfortable.

Martin
Messkirch, Swabia, 1901

The Little-Bridge Fake

It's Sunday afternoon. Martin is playing soccer in the meadow. He's quite proud of devoting his time to a sport that Germans have taken up only in the last thirty years.

The field is soaked; it has rained. Soil sticks to the shoes. Martin doesn't dislike sinking in the mud and hearing it squish beneath his soles.

Martin is the outside left, on the edge of play, always on the alert, ready to send the ball back with a long cross. He wouldn't like to be the goalkeeper. He wouldn't be able to stop the ball.

He loves having the laced-up leather globe at his feet, loves to feel it obey him. He hates the idea of touching it with his head. He loves to score, when he can. To shoot the ball toward the sky and soar with it.

He's not big, but he's quick as lightning. He's not very strong, but he's sharp at judging distances. And Martin knows the fakes, especially the little bridge. What fun! He slips in front of some great oaf whose thighs are open and he sends the ball right between the fellow's legs. To guard against a little bridge, you have to be smart enough to squeeze your calves together in a flash, and there's no one speedier than Martin. The little bridge is his favorite maneuver, nothing like it, a joy shared with no one.

The referee is about to blow the whistle. The game begins. Martin hops and skips, eyes glued to the round object ferreting between the players' legs. The ball has a life of its own: it escapes, it stays close, it bounds, it rises to the thighs. A throw-in, and the elusive object steals away, vanishes, leaps up, leaving a white trail in the retina. The eye is blind to everything but the path of the ball. It's coming!

I have it. At my feet. Rough pushes and jabs, bodies, hips, elbows, I resist. Keep going, ball, I'm right with you. Dribbling, releasing, sliding, pushing, stopping, almost there. Down to the end. I poise my foot, I shoot. . . .

A perfect orbit, no stopping it. The ball goes between the goal posts, strikes the netting.

"A goal for Messkirch," says the referee.

"Hurrah!" shouts Martin.

The other team is pouting. Those on the scoring side clap, jump up and down, a goal, a goal.

Kickoff. The ball flies, Martin does not take his eyes off it. And suddenly a colossus, all muscle, looms up in front of him, legs spread apart. It's Hans the simpleton, an awe-inspiring brute. Martin sticks to the ball and executes his maneuver. The ball slips between the adversary's legs. The little bridge!

In a rage, Hans kicks Martin in the ankle. The whistle blows.

"Hans, disqualified."

Martin has flopped down in the mud. The smell of earth fills his nostrils, and he stays where he is, happy. The damp soil smells good. A cesspool with an animal stench, an aroma of woman. Mud is nice.

"Get up! Come back, Martin," a distant shout from the referee.

To leave the ground is an ordeal. Heavily, Martin raises himself up a bit and wipes his eyes. He is blinded by mud. The harder he rubs, the darker the world becomes.

Finally, he sees through the brownish blur. The referee is gone. The team is gone. There's nobody left on the playing field but Hans the simpleton. Before Martin can stand up, the brute delivers shattering kicks to his head.

Under the blows, Martin opens his eyes.

⇜

Don't give in. Fake. . . . Slip in, between the legs. Quick, the little bridge. The ball, don't share the joy. Fall instead. Stay on the ground. Smell the odor between the legs. Disqualified? Why?

Elfriede

Elfriede shuddered. Martin did not like to share, least of all his dreams.

Martin's dreams: her major worry. The chasm into which he could topple at any moment. The same feverish excitement had first pushed Martin into Hannah's arms, then into the arms of the monster, the deceitful hero. Yes, his obsession with disclosure of the world often led Martin to the abyss. What lay in the abyss? Elfriede had never learned.

The first few times Martin's eyes took on their faraway look, she had loved him like that, wandering astray. His gaze came back to rest on her, still a somewhat peculiar gaze, then it found repose. But soon the gaze did not return so readily. Martin would stare into space for hours. It was disturbing. Yet Elfriede noted that after these interludes of vagueness Martin worked better. For longer stretches, anyway. When she finally held Martin's first book in her hands, she read assiduously.

The language was disconcertingly new. Martin's German violated the rules of grammar. Elfriede found Martin's writing very hard to understand. The vocabulary of philosophy eluded her; the references to Parmenides, Plato, Hegel conveyed almost nothing to her; Martin's ideas were very difficult. She fastened on to the parts she found meaningful.

"Being-toward-death," maybe that referred to the moments Martin turned his gaze inward, his head bowed with anxiety. Elfriede also had some familiarity with the key concept that so thrilled Martin's colleagues in philosophy: *Dasein*, "Being-there." She understand *Dasein*'s absurd weightlessness: it was the void which Martin stared at so fixedly. And Elfriede saw the dangers of the "chaos of gaping-open." In total darkness, twisted together in a vipers' nest lay *Dasein*, death, and possibility. When he thought, Martin danced above the snakes, invulnerable and exhilarated. But he traveled the road of everyday life as a sleepwalker and would often teeter dangerously on the edge of a precipice, where he might take leave of himself. Deep in the chasm, anxiety awaited him.

In the early days of their life together, when Martin's gaze strayed, Elfriede recalled him to reality: "Where are you Martin? Come back!"

Lashed by the familiar voice, he trembled. Too much suffering. Elfriede learned to speak quietly and gently, then to whisper, and finally, to say nothing at all.

"Thinking is going on inside me," he'd say, chagrined. "I can't stop it."

It was not good to call Martin back to the world. A sleepwalker should not be awakened abruptly; he might die, or he might never recover. One must go along with someone who flees, be there for him, remove obstacles, remain silent. Elfriede learned to stay in the background.

Martin would always return. In his own time, for dinner. Or sometimes later. Once, he foundered. After the humiliation, his gaze vanished for good. A person no more, just a void. The psychiatrists who took care of him gave a name to his not being there—depression. They administered so-called therapy—conversation and medication. Ridiculous! Waiting would have been sufficient.

For Elfriede knew better than anyone that Martin desperately needed this return to the roots of Being. Without it, no more ideas.

She was sure of that. To write his Genesis in his language, Martin had needed to withdraw deep within himself. He was not in a state of depression, he was withdrawing. A necessary precaution! Martin was not like other people.

There dwelt in him the strange threat of the divine; and indeed, in reading his works over the years, Elfriede had seen it down in black and white: "The threat of a god." Sometimes, "The light of a god," Elfriede sensed Martin's need to cut himself off from human beings to evade the threat. When in withdrawal, Martin was not in danger. Similarly, before prophesying, the priestesses of old would sequester themselves deep in a cave, out of the sight of the community, opening themselves to their particular god. For if he were to inspire them in public view, those mortal women would be shattered by his force.

And a god did loom up one day, in the guise of Hitler. Martin left his cave, the real and the dream came together. Martin's spirit exploded.

But Martin survived—barely. The psychiatrists did not keep him long. Little by little Elfriede absorbed the anxiety and saved him. It was not easy. To reestablish a peaceful passing of time, a rhythmic unfolding of hours. To maintain the house so he could have access to another house, "the house of Being," in which there was no room for Elfriede.

Hannah had found a room in the house of Being. It was so unfair! No effort, no preparation, and Hannah had access to the joyful, unshared place. Why her? Through what kind of spell? Through what sovereign right?

Hannah
Königsberg, East Prussia, 1922

A Beggar Arrives in the Night

Her usual nighttime routine. She reads and then it's time for sleep. Hannah has just finished high school and has taken her matriculation exam, so she doesn't have much else to do. When she turns off the light, ideas starts going round and round in her head. Finally she drops off.

Hannah dreams there is someone at the front door. A muffled knock.

Another knock. She awakens with a start. Somebody did knock, it's not a dream. In the master bedroom, her mother is up. Uneasy, Hannah jumps out of bed and goes into the hall.

"Did you hear it, Hannah?" her mother says. "At one in the morning. Who can it be?"

"There was a knock, no doubt about it," Martha's husband chimes in. "We have to go see. Maybe someone needs help."

Hannah respects the man her mother married after the death of Hannah's father, Paul Arendt. Martin Beerwald is broad-minded, courageous, and kind. It hasn't occurred to him that a thief might be trying to gain entry to the house.

Martin Beerwald goes downstairs in his bathrobe.

Leaning over the banister in their nightgowns, the two women wait to see who has arrived on their doorstep.

He isn't old. In his thirties. He wears a suit that has seen better days. He is unshaven, quite pale.

"I didn't want to disturb you, sir," he says humbly, removing his hat. "I know it's very late. I'm sorry."

"What do you want?" Herr Beerwald asks grouchily.

"It's because of inflation. I have no money, sir. I've lost everything. I . . . well, if you'd be so kind as to give me a cup of coffee, I'd be very—"

"Come in, sir." Martin places a hand on the man's shoulder. "Martha! Get dressed and make coffee!"

The two women rush to their rooms. Coming out again, Hannah nearly collides with her mother, who is hurriedly fastening her sash.

"Another unfortunate person reduced to begging!" laments Hannah. "There's so much injustice."

"Don't raise your voice," says her mother. "We mustn't humiliate him. Poor Germany."

Then she goes downstairs and puts the kettle on. Sitting shyly on the edge of a chair, the man lowers his eyes. Finally he speaks up: "You are kind, ma'am."

"It's nothing," she answers. "Would you like something with your coffee? We have bread, cold chicken."

The man hesitates.

"You look hungry," she says. "There's nothing shameful about filling up, you know."

"I would like that," the man says with a sigh.

He doesn't eat, he gobbles, from time to time casting a distraught glance at the three bathrobes—Martha, who is seated; Beerwald, who is watching him; Hannah, off in her corner. When he is through, the man gazes at Martha beseechingly.

She simply says, "I'm going to fix you a nice omelet."

"Thank you," says the man, looking at his shoes. "Without you, I don't know what—"

"Now, now!" says Martin Beerwald, gruffly. "In the times we live in, we have to help one another."

"Especially when we're lucky enough not be in need," Martha puts in. "You are starving, and we have plenty."

The man shivers. "I hadn't eaten all day. To think I am forced to ask for charity, ma'am! I never would have believed that could happen. How can I thank you? I'm not at all used to—"

A beggar, that's what he's become. No one asks any questions. They don't even ask his name. And since he doesn't know how to thank them, he weeps.

"Once in a while, it is quite all right to share," Martha says.

Hannah was stirring her coffee, but the cup was empty. Elfriede thought she'd better recall her to reality. "Hannah! Where are you? Come back!"

Hannah reacted with a start. "That . . . What? What did you say?"

"You, too, were dreaming."

"I was," said Hannah. "I just dropped off. I felt so weary all of a sudden. I haven't eaten anything today."

"What, you've had no food? But that's insane! Why didn't you speak up?"

"I didn't think of it."

Elfriede was already rummaging through her food supply. A few slices of ham, black bread, butter. Ham? No, Jews weren't allowed to eat pork. She was looking for something else when Hannah intervened.

"I eat it," she said with a smile. "Ham, that is. I don't keep kosher."

Elfriede frowned. She didn't understand.

"I don't observe Jewish dietary laws," Hannah explained benevolently. "The word for those rules is 'kosher.' I don't want little slivers. I love ham."

Elfriede frowned even more. With Hannah, always better to stay on your guard. Mistrustful, she set everything on the table. "Fine, since that's how you want it," she muttered.

Hannah folded a piece of ham, put it between the thick slices of pumpernickel she'd just buttered, looked with appetite at the grains of wheat embedded in that German bread which always melted in the mouth. Then she gobbled her sandwich. "I think I was hungry," she said, wiping her lips. "I do feel better. If it's not too much trouble, I'd like more coffee."

Silent, Elfriede put water in the kettle, placed it on the stove and lit the burner. "If you don't mind, I'll just step out for a few minutes. I won't be long."

Then, with her graceful step, she scurried to the door and closed it carefully behind her.

Hannah watched this departure enviously. Efficient Elfriede walked through life without a superfluous gesture.

Hannah

W hen Hannah cooked, everything went wrong. Oil spattered, the stove would not obey, the pot of cabbage would foam up and boil over, putting out the gas. And when Hannah shut a door, she was likely to pinch her fingers. While Elfriede! The perfect homemaker. For her, objects would materialize when and where they were supposed to. Elfriede had a talent for the tempo of everyday life.

Martin didn't. Except maybe when it came to walking.

When Hannah and Martin walked through the fields, Martin's feet took on a life of their own. Martin's shoes had the fast, strong rhythm of a pounding heart. He walked as if propelled by the wind and sometimes Hannah found it hard to keep up with him. One day, in the hope he would pull her along at his pace, she had offered him an outstretched, loving hand.

But he had stared at Hannah's fingers in amazement. What were they doing there? Martin tried to figure out what Hannah wanted. Finally, recovering his composure, he stroked Hannah's hand awkwardly, but he did not take it in his. Then he started out again, faster than before.

Hannah stood there stupidly and contemplated her hand—an unfamiliar part of her without the man she loved gripping it.

Martin walked all alone, with Hannah trailing him. And nothing stopped him until he saw it was time to go home. She remembered vividly the breathless pace of those walks. What compelled him? The weather? The road? The land? His body, or Hannah's? Why did she follow this man who refused to take her outstretched hand? What did she get in return?

Almost nothing. A few poems. A gaze that rested on her and enveloped her. The promise of future meetings, tomorrow, later, not now, whenever her lover decided the time was right.

For the pact between Martin and Hannah stipulated it was solely up to him, her lover, to arrange their rendezvous. He, the lover, had an official mate, children, a home life: only he knew when he could get away. All this went without saying, and indeed, was never put into words. Hannah would receive coded messages: lamp lit at 6 P.M., I'll be coming to your place. Her student quarters awaited Martin. So, no talk sessions with friends. She accepted loneliness.

By staying in so much, she flushed out a companion, a gentle and attentive creature. Its nest behind the wardrobe, Hannah's mouse emerged at the coffee hour, when there were bread crumbs. Hannah would crouch down and stay quiet. Its whiskers atwitter, the tiny gnawing thing would look at her and tremble before stealing under the breakfast table. Hannah and her mouse had all the time in the world to become domesticated.

If Martin should happen to be home alone, she was to await a signal from the Heidegger house, the lamp turned on and off three times. Not for her to decide. Hannah, ready at any moment. A voluntary recluse, Hannah was the lamp turned off then relit at the arrival of the nocturnal Lover. For twelve all-too-short months, waiting for Martin led to infinite excitement and delight for Hannah.

At the end of 1925 she left Marburg.

Martin thought it would be better that way. Living far away, Hannah would not have to sit and wait and suffer, he said. She could even take a lover if she wished: Martin would not be jealous, quite the contrary. It didn't bother him a bit when Hannah found herself a husband. Their passion was beyond ordinary feelings, and Martin was unselfish.

They met between Marburg and Berlin, in towns along the railroad line. The pleasure of waiting kept its savor of forbidden love. They would meet on the station platform, he would take her to a hotel. With their bodies, it was the same as ever, but there was still the time apart. So long, so nonsensical. Martin would put his clothes on and leave. When will we see each other? One day soon? Just what does that mean, "soon"? The looming up of Being. But when, can't you tell me? No answer. Not now, not forthwith.

"You know my time isn't my own," he'd say.

Martin assigned Hannah to sentry duty. She complied. Waiting exacerbated love to the point of pain, like the scab the injured child enjoys picking until it bleeds. Much blood flowed under the bridges spanning the railroad stations, and in return much delight. The scab did get infected, but it was only local.

Until that day at the Heidelberg station when he didn't make it. Fulminating gangrene, love amputated. The wound healed over, forming a thick scab Hannah left alone. Operation a success.

Hannah no longer picked at the wound she thought healed. After they had broken up, one day Martin visited Hannah's young husband in Berlin. And the wound was reopened.

Hannah
Berlin, October 1929

The Dwarf's Nose

At last the visit is over. Professor Heidegger is about to return to Freiburg accompanied by Hannah's husband, Günther Stern. And it's none too soon. Hannah can't take any more.

The professor is extending a special courtesy to the young couple. He arrived by train for a brief stay, he's leaving that very evening, and by coincidence Günther is going to Freiburg for his university *Habilitation*. The professor has invited the young man to ride with him so they can continue their conversation.

Martin is fatherly, perfectly proper, nostalgic. Innocent Günther knows nothing, sees nothing. Overwhelmed, Hannah watches her husband help Martin into his brown loden coat with the respect owed one's elders.

"We'll walk to the station, won't we, my boy?" asks Martin.

"Yes, indeed, Herr Professor. Let's walk," says Günther, eager to please.

They make a fine pair, those two. But she is left out!

"Oh, I'm so sorry!" she says with false cheer. "I just remembered an errand I have to run right away. I'm deserting you. You won't hold it against me, I'm sure."

"Oh, not at all," says Martin with a slight bow. "Until we meet again, dear Frau Stern."

Hannah is already racing downstairs. Once on the sidewalk, she runs. She'll be at the station ahead of them. She's planning a little surprise. With Martin and Günther still on their way from the house to the station, she reaches the platform and hides behind a doorway. She's waiting for them.

They will pass by her, enter the car, and—hurry, hurry—Hannah will step forward, and they will see her from the train. What a clever idea!

Martin and Günther pass by Hannah, enter the car, and—hurry, hurry—Hannah rushes along the platform. The engine is starting up. She has her smile ready.

Martin and Günther are at the window, deep in lively conversation. Their car slowly passes by Hannah, she waves, she calls out . . .

Martin's eyes rest on her but do not see her, and the train accelerates. Hannah's smile fades. Martin didn't recognize her. Neither did Günther.

It can't be, she says to herself.

When she was a child, her mother would terrify her with the story of the dwarf whose nose grew so large nobody could see him. Then, to tease her, Martha would pretend she couldn't see Hannah, and the frightened child would yell, "Mutti, I'm Hannah! I'm here!" But no, Hannah had become invisible to her mother.

Without thinking, Hannah touches her nose. It hasn't grown. The train has left. Hannah is alone on the platform. Invisible to her one and only love, who passed right by her as if she didn't exist.

"I'm Hannah," she whispers. "I was here, I really was."

Hannah

Hannah remained on the platform a long time, lonely enough to die. She'd forget Martin someday. But not here in a station where the trains come and go. Wait, wait a little longer.

But should she linger at the edge of the field while he walked on ahead and didn't stop for anything?

Wavering and hesitation. To take Martin away from his life was a heroic undertaking. Hannah didn't have the strength for it. Martin was a departing train, Hannah the passenger, the destination nowhere. Should she risk her neck by jumping from a moving train?

In the long run, yes. For when confronted with the future, Martin fled. The notion of "future" belonged to human concerns, to the "they" of everyday life whom Martin so disdainfully labeled "public." The future? No need for it. The future offered nothing but an enervated world, that is, a world without nerve, without spirit.

Martin rejected the love of the world. Nothing frightened him more than the middle road of the community, the "they-say" that made him take flight. Martin would never be his own contemporary.

In his philosophy, the "I" of the first person had no substance. Martin could not say "I love you." If someone said "I," that was not accurate. It was the "they" speaking, and the "they" did not think. "Thinking is going on inside me. I can't help it," Martin would say ecstatically. So thinking was not up to him. The "I" could do nothing; the "I" was passive.

No one could envisage living "with" Martin, not even his wife. No one with him. Besides, he hadn't made any promises.

Yet he started it, he led the way.

After Martin had granted Hannah an interview in his university office, he sent her the first of his missives. His wording solemn and formal, *Privatdozent* Heidegger offered to serve as mentor to the young lady philosopher with the brilliant future. Right off, Hannah was flattered by this attention from the famous philosopher. But the letter didn't stop there.

In return, the professor was asking that Fraülein Arendt be a solace to him in his terrible loneliness. Hannah was deeply touched. Heidegger was isolated, suffering, and she could console him!

"Future," the word was there. And also, "loneliness."

Loneliness was the gleaming key that opened the door to love. Hannah rushed through that door with no concern for the future.

Even though he lived with a wife, Martin suffered from loneliness. Why had he married? A mistake. There was no other explanation.

But, to her great dismay, Hannah realized there *was* another explanation. Martin didn't share his isolation with a living soul. When he abandoned it, it was for a moment of Being, such as thinking, snow, or sex. A brief exit, then shut away again.

"In every now there is a just-now and a forthwith," Martin had written. That is, the present, the future, and the past are lines of flight. For Martin, time had no meaning.

Something else: the whole question of meaning! "The absurd is a challenge to meaning," he said, and Martin rose to that challenge.

He sought the absurd, with its dearth of landmarks: no ordered world, no highways, no houses. He wanted to stray down paths. For Martin, thinking required "not-being-at-home." That is, being nowhere.

Something else: when he saw Hannah again after all those years, it wasn't to his "at-home" he brought her. Instead, they were under Elfriede's roof, in the family dwelling that was not his "at-home." Sly Martin had managed to transform the house where he lived into nowhere in the world. Somewhere else.

So many somewhere elses, something elses! With Martin, all that was inevitable. Absence, breakup, silence, Nazism, and something else: you're the passion of my life. Stay, go away, come back, or something else.

And the letters that followed! Sixteen in 1950. Well, what did he have to say?

That he loved her as before, that from afar he longed to run his fingers through Hannah's hair, he could almost feel it. That their hearts still belonged to each other, that in the night he dreamed of her beside him.

From afar. In dreams. From somewhere else.

He had asked for a recent photograph, and Hannah sent one that had turned out rather nicely. Serious, head tilted to one side, a cigarette in her hand. And Martin gazed long and thoughtfully at Hannah's portrait. Her eyes had lost nothing of their sadness, he said. The passing of the years was marked in them, but the young girl could still be seen in the face of the mature woman. But all in all, Martin wrote, Hannah's portrait was too beautiful to be true.

Might as well say that Hannah looked perfect in the photograph because she couldn't move. She wondered whether Martin might really have liked her better dead.

Martin
Marburg, Hesse, 1924

Music

He's arranged a rendezvous for today. He'll turn the living room lamp on and off three times. The signal will tell her that Elfriede has left the house with the children, the coast is clear.

There is the sofa, as vast as the sea. The coast is here already, now. Martin strokes the fabric. Hannah is not here yet. Just now.

She rings. She's coming.

Forthwith. And time disappears.

After making love, Martin always wants to hear Beethoven. Hannah's frail body stirs; she is alive, seated at his feet. Martin tightens the vise of his thighs around her neck. She whimpers. She may well come out with some of her heavy sighs and break the silence. But no. She is quite still, receptive to Being-with the music. Hannah is a good little girl, and she will not disturb the music. Martin quivers.

The blissful clearing comes. And its ecstasy. With no one other than Hannah. Martin's secret name for Hannah is "Person-with-me."

End of the last movement. Forthwith, time is to start up again. Now, the music stops. Silence. Martin leans over and kisses Hannah on the mouth.

Hannah's lips are stone cold, and her wide-open eyes stare into space. He strokes Hannah's icy hands. She is not breathing. Hannah is dead. Here, forthwith.

Martin sits with Hannah hunched up in his arms and observes the stopping of her life, a simple thing really. Hannah has left the world. She has finished being with him and has begun being no more. Martin holds against him something unalive, called a corpse. He shudders with fright. He didn't kill her!

It wasn't he! These are not his legs around her. It is Beethoven who made the blood flow from the tiny fairy ears. Hannah changes before his eyes. The tongue he loved to kiss hangs out of her mouth, the head crowned with black tresses falls off and rolls on the floor. Martin's foot dribbles.

Martin utters a stifled cry.

He runs away, bangs into the door, and wakes up.

⌒

The head. Not deceased. Not her. Not now! Just now, maybe. Someday. Which one first? She, or he?

See her again, just once. Get up, go, walk. Try it, no help. Too hard . . .

Hannah

In 1950, sixteen letters. Only six letters in 1951. Martin didn't ask for more photos of her, but he wanted one of Martha, her mother, whom he never met. He advised her to be discreet when she wrote him. He warned that on her next visit to Freiburg, she might witness some incidents that . . .

⬭

Elfriede had regained the upper hand.

Hannah hemmed and hawed before she left for Germany. When she talked to her husband about visiting Martin, Hannah no longer used names, but spoke of "Freiburg," the city where Martin's wife had her house, with Martin shut up inside. Hannah said "Freiburg" in the tone one refers to a prison and the shame of incarceration.

Would she see Freiburg? Undecided. What would Freiburg say if she appeared? Freiburg would make scenes, and Freiburg would suffer. Freiburg would not stand for her being there, and Freiburg would look at her with a hangdog expression. Freiburg was a couple and she, Hannah, the intruder.

In 1952—all in all, three letters from Martin—Blücher made her go. Urged on by her husband, Hannah saw Freiburg again. Elfriede made scenes. Martin suffered. Hannah backed off. Break. In New York, whenever she talked the incident over with Blücher, remembering Freiburg would depress Hannah.

In 1967, the personal name reappeared— *Martin*, in blue ink, at the end of a letter. This was the signal: Hannah knew she could now return to Freiburg, a German city where Martin awaited her. Freiburg had calmed down. Years of respite. And now, late in the day, Freiburg was nothing more than Elfriede, Martin's better half.

Someday Martin and Hannah would both be gone.

Then, life's interminable waiting, as Martin Heidegger put it, would be over. He would end up having dwelled on "Being-toward-death" at every step in his philosophy, all the time. With his peasant heritage, Martin always quoted the Bohemian plowman's saying: "As soon as a man is born, he's old enough to die." Someday, Martin and Hannah, both of them, would reach their last. Hannah merely shrugged at the thought. Not something to be obsessed with. After death, there was the void, the Sheol of the Old Testament. No more, no less.

Should one dwell on death or on life? Hannah had made her choice. Life, definitely. Nobody could do anything about death. One could hold on to life. Underwater, Hannah had always been able to kick hard enough to come up for air. Hold fast! Resist! Don't give in! Even in the French concentration camp, Hannah had not let mud and hunger defeat her.

Take risks, assume them. Carry papers coded in Greek under the nose of the German police, tell the nice police interrogator some nice little fibs, cross the border secretly. Turn into a pariah in France, a pariah in the United States, a foreigner everywhere. Unwittingly risk all, ponder the Eich-mann matter, bring out his banality, his terrifying obedience, and turn into a pariah among the Jews, a pariah in Israel, pain and sorrow. Hannah had done so many things. And she still had more to do, under this roof in Freiburg.

She was going to go for forgiveness, accepting Martin for what he was, and Elfriede, too, for that matter. To carry through, she'd have to be tough! So be it—hold on, don't give in.

While Martin would end up having spent his life in flight.

He had even written something about the musical form embracing the concept of flight, the fugue, in which two voices go their separate ways before joining in counterpoint.

In thinking, too, Martin ran away. The impostor! Hannah had never run away.

Never?

Oh, my God, she sighed.

Hannah
Königsberg, East Prussia, Summer 1920

She Runs Away to Stolp

"**H**annah is missing!"

That's what her mother will say. Or: "I've lost my daughter!" Or maybe she won't say anything. She will weep and moan. Too bad!

Hannah puts those burdensome thoughts out of her mind. She's going to do it. Everyone is asleep. That's essential to her excursion. Secrecy in the night, while the family slumbers.

She pulls her sheets aside very, very carefully, as if somebody might hear the fabric rustle. Her dress is draped over a chair. She puts it on over her nightgown, which is longer—a bit of *broderie anglaise* showing, so what. She fastens buttons in the dark, she does them up wrong, she starts over. Keep calm, Hannah, keep calm. Now for the most important item: to cover her curly mop, a little black veil snitched from her mother's dresser.

Barefoot, she goes downstairs carrying her sandals. One step at a time, she mustn't fall. She puts out her hands and gropes her way along: on the left, the buffet; opposite, the table, the chairs around it; then, the corner of the wardrobe, and directly in front of it, the door. Before going to bed, Hannah oiled the keyhole, a task assigned by her mother.

That's how she got the idea. Oiled, the lock makes no sound. It opens smoothly and tempts one to go out. What fun, to take off while the others are sleeping!

To leave the house when the moon is full and go to Stolp, the home of Anne Mendelssohn, a girl her own age whom Hannah doesn't know.

She's outside. Pointless to close the door. Her mother will know she's gone. Hannah puts on her sandals, sniffs the night odors of Königsberg. Tonight it's definitely not a full moon. Just a thin crescent, no more than a sarcastic smile, and she must crane her neck to see it above the rooftops. But stars abound, benevolent. It's warm. Hannah knows where she's going. She picks up a pebble near the doorstep and puts it in her pocket.

She walks through the streets.

There's no one about at this hour. Hannah feels liberated from daytime, home, school vacation. The streetcar is late. It's taking a long time! At last, wheels come squeaking along the tracks, a bell rings, cars rattle, here it is. The streetcar is at the stop. Hannah boards, lighthearted. The conductor eyes the black veil and the *broderie anglaise* showing below the dress of this frail young girl.

"A ticket for Stolp," says Hannah with assurance.

"All by yourself so late at night?" The conductor is surprised and suspicious.

"My grandmother is ill," she answers, sounding properly gloomy. "I have to go to Stolp. A ticket, please."

True or false? The kid's playing sweet and innocent. The conductor shrugs and starts up again.

There are a few workers on the streetcar, dozing. They're returning home or going to their factories. Hannah feels sorry for them. It's not often she sees Königsberg asleep. Hannah is wide awake, on the alert. Then she nods off. Stolp is not far from Königsberg, but in the dark she doesn't see the countryside.

Suddenly things look different. Between buildings, she glimpses a horizon fringed with gray. Already! Oh, no! It can't be morning, not yet! She presses her veiled forehead against the window and concentrates on the lightening of the gray. The streetcar moves along unhurriedly: stops, tickets, more and more passengers. Heavy with the life of the coming day, light prepares for a rebirth. Fast, faster!

She gets off the streetcar in the whiteness of dawn. The Mendelssohns live on the other side of the street, around the corner on the left. Anne Mendelssohn, the daughter of the family, has her shutters closed. Hannah doesn't even know whether she is dark or blonde.

Hannah's mother will not allow her to associate with the Mendelssohn girl. Anne's father is in prison because he supposedly seduced one of his patients. It is true that Doctor Mendelssohn is strikingly handsome. It isn't certain that the accusations against the unfortunate doctor are completely justified; anti-Semitism is rumored. But when it's a matter of morals, Martha doesn't fool around.

Hannah takes out her pebble and throws it. A shutter opens. Hannah removes her veil. "I've come to get you up!" She shouts at the top of her lungs.

"Who is it?" Anne's voice, sleepy.

"You don't know me!" yells Hannah. "I'm a friend of your sweetheart, Ernst Grumach!"

"At this hour? You're totally insane!"

"Let me in, or I'll break a window!"

Anne's dainty steps on the stairs and in the tiled entry.

Anne opens the door halfway, revealing a tired face. She looks annoyed.

Hannah throws her arms around Anne's neck.

If Ernst Grumach hadn't talked so much about his girl-friend, Hannah wouldn't have wanted to meet her. And if Hannah's mother hadn't declared the Mendelssohn house off-limits, Hannah wouldn't have decided to help fate along. Now, it's done. Because of a young man named Ernst Grumach, Anne and Hannah have met. They will be friends for life.

In Königsberg, Martha opens the door to Hannah's room and sees the unmade bed. Her heart skips a beat.

Hannah is incorrigible. Where has she gotten to? Is she on the street, all alone, in the woods, in the fields? Martha is furious. She is not worried. Well, not very. An hour goes by. Martha waits.

Hutzpah Hannah, she thinks, more and more restless. *Hannah the smarty. Just wait until I get my hands on you, my girl.*

Hannah the runaway. Tidying up her dresser drawers, Martha discovers that Hannah has made off with a black tulle veil. Her favorite.

Hannah

When Hannah returned home, Martha was angry but not tearful. Rather proud of her coup, Hannah explained she had been tempted by the starry June night and a desire for secrecy. Martha gave her a stern scolding. Once again, Hannah was proving that blood always tells.

Martha called up the ghost of her aunt, notorious in the family for conspiring with anarchists while disguised in a black veil. Same shape, same height, same melancholy eyes and love of secrecy as Hannah. No more mysteries, Martha said. No conspiring.

Not now, anyway.

Later Doctor Mendelssohn was released from prison, and he resumed his medical practice. Martha admitted he had been the victim of false rumors, and the two families got to know each other. Hannah and Anne were separated no more. Annchen, her beloved friend.

All the same, after the flight, Martha had shouted so loud that Hannah didn't run away again, except by writing her first poems. One wrote poetry on one's own, and in solitude. One surprised oneself creating. One did not publish, one concealed one's work. One hid inside it. Yes, poetry was an acceptable flight: a veil for thinking.

So Martin and Hannah did share a taste for running away. Like all lovers, they had run away, separately but together, as if performing their own fugue.

Two runaways who loved each other for life and beyond the grave. What a charming tale! Martin and Hannah could have turned into Tristan and Iseult, joined in death far from their respective spouses. "Tragedy," Martin would have deemed it. But instead, they were playing the last scene in a comedy of petit bourgeois life. Could anyone imagine a Tristan old and deaf, and an Iseult hobbling along on bad legs?

I wanted it that way, Hannah thought. *What exactly did I want?*

To avoid a breakup. To hold tight the thread of his life. To fill the absence that blotted out none of it, not Beethoven or the rumpled sheets of love, not the ecstasy or the waiting.

Or the swastika on Martin's lapel.

And, like a jellyfish defending itself in the deep sea, Hannah had sprayed a cloud of black ink over that damned cross.

Enough dreaming of the past! The teakettle was whistling. Elfriede wasn't back yet. Where had she gotten to? Was she with Martin? In her room, taking a pill? In the bathroom? The teakettle was about to boil over. Annoyed, Hannah told herself she had to turn it off. But which knob? There, the upper one, on the right? Which way?

"**N**o!" shouted Elfriede from the doorway. "You're turning the gas on instead of off. You'll asphyxiate us, Hannah!"

Flustered, Hannah turned the wrong knob.

"Let me do it," Elfriede said.

"I'm not very good in the kitchen."

"So I see." Elfriede smiled. She carefully spooned the black powder into the coffee filter, then added the boiling water and waited as it seeped through the holes. Efficient woman, not a superfluous gesture.

The time had come to learn the truth about Elfriede.

"Here's your poison." Elfriede served the coffee.

"I don't want it. Well . . . yes, I guess I do." Hannah swallowed the brew in one gulp. Elfriede wore an enigmatic little smile.

Hannah slammed her cup down on the table. "Oh, thank you. I don't feel a bit tired now. Let's go on, Elfriede. With our chat, that is."

"I think we've talked enough. I'm somewhat weary, Hannah. I admit your role in Martin's life. And you've come to understand mine. Everything has been said."

"Not quite."

"What's left?" asked Elfriede, surprised.

"You. Explain to me, honestly and sincerely, why you dragged Martin into Nazism."

Elfriede's gaze was icy. She collapsed in her chair. "Not again," she muttered. "You'll never be done with it!"

"About Martin's motives, I have some idea. But about yours, no."

"Mine? Do they matter?"

"You supported the National Socialist Party before he did.

I can't help thinking that he followed your lead. You're well aware of your influence, Elfriede. Your commitment."

"I didn't do much," she said defensively. "I was—"

"A Nazi," interrupted the pitiless Hannah. "The only woman who can explain to me how people could support those ideas."

"Not for long! We soon realized that—"

"In 1933, as soon as he is in power, your Führer promulgates anti-Jewish laws. Jews out of the universities. Jews out of the civil service. You were a party member."

"We never thought things would get to—"

"We've heard that before. Everybody's innocent."

"Would you please let me finish my sentences?" Exasperated, Elfriede stood up and paced the floor.

"Oh, do sit down, Elfriede. I won't interrupt you again."

No answer.

"I'm here to understand. To listen to you. This isn't a court of law—"

"Oh, yes it is!" Elfriede confronted her. "You just won't stop. Do I feel remorse? No! Am I guilty? Leave me alone!"

"Whatever you say." Hannah got ready to depart. She retrieved her cigarettes and put her purse over her arm.

"You aren't leaving!" Elfriede was indignant. "What about Martin?"

"You're the one I want to hear. You don't want to talk, so I'm leaving."

Elfriede sat down on the edge of her chair, defeated. "You really want to understand?"

"I want to understand everything, Elfriede. Even you."

Elfriede hesitated.

Hannah's dark eyes were inscrutable. Chin resting on her hand, Elfriede's enemy had assumed the air of the objective listener. She raised her eyebrows and said encouragingly: "Try, Elfriede."

Elfriede began. "You know that I was a student before I got married. Martin must have told you I was deeply involved in women's issues in those days. Do you remember his mentioning it?"

"Quite well. But I've never gone along with feminism. We can't overlook that little difference between men and—"

"Don't get started on your fancy theories! Or I'll just stop."

"I'm sorry." Hannah bit her lip.

"In my family, we had a sense of responsibility toward others. I was raised in the Lutheran faith, with its principles of social commitment. Martin's background was different. Being born a Catholic in Germany doesn't help you get ahead at the university. It's harder to have self-confidence. Martin has no notion of community. Martin was so shy, so put down—"

"Stick to yourself, please."

"Well . . ." Elfriede paused. "I was a member of the Youth Movement, which Martin joined and also Elisabeth Blochmann, who is Jewish, and a friend of ours. Martin helped her greatly during the war, by the way."

"I know. He found her a place in England. And you?"

"I worked in education and later I took up the cause of women workers. Germany's decline was impoverishing them."

"Decline." Hannah took special note of the word. "You're talking about the Weimar Republic."

"You're not going to defend. . . . Well, let's put it this way. Inflation hit working women quite hard. There was terrible unemployment. Where were you in 1929, Hannah? At the height of the crisis?"

"In Berlin. I'd just married Günther Stern."

"And you were a student."

"Right. But I was active, also."

"Not in quite the same way. Meetings, leaflets, demonstrations, talk until all hours. What did you do for the poor? I was educating. When the Nazi Party urged German women to join them and struggle in dignity, I didn't hesitate. I became a member."

"Simple as that," said Hannah. "Had you talked it over with Martin?"

"Martin was very proud of my independence. The man who was incapable of commitment delegated the commitment to me."

"Finally, we've gotten to the point," Hannah exulted. "So it's because of you he ended up a party member."

Elfriede couldn't let that stand: "He made up his own mind. The development of his ideas led him to. . . ." She stopped. Could she explain why Martin had become so fired up, so enthusiastic? It was hard, but she finished her sentence: ". . . to seek the regeneration of the world. Germany . . . you remember how it was. Our universe was disintegrating, the stench of moral decay was everywhere. And then there was an opening. A torch in the darkness."

"Always the same rhetoric," said Hannah, unmoved. "The bonfires in the night, the masses orderly and united, the SS on guard in black with daggers flashing bright, and so on."

"We believed it. The people believed it. The party was an opening to another world. Martin jumped in. I demanded nothing from him!"

"But you were happy to see him a Nazi."

"I was surprised. Martin was a different person. He was in a constant state of excitement. He talked nonstop, his eyes were bright, he didn't sleep, he was like a madman. For the first time since I had met him, Martin was doing something.

My duty was to support him, and that's what I did." Elfriede paused. She wanted to be done with it, so she added breathlessly: "I held out to the end, longer than he did."

"How interesting," said Hannah. "What do you mean?"

"After he resigned the rectorate in 1934, I kept on," she said, raising her head. "During the war, I defended the rights of women. I struggled so they would be allowed to dig trenches. My women obeyed me, even when they were pregnant or sick. It seems I terrorized them."

"I don't doubt it," said Hannah. "To command, the Prussian ideal!"

"I am Prussian by birth, Hannah. I'm not ashamed of it. I was working for the German nation. Think what you like, but I didn't do anything bad."

Hannah was silent. Elfriede's innocence was indefensible. There was a naive look of defiance in her eyes. She was within her rights, German to the core. Incapable of repentance. Eichmann in skirts. Hannah would have to start over: "Early on, when you saw Jews beaten, their houses ransacked, what did you think?"

"That it was very sad for them."

"That's not what I mean by thinking, Elfriede. Weren't you concerned about the injustice?"

"Yes, but it was inevitable. Some Jews said so themselves! They agreed that Jews had become too prominent in business and at the universities!"

"That was the opinion of a handful of irresponsible people!" Hannah was incensed.

"Maybe, but Jews put up with the new laws! And some of them even thought the laws were good ones! As for us, how could we have realized what was in the works?"

"Wait a minute," said Hannah. "In 1933, the first decree

came out barring non-Aryans from the civil service. That was the beginning. and you didn't even flinch, Elfriede."

"And neither did the Jews!"

"But when Jewish professors were dismissed, you didn't say a word."

"Martin said that a new world couldn't come into being without some losses. We decided to control the damage as much as we could. To ease the pain for our Jewish friends. Believe me, we didn't approve."

"I think you were an anti-Semite, Elfriede," said Hannah, uttering the term slowly and deliberately.

"And I say no!" Elfriede was mad. "Prove it!"

"Why did you turn your back on Günther Stern?"

"That's a lie. I don't even recall ever . . ."

Suddenly the memory came back, full force.

Elfriede
Todtnauberg, Black Forest, Summer 1924

Günther Stern by Firelight

The students sit in a circle, listening to Martin's every word. Night is falling over Todtnauberg. It is the hour the mountains come alive. Elfriede is standing ready with a bundle of sticks. Very soon, Martin will light the fire.

He speaks slowly, the magician they gaze at in fascination. He conjures up the Greek roots of Being, that gleam in the night. He quotes Hölderlin, he is fired up.

The young people wear shorts, and the girls have braids. Elfriede looks at them like a tender mother hen. After the collapse of Germany, the shame, the reparations, hope lives in them. They are beautiful, some frail, a little too frail. They need to be properly fed, built up. The destiny of Germany depends on these ecstatic youngsters.

Martin gives the signal. Elfriede piles the branches in the form of a cross. He puts a match to the wood, and the flames rise. Too many to focus on, they burn swift but not high. Tension is broken, backs unbend, the students laugh. One stands up and stretches, with a natural grace that takes Elfriede's breath away. Magnificent muscles gleam on his bare arms. What a fine, handsome German, this young stranger!

Elfriede can't take her eyes off him. He walks back and forth, strong and graceful. He is Nature. Abruptly, Martin dares him to stand on his head. The boy sits on the grass and in a split second his feet are high in the air. He is standing on his head, his back lit up by the dying fire. He holds the position for a long while. Effortlessly, he endures. Martin congratulates him, astonished, and the agile boy comes back to earth.

Elfriede can no longer contain herself. She comes out of the shadows, she draws closer. The boy is right in front of her, hands in his pockets. He has perfect, regular features.

"What is your name?" she asks.

"Günther."

"Like the Wagner hero. What a coincidence!"

"Wagner!" The boy frowns.

"Come with me," she says, taking his hand. "We have to go back to the real world, return to the house. See, there's Martin signaling me that the evening is over."

The embers glow. The young people rise and go down the hill. Elfriede walks hand in hand with Günther. The night is for confidences. She doesn't hesitate: "Someone like you, don't you want to join the National Socialist Party? You're young, strong, healthy, just the kind of shining child we need."

"I'm Jewish. My family name is Stern. It's Günther Stern. That means 'star.'"

Horrified, Elfriede claps her hand to her mouth. This perfect German is a Jew. He bears the name of the star that adorns the synagogue!

Before she turns her back on him, the boy flashes her a proud smile.

Elfriede can't stand reading in the young Jew's eyes her ill will, her revulsion. She can't bear that smile. She retreats into the shadows.

Never again. Never again will Elfriede reveal anything.

As they get ready for bed, Martin talks of a bonfire that would rise to the sky, an unforgettable blaze. To regenerate philosophy, vigorous action is needed, even if it means ruthlessly cutting off decayed limbs. "Thick log, thick ax," he says.

Henceforth, Elfriede shall prepare a fortress of logs. No more of those little branches that blaze up with a brief, puny flame.

Günther's muscles rippling in the firelight. Elfriede remembered those shoulders.

"I see it's coming back to you," Hannah said.

"Oh, no, it's a blank. I'm trying to attach a face to that name." Elfriede was blushing.

"Odd, isn't it? We forget so much!"

"Martin and I never hurt our Jewish friends," Elfriede reiterated. "Quite the contrary. We felt terrible—"

"But when old Husserl died, Martin didn't attend his funeral. His own professor, his mentor! A Jew Martin had let them drive from the university! A giant of a philosopher! Showing up at the services would have been dangerous, I suppose!"

"Martin was sick in bed! He was shaking with fever—"

"But you weren't there either. He could have asked you to represent him! You didn't. You didn't even send his wife a letter of condolences!"

"Afterwards, Martin regretted his behavior," said Elfriede. "It's just that he was ashamed."

"I'm not talking about Martin." Hannah was enraged. "Where were you?"

"Taking care of Martin." Elfriede, shaking, was barely audible. "This is ghastly. When Professor Husserl died . . ." Elfriede couldn't finish her sentence.

Elfriede
Freiburg im Breisgau, April 23, 1933

Flowers for Malwine

When Martin arrived home from the university, he gave her the sad news: Professor Husserl has been dismissed, in accordance with the decree on non-Aryans in the civil service. The decree dates from April 7.

"Well, it's to be expected," said Elfriede. "Since he and his wife are Jewish. Poor Husserl!"

"It's the new law of the Reich," Martin replied with a sigh. "And by definition, laws are merciless."

"And their son was arrested by the Gestapo recently," she reminded him. "Do you want to go visit? That might console them a bit."

Martin was hesitant. "I don't know. The last time we got together, Malwine Husserl didn't hide her feelings. I think she holds our political involvement against us. She's likely to consider our calling on them a provocation. No, no visits. Send them flowers, let that speak for us."

Elfriede decides she'll write a letter to accompany the flowers. It's time to say something.

Nothing could alter student Heidegger's debt to his mentor, Edmund Husserl. No path taken will extinguish that gratitude, so difficult to put into words especially in light of recent events, and so on. More than likely, swept up in the overall excitement, some petty bureaucrats erred and went too far, as happened in the 1918 Revolution, when enraged Reds executed willy-nilly.

Nobody can keep idiots from making mistakes. Professor Husserl is a national treasure, and the Reich would be wrong to deprive the country of a such a man. Simply an error, which will be corrected. The Reich cannot attack Germany's worthy Jews. If the others are driven out, that's all right. But Malwine Husserl?

Malwine is a good Jewess. Not like those brazen students who used to flock around Martin in Marburg. What was her name, the girl from Königsberg? Sarah, or something like that. Sarah Arendt. Or maybe it was Hannah. Trashy little thing! A come-hither look, bobbed hair, tight skirts, and high-heeled boots! No, Malwine was never like those girls. And her husband is a respectable Jew. They should have made an exception for Professor Husserl.

She signs the letter for both Heideggers.

At the florist's, Elfriede makes her selection with special care: iris, peonies, nothing yellow. A simple, tasteful bouquet. She will drop the flowers off at the Husserls herself. She has done her duty. And she loves Malwine with all her heart.

Elfriede

Two memories flooding back, one right after the other!

Martin had never been anti-Semitic. He didn't think about Jews; he didn't notice anything. The most telling signs seemed to elude him: the name, the nose, the dark and melancholy eyes, the gift for music, the insolence, the grace. In his hometown Martin had never run across Jews from the East, emerging from squalid shtetls with their frock coats, sidelocks, and beards. And when Hannah appeared, he hadn't recognized in her the deadly Jewess, seductress of married men. Elfriede was sure of that. Otherwise, Hannah would not have had Martin.

Thus, when it came to anti-Semitism, Martin was above suspicion. And Elfriede had thought she, too, was irreproachable, until those memories rose up and made her cheeks burn.

Elfriede was quite astonished. Yes, the encounter with that boy showed she had been anti-Semitic, one time at least, if not more. No getting around it. By her very presence, Hannah was bringing to the surface what had been buried under the layer of time. Sorceress!

But Elfriede merely shared a sentiment widespread among the German people; indeed, if it had not been general, the nation would not have gone along with the first anti-Jewish laws! The evil didn't come from her. It was collective. Germany's difficult history was the cause: Was it *her* fault if the rest of Europe had oppressed the Weimar Republic after the

First World War? Was Elfriede supposed to be responsible for decline, unemployment, and a poverty that contrasted cruelly with the outrageous wealth of the Jewish international bankers?

Besides, the bouquet sent to the Husserls proved that Elfriede did change. As a warm-hearted German woman, she was not insensitive to the suffering of others. And it was too easy for Hannah to cite their eternal disputes as a sign that Elfriede was anti-Semitic. Hannah was Jewish, of course. Arendt. But more significant, she was Martin's passion. If she'd been a blonde Aryan, Elfriede would have followed the same course: war to the last.

A long conflict. Elfriede had succeeded in making Martin's passion difficult. As for the other woman herself, Elfriede kept her at bay with a stick, as one would a snake.

Except now, in the kitchen. The snake had coiled about the stick and was spitting her venom.

Anti-Semitic, Frau Heidegger? Elfriede would not confess to anything. She would wield her stick and strike a few blows.

"So, when Husserl died?" Hannah was tired of waiting for the rest of the sentence. "What were you going to say?"

"Nothing important." Elfriede could barely speak.

"Why such a face?" Hannah was concerned. "Does your stomach hurt?"

"It's a problem I have." Elfriede sounded grouchy. "Heartburn. I have to take pills. That's what I was doing just now."

"With me, it's lung trouble. What you'd expect from smoking. Bad legs, too. It's hard to walk."

"At least old age brings a measure of tranquillity," commented Elfriede. "See how calmly we're talking."

Allay Hannah's suspicions. Wait a minute or two. The old lady was lighting another cigarette.

Launch the attack. Elfriede's tone was casual: "Incidentally, Hannah, weren't you yourself accused of anti-Semitism?"

"Forget it," Hannah snapped. "The topic was *your* anti-Semitism, I believe."

Hannah wasn't lowering her guard. A setback. Wait, dodge. "I can prove I have nothing against Jews. When Professor Husserl was dismissed, I took his wife flowers and a letter I'd written."

"Yes, my old friend Jaspers told me. So you sent a bouquet. But you didn't protest publicly."

"They would have thrown us in prison."

"Then what? If all Germans had done the same, would Hitler have thrown the entire nation in prison?"

"Martin protected several Jewish faculty members. Why, Elisabeth Blochmann went—"

"You told me already," Hannah interrupted. "And that's not the point."

"What? You mean helping Jews wasn't the point?" Elfriede was offended. "And what should we have done?"

"I'm going to spell it out for you, Elfriede. Let me tell you about an experience I had."

"Not again!"

"You don't know this story!" Hannah slammed her hand on the table. "It would be good for you to hear it. When I was first in the United States, I spent some time in Massachusetts studying English, which I didn't speak. They put me up at the home of a Mrs. Giduz, an unremarkable person. But when the United States entered the war, this ordinary American woman fired a letter off to President Roosevelt because she was shocked by the internment of Japanese Americans."

"Martin wrote letters to the government, too!" Elfriede exclaimed.

"Letters of recommendation, not protest! Mrs. Giduz simply referred to fundamental liberties. She didn't assume a begging tone, she didn't try to arouse her government's pity, she wasn't requesting a special favor. She was indignant! That's the difference between you and a good American citizen, Elfriede."

"I'm not an American. I'm German."

"Exactly," said Hannah curtly. "You're German. What were you supposed to do, Elfriede? Sound the alarm, that's what! Refuse to obey. But that didn't even cross your mind. Why not? Because your anti-Semitism is so deep-rooted it blinds you to everything else. You were very sad. Well, how nice! Is it possible to save someone by feeling sad?"

Hannah had finished her tirade. Elfriede was weighing her reply. She sighed and went ahead. "If I'm an anti-Semite, then Martin is, too."

"Him? Of course he isn't. I'm living proof!"

"In 1933, he said a new chapter in the history of Being was in the works. That only the Führer himself was the new Germany's law and reality."

"Don't hark back to what we already know. Martin was stricken with a bad fever, an attack of romanticism."

"To the point of extolling the person of the Führer?" Elfriede was taunting her. "To the point of telling his friend Jaspers that Hitler's lack of culture didn't matter because he had wonderful hands?"

"And how do you know about that? What next!"

"Jaspers told you in a letter, then you mentioned it to Martin, and Martin told me. He was very upset. If your correspondence with Jaspers were ever published the remark would appear in print and be taken the wrong way."

"My correspondence published! An honor I don't deserve."

"No. But this shows that Martin is still afraid of you. Even when it's a matter of an insignificant comment. It was just a joke!"

Hannah looked thoughtful. "I don't think Martin was joking. Once again, he was dreaming. The Third Reich, dream of greatness with a supreme leader as hero. Enthusiasm excites, embellishes. Adolf Hitler was an exceptionally ugly man, and you people all saw him as handsome. So, the hands—"

"That's right. Martin was dreaming a waking dream. And so was I. We all were. I don't see why you accuse just me, and not my husband."

"Because he's a dreamer and you aren't," said Hannah. "I don't know anyone who is more of a reasoner than you. Realistic, shrewd, the opposite of Martin."

"Concede that it was a collective dream," said Elfriede with a sigh. "Agree, and that should settle matters. You have to believe I wasn't as reasonable as you think. Nobody is beyond dreaming when the dream brings hope."

"And harms the Jews? And is built on their blood? There's your racism, right there!"

The moment had arrived. Go on the offensive, now. Elfriede took a deep breath and plunged ahead: "Speaking of racism, why did they accuse you, a Jew, of being anti-Semitic?"

"So we're back to that." The cigarette shook in Hannah's fingers. She spoke slowly: "It's true I was the subject of a controversy in the United States. I have no desire to discuss the matter with you, Elfriede."

"What right have you to refuse?"

"In the name of right itself! You're in no position to act as judge and jury. And I've had enough. Since it's come to this, I'm leaving."

She jumped up in anger. The door banged behind her. Elfriede was alone. Hannah had left without her purse.

That meant Hannah would have to come back. Just a matter of time. For sure, Madame Arendt would take advantage of the little explosion and make a big thing of it with Martin.

Patience.

Martin
Freiburg im Breisgau, December 1944

The Piano

It is Saturday evening. The bombing of the city has begun. The enemy armies are invading Germany. Tomorrow Martin goes away. He has to leave before they arrive.

Tomorrow he will say goodbye to his wife and travel to Messkirch. Awaiting him there is his brother Fritz, to whom he turns in times of trouble. The two of them will devote themselves to an urgent task: putting Martin's philosophy manuscripts in order. The war is nearing its end, the Reich is doomed, Martin is leaving. Elfriede will watch over the Freiburg house.

But Martin wants to spend tonight with his friends Georg and Edith Picht. Like Martin, Georg is a philosopher. Edith is a pianist. Martin had a sudden, overwhelming urge to see them. He has entered their house as if it were an ordinary visit, feeling rather awkward for coming. He looks tired.

Two months earlier he was drafted into the militia and sent to protect a bridge over the Rhine, at Breisach. Decree from the Führer, October 18, 1944: call-up of all males sixteen to sixty. Martin has been home just a week. When his detachment set out on its mission, the bridges had already fallen. Too late. The end is at hand.

Martin has a hard time expressing himself. Before he flees, he would like to . . . He wants to . . .

Martin can't finish his sentences. Silently, Edith stands behind his chair and puts her hands on his shoulders. Martin gazes at her concert grand. The gleaming top is raised high to reveal the felt-covered hammers and the taut strings. A famished mouth clamors for its music.

"Play me something, Edith," he begs.

Edith sits at the piano, places her fingers on the keys as she tries to choose. "Schubert's Sonata in B-flat Major," she says.

Martin nods.

Edith's hands move swiftly over the keys and the melody rises.

The storm is over and the sun has just reappeared. The first movement sheds golden light over a now-peaceful world. The caring music caresses the lost children, the scratched cheeks. It is a clear sound that ends as it began, in all simplicity.

The second movement weeps the tears of rain. Thunder still rumbles in the distance. The downpour has soothed the black piano, the hail has softened the earth. The notes dig deep, sow the seeds scattered by the winds and prepare the tomorrow of the plants. The now is nothing. A just-now, there will be. Forthwith is but an interval of brightness with drops of water falling against the newly returned sun. The music of the third movement gathers up the remnants of the storm and renews.

Lively as a blue jay, the last movement flies joyfully above the restored ruins. A determined, insistent octave repeats a warning—a knell. Sweeping, airy flights between the beats of the measure . . . Then, any obstacle fades away, and a present emerges, the Sunday of Care, the return of peace.

At the last chord, Martin closes his eyes. The echo ripples and disappears. Deep silence fills the Picht house.

Martin looks at Georg and smiles. "That's something we can't do with philosophy," he says.

In the distance, a low rumbling shakes the vigilant city.

"That is constant," says Georg.

That, music; that, bombs. In terms of the passing of time, the "that" doesn't count.

"I have to go home," says Martin, with a brief sigh. "I leave before dawn tomorrow."

"When will you return?" Edith asks.

Martin evades the question with a vague gesture. *When it's all over.*

"Write something in our guest book," she says. "We'd like that, Martin."

With a sure hand, Martin puts down the words: "A fall is not final."

His fingers around the pen, he hesitates momentarily, then continues. "Within every fall there is the assurance of rising again."

Then he says goodbye to his friends and steps into the cold December night.

Barely outside, he hears the roar of the tempest that shatters the piano, twists the vibrating strings. The music breathes its last and Martin runs in the snow, he knows not where.

He is no longer there. He is spared. He is asleep.

But Hannah had still not returned.

Elfriede began to worry. Would she have left without her purse? But how? On foot, in the rain? Hannah was crazy enough to—

The door flew open. Hannah said, "I forgot my purse."

"You can't go off so impulsively!" Elfriede exclaimed. "Stay—"

"Out of the question!"

"You are afraid, then." Elfriede sighed.

"Me, afraid? Not a bit! If you hadn't taken that tone, I'd be willing to explain what happened."

Elfriede said nothing.

Hannah went on: "Don't be so Prussian. Or I will leave."

Silent, Elfriede buried her face in her hands.

"Is that too much to ask?" Hannah sounded impatient. "Are you listening? Are you going to answer me?"

"I don't know how to talk to you any more," Elfriede whispered. "So I'm keeping quiet."

Hannah paused, perplexed. Unshed tears glistened in the enemy's eyes. "All right, Elfriede. Give me one good reason why I should explain the controversy I was embroiled in." Then Hannah sat down.

A timorous Elfriede pushed her own chair back. "Have you talked to Martin about this?"

"No, but he hasn't brought it up."

"Well, *I* am asking for some explanation." Elfriede could barely get her words out. "To me, that's only fair."

"Fair?" echoed Hannah, frowning.

"I've explained how I see things. Now it's your turn. The rules of war."

"Good enough!" Hannah's voice rose. "I shan't be evasive."

"That's nice of you, Hannah."

"I'm not being nice! I'm trying to be fair."

Elfriede's reply was a firm, approving nod.

Hannah began nervously: "They accused me of slandering the Jews. You can see how preposterous that was. The debate was about my report on the Eichmann trial in Jerusalem."

"I'm familiar with your book," Elfriede said abruptly.

"It's a painful subject, Elfriede. I'd like a little coffee."

Elfriede jumped up.

"It's almost cold," she said, embarrassed.

"I'll drink it anyway."

The taste of the lukewarm coffee intensified Hannah's own bitterness. She gulped down the whole cup. Then she spoke, controlling her emotions: "When I wrote my account of the trial, I'd no idea of the fuss it would cause."

"Oh, yes, I'm sure you had no idea."

"Another remark like that, Elfriede, and I'm leaving!"

"I'm sorry," Elfriede said. "It was unintentional."

"Well, you should make it your intention to keep quiet," Hannah grumbled. "The scandal grew out of a misunderstanding. They took me to task for asking the Jewish witnesses: 'Why didn't you resist?' "

"A legitimate question."

"But I'm not the one who asked it! I was quoting the Israeli prosecutor, whom I attacked in no uncertain terms. He asked all the surviving witnesses that horrible question—how outrageous! They accused me of disrespect toward the Jews. Me!"

"While you were merely stating the facts," Elfriede said.

"I didn't implicate the Jews, Elfriede! I simply tried to understand what had really happened."

"What happened is beyond understanding," Elfriede said.

"Oh no, that isn't true. In April of 1933, they promulgate the first decree. Nobody objects. In 1935, they pass the Law for the Protection of German Blood and German Honor. The machinery is set in motion. They revoke, they expropriate, they comb genealogies, they set up categories of Jewish ancestry, they take note of half and quarter Jews. Nobody objects."

"But, Hannah, when you say 'they,' who do you mean?"

"All of you!" Hannah exploded. "The 'they' who make the decisions, the 'they' who accept them, and I'm talking about you, Elfriede! Do you understand?"

"Yes," she whispered.

"Then they do more. They enact the Racial Shame Law and they throw Jewish men in prison for having Aryan wives. Nobody protests. They expel the Jews to the marches of the East. And since the Jews have to be put somewhere, they put them behind walls. They create ghettos. That's where Eichmann comes in. Are you following me?"

A tense Elfriede nodded, "Yes."

"I see that you've followed." Hannah's tone was sarcastic. "Eichmann followed, too. For Nazism to work, everything had to run perfectly. And all Adolf Eichmann did was carry out orders to perfection."

"To perfection!" Elfriede was surprised. "That monster?"

"No! Just a conscientious petty bureaucrat."

Hannah
Jerusalem 1961

The First Day of the Trial

She's holding her notebook on her lap. Tension in the auditorium is high. The bulletproof glass booth is awaiting the accused. He is about to enter. Excited, Hannah drops her pen. By the time she's retrieved it, the accused is there. A side view, behind the window.

He is a sharp-featured individual, one of those skinny old men who sit under the lindens in German village squares on balmy days. He wears black-rimmed glasses. He must be far-sighted, or nearsighted perhaps—anyway, his sight is poor. The photographers' flashes make him blink. He seems to have tears in his eyes.

The man is remorseful or his eyes wouldn't be moist. Hannah leans forward for a better look. The accused is taking out a handkerchief. So he really is crying.

No. He brings the handkerchief to his nose and blows loudly. Somewhere in the auditorium there is a stifled nervous laugh. "Shhh," go the indignant whispers. Judges are silent.

The man in the glass booth has a cold. Unruffled, he folds his handkerchief, rearranges it in his pocket, settles in his chair again, all without lifting his head.

This isn't the monster she was expecting. That the world was expecting.

"*Beth Hamishpath.* All rise!" shouts the bailiff.

Hannah rises with the spectators. Enter the judges, three black robes. The man is standing, calm.

Hannah is gripped by fear. The trial of the century is beginning, with a phantom defendant. She wanted to see for herself the only surviving Nazi war criminal as he faced the judges of Israel, and the moment has arrived! The man is a nonentity. The proceedings are underway. He answers the questions docilely, in the nasal voice that accompanies a cold.

Hannah tries to take notes. But it's no good; she can't write. She lays down her pen and contemplates the man in the glass booth, the animal responsible for millions of Jewish deaths.

The penned sheep, bleating. Distraught, she realizes that her fear comes from her. Because of the banality of a court trial when she was expecting the grandeur of Greek tragedy, with all its solemnity of punishment. She is afraid of the banality of mankind and of the banality of the defendant, the state prosecutor, the public, even the unfortunate witnesses.

Above all, she fears discovering the worst: the banality of evil itself, for this colorless little man certainly must have been touched by evil. Not for a moment does she doubt the defendant's guilt. And not for a moment does she believe she is face-to-face with the real culprit.

The real culprit is in everyone. Without exception.

They caught the accused in Argentina, where he was leading a happy and uneventful life. He surrendered without resistance. He is sure to be hanged. He has already said that public hanging in Jerusalem is fine with him.

Suddenly Hannah realizes that he is obedient. Even here in Jerusalem, answering questions behind glass, willingly and with such ease.

Guilty of being normal.

She will say so.

"**I** can still see him in his glass booth in Jerusalem," Hannah said. "Reasonable, serious. Yes, the great Nazi war criminal was a petty bureaucrat. Eichmann had followed the Führer's orders, meticulously and obediently."

"Blindly," said Elfriede. "Like all of us."

"Eichmann wasn't blind. Nor was he a vicious man. At first, he was in charge of rounding up the Jews from the East, which he did. Correctly, as he did everything."

"I don't see how you can murder correctly!" said Elfriede.

"In the beginning, Eichmann wasn't supposed to murder the Jews; he just had to send them away. He dreamed of finding them a place, Madagascar, for example, or lands farther to the East—somewhere else, anyway. He was even rather nice to his Jews. He had friendly feelings toward his 'clients,' as he called them."

"Like us," said Elfriede softly.

"God in Heaven! I never said you were a war criminal. But I do say anyone is guilty who doesn't protest a racist act."

"Let's get back to the accusations against you," Elfriede countered.

"Don't use that tone with me, Elfriede!"

"I'm sorry."

Her hand trembling a little, Hannah slowly extracted a cigarette from the package, lit it, and set her lighter down. Then she took the first drag and blew smoke in Elfriede's face. "Let's continue. When he got the order to transport the Jews to Auschwitz, he felt betrayed. They were stealing his Jews! He tried to be cunning, to negotiate. He realized what he would be doing with his trucks and railroad cars, his shunting of the trains. In the end he obeyed, like a good German."

Elfriede looked deathly pale. "You're exaggerating."

"Not in the least. You say you've read me? It's all there! Eichmann fought for reduced train fares, so the operation would cost as little as possible. He signed invoices, he stamped great stacks of forms. And he transported his dear Jews to Auschwitz."

"But he wasn't there," said Elfriede.

"Oh, yes, he was. Eichmann visited Auschwitz several times. He himself wrote up the proceedings of the Wannsee Conference of 1942, which worked out the Final Solution; he knew all the details of the plan. He knew what he didn't want to see at Auschwitz. He avoided the gas chambers. He inspected the barracks, the sheds, the dining halls, the offices. Eichmann's Auschwitz—for him just a prison camp."

"Yet he suffered mental anguish," said Elfriede.

"Yes!" Hannah sounded bitter. "That makes it worse. He was a kindhearted person, like you. But he let it happen. Like the police, the conductors, the stationmasters, all of you. And there's your German guilt!"

"But we didn't know what was going on! If we had—"

"Same old refrain." Hannah was annoyed. "In 1934, I can understand it. But in 1944, Elfriede."

"No one knew what was happening in the camps, Hannah. Not even you."

Yes, in New York, the first time Heinrich and Hannah heard the unpleasant rumors, they couldn't believe their ears. What, the Nazis had decided to exterminate all the Jews in Europe? Unthinkable. Militarily, there was no need. It was disinformation, mad ravings. What would be their motive? Was it gratuitous?

But why the deportation of so many German Jews back in 1938? That had already been done, and gratuitously. In late 1942, Hannah and Heinrich saw with their own eyes a document sent by the Jewish community in Vienna: a copy of a memorandum on gas chamber procedures. There was no longer any room for doubt. Henceforth, the unthinkable was part of the real world.

⟨⟩

"We found out in 1942, Elfriede." Hannah spoke firmly. "And *we* were in New York!"

Elfriede looked skeptical.

"I assure you that we knew!" said Hannah. "We joined the struggle in America. We organized public marches, we alerted—"

"But that's not why they got after you, Hannah," Elfriede said, sweet as could be. "Am I right?"

"You won't leave it alone! But who is after me? Nationalists! And Jewish nationalists at that!"

"Now we're making progress," said Elfriede coolly. "They attacked you because you pointed a finger at the part Jews played in their own massacre. I did read your book."

"Then, may I ask why you're questioning me?"

"Because I want to hear it from you!"

"Oh, really!" Hannah was enraged. "You can't be serious!"

"Then I'll speak for you," Elfriede persisted, her voice low. "Some of the Jewish councils agreed to make up lists of Jews for the Nazis. If they had refused—and this is what you wrote—the task of extermination would have become complicated. The executioners wouldn't have been able to massacre such great numbers of human beings. You're the one who said it. That thousands of lives would have been spared. That Jews are guilty of not resisting, of letting themselves be killed. And it's not my fault."

Elfriede had limited herself to reciting the facts, sadly, without rage. Her pain-filled eyes seemed to say: *Understand that we are all guilty. Mankind is like that. It is not us. It is not I. It is not he. It is others, all the others, even the victims.* Elfriede's voice had contained no note of accusation. Nothing but an unbearable compassion.

Hannah looked for something that could serve as a judge's gavel. The sugar bowl. Hannah pounded it on the table, three times, as in a courtroom

Elfriede jumped.

"I cannot let you get away with that," said Hannah. "Who did the killing? The Jews or the Germans? I refuse to be considered a 'guilty party.' Absolutely not. It's a question of the categorical imperative and the moral law, Elfriede."

"Morality, philosophy. Do they serve any purpose? What philosopher could have prevented those horrors?"

Hannah, on the rack, trembled.

Hannah
Basel, March 4, 1969

She Bids the Philosopher Farewell

Standing stiffly in a black dress, Madame Arendt holds her speech in her hand. She has prepared five pages of notes, and she would prefer to talk without them. But she is overcome by emotion. So much so that she cannot be spontaneous.

Jaspers died a week ago. In her purse, Hannah has the telegram she received from Basel: "Karl died at 13:43 today, Trude." Poor Gertrud, whom Karl loved his whole life, he so tall, she so tiny. Hannah quickly boarded a plane, and now she is here, about to deliver a eulogy for Professor Jaspers.

He was destined to live with illness his whole life. Weak lungs, colds, often bedridden, the great philosopher was destined to survive the threats of the Nazis. Gertrud is Jewish. Because of her they went into exile in Switzerland. After the war, Karl Jaspers accepted Swiss citizenship, an honor rarely offered. He, the perfect German, died abroad, in the country he had chosen.

Jaspers, the resistance of the powerless, perseverance, courage. The honor of German philosophy under Nazism. Lover, husband, worthy on all counts, he will remain Hannah's best friend.

Friend! That does not begin to describe it.

Friends, Hannah is inundated with them. Dinners, phone calls, letters, gossip, squabbles, displays of affection, all that. Cave chatter, Plato would have said it. After the Eichmann controversy, Hannah lost some of her dearest friends. Which means they probably weren't really friends. But with Karl and Gertrud, never the slightest shadow of a doubt.

Nothing damaged their friendship. Not even the cruel separation of the war years, the long silence between Hannah's flight and the end of the war, a period when she did not know whether they were still alive and when the Jaspers had no news of Hannah. Peace arrived, and the professor became the friend of his former student; Hannah met Gertrud, and the three of them were bound together with a sure affection.

Jaspers was not only a "friend" to Hannah: he was the incarnation of friendship, in the Greek sense of *philia,* that victorious love with no defeats or betrayals, no pretenses, no neglect. A steel cable across life's abysses, friendship is by definition strong and solid.

With him, Hannah partook of the world. There is no other definition of friendship. Without Karl Jaspers, the world is less: she will have to partake of it without him, with Trude alone.

What remains are the memories. His office, where the girl Hannah worked on her dissertation. The armchair in which he sat and cast his kindly gaze upon her, one eye nearly shut and the other wide open. Indignation, reflections, heartbreak over Germany, unanswerable questions, private jokes, picnics, birthday presents, baskets of blue hyacinths—in short, life. And their endless discussions on the subject of Martin.

Hannah runs her eyes over her mourning outfit, fiddles with the white cuffs, clears her throat, and begins:

"We are gathered here in the public arena he so loved . . ." Karl was a fighter. Hannah continues, stirred up, but in control. He was a citizen of the community, willing to be a man without a country. For Jaspers, the compost of philosophy demanded of the philosopher physical frailty, exile, or "an insignificant little country where one's activities do not bring notoriety."

Jaspers chose the third alternative: Hannah does not uses those words in Basel. She says Karl Jaspers left Germany to remain a philosopher.

Like her. Everyone knows that.

The applause upsets her.

Once Karl wrote her: "We always bid each other farewell without ever leaving each other." In advance, he had a say in the mourning Gertrud would wear—a black dress to satisfy convention, a white collar to signify a good death. Tomorrow Hannah will put on the white collar, too, but she will add a touch of red to symbolize his active mind.

Did Jaspers serve some purpose? Yes, he personified the strength of the weak.

Two men had been there to support Hannah during the Eichmann controversy. The friend and the husband, Karl and Heinrich. Two partners taking responsibility for the same planet, concerned about the city and about truth. Karl had died, then Heinrich. Martin and Hannah were left, the philosophers.

ᗡ

"You're wondering whether philosophy serves a purpose, Elfriede?" said Hannah. "It's funny you should ask. What would Martin say?"

"That philosophy has no political utility," was Elfriede's ready answer. "It serves no purpose."

"If that's the case, how will anyone understand the Eichmann story? Courts don't think, they follow procedures and apply the law. Guilty or not guilty, that's the only question of interest to them. But that's not enough for the philosopher! Look at me, for example—I had to bring out the banality of evil. And they haven't forgiven me."

"Really? I don't see why not."

"It's so much easier to believe in a diabolical plot! But it's not like that! Evil is most unassuming."

"All the same, without the Jewish councils, the Führer's entourage couldn't have achieved its ends," mused Elfriede. "Dreadful."

"The Führer's *entourage*? And him, you've forgotten? You did read *Mein Kampf* before joining the party, Elfriede!"

"Nobody took seriously the business about annihilating the Jews," Elfriede said. "It didn't make an impression on me at the time."

"Yes, nothing out of the ordinary there. Terribly banal, in fact."

"What stayed with me were his ideas about the rebirth of the German people. And, too, there's no proof Hitler was told about—"

"You'll always be just what you are!" shouted Hannah. "Incurably German."

"Incurably! But loving your country doesn't make you ill."

"It can. The disease is called nationalism. And I underwent a successful cure, among my people. I'm talking about the Jewish people. As soon as the Eichmann trial began, I realized that the state I had been dreaming of was a Utopia. A state is by definition unjust."

Elfriede brightened up: "That's just what Martin said in 1933."

"But *he* obeyed. Not I. I needed a thorough purging to get the state of Israel out of my system. I called that cleansing *Cura Posterior*. My long-delayed cure."

Elfriede's blue eyes were wide with astonishment. "Cured of what?" she inquired.

"Of the nation," replied Hannah.

"I don't understand. You no longer love Israel?"

"Let's go over it, Elfriede." Hannah sighed. "It's true that I loved the idea of the state of Israel. I had been a passionate Zionist, but what I saw with my own eyes in Israel disturbed me. The idea shattered when it came up against reality."

"A state organizes, orders, forbids, governs," said Elfriede. "I don't think that a state dreams. It is ruled by reality. So what disturbed you?"

"I had defended the right of Jews to have their own territory but not as a means for perpetuating military values. When I was there, I saw boys singing around a campfire. I hated that moment."

"Why?" Elfriede asked in all innocence. "At Todtnauberg, Martin and I had some magnificent bonfires for our guests."

Martin
Freiburg im Breisgau, May 27, 1933

He Makes a Speech

The big day is here. Martin has carefully prepared his inaugural address; he wants it to create an impact. A printed version is to be distributed by the official press of the Third Reich. His colleagues and the student body are waiting: He is about to be tested. A moment of truth for Germany's future, the investiture of Freiburg's new rector will be a memorable ceremony.

With that it mind, Professor Heidegger sent his colleagues a memorandum from the rector's office stating that at the conclusion of his address the audience would rise, give the Nazi salute as they sang the "Horst Wessel Lied," and finish by hailing victory with the customary shout, *Sieg Heil*.

That was four days ago. His directive was not well received. The new rector sent out a second one, stating that the salute would be reserved for the fourth stanza of the Nazi anthem. Everything is in order.

In the anteroom, Martin holds his notes in a hand that trembles.

"Your hands are shaking," Elfriede says.

"This is like taking an exam." He makes a joke of it.

"Come on, have a little drink of water."

"No thank you," he says, smoothing his hair. "I have to march into battle now."

And he walks toward an amphitheater that is full to bursting. The applause is intoxicating. He sets down his papers, collects himself briefly, raises his head and begins.

The essence of the university does not lie in the training of students! Those who endeavor to promote the mere advancement of knowledge degrade the university. The essence of the university is learning, as discovered by the Greeks in the early days of philosophy, when the brightest of light shone between the columns of their temples. Yes, like the Greeks, we must be heroic, or the university can no longer be called a university.

Truth is a challenge, a battle won by mounting the attack, the great cleansing of war! Without the magnificence of the National Socialist revolution, Germany would lose the battle for truth, as before . . .

Martin senses the shivers going through the audience and his excitement grows.

God is dead! he shouts. The culture died with him. We must march into battle and fight, with no rear guard. We must stand alone if need be, heroically!

He is straining his voice, raising his arms.

The absurd is a challenge to meaning.

The students rise in unison and sing the song about Horst Wessel. "Flag raised, ranks closed, the storm troopers march on, firm and calm, / Comrades who gunned down the Red Front, the Reaction, you are with us in spirit, you march in our ranks. / The way is free and clear for the brown battalions . . ."

Tears in his eyes, Martin sings with them of the glory of

the young hero who sacrificed himself for his party. "Millions, full of hope, to the swastika turn their eyes . . ."

Martin wants to be the first to raise his hand in salute and he whispers *"Sieg Heil,"* his voice cracking with emotion. He has passed his exam in Nazism.

Then, bonfires from deep within the forest blaze up in all four corners of the hall and the flames devour the benches, the desks, the paneling, all the wood in the university, while an impassive audience gives the Nazi salute.

Even unto death. Students, professors, the fire has reduced them to ashes, and the fire reaches the platform. Martin sees the flames licking about the steps, he feels burning heat sweep over him, he must stand alone, his arm raised.

The hand catches first. Then the arm. Then the collar of his suit. Martin stands alone, arm raised.

Before the fire makes his head explode, he wakes up.

⟨⟩

Again? Why? The head . . . Nightmares. The women's fault. Abandoned me!

Nazi? Explain, Professor. Card, insignia, salute, yes. Mistake? Do I say it? Never. Stupidity—one word, even one. Not to talk about. Be quiet. Tell us, Professor! Question? Silence.

Don't sleep. Watch fire. Don't give in. Eyes open. No, don't close! No strength. Defeated.

Elfriede

The bonfires at Todtnauberg, magnificent!

Once again, Elfriede was all admiration. A few feet from Stern's muscular legs burned a small but stubborn fire. The flames rose, high under the stars, and Martin held forth, lyrical before his uniformed students.

For this had been his idea. A nighttime gathering of the best from the university, future Nazi Party members, serious, promising, disciplined young people, seated around the pure flame that would destroy the old world. In these surroundings, Martin's image and voice would chant the Genesis that was his dream.

What splendor in the dark sky! The night of the first fire, Elfriede had promised herself she would never forget the sight of Martin as a Germanic divinity. Her prophet had awakened, and German greatness was his! Kneeling on the ground, Elfriede had addressed him a pagan prayer, a hymn to the hero he was becoming before her very eyes. Over the crackling of the fire, this man who inspired youth was announcing the renewal of the world. She would not forget that evening.

Later, there had been the torches in Nuremberg Stadium, the consecration of the Führer, an event worthy of antiquity. The orderly masses raised right arms stiffly toward the sovereign guide. The standards formed a single line of red and black flags stamped with the new cross. Amplified, the voice thundered, hammering heaven as if it were a forge: the German, at odds with himself . . . a new order . . .

In those days Martin said that Hitler personified Germany. Such ardor, such drive! The bonfires of Todtnauberg had burned high, reaching for the supreme power. Martin was right, and Hitler was great.

Elfriede could not forget those splendid fires.

Nor could she forget the showers of sparks she'd never seen that flew out of the crematoria chimneys. *Oh, dear God, keep Hannah from thinking about them! I'm renouncing fire.*

Not a problem. Cigarette in her hand, Hannah was pursuing a different train of thought.

"About the bonfires at Todtnauberg," she said, waving away the smoke. "Just imagine, Elfriede, I saw the very same thing in a kibbutz. Young people sitting around a campfire, singing, that's how the downhill slide begins. You don't see the harm, but it's there! The harm is in exalting collective values at the expense of the individual. Joining up."

"But didn't you join up, too, when you became a Zionist?"

"That's why I had to undergo my cure. Do you know the meaning of the word in Latin? *Cura*: care. Does the word ring a bell?"

" 'Dasein's Being as Care,' paragraph 41 of *Being and Time*," Elfriede recalled.

"Congratulations. But my concept of Care is not the same as Martin's. My Care is not metaphysical. It brought me to some serious thinking about my youth as a joiner. My husband and I remembered young people's organizations in Weimar Germany. We were afraid of them, and for good reason. Nazi youth set the stage for extermination. And you in your way unknowingly contributed."

"Then all mankind is guilty," said Elfriede.

The sugar bowl struck the table three times.

"The Jews were in a state of innocence regarding the gas ovens." Hannah's voice was loud. "That's indisputable, Elfriede. I've already said you can't lump murderers and victims together."

Elfriede heard the verdict without flinching.

"Guilty," declared Hannah. "I can't help that. Do you have something to say in your defense?"

"No," said Elfriede. "Wait, yes I do. It's not Germany that is guilty, but the destructiveness of negation. That's what is at work today. Martin isn't to blame."

"Who said anything about Martin? It's you I'm after!"

"I can't convince you I did nothing!"

"Oh yes you can, Elfriede. That's just it. I'm well aware that you did nothing."

"Was my behavior worse than Rabbi Baeck's at Thereienstadt?" Elfriede was angry. "He, too, did nothing and *he* knew what was happening!"

"Elfriede!"

"What? Am I shocking you, maybe? How is an ignorant German woman any more guilty than the head of a community in a camp, who *knew*?"

"Watch out!" Hannah picked up the sugar bowl.

Instinctively, Elfriede protected her head.

It was hard for Hannah to put the object down. She had come close to knocking out the enemy. Comparing herself to the Head Rabbi of Berlin! She, the Nazi!

"I was wrong to say that. I shouldn't have," said Elfriede, lowering her arm.

"Tell me where you got that dreadful idea!"

Elfriede, her head down, was barely audible. "I knew that you had questioned Rabbi Baeck's behavior. You yourself, Hannah. That's why I brought it up."

"Me? Well, it's true. But *I* had a right to do so."

Confident, arrogant, her usual demeanor. Isolated, like Martin. In Hannah's eyes, Elfriede would always be wrong.

"Besides," said Hannah pensively, "I'm no longer so sure of my judgment."

Elfriede looked up in surprise. Hannah was thinking out loud. "Chief Rabbi Baeck knew what lay in store for his community. He chose to say nothing to the Jews at the Theresienstadt Camp and to let them leave for Auschwitz uninformed because he hoped their docility would make their deaths easier."

"I think he was right, " Elfriede said.

"Certainly not! The executioners, they, too, were unfortunate Jews! Their survival depended on their obedience! The Nazis had turned them into hangmen!"

"Calm down. I know all that. The setup at the extermination camps didn't leave any way out for the . . . the victims."

"There was a way out!" exclaimed Hannah. "Being able to choose the moment of one's death, freely! To die on one's feet. Not like an animal in the slaughterhouse. I respect Rabbi Baeck's choice, but . . ." Hannah stopped. The sentences she had written about Rabbi Baeck were so many arrows released only to fly back to her. Choked with emotion, she continued: "I wasn't there. I have no right to judge what happened. Nobody has the right. You least of all."

"But I'm not saying a thing," Elfriede protested. "Not a thing."

"Well, you've said too much already! I shouldn't be explaining myself to you. It's shameful!"

"Let's stop. You're angry."

"The Jews should have armed themselves! That's what I thought before the war. There were a few of us who supported the idea of a Jewish army. We could have fought the Nazis. See what happened instead?"

"Hannah, *please*," Elfriede begged.

"No, I won't stop! You wanted to understand, so you'd better try. I'll tell you about it. Because of my book on Eichmann they came up with the name 'holocaust' for the extermination of the Jews of Europe. Do you know what 'holocaust' means? A sacrifice. Do you see the significance?"

"I think so," said Elfriede, shaking. "An appalling sacrifice."

"You're such an idiot! The Jews' destiny is always sacrifice, then? But one fights; when there's an enemy, one fights. Too many Jews take pleasure in the holocaust idea. Even the prosecutor at the trial in Jerusalem, the man to whom Eichmann was evil incarnate!"

Elfriede said timidly, "I don't really understand."

"You don't understand that an Israeli prosecutor, proud of his role, would want to transform an ordinary little bureaucrat into a sadist? That, under orders from the Israeli prime minister, he would be willing to paint a portrait of the eternal anti-Semite facing the persecuted chosen people?"

"No," she said, frightened.

"It's all too easy! They hang Adolf Eichmann, and once and for all they've wiped out the drastic evil that has always threatened the chosen people."

"You would have wanted him pardoned?" Elfriede was astounded.

"You're insane! But there is no drastic evil. There are just conscientious cogs in the machinery. There is just indifference and banality, which will kill once again!"

"For certain," said Elfriede nervously. "Calm down."

Hannah's eyes flashed lightning bolts. Deep in her tar-filled lungs, the bellows of the forge shook. Go, fire; go, fire; go, fire. Heat the iron red hot. Don't stop, keep pumping. Stronger and stronger. Again. Anger that will not be extinguished, that has to come out!

Breathing hard, Hannah clenched her fists. Against whom, the anger of her life? Whom does she strike?

"This isn't good for you, " Elfriede puts in. "Think about your heart."

"Shut your mouth!" Hannah was infuriated.

Elfriede pushed her chair back and went to the other side of the kitchen, terrified.

Hannah
Jerusalem, August 1961

She Meets Golda Meir

The Israeli foreign minister wears her hair parted in the middle, as Hannah once did. Silvery strands crisscross Golda Meir's immense head, some escaping free and wiry on her cheeks. Other than that, mannish, with steely eyes and a deep voice. Hannah looks admiringly at this Jewish heroine who resembles her, except when it comes to femininity.

"Well, how did the session go today?" asks the minister.

"Quite wearing," Hannah replies. "The prosecutor introduced all the evidence from Treblinka. Horrible."

"Horrible, but necessary, Madame Arendt. I'm tired too." And indeed, the great woman does look weary. With a hostess's gesture, she points out the refreshments—cookies and a thermos of café au lait. "If I had time," she says, "we could have shared a meal in my kitchen. I would have made apple strudel to remind you of home."

"I wasn't born in Austria. I'm from Königsberg."

"How stupid of me!" says Golda Meir. "Your accent is German, of course. And I'm sure you've noticed all the different accents in the auditorium. A veritable Tower of Babel, when they're not speaking Hebrew."

"That's right," says Hannah. "But they could have done without a German interpreter for the defendant. Everyone at the trial understands German."

"That's not the point," says the minister, frowning. "Israel's official language is Hebrew. Otherwise, how could we unify our people, I ask you?"

Hannah does not have an answer.

"Founding a state is hard enough as it is!" sighs Golda Meir.

"To begin with, church and state should be separate," says Hannah. "Otherwise, we'll have trouble with the atheists."

"Oh, I don't care!" says Golda Meir. "All that matters is Israel, whether you're an atheist or not."

"And if you don't believe in God?" says Hannah. "That's my situation."

"Mine, too, of course," says the minister, surprised. "You realize that as a socialist, I obviously don't believe in God. I believe in the Jewish people. And you do, too, Madame Arendt."

"I believe in the Jewish people?" Hannah is shocked, but she doesn't understand why.

"Oh yes, " says the minister. "Naturally, you believe in the Jewish people, Madame Arendt. You love them. Otherwise, you wouldn't be here at the Eichmann trial."

No! thinks Hannah, rebellious.

Hannah does not believe. She does not love. She is Jewish, that's different. She neither loves nor believes, she belongs to the Jewish people, that goes without saying. Hannah detests belief. So now she's being asked for a profession of faith? Out of the question. A profession of love, as for a person? No, not that either.

"And what's more," says Golda Meir, "Israeli justice is

showing the world that we exist as a state. It shows the force of our belief in Israel. The Jewish state is strong, armed, sure of itself from now on. Think of . . ."

The minister goes on, a monologue. Hannah is barely listening. She is terribly sleepy. Where has she heard these words before? God in Heaven, where? Her eyelids are heavy.

We shall exterminate our enemies. . . . Our power is indestructible.

How can she make the Israeli foreign minister stop talking? How can she tell her it's late, so late that Hannah needs to go to bed and forget this unpleasant feeling of déjà vu?

Only her dear Heinrich had understood how horrified Hannah was by Golda Meir's pronouncements.

Israeli justice, confident, powerful, indestructible. The exterminating force.

Hannah face-to-face with Elfriede.

Suddenly, all of Hannah's anger faded away. The forge grew cold. Hannah got her breath back but it wasn't easy. Her heart went on pounding, choking her, go fire, go . . .

She was overcome with shame.

Elfriede skulked in the corner.

"You're acting as if I were at death's door," said Hannah, uncomfortable. "That's right. You're treating me the way you do Martin. . . ."

A shaky Elfriede was rummaging through the kitchen cupboard.

Hannah felt dizzy. She saw spots before her eyes, tiny moths. Muddled, she said to Elfriede, "Come and sit down."

Elfriede turned around and stood against the cupboard.

"I won't pull a heart attack in your kitchen, Elfriede. How about a little more coffee?"

Elfriede moved closer. The coffee pot was right in front of Hannah. "Help yourself," was all she said.

"Thanks," said Hannah, lifting her cup with a shaky hand. She made a face as she downed the cold coffee. "I shouldn't have gotten so angry. I guess you really unhinged me."

Elfriede sat down. The crisis was over.

"There is one thing," said Hannah, ill at ease. "I don't understand why—"

Her right ear had started ringing, then the sound stopped. Just some inconsequential tinnitus.

"—the anger," she finished. "There was a time when I thought I had arrived at true detachment."

"You, detached?"

"Yes, it did happen," she replied. "By accident."

Hannah
New York, March 19, 1962

She Makes a Choice

"She's coming to," says a voice.

Hannah tries to open her eyes and can't. The swollen lids reject sight. Her head is heavy, her neck hurts. Why is she stretched out in a van? Why the sirens? An air raid?

An ambulance. She's in an ambulance with a doctor and a white-coated medic. There was a crash, the screeching of brakes, the smell of hot metal, then blackness. An accident.

"You mustn't move, ma'am," says the voice.

That means she is probably able to move. Imperceptibly, Hannah bends a knee, an elbow. She can do it. Not paralyzed. Now the eyes. She makes an effort, and she sees the doctor's concerned face.

"Don't be alarmed," he says. "The scalp always bleeds a lot."

So, there's blood, and a bump on the head. Better test herself. First, her poems: "My winged feet dance in mournful radiance."

Poetry, that's a start. Now, Greek. German. English. No head injury. Her phone number, just to be sure. Very good. Her brain is functioning.

Now she can let go, float. It's all right if her body is smashed, because the things that matter are sound. The ambulance heads for the hospital. The stretcher is lifted down; Hannah is in pain. Off to X-ray.

"Nothing catastrophic, but you're in bad shape," says the doctor serenely. "You could have been killed."

The mouth forms words: "For . . . how . . . long?"

"Don't be in a hurry. It will take a while. Hemorrhages in both eyes, broken teeth, concussion, not to mention bruises, broken ribs. And I'm waiting for the results of your electro-cardiogram. Right now, let's say two months."

"Two months," the words breathed through swollen lips. "Perfect."

Bandaged, treated, stuffed with painkillers, Hannah waits for her husband. She is serene. She no longer fears anything. Happy, she lets life take over.

When it happened, she wasn't afraid. When what happened? She doesn't remember.

Gradually, it comes back to her—the fleeting moment when she was outside herself. A moment of calm, of peace. She was presented with a choice between life and death. She could go forth luminous and weightless or assume again the burden of flesh and blood. Hannah made her choice. She came back to her body, she is alive.

Because of that moment, peace and calm will be with her forever.

"An accident?" Elfriede was astonished.

"I was in New York, hard at work on the Eichmann report. I had an important appointment and a truck ran into my taxi in Central Park."

"I didn't know. Was it serious?"

"Quite," answered Hannah gloomily. "Eye injuries, broken teeth, bruised face, and so on."

"You'd never know it, though." Elfriede was trying to be nice.

"I asked for a veil to hide behind, but that didn't work out. Then I put a black patch over one eye, like a pirate. No, the worst was the damage to my heart. I saw that when I had my coronary."

"And this accident made you detached?"

"Me?" Hannah seemed surprised. "Oh, right, yes. You see, when something so extreme occurs, one can no longer be judgmental. I returned to my work on Eichmann in a different state of mind. I was quite serene. And lucid. After my trauma, I understood the banality of evil."

Elfriede frowned, perplexed.

"Yes, it is complicated," said Hannah. "When one has an unforeseen choice between life and death, one becomes oneself. It's hard to explain. I had arrived at . . . I don't quite know how to put it. A taste for living, probably."

Elfriede's eyes opened wide.

Hannah went on. "Despite everything, life was beautiful. Evil was banal, and I had survived. Embodied in me alone was my share of humanity."

"That goes without saying," whispered Elfriede, stunned.

Little by little Hannah's head had cleared. No more moths in front of her eyes.

Of course. For Elfriede, it did go without saying. Of course, she'd never had any doubts about living. Elfriede had no doubts about anything. Determinedly banal, and basically not a mean person. Useless to belabor the point.

"Let's go on," she said brusquely. "Whatever the reason, I have changed. I don't want to fight for a state any more, a nation—or even a people. I have replaced love of Israel with love of people—the only love worth anything. Whatever the group or entity, loving it is irresponsible."

"There's no more homeland then." That bothered Elfriede. "I no longer have the right to be German!"

"So what? You are a person! Why, when Blücher died . . ." What was she going to say now? That had nothing to do with Elfriede!

"Well?" asked the enemy. "When your husband died?"

"Nothing." Hannah's face had clouded over. "I'd like some ice in my water."

Docile Elfriede rose and went to the refrigerator for ice cubes. Outside, the sky looked threatening again. Hannah sat hunched over, waiting for the thunder. Caught by the light, Elfriede's face was tawny and as gentle as Eichmann's. What a thought! Why wasn't it thundering?

"The storm is far from over," Elfriede said. "You're won't be able to leave any time soon. Look out there! It's as dark as night."

"Dark as night," Hannah echoed absentmindedly.

Hannah
New York, November 4, 1970

She Says Kaddish

On the casket there will be no Star of David beneath the name HEINRICH BLÜCHER.

Hannah wanted one, but it is out of the question. For Heinrich is not Jewish.

Her friends are here, crowded into the chapel. Hannah doesn't see them clearly, but she feels their presence, that of a kind of family come together for a religious observance. It is not the Jewish ceremony she envisioned for Heinrich.

She will not have the right to say Kaddish for her husband: "Ysgadal veyikadach chemey rabo, beolmo dievro' hiroussay vehamil' h . . ."

Pronounced solemnly by a male voice, the sacred lines would have piled up on Heinrich's casket. They would have burrowed deep inside it. With no man here to speak the words, Hannah recites the Kaddish in a low voice, for Heinrich: "Oh, God, our heavenly father, you who have the power of life and death. You who reveal yourself to us as the God of love and mercy, give to the souls of your servants light and peace . . ."

Heinrich was struck down the day before. Hannah does

not feel anything yet. Empty, even of tears. She is stone eroded by the rains. She knows grief will come. Tonight, tomorrow, now, forthwith, or just now.

No memories rise up. Hannah is the casket, that long box of gleaming wood. And she is the words of the homages that fade away into whispers. Hannah is no longer herself, she is just a thing, like Heinrich.

For a long time Hannah has not believed in God.

But the Kaddish is not the prayer of the dead. It is a song to the glory of God. Do not lament if something is taken from you that was not yours. That did not belong to you. Heinrich does not belong to Hannah. He has been taken back, that's all. The words of the Kaddish are appropriate no matter who has died. He has been given to me, he has been taken back, he does not belong to me.

But Heinrich is not Jewish. Hannah's dream has not been realized.

Hannah does not shout. She would like to. Heinrich would be entitled to such mourning, if she had the strength. But no. He is gone, and Hannah remains. She is keeping vigil over her husband, who is not Jewish. Who has been taken back.

Who *was* not Jewish. Who *was* taken back. She must learn to speak of Heinrich in the past tense.

Tonight she will light the candle that Jews place before the portrait of the departed, a candle that is to burn for a year. It is customary.

And then, Hannah will break with tradition.

She will say the Shabbat prayers, as her grandfather did in Königsberg. "Blessed are you, our Lord God, king of the universe, who have sanctified us by your commandments and have given us the order to light the lights for this day."

Unheard of. It is neither the day, nor the time. It is up to the men to say the Shabbat prayers. Too bad. Since one light has gone out, it is for her to light another, so she can go on.

Hannah

As a child, she didn't really know she was Jewish.

The middle-class Jews of Königsberg had nothing to fear from their fellow citizens. They were German, patriotic, and that was that. They had fought during the Great War, they had received medals, they had often died for their country, Germany. Their religion had nothing to do with their nation. It was simple.

On Saturdays Hannah would go to synagogue with her grandmother. The little girl rather liked the lighted candles, the men's chanting and their striped shawls, the fringed scrolls of the Torah, but she also enjoyed the flowers on the altars of the churches she attended with the Arendts' maid. Rabbi Vogelstein came regularly to teach her the basics of Judaism, and at school, catechism class was mandatory. Jesus, Yahweh, the cross, the scrolls, the canticles, the star, it all enchanted her.

Children always hear these things from other children. At catechism one day, another little girl said that Hannah's grandmother had killed Christ. Hannah was quite shocked and went home to ask her mother if it was true. What was Martha Arendt's reply? Probably something like: "Don't listen to your schoolmates," or "That's just talk," or "What nonsense!"

Oh, yes, Martha did say: "Never let anybody talk to you like that again." Which upset Hannah.

Thus, in elementary school Hannah had learned she was Jewish.

What she remembered more vividly, as though it had been yesterday, were the instructions given by her mother when she entered high school: If one of her professors dared say a single word against the Jews, Hannah was to stand up immediately and come home, remembering exactly what had been said.

The remarks her mother did not allow furnished Hannah an excuse for some nice days off. Several times Frau Arendt received letters from the school apprising student Arendt, Hannah, of the rules and regulations. Cutting school was a serious offense, and student Arendt had left class. Frau Arendt always answered the headmaster's letters, replying with a full explanation.

As for anti-Semitic remarks uttered by children, the instructions were no less clear: Don't bother about them, don't leave class. Between the insults of the teachers, which she had to counter by walking out, and the students' nonsense, which she was not supposed to counter, Hannah became familiar with the anti-Semitic line: grating, fierce, murderous. It soon dawned on Hannah that being Jewish was no joke.

She was totally ignorant of Zionism. Paul and Martha Arendt were socialists, and they were Germans; they had no Zionist sympathies whatsoever. Yet, on one point, Hannah's mother was quite specific: no looking down on poor Jews from the East, those of Galicia, Bukovina, Poland, border Jews. No making fun of their griminess, their long caftans and their sidelocks. Ghetto Jews had to be treated with respect, even if one did not approve of their rejection of modern ways.

Hannah had always found it hard to follow that particular

order of her mother's. At the Jerusalem trial in 1961, she watched the crowds milling about the House of Justice, and everything in her wanted to reject the Eastern-looking passersby, the Jews from elsewhere, with their nonchalance, their sloppiness. To think that Uncle Rafael had been awarded a posthumous Iron Cross during the Great War of 1914–18, and that these uncouth creatures were jostling her in the street, in Jerusalem! She, a European Jew! Ghetto Jews!

Then Hannah had suddenly remembered her mother's instructions, and she felt ashamed.

Still the same old reflex. The respectable German Jew didn't let go of her prey easily.

It had taken her some time to straighten out her thinking.

There existed only one Jewish people, to which Hannah belonged, whatever her background. Hannah was of Israel. That was that.

Although. Was it really over, the interminable story of Hannah and the Jews? As a girl, she had decided two things. One, that she was an atheist, like her parents. Second, that she would be a Zionist. Unlike her parents.

As for atheism, Rabbi Vogelstein had removed the main obstacle. To hear her mother tell it, the little Arendt girl wanted to grow up to marry the rabbi who was teaching her Hebrew. Emboldened by this innocent love, Hannah the smarty told him she could not believe in God. Calm as could be, Rabbi Vogelstein looked at her over his glasses: "And who asked you?"

A moment to remember. Fine and good. You could be a Jew and not believe in God. She hadn't budged an inch from that position.

As for Zionism, the choice was clear-cut. In Hannah's student days, German Jewish youth didn't discuss its pros and cons. A state for Jews in Palestine was absolutely essential, and the state of Israel must be secular and socialist, period, end of discussion.

But in 1948, the state of Israel was not created secular. It had turned out to be impossible to draft a constitution, for there was no consensus on secularism for the Jewish people. One was a Jew by birth, and the birth of Israel had been writ in the Bible. No way out. The principle of secularism was at variance with the existence of a Hebrew state. Accordingly, the founding fathers passed over the question in silence. No constitution.

"And who asked you?" No one. Israel would be a democracy without a constitution.

The more it developed, the more Hannah feared what the state of Israel would become. Its penchant for brigades, its wars, its manly chants, all that, unpleasant echoes. Its nationalism, its inability to federate the Jews, and the Arabs of Palestine. The socialism of the founding fathers had melted in the sun like the snows of Central Europe.

The Eichmann trial in Jerusalem had broken Hannah's last ties to the Jewish state. The proceedings had one objective: to condemn the monster publicly, avoiding the reality of what had taken place. Anger. Hannah had expressed it. She was declared a pariah. The greatest torment of her life.

Two Jerusalems dwelt in her.

The first she had encountered during her Zionist period, when she lived in Paris and militated with Youth Aliyah for the return of Jews to Palestine. Hannah was very anxious to accompany one of the trainee groups sent to Jerusalem in Palestine. In 1935, the long-awaited day came.

The boat sailed from Marseille to the port of Haifa, whose hills she looked upon with great excitement. The land of the

Jews! And then Jerusalem. The climb to the Arab city, the white stones in the sun, the thousand-year-old Jewish tombs in the ravines of Hebron, the Western Wall, and the caftaned Jews bewailing the Exodus. The state of Israel did not yet exist. In 1935, Jerusalem was a city of antiquity, imbued with meaning.

She was less pleased with the kibbutzim, where she could see right away that a new aristocracy had been created. The pioneers were lords. At the time, Hannah said nothing about her uneasiness. Had she only felt it while she was there? She couldn't be sure. The socialist equality of the kibbutzim impressed her. In spite of her instinctive recoil, the Jerusalem of Palestine remained dear to Hannah's heart.

Her second Jerusalem was the city in the state of Israel where Eichmann stood trial. In 1948, when the UN passed the resolution creating the new nation, Hannah had hoped for an agreement between Arabs and Jews. But instead, war. And then more war. A cloud hung over Hannah's Zionism.

Between 1935 and the start of the Eichmann trial, much blood had been spilled. Hannah set out for Jerusalem with a heavy heart. And a surprise was in store.

Fond memories of her first trip were rekindled. Once again she was thrilled by the grandeur of ancient times. Not in Jerusalem, which was now imbued with might rather than meaning.

No, it was at Petra, in what was then Transjordan. There, set in the rocks stood a Roman temple, fragile and eternal. The silent columns were as moving to her as the Greek temple she had visited on her stopover in Syracuse.

Yes, Hannah preferred dead antiquity to what the state of Israel had become. But ruined temples were convenient: philosophizing in the presence of a vanished past was all too easy.

She had occasional twinges of remorse. Never for very long. She was Jewish, secular, socialist, that wasn't going to change. Zionist, that was another story, full of contradictions.

So much so that Hannah found herself in more or less the same position as the Jews of the Exodus during the endless centuries when Israel slept and they longed to return to Jerusalem.

Those Jews did not think up the Jewish state. No, it was born of the dream of an elegant Viennese intellectual, Theodore Herzl. This late-nineteenth-century visionary combed through the countless names of the city of Jerusalem, deciding upon "Zion" for the state that did not exist. Ridiculed by middle-class urban Jews, Zionism inflamed the hopes of other Jews, the poor ones.

How had such a dandy become such a luminary? How had a journalist and member of the upper middle class become the new Messiah of ghetto Jews?

Very simple. By following the Dreyfus trial as a correspondent in Paris. French anti-Semitism created the Zionist ideal. When Hannah discovered she was Jewish, she had studied up on the Dreyfus Affair. Herzl was right on two counts: a Jewish state was necessary, and any trial involving Jews needed to be closely monitored.

So Hannah became an ardent Zionist, until the dream became reality. Hopes for peace dashed. A state must be strong, said the heroes of Israel.

Hannah gave up. Zionism was an ideal, just an ideal, nothing more. But in 1973, when Israel was attacked in the Yom Kippur War, she was shocked to find she still had nationalistic sentiments. She gave money, became a sponsor of war. Madame Arendt had answered the call to arms.

But it was better before, when century after century they

would sing "Next year in Jerusalem," with wild hope in their hearts and no date set for boarding a plane to Tel Aviv. Go back to Jerusalem? The mythic return was now no more than a reservation marked on one's calendar.

The Jews of the past were speaking to the heavenly Jerusalem that no one could take away. It was the one true Jerusalem. The enchanted castle. Heavenly Jerusalem lived in the Jewish love for music, in the Yiddish tongue, in love of children, love of trees. The Jerusalem of the Exodus was a whirlwind, a celebration with a touch of sadness and a touch of joy, made up of swaying rhythms, violins, and melancholy.

And the German language, too.

Hannah had been taken aback the first time her friend Blumenfeld told her: "I am a Zionist by the grace of Goethe," adding, deadpan: "Yes, indeed, Zionism is Germany's gift to the Jews." But Hannah soon understood.

The real Germany, it was she, Hannah. Jewish, philosopher in German, carrying around in exile German fir forests, hearty broths, the steam of trains, snug domesticity. She had brought with her the poets of Germany, Hölderlin, Schiller, Goethe, Lenz, Buchner. Because of Adolf Hitler, they were no longer at home in their land.

Like her, the German poets had become pariahs.

Once free of all attachments, Hannah felt free to criticize Jews if they should falter. As she did others.

No, more harshly. For Hannah realized she was tougher on Jewish mistakes than on those of the goyim, the non-Jews. Non-Jews had an excuse: they were not Jewish. While they, the Jews, had duties to humanity. They were not entitled to error.

It was very odd. The goyim had always seduced Hannah. Such innocence and good will! So many unconscious prejudices, under the very nose of reason! Their naïveté was unshakable. Martin was like that. Blücher, too. Hannah still found it amazing that the two real loves of her life were men who were not Jewish.

And it wasn't for lack of trying. Her first husband, Stern, was Jewish, and Hannah hadn't loved him. She'd loved only two men, each one unique; Martin, Heinrich, both goyim. Hannah was forced to admit she had needed them. Out of contrariness? Maybe. That was like her.

And now, she pictured herself as an old sage of the Polish ghetto, an impish Hasid, mystic, indulgent toward human weakness.

And even here, face-to-face with her old enemy, Hannah found herself being understanding in a way that she didn't like. That was why she had to stand firm.

Was she going to explain to Elfriede that the real German was her Jewish rival? And to throw up to her that the Germany of the spirit bore the name Hannah Arendt? Wait a minute. She was being a bit silly.

But she couldn't help it. Hannah burst out laughing.

"What's so amusing?" Elfriede snapped. "The idea of staying here on account of the storm?"

"Maybe. You have to admit it's funny, our being in prison together."

"You *can* leave in the rain, you know. I don't see any problem. Just say goodbye to Martin and you're off! Good riddance!"

"I was joking. The two of us in the kitchen, without Martin, that's rich!"

"Leave Martin in peace, and if you're hungry, eat." Elfriede was annoyed.

"You are amazingly thoughtful," Hannah observed. "Now, what were we talking about?"

"About you, remember. Now, don't take my question the wrong way, Hannah. But is it true that when the Eichmann book came out, a French weekly featured a story on your anti-Semitism?"

"No. The headline of their article was a question: 'Is Hannah Arendt anti-Semitic?'"

"Poor Hannah. If I understand correctly, you imagined Jews were better than other people. And you found out they weren't."

"For the state of Israel, that's true. I don't deny it. As for the Jewish councils, please remember that some of their leaders chose suicide. Czerniakow in Warsaw, for example."

"I understand," Elfriede said.

Inexplicably, the hostilities had ceased for a moment.

"And yet, Elfriede, and yet . . ." Hannah paused, reflecting. "I know the mechanisms that can transform a human being into a beast, a bureaucrat into an assassin. But why? It's unpardonable. Auschwitz ought not to have happened."

"Now you see what it was like for us!" Elfriede was gloating.

The woman was an idiot. Why did she spoil things with these smug exclamations of hers? Hannah spoke up: "Enough pleading your case. It's quite unpleasant."

Elfriede was panicky. "No, no. You're wrong. I was trying to make you understand what I felt in 1945. When I found out, what an ordeal!"

"Finally, a bit of remorse."

"Stop it! I was devastated."

Once more Hannah foundered as she contemplated Elfriede's case. With the jealousy cleared away, only good feelings remained.

"And Martin, what did he say?" Hannah's voice was a whisper.

"Obviously, we hadn't believed any of it. Then afterward . . ."

Elfriede
Freiburg im Breisgau, September 1945

They See the Photographs

Defeat has come and with it denunciation. In Freiburg, the onetime rector is an outlaw. Martin is friendless.

But the young soldier has come to see them again.

Martin is fond of this French intellectual who is acquainted with his thinking and who treats him with consideration when the Germans have their backs turned.

But today the young Frenchman isn't wearing his respectful smile. He has an air of authority. A bit too determinedly he places a thick folder on the table. There is one word on the cover: *Dachau.*

The young man is about to do something with the unopened folder; Elfriede guesses the ordeal to come and is uneasy. Impassive, the young Frenchman glances at her. He is going to open the folder. He opens it.

It contains photographs.

So, the Frenchman wants to show the pictures, exhibit the evidence, and get Martin to look, if he's up to it. Elfriede brings her chair close to her husband's, as close as possible. Courage, Martin. The moment has come. They have to see.

Dried up cadavers, piled like logs. Survivors, skin and bones. Great, lifeless eyes.

Martin and Elfriede say nothing. Not a word, not a breath escapes their lips. The young Frenchman doesn't say anything either; he waits. Elfriede lowers her eyes, rubs her hands against each other, as if she were a fly. Martin is going to have to say something. . . .

Martin has a vacant look. Elfriede pulls herself together. "No one informed us what was happening in the camps," she says, the sound of her voice echoing unheeded.

The young Frenchman glances at her furtively, then his eyes fall on Martin. It's his words that are awaited, not hers.

She goes on, desperate. "We didn't know a thing!"

Useless. The young man's eyes are riveted on Martin.

Finally, a whisper from Martin, his eyes half-closed: "There are no words for it."

The young Frenchman looks relieved for a moment. *Go on, Martin, go on.*

"We have been deceived by criminals," Martin says slowly. "All the German people."

The Frenchman's face tenses up. Martin notices.

"The threshold of the inhuman was reached," he continues. "Man was transformed into an object. There were no longer men, just things. There is no name for . . . that."

He is finding it hard to breathe. The young man does not interrupt.

"A plan," says Martin, speaking faster. "A plan for efficient mass killing. This is what comes of nihilism, the death of thinking. A threshold has been crossed."

The young man nods. Elfriede is relaxing a little, imperceptibly.

"But once the threshold of inhumanity is crossed, time does not stop," Martin continues. "Nothing guarantees that it is over."

The young man looks intrigued.

"The plan can be set in motion again," sighs Martin.

Elfriede scurries away quietly, her heart pounding.

Maybe the young French intellectual understood Martin's thinking. Flushed, Elfriede dries her damp hands. Of one thing she is certain: neither she nor Martin knew what was going on. If they had known!

If we had. She sighs and collapses into a chair.

Elfriede

Martin had decided never to explain his period of Nazi involvement.

Not to give in to the world that came after. Not to demean himself before the moderns. No response, as long as he lived. The insult was too great, and Martin too shattered. The proper response to questions is silence. Elfriede had accompanied him in his muteness. No one had ever gotten after her, except Hannah. And that was the only ordeal she could not handle. The rest had already happened.

For Elfriede went through the worst without Martin.

In spite of his age, he had not avoided the Third Reich's final mass conscription, its last-ditch effort. Five years older and Martin would have been over the limit, sixty. No intervention on his behalf did any good. The enemy armies were advancing through Alsace, less than fifty kilometers from Freiburg. Martin was drafted; then, thanks to the chaotic situation, he came home.

In November, American aircraft pounded Freiburg. In December, the bombs still rained down. Teeth clenched, Elfriede was there. But not he.

Martin had fled. He had taken his manuscripts to his birthplace, the town of Messkirch, where his brother awaited him. Fritz had always classified Martin's notes. While the enemy invaded Germany, Martin and Fritz spent the winter sorting and filing. In Freiburg, the occupation began.

Then the university fled also, joining the master in the highlands of Swabia. Professors and female students took to the Messkirch road, by bicycle or on foot, carrying their precious books. In Freiburg, Elfriede guarded the house.

Under the aegis of the great philosopher, the university folk in exile settled down after a fashion, either at Wildenstein Castle or in the nearby village. Every morning Martin headed to the castle to teach his final course, in the kitchen. He had taken refuge on the high peaks of Hölderlin's poetry, a safe place for him.

Up at the castle they knew battles were raging down below; they knew the wounded lay close by, in a makeshift hospital at the Beuron Monastery. They knew Freiburg was occupied. Free as an acrobat walking a tightrope, Martin profited from the last days of the Reich to elucidate Hölderlin, the poet who had ended his days in a tower beside the Neckar because he had been declared mad. Surrounded by disaster, Martin was dancing on the edge of an abyss into which he was about to tumble.

The days dragged on; French troops went to the eagle's nest of the Führer to capture the remnants of the Vichy government, whose members had been holed up at Sigmaringen in Bavaria. The fall was imminent.

It came, with the harvests. And there in the countryside, the university people helped bring the crops in. Famine was threatening, and they received food in exchange for their labor. Since the Reich was collapsing, these good intellectuals retreated into the rhythm of the seasons. In Swabia, as elsewhere, the harvest season had its festivities. There was a party at the castle, with theater, dancing, bread, and wine. Following a piano concert, Martin gave a last lecture, and then it was over. And the whole time, Elfriede had to struggle in Freiburg.

Her memories of those days were rather muddled: the boots of soldiers who were not German, the bowed heads of the Germans on the streets, piles of rubble, brief shouts, songs of victory, despondency alternating with wild hope, distress, the end of the world.

Her house requisitioned, like the dwellings of all Nazi party members. The library seized, that was far more serious. About the requisitioning, Elfriede could do nothing. She battled for the library at every step. The books gone, Martin's thinking would be gone with them.

That is how Frau Heidegger got to know the French officers with the occupation troops. Martin's library wasn't their first concern. Because she was putting up a fight she was not afraid. She was sure she was within her rights: Martin was not guilty. She? They scarcely bothered with her. The Heidegger wife was nobody important. Elfriede negotiated a postponement; she got it. In July, Martin was back in Freiburg.

But the French were not his worst enemies.

In no time, there surfaced Germans to bring charges against the Nazi professor. The nightmare started slowly. Proving he had held no posts in the Nazi party was easy: it was the truth. But once denazification was underway, there was no stopping it. The denazification committee summoned Professor Martin Heidegger in July 1945, a month after the summer harvests in the fields around Wildenstein Castle.

Alfred Lampe, one of the three professors on the committee, had been treated badly during Martin's rectorate. A petty academic squabble, dangerous in those troubled times: Lampe was looking for revenge. The war over Martin's survival as a philosopher seemed lost in advance; contrary to all expectations, however, Lampe did not succeed in having Martin dismissed. In August 1945, the denazification committee merely banned Martin from participation in university affairs.

No, It was not Lampe who played the role of traitor in the tragedy, but Martin's oldest friend, Karl Jaspers.

Karl's wife, Gertrud, was Jewish. One day she confessed to Martin that she often cried because of Hitler. Martin had answered affectionately: "There's nothing like a good cry." Gertrud had not taken it well. Cautious, Martin kept out of her way.

Because of Gertrud, in 1937 Jaspers had lost his post. Unlike Malwine Husserl, Gertrud didn't receive a single bouquet, or a letter. Ever since, Karl had been waiting for a word of regret from his friend Martin.

None came. Why say you're sorry when you're not guilty? When the senate rejected the verdict of the denazification committee, Martin did not hesitate for a moment. He was so sure of Karl's loyalty that he asked him to draw up a report for the senate's commission of inquiry. His friend Karl Jaspers would set them straight.

Karl could testify that Martin had broken with the Nazi authorities back in 1934, after the massacre of storm troopers by Hitler's militia, the SS. Karl knew that after the bloody "Night of the Long Knives," Martin had condemned the violence privately; then he had distanced himself and resigned his post.

Very soon. Jaspers could certify that afterward Martin had been spied on, threatened, distrusted. It was true. It was also true that Martin as well as Elfriede had renewed their party membership annually, but that was an insignificant detail. Jaspers would understand.

Jaspers asked nothing of Martin. No disavowal, no remorse. Nothing. In his report, he explained that Martin's brief Nazi involvement was not the issue; more significant was that Heidegger's mode of thinking would be harmful to Germany's defenseless young people. Dictatorial, the master's philosophy. The concept of freedom had no place in it. The "Being-there" so important to Heidegger ranked the notion of responsibility on the level of mundane human concerns, themselves contemptible. Heidegger's teaching would endanger German moral reconstruction; it did not answer to the needs of the community. The verdict of the philosopher friend was not subject to appeal.

Jaspers turned in his report in December 1945, a year after the evening of the Schubert sonata at the Pichts'. The following January, upon the recommendation of the faculty senate—Germans—the French military government relieved Heidegger of his teaching duties, took away part of his salary and, later, his pension. Livelihood cut off. Because of the friend Karl, who was still waiting to hear a word of regret.

That marked the beginning of Martin's uncompromising silence. Never explain, never complain. Jaspers would continue the fruitless wait.

But his arrow had struck its target. Once the lengthy proceedings were over, Martin finally plunged into the abyss on whose edge he had so long danced. He didn't complain, he didn't explain. Elfriede took care of the endless paperwork, dictating to him and sometimes doing the writing herself. She would get him moving so he could appear at his hearings. He still did not complain; he was wandering. In the spring of 1946, his vacant look would not go away.

Elfriede appealed to the dean of the School of Medicine. Martin had to be hospitalized in a special clinic. Like his master, Hölderlin, Martin had chosen madness. Perhaps he dreamed of ending his days in an old tower on the banks of the Neckar, but he was not living in the Romantic age. He may well have had the tortured spirit of the nineteenth century, but—alas—Martin was not crazy.

In three weeks, his steady gaze was back, and so was Martin. Cured. Without a pfennig. A miserable wretch.

Of those days, Elfriede retained only the sequence of events. Once upon a time there was defeat, bombing, occupation. There happened what happens in wars: revenge, cleansing, punishment by the conquerors. Elfriede did what women do in wartime: she looked ahead to better days, held on, hunted up food, rummaged for fuel. She would open the American rations and taste the canned Spam without knowing it was meat she ate.

Elfriede had buried the occupation under a sullied glacier. The snapshots of memory would never come back.

All that rose to the surface was her vivid recollection of the young French intellectual, unforgettable bright spot in those difficult times. Elfriede could not forget his sunny presence, no questions, no suspicions. Martin's hope was no longer Germany but France. With the French, Martin's thinking would live on. As Martin put it, collapse signaled the passing of the night.

But that was before Karl's report. Then there was the painful scene Elfriede was to hear about only later.

Besides asking Jaspers to write a statement, Martin also sought the help of the churchman who had guided him during his years in the seminary. Conrad Gröber had ended up Archbishop of Freiburg: Like Martin, he had believed in the national renewal, but he soon turned against it. After the war, he was not under suspicion.

According to the story, Martin ran into the prelate's sister Marie in the archbishop's waiting room. She remarked rather nastily that they hadn't seen Martin for twelve years or so. And Martin allegedly replied: "Marie, I've paid a high price. It's all over for me now."

Elfriede doubted the story. By those two sentences, Martin would have acknowledged the attacks against him. That was not his style. And besides, at the time, he was already without the power of speech, as naked and defenseless as Adam under the angel Gabriel's sword. In those days, Martin wept.

"I remember," Elfriede mumbled. "The first time we saw the photographs. Those living dead with their empty eyes. They were no longer human. Really, you know him—do you think Martin could have been a party to such insanity?"

"No, Elfriede, I don't think so."

"Martin was stupid! Stupidity! That's the only word I've heard him use for it."

"Really?" said Hannah. "I prefer 'idealistic.' Martin, stupid! Could he have suffered a temporary loss of intelligence?"

"Also, he likes to take risks. Or didn't you know?"

"I don't know anyone more cautious," said Hannah. "That's one of his faults. He's afraid of his own shadow! He's even afraid of you!"

"And what about his skiing?"

"Sport doesn't count." Hannah shrugged.

"You don't know Martin," Elfriede said quietly. "He loves danger. In 1914, he showed me the poem with those fearsome words, 'The god of war unleashes his indestructible spirit.' And the slaughter about to begin, Hannah! Wake up! Martin isn't the person you think he is!"

Hannah shuddered. *The god of war. Martin can think in those bellicose terms, I know that. He has a bloodthirsty streak. She's right.* Aloud, she said, rather annoyed: "You must have encouraged him. I can't help thinking that without you—"

"That isn't so!"

"He often told me he had acted on his own," said Hannah, thinking back. "That you had supported him loyally. But *I* think you were proud of Martin's title. Rector of the university! A triumph, wasn't it?"

"And what a price!"

"But on the day?"

"Yes, that day . . . He made such a fine speech."

"The regeneration of Germany?"

"No, Hannah. Martin only wanted to revitalize the German spirit. You should know that better than I, considering you cut your teeth on his lectures."

Hannah said in a loud voice, "I repeat, Elfriede. The spirit knows no country."

Elfriede objected. "We have to be born somewhere. We are never really separated from our native soil. Our childhood is there, our memories of the morning air, the countryside, the sound of the wind in the trees—"

"Or the cries of the Cossacks," said Hannah calmly.

Throwing up her hands in anger, Elfriede knocked over the sugar bowl.

"We'll never get away from this, my dear," Hannah commented as she picked up sugar cubes. "Even when we don't mean to, we are hurting each other. We must make peace, once and for all."

Elfriede did not answer.

"We are complete opposites," Hannah went on.

Muteness. The god of war wouldn't call it quits.

"That's why Martin has loved us both," said Hannah. "I was wrong to be suspicious of you, I admit. Yes, after all, maybe you are not the cause."

"You're just too relentless in hunting down the truth," said Elfriede. "Martin, now, knows how to keep quiet."

"Truth." Hannah was barely audible. "The truth is that he passed on to me something infinitely precious. A part of Germany that eludes you."

"You're talking to yourself!"

"Elfriede, let me go see if he's all right."

The forget-me-not-blue eyes clouded over.

"I beg of you," Hannah said humbly.

Elfriede looked at her in surprise. Arrogance was losing ground!

"It's probably the last time, Elfriede."

"Go ahead. But don't stay long."

Martin
Messkirch, Swabia, 1900

The Alarm Bell

It is Sunday. The child has grown; he dresses himself now. The mother has placed the lighted candle in Martin's hand.

"Listen, Martin," says his mother. "You are old enough to know why you are allowed to carry the candle to the church. Not so long ago, Catholic children were beaten up. The Old Catholics would push their heads into the water trough, to rebaptize them. They called us the 'sickly black ones.' They even took away our church. You did not know those days. After you were born, they were forced to give the church back to us, the Roman Catholics. When he departed, the last of the Old Catholics didn't know what he should do with the consecrated candle. You were playing on the square, you were very young. He gave it to you. Don't forget."

She has spoken without a pause.

Martin hears her every word, repeating the story to himself as he walks down the hall, the light in his hand. They used to submerge his head in the trough. They used to beat him up. He used to play on the square, and someone gave him the candle. He was born black and sickly. Now he understands that he is the witness of the flame. He will hold it always.

The door opens onto the town square. The Messkirch church is massive, enormous. Beside it, you can see the road to the castle. A tempting path, which you can't take while carrying the candle. Your duty, to walk from the house to the church.

But the child succumbs. He runs off, takes the castle road. The ancient lindens are sending out their first shoots. The air is cold, but wild hyacinths show bright blue through the undergrowth. Martin, enthralled, walks across meadows already touched with green. The candle still burns; there seems no end to it nor to the road, which, indeed has none. The foresters traced a labyrinth of trails when they came to fell the trees. Martin proceeds along the paths because they lead nowhere.

Suddenly, he hears the alarm bell. It is four in the afternoon.

This is the fourth bell of the church's seven, the one dreaded by those who nap, for it startles them awake. Naps are not for Martin. While the world sleeps, Martin keeps a vigil. An alarm, that's for others, who doze.

He himself does not dread the fourth bell, nor any of the other six. He reveres them all; they tell what time has come. There are bells for dawn, for noon, for night, for the dead, for celebrations, that one intoxicating.

The alarm bell does not make him retreat. He will not return home, he will not retrace his steps.

He will walk, candle in hand, looking at the blue sky.

Why are his eyes black? He so loves blue! When Martin looks in the mirror, he sees a little imp whose eyes are not blue.

He will walk as long as need be but knows not where he is going.

Suddenly, a shape bars his way. From where did this black-eyed old woman spring? Why the piercing gaze? What has he done? Is it time to return? She takes his hand. He thrashes about, struggles. She pulls him, she is strong, she drags him and, lo and behold, her eyes are now blue. Gigantic, luminous eyes. "No," he groans.

The woman is nowhere to be seen. It's over.

Which of the two is here? Who wants my hand? Those two, the "I" again. They want. To have, to possess . . .

Not here yet, the right time. No, stay. Passive. Be bright flame under the palm. Hold the candle. Rub the wax.

Dazzling, the blue, too blue, lake of fire! Penetrating, the black orbs. So gentle. Drown in them. . . . Important to close my eyes. Go back to sleep.

One last glance at the sleeping Martin, and Hannah shut the door behind her. She walked slowly to the kitchen.

"Well?" said Elfriede, anxious.

"He's still asleep. He didn't even wake up when I touched his hand."

"Sometimes he talks in his sleep. Did he say anything?"

"Oh, look, it's not raining now," Hannah observed.

"Oh my, you're right," said Elfriede. "But the thunder sounds close. The storm must be about two kilometers away. There's no guarantee it won't get us—"

"Dammit. I'm stuck here."

"You seem pleased about it, for once."

"This conversation should have taken place sooner, Elfriede. Instead of squabbling, we ought to have talked openly and honestly, as we've done today. Without hiding anything."

"I'm somewhat at fault," Elfriede said. "I was so resentful, so jealous!"

"And I didn't do much better," Hannah admitted, feeling at ease. "I wanted you to be in the wrong."

"So, we've made peace?"

"Peace," said Hannah.

They exchanged smiles.

"If Martin could see us, he'd be happy," Elfriede said, breaking the silence. "Oh, that reminds me. You haven't answered my question. Did he talk in his sleep?"

"I think so. When I took his hand, I thought he mumbled, 'yes.' "

"Because you took his hand," Elfriede noted. "A minute ago you said you had only touched it."

"Touched, taken, you're not going to fret over something so minor!"

"No, but he said 'yes,' right at that moment." Elfriede was worried. "You can still get him stirred up, Hannah. I knew that would happen!"

Hannah clicked her lighter and focused on the flame.

Hannah

Deceitful Hannah.

Squeezing Martin's hand, Hannah had heard distinctly the "no" he muttered in his sleep. He had not said the "yes" that so upset Elfriede. Hannah was being deceitful.

As a child, when she didn't want to spend vacations with her grandparents, she would manage to fall ill. Sore throat, bronchitis. She had a knack for deceit.

In her school days, they said she was brilliant; but she would memorize the subject matter that bored her, pretending to understand it. To get through life she needed deceit.

It had started during her father's last weeks. He was in such pain that Martha would sit at the piano to soothe him. His face distorted by illness, Paul would manage a little twisted smile. Music deceived. Her father was going to suffer an agonizing death. To be aware of that was not allowed. When he did die, deceitful Hannah played insensitive.

To commemorate the first anniversary of Paul Arendt's passing, Martha planned a heroic outing: mother and daughter would go to the deceased's favorite restaurant for a candlelight dinner in his honor. The joyful celebration had a hollow ring. Hannah had choked back her tears.

And as for love, good God! The first boy in her life was named Ernst. It was because of him she ran off to Stolp, to get to know his sweetheart. Then, for no earthly reason, Hannah swiped Ernest from her friend Annchen. Without telling her.

And that wasn't all. To meet her lover, she would leave class by feigning headaches. Hannah suffered many migraines that year. She had still not taken her matriculation exam, for which she had been studying independently. When the time came, she passed in spite of her secret trysts. Neither her mother nor her girlfriend ever learned that she was sleeping with Ernst.

When was she ever sincere? Not even in her mind. Didn't that come from her mind, the desire to sleep with Annchen's boy friend? And did it come from her mind, the driving need to crush the arrogance of the state of Israel? Was the cure— for her, the great Care—authentic? Martin's favorite word. The authentic was there, innate in Being, ready to be disclosed. But when?

Looking back, she could find three or four instances of authentic Being in her life. The accident in Central Park. And her poems. The first, just before meeting Martin. Let us find each other, the white lilac is in flower.

The poems from her days with Martin. Ah, if you knew the smile with which I surrendered.

The poems after Martin. Why do you hold out your hand so shyly, so discreetly? Is your homeland so far away?

And Martin in his entirety . . .

With him, had she been authentic? In bed, yes, but what about the rest? When she would curl up at his feet and gaze at him adoringly, Hannah waited to hear the word that would unite them forever. Not the "come to me" of making love. Something else.

And when she returned to Germany . . . Why that sudden urge, why the letter to Martin? She knew for certain he had been a Nazi. Why the intentional memory lapse? Why the pretense about Martin's Nazism? "Escapade"— the word sprang from a lover's forgiveness.

To justify herself, she constructed some long, complicated arguments that boiled down to Elfriede's having led Martin to his fall. Poor Martin. But Hannah knew this was not true. Elfriede had not written the Rector's Address for Martin. To excuse Martin, Hannah was once again deceitful.

And Karl Jaspers was also to blame! Why did he make that blasted comment?

No one was harder on Martin than the man whose damning report had resulted in his dismissal. But some years later, Karl turned out to be deceitful, too. For when Hannah confessed the long-ago liaison, what did Jaspers say? "How exciting!"

The excitement of the past then took hold of Hannah. And that explained the unsigned letter to Freiburg. She kept dear Karl abreast of her reunions with Martin, and dear Karl melted. You old lovebirds! What a tangle of mixed feelings for the two moralists, Karl and Hannah.

And then, out of the blue, Karl was belatedly making excuses for Martin. Martin had been caught up in the unhealthy excitement of those days. Maybe Jaspers had been too hard on him. Back in 1945, after years of being ostracized, it would have been difficult for him to act otherwise. Now, however, he had no choice but to conclude that Martin was a significant philosopher, despite his momentary mistake. And so on. In conclusion, Karl called Martin the last of the romantics.

Romantic, Martin! For certain. He loved thunder and lightning. Stormy waters, bonfires. The unexpected, surprise, turmoil. He loved the calm after the tempest, and the drawing in that follows love. Martin needed to go back and forth between blackness and Being, the nothing and the light. And when everyday life resumed once more, he could cope with it only through sentimentality.

Emotion, effusion. And the best part was that Martin the philosopher had always inveighed against feelings! The "I" of feeling, he wrote. The obstacle to the emergence of Being.

Yet sentimental Martin was forever awash in feelings. I, I've always loved you, you, passion of my life, he would say. In spite of his denials, Martin could not see beyond his feelings. He even went so far as to join the hands of his two women in his!

Hannah did an objective inventory. Her scars. The wife's hurt pride. Martin's slyness, his phony naïveté. The setting up of the ménage à trois, with romanticism as an excuse.

Hannah's tongue had savored the taste of romanticism. The ecstasy of whispered words entering her mouth and passing through her body. And afterwards, the letdown when life resumed. The deceitful trickery of time passing away.

Heinrich, on the contrary, was not deceitful. Ever.

But of course Hannah's second husband was not a philosopher. No one can deceive like a philosopher. But Heinrich, no. An anarchist revolutionary and a worker, he was gruff, unpolished, dependable, and faithful to truth. No deception. When there were other women in Blücher's life, it was all out in the open. Their union was totally honest. Then Heinrich had died.

Afterward, her friend Anne came to stay with her in New York. Hannah had long before stopped being deceitful with Annchen. One day, however . . . For convenience, Annchen had taken Blücher's keys, and the first time she used them to enter the apartment, Hannah yelled from the living room: "Heinrich, leave your overshoes at the door!" But it was not he who walked in. Seeing Anne, Hannah was startled. Yet, just as when her father died, she said nothing.

And what kind of deceit was she up to now, here in this

kitchen? Martin was going to die, and she . . . Over a chance word mumbled in sleep, over a "yes," or a "no" from Martin, she was lying. Why?

To keep Martin from dying. To hold on to him. Because he was hers. And even that was no longer true.

The day of the accident in Central Park, deceit had just faded away. And now here it was, backfiring on her as she faced Elfriede. Time to be rid of it!

"Martin definitely mumbled something in his sleep." It was hard for Hannah to speak up. "But I don't know whether he said yes or no. I think it was 'no.'"

"You always tell the truth, Hannah. You're really sure he said 'yes.' You're lying to make me feel better!"

"Truth! You know Martin's thinking on the subject. Truth is uncoveredness. It has nothing to do with a yes or a no. It is not dependent on facts. Forget that."

Thunder rumbled, closer.

"Just as I said," observed Elfriede. "A storm is coming."

"Your flowers will be ruined," said Hannah.

"That's no disaster. You cut them back and they grow again. Martin is devoted to the garden. The change of seasons delights him! But next spring, I don't know . . ."

"Don't think about it. Instead, tell me how he occupied himself when he was well."

"He wrote. He had many visitors. Strangers would come to the house as if it were a monument. He was invited to ceremonies. All that sort of thing."

"You wanted him famous," said Hannah. "And so he is."

"He's crazy about soccer matches on television. He can't take his eyes off the screen. Just like a youngster. Martin was a fair soccer player in his youth."

"Well," said Hannah. "Skiing, soccer. That would make a fine subject for a dissertation: 'The role of sports in Heidegger's thinking.'"

"Nothing complicated about it. Thanks to sports, Martin grew strong. He developed muscles. Then he developed his thinking, as muscular as his body."

"Muscular!" Hannah exclaimed. "You come up with funny words! Martin's thinking is founded on the fragile, the uncertain. On his roaming roads that lead nowhere. I'm quoting him, Elfriede."

"And where do his roots fit in? The country, the rejection of the city? Because everything came out of Martin's shrinking back from city life. In Konstanz, while he was at the seminary, he hated the flirtations, the parties with sweet wine, the easy ways."

Hannah smiled, "But the seminarians were cloistered. I think he was frustrated."

"Martin is a peasant," said Elfriede. "That's why I had the mountain cabin built. Because town life was suffocating him. Too modern, too fast. Time disappears in technology."

"Ah, yes, technology. I forgot his obsession. Martin is against progress."

"And where is progress headed? And where has it been? According to Martin, those death factories, the gas chambers, came out of technology, industry. It took a lot of trains!"

"That's idiotic," said Hannah. "Trains don't run by themselves. They have conductors, who receive orders. And in the camps, there were SS men to release the gas into the ventilators."

"Eventually you'll see him proven right," said Elfriede, shaking her head. "People will recall that Heidegger viewed technology as man's worst enemy. It's nihilism! The plan, as he calls it."

"You're making him out to be a reactionary. Martin's work has nothing to do with the real. It's clear that Martin doesn't live in the world."

"Because the world is becoming lost in technology," said Elfriede, insistent. "Martin is rooted in the earth where I plant my flowers. You have wandered too much of your life, Hannah. It's not your fault if you have no roots. You can't understand."

"Oh, yes I can. I was born here in Germany. I have my memories. Odors, for instance. Soup with dumplings, verjuice in September, steam from the trains. And then, my mother tongue."

"Is that why you come to see Martin so often?" Elfriede asked quietly. "For Germany?"

"Certainly not!"

Hannah had sounded abrupt. Elfriede flinched.

"No," Hannah went on. "Blücher was German, remember. Terribly so! My husband was my portable homeland."

"Too bad," said Elfriede. "In that case, I might have understood."

A sharp crack of thunder over the roof. Hannah looked up instinctively.

"It's here," said Elfriede. "The storm. Let's hope it doesn't wake Martin."

Martin
Breisach, Baden Württemberg, October 1944

The May Bug

He is in step, boots on his feet, helmet on his head, pack on his back. A line, no straying. He never would have believed this could happen.

He is in uniform. Professor Heidegger, an ordinary draftee. He's a soldier, at his age. And the gun, above all, the gun . . . Why have it? Martin has never learned to shoot.

The technology of death.

The detachment is to take up a position beside the bridge, to protect it. There are three cannons. On the other side of the river, you can make out Alsace—sometimes French, sometimes German, it's about to change countries again.

The river has a name, the German Rhine. The water flows, oblivious to frontiers. According to orders, the detachment is entitled to a break. The sun beats down, the soldiers sweat and wait to resume the march.

Beside Martin, a soldier picks a dandelion flower and pulls off the petals one by one, singing "Fly, little May bug, fly, / your papa's gone to war, / your mama's in Pomerania, / Pomerania has burned, / fly, little May bug . . ."

He is smooth cheeked, blond.

"How old are you?" asks Martin.

"Me? Sixteen," says the kid. "And you?"

"Fifty-five."

"Oh," exclaims the boy. "You poor old man!"

"Right you are," Martin sighs.

The kid goes back to his painstaking task. "Fly, little May bug . . ."

"There are no May bugs in summer," says Martin.

"But I am from Pomerania," says the boy. "And when it's the season, in May, I always catch a May bug and let it fly from the end of a string."

"You're far from home."

The adolescent shrugs. "Fly, little dimwit. / Fly to the baker's shop./ Bring us back a great big cake, / and you will be a little dimwit. . . ." He stops. "That would be terrific. A May bug bringing us a cake."

"Would you care for a cookie?" asks Martin. "I have some in my bag."

"Yes!" The boy's eyes sparkle.

"But you have to sing me your song," teases Martin, holding up the cookie. "Otherwise . . ."

Laughing, the boy lunges toward him and grabs the cookie.

"You have to admit I'm a good May bug," says Martin mischievously.

"Not bad," says the adolescent, his mouth full.

Life can be delightful at times. Martin looks at the peaceful water, the deep blue sky. He sets down his rifle. The boy smiles at him.

Suddenly the fractured bridge explodes under shellfire, the water of the Rhine splashes up, red. The boy has fallen, at Martin's feet. A shattering, no more head, mush. He still has a piece of cookie in his hand.

⌾

Open my eyes. War, enough! Anxiety, still! So far . . . Why? No more dreaming. Thinking, instead . . . Try!

All lies. No bridge, no Rhine. Time, no. Explosion, not true. Terrible dream, not real. Un . . . real. Being, no. Retreat. Return. Alive. Messkirch, Freiburg. Shout. Call for help.

Martin cries out.

Elfriede pricked up her ears. "Listen. I think someone cried out."

"I didn't hear anything," said Hannah. "But the storm is—"

"Shhh," whispered Elfriede. Between two claps of thunder, rain began to beat on the windows. "I guess I was mistaken. I thought it was he, yelling."

"On watch your whole life," Hannah noted. "Do you never have any rest?"

Elfriede slumped in her chair. Each thunderbolt was less menacing than the one before. The downpour became heavier, rain streaming down the branches. Then the drops stopped falling. Here and there water dripped from the leaves where it had collected.

Elfriede opened a window. She murmured, "The smell of damp earth after a summer shower."

"Ah, yes. I have to admit it's nicer than on Fifth Avenue!"

"And we needed some air. You've nearly smoked us out."

"I know," said Hannah gloomily. "I can't do without tobacco. Even in the hospital, I smoke. Very bad habit."

"You didn't smoke after your heart attack, I hope!"

"I did, once they removed the tubes," Hannah admitted. "Doctors don't agree about the dangers. Some say, no smoking; others say, smoking in moderation. I decided to live as I wanted to."

"Very foolish," Elfriede said.

Elfriede stood at the open window and filled her lungs. Lost in thought, Hannah took one last drag before she crushed her cigarette in the ashtray.

Without turning around, Elfriede asked abruptly, "Tell me about Günther. The young man I supposedly humiliated."

"And what do you want to know?"

"What I don't know. Why you married him."

"Let's see . . ." Hannah paused, then began her tale: "I first met him in Martin's class at Marburg. And I ran into him later, in Berlin, at a ball at the Museum of Ethnology. It was a fundraising event for a Marxist journal."

"Marxists dancing for the revolution. That's a fine mess!"

"And what's worse, it was a masquerade ball! I went as a harem girl."

"Bare midriff?"

"Yes, indeed. And I wore a little black veil, which showed off my eyes. That's what Günther said, anyway."

"I can believe it." Elfriede felt a certain envy. "And when was this ball?"

"We got married in 1929," Hannah said hurriedly.

"In 1929," echoed Elfriede. "A year after your breakup with Martin. You married on the rebound, Hannah."

"You think so? My dear, I slept with him the night of the ball. In 1927."

"In 1927. But that means you were unfaithful to Martin!" Elfriede was outraged.

Hannah smiled. "Right you are. You're not going to throw a fit, I hope! Besides, Martin knew it. And he even—"

She paused. Elfriede wouldn't be able to handle the rest.

"Don't stop when you're doing so nicely!" said Elfriede. "I think I can take anything now."

"All right. Martin encouraged me to do it. For my own good."

The words had been spoken. Hannah waited for the wife to react.

"Some nerve," said Elfriede.

"That's all you have to say?"

"Do you think I'm unaware of his indiscretions? It was a pattern with him. My jealousy of you had nothing to do with that."

The two women looked at each other uncertainly. Disconcerted, Hannah thought of two bodies moving, the one penetrating with its organ, the other opening and receiving, one inside the other, an act often the same, always the same, never the same. And never again.

"All that's over and done with," said Elfriede. "Let's get back to Günther. You take a lover, fine. Martin abandons you, you marry the lover. And you say it wasn't on the rebound?"

"It was a Jewish marriage, my dear. A Jewish woman marries a Jew, not a goy. Both sets of parents were pushing us. It was the work of a little committee."

"A quickie wedding," said Elfriede. "No celebration, no white gown, I would imagine."

"Those things meant nothing to us. A civil marriage was a legal formality of no consequence. The really happy ones were our parents. We were young and lighthearted."

"You could have had a baby," Elfriede interjected.

Hannah answered a little thoughtlessly, "No. I didn't love Günther."

"A-ha. There you are! Married on the rebound, just as I said!"

Hannah had fallen into the trap. She lowered her head. *I never should have uttered those words. And what's more, I'm being deceitful again.*

Hannah
Berlin, January 1927

The Basket of Lemons

She is sick. Snuggled in the comforter, she keeps her feet under her so no air will hit them. She is feverish. A sore throat, as usual. She caught cold at the ball. She is alone.

When they were leaving the ball last night, Günther wrapped her in his cape, but her throat was exposed, and her shoulders were bare. Serves her right. The harem girl . . . As if Martin could see her from his cozy nest in Freiburg!

Heidegger's harem girl—Hannah couldn't put the thought out of her mind. This morning, at dawn, she slept with Stern. One more, one less. And now, tonight, her throat is killing her.

Three taps on the door.

"Come in," she croaks.

Günther's head appears. Just his head and a hand extending a basket that contains something wrapped like candy.

"I thought so. You trembled too much in my embrace. May I come in, my little Jewish princess?"

Glowing, he approaches on tiptoe and places the basket on her bed.

"Fruit paste?" groans Hannah, in pain.

"Not to treat a sore throat. I'd say you don't know much about medicine."

He sticks his hand in the basket and comes up with a gorgeous lemon. "Vitamins, and besides, it's pretty. Look at that shiny skin. Doesn't seem real, does it? I polished each and every lemon."

Hannah starts to laugh but stops.

"Ouch," he moans, making a face. "Don't laugh, my princess, you'll hurt your throat. Today I'll peel a lemon instead of peeling off your clothes. Where do you keep the knives?"

With a gesture of desperation, Hannah indicates the pile of dishes in the sink. Günther carefully pushes the plates aside, delicately lifts a fork, uncovers a dirty knife, washes it, and returns to peel the lemon. The skin comes off in a perfect, unbroken spiral.

"That's the way to do it," he gloats. "Suck on this fruit of love for me, Princess. Faster than that."

Taking in the acidy juice, Hannah looks at Günther. Light as the air of a fine winter day, he hovers nearby, concerned.

"I wouldn't mind taking care of you all my life," he says, as serious as can be.

At that very moment, Hannah had thought of marrying Günther Stern to put an end to the business of losing Martin. To her mind, Günther was delicately peeling the rind of sorrow, without a break, and inwardly she had said *yes*. A fantastic memory, which the aftermath did not spoil. And, now, what right did she have to judge? After all, Günther had been her first husband.

〜〇〜

"Actually, Günther was a delightful person," she said sadly. "Maybe I'm being unfair to him. I wanted to settle down."

"So, you became happy newlyweds in Frankfurt—"

"No. Günther's candidacy was rejected. He took up novel writing, to my great disgust. I could do nothing to keep him from starting down that slippery slope! He abandoned philosophy."

A smile from Elfriede. "The traitor."

"But he didn't sign his works Stern. He wanted a pseudonym, so he hit on 'ander' because it means 'other.' And Anders is the name he goes by to this day."

"Anders," mumbled Elfriede, turning pale. "He wanted to be other, didn't he? So that means he abandoned the star?"

"He did choose to be called 'Other,' that's true. He lives in Vienna. He's a nice fellow."

"A nice fellow," Elfriede echoed. "What a shame you didn't have a child with him. It would have had those handsome, regular features, and maybe that nice mop of hair. And the muscular back."

Hannah smiled. When it came to the famous episode of Stern at the Todtnauberg bonfire, Elfriede obviously had total recall. Of course, Elfriede had not forgotten Günther. She was as deceitful as anyone else.

Suddenly Hannah remembered that she had been called "Frau Stern," the wife of a husband who had exchanged his Jewish name for another, "Anders," a name for novels. Yes, Anders had forsaken the star that symbolized who he was. Hannah had kept Günther's Jewish name for a long time, longer than he, the deceitful fellow. But could he have done otherwise?

The truth was somewhere in the middle, neither said nor unsaid. The truth was in the intervals, between rain and sun, like Elfriede's tiny sighs. Or their hands joined in Martin's.

"And then?" asked Elfriede.

"A dull story. We had no money, we managed catch-as-catch-can. Günther did an article on Brecht and was involved in his theater. He became a journalist. Our lives took different paths. It wasn't planned that way. I was working on my dissertation—"

"You're always working," Elfriede interrupted.

"Intellectually, we got along fine, but—"

"Not in bed," said Elfriede, stifling a laugh.

"Elfriede!"

"At our age, we can say what we want," said Elfriede, pleased with herself.

Hannah was stunned. "You seem to be taking your revenge."

"It's our truce," said Elfriede, her eyes sparkling. "The rain has stopped, we're having a chat. Martin is sleeping . . . and I'm taking advantage of the moment."

Bewildered, Hannah looked at the wife, who was stretching.

"I see you've lost interest in Stern." Hannah was offended.

"Oh, no," said Elfriede, stifling a yawn. "But I know the rest. You ended up divorcing."

"In the meantime," said Hannah dryly, "in 1933, my young husband fled, threatened by the Gestapo because he was in Brecht's address book. Stern, whom you claim to have forgotten."

"Well, I guess the truce is over," said Elfriede regretfully.

Elfriede
Freiburg im Breisgau, 1950

She Is Angry

It is the second time they've seen each other. The first time did not go well. Today, Martin insists they exchange kisses. They have retired to the living room. Martin waits on the other side of the wall.

Hannah and Elfriede have their backs to each other. Continuing silence. One coughs, the other sighs. This will never be over.

"Well?" says Hannah.

Elfriede shouts. She can't help it. "Martin would have gotten nowhere if he hadn't married me!"

Fists clenched, the other keeps quiet. Foul creature.

"I was from a good family, and he was a nobody! The son of a cooper. That's something *you* should be able to understand!"

"Perfectly," says Hannah. "An alliance between the mob and the elite. I've always been on the side of the mob."

Trapped. Elfriede is afraid of her own words. "That's not why he married me! I wasn't rich! Don't go getting the wrong idea."

"Of course not," says Hannah.

Her stinging tone! With effort, Elfriede unclenches a fist.

"Suppose he'd left me for you." She's speaking more calmly now. "He would have ended up like old Husserl! Living with a Jewess. Martin would have lost his job, and—"

Elfriede stops.

"It just would have happened a few years sooner," Hannah observed. "And he would not have been denazified. Anger makes people say stupid things."

Frau Arendt is always right.

Kill her. Squeeze that once-slender neck. The neck Martin caressed. Pop from their sockets those piercing eyes, as black as Martin's. Strangle that husky, velvety voice. Destroy Arendt's words, as if cracking eggs. Remove the white, find the yolk. Vermin.

Sitting down. Crying.

"Fine," says Hannah. "We've been here fifteen minutes. A long time. Let's get it over with."

Don't answer her.

"Make an effort," says Hannah. "Martin wants us to be friends. I don't like it any more than you. But let's not walk away from it."

"I can't do it," says Elfriede, sobbing. "Too much at once. I learned of your existence day before yesterday, yesterday I saw you, and today you're still here."

"It's not my fault," says Hannah.

"It's never your fault!" Elfriede shouts. "It's always someone else's fault, Frau Arendt!"

"Now, now," says Hannah. "Don't lose control."

"Control over what? I've never had anything!"

Distress. Hannah's hand on her shoulder.

"I don't want your pity," she says, pushing the other away. "I'll be fine."

She stands up, grits her teeth, approaches Hannah and kisses her, once on each cheek, without touching. It's done.

"Congratulations," says Hannah. "My turn."

On her skin, those full lips. Sickeningly soft.

War to the end.

"Now, we'll have to do the same in front of Martin," says Hannah. "Because he wants it. Let's go, Frau Heidegger."

Hannah patted Elfriede's tight fist and said, "I'm asking you to forgive me. I have a sharp tongue, and when it's unleashed, I say things I don't mean."

"I'm no match for you in battle," mumbles Elfriede.

"Neither battle nor truce, Elfriede. Let's make it a lull."

"If that's your pleasure. The word changes nothing. You have a grudge against me because of Stern—or Anders, that is. Just when I was feeling comfortable with you!"

"Give me your hand. Let's not talk about Stern any more. Since you've obviously forgotten the incident, I can hardly hold it against you. Your hand, Elfriede."

Hannah released her prey. Elfriede unclenched her fist. She did not extend her hand. Hannah crossed her arms and waited.

Elfriede stared at the sugar bowl. Suddenly she spoke, quietly, lowering her eyes. "How many men have you been with? For me, it's just the one."

Hannah saw a whirl of faces. How many? Ernst, Martin, Benno, how many? Four, five, more? Not counting the one whose name escaped her. Was he called—

"You're not answering," said Elfriede. "So there were that many!"

"Let's say several. Is it important?"

"I think so." Elfriede exhaled. " Yes, I do believe I envy you. Changing must be . . . how should I put it? A bit dangerous. At the same time, no."

"Exciting," said Hannah.

"Not any more," she mumbled. "What do you call the surge that began in the legs and made them so weak?"

"Desire," said Hannah.

"That's it. Change must arouse desire."

"Sexual desire." Hannah had gone one step further.

"Sex?" said Elfriede, hesitant.

"You must know the word!"

"The act, too," said Elfriede.

"We do have some odd conversations, my dear. If Martin could hear us!"

Hand over her mouth, Elfriede stifled a giggle. "Be serious, Hannah! If Martin were here, we wouldn't be talking like this."

"I know, but I don't see why not, " Hannah answered, lighting a cigarette. "Philosophers have often written of desire. Spinoza, for example. Martin, very little."

Soaring, aspiration, light, inspiration, appearance, disappearance—Martin's words fluttering around desire while the word was absent. Desire.

"Martin, philosophizing about sexual desire!" exclaimed Elfriede. "Unthinkable."

"I like the unthinkable. My rule is, leave nothing in the dark."

"One cannot ponder sex," Elfriede said decisively. "Some things are just not done."

"But they are being done already, under your very nose! In Germany, in France, all over Europe. Young people are devoting their attention to sexuality!"

"That's not very wise," said Elfriede. "Too much talking and the mystery vanishes."

"Result, you desire it, that mystery. You're curious, aren't you? You act as though you haven't experienced much—"

"Not like you," Elfriede retorted. "In Berlin, and in America."

"And what am I supposed to have experienced in America?" said Hannah, intrigued.

"Freedom, I imagine," said Elfriede. "The forbidden fruit."

Hannah crushed her cigarette in the ashtray. "People don't live that freely in America. I ran into narrow-minded people everywhere, and I often felt restrained."

"But you had lovers there, I'm sure," persisted Elfriede.

"Me? No, I was never unfaithful to Blücher."

"Oh," said Elfriede. "Never mind. By the way, why do you always refer to your husband as 'Blücher'? I never hear you say 'Heinrich.' "

"Out of propriety," she answered, expressionless.

"But you called him Heinrich, didn't you?" Elfriede persisted.

I still call him that, Hannah said to herself. *When Martin dies, she'll see. . . .* Aloud, she said, "Blücher is a magnificent name. So Germanic."

"Tell me about him. I'd like to get an idea of him."

"You're asking the impossible."

"At least tell me how you met!"

"I beg of you!" Hannah cried. "Don't keep on!"

"Hannah, what are you afraid of? That I'm going to repeat to Martin—"

"*He* is alive!" she cries, distraught. "Blücher—"

She couldn't finish.

Hannah
Gurs, 1940, in France

The Muddy Camp

They're yawning on the straw mattresses. The day is beginning, and this is its only normal moment. When you wake up, you don't remember, until the world pieces itself together again. You stretch, you rub your eyes, you open them, and here is the world in all its glory. A concentration camp in France, in 1940.

A sleeper stands up, pulls back the fabric that serves as a curtain. It rained in the night. The mud won't have dried up yet. In the shelter, they're sighing, they're emerging from the dark, and in the light of day they become a group of women, just a few of the 6,356 internees at this camp at Gurs in France, 2,000 of whom are women from Paris, one of whom is Hannah, now awakening.

Before they rounded up the women up at the sports palace, the Vélodrome d'Hiver, Hannah was able to visit Blücher. But at Gurs, no news.

After war was declared, Heinrich spent two months in the Villemalard camp, a rainy place with piles of straw for beds. He endured by reading Immanuel Kant and talking with his friends, Peter and Erich. Erich missed his son and he worried. Childless

Heinrich tried to keep the father's morale up. In Berlin, Heinrich had been through worse, but there he had a gun. In France, Heinrich is disarmed. He has only his fighting spirit.

Finally, thanks to Hannah's efforts, he got out of Villemalard. A feigned attack of kidney stones, the intervention of a major's widow, a narrow escape. Heinrich returned to Paris.

Heinrich and Hannah took advantage of their reunion to be married. For the United States does not grant emergency visas to unmarried couples, and the newlyweds are hoping to depart for America.

The phony war was still on. The Germans had not yet invaded France. In May, the French authorities rounded up all enemy aliens. Hannah is German, therefore an enemy. France has betrayed her.

Married women were separated from their husbands. Hannah's train went off to Gurs where her comrades weep at sunrise. As for Blücher, Heinrich, he is nowhere to be found.

The Spanish woman, who has seniority here, is holding up well. She will be the first at the water bucket, no doubt of that. She belonged to the International Brigade; she is an anarchist. Stubborn, haughty. And, actually, she has already gone outside. Hannah's neighbor crouches on the floor, sobbing.

"You mustn't, Kaethe," says Hannah. "On your feet!"

"Why? So we can do nothing all day and empty buckets of shit at night? Leave me alone."

"There is codfish to prepare," Hannah scolds. "And bedding to straighten up. Go wash!"

Kaethe covers her ears and stretches out on the floor. The others look at her, tears in their eyes. Hannah kneels beside the disconsolate one and tells her: "You have to rub your skin with soap and water. Don't fall apart; that's what they want. Get up!"

It doesn't work. Kaethe sobs so loud her hiccups drown out all other sounds. Her despair infects the others. Hannah is getting panicky. "Washing is absolutely essential," she shouts.

"Maybe so, but they've put us here to croak," says Kaethe.

It has been said. Crushing silence. The idea goes around in their heads. *Yes, maybe we ought to do ourselves in,* thinks Hannah. *Make up our minds and do it, forthwith.*

For the past few days, the idea has been spreading through the camp. A collective suicide, to raise the alarm. A thousand women choosing to die in the mud of Gurs. They're all thinking about it as they listen to Kaethe's sniffles.

Suddenly, rebellion.

"If that's what they want, I'm not going to take it lying down!" shouts Camilla. "I'm going out and wash. Coming, Lotte?"

Lotte and Camilla are on their feet. In the twinkling of an eye.

"You're right," says Rachel. "Why give them the satisfaction?"

Murmurs. The women rise. Now they have all gone out. Only Hannah and Kaethe are left.

"So, do you die or do you live?" Hannah challenges her. "Make up your mind!"

No answer.

"Quitter," says Hannah. "Stay in your own little hell. I'm leaving."

She opens the door and looks out on mud. Outside, the others are soaping up. To find the courage to live, all you need do is conjure up death.

She concentrates: get that shoe on without touching the foot to the ground; stand on one leg like a wader bird. The prisoners are mud splattered. Lotte has black splotches on her belly, Camilla wipes off her navel. They laugh.

Hannah's turn now. Cold water on sleepy skin, morning shivers. Hannah straightens her spine. She washes her eyes and opens them to see clouds, and the clouds scurry in the wind. With a little luck, the sun will return.

She has to pass the time without Blücher, who may be dead. Heading back to the shelter, Hannah meets up with Kaethe, outdoors, her feet sunk in the mud.

Kaethe, Camilla, Rachel, and the Spanish woman—
Hannah had not seen any of them again. Erich had a second
son, a delightful little carrot top, then he emigrated to the
United States. The family of friends was reunited there.
Erich's little carrot top grew up to be a revolutionary in Paris
in 1968, to the great delight of Hannah, who offered him
financial help. Then he was expelled from the country
because he was German. History repeating itself.

"Excuse me, said Elfriede, embarrassed. "I was forgetting your
husband died."

"It's so hard, you'll see," Hannah said. "And there were the
times I thought I'd lost him. When he had his ruptured
aneurysm—but he regained consciousness almost immediately. And when I was at Gurs, with no news."

"When did you see him again?"

"You won't believe this. We met by chance on the street.
Along with everyone else, he had walked to Montauban, in
the southwest. I was there too."

"What, you too?" Elfriede was confused. "After your
release from Gurs?"

"It was more like an escape, Elfriede. After the defeat,
France had fallen apart. In the general confusion, we managed to round up papers and we took to the road, kerchiefs on
our heads, toothbrushes in our pockets. And we'd done the
smart thing, for order was restored a few days later. Those who
had stayed at Gurs were snatched up by the Germans."

"By the Gestapo, you mean," said Elfriede.

"Yes," said Hannah. "Chaos is not unproductive, you see.

Without that disorganization, I would have been gassed. And thanks to the chaos, I ran across Blücher in Montauban."

"What an extraordinary story!" Elfriede was touched.

"Isn't it?"

Hannah
Montauban, France, July 1940

Light Shines on the Rooftops

For a long while they tremble, clinging to each other, eyes closed, lips parted, speechless. They can hardly do more, so overwhelming is the end to anguish. They hardly know who they are, a man, a woman, a couple, laughter, tears, joy, one and only. They stand on the street in an embrace that lasts forever. Then it has to end, and life must begin anew.

Which one plants a kiss on the skin of the other? Which one extends fingers to feel the muscles, absorb the odor of the skin in the hollow of the throat, pat the rough chin, grasp the buttocks, cup the breasts? Heinrich keeps touching Hannah's body to prove she is real. She, usually so reserved, utters little animal moans. Finally he raises his head for a first quick look into her eyes before continuing the caresses. They have no need of words.

What returns them to their surroundings? The sound of a cooking pot dragged along the pavement, an infant bawling, the shrieks of men pulling handcarts, the bell on a bicycle, the neighing of a balky horse? Looking over Heinrich's shoulder, Hannah sees a child perched on a mattress, sucking his thumb. A great crowd moving in all directions, chaos and shouts everywhere. People! People no more, but searchers. "Do you have milk for my baby? He's hungry." "Do you know where we can find meat?" "I need a bed. I can't take another step." "Mommy, I want . . ." "You wouldn't by any chance have a cigarette?" "This is absurd. Where are the gendarmes?" "I saw an overturned truck on the road, blood everywhere. Which way to the hospital?" "If only we had some news . . ." "How can I manage, on my own with the kids?" "Where is my father? He's eighty, wears a beret, glasses. You don't know where he might have . . . ?"

The retreat.

Nobody bothers the two who have found each other.

"Poor France," says Hannah. "Are you OK?"

"I have a hell of an earache," says Heinrich, and they laugh.

They observe the people and their sad plight. Then, hand in hand, they walk alongside the river of exiles.

"They look lost," says Hannah, "Where are they all going?"

"And us," he says. "What are we to do?"

"I can answer that. We're going to Lotte's house. Erich is there. For now, don't worry."

"This is definitely a liberated zone?" he says, frowning.

"Have you noticed the light on the rooftops?" Hannah asks. "Amazing!"

As they were talking, life had returned of its own accord.

"Have you noticed the light on the rooftops?" she whispered, far away.

Elfriede took her hand. It was icy.

"Where are you, Hannah?" she said softly. "Come back. . . . Don't stay in the past."

"In the past? What did I say?"

"You called me '*du.*' You were somewhere else."

Hannah sighed. "Yes. My memory is really out of control. I was reliving the day I found Blücher, in Montauban. An unbelievably beautiful summer day."

"A very happy moment for you," said Elfriede.

"Very. But I seem to spend my time leaving the present. It's not normal. I wonder if I'm about to die."

Elfriede shuddered. Hannah, dying before her?

"Bah!" She exclaimed with forced heartiness. "Abandon the present, if it's for a happy memory. There's no harm in that! Martin does the same thing when we talk about our trip to Greece. Just like you. I take out the pictures, and he's off in his dream world. In Delos, because of the fallen columns, he said, 'A great beginning speaks to us here, from every side.' "

Hannah smiled. "So he finally made up his mind to see his Greece. And it wasn't an easy decision."

"Twice he canceled reservations for no apparent reason! At the last minute, it was not his royal highness's pleasure."

"I'm not surprised. He was afraid of being disappointed."

"That is what happened at first. Tourists everywhere. He did not find the Greece of his imagination."

"But the Acropolis in the moonlight, amazing!"

"Even in broad daylight, it is superb. But Martin didn't see much of the Acropolis. Too many people. He pouted. I felt guilty for enjoying Greece so much."

"It wasn't the true Greece," said Hannah. "Martin's Greece cannot withstand the men of today. As for me, Sicily was where I encountered Martin's Greece. The ruined columns against the sky, and amid the blue, the absent god. I was inspired."

"Alone?"

"Yes, but I went there with Blücher, too."

"You really loved him. And I sense that what you feel for Martin now is quite pure."

"Quite," said Hannah. "Do you have any cookies? I need something to munch on."

Elfriede opened the storage cupboard. "There's marzipan."

"Marzipan! How delightful. Give it to me, quick."

Slowly, she licked the sugary crust before biting into the finely ground almonds. "How I could gobble marzipan when I was little," she said with her mouth full. "You can't imagine how happy you've made me."

"You have crumbs on your chin."

"But that's the fun of marzipan. Understand, it's my childhood, the taste of sugar and spice. My grandmother always had some for me. This is so good!"

"Wait," said Elfriede, offering her a napkin. "Wipe your mouth."

Hannah pretended she hadn't heard. The crumbs whisked away, the napkin at hand, that was Elfriede's Germany. Clean. Nothing soft, nothing crumbly. Hannah's Germany smelled of boiled beef, bright red jelly, ground spices, marzipan. Since childhood, her Germany had been bits and crumbs to savor.

"Is there more?" she asked.

"A morsel, but it's too dry. Fit for the trash can."

"You're not going to throw it in the garbage! Marzipan, the essence of Germany. No!"

Elfriede at her most innocent. Too late, one toss, and it was done!

"You shouldn't have," Hannah reproached her.

"And why not?" Elfriede was surprised.

Hannah saw a blinding flash.

Hannah
Paris, April 1939

The Trash Can

M artha is clutching the corpus delicti in her right hand. "No," she says. "I cannot part with it."

"Mutti, be reasonable," Hannah says. "We're refugees here, and we're German. Suppose war breaks out—"

"France will protect us."

"France will be suspicious of us! There are phony refugees, Nazis in disguise, fifth columnists. The police have the power to raid our apartment. What if they find it?"

"An old military medal," says Martha.

"The German Iron Cross! They would deport us. Come on, give it to me."

Martha Beerwald arrived in Paris yesterday without her husband, who has remained in Königsberg despite the danger.

After fleeing to Prague with Hannah six years ago, she has now left Germany a second time. But this time, it is for good.

In 1933, when Martha returned to Königsberg, she had hoped Hannah would come back to her homeland. Perhaps it was only one of those bad periods through which Jews had so often passed; the situation might improve; Hitler might be pacified.

Until November 9, 1938, the day a young Pole killed the third secretary of the Germany Embassy in Paris. That very night, all over Germany, the Nazi militias received their orders: burn the synagogues, demolish Jewish stores, ransack their houses, bludgeon and arrest as many Jews as possible. The operation, directed by Goebbels, kept the name derived from a fairy tale: *Kristallnacht*.

The horrified residents of Königsberg were appalled at the fate their Jews had suffered. Martin Beerwald saw no reason to worry, since the Jews of Königsberg could count on their German fellow citizens. Aging rapidly and lacking the energy to emigrate, Martha's second husband nourished false hopes. Martha, no. Hannah's letters were more informative than the official propaganda. Martha finally realized her daughter would not be coming back to the land of Hitler.

Heartbroken, Martha decided to join her. It took several months to arrange the departure.

Martha has brought with her the most precious Arendt family possessions, including gold coins disguised as buttons. This morning, Martha unpacked her wedding veil, her photos, and Hannah's baby book. And Uncle Rafael's old Iron Cross, awarded during the 1914–18 war.

Martha is without her husband, she does not speak French, and has never before met Hannah's companion, Heinrich Blücher. In a single day, she discovers exile, Paris, Blücher, and she is reunited with the daughter she has not seen since 1933.

Martha sits on the edge of her chair. She has nothing to hang on to here but her daughter and the odds and ends she so reverently wrapped before leaving her country. To think that this glorious trinket from a dead Germany, this fragment of the past, has to be snatched out of her hands. What a shame!

Hannah has no choice.

After *Kristallnacht,* the Jews of Paris panicked. The dignitaries of the community hastened to reassure them. Above all, don't make a move. The watchword of the Jewish community was quite clear: no politics. The assassin was not French. Rumor had it that he was a homosexual, a shady character who solicited at the German Embassy. Not a worthwhile cause, better keep quiet.

The rabbis launched eloquent appeals for a return to the values of the ghetto. Keep to yourselves.

The hell with the rabbis! Hannah is active in the movement for the return of the Jews to Palestine, the only escape for her people. She doesn't delude herself. In France, hatred of Germany is at its height; and anti-Semitism is alive and well in the land of the Dreyfus Affair. Therefore, German Jewish refugees will be the first to suffer.

And here she is, the mother, clinging to an object she doesn't want to part with.

"Listen, Mutti. You are going to live with us in this apartment. Heinrich is a Communist and he has false papers. You have no right to put us in danger!"

"But it's only my brother's cross."

"And it's a symbol of the German Army, Mutti. When war comes—"

"I understand," says Martha. "I'll hide it."

"Go ahead," sighs Hannah.

Martha scurries to the storage closet, where she places the Iron Cross under a pile of sheets. The first place the police will look.

"There," says Martha, reassured. "That would be the last straw, if they took Rafael's cross. Don't forget that it was—"

"Awarded posthumously, I know. Go to bed, Mutti. I'll come and kiss you goodnight."

Once Martha is asleep, Hannah lifts the pile of sheets and retrieves the black metal cross with the white border. A fine object, pride of the Jewish officers who fought valiantly for their country.

Hannah finds a rag in the kitchen, wraps up the cross, and goes out in the night. Where should she dump her little package? Under a door. Dangerous for the people in the building. Throw it in the gutter? Hannah hesitates. The Seine is too far, it's growing late. She has to act quickly. At the corner of Rue de la Convention and Rue de l'abbé Groult there is a metal trash can.

Better do it, no choice. Raise the cover, toss in the object, close the can, hurry home. Uncle Rafael's military medal is now buried in a tomb of garbage. Hannah does not know whether it lies under potato peels, chicken bones, or rotten eggs.

"Elfriede." Hannah was breathless, deathly pale. "I don't feel well."

"Are you sick to your stomach?"

"I'm dizzy," Hannah said, bringing a hand to her chest. Twinges on the left side. Methodical, Hannah analyzed the throbbing. The twinges were concentrated in the diaphragm. Was this a heart attack? "A stitch in the side, I think. Anyway, that's what I'm hoping."

"Go lie down." Elfriede's tone was firm.

"Yes."

The nearest place was the couple's bedroom.

From the doorway, Hannah could see the reading glasses, the pill bottles, the clutter on the night tables, Martin's shoes at the foot of the bed. She stopped.

"Don't be silly," Elfriede said. "Lie down. Take off your watch. I'm going to loosen your blouse."

Gentle Elfriede with the light touch. Hannah let herself go, marveling at life. The pillow was edged with simple lace, the quilt was smooth, here on Martin's bed. But her stitch did not go away.

"Marzipan is filling, and you gobbled it down," Elfriede said reproachfully. "That would explain the stitch. Close your eyes and try to relax."

"I have too many memories today. I don't know what kind of tricks my mind is playing."

"None, I'm sure! After all, you are sixty-nine! You ought to stop traveling."

No. Hannah would not give up trips or tobacco. She would die suddenly, struck down as she soared. One day or one night.

"Do you know what Pope John XXIII said?" Hannah

asked. " 'Every day is a fine day to be born, every day is a fine day to die.' He's right. I will not change the way I live."

"You chatterbox!" Elfriede was teasing her. "Be quiet now."

"If I don't talk, I die."

"Not here! Please wait!"

They laughed. Outside the window, the newly returned sun shone bright on the snapdragons. Elfriede took Hannah's wrist and felt her pulse. "It is a little fast." She frowned. "But, honestly, I'm not worried. Rest a while! I'll leave to keep you from talking."

Hannah was alone in the room.

Hannah
Königsberg, East Prussia, January 15, 1919

The Death of Rosa the Red

The key turns in the lock, the door bangs. Martha is home. Hannah is quietly reading in her room, when her mother enters and sits down on the bed, handkerchief knotted in her hand. Mutti's eyes are red, she has been crying. Hannah closes her book, snuggles up in her mother's arms, and Martha bursts into tears.

"Hannah, I have to tell you . . ." she begins.

"Somebody died?" Hannah is alarmed.

"Yes. Do you remember the time the two of us ran through the streets?"

"Through the streets?" echoes Hannah. "Right before Christmas?"

"No," says her mother. "It was in January, when there was the general strike, before the insurrection."

"Strikes, that's when workers demonstrate against the bosses," says Hannah. "You told me they were right. So, they won?"

"No! Try and remember what I told you the day of the demonstration."

Concentrating, Hannah recalls.

They had entered a café and squeezed into a back room jammed with people talking loud and smoking. Mutti had taken part in the discussion. Then everyone went outside to join the workers. At one point, Mutti grabbed her hand and said they had to run fast. They hid under a porch, and that's when Mutti told her something. . . . But what?

"You are thirteen, Hannah. I told you not to forget that moment."

"A historic moment, Mutti." she exclaims, beaming. "You see, I do know! 'Remember this event, Hannah, you are living a historic moment.' "

"Fine," says Martha. "Then you must also remember Rosa Luxemburg."

"Yes, the revolutionary who fights for the workers. Like Spartacus, the ancient Roman slave who struggled against his masters. You told me about her in the fall, when she was released from prison."

"Her hair had turned white," says Martha.

"But you said she would succeed this time."

"She is dead," sobs Martha, folding Hannah in her arms.

Upset, Hannah holds Mutti as tight as she can.

"Maybe she was sick. Like Papa. You mustn't cry, Mutti. Stop!"

Martha blows her nose hard. "She wasn't sick. They found her body in a canal in Berlin. That innocent, beautiful woman!"

"How did she fall into the canal?" Hannah is surprised.

"They shot her in the head. Then they threw her in the water."

They, thinks Hannah. *They, that means the bosses, the bourgeoisie. The Romans, the masters. The revolution of Spartacus is* over. We can't forget it. Remember this event, Hannah, you are living a historic moment, the aftermath of the murder of the Red Rose.

"Rosa Luxemburg," says Martha. "Do not forget her name."

Hannah

After Paul Arendt's death, Martha sought consolation through involvement in the German revolutionary movement Spartacus. While he was alive, Paul had supported the Spartacists. Although not enthusiastic about the tactics of popular uprisings, Hannah's father liked communist ideas. To bring down the bourgeoisie and turn their power over to the working class, that was fair. Paul Arendt had no love for guns, but revolution required them.

His widow picked up the torch. Mother and daughter were so close that Hannah partook of Martha's every emotion. After Rosa's death, Hannah wept, like her mother.

Then Martha Arendt changed.

Counterrevolution wiped out the workers' movement, whose leaders were murdered. No more meetings in cafés, no more demonstrations or running through the streets, no more excitement. The reactionaries crushed liberties. It was not the season for armed struggle by the Reds.

The Spartacist rebellion and the mourning for Paul Arendt ended simultaneously. Martha retreated into herself. The next year, 1920, she accepted a marriage proposal and took as her second husband Martin Beerwald, whose wife had died of diabetes five years earlier.

It was not a bad development, inasmuch as Martin Beerwald already had two children, Eva and Clara. Two new sisters for Hannah. Predictably, a few scuffles broke out between the three daughters of the house. But not for long.

Clara was a fantastic pianist, but she was extremely sad, and at the age of thirty Clara killed herself. Eva played the cello, and Eva had a sunny disposition. Eva emigrated to England after the death of her fiancé, shot during *Kristallnacht*. Martin Beerwald had the good fortune to die before 1942, the year the gas chambers were introduced.

At the time of his passing, Martha had already left Paris, along the same escape route as Hannah and Heinrich, going through Spain, then sailing to the United States from Lisbon. She moved into the Blüchers' apartment and lived with them until her death, several years later.

Of the family, now there remained only Hannah in New York and Eva in London. Günther Anders was spending a quiet old age in Austria. There was no one left in Germany.

Hannah did not forget Rosa Luxemburg. She had gradually become acquainted with her, the frail and sickly girl who was such a fine student but so rebellious that in high school she was denied her gold medal. Rosa's strong will dominated a body racked by ill health.

Lame Rosa was the editor of the Spartacist newspaper, the *Red Flag*. Rosa was good at denouncing the imperialism of the First World War, the conflict that Germany's Social Democrats had voted to fund. Rosa had foreseen the despotism of Lenin and the flaws in Marxist thought. She was stubborn, tenacious, and a prisoner.

Hannah had traced Rosa's path, her enthusiasm for the natural sciences, for plants and birds, her participation in the Socialist International, her speeches, her articles, her years in prison. Her compassion for her women comrades, her fiery gaze. Rosa became Hannah's ideal sister, a sister who was not Clara nor Eva, but daughter of Martha Arendt and the revolutionary spirit.

When Hannah was first teaching in the United States, a student once shouted from the rear of the lecture hall, "Rosa Luxemburg has returned!" Hannah blushed, embarrassed.

Hannah and Rosa, two Jewish women who believed in the primacy of the spirit.

Rosa Luxemburg had an epithet: "The Bloody." Hannah had hers: "The Jewess who didn't like Jews."

Rosa the Bloody played with the children of Spartacist leaders, trimmed a Christmas tree, and cooked, an activity she hated. At midnight Rosa the Bloody might sing a Mozart aria or the "Internationale." Rosa the artist led her life according to the ideal: "One must be a candle burning at both ends." Rosa had had no children.

Hannah sang off key. But she had not had children, she hated cooking, and she was a good writer. Rosa's and Hannah's candles had burned at both ends. For Hannah, death was still to come.

Die a victim of murder, that was the best scenario. But who might shoot Hannah? A Jewish madman? A gangster? That would be a miracle. Even the rebellions of 1968 were over—not an assassin in sight. The heroic death of Rosa Luxemburg was not available.

What about dying here, forthwith, in Martin's bed?

Martin would rise from his armchair, enter the bedroom, see Hannah lifeless, and lean over to revive her. He would shout "Hannah!" several times. He would plead with her. He would finally comprehend. Martin would place his hand on her warm forehead and close her eyes.

No. Elfriede would return to the room and utter a terrified cry. She would pick up the phone and call emergency. And after the ambulance had left for the morgue, Martin would comprehend. He would sit in his armchair and perhaps he would cry.

Martin
Delphi, Greece, May 1960

The She-Goat

Olive trees everywhere. In the hazy distance rises the sanctuary of Apollo. Last night Martin reread the hymns of Callimachus and Pindar. He became imbued with the force of the god whose arrow killed the serpent Python at Delphi. It is here, near Apollo, that he will find the Greece invisible in Athens.

The car stops. From afar Martin can see the tourists crowded about the busses, camera bags over their shoulders.

"I'm not going up there. Too many people."

"Martin, please," says Elfriede.

"The need to concentrate is asserting itself. I'd rather stay here and think."

"The tourists aren't arriving, they're leaving. Look."

Skeptical, Martin waits for the busses to start up. When the dust settles, the sanctuary grounds are nearly empty. It is 4 P.M. An occasional visitor rushes down the steps of the ruins. By sunset Delphi will be deserted.

"All right," he says. "Let's try."

A brief walk under the shade of the plane trees. Lower down, to the right stands a small round temple rarely visited.

Then, harsh sunlight. He has to climb the worn stones, let bits of rock roll underfoot, hoist himself up. Martin is out of breath and he stops. A lone voice coos in Italian, empty words cast to the winds, "Vieni, e tarde Benito!" No silence here. Cave chatter! The god will avoid the encounter. The rendezvous at Delphi has failed in advance.

Seated on a block of marble, Martin contemplates the enormous amphitheater beneath the steep rocky cliff. Apparently it is beautiful; at least, that's what "they" say. But the columns do not rise as grandly as those of Olympus. Despite its ancient stairs, the ruins of Delphi provide no glimpse of the divine. At what spot did Apollo draw his fearsome bow? Where did he take possession of his priestess? A veiled woman inhabited by the god, on her tripod, breast bared to the trance delirious . . . This is a hopeless dream! Where is the Pythia, who uttered the prophecies with double meanings?

Nowhere. It continues hot. Martin fans himself with his hat.

A she-goat is frolicking on the rocks below. What an agile creature! Her hooves do not touch the stones but barely brush them. On her hind legs, the animal stretches gracefully to the top of a bush then leans her muzzle forward to nibble daintily on the leaves. Her beard shakes a little. The left paw, bent back, is in the air. Then, effortlessly, she is on all fours again. She stops, bounds ahead, and suddenly she is in front of Martin.

Her head slightly cocked, she stares at him with her almond-shaped eyes. She is perfectly motionless. Martin returns the look and examines her pupils, strange vertical slits across the center of the green orbs. The goat's gaze asks silent questions and the damp muzzle shudders as if endowed with the power of speech. Moved, Martin grabs the hairs of her chin, holds her tight.

"And maybe you're the face of the God?" he whispers.

"You don't know how right you are," replies the goat, who lowers her horns and charges.

Stunned, Martin rolls on the ground and the horns will not let him be. They pierce a hand, they penetrate a thigh. With one powerful butt, the animal hurls Martin onto her huge back and flies away with him. The wind whistles in his ears.

"This is the price mortals pay when they resist," shouts the goat. "You wanted to partake of the divine that is no more, so you should be happy now! I'm carrying you off. And since you want to see the clouds illuminated, become a star among stars. Shine! You shall never see the earth again. High up, it is all lifeless gleam."

Martin sees tiny white spots on the water, sails of ships heading out to sea. The horizon blends into the ocean; the goat heads straight toward the blinding sun. Overcome with panic, Martin utters a cry that rends time.

"Mortals are cowards," whispers the voice. "We have always known that. They defy us and lose their grip. Mortals are incapable of acceding to the divine, when it kills. You are like the others, you, lacking in courage—"

"Who are you?" he cries, despairing.

"I am your other," shouts the obstinate voice. "I am the force that strays off the path, swerves. I am the god's arrow, which aims at the heart and breaks it. I am the one you have always driven away. I am the one who flees and always returns, the Stranger in your world. I am your one and only, and your death."

"Help!" Martin shouts.

"Poor Martin." The voice is familiar. "You never could

choose. The moment the long-awaited sign appears, you are frightened. You want to fall away? That's fine. Go ahead!"

The goat bounces and casts off her burden. Martin falls into a gray desert of a great simplicity. His mangled body whirls. It encounters eternally rolling stones, lost lances, stray guns, shrapnel, train wheels, ashes. There is no more world on which to land. His fall is without end.

Martin awakens with his temples throbbing. His wife is leaning over him. Elfriede kisses him on the forehead. "Go back to sleep," she whispers. And she leaves.

But Martin does not go back to sleep.

⤏

No more sleep! The two together; queen bees without a drone. Words, venom. Me-I . . . No, Me-I. The One and the Other.

The Other. Eighteen years old, little wild thing, serene eyes, sweet down on her lips, incisive creature, frightened, repressed cry, terrier . . . But with him, arms opened wide, feathers, soaring, pleasure, magnificent lark. Afterward, no talk. Shush her . . . "I love you?" What? Three words? I-You-Me, tied together? Leave, fast as I can! I'll return. You're sure? she wants to know. Yes, yes . . . When, tell me?

The one. First, always, official. Blue light, vast lake. Silence, violence. Gliding, her dress; smooth, her skin. Offended, sometimes. Anger. And the sheets, the bed. "I am here." I am, she is, here, all the time. Never far away.

Between the two, choose? No, no! Go, come, enter, leave. Smile, why not! Bright sky, green fields, wind, peaks, climb them . . . No?

Yes! Need air! Hike, scale, up and up, breathe. Without a word . . . Heart at peace, here, here . . . Gentle . . .

Do, touch, feel, lick, enter, farther, deeper, there . . . "*Being-there.*"

And die, some fine day. Now, already? No, no! Check . . . *Deaf ears. Shaky hands. And the heart? Strong. Smile, just to see? Let's try. Yes!*

I smile, therefore I live. In the background. I don't live here. Where I live, I don't . . . *I?*

Yes, Yes! I've retrieved the "I"! I am here. My name is . . .

⟨✣⟩

"Come!" Martin shouted.

They didn't hear. Get up by himself. Walk.

"I want to walk," said Martin aloud. "I need air!"

Hannah heard Elfriede's regular footsteps, saw the door open.

"Well," said Elfriede, "how are you feeling?"

"You were right. It wasn't what I feared. It's gone, and I'm getting up."

"Careful! I'll help you."

Hannah was on her feet, legs numb. She walked slowly to the mirror and patted her hair in place. "I look absolutely terrifying," she lamented.

"Come back to the kitchen," said Elfriede. "A little mint liqueur will do you good. On a sugar cube."

They left the room side by side, one scurrying, the other panting and puffing. The path to the kitchen seemed endless. Where the hallway turned a corner, Elfriede leaned on Hannah's arm. "I have to watch out here," she said, stopping. "I often bang myself."

"Yes, bruises. I get them too."

"But you, you're young," observed Elfriede.

"So silly! I'll always be younger than you!"

"That's not what I meant, and you know it. Even now, you never miss a thing, Hannah."

"That's not my fault, either. On our way, then!"

A few more steps, and they were in the kitchen. Hannah sat down. The teakettle still sang on the burner. Elfriede bent over a brightly colored metal canister, took a flask from a drawer. Hannah bit into the soaked sugar cube contentedly.

"Do you have these spells often?" Elfriede asked.

"Only since my fall."

"A fall! When?"

"Recently. There was a hole in the pavement, I caught my foot, people crowded around. They wanted to take me to the hospital, no thanks! They helped me up and I went home. I don't like being the center of attention."

"You did see a doctor, of course!"

"No."

"Too much pride. You don't consider yourself an ordinary mortal."

"Maybe not," said Hannah, smiling. "And furthermore, I'm going to smoke."

The thought came to Elfriede that Hannah was getting ready for death. "After all, it's your life. What will you do after Freiburg?"

"Meet my old friend Anne in Tegna, in Switzerland. I also have a Kant project to finish. Then, it's back to New York, which doesn't thrill me."

"You're all alone there," Elfriede remarked.

"No, I'm not. Just a phone call, and friends will stop by, we put together a meal, we talk. No, it's something else. There are a lot of assaults in my neighborhood now, and I don't feel safe any more."

Something was creaking in the room where Martin slept. Like the wind rattling a door.

"Listen," said Hannah anxiously. "There's a noise down his way."

"But surely it's nothing," said Elfriede. "I just came from there. He was still dozing."

"I tell you, I hear something. What if he's fallen out of his chair?"

"I'll go check, if it makes you happy," Elfriede said.

She went out. Soon Hannah heard her exclaim, "But what are you doing? You should have called, Martin!"

Hannah unwound her legs. She didn't walk. She ran.

Martin was a little shaky, but he was on his feet.

Standing between Elfriede and Hannah, he was silent. His eyes traveled slowly from one to the other, glancing briefly at each face without resting on either.

"Sit down," Elfriede ordered. "You're going to fall."

He raised his bushy eyebrows and took a step.

Hannah intervened. "You should listen to Elfriede."

Head down, he took another step.

"You're so stubborn," Elfriede said. "You're in no condition to walk."

"Be sensible!" exclaimed Hannah.

⌒⊙⌒

The one and the other, together. The two of them, relentless. You-this, you-that. You must, you mustn't. Me-I. Don't dare talk . . . Leave me alone. Walk, yes! Third step, fourth. Go. Outdoors!

⌒⊙⌒

The two women shrieked in unison. Quicker than Elfriede, Hannah grabbed the old man by the arm and clasped him tight. "I have you," she said, "and I won't let go."

Petrified, Elfriede watched Martin and Hannah slowly head for the front door.

"Would you open the door for us, Elfriede?" Hannah asked.

And Elfriede did so, wordlessly handing Martin's cane to Hannah. Then she stepped aside as they walked by her arm in arm.

Outdoors, the leaves on the rosebushes glistened with

rain, and the few roses spared by the cloudburst opened their hearts to the sun. Leaning on Hannah, Martin walked down the steps. Once on the flat, he grabbed his cane. Hannah felt Martin pull away from her. Time stood still.

Hannah
Königsberg, East Prussia, 1911

Her Father Falls

She is seven, she is holding her father by the arm, and he is staggering.

Martha has asked her daughter to take Paul Arendt for a stroll in the park, the Tiergarten, a daily ritual. He can barely walk. He has lost his sense of balance, he might fall down any time. Twitching convulsively, his legs do not work well. Left to himself, he falls.

Hannah will talk to him in a low, soothing voice. These are Mutti's instructions: whisper, take his arm, and this time don't let him go for a second.

The other day, the little girl's mind wandered during the walk. She loosened her grip on her father's arm, one leg twisted, her father clung to her, but it was too late. He fell hard. She could not raise him up. She had to ask passersby for help. Because his arms flailed about in every direction, they had trouble getting him to his feet.

One of the passersby, an elegantly turned out young man, offered to call a taxi, but Paul Arendt glared so angrily that his daughter said, "No thank you, sir." A woman walked away muttering, "How awful!" The young man gave the little girl a pitying look that her father intercepted.

Humiliated, Paul Arendt shook all over. While the child brushed the dust from his suit, he shouted nonsense, drooling. Then he started off, on his daughter's arm, his legs splaying out at each step. A jumping jack.

Since leaving the hospital, he hasn't been right in the head. Martha warned Hannah: your father is very sick, it's serious. Mutti did not say that Paul was about to die, but Hannah has guessed. What is he dying of? When Hannah asks the question, Mutti does not answer. For now, he is alive. Martha insists they act as if nothing were wrong.

Paul Arendt can still play cards with Hannah, but he loses control and is distraught when the cards slip out of his hands. The little girl speaks to him in a low voice, gently, as if he really were going to die. Quiet, Papa, easy, there, there . . . Hannah has unlimited patience for her father.

At each step he takes on the flagstones of the Tiergarten, Hannah shudders. If he falls, it will be her fault. He is not responsible.

Martin and Hannah

Hannah tightened her grip on Martin's arm. He pushed her away with his trembling hand.

"By myself," he mumbled.

Hannah stepped back.

Martin walked, taking short steps.

Elfriede joined Hannah at the foot of the stairs. Here and there, Martin stopped before the broken snapdragons. Then he would set off again.

"He'll slip, the flagstones are wet," Elfriede said.

"Let's leave him be," said Hannah. The sound of her own voice shocked her. They ought to whisper while he was walking. Martin pursued his path, methodically, looking down at the grass, the plants, the leaves scattered by the storm.

"He'll catch cold," Elfriede said.

"It doesn't matter." Hannah kept her voice low. She started down the path, bathed in light. Martin had his back to her. She reached him but did not touch him.

"Martin," said Hannah.

He turned to face her. He was blinded by the rays of the sun. Leaning on his cane, he shielded his eyes so he could see Hannah standing at the Occident of the world. In the sky a rainbow was forming.

"God willing, I'll love you more after I'm dead," said Hannah.

From beneath the visor of his fingers, Martin saw nothing but the eyes that shone with tears. He staggered.

Hannah did not move. "You won't fall, Martin. I am here."

His stubborn goat, his Greece, his one and only other. He smiled at her.

Elfriede called out, "What is he saying?"

"Nothing!" Hannah yelled back. "He is walking all by himself!"

The old man gave her an impish wink and headed for the rattan chair under the cherry tree.

"Help him sit down!" Elfriede shouted.

Hannah nodded but did not move. With a sigh of satisfaction Martin seated himself. One last time, Hannah looked lovingly at the forehead with its prominent veins, the short white curls under the black cap, the eyes filled with boundless rapture. He made a sign with his head, maybe a "yes."

"Goodbye, Martin," she said, and she retraced her steps.

A smile, a wink, a nod—so much. There would never be a last kiss. Just the sun between them, a look, last words, "By myself."

Reaching Elfriede, Hannah said. "There. He made it."

"He's safe where he is," said Elfriede, relieved. "I'll cover his legs with a blanket."

"Good idea," said Hannah. As she went up the stairs, Hannah could see Elfriede fussing over Martin, arranging the blanket on his lap. She looked at her watch. Elfriede was coming toward the house. What time was it, then? So late, already!

Her purse was in the kitchen, her coat and umbrella in the entry. Her shoes were there, too, and she sat down to put them on.

Elfriede pushed open the door and asked, "What are you doing? Are you leaving already?"

"Would you phone for a taxi, please? I don't want to miss the next train."

"You could stay for dinner. I'm sure Martin would be delighted."

"No," she replied, tying her laces. "Now that he's better, I can go."

"He didn't say anything, did he?" asked Elfriede.

"Not a single word," said Hannah. "But he did walk."

She tried to get up, but her knees gave way. Elfriede leaned over to help her.

"He walks better than I do," Hannah said. "My legs are in terrible shape. So, what about the taxi?"

"You really are leaving us," said Elfriede, looking sad.

"Really." Hannah smiled.

Elfriede dialed the number. "Fillibachstrasse, 25, Heidegger. For Frau Arendt. A, as in Augsburg, yes. No H. Fifteen minutes? Fine."

"Fifteen minutes," she said, replacing the receiver. "Come and sit while you're waiting."

Next to the window was Martin's empty chair. Hannah and Elfriede sat side by side on the sofa.

"With my people," said Hannah, "when you were going away for a long time, you'd throw salt over your shoulder. To guarantee you'd return."

"No need for salt. You'll be back next year."

"Next year," echoed Hannah pensively.

"Even if Martin is no longer here. We have so much to say to each other."

"What if I die before he does?"

Elfriede laughed a forced laugh, and she put a hand on Hannah's knee.

"One or another of us has to be the first to pass on!" said Hannah. "I don't see anything comical about it."

"No! What's funny is that you're the youngest! Good heavens, why would it be you?"

Why? A question to be answered with silence. To put it simply, Hannah had had her share of life. They would bury her beside Blücher, they would say Kaddish.

"But if it does come to that," she said, "I would like to ask you a favor, Elfriede. Have Martin light a candle to my memory."

Taken aback, Elfriede stared at her. Hannah was not joking. "A candle," she said. "Just one?"

"Yes. Thank you."

"I shall do so."

Hannah coughed delicately. Through the window, there appeared a perfect rainbow, an arch of color after the rain. The light would soon fade away. Tomorrow, a new day would dawn, a fine day to die.

"What's happened to the taxi? It's late," said Hannah.

"Don't be in such a hurry. Wait . . . I hear a car engine. It's here."

"He came fast," said Hannah. "Well, goodbye, Elfriede."

"Goodbye, Hannah."

They were not ready to move. Seated in the shadowy light, Elfriede squeezed the hand that Hannah held out to her.

"You must get Martin," said Hannah. "The sun is setting, and it will be damp. Now he could catch cold."

Elfriede tightened her grip on Hannah's fingers and shook her head.

"You must," said Hannah. "Go ! Get up! I'll follow you."

Elfriede let go of Hannah's hand and obeyed.

Another minute opposite the empty chair. Outside, the taxi waited and Elfriede was on her way to the garden. The time was up. Hannah went to the entry, put on her coat, picked up her purse and her umbrella, and walked carefully down the stairs.

Standing behind Martin's chair, Elfriede waved. Hannah nodded to her, opened her umbrella and unlatched the gate to the street.

"Why is she opening her umbrella?" Elfriede said to Martin. "She's out of her head! It's not raining now."

Hannah closed the useless object and climbed in the taxi. As the engine started, she lowered the window and nodded one last time. Elfriede stood with her hands on Martin's shoulders.

"To the station," said Hannah.

Hannah
Paris, May 23, 1940

At the Vél d'Hiv

They have been here a week.

The announcement appeared in the newspapers on May 5: on the fourteenth day of the month of the May bug, all foreigners from Germany, the Saar, and Danzig, seventeen to fifty-five years of age, were to assemble in the principal stadiums of Paris, men at the Buffalo, women at the Vélodrome d'Hiver. Martha Arendt is over the age limit. She has stayed at the apartment, Rue de la Convention.

The women were allowed to bring enough food for two days, their forks, knives, and spoons, and thirty kilos of baggage. At the Vél d'Hiv, they were divided into groups of four, assigned spots in the bleachers, and issued straw mattresses. Hannah is billeted with a woman named Franze, and two women she doesn't know, enemy aliens like herself.

After the first two days, they were given food. The sun of summer 1940 is relentless. The women swelter under the glass roof of the Vél d'Hiv. And there they stay, standing up often to stretch their legs, unable to do more, because walking is not allowed. One night a plane shook the panes of glass over their heads, a bomber perhaps. They were terrified. Since then, they have been waiting to hear their fate. Destination unknown.

French police guard them. No, the women aren't mistreated. Just confined. So they can be sent where? No answer. Today, tomorrow, in three days? It's already been a week.

A police captain enters the stadium. Assemble! Line up by twos! Today is May 23.

They are leaving Vél d'Hiv, all the enemy aliens packed into busses.

Off they go. . . . As they cross Paris, Hannah looks out at the city where she has spent seven years of her life.

Seven years of mutual aid and support, of friendship and conflict. Seven years of fatigue and catch-as-catch-can. Seven years of temporary work, secretary, researcher, seven years with time to be a lady's companion to the Baroness Rothschild, who dressed in red silk to cheer up Jewish orphans.

Seven years of meeting people and four years of Blücher, who courts her. Four years with Heinrich, I think I love you. Four years of hesitation, four years of growing accustomed, rough and tender years. Four years of popular French melodies of love and disaster: "La fille de joie est triste, au fond d'la rue là-bas, son accordéoniste, il est parti soldat"; "Tout va très bien, madame la marquise." Four years of longing, with the melody of lost love, "Vous, qui passez sans me voir, sans même me dire bonsoir"; and the refrain of the young lovers who hear the golden wheat fields sing: "Nous irons écouter la chanson des blés d'or."

Four years of walking along the Seine and down avenues lined with chestnuts in bloom. Four years of passing Notre Dame, the Jardin des Plantes, and the absurd belfry of the Gare de Lyon, which is now before her eyes.

Relief. Trains from the Gare de Lyon go the south, not to

the east. The women in Hannah's bus cry out, we're not going to die!

Here are the platforms.

There are the trains, among them, Hannah's.

When she steps into the coach, Hannah is liberated. Wherever she's going, it is in France, the South of France. Nothing can happen to her.

The train starts, picks up speed, the windows shake, the houses display blind windows, laundry on balconies, pots of geraniums. Paris is left behind. The train passes stone houses, red roofs, climbing roses, small gardens, cottages. The suburbs thin out and here is the country with its poplars. When the wheat fields appear, Hannah grows gloomy. Harvest time is near. The wheat fields will be golden, but Hannah will not hear their song.

Maybe she will never see Paris again. Nor her mother, still on Rue de la Convention.

Nor Heinrich: he, too, departing. No matter what happens, this train is leaving Paris and carrying its cargo of women nowhere, without Blücher.

Separate destinations.

"Again," she whispered. "It's not over with!"

"Oh, yes it is," said the taxi driver. "The storm's finished for tonight. In these parts, the wind dies down at sunset. I know, I was born here."

"I see. And when was that?"

"In bad times, ma'am. I came into the world in 1946. My mother almost died when I was born. Tough having a baby during the Occupation!"

"The postwar period, " Hannah corrected him.

"By the way, did you see old Heidegger?" the driver asked. "They say he's very tired."

"Yes," said Hannah. "But fit as a fiddle."

"Good. Such a credit to us. Think of it, the greatest German philosopher of the twentieth century! People come here just to see him."

Hannah closed her eyes.

After a brief silence, the driver spoke up again: "Have you known him a long time?"

"A very long time. Since 1924."

"Wow, that is something! An old acquaintance then. You were just a kid!"

"More or less." She smiled. "I was eighteen."

"I'll bet he put the make on you," said the driver.

"What colossal nerve!"

"OK, I didn't mean anything by it. Just paying you a little compliment."

Hannah rested her head on the back of the seat and let it sway with the motion of the cab.

Hannah
Marburg, Baden Württemberg, 1924

The First Time

Intimidated, she entered on tiptoe. He held the door and stepped aside to let her pass. Now he is looking at her so closely that she stands still and lowers her eyes.

"Do sit down, Fraülein Arendt," says the professor. "You wished to have this interview. I am listening."

Hannah raises her head and meets the bright, relentless gaze. Like a statue. She is silent.

"I am listening, Fraülein Arendt," the professor sighs. "Come now, do not be afraid. I am not an ogre."

A terrified shudder and she puts her hands in her lap. She cannot utter a sound.

"Stand up," he says softly. "I want to see you in the light."

Hannah complies with the order. The sun is in her eyes. She shields them with her hand.

"That's fine," he says, satisfied. "Now the rays of the sun pass right through you. You are different in the light, Fraülein Arendt."

Suddenly she wants to run and to laugh. Her legs buckle, but she holds on, standing in his presence.

"You cannot see me, but I am getting a good look at you,"

says the professor, enjoying himself. "Under that cloche, you are not just anybody."

Impulsively, she takes off the hat and reveals her unruly curls. Then she lowers her head sheepishly. What has she done!

"I can't see your eyes," Heidegger whispers. "Don't keep your head down. Why are you trembling?"

Hannah is no longer afraid. She dares to face the dark, fiery look.

"What is that Orient in your eyes?" he says. "From where have you come to me? Why you?"

Hannah parts her lips to answer that she does not know, but she cannot speak. Suddenly the answer is apparent. The sun blinds her. The beginning of everything.

"God in Heaven," she muttered. "When all is said and done . . ."

"What did you say?" asked the driver.

"Nothing," she answers, rummaging through her purse. "I'm hunting for my cigarettes. I think I must have left them in the kitchen."

"You can pick some up at the station."

The station, where the trains are. A separate destination. A fine day to leave Freiburg.

*F**our months later Hannah Arendt died suddenly, suffering a fatal heart attack as she talked with friends in her Manhattan apartment on the evening of December 4, 1975. She was sixty-nine. She was cremated at Ferncliff, near Hartsdale, New York.*

Martin Heidegger died in bed at his home in Freiburg sometime after dawn on May 26, 1976. He was eighty-seven.

Elfriede Heidegger, née Petri, passed away on the morning of March 21, 1992. She was ninety-eight. She rests beside her husband, in Messkirch.

Author's Note

"Despite the debacle of her 1974 visit, Arendt decided to visit Martin Heidegger in Freiburg on her way to Tegna. She found him unwell. Concerned about her husband, Elfriede Heidegger was cordial to Hannah Arendt, and at long last a truce was reached between the two women, a reconciliation."

That is how Hannah Arendt's biographer, Elisabeth Young-Bruehl, describes the last meeting between Arendt and Heidegger, which took place in 1975. Those lines were the inspiration for my novel.

Without attempting an exhaustive bibliography, I wanted to list works I found especially helpful in providing material on the ideas and events marking the passion of two tortured existences, in whose story ideas and events are of equal weight.

The reader should keep in mind that the history of the Jews during the period from the beginning of the century to the present had been little studied in the era of the fictional conversations between Elfriede and Hannah. In 1975, the countless examples of Jewish resistance to the extermination were virtually unknown, as Simon Epstein points out in his work *Histoire du peuple juif au XXe siècle* (see bibliography below), in which he takes Hannah Arendt to task for failing to provide adequate documentation for her conclusions. Nineteen seventy-five was another world: the one inhabited by the protagonists of this book.

BIBLIOGRAPHY

ABOUT HANNAH ARENDT

Courtine-Denamy, Sylvie. *Hannah Arendt*. Paris: Belfond, 1994.
Even-Granboulan, Geneviève. *Hannah Arendt, une femme de pensée*. Paris: Anthropos, 1990.
Young-Bruehl, Elisabeth. *Hannah Arendt: For Love of the World*. New Haven: Yale University Press, 1982.

ABOUT MARTIN HEIDEGGER

Biemel, Walter. *Martin Heidegger: An Illustrated Study*. Translated by J. L. Mehta. New York: Harcourt Brace Jovanovich, 1976.
Cahiers de l'Herne, 1983. *Heidegger*.
Farias, Victor. *Heidegger and Nazism*. Edited by Joseph Margolis and Tom Rockmore. Translated by Paul Burrell and Gabriel R. Ricci. Philadelphia: Temple University Press, 1989.
Safranski, Rüdiger. *Martin Heidegger: Between Good and Evil*. Translated by Ewald Osers. Cambridge: Harvard University Press, 1998.
Towarnicki, Frédéric. *A la rencontre de Heidegger, souvenirs d'un messager de la Forêt-Noire*. Paris: Gallimard, 1993.

ON ARENDT AND HEIDEGGER

Ettinger, Elzbieta. *Hannah Arendt / Martin Heidegger*. New Haven: Yale University Press, 1995.

Taminiaux, Jacques. *The Thracian Maid and the Professional Thinker: Arendt and Heidegger*. Translated and edited by Michael Gendre. Albany: State University of New York Press, 1997.

Villa, Dana R. *Arendt and Heidegger: The Fate of the Political*. Princeton: Princeton University Press, 1996.

BY HANNAH ARENDT

Between Friends: The Correspondence of Hannah Arendt and Mary McCarthy, 1949–1975. Edited and with an Introduction by Carol Brightman. New York: Harcourt Brace, 1995.

Between Past and Future: Eight Exercises in Political Thought. New York: Viking Press, 1958.

Eichmann in Jerusalem: A Report on the Banality of Evil. New York: Viking Press, 1963.

Hannah Arendt / Karl Jaspers Correspondence, 1926–1969. Translated by Robert and Rita Kimber. New York: Harcourt Brace Jovanovich, 1992.

The Human Condition. Chicago: University of Chicago Press, 1958.

Men in Dark Times. New York: Harcourt, Brace & World, 1968.

The Origins of Totalitarianism. New York: Meridian Books, 1958.

Was ist Politik? Munich: Piper, 1993.

BY MARTIN HEIDEGGER

Being and Time. Translated by John Macquarrie and Edward Robinson. New York: Harper & Row, 1962.

Correspondances avec Karl Jaspers; avec Elisabeth Blochmann. Paris: Gallimard, 1996.

Holzwege. Frankfurt: V. Klostermann, 1977.

Introduction to Metaphysics. Translated by Ralph Mannheim. New Haven: Yale University Press, 1959.

"Letter on Humanism." In *Martin Heidegger:Basic Writings*. Edited by David Farrell Krell. San Francisco: Harper, 1993.

HISTORICAL BACKGROUND

Cahiers Spartacus, May 1948. *La Vie heroïque de Rosa Luxembourg*.

Courtine-Denamy, Sylvie. *Three Women in Dark Times: Edith Stein, Hannah Arendt, Simone Weil*. Translated by G. M. Goshgarian. Ithaca: Cornell University Press, 2000.

Epstein, Simon. *Histoire du peuple juif au XXe siècle*. Paris: Hachette Littératures, 1998.

Friedländer, Saul. *Nazi Germany and the Jews*. Vol. 1, *The Years of Persecution, 1933–1939*. New York: Harper Collins, 1997.

Hilberg, Raul. *The Destruction of the European Jews*. Chicago: Quadrangle Books, 1961.

Löwith, Karl. *My Life in Germany before and after 1933*. Translated by Elizabeth King. Urbana: University of Illinois Press, 1994.

Reichl, Peter. *Der schöne Schein des Dritten Reiches: Fazination und Gewalt des Faschismus*. Munich: Hanser, 1992.

Rovan, Joseph. *Histoire de l'Allemagne*. Paris: Seuil, 1984.

Circus Galacticus

Circus Galacticus

DEVA FAGAN

HARCOURT
Houghton Mifflin Harcourt
Boston   New York   2011

Harcourt is an imprint of Houghton Mifflin Harcourt Publishing Company.

www.hmhbooks.com

Text set in 12-point Classical Garamond BT

LIBRARY OF CONGRESS CATALOGING-IN-PUBLICATION DATA
Fagan, Deva.
Circus Galacticus / Deva Fagan.
p. cm.
Summary: Trix's life in boarding school as an orphan charity case has been hard,
but when an alluring young Ringmaster invites her, a gymnast,
to join Circus Galacticus she gains an entire universe of deadly enemies
and potential friends, along with a chance to unravel secrets of her own past.
ISBN 978-0-547-58136-1
[1. Science fiction. 2. Circus—Fiction. 3. Gymnasts—Fiction. 4. Orphans—Fiction.
5. Identity—Fiction.] I. Title.   PZ7.F136Cir 2011
[Fic]—dc22   2011009594

Manufactured in the United States of America
DOC 10 9 8 7 6 5 4 3 2 1
4500319502

For Maureen,
who has always been a stellar friend

Freak

MY PARENTS always told me I was special. The trouble is, I believed them. Just like I believed they'd always be there, and that real monsters didn't exist. Right.

I guess in a way it's true. I'm not like the other girls at Bleeker Academy. But nobody calls me special here. They have plenty of other names for what I am.

"Hey, freak!"

I stop on my way into the gym, turn, and give Della my best guns-cocked-and-loaded stare. Yeah, I've heard the bit about walking away. Trust me; it doesn't work with Della. She's a shark, and I've learned not to bleed.

The hall is crammed with girls, most of them crowding around the large bulletin board. Excited chatter floats across the sea of navy blue jackets and plaid skirts. Della and her cronies have staked out a prime spot right in front of the shiny new poster decorating the board. Two gleaming, golden words sprawl across the top of the page: CIRCUS GALACTICUS.

"Don't look like that, Trix," Della says, sweet and nasty as cough syrup. "We all know you don't really like it here, so we found you a new home, with the rest of the freaks."

I've got a half-formed insult almost ready to fire. It sputters out as I get a good look at the poster. Garishly painted faces leer at me, grotesque and gorgeous. But it's not the alligator man or the green-haired girl who catches my gaze and freezes me there, making me forget even to fight back.

It's the guy in the center, the one in the electric-blue top hat, reaching out as if he could take my hand and pull me right into that glittering page. I swear his smile has more wattage than every billboard in the city. And those eyes . . . It's only a poster, but they remind me, somehow, of the sky out in the desert. Dark and deep and glittering, blazing with possibilities.

Dimly, I'm aware of one of the other girls complaining. "I still don't see why we're going to some stupid circus. This stuff is for kids. They should be sending us to a concert or something."

"At least the ringmaster's hot," someone says, giggling. "Too bad he's stuck in the sequined freak show. He could totally be in the movies."

Bright spots fuzz against my eyelids, and I blink, trying to get back to reality. There's something else at the bottom, under the performance information and promises of popcorn and cotton candy. I lean closer, squinting to read the odd, silvery print.

Feeling alone? Misunderstood? Strange things happening? We have answers! Visit the Hall of Mirrors and find your True Self!

If only. I shake the crazy thought out of my head. It's a line to drum up desperate idiots looking for answers. It's not like some circus mirror can fix my screwed-up life. It can't bring *them* back.

"What's your problem now?" says Della.

"Just reading the fine print," I say, tapping the poster.

Della looks from me to the poster. "There's nothing there, moron."

"Check your eyes, princess. This bit. Right here."

Della turns to her pack and circles her finger beside her ear.

"You seriously can't see this?" I'm too surprised to stay on the defensive.

"God, you really do belong in the freak show," says Della. The rest of the girls crack up.

I'm not sure what Della's playing at, but if I don't start fighting back, this is going to turn into a feeding frenzy. I step away from the poster and shrug. "Thanks for the career counseling, but I've got other plans."

"Other plans?" Della says dangerously. "You mean state finals? As if you have a chance. Especially if you show up looking like some reject from the League of Supergeeks." Her lip curls at my neon-green tights.

Okay, so they have silver lightning bolts running up the side. Sometimes a girl needs to feel like a superhero. It sure beats feeling like the resident crazy girl who has no friends. I cross my arms, matching Della's sharp smile. "At least *I'm* going."

Score. I catch Della's wince before she can shrug it off. "Whatever. *I'm* not some orphan charity case begging for a scholarship," she says. "And I'm not delusional. I hope you still buy your own hype when you're slinging fries."

The other girls giggle. Not only Della's pack, but the rest of the average Janes trying to hold their place in the food chain. If I were a better person, I'd forgive them. Right now I'm just trying not to let Della see how deep that cuts.

"Oh, poor Trix," says Della. "I made her cry."

That's it. If I don't get out of here soon, she's going to be eating that stupid poster and I'm going to be on the fast track to a life of fries. I start off down the hall to class. Okay, so maybe I brush into Della on the way. Just a little.

The next thing I know, I'm flying through the air with the heat of Della's shove burning into my back. I roll, letting my body do what I've trained it to do, even though this is hard linoleum, not padded mats.

I scramble to my feet and throw myself at Della, smashing her into the wall. I pull her back. My fingers twist into the collar of her shirt. Scarlet drops spatter the white cotton. Blood trickles from her nose. I freeze.

It's not a last-minute attack of remorse. It's the look on her face. Triumph. Then a voice speaks.

"Beatrix Ling! What in heaven's name are you doing? Unhand Miss Dimello at once!"

I force my fingers to unclench, even as Della puts on a look of injured innocence.

Headmistress Primwell minces forward, her soft cheeks quivering as she regards the pair of us. Lips compressed, she hands Della a tissue. "Miss Dimello, please explain."

"It was an accident, Headmistress," says Della, slightly muffled as she presses the tissue to her bloody nose. "Trix tripped."

"You pushed me!"

I swear, if Della looked any more innocent she'd have forest creatures frolicking around her feet. "The hallway was crowded," she says. "I tried to help, but she went kind of crazy." Over Della's shoulder I see the ring-master smiling above his invisible promises. My pulse hammers in my ears.

"I'm *not* crazy!"

"Enough, Miss Ling. I think we had best continue this conversation in my office."

* * *

The headmistress's office is a lot like the rest of Bleeker Academy for Girls: shabby, uptight, and depressing. It's November, so it's already dark. The sickly yellow light of a streetlamp trickles in through the dusty window.

I don't sit. Neither does Primwell. The wide oak desk between us holds a writing mat, three pencils sharpened to needle-fine points, and a bowl full of what look like hard candies but are actually nasty menthol throat lozenges.

I wait for her to say something, but she turns her back to me, moving to one of the olive-green filing cabinets lining the back wall. The drawer slides open with a bang that makes me jump. Primwell thumps a hefty file labeled LING, BEATRIX onto the desk, sighing like it's her burden, not mine. "Do you know what this is?"

"My records."

"And do you know, Miss Ling, that your file is approximately five times as thick as that of any other student?"

"I guess I'm just more interesting."

"I should think a girl who owes her room, her board, and her very future to the charity of others would try a bit harder to conform to our standards of behavior." Primwell looks at me like I'm some sort of mangy dog at the pound, the type that's about to get put down because it's too much trouble and no one wants to bother with it any longer. Maybe she *is* sorry for me, but I think she's more sorry for herself.

"Is that too much to ask?" she says. "Can't you try a little harder to make this work?"

"It's not my fault! Della and the rest of them, they act like—"

Primwell cuts me off with a wave of her hand. "Personal responsibility, Miss Ling. That is something we value highly here at Bleeker Academy. Perhaps instead of blaming Miss Dimello and the other girls, you should be asking yourself what you can do to make your life—all our lives—easier."

I set my fists on the desk. "You think this is my fault? You think I can make Della like me? No way. She hates me. It's not my fault I'm going to the finals and she isn't."

"Not anymore," says Primwell.

"What?" She can't mean what I think she means. No. Please no.

"We have had enough of your disruptions. The other students deserve better than this. I'm sorry, Miss Ling, but I'm afraid you will not be attending the state finals. I am removing you from the gymnastics team."

The air in my lungs vanishes, like I've been dumped in a vacuum. "P-please," I finally stammer, "give me another chance. I need to compete. I can get a scholarship, go to college, become an astr—"

She shakes her head. "You dream too large, Miss Ling." She steeples her fingers and looks at me with what she probably thinks is a kindly expression. "Your grades aren't bad. Some are even quite good. But with your history of behavioral issues and"—she coughs—"your financial situation, you have to be realistic about your options. It's not as if you have other prospects."

"I do, too," I insist, reckless with my fear.

Primwell's expression softens for a moment. "Your parents are dead, Beatrix. Clinging to false hopes does you no favors." She flips open my file. I turn away, but not before I see the harsh black headline of the news clipping. TRAGIC ROCKET ACCIDENT CLAIMS LIVES OF ASTRONAUTS.

My heart races. I'm eight again, the little girl in a field in Florida, watching fire and light rage across the sky. I don't quite understand the shrieks and cries from the grownups, except that something is horribly wrong. I'm trapped in that moment when my insides collapsed, a black hole about to suck all the light and joy from my life.

I gulp, hard, forcing the monster inside back into its

cage. I won't let Primwell pity me. I keep it together until I'm back in my dorm room. I force open the dusty, creaky old window with shaking fingers, then collapse against the frame.

Cool air slides over my hot cheeks. I keep my eyes on the lightning bolts decorating my ankles. In my mind, I run through my floor routine. Back handspring, step out, round-off. Twist and flip and whirl. I'm perfect, flawless. The judges applaud. I stand on a step, and someone slings a medal around my neck.

But only in my dreams. I brush a hand across my face. I'm no crybaby, but that scholarship was my last chance, and now it's gone. How can this be my life? Were my folks lying? How could they leave me in this horrible place, thinking I'm something special? Maybe I *am* a deluded freak. I lift my head and stare out the window. The city lights stain the night sky orange. It doesn't stop me from squinting at the fuzzy specks above.

I was six years old the first time I really saw the stars. They hung sharp as broken glass in the desert sky. I jumped, trying to reach them—they looked so *close*. I begged my dad to hoist me up on his shoulders, but even he wasn't tall enough. God, I can still feel that ache. I'd never wanted anything that bad.

Dad smiled and tried to make me laugh away my tears. But Mom understood. She held me so tight I can almost feel her arms, even now, nine years later. I think she was crying, too. *You'll reach them someday, Beatrix,* she said. *I promise.* Then she spun me around until my head swam with stars. That's all I have left of my folks now.

The stars . . . and the rock.

Dad gave it to me that same night. Here's the funny thing: What I remember best about my dad is his smile. He was this big bear of a guy who loved practical jokes and silly puns. But that night he was totally serious.

It's from up there, he said, pointing to the swirl of light above us. *And it's very, very important. There are people who want it. Bad people. You have to keep it secret. You have to protect it. Can you promise to do that, Beatrix?*

So I promised. Crossed my heart, and all that. Mom gave me another hug, then whispered in my ear, *You're our special girl, sweetheart, and only you can keep it safe.*

I wonder sometimes if it was just another of Dad's practical jokes. Maybe it didn't mean anything. Sure, the rock is real enough. And it's not like any meteorite I've seen: smooth and black and glossy, more like something spat out of a volcano. But it's not as if ninjas have been breaking into my dorm room to nab it.

I pull the meteorite out of my sock drawer and set it on the window ledge where it can catch the almost-starlight. I hope they can see I still have it, if they're watching.

"Hey, Mom. Hey, Dad. I don't suppose you guys

could give me some help?" I lean out, trying to catch a glimpse of Orion, my mom's favorite constellation. "I think I screwed up, bad. It's hard, you know, when—"

The words die in my throat as I realize there's a guy across the street watching me. I'm pretty sure it's a guy, even in that long gray coat. He's standing just beyond the ring of yellow light cast by the nearest streetlamp. I can't make out his face. There's a scarf muffling the bottom half, and he's wearing these weird mirrored sunglasses. A thin coil of smoke twists up, catching the light, but I can't see his cigarette.

Okay, maybe he's not watching me. Maybe he's having a smoke. It still creeps me out enough that I shut my window. There are better places to see the stars.

Heat sears my hand as I pick up the rock. I throw it onto the bed. How did it get so blazing hot? I blow on my stinging fingers. I must have put it down too close to the heating pipes.

Wrapping the rock in my blanket, I throw it over my shoulder hobo-style and slip out of my room. If Primwell catches me out, there'll be hell to pay, but it's worth the risk to get closer to the stars. Besides, no one knows about the unlocked door to the roof except me and Eddie, the night janitor. He isn't allowed to smoke on school property but likes to have a quick one at the end of his shift, watching the sun come up over the city. Works for me. I only come up here when it's full dark.

It's not much better than my dorm-room window,

but there's one spot where I can curl up and tilt my head against the chimney and see nothing except the sky. My blanket's thin and ratty, but the rock is still warm, so I press it to my chest and huddle down. I slip into happier memories of spinning under the stars. In this half-dream state I can almost remember what my mom's voice sounds like. *You're our special girl, sweetheart.*

I wake to fuzzy grayness. Thick fog blankets the rooftop, smelling like the sea. It's still the middle of the night. Better get back to my own bed before Primwell catches me and decides to expel me from the school as well as the gymnastics team. I roll upright, bundling the blanket and sticking the meteorite back in my pocket. It's ice-cold now.

Cautiously I find my way to the doorway through the fog, then hustle down the stairs and back to my dorm. I'm two steps through the door when I realize the window is wide open. I spin around as the door thumps closed behind me. A figure steps from the shadows.

I take it back. Ninjas *have* broken into my room.

#

 GRAB for the nearest weapon, an old hockey stick propped by the foot of my bed. I whip it through the air and slam it into the intruder. There's a dull clang. The impact jitters into my arms.

I don't waste time. I'm pulling back for another swing when a word cuts through the dark air.

"Wait." His voice is raspy, like he's talking through an old pipe.

"Yeah, right." I swing. An arm shoots out, seizing the shaft of the hockey stick.

It's him. Creepy smoking guy. I still can't see his face, only the close-clipped black hair, gleaming gray at the temples. His mirrored lenses catch glints of yellow street-light as he twists, tearing the hockey stick out of my grip. He snaps it in two in midair, then tosses the broken shards across the room. "Don't fight me, Beatrix. I'm not here to hurt you."

I take a step back. My panic-quick pulse beats in my ears. "How do you know my name?"

"I know more than your name. I know you are unhappy. I know who your parents were."

The meteorite suddenly feels heavy in my pocket. "Who *are* you?"

"You can call me Nyl."

"And you're what? Some sort of long-lost family friend? Fairy godfather?"

The choking, wheezing sound nearly jumps me out of my skin before I realize he's laughing. "In a manner of speaking."

"I'm not looking for a prince." Yeah, keep up the banter, I tell myself. Don't let him see how scared you are.

Nyl cocks his head, his voice smoother now. "What about a place where you belong? I can give you that. They left you alone, with so many questions and no answers. I can help you."

I slip a hand into my pocket to grip the meteorite.

The weird silvery words from the poster come back to me. *Strange things happening? We have answers!*

"Are you from the circus?"

"No!" He recoils so violently the scarf slips free from his face. My breath catches at the sight of what's beneath: a chrome faceplate, like some sort of funky gas mask, studded with hoses that curve off over his shoulders. Threads of white smoke rise from behind his back as he draws a rustling breath.

I open my mouth, but it's a long moment before anything comes out. "What—who are you?"

"Someone who knows you can't cover lies with bright lights and sequined costumes." The bitterness in Nyl's voice crawls along my skin. "Don't trust him. That boy may glitter and enchant, but he is far more dangerous than you can imagine. You will find no answers there. Believe me, it will only end in pain."

As I back up another step, I hit the edge of my bed and stumble. The direction of Nyl's gaze shifts to my hand, raised to steady myself. And the meteorite I'm holding.

Smoke twists up from Nyl's silver mask as he growls something I can't make out. His fingers twitch, and I think I see a crackle of blue light in his palm, just for a moment. "That stone. Beatrix, did your parents give that to you? Did they tell you how dangerous it is?"

"My parents wouldn't give me something dangerous," I say fiercely.

"You must give it to me."

Nyl moves so fast I don't have time to run. His cold fingers clamp onto my shoulders, pulling me close. The mirrored lenses of his goggles reflect fragments of my face: a wing of shiny black hair, a dark, terrified eye. His breathing is as loud as a hurricane in my ears.

You have to keep it secret. You have to protect it. Can you promise to do that, Beatrix?

I struggle against his hard, cold grip, wrenching my arm up. The meteorite crunches into his monstrous face. He catches my hand before I can land another blow. Crackling blue flames lick from his fingers, biting into mine. I hiss as pain lances up my arm. The meteorite falls to the floor, skittering off under the bed.

He tries to push me away then, going after the rock. I bring my other arm up. Maybe I can get his eyes, hit a weak spot. My fingers slip across one of the tubes. I grab it and pull. It doesn't give.

Nyl roars, shaking me until my teeth rattle. I bite my tongue and taste blood. Just do it! I scream silently to myself. You promised! You need to keep it safe!

I yank on the tube again. A stream of pale smoke hisses into the air. I twist away as Nyl scrabbles at his face, croaking and gasping.

"You will regret . . . your choice." He sounds like he's about to keel over. He backs away, toward the window. "One day . . . you will beg us . . . for help."

He turns, slipping out the window like a ghost. By

the time I stick my head out to see where he's gone, there's no sign of him. How did he even get up here? My dorm is on the third floor. I slam down the window anyway, busting my fingers to close the ancient lock.

I slump onto my bed. Now that he's gone, now that it's over, I start to shake. Some maniac in a silver gas mask just broke into my dorm room and attacked me with a glowing handful of blue lightning! If there weren't a shattered hockey stick lying in the corner of the room, I'd think I was going crazy. All my life I've been afraid it was all a big joke, my folks saying I'm special and giving me the rock to keep safe. Well, I guess it's not a joke, at least not the part about keeping the rock safe.

The meteorite! I scrabble under my bed until I find it, then slump down to the floor, hugging it to my chest. Breathe, I tell myself. Just breathe.

I curl into bed, trying to push down my host of fears. I can do this. I'll find answers. Things will look better tomorrow; I know it.

When I wake up the next morning, my hair is pink.

* * *

A girl with hair the color of cotton candy stares back from the mirror. I raise a hand to my cheek. So does she. I tug a lock of my hair forward so I can see that, yes, it really is *bright pink*.

At first my mind spins elaborate explanations. Maybe

I got something on me yesterday in chem class that caused a weird reaction. Or Della snuck in and dyed it while I was asleep. Maybe I ate a piece of radioactive bubblegum.

Was this was what Nyl was warning me about? Did the rock somehow cause this? I pull the meteorite from under my pillow. I frown as my fingers catch against a slight imperfection. What the—?

A thin crack runs halfway around the rock. It's barely noticeable, but that doesn't stop the guilt hammering into me. They gave me one thing to do, and I screwed it up. It must have happened when I bashed it into Nyl's face. Or maybe when I dropped it. Doesn't matter—it's still my fault.

All things considered, it's been a pretty miserable twenty-four hours. Getting kicked off the gymnastics team means my ticket out of this sorry excuse for a life is toast. I've got a crazy gas-mask-wearing stalker who can toss around blue lightning with his bare hands. And Primwell is going to flip out when she sees my hair.

Honestly, though, the pink isn't bad. It'd be cute if it weren't so freaktastic having it change color all on its own. What's next, paisley? Or worse, plaid?

That's right, Trix, I tell myself. Hold on to your sense of humor.

I dig out a scarf and tie it kerchief-style over my head. My bobbed hair is short enough that I think that'll do the trick. It's Saturday, so at least there aren't any classes. And since I've been kicked off the team, no practices, either.

I slip downstairs, hoping I don't meet anyone, especially Primwell. But the hall is empty. Just me and my pink hair, and the ringmaster's smile daring me to dream.

I study the poster. What did Nyl say? *Don't trust him. That boy may glitter and enchant, but he is far more dangerous than you can imagine.*

Was he talking about the ringmaster? He looks too young to be dangerous. Too young to be a ringmaster, for that matter. But there's something in his eyes, something ancient and timeless and, yeah, maybe a little scary. Again, I think of the desert sky. Are the stars dangerous?

I wonder what my parents would say.

I shift my gaze down. At the bottom of the page, the silver words still promise answers. And today's date. The school trip is tonight.

"Let's hope for some truth in advertising," I tell the poster. Because you can bet I'm not going just for the popcorn.

* * *

Our buses pull up in front of a giant red striped tent that rises up from a cloud of spinning spotlights. At the top sits a ringed ball, like the planet Saturn, proclaiming

CIRCUS GALACTICUS! with each revolution. I've spent the entire ride scrunched down in my seat, praying Primwell doesn't decide my kerchief is a dress-code violation and discover my pink hair.

I make it off the bus safely, lagging at the rear of the group. An army of smaller stands lines the approach to the big top, decked out in stripes and neon. There's still a ton of people outside, sucking down sodas and cramming popcorn into their mouths. At least I think it's popcorn. It looks blue in this light.

I ditch the school group as they head for the ticket booth. I hustle along the midway, searching for the Hall of Mirrors. Music buzzes against my skin, matching the jittery excitement inside me. I think I see Primwell, so I duck behind a big guy in front of one of the refreshment stands. He doesn't notice; he's too busy shaking his tub of popcorn angrily at the boy inside.

"But it *is* popcorn," the boy is saying. He rubs a hand over his crest of bright red hair. He's got a crazy clown grin slathered over his lips and asymmetrical white diamonds on his cheeks.

The man scowls. "It's blue!"

"Doesn't it taste like popcorn?" says the clown boy, sounding disappointed. "Anyway, that other stuff is blue. The frozen drinks. Slooshies, or whatever you call them. I figured you Earthers liked your food blue."

Earthers? That's carrying this whole space theme a

little far. The boy is trying to soothe Mr. No Blue Popcorn with complimentary "slooshies" when I spot what I'm looking for: a long, low tent slung up alongside the big top. The sign on the front says HALL OF MIRRORS, under a larger neon light that blares FREAK SHOW. I guess the universe has a sense of humor.

I'm about to go for it when I see Primwell. She's patrolling the open thoroughfare between me and my answers with a searching look on her face. And I kind of doubt she's on the prowl for blue slooshies. I bounce on my toes, my stomach a churning ball of frustration.

A loudspeaker crackles. "Ladies and gentlemen, the show is about to begin! Please make your way to your seats, and let us take you out of this world!"

I stop bouncing, mesmerized. It's a voice that makes you want to look up into the starry night sky and spin, or to run a mile to see the first snowflakes falling over the bay. As a tide of bodies surges toward the big top, I lose sight of Primwell. I shake off my daze. It's now or never. I run for it.

Gulping down air, I crouch inside the Freak Show tent, letting my eyes adjust. The only light is the weak golden glow from the glass display cases jammed in everywhere. I move farther in, checking out the labels as I go. It's some crazy stuff. CONSULT THE DRAGON ORACLE. WONDER AT THE LAST BREATH OF PASHFALLASARDOO. There's some disgusting green oil that's labeled OOZE. But no Hall of Mirrors. Probably way at the back. This place is bigger than I thought.

The gold lights near the front of the tent flicker. I duck instantly behind the nearest display, holding my breath. Was that a footstep? I retreat deeper into the tent.

I'm backing up, eyes peeled wide, when my heel crunches onto an empty popcorn tub. The breath catches in my throat as some instinct throws me down. A dark shadow whooshes over me. I come up with my fists clenched to confront my attacker. It's Nyl.

"Oh, wonderful. I needed a few more dire-yet-vague warnings." That's right, Trix, keep up the snappy lines, and maybe you'll forget how terrifyingly weird your life is.

Nyl stares at me. I realize my kerchief is gone, lost in the shuffle. "Your hair . . ." His shoulders droop slightly. "You should have given me the stone when I asked for it, Beatrix. I could have stopped this."

"Don't tell me my pink hair is going to destroy the universe. I mean, it's a little bright, but it's not radioactive."

"If you understood what is at stake, you would not joke."

"Okay, then enlighten me. Are you trying to tell me some space rock turned my hair pink?"

"Yes. And now you need to give it to me before it

corrupts you further. I can still help you, Beatrix. We can cleanse you of the taint. You can be one of us."

"Cleanse me, huh?" I take a step back. He's trying to sound smooth, but I can hear the teeth in his words. This is about to get ugly. "How 'bout I get back to you? I'd like a second opinion, preferably from someone who isn't attacking me."

"There is no more time!"

As he makes a grab for me, I kick the legs of the nearest display. Glass crackles across the ground. A tide of oily green ooze slops out from the smashed display. Nyl sees it, but not in time to avoid it. His foot lands right in the middle of the puddle, and the next moment his legs go flying out from under him.

I run. I don't care about the Hall of Mirrors anymore. I just want out of here. Please, please, let there be an emergency exit.

I can see the rear wall. There's no way out. Only a red-curtained doorway under a big, shimmery sign that says HALL OF MIRRORS. Do I dare go in? What if I get trapped inside? Nyl's breathing rasps so loud I could swear he's right behind me. I risk a look back. Nothing.

In the distance, something clicks, and a whole row of display cases go dark. *Click.* Another row blinks out. *Click.* And another. Pretty soon it'll be pitch-black in here. He's driving me with darkness. I've got nowhere else to run. I push through the curtain.

Warped reflections goggle at me. Turning one way, I see myself impossibly thin with a head like a watermelon. Another, and I'm a potbellied string bean. There's a wiggly Trix, a short Trix, a tall Trix. The only thing they all have in common is hot-pink hair and desperate eyes.

"Okay, I'm here," I whisper to the mirrors. "Where are my answers?" I spin, searching the reflections. "Come on! There was secret writing and everything. It must have meant something. I can't just be going insane."

Nothing happens.

"There's nowhere to run, Beatrix. Stop fighting me."

I bite down hard on the scream that tries to force its way out of my throat. It sounds like he's right on the other side of that red curtain. I back away, until my shoulder blades meet the undulating coolness of the farthest mirror. Nowhere else to run.

The curtain trembles. A gray-gloved hand pushes through. My splayed fingers brush the smooth surface behind me. Then, suddenly, I'm falling backward. Right through the mirror.

CHAPTER 3

Through the Looking Glass

 STUMBLE, trying to figure out what happened. Narrow corridors twist away on either side, cluttered with boxes and bins. An oblong of dark glass fills the wall in front of me.

You dork, I tell myself. It's not a magic portal. It's some kind of secret sliding door. Judging by the jumble of sequined costumes, hoops, and bowling pins, I must be somewhere backstage, inside the big top itself maybe, since I can hear the distant beat of music. Question is, am I safe?

I lean closer to the dark glass, trying to see the room beyond, then leap back. Nyl's right on the other side of the glass, staring at me.

My heartbeat throbs in my ears, the only part of me that isn't frozen, for a long, long moment. Nyl lifts a hand toward the glass. I get the impression he's trying to touch it. Then he clenches his fist, swinging it down to his side.

Can he even see me? I force one arm to move, waving it in front of the mirror. Now that I think about it, this stuff looks a lot like that one-sided glass you see in cop shows.

No reaction. Nyl stands there, staring. Then he turns and stalks out of the room. I don't breathe until the red curtains swing closed behind him. I back away from the mirror door. There's no way I'm going out that way. Besides, the poster promised me answers, and I'm not leaving until I've got some. There's got to be someone here who knows something. The music seems louder to the left, so I head that way.

As I pass the heaps of boxes, I squint at them. The labels are in another language, some crazy alphabet I don't even recognize. But it's that same silvery paint as on the poster. I reach out to touch the letters, only to snatch my hand back. The gibberish is gone, replaced by a perfectly recognizable word: FRAGILE.

Whoa. I try another. HIGHLY DANGEROUS. I back away,

and not only because of the warning. This is freaking me out almost as much as the stalker in the gas mask who wants to "cleanse" me. Maybe it's some kind of optical illusion. I keep going, but I make a point of checking all the boxes as I pass by. Who knows? Maybe one of them will be labeled ANSWERS.

The music is louder, so I must be getting somewhere. I've just found a large barrel to be used IN CASE OF WEEVIX INFESTATION when I hear voices. I can't make them out at first, but as I get closer the words grow clear, like I'm tuning in to the station. I skulk behind a tower of hatboxes labeled PROPERTY OF THE GRAND WAZEER OF DENEB-5, listening.

"I said I would take care of it! Don't worry. No one will find out," says a girl's voice. "I have to go. I'm on next, and they'll miss me if I'm not back soon." A buzz of static crackles, then winks out.

I scope things out over the topmost hatbox. After Nyl, I'm not taking chances. Thankfully, this girl seems relatively normal, or as normal as a person can be wearing a skintight sparkling body suit. She doesn't look very menacing, slumped against the wall with her head in her hands. I think she's crying.

I step out, clearing my throat. "Um. Hi. I'm sorry, but I'm sort of lost back here, and I was wondering—"

The girl whips around, her long black braid lashing the air, trailing red sparks. "Intruder!"

"Hey, I didn't mean to! I'm trying to get out."

"Too late for that, spy. What did you hear? Who are you working for?"

"Nobody!" I back up, closer to the hatboxes. "What, you think I'm some sort of Ringling Brothers secret agent? Look, if you don't want random people showing up backstage, you shouldn't put hidden doors in your Hall of Mirrors."

The girl stares at me. She shakes her head, setting fire to the crimson fiber optics again. "That's impossible. You're an Earther."

There's that word again. "Fine. I guess I'm not finding any answers here. I'll keep looking." I turn back the way I came.

I've gone three steps when something whooshes overhead. The girl lands lightly in front of me, blocking the way. I stare. That was one amazing leap, even for an acrobat.

Sparkles crosses her arms. "No, you're coming with me. You've got questions to answer, Earth Girl."

"I don't know anything! That's why I'm here. You guys said you had answers!"

The girl's eyes narrow. When she jumps this time, I'm ready for her. I scoop one of the hatboxes off the pile and hurl it at the figure flying toward me.

Sparkles tries to twist out of the way, too late. The hatbox explodes on impact with her nose, filling the air with brilliant blue-green feathers. The girl crashes onto the floor. I spin around and hightail it down the corridor.

Each footfall jabs my fury into the ground, propelling me forward. I can't believe I was such a moron! All I've learned about my true self is that I'm angry as a hornet's nest and probably going insane. Nyl was right. That poster was one big lie wrapped up in a pretty package.

I check over my shoulder. Sparkles is chasing me. What's she going to do, turn me over to security? Send me back to Primwell? No way. I put on a burst of speed, skidding around a corner and right smack into someone.

All I see is a pair of eyes that glitter like my memory of the desert sky. Then we collapse in a tangle of elbows and flashy clothing. I struggle to get free. My feet connect solidly with something.

"Have a care—that's fine Denebian silk you're treading on." Even without the loudspeaker, his voice fills the hallway with liquid sound.

I stare. I can't help it. That poster was *nothing* compared to the real thing. Della and her girls got one thing right: He could totally be a movie star. He'd melt a million hearts with that smile. It's not only good looks; it's something more, a spark so raw and powerful it shakes my core. I feel like my universe suddenly got a whole new dimension.

"And who do we have here?" he asks, quirking a brow at me. Pounding feet announce Sparkles.

"Ringmaster!"

He looks away from me, finally, and I try to shake off the feeling that I've been standing there for hours rather than seconds. "Yes, Sirra? Is there a problem?"

"This Earth girl was snooping around the back corridor!"

"Snooping isn't necessarily a bad thing. I encourage a good snooping now and again. Keeps us on our toes." He doffs his electric-blue top hat, bowing low. "Welcome to the Big Top. I'm the Ringmaster. And you are . . . ?"

"Beatrix Ling," I manage to get out.

"She's a spy," insists Sparkles—or Sirra, if that's her name. Her nose is red and starting to swell, and she's got blue-green feathers stuck in her hair. She looks like an angry parrot. "And she's a liar. She said she came through the mirror."

"Did she? That *is* interesting."

"It's impossible. She's not one of us!"

"The Tinkers' Mirror never lies. And it's time we had a new recruit to liven things up around here."

"No," protests Sirra. "You're going to bring her *with* us? We're in enough trouble already without taking home souvenirs."

"Hey!" I interrupt. "Nobody's bringing me anywhere! First you make me think I'm crazy with your secret messages, and now you're going to kidnap me? *We have answers,* hah! For all I know, you're the ones who gave me this bubblegum dye job, not my—" I stop myself before I mention the meteorite in my pocket. I've got enough trouble without these bozos coming after it, too.

The Ringmaster cocks his head. "You mean to say your hair isn't normally pink?"

"Of course not! No one has pink hair *naturally!*"

"I grant you it is rare, yes. The Mandate were so dreary in their color choices." He tugs out a lock of his own dark brown hair and studies it mournfully.

My anger is starting to wear off, which isn't a good thing, because that'll leave me with just the fear. My legs tremble. "Please, let me go. I won't cause any trouble."

"I find that hard to believe," says the Ringmaster, casting aside his lighthearted humor with such absolute suddenness it catches the breath in my chest. "You've been causing trouble all your life, haven't you? Asking questions that weren't in the textbooks. Saying things other people were afraid to say. There was always something off about you, something different, something that made other people stare and whisper and maybe even laugh . . . Isn't that right?" His eyes pull on mine, demanding an answer.

I swallow against the boulder that seems to have lodged in my throat. "How . . . how do you know?"

"I know because it's the story of every person who walks through that mirror. It's the story of the Tinker-touched. That's what we are. That's what you are. It's why your hair is that remarkable and quite fetching color, and why you were able to find your way into the Big Top."

I shake my head. "I don't know what you're talking about. I'm . . . nobody. A weirdo. A freak."

"Just like the rest of us."

Sirra snorts. The Ringmaster ignores her, his eyes fixed on mine. Then he grins, twirling his jeweled baton from hand to hand. "But I've gone about this all wrong. You should see the show first. Speaking of which—you'd better get back to the stage, Sirra, before Nola has a fit looping that intro."

I realize that the music has started to repeat, going from a trembling hush to a triumphant burst of synthesized trumpeting over and over again, with a grating fuzz of static in between. Sirra hurries away down the corridor, shooting me a backward glance that says pretty clearly she'd rather be bashing my face in.

"Well? Do you want to see the show?" The Ringmaster waves for me to follow.

I cross my arms. "Who are you guys, really? You said you had answers. I want answers before I go anywhere."

"We're exactly what it says out front. The Circus Galacticus, bringing acts to delight and amaze across the universe."

"Across the *universe*. Seriously?"

"Of course not!" He gives a huff of disdain. "Do I look like the serious sort? Across the universe stupendously. Across the universe *insouciantly*. Wonderful word, *insouciant*, isn't it? I love Earth. All the brilliant, maddening words. Did you know there are more than six thousand languages on this planet? Drives the translator to distraction."

"Wait; back up. So you're saying you're aliens? I don't . . . I can't . . ."

"Of course you can," says the Ringmaster. "Is it so hard to believe there might be something more out there?"

"No. I mean, my parents always said there was. But . . ." I flap my hands, unable to express just how different this all is from the sleek rocket ships and wise visitors from the stars that figured in my bedtime stories. "A *circus?*"

"You would have preferred an invasion fleet? Flying saucers and death rays?" He gives me a cheeky grin. "Come to the show. You won't regret it."

I feel like I'm standing on the edge of a very deep chasm, and I'm not sure yet if I'm wearing a parachute. I stuff one hand into my pocket, feeling for the reassuring heft of the meteorite. "All right. I'll watch the show."

"Brilliant!" The Ringmaster seizes my hand. The next moment we're careening along the hallway in a madcap dash. I feel giddy, like I've got soda fizzing through my veins. We come to a halt in front of a wide doorway. It opens to reveal a vast darkness sprinkled with blazing lights.

"Welcome to the Big Top," says the Ringmaster, leading me out. We're in a kind of alleyway between two banks of bleachers. Craning my neck, I catch glimpses of sneakers and jeans above. Drifts of blue popcorn and discarded candy wrappers litter the sheet-metal floor on either side. Ahead, a ring of red and blue lights marks the open center of the tent. It's empty. The Ringmaster points his baton upward. "There."

Two silver figures spin through the air, swooping and falling. Spotlights arc across the darkness, tracking the aerial dance. Sirra flips off her trapeze, spinning through the air, once, twice, and she's still going. I count each somersault, amazed. What, does gravity not apply to this girl?

I exhale as she catches hold of her partner's arms, and the crowd erupts with cheers. "Seven midair somersaults? That's impossible. She's . . . she's not flying, is she?"

"Not exactly. Sirra does have a special relationship with gravity, though. It's a remarkable gift, but not everyone in the universe would see it that way. That's why she's here. That's why we're all here, in the Circus Galacticus. Have you ever heard what the best place is to hide something?"

"In plain sight?"

He grins. "Precisely. Out on the street a man with scaly green skin is a monster, a danger, something to be locked up and studied. But stick him under a tent and call him the Spectacular Dragon Boy, and everyone is perfectly willing to believe it's only special effects and makeup. That it isn't real."

I tear my gaze from the aerial display. "Okay, let's say I believe you're aliens and all that. Aren't there planets full of dragon people?"

"Not many," says the Ringmaster. "Not since the Mandate."

"The who?"

"An ancient and terrible power. They held the entire universe in their grasp, once upon a time. They shaped it for eons, molding conformity, establishing law, dictating order on even the most basic genetic levels. It's thanks to them that you and Sirra look like you could be schoolmates, even though you were born in different galaxies."

"Except I've got pink hair now."

He nods. "The Mandate were not the only power at work. There were others who saw diversity as a strength, not a weakness. Where the Mandate created order and conformity, the Tinkers spread color, vitality, and variation. The seeds of their genetic manipulation have been passed down through generations. And when those seeds bloom, you get someone like Sirra. Or someone like you, Beatrix."

"You think my pink hair is some kind of mutation? Are you sure it's not because of something else?" Like, say, a mysterious black meteorite?

He hesitates, but only for a moment. "The Tinkers' Mirror is keyed to specific genetic patterns. There's no way you could have come through it if you weren't touched by the Tinkers."

"But my hair only changed color last night!"

"Right on time, then. Most of the troupe had their gifts flare up in their teens."

Okay, so maybe I'm not a big fake with a space-rock makeover. Maybe I really do belong here. The sharpness of how badly I want that scares me enough that I figure I better change the topic. "So, I'm guessing the Mandate and the Tinkers weren't best friends."

"No. Not at all." The Ringmaster looks down, buffing the brass buttons of his blue tailcoat. "There was a war. A terrible war. And when it was over, they were both gone. All that remained were their children, those carrying the genetic inheritance of the ancients. And the younger races, who banded together, set themselves up a government, and confiscated anything touched by the Tinkers or the Mandate. If they knew what we were, they might lock us away. Or worse, use us, control us, make us their tools."

"So you're outlaws. Mutant outlaws. And now I'm one, too?"

"Exciting, isn't it? Admittedly, it's unlikely the Core Governance will be waltzing in to arrest you anytime soon. Earth is in the Excluded Territories, outside their domain. You could go on with your life, dye your hair so no one notices. Live so no one notices."

"Or . . . ?" I desperately want there to be an "or."

"Or you could come with us. Travel the stars! Spread wonder and amazement across the universe!"

Something deep inside me unfolds, like a crinkly butterfly testing its wings. I still have questions, though. "Hold on. If you really are an intergalactic circus, where's your spaceship?"

"Here." The Ringmaster spins to take in the bleachers, the ring, the tent. "The Big Top can be a slow old girl, but she's reliable and spry when she needs to be." He pats the wall. "She's our home. And she could be yours, too."

A wild burst of applause drowns out anything I might say to that. Sirra and her partner slither down from the heights on ropes of light.

"Time for the grand finale," says the Ringmaster. "Think about it, Beatrix. The choice is yours."

He bounds off toward the ring. The spotlights leap onto him, catching in the large gem at the top of his baton. He twirls it from right hand to left and back again.

I can feel that entire tent watching him. Hundreds, maybe thousands of people. He's like an eclipse: You don't want to look away, even if it dazzles you forever.

"Ladies and gentlemen!" His voice booms out to fill the tent. He turns to take in all the crowd, blue coattails flaring. "It has been our honor to entertain you. If you have learned one thing this night, let it be that anyone can reach the stars. Choose your own destiny, and the universe is yours."

He stops, the tip of his baton pointing directly at me. He gives the slightest nod. "But for now, good night, and may your skies be always bright with stars."

The pulsing music reaches into my chest and grabs my heart, sweeping it away. Figures spill into the ring, colorful and chaotic as a kid's finger painting, cartwheeling and backflipping and dancing. Girls toss rings, leaping through them. Everywhere I turn there's motion and light and life.

Trying to take it all in is like watching a dozen TV screens at once. My feet are stuck fast to the ground, but my heart swoops up into the sky. I could be one of them. If I dare. What have I got to lose?

I spot the redheaded clown who was selling the popcorn. He springs up into the air to land at the top of a pyramid of performers. A gasp reverberates through the stands as every one of their costumes turns silver. It's a rocket. They're forming a human—alien—spaceship. Sparks blossom along the base. A lump clogs my throat.

I close my eyes. I can't watch. My mind is in that Florida field, my eyes seeing that fire again and again and—I can't breathe. I want to run. Lights flare so bright I can see them through my eyelids.

The thunder of applause fills the tent. Then some jolly please-leave-in-an-orderly-fashion music comes on. I open my eyes in time to see the Ringmaster returning from the now-dark ring. I turn away quickly, before he can see my brimming tears.

"Beatrix?"

He actually sounds worried. I allow myself one shuddering, breathless sob. My parents might not have reached the stars, but I can. And I will. I brush my cheeks, put on my smile, and turn back around.

"I'm coming with you. I'm running away to join the circus."

CHAPTER 4

Up, Up, and Away

THE DOORS SKIM SHUT, cutting off the boppy music and the chatter of the departing crowds. "So what happens next?" I ask. "Don't tell me I need to wear one of those skintight glitter suits."

The Ringmaster laughs, twirling his baton. "A tour first, I think. You'll want to get to know your new home and meet the rest of the troupe."

Running footsteps approach along the corridor. There's a girl pelting toward us. She doesn't look any more like an alien than the rest of them. Wavy brown hair, medium brown skin. No tentacles.

"Am I late? Is this her? Did you hear Sirra's intro, Ringmaster?" The girl makes a disgusted face. "I tried to loop it, but the join was all scratchy. It'll be better next time. I know exactly how to fix it . . ." She spews a breathless stream of what sounds like alien gibberish except for a few recognizable words like *wavelength* and *harmonic*.

The Ringmaster lets her babble on, nodding and smiling in a way that makes me think he doesn't understand her any better than I do.

"So that sounds like it ought to work, doesn't it?" she finishes brightly.

"We are fortunate to have your technical genius on board, Nola. I shudder to think what we would do without you."

"Me, too," says Nola cheekily. "We all know you're hopeless without the autosalon. I saw your hair last time the system went haywire. Do you even know how to use a comb?"

The Ringmaster stifles a choking sound. "Right, then. Nola, this is Beatrix, the newest member of the Circus Galacticus."

The girl beams. "Hi! Nola Ogala. I'm a Tech." She points out a gold patch on the shoulder of her black jacket, which looks like a wrench giving off a shower of sparks. "So are *you* the one who bopped Sirra on the nose?"

"Um, yeah." My stomach drops. Don't tell me everyone here is on Team Sirra and I'm just trading one personality cult for another.

She grins. "Hah! I wish I could have seen it. So, do you have a roommate yet? Because I've got a double right now, and it's only me."

Okay, this is *so* much better than Bleeker already. This is where I belong. I can't believe I even listened to that garbage Nyl was trying to—

Nyl. Who couldn't get through the secret superhero door. Who is probably one of the bad guys. Who is *right outside this ship.*

"The Mandate," I say. "I think they're here."

Nola's eyes go big as spotlights, matching her open mouth.

"The Mandate?" repeats the Ringmaster in a tight voice. "Are you sure?"

"Well, it wasn't like he was wearing the T-shirt, but based on the things he said, yeah."

"What sort of things?" asks the Ringmaster.

"For starters, he really doesn't like you. He said you were dangerous."

A hint of a smile pulls at the Ringmaster's mouth. "Hmm. Well, I won't argue with that. Anything else?"

"He"—I almost mention the rock, but chicken out—"he said that my pink hair was a taint he needed to cleanse. Not that he's the picture of normal with that gas mask thing. Plus, he was pretty much the walking definition of creepy. He showed up in my dorm room in the middle of the night! And then he turned up here again, right before the show. My own personal crazy masked stalker."

All the humor washes out of the Ringmaster's face. "Masked? Did he tell you his name?"

"Nyl. Does that mean something to you?"

"It means the Mandate *are* here. And it's time we were leaving." The Ringmaster taps his baton. The jewel on top springs open. There's a panel underneath that looks kind of like a TV remote. As he punches buttons, the lights along the ceiling turn orange and a siren begins wailing somewhere. When he speaks, his voice echoes on all sides.

"Galacticus Crew, this is the Ringmaster speaking. I'm afraid we've run into a small wrinkle. Please prepare for immediate departure and possible evasive maneuvering." He takes off down the corridor.

"Come on," says Nola. "We'd better go, too. He'll need help."

The Ringmaster doesn't slow down, not even when we round a bend and hit what looks like a dead end. The doors peel back, revealing a large space full of light. The Ringmaster darts inside, waving his baton as if directing an invisible orchestra. Lighted panels wink and blink in nonsensical patterns.

"Where are we?" I ask.

"The bridge." Nola pulls me to one side. "Better buckle up. Quick getaways aren't usually the smoothest."

She runs a hand across the wall. An instant later, the surface folds open, revealing two seats. Nola prods me into one of them.

The moment I sit, a belt snakes out across my waist, followed by two more crisscrossing my chest. "Hey!"

"Stay there, where it's safe!" Nola races off to one of the panels and begins tapping at it. "I've got the drives coming up, Ringmaster. We'll be ready in ten."

The Ringmaster is talking into his baton again, sounding as relaxed and cheerful as ever, all while jumping around like a madman at the consoles. "Ladies and gentlemen, in thanks for your splendid patronage, the Circus Galacticus is pleased to offer you free refreshments outside! So hurry up and exit the main tent to claim your popcorn, cotton candy, and slushies. Thank you, and we hope you enjoyed the show!"

"That did it," Nola says after a minute. "Everyone's out. Closing the main doors now."

I tug against the straps holding me in the chair. *Safe* is apparently the alien word for *stuck*. And I can't shake the feeling that somehow this is all my fault. "Can't I do anything? I feel stupid just sitting here."

"First day and she's already raring to go," says the Ringmaster. "I like it." He waves the baton in my direction. "Mind your head." A screen drops down, barely missing my nose. "There. If you could locate our Mandate visitor, I would be most obliged."

It looks a lot like a video game console, complete with joystick, but the screen is dark and the buttons are covered in more alien script. Gingerly, I tap the edge of the display. The gibberish blurs, then reforms. One button now reads POWER. I push it, and the screen crackles to life. I'm looking out at the street, at a line of buses.

Tweaking the joystick shifts the image. Now I'm goggling down at the people in front of the Big Top as they crowd around the refreshment booth. The red-headed clown is handing out striped bags of popcorn and billowing cones of cotton candy.

"Jom, time to fly," says the Ringmaster. On my screen, the boy nods, tossing the last few bags at a pack of little kids, who cheer. He sprints off the screen into the Big Top.

I spin the joystick and curse myself for not saying something sooner. This is my fault. The Ringmaster handed me a ticket to the universe, and I returned the favor by leading his biggest enemy right to him. Nyl could have called up a whole army of other nasties by now. I clench the joystick tightly. No. I *refuse* to lose all this, not after I've just found it.

I'm passing over the chain-link fence along the rear of the circus grounds when I catch a flash that doesn't belong. A sleek black shape sits nearly hidden between a couple of trash bins. "Whoa. Now *that's* a spaceship."

The Ringmaster looks up, frowning. A tap on his

baton, and suddenly one whole wall vanishes, replaced by the image on my screen. "The Mandate have such mundane concepts of spacecraft design."

"It's only one guy." I breathe a sigh of relief. Jiggling the joystick, I zoom in on the dark figure standing near the arrow-sharp nose of the craft. Nyl.

"One is enough."

"You're a million times bigger than he is. And you've all got superpowers. Can't we just . . . fight him? Or something?"

I'd swear the Ringmaster looks afraid for a moment. "We've done what we came here to do. Time to be off. The universe awaits!" He gives the baton a last twirl, ending with a triumphant jab at the console.

The walls shudder. The overhead lights blink from orange to purple. Nola throws herself at the seat beside me. The small screen slides up into the ceiling. On the wall, Nyl's rocket starts giving off sparks from its tail end.

"He's going to follow," calls Nola.

"Let him try." The Ringmaster holds his ground, even as the entire room shifts. "Off we go!"

A huge weight presses down, stealing away my breath. I grip the arms of my seat.

"It's okay," Nola says through chattering teeth. "All perfectly normal."

Suddenly the weight is gone. My insides lurch as gravity shifts. The room spins. Please, please, don't let me get sick.

Then I forget about my stomach entirely as a field of stars opens up across the wallscreen. In one corner looms a gray, pockmarked surface, more detailed than I've ever seen, even through Dad's telescope.

"The moon!"

"Yes, one does tend to run into such things in space," says the Ringmaster. His smile drops away. The gleam in his eyes catches me like the flare of a comet across the sky. "What do you think, Beatrix? Are you glad you came along?"

My heart is too full. I feel like a tongue-tied little kid. I'm such a dork. I can't even speak—all I can do is stare, at him, at the stars.

And then at the sleek black arrow racing onto the screen. "He's back!"

"Drives full up, Ringmaster," calls Nola.

I lean forward as blue light flares along the nose of the Mandate ship. "He's shooting at us!"

"Too late," says the Ringmaster. "Say goodbye to the Earth, Beatrix."

I get one glimpse of a blue and white marble hanging against the blackness of space. Then everything melts: the stars and the bridge and the ship about to shoot . . .

* * *

I blink crud from my eyes. I'm still in the chair on the bridge, but the straps are gone.

"Do you feel okay?" Nola's voice buzzes in my ear.

"Sure. If 'okay' covers feeling like you've been dunked in glue and held upside down for a few days." I groan.

"Jump sickness is always worst the first time. You'll get your space legs quick enough."

"So I guess we got away. Where's the Ringmaster?"

"Oh, you know. Well, actually you *don't*, being new. The Ringmaster never stays in one place very long. He knows the Big Top better than any of us. Always off doing something." She shrugs. "He asked me to take you on a tour. If you feel up to it, that is."

"I am the uppest of the up. If I spend another minute in this chair, I'll grow a drink holder."

"Good! What do you want to see first? There's the common room or the biohabitat or the infirmary or—"

"Can we see outside? Can we see real space?"

"The viewing deck it is!"

A few minutes later, I'm gripping the viewing deck railing and taking deep breaths. I am *not* starting my new life on the Big Top as the girl who faints at the first sight of space. But it's so huge, and I'm so small. Yet at the same time, here I am. In a spaceship! In the middle of it all! Wherever that is.

"What system is this?" I ask. "I don't recognize anything."

Nola taps into a small console along the railing. Lines of blue alien gibberish fly up across the transparent bubble of the viewing deck, labeling each of the stars. "Oops!" She taps a few more buttons. "There, can you read that?"

"Um. Yeah." Most of the stars don't even have labels, and those that I can see are nothing but strings of numbers and letters. "We must be pretty far from Earth if they ran out of names. Are we even still in the Milky Way?"

"Oh, no. That's all part of the Excluded Territories. We're back in Core space now, all quarter-million inhabited systems of it. But here, we can zoom out." She fiddles with the console. The blue lines dance around, reforming a sort of inset star chart. Squinting, I see a tiny blob in the corner labeled *Milky Way*. The larger area is now labeled *ACO 3627*. Good thing I did my last science project on the Great Attractor. At least I recognize something out here.

"We're in the Norma galaxy cluster? We just traveled 250 million light-years? This is one fast ship. Like, impossibly fast. How do you beat light speed?"

"It's more like bending space than going really fast. And we're not sure exactly how it works," admits Nola. "The Tinkers and the Mandate knew how, and this is a Tinker ship. The only one left, as far as we know. Most everything was destroyed in the War. There are a couple of Mandate ships kicking around, too, we think."

"You think? I thought they were, y'know, your big ancient enemy."

"Yeah, but they keep a pretty low profile. They don't

want to get nabbed by the Core Governance any more than we do."

I tap my fingers against the railing. "So what are they doing?"

Nola shrugs. "Gathering strength. Trying to stay in one piece. Same thing as we are, but without the sequins and popcorn. The Core may not like either of us, but it doesn't stop the officials from appropriating any Tinker or Mandate tech they can grab. They'd love to get their hands on the Big Top, if they could find a way around the Ringmaster's lawyer."

"So if there are only a few of these space-bending ships, what does everyone else do? Hitchhike?"

"They use the pipelines. The Mandate set them up eons ago, using some sort of wormhole technology. Regular ships pop in one end and out the other. Most systems have at least one, except where the fighting was really bad during the War." Nola frowns. "You look confused. Is the translator going wonky? Sometimes it takes a while to come back to speed after a jump."

"No, I got it. It's just . . . mind-blowing. I mean, interstellar plumbing!" I wave at the star field. "Which one's yours?"

"Oh." Nola coughs. "It's that one." She zooms in on one of the oblong galaxies in the midsection of the cluster, then points to a star along the edge. "Yamri. Pretty humdrum. The only thing we're famous for is agricultural machinery."

"How long since you left?"

"Five hundred and twenty-three days." She sighs. "I don't even remember what it smells like in the spring. That's when all the fields start blooming up, all green and gold. It was my favorite time of year."

She has a look on her face like Dad used to get whenever I begged him to tell me stories about growing up in Taiwan. He'd tell me about lanterns that asked riddles and filled the night with color, about hiking through misty green mountains, and the sweet crispness of sugarcane juice on a hot day. It was like this magical fairyland that he'd never get back to, not really. "Sorry," I say. "I guess you miss it?"

She shrugs it off. "Oh, it's not that bad. I love the Big Top. I've seen things a colony girl from Yamri would never even imagine. This is where I mean something. This is where I belong." She taps her sparky wrench badge proudly. "Speaking of which, we ought to get you some things. Come on."

CHAPTER 5

The Arena

NOLA LEADS ME THROUGH a maze of wheezy lifts, twisty corridors, and slithery ladders. I don't know how she keeps track of where we are. At one point I'm sure we're about to head back onto the bridge, but instead we end up in an oval room lined with giant iridescent kites.

"Spacewings," says Nola, pausing. She tucks back her wavy crop of brown hair. For the first time I notice the black gadgetry thing looped over her right ear. She fiddles with it. A slip of something dark and flexible slides out to cover her eye, like an odd black eye patch. As I watch, Nola waves her hands in the air, says "Dispensary," then waves some more. She nods and the eyepatch snaps back.

"Okay, we should be able to go this way." She pushes aside a pile of the spacewings, revealing a doorway. "Sorry for the roundabout route, but we're still decompacting after the performance and the jump. Lots of rooms are still smashed flat."

"Decompacting?"

"To make room for the inside of the tent and the jump burst."

"You mean every time you perform, you have to squash down half the ship?"

Nola nods. "And even more when we need to jump. I helped fix some of the compactors after I came on board. We're up to sixty-eight percent now," she says proudly, leading me down yet another tunnel-like corridor. "If only the Ringmaster weren't such a pack rat, we could do much better." She wrinkles her nose. "Plus, there are parts of the ship even the Ringmaster can't get into. Who knows what's in there, gumming up the works? Poor Big Top." She pats the nearest wall.

The wall hums back.

I stop walking. "What was that?"

"Oh, you know, the Big Top likes being appreciated."

"Are you telling me it's *alive?*" I flinch away from the walls slightly.

"Honestly, we don't really know what the Big Top is. I mean, she's older than some planets. But the Tinkers made her and she's partly organic, so . . . yeah, she's alive. Okay, here we are." Nola leads the way through an arched doorway that suddenly looks a lot more like an esophagus than it did a moment ago.

I can't actually see the walls. It looks like someone crammed the contents of about twenty thrift stores into a single room. I step gingerly around a set of giant-size Tinkertoys, a stack of holographic photographs, and a pile of orange bowling pins.

"Sorry about the mess." Nola pushes aside a rocking chair that's got tiny wings sprouting from its back. It rolls back and forth, knocking into a box covered in pipes, which starts tooting off-key and letting out puffs of purple steam.

"What *is* all this stuff?"

"This is people—and by people I mean the Ringmaster—getting carried away with the dispenser." Nola plucks an umbrella off a freestanding console near the center of the room and glares at it. "Oh, I need a new acid-proof umbrella," she goes on in a fake drawl. "No, that's not the thing. What about something in mauve? No, that won't do. Let's try lime green this time, to match my costume." Nola tosses the umbrella aside. "I keep telling people we shouldn't use it willy-nilly until we figure out how to put things back if we don't want them. When we all die smothered by acid-proof umbrellas, then they'll wish they'd listened."

She looks so fierce I hold up my hands. "Um, maybe we shouldn't bother, then. I don't need an acid-proof umbrella. Do I?"

"No." Nola smiles. "But you'll definitely need a know-it-all." She taps the black thing curled around her ear. "Your insignia will have to wait."

"Insignia? You mean that?" I point to the patch on her jacket.

"Right, I'm a Tech. The wrench is our symbol. One sec." She scrambles over to a monstrous pile of clothing and begins rooting through it. A few moments later she's back with her arms full of fabric. "There are four different insignias. See, this one's for the Clowns." Nola holds up a purple jacket with a patch on the shoulder that looks kind of like a Mardi Gras mask. "And this one's for the Principals." She points to the star decorating the end of a long scarf. "And then there's the Freaks," she finishes, holding up a poncho with a decoration that makes me shudder.

"I am *not* wearing an eyeball."

"You won't be wearing anything until we figure out where you belong."

"Didn't the mirror-door whatsit do that already?"

"Coming through the door means you're Tinker-touched. It doesn't tell us anything about how you'll fit into the show. Like if you'll be technical crew, or a supporting performer, or whatever. Can you do anything really neat? Bend gravity or turn water to ice? Oooh, can you control electricity? That would be amazing!"

I swallow a sudden lumpy feeling in my throat. What if I can't do anything? What if I'm not the real deal, just some wannabe spiffed up by my meteorite somehow? Are they going to drop me off with a "Sorry, go back to school, get a job selling pizza, have a swell life?" Or worse, will I end up stuck in a glass box under a sign: MARVEL AT THE PINK-HAIRED GIRL?

I shrug, hoping it looks casual. "My hair turned pink. That's it so far. Anyway, what do you do? I mean, how did you figure out you were a Tech?"

"I've always been good with machines and that stuff. My aunt swears I fixed her combine when I was only five. By the time I was twelve, they were hiding me whenever Core inspectors came around. Didn't want them to see me doing this." Nola holds out her hand.

I gasp. Tiny silver ridges appear across her palm. In a moment her whole hand looks like something from the inside of a computer. Nola wiggles her fingers, laughing. "Weird, huh? I thought everybody could do it at first. I did all sorts of neat stuff. I programmed our auto-cook to put extra syrup in my porridge; I set the video-com to switch over to *Love Among the Stars* whenever a new episode came online. It was great!"

Nola heads for the birdbath-shaped console poking up from the center of the room. "We'll have to request your know-it-all from the dispenser," she explains, laying her still-silvery palm on the console. "Now you put your hand there, so it can read your genetic signature."

I set my hand alongside Nola's. With a snick of sliding metal, the hollow opens, popping out a small pile of black gadgetry.

"Go on," says Nola. "Try it out."

Gingerly, I hook the loop over my ear.

"WELL, HELLOOO, PARTNER!"

"Aaagh!" I try to pull it off, but the band clamps into place along my forehead.

The synthetic voice babbles on. "I know we're going to be the best of friends, dear! I can't wait to tell you *everything* about the universe! Are you excited? I know I am! Now, what should we cover first, hmmm? Ooooh, you must be *dying* to know the latest dish from *Love Among the Stars;* am I right? In the last episode, we saw Dalana admit her true feelings to Kel Starstrike, just before the space pirate Zendalos tossed them both into a black hole."

"Shut up!"

"I know! *What* a plot twist! But it gets better,

because meanwhile, Dalana's evil twin, Talana, was scheming to take over the galactic empire by—"

"No, really," I say. "Shut. Up." I yank at the earpiece, but it won't budge.

Nola's doubled over, giggling.

"A little help, please?"

"Wow. I knew the know-it-alls have personality chips, but I've never seen one like that."

"It's not funny! How do I get the stupid thing off? I need a new one."

Nola wipes her streaming eyes, no longer laughing. "Oh, Trix, I'm sorry, but I can't. We only have so many blanks, and once the dispenser imprints it to your genetic code, it can't be reused except by someone from your planet. We can't just make a new one."

"Well, then, can you at least give this one a new personality chip?"

"Not easily. But I'm sure this one will settle in, given a few days."

"Given a few tranquilizers, maybe."

"You can turn it off, if you want to." Nola indicates a button on her own.

"Wait!" protests my know-it-all. "We need to talk about what you're going to wear tomorrow. It's your first full day on ship! We have to look our best, don't we?"

"No, we don't!" I flick the switch. Blessed silence follows. "Hallelujah."

Nola swallows a last giggle. "Seriously, though, Trix. You need a know-it-all."

"Yeah. Because it's vitally important that I know the latest plot twists on *Love Among the Stars*?"

"It's a good show," Nola says with an injured expression. "You ought to try watching. Anyway, it's more than that. Your know-it-all will help you find your way around the Big Top, and you can use it to send messages, like if you need me. Have your know-it-all patch you through to mine. They've got access to the whole datanet."

"I think I'll fly solo for a little longer. So what now?" I yawn. "What time is it, anyway?"

"Your know-it-all could tell you," Nola says with a cheeky grin. "It's ten. Breakfast is at eight."

"So do you sleep in normal beds or what? Don't tell me it's some kind of weird pod thing."

"No, the dorms are really nice. And I meant what I said before. I've got a double. You can room with me if you like."

"Seriously? You mean it?"

"Sure. What, do you snore or something?"

"No, it's just . . ." No one's ever gone out of their way to be friendly to me. I mean, there were some girls at Bleeker who were nice enough—but only when Della wasn't looking. Part of me doesn't think Nola could really want to hang out with me. Crazy, huh? I'm on a spaceship, in another galaxy, and the thing that's hardest to believe is that I've got a shot at my first real friend.

"I'd love to be roommates," I say finally.

Nola beams. "Wait until you see our room. It's the best! I've put in a ton of customizations. You'll love it! I mean, I hope you will."

"I bet it's amazing. So, is that our next stop?"

She shakes her head. "There's no way to reach the dorms right now. We have to wait for the decompaction bell. Everybody's probably hanging out in the commons. Come on, I'll introduce you."

Nola's know-it-all leads us back out past the space-wings, then up two sets of ladders and down a pearly white corridor that spirals like a giant snail shell. We come out into a large round room with mirrored walls, like an inside-out disco ball. About thirty other kids are gathered around a raised platform lit by orange lights. Inside, a figure jumps and catapults as puffs of smoke, bursts of flame, and several nasty-looking metal mallets chomp through the air. I guess "hanging out" in an intergalactic circus involves more than flopping onto the sofa and watching bad TV.

"Someone's in the Arena!" says Nola, clapping her hands together. "Oh. It's Sirra. Well, it's still fun to watch." She leads the way to a spot along the side with a good view. With Sirra putting on a show, nobody pays us much attention.

The Galacticus crew all look about my age or a few years older and oddly normal, for aliens. You could have pulled most of them off the street back home, if you were in the artsy, punked-out part of town. And then there are the really weird ones.

I try not to stare at the guy who looks like a walking boulder, or the one with antennae like a moth. Far out! I wonder how much of it is thanks to the Tinkers. Or are there entire planets of rock people?

"I guess I wouldn't mind watching Sirra get pulverized," I say, turning back to Nola. "What is it, some kind of training machine?"

"More like a game. People play one another to see who can stay in longest. I once pawned off a whole week's bilge-cleaning duty to Jom on a bet that Ghost would beat Etander. And it's fun. Sirra won't get pulverized, though. She's too good. Watch."

Sirra cartwheels over two smashing metal plates and hangs in midair for a long moment, arms flung out artistically. Even with a giant deathtrap trying to take her out, she's going for the glamour shots. I'm kind of impressed, in spite of myself.

The lights in the Arena abruptly switch from orange to blue. The flames wink out. Sirra flips down to land triumphantly outside the Arena.

"She's good, isn't she?" says Nola, sounding wistful.

"You could totally take her, with your Tech mojo."

"Oh, they'd call it cheating."

"She's using her superpowers. Who says you can't?"

Nola ducks her head. "I couldn't go in there, anyway. It's too dangerous. Look." She points at a dial on the side of the ring. "That was only level five, and did you see those fire jets?" She shudders.

"Eh, it doesn't look too hard."

Me and my big mouth. My words ring out into one of those weird lulls in the conversations around us. Every single person hears me. And stares.

"Hey, everybody," says Nola, doing her best to cover for me. "This is Trix. She's new. Trix, this is . . . uh . . . everybody!"

"Not too hard, is it?" Sirra bounds down from the platform, arms crossed, chin high. "I'd like to see you last three minutes, Earth Girl."

No backing down now. "Sure. But only if we make it interesting."

"Interesting?"

I march over to the panel and spin the dial as high as it goes. Excitement buzzes through the crowd. Sirra's eyes go wide.

"Trix!" says Nola. "Are you sure? Level thirteen?"

"It's okay. I know what I'm doing." I lower my voice. "If we stick to the easy stuff and Sirra beats me, I'll look like an idiot. Even Sirra is scared of level thirteen."

"And what about you?"

I try to smile. "I'm more scared of looking stupid."

"Sirra, don't," says a boy with the same coppery skin and slippery dark hair as Sirra. "You don't need to prove—"

"I do, Etander. Someone needs to show the new girl how things work around here. She obviously doesn't know her place. She probably can't even do a cartwheel."

I say nothing. Instead I try to shake out some of the tension from my arms, roll my neck, and wiggle my toes.

"Trix," whispers Nola, "don't do it!"

I'm already moving, taking the three bounding steps that propel me into a front handspring, step out, round-off, back handspring. As I slam down from my double twisting layout onto the edge of the Arena, the crowd erupts in whoops of surprise. I wink at Sirra. "Ready when you are, Sparkles."

Sirra grimaces, then vaults over the steps, pulling a midair somersault to land on her hands beside me. Supporting herself one-armed, she waves. The onlookers cheer even louder.

"Watch out in there," says Sirra, bobbing upright. "This is no place for newbies."

"How's your nose?" I don't wait to see her reaction. It's time to face the Arena.

Someone, probably Nola, shouts, "Go, Trix!"

As soon as my feet touch the floor, about five billion things start trying to kill me. I duck under a giant rolling pin studded with jabby spikes. I twist out of the way of shooting flames. I leap up to grab a dangling hook, narrowly avoiding a pit that falls away under my feet. It's taking all my energy just to stay in the game. I've got to focus. I only need to last three minutes.

It feels like it's been an hour already. Sweat streams down my neck, tickling my skin. I throw myself under another swipe of the giant rolling pin. I may not be posing, but I'm surviving.

Then the net gets me.

Threads of fire burn through my body. It catches me by the legs and one arm. It's going to toss me out. I claw with my free hand for anything that can keep me inside the Arena.

My slippery fingers scrabble against smooth metal, then catch. I grit my teeth against the crackling pain that pulses from the net. I'm holding one of the spikes that pokes up from the floor. All I want is to let go and escape the pain, but I can't. I won't give up.

"You'll never make it, Earth Girl!" Sirra pirouettes aside, evading a blast of flame. "Let go!"

"Make me."

"Fine. If that's what it takes." Sirra leaps, soaring over the intervening obstacles to thump down in front of me. "What do you think of the Arena now?" Her eyes glitter with the reflected blue sparks popping off the net.

"Not . . . so tough," I huff. "Might . . . take . . . a

nap." I force a grin. I can tell her patience is running out. I only need her to come a little bit closer.

Sirra snarls, reaching for my fingers. Before she can wrench them free, I let go and grab her instead. She shrieks and kicks, but I've got a good grip. I hold tight as the net flips me up into the air, so that we both go flying out of the Arena. We slam to the ground in a tangled heap.

Sirra throws herself off me, planting an elbow in my gut along the way. I don't care. I made it a tie. That's good enough.

The translator can't handle whatever it is Sirra's saying as she stalks off, but I get the picture. I start to laugh, but it hurts.

"Trix!" cries Nola, popping up over my head. "You were amazing!"

I manage a smile, barely. All I want is to lie there for a few years enjoying my victory and waiting for my body to feel less like a sack of jelly.

A weird wailing echoes from the ceiling. All at once everybody's moving, heading for doors and chattering.

"Trix?" Nola asks. "Are you all right?"

I shake myself. "Considering that the day started with my hair turning pink and ended on a circus space-ship filled with mutant outlaws, yeah, I'm surprisingly all right."

"Come on, then. Let's check out your new home."

My new home.

CHAPTER 6

Breakfast of Champions

THE NEXT MORNING I'm still tucked into my bed yawning as Nola bops around showing off the different gadgets she's installed "for fun." She tried giving me the rundown last night, but I was so wiped I fell asleep pretty much as soon as she popped down my foldaway bed. I'm still not entirely sure this isn't all a crazy dream, except that if it were, the dorm would probably be bigger. It's actually smaller than my room at Bleeker, but about a million times more comfy.

The walls are chock-full of all kinds of stuff. A woman

sitting on a giant thresher waves from one picture. It could be a cornfield in Iowa, except there are two moons in the sky. One whole wall is filled with engineering schematics. And there's a pair of impossibly beautiful identical women gazing smolderingly from a poster right beside Nola's bed. I can't read the alien script above them, but I'm pretty sure it says *Love Among the Stars.*

"And see this?" Nola gives her desk a push. It flips up, disappearing into the wall. "All the furniture is foldaway. Oh, and check this out." She presses her palm to the wall. It changes color, from green to bright pink.

"To match your hair," Nola says. "Or try this." The walls go dark, speckled with stars. "It's what you'd see if we were outside. The program patches in from the external sensors, so it's all live feed. It took me three days to work out how to integrate them, but isn't it neat?"

"Whoa!" I pull myself out of bed to spin around, taking it all in. "You even did the floor." Stars drift below my feet. It's kind of freaky, but amazing.

"So you like it? You think you'll be okay here? I mean, rooming here?"

"Absolutely. Who wouldn't be? I've got supergenius Tech Girl to show me the ropes and the cushiest bed in the galaxy."

But as I stare out into the limitless expanse, I can't help shivering. Nyl is out there, somewhere, waiting to get his hands on my meteorite. What if he finds us? Just how safe is my fabulous new life?

"What?" Nola glances around. "Is it making you space-sick?"

I shake off my fears. There's no reason to worry Nola. Nyl's probably light-years away. "No. It's great. So where do we get breakfast? I'm starved. Please tell me you don't live on weird energy drinks and protein pills."

"Oh, no—the food here is amazing! Jom isn't even a Tech, but he's got the culinary protocols figured out better than any of us, what with the family business and all that. You just have to be careful with his experiments . . ."

Nola trails off, her eyes wandering. She cocks her head, raising one hand to her know-it-all. She nods, then says, "Got it, Miss Three. I'll be there quick as I can. I need to drop Trix off for breakfast." Her conversation apparently finished, she looks at me, a hint of worry in her eyes.

"What's up?"

"I need to help with the test setup. They want to run you through after breakfast, to find out what you can do. Don't worry; you'll be fine."

A pang of fear twists my stomach. Breakfast suddenly sounds a lot less appealing. "Sounds like fun. Can't wait."

My insides don't quiet down, even with the distraction of Nola showing me the bathrooms, the storage lockers, and the laundry chute. By the time we reach the cafeteria, I feel like a pair of boa constrictors is having a fight in my stomach.

The rest of the troupe crowds around four of the tables, helping themselves from the army of steaming platters. There's a fifth table standing lonely in the corner, completely empty. Yeah, that's a good sign. Social failure, here I come.

"I'm sorry," Nola says, twisting her hands together. "I feel horrible setting you loose in the cafeteria by yourself."

"Are you worried about me or the rest of the troupe?" I say, smiling so maybe she won't see how nervous I am.

"Heh. Maybe both. But seriously, you'll be fine. You could sit with the Techs. They wouldn't mind."

"Yeah." I follow her gesture to the seven kids at the nearest table. "I don't think they'd even realize I was there." Every one of them has a sparky wrench insignia and is wearing what look like large wraparound sunglasses. They sit staring straight ahead, eating in complete silence.

Nola winces. "It's easier to talk and eat at the same time if you do the talking virtually. No choking."

"Smart. It's okay; I can handle this. Go on. I'll see you later."

Nola still looks worried, but she nods. "You really

better turn on your know-it-all, Trix. You'll need it to find the testing room."

"Okay, okay. After breakfast. I'm not eating with that thing babbling in my ear about evil twins from some silly soap opera."

I watch Nola head off, glad for an excuse to keep my back to the room while I come up with a plan of attack. I'll turn around, walk past each of the tables, and see if anyone looks friendly. If they completely ignore me, I'll sit at the empty one and make it my own.

I really hope they don't ignore me. Please let just one person give me a smile. Even a smirk! I can work with a smirk. All right. Here I go. I straighten my shoulders and turn around.

The Techs are a lost cause, so I move on to the next table, where a dozen or so boys and girls lounge like a pack of lions in the sun. Stars glitter from the patches decorating their jackets, shirts, and scarves. Sirra doesn't ignore me, that's for sure, but her look hardly says "Come sit at my table and we'll make up." It's more like "Get out of my spaceship and never come back." I keep walking.

The third table is the smallest, and the collection of people around it is definitely the oddest. A boy who looks a lot like a giant snail sits snuffling a plate of spongy brown cutlets. He's flanked by the rock boy I saw last night and a kid who looks like a walking alligator. The most normal of the group is a girl with a crackling haystack of white-blond hair who stares at me through thick, dark-rimmed goggles.

I guess I better give it a shot.

"Hey," I say. "I'm new here. My name's Trix."

The blonde tilts her head. "One thousand three hundred forty-nine. Go and find it. Go!"

I back away. "Ahhh. Okay. Table's full. Got it." Great. Even the Freaks don't want me. One more left before I'm doomed to the Siberia of table five.

I can't see much of the fourth table, because there are about twenty kids packed around it. Popcorn Boy is there, with his cockatoo crest of red hair. He's balancing three knives end to end as he tilts back in his chair. A girl with curly green hair sits perched on the back of her own seat, juggling what look like blueberry muffins. As I watch, she bounces one in a very unmuffinlike way off the table. The only person who isn't joking, juggling, laughing, or dancing is the girl in black at the very end of the table, who's completely ignoring the rest of them.

"Hey, Theon, do you like my new act?" asks Popcorn Boy as he adds a fourth knife to his tower.

"You call balancing a few knives an act?" says the green-haired girl. "Give it up, Jom. And while you're at it, try not to rubberize the muffins next time."

"They taste fine. Besides, this way no one will notice if you drop one." He gives her a cheeky grin.

"You are so going to regret that." The girl, Theon,

begins pelting the redhead with her muffins. He yelps and topples backward.

Everyone ducks as the cutlery goes flying, except the goth chick at the end of the table. She just looks bored, even with one of the knives flying right into her forehead. No, *through* her forehead! Like she's a ghost or something! Unbelievable! The knife clatters onto the floor behind her. She picks up one of the muffins, dusts it off, and takes a bite.

This is *definitely* where I belong.

I run through possible lines. *Hi, I'm Trix. Please let me sit with you so I don't look like a dork.* No, definitely not. *Hi, I'm Trix. I've got no idea what I can do, but you guys look like the most fun bunch, so here I am.* I sigh. It might work.

I'm about to try it out when someone taps my shoulder. It's the boy who tried to call Sirra off last night. "Hi," he says, smiling. And it's an honest-to-goodness smile, too. "Do you need a place to sit?"

I shoot one look at the empty fifth table. "Um. Yeah. Guess it's a little obvious I'm new here. Trix. Is my name, I mean. Beatrix Ling. But you can call me Trix." Man, could I sound *any* dorkier?

"I'm Etander. Come on, you can sit with us." He starts back toward the Principals' table. Okay, I can do this. I slide into the chair Etander offers and hope I'm not smiling like a maniac as he introduces me to the Principals.

I'm sure my know-it-all would be happy to record

their names, but I am *not* ready to deal with that level of crazy right now. Within five minutes about the only thing I can remember is that the black and white spotted girl who bends light is named Dalmatian, and she only joined the troupe a few months ago herself. The others are a mixture of flashy outfits and exotic colors who do things like contortion and tightrope balancing and sound sculpture, whatever that is.

"And you already met my sister, Sirra Centaurus," Etander finishes.

Sirra looks like she's sucking on a lemon. "This is the Principals' table, Etander. Not a home for strays."

"Don't mind her," says Etander, rolling his eyes. "She's not used to anyone matching her in the Arena. You did very well."

"Not as well as your sister," I answer, feeling generous now that I have potential allies. "So does that mean you're from the Centaurus galaxy cluster?"

Etander clears his throat, glancing at Sirra. "Yes."

"Ignore the humble act," says someone at the end of the table. "It means their family *owns* it."

"The Centaurus Corporation owns it," snaps Sirra. "And we're here now, like it or not. So it doesn't matter. Drop it. We're neglecting our guest of honor." She pushes a platter of bright yellow curds across the table. "Try the scrambled pepper-eggs, Trix. They're delicious."

"You ought to check with your know-it-all," says Etander. "It might not be safe."

"Oh, I'm sure Trix is up for anything." Sirra smiles. "She did match me in the Arena."

"Yeah, but I'm not stupid." I tap the button on my earpiece. Nothing. "Um. Know-it-all? Are you there?"

"Oh, so we're talking again, are we? You invite me in and then you shut me out. Don't you care about *my* feelings?"

"Not really," I say. "Are pepper-eggs safe to eat?"

My know-it-all huffs. "For that, my dear, I very well might keep the latest *Love Among the Stars* scoop to myself."

"Good. I've heard enough about that stupid show already. Just tell me if I can eat the eggs."

"Are you sure? It's quite the shocker! Oooh, the plot twists!"

"Just. Yes. Or. No."

"Yes." My know-it-all goes silent. If it had a body, I bet it would be crossing its arms and looking point-edly away. I flop a spoonful of the eggs onto my empty plate. My stomach grumbles. I hope they taste as good as they smell.

I pause, fork raised partway to my lips. Sirra is giving me an awfully strange look. I wonder if she's planning to wig me out by telling me these are bug eggs or something. But I've already seen half the other kids eating them. And my know-it-all said they were safe. I take a bite.

My mouth bursts into flames. Seriously, it feels like

someone is rubbing hot coals along my tongue. I sputter, forcing myself to gulp down the bite rather than risk spewing it on everyone else. Not that Sirra doesn't deserve it.

"Little spicy?" Sirra asks, taking a bite of her own, hoity-toity as a lady eating tea sandwiches.

I try to say something rude, but it hurts too much. I grab a glass of green juice and suck it down so fast I don't even taste it. Maybe the pepper-eggs already burned away my taste buds.

"Mmmphhhagh! Stupid overgrown encyclopedia!" I slap my earpiece. "What was that, Britannica? You said they were safe!"

"They are," chirps the know-it-all, rather smugly. "You're alive."

"Why didn't you *warn* me it was going to burn my mouth out?"

"Yes or no. I believe those were your exact words."

I fume incoherently. It doesn't help that half the table is giggling. No way. Not here. Not again. I will *not* be the loser everyone else laughs at.

"Come on," says Sirra, rising. "Time for those of us who belong here to get to work. Miss Three is waiting for us."

The rest of the table filters away, leaving me rubbing my streaming eyes. As I'm fumbling for more juice, someone pushes something crusty and crumbly into my hand.

"Eat that," says Etander. "It should cut the heat. According to my know-it-all, that is."

I blink at the thing in my hand. It looks like a piece of toast. I figure things can't really get much worse, so I take a bite. It doesn't make everything magically all better, but he's right: It does dull the pain. I look up to thank Etander, but he's gone already, disappearing out the door with his sister.

"Listen up, you demonic thing," I inform my know-it-all. "You are going to take me to Nola. You are not leaving out any more important details. You are not letting me make a fool of myself."

"I'm a know-it-all, dear, not a miracle worker."

"I mean it. Or I'm cutting your feed from *Love Among the Stars.*"

"You wouldn't *dare!*"

"Try me."

"Hmmph. Very well. Stand up from the table. Turn left. Walk twenty paces. Go through the door. Turn right—"

"You're pushing it, Britannica."

"They *are* important details."

I groan. "After this, being tested for superpowers'll be a picnic." I stand up, turn left, and walk twenty paces out the door.

CHAPTER 7

Placement

SO WHO'S MISS THREE?" I ask as I do yet another lap around the common room, too nervous to sit. I feel like a pinball, rattling around waiting to be bounced in or out of the game. "I thought she was training the Principals right now."

"She is," says Nola. She sits cross-legged on the floor, fiddling with a bundle of blinking wires and mechanical guts that hang from the wall. "She's an artificial intelligence, but she's got three different simulacra. Did that translate? You know what I'm talking about, right?"

I stop pacing. "In the movies on Earth, the AIs are usually the bad guys."

"Well . . ." Nola twiddles with one of the wires, zapping it with her wrench.

"I don't like the sound of that."

"She *is* a bad guy. Was, I mean. She was created by the Mandate, years and years ago."

"And you invited her onto your Tinker ship? I thought the Mandate were the Big Bad?"

"The Ringmaster reprogrammed Miss Three himself. He wanted to learn about the Mandate, and Miss Three can teach us."

"So you can fight them?"

"You cannot fight the Mandate," says a voice that bites my skin like a static shock. I whirl around to see a ghostly figure in a dark suit that definitely was not there a moment ago. The hologram holds a clipboard and stylus as insubstantial as herself. With her slicked-back hair and perfect bone structure, she reminds me a lot of a department store mannequin.

Nola stops fiddling with her wires and scrambles to her feet. "Miss Three, this is—"

"Our beloved Ringmaster's newest recruit. Beatrix Ling. Lately of Sol-3, commonly called Earth by the distressing melange of individuals that live there," says Miss Three. "Currently unclassified."

I straighten my shoulders. "I'm ready for your tests."

"Convinced you're something special, are you? No doubt he's already filled your head with dreams of being a star."

I stare right back. No way some microchip is getting me riled up.

She gives a little shrug, then runs a stylus across her clipboard. "Let's get started, then. We'll begin with the medical examination."

An hour later, I've been poked and pricked and prodded enough for a hundred checkups. I lift weights, run on a treadmill, jump, tumble, balance, and throw darts at a screen. All the while Miss Three watches, like it's all some faintly amusing practical joke.

Nola hustles around silently, fetching this or that instrument when Miss Three requests it, occasionally shooting me reassuring looks.

I'm trying harder than I've tried for anything in my whole life. I know I nail the physical tests. But I don't warp gravity. I don't shoot lightning out of my fingertips. Aside from my pink hair, I'm depressingly normal.

"That's enough, Nola," says Miss Three. "Clearly Miss Ling has only an average degree of visual recall."

Nola gulps and flicks a switch. The shapes vanish from the wallscreen.

"Wait! Let me try again! I *do* have a good memory. I've got practically every constellation memorized."

"All well and good, Miss Ling, but I'm afraid our

audiences are unlikely to be entertained by a recitation of crude astronomical nomenclature pertaining to a sky they will never see."

"But Miss Three, there are still other—" begins Nola.

"No. It's clear to me you have no extraordinary abilities. There is no need to resort to extreme measures. Now you see how empty the Ringmaster's promises are." She gives me a plastic smile. "Not everyone can be a star. I regret that he has raised such false hopes, but it is better to learn the truth now, while you can still return to some sort of reasonable life."

I am *not* settling for some secondhand clunker of a life when I can get the newest, snazziest model. "Hang on a minute. Why isn't the Ringmaster here? Maybe he ought to judge for himself what I can do. He's the one who asked me to stay."

"The Ringmaster is a busy man and does not have time for trivialities."

"This is my future we're talking about. It's not trivial to *me*." I flick my know-it-all. "Hey, Britannica, get the Ringmaster on the line, will you? Tell him Beatrix is getting fed up with these stupid tests."

"So sorry, dear, the Ringmaster is unavailable right now. Would you like to hear his away message? It's *so* amusing. Though not as amusing as what Dalana says when the space pirate Zendalos surprises her in—"

I grit my teeth and switch it off. Miss Three raises her brow in an arch so perfect it looks like it was drawn with a protractor.

I turn to Nola. "You said there are more tests."

"Yes, but Trix, they're dangerous! Maybe we should wait—"

"I want to get this over with. Got that?" I say to Miss Three.

"If you are willing to risk so much in this foolish quest, then by all means, proceed."

"Do it."

Nola nods and lays her silver hand against the wall. In the middle of the room, the Arena springs to life with a wheeze of grinding metal. The dial on the panel is gone, replaced by a single flashing purple word: OVERRIDE.

"What do I have to do?"

"Step inside," says Miss Three. "And survive."

I strip off my jacket, feeling the heavy lump of the meteorite in one pocket. What if Nyl was telling the truth? Maybe I'm not really Tinker-touched, just a normal Earth girl jazzed up by a space rock. Miss Three seems to think I'm nothing special.

With my back to the others, I close my eyes for a moment. No. My parents promised. And I got through that door. That must count for something. Come on, Tinkers. You must have given me more than pink hair.

I'll take anything. Gravity, fire. Okay, maybe not a snail shell. But let me stay here. Let me be something more.

I step into the Arena. The ground disappears. I fall, twisting aside in time to avoid being skewered by spikes lining the pit.

If I thought last night was bad, this is a million times worse. I dive and jump, my legs and arms already weak from all the other tests. I'm too slow. I'm not going to make it. Miss Three is right. I'm an idiot.

Faint bluish light haloes the mallets and spikes and every other instrument of death racing to take me out. I'm shaking; it's not only fear and complete exhaustion. Energy jolts my bones. The whole Arena hums with power. My hair's in my eyes. I try to brush it back, but it sticks to my fingers, crackling with static. A jolt of pure agony spills me onto the floor. I scream. My hands feel like I've dunked them in acid. Nola's voice echoes dimly through a fog of pain.

"Miss Three, we've got to stop it!"

"You heard Miss Ling, Nola. She asked for this."

I open my lips to scream, but nothing comes out. All I have is pain.

It stops. For a brief and glorious moment I think it's me, that I've found some Tinker-power to switch off the light show. Then I open my eyes and see him.

"Ringmaster. I didn't . . . I was trying . . ." The words choke me. I don't want it to be real. I've failed. One day, and I've already trashed the biggest dream of my entire life. I don't belong here.

"I understand," he says, holding out a hand to help me up off the floor. "But I think that's quite enough for now."

"Ringmaster," says Miss Three, "you should know that this was all at her own request. She understood the consequences and insisted that we proceed. It is unfortunate that such extreme measures were necessary to convince her of her lack of—"

"Thank you, Miss Three, Nola. I'd like to have a word with Beatrix now."

Miss Three's simulacrum winks out, her taunting smile lingering in a ghost of photons. Nola starts packing up her tools, moving about as slow as molasses. She gives me an encouraging nod, but there's a worried crinkle between her eyes. I try to smile back. Then finally she snaps the toolbox closed. The door shuts behind her, and I'm alone with the Ringmaster.

I stand miserably, trembling all over from the aftereffects of the test and the fear of what he's about to say.

"So, would you prefer nachos or cake?"

"What?"

"Ah, you're quite right. Why choose? We'll have both. Excellent!"

I stare at him, wondering if one of the aftereffects of my thrashing is hallucinations.

"For brunch," he says. "Another fabulous word: *brunch*. Not quite one thing or the other, but sometimes it's exactly what you need. Come along." He sets off briskly toward the door. "There's something I'd like you to see, so you can begin to understand."

"Understand what?"

The Ringmaster spins around, arms flung wide. "All of this. The Big Top, the rest of the troupe, the show itself."

"But I don't have any superpowers. Aren't you going to kick me out?" My voice cracks.

"I didn't travel three hundred parsecs to Earth just for the avocados."

"You really mean it?" I'm going to cry at any moment, but I've got to say it. "You're not sending me away? I mean, it's crazy, I know, but . . ." I squeeze my eyes shut on the tears and whisper, "I'd die if I had to go back."

Cool fingers touch my cheek, making me jump. "Beatrix, I swear to you on . . . on the honor of my name, I will never, ever ask you to leave the Big Top. This is your home now. Please believe that."

My shudder of relief nearly topples me. The Ringmaster's hand slips lower, catching me around the shoulders. "I'm not sure which of us is a bigger fool. You, for nearly killing yourself trying to prove you belong. Or me, for not expecting you'd do that." He gives me an inscrutable look.

"I'm sorry I can't do anything," I say when I find my voice again. "All I have is this stupid pink hair."

"Pink is an underrated color," he says. "Some of the best things in the universe are pink. Sunrises. Erasers. Flamingos. And . . . well, there are those shellfish you can get potted with brown butter."

"Thanks. I feel so much better knowing I remind you of a prawn."

He grins. "That sense of humor will serve you better than any Tinker power. Now, can you walk? Good. Follow me."

We travel along several corridors, then down something like a firefighter's pole that puffs out a cushion of air at the bottom. I walk out into a room that definitely does not belong on a spaceship.

Gilt-framed paintings and old-fashioned green lamps fill the few bits of wall that aren't crammed floor to ceiling with bookshelves. A bunch of study carrels fills the far end. I see the blonde from breakfast in one of them. She doesn't even look up when we come in. Her carrel is filled with a dozen video screens, each of them playing something different. There's no one else in the room.

"The library," the Ringmaster announces.

"We're eating in the library?"

"Don't tell Miss Three. She'd like to have a rule against eating anywhere outside the cafeteria. But I defy anyone to read the picnic scene in *Moons over Mizzebar* without a snack. It's impossible."

"You brought me here to read about a picnic?"

"It's a brilliant book, picnics aside," he says. "But we're here for something else." He leads the way to a low table bearing matched silver-domed platters. As I sink into one of the pudgy armchairs, he pulls the covers away with a flourish.

Two heaping servings of nachos lie drenched in cheese and salsa and beans, sprinkled with black olives, and decorated with giant dollops of guacamole. The cake stands proudly alongside, topped with candied pineapple and ruby-red cherries, oozing caramel.

"Help yourself. I've got to find something."

He doesn't need to tell me twice. Now that the terrible knots are starting to unwind, I'm starving. As I chow down, the Ringmaster flits along the shelves, muttering and occasionally resting a hand on a volume, only to pull away.

"Aha! *A Treatise on the Social Conventions, Taboos, and Millinery of Deneb-5.* Perfect!"

"You want me to read about hats?" I ask around a mouthful of cheese and beans.

"What? No, the book's rubbish," he says as he returns to the table. "Miss Three insisted I read it before our last—and consequently only—performance on Deneb-5. But it's perfect raw material for the replicator."

I watch in alarm and fascination as he piles a mountain of avocado and beans onto a chip, all while balancing the book atop his baton, defying both gravity and common sense. Maybe that's his superpower. That and the ability to wear a bazillion sequins without looking like an ass.

After piloting the loaded chip into his mouth, the Ringmaster heads for the nearest painting. The stern lady in the portrait disappears, to be replaced by a slot like a library book drop and a glowing screen. The Ringmaster pops his book into the slot, then taps the screen. A loud whirring and clacking echoes from beyond the wall. With a triumphant trill of beeps, a dark oblong pops out. The Ringmaster stares at the cover for a long moment.

"Didn't it come out right?"

He sighs, so faintly I almost think I'm imagining it. "No, it's fine." He hands me the book, then plops down and begins polishing off the rest of his nachos.

I can barely make out the title. *The Programme of the Circus Galacticus, Twelfth Edition.* Someone used up an entire lifetime supply of gold curlicues decorating this thing. I flip to a random page and read aloud. " 'Act Nine: Firedance. Having gained the Seeds of the Tree of Life, the Dreamers seek to Kindle the Seeds in the Fires of the King. As the Trickster confuses and beguiles the King, the Dreamers carry out a series of foudroyant escapades . . . ' " I look up. "Is *foudroyant* a real word or is the translator being goofy?"

"It's most certainly a real word, and an excellent one at that. It means *dazzling.*"

"And you didn't think it might be easier just to say *dazzling*?"

"You can never have too many words that mean *dazzling*. Besides, I didn't write it. The Big Top did."

"The spaceship takes notes on your performances?"

"The Big Top is more than a spaceship. And it's not notes; it's a script. A performance by the Circus Galacticus is more than death-defying feats and amusements. It's a story."

"Like a musical, but with clowns and acrobatics?"

He taps his nose. "Exactly."

"Do you mean the Big Top writes the plot? Is it always the same?"

"Yes and no," replies the Ringmaster vaguely as he carves off a chunk of cake and wraps it in a napkin. I crunch down on my last handful of chips, waiting for more answers.

"But you should read *The Programme* before we continue this conversation," he says, standing. "You do that, and I'll be back before you miss me." He winks, toasting me with his slice of cake, then disappears out the door before I can do more than sputter through my mouthful of corn chips.

The blonde is watching me. "You don't fit," she says. "You have to find it."

"Um. Okay." I slouch down, open *The Programme* to page one, and begin reading.

It starts with a cast list of a dozen characters. First up is "The Ringmaster: Madcap and Mysterious, he awakens Dream and Color in the grim world of the sleepers held fast within the hold of the Iron King."

I read through the rest of them, my brain struggling under the onslaught of melodramatic word choices and capital letters. Some of the entries don't make a lot of sense. There's one for a character called the Trickster: "Veiled in Shadow, he may be Friend or Foe." I've got no clue who that is.

Others are clear enough. "The Stardancer: A Graceful Voyager who cavorts among the Stars, her Beauty and Power inspire the Dreamers to hold fast to their Hope." Sirra's got beauty and power all right, but what she inspires in me isn't hope. More like loathing.

The last entry is for "The Lightbearer: Dappled in Light and Dark, she Illuminates the Treachery of the King." That must be Dalmatian, with her spotted skin and light-bending powers.

It goes on into descriptions of each act. I skim the entire book pretty quickly. By the time the Ringmaster comes back, I'm rereading the last few acts.

He's changed his coat to a blindingly lime-green version, and there's something that resembles a singed bullet hole in the crown of his top hat. But he slides gracefully into his chair with the air of someone who's just taken a refreshing stroll in the park.

"So?" he asks. "What do you think?"

"It's sort of like a fairy tale or something. But it's—sorry—a little weird."

The Ringmaster nods and mm-hmms in a way that doesn't tell me anything useful, so I continue. "These Dreamer people want to reach the stars, so they try a bunch of different things. But the King and his Minions stop them every time, and then finally the Oracle tells them to go to the Tree of Life. So they go and—is there *really* an act that involves dancing fruit?"

"It's quite a crowd pleaser, actually," says the Ringmaster.

"If you say so. Anyway, they get the magic beans. But for some reason, they need to dunk them in the King's fires to make them grow, so the Trickster helps them do that. And then he disappears, and so does the King, and everyone lives happily ever after, which makes no sense."

He leans forward, drumming his fingers against the jeweled top of his baton. "Why?"

"There's something missing."

"Ah." He leans back again, looking remarkably pleased with himself. "I knew you were clever. Please, elucidate."

"Well, for one, the Iron King fellow causes all this trouble and then what? He just goes away and lets them fly up into the stars at the end? There ought to be a big fight or something. And the description of the Light-bearer talks about her revealing treachery, but that never happens." I thump the book down on the table. "Why are there twelve editions? There's something you're not explaining."

"Many things, in point of fact," says the Ringmaster. "Infuriating, isn't it? But if I sent you to the corner market to buy bread, you'd go straight to the bakery section, pick up your loaf, and be off. There might be perfectly ripe tomatoes and cans of curried sardines, and you'd walk right on by without even taking notice."

"If I saw curried sardines, I'd *definitely* keep walking," I say. "And what if you really needed bread?"

"The point is, most people become blind if they're told what to do."

"Are you going to explain about the twelve editions or not?"

"Twelve editions," echoes a clear, sharp voice from across the room. It's the blonde. "Twelve characters."

"Oh, now, that's cheating," protests the Ringmaster, but I'm already opening the book to the front and peering at the cast list.

"She's right. There are twelve of them." I tap my finger under the last entry. "The Lightbearer is Dalmatian. And she was the last one to join, before me. So the Big Top creates a new *Programme* whenever a new person comes on board? No, that can't be right, because there's more than twelve of us. What? Why are you smiling like that?"

"You said 'us.'"

"Maybe I shouldn't have. I'm not in *The Programme*."

"Not every new member of the troupe produces a new edition of *The Programme*."

"But you thought I might." Now I understand that look he'd had, earlier, staring at the book. My insides sink, dragging me deeper into the chair.

"Chin up, Beatrix. You'll make a brilliant Clown, for the time being."

"For the time being?"

"Until something changes. No, don't ask. Remember the sardines."

"I don't understand, though, why you bother calling people Clowns and Principals and Freaks. They're all in here in *The Programme*, one way or another."

He pauses, like he's not sure which answer to give me. Finally he says, "Those labels—they're meant to help you work together, not to divide you."

"Hmph. Tell that to Sirra."

He raises an eyebrow. "None of us is perfect, Beatrix. Everyone here deserves to be given a chance, including Sirra. You're not the only one I invited onto this ship."

What? He's taking *Sirra's* side? Has he not been paying attention?

"So you're okay with it all? You like having everyone sitting at their own special table?"

"Of course I don't like it," says the Ringmaster sharply.

"Then do something about it! Can't you make them—"

"No!" The bullet-crack violence of the word sends me cringing back in my seat. "It doesn't work that way. That's what *they* do. It's not why I'm here." The Ringmaster is on his feet, hands clenched to white knuckles on his baton, all trace of the lighthearted jester snuffed out.

My mouth is dry, but I force a question out, to release the painful tension that fills the air. "Then why *are* you here?"

Something seems to break in his eyes, and he sinks back into his chair, the baton now loose in his hands, resting across his sharp knees. He laughs, but there's a bitterness to it. "That, Beatrix, is an exceptionally good question. And I'll give you one in return. How do you free someone when he doesn't even realize he's in a cage? Sometimes we like our prisons. They can be very comfortable. What would you do?"

"I'd bust them all. Every one."

"Somehow I believe you could do it," he says, smiling for real. He springs lightly to his feet and pulls me to join him. "Enough philosophizing. It's time for the Clowns' afternoon training session. Let's go and show them how *foudroyant* you can be."

CHAPTER 8

Firedance

APPARENTLY even on a spaceship the size of the Big Top there aren't a lot of open areas, so we head to the main performance ring for the practice session. It's a little different than I remember it. The "tent" walls still swoop up into dark heights, but most of the bleachers are collapsed into heaps of metal along the sides.

There are other differences: Bottles of water and shoes lie in scattered heaps outside the Ring. The lights are steady and bright, and the soundtrack is the drumming of feet and the counts and calls of the performers. The fantastic costumes and makeup are gone.

And it is *still* damn impressive. I hang back by the doors. Am I crazy? Can I really do this?

The Ringmaster turns to me. "Nervous?"

"No! I mean, yeah, a little. It's just . . . I don't know the routines." And they might all hate me.

"Never fear. You'll shine."

"Yeah, I can see it now. A big, shiny fall on my ass."

He laughs, which somehow makes it better. "We all fall sometimes. I once tripped clear out of the Ring right in the middle of the grand finale. Ended up in the lap of the ambassador from the Thenx Syndicate. Nothing can be as bad as that, believe me."

"Why? Was the ambassador upset?"

"No. She wouldn't let me go! Kept shoving universal credit chits down my shirt front."

"That doesn't sound so—"

"With her tentacles."

"Okay, okay, you win." I take a breath and raise one hand to the Clown insignia newly clipped onto my jacket. "Let's do this."

Now it's the Ringmaster's turn to hesitate, like an actor about to step onstage. He closes his eyes, just for a moment. It's funny, he's so effortlessly dazzling—so *foudroyant*—but how much wattage does it take to keep that charm blazing? What happens when the batteries need recharging?

I'm about to ask if he's okay, but by the time I open my mouth, he's plunging ahead into the room. The moment he steps into the Ring, every eye is on him. Seriously, I even check up top for a spotlight, but there's nothing. It's all him. The Clowns break off their practice and surge toward us in a mob.

"Hello, hello, my jongleurs and jollies," he calls out as the tide of performers crashes into him, then breaks apart to surround us in an excited and slightly sweaty pool. "Practice goes smashingly as ever, I see. Theon, that last leap was excellent. You'll have the crowd on its feet."

At this, the green-haired girl who was juggling muffins at breakfast grins. Another girl gives her a high-five. Her smile fades quickly, though. "They'll be on their feet walking out if we don't fix the rest of the act," she says, crossing her arms. "It's crap, Ringmaster. It doesn't work without the Trickster. And now the King's broken down again. Half the time the light and smoke don't even work. You need to do something."

"Ah, well, there are always a few hiccups, aren't there? But first, let me introduce the newest recruit to the Clown Corps. This is Beatrix Ling."

Most of them actually smile, or at least look curious. The only one who doesn't is the goth chick, but I'm guessing it would take an event bigger than me to crack a reaction out of that amount of sullen.

The green-haired girl gives me a calculating once-over, then holds out a hand. I grit my teeth and match her viselike grip. "Good, we can use some new blood. I'm Theon. I make things frictionless." Suddenly her fingers are like oil in my hand, slipping free and leaving me clutching air. "So," she says, "what can you do, Beatrix?"

"Um . . ."

"She can hold her own in the Arena, for one thing," says the boy with the brilliant red hair. "I'm Jom," he adds, giving me a wave. "Welcome to the Clown Corps, Beatrix."

"Just Trix is fine," I say. "I've got pink hair. And . . . um . . . spunk." Did I really say that? I am the definition of lameness. "But, um, I'm totally up for learning the routines. You guys look amazing out there."

"We work hard," says Theon, but she smiles, which makes her look a little less like a drill sergeant. "And don't worry; you'll catch on. You're quick. I can tell."

"Very good," says the Ringmaster. "And now . . ." He pauses, his eyes distant.

Theon groans. "Not again."

The Ringmaster comes out of the momentary daze, but he still looks distracted, like he's doing calculus in the back of his brain. "I'll be off now."

"But, Ringmaster," Theon protests, "you *promised* you'd actually stay for this practice! We wanted to show you the new bit Asha and Leri worked out. And what about the Trickster? And the King?"

"I have every confidence you can work things out, Theon. I promise I'll run through the video feeds later. But you know how these things are. We're coming up on a stellar dust field. There may be leeches. The Big Top needs me."

"So do we," mutters Theon. But he's already heading for the door. "All right, I guess we're on our own. Let's take it from the top, people. Jom, have Trix shadow you until she's got the basics."

"Don't let Theon get to you," says Jom as he leads me to the far side of the Ring. "She's got kind of an obsession with people's powers. Maybe because the best thing about hers is that she never has a bad hair day. Not that I should talk. I mean, all I do is make smells."

"Smells?"

"Yeah." He rubs a hand back across his scarlet crest of hair. "It was pretty miserable for a while. Couldn't control it. Made everything smell like rotten pepper-eggs. I think if the Ringmaster hadn't shown up, my parents were going to disown me."

"The Ringmaster helped you control your stink?"

"Yep. And now . . ."

A rich scent like the most absolutely amazingly wonderful brownie floods my nose. Seriously, I nearly fall over; it's that good. "Whoa! That's amazing. And cruel."

"Food is my forte. And don't worry; I'm doing something special for dessert tonight!" Jom winks. "Here's our starting mark," he adds, pointing out a glowing symbol on the floor.

I give a little test bounce. The entire Ring is a kind of giant trampoline. No wonder the Clowns could manage those phenomenal leaps. A little ripple of excitement fizzes through me. I can do this. It might even be fun. A bunch of other marks illuminate the floor, like a crazy-complicated set of dance steps. Jom gives me a rundown, but even so, I finally cave and flick on Britannica to help me keep track. Fortunately she seems to consider it a matter of personal honor that I nail my moves, so there's a minimum of space-opera small talk.

We run through the sequence a half-dozen times. The third time Jom has me take over his part so he can see what I make of it. After that we alternate. The translator doesn't catch everything Jom says, but it must be positive, since he's smiling. Even Theon gives me a "Nice one!" after I finally land the tricky third midair tumble without a falter. It's almost enough to bust me out of my doubts, to make me start believing the Ringmaster that this is where I belong.

As I watch the Clowns running through the Firedance for the sixth time, two things stick out. One is: These guys have some absolutely mad energy and talent. No way are they second string, even if they aren't Principals. Two is: Theon was right about the routine. It's not working.

The Programme has us Clowns divvied up, half as Dreamers, half as Minions of the Iron King. From what I remember, this act involves us trying to dunk the magic beans into the King's fire. It ends when the Trickster finally succeeds, then vanishes in a puff of smoke.

I watch the glowing dance-step symbols rippling across the stage and realize why things are so weird. There are two sets of symbols that nobody's following. When Theon calls for a rest break, Jom and I head over for a chat.

"We don't have a Trickster anymore," says Theon, popping the cap from her water bottle so hard it shoots off across the room. "And we never had any King other than old Rustbucket there." She jerks a thumb over her shoulder at the mechanical "King" at the center of the ring. I can see what she means. He's cool-looking and all, with the black spiky crown and clawlike hands. But one of his red glowing eyes is on the fritz, which makes him look like he's winking at us. And most of the time his grand gestures get stuck on repeat until someone manages to give him a thump on the back. Plus, he's supposed to be moving around, according to the choreography. I think this old guy would collapse if he tried to move an inch.

"So where are they? They're in *The Programme*."

"The way we figure it, there's never been a flesh-and-blood King," says Theon. "At least, we've been using the rustbucket since anybody can remember. But we did have a Trickster, once. He left."

"That's crazy. I mean, look at this place. Why would anybody leave?"

"I don't know the whole story," says Jom, "but the way I heard it, he ran away and joined the Outcasts."

"The what?"

"There are a lot more Tinker-touched in the universe than us," says Theon. She swigs her water, a dent deepening between her brows. "Some of them try to hide, some of them get taken by the Core or the Mandate, and some of them fight back."

"So aside from the Core Governance that wants to use us and the Mandate agents, who probably want to do something equally nasty to us, there's some sort of League of Evil Mutants out there?"

Theon nods. "I was pretty new when it all went down, but I guess Reaper thought we should be doing more, fighting the Mandate and even the Core Governance. There was a big blowup between him and the Ringmaster, and the next day he was gone. The Ringmaster never talks about it, but people say Reaper joined up with the Outcasts and—what are they doing here?"

I turn to see Sirra and Etander crossing the floor toward the Ring. Sirra steams ahead; I can almost see her flags flying for battle. Etander lags behind like an anchor trying to slow her down.

We gather into a united Clown front. Even Ghost lurks near the back of the pack. Theon is gritting her teeth, and I catch a whiff of smoke and hot metal as I take a position between her and Jom.

"We need to use the Tent," says Sirra.

"We've got another hour of practice scheduled," says Theon. "After that, it's all yours."

"We need it now."

Jom's checking something on his know-it-all. "You guys are scheduled in the small practice hall."

"The lifters broke down. Again."

"So call a Tech," says Asha, narrowing green eyes slitted like a cat's. Her twin sister nods in agreement.

"I did. But it's going to take an hour, and we need to practice."

"So do we," I say.

"That's for sure," Sirra says. "But Etander and I are Principals." I feel her eyes latching onto the Clown insignia on my collar. "People actually care about our act. The Firedance is nothing but filler now. Everyone knows it."

"Oh, really?" I cross my arms. "Want to make a bet? Our new and improved Firedance is going to blow your Skydance out of the . . . sky," I stumble over my metaphor, but I think she gets my drift.

"New Firedance?" Jom's scarlet brows arch in surprise. The hot-metal smell turns abruptly to a light peppery scent that makes my nose itch. I give him a sharp look. "Oh, right," he says. "Our new Firedance. That we've been practicing. Just now."

"I'm calling the Ringmaster," says Theon, shaking her head. "He can sort this out."

Sirra shakes her head. "There's nothing to sort out. We need the practice space."

"Sirra," says Etander, "we can wait. There's no need to—"

"Yes, there is! You know we need to work on it. You nearly missed your catch last show. We can't afford that kind of mistake!"

By this time, the rest of the Clowns are in on the action, calling out and shouting. Theon's trying to leave some kind of message for the Ringmaster. Jom is waving his hands and telling everyone to stay calm, but the cool spring rain scent he's putting out isn't settling anybody down. Even Etander's hands are shaking, though to give him credit, he still looks like he'd rather be anywhere else.

I ball my hands into fists. "You don't want this fight, Sirra. We were here first."

"You?" She laughs. "You haven't been here a week. You don't know anything about how things work around here. You're a Clown. I'm a Principal. And that's—"

"Sirra!"

Etander's choked call spins his sister around. I blink, not sure I'm seeing clearly. Something's wrong with his hands. Sharp spines pierce the skin. In a ripple of shimmering charcoal, they become something monstrous. He grimaces, lips twisting, teeth clenched. I only meet his eyes for a moment. He closes them before I have to look away from the agony and shame.

"What's wrong with him?" I ask. "Do we need to get—"

"Stay back," Sirra snaps. "He's fine!" Heedless of the spines, she takes his hands in hers. "Etander, listen to me. It's all right." She makes a gentle shushing noise, all while gripping his monstrous claws. Scarlet drips from her tight fingers to splash on the floor between them.

A growling bellow rips from Etander's twisted lips. Spines are starting to bristle along his cheeks. I flinch. Sirra doesn't. "Come back, Etander. Please." The last word is a bare whisper of desperation.

Silence holds the rest of us so tight we barely breathe as Sirra fights to pull her brother from whatever this is. The change halts, then reverses. The spines diminish. And finally Etander stands trembling and hunched, himself once more. Sirra gives a ghost of a cry and hugs him tightly, speaking too low and quick for the translator to follow.

Then, without a word or even a look, Sirra pulls Etander away, toward the exit. No one speaks until the door closes behind them.

"Okay," I say. "What was that?"

Theon clears her throat. "Etander's Tinker-touch.

Gives him a pretty rough time when it starts up. But he'll be okay."

I'm not sure what definition of okay includes turning into a monster. Poor guy. Poor Sirra. I never thought I'd be sorry for her, but I can still hear the fear in her voice. *Come back, Etander. Please.* She thought she was losing him. "Does it happen a lot? What do you do if he spikes out like that onstage?"

Jom waves a dismissive hand. "Onstage no one blinks an eye. They think it's part of the act. No more real than the Mizzebar Moon Monster."

"Hey!" says Asha. "I'll have you know our uncle has a real, live video of Mizzy. You can see her wings and everything."

Jom rolls his eyes. "Anyway, it doesn't even happen that much anymore."

"Only when he gets upset," says Theon. She scuffs a foot against the floor, looking down for a moment. When she lifts her chin, she's all business. "So what was that about a new Firedance, Trix?"

Everyone seems glad for a change of topic. Next thing I know, I've got all eyes on me. I hope I'm not about to make a huge fool of myself.

"Um . . . well, it's like you said. The routine is crap as is. Not because of you guys," I add quickly. "You're brilliant. But the missing parts are ruining it. So . . . we need to fill them in."

"You mean have one of us play the King?" Jom asks.

There's a note of excitement in his voice that tells me my crazy brainstorm might work.

"And the Trickster. We'll need to alter the choreography a little, though, since none of us can whip up shadows. So then we can do it like this." I start sketching the moves in the air with my hands, only to be met with a wall of blank looks.

"Just a moment, dear," says my know-it-all. "You look like you're swatting flies. If you'll allow me to consult with the Big Top . . . there, that's better."

More glowing symbols appear under our feet. It's the entire act, straight from *The Programme*. "Perfect! I owe you one, Britannica."

"Good," purrs the infernal device. "Then from now on we'll have no more of that particular color eye shadow. Green and pink have no business getting that near each other except on a watermelon."

I ignore the lecture and focus on my plan. "These bits will have to change," I say, pointing. Then I have my know-it-all display my alterations.

Theon shakes her head. "I don't know. *The Programme* says—"

"*The Programme* can change. Do you want us to look cool or not? Let's show them you don't need to be a Principal to get applause. Who's with me?"

Jom already has his hand raised. Then one of the cat-eyed twins, Leri, gives a shrug and raises hers. Then

Frex, the boy who can stick to walls, and then the goth-girl Ghost.

Theon is the last. "Okay. Let's do it." She punches the air and grins. "Let's show them what the Clowns can do!"

The first thing I do is call Nola. No way we're sticking with the clunky old Iron King. Nola works her magic, rejiggering the King's arms into a set of bracers that throw off fake flames. I turn these over to Jom.

"Excellent!" He backflips across the Ring and lets off a great gust of flames. "Nola, these are amazing!"

Nola beams, then tosses him the crown, which she's enhanced so that it gives off little flickers of light from the hedge of spikes that encircles it.

"Okay, so we've got a King," says Theon. "And we're set with the other changes. But what about the Trickster? Some of this stuff is pretty complicated." She taps the glowing choreography markings with her foot. "Even I would have trouble with that bit at the end. The moves are tough enough without having to worry about throwing the seeds into the flames and catching it at the end. But it's got to be spot-on, or we'll look ridiculous."

"Here, let's try it. I'll show you what I was thinking."

My snazzed-up routine isn't perfect. Theon has to tweak part of it so Asha and Leri don't slam into each other, and it takes Jom a couple of runs to get comfortable with the crown. And, yeah, I fall on my ass. Three times. The Trickster part is tough, no question. Even by the end I don't have it down, but I can feel us getting sharper. I know we can make this work.

So do the rest of the Clowns. I thought they had some crazy energy before, but that was nothing compared to this. It's like there's a current running through each of us, electrifying our lives, linking us. We are going to be freaking amazing. With enough practice.

We go late, jazzed on the joy of it all. Finally Theon calls a halt. "That's enough, guys. Good work, everyone. I think we've really got something here."

Jom claps his hands together. "All right, folks, dinner's in an hour. And in honor of our newest Clown and her brilliant new Firedance, there'll be Chocolate Supernovas all around!"

A cheer rises from the crowd. I'm buffeted by good-natured cuffs to the shoulder and slaps on the back. I promise Nola, Jom, and Theon that I'll see them in the cafeteria. "I want to run through that last move once more," I tell them.

"Don't burn out on your first day," says Theon. "Seriously, Trix. We need you to stick around. You did good today."

The glow of Theon's words takes me through another three runs. I'm too worn out for it to really help, but I can't stop. I need to do this, to make myself believe this is all real. I'm here. My crazy suggestion worked. People might even be starting to like me. I might, *finally,* belong somewhere.

By the time I'm done stretching, everyone else is gone. I'm sure my know-it-all would be happy to direct me back to the dorms, but I am so not ready for another dissection of Dalana's wardrobe. And anyway, I should be able to figure it out myself, with a little trial and error. If this really is my home now, I'd better start getting to know it. Despite one wrong turn that lands me in some kind of giant greenhouse, I get back to my room with just enough time to wash the stink off before heading to the cafeteria.

CHAPTER 9

Supernova

DINNER IS GOING MUCH BETTER than breakfast so far. The dumplings are delicious, and Nola is sitting with us at the Clown table. "What a day!" she says. "You guys are going to be amazing! When are you going to tell the Ringmaster about the changes?"

"Next time he sticks around for more than three minutes," says Theon, impaling one of her own dumplings on a chopstick, then dipping it in a bowl of dark purple sauce.

"He spent more than three minutes with Trix," says

Nola, giving me a wicked smile. "I still can't believe the Ringmaster actually invited you to have brunch with him. Alone!"

"He did leave for part of the time. And we weren't alone. That girl, the one with the glasses, she was there, too." I jerk a thumb in the direction of the Freak table.

"Good as alone, then," says Theon, "if you mean Syzygy."

"That's her name?" I wonder if the translator is working.

"A lot of us call her the Oracle," says Jom. "That's her part in the show."

"Can she really tell the future?"

"Yes," says Jom.

"No," says Theon.

"Sort of," says Nola, adding, "It's complicated. She's like a super-fast, super-powerful computer. She absorbs information and doesn't forget it, ever."

"You mean she has a photographic memory?"

"More than that. She can process it, find connections and patterns. Calculate probabilities. So it's sort of like predicting the future. In a way."

"In a freaking weird way." Theon shivers. "She once told me I'd be the last Gendari to see the Moons over Mizzebar. *And* she said I was going to—well, it was stupid. And impossible."

"Syzygy isn't bad," says Nola. "She's different, like

the rest of us. Anyway, I'd rather hear more about Trix and the Ringmaster's *private brunch*."

"There's nothing more to say." I squirm under the many eyes. "I mean, there were nachos and pineapple upside-down cake, and he showed me the *Programme*. He told me I could be a Clown. It wasn't a big deal."

From the way they're looking at me, I can see they have a different opinion. "What's his deal, anyway?" I ask. "I mean, where's he from? What's his Tinker-touch? How did he end up as Ringmaster of a mutant intergalactic circus?"

The response is a whole lot of shrugs and some off-the-wall story Asha swears is true about how the Ringmaster is secretly the long-lost son of the actress who plays Dalana on *Love Among the Stars*.

"It's just weird, don't you think?" I say. "He looks like he's twenty, tops, and acts like it, too, some of the time. And then other times . . ." I trail off, not even sure what question I'm trying to ask, or why.

Jom saves me by suddenly jumping to his feet, raising a hand to his know-it-all. "They're done! Okay folks, you know the drill: get your spoons ready!" He bounds over to the dumbwaiter.

A stir of excitement runs around the table, rippling out to the rest of the cafeteria. The Techs take off their wraparound goggles, and even the alligator boy swishes his tail and clicks his long, curved talons against the tabletop.

"Ready for what?" I grab my spoon, eyeing it dubiously.

"Jom makes the Chocolate Supernovas with paccadi nuts," says Nola. "They do fine in the oven, but when they start to cool, they get unstable. If you don't find the nut in your dish and get it out in time, it'll explode."

"Thus Chocolate Supernova," finishes Theon, twirling her spoon and grinning. "Bet I find mine first. After Ghost, of course."

I follow her look to the end of the table, where Goth Girl is in her normal spot, her chin cupped in one hand and the viewscreen of her know-it-all covering her right eye. I wonder if she's watching *Love Among the Stars*.

Jom comes back a moment later balancing five large trays—two on each arm and one on top of his head—and starts dishing out the contents. "Work quick, people!" He skids the bowls down the table into the dozens of eager hands.

"There you go," Jom says, setting the last dish in front of Nola. I can't help but notice that Nola's Supernova is about twice as big as anyone else's. The smile Jom gives her is twice as wide, too. Good for Nola. Jom seems like a nice guy. And he can cook.

Nola doesn't notice. She's busy telling me what to do. "Go on, Trix! You have to sort of bash the coating and then dig for the nut."

On my other side, Theon is already scooping out

spoonfuls of molten chocolate with a look of intense concentration. At the end of the table, Ghost reaches right into the chocolate, coming out holding a perfectly clean, acorn-shaped nut. She tosses it into the garbage chute at the center of the table and begins to eat her Supernova.

A *pong, ping, pong* of paccadi nuts rattling into the trash processor is the only noise as we all focus on defusing our desserts. The first bang makes everybody jump, but it's from down in the bowels of the trash system. More bangs follow, and I'll admit I'm starting to get nervous.

A sudden trill from the center of the cafeteria sets off a stir that has nothing to do with dessert. A screen slips down from the ceiling, filled with a Venn-like image of four interlocking rings against a gold background. "What is it?" I ask.

"A governance alert," Nola says as the screen switches to a polished woman in a dark green suit. Her plasticky voice fills the room.

"Citizens of the Core, we can now confirm reports that an uncontained genetic anomaly, one of the so-called Tinkers, is responsible for the recent devastation on Circula Fardawn Station."

On the screen, an image appears of a gray oblong hanging against a starry sky. Two curving arms sweep out from the main body, like the arms of a twirling dancer.

Suddenly one of the arms brightens, flaring red, then blinding white. It explodes, sending a shower of glittering debris across the sky.

Nola gasps. Theon swears. Everyone in the cafeteria is riveted to the devastation on that screen.

The reporter goes on. "The official death count stands at 253, but is expected to rise. Dunosse Frexim, President of the Core Council, had this statement on the tragedy."

The image switches again, now showing a man standing at a podium and speaking vigorously. "I call on all citizens to report any suspected genetic anomalies to their local Governance Authority. We must ensure that these random and dangerous elements are provided the guidance and control they need to be productive members of society."

The woman with the plastic voice comes back on. "Our hearts go out to all those affected by this tragedy. The Red Hands have set up a dedicated netlink for those seeking information about survivors or interested in giving a donation. Thank you, and good night."

The screen winks out. Silence fills the room. Then Syzygy turns her mirrored eyes toward the Clown table and raises one hand to point right at me. She clicks her thumb and says, "Bang!"

I stare back in confusion for a split second. Then my Chocolate Supernova explodes, covering me in sweet, sticky syrup.

* * *

"How long do you think it'll be before they stop calling me 'Supernova'?" I groan, tossing myself down on the bed.

Nola, perched cross-legged on her own bed, winces. "People *still* call Jom 'Mooner.' It was right after he came on board and he'd just started fiddling with the autocook. He was trying to make salad dressing, but it came out as some sort of acid. And then he didn't realize and wiped his hands on his pants and, well . . ." Nola blushes, ducking her head slightly.

I can't help giggling. "Okay, I'll take being publicly drenched in chocolate over that any day. I wish I could get the stuff off, though." I sigh, noticing yet another smear of chocolate on my elbow. Three runs through the sonic showers apparently were not enough. "Too bad for Jom, though. He seems nice." I watch Nola carefully.

"Oh, he is!"

"He's *especially* nice to you."

"What? No, he's just . . . really? You think so?"

"Did you not notice the ginormous Chocolate Supernova he gave you?"

"That was an accident. It didn't *mean* anything."

I snort. "If you say so." I lift up the covers and crawl into bed. On the other side of the room, Nola does likewise after hanging her know-it-all carefully from a hook beside her bed. I toss mine onto the floor.

The lights flick out, leaving the room in a starlit darkness.

I stare into the spangled blackness, fidgeting as I try to get comfortable with the lump of the meteorite under my head. I don't dare leave it out. I already almost lost it when Nola got carried away showing me how to use the laundry system. She probably thought I was insane, throwing myself down the chute to grab my chocolate-covered jacket. Maybe I should show it to her. She's nice, and smart, and I don't want to keep secrets from her. But . . .

You have to keep it secret. Can you promise to do that, Beatrix?

I need more information. I wonder if there are any books on it in the library. *The Dummy's Guide to Mysterious Family Heirlooms.* But am I really keeping it secret because of my promise? Or am I scared I might find out I don't really belong here, that my pink hair is all some weird side effect?

"What is it?" Nola asks.

"Huh?"

"You groaned. You aren't still worrying about the Supernova thing, are you?"

"No, I—" But I can't say it, not yet. I curl my fingers around the meteorite, clutching it to my chest. "I was thinking about that news report. Do you really think it was a Tinker-touched person who blew up that space station?"

"Some of us have some pretty, well, terrifying powers. I mean, look at what Sirra can do. If she wanted to, she could cause some serious damage."

"You think someone *wanted* to blow up the station?"

"It could be. Not everyone joins the circus. And not everyone stays."

"Right. Theon told me about the Outcasts. You think they blew up the space station?"

"Maybe," says Nola. "Or it might have been someone who didn't even know they were Tinker-touched, and woke up one day like you did, except instead of pink hair, they . . ."

"Blew up a space station," I finish. "Sounds like it might've been better all around if you guys had found them instead of me."

"No, don't say that, Trix. We don't know. Even Syzygy doesn't know. You're the one we got, and I'm glad you're here. Besides, who knows? You might manifest an even worse power."

"Gee, thanks. No need to sound so cheerful about it. Aren't you worried I might blow you up in the middle of the night?"

"Of course not," says Nola in a falsely serious voice. "I patched an auto-ejector into your bed to spit you out into space if you start going supernova on me."

I giggle, and my grip on the meteorite relaxes. I still can't get over the fact that I've got a friend. I've seen other Bleeker girls laughing like this, teasing and joking with one another, the way you can only pull off when you know you're friends underneath it all. "Hey, Nola. Thanks. For everything."

"S'okay. Good night, Trix."

"Good night."

* * *

The next week is pretty much the best week ever. The new Firedance smokes the old one. Sure, it's going to take twice as much work to get it down, but we're all jazzed about it. I have a table to sit at. I have friends. People still call me Supernova, but I don't care. I love it all. The only downside is the pile of schoolwork Miss Three saddles us with.

I slump down in my chair in the library, letting my head thump back against the smooth metal. About a bazillion pages of tiny print scroll by on the screen in front of me. I flick on my know-it-all and get Britannica to patch me through to Nola. "Remind me again why I'm busting my ass to write an essay on Core Governance Mining Regulations?"

"For your second career as a prospector?" says Nola.

I wince as a shriek of grinding metal bursts out of the

earpiece. "Are you tearing the autosalon apart with your bare hands? Weren't you only giving it a tune-up?"

There's another distant crash. "Yes," she replies, but I'm not sure which question she was actually answering.

"Seriously, though. Give me one good reason I need to know this stuff."

"Because if you don't, Miss Three won't give you your stipend and then you won't be able to come out with me and have fun at the Hasoo-Pashtung Bazaar?"

I sigh. "I can't believe the Ringmaster puts up with this."

"I don't think he puts up with it so much as he runs screaming in terror from the prospect of being responsible for anything so mundane." The clatter in the background sounds like a freight train dancing the tango. "Listen, Trix, I have to go. But I'll help you with the essay tonight if you want."

"Thanks, Nola."

She clicks off. I spend about a half-hour trying to make sense of a single subclause about the use of sonic liquifiers before I start to feel like someone used a sonic liquifier on my brain. Leaving the study carrel, I decide to check the shelves again for anything that might give me a clue about my meteorite.

Last time it took me an hour to get through a single shelf. Nothing is in any sort of order. I guess I could check out the catalogue window thing, but honestly, it's kind of fun looking through this stuff. Some of it I recognize: the collected works of Shakespeare, a bunch of shonen manga, and the Time-Life "Supernatural" series. Most of it, though, is stuff like *Pipelines: Miracle or Menace?* and *101 Recipes for Paccadi Nuts* and *A Brief History of the Centaurus Corporation* (which is, I kid you not, a foot thick).

A muffled thump turns me toward the door, wondering if I've got company. I don't see anyone. The next moment I yelp as Miss Three materializes right in front of me. She smirks at the book in my hands. *Love Among the Stars: The True Story.*

"Hard at work on your essay, I see." Her eyes track the room like laser beams, then return to my face. "Where is he?"

"Who?"

"The Ringmaster. He knows how important it is that we review the accounting records in a timely fashion, and yet he insists on running off, when we're already five performances behind, and—what is it, Miss Ling?"

I could swear I saw a flash of sequins around the edge of the doorway, but I latch my gaze back onto Miss Three.

"Nothing. There's no one else here. Just me, doing my essay."

She frowns. A spider web of static crosses her ghostly face as she spins, slowly, toward the door.

"Hey, have you checked the autosalon? Nola's working on it. Maybe he's over there. Supervising."

It's a lame excuse, but she halts, studying me.

"You should check over there," I say.

I almost smell the ozone crackling off her response. "I know his ways, Miss Ling. He can't hide forever." Then she winks out.

"You can come out now," I say. "She's gone."

The Ringmaster steps out from the entryway gingerly, his eyes darting around the room. Then he pulls the top hat from his head, brushes back his mane of dark hair, and heaves an enormous sigh. "Thank you, Beatrix, for saving me from a fate that requires only the barest smidge of hyperbole to merit the term 'worse than death.'"

"No problem," I say. "Not that I'm a fan of crunching the numbers, either, but how long do you think you can play hide-and-seek?"

"Oh, I suppose I'll have to deal with it eventually," he says, leaning against the wall. He quirks one brow at me. "Rather like your essay, I imagine."

"Don't remind me."

He twiddles his hat in his hand for a moment, giving me a speculative look. "Would you care for a break? A little excitement and mystery and quite probably danger?"

I toss my book aside. "As long as it doesn't involve the twelve subclauses on the Shovel Hygiene Ordinance, I'm good to go."

CHAPTER 10

The Lighthouse

WHOA." MY BREATH FOGS the viewport glass as I press myself against it, staring at the needle of gold hanging in the black void beyond. "What did you say it's called?"

"The Lighthouse," says the Ringmaster. He's more jittery than I am, spinning his baton from hand to hand like it might burn him if he holds it too long.

"And why did the Tinkers build it?"

"This particular lighthouse once helped to guide ships through the Anvaran dust clouds. But all the lighthouses served as strongholds for the Tinkers. They were places of learning and teaching: way stations from which to reach out across the universe."

"Then there's more of them?" I squint. The Lighthouse is a lot closer now. It's hard to judge size, but it looks big. Like, city-skyscraper big.

"So the legends say. This is the only one I've found." The Ringmaster stares fixedly out the viewport, as if the whole entire ginormous Lighthouse might vanish if he looked away for even a millisecond.

"I don't get it, though. If it's a Tinker clubhouse, why is it so dangerous?" Outside, the boarding tube snakes out from the Big Top to link us to the Lighthouse.

"If the light itself were to activate while we were on board, it would be rather like sunbathing on Venus."

I cross my arms. "So will it hurt the Big Top if it lights up?"

"No, the Big Top has solar shielding. Out there we'll be unprotected. But it's probably completely inactive now." He gives an airy wave.

"Probably? So, what, we have only a five percent chance of getting burned to a crisp?"

"It wouldn't be fun without a little danger, now, would it?" The Ringmaster's smile is like the noonday sun, so bright you're sure nothing terrible could ever happen as long as it's blazing down on you. "Besides, you can hardly expect to find anything interesting somewhere safe."

A shiver runs through the floor as the far end of the boarding tube clamps onto the golden needle. The doorway to the tube hisses open, waiting for us. The Ringmaster holds out a hand. I take it, and together we race along the passage to the airlock that will take us onto the Lighthouse.

The Ringmaster hands me a breathing mask. "Just in case," he says lightly. He's got another stuffed into one of his sequined coat pockets. "Think of it, Beatrix. We're about to walk in the footsteps of the ancients. Are you ready?" He rests a hand lightly on the sealed tunnel before us. He's grinning like a madman. And maybe he is mad, and I guess I am, too, because I can feel the enormous goofy smile plastered on my own face. But come on, we're about to explore an ancient alien space station. I think a little madness is understandable.

As the door hisses open, the Ringmaster pulls out what looks like an old-fashioned gold pocket watch. He flips it open briefly, then slides it back into his coat. He glances back, toward the Big Top, and for a moment he looks almost . . . guilty.

"I really don't think an hour is going to make a difference," I say.

"What?"

"Miss Three. You know, the number crunching. You looked worried. But this is more important, right?" I frown. "Is the translator not getting this?"

"Miss Three, of course. Yes," he says, talking rapidly, as if trying to escape the conversation. "Right, let's go."

Man. The Ringmaster isn't the easiest book to read, but today I feel like he's written upside down, backwards, and in Swahili. I shrug it off and follow him into the Lighthouse.

We move slowly at first, as the Ringmaster lingers over every niche, every scrap of metal, even the light fixtures. "Hah, still on standby! And the artificial gravity is working," he says, fiddling with a panel in the wall. A murky amber glow fills the corridor. "Good old Tinker technology. And they say we're not reliable." The light begins to sputter. The Ringmaster gives the panel a thump, and the flickering stops.

"And look at this!" He darts forward to jam nearly his entire upper body into a shadowy recess. His voice echoes from the wall. "The recycling system! Imagine it, Beatrix! The first Tinker might have once stood here, tossing away a candy wrapper."

I cross my arms, leaning against the wall while he extracts his head. "So you brought me to see the ancient alien garbage disposal. You sure know how to show a girl a good time."

He gives me an injured look. "Recycling systems can be quite fascinating, I assure you. You should visit the one on the Big Top. It's an experience you won't forget."

"Sorry," I say, hastening to catch up as he takes off

again down the corridor. "I guess I was expecting something a little more . . . whoa."

"Like this?" The Ringmaster leads the way out into a massive open space. Bigger than the Big Top tent. So big I can't see the far side. A narrow walkway edged by softly gleaming lights stretches out into the void. The Ringmaster lifts his baton, the gem on the top flaring to life.

Suddenly a thousand lights are winking back at us, reflected in the glossy walls that swoop up into unseen heights and down into the abyss. I can make out the distant sparkle of the far side now.

The entire center of the Lighthouse is hollow. "What is this place?" My voice comes out as a whisper. It's like being in a church, somehow. The age, I guess, and the silence. The feeling that I'm standing on top of generations of pain and joy and striving.

"This is the lantern chamber, the source of the light itself. When the Lighthouse is active, this chamber reflects and concentrates the beacon. And consequently would burn us to a crisp."

"And that?" I point to the slice of darkness hanging in the center of the chamber, tethered by the narrow walkway.

The Ringmaster grins. "That is the heart of the entire station. The Keeper's Watch. If there's anything interesting here, that's where we're going to find it."

We cross the walkway in the golden circle cast by

the Ringmaster's baton. I glance over the edge. It's enough to lodge a bowling ball in my throat. Anybody who falls here is going to have a long, long time to regret it.

When we're about halfway across, I think I see something. A flicker in the reflected lights, like something's moving in front of them. Then nothing. I shake myself sharply. Come on, Trix. Next you'll be saying you saw the Mizzebar Moon Monster.

Still, I can't help but sigh a little in relief when we duck into the black dome of the Keeper's station, away from the abyss and the chilly gusts that flow up like the breath of some nasty monster waiting below.

We find out soon enough that the monster has already been and gone and left his calling card. Panels hang open, revealing banks of blackened wire. Screens sit dead and dark, drifts of shattered glass littering the floor around them. The room is totaled.

With a savage curse, the Ringmaster kicks aside a pile of broken metal, sending it rocketing out of the room. The violent clatter turns to utter silence as the debris tumbles off the edge of the walkway and into the void. It makes my skin crawl.

"What do you think happened?" I ask.

The Ringmaster whips around, teeth bared, baton raised as if to smash the long-gone vandals. It's more than a little terrifying. "The Mandate. They destroyed it, as they destroy everything!"

"Hey!" I catch hold of his arm before he can bash anything else. He starts to shake me off, but I hang on. "I like to hit things when I get angry, too, but can't we use any of this stuff?"

The fury washes out of his face like I socked him with a bucket of cold water. He drops his arm, digging the end of the baton into the floor and leaning heavily against it. "I thought—hoped—there might be . . ." He coughs, and I can't make out the last word. It might have been "answers."

The Ringmaster raises a hand to his throat, his breath rasping. Slumping against the wall, he pulls the breathing mask from his pocket and presses it to his mouth. Closing his eyes, he draws a long, rattling breath. He takes three more hits, then lowers the mouthpiece and rests his head back against the wall. I've never seen him look so young, or so . . . fragile. It scares me enough that I scramble for a joke.

"You okay?" I ask. "Or do you need a time-out?"

He winces, then chuckles. "I suppose I deserved that. No, no more tantrums. Only . . . regret."

"Are you sure there's nothing here?" I search the floor around us for anything that isn't blackened, smashed, or shattered. I spot a few bits of crystal that look like the datastores Nola gave me to download onto from the universal net. "What about those?"

His lips twist as he scoops up a handful. "Broken. I

suppose Miss Three might be able to recover something, but the chances are—"

I stiffen upright. "Did you hear that?" A slithering noise whispers against my ears. "There!"

The Ringmaster pushes himself away from the wall, searching the darkness. His eyes widen, looking past me.

I follow his gaze in time to see something bleed through the darkness, a darting crimson needle. The Ringmaster pulls me closer, to the center of the circle of light that falls from his baton. "Stay in the light, Beatrix."

"What are they?"

"Imagine every quality that would be desirable in a living weapon, culled by the Mandate from a universe of deadly genetic potential. Put them all together, and you have the Vycora. They are fast, they are implacable, and they can slice us through before we even feel the pain of it. They have only one weakness. Light."

"So we're safe here?" I spin around, searching the edge of the pool of golden light.

"For now. But I can't—" Another fit of coughing doubles him over. As the baton dips, our frail circle of protection shifts. I step sideways, grabbing the Ringmaster's arm to keep him upright. Something slithers over my foot. I kick it away, terror digging sharply into my spine. But it's only a coil of blackened wires.

The Ringmaster raises the mask to his face again. For a long moment the only sounds are his strained breathing and the skin-crawling slither of the Vycora. Then he puts the mask aside and looks at me intently.

"Beatrix, do you trust me?"

It feels, somehow, as if this is the most important question anyone has ever asked me. "Yes."

He gives me a brief, dazzling smile before scrambling upright and heading for the nearest of the smashed consoles. He begins ripping through them, pulling out the innards.

"Um. But I'd still like to know what you're doing."

"Turning on the Light. Aha!" He brandishes a handful of colorful wires, then begins twisting them together, like he's hot-wiring a car. "It should drive off the Vycora."

"I thought you said the Light would fry us."

"Only if we don't get back to the Big Top before it reaches full power."

"Which will take how long?"

"Twenty-three seconds. Plus or minus."

"Getting burned to a crisp is a definite minus." I bounce on my heels. All I can think of is the time I spilled hot grease on my hand as a little girl, helping my mom fry spring rolls. And how much it hurt. But crazy as it sounds, I do trust the Ringmaster. "Starting when?"

"Now." He dances back from the console as a hum pulses through the floor. Light begins to pour out from somewhere above us: a pure, white brilliance that makes me blink.

We run, racing between the killing darkness and the blinding light. My mind is empty of everything but the pounding of my feet and the dark outline of the distant door. Scarlet threads slide across our path, but the claws of brilliance tear them away.

A moment later the light begins to tear at us, too. I hear the Ringmaster hiss. Spines of white-hot fire jab into my skin. Tears stream down my cheeks, burned out of my eyes.

The light chases us all the way back to the Big Top. Even as the airlock hisses closed, I can see bright beams reaching out from the Lighthouse. It's like a star being born. The terror and the wonder of it nearly knocks me to the floor. Relief turns my knees to jelly, but at the same time there's an ache deep inside. It's like someone handed me a book of secrets and only let me see one page before snatching it back again.

I punch the control panel beside the windows, darkening the glass. The light streaming through the viewport dies to a distant glow. The Ringmaster leans against the wall, resting his head against the gently humming metal and drawing a long breath. "I'm sorry."

For a moment, I'm not entirely sure he's talking to me. "Are you hurt?" he asks.

"No. You?"

He shakes his head. "We achieved a dazzlingly successful escape, if nothing else." He sighs, extracting a handful of broken crystal from his pocket. It's the crushed datastore.

"What did you expect to find?" I say at last.

The Ringmaster smiles faintly. "Oh, the usual things. Answers to the eternal questions. The meaning of life." He turns the bits of crystal in his hand. "The trouble with being the leader is that people tend to expect you to be leading them somewhere in particular." He looks up then, and for once his eyes don't hold galaxies, only uncertainty and pain. He's never looked more human.

I feel like somebody's offered me a key, for this brief, fragile moment, to unlock a part of the mystery that is the Ringmaster. I don't know how long it will last, and there's so much I want to ask. When I open my mouth, the question that comes out surprises even me.

"Are you happy being the Ringmaster?"

He closes his eyes and rests his palms against the wall. The Big Top hums. His lips tighten.

"It wasn't supposed to be a stumper," I say finally.

The Ringmaster's eyes stay closed. "Life is about choices, Beatrix. But when you choose one road, it means there are others you may never walk. Things you sacrifice . . ."

"What kind of things?"

He looks at me then. "It's more than a title, being the Ringmaster. The Big Top is my responsibility. She is mine and I am hers. Which means I can't be . . ." He stops himself, giving a sort of half-shrug. "But it was my choice. I've seen things, done things, been things I could never have otherwise. And I would never give it up. *Ever.*" The Big Top thrums again, more loudly. His lips twist. "Though perhaps she deserves better."

"No," I say. "I'm just the new girl and all, but from what I've seen, I think the Big Top is lucky to have you. We all are."

The Ringmaster cocks his head, speaking to the walls. "You hear that? I take her out and nearly get her burned to a crisp and she says I'm doing a good job." He sighs, glancing down to the crushed datastore bits. "And I thought I might find answers. It was foolhardy, but I'm a fool if nothing else."

The meteorite weighs in my pocket as if it's trying to compact into a black hole. I hear Dad's warning, as clear as ever. *You have to keep it secret. You have to protect it.* But the Ringmaster has given me his secrets, or at least some of them. I want to . . . honor that. To share a secret of my own. I can't find the right words, so in the end I just stick out my hand, the black oblong smooth in my palm.

There's a flicker of something in his face, too quick for me to catch. He brushes the tip of one finger over the meteorite, tracing the thin crack.

I force myself to speak. "My parents gave it to me. I thought maybe . . . maybe it's important. They made me promise to keep it safe, and Nyl sure wanted to get his hands on it, so I figure it must be the real deal."

He's still staring.

"Or maybe it's a pretty rock," I add.

"No. The Tinkers made this. But made it for what?" He takes it, holding it aloft and frowning.

"And why did my parents have it?" I search his face for answers. "They must have been Tinker-touched, too." My hands are shaking. "Right? That must be it. Why else would they have it?"

"Indeed." The Ringmaster gives me an inscrutable look, then presses the meteorite back into my hand. "Thank you. For trusting me enough to show me this." He hesitates, then adds, "It might be wise to allow Miss Three to study it."

"No! I mean, why? If it's a Tinker antique, what would she know? Besides, she's from the Mandate. I don't—"

"Trust her?"

I fiddle with the meteorite, tumbling it between my fingers. "Not yet. But I've got someone else I want to show it to."

*　*　*

"It looks like a rock to me," says Nola. She turns the meteorite to catch the brightest beams from the lamp, then shakes her head. "If the Ringmaster didn't know, I'm not sure I can do any better."

"The Ringmaster isn't a Tech genius," I say, bouncing on the edge of my bed.

"I guess I could run some tests," Nola offers. She roots around inside one of the flip-out drawers beside her bed, pulling out a selection of tools. "There must be something inside, if it heated up. But you said that was the first time?"

"Yeah. I wonder why? Maybe it was reacting to my Tinker-touch. It happened that same night my hair turned pink. The same night Nyl found me." I suppress a shiver at the memory, and try not to think about where he might be now.

Nola shrugs. "Could be that. Could be chance. Could be something else completely." Nola slides one of her tools over the surface of the rock, frowning. "Has it always had the crack?"

"No." I fill her in on my first encounter with Nyl. "So if bashing him in the face with the meteorite didn't bust it, dropping it onto the floor must have."

"Hmmm. It's not actually a meteorite. It's artificial. A pretty durable composite." By this time Nola has gone through a half-dozen scanners, gauges, and something that looks like an eggbeater, but the furrow between her brows has only gotten deeper. "I'm surprised it cracked at all. Hey, what's this?"

"You found something?"

"Maybe." Nola squints at the display on her egg-beater. "I'm picking up some microwave radiation."

"So . . . I can use it to make a bag of popcorn?"

Nola frowns, twiddling a dial. "It could be a signal, or a message. Or a beacon." She lifts her eyes. "But I know one thing it definitely is not."

"What?"

"An essay on Core Governance Mining Regulations."

I groan, flopping back onto the bed. "It's going to be a long night."

CHAPTER 11

Secrets in the Dark

I'M ON FIRE. Struggling out of sleep, I find myself twisted in my sheets, slick with sweat. Even through my pillow I can feel the warmth pulsing from the rock. I throw back the covers, feeling disgustingly damp.

I fumble for the rock. It's warm, but not too hot to handle. Across the room Nola mumbles something in her sleep. We were both up late: me because Core Mining Regulations make zero sense, and Nola because she's a saint and helped me with the essay. I'm not keen on making her miss any more sleep because of me, so I slip out into the hall as quietly as I can.

It might be my imagination, but I could swear the rock is getting warmer. I head down the hallway. My fingers flinch from the heat cupped in my hands. It's definitely getting hotter. I head for the bathroom, in case I need to play firefighter.

Except that now the rock is cool again. What kind of game is this? Is it trying to drive me insane?

Or is it trying to send me a message? I back up. Heat stirs against my palm. Gotcha! I take another step, letting the heat lead me along the corridors, out of the dorms, all the way to—

A hallway. A really *boring* hallway. I don't get it. The rock is so hot now I have it bundled in the hem of my shirt. But there's nothing here. I spin around, searching. Then inspiration strikes. I kneel down.

An even stronger wave of heat flows off the rock, pushing me back a step. So maybe it *is* leading me somewhere. I'm just not on the right level. As I stand there, trying to decide how seriously Nola would bust my ass if I started pulling up floor panels from her ship, I realize the rock has gone cool. Wonderful.

I'm about to try to find my way back to my room when I hear a noise. Someone else is moving along the corridor, somewhere beyond the next curve, out of sight. I shrink back against the shadowy arch of the hall. Muffled footsteps pad away. Whoever it was, she's going the other direction.

There's nothing for it. I have to find out what's up.

Rounding a curve in the corridor, I catch a glimpse of someone with long dark hair. Sirra. And I've got a good guess where she's headed.

I keep my distance, trying to walk as quietly as I can. It gets harder as we move into the really cluttered corridors.

Something tickles my toes. Feathers. I spot the remaining hatboxes, still piled against the wall. Somewhere in the distance a burst of static crackles. I stay skulking behind the hatboxes, listening hard. This time I'm going to find out what Sirra is up to.

I can barely make out her silhouette under the dim blue track lights that run along the ceiling. The noises coming out of the wall are still gibberish, but I can hear Sirra well enough.

"No, not yet," she says. "I need more time. I have a plan. Send it to me. But not there. It'll take too long."

More gabble, then Sirra again, sounding annoyed. "Fine, never mind. Make it Hasoo-Pashtung. I'll figure something out."

Hasoo-Pashtung. It's one of the scheduled performance stops, a couple of months down the road, the one Nola keeps talking about because it's got some ginormous shopping bazaar.

There's another sputter from the wall. "I know! I know it's my fault! But no one else will find out. I need to get her alone, and then I can settle everything, I promise. It'll all be over soon." Silence fills the corridor, broken only by a gulping breath.

Something prods me in the shoulder. I bite down on a yelp of surprise as Nola's round face emerges from the shadows. "Trix, what are you doing?" she whispers.

"Better question is, what's Sirra doing?"

"Coming this way! Quick, in here." Nola lays a hand on the wall beside us. The metal scrolls open, revealing a dark recess. We tumble inside.

The walls zip closed, leaving us in near total darkness. A small slitted window lets in a slice of the dim blue light from outside. We watch in silence as Sirra marches past our hiding spot.

"What is this?" I ask, after I'm sure Sirra is gone.

"Storage closet. Though obviously *some* people have a different notion of what that means. Did you see all that clutter out there? And here's this perfectly good closet, not a foot away, empty!" Nola taps the wall. It folds open obligingly.

"Lucky for us," I say, following her out. "I don't think Sirra would have been happy to find someone eavesdropping, even if we only heard half the conversation. Why wasn't the translator handling the other voice?"

Nola frowns. "Some sort of scrambler, maybe. Come on, I'll take a look."

I pace back and forth, scuffing up clouds of feathers, while Nola studies the communication panel. "Yeah, someone definitely didn't want anyone listening in on that call."

"Can you tell where it came from? Who it was?"

Nola shakes her head. "Someone off-ship. What was she saying? I only heard the last part."

I fill her in, describing the most recent conversation as well as the one I stumbled into when I first came on board.

"I wonder who she needs to get alone?"

"And why." I frown. "She's up to something."

"Do you think we should tell the Ringmaster?"

"No," I say quickly, remembering his attitude at brunch. "First we get proof."

"That's about all I can do right now. I guess we should get back to the dorm. If we can even find the way." Nola grimaces. "I was in such a rush to follow you, I forgot to grab my know-it-all."

I point down the corridor. "It shouldn't be too hard to go back the way we—"

An eerie wailing cuts off my words. A moment later, the corridor I was pointing at is gone, replaced by a blank gray wall.

The hallway lights turn orange. Nola yelps. "The ship's compacting! We've got to get out of here!"

Only one choice. We race down the remaining corridor. Metal crunches and slams behind us. I keep my eyes ahead, willing the walls to stay put just a little longer. "What's a safe spot?"

"Our beds get capsuled, but they're probably cut off already."

"Where else?"

"The bridge, the library, the commons, the bio-habitat."

"Great. Where are they?" We've reached a junction. Two orange-lit corridors twist away, right and left.

"I—I don't know. I don't know where we are, Trix. I don't have my know-it-all. We're going to get smashed!" Nola's voice spirals up into a squeak of fear.

"No, we're not!" I scan the walls, looking for anything familiar. "What about another closet?"

"If I knew where one was. Maybe—eeeee!" Her voice ends in another squeal as the right-hand hallway slams shut.

"It's okay. I know how to get out of here! This way!" Seizing Nola's hand, I pull her with me down the remaining corridor. "I was in this hall the other night. I remember that light was out, see there? A little farther there's a turn . . . aha! And then there was a door that goes into—"

We burst out into an open green space. One last crash of compacting metal echoes behind us. Both of us go sprawling across the grass of the biohabitat. I have just enough time to enjoy my three-dimensional state before everything melts to the familiar blackness of the jump.

* * *

"See? It's better than last time, isn't it?" says Nola.

"Oh, sure." I rub my gummy eyes. "This time I only feel like I've been dipped in glue and hung upside down for a few hours. Much better." I stand up shakily.

The Ringmaster's voice echoes from the walls.

"Attention, Galacticus Crew! As you may have noted, we took a bit of a detour. I'm afraid the Big Top took it upon herself to jump us into the Jerrindar System."

Nola gives a low whistle. "That's not good."

"While it's my hope this is merely the result of the Big Top conceiving an urgent and inescapable craving for Jerrindarian Toffee, you may be assured that Miss Three and I will be investigating fully. In the meantime we ask you all to remain in your dorms. Please, go back to sleep; you'll need your strength in the morning. We've acquired some leeches, and you know what that means."

Nola groans.

"Leeches?" I ask. "Like the nasty little things that suck your blood?"

Nola makes a face. "No, like the nasty *big* things that suck on the Big Top's energy field. They're disgusting." She shivers. "But leeches bother me a lot less than the Big Top jumping on her own."

"Do you think Sirra had something to do with it?"

Nola taps a finger against her chin. "It's possible. If the Big Top detected a gravity well, it might set off the proximity warnings for a black hole, and that would cause a jump. But why would she do it, Trix?"

"I don't know," I admit. "Still, it's pretty suspicious that she was the only one prowling around when it happened."

"Actually, she wasn't the only one." Nola gives me a meaningful look.

"Oh. Right. But we didn't do anything."

Nola doesn't look entirely convinced. "I'm not sure Miss Three would see it that way."

"No, as a matter of fact. She does not."

"Uh-oh," says Nola.

Yeah, we're toast. Miss Three flickers into view, a severe, dark ghost floating above the greenery. "Would you two please explain what you are doing out of your dorms in the middle of the night?"

"Ahh . . ." Nola opens her mouth and flaps her hands, looking like a fish out of water.

"It was my fault," I say. "I was sleepwalking. Nola came after me to wake me up, but then the alarm went off, so we had to come here to not get squashed. Sorry," I add, aware that I don't sound particularly apologetic.

"And I suppose you had nothing to do with that unplanned jump?"

"No," says Nola, her nervousness bubbling over. "How could we? Even I don't know how to make the Big Top jump. I've tried to see what the Ringmaster does, but it's something with that baton of his, and I can't quite make it out, so you see we couldn't—"

"Enough, Miss Ogala. I assure you we will be getting

to the bottom of this matter soon enough. For the time being, kindly return to where you are supposed to be, and stay there. We will see about suitable recompense for curfew violations tomorrow."

Thankfully the decompaction bell sounds. Nola and I beat a hasty retreat back to our dorm.

CHAPTER 12

Leeches

T'S A PUNISHMENT, that's what it is," says Nola glumly. "If this was a random chore assignment, I'm the Wazeer of Deneb."

"Is it really that bad?" I grit my teeth as I shove my foot into one of the tall white spaceboots. I'm already wearing the suit; it's hard to believe something so crinkly-thin is going to keep me safe in the big black void.

"Is it that bad? Hah!" says Theon as she buckles on her own boots. "Ask your know-it-all to find you some pictures of Anvaran dust cloud leeches. No, wait; ask for pictures of the sucker scars, so you see what you're really getting into."

Besides the three of us, there are five others on leech-removal duty: Sirra, Etander, Ghost, a Tech boy named Toothy, and the walking boulder I've seen at the Freak table. He introduces himself as Gravalon Pree in a voice as rich and rumbly as Rocky Road ice cream. He's the only one besides me who seems excited about the mission.

"But we get to fly around with those spacewings," I say. "That's got to be amazing!"

Nola shudders. "That's the worst part."

"But it sounds like fun. Isn't it?"

"Maybe for you. I get sick."

"You should stay midship, Nola," says Sirra. "Trix can handle the aft section on her own. She's always up for a challenge."

Right, like Sirra's suddenly some kind of guardian angel. It has nothing to do with getting me alone out on the hull. Nola looks at me, clearly thinking the same thing. "No, I'm Trix's partner. I'll stay with her."

Sirra shrugs. Clicking down the seal on her helmet, she heads for the airlock, where the others are waiting. She doesn't have any spacewings. I guess with her fancy gravity-bending superpowers, she doesn't need solar-powered jets. Gravalon Pree, on the other hand, doesn't seem to need a spacesuit, but with his extra-large space-wings he looks like some sort of overgrown rock fairy.

While Nola is off checking something on the airlock,

I pull on my own wings. They slip on over my shoulders, but I can't lower my arms. I crane my neck, but I can't see what's wrong. Worse, they won't come off. I'm stuck looking like a complete idiot, flailing around with my arms in the air.

I'm about to do something supremely violent to the wings when suddenly they slide down into place. I turn to see who saved me, expecting to see Nola. "Thanks. I was afraid I'd be stuck that way for—"

It's Etander. "—ever."

Immediately my eyes go to his hands. Today they look perfectly normal. I wrench my attention back to his face. "Oh. Hey. Thanks."

"They were caught up in back," he says quietly.

"Um . . ." Should I ask how he's doing? Or would that only make things more awkward?

He saves me from my social disorder by going on. "About what happened last week . . . we shouldn't have tried to kick you out of the Ring. I'm sorry about . . . about everything that happened."

"Hey, no problem. We're good," I say. "I mean, if you're all—"

"Are you looking forward to testing out the space-wings?" he interrupts, eyes darting away from my unfinished question.

Okay. I guess we're done with that topic. "Sure," I say. "Sounds like fun. And a little dangerous."

"You don't seem afraid."

"Hey, as long as I don't end up covered in chocolate with a new nickname, I think I'll be happy."

That wins me a smile. "Good luck, then."

Theon calls for everyone's attention. "All right, people, time for a safety-procedure chat. I know everyone else has heard it before, but we've got Trix with us for the first time, and you all can use a reminder, so listen up."

"Yes, Miss Three," says the Tech boy in an undertone. Theon scowls at him.

"In case you've forgotten, Toothy, we almost had Dragon doing a space dive into the nearest star last time we went out on spacewings. This is seriously dangerous."

I can feel Etander's eyes on me, and I ignore them.

"Now, there are three rules to remember: First, don't get too far from the ship. This isn't the time for joyriding. Second, don't use your blasters"—she pats the blunt black rod hanging from her belt—"until you pry the leech free. We don't want to accidentally breach the hull.

"And third, if someone gets suckered by a leech, remember to use your beacon." She taps the palm-size disk hanging beside her blaster. "Press the button and give it a good throw, as far away from yourself and the Big Top as possible."

"What does it do?" I ask.

"Lets off an energy signal that attracts the leeches," says Toothy, his grin showing a large number of his namesakes. "I designed it."

"So why can't we trigger a bunch of them to get all the leeches off?"

Toothy's grin fades.

"They have a few side effects," says Nola. "We're working on it."

"What kind of side effects?"

"Well, the worst part is that the energy burst upsets the Big Top's jump system," says Nola. "So we wouldn't be able to jump for at least six hours. It also gives everyone hiccups. We're really not sure why that is."

"So only use it in a real emergency. Everybody got all that?" Theon crosses her arms, looking more than a little like Miss Three. "Good; let's go blast some leeches."

A hiss of decompressing air raises goose bumps along my arms. This is it. In a moment, I'm going to be in space. No glass, no screen; only a thin layer of some wacky alien super-fabric between me and the universe. Okay, so I'll be spending the morning pulling giant leeches off the hull. But I'll be in space! I'm going to fly!

I start to bob as the pull of the ship's artificial gravity ebbs away. Theon and Ghost fly out into the void, followed by Sirra, Etander, and Toothy. With the underwater grace of a humpback, Gravalon Pree dives smoothly through the door, executing an elaborate curvette as he heads off along one finlike ridge of the ship's hull.

Nola pauses, clinging one-handed to the exit, to look back at me. She's saying something. I rap at my helmet.

"Hey, Britannica! I turned you on for a reason. Come on, give me a link to everyone else."

"I beg your pardon," comes the voice of my know-it-all. "I thought you said to be quiet. I was trying to oblige."

"Nola, I want to hear. You, I want quiet. I'm going to hear too much about that stupid show as it is." I stifle a groan. I have *got* to figure out a way to deal with that thing. It took some serious bribery to get it to do what I wanted this morning.

"And you won't regret it!" shrills my know-it-all. "We are going to have *such* a good time watching the marathon! But have a care with those leeches, dear. You've enough of a challenge with that hair. You certainly don't need a sucker scar to worry about."

"Okay, okay, I'll be careful. Now, patch me through."

"—you going to be okay?" Nola's voice comes through so loudly it's like she's right inside my helmet.

"Piece of cake!" I give her a thumbs-up in case the translator doesn't know how to handle that. It's true. I really feel good about this. For as long as I can remember, my sleep has been full of flying dreams. I've probably spent half my nights swooping over trees and into the clouds. I figure it might even have been part of my Tinker-touch. Maybe all those dreams were preparing me for this.

I pat the slight bulge along my side where the rock lies tucked in the pocket of my shirt, under the tinfoil spacesuit. It's not only the rock that got me here. I *am* special. This is what my parents were trained for. This was what I was born for. Space.

Gripping the handholds of my spacewings, I give the thrusters a trial burst. For one glorious moment I'm perfect, an eagle, a comet in the night. Then one wing dips. My hands clench instinctively. Suddenly I'm rocketing forward, careening past Nola and out into space.

It's like flying twelve kites at once in a hurricane. I swing my arms around, trying desperately to stop myself. All I accomplish is turning my flight into an end-over-end tumble. I feel like I left my stomach back on the ship.

Finally I steady myself and come around into a shaky glide. Nola flies over to join me. "Are you okay?" She looks a little green herself, but at least she's staying right-side up.

"Yeah. Just getting a feel for these things." I give the thrusters a gentle tap, enough to keep up with Nola.

"You're doing great. Much better than my first time. Come on, our section is this way."

I grit my teeth, struggling to stay with Nola as she heads off along the rippling red striped hull of the Big Top. So much for my fabulous inborn talent for flying. I'm barely holding my course steady, and it's not like Nola's a speed demon.

But by the time we reach the tail section, I'm a little more confident. I swoop along the ridges and up into the emptiness beyond, trying to get a glimpse of the entire massive ship. Now that I can see it, the Big Top reminds me of some weird undersea creature, like a jellyfish or maybe a pudgy squid. With red stripes.

"Trix, don't go too far!" Nola's voice echoes in my ear. "Remember what Theon said. Anyway, I found some leeches. We'd better get to work."

Reluctantly, I fly back. Nola has already clamped her magnetized boots onto the hull and is hard at work pulling on something that looks like a giant purplish-gray slug. The thing narrows, stretching like a piece of taffy.

It pops free. "Take that!" Nola says, directing her blaster at the leech. It twitches in a halo of crackling blue light, then drifts off into space. She turns to me as I land. "Did you see how I did it? You have to be careful when they let go; that's when they're liable to attack. Want to try one yourself?" She gestures to the hull on either side. About a dozen more leeches have clamped onto the Big Top. The smallest is as long as my forearm. The largest is almost as big as I am.

As we work, Nola chatters away, telling me stories about life on the Big Top. Considering I'm prying giant leeches off a spaceship, I'm having a great time. It's funny; when the Ringmaster offered me this shot at joining the circus, I thought the best thing would be space itself. And it *is* pretty freaking spectacular. Right now I can look up at that dome of stars and know—not just hope—that they're full of life. It's a feeling I can't even put into words. Mom and Dad would have understood it.

But you know what else is just as freaking spectacular? Nola. Here she is, telling me her stories, inviting me into her life like I'm her sister or something, not a random pink-haired tagalong from a boondock galaxy. I'm not all that used to people being nice to me. Pretty much everything that's made me happy since I lost my folks has been something I've made or grabbed for myself.

Nola also fills me in on what she's learned about last night's unplanned jump. Turns out it was a gravity anomaly. And guess what? Our new course means we're headed for Hasoo-Pashtung next. Sirra is *definitely* up to something.

"That's the last of these," says Nola, watching the remnants of the largest leech drift away. She heaves a sigh. "I guess we'd better fly over to the other side and check there, too. I hope I make it without getting sick."

Poor Nola. From the look on her face, I don't think she's exaggerating the danger. There must be something I can do to make this easier on her. "How about you stay here?" I say. "I'll go check it out and come back. No sense in you making yourself sick if there's nothing there."

"Are you sure? It's your first time out on spacewings. And what about Sirra?"

"Positive. I'm practically an expert with these things now, and Sirra's at the other end of the ship. Be back in a flash."

"Okay. Thanks, Trix. But keep the link open. Call if you need help."

I wave, then set off over the ridge to the next valley. Finding it leech-free, I move on, winging up away from the hull to get a better view.

I spot a cluster of leeches. There aren't too many, and the biggest is only about two feet long. "Hey, Nola," I say into the link. "I found a few more, but I can handle them. You stay there, and I'll be back when I'm done. Okay? Nola?"

I tap my helmet. "Nola? Can you hear me?" I wait for a long, silent moment. "Hey, Britannica, want to fill me in on what the space pirate Zendalos has been up to?"

Something is definitely wrong. I better head back, before Nola gets worried.

A web of blue light springs up in front of me. I backwing into a somersault, but the blue light is every-where, caging me in. I pull free my blaster.

"Nola!" I shout into the link. "Something's happening! I need help!"

"Your friend can't hear you." A familiar voice crackles in my ear. I never thought I'd miss that screechy know-it-all, but right now I'd take all the *Love Among the Stars* factoids in the universe over this voice. "I suggest you not attempt to escape the energy cage. You will find the experience both futile and rather painful."

I whirl around. The tip of one spacewing brushes against the interlacing blue light. "Aaaagggh!" I curl against the agony that tears into me. My fingers spasm. The blaster flies free, spinning off beyond the curved wall of my prison.

"As I said."

My hot breath fogs my helmet as I turn, searching for him. There. Nyl floats a few yards beyond my cage. His batlike spacewings blot out the stars.

"What do you want?" I demand.

"To talk."

"Right. You're one of the Mandate, and all you want is a chat? Next you'll be inviting me in for tea and cookies."

"I see he's gotten to you already with his fairy tales." Nyl drifts closer. Starlight gleams on his mask as he tilts his head. "Don't be so quick to assume you know who is the villain and who is the shining hero."

"Call me crazy, but I'm going to say the villain is the guy who keeps attacking me."

"I am trying to help you. You are on a dangerous path, and if you don't turn back now, you will be lost forever. It may even be too late."

"Thanks for the oh-so-helpful warning, but I'm right where I want to be."

"This isn't a joke! I know the lies the Ringmaster trades in, but you must not believe them. You don't belong here."

"I do, too! He said it himself! He said I'm—"

"Of course," cuts in Nyl. He sighs. "Listen to me, Beatrix. I understand how bewitching that can be. The idea that you are somehow better than others. That you are shaped for some brilliant future. Others may toil and scrabble in menial occupation and mundane lives, but not you, never you. You are . . . *special*."

On his lips it sounds like a curse.

"Have you ever considered the pain that proceeds from disparity, from difference? You've seen it on your own planet. The wars fought over the color of one's skin or the choice of one's god. That is what comes of this. Is that what you want?"

"Of course not!" I protest. "But you're twisting it all up! I'm not saying I'm better than anyone. I mean, even if I am, I'm not saying they should . . . aaagh! Look, I'm not a lawyer. I can't make it sound all pretty and convincing, but I know you're wrong. That isn't what the Ringmaster is about."

"You seem to think yourself an expert on the Ringmaster. Do not be so certain you know the truth. How much of his precious ship has he even allowed you to see? You don't belong here."

"Yes I *do!*" My voice rises like a little kid's. "My

parents were Tinker-touched, and so am I. This is where I belong!"

"Is that what he told you?"

"Yes!" I snap, even as a part of my brain sifts through the words cluttering my memory. Had he said it? Or only let me think it?

"He deceives you. He does it to protect you, but he only makes you weak. Come with me now." Nyl drifts closer to my cage and extends one arm. The blue fire pulls back, allowing his gray-gloved fingers to slip past. He holds out his hand. "Abandon this folly. Let us cleanse you of the taint before it destroys you. Let me show you that you need not cover your life in spangles and glitter for it to be something glorious. Something happy. I promise you this, Beatrix. If you stay on this ship, it will break your heart."

"You're wrong." The words tear out of my tight throat. I spin around, searching the remorselessly empty sky. Maybe I can force my way through the web, take the pain, and hope I don't black out before I'm free. "I'm staying here. I belong here." I ignore his outstretched hand.

He is silent for so long, holding that pose, I wonder if maybe I've found a way to freeze time. When he finally does speak, it's like a whip crack on my nerves.

"How unfortunate. We had hoped you would come willingly." He balls his fist and pulls it back out of the blue-fire cage. "But willingly or not, you will come."

The orb of light begins to shift, to float upward, away from the Big Top. Crackles of agony dance along my arms as I try and fail to stay away from the walls. I want to scream, not from pain but from frustration. If only I hadn't dropped the stupid blaster, I might be able to fight back!

Wait. I'm *not* completely defenseless. And we're still close enough to the ship that it might work! I grab the leech beacon from my belt. Punching the button, I throw it as hard as I can, right at Nyl.

He grunts as it catches him in the midsection. The flash of light makes me look away. An odd, fizzy feeling runs along my skin.

"Beatrix, you must—*hic*—" he begins. Then the leeches are on him. He disappears under a writhing mass of gray-purple. The blue web winks out. I spread my spacewings and take off.

As I speed over the next ridge, I catch sight of two other white-clad shapes winging toward me. Static crackles in my ear, followed immediately by Nola's voice. "—happened? Trix, are you—*hic*—okay?"

"Nola? I'm—*hic*—all right. Can you hear me?"

"Thank the First Tinker! When I saw the—*hic*—leech beacon go off and you didn't answer, I thought . . . well, it was—*hic*—horrible, so I'm not even going to say it. Are you—*hic*—sure you're okay?"

"What happened?" asks Theon. "Did you—*hic*—get leeched?"

"No."

"Then why did you set off the—*hic*—leech beacon?"

"There was a Mandate ship. The same—*hic*—one, from Earth. Over there."

Theon takes off over the ridge, holding her blaster ready. I follow.

There's nothing. No ship, no dark-winged Mandate agent. Not even any leeches.

"He's gone!"

"Are you sure he was here?" Theon soars up away from the hull to survey nearby space.

"I didn't—*hic*—imagine it! He was here! He was trying—" I cut myself off. My body feels like I just put it through a round in the Arena at level bazillion. And that's nothing compared to the crazy thoughts battering my brain. I won't believe it. I can't.

"Trying what?" asks Nola.

"It was lies," I say, my voice cracking. "Only—*hic*—lies."

CHAPTER 13

Restricted Area

THEY DON'T HATE YOU," says Nola. We're heading for the common room, several days after the de-leeching incident. "It all worked out okay. It didn't slow us down—very much—and everyone stopped hiccuping yesterday."

A rumble like a distant rockslide echoes along the corridor. "Everyone except Gravalon Pree," amends Nola. "But at least they're not calling you Supernova anymore."

"Right. And Leechbomb is *so* much better," I say.

"You're the only one who isn't acting like I'm insane." Toothy hustles past, glaring at me with sleepy, dark-circled eyes. I can't really blame him. He's Gravalon Pree's roommate. "Or giving me the evil eye."

"If you say you saw a Mandate ship, I believe you. There's a lot of strange stuff going on around here lately."

"Coming through!"

We plaster ourselves against the wall as Jom and Frex come barreling along the hallway, whooping and juggling a pair of fluffy lavender slippers between them as they go.

One of the Principals thunders after them, bellowing, "Give them back, you idiots!" He makes a lunge for Frex, who leaps clear at the last moment: onto the ceiling. He races onward, upside down, and doesn't even skip a beat juggling. The slippers continue sailing back and forth between him and Jom.

A crowd follows after them, shouting encouragement to both sides and uniformly ridiculing the slippers. Catching Nola's eye, I can't help but laugh. "Only lately?"

As the mob rampages away down the hall, Nola lifts a hand to adjust her know-it-all. "The recycling system? Are you sure?" She shudders. "I hope this isn't going to involve a visit to Rjool's lair. No, it's fine, I'll check it out." She straightens her shoulders and sighs.

"Trouble?"

"A Tech's work is never done. You'd better go on without me. This shouldn't take long, but the marathon starts in ten minutes, and you don't want to miss the recap show or you'll be completely lost. I'll catch up with you in the common room." With a hasty wave, Nola sets off back down the hallway, leaving me alone. Or nearly alone.

"Don't you worry about getting lost, dear," chimes my know-it-all. "I've got all fifteen seasons indexed by character name, key plot points, and location. I've also cross-referenced every costume item to the appropriate mercantile dynasty and catalogue, customized to your size and coloring. I think you'd look lovely in this blue number Dalana wears in season eleven, episode five."

I blink as the viewscreen scrolls open in front of my eye, displaying a hideous monstrosity of skintight skirts and hugely puffed sleeves. "Isn't that gorgeous?" burbles my know-it-all. "It's from the scene where Dalana confronts Zendalos at the Governance Ball and discovers the true identity of—"

"Over my dead body." I continue along the corridor.

"Really? I do think it's more suited to a ball than a funeral, but of course it's your choice. I'll update your registered last will and testament as soon as I can contact Core Legal Records Bureau."

"I have a will?"

"Oh, yes. Birth certification, school records, everything. Of course it's all forgery; part of the Ringmaster's false identity protocol, since you're actually a heathen from the Excluded Territories. No, dear, not *that* way!"

"Isn't the common room this way?"

"Heavens, no. You should have gone left at the last intersection. This is a restricted area."

I study the hallway before me. It looks like all the rest: curving, gray-brown, lit by recessed orange lights. The flattened remains of a box labeled FRAGILE lean against one wall, the apparent victim of a compaction. "Why is it restricted? Is it dangerous?"

"That information is restricted."

"Says who?"

"That information is restricted."

"And you call yourself a know-it-all."

"I do know it all," says the device. "I just don't tell it all."

I'm about to return to the unrestricted corridor when Nyl's words whisper from my memory. *How much of his precious ship has he even allowed you to see?*

That's it. I click off the know-it-all and march onward.

* * *

You'd think something called a restricted area would be at least a little bit exciting. You know, maybe some captive alien monsters, or top-secret science experiments, or maybe even the Ringmaster's personal quarters. So far I've found a room full of feathered fans, another chock-full of rusty old gears and springs, and lots and lots of long, monotonous corridors. The only danger here is that I might die of boredom. I'm starting to think I'd be better off watching the six-hour *Love Among the Stars* marathon. One more corridor; that's as far as I'm going. If it's more of the same, I'm done here.

I turn the corner and stop, staring at a hallway that is *definitely* not more of the same. It's more like a tunnel than a corridor. The curved walls glow pink. I can't find the light source. It's like the whole place is . . . alive. Ridges ripple along the walls, reminding me in a nasty way of the pictures of brains from my bio book. Or those things in your lungs that get all crusty and gross in smokers.

Well, I *was* looking for something interesting. Better check it out while I have the chance.

I go about five steps before I realize my pocket is giving off heat. I pull out the rock. It's definitely warm to the touch. Hmm.

I take a step back. Like magic, the rock cools down. A step forward, and it's warm again. I hold the infuriating thing up in front of my nose. "So you want to play hot and cold again? Fine. I'm game."

The cerebral tunnel takes me past two arched doorways. By the time I reach the third, the rock is so hot I need to bundle it in a corner of my jacket. As I move on, the heat dies away.

I spin around, facing the third doorway. There's some kind of panel above it. I can't read the funky alien script. I try tapping at the door. All that happens is that the squiggles above it reconfigure into numbers: 1349. Great. That's a lot of help.

There's no lever or knob or anything. "Come on," I tell the door. "I followed the bread crumbs and everything. Let me in!"

The door ignores me. I'm about ready to give it a good kick when I hear voices echoing from back down the corridor behind me. There's only one person on the ship with an electronic buzz to her voice: Miss Three. And I am *not* getting lectured again. I've got no choice but to keep going and hope there's a way out farther down the tunnel.

It sounds like a good plan, except that when I skitter around the next curve, there is no more tunnel. The brainlike walls widen out to encircle a dimly lit open space. It's a dead end.

"It's too great a risk, Ringmaster," says Miss Three behind me. My heart thumps even faster. Bad enough to be caught sneaking around a restricted section by Miss Three. But how can I explain this to the Ringmaster? I've got to hide. But where?

I check out the corrugated walls. The ridges are deeper here, twisting in patterns that almost make sense if you tilt your head and squint. It's my only choice.

Jamming my fingers into one of the grooves, I pull myself up and scramble into the deepest crevice I can find. Ewww. Spaceship walls are not supposed to be damp. Or warm. Or *spongy*. Gah.

I hold my breath as two figures walk into the room below.

"She hasn't caused any serious trouble so far," the Ringmaster is saying.

"The jump systems were offline for nearly eight hours. If we'd been attacked—"

"But we weren't. And if there was a Mandate agent in the area, she can hardly be blamed for panicking."

Hmmph. I did *not* panic. I used the resources I had on hand. That's being clever, not panicking.

"The Big Top sensors reported no such presence," says Miss Three.

"Sensors can be deceived."

"Then I suppose you'll say it was a coincidence I discovered her sneaking around the very same night the Big Top made that unprecedented jump? And how do you propose to explain the strange communications we've been tracking? Someone on this ship is sending illicit messages. Miss Ling is a threat to everything you've built here. The ship itself has not recognized her. I've seen the *Programme*. She's no Principal, whatever you may have hoped. You can't allow her to stay. You know what she *really* is. Why won't you tell her the truth?"

"Only Beatrix knows what she really is, and what she's capable of. I intend to give her the chance to discover that. And whatever the case, she deserves a place on the Big Top as much as I do," says the Ringmaster, a harsher note entering his voice. "Though perhaps that's not the best of arguments." The echoes of his laugh grate against my skin.

"This is hardly the time for laughter."

"Indeed it is! Danger and destruction are everywhere; enemies confront us at every turn; all that we've worked for might come to nothing. It's exactly the right time for a bit of humor. Keeps one sane, you see."

"With such a model of sanity before me, how could I not?"

This time the Ringmaster's laugh holds no sharp edges. "A joke! Very good, Miss Three! You see, you're learning something from me."

"And you would do well to learn from me, Ringmaster. It's why I am here, is it not? That girl is a danger you cannot ignore. She could jeopardize everything."

"Believe me, Miss Three, I'm aware of the danger. But also of the potential. If the former outweighs the latter, I'll know how to act."

"And you are prepared to take extreme measures?"

"Yes."

What? What does that mean?

"Good. Shall we proceed, then?"

"By all means. Let's have some action."

With a sweeping gesture, the Ringmaster brandishes his baton. The gem catches the light, winking. He dips smoothly, as if bowing, and thumps the baton against the floor. Two panels scroll open, revealing a spiral stairway that leads down into darkness. "Aha! I thought that would do it. Now, let's see if this answers some of our questions. After you, Miss Three."

As soon as the floor closes over them, I jump down from my hiding spot and book it out of there. But as fast as I run, I can't escape my fears. It's like someone took all those little doubts that have been cutting at me and turned them into a single horrible spear. I swear I can almost feel it, struck right through my heart.

I don't want to think about any of this, not about secret rooms or extreme measures or whether or not I belong in the new life I was promised. All I want is to find Nola and eat blue popcorn and watch some stupid mindless space opera. I can come back later to find out what's behind door number three.

CHAPTER 14

The Hasoo-Pashtung Bazaar

URNS OUT "LATER" is an understatement. The midnight detour and the leech-bomb incident threw our schedule to bits, but now that we're getting back into settled space again, we've got a full roster of performances coming up. And that means practices and more practices, as well as costume design and fitting, prop and set prep, and a host of other details. Not to mention our normal share of schoolwork, courtesy of Miss Three and Core educational regulations. To be honest, I'm kind of relieved. It helps keep me distracted from the ache of all the questions and doubts I'm lugging around. Like what Miss Three meant when she said I didn't belong here. And whether Nyl might have been right.

Even if I weren't up to my ears in rehearsals and physics labs, it would be hard to unravel the mystery of the Restricted Area, because I can't find it. Five times I've gone out, retracing my steps. Once I ended up in the common room, and another time in the biohabitat. Once it was a room full of broken teapots. I tried to get my know-it-all to show me where it was, but the stupid thing refused, even when I threatened to melt it down and turn it into a potato peeler.

The Ringmaster is making himself pretty scarce lately, too. Sure, he'll wander into our classrooms and practice sessions now and then. Occasionally he'll take over, spinning the entire class off on a wild tangent about the taboo on eating fruit in public on Voxima-3. Or he'll have the Clown corps run through a scene in slow motion to "perfect the emotional tone." Some days I only realize he's watching by the weight of his stare. When I look up, he's already slipping out the door.

Then there was the time I was running down the hall late for Astrophysics and nearly bowled him over like I did the day we met. He twinkled that smile at me and said something silly about rabbits. I *wanted* to ask about the conversation I'd overheard. To trust the promise he made me. To find out the truth. But like a dork I stammered something about gamma radiation and ran away.

The truth is that I'm terrified. The truth is, I'm in love. With the Big Top, and with this life: the madcap antics of the other Clowns, Nola and her jokes and her kindness, the weird and wonderful meals Jom conjures from the culinary system, the stars swooping by over my bed at night. I can't bear the thought that someone might take that away. I love all of it too much.

Okay, not *all* of it. I don't think anyone could love the ridiculous costumes we Clowns have to wear for the Tree of Life act.

"It only makes sense. We're part of the Tree," says Theon. "It doesn't look *that* bad."

"Easy for you to say. You get to be a leaf. I look like I belong on Carmen Miranda's head." I prod one of dozens of puffy pear-shaped fruit decorating my green body suit.

"What? The translator didn't get that."

"Never mind." I sigh. "At least I get a cool costume for the Firedance."

Maybe I'm a little prejudiced, but the Firedance is going to be freaking *amazing*. We've been spending every day practicing for it, and I've put in a buttload of extra early-morning sessions. It's tougher than anything I've done before. The fact that I made up the choreography isn't much of a consolation, especially since I *still* haven't nailed the most important bit, that last throw-leap-catch, where I trick the King into kindling the seeds of the Tree of Life.

"How many people are going to be watching?" I ask, trying to ignore the knots that have taken up permanent residence in my stomach.

"Oh, it's only a mid-size show. Five thousand."

"For real? I'm going to be up there in front of five *thousand* people? Parading around with purple pears on my—"

"They're patching it into the local entertainment net, too," says Asha, from the cosmetics station, where she's testing out new makeup designs with her sister. "So there could be up to a hundred thousand watching the feed. Isn't that great?"

I open my mouth. No words come out. I can't breathe. Did my bodysuit suddenly get tighter?

"It's okay, Trix," Theon says. "You'll do fine. You've really been working hard."

"Not hard enough. The end of the Firedance—"

"Will be perfect. You've still got practice tomorrow morning."

I groan. "I need more. Maybe I could skip this bazaar thing and run through it a few more times this afternoon."

A chorus of protests slaps me down.

"You can't miss the Hasoo-Pashtung Bazaar," insists Asha, waving her airbrush.

Leri, one half of her face bright green, leans away from the mirror to tell me, "It's *amazing!* There's stuff there you can't get anywhere else in the universe! I found a set of antique Haitren dynasty beads last time."

"And a life-size hologram of Kel Starstrike," Asha adds. "*With* personalized audio." She pitches her voice low and dramatic. "*The universe is an empty void without you, my darling Leri. But you, my love, are the brightest star in*—mmmph!" She ducks as Leri directs one of the airbrushes at her, but not quickly enough to avoid a streak of orange across her cheek. Asha yowls and raises her own airbrush in retaliation.

"Hasoo-Pashtung really is something," says Theon, watching the antics of the sisters with a frown. "Hey, don't waste all the paint!" She returns her attention to me. "No one misses it. Everyone goes to the bazaar."

"What about the Ringmaster?"

Theon rolls her eyes. "Oh, no, he never leaves the Big Top. You'd think he was chained to it. But Miss Three has a mobile projection, to keep an eye on us."

"You mean to stop us from having any fun," says Asha. "First Tinker forbid we have a good time." The battle seems to have ended in a draw; both sisters are streaked in a clashing array of paints.

"To make sure we don't jeopardize the Circus," says Theon. "If the Core Governance starts sniffing around, they might find out what we really are. And if that happens, none of us is going to be having much fun ever again."

* * *

Nola and I meet up with Theon, Asha, and Leri inside the Big Top's main entrance for our escapade. The ship is parked in an assigned lot on the edge of the bazaar, the better to draw in crowds. With the doorways thrown open, a thousand scents and sounds flow into the Big Top. It's downright intoxicating, and I'm already glad I decided to take the break. This is my first chance to be on an actual alien world! We're weaving our way through the velvet ropes and pylons toward the door when someone speaks.

"Have a lovely time, ladies. Make the most of your freedom."

The Ringmaster leans against the ticket booth inside the doorway. With his features cast into shadow by the brim of his top hat, he seems oddly morose, even somber. Then he tilts his head, flashing white teeth. "And go ahead, get into a little trouble if you like. I won't tell Miss Three."

The other girls laugh and continue on. I pause a moment.

"Don't you want to see the bazaar?"

He drums thin fingers against his baton, silent. I get the impression he's trying out several answers in his head. "Oh, you know how it is," he says finally. "There's always something that needs looking after around here. And

I've seen bazaars before. I'll survive. Thank you," he adds, then waves to the door. "Better hurry on. Marvels to see, delights to sample. Be sure to try a sundae from Supulu's Stellar Scoops. Your mouth will be thanking you for the next year at least."

"Aliens have ice cream?"

"Everyone has ice cream. One of the very few things the Mandate got right."

"Okay, thanks for the tip." I start for the doors again, then stop. "Well, if you can't go, do you want anything? I mean, from the bazaar. Curried sardines?"

The Ringmaster chuckles. "Since you ask, I could use a good teapot. Never have found one that works quite properly. Always too big or too small, or worse yet, they dribble when you try to pour and you end up with stains all down your trousers." He gives a wan smile. How can the same person look so kindly one moment, and the next be "prepared to take extreme measures"?

"What's wrong?" he asks.

"You're just . . . confusing," I admit, startled into honesty.

"Well, I confuse myself sometimes, so that's no surprise. But Beatrix, is there something you want to ask?" He leans forward.

"I—" Questions hover on my lips. Then I catch sight of a shadow behind him. Miss Three. "Um . . . what's your favorite color? For the teapot."

"Today I'd have to say my favorite color is pink."
He winks. "Go on. Have fun."

I go, hurling myself into the chaos and wonder of
the Hasoo-Pashtung Bazaar.

* * *

Two hours later, Nola and I duck under the lavender
and green striped awning at Supulu's Stellar Scoops,
bone-tired but over the moon with the wonder of it all.
When I close my eyes, I can still see the dazzle of the
light fountains. Scents of wood smoke and spun sugar
and ozone cling to my skin. I've got a new pair of iridescent black boots, a freebie fiber-optic hair ornament
some huckster shoved into my hands, telling me I was a
"pretty pink lady," and a fuchsia teapot I haggled over
for fifteen minutes. Silver ribbons stream down from my
jacket, announcing my high scores at the gigantic Hasoo-
Pashtung Arcade.

"It's just as well we're not old enough for the club,"
I say as I slide into a booth. I stretch my legs out. "My
feet need a break, and my stomach needs ice cream."

"I guess," Nola says. She stands looking out across
the street at Retrograde Station, bouncing slightly on her
heels to the beat that we can feel even over here. "It's
not fair. My birthday's next month! And I love dancing!" She spins around, gyrating to the distant music.

"Whoa. You've got moves." She does. I'm not just being nice. "Can't you, y'know, do your mojo to the ID station so it thinks you're older? Or someone else?"

"Oh, no! I mean, yes, I could try. But I wouldn't dare, not here. There's a Governance Guard on every corner, practically. And if I got caught . . ." Nola shivers.

"Next year, then. We'll get totally glammed." I dig in my bag for the hair extension and toss it across the table. "Then they'll see what they've been missing."

Nola clips on the glittering swatch of purple and models it with a snooty fashion-mag hauteur. Then we both dissolve into giggles.

"What should we get?" she asks, after we've recovered.

I study the tabletop, where a list of flavors scrolls by in a swirl of alien script my portable translator can barely keep up with. Every so often there's an advertisement showing a chubby redheaded toddler trying to stuff a giant ice cream cone into his mouth. "I can't tell what half this stuff is. How about we split one of these Asteroid Belt Blaster thingies? It's got a scoop of every flavor."

While Nola places our order, I check out the people hustling by on the street. It's freaky how human they look. The Mandate really did a number on the universe. Everywhere I look I see two eyes, ten fingers, two legs. But they've got differences, too, just like on Earth. They have skin, eyes, and hair of every color. Some folks have buck teeth or beaky noses, freckles or dimples. Others are rigged out in outlandish costumes, feathered head-dresses, and colorful tattoos.

A tall boy with a lumpy but genial face waves at me. I do a double take when I realize it's Gravalon Pree, his rocky features hidden by a holographic projection. Miss Three tried to get me to cloak my pink hair, but I refused. They've got hair dye in space, after all. It's funny, but I'm kind of attached to my bubblegum mop now. It's still my only proof that I'm anything out of the ordinary.

A whir of hydraulics pulls my attention back to the table as the robotic dessert cart trundles up with our order. Wielding a lobster-claw serving arm, the waitbot sets down a ginormous dish. A mountain of ice cream only slightly less impressive than Mount Everest rises up, its mottled colorful heights swathed in drifts of whipped cream and sprinkled with candied nuts.

I have to shift sideways to peer at Nola around the delicious monstrosity. "How many different flavors *are* there?"

Nola blinks wide eyes. "Forty-seven."

"I'm going to need a bigger stomach."

"I'm not even sure where to start," says Nola, her spoon hovering over the mountain.

"Tachyon Toffee Swirl, definitely. It's amazing." Jom slides into the booth beside Nola. He's wearing a wide, sombrero-like hat that I assume is intended to hide his bright red hair. His wraparound sunglasses, on the other hand, make him kind of dorky. "Hey, Nola," he says, smiling. "Looking good. Purple's my favorite color."

Nola flushes, raising one hand to the fiber-optic swatch.

Jom continues on, pointing out different scoops in the tower. "The Beta Berry Burst has a good flavor, but the texture's icy. Fudge Freefall is risky; if the under-chef did the fudge, it's brilliant, but if not, it's nasty. White Dwarf is the creamiest, but too bland. If it were me, I'd add a bit of tangelo zest. Radioactive Ripple and Dark Matter are pretty reliable. Definitely steer clear of the Cosmic Nut Crunch, though."

"Whoa. So I guess you eat here a lot," I say.

"Of course he does," says Nola, "his grandmother—"

"Shh!" Jom cuts her off. "I'm incognito."

"Incognito?" I snicker. "In *that* get up?"

Jom pulls off the sunglasses. "Don't laugh. If the local management finds out who I am, they'll freak. It happens all the time."

"Find out what? That you're Ti—" I lower my voice. "I mean, that you're in the circus?"

"Worse," says Jom. He taps the tabletop as the advertisement with the ice-cream-slathered toddler scrolls by yet again. I look from the kid's scarlet curls to the bright red hair poking out from under Jom's hat.

"That's *you?*"

Jom sighs. "Good old Grandma Supulu. Why spend money on an actor when you can embarrass your own grandson in front of the entire universe?"

"You mean your grandmother *owns* this place?"

"This and 257,584 others. Normally I stay as far away as I can."

"So why are you here now?" Nola asks.

"Well . . . um . . ." A panicky look enters Jom's eye.

I nudge Nola's foot under the table. "Obviously he's here to save you from the evils of Cosmic Nut Crunch. The least you can do is thank him. Or maybe invite him to stay and help us eat this monster." Now if only Nola takes the hint. How such a smart girl can be so clueless is beyond me. Clearly Jom has one and only one reason for entering the confectionery danger zone. And if purple was really his favorite color before he sat down, then I'm the Wazeer of Deneb.

"Oh!" Nola flushes and sits up straight, shooting a sideways glance at Jom. "Trix is right. You have to help us with this thing. Which one did you say was the Beta Berry Burst?"

Under Jom's expert guidance we navigate the perils and delights of the Asteroid Belt Blaster. We sample scoops of every color and flavor imaginable (including a few that maybe should have stayed imaginary). But there's still at least half the mountain left when my stomach finally tells me enough is enough and that one more bite is going to bust my gut.

"I guess that's why they call it the Belt Blaster," I say, leaning back and groaning. "I can't believe I have to do backflips tomorrow." Then I catch sight of something that drives all my worries about tomorrow's performance away. "Is that Sirra?" I squint at the figure lurking in the alley across the street.

"Now *that's* how you go incognito," says Nola, giving Jom a meaningful look.

Incognito is right. I almost didn't recognize her in those drab brown coveralls with her hair stuffed under a gray cap. "What's she doing?"

"Maybe she wanted to find out how real people live," says Nola.

"Maybe she's got a secret boyfriend," says Jom. "Has to meet him on the sly."

"Looking like a street urchin?" I shake my head. "Huh. What's she got in her hand? Wait—she's headed into the alley now." I spring to my feet.

"You really care that much about Sirra's love life?" asks Jom.

"I'm coming, too," says Nola, sliding past Jom and out of the booth.

"Wait up, Nola!" calls Jom. "I can help—whoops! Sorry, ma'am, I didn't see you there. Stupid glasses. What? Um, yes, that's me, Jom Supulu. No, no, I'm only passing through. This isn't an official visit. *No, I don't need any samples!*"

I look back to see Jom fending off the advances of a woman who must be the store manager. Jom gives us a helpless wave as an army of lavender and green striped soda jerks whisk him off into the interior of the shop.

"Poor Jom!" says Nola with a giggle.

We head for the alley, skirting around the long line still queued up for entry to Retrograde Station. As we make our way along the passage, the dance beat thrums through the wall. From behind a large recycling bin, we watch as Sirra paces back and forth, down at the far end of the alley, beside what must be a back entrance to the club.

"What do you think she's waiting for?" asks Nola in a low voice.

"You mean who." I jerk my chin at the scene. A second figure slouches out of the shadows beyond Sirra. I can't make out his face under the dark cowl of his hood, but I think they're talking.

"I can't hear anything," I whisper, leaning closer, as if a few inches might reveal their conversation.

"She's handing him something. Looks like a bag. Wow. She does not look happy, though."

Sirra's hands flash like knives, cutting the air with angry gestures. Mr. Hoodie isn't impressed. He holds up a finger—no, two—then shakes his head.

Spinning on her heel, Sirra stalks away, continuing

down the alley. Mr. Hoodie watches until she reaches the far street. Then he heads up the stairs and into the club. The burst of music from the opened door dies away as it swings shut with a heavy thump, leaving Nola and me alone in the alley.

"Did you see his face?" I take the steps two at a time up to the door. I tap the panel but nothing happens. "Open up! Nola, we need to follow him."

"Trix, be careful!" Nola joins me on the landing, looking like she'd rather be anywhere else. "We can't break into Retrograde Station! Remember what I said? If we get caught, if we get noticed . . ."

"We won't get noticed. Come on, you can do it. You're a supergenius."

Nola gives a watered-down smile. "I don't know . . ."

"Please, Nola. Sirra's up to something. You know that. This is our chance to find out the truth!"

"Okay, I'll try." Nola closes her eyes for a moment, then raises her silver-palmed hand to the panel. She frowns, her lips twitching. "It's hard. I don't know if I can disable the protocols fast enough."

"You can!" I bounce on my heels, calculating how far the guy could have gotten by this time. "We've still got a shot at—"

The alarm shrieks across my words. Nola jerks back from the door, bashing into me. "Oh, no, no, no," she whispers. "I knew this was a mistake. We've got to get out of here. We can't get arrested. Hurry!"

We flee down the steps and start back along the alley. Too late. A pair of gray-capped Core soldiers pelt toward us. Both of them have stubby black rods pointed at us. "Halt and identify yourselves!"

Everything's falling apart, and all I can think is that it's my fault that Nola's here. I grab her hand, pulling her back the other way.

Nola stumbles. Her hand pulls free from mine. I look back in time to see her crumple, pressed to the ground like there's an invisible giant holding her there. She shrieks, pinned and helpless.

"Nola!" I beat at her invisible prison, but my fists bounce back. "Can you get yourself out?"

"I don't know. Oh, Trix, run! Get out of here. Please!"

"Not without you. There must be a way to break it. Maybe I can—"

"You're not going to do anything," snaps one of the guards, bringing her weapon up to point at me. The other guard still has his weapon trained on Nola.

I tighten my fists, my nails biting into my palms. After all the warnings about the Core, here I am about to get nabbed, and I've got Nola mixed up in it, too. I'm the worst roommate in the universe. The worst *friend* in the universe.

Maybe if I can take out the guy, bust that gizmo he's using, it'll free Nola. I'll take the fall, no question. Just please let Nola get away. I sink into a crouch, prepared to launch myself at him.

But someone else gets there first. It happens so easily, so quickly, that I don't have time even to blink before the two guards are on the ground.

Nola gasps, pushing herself to her knees. I scramble to her side, helping her up. Our rescuer drifts down from above like a slice of shadow.

"M-miss Three?" Nola stammers. "I—"

"'Thank you' would be the appropriate response." The simulacrum's voice sounds tinny, more distant out here in the street. "Perhaps followed by an apology for necessitating such extreme measures."

I look to the still bodies of the guards. "You didn't—"

"No, Miss Ling, they are not dead. Sadly that is not within my . . . mandate . . . to effect under the current situational parameters."

"So what now?" I ask.

"They will awaken shortly with headaches and a temporary blurriness of vision. I have already wiped all mobile data receptors and jammed local transmissions from this alley. Sadly they *will* retain their memories, so I suggest you remove yourselves and return to the Big Top. You've done enough to endanger the rest of the troupe already. I can only hope we will be able to prevent this from turning into a disaster."

CHAPTER 15

Break a Leg

BACK ON THE BIG TOP, Nola and I spend
the rest of the day waiting for the storm to hit, but nothing happens. And what with the million and one things
we still need to do to get ready for the show, we don't
have much time to obsess over it. Honestly, I'm a lot more
worried about falling on my ass during the Firedance
than about Miss Three's congenital pessimism.

By the next day the butterflies in my stomach have
turned into a freaking plague of locusts, despite the fact
that I finally nailed that tricky Firedance move during

my morning practice. I sink down onto the red velvet carpet for the full-cast meeting and bend forward to stretch the stiffness from my hamstrings. I wish it were as easy to relax my nerves.

From the far side of the tent, Lorlyn, who does the music for the show, sends warm-up trills and odd high-pitched laughter across the empty stands. The lights high above twinkle as Toothy runs through a last set of tests. It's nearly showtime.

Nola plops down beside me, purple sparks glinting in her hair. I told her to keep the hair swatch. It looks cute on her. And it's not like I need more color. "Hey, Trix," she says. "Have you seen the Ringmaster? Did he say anything about yesterday?"

"No. Haven't seen him." I pull the sack beside me into my lap and double-check the contents. The teapot lies in pink splendor, remarkably uncracked despite yesterday's adventures. "Do you think he'll be mad?"

"He doesn't *look* mad." Nola nods to the doorway.

The Ringmaster strides to the center of the Ring, moving with a frenetic, almost manic energy. But Nola's right; he doesn't look angry. Distracted, maybe. The knot in my gut starts to relax, replaced by a fizzy feeling of excitement. I see it on the faces around me, too. We're like a soda given a good shaking, and we know the Ringmaster's about to open the bottle.

The chatter dies to silence as he searches the crowd,

his gaze catching each one of us in the net of his attention. "Ladies and gentlemen of the Circus Galacticus, this is it! There's a world out there waiting for you to wake up their hearts and dazzle their souls. You have worked hard, and I want you to know how deeply I appreciate that. You are all stars."

I don't usually go in for big speeches, but I have to admit it: Chills race up my spine. I'm not even that nervous anymore. I might be shaped like a girl, but I feel like a piece of lightning.

"Now, I have a few last-minute notes," he says, and begins reeling off a list of technical jargon. My attention drifts as he launches into a highly detailed discussion of the "emotional resonance" of Lorlyn's set piece, and how to work in some new thematic elements throughout the score for the show. I run through the Firedance choreography in my head, trying to remember the feel of landing the moves earlier that morning.

"And that leaves one last alteration," the Ringmaster is saying, "to the Firedance."

I jerk my attention back. Something about his voice sets me on edge. I realize I've got the teapot in a stranglehold.

"Due to some . . . technical difficulties, I've decided to return to the original Firedance choreography for this show. Beatrix, we can use your assistance backstage with the special effects. I trust Nola will be able to fill you in on that." He claps his hands, turning away. "All right, then! Time for the good luck circle. Gather round, everyone!"

"What?!"

It's not just me. A chorus of protests cuts across the room. Theon stands; Jom is waving his hands. But I'm the one the Ringmaster looks at when he finally faces us.

"You can't," I say. "Not after all the work I—we—put in. Do you think we're not good enough?"

"No, quite the opposite," he says, but his thin smile fades the next moment. "It's not that. It's what happened yesterday. We can't risk drawing the attention of the Core Governance."

"You want me to hide because I had a spat with some guards in an alley?"

"It was considerably more than a spat. If they recognized you and started asking questions, it would jeopardize the entire Circus. The Big Top is never more vulnerable than during a performance. Anyone can buy a ticket. Anyone can come in and see the show." He shakes his head. "I'm sorry, but Miss Three is right about this. In fact, it would be best if you remained behind the scenes completely. Especially with the additional danger of the Mandate attempting to—"

"Miss Three? This is *her* idea? So now you're letting her tell us what to do? I thought you didn't do that. I thought you wanted us to break out of our cages!"

The pain in his eyes kills me, but I'm too angry to stop now. If I hadn't gone into that damn alley in the first place, none of this would have happened.

"Beatrix, you have to understand—"

"Fine," I cut him off. "I get it." I spin around and head for the doors.

"Trix, wait!" Nola pelts after me.

I keep walking. "You heard him, Nola."

"But it's not like he's saying you're not good enough."

"Whatever. I've got to get out of here." I tear my eyes away from the circle gathering at the center of the tent.

"Trix, wait. It's tradition. We do the circle before every show, for luck."

"I don't need luck if I'm stuck doing some mindless behind-the-scenes garbage."

Nola looks at me with a stunned expression, like I disemboweled her favorite teddy bear.

"What?" I ask.

"That's what you think we Techs do? Mindless garbage?"

The catch in her voice stings me. I groan. "That's not what I mean, Nola. I think it's great that you're a Tech."

"Don't patronize me, Trix. I get enough of that already." Nola's voice breaks, recovers, breaks again. She turns around stiffly and heads for the crowd around the Ringmaster.

God, I'm screwing up *everything* I touch. I want to run after her, to explain, to make things right. But I can feel the tears burning in my eyes, and there's no way I'm letting anyone see them. I run out the door. Out in the hall I ditch the pink teapot in the nearest recycler. I never want to see that thing again.

* * *

I throw myself into the last-minute preparations. It's the best way to stop people from trying to talk to me. Don't get me wrong; I know they're trying to help. But I need work, not comfort. When the Ringmaster breezes through, I make myself scarce. There's no way I can speak to him without yelling, and that'll only make things worse.

What I do need is to apologize to Nola for putting my foot in my mouth so spectacularly. I have a pretty speech all worked out and everything. But there's no sign of her. Maybe she's doing some avoidance of her own. I wouldn't blame her.

The worst part isn't even that she might never want to see me again. I've been on my own, and it sucks, quite frankly. But I'd take that any day over hurting Nola, over making her doubt herself. My gut twists at the thought. Please let me have a chance to make this better.

Finally it's showtime. I lurk backstage, helping

Toothy with the special effects, trying not to look at the other Clowns out in the Ring. There's a special kind of pain in watching other people get something you want. It's not that I want them to fail, except maybe down in some deep nasty part of my self, a part I try to keep locked away.

I just . . . want it for me, too. And that feeling is like a hot razor slashing at my chest. I want the sweetness of the applause and the lights dazzling down and to know that I'm something bigger than my skin. I even want to be one of the stupid dancing fruit.

I thunk my forehead into the wall, running one hand back through my hair miserably. How pathetic am I?

"If you're going to sit here blubbering, I'd appreciate it if you'd shut me off again. Pity parties are *so* boring."

What the—? I feel for the know-it-all earpiece and realize I must have flicked it on accidentally. I'm about to shut it off, but a spark of outrage holds my hand back.

"Maybe I've got a good reason to be upset. Missing out on being a dancing fruit is one thing, but the Firedance was my big chance to . . ." I gulp.

"Show off?"

"No! To show what I'm capable of. To prove myself!"

"All you're proving right now is that you can pitch

a fit, dear. You'd never catch Dalana wallowing like this, letting her friends down because she suffered a disappointment."

"How exactly am I letting anyone down? The Ringmaster made it pretty clear they don't really need me."

"You're lucky I haven't got a corporeal form or you might have gotten your nose tweaked for that. How an otherwise clever girl could draw such a ridiculous conclusion is beyond me. Did you even try to understand the situation? No, of course not. Easier to be angry and upset than to do something productive."

"Are you calling me a coward?"

"What is that delightful phrase from your planet? If the shoe fits—"

I hit the "off" button. I so do not need this right now. But Britannica has one thing right. It's time to do something. The Tree of Life scene is just ending now. I still have a shot.

I find Jom and Theon and a couple of the other Clowns over by the costume racks. "You guys looked great out there," I say. "But you know what would really blow them away? Our Firedance. The new one."

Jom lifts his head. "Really?" I catch sparks of attention from some of the others, too.

"But we can't," says Asha.

"Yes, we can!" I say. "We've busted our asses getting ready for it, and a few Core nimrods aren't going to stop us. Don't you guys want this? Don't you want to show them what Clowns can do?"

There's a handful of cheers. And Jom, my hero, is already pulling out his fiery gauntlets and crown from a box behind a pile of stuffed fruit.

"But you can't go out there," protests Theon. "The Core guards might recognize you, like the Ringmaster said."

"Not if I look like someone else."

"How?"

I gesture around us. "This is the Circus Galacticus. We've got wigs, makeup, even freaking mobile image projectors. There's got to be a way."

"There is."

I turn to see Nola, standing with arms crossed, over by the makeup station. She doesn't look at me. "Jom, you guys better get that rustbucket off the staging lift and reset the floors for the new Firedance. I'll take care of Trix."

The rest of the Clowns dash off, buzzing with excitement. I *knew* they wanted this as much as I did. Only Theon is still frowning. Well, her and Nola.

Nola takes something out of her pocket, tapping at it with one silvery finger. It looks like the gizmo Gravalon Pree was using to go incognito in the bazaar. I can't believe she's actually helping me, after what I said.

I stop trying to remember my pretty speech. A jumble

of words spills out. "I'm sorry for what I said, Nola. I'm an idiot. I was upset, but I shouldn't have said that. I know you do an amazing amount of work for the show. Stuff I couldn't do if you sat me down for a year to teach me."

She sort of nods, her eyes fixed on the gadget.

"I'll make it up to you," I babble on. "I'll bribe Jom to make you Chocolate Supernovas every day. I'll do your chore section for the next month. I'll tattoo *Techs Rule!* on my forehead. But please, Nola, don't be mad. You're my best friend."

At that, she finally turns around to face me. She's biting her lip. "Okay," she says. "I'll forgive you. But only if you get the tattoo." Then she laughs, and everything is a million times better.

"I really will make it up to you," I say. "I promise."

"Well . . . I *am* scheduled to clear the auxiliary recycling system filters for my chore section this month. Nothing says 'I'm sorry' like slopping out trash for a friend."

"You got it." I try not to think too hard about what sort of disgusting things a spaceship full of teenagers can find to toss down the garbage chute.

"Here." She clips the image projector onto my belt, beside the bulge where I have the rock stuffed under my outfit. "I gave you brown hair, and—sorry—kind of a big nose. But no one should be able to tell it's you."

A series of thrilling chords booms out into the vastness of the tent. "That's your cue," Nola says. "I need to get back to the lighting booth. Good luck!"

As Nola heads off, I catch a glimpse of sequins. The Ringmaster. I duck around one of the screens, hiding out in the changing area until the coast is clear. I'm about to head over to my starting mark when Sirra comes around the corner, jostling into me.

"Watch where you're going," she snaps. "Some of us have to get ready to perf—" Sirra stops and stares at me. I realize she doesn't recognize me.

"Don't rush," I say, flicking off the image projector before she can start screaming about spies again. "Those folks are about to get blown away."

Her eyes widen. "I thought you were supposed to be backstage pushing buttons."

"Change of plans."

"Oh, really? Does the Ringmaster know about it?"

"He will in a moment." I consider a more violent response, but I've got more important things to do. Plus, Syzygy is standing over by the rack of spare costumes, repositioning one of the orange unitards between the reds and the yellows and carefully not watching us out of the side of her enormous glasses.

Sirra rolls her eyes. "Whatever. I have to get ready. The crowd will need some actual entertainment after they're done laughing you out of the Ring."

"Right," I say sarcastically. "Good luck."

Sirra continues on. I turn on the image projector again and check my reflection in the mirror. Man. That is one big schnoz.

"Break a leg," says Syzygy as I head on out to the Ring.

"What?"

She rearranges two shirts that both look blue-green to me and says, "It means good luck. In the idiom of your language. Is that not correct?"

"Yeah, I guess so," I say. "Good luck to you, too."

* * *

The Firedance is *amazing*. I'm talking write-it-in-the-sky, shout-it-from-the-mountaintops, utterly freaking amazing. We are on *fire*. Not literally, I mean, except for Jom as the King. But we smoke the house. They love us. They clap. They cheer. It's the sweetest thing I've ever heard.

It's *so* awesome, I'm pretty much in a daze by the time I dance offstage, the applause singing in my ears.

Something slams into me. An arm clamps across my chest; another grips my waist. Grinding breaths brush against my cheek. It's Nyl. The image projector crunches under his grip, and suddenly I'm back to my pink-haired self.

"Quite a performance, Beatrix," he says. "Maybe

you do belong here. But I can't allow you to jeopardize everything we've worked for."

I kick out, but my feet only catch the hem of his long coat. His cold hand slides along my waist. Something rips. Air whispers against my skin. He pulls away, holding something.

I brush my fingers over my side, feeling for the injury, but there's nothing, not even a cut. It's a more terrible wound than that. He's got the rock.

Grabbing hold of one of the costume racks, I drive it across the floor toward Nyl. It catches him in the chest, slamming him back into the special-effects station. Metal crunches. Something sizzles. I smell burnt plastic.

Nyl pulls himself up, tearing free a half-dozen hoses from the FX station. They hiss puffs of artificial smoke into the air between us. He runs.

I hurl myself upright and take off after him. He's heading for the emergency exit. I shout, the words garbled by rage and desperation. I put all my energy into one last lunge.

Nyl swivels toward me as I leap. My hands lock into fists. He flicks something into the air between us. I catch one last glimpse of that mask before blue fire webs lace across my vision, dragging me down to the ground. I scream. The physical agony is nothing compared to what I've lost. How could I let this happen?

Lorlyn's soaring voice fills the Big Top, mocking my

loss with a song of triumph and victory. As I stare wildly up, I see two silver figures flying among the clouds.

Not clouds. Smoke. Billows of it jet upward from the busted mess of the special-effects station. Sirra flips out into the void, just as a great gust of smoke hits. Then she's lost in it. All I can see is Etander, hanging from his own trapeze, arms out to catch her.

The music is too loud. I can't hear his shout, but I see it: his lips pulling back, his sudden jerkiness as he reaches for something that isn't there.

A single silver arrow plummets from the clouds like a fallen angel, already limp as a rag doll. Did she hit something? Get knocked out by the smoke? My fingernails dig into my palms as I scream for her to wake up and save herself.

The vibration of the impact ripples through the flooring, sending an answering tremor through my body. The music stutters out, punctuated by cries from the stands. Somewhere above I hear Etander shouting his sister's name, but the huddle of silver in the center of the Ring doesn't move.

CHAPTER 16

Fairy Tales

T BREAKFAST the next morning, I slump into one of the seats at the fifth table. Life moves on around me. The Clowns chatter and joke, the Techs visit their virtual world, the Principals lounge and preen. The Freaks are playing some sort of board game with armies of little toy soldiers. I'm still stuck in yesterday, my mistakes on infinite repeat in my head. I haven't slept, and my mouth fills with sawdust at the thought of food.

"You should go back to the Tech table," I tell Nola. "*You* didn't send Sirra to the infirmary with a broken leg and a concussion, saddle the Ringmaster with a ginormous fine, and lose the one thing your dead parents told you to keep safe. I deserve to be exiled so I can wallow in my guilt. You don't."

"Oh, go right ahead and wallow," Nola says with a sly look. "I'm here because I need room to clean out my toolbox."

I can believe it. By the time she's dumped everything out, there's at least three dozen gizmos, gadgets, and doodads laid out on the table between the bowl of fruit and the platter of pancakes. I shake my head at the now-empty toolbox in Nola's lap, which is about as big as a textbook. "I don't see how it all fits. Unless that thing is bigger on the inside than the outside."

"Give me a few years and maybe I'll figure out dimensional transcendence. For now it's all about organization. Everything has a place." She slides a small wrench into one corner of the lid.

"Yeah," I say. "Right."

Nola looks up sharply. "Trix. You have a place. You're still a Clown."

"They all hate me. You should have seen the look I got from Theon. Urrgh." I slice one of the muffins in half, then in halves again.

Nola spins the screwdriver she's been cleaning between her fingers. "Did they *tell* you not to sit with them?"

"No," I admit. "But I don't deserve to sit there. It's all my fault this happened."

There's enough of a pause that I know I'm right. Nola clears her throat. "When the Ringmaster is done smoothing things over with the Hasoo-Pashtung authorities, I'm sure he'll figure out a way to—"

"It's not his problem to fix," I say. "Enough with the wallowing." I shove my diced muffin down the recycler. Across the room, Etander is sitting quietly at the Principals' table. Maybe I shouldn't bother him. I might rile him up into Hedgehog Boy, talking about the accident.

It's a nice excuse, all thoughtful on the surface. And all cowardice underneath. No, I've got to do this. I leave Nola to finish organizing her toolbox. She looks up with worried eyes. "Are you sure you don't want me there for moral support?"

"Thanks, but groveling goes better without moral support." I draw in a breath and head for the Principals' table.

They all look at me, except Etander. He stares into his empty plate like it's a crystal ball. "Hey, Etander," I begin. Man, my voice sounds creaky. I cough. "I wanted to apologize for screwing up the smoke machine thing."

He looks at me then, and I kind of wish he hadn't. It's not an accusing or angry look, but it still makes me feel about an inch tall. I'm a pathetic worm. He gives a small nod but says nothing.

"I swear it was an accident."

"I believe you," he says finally. "But I'm not the one you should be apologizing to."

Ouch. All right, I deserved that. I mumble something and start to walk away, then stop. "Sirra's still in the infirmary, right?"

Etander nods. "Miss Three said it would be another day before the bone had regenerated enough for her to risk moving around, even using her powers."

"Okay. Thanks."

I practically run from the cafeteria. Nola catches up with me in the hall outside. "Trix, where are you going?"

"To do more groveling."

She falls in step with me. "Don't worry; I'm not here for moral support. I figure someone better be there in case she goes for your head. Plus, you'll get lost otherwise, since you still refuse to be sensible and use your know-it-all."

"I remember the way. Mostly," I add as Nola grabs my elbow to redirect me at the next junction.

A few minutes later we're standing outside a door marked with the linked-hands symbol that's apparently the intergalactic version of the Red Cross. Nola is about to touch the entry pad when I motion for her to stop. "I hear voices. She's talking to someone."

"So?"

"I don't want to grovel in front of Miss Three. Or the Ringmaster."

"And I thought you were supposed to be brave,"

Nola says teasingly. "Don't worry; it's not either of them. Can't you hear the static? That's some sort of audio feed. Probably her parents checking in on her. It was all over the news about the accident."

Sirra's voice suddenly rises in volume, so that every word rings clearly even through the door: "—you hateful, manipulative bastards! I did what you asked! Leave us alone!"

Nola winces. "Maybe she doesn't get along with her folks?"

"Or maybe it's not her parents."

The conversation seems to be over. Someone's moving around inside. I lean toward the door to listen, only to have it slide open under my palms, sending me tumbling into the room.

I guess if I'm going to grovel to a girl who hated me even before I broke her leg, falling flat on my face is a good way to start. Nola gives me a cheery wave as the door skims shut, leaving me alone with Sirra.

She looks less like an invalid and more like somebody caught in the act of doing something she shouldn't. The hem of her black nightgown drifts around her knees, revealing one normal leg and one that's covered in a layer of something resembling marshmallow fluff. Her hands are tucked behind her, and she's pressed herself back against the wall. Neither of us says anything, but I hear a distant rattle and a click. Did she throw something down the recycler chute?

By the time I've got myself vertical again, Sirra's back in her bed, the viewscreen of her know-it-all covering one eye. Huh. She's ignoring me completely. I'd have thought she'd be enjoying this.

I clear my throat. "I'm sorry I messed up your act," I say, shoving the words out. "And that you got hurt."

She gives a little shrug, like I'm a fly buzzing in her ear. "Sure. Whatever."

Something's definitely wrong. I was sure she'd have me licking her boots by this time. "Okay, then." I head for the door.

"Trix."

I stop. Here it comes. "Yeah?"

"Is Nola out there?"

"Um. Yeah. Why?" Maybe she wants to ream me out in front of an audience? Okay, if that's what it takes.

Sirra opens her mouth, then snaps it shut. "Never mind. Go on. Try not to break any of *her* bones."

Honestly, I'm kind of relieved when she says that. For a minute there I was afraid the fall busted more than her leg. But this is the Sirra I know and don't love.

Once I'm out in the hall, I fill Nola in. "Weird, huh? I'm still not even sure she noticed me apologizing."

"She has been acting pretty strange lately, making all those mystery calls off-ship. I wonder . . ."

"What?"

"Well, you said she saw you getting ready for the

Firedance. She knew what you'd look like, even with the image projector. So I'm wondering if maybe . . ."

"She tipped off Nyl?" I lean back against the wall as it all clicks into place. "Nola, you're brilliant."

She grins, but her smile fades after a moment. "But Trix, that's horrible. To think she'd sell us all out. I mean, she's one of us. She needs the Circus as much as anybody. It can't be true."

"I dunno." I shake my head. "Her family has money and power. That can hide a lot of dirty laundry. Plus it's not like she's got three eyes or antennae or pink hair. Sirra can pass for normal."

"But Etander can't."

"Yeah." I shake my head. "The Tinkers sure handed out some crazy gifts, didn't they? I mean, what's the point of turning into a porcupine like that? Or pink hair, for that matter?"

Nola shrugs. "Maybe there is no point. This is the Tinkers we're talking about, after all. Who knows if they were trying to do any of this? Your pink hair, my tech-interfacing, it could be intentional or it could be recycled bits of old lab experiments."

Recycled. "I think Sirra was throwing something in the recycler, right when I came in. If we could find it, maybe we could figure out what she's up to."

Nola frowns thoughtfully. "The reclamation system will be down for the filter cleaning, so whatever she threw away will still be in the tanks until tonight. But Trix, we don't even know what we're looking for. And the Big Top makes a *lot* of trash. I can only think of one way this might work."

"What?" I ask. Nola looks suddenly queasy, like she just came back from a long spacewings flight.

"We'll have to convince Rjool to help us."

"Rjool? Is he one of the Freaks?"

"No, Rjool isn't Tinker-touched. He isn't even . . . well, you'll have to see for yourself. He never leaves the engineering zones. Oh, I really wish there was another way."

"Why? What's wrong with him?"

Nola opens her mouth, but before she can say more, we both become aware of footsteps approaching.

The Ringmaster comes around the corner and halts at the sight of us. "Ah. Beatrix. Good. Nola, if you'll excuse us?"

I fight the urge to grab Nola's arm and cling to her like a life preserver. The Ringmaster doesn't actually look angry. But he does look serious, and there are shadows under his eyes.

I wave Nola off. "Meet you after lunch for chore section." Then I'm alone with the Ringmaster. He has his hands shoved into his pockets, his chin tucked down into his collar.

All my mistakes hang in the air between us. The

silence goes on long after Nola's footsteps have faded. The words finally burst out of me. "Aren't you going to yell? Ream me out for being such an idiot and nearly getting Sirra killed? Not to mention losing the ancient Tinker artifact?"

"No," he says. "You aren't the only one who's made mistakes. There are things you need—" He falters. "Things I need to tell you."

"Is this about the rock?"

He hesitates. "In part. But I think this conversation would benefit from a change in venue."

I follow him silently down the hall and along several others. We don't talk. I hate this feeling, like I'm headed off to take a test I didn't study for. And there's no more time to cram. Do or die.

It's a relief when we finally get to the viewing deck. The Ringmaster walks slowly to the windows and sets his elbows on the railing, staring out into space. I clear my throat. "You're not going to tell me the rock is dangerous, are you? I mean, Nyl said it was. But he's one of the Mandate, so that's just a bunch of bad-guy talk, right? I mean, it's not true. He was trying to scare me."

The Ringmaster turns his back to the stars, locking me in place with his gaze. "A villain can speak the truth as well as any hero. Perhaps better. There are truths that can be hard to hear. Things you might not want to believe."

I have a nasty feeling there's a pit about to open

up under my feet. "You know something you're not telling me."

"Oh, many things, no doubt. Would you like to know the secret ingredient in Tachyon Toffee Swirl? The last words of the Hermit of Pergola-7? The absolutely best place in the universe to have a spot of tea?"

I try to smile but fail. "I want to hear about the rock. You found out what it is, didn't you?"

"I have . . . an educated guess." He pauses. "Did your parents tell you fairy tales?"

"Huh?"

"Bedtime stories, old legends of faraway places? Heroes and quests and curses?"

"My dad learned all sorts of crazy folktales from his grandma. Frogs trapped in wells and monkey kings leaping across the clouds. They always made him sad, though." I hadn't understood why, back then. Now I blink my eyes and wonder if the Ringmaster can see that same look in my face. I cast my mind back through layers of tears and bleakness to happier times. "My favorites were these amazing stories he made up about aliens. I figured out later that he stole half the plots from old movies, but I loved them so much it didn't matter. Reaching the stars was my happily-ever-after." I shake my head. "What do fairy tales have to do with my rock?"

"Let me tell *you* a fairy tale, Beatrix, and see what you make of it. Some of it Miss Three recovered only recently, from the datastore fragments we found on the Lighthouse. Some I already knew. Some may truly be only a fairy tale." He clears his throat, then begins in something closer to his stage voice.

"Once upon a time there were two powers, the Mandate and the Tinkers. They battled each other in word and deed, both convinced they knew what was best for the universe. Great and terrible were their battles as they warred across the universe. But in time, each faded, drained by the endless conflict. And eventually they disappeared. Some say they died out. Others whisper that they will return one day, to wage their battles anew. All we know for sure is that they left behind their children, raw and inexperienced, to forge a new world from the ashes. And they left an inheritance: of technology, of ships, of gifts hidden in the blood and bones of the new generations.

"But the greatest treasures—their greatest weapons—they hid away in secret. Perhaps to await their own return. Perhaps to await future generations wise enough to use them."

I can't help interrupting. "Weapons? What kind of weapons?"

The Ringmaster drops his storytelling air to give a bemused sigh. "It's an old, old story, worn with time and translation. All we have left are the names and a handful of maddeningly vague details. The Mandate's Treasure is called the Cleansing Fire. I will leave it to your imagination to consider the implications of that delightful name."

"And the Tinkers' Treasure?"

"The oldest stories call it the Seed of Rebirth. They say it holds the essence of the Tinkers' Touch. A power that can reshape a living being, granting it new abilities, new life, whatever it needs to evolve and grow. The pinnacle of their genetic technology."

I have a horrible suspicion of where he's going with this. "And the maddeningly vague details? Let me guess. It's a shiny black stone."

He gives a faint sad smile and taps his nose.

"My rock. You're saying my rock is the Tinkers' Treasure."

"Yes."

"And now the Mandate has it. Because I couldn't keep it safe." I sag against the railing. "How did my parents get their hands on something like that? A pair of scientists on some podunk planet in the Exclusion Zone just happened to find an ancient alien treasure?"

"Your parents were more than that."

"So they *were* Tinker-touched? Right? That must be it."

The Ringmaster is silent for so long I start to quiver. I want to pace, but I refuse to walk away. I have to see his face when he says what's coming.

"Once upon a time," he begins, "there was young woman, the daughter of an ancient household of great power. This young woman saw much of the ways of her kinfolk, and did not like them. She wished to walk another path. Then a day came when her people captured a grand prize, the greatest treasure of their enemies, bought with blood and death and pain. Terrible pain . . ."

"Ringmaster?"

He shakes himself, continuing on. "The girl's people threw a grand celebration. They held the future of their enemy in their hands, and they planned to crush it. To destroy it.

"But the girl had already looked upon the treasure and seen its beauty. She could not let it be destroyed, even if it meant defying her family, her blood. So she stole the treasure and ran far, far away. She found a world that knew nothing of her kind, a place where she herself was a fairy tale. And she met a young man who had stars in his eyes. She shared her secret. They fell in love. They had a daughter." He looks at me.

"No. Freaking. Way. My mom was one of the Mandate?"

The Ringmaster eyes me quizzically. "I'll admit to taking some artistic license in the telling of the tale, but between what you've told me and what I've gathered, I believe it's true."

My feet carry me back and forth along the viewing deck, beating into the metal flooring with a reliable, sensible *thunk, thunk, thunk.* It's about the only thing in my life that is reliable or sensible right now.

"How did I get through the mirror?" I say suddenly, seizing on the first of the hundred questions fogging my brain. "The only reason my hair turned pink was that rock. Right?"

"We don't know that," says the Ringmaster, but the doubt in his voice punches me in the gut. "It could be that you inherited the genetic markers from your father. And even if it is the result of the Seed, what does it matter? You still bear the Tinkers' touch."

"It matters because I don't really *belong* here." My voice is so sharp now I half expect my lips to bleed. "That's why Miss Three said I was a danger."

"When did Miss Three say you were a danger?"

I halt, crossing my arms. "When you two were in the Restricted Area talking about using 'extreme measures.'"

"Ah. That." The Ringmaster gives the jeweled top of his baton an unnecessary polish. "Miss Three is truly one of a kind. Or three of a kind, to be perfectly accurate. I trust her opinions on a great many things. But where you're concerned, she's hardly an impartial judge. Please believe me when I say that I do not, and never have, believed you to be the enemy, no matter your parentage. And I blame myself for not telling you the truth sooner. I thought . . . I was afraid it might hurt you. That it would make you doubt yourself."

"You were right." I press my palms to my temples.

My skull feels heavy, stuffed with iron and nails. I run my fingers back through my hair, gripping handfuls. My scalp prickles with pain. "Talk about fairy tales. Here I was, believing I was one of the superheroes, that some ancient power chose me to do great things. But I'm one of the bad guys." A bitter laugh spills out of me.

"Beatrix, I—"

"No! No more lies." My voice cracks. The tears start to leak through. I grab hold of the railing to keep me strong. "You told me I was special. You made me believe it, even when I flunked all the tests. You handed me a dream, even though you knew it was a lie."

"But you are—"

"Don't you dare say it!" I rip my hand away from the barest brush of his fingers. "Don't you dare lie to me again. I can't take it. Really. I try to be tough and all that, but this is too much. I'm in too many pieces. You can't wave your baton and dance them all back together again like that."

I don't bother brushing the tears from my eyes anymore. I run, leaving the Ringmaster and his false dreams where they belong, with the stars that are always going to be beyond my reach.

CHAPTER 17

Rjool

THE NEXT FOUR HOURS ARE TORTURE. The Ringmaster's fairy tales grow sharp claws and tear my thoughts apart. There's no way I'm going to Miss Three's lecture on Core Governance Trade Law, or even the symposium one of the older Techs is giving on Strong and Weak Nuclear Forces. I go to the common room instead and run myself through the Arena at level eleven. Maybe if I can squeeze all the sweat from my body, there'll be nothing left to feed my tears. On my seventh run I make it five minutes, a new personal record.

But the truth of who I am turns the victory as hollow as my stomach.

I grab what I can from the vending machines on the way back to the dorms rather than face lunch in the cafeteria. I'm not a coward, I'm . . . establishing a defensive position. Marshaling my resources for a big comeback performance.

Yeah, I don't really believe it, either. But it's a lie I need right now.

Back in the dorm, I mechanically down a half-dozen energy bars and protein drinks. My stomach rebels at first, but I keep going. I'm going to need my strength to get the Tinkers' Treasure back.

It's my only choice, really. It's not like I'm going to run off and sign up with the Mandate, no matter who Mom was. And sure, I could hightail it back to Earth, make some sort of lame life for myself. It's probably where I belong, but I can't leave yet, no matter how much I want to get away from everything that reminds me of my broken dream. The Big Top may not be my place anymore, but I can't leave it like this, suffering for my mistake. And the next step to finding the Tinkers' Treasure is figuring out what Sirra is up to.

By the time Nola comes in, I'm practically bouncing off the walls between the sugar and my need to do something constructive. Or destructive.

"Trix," she starts off, "have you been hiding in here

all—what's wrong?" She steps closer, looking way too intently into my eyes. "Have you been crying? What did the Ringmaster say?"

"It doesn't matter," I say, bounding upright and starting to sweep up the layer of wrappers and drink cartons from the bed.

"Are you sure?"

"He found out what the rock was," I admit. "He called it the Tinkers' Treasure."

Nola gapes for a moment. "As in, the long-lost artifact that holds all the secrets of the original Tinkers?"

"That's the one. So it's pretty much the last thing you'd ever want the Mandate to get their hands on. Basically, I screwed up royally, and we need to get it back before they destroy it. Please tell me this Rjool character is going to need a butt-kicking. I am crazy-ready to thwack something."

"That'll be hard, since Rjool doesn't have a . . . well, you'd have to find something else to kick. Here, I brought gear." She tosses me a set of yellow coveralls and a pair of rubbery black gloves. "But we don't want to fight him. He's a Loranze."

"A what?" Following Nola's lead, I pull on the coveralls over my clothing, relieved to finally be doing something. Even if I don't get to thwack anything.

"Ask your know-it-all to show you."

"Oh, my stars," says Britannica when I put the question to her. "A Loranze? That won't do, not at all. Nice young ladies shouldn't be associating with creatures like that."

"No worries for me, then."

My know-it-all tsks me. "I admit that you're a work in progress, dear, but there's potential. So it would be highly unfortunate for you to be fraternizing with one of the Untouched."

"The Untouched?"

"One of the very few races in all the universe not tampered with by the Mandate or the Tinkers. Highly dubious characters, in my opinion. Look."

The viewscreen slides out over my eye. I nearly jump out of my big yellow boots. "Whoa. Now, that's what I call an alien."

Hovering in front of me is the frozen image of something that looks like it belongs on one of those nature programs about deep-sea critters. "Are those tentacles? But those numbers can't be right. Average weight five tons? Average height fifty feet? How did something that big get in here?"

As we make our way to the engineering sector, Nola fills me in. "You can mail-order Loranzelli eggs over the universal net. They come with a tank and everything. It's a big gimmicky thing, and half the eggs don't even hatch, and the other half aren't even real Loranzelli, just some sort of genetically altered cephalopods. The rumor is somebody on the Big Top got a real one, and when they realized it, they tossed it down the recycler. By the time they found Rjool, he was too big to get out easily. No one's ever admitted to being the one who tossed him, though."

We're headed through an unfamiliar part of the ship now. The halls are narrower, and half the doors are plastered with dire warnings about electrocution, radiation, and cataclysmic polarity reversal.

"Anyway," she goes on, "Rjool does a good job keeping the recyclers running. He can handle everything except the one set of auxiliary filters that's on the other end of the recycling zone, and we have those in chore rotation. I've spent about five minutes, tops, down here in the past month, now that he's taken over the water reclamation system, too. But believe me, five minutes is more than enough."

"So he *is* dangerous?"

"Well, in a way. He likes to talk, and ask questions. Personal questions."

"So, like, he wants to know your favorite color? How does that qualify as dangerous? "

"I'm serious," Nola says. "You won't be laughing five minutes from now. He knows things about all of us from going through the trash. It's like he can read your mind, like he knows all your worst secrets. You step one toe into his lair, and the next thing you know he's pulling out a dirty sock and asking you about the fight you had with your mother last Tuesday. It's amazing. Well, repulsive and amazing." She pauses in front of a large door. "Ready to see for yourself?"

I am suddenly way less interested in meeting Rjool. All my worst secrets? But I need to find that rock. I sigh. "Are you sure we can't just kick his—tentacles—and make him help us?"

Nola opens the door.

"Never mind," I say. Because by then, I've seen Rjool. He's hard to miss, since he fills up at least half the room. It reminds me of the banyan tree I saw once on a nature special. It looked like a huge grove of small trees, but it was really this one massive tree with all these weird roots dripping off it.

Rjool is like that, except the trunk in the center has five globby eyes and a clattering beaky mouth, and the things dripping out of the air everywhere are tentacles, not roots. They *slither*. If you can imagine a room with snakes plastered over every bit of floor and wall, you can get how creepy this place is.

Two of the eyes turn in our direction. There's not a lot of space left that isn't full of whispering tentacles, but Nola finds us a bare spot near the center of the room. A hollow, boomy voice fills the room.

"Nooooola. How good to see you again. How is the new skin treatment? Taking care of all that pesky acne?"

A thin tentacle wriggles forward, holding an empty jar emblazoned with the animated face of a boy peppered with zits that shrink as he lathers on a blue goop.

"Yes," says Nola in a tiny voice. She looks ready to melt into the flooring.

"And what about that other new cosmetic cream? I know I have the bottle here somewhere . . ." Tentacles slither around us. Nola gives a low moan. "You know the one," he continues. "The label says it will increase the—"

"Hey," I interrupt. "Do the words *not your business* exist in your language or what?"

Three of Rjool's eyes turn to ogle me. "And you've brought me someone new. Mmmmm . . ."

I'm no expert on reading the expressions of banyan tree–squid aliens, but I think he's looking at me like I'm something good to eat.

"We're here to clean the filters," says Nola, rallying herself. "And to ask a favor."

"A favor? *Hooohoooohoooo . . .*"

I realize after a moment that he's laughing. It makes all the tentacles shiver. And me.

"There are no favors," says Rjool. "But introduce me to your friend. I looove meeting new people." He clatters his beak.

"I'm Trix," I say, "and we need to get whatever it was Sirra ditched in the infirmary recycling system this morning. And that's all you need to know."

"Oh, ho . . . It sounds as if someone has something to hide. A few sordid little secrets, hmmm?" Now all five eyes are staring at me, like they can see right into my soul. Or worse, into my DNA.

I shake myself. Rjool couldn't possibly know about my parents. Even *I* didn't know until today. He's playing me. "Listen, you overgrown squid, this is important. There might be a Mandate spy on the ship, and this is evidence."

"You care a great deal about this ship, considering you've only lived here for six weeks. Aren't you afraid to love something so much? What if you lose it?"

Nola steps in, which is good, because I swear I'm about to start tearing off tentacles. "Okay, Rjool," she says, "you know what we want. So are you going to help or not?"

Two large tentacles twist forward across the trunk, like crossed arms. "I can find your evidence. But first, your friend will answer three questions."

"What kind of questions?" I demand.

Rjool waves three small tentacles in the air around me. "Interesting. Your pulse rate has increased considerably since you first entered my domain."

"Fine. I'm not scared of you, or your questions. I just don't want to waste any more time."

"Trix, you don't have to do it. I can find something to bribe him with," says Nola, lowering her voice. "I'll offer him my signed poster of the twins. He's a huge fan of *Love Among the Stars*."

"No, we're here now, and we need that clue. I'll do it."

"Oh, gooood," says Rjool, clapping two tentacles together. A shiver runs through the rest of the snaky mass. "Now, let me see what I have here. Ah, yes, that's a good starting point." A tentacle curls out, holding a ragged piece of cloth embroidered with a golden letter *B*. "Tell me about this . . ."

I lick my dry lips. "It's the insignia from my old school. Bleeker Academy."

"It was the very first thing to come through the system bearing traces of your genetic material. "Why were you in such a hurry to throw it away?"

"It was coming loose, anyway."

"But some of these threads were cut. You went to the effort of removing it."

"Okay, fine, I cut it off. I'm done with that place, with Primwell and the rest of them. It was a nasty, horrible cesspool of a school. And I am not going back. I'd rather get pitched into a black hole."

"You aren't planning to stay on the Big Top, then?"

"I can't—"

Nola's expression freezes the words on my lips. I switch gears. "Is that another question?"

"Only if you want it to be," Rjool says in a voice that runs over my skin like oil.

"Give me another, then. Let's get this over with."

Rjool rumbles with laughter. Creep. "Here's a promising little trinket," he says. Something sails toward us along the sea of tentacles, bobbing like a round, hot-pink boat.

"Trix, that's the teapot you got for the Ringmaster. But you worked so hard bargaining for it! Why did you throw it out?"

"Yes, Trix, why?" echoes Rjool.

"It's broken. Look—the handle has a big chip in it."

"Mmm-hmmm, yes." Rjool nods, and I think I'm off the hook until he adds, "But that chip came from rough contact with the recycling system filters. In other words, after you threw it away. If you want my help, stop lying and answer my question."

"Why do you care? What's it matter to you?"

"I simply find it intriguing that someone would go to the effort of acquiring an object so calculated to please a particular someone, and then immediately throw it away. It bespeaks a troubled relationship, veering from intense friendship to petulant rage."

"I am *not* petulant," I snap. "He lied to me! He made me believe—"

"Yes?"

"That's your answer," I say. "That's what you get. You want more, make it question number three."

"Very well. I think you've made it clear. That leaves one question." Rjool's eyes quiver, all five of them goggling at me like I'm a freaking science experiment. "It so happens that an odd recycling deposit came down from the infirmary earlier today. The dusting of skin cells I took matches the genetic signature of Sirra Centaurus." He holds something in one loop of tentacle, but it's so small I can't make out what it is.

"So you've got what we want. Give me the question already."

"You're very eager to prove she's the spy. Why is that?"

"That's a no-brainer. Of course I want to find out who's feeding information to the Mandate. You remember them, right? The enemy who wants to destroy us all?"

"But you seem *particularly* eager to prove that Sirra is the spy. You're even willing to go through her garbage to do it." He brandishes the thing in his tentacle. "This could be something perfectly harmless. It could even be quite personal. And yet you're prepared to sweep that all aside to indulge your own curiosity. Maybe what I should be asking is whether the words *not your business* exist in *your* language."

"It's not the same thing!"

"Isn't it? Please, explain . . ."

"It's—Well, at least I'm trying to keep this ship safe. You're doing it for kicks."

"But you would be happy if you could prove Sirra was the spy, wouldn't you?"

I bat aside a tentacle as it tries to slide up along my arm. "Okay, yes! Maybe because then I don't need to feel so guilty for landing her in the infirmary. There, you've got it, proof I'm a rotten person. Happy now?"

"Yes, this is quite stimulating. Much more entertaining than the usual games. But I still need the truth."

"She's just so—" I clamp down on the words, holding them in. Oh, Rjool is clever all right.

"Perfect?" he finishes. "You can't stand to see someone shining so brightly, when you're worried your own light is only a reflection."

I open my mouth to protest, already shaking my head. "Yes." The word slips out before I can catch it and stuff it back deep inside.

"Hmmmmmm . . ." is all Rjool says.

I draw a long breath, trembling with adrenaline. Remember the mission, I chant to myself, curling and uncurling my fists.

"Okay," says Nola abruptly, "that's three. We're done. Hand over the clue, Rjool."

A single tentacle slips forward to drop a small nub of metal and plastic into her outstretched hand. "A pleasure, Trix, Nola. Do come again."

I force myself not to run from the room under those five goggly eyes. Out in the corridor I let myself sink against the wall. I'm shaking even worse now. Nola's looking at me like I'm some broken gadget she doesn't know how to fix.

"I'm okay," I say. "Is he always that twisted?"

"I guess it's the only entertainment he's got, stuck down here. But Trix, are you *really* okay? Do you need to . . . talk about anything?"

"No!" I wince. "Sorry, didn't mean to shout. But the last thing I want right now is more talking. Let's see if it was worth it. Is that a datastore?"

"Looks like one." Nola searches the wall with a slight frown. "Need to find a port, and we can see what's on it. There's one, down that way."

We head back along the corridor. Nola taps the wall, revealing a screen, keypad, and various other mysterious buttons and lights. "Ready?" She looks to me, holding the datastore up, ready to plug it into one of the sockets.

I nod. "Let's see what Sirra's been hiding."

"Huh. It looks like a bunch of medical files."

Images begin flipping across the screen. They look like EKGs and MRIs and all those other funky medical acronyms. Then I spot an X-ray of a hand, with a shadowy overlay of spikes along the back, and recognize it, even before we get to the videos of his face. Etander, smooth-skinned and gorgeous, changing to Etander, tormented and bristling with spines.

"What *is* this?"

Nola shakes her head. "There's a pre-recorded videostream. Here, I'll play it."

The gray static clears to an image of a man's face, hidden by a featureless mask. When he speaks, his voice is deep and oddly off-kilter. "We're disappointed, Miss Centaurus. We thought you understood our position and were prepared to deal seriously with us. But you have not delivered the promised payment in full. You know what is at stake. Do you want the entire Core to learn the truth about your brother? If you value your mother's position and the reputation of your family, you will transmit the remaining funds at once. You have one week, or we release the files."

The screen goes dark.

"Whoa," is all I can say. I slide the datastore out of the wall.

"So," Nola says, "I guess she's not the Mandate spy?"

"No," says a sharp voice behind us. "She's not a spy. She's being blackmailed."

"Sirra!" Nola nearly shrieks.

Sirra floats in the middle of the hall, her one leg still covered in marshmallow padding, though she's ditched the dressing gown for pants and shirt. Her face is almost as masklike as the man in the video.

"So that's what it was all about?" I ask. "The sneaking around and making secret off-ship communications in the middle of the night?"

Sirra stares at me. "I'd like my datastore back." She holds out her hand.

"And the midnight jump? Was that you, too?"

She gives a short nod. "There aren't a lot of places you can withdraw the amount of hard credit I needed without someone noticing. Hasoo-Pashtung is one of them."

I shake my head, trying to make sense of it. "But if you're not the Mandate spy, why did you care about getting me alone?"

Sirra snorts. "I wasn't trying to get *you* alone. As if you'd be any help. It was Nola I needed. I thought a Tech might be able to do something, and she's the best, so I was going to ask . . ."

"I could!" Nola pipes up. "I could track them down on the net, maybe even make a hunter app to go after the data itself. I'll start working on—"

"No!" Sirra shouts, her mask crumpling, making her look suddenly younger. She also looks angry, which doesn't surprise me, and terrified, which does. "I've had enough help from the two of you. I'm better off on my own. I'll pay what they want, and then this will all be over. And you are never, *ever* going to speak about it again. Especially not to Etander. Got it?"

"Got it," I say. "Here."

Sirra stares for a long moment at the nub of black

and gray in my outstretched palm. She raises a hand, but she doesn't take it. She makes a fist, and as her fingers clench, the datastore crumples, collapsing in on itself.

When it's the size of a gumball, Sirra drops her hand, turns around, and walks away.

Captured

 SIT ON MY BED, staring at the metal gumball. A flock of images circles my thoughts. Sirra in the hallway, Rjool gloating over my secrets, Nyl with the Tinkers' Treasure in his hands. My own face in the mirror, pink-haired and hopeful, full of grand dreams of being a star. The Ringmaster telling me the truth.

If I sit very, very still, and try really hard, I can drive them away. The sound of Nola typing at her keypad grows dull, the world turns gray, but I'm still in control. I can't afford to break apart. I have a mission.

"Okay, that ought to do it," says Nola, catching another datastore as it ejects from the wall. "All we need to do is get this to an unprotected netlink and upload it. It'll search out any data matching the parameters I gave it and destroy them. Of course, the blackmailers might have an off-grid backup. But hopefully the hunter app can find them first and cause them enough trouble that they'll think twice about messing with Sirra."

"Sirra was right. You are the best," I say, still rolling the marble in my palm. "Feel any less guilty?"

Nola sighs. "Nope. You?"

I shake my head. "I've racked up enough bad karma at this point I'm coming back as a slug, even if we take care of Sirra's blackmailer. So where do we find an unprotected netlink?"

"That's the trouble. There aren't any, not in public. Only in Core Governance Communication offices, under high security."

"I guess that's my part, then. Is there one here?"

"On Hasoo-Pashtung? Yes, I think so. But we need a plan, Trix; you can't just walk in. And you saw the announcements this morning. We're leaving this sector after tonight's show."

I thunk my head back against the wall and groan. "Just once, I'd like something to work out. We've got no lead on Nyl and the rock, and no way to fix this mess with Sirra." *And you still don't belong here,* hisses a nasty voice in the back of my brain. *Maybe you ought to give up and go home.*

"There's one thing I don't understand," says Nola. "I can see Nyl managing to sneak into the Big Top during the show. It's not hard to lose one Mandate agent in a crowd of five thousand. But how did he know it was you, with the image projector on? If Sirra wasn't the spy, could it be someone else? Or *something* else?"

"You mean like a bug? Electronic surveillance?"

Nola bounces up and starts rooting around in her tool drawer. A few minutes later, the room is filled with the stench of hot metal and she's holding up a black wand trailing a spray of wires. She fiddles with a dial along one side of the thing. "There, this ought to detect any odd transmissions. We'll take it to the stage area and see if we find any—oh."

"What? Isn't it working?"

Nola looks up with big eyes. "Yes. And it's registering a signal. Here."

She starts waving the thing around the room, running it over the walls, the beds, even her *Love Among the Stars* poster. I hastily join her, peering over her shoulder at the bug sniffer. There's a small lighted display with a bar of light that wavers up and down as Nola directs the device around the room.

"Check our clothes. Maybe they planted something on us in the bazaar?" I pull out my jacket, still emblazoned with the silvery trophies from my high scores at the arcade. "Check the ribbons!"

She holds the wand to my jacket, but the display doesn't change. "It's not the ribbons." Nola shakes her head, setting purple sparks glittering.

I stare at her. "Here, let me try something."

Taking the bug sniffer, I raise it up to Nola's head. The red bar gets bigger and bigger, and the thing starts beeping like an insane microwave. I'm pointing it straight at the purple fiber-optic swatch she's been wearing ever since Jom said he liked it. The one I gave her. The one that guy at the bazaar gave me.

Nola tears it out of her hair and checks the readout. Then she stares at me. In a rush of motion she flings herself over to her drawer, pulls out an opaque black jar, thrusts the purple hair swatch into it, then slams the lid on it. "Give me an hour," she says. "I'm thinking our luck has changed."

A half-hour later, Nola is muttering under her breath and looking bloody murder at the fiber-optic bug. But she won't rest, and she won't give up. "If they're watching, they know we're onto them," she says. "We don't have long to track them down."

Another half-hour and Nola's got a dusting of metallic powder across her nose and singe marks up one arm, but she's grinning like a mad scientist. "That'll do the trick!"

I check out her newest creation, which looks a lot like a divining rod, except for the rippling lines of electricity that fill the V between the two metal arms. "What is it?"

"It should allow us to locate the receiver for that bug. There must be a relay somewhere nearby, probably out in the bazaar."

"Brilliant! Let's go!" I move for the door.

"Wait, Trix. Shouldn't we tell someone?"

I hesitate. The thought of facing the Ringmaster right now twists my stomach. Besides, it's not like we're after trouble. Just information. "No. We'll look like idiots if we bring a whole war party and there's nothing to find. Don't worry; it's a reconnaissance mission. No heroics, I promise. If we find them, we'll come back for help."

We head out into the bazaar, which is as crowded as ever. I plow into the throngs, giving Nola some space to do her thing. I try to hold my tongue, but after we pass by Supulu's for the third time, I have to ask, "Is it working?"

"Can't get a decent fix," Nola says, grimacing at the divining rod. "Time to try something else." She pulls a fist-size disk out of her pocket, twists a dial on the front, and hands it to me. "Take that. You'll have to get a good distance away from me, though."

"Why? What's it do?"

"It'll help triangulate the receiver location. I left one at the Big Top, too."

"Got it. I'll head for the spice market. Stay in touch."
I flick on my know-it-all.

"Be careful, Trix," she says. "Remember why we're here. Reconnaissance. Don't go picking fights."

"Who, me?" I wink as I head off down a side street, following the scent of alien spices.

I convince my know-it-all to show me our locations, overlaid on a map of the bazaar. The triangle between the Big Top, Nola, and me covers about a quarter of the region. "Needle in a haystack," says Britannica, "isn't that the saying on your planet? You really ought to go back and speak to the Ringmaster, dear."

I ignore her. "Hey, Nola, you see anything?"

Nola's voice crackles in my ear. It sounds like she's standing next to a racecar revving its engine. "Sorry for the—*rrrpphsst*—outdoor concert. It's crazy! But I think I've got—*vvrrrroooshhht*—getting a reading nearby!"

"Good work! I'm on my way. Hang back, though, Nola. Reconnaissance, remember?"

"*Wrrrrr*—here somewhere—*squeeee!*—very close!"

The sudden silence is almost a physical blow. "Nola? Nola?"

On the viewscreen, the light marking Nola's position suddenly winks out.

"Nola?" There are screams hidden in my voice, but I won't let them out. This isn't happening. "Britannica, where is she?"

"Dear me. Miss Ogala's know-it-all has gone offline."

I'm already sprinting, taking the fastest route I can find to the spot where she disappeared. Please be there, Nola. Please let it be the concert interfering with the signal. *Please.*

The square is jammed with people, rocking out to the racecar band. I search for Nola. Nothing. I keep moving, fighting my way to the light fountain at the center of the plaza. A lanky ebony-carved figure rises from the pool of luminescence, showers of color falling from its hands to dapple everyone and everything in rainbow light. I'm about to hoist myself up onto the statue's shoulders when I catch sight of something shiny on the flagstones. I jump down from the ledge of the pool to snatch it up.

It's the divining rod.

A roll of thunder drowns the caterwauls of the band. All around me people point, gesturing at the sky. I turn, following the fingers, to see a familiar sleek black ship rocketing into the heavens. Nyl's ship.

Nyl's got her. The Mandate has Nola.

* * *

"What's there to talk about?" I sputter. "We have to rescue her!"

"I simply said we would do well to consider the best course of action," says Miss Three coolly.

"I guess I shouldn't expect somebody with no heart, and no body for that matter, to get riled up. But I don't get why *you're* just standing there," I say, turning on the Ringmaster.

"I assure you I am doing considerably more than that." He speaks through gritted teeth. I recognize, belatedly, the look of intense concentration on his face as he stands with hands splayed across the console. We're on the bridge, which is where Britannica led me when I came rampaging back onto the ship less than ten minutes ago.

"Shouldn't we follow them?" I say, jittering my toes against the floor. "We need to do something."

"It seems to me you've done quite enough, Miss Ling," says Miss Three.

"Don't you think I know that?" My voice echoes from the walls, so hot it should be raising sparks. "I figured if they went for anyone, it'd be me. They *should* have come after me. I'm the expendable one."

Miss Three's thin lips twitch. "At least we agree on something."

"Enough." The Ringmaster's words crack like a whip. "We're about to jump. I suggest you prepare yourselves." The lights blink to orange as the compaction bell begins to toll a warning.

I hastily slide into one of the flip-out chairs, remembering with a twist in my gut that it was Nola who first showed them to me. "So we *are* going after them?"

"No. They're too far ahead, and the Big Top isn't prepared for an out-and-out fight in any case. We need more information. So we're going to visit informative friends."

"You mean to seek the Outcasts?" asks Miss Three. "Ringmaster, I must protest. They are too far outside our sphere. Their ways are too different. You cannot hope—"

"Yes, Miss Three, I can." The lights blink to purple. I stiffen, gripping my armrests as the sickening sensation of reality turning inside out takes over, and everything fades to black.

The Outcasts

E WAIT FOR THEM ONSTAGE. Even partially compacted, it's still the biggest space on the Big Top. The entire troupe is here to meet our mystery guests. We've been docked to their vessel for what feels like hours. I pace between the bleachers, keeping my distance from the others.

"It's only been thirty-point-four-five minutes," says my know-it-all. "Have some patience. Why don't you go sit with your friends?"

"Haven't you been paying attention? I lost my only friend. And anyway, I don't belong here."

Britannica tsks me. "My, my, it sounds to me like someone's feeling guilty. You belong here as much now as you ever did. Open your eyes, dear."

"Whatever. We're wasting time," I grumble, sticking my hands in my pockets and leaning against the railing. Something cool and metallic meets my hand, and for a moment I think it's the rock. I pull out the datastore with the hunter app, the one Nola made for Sirra before getting taken.

I look for Sirra, expecting to find her sitting pretty with her court of Principals in attendance. When I finally spot her, she's up on top of one of the bleachers, sitting with Etander and talking quietly and intently.

On the way up the stairs, I catch bits of their conversation.

"—should have told me," Etander is saying. He's not Hedgehog Boy, but he's on his way, flushed and tight-lipped.

"I'm taking care of it," Sirra retorts. "It's got nothing to do with you."

"It's my fault! We went to those doctors because I couldn't control—" He sees me and breaks off.

I clear my throat. "Hey. Sirra, can I talk to you?"

She's breathing fast, her fingers driving into the spongy stuff covering her leg, leaving deep dents. "I doubt it's anything I want to hear."

"Okay, don't listen. But take this." I hold out the datastore.

"What is it?" She narrows her eyes at me.

"Nola made it. To help with your . . . problem." I flick a look to Etander. "She said it needs to get uploaded on an unsecured netlink port. Dunno where you can find something like that, but I figure with your connections, you've got a better shot than me. Anyway, she wanted to help. So here. Take it."

I turn and retreat down the stairs as a distant clang shivers through the air. The whispers start the next moment. *They're here. The Outcasts.*

Returning to my skulking spot between the bleachers, I survey the crowd. Some look excited. Others look worried or afraid. Even the Ringmaster looks nervous. The door opens.

I take a step back. Talk about stage presence!

There's a vibe you get when someone is performing and you can feel that they're trying to reach out. You know they're performing to *you,* that everything is connected. It's why I still can't help but seek out the Ringmaster's gaze, even as angry and ashamed as I am right now.

The Outcasts aren't like that. They don't care what we think. At all. They want us to take a step back, to look away. They want us to *disconnect.*

There are three of them. The one in front is in his late teens maybe, with a topknot of white-blond hair that sweeps down over his black patch-elbowed duster. On his right hulks something I can't even identify, except that it's big and ugly. It moves with a wheezy groan of hydraulics, swiveling its metallic faceplate to take in the gathered crowd. A lump clogs my throat as I spot a patch of skin near the shoulder, oddly shiny and red. It's not a robot. It's a man, burned and buried under layers of metal.

The third Outcast is a girl. Her pigtailed hair bristles with metal skewers that I'm guessing are more than just decorative. And she's blue. All over. Trust me; her outfit doesn't leave much room for doubt on that point.

All three of them are painted and tattooed with sharp swirls of black and white and dripping with heavy metal chains and studs. It's a little over-the-top, but they pull it off without looking like rejects from a bad post-apocalyptic movie. Mostly.

The Ringmaster dips his top hat to the trio. "Welcome home, Reaper."

"This isn't my home," says the blond one, "not anymore. Looks like you've found plenty of new blood, though." He surveys the bleachers. Someone gives a half-wave. Reaper doesn't react. "I'm glad to see the old girl's still in one piece." He looks around the stage like a kid checking out his nursery, fond and disdainful.

"Barely," mutters Pigtails, around a gob of chewing gum. Tell me the blue girl did not just diss the Big Top in front of the Ringmaster.

"Ringmaster, this is Amp," says Reaper.

The blue girl gives the Ringmaster a look that makes me flush. "Mmm, the ship may be nothing to look at, but the captain's not bad. I could get used to sequins."

I'm indulging a colorful fantasy involving Amp and a few dozen space leeches when she snaps her gum. The crack is as loud as a bolt of thunder. I guess her super-power is more than blue skin and the ability to wear minimal clothing. She seizes the Ringmaster's hand in hers, sidling closer. "I make things loud."

"Charmed, I'm sure." The Ringmaster slips free from her grasp and gives Amp a carefully measured smile. I'm not-so-secretly pleased to see her pouting. Guess that bad-girl schtick isn't working the way she hoped.

Meanwhile, the Ringmaster has moved on to the third Outcast. Metal squeals against metal as the giant raises one bulky hand to flip up his faceplate.

I'm not the only one who hisses in surprise and—I'll admit it—disgust. The face beneath is a mass of scars and raw, flaking skin. The scarred man bows, stiff as a soldier. "Ringmaster, I have long aspired to the privilege of meeting you. We may have chosen differing paths, but there is none who can say you have not sacrificed all for our people. My name is Schadenfreude."

What the blazes? This translator must have a screw loose. I sure hope my name doesn't translate into something weird like that.

"That is a refreshing sentiment, Mr. Schadenfreude,"

says the Ringmaster. "And I'm grateful to all of you for agreeing to this meeting. I wouldn't have risked contacting you had the need not been very great."

"I haven't forgotten my debt," says Reaper. "But there's not much to go on in the details you sent. What makes you think we know where she is?" Reaper flicks a cool look at Miss Three, who's been hovering silently in the Ringmaster's shadow. "You've got an expert on the Mandate here. Good chance for her to finally earn her keep."

"I've already stated my opinion," says Miss Three. "The girl is beyond our reach. In all likelihood she's already dead, or converted."

"No!"

My shout is still echoing from the heights as I bound up into the Ring to confront them. "We're getting Nola back."

The Ringmaster, courteously smooth as usual, presents me with a wave of his baton. "Reaper, Miss Amp, Mr. Schadenfreude, this is our newest troupe member, Beatrix Ling, of Earth. She is also Miss Ogala's roommate and was in the vicinity when the abduction took place."

Amp snorts. "You couldn't stop them from taking her, and you think you're going to be able to get her back from inside a maximum-security Core station? Good luck with that."

"I'll get her back from a black hole if I have to," I snap, taking a step toward the blue girl. "Watch me."

Amp draws one of the steel needles from her hair. The Ringmaster tugs me back by one elbow. At a look from Reaper, Amp starts cleaning her nails with the thin spike.

"A Core Governance facility?" asks the Ringmaster. "But she was taken by an agent of the Mandate."

Reaper grimaces. "You see what happens when you spend your time pandering to a universe full of mindless drones? You're never going to do it, Ringmaster. They don't want to be saved. You've wasted too much effort on them already, when you could have been helping our own kind. If you had, maybe the girl would still be free."

The Ringmaster grips his baton, white-knuckled. "Let's put aside the philosophical debate for a time of greater leisure, shall we? Please, tell us what you know."

It's Schadenfreude who speaks then. "According to our sources, agents of the Mandate have infiltrated some of the highest levels of the Core Governance. They do not control it, though that may be their ultimate goal. But there are certain facilities under their total or near-total control."

"Circula Fardawn Station?" asks the Ringmaster.

"So you have been paying attention," says Reaper with a feral grin. "Yes, that was a blow the Mandate won't soon forget."

"Nor will the families of those who died there," says

the Ringmaster. "Or are you going to tell me all 567 sentients on that station were agents of the Mandate?"

"Collateral damage is part of war."

"That wasn't war. That was terrorism."

Reaper's lips curl. Amp starts tapping her skewer against one of her wide metal bracelets with a *ting, ting, TING* that's loud enough to rattle my bones.

"Enough," snaps Reaper. "I'm here to repay a debt. We have word that a prisoner was delivered to the station at Vargalo-5, and that the incoming flight originated from Hasoo-Pashtung. If that's not your girl, I don't know where she is. But Ringmaster, for once I agree with Miss Three. This isn't a fight you're going to win. Even the Outcasts aren't ready to take on Vargalo-5. It may look like a Core station and play by the Core rules, but it's Mandate through and through."

"We are fairly certain it's their main research facility," adds Schadenfreude. "We've . . . lost some of our own to that place."

My lips are stiff as cardboard, but I force the question out. "Lost, as in dead?"

"Not always. More often changed. Conformed. Broken." Schadenfreude shakes his head. His eyes are two pools of sorrow in a desert of twisted flesh and jagged metal.

"Then I guess we'd better get moving. Right?" I turn to the Ringmaster.

"Yes, of course. I've already plotted a route to the

Jorlax Nexus. If I can gain an audience with the right people, I'm sure we can arrange sufficient political pressure to—"

"*Political* pressure? They might be melting Nola's brain right now, and you want to chitchat? We need to go get her out!"

"I like this one," says Reaper. "Maybe she belongs with us."

"Yeah? And what are you going to do about Nola?" I ask.

His superior smile wavers. "We have plans to deal with Vargalo-5, eventually."

"Great. Another contender for the Who Can Be Most Useless title."

Reaper laughs. "You'd better watch her, Ringmaster. She'll give you almost as much trouble as I did."

"Oh, a good deal more, I suspect. She isn't a coward."

"Careful." Reaper's voice is low and dangerous. "I'm not your painted puppet anymore. I'm more powerful than you remember."

I stare at the Outcast. Was his long coat always that dark? Were there always drifts of shadow swirling around his feet? No, I'm not imagining it. They're moving, slithering along the floor toward the Ringmaster and me. With a suddenness that makes me gasp, my feet go numb. There are dim cries of alarm, but my world has turned dull and gray. I try to move, but everything is ice and stone.

"More powerful, yes," says the Ringmaster, "but no wiser."

Light bursts, brighter and brighter, burning into my eyes and bringing color to the world again. I blink, tears stinging from the brilliance, to see the Ringmaster brandishing his baton like a sword. Every light in the entire tent is blazing.

Reaper retreats, raising one hand to shield his eyes. When I blink again, there are no strange shadows darkening the floor. "We're done here," growls Reaper. Spinning on his heel, he heads for the door. Amp snaps her gum one more time, then follows.

The rest of the troupe are on their feet, chattering and calling out and stumbling woozily down from the bleachers. Whatever Reaper did, it affected everyone, though it looks like Theon made it halfway to center stage before getting knocked loopy. Jom's helping her up. I spot Gravalon Pree and Ghost, of all people, blocking the doors.

"Step aside, Gravalon, Ghost," calls the Ringmaster. "Let them go. The show's over."

Reaper and Amp leave and don't look back. Good riddance.

Schadenfreude still hasn't moved. "My apologies for the conduct of my associates," he says, dipping his head with a rasp of protesting metal. "I'm afraid you bring out the worst in him, Ringmaster. Even as you bring out the best in others." It takes me a minute to identify the grotesque spasm that crosses his face as a smile.

He turns to me. "I hope you can recover your friend unharmed. Perhaps this will help." He holds out a battered datastore. "This is all the information we've gathered on the station itself."

I take it, trying not to flinch as my fingers brush the cracked flesh and warped metal mosaic that is his palm. Schadenfreude flips down his faceplate, salutes the Ringmaster, then follows after the other Outcasts. The door closes behind them.

The Ringmaster sighs. "Relieved?" I ask.

"No. Regretful." He shakes himself. "But we've places to go and people to see. Move smartly, you lot. We'll be jumping to the Jorlax Nexus as soon as I'm back to the bridge."

What? Still?

Nods and calls of *Yeah!* and *Got it!* percolate through the rest of the troupe. "What about Vargalo-5?" I say loudly as the Ringmaster heads backstage.

He halts, shoulders slumping slightly. "Beatrix, I want to rescue Nola as much as you do, but there are better ways to go about this."

"I thought the whole point of this circus was to fight back. Isn't it?"

"Yes! I mean, no, not that way. It's more complicated than that. This isn't a battleship. It's a school, a home, a hope for the future."

"Then we leave the Big Top somewhere safe. We go there and get her out!"

"I . . . can't do that, Beatrix. My first duty is to keep this troupe safe."

"That worked real well for Nola." It's a cheap shot. I regret it as soon as the words are past my lips.

He whirls around with a terrifying suddenness. "I wasn't the one who led her into danger!" The fury in his voice tears into me.

I stagger back, gulping down air, digging fingernails into my palms. Stay focused. And damn it, do *not* cry. The acid of my guilt and anger churns through my veins, chewing at my insides. With visible effort, the Ringmaster relaxes, although the knuckles gripping his baton remain white and hard as diamonds.

"You're right," I croak, finding half my voice. I cough, but the lump in my throat won't go away. "I'm sorry. I know I messed up with the Firedance, but this isn't about showing off. This is about getting Nola back before they destroy her."

The Ringmaster lifts his head. There's something fragile in his eyes. When he speaks, his voice is a whisper. "I know. And if I could . . ."

I remember our trip to the Lighthouse, how he

checked that pocket watch, and the guilt on his face when he looked back at the Big Top. Then later, coughing like he was . . . like he was at death's door. He would get Nola back, if he could. But he *can't*. The realization staggers me.

"You can't leave the Big Top," I say, speaking low so only he can hear it. "When we went to the Lighthouse, it wasn't the atmosphere making you sick. It was being away from the Big Top. That's what you meant about choices and sacrifice. Being the Ringmaster means you can't leave her."

He lowers his gaze so I don't need to see what's breaking inside of him. "Not for long. Not for long enough to save Nola. I'm sorry."

I reach out and grip his hand, just for a moment. "That's all right," I say, loud enough so everyone can hear. "I'll save her. And I just might get the Tinkers' Treasure back, too."

My attempt at bravado misses the mark. He reaches for my arm. "Beatrix, no. That isn't what I meant. It's too dangerous. I can't let you to risk yourself that way."

"Don't worry." I'm all business now. Time to get this over with. "This is for the best. Your job is to keep the Tinker-touched safe. Not half-Mandate screwups who do more harm than good."

Startled exclamations batter my ears: Theon telling me not to joke, Jom insisting it's not true. Even Sirra looks surprised. Only Miss Three seems happy.

I take one long look around, fixing the stage in my memory, only the good parts. The sweetness of the cheers for my one-and-only performance. The Ringmaster blazing that heart-stopping smile, just for me, the first night I stepped onto this ship. Nola, being a better friend than I can ever deserve.

I have to remember it all. I don't expect to be back.

* * *

I spend the next twelve hours going through the information on the datastore from Schadenfreude. It's going to be tough; that's for sure. The Vargalo-5 station has security I've never even heard of. Gravimetric field inducers. Multiphase laser grids. Vuolu scent hounds. If I had a month to plan and a crack team of ninjas, I might stand a chance. Instead I've got a few hours, a soap-opera-addicted know-it-all, and me, the pink-haired wonder.

I've got to give Britannica credit, though. I don't know if it's all the *Love Among the Stars* or what, but she's got one devious mind hidden in those microchips. Between the two of us, we cook up a pretty decent plan. There's only one problem with it.

"Aaaaugh!" I throw my viewer onto the bed. "There must be some way onto the station. Maybe I can get close enough to use spacewings. Or find a transport to sneak onto. You guys have pizza delivery, don't you?"

"Let's stay focused on rational options, dear. Now,

have you considered disguising yourself as a snappy, up-and-coming junior officer of the Core Governance? Dalana does that in season twelve, episode thirty-two, in order to liberate the scientist wrongly convicted of espionage."

"I'm so glad we're sticking to rational options." I groan and flop onto the bed. Maybe I ought to sleep. But we'll be docking at the Jorlax Nexus in less than an hour. That's my one shot. I've got to have a plan ready for action. Maybe I should ask the Ringmaster for help. Then again, he might just try to stop me. We haven't spoken since the Outcasts left. I wish—

The door chime pulls me back from these thoughts. Finally! I spring up, race to the door, and slap my palm on the pad. My pulse thrums loud in my ears. "Ringmaster, I—Jom? What are you doing here?"

I search the hall, but there's no one else. Jom runs a hand back over his crest of red hair, looking sheepish. "I'm here to help. You're going after Nola, right?"

"Um, yeah, but—"

"Then I'm going with you." He pulls his shoulders back. A whiff of some sharp, minty scent hits my nose. "I'm not letting them change her. I don't care how dangerous it is."

"Are you sure? That was the truth, what I said in the Ring. About who I am."

"You're her friend. You're not abandoning her. That's

what really matters. Besides, the way the Ringmaster explained it to us, you're a Tinker, too. The Big Top let you in, and that's good enough for me. And . . ." He crinkles a smile at me. "I've got the perfect way to get onto Vargalo-5. So what do you say?"

"Ask him if it involves disguises," pipes Britannica. I ignore her and stick out my hand.

"I say welcome to the Nola Liberation Army. So, tell me about your plan . . ."

CHAPTER 20

E**S**c**a**p**e**

BY THE TIME we do dock at the Jorlax Nexus, I'm feeling almost chipper. Jom's plan is . . . innovative . . . but it's better than nothing. I'd feel better with a few ninjas, but I'll take what we've got.

The Ringmaster never does come calling, at least not in person. Britannica takes a couple of short voice messages, and then one long one. They're all variations on a theme: Please stay here. Stay safe. Diplomatic channels. Time. I delete them before they make me chicken out.

A half-hour after we dock, the Ringmaster is deep

into negotiations with his contacts, and it's time for Jom and me to make our move. We head for the airlock that links ship to station.

"Looks clear," I say.

We make it about three steps when a ghostly figure shimmers into focus, barring the way.

"Miss Ling, I've been expecting you," says Miss Three. "The Ringmaster suspected you would not listen."

"Trix," says Jom in a low voice, "we need to get to the distribution center by twenty-one hundred hours or this won't work."

"Get out of our way, Three." I step forward. "Or I swear I'll find your motherboard and stomp it into itty-bitty pieces."

She arches a perfect brow at me, then glides to one side. "You mistake me. I'm not here to stop you. Go. This ship is better off without you. *He* is better of without you." Then she's gone, winked out.

"Let's go!" Jom pulls me out the door.

After the Hasoo-Pashtung Bazaar, the Jorlax Nexus station is a little disappointing. It reminds me of an airport, or one of those old indoor shopping malls, with stands selling JoJoPop and Supulu's Scoops every fifty feet and bubbly, inoffensive music piped in. The people look like regular sorts, out for a stroll, on business, shopping. The view, though—that's pretty freaking amazing. If I survive the next six hours, I am definitely coming back here. The outer walls are clear, floor to ceiling. On the other side is a Hubble image come to life. Not as colorful, maybe, but much, *much* bigger. Swirls of bronze and gold filter the light of a dying star. It's a sight to hold on to.

We hit our first roadblock, literally, when we're about halfway to our destination. A security checkpoint chokes the flow of traffic to a standstill. There's a single archway that I take to be a high-tech metal detector, and the line waiting to pass through it must be a hundred people deep.

"Gotta love the Core Governance in action," says Jom, grimacing. "We've got ten minutes."

"You think we should jump it?"

"I'm sure you'd love another chance to show off," says a voice beside me. "But if you're serious about saving Nola, you're probably better off without the attention."

"Sirra?" Jom asks. "What are you doing here? Taking tea with the Wazeer of Deneb?"

He's right. She looks ready for a state event. The marshmallow cast has been replaced by a close-fitting brace that blends into her dark velvety pants. Her tall boots shine as if daring one speck of dust to land on them. Golden insignias glitter with gems, decorating her fitted scarlet coat. She's even wearing something that, I kid you not, looks like a tiara.

"You two clearly need help," she says. "And I need

an unprotected netlink upload site." She holds up No-la's datastore.

"So you want to come with us?" I say. "Risk everything?"

"I've got everything to lose if I don't do something," she says, clenching the datastore in her fist. "So, do you want to stand here all day or what?"

"I'll take the 'what' option," says Jom.

"Follow me, then, and keep your mouths shut." Sirra marches forward, limping slightly. Jom and I look at each other and abandon our spot in line.

Sirra's not even halfway to the checkpoint when the flurry of activity starts. The guards look as if someone set loose a swarm of bees on them, rushing back and forth, waving hands in the air. I spot one guy ducking behind a potted plant to tuck in his shirt and straighten his jacket. The excitement spreads to the people waiting in line, who point and watch open-mouthed.

By the time we reach the checkpoint, there's a line of uniformed guards standing at attention. They even *salute*. I'm starting to see how Sirra turned out the way she did, if this is the kind of treatment she's used to.

"Lady Centaurus," says a guard with a silver star on her cap, saluting again. "This is a great honor. We had no word that one of your family would be visiting the Nexus. Is the President traveling with you?"

"No, my mother isn't here. But I'm sure she would

be glad to know the security of Nexus is in such capable hands."

The guard looks so happy at this you'd think Sirra had handed her the winning lottery ticket and a puppy. Sirra continues on, "But I do have some *rather urgent* family business to attend to, if you understand."

"Oh, yes, of course, Lady Centaurus. You, there, clear a path. Quickly, now, let's not keep the lady waiting."

Sirra slips a coy look back at Jom and me, then resumes her regal coolness. Within a minute we're being waved past the checkpoint. Jom and I get some odd looks, mostly focused on our . . . unusual . . . hair. But one sweet little smile from Sirra and an "Oh, these are my assistants," and we're free and clear.

Sirra keeps up the empress-of-the-universe act until we round the next bend in the main walkway. Then she ducks into an alcove beside a potted palm. She pulls off the dozens of gold emblems and tiara and stuffs them into a pouch, then shakes the elaborate hairstyle down and ties it back in a simple ponytail.

"Please tell me you have a plan to get to Vargalo-5," Sirra says, fiddling with a tiny dial on the sleeve of her coat. As she spins it, the color of the jacket darkens from the brilliant scarlet to a muted burgundy. The empress is gone, replaced by a polished but not particularly eye-catching young woman.

"Can't you snap your fingers and get your minions to help?" I say as we head off down the walkway.

"Even I can't just walk into a high-security military research facility."

"Don't worry," says Jom, careening around a corner and leading us down a side hall. "I've got us our ticket to Vargalo-5 right here." He points ahead to the doorway emblazoned with the image of a gigantic ice cream cone and the words SUPULU'S SCOOPS DISTRIBUTION CENTER. Jom presses one hand across the identification panel. The door slides open with a cheery "Welcome, Master Supulu!"

We follow Jom into the chilly maze of shelves packed with tubs labeled Tachyon Toffee Swirl and Cosmic Crunch to a loading bay. A stubby shuttlecraft emblazoned with the Supulu logo and the words DELIVERY SERVICE sits proudly on the flight deck, being prepped by a crew of robotic loaders. As we watch, one of the mechanicals deposits a final pallet stacked with tubs into the delivery shuttle. Everything, from the tubs to the robots to the shuttle, is striped in pale green and lavender.

Jom comes out from the cockpit with a bundle of lavender and green fabric in his hands. "Um . . . I hope you guys like stripes."

* * *

I squirm in my seat, looking out the window at the Vargalo-5 station below. The white domes bubble up from the blasted lunarscape of the small moon.

"Don't worry," says Jom from his spot at the controls. "There's another two transports ahead of us. We'll get our clearance eventually."

I blow out my breath, but it doesn't help with the tight feeling in my chest. The air in here is too thin. And this uniform isn't helping. "How do they expect you to work with this—this *thing* flopping into your face every time you turn around?" I try for the umpteenth time to reposition the peaked lavender and green cap so the pompom on the end isn't tickling my nose.

"Oh, it's not that bad," says Jom, giving the fluffy tip of his own hat a practiced flick to send it back over one shoulder. "My grandfather designed the uniforms, you know. The cap's supposed to look like an ice cream cone. Get it?"

"Enough of this," I mutter. Pulling off my cap, I give the pompom a good yank. It pops free. I toss it into the aisle.

In the seat across from me, Sirra's been waging her own war against the hat. She stops to watch the de-pomming. Catching my eye, she grins. A moment later her own cap is pompom free.

"And listen," says Jom, "I know this is a deadly dangerous mission and all that, but my uncle's going to kill me if anything happens to this stuff. So try to keep the uniforms clean, if you can. What? Why are you both giggling?"

Sirra slaps a hand over her mouth, but her shoulders keep shaking. I sweep the two discarded pompoms off the floor and make a show of dusting them off, which only makes Sirra laugh harder.

It's a weird, weird world. A week ago Sirra and I hated each other, and honestly, we probably still do. But right now I'm just glad to have someone to laugh with, to loosen the bands of fear that clamp me down whenever I think about what's coming.

Jom leans forward, taking the manual controls as a voice crackles from the comlink. "Supulu Shuttle 8552, please hold your position. We have an incoming flight that has priority."

I sink lower into my seat. Wonderful. More waiting.

"Copy that, Vargalo-5," replies Jom cheerfully. Then he lets a note of doubt into his voice. "I sure hope I don't lose any cargo, though. Freezers won't last much longer."

There's a pause. Then the same voice, but less clipped and formal. "You got any of that Limited Edition Love Among the Starberries on board?"

"Sure do!" says Jom. "Tell you what, if you can get us down sooner rather than later, I'll even set aside a pint for you."

There's another, longer pause, then "Supulu Shuttle 8552, you are cleared for descent to platform North Gamma-5. Please report to the deck officer upon landing."

"Thank you, Vargalo-5 Control," says Jom. He clicks off the comlink and winks back at Sirra and me. "Ice cream: better than a universal lockpick."

Jom works more of his magic on the deck officer after we land, distracting him with a tub that's "exceeded optimal storage temperatures" and can't be refrozen without violating some Supulu taboo. While the officer takes an ice cream break, we get to supervise the unpacking of the remaining tubs.

The moment the guard is out of sight, I head for the nearest com station. Sirra beats me to it, only to slam a fist into the wall. "Internal only! No netlink. It's not enough."

"It's enough for me." I edge around her and flick on my know-it-all. "Britannica? You in?"

"Of course. Bringing up schematics now."

The screen blinks on, showing the now-way-too-familiar layout of the station.

"There," says my know-it-all over the shared com channel. "Miss Ogala is in the detention wing, as expected. Records indicate she has been subjected to only minimal processing."

"Thank the First Tinker," says Jom, jogging over to join us, having finished with the unloading.

Britannica goes on, "You should be able to proceed with the original plan of making your way around the outer maintenance passages and then . . . Oh, dear."

"What's wrong?"

"I'm afraid Miss Ogala is scheduled to be transferred to a treatment chamber in approximately thirty-three minutes."

"What kind of treatment?" asks Sirra.

"Full-scale genetic cleansing."

"Even in a best-case scenario, our planned route will take forty," says Jom. He pulls off his cap and twists it so roughly I hear a rip. "And the backup plan isn't much better."

"Then we'd better find a backup for the backup." I glare into the sea of thin green lines that stand between me and Nola. I point to the schematics. "Look here, there's a passage that runs almost straight from where we are to the detention block. It's the only way."

"That's the passage with the Vuolu scent hounds," says Jom, continuing to mangle his hat.

"You said you had a way to get past them."

"I said I had an idea. That's not the same thing. And I can't do anything about the variable gravimetric fields."

"Good thing we've got Gravity Girl with us, then." I point to a spot near the blinking light that marks Nola's cell. "And look, Sirra, you're in luck: There's a full netlink station right here."

Sirra doesn't move. For a moment I think I might have to come up with an inspiring speech. Then she shakes herself, gives a tight nod, and heads for the wall panel that leads to our backup backup route.

The first part is tense and boring, not a good combination. All we find are seemingly endless tubelike passages that make me feel like a gerbil. We scuttle along the Habitrail, hunched and ready for attack, for sirens and wailing alarms. It's a dangerous feeling when you start hoping for something to happen to relieve the numb fear slowly paralyzing your thoughts.

I notice the tube widening, feel an odd heaviness in one foot. Britannica starts to say something, but it's too late. Suddenly my entire body has turned to lead. I slam down onto the floor. A hum of power buzzes in my bones.

"Graphimephric . . . m-field," says Jom, the translator barely un-garbling the words. With great effort I twist my head a fraction of an inch so I can see him splattered flat as a pancake against the floor.

"Sirra," I gasp out. "Your . . . cue."

The field shifts sickeningly. Is this how the ocean feels in a storm? Whipped by waves that shift it and slop it around until up is down and inside is out? I grit my teeth, my entire focus boiling down to one thought: Don't hurl.

When it stops, I'm on the ceiling. My lead bones have become clouds. Jom careens into me and grunts. "Sirra! Do something!"

I twist so the momentum of the jolt from Jom spins me around to face Sirra. She's floating, arms outstretched, her dark hair coiling in a halo around her frightened—yes, frightened—face. "Sirra, can't you stop it?"

"No . . . I mean, I don't know. It's too much. Changing too fast."

On cue, I slam back down to the floor. Jom bellows in pain.

"If I get it wrong, it might backlash. It could tear us all into pieces."

"If it's a choice between that and getting beaten to a bloody pulp, I'll take the chance," calls Jom.

"I don't think I can do it."

"Come on, Sirra, you're the star of the Circus Galacticus. You perform for bazillions of people. You're the definition of overachiever. Everything you do is perfect. Believe me; I noticed. So do this! Get another gold star for your collection."

Nothing. I think I hear her breathing, fast and desperate.

"I'm afraid Lady Centaurus won't be able to be of further assistance," pipes my know-it-all. "I don't suppose you can reach that control panel on the far end of the chamber?"

I'd laugh, but there's no air in my chest. I can barely move an inch, let alone cross the ten feet to the panel. But I try. Not much else to do. "I guess I finally found one thing I can do better, though," I say. "At least I'm not giving up without a fight."

Sirra's voice is faint. "You're trying to make me angry."

"Well, yeah," I admit.

"It's working." The words are sharper, stronger.

I can't see what's happening, but suddenly my body feels cloudlike again. Jom groans. "Hold on," says Sirra. "Don't move."

The clouds turn to marshmallows, then to solid flesh. My heels sink onto the floor. I catch myself against the wall. Don't hurl, don't hurl, chants my brain. Sirra flies past and taps something into the control panel. The humming stops.

"Good work," I say, once I find my lips. "Remind me to give you that gold star."

Sirra smiles. "If we get out of here, it's gold stars all around."

"Ah, isn't it wonderful how a little adversity can make bosom friends out of former enemies?" says my know-it-all in a dreamy voice.

I snort. "Bosom friends?"

"Hardly," says Sirra, dropping her smile like a hot coal. "Let's call it allies for now."

"Sounds good to me." I move to join Jom over at the hatch that will take us out into the detention wing.

"I'll go first," he says. "If there are Vuolu hounds, I'll distract them. You two get Nola out. Okay?"

"As long as distracting them doesn't mean letting them chew on you."

"No." Jom cracks the hatch, peering out. "But it does involve a bit of acrobatics and making myself smell like a fresh Denebian sausage. Nothing a Clown can't handle. All right, it's clear." He ducks out of the hatch.

Sirra and I follow, emerging into a gray corridor lined with narrow doors that remind me uncomfortably of tombstones. It takes me a moment to get oriented. "It should be this way," I say, pointing to the right.

"Shhh!" Jom raises a warning hand. In the silence that follows, the *click-click-click* of claws echoes from somewhere around the corner to the left. "Go! Find her!"

Then he's gone, slipping off down the left-hand hall, trailing a faint whiff of smoked meat. I hesitate. It feels wrong, but we're running out of time.

"You heard him," Sirra says.

We move on. I'm listening so hard for growling and screaming in the distance, I miss the cell. Sirra catches my elbow and points to the number glowing from the keypad beside the nearest door. "This is it."

"And there's the netlink." I point up the hall. "Go do your thing." Leaning closer to the door, I call out, "Nola?"

A long moment ticks by, and I swear I lose about a year of my life before I catch the faint "Trix? Is that really you?"

"Pink hair and all. I've got Jom and Sirra here, too. Don't ask; I can't explain it, either. We're here to rescue you, but we're going to need help. Can you get this door open? You know, with your Tech mojo?"

"I can try. But everything keeps spinning. Whooa, one step in front of the other." There's a muffled thump from inside the cell. "Hello, there, Mr. Door. How do you feel about opening? Good? Oh, do you really have to? Well, okay, then . . ."

The next moment the door slides open, Nola falls out, and sirens start blaring.

Sirra rejoins me, her face sharp with fear. "They're coming!" The thud of running footsteps pounds toward us.

Jom rounds the corner, running like he's got a pack of Vuolu hounds on his trail. Relief breaks over his face like a sunrise when he sees us. "You found her! Is she okay?"

"She's fine. Pretty loopy, though. I think they drugged her. She's not going to make it out on her own."

Jom doesn't hesitate. He scoops Nola up and keeps running. Sirra and I follow. We hurtle around the corner and skid to a stop. Three gray-uniformed soldiers block the hall, brandishing familiar stubby black weapons. Sirra sweeps her arms up, and suddenly all three are floating into the air. We duck under their flailing legs and race onward and into our hatch.

Gravimetric chamber, Habitrail, it all whips past now as we flee, driven by the shrieks of the alarms. I roll out the last panel into the landing bay and spring upright, fists clenched, ready to fight. But all I see is the striped

Supulu shuttle. Jom goes right for the ship, still carrying Nola. A moment later the thrum of the engine starts up. Britannica helps me spin the landing deck, positioning the shuttle for takeoff. I can't believe it. We're going to do this crazy thing. We're going to make it out of here!

But one look toward the hangar bay doors, and everything falls apart. The slice of stars is narrowing. They're trying to trap us here. "Jom!" I call over my comlink.

"I see it! I can't stop it. Signal isn't getting through!"

"I believe you'll find a manual override on the far wall," offers my know-it-all. "Yellow panel, red switch."

"Don't worry, Jom; I'll handle it. Start the pre-burn."

"Are you sure you'll have time—"

"You worry about Nola. Got it? Nola." Then I have Britannica kill the link so I don't have to lie.

I dash across the room and slam the red switch. The slice of stars begins to widen again. Sirra's raising the ramp. I'm about to make my last wild sprint for the shuttle when a flicker of movement catches the corner of my eye.

A dozen gray-uniformed guards boil out from the corridor into the landing bay. At their center stalks a single figure in a long charcoal coat with a glinting face.

"Sirra, go!" I shout. Sirra opens her lips; she's saying something, but I can't hear it over the pre-flight burn. I turn away. No time. Nyl is pointing at the shuttle, his hand wreathed in blue fire.

My body moves before my mind, sharp and sure as an arrow. I launch myself at Nyl, catching his hand as it explodes with blue fire, driving it down, away from the shuttle. Pain rips through me, tangling my nerves into knots of agony that leave me huddled and breathless at Nyl's feet.

When I look up, though, all I see is that ridiculous striped shuttle, shooting out into the stars. *Go, Jom,* screams my mind. *Get her out!*

Then a silver monster fills my vision, and his terrible words fill my ears, and I retreat into the blackness, where he can't find me.

CHAPTER 21

The Mandate

BLANK WHITE WALLS and a piercing headache greet me when I wake. I batter my fists against the cell, searching for any weakness and finding only my own. I black out again.

I wake up sprawled on the floor. Time slides past, featureless as the walls of my prison. Food appears on a tray through a narrow slot in the wall. Britannica remains silent, muffled or dead.

For a while I live on flavorless pudding, dry biscuits, and the memory of happier times. I summon up starry desert nights and bedtime stories. I try to tease hidden meaning from the past. What were my parents planning? Why did they leave me the Tinkers' Treasure? What did they expect me to do with it?

I begin to realize that the worst part isn't the things I miss: friends, freedom, decent food. It's what I've got locked in here with me: my mistakes, the things I've said, the people I've hurt or disappointed.

"I tried," I whisper into my hands. I know Nyl's watching me. Tiny red eyes wink at me from the corners of the room. It's those eyes that keep me going. I may be dying inside, but Nyl is not getting a piece of that.

At last he comes, like I knew he would. The door whispers shut. He's alone.

"That was quite the martyr act," he says. "And all for one little girl? Or perhaps there is a part of you that knows your place is here, with us."

"Like hell it is." I stand to face him. "My mother didn't think so, and neither do I."

"So he finally told you? If you know the truth, that only makes the situation clearer. You have no other options. Suppose I opened this door and set you free, right now? Where would you go? Back to the Circus? Back to him?"

I curse my own silence as he chuckles. "Perhaps you'd like to return to that pit of a world where I found you, to that shabby little room and that shabby little life?"

He crosses his arms, tilting his masked face consideringly. "There is still a place for you with us, Beatrix. You have family here, you know."

A noise crawls from my throat before I can stop it, a sort of whimper.

"True family," he says. "They are waiting for you to return and take your mother's place. Don't you want that?"

Damn me, but I do. "No," I say, to myself as much as to Nyl. "She left for a reason."

"She left because she wasn't strong enough. She wasn't a fighter, like you. But time is running out, Beatrix. Not all my associates are as patient as I. If you don't join us now, I won't be able to protect you much longer."

I raise my chin. "My blood may be Mandate, but I am *not* one of you."

He cocks his head. "Ah. Despite everything, you still think you're one of *them*, do you? Well, then. Here. Let's test that hypothesis." He tosses something at me.

My hands rise instinctively, catching it. I blink at the familiar black lump cradled in my palms.

"That's what started this all," he says. "The so-called Tinkers' Treasure. Your sacred charge." He laughs. "It's nothing but a joke, Beatrix. You are no Tinker. It isn't meant for you. Go on, try. You can't even open it. If you truly belonged with him, don't you think you would have unlocked its secrets long ago?"

My fingers tighten. "You're wrong. My parents gave it to me for a reason. Just because I don't know what it is doesn't mean there isn't one." I grip the rock in both hands now, ignoring the slippery echoes of doubt twisting in my thoughts. What's wrong with me? I cracked it once just by bashing it in his face and dropping it on the freaking ground.

"This is the folly of such dreams," says Nyl. "In his world, there are always going to be those who shine more brightly than the rest. We can take that all away. Think of it, Beatrix. A world without jealousy or war. All peoples working together to create a bright future for all. You can help us make that happen. Aren't you tired of wishing to be better? Of jealousy clamping you in its sharp fangs and filling you with its poison?"

"Yes." The word slips out before I can stop it. I stare down into the glossy blackness of the rock. Then I look up again, into his mirrored glasses. I can't see his eyes, but I know I'm staring straight into them, holding him with the power of my resolve. "But I'll take painful dreams over empty comfort any day."

Nyl shakes his head. "A pity." He clenches his hand. A few flickers of blue flame flare angrily.

And with that, something in my brain clicks into place. I remember that first night in my dorm, the blue flames flickering in Nyl's hand as he wrestled me for the stone. It *wasn't* me bashing the stone into his face that cracked it. It was those flames. Just like the King's fire wakes up the seeds of life in the Firedance. I know what I need to do.

I slam my fist into his face. Something cracks. Nyl stumbles back, his mirrored glasses broken. Brushing them aside, he gives a roar of anger that raises goose flesh on my skin. His hand thrusts out, sending a bolt of blue flame right at me.

I launch into my routine, diving, flipping, tumbling, as bursts of fire erupt on all sides. I hiss as pain licks my heel. These aren't FX now, and I have to nail it, not for applause, but for my life, and for the future. Nyl shouts in fury as I dance around him.

Time for the last set. Backflip, round-off, spring onto the cot, and dive through the air.

After all my doubts, all the second-guessing, I am exactly where I need to be, in this one perfect moment. Nyl roars, releasing a tide of fiery blue death. I toss the rock free, so that it sails ahead of me, into the heart of the blue flames, even as I duck and tumble to escape them.

Almost. I scream as the agony rips up my left arm and into my chest, doubling me over. My legs buckle, sending me sprawling. I grit my teeth, wrenching my other arm out to catch a falling star. The Tinkers' Treasure smacks into my palm.

I lie panting, my left arm limp and lifeless, my right hand buzzing with warmth, spreading a slow honey through my fingers, into my bones.

Nyl looms over me. With his broken glasses gone, I

see his eyes for the first time. They hold me, dark and merciless, and somehow it's all the more terrible because he isn't a monster under that mask. Just a man.

Threads of smoke trail from his breathing mask. Blue flames dance along his skull, skittering down his shoulders and into his outstretched hand. "Clever girl. And you got so close to victory. All the power of the Tinkers' Touch, in your hand for the taking. It's what you wanted all along, isn't it? To be a brighter star than any of them. A shame no one will ever see it."

I try to move. My body isn't mine anymore. I manage a tremble, a shiver, a whispered name.

Nyl pauses, holding my death in his hand. Outrage flares in his dark eyes. "Stupid girl! That boy is a broken soldier, pretending he has tricks up his sleeve when it's only smoke and mirrors. He could never have saved you, even if he wished it."

With a thunderous crash, the ceiling caves in. I blink, hope stirring, pulse racing, as a glittering figure falls from the heavens.

"Would you care to bet on that?" The Ringmaster sweeps his baton in a level arc, filling the room with a crackling web of light. I catch one glimpse of his eyes, fixed on my own, before everything bleaches away.

A hand finds mine, pulling me up. My legs are trembling, but he moves closer, supporting me. When I can see again, I'm on the far side of the cell. Nyl stands at the door.

"You! How—?" Nyl shakes his head. "Impossible! You would never leave that ship . . ."

"I didn't." The Ringmaster jabs his baton up, pointing up at the stars—no—the lights! The glorious, light-spangled vastness of the Big Top rises over us, fully enclosing the cell. They landed right on top of the station!

The door behind Nyl slides open, releasing a tide of soldiers. "You can't escape," says Nyl. "Not on that decrepit artifact. Not alone."

"Spoken like a true agent of the Mandate. You never have any faith in what you can't understand or control," says the Ringmaster. "And I'm not alone."

An avalanche cascades into the room, bowling into a handful of soldiers and knocking them aside. No way. Gravalon Pree? And he's not the only one. Jom barely hits the floor before he's leaping at the nearest soldier.

Theon slams down between two others, and suddenly they can't hold on to their weapons. Another soldier yelps as he sinks into the floor and disappears. Ghost rises up a moment later, and I swear she's actually smirking. There are others, a good dozen of the troupe. Principals, Clowns, Techs, Freaks. Nola, wielding a gun bigger than she is, shooting gobs of paralyzing goop.

"You—you came," I stammer.

"We came, we saw, and we knew when to make our getaway," says the Ringmaster, winking. "Let's be off," he calls out. "I think these ladies and gentlemen won't require an encore."

The next minute we're all floating. I catch a brief glimpse of Sirra, arms outstretched, lifting us all from the battlefield. Panels of metal fold out to re-form the floor, cutting off our view of the station below.

Miss Three flickers into sight as Sirra is setting us back down again. "Ringmaster, a full squadron has launched. We must jump as soon as possible."

The Ringmaster sprints for the door. "Buckle up, troupes. And give the Big Top some encouraging thoughts. We're going to need them, I'm afraid."

Everyone scatters. I follow the Ringmaster. So does Nola.

"We're not fully compacted, Ringmaster," she calls out as we run. "We can't jump."

He hurtles onto the bridge. "And that's why they invented these lovely things known as evasive maneuvers. I've asked Syzygy to provide some."

The blond girl stands beside one of the consoles, her thick goggles reflecting a stream of green and red flashes. As Nola and the Ringmaster race around the bridge, I'm left standing, shaky and silent, watching a dozen shapes winging toward us on the viewscreen.

Weariness drags at me. My whole body feels numb, except for my right hand, gripping the Tinkers' Treasure. I grit my teeth and look around for something, anything I can do. "Are there shields? Weapons? Can't we fight back?"

"No weapons," says the Ringmaster, his voice grim.

"No shields, either," adds Nola.

Syzygy stares at me. "Not yet."

I look down at my hand. Does she mean I should use the Treasure? Even Nyl said it. *All the power of the Tinkers' Touch, in your hand for the taking. It's what you wanted all along, isn't it? To be a brighter star than any of them.*

The first bolts are almost graceful, bursting from the wings of one of the enemy craft, arcing like a golden rainbow across the screen. Then the world spins, metal groans, and the entire Big Top shudders like an old woman caught in a cold, cold wind.

"Close call," Nola says, then cries a warning as three more missiles spin toward us.

"Hold on! It's going to—"

The impact throws me to the ground. The Ringmaster is the only one who keeps his feet. I doubt there's any power in the universe that could pull him from that console. I look at his face and wish I hadn't. He knows the Big Top is dying. And I know, with a certainty that shakes me to the core, that he's dying, too. She's a part of him, or he's a part of her. The details don't matter. He can't leave her. He can't live without her.

Warmth tugs at my hand. I look at the rock. The glossy blackness is cracked with lines of red and gold. Inside, a light pulses, beating like a trapped hummingbird.

A faint chiming calls to me. It wants to be used. It wants to grow into something new and glorious. It's there for me to take, if I want it, like Nyl said. The vision catches me with a suddenness that makes me gasp. I see myself, powerful, brilliant. Shining brighter than any star. I am the pinnacle of the Tinkers' art. The Tinkers' Treasure can save me.

But I'm not the one who needs saving. I close my smarting eyes. I don't know what to do. It's a gorgeous, dazzling dream but somehow . . . false. Because it's not only me. It's Nola, working her magic behind the scenes, showing up to help me even when I didn't deserve it. It's Sirra, sharp and hard as diamond, willing to risk everything for her brother. It's Jom and Theon and all of them, the madcap, rampaging, brilliant troupe. And it's the Ringmaster and his Big Top, coming to take me away, giving me a dream to believe in. A dream I *still* believe in.

Syzygy's voice breaks my reverie. "One thousand three hundred forty-nine. There is still time."

1349. The room the rock was leading me to. "I know what to do," I say, quietly at first, to myself more than anyone else. Then louder. "Ringmaster! I need to get to the Restricted Area. I know how to save the Big Top."

He doesn't ask questions, though I see them in his eyes. He takes my hand, turns, and runs for the door.

Five times we're thrown by the sudden tilting of the floor. I start to smell smoke. The Big Top shudders and groans. I run faster. By the time we get to the section with the corrugated walls, I'm leading the way. It's like the rock itself is a magnet, pulling me along, unerringly, to its destiny. Outside door 1349 I pause for a breath, then press my palm against the spongy surface. The door folds back in pleats. The room on the other side is nothing I could have imagined.

It's a little like stepping into a giant brain, complete with the ick factor. Except it's more than that. The curving walls shimmer with golden light. Ghostly images flicker at the corners of my eyes. Sparks glitter, leaping between the stalactite-like growths that decorate the room, if *room* is even the right word.

The Ringmaster stands motionless. "Beatrix," he says, "this is the heart—the brain—the soul of the Big Top. I always knew you had a heart of gold, old girl," he adds quietly.

A shudder shakes the room. The Ringmaster stumbles, nearly falling. He steadies himself against a stalagmite.

"Ringmaster?" Nola's voice comes over the com, cracking with fear. "They're all over the place! They keep coming and coming. I don't know what to do!"

"Nola," I say calmly, "it's going to be okay. Listen. You got that? Breathe." I look down one last time at the Tinkers' Treasure, pulsing in my hand like liquid gold. Then I throw it into the air.

It hangs for a moment, growing brighter and brighter.

With a tinkling like a roomful of breaking china, it explodes, scattering flakes of golden light. I rub my eyes, and when I look again the entire room is glowing, rippling. Changing. The walls tremble. My skin prickles, goose bumps rising. Even my scalp tingles.

The Ringmaster stands frozen, staring around in bewilderment as if someone just threw him a surprise party and it wasn't even his birthday.

"Where did that come from?" Nola's voice rises, alarmed. "The Big Top doesn't have shields. Or polarity-reversal canons. What's going o—ooooh! The Big Top has shields! Hah! And polarity-reversal canons! Yeah, you better run away, Mandate scum. And don't come back."

CHAPTER 22

Principles

IT'S STILL THE SAME old Big Top, even with a Tinkers' Treasure makeover. Sure, the doors are less wheezy, the lights shine a bit brighter, and the Techs say it'll take days to catalogue all the new defensive systems. But I still trip over piles of feather boas in the halls, and Nola's still the only one who can program the autosalon.

When I go to dinner the first night after it all went down, I prepare myself to sit alone. I figure it's better that way. Less attachments, less hurt when I go. I don't count on Nola, Jom, Theon, Gravalon, and a half-dozen others crowding around table five to join me. Jom even gives me the second-largest Chocolate Supernova for dessert, nearly as big as Nola's.

I won't lie. I love it. And hate it. They don't even say the word *Mandate,* but it's there, hanging in the air like the stench of a forgotten lunch, left to rot under the table. I let Jom tell the story of Nola's breakout, and when they ask what happened to me afterward, I shrug and mumble something about being questioned.

As if it were that easy.

* * *

There's one conversation I can't run away from, though, even if it scares me stiff. When I find the Ringmaster, he's looking out from the viewing deck at the whorls of light and color drifting past. In a strange way it makes me feel better. Last time we were standing here, my world was breaking apart and I was furious with him. Now it's time to put it back together and apologize.

"Hey," I say. "I've got something for you."

He turns, his expression scrupulously mild, like I'm a rabbit he expects to bolt. I hold out the pink teapot. "I'm sorry it's chipped," I say. "It kinda took a detour."

Yes, I went back and got it. From Rjool. And trust me, there's no power in the universe that's going to make me tell anyone that story. *Ever.*

The Ringmaster looks between the teapot and me. Before he can say anything, I blurt it all out. "I'm sorry, Ringmaster. You took me up here, gave me all of this" —I wave out the window—"and I . . . I've been nothing but trouble. I'm so sorry." I study the pattern of the floor panels with such intensity that his touch on my arm makes me jump.

"Beatrix, the Mandate are the ones who want only to avoid trouble. Nyl and his ilk would have us all following rules blindly, accepting what we're given. I meant what I said to Reaper. I like a bit of trouble in my life." This time he doesn't wink when he says it. At that moment my elbow is my connection to everything that matters.

"If you hadn't acted when you did, Nola might have been lost to us, utterly. I hesitated. I was confused. I wanted to be sure. I was . . . afraid." His face darkens.

"You had more to lose. I get that now," I say, wanting to chase the shadows from his eyes. "It was easier for me to take the risk. I'm nothing sp—"

The word dies unspoken as the Ringmaster presses one finger to my lips. "No. I knew exactly what I was doing when I asked you to join the Circus Galacticus. Special isn't only what you can do. It's the choices you make. You don't go through the universe looking for a place that's ready-made for you to fit into, a round peg for a round hole. You have to make your own place. Do you understand?"

I nod, and his finger falls away, leaving a ghost of warmth. He sighs. "My mistake was not realizing I needed to do the same . . ."

"What do you mean?"

"I don't know what this is all for." The Ringmaster waves to the room. "The Tinkers left this ship for us, but for what purpose? Am I truly doing their work, gallivanting around the universe?"

All this time I've been thinking about how much I need this place, this life. I looked to the Ringmaster to show me the way. Now, suddenly, the world has shifted. There's a desperation in his eyes that kills me. "That's not the right question," I say. "Those ancient long-lost Tinkers, they're gone. They retired, quit, whatever. You're the one who's here now, reminding people they can reach the stars and choose their own destinies. That's the real way to fight the Mandate. That's the real way to bust those cages. And I think the universe needs that pretty badly right now. I—" My voice breaks. "I know I did."

He meets my gaze for a long moment, then nods as the terrible tension in his face ebbs away.

"So that's our place," I say, smiling. "That's what we do."

The Ringmaster's eyebrows rise toward the brim of his top hat. "We?"

"If you'll still have me. Even if I'm never more than a pink-haired-clown dancing-fruit person. This is where I belong."

"I'm . . . glad to hear it." There's a catch in his voice. The Ringmaster doesn't look at me, but I can almost feel the shape of the space between us, no longer filled with fear, but with possibilities.

He clears his throat and continues on breezily. "But don't abandon all hope. You had the Tinkers' Treasure in your hands. You may not have used its power for yourself, but that doesn't mean it hasn't left its mark. And then there's this."

He holds out a familiar, gold-filigreed book. The cover reads *The Programme of the Circus Galacticus, Thirteenth Edition*.

"Thirteenth? How? What changed?"

He grins, flipping it open. And there it is, at the bottom of the cast list.

"The Champion: She who guards the Dreamers and stands undaunted before the King of Iron and Flame." I skim the rest, not quite taking it in.

"No way. Really?"

"Unless you know someone else with a 'brave spirit and hair like a sunset sky,' I think there's little doubt who it's referring to. So," he adds, "Clown or Principal? You'd be within rights to trade in for a star." The Ringmaster's smile is a riddle, but I know the answer.

We stand there, our faces turned to the galaxies wheeling past. It's not the desert, and I can't forget what I've lost. But that's okay.

"I've got all the stars I need right here."

Acknowledgments

I wrote this book in an attempt to capture some of the wonder and awe I feel every time I look up at the stars. I would like to express my deepest thanks to the scientists, astronauts, and all the other men and women who have worked over the years to understand and explore our universe. I'd particularly like to thank (and recommend!) the folks behind www.astronomycast.com, who provide a wealth of fascinating, inspiring, and accessible information about all sorts of topics related to astronomy.

Many thanks are also due to Karen Jordan Allen, R. J. Anderson, Geoff Bottone, Melissa Caruso, Megan Crewe, Erin Dionne, Robert Dunham, Megan Frazer, Robin Merrow MacCready, Patty Murray, Cindy Pon, Jon Skovron, and Luanne Wrenn for reading various versions of this manuscript and helping me to make it better.

I remain grateful to my agent Shawna McCarthy for being my advocate and adviser, and to my editor Reka Simonsen for her wise insights and attention to detail. Many thanks to everyone who helped produce this book, including Sarah Dotts Barley, Ana Deboo, Su Box, and the team at Harcourt.

And last but not least, I thank my wonderful, amazing family. Mom, Dad, Dave, and my beloved Bob, thank you for your support. You are my stars!

Biography Today

Profiles of People of Interest to Young Readers

Scientists & Inventors

Volume 11

Cherie D. Abbey
Managing Editor

Kevin Hillstrom
Editor

Omnigraphics

615 Griswold Street • Detroit, Michigan 48226

Omnigraphics, Inc.

Cherie D. Abbey, *Managing Editor*
Kevin Hillstrom, *Editor*

Peggy Daniels, Sheila Fitzgerald, Jeff Hill,
Diane Telgen, Rhoda Wilburn, and Tom Wiloch, *Sketch Writers*

Allison A. Beckett, Mary Butler, and Linda Strand, *Research Staff*

* * *

Peter E. Ruffner, *Publisher*
Frederick G. Ruffner, Jr., *Chairman*
Matthew P. Barbour, *Senior Vice President*
Kay Gill, *Vice President—Directories*

* * *

Elizabeth Barbour, *Research and Permissions Coordinator*
David P. Bianco, *Marketing Director*
Leif A. Gruenberg, *Development Manager*
Kevin Hayes, *Operations Manager*
Barry Puckett, *Librarian*
Cherry Stockdale, *Permissions Assistant*

Shirley Amore, Kevin Glover, Martha Johns,
Kirk Kauffman, and Angelesia Thorington, *Administrative Staff*

Contents

3

Preface

Welcome to the eleventh volume of the **Biography Today Scientists and Inventors** Series. We are publishing this series in response to suggestions from our readers, who want more coverage of more people in *Biography Today*. Several volumes, covering **Artists, Authors, Business Leaders, Performing Artists, Scientists and Inventors, Sports Figures, and World Leaders,** have appeared thus far in the Subject Series. Each of these hardcover volumes is 200 pages in length and covers approximately 10 individuals of interest to readers ages 9 and above. The length and format of the entries are like those found in the regular issues of *Biography Today*, but there is **no duplication** between the regular series and the special subject volumes.

The Plan of the Work

As with the regular issues of *Biography Today*, this special subject volume on **Scientists and Inventors** was especially created to appeal to young readers in a format they can enjoy reading and readily understand. Each volume contains alphabetically arranged sketches. Each entry provides at least one picture of the individual profiled, and bold-faced rubrics lead the reader to information on birth, youth, early memories, education, first jobs, marriage and family, career highlights, memorable experiences, hobbies, and honors and awards. Each of the entries ends with a list of easily accessible sources designed to lead the student to further reading on the individual and a current address. Obituary entries are also included, written to provide a perspective on the individual's entire career. Obituaries are clearly marked in both the table of contents and at the beginning of the entry.

Biographies are prepared by Omnigraphics editors after extensive research, utilizing the most current materials available. Those sources that are generally available to students appear in the list of further reading at the end of the sketch.

Indexes

Cumulative indexes are an important component of *Biography Today*. Each issue of the *Biography Today* Subject Series includes a **Cumulative General Index,** which comprises all individuals profiled in *Biography Today* since the series began in 1992. The names appear in bold faced type, followed by the issue in which they appeared. The Cumulative General Index also contains the occupations, nationalities, and ethnic and minority origins of individuals profiled. In addition, we compile three other indexes: Names Index, Places of Birth Index, and Birthday Index. These three indexes are featured on our web site, www.biographytoday.com. All *Biography Today* indexes are cumulative, including all individuals profiled in both are General Series and the Subject Series.

Our Advisors

This series was reviewed by an Advisory Board comprised of librarians, children's literature specialists, and reading instructors to ensure that the concept of this publication—to provide a readable and accessible biographical magazine for young readers—was on target. They evaluated the title as it developed, and their suggestions have proved invaluable. Any errors, however, are ours alone. We'd like to list the Advisory Board members, and to thank them for their efforts.

Gail Beaver
Adjunct Lecturer
University of Michigan
Ann Arbor, MI

Cindy Cares
Youth Services Librarian
Southfield Public Library
Southfield, MI

Carol A. Doll
School of Information Science and Policy
University of Albany, SUNY
Albany, NY

Kathleen Hayes-Parvin
Language Arts Teacher
Birney Middle School
Southfield, MI

Karen Imarisio
Assistant Head of Adult Services
Bloomfield Twp. Public Library
Bloomfield Hills, MI

Rosemary Orlando
Director
St. Clair Shores Public Library
St. Clair Shores, MI

Our Advisory Board stressed to us that we should not shy away from controversial or unconventional people in our profiles, and we have tried to follow their advice. The Advisory Board also mentioned that the sketches might be useful in reluctant reader and adult literacy programs, and we would value any comments librarians might have about the suitability of our magazine for those purposes.

Your Comments Are Welcome

Our goal is to be accurate and up-to-date, to give young readers information they can learn from and enjoy. Now we want to know what you think. Take a look at this issue of *Biography Today*, on approval. Write or call me with your comments. We want to provide an excellent source of biographical information for young people. Let us know how you think we're doing.

Cherie Abbey
Managing Editor, *Biography Today*
Omnigraphics, Inc.
615 Griswold Street
Detroit, MI 48226

editor@biographytoday.com
www.biographytoday.com

ASA Odor

George Aldrich 1955-
American Chemical Specialist
"Space Sniffer" for NASA

BIRTH

George Aldrich was born George Eugene Loveless on August
13, 1955, in Fort Benning, Georgia. At the time, his father,
Thomas Gene Loveless, was stationed there as a soldier; his
mother, Angeline (Burton) Loveless, had wanted to be with
her husband for their first child's birth. Thomas Loveless spent
his career working on electrical and electronics systems for
military and government airplanes. (These planes included Air
Force One and Two, which serve the President and Vice-Presi-
dent of the United States.) The family, which grew to include
George's two younger siblings, Debi and Thomas, soon moved

to Oklahoma and then Colorado. When George was seven, his parents divorced.

In 1964, George's mother married Marv Aldrich, who worked in engine and materials testing for the National Aeronautics and Space Administration (NASA). Aldrich adopted George and his two siblings, giving them his surname. Angeline Aldrich kept busy as a homemaker as she and her new husband added two more siblings to the family, George's half-sisters Jamie and Kelly. Thomas Loveless also remarried and had more children. Although George did not live with his biological father's family, he gained a stepsister, Leona, and three more half-siblings: Dodi, Greg, and Pam.

YOUTH

After his mother's marriage to Marv Aldrich, the family moved in 1964 to Las Cruces, New Mexico. There his new father worked for NASA's White Sands Test Facility, a branch of the Johnson Space Center. George grew up enjoying the wide-open spaces of the New Mexico outdoors. The senior Aldrich took him fishing, hunting, and hiking, hobbies Aldrich would also pursue as an adult—he has owned his own hunting weapons since the age of 19.

Although he was tall and enjoyed playing basketball in elementary school, Aldrich didn't consider himself very athletic. As he entered high school he bypassed sports teams in favor of schoolwork and after-school jobs. He worked at a Safeway grocery store all through high school. When he was younger, he had caught the eye of the store's manager while doing odd jobs around the trailer park where he and his family lived. His work ethic impressed the man, who told him there was a job waiting for him as soon as he turned 16.

EDUCATION

Aldrich was a reliable worker in school as well. He considered himself "an average to above-average student," depending on the class. His favorite subjects were math and science, especially chemistry. "I liked math and science," he explained, "so I took as many of those classes in high school as I could." But at that point he had no specific plans for his future career. As a youth, Aldrich considered working as a heavy equipment hauler—he could "sit for hours" watching the front-end loaders move dirt into flooded areas of his family's trailer park during the rainy season. Civil engineering also appealed to him, but he would have needed a college education to enter that field. In any case, he had no clue that he had a special ability to detect scents—an ability that would bring him recognition and notoriety in the future. "I never noticed I had a good sniffer," he said. "I thought I would be a heavy equipment hauler, civil engineer, or helicopter pilot."

Aldrich graduated in 1973 from Mayfield High School in Las Cruces, New Mexico. He did not continue on to college at that point, but since then he has taken occasional college courses and classes in real estate.

MARRIAGE AND FAMILY

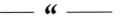

Aldrich first met his wife, Pam Heath, at church when he was in the tenth grade and she was in the ninth. The high-school sweethearts married on September 6, 1974. They have three daughters: Shawna Jean, Amanda Renee, and Jennifer Lee Ann. Pam Aldrich is a homemaker who frequently looks after the couple's five grandchildren.

"I never noticed I had a good sniffer," Aldrich said. "I thought I would be a heavy equipment hauler, civil engineer, or helicopter pilot."

CAREER HIGHLIGHTS

Climbing the NASA Career Ladder

Coming out of high school in 1973, Aldrich looked for a full-time job, and his adoptive father helped him with his search. Marv Aldrich still worked at NASA's White Sands Test Facility (WSTF) as a steam generator operator, helping simulate the conditions of space to test materials and engines for NASA rockets and vehicles. In November 1973 he alerted his son to a temporary position at the facility performing odd jobs. Aldrich got the job, and within three months he obtained a full-time position as a firefighter and guard. In 1975 he moved from the fire department into warehouse work, hoping he could eventually work his way into the testing labs at WSTF. In 1978, aided by his strong background in chemistry and good work ethic, he finally won a position as a technician in the toxicity and odor testing labs.

Aldrich has spent most of his NASA career in the toxicity testing labs, running instruments that perform chemical analyses on spacecraft components. In any enclosed, unventilated area, such as a spacecraft—or even a car with rolled-up windows—an object can heat up and give off gases. This process is called "outgassing." Some of these gases can be dangerously flammable or poisonous. The labs at White Sands test everything that goes into space for these potential hazards. They begin with an instrument called a gas chromotograph (GC). The GC separates a complex gas mixture into individual compounds by passing it through a barrier called a column. After isolating compounds with the GC, the lab can run a variety of chemical analyses on their samples.

One type of chemical analysis uses the flame ionization detector (FID), which detects specific chemicals by burning a sample with a hydrogen and

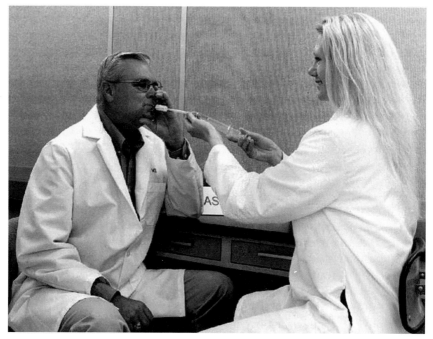

Working on the Odor Panel, testing for toxic chemicals in the lab at NASA.

air flame. Any hydrocarbons in the sample will burn and give off ions (an atom or molecule with an electrical charge). The GC/FID instrument can detect these ions and thus measure the amounts of carbon monoxide (a poison gas) and methane (a combustible gas), or the total amount of organic (carbon-containing) compounds. Using these measurements to determine how flammable a sample is can prevent fire, which is a big concern in a spacecraft. In 1967, for instance, NASA's Apollo 1 mission ended in tragedy when the capsule caught fire during a launch pad test. Astronauts Virgil "Gus" Grissom, Edward White, and Roger Chaffee all perished before rescue teams could reach them. The GC/FID is crucial in NASA's efforts to detect and avoid materials that could catch fire easily.

Equally important is detecting and avoiding any materials that could prove toxic when enclosed in a space capsule. To help analyze the chemical compounds in a sample, Aldrich can run the GC with a mass spectrometer detector (MSD). Once the GC separates a sample, the MSD uses magnetic fields to determine the mass of these different compounds. Because chemists know the mass of different chemicals, a mass spectrometer can identify simple but potentially dangerous compounds. These include formaldehyde, an irritant and potential cancer-causing agent in higher concentrations; acrolein and phosgene, both used as a chemical weapons in World War I; perfluoroiso-butylene, a lung irritant Aldrich calls "one of the nastiest compounds known to man"; and various poisonous or irritating sulfur compounds. Another instrument, the infrared detector (IRD), can identify and quantify ammonia, a flammable gas that can irritate the eyes and respiratory system.

Aldrich has worked in other positions at NASA's White Sands facility. In 1981 he was promoted into the self-contained atmospheric protective ensemble (SCAPE) unit. A SCAPE is an enclosed suit that has its own air supply, held in liquid form in a backpack. Astronauts wear a SCAPE while entering a spaceship because of the potential danger from the rocket's flammable fuels, particularly liquid hydrogen. Technicians servicing the rockets will also wear a SCAPE for protection against these fuels. Because the suits are bulky, the wearers cannot seal the suit unassisted. Aldrich's job during his four years with the SCAPE unit was to assist wearers in donning the suit and to monitor them during operations. He also helped maintain the suits, checking for pinhole leaks and repairing or replacing worn out parts.

> An awful stink "may not make an astronaut sick, but it's distracting if there's a bad odor floating around," Aldrich explained. After all, in space an astronaut "can't just roll down the window" to clear the air.

In 1985 Aldrich returned to the toxicity labs, but in 1988 he moved to the test stands section of WSTF. This is the area where scientists simulate the vacuum of space in order to test engine performance. Aldrich's father Marv worked in this section; during the 1960s, the facility tested all of NASA's engines, except for the huge Saturn rockets that powered the Apollo missions to the moon. Although the younger Aldrich didn't work directly with his father in this section, he also supported engine testing and firing during his three years there. In 1991 he returned once again to the toxicity labs. By 1998 he had achieved the center's highest rank for a technician, Chemical Specialist; he continues contributing to America's space program by preparing and testing samples for chemical analysis in the Molecular Desorption and Analysis Laboratory. The efforts of his lab help keep astronauts safe in space.

In addition, Aldrich spent 20 years as an auxiliary (volunteer) fireman at the White Sands Testing Facility. During the last five of those years he was part of the Hazardous Materials (Hazmat) Team, trained to clean up dangerous material spills wearing a suit with a self-contained breathing atmosphere. "It was a great experience for me to have training with fighting fires, rescue, Hazmat, CPR, and so many numerous things," he commented.

Working on the Odor Panel

It is Aldrich's other position at NASA that has brought him the most attention, however. He had no sooner joined the fire department at White Sands than his boss informed him of the existence of the NASA "Odor Panel." This all-volunteer group is responsible for sampling the scent of every single object that goes into space for NASA. It is a relatively simple matter to use chemical analysis to identify hazardous compounds that could endanger the astronauts. Detecting unpleasant smells, however, takes a keen human nose. In 1974 Aldrich qualified for the panel by passing a physical (volunteers must be free of allergies and sinus trouble) and earning a perfect score on the nose certification test. Over the next 30-plus years, he has continued to identify correctly all 10 of the sample scents used to "certify" his nose three times a year.

Testing the smells produced by outgassing can be as important for the astronauts' health as testing for toxic chemicals. For instance, after the Apollo 13 mission in 1970 narrowly avoided disaster following an oxygen tank explosion, the flight plans for the next Apollo missions were rewritten. "But they were printed with a different ink," Aldrich related. "Those manuals stank so badly that all the judges got blisters in their noses. They had to reprint the thing with a different ink. It almost delayed Apollo 14." Space programs in other countries (except for Japan) do not test for odors, which can lead to problems. In 1976, Soviet cosmonauts on the Soyuz-21 mission had planned to spend two months on the Salyut-5 space platform. They were forced to return to Earth ahead of schedule because of an unpleasant, acrid odor of unknown origin. Even if an obnoxious smell doesn't produce any physical side effects, it is still important to detect it before it goes into space. An awful stink "may not make an astronaut sick," Aldrich noted, "but it's distracting if there's a bad odor floating around." After all, in space an astronaut "can't just roll down the window" to clear the air.

Aldrich and the team at the toxicity labs first prepare samples by putting an object in a test can, sealing it, and then pumping in purified air. The sample is baked for three days in an oven at 120°F. Then the sample is run through chemical analysis and checked for flammability and toxic compounds. Only after it is certified non-toxic does it go before the Odor Panel. There five judges are given gaseous samples to smell through a breath mask. They rate things on a scale of zero (no scent) to four (offensive). Anything that averages higher than 2.4 gets rejected—and anything can be tested. The "nasal-nauts" check such ship components and tools as circuit boards, wires, epoxy glues, and paints. (One refrigerator flunked the test—it had been used to store urine samples.) They clear clothing and personal hygiene items, from tennis shoes and socks to shaving cream, cologne, make-up, tampons (deodorized and non-deodorized), and the adult diapers used on space walks. Any personal items that the astronauts might wish to take into space also must pass the Odor Panel, whether a guitar, a stuffed toy, or a photo album.

The Odor Panel's work continues to be important as NASA contributes to the International Space Station (ISS), which several countries help build and maintain. A potential problem occurred on the ISS in 2000, after time constraints meant some items had been tested for toxicity but not odor. On this mission, the astronauts began to energize a previously unused part of the station and started by stowing several bags of supplies. Unfortunately, they discovered a "funky, putrid smell," similar to that of a cut onion, coming from the Velcro straps used for stowage. The astronauts quickly put away the straps and were able to continue with the mission, but a more crucial item could have presented a serious problem. Thus Aldrich's work is critical to the success of NASA missions in space and also to the U.S. Navy's missions underwater: he also contributes to similar tests carried out for the Navy's submarines and other underwater facilities.

"I don't have a great sense of smell," Aldrich remarked, "but I don't have allergies likes some people do, so perhaps I can smell more clearly than the average person."

Receiving Recognition as a "Super Sniffer"

NASA astronauts appreciate the years Aldrich has devoted to the Odor Panel and his job at White Sands. In 2004, he received the prestigious "Silver Snoopy Award," a recognition of outstanding performance in contributing to flight safety and mission success. One of NASA's astronauts presented him with a Silver Snoopy pin that actually flew into space, on the shuttle *Columbia* in 1998. The award acknowledged Aldrich's efforts working in the toxicity labs, as well as his years volunteering for the Odor Panel.

Since 2000, Aldrich has also used his super sniffer in the service of the National Rotten Sneaker Contest, sponsored by the manufacturer Odor-Eaters. He began by volunteering as a judge for a local contest at the White Sands Missile Range, rating each contestant on the scent of their shoes. He was then offered a position judging in the national contest, which is held each year in Montpelier, Vermont. Billed as the contest's "Master Sniffer," Aldrich gives each sneaker a score from 1 (awful) to 5 (new sneaker). "This contest is a huge shock to my sense of smell," he noted. "I'm usually still smelling them several hours after it's over."

Judging the stinky sneakers in the Odor-Eaters contest requires a lot of stamina.

His unusual job and his participation in Odor-Eaters' national contest have brought Aldrich a measure of media fame. He has been profiled in national and international magazines and has been interviewed by television journalists from as far away as Liverpool, England, and Sydney, Australia. He has appeared on talk shows, including "The Caroline Rhea Show," and on such game shows as "I've Got a Secret" and "To Tell the Truth." Aldrich remains modest about his nasal abilities, however. "I don't have a great sense of smell," he remarked, "but I don't have allergies likes some people do, so perhaps I can smell more clearly than the average person." He is sensitive to odors in public, so his favorite scents are those that are clean and fresh: New Mexico's mountains after a rain, or the smell of pine needles. His least favorite scents are strong perfumes, the smell of newly laid tar, and the odors coming from chicken farms and dairies near his New Mexico home. "Luckily, I have a strong stomach," he noted.

His unusual volunteer work has brought him notoriety, which has been fun. But for Aldrich, the most important thing is helping NASA send astronauts safely into space. He witnessed a Space Shuttle landing in March 1982, when *Columbia* landed at White Sands because of wet conditions at California's Edwards Air Force Base, where it had been scheduled to land. "Hearing the sonic boom as it re-entered the atmosphere was one of the high points of my job," he said. The low point, he recalled, was the tragic loss of *Columbia* 21 years later when it disintegrated upon re-entry, killing all seven crew members aboard. Striving for safety is the reason behind his work as a "nasalnaut." "Astronauts are heroes," Aldrich noted, and if his efforts help keep them safe, "it kind of makes you proud."

HOBBIES AND OTHER INTERESTS

Aldrich enjoys spending time outdoors. Although he can't be as active as he was before undergoing heart surgery in 2004, he can still take walks of four or five miles. His outdoor activities also include occasional bird hunting trips. He has made speeches in local schools about the importance of studying science, and he is writing a book about his life as a Super Sniffer.

FURTHER READING

Periodicals

Baltimore Sun, Nov. 27, 2003, p.A2
El Paso Times, Nov. 26, 2000, "Borderland" section, p.1
New Scientist, June 30, 2001, p.44
Scientific American, June 2001, p.106
Wired, Mar. 2004, p.106

Online Articles

http://www.nasaexplores.com (NASA Explores, "The Nose Knows," Aug. 12, 2002)
http://spaceflight.nasa.gov/shuttle/support/people/galdrich.html (National Aeronautics and Space Administration, "Behind the Scenes: Meet the People," Apr. 2003)
http://www.hq.nasa.gov/osf/sfa/snoopy.html (NASA Spaceflight Awareness, "Silver Snoopy Award," 2005)
http://www.odoreaters.com/rsc.shtml (OdorEaters, "Rotten Sneaker Contest," 2004)

Other

Information for this profile was also taken from a phone interview with *Biography Today* conducted on Aug. 9, 2005.

ADDRESS

George Aldrich
NASA–White Sands Test Facility
12600 NASA Road
Las Cruces, NM 88012

WORLD WIDE WEB SITES

http://www.wstf.nasa.gov

Paul Farmer Jr. 1959-
American Doctor and Medical Anthropologist
Advocate for Health Care and Social Justice for the
Poor
World Leader in the Treatment of Tuberculosis and
Other Infectious Diseases

BIRTH

Paul Edward Farmer Jr. was born on October 26, 1959, in
North Adams, Massachusetts. (His nicknames are "P.J.," for
Paul Junior, and Pel.) He is the second of six children of Paul
Edward Farmer Sr. and Ginny (Rice) Farmer. His father was
an on-again, off-again teacher and salesman. His mother was
a grocery store cashier. After the children were grown, Ginny

Farmer earned a literature degree at Smith College in Massachusetts and became a college librarian. Farmer has an older sister named Katy and four younger siblings: sisters Peggy and Jennifer and brothers Jim and Jeff. Jeff is a professional wrestler known as "Sting" or "Super J." who likes to hoist Farmer above his head.

YOUTH

Farmer had an unconventional upbringing that helped him learn flexibility and compassion for people outside the mainstream of society. Farmer's father was so strict that his children called him "The Warden." Yet he also had a restless and adventurous spirit that inspired him to move his family into a converted bus, and later onto a boat. "His dream was to live on an island and have the children around him in a compound setting," Farmer's mother said. "So we did have some very strange adventures."

When Farmer was about seven years old, his father moved the family from western Massachusetts to Birmingham, Alabama. His father planned to get a high-paying sales job, but he eventually had to settle for a modest teaching position. Even as a young boy, Farmer was clearly intelligent, and the local school authorities enrolled him in a class for gifted children. As a fourth grader, he started a club devoted to herpetology (the study of reptiles and amphibians). He made detailed charcoal drawings of the animals and prepared lecture notes on their diets and characteristics.

Farmer was raised as a Roman Catholic, and his family went to church every Sunday. But he preferred to find out about right and wrong in books. One of his favorite works was *The Lord of the Rings* trilogy by English author J.R.R. Tolkien. At age 11, Farmer read all three books in a couple of days, and then read them all again. He then read *War and Peace*, a long, complex novel about good and evil by the 19th-century Russian author Leo Tolstoy. It's a difficult book, one that would be challenging for many adults, let alone an 11-year-old boy. But Farmer loved it.

In 1971, the family packed into their converted bus and moved to Brooksville, Florida, on the west coast of the state, near Tampa. Paul Sr. hoped to move them into one of the pretty local houses. But instead, the family spent five years living at a trailer park in their cramped bus. In a raised part of the bus's roof, he built a stack of three bunk beds, with Farmer's bed on top. Farmer would lie on his bunk to read or do his homework—while down below his brother Jeff practiced the drums, and his four other siblings got on noisily with their activities.

When Farmer was about 14, his father bought a damaged, 55-foot-long wooden-hulled boat that he named *Lady Gin*, after his wife. He planned to take a year off from his paying job to renovate it. The renovation took three years. But eventually the Farmers moved out of their bus and onto the *Lady Gin*, which they docked in a marshy, wildlife-rich inlet called Jenkins Creek.

Farmer loved the seclusion of the new surroundings and the many birds and animals that lived there, including osprey, otters, and alligators. But in some ways, life was harder than ever. The *Lady Gin* had no plumbing. The family had to fetch water from a tap miles away, wash clothes at a laundromat, and bathe in the creek, summer and winter. Money was scarce. Their mother brought home discounted, damaged canned goods from the Winn-Dixie grocery store where she worked. Their main meal frequently was soup made of baked beans and hot dogs. Farmer said he never felt underprivileged growing up. But he noted, "It *was* pretty strange."

> "My parents clearly believed in helping the underdog," Farmer said. "My dad, especially, was forever keeping an eye on the elderly, on the mentally challenged,... or on just about anyone who needed a hand. My mother, of course, was keeping an eye on my dad, who needed a lot of tending, and on her six young kids."

The Farmer children often saw their parents helping people whom they referred to as the "*truly* poor." "My parents clearly believed in helping the underdog," Farmer said. "My father was always collecting lost causes and wounded types. My mom is the same way." He remembered them being engaged in "the quiet activism of the trailer parks: my dad, especially, was forever keeping an eye on the elderly, on the mentally challenged, . . . or on just about anyone who needed a hand," he said. "My mother, of course, was keeping an eye on my dad, who needed a lot of tending, and on her six young kids."

Besides compassion, education was a key value in the household. The Farmers required their children to read for two hours each day. "No matter how small an area we lived in, we always had bookcases with classics. It wasn't junk. We had good literature," recalled Farmer's youngest sister, Jennifer.

EDUCATION

High School

At Hernando High School, in Brooksville, Florida, Farmer was known for being smart and funny. His intelligence was striking: he received "A" grades on papers he wrote during his lunch hour. In a televised high-school quiz show, he hit his buzzer before he knew an answer, because he was sure he could think of it. Farmer had a mischievous side as well. For example, he loved to organize elaborate food fights. When he was asked to set up the school Christmas tree, he displayed it upside down. Besides that, he was unusually sensitive to people of all ages. A friend remembered that he would always take time to chat with his bed-ridden mother. "And it was out of deep concern," Sam Griffin said. "It wasn't like he was trying to make points." He was elected "most popular" senior and class president, and was the valedictorian of his class of 1978, an honor given to the top student.

College

Farmer won a full scholarship to Duke University in Durham, North Carolina. There he became interested in medical anthropology. This field takes elements of anthropology—the study of the environment, social relations, and the culture of a group of human beings—and applies it to everything that affects health and illness in that society. For example, a medical anthropologist might look at how a society's religious beliefs influence the diagnosis or treatment of an illness, or how local transportation affects a community's medical systems. "As strange as it seems now, I have to say I just loved the topic," Farmer recalled. "I loved the readings, the suggested research (I volunteered in a big emergency room), the faculty, the broad view. By the time I was 21, I was dead sure I wanted to be a doctor and an anthropologist. Where that surety came from is now a mystery, but there's no doubt it was there." Farmer received his bachelor's degree in anthropology from Duke in 1982.

During college, Farmer was influenced by the work of Rudolf Virchow, a 19th-century German doctor and anthropologist. Virchow believed that social problems, like dirty water or poor nutrition, went hand in hand with disease. Farmer was powerfully drawn to Virchow's philosophy that it was the doctor's job to cure both. Farmer was also influenced by liberation theology. This is a branch of the Roman Catholic religion that was established in Latin America in the 1960s. Liberation theologists declared that the oppression of the world's poor was no less than "institutionalized sin." They called on the Catholic Church to provide a "preferential option for the poor." This moral stance—put poor people first—has guided much of Farmer's work. In recent years, he said that the Catholicism of his boyhood had little impact on him. "But emotionally and intellectually, liberation theology has been, well, a Godsend," he said, "a resource for living and thinking and writing."

Farmer found a focal point for his ideas and his academic interests in Haiti (*see* sidebar on Haiti). He began to learn about the country after meeting a

21

Belgian nun who helped Haitian emigrant farm workers in North Carolina. Farmer became fascinated by the Haitians, their rich culture, their tragic history, and their native language, Creole, which he learned to speak fluently on his first trip to the country. He wondered how circumstances in Haiti could be so bad as to force Haitians to work under horrible conditions for low wages in the United States. He set out to learn everything he could about the country.

——— " ———

"I have to say I just loved the topic," Farmer said about studying medical anthropology. *"I loved the readings, the suggested research (I volunteered in a big emergency room), the faculty, the broad view. By the time I was 21, I was dead sure I wanted to be a doctor and an anthropologist."*

——— " ———

Graduate School

After he graduated from college in 1982, Farmer went to live in Haiti for a year. He worked as a volunteer in eye clinics serving poor people. Working in Haiti and helping the sick and desperately impoverished people there was "an area of moral clarity," he said.

In 1984 Farmer entered Harvard University in Cambridge, Massachusetts, to study medicine and anthropology. But he continued to visit Haiti. He worked there much of the time he was in school, returning to Cambridge mainly for lectures and exams. He was away from campus so often, his fellow students called him "Paul Foreigner." But he still earned excellent grades. In 1990, Farmer received two graduate-school degrees at the same time: his medical degree (MD) and a doctorate (PhD) in anthropology.

Farmer is a dedicated academic. But he makes it clear that the experience of life in Haiti was his best teacher. "I would read stuff from scholarly texts and know they were wrong," he said. "Living in Haiti, I realized that a minor error in one setting of power and privilege could have an enormous impact on the poor in another." He cites as an example a large dam that international development agencies built in 1956 in central Haiti. It was designed to supply electrical power to the far-away capital, Port-au-Prince. It may have boosted the city. But the flooding drove local poor families in the village of Cange (pronounced "Cahnj") from their homes. They were forced to live as squatters on dry, unusable soil. Farmer chose Cange, among the poorest of Haiti's deprived villages, as the center of his work.

Haiti

Location and History

- Haiti lies on an island called Hispaniola in the Caribbean Sea, about 700 miles south of Miami, Florida. The eastern half of Hispaniola is occupied by the Dominican Republic, a separate country.
- Haiti began as a French slave colony in the 1700s. A third of the slaves transported from Africa died within a few years of arrival.
- In 1791, the slaves in Haiti revolted against the French. In 1804, they won. Haiti became the only nation ever born of a slave revolt.
- Since 1804, Haiti has suffered recurring political upheavals and difficulties, including dictatorships, military-backed governments, and controversial intervention by foreign governments, particularly France and the United States.

Conditions Today

- Haiti is the poorest country in the western hemisphere.
- The official unemployment rate is 70 percent.
- Very few Haitian households have electricity.
- Fewer than half of Haitian adults can read.
- Average life expectancy for Haitians is only about 50 years.
- A quarter of Haitian adults die before age 40.
- Half of all deaths in Haiti are of children five years old or younger.

CAREER HIGHLIGHTS

Over the past 20 years, Farmer has worked around the world as a health-care provider and advocate for the poor. His philosophy is simple: "The well should take care of the sick." His medical specialty is infectious disease, including HIV/AIDS. He is a world authority on treating and controlling tuberculosis (*see* sidebar on infectious diseases). "It's a human-rights issue that people are dying of these readily treatable illnesses," Farmer said. Health officials are skeptical that modern health care—especially complicated courses of medication—can be delivered in wretched conditions. Through the example of his work in Haiti, Farmer has shown that it can be done. In fact, he has demonstrated that improving living conditions of the poor must be a responsibility of the health-care givers. His writing and campaigning have helped to lift the standard of health care for poor people all over the world.

Bringing Free Health Care to Cange

Farmer's year of volunteer work in Haiti in 1983–84 taught him that poor people there couldn't get medical treatment. There was only one doctor for every 20,000 people. Yet hospital beds were often empty, because people couldn't pay. Disease and death were everywhere. Farmer was haunted by patients like a pregnant young woman who died when her sister couldn't raise the money for a blood transfusion. Her five young children were left orphans.

Influenced by the ideals of liberation theology, Farmer decided to bring free health care to the poor of Cange. He teamed up with Fritz and Yolande Lafontant, who had provided schooling and other help for the village's displaced people since the 1970s. They also had the support of Ophelia Dahl, an 18-year-old volunteer from England. She had come to Haiti at the urging of her father, Roald Dahl, the author of *Charlie and the Chocolate Factory* and other classic children's books. She and Farmer formed a close friendship and a budding romance. Together with the Lafontants, they established a health project based in the community. They saw it as a springboard to help close the gap of "inequality to access" in Haiti. For them, the term 'access' meant access to health care, education, clean water, and whatever else people needed.

Farmer first set out to discover the needs of local people. He employed Haitians to help him go from hut to hut, noting information about the occupants, including recent births, deaths, and illnesses. Key measurements, like the number of deaths among babies, were even worse than Farmer expected. It was obvious that Cange's biggest health problem was the lack of food and safe water. "Half or more of the patients that . . . we see in clinic are patients who really are sick because they don't have enough to eat, or clean water to drink," Farmer said.

Foreign supporters helped to pipe in safe water. Next, they provided for sanitary latrines in the village. Meanwhile, the team built a clinic called Clinique Bon Sauveur. They trained local people as health workers to travel to villages to help people with their medication. A mobile unit was acquired to screen people in surrounding villages for preventable illnesses.

Farmer quickly became known as a kind, tireless friend to the hundreds of poor people who lined up at the clinic for care. This work in Cange was described in an acclaimed biography, *Mountains Beyond Mountains: The Quest of Dr. Paul Farmer, a Man Who Would Cure the World*, by Tracy Kidder. Kidder described the doctor's warm rapport with his patients and his sense of humor: "He has [patients] sit in a chair right next to his, so that, I figure, he can get his thin, white, long-fingered hands on them. He calls the older women 'Mother,' the older men 'Father.' Many bring him presents. Milk in a green bottle with a corncob stopper. . . . 'Thank you, thank you!' Farmer says [in Creole]. He smiles and, staring at the bottle on his desk, says in English, 'Unpasteurized cow's milk in a dirty bottle. I can't wait to drink it.' He turns to me. 'It's so awful you might as well be cheerful.'"

At the clinic, Farmer was busy seeing patients from sunrise until after dark. Yet it was not uncommon for him to walk hours over rough, hilly trails to attend personally to a needy patient—a practice he still maintains. When asked why he spends his valuable time this way, he answered, "I do it because it's my favorite part of the work, the clinical work and visiting patients in their homes. Really, they're not homes, they're huts. . . . [We] get some of our best ideas by walking the long way and thinking about what our patients must be going through."

——— *"* ———

Establishing Partners in Health

Farmer relied on a small group of supporters to fund the Cange project. In 1985, he met Thomas White, a wealthy construction-company owner from Boston. White was looking for a project worthy of the fortune he wanted to give away. After visiting Cange, White began to donate heavily to the project, giving more than $30 million to date. Two years later, he helped Farmer es-

"The well should take care of the sick," Farmer once said. "It's a human-rights issue that people are dying of these readily treatable illnesses."

——— *"* ———

tablish Partners in Health (PIH), a public U.S. charity that would support work in Haiti and elsewhere. Partners in Health would have a Haitian sister organization called Zanmi Lasante ("Partners in Health" in Creole). Also among the charity's founding members and board of directors were Dahl, businessman Todd McCormack, and Jim Yong Kim, a Korean-American medical-school classmate of Farmer, who shared his ideals and passion for healing. In addition to their initial primary work in Haiti, PIH also funded small health initiatives in poor sections of Boston and in Mexico.

Community-Based Treatment for TB and HIV

From the start, Farmer and his colleagues set out to deal with of one of the most common and deadly diseases in Cange: tuberculosis (TB). Treatment required drugs that were too expensive for most Haitians. The team found a way to provide them for free. At one point, they simply "borrowed" needed drugs—about $92,000 worth—from the Boston hospital where Farmer studied. (His benefactors always paid back what he borrowed.)

Farmer with an AIDS patient and a nurse during a home visit.

Another challenge was getting the Haitians to follow the course of medication prescribed. "Directly observed therapy" became an important part of Farmer's strategy. It meant that community health workers were paid to visit patients at home, to watch and make sure they took the right medicines at the right time. If patients didn't show up for appointments, someone went to find them. Importantly, each patient also got a small amount of money each month. This helped provide vital extras like a bit more food, childcare, or transportation to doctor's appointments. From the time Farmer's team started treating patients for TB, they didn't lose a single one.

Farmer and Partners in Health applied community-based treatment when treatment became available for HIV/AIDS (*see* sidebar on infectious diseases). The drugs to control AIDS—a group of medicines often referred to as a "cocktail"—are very expensive. Farmer and his team worked to reduce the cost of treatment from about $10,000 per patient in the United States to $1,500 per patient in Haiti. PIH hopes to reduce the cost even further. Meanwhile, counseling and testing, especially of expectant mothers, helps to prevent the spread of HIV/AIDS.

The disease is still a major public-health problem in Haiti. But today the country's AIDS epidemic is on the decline. Over 10 years, the rate of mother-to-baby transmission of HIV fell from 22 percent to four percent.

HIV screening happens seven times as often. Over almost 20 years, condom use increased from zero in the mid-80s to 15 million in 2003.

The medical world took notice when Farmer and his team got better results treating HIV/AIDS than many inner-city hospitals in the United States. "We don't need big infrastructures to treat AIDS or tuberculosis for that matter, or drug-resistant malaria," Farmer said. "What we need are the medicines, and the community health workers, and to make sure that the community health workers are paid at least a modest stipend so that they can do this job and not another job, such as planting corn or millet for their family to eat."

Partners in Health's pioneering approach to treatment of AIDS and other infectious diseases helped Haiti qualify in 2002 for money from the Global Fund to Fight AIDS, Tuberculosis, and Malaria. Because of the award, Zanmi Lasane has been able to expand treatment to nearby communities, caring for hundreds of thousands of peasant farmers in the central plateau. In 2004, PIH served almost a million patients in Haiti. They also helped to provide school tuition, clean water, homes, and jobs for patients and their families.

"Half or more of the patients that we see in clinic [in Haiti] are patients who really are sick because they don't have enough to eat, or clean water to drink," Farmer said.

The clinic in Sange, Clinique Bon Sauveur, began as a one-building facility. It now includes a hospital of more than 100 beds, an infirmary, a surgery wing, a training program for health outreach workers, a primary school, and a special facility for children's health-care. In 2002, PIH opened a new clinic in the town of Lascahobas. That same year, the Bon Sauveur hospital conducted its first open-heart surgery. Farmer said, "Well, we've worked with our friends in Haiti to establish nothing short of a modern medical center in one of the poorest parts of that country. It works!"

Treating TB in Peru, Russia, and Africa

Beginning in 1994, Partners in Health applied their community-based treatment method to reduce Multidrug Resistant Tuberculosis (MDR-TB), a form of the disease that resists many TB drugs. At the time, many experts, including those at the World Health Organization (WHO), said that if poor people in the developing world got this form of TB, most would die.

Infectious Diseases in the Developing World

Paul Farmer specializes in infectious diseases—diseases that can easily be passed from one person to another. These diseases thrive in crowded, unsanitary conditions typical of the developing world. Several infectious diseases are of greatest concern to public health officials:

Tuberculosis (TB)

TB spreads when an infected person sneezes, coughs, or spits. Infected particles are released into the air to be breathed in by others. TB most often affects the lungs, eventually destroying them, but can attack almost any organ of the body. About nine million people, mainly in the developing world, come down each year with the disease. It is preventable and usually treatable with antibiotics. In developed countries like the United States, it rarely occurs.

Multidrug-Resistant Tuberculosis (MDR-TB)

MDR-TB occurs when TB bacteria develop resistance to drugs. The resistance can build up when a TB patient is treated with only one antibiotic, or too-small doses of several antibiotics. In the worst cases, the TB bacteria grow strong enough to resist even the most powerful drugs. MDR-TB patients usually require a variety of drugs, tailored to their needs, and a lengthy course of treatment. Such specialized care is often expensive and difficult to deliver. Until the late 1990s, when PIH challenged them, world health officials considered it virtually impossible to attempt MDR-TB treatment for poor people in the developing world.

HIV/AIDS

These initials stand for "human immunodeficiency virus" and "acquired immune deficiency syndrome." The HIV virus causes the disease AIDS, which attacks the body's immune system and destroys its ability to fight off infections. It can pass from person to person through bodily fluids like blood and semen. It is most often transmitted between sexual partners or drug users sharing needles. By the end of 2002, it was estimated, 42 million people were infected with HIV worldwide, the vast majority in developing countries. Some 25 million people have died from AIDS. AIDS can be managed by such drugs as protease inhibitors. But, as is the case with MDR-TB, treatment is expensive and often complex. PIH and others are working to deliver appropriate treatment to the many poor people who need it.

According to conventional beliefs, the medications would cost too much and the treatment would be too complicated.

To disprove them, Farmer, Kim, and their PIH colleagues went to a shantytown near Lima, Peru, in South America. Locals were skeptical—what could Farmer, an American "gringo," know about TB when it barely existed in his country? "He *looks* like a gringo," a health official replied. "But he's a fake gringo." PIH devised a program where each patient had a drug therapy tailored to his or her needs. Community members were trained to deliver the drugs—as many as seven antibiotics—to the patients' homes. Often the therapies lasted for a longer period than conventional treatment. After a two-year course of treatment, 100 people were cured.

As a result of the program, WHO began to reconsider its policy on treatment of this form of TB. In 1999, it appointed Farmer and Kim to set up further community-based treatment programs for drug-resistant TB as part of an international response. (Farmer declined any salary for the post.) A year later, the Bill and Melinda Gates Foundation gave almost $45 million to PIH and Harvard Medical School to research and treat TB in Peru, Haiti, and the former Soviet Union (with a focus on prisoners in that region). Some patients also needed HIV treatment along with TB therapy, which the team provided. Increasingly in recent years, Farmer is involved with international groups that work on solving the problems of AIDS and tuberculosis.

———— " ————

"We don't need big infrastructures to treat AIDS or tuberculosis for that matter, or drug-resistant malaria," Farmer said. "What we need are the medicines, and the community health workers, and to make sure that the community health workers are paid at least a modest stipend so that they can do this job and not another job, such as planting corn or millet for their family to eat."

———— " ————

In 2005 Farmer and PIH gained the support of former President Bill Clinton's charitable foundation, which enabled them to take their health strategy to eastern Rwanda in Africa. About half a million Rwandans suffer from HIV. The team, including workers from Haiti, traveled to Rwanda in order to establish health models that can be used in the rest of Africa and in Asia. "It seems to me that making strategic alliances across national borders in order to treat HIV among the world's poor is one of the last great hopes of solidarity across a widening divide," Farmer said.

Farmer with Dr. Howard Hiatt and a 104-year-old patient in Haiti.

Reaching a Wider Audience

In addition to his work with Partners in Health, Farmer has important affiliations in the United States. These help him spread his message to key audiences, as well as exchange information and share resources. He holds two positions at Brigham and Women's Hospital in Boston: attending physician in infectious diseases and chief of the division of Social Medicine and Health Inequalities. At Harvard Medical School he is the Presley Professor of Medical Anthropology. He also directs Harvard's Program in Infectious Disease and Social Change.

Farmer has written or co-written more than 100 scholarly books or articles. He often explores how poverty affects the treatment and cure of easily controlled diseases. In his writing and speaking, he also has been an advocate of justice for Haiti. In particular, he criticizes governmental policies from the U.S. and other countries that have withheld much-needed aid from the country. Farmer says that all his work—writing, clinical, advocating, and charity—grows from what he learned in Haiti: that poverty, inequality, and political turmoil always lead to inferior medical care and lower cure rates for those who most need help.

Paul Farmer is known to a much wider audience since the publication of his biography by the renowned author Tracy Kidder. *Mountains Beyond Mountains: The Quest of Dr. Paul Farmer, a Man Who Would Cure the*

World appeared to much praise in 2003. While the book gained supporters for him and for PIH, Farmer seemed embarrassed by the personal nature of the book. He was troubled that it under-emphasized his colleagues and their important role in his work. "I work with hundreds of community healthcare workers and doctors," he said. "Basically our [goal] has been to make this more of a movement."

Farmer has won several prestigious awards, including a MacArthur Foundation Fellowship, or "genius" grant, of $250,000. He has been mentioned as a contender for the Nobel Peace Prize, one of the world's highest honors. But he is concerned only with furthering his work. "I want to show how poor people are put at risk for being sick and then denied access to health care. That's all I really care about," he said. The health and social problems he aims to tackle are enormous. But he doesn't want that to stop anyone from trying. "It's unrealistic to think that we can save everyone," Farmer said. "But it should still be our goal."

——— **"** ———

"I want to show how poor people are put at risk for being sick and then denied access to health care. That's all I really care about," Farmer said. "It's unrealistic to think that we can save everyone. But it should still be our goal."

——— **"** ———

With all of the fame and awards that Farmer has earned, helping his patients remains the best reward for his work. "I get the satisfaction of seeing someone who would otherwise die, do well," he said. "That is very satisfying."

MARRIAGE AND FAMILY

For several years in the 1980s, Farmer was romantically involved with Ophelia Dahl, co-founder and executive director of PIH. After they broke up, they remained close friends. In 1996, Farmer married Didi Bertrand, an anthropologist and the daughter of the schoolmaster in Conge. They met when Farmer treated Bertrand's mother at his clinic. They fell in love after she became his research assistant. They have a daughter, Catherine, born in 1998. Bertrand and Catherine divide their time between Cange and Paris. Farmer considers Cange his home, though he travels around the world almost constantly for his work.

HOBBIES AND INTERESTS

In his rare spare moments, Farmer likes to read *People* magazine, which he refers to as "J.P.S."—Journal of Popular Studies. His brother Jeff, the pro wrestler, has encouraged him to watch action-adventure films as a form of stress relief. Tracy Kidder reported that Farmer occasionally enjoys a good dinner with a fine bottle of wine. But most of Farmer's waking moments (he usually sleeps only four hours a night) are devoted to his work.

SELECTED WRITINGS

AIDS and Accusation: Haiti and the Geography of Blame, 1992
The Uses of Haiti, 1994 (updated edition, 2003)
Women, Poverty, and AIDS: Sex, Drugs, and Structural Violence, 1996
    (co-editor, with Margaret Connors and Janie Simmons)
Infections and Inequalities: The Modern Plagues, 1998
The Global Impact of Drug-Resistant Tuberculosis, 1999 (co-editor)
*Pathologies of Power: Health, Human Rights and the New War on
    the Poor*, 2003

HONORS AND AWARDS

Wellcome Medal for Research in Anthropology as Applied to Medical
    Problems (Anthropological Institute of Great Britain and Ireland): 1992
MacArthur Fellow (John D. and Catherine T. McArthur Foundation):
    1993
Eileen Basker Prize (American Anthropological Association): 1996,
    for *Women, Poverty and Aids: Sex, Drugs, and Structural Violence*
Margaret Mead Award (American Anthropological Association): 1999
Nathan Davis Award for Outstanding International Physician (American
    Medical Association): 2002
Heinz Award for the Human Condition (Heinz Family Foundation): 2003
Award of Excellence (Ronald McDonald House Charities): 2003
Inductee into the Medical Mission Hall of Fame: 2005

FURTHER READING

Books

Directory of American Scholars, 2001
Kidder, Tracy. *Mountains Beyond Mountains: The Quest of Dr. Paul
    Farmer, a Man Who Would Cure the World*, 2003
Who's Who in America, 2006

Periodicals

Biography Magazine, Sep. 2001, p.82
Current Biography Yearbook, 2004
Hendersonville (NC) Times-News, Nov. 21, 2000

New York Times, Nov. 30, 2003, section 1, p.1

New Yorker, July 10, 2000, p.40

Salt Lake City Deseret Morning News, Mar. 25, 2005

St. Petersburg Times, Feb. 22, 2004, Hernando Times section, p.1; Feb. 22, 2004, Floridian section, p.E1

Online Articles

http://www.ucpress.edu/books/pages/9875/9875.auint.html
(University of California Press, "Championing Health Care as a Human Right: An Interview with Paul Farmer," undated)

http://www.inequality.org/farmer2.html
("Interview with Paul Farmer: At a Clinic in Haiti, a Doctor Practices What Others Preach," undated)

http://www.satyamag.com/april00/farmer.html
(*Satya*, "The Potential for Global Human Solidarity: HIV through the Eyes of a Physician on the Front Lines. The *Satya* Interview with Paul Farmer," Apr. 2000)

Online Resources

Biography Resource Center Online, 2005, article from *Directory of American Scholars*, 2001

ADDRESS

Paul Farmer
Partners in Health
641 Huntington Avenue, 1st Floor
Boston, MA 02115

WORLD WIDE WEB SITES

http://www.pih.org

Donna House 1954?-

American Co-Designer of the National Museum of
the American Indian

EARLY YEARS

Donna House was born in about 1954 in Washington, DC. At
that time, just after the Korean War, her father was a guard at
the Pentagon, the headquarters for the U.S. armed forces.
House was the oldest of her family's nine children. A Native
American, House can trace her ancestry to both the Oneida
Nation of the northeast and the Navajo Nation (or Dineh, as
they call themselves) of the southwest.

House grew up on a Navajo reservation in Oak Springs, Arizona, about four hours west of Albuquerque, New Mexico. The reservation was so small that Shiprock, New Mexico, a nearby town of 8,000 inhabitants, "seemed like New York to us." Her extended family lived on the reservation, and she learned much from them. Family members who were healers taught her about the land as she helped them gather sacred plants. She learned about their different uses, and how the time of day, temperature, wind, phase of the moon, and night sky at the time of gathering could affect their use. Her family used these plants to practice Dineh medicine. (The nearest hospital was 100 miles away.)

EDUCATION

To attend school, House had to ride a bus two hours each way. When she got older, the family moved to Fort Defiance during the school year to make the journey easier. Summers were spent back in Oak Springs, where they used kerosene instead of electricity, raised sheep, and hunted the occasional prairie dog. Native Americans' experience with government schooling has a mixed history. In the past, it was common for the U.S. government to forcibly remove Native American children from their homes and send them to distant schools. This process was intended to sever the children's connection to their families and their culture. House's own grandfather was only eight when government agents removed him from his home and sent him to a Bureau of Indian Affairs school far from his family. Nevertheless, House enjoyed attending school off the reservation and found herself attracted to science. "There was a sense that Western knowledge was a curiosity, like the curve in a canyon you're hiking."

> *"Recognizing the diversity of plants is no different than recognizing the diversity of people," House explained. "All seeds have stories. The evolution of stories, knowledge, and memories of our ancestors are embedded in them."*

House enrolled at the University of Utah, intending to concentrate on a pre-medical program that would lead to a career as a doctor. Because her beliefs would not allow her to dissect animals or insects, however, she decided to switch her major to environmental science. She focused on botany, the study of plant life, because she hoped to keep alive the lore she had learned from her family. "I respect the Dineh—I respect the knowledge," she said. "I want to keep that ethos and knowledge continuing." When House graduated from college, she was the first person from Oak Springs to do so.

MAJOR ACCOMPLISHMENTS

Relating Plants to People

Throughout her career, House has worked as an ethnobotanist: someone who explores the characteristics of plant species as well as their cultural significance. She often works to protect rare and endangered plants by teaching people about their cultural and ecological importance. "Recognizing the diversity of plants is no different than recognizing the diversity of people," she explained. "All seeds have stories. The evolution of stories, knowledge, and memories of our ancestors are embedded in them." House has worked with local tribes, national environmental groups, and government agencies, seeking ways to protect endangered plants. Her clients have included the Navajo Nation, the Nature Conservancy, the U.S. Fish and Wildlife Service, and the National Park Service, among others.

> "I see a relation between the loss of plant species and the loss of native people. Without these plant species, we wouldn't have our culture, we wouldn't have our songs, and we wouldn't have our dances."

While working with the Nature Conservancy, for instance, House conducted research on Kearney's blue star, a wildflower that only grows in southern Arizona. In the 1980s, a federal government survey found just eight specimens of the plant. House worked with members of the Tohono O'odham (Papago) Nation, on whose lands the Kearney's blue star is found. Consulting with members of the tribe, she located a canyon with dozens of the endangered plants. "They knew more about their ecosystem than I did, no matter how much I read," House said of the Tohono O'odham. "Elders know the birds, the paths the animals take, the plants. A lot of knowledge you can't find in a library."

House has also worked with various conservation groups, tribal groups, and local ranchers to limit oil and gas development at the El Huerfano Mesa in northwestern New Mexico. Known as Dzil Ná'oodilii to the Navajo, the Mesa is a sacred place in the tribe's mythology. Protecting the landscape can help protect the native culture, House explained: "I see a relation between the loss of plant species and the loss of native people. Without these plant species, we wouldn't have our culture, we wouldn't have our songs, and we wouldn't have our dances."

The ethnobotanist also contributed to the Navajo Nation's Showcase of Culture at the 2002 Winter Olympic Games, held in Salt Lake City, Utah.

The National Museum of the American Indian, part of the Smithsonian Institution in Washington, DC.

She helped plan landscaping for this 11,000 square-foot facility, which was shaped like a hogan (the domed, one-room homes built by the Navajo). Her job was "significant not only to make it look natural," she explained, "but significant in explaining how the environment is important to indigenous people." House also serves her tribe as a member of the Navajo Nation's Committee of Scientists. Her work as an ethnobotanist helps preserve native knowledge. Territories controlled by Native Americans have some of the best quality air, water, and forests in America, she explained, for indigenous peoples "have developed a relationship with the environment for thousands of millions of years." Because "Indian lands haven't been inventoried," she remarked, "it is important to explore their relationship to the land before knowledge is lost."

Helping Design a National Museum

House's most visible project has been her work on the National Museum of the American Indian (NMAI), located on the Mall and part of the Smithsonian Institution in Washington, DC. Congress approved the creation of the NMAI in 1989; it took another ten years to raise funds and gather input for designs. Groundbreaking on the facility took place in September 1999, and five years later the museum was officially opened to visitors. House was an integral part of the museum's design team, which also included Native

American architects, designers, and curators. House led the design of the museum grounds, directing the landscaping for the 4.25-acre site.

Creating the environment for the NMAI proved to be a massive undertaking. Not only did House consult with botanists familiar with the region, she also canoed tributaries of the nearby Potomac River in order to get a feel for the countryside. Although the NMAI explores the cultures of native peoples throughout North and South America, the botanist stuck with local flora of Potomac River area in planning the exteriors. "The philosophy was going to be of this area; land has memory, land has spirit," she noted. "In order to honor the people that were extricated and the species that were extricated, one of the things that was so important is to bring back and have respect and honor the people that have disappeared by having native plants and just recognizing the Eastern vegetation." This proved more difficult than expected, because most people stock their gardens with exotic species and suppliers didn't have many native plants on hand.

—— " ——

"In the native philosophy,"
House observed, "there
should not be any line
between the building
and the landscape."

—— " ——

In the end, the NMAI site was landscaped with four different habitats and some 33,000 individual trees, shrubs, and other plants from 150 different species. The habitats include a hardwood forest like that of Rock Creek Park in Washington, DC; a wetlands area with water lilies, silky willow, and rice; a meadow with species native to the Potomac River Valley; and an area with corn, beans, squash, other traditional crops domesticated by Native Americans, as well as medicinal plants. The interplanting of corns, beans, and squash demonstrates the Indian's understanding of nature: the corn's stalk supplies a pole which the bean vine can climb; the bean feeds the soil with nitrogen; and the low leaves of the squash keep weeds away and provide shade for the other plants' roots. None of these plants are labeled, however. "That's not a native experience. It's putting a tag on beings," House explained. "When you take a piece of tree to use, you acknowledge them, thank them. You don't learn that in architecture school."

The NMAI grounds also contain some 40 "grandfather rocks," large granite boulders that symbolize the Native peoples' long relationship with the environment. The grandfather rocks, weathered over millions of years, were blessed by Native tribes. In addition, the site includes four directional stone markers, gathered from Native communities. The stones, which identify the four cardinal directions (north, south, east, and west), stand as

A grandfather rock from the eastern side of the Smithsonian NMAI,
with the U.S. Capitol building in the background.

a metaphor for the indigenous peoples of the Western Hemisphere. The stones were gathered from Native communities in the Northwest Territories, Canada (northern stone), Isla Navarino, Chile (southern stone), Great Falls, Maryland (eastern stone), and Hawaii (western stone).

While traveling the country talking to Native people, House met a Northern Cheyenne elder who spoke of "the significance of the ancient people, the ancient people being of stone, of boulders, or rocks, and how they were here before human beings, before the five-fingered people." This "strong statement" of the rocks greets visitors, as well as a cascade of water. "Water plays a great role with native people, and the water has different voices, so we have a cascade that breaks down into different heights," House noted. It creates visual interest and the impression of listening to different voices. "When people come onto the land, they are going to be greeted by water and boulders—ancient boulders that are the ancient people of the Earth. This museum represents a past that hasn't been in history books." Overall, the botanist strove to create a design that would create a sense of wholeness: "In the native philosophy," she observed, "there should not be any line between the building and the landscape."

—— *"* ——

"The plants, and the animals, and the stars and the water are who we are, and those natural elements have to be a part of the landscape.... The natural world doesn't only belong to indigenous people. It belongs to all."

—— *"* ——

The NMAI opened on September 21, 2004, with 25,000 Native Americans participating in the opening ceremonies. Although the museum addresses historical issues concerning Native Americans, "it's a living museum. We're still here," House noted. The designers have created a positive atmosphere not just to commemorate the Indian past, but celebrate the present. Among the Dineh people, she said, "We let go of that negative energy. You sing reality into being."

The museum is expected to be very popular with tourists, but House hopes that, in addition, there will be "visitors besides the five-fingered people: dragonflies, damselflies, hawks, ducks." She explained: "When I look at the National Museum of the American Indian's landscape, I see habitats for butterflies and everything else that will be partners for these native plants. The landscape's foundation is not only of native philosophy and our relationship with the environment but to educate people about the importance of protecting biodiversity: the importance of native plants of the Americas." In the end, House hopes that human visitors to the NMAI will gain a spiritual understanding of nature: "The plants, and the animals, and the stars and the water

This cardinal directional stone at the NMAI, from a Native community in Hawaii, represents the indigenous peoples of the west.

are who we are, and those natural elements have to be a part of the land-scape.... The natural world doesn't only belong to indigenous people. It belongs to all."

HOME AND FAMILY

House lives in an adobe house set on a ten-acre farm in New Mexico, where she encourages the growth of native plants. Besides devoting time to gardening, she has volunteered with the Hispanic community in Espa-nola, a town south of her home. There she works in a community college to help students develop prototype solar "low-rider" vehicles.

FURTHER READING

Periodicals

Denver Post, Aug. 15, 2004, p.F1
Los Angeles Times, Jan. 9, 2000, p.4
Minneapolis Star-Tribune, Sep. 19, 2004, p.A1
Navajo Times, Nov. 4, 1999, p.9; Jan. 31, 2002, p.2
New York Times, Sep. 9, 2004, p.F1
Time, Sep. 20, 2004, p.68
Washington Post, Apr. 25, 2002, p.H1; Sep. 20, 2004, p.C1

Online Articles

http://news.nationalgeographic.com/news
(National Geographic News, "New National Indian Museum Is Native by Design," Sep. 24, 2004)

Other

"Talk of the Nation," transcript from National Public Radio, Sep. 20, 2004

Information for this profile was also taken from an email interview with *Biography Today* conducted in Sep. 2005.

ADDRESS

Donna House
PO Box 19
San Juan Pueblo, NM 87566

WORLD WIDE WEB SITES

http://www.nmai.si.edu

Dean Kamen 1951-

American Inventor, Engineer, and Entrepreneur
Creator of Specialized Medical Equipment and the
Segway Human Transporter

BIRTH

Dean Kamen (pronounced KAY-men) was born on April 5, 1951,
in Rockville Centre, New York. His father was Jack Kamen, who
worked as a comic-book illustrator and commercial artist, and
his mother was Evelyn Kamen, who worked as an accounting
teacher. He has an older brother named Barton, a younger brother named Mitch, and a younger sister named Terri.

YOUTH

Kamen grew up in Rockville Centre, a small town on Long Island that serves as a suburb for New York City. By his teen years, he was becoming obsessed by science and engineering, and he seems to have been interested in little else. He did become a member of the wrestling team in high school and attempted to join the football team, though his small size (he weighed just over 100 pounds at the time) convinced him that he didn't belong on the gridiron. In some ways, Kamen seemed to have grown up in the shadow of his older brother Bart, who did very well in his studies. Bart became a Westinghouse scholar while in high school and later became a doctor.

——— **"** ———

"I was a terrible student. I just remember thinking school was humiliating and intimidating and frustrating," Kamen said. "I don't like people telling me what to do. I didn't like teachers judging me.... I just tried to get through it each day and get away."

——— **"** ———

EDUCATION

Though his knowledge of scientific principles has been a big part of Kamen's success, he had a difficult time with formal schooling. "I was a terrible student," he said. "I just remember thinking school was humiliating and intimidating and frustrating.... I don't like people telling me what to do. I didn't like teachers judging me.... I just tried to get through it each day and get away." Sometimes Kamen's dissatisfaction caused him to challenge his instructors. "I would always question what the teachers said," he explained. "They used to get furious with me. But I was very frustrated and became pretty belligerent." Kamen has even claimed that he purposefully attempted to get low test scores just for the fun of it. While he may have disliked his classes, he loved to study on his own, and his favorite subject was science. He analyzed the discoveries of Albert Einstein and read such important works as *Principia* by Sir Issac Newton and the writings of Galileo. These books unlocked his imagination in a way that his school classes never did. "The thing I liked about science was that you could count on it—not like the law or other fields that are constantly changing," he said. "I mean, no one is going to repeal Ohm's Law or Newton's Law."

After graduating from high school on Long Island, Kamen enrolled at Worcester Polytechnic Institute in Worcester, Massachusetts. He still had little respect for tests and grades: he sometimes didn't bother to take the required examinations, so he failed a lot of classes. He did learn a lot at Worcester, but mostly by spending long hours talking with professors about physics and engineering. "Dean was one of those rare kids who really wants to understand and get to the bottom of things," said Dr. Harold Hilsinger, one of his professors. "He was in my office every day for as many hours as I could stand." Kamen left college after five years and never earned a degree. Still, he treasured the information that he had gained at Worcester. "There is a big difference in saying I didn't get a diploma and didn't get an education," he later pointed out. "I owe my success to education." In the early 1990s, after he had made his name as an inventor, Kamen received an honorary degree from Worcester Polytechnic.

CAREER HIGHLIGHTS

Kamen's casual attitude toward grades may have come partly from the fact that he already knew how he was going to earn a living—he was going to be an inventor. In fact, by the time he was in high school, he already *was* an inventor and was making good money from his creations. He began by designing solid-state electronic units that would make lights flash in time to music. He sold these to local rock bands that used them in their performances.

"The thing I liked about science was that you could count on it—not like the law or other fields that are constantly changing," Kamen said. *"I mean, no one is going to repeal Ohm's Law or Newton's Law."*

At age 16, while working a summer job at the Museum of Natural History in New York City, Kamen boldly asked the museum's chairman if he could upgrade the lighting system for the Hayden Planetarium. The chairman ignored him, so Kamen took matters into his own hands. He built a sample control unit, or "box," and wired it into the planetarium's system on his own—without permission. The chairman was shocked at what Kamen had done, but when he saw the light show, he hired the teenager to redo the lights in four museums for a total fee of $8,000. By the time Kamen was in college, he was earning $60,000 a year from his expertise in electrical engineering. He performed most of his work in his parents' basement, which required him to travel from Worcester to Long Island each weekend.

Inventing the AutoSyringe

Kamen soon turned his skills toward medical technology. His brother Bart was then studying to be a doctor, and he urged Dean to look into the problem of automatically providing medication to hospital patients. Combining common parts such as timers and circuit boards with precise elements that he learned to mill out of aluminum himself, Kamen created what he called

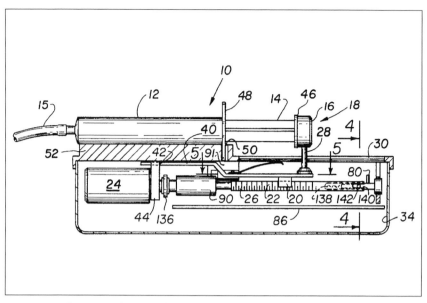

*The patent drawing for Kamen's medication injection device,
which became the AutoSyringe.*

the AutoSyringe. It was a drug-infusion pump that could provide precise doses to patients at precise times. Once doctors learned of the device, they phoned the 20-year-old inventor hoping to place orders.

Kamen's scientific career was off and running, but first there were a few problems: he had no place to manufacture the devices, and he had no employees. He solved the first problem by enlarging his parents' basement. (According to legend, he had the construction done while they were out of town, tearing up the neighbor's lawn in the process.) He solved the second by putting members of his family to work, including his mother, who did the bookkeeping, his younger brother, Mitch, who assembled the devices, and his father, who did the illustrations for the instruction manuals and also drew up the new product designs that Kamen envisioned. "I was like a police artist," Jack Kamen said. "Dean knew what he wanted in his head but he isn't an artist. So he'd tell me what components to draw. 'Put a switch here, a display there,' he'd direct me." Kamen also began hiring other aspiring engineers that he had met at college to help him expand the business. They developed automatic pumps for use in chemotherapy, diabetes treatment, and other specialized uses, all bearing the name of Kamen's self-made company, AutoSyringe Inc.

When the business outgrew his parents' basement, Kamen moved operations to a nearby office on Long Island. Then, in 1979, he relocated the company to Manchester, New Hampshire. He was attracted to the New England state because it had "more space, more freedom, and less taxes." Kamen is a vocal critic of official bureaucracy and believes that most state and federal governments place too many regulations on businesses. Because New Hampshire avoids some of this red tape—and because it collects less of his money in taxes—he believes it one of the better places to do business in the U.S.

AutoSyringe grew to include 100 employees, but even then the company was having difficulty meeting demand. Kamen was more interested in researching new inventions rather than manufacturing his old ones, so his enthusiasm began to wane. In 1982 he sold AutoSyringe to Baxter Healthcare, a larger company. The exact price of the sale is unknown, but Kamen has mentioned "tens of millions" of dollars, and some estimates place the figure at $30 million. Whatever the case, at age 31, Dean Kamen was a very rich man, and he was soon looking for his next challenge.

——— " ———

"Dean possesses the fundamental quality of most very successful people," said Bob Tuttle, his financial advisor: "a very high energy level and a boundless, almost ridiculous work ethic."

——— " ———

Millionaire and Working Man

Kamen immediately founded a new company, which he named DEKA by taking the first two letters of his first and last name—DEan KAmen. The company focuses on research and development. In other words, Kamen and his staff come up with ideas for new products and build the initial models, or prototypes. The actual manufacturing and sales are usually handled by other firms that pay him for the right to sell the devices. Like AutoSyringe, DEKA often focuses on medical technology. One of the most notable devices DEKA has created is a small, portable machine that allows people with kidney problems to undergo dialysis treatment at home, rather than traveling to a hospital. Known as HomeChoice, the portable dialysis machine uses fluid management system (FMS) technology—machinery and control devices that precisely measure and transfer tiny amounts of liquid. DEKA has applied this same technology to a range of other products.

Running one company was not enough for Kamen, however. He took up several other business enterprises beginning in the 1980s, some of them more or less by chance. He had been interested in helicopters since childhood, so he bought one and learned to fly it. (He uses it daily to get to and from his office and also owns and flies his own jet.) He soon came up with

Kamen hard at work on a metal lathe at his machine shop at home, 1994.

ideas on how to improve the helicopter's performance, so he bought the Enstrom Helicopter Corporation. (He sold that company in 1990.) Seeking a new headquarters for DEKA, he purchased several historic mill buildings in Manchester and renovated them. Unhappy with the technology that was available to operate the heating and cooling for the offices, he formed another company, Teletrol Systems Inc., which handles climate control for large buildings all across the country.

Despite all of his business interests, Kamen does not look like a corporate leader. He refuses to wear a suit and tie and instead dresses in the exact same outfit everyday: blue jeans and a blue denim work shirt. He is said to own 25 of each, and he dons this uniform whether he is tinkering in his machine shop or meeting with the chief executive of the United States. (Kamen has met three presidents: George H. W. Bush, Bill Clinton, and George W. Bush.) Kamen has explained that he dislikes the "thin, delicate material" of business suits. "If you do anything, by the end of the day those delicate things get dirty and ruined," he once said. "So I wear these clothes [jeans and work shirt] because I work. And frankly, the message sent by suits and ties—which is 'I don't really work'—is offensive to me."

No one has accused Kamen of not working. It's not uncommon for him to spend as much as 20 hours a day on the job. Sometimes he's attending to the details of business operations, sometimes he's bounding around the

DEKA offices to check on the progress of the other engineers. He also performs hands-on tasks himself, both in the office and in the machine shop he has at his home, where he sometimes continues to experiment with designs long after midnight. "Dean possesses the fundamental quality of most very successful people," said Bob Tuttle, his financial advisor: "a very high energy level and a boundless, almost ridiculous work ethic." Sometimes described as "tightly wound," Kamen moves fast, but he is also famous for launching into lengthy talks that often touch on his vast knowledge of science and many other subjects. His business associate John Doerr said that "if you ask Dean the time . . . he'll first explain the theory of general relativity, then how to build an atomic clock, and then, maybe, he'll tell you what time it is." President Bill Clinton has also joked about Kamen's long-winded talks. "If you do not want to hear about what he does," Clinton said, "do not ask—or stand within a four mile radius."

> **"If you ask Dean the time,"** **said his business associate** **John Doerr, "he'll first** **explain the theory of general** **relativity, then how to build** **an atomic clock, and then,** **maybe, he'll tell you what** **time it is."**

While sometimes amusing, Kamen's high-octane personality can be overwhelming in certain cases. "Sometimes his intensity is almost frightening," explained Bob Gussin, chief science officer at Johnson & Johnson, one of the companies that Kamen contracts with. "Dean is so intense and so aggressive that you always have to worry whether he'll get frustrated at not moving fast enough." Woodie Flowers, a professor at the Massachusetts Institute of Technology and one of his close friends, has seen some of the top engineering graduates from his college fall to pieces once they go to work for Kamen. "Dean occasionally runs over people," Flowers said.

For other DEKA employees, however, the intensity and the freewheeling atmosphere are what make their jobs satisfying. "DEKA is one of the highest-morale operations I've ever seen," said Ray Price, president of the Economic Club of New York. "There's no bureaucracy, and very little structure. Dean expects performance, but how [the employees] get solutions is up to them." Many DEKA employees take the job because they want to work alongside Kamen, who has a reputation for being one of the best in his field. "Dean is one of the premier electromechanical engineers in the world," said Jerry Fisher of Baxter Healthcare. "There just isn't a problem he can't attack. He invariably comes up with a half-dozen ideas that can make inroads into a problem. And he's relentless." Kamen admits that he's demanding and driven, but he believes that these qualities are essential in his line of work. "People accuse me of being unreasonable," he argued. "But I think being unreasonable is good. Being unreasonable is how things change." He also insists on personally overseeing most of the activities at DEKA. For most of the company's projects, this tight control has worked well, but in the 1990s his team began to work on a new type of technology that would prove quite different from what they'd done before.

———— " ————

"Dean is one of the premier electromechanical engineers in the world," said Jerry Fisher of Baxter Healthcare. "There just isn't a problem he can't attack. He invariably comes up with a half-dozen ideas that can make inroads into a problem. And he's relentless."

———— " ————

Fred and Ginger

It began with a man in a wheelchair that Kamen observed at a shopping mall. Kamen noticed the difficulties the man had in getting his chair up a curb and decided he could build a better wheelchair. Soon, he and some of his best engineers went to work on the problem. As usual, he encouraged his team to come up with wild, unconventional ideas, even if they seemed impossible. This approach is standard operating procedure at DEKA because Kamen believes it results in new and better ways of doing things. He knows that a lot of the experiments will go nowhere but that one of them could lead to a real solution. In explaining this process, he noted that "if you start to do things you've never done before, you're probably going to fail at least some of the time. And I say that's OK." He has a motto that sums up this attitude, and it is a guiding principle at DEKA: "You gotta kiss a lot of frogs . . . before you find a prince."

The primary goal was to make a chair that could climb stairs and curbs, but the initial designs by the DEKA engineers all had the same problem: they became unstable when they climbed and often toppled over. After much trial and error, they hit upon the idea of using gyroscopic tilt sensors to keep the chair upright. The rapidly spinning gyros sensed when the chair was beginning to become unbalanced, and onboard computers used this information to adjust the chair's wheels to keep it in equilibrium. One of the early prototypes of the chair had the tendency to move around as if it were dancing. The engineers joked that it looked the famous dancer Fred Astaire, and Kamen began to call it Fred *Up*stairs. Soon the product was known by a simple code word: Fred. In addition to its mobility, Fred also had the ability to raise its passenger to an upright position. Rather than

*Kamen at the top of the Empire State Building, pointing out
the sights to a 16-year-old user of the iBot.*

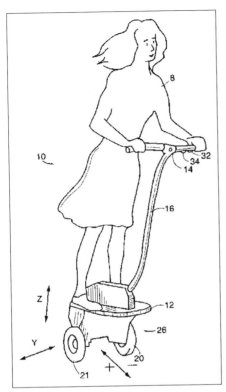

The patent drawing for "Ginger."

continually looking up at others, a wheelchair-bound person using Fred could meet people eye-to-eye, which could enhance their authority and self-esteem. These were huge breakthroughs, but implementing them into a finished product and getting that product approved by the Food and Drug Administration took a long time. Work began on Fred in the early 1990s. The chair, now renamed the iBot 3000 Mobility System, finally went on the market in 2003—more than a decade later.

While working on Fred, the engineers made another discovery. Just for fun, one of the DEKA workers began standing on the wheelchair's platform as he rode around the laboratory. Observing this, Kamen and his colleagues realized that they could use Fred's technology to make another type of transportation device—one where the rider stood rather than sat in a chair. Its use wouldn't be limited to those with disabilities, but would also extend to the general public. Soon, the DEKA staff created a two-wheeled prototype designed specifically for standing travel. Like Fred, the device used gyroscopic tilt sensors to keep itself oriented, so it was able to remain upright on its two wheels even when standing still. They named it after Ginger Rogers, Fred Astaire's dance partner. By the late 1990s, the Ginger project had become DEKA's number one priority. In a top-secret area in his company's Manchester headquarters, Kamen devoted large amounts of money and manpower to the new product. He was convinced that Ginger had the ability to change the world.

Revolutionary Transportation

Kamen based his high hopes on several facts. His new machine was small enough to fit on a sidewalk but could transport a person at a brisk 12 miles per hour—about four times the speed of walking. Its electric motor didn't emit air pollution. And most important of all, Ginger was amazingly responsive and fun to ride. Since it worked on the basis of balance, a rider simply leaned forward to go forward, leaned back to slow the machine or stop it, leaned further back to reverse it. Ginger's ability to interpret and adjust to a person's center of gravity left riders amazed. Most people said that the machine seemed to read their mind. Kamen believed that Ginger would help solve the transportation problems common in most large cities, where automobiles pollute the air and create time-consuming traffic jams. He confidently predicted that his new transporter would "profoundly affect our environment and the way people live worldwide."

Kamen was so excited about Ginger that he decided to change the way he normally did business. Usually, DEKA would license its products to another company, which would handle the manufacturing, marketing, and distribution. For instance, the iBot (Fred) was actually put out by Johnson & Johnson. But with Ginger, Kamen wanted to control as much of the process—and the profits—as possible. This required him to take on a lot of responsibilities he wasn't used to, such as building a factory and hiring marketing and sales personnel and a chief executive officer (CEO) to oversee the project. While he felt he didn't need a corporate partner, Kamen did need money. He had financed the development himself up until 2000, but Ginger was getting expensive: $100 million would be spent before the product was ready for mar-

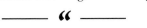

"Nothing has happened at the level of the pedestrian to improve transportation since we invented the sneaker.... We think if you could integrate Segway technology into cities it would be a universal win for everybody."

ket. Kamen began looking for investors, wowing them with demonstrations of what Ginger could do. Eventually, he lined up several prominent backers, including Credit Suisse First Boston and Kleiner Perkins Caufield & Byers. Such technology experts as Jeff Bezos, founder of Amazon.com, and Steve Jobs, head of Apple Computers and Pixar, served as advisors to the company. The investors were so excited by the transporter that they agreed to lay down about $90 million in total. In return, Kamen gave up just 15% ownership of the company—a very good deal from his standpoint. "I did it the way I usually do," Kamen said of the financing. "I figure out what I think is fair, and then make sure everyone compromises and does it my way."

Up until 2001 Ginger remained a well-guarded secret. Kamen was reluctant to let the public know about the machine before its debut because he feared other companies would try to steal the idea or that potential competitors, such as car companies, would try to create problems for the new product.

Two Segway riders glide along the sidewalks of Atlanta.

But suddenly, in January 2001—a year before the planned launch of the product—everyone seemed to know about Ginger. The web site Inside.com managed to get hold of a book proposal from author Steve Kemper, who had been documenting the development of Ginger with Kamen's permission. Kemper's proposal hadn't said what the mysterious product was—it was known simply as "IT"—but it did include quotes that got everyone's attention: Steve Jobs said IT would be as important as the personal computer; John Doerr, one of the venture capitalists backing the product, said IT was the most important piece of technology since the Internet. The story was splashed across newspapers, television programs, and the Internet. Several web sites were created with the sole purpose of speculating about IT. Some of the wilder theories proclaimed that it was a time-travel machine, an anti-gravity device, and a robot that could read minds.

Kamen was very upset about the news leak and said that the theories were "beyond whimsical," but IT remained a hot news story. Later in 2001, when the product was finally unveiled, Kamen appeared on the television program "Good Morning America." Ginger, now officially renamed the Segway Human Transporter, was wrapped in a sheet and lit by spotlights. When the wrapping was lifted, the world saw a rather humble sight: "two wheels, a platform, and a T-bar," as Steve Kemper describes it in his book *Code Name Ginger*. In other words, the Segway looked far less impressive than people had expected after all of the buildup. "That's *it*?," asked the show's host Diane Sawyer. "But that *can't* be IT."

Like most other people who were first introduced to the Segway, Sawyer didn't really understand the machine until she rode it. Then its ability to balance and maneuver became clear. Other journalists who got the chance to try a Segway had a similar experience. "All it takes to be convinced is one ride," wrote one reviewer. "It's the perfect middle ground between feet and cars." Kamen, meanwhile, continued to promise that the Segway was going to be the transportation device of the future, vowing that the transporter "will be to the car what the car was to the horse and buggy." He also said that "nothing has happened at the level of the pedestrian to improve transportation since we invented the sneaker. . . . We think if you could integrate Segway technology into cities it would be a universal win for everybody."

A Slow Start

Despite the glowing reviews and brash predictions, the Segway has not become a smash hit. Sales began slowly and have yet to reach the levels that Kamen and his investors expected. Though definite figures have not been released, Steve Kemper estimated that about 10,000 Segways had been sold by late 2004; if true, that's 10 to 20 times less than the company had predicted.

Analysts have noted several reasons that may explain the lackluster sales. First, availability has been a significant problem. The Segway designers often say that the machine needs to be ridden to be appreciated, yet that was hard to do in the first few years after the transporter was unveiled. Trial models were tested by business customers beginning in about 2001, and the consumer version was released in late 2002. Even then there were almost no dealerships where potential customers could take a test drive. Retail outlets didn't begin to open until 2003 and are still rather limited. Also, the Segway is expensive. When the consumer version was initially released, its list price was nearly $5,000. A smaller and lighter version now retails for about $4,000.

> *"I'm looking to give people alternatives and options that give them a better quality of life,"* Kamen said.

Some of these shortcomings have been blamed on management problems at the company. Segway has already gone through several presidents and CEOs, and it lacked a sales manager for an extended period. Some observers believe that Kamen himself is the source for most of these difficulties—perhaps because he has little experience with manufacturing and marketing. Steve Kemper, for example, feels that Kamen tries to maintain too much control over Segway operations rather than trusting his managers. Kemper also believes Kamen's slow decisions have harmed production and hurt sales. To some extent, Kamen agrees with these judgements: "Having less experience at building companies than we had at inventing life-saving products, . . . we certainly made mistakes," he admitted in *Wired* magazine.

Other criticisms involve the design of the Segway. Paul Saffo, director of the Institute for the Future, believes the weight of transporter (70 pounds for the lightest model) is a problem, making it difficult for owners to move it up and down stairs and to load and unload it from a car or truck. The Segway is "about 40 pounds too heavy," according to Saffo, and it "costs three times what a consumer device should cost." The transporter's power source is another concern: the basic battery originally supplied with the transporter lasts for only 10 to 12 miles of travel under normal conditions. After that, a new battery is needed or the original has to undergo several hours of recharging. An enhanced lithium-ion battery has recently been introduced, which is said to increase the range to 24 miles. Finally, questions of safety continue to swirl around the Segway. Because the device is primarily intended for travel on sidewalks, some people see it as a dangerous hazard to slower moving pedestrians. While many cities and states have approved its use on sidewalks, a few have banned it. There were also a few reports of Segways shutting down when they ran out of battery power, which tossed their riders to the ground. These incidents were quite rare, however, and the company has addressed the problem with a software update.

> "Instead of building vacation homes and second BMWs and trinkets and jewelry, let's make devices to give people water and electricity and education," Kamen reasoned. "The solution ... is to give people hope. Everybody has to be able to participate in a future that they want to live for. That's what technology can do."

Such setbacks didn't diminish the engineering community's enthusiasm for the transporter. In 2002 Kamen was named the winner of the prestigious Lemelson-MIT Prize for his innovative design work on the Segway. Kamen himself still believes in his creation and its ability to revolutionize travel. He's especially hopeful that it will be adopted in developing countries. "Most people in the developing world today can't afford cars and don't really need cars," he said. He added that "if they had them, it would be an environmental disaster" because of the huge amounts of added exhaust that would be emitted by the vehicles. Therefore, Kamen hopes that the low price and more environmentally friendly Segways may be the answer. Overall, he feels that the transporter will become more popular over time. "[Certainly], I would like to see the rate at which it gains acceptance continue to grow, but when you look at most really big ideas that change the way people think about how they do things, like how they move, ... those things take time."

The Segway isn't Kamen's only project that holds out promise for underdeveloped countries. DEKA is hoping soon to market a viable version of the Stirling engine, which was originally devised by inventor Robert Stirling in 1816. The engine works on a novel external-combustion principle and can burn a wide range of substances for fuel, including wood, grass, and animal manure. Kamen's version is designed to generate electricity and also to purify drinking water. Both tasks would be well suited to poor countries where both power and clean water are in short supply. The engines are expensive to build at present, which is one reason Stirling's invention has never proven a feasible power source. But Kamen hopes that costs will drop once the engines are produced in large quantities. If so, it may be yet another case where his expertise and innovation has made a big difference in people's lives. According to the famous inventor, that's all part of the plan. "I'm looking to give people alternatives and options that give them a better quality of life," he said. But he also makes it clear he's most interested in providing essential goods to the poorer inhabitants of the globe rather than luxury items to wealthier countries. "Instead of building vacation homes and second BMWs and trinkets and jewelry, let's make devices to give people water and electricity and education," he reasoned. "The solution . . . is to give people hope. Everybody has to be able to participate in a future that they want to live for. That's what technology can do."

"Our culture celebrates one thing: sports heroes," Kamen said. "You have teenagers thinking they're going to make millions as NBA stars when that's not realistic for even one percent of them. Becoming a scientist or an engineer is."

HOBBIES AND OTHER INTERESTS

Since the mid-1980s Kamen has been dedicated to promoting science to schoolchildren. He began in 1984 by founding Science Enrichment Encounters, a science museum in Manchester, New Hampshire. A much more ambitious plan was launched in 1989 when he formed U.S. FIRST—the U.S. Foundation for the Inspiration and Recognition of Science and Technology—an organization he has called "my most important invention." The foundation's primary activity is to sponsor an elaborate science contest each year where teams of students build robots to accomplish specific tasks. Matches are held all across the country and culminate in a championship game that takes place in front of tens of thousands of spectators. Winners go home with college scholarships and other prizes.

Kamen devotes lots of time and money to U.S. FIRST because he thinks it's a great way to change society's values. "Our culture celebrates one thing: sports heroes," he said. "You have teenagers thinking they're going to make millions as NBA stars when that's not realistic for even one percent of them. Becoming a scientist or an engineer is." Kamen believes that he

can put students on the right track by promoting science as a fun and rewarding activity—both personally and financially. If that doesn't occur, he argues, the United States will soon lose its technological edge over other countries. "In 10 years, unless we dramatically change our priorities and our standards, we will become a second-tier country. . . . U.S. FIRST is my way of attempting to fix that."

HOME AND FAMILY

Kamen has never married and has no children. "DEKA and FIRST are my work, my family, my hobby," he has explained. "They're everything." Kamen once admitted that he found science far less threatening than romance. "I can start the biggest [technical] project in the world," he said, "but I think getting in relationships is riskier and to me scarier."

Though his business and charity commitments take up most of his time, Kamen does have two comfortable homes where he spends his few leisure hours. His main home is a hexagon-shaped mansion named Westwind that sits on a hilltop in the town of Bedford, New Hampshire. The house says a lot about its owner: it's filled with portraits of Kamen's hero Albert Einstein and also includes vintage steam engines and other historic machinery. There are secret passageways and lots of luxurious touches, including an indoor pool, a film theater, and a regulation-size baseball diamond. But Kamen probably spends more time in the machine shop loaded with much of the same industrial manufacturing equipment found at his office. "I just like running those machines," he said. "It's relaxing." His second home is actually an entire island—North Dumpling Island. Located off the coast of Connecticut, it came complete with a mansion and lighthouse. Kamen jokingly refers to it as an independent kingdom and has taken the official title of Lord Dumpling. The "kingdom" has its own national anthem, and his friends have been appointed to official government posts. For instance, the founders of Ben & Jerry's serve as the Joint Chiefs of Ice Cream.

HONORS AND AWARDS

Medical Product of the Year (*Design News*): 1993, for the HomeChoice
    dialysis machine
Engineer of the Year (*Design News*): 1994
Kilby Award: 1994
American Institute of Medical and Biological Engineering Fellow: 1994
Hoover Medal: 1995
National Academy of Engineering Member: 1997
Heinz Award for Technology, the Economy, and Employment: 1998
National Medal of Technology: 2000
Lemelson-MIT Prize for Inventors: 2002
Green Cross International Award: 2003
Inductee, National Inventors Hall of Fame: 2005, for the AutoSyringe

FURTHER READING

Books

Brown, David E. *Inventing Modern America: From the Microwave to the
    Mouse*, 2002
Kemper, Steve. *Code Name Ginger*, 2003

Periodicals

Current Biography Yearbook, 2002
Design News, Mar. 7, 1994, p.66
New York Times, Feb. 14, 1993, sec.3, p.10; Dec. 3, 2001, p.C1
Newsweek, May 27, 2002, p.56
PC Magazine, Oct. 15, 2003
Smithsonian, Nov.1994, p.98; Sep. 2003, p.95
Time, Dec. 10, 2001, p.76
Vanity Fair, May 2002, p.184
Wired, Sep. 2000, p.176; Mar. 2003, p.123

Online Databases

Biography Resource Center Online, 2005, articles from *Biography Resource
    Center Online*, 2001, and *Newsmakers*, 2003
H. W. Wilson Company/Wilson Web, article from *Current Biography
    Yearbook*, 2002

Online Articles

http://www.cbsnews.com/stories/2002/11/12/60II/main529072.shtml
    (CBS News, "60 Minutes: The Great Inventor," Aug. 27, 2003)

http://www.gartner.com/research/fellows/asset_55323_1176.jsp
 ("The Gartner Fellows Interview: Inventor, Physicist, Entrepreneur
 Dean Kamen," Oct. 30, 2003)

ADDRESS

Dean Kamen
DEKA Research and Development Corporation
Technology Center
340 Commercial Street
Manchester, NH 03101

WORLD WIDE WEB SITES

http://www.dekaresearch.com

Cynthia Kenyon 1954-
American Geneticist
Conducts Breakthrough Research into the
Genetic Process of Aging

BIRTH

Cynthia Kenyon was born on February 18, 1954, in Chicago,
Illinois. Her father, James, was a professor of geography at the
University of Georgia, and her mother, Jane, was an administrator in the physics department there. Kenyon is the oldest of
three children.

YOUTH

Kenyon spent her childhood in Illinois, Georgia, New York,
New Jersey, and Connecticut. When she was born, her father

was attending graduate school in Chicago, Illinois. The family left Chicago after James completed his degree. They lived in various places and finally settled in Athens, Georgia, when James began teaching geography at the University of Georgia.

Growing up in Georgia, Kenyon loved reading and could often be found at the river near her house, absorbed in a book. She was interested in a wide variety of subjects and read anything and everything available to her. Her parents encouraged her love of reading, her curiosity, and her desire to learn about the world around her. Kenyon's parents were intellectuals who "never asked . . . a question that ended in a yes or no answer," her mother Jane remembered. In this way, Kenyon began to learn how to think independently, to make connections between information from different sources, and to form her own conclusions. These would become important and useful skills later in her career as a scientist.

EDUCATION

Throughout her school years, Kenyon's favorite subject was music. She played the French horn and loved being a part of the school orchestra. By the time she reached high school, she wanted to become a professional orchestra musician. She worked hard at her music and practiced for several hours every day. Eventually she moved up to first chair in the school orchestra's French horn section. (Each instrument in an orchestra has a first chair, a special place usually given to the best musician in that group.)

—— " ——

"I didn't know it at the time, but I was terrible at the French horn," Kenyon admitted. "I would miss notes and people would get mad at me. It was so unpleasant that I finally quit. I love the thrill of playing something and having it sound beautiful, but I just wasn't very good at it...."

—— " ——

In spite of her progress and her love for playing music, Kenyon came to realize that her dream of a career in music was not to be. She gave up the idea while she was still in high school. "I didn't know it at the time, but I was terrible at the French horn," she admitted. "I had almost no talent. I would miss notes and people would get mad at me. It was so unpleasant that I finally quit. . . . I love the thrill of playing something and having it sound beautiful, but I just wasn't very good at it. I finally realized that, and once I gave it up, I felt like I could fly, everything else just came so easily. . . . It taught me that what you should try to find is not only something that you like, but something that you're good at. It's not enough to just work hard; you have to have some talent for it."

After high school, Kenyon enrolled in the University of Georgia. She struggled to decide which subjects to study and which area to focus on for her degree. Her interests were so varied that she had trouble even narrowing down her top choices, which at one point included dairy science, veterinary medicine, mathematics, philosophy, Russian literature, and English literature. She was looking for something that would capture her complete interest, something she could become passionate about.

> ———— " ————
>
> *"I finally realized that, and once I gave it up, I felt like I could fly, everything else just came so easily.... It taught me that what you should try to find is not only something that you like, but something that you're good at. It's not enough to just work hard; you have to have some talent for it."*
>
> ———— " ————

After three years of disorganized studies, Kenyon was still interested in such a wide range of subjects that she was unable make a decision. University students are required to choose a degree program in order to graduate, and she was running out of time. She finally decided to take a break from school. Kenyon dropped out of college with a plan to work for a while, and took a job helping out on a farm.

Choosing a Career

Although she was no longer enrolled in classes, Kenyon had not abandoned her love of learning. She continued to read about many different topics, and was still thinking about what she wanted to do with her life. She did not enjoy working on the farm, and knew that was only a short term situation.

Everything changed the day that her mother brought home a copy of the book *Molecular Biology of the Gene* by James Watson. Watson is a scientist who discovered genes (DNA), the basic units of heredity. He discovered that the genes of living creatures are arranged in a linked spiral pattern called a double helix. In this book, Watson describes the science of genetics and how genes work.

The science of genetics focuses on deoxyribonucleic acid, or DNA. DNA is a chainlike series of proteins that guides the organization and function of living cells. The DNA within every cell is divided into chromosomes, each of which includes a specific number of genes. Genes are the distinct parts

biology at the Massachusetts Institute of Technology in 1981. Kenyon performed her postdoctoral work at the Medical Research Council Laboratory of Molecular Biology at Cambridge University in England. At Cambridge, she discovered what would become the focus of her life's work as a scientist.

CAREER HIGHLIGHTS

When she first arrived at Cambridge in the early 1980s, Kenyon was researching the DNA-damaging affects of such bacteria as E. coli. The laboratory next to hers belonged to H. Robert Horvitz, one of three 2002 Nobel Prize winners in medicine and physiology (the study of the internal functions of living organisms). Horvitz was conducting research with the microscopic worm Caenorhabditis elegans, also known as C. elegans, nematodes, or roundworms.

> ——— " ———
>
> *One day in the lab, Kenyon found an old dish of C. elegans worms that should have been thrown out. "There were all these worms on the plate; I had never seen an old worm. I had never even thought about an old worm. I felt sorry for them, and I felt sorry for myself, 'Oh, I'm getting old too' and right on the heels of that, I thought, 'Oh, my gosh, you could study this.'"*
>
> ——— " ———

C. elegans generally live in soil and are often used for scientific study, especially genetic research. These worms make good research subjects for a number of reasons. They live their whole lives in just two to three weeks, allowing scientists to quickly see the results of an experiment. They are transparent, so scientists looking at C. elegans under a microscope can see inside the worms' bodies. This makes it very easy to study cells and to see any changes that result from an experiment. C. elegans share genes and genetic processes with humans, and their genetic structure is completely documented. Kenyon was fascinated. She explains, "In Caenorhabditis elegans you have only a thousand cells and people knew where they all came from in the cell lineage, starting from the fertilized egg. It was the most amazing thing I'd seen . . . and I thought, wow, that's what I want to do."

At Cambridge in 1982, Kenyon began working with C. elegans. She was studying developmental biology with direction from Sydney Brenner, who shared the 2002 Nobel Prize with Horvitz. Their work explored the genetics of developing worms. One day in the lab, Kenyon found an old dish of C. elegans that should have been thrown out. She had forgotten about the dish and was surprised by what she saw in it. "There were all these worms on the plate; I had never seen an old worm. I had never even thought about

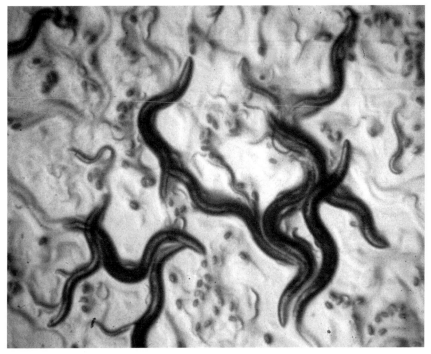

A microscopic view of the worm Caenorhabditis elegans, *or* C. elegans, *the subject of Kenyon's intensive study of aging.*

an old worm. I felt sorry for them, and I felt sorry for myself, 'Oh, I'm getting old too' and right on the heels of that, I thought, 'Oh, my gosh, you could study this.' "

The Study of Aging

Kenyon began to study how C. elegans aged and the changes that happened as the worms got older. She believed that the aging process was controlled or at least influenced by genes. This belief was based on a simple observation of the world around her. "All animals age, but at different rates: maybe there's a regulatory mechanism that controls the rate of aging and it can be set differently in different species, and that's why a bat lives for 50 years and a mouse lives two years. So we set out to find genes that regulated aging."

Although Kenyon and her colleagues knew they were doing valid research, the scientific community thought otherwise. Reactions from fellow scientists ranged from amusement to ridicule. The last thing any scientist wanted to do was study a subject that had already been fully explored. And in the area of aging, most molecular biologists believed that there was nothing left to study. Kenyon recalls, "The thing about aging was that everybody thought, 'Well, you know, the animal just breaks down, and what's to study, really? It's not going to be very interesting.' It was embarrassing to say we were working on aging. The field had a reputation for going nowhere." Looking for the cause of aging was believed to be as useless as verifying that the Earth is round and not flat. Kenyon remembers that one person warned her to "be careful . . . you might fall off the end of the earth."

In fact, many of the other research projects on aging were not high quality work. For centuries, people have wanted to know why we grow old and what can be done to stop the aging process or at least slow it down. And so for centuries, there have also been people ready to make money selling "cures" and "treatments" for aging. In the beginning, Kenyon found her research was being seen the same way—her work was not taken seriously, and it was difficult to find support for what she was doing. At one point, she even forbid her colleagues from using the word "aging" on applications for the grants, in the hope that it would increase their chances of getting money to fund their research.

> "When I looked at it, I could see that different animals have different life spans. The mouse lives two years and the bat can live 50 years and the canary lives about 15 years. They're all small animals. They're warm blooded. And they're not that different, really, in such a fundamental way from each other."

In spite of all this, Kenyon was still convinced that her work had value. She was as determined as ever to solve the aging puzzle. She wanted to understand when and why the process of aging began, using the relatively simple genetic structure of C. elegans as a starting point. She believed there was much more to growing old than a simple decline of health and mobility. "When I looked at it, I could see that different animals have different life spans. The mouse lives two years and the bat can live 50 years and the canary lives about 15 years. They're all small animals. They're warm blooded. And they're not that different, really, in such a fundamental way from each other."

Because the genetic structure and processes of C. elegans are closely related to those of humans, Kenyon also suspected that anything she learned could then be applied to human aging. Her goal was not to extend life or to prevent the changes that come with old age—unlike the researchers whose questionable work had made it difficult for her to gain acceptance in the scientific community. Instead, Kenyon wanted to understand aging in order to explore the possibility of improving the quality of life for older people. She thought that understanding why animals have such dramatically different life spans could help us understand why some people are healthier than others in old age.

In 1986, Kenyon left Cambridge and joined the faculty of the University of California-San Francisco (UCSF) as an assistant professor in the biology department. She moved her research projects to San Francisco and continued her work there.

The First Breakthrough

Exploring the idea that aging was genetically controlled, Kenyon had been working on manipulating various genes in C. elegans and watching the results during the worms' short life spans. After almost ten years of research and study, she and her team finally had a breakthrough: they identified a genetic cause for aging. "People have always thought that, like a car, our body parts eventually wear out. But we found that over time, when one gene was manipulated, the worm actually remained youthful—in all ways—so that the age-related diseases were also postponed." Kenyon published the results of her research in the December 1993 issue of the scientific journal *Nature*.

> "People have always thought that, like a car, our body parts eventually wear out. But we found that over time, when one gene was manipulated, the worm actually remained youthful— in all ways—so that the age-related diseases were also postponed."

The startling announcement informed the world that a single gene could be manipulated to double the life span of C. elegans. Kenyon told *Discover* magazine, "There was already a mutant worm that was reported to live 50 percent longer. It had been isolated by Michael Clas 10 years earlier and been studied by Tom Johnson's lab [at the University of Colorado at Boulder]. They thought maybe the mutant lived long because it didn't eat well or didn't reproduce well, but I thought there's a real set of dedicated genes for aging and that was the reason why. So we looked for these mutants and, in 1993, we found the daf-2 gene. It was a gene that controlled aging. Scientists didn't think there were going to be genes that controlled the aging process."

By changing the daf-2 gene to stop most of its activity, Kenyon found the worms lived twice as long. This proved that the worms weren't living longer because of differences in feeding or reproduction, two possible explanations that she called "boring." And even more exciting was the discovery that the long-lived worms stayed healthy and active far longer than normal worms did. "After two weeks, the normal worm is basically in a nursing home or dead already. It's lying quietly, it looks old. In contrast, the altered worm is still active. It isn't just hanging on to life; it's out on the tennis court."

—————— " ——————

"After two weeks, the normal worm is basically in a nursing home or dead already. It's lying quietly, it looks old. In contrast, the altered worm is still active. It isn't just hanging on to life; it's out on the tennis court."

—————— " ——————

As silly as it may be to imagine a worm playing tennis, Kenyon drew the comparison to help people understand what this research could mean for the human life span. The daf-2 gene in C. elegans works with hormones that are found in all animals and also in people. If slowing the work of daf-2 in C. elegans could make the worms stay healthy longer, Kenyon suspected that there might also be a way to extend the healthy years of people. If humans lived to be 150 years old, at age 90 a person would look and act like a 45-year-old. And Kenyon says that when she first saw the healthy old worms, "I wanted to be those worms.... If I were a worm, I would rather be the long-lived mutant than the normal worm, that's for sure."

A Further Understanding of Aging

In 1999, Kenyon and her team discovered another genetic factor that controls some aspects of the aging process. This time it was the reproductive cells, which also speed up the aging process. Removing the reproductive cells in C. elegans resulted in worms that lived 60 percent longer than normal, just over twice as long. This means the worms live a very long time but are not able to reproduce. The dramatic increase in life span surprised the scientific community, but the side effect of infertility did not.

Many believe that an extended life span comes with a biological price tag. For example, a longer, healthier life costs the worm its ability to reproduce. Once again going against the majority, Kenyon believed it would be possible to manipulate the reproductive cells so that the worm lived longer while still being able to reproduce. She pointed to evolution as proof that this is possible. "People think that if you extend life span there has to be a trade-off, but how

Kenyon prepares a sample for viewing while working in her lab at the University of California-San Francisco.

could that be true? Think about it, evolution started with this little tiny primitive animal that is one of your ancestors and that gave rise to C. elegans and then to some animal that gave rise to you. If every time you changed genes there was a trade-off, we would never be so much superior. We are amazing. If every time there was some downside, we would not live 1,000 times longer than the nematode worm . . . and we are not 1,000 times worse off."

In 2000, Kenyon co-founded a company called Elixir Pharmaceuticals with fellow researcher Leonard Guarente. Elixir focuses on research and development of drugs to treat age-related diseases and to slow the effects of aging. This research is redefining preventive medicine to include certain diseases that were once thought to be an inevitable part of growing older. Kenyon believes that it is possible for people to be healthy longer in their lives. "We're not just talking about extending life span, but also extending the good years; what we call the 'health span.'" In February 2003, Elixir merged with Centagenetix, a company that had been studying the chromosomes of people who live to be 100 years old.

> "Many of the most successful scientists are gregarious people who love other people," Kenyon said. "They enjoy making other people happy, and it shows in the way they love to teach, the way they give great talks. It's a very social environment."

In 2003, Kenyon published the results of her study on the beginnings of age-related disease. She wanted to find out why older people seem more likely to have certain diseases. Once again, she found the daf-2 gene was responsible. She learned that daf-2 directs the activity of about 100 other genes. Changing the function of daf-2 in earlier experiments caused the life span of C. elegans to double. This time, Kenyon changed daf-2 in a different way and found that the worms lived six times as long as normal. This would be the same as a human living an active life for about 500 years.

Overall, Kenyon and her team have discovered that it is possible to extend the life span of C. elegans by manipulating any one of more than 30 previously unrecognized genes. Some of these genes have a direct affect on the aging process, while others are agents that help or block different biological processes related to aging.

Becoming a Respected Scientist

When she was beginning to study aging, Kenyon was often dismissed by scientists working in other areas, and she couldn't convince postdoctoral fellows to work on her project. Now, she is one of the most respected geneticists in the country, and she has more applicants than there are available spots on her team. "Kenyon is part of an elite core of researchers," said Andy Evangelista in *UCSF Magazine*, "an internationally recognized pioneer who has helped thrust the science of aging to the research forefront."

Many skeptics have been converted by the results of Kenyon's work. As explained by Arjumand Ghazi, a postdoctoral fellow who worked with her in 2003, "When I first saw the mutant daf-2 worms, I became a believer. This is not just fantasy. [Kenyon] is definitely a pioneer. Her enthusiasm and passion are infectious. . . . I have grandparents and parents who are getting up there in age. I can relate to this research and see myself still working in this field in 20 years."

Kenyon has elevated the once-questionable field of aging research to a respectable scientific pursuit. She recalls that "there wasn't a field when we started. Now, there are a lot of people working on aging." According to Gordon Lithgow, a molecular biologist at the Buck Institute for Age Research in California, "The field needed an injection of fantastic talent, people like Kenyon. There's some great science coming out of this area." David Sinclair, who studies aging at Harvard University, credits her work for the recent growth in the field. Sinclair said that "Few people were expecting single genes to have a huge effect. . . . [Because of Kenyon's work] the field is exploding."

—— *"* ——

"I stopped eating carbohydrates the day we found that putting sugar on the worms' food shortened their life span. . . . I don't eat sweets, bread, pasta, potatoes, or rice. I actually do eat lots of carbohydrates, just not starchy ones, the ones that turn into sugar quickly in your body."

—— *"* ——

Kenyon has published numerous scientific articles and is currently writing a book on aging for non-scientists. Because of her talent for translating complex scientific topics for non-scientists to understand, she has appeared on numerous television and radio shows. She is a full tenured professor at UCSF. In 1997, she was appointed the Herbert Boyer Distinguished Professor of Biochemistry and Biophysics, and also became director of the Hillblom Center for the Biology of Aging at UCSF. In 2003, she was one of six people invited to speak at the celebration of the 50th anniversary of the discovery of DNA. A member of the American Academy of Arts and Sciences, the National Academy of the Sciences, and the Institute of Medicine, Kenyon was also the president of the Genetics Society of America in 2004.

Kenyon has devoted her life to genetics. She is proud of her work and the students she teaches. She enjoys the thrill of discovery and loves the collaboration and social aspects of her work. "Many of the most successful scientists are gregarious people who love other people," she said. "They enjoy making other people happy, and it shows in the way they love to teach, the way they give great talks. It's a very social environment." Her closest friends are among a group of biologists from all over the world.

Speaking of her own work, Kenyon told *Discover* magazine that her most important discoveries so far have been, "That aging is regulated by hormones, that it's plastic. That it's run by the endocrine system and that the endocrine system evolved early. That there's a universal hormonal control for aging." She believes there is a great need for aging research to continue. "The process of aging influences our poetry, our art, our lifestyle, and our happiness, yet we know surprisingly little about it. . . . I think it would be fabulous to live to be 150. Remember, if you're like these worms, at 150 you would be just the same as a normal 75-year-old. Of course you want to be in good health. . . . These long-lived worms stay young longer. That's the thing that's so hard for people to grasp: it's not just being healthy longer. It's being young longer. The worms have told us it's possible."

HOBBIES AND OTHER INTERESTS

Although she once dropped out of the school orchestra, Kenyon never lost her love of music. She still plays the French horn, the Alpine horn, and the guitar. Her work has influenced her whole life—she stays physically fit and maintains a healthy diet because she believes doing so will increase her own life span. "I stopped eating carbohydrates the day we found that putting sugar on the worms' food shortened their lifespan. . . . I don't eat sweets, bread, pasta, potatoes, or rice. I actually do eat lots of carbohydrates, just not starchy ones, the ones that turn into sugar quickly in your body."

SELECTED WRITINGS

Cynthia Kenyon has published her research in more than 70 scientific journal articles. The following selections represent some of her most important research.

"A C. elegans mutant that lives twice as long as wild type," *Nature*, 366, 1993
"Cell non-autonomy of C. elegans daf-2 function in the regulation of diapause and lifespan," *Cell*, 95, 1998
"Signals from the reproductive system regulate the lifespan of C. elegans," *Nature*, 399, 1999

"Regulation of lifespan by sensory perception in C. elegans," *Nature*, 402, 1999

"Rates of behavior and aging specified by mitochondrial function during development," *Science*, 298, 2002

HONORS AND AWARDS

Herbert Boyer Distinguished Professorship (University of California San Francisco): 1997, 2004
Ellison Medical Foundation Senior Scholar: 1998
King Faisal International Prize for Medicine: 2000
Elected to National Academy of Sciences: 2003
Elected to American Academy of Arts and Sciences: 2003
Discover Award for Innovation in Basic Research (*Discover* Magazine): 2004
Elected to Institute of Medicine: 2004
Wiersma Visiting Professorship (California Institute of Technology): 2004
Award for Distinguished Research in the Biomedical Sciences (Association of American Medical Colleges): 2004

FURTHER READING

Books

Who's Who in America, 2006
Who's Who in Medicine and Healthcare, 2004

Periodicals

Current Biography Yearbook, 2005
Discover, Nov. 2004, p.78
New Scientist, Oct. 18, 2003, p.46
Science News, Aug. 2, 2003, p.75
Smithsonian, Mar. 2004, p.56
U.S. News & World Report, Dec. 29, 2003, p.74

Online Articles

http://www.sciencenews.org/articles/20030802/bob9.asp
   (*Science News Online*, "Old Worms, New Aging Genes: Biologists Look into DNA for the Secrets of Long Life," Aug. 2, 2003)
http://www.pbs.org/safarchive/3_ask/archive/bio/103_kenyon_bio.html
   (*Scientific American Frontiers Archives*, "Ask the Scientists: Scientists from Previous Shows," undated)
http://pub.ucsf.edu/magazine/200305/kenyon.html
   (*UCSF Magazine*, "Cynthia Kenyon: Probing the Prospects of Perpetual Youth," May 2003)

ADDRESS

Cynthia Kenyon
University of California San Francisco
Genentech Hall
600 16th Street, Box 2200
San Francisco CA 94143-2200

WORLD WIDE WEB SITES

http://www.ucsf.edu/neurosc/faculty/neuro_kenyon.html

Clea Koff 1972-
English Forensic Anthropologist
Studies Forensic Evidence to Investigate War Crimes
and to Identify Missing Persons

BIRTH

Clea Koff was born in London, England, on September 14,
1972. Her parents were documentary filmmakers. Her father,
David Koff, is an American, and her mother, Msindo Mwinyi-
pembe, is a Tanzanian. Clea has a brother named Kimera.

YOUTH

Growing up with documentary filmmakers made for an unusual childhood. "My parents, David and Msindo, made documen-

tary films about subjects like colonialism and resistance in Africa, the Israeli-Palestinian conflict, and the intersection of race and class in Britain," Koff explained in her book *The Bone Woman: A Forensic Anthropologist's Search for Truth in the Mass Graves of Rwanda, Bosnia, Croatia, and Kosovo.* Clea and Kimera normally accompanied their parents when they were filming overseas. "Our parents took us with them even when they traveled for filming," Koff recalled, "and we were participants at our destinations, not tourists."

Koff's upbringing was different from the norm not only in the traveling she did, but also in the things she was not allowed to do. Her parents were activists who imposed certain beliefs and behaviors upon their children. She and her brother could not watch television until they were ten years old. Koff never attended a music concert. "I almost went to a David Bowie concert," she recalled, "but that was taken away at the last minute." Still, her parents' strict control of her behavior never struck her as being unfair. Though coaxed by a school friend to rebel, Koff refused: "I was a pretty good kid."

> —— " ——
>
> *"I was burying dead birds in plastic bags so I could dig them up later—I was curious how long it took them to 'turn into' skeletons,"* Koff recalled. *"I took the stinking bags to my (somewhat horrified) science teacher for extracurricular and wholly self-motivated death investigations."*
>
> —— " ——

As a child, Koff remembers being interested in the skeletons of dead animals and birds. "I was burying dead birds in plastic bags so I could dig them up later—I was curious how long it took them to 'turn into' skeletons," she recalled. "I took the stinking bags to my (somewhat horrified) science teacher for extracurricular and wholly self-motivated death investigations."

EDUCATION

Koff attended elementary school in England. Her family then moved to Washington, DC, and later to Los Angeles, California, where she attended Ulysses S. Grant High School. In high school, she saw a television documentary about the human remains preserved during the volcanic eruption at Pompeii. The account so impressed her that she decided to study archeology at Stanford University. During a college archeological dig in Greece, however, she found that she did not want to research the remains of ancient bodies. Instead, she wanted to study the remains of crime victims to determine their identities and the circumstances of their deaths.

Koff was inspired to study forensic anthropology by Clyde Snow's book *Witnesses from the Grave: The Stories Bones Tell*, a memoir of his work identifying the dead bodies of government opponents in Argentina. Thousands of Argentineans were killed and buried in mass graves during a dictatorship that lasted for many years. When democracy returned to Argentina, Snow and other scientists used new forensic methods to identify the victims of the old regime. Koff was fascinated by how much information could be obtained. Following her graduation from Stanford with a bachelor's degree, she went on to study forensic anthropology at the University of Arizona and earn a master's degree from the University of Nebraska.

CAREER HIGHLIGHTS

Traveling to Rwanda

In 1996, when she was still a student in graduate school, Koff was contacted by Physicians for Human Rights, an organization based in Boston. They had been asked by the United Nations (UN) to assemble a team of forensic experts to investigate alleged acts of genocide in Rwanda, a country in east Africa. The nation had been wracked by a racially motivated war between the Hutu and Tutsi tribes. In 1994, members of the Hutu tribe had murdered an estimated 750,000 Tutsis in what the UN described as an act of genocide. The UN wanted a team of scientists to find evidence for the UN International Criminal Tribunal for Rwanda. Their specific goal was to determine whether those killed in Rwanda were soldiers who had been legitimately killed in combat or civilians who had been murdered. Koff was one of 16 scientists on the UN team who traveled to Rwanda to investigate the killings.

> *The UN report on the genocide in Rwanda concluded the following: "Approximately 800,000 people were killed during the 1994 genocide in Rwanda. The systematic slaughter of men, women, and children which took place over the course of about 100 days between April and July of 1994 will forever be remembered as one of the most abhorrent events of the 20th century."*

The team began their investigation by finding the sites of mass graves, either with the help of local villagers or by examining differences in soil color and texture that showed where the ground had been disturbed. They would then don gloves, overalls, and heavy boots and dig up the remains of those buried at the site. Everything found was carefully cleaned and documented. Bodies were identified in a number of ways: from DNA sam-

In The Bone Woman, *Koff described her work documenting the genocide in Kibuye, Rwanda. "Part of our work at Kibuye was cleaning and documenting clothing and other personal belongings that could help identify bodies. Later, we held a 'Clothing Day,' on which survivors came to help identify the dead, who were often relatives. Clothing Day allowed me to see our work in a humanitarian, rather than solely forensic, context."*

ples and also from documents, keys, and jewelry found on the bodies. Autopsies determined how the victims had been killed. Many of the Rwandan dead had been civilians who were killed with machetes. Because of the evidence unearthed by Koff and the others, 20 Rwandans have been tried and found guilty of murder, including the former head of the Hutu government. Some 35 other people are awaiting trial. Although the work in Rwanda was difficult and gruesome, Koff believed it was also worthwhile.

Following its investigation, the UN report concluded the following: "Approximately 800,000 people were killed during the 1994 genocide in Rwanda. The systematic slaughter of men, women, and children which took place over the course of about 100 days between April and July of 1994 will forever be remembered as one of the most abhorrent events of the 20th century. Rwandans killed Rwandans, brutally decimating the Tutsi population of the country, but also targeting moderate Hutus. Appalling atrocities were committed, by militia and the armed forces, but also by civilians against other civilians. . . . The failure by the United Nations to prevent, and subsequently, to stop the genocide in Rwanda was a failure by the United Nations system as a whole. . . . The lack of will to act in response to the crisis in Rwanda becomes all the more deplorable in the light of the reluctance by key members of the International Community to acknowledge that the mass murder being pursued in front of global media was a genocide. . . . As the mass killings were being conducted in Rwanda in April and May 1994, and although television was broadcasting pictures of bloated corpses . . . there was a reluctance among key States to use the term genocide to describe what was happening. The delay in identifying the events in Rwanda as a genocide was a failure by the Security Council."

Koff experienced a terrible reaction to one young man's body, which showed evidence of gunshot wounds. "I felt so awful, so full of hurt and emotion, and mixed in with that was a knee-buckling sense of privilege that I was touching the bones of someone whose family was out there and wanted more than anything to have him back."

Traveling to the Balkans

Koff soon volunteered to assist five more UN missions to investigate mass graves in Bosnia, Croatia, and Kosovo, part of a region in Eastern Europe known as the Balkans. The area was populated by many different ethnic groups—Albanians, Bulgarians, Greeks, Romanians, Serbs, Croats, Slovenes, Bosnians, Macedonians, and Montenegrans. Following the break up of

Working near Vukovar, in Croatia, to locate the edge of a mass grave.

Yugoslavia into a number of smaller nations in the early 1990s, a number of regional wars broke out. These wars were spurred by long-repressed antagonism among the various ethnic groups. There were widespread atrocities, including "ethnic cleansing," a form of genocide that included the deliberate murders of a group of people based only on their ethnicity. Ethnic cleansing was commonly practiced to remove unwanted ethnic groups from a territory now controlled by a rival ethnic group. The UN again sent in teams of forensic experts to determine the extent of these atrocities and to find who had been responsible for the crimes. Evidence for wholesale murder was easily discovered. In many cases, the dead bodies had their hands tied behind their backs, wore blindfolds, and had multiple gunshot wounds.

After a one-week vacation in mid-1996, during which she recovered from her experience in Rwanda, Koff set off for two months in Bosnia. Her first mission was to work with a team of forensic experts trying to discover what had become of 8,000 men who had disappeared near the small Bosnian town of Srebrenica. The team soon located a spot where a mass grave had been dug and covered over. This grave site was similar to other such sites, Koff explained, because it looked deceptively peaceful: "Often the place will look like a good spot for a picnic because it has sun and shade, a stream, and is quiet enough to allow one to hear the rustle of high leaves in the trees when a breeze comes through."

During the Bosnia mission, Koff experienced a terrible reaction to one of the bodies she unearthed. It was a young man who, Koff could tell from the bones, was only about 16 years old. His body showed evidence of gunshot wounds. Koff was unable to keep her emotions in check while doing her gruesome work: "I felt so awful, so full of hurt and emotion, and mixed in with that was a knee-buckling sense of privilege that I was touching the bones of someone whose family was out there and wanted more than anything to have him back."

"If someone had asked me about my career goal on my first mission to Rwanda," Koff wrote in her memoir, "I would have said that I aspired to give a voice to people silenced by their own governments or militaries, people suppressed in the most final way: murdered and put into clandestine graves."

In August 1996 Koff joined the UN forensic team in nearby Croatia. The mission was to investigate a grave site near the town of Vukovar. Unexpectedly, they ran into a protest from the local women in the village. The women were convinced that their missing husbands and sons were not dead and buried but still alive in Serbian prisoners-of-war camps. They did not want any useless digging to be done. But two months later, when the bodies had been successfully unearthed and identified, the women in Vukovar finally came to believe the worst. Koff remembered: "One women believed when she saw the front-door key to her old apartment, found in the pocket of the trousers worn by the man anthropologically identified as her husband."

In 2000 Koff embarked on the last of her UN missions, this time to Kosovo, another country in the former Yugoslavia that had seen years of war. The one-time province of Serbia, Kosovo had endured violent ethnic cleansing by both sides. The Serbian government forced Albanians out of the area and allowed Serbs to move in. Following NATO bombing of the Serbian Army and their subsequent withdrawal, some 100,000 Serbs were then forced out of the region. After the fighting was over, several thousand civilians were missing and presumed dead.

The UN mission encountered difficulties in locating the bodies of those who had been murdered during wartime. Groups of bodies had sometimes been buried in local cemeteries, the sites disguised to look like regular burials. Other times, locals found their murdered relatives lying in fields and buried them properly. These incidents made it difficult for the team to carry out its mission to locate and document victims of war crimes. Koff remembered that she was speechless whenever a relative was present when they exhumed a body from the ground: "There I am, on the one hand in a deeply personal situation with someone because I am involved with his or her dead relative, and yet on the other hand we are strangers. So I say nothing because it is only my actions that can help."

—— " ——

"When there's a disappearance, people are living with loss and grief and not knowing what's actually happened to their relatives," Koff said. "That is what people in our communities here in the U.S. are actually dealing with. It's a disappearance."

—— " ——

New Approaches to Her Work

During her UN missions, Koff kept a journal recording her experiences. Upon her return from Kosovo in 2000, she began reworking these journals into a memoir. In 2004, she published *The Bone Woman: A Forensic Anthropologist's Search for Truth in the Mass Graves of Rwanda, Bosnia, Croatia, and Kosovo.* The book details both Koff's experiences doing forensic work and her ideas about the motivations behind the horrible crimes she uncovered. "If someone had asked me about my career goal on my first mission to Rwanda," she wrote in her memoir, "I would have said that I aspired to give a voice to people silenced by their own governments or militaries, people suppressed in the most final way: murdered and put into clandestine graves."

Response to the book was positive. Caroline Moorehead of the *Independent* admitted that *The Bone Woman* "is not for the squeamish." But Phil Whitaker in the *Guardian* called the memoir "a humane, hopeful and involving book." Writing in *Library Journal*, Joan W. Gartland concluded: "This is a brave book, presented in a clear voice by a scientist who is confident that her missions will get to the truth and yet human enough to cry at the horror of it all."

Koff now finds herself on a new mission. After spending the past years working overseas, she has turned her attention to the United States. She has formed the Missing Persons Identification Resource Center, a nonprofit organization in California set up to support the families and friends of missing persons. "When there's a disappearance, people are living with loss and grief and not knowing what's actually happened to their relatives," Koff said. "That is what people in our communities here in the U.S. are actually dealing with. It's a disappearance." The Center will create anthropological profiles of missing persons to assist law enforcement efforts to match them with the estimated 40,000 unidentified bodies in coroners' offices nationwide. "I'm not saying we're going to match everybody up," Koff admitted, "but we will improve the probability that somebody will be found. . . . Whether it's a war or whatever—it's still people looking for the remains of their family. People need to know." As of early 2006, the Center was still in the preliminary fund-raising stage.

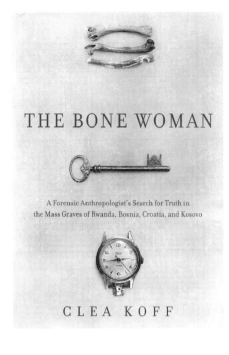

WRITINGS

The Bone Woman: A Forensic Anthropologist's Search for Truth in the Mass Graves of Rwanda, Bosnia, Croatia, and Kosovo, 2004

FURTHER READING

Books

Koff, Clea. *The Bone Woman: A Forensic Anthropologist's Search for Truth in the Mass Graves of Rwanda, Bosnia, Croatia, and Kosovo,* 2004

Periodicals

Booklist, May 15, 2004, p.1583
Current Biography Yearbook, 2004
Guardian (London), May 22, 2004, p.12
Herald (Scotland), Apr. 10, 2004, p.19
Independent (London), Apr. 30, 2004, p.25
Library Journal, June 15, 2004, p.83
Los Angeles Times, June 9, 2004, p.E1
New York Times, Apr. 24, 2004, p.A4
Times (London), Apr. 3, 2004, p.4

Toronto Sun, July 25, 2004, p.S22
Washington Post, May 9, 2004, p.T7

Online Articles

http://abcnews.go.com/WNT/Science/story?id=934304
   (ABC News, "'Bone Woman' Digs Up Remains to Foil Killers: Woman
   Who Found Evidence on Killings in Rwanda, Bosnia, and Kosovo Now
   Turns to U.S. Missing Persons," July 10, 2005)

ADDRESS

Clea Koff
MPID
PO Box 65922
Los Angeles, CA 90065–0922

WORLD WIDE WEB SITES

http://www.mpid.org
http://www.thebonewoman.com

Marcia McNutt 1952-

American Marine Geophysicist
Director of the Monterey Bay Aquarium Research
Institute

BIRTH

Marcia Kemper McNutt was born on February 19, 1952, in Minneapolis, Minnesota. She is the daughter of Patricia Suzanne (McClain) McNutt and Richard Charles McNutt, who ran a family plate-glass business. McNutt grew up with no brothers and three sisters.

YOUTH

McNutt fell in love with the ocean early on. Although she was born and raised in landlocked Minnesota, each spring she would travel to La Jolla in southern California, near the Pacific Ocean, to vacation with her grandmother. "I can still remember the smell of the ocean after getting off the plane in San Diego from Minnesota, the warm humid air of March, the brilliant sunshine," McNutt said. "It was such a different world."

When McNutt was six, she visited the Scripps Institution of Oceanography in La Jolla and decided to become an oceanographer. (She would later earn her doctorate degree at Scripps.) She was fascinated by "this world going on down there with very little intimate contact with people." She never forgot seeing "all the unusual fish in tanks and realizing that except for this unusual opportunity to display them, it wouldn't be possible for the average person to see them."

> "I wasn't interested in playing with dolls. As I got older, I didn't like jobs that involved babysitting," McNutt said. "Mother always tried to dress me in pink. But I loved the outdoors and animals."

All through her youth, McNutt was a confirmed tomboy. "I wasn't interested in playing with dolls. As I got older, I didn't like jobs that involved babysitting," she said. "Mother always tried to dress me in pink. But I loved the outdoors and animals." McNutt thought in terms of black and white—never in between. Science, with its reliance on facts and data, had a natural appeal to her, even in elementary school. "In my own naïve way, I equated science as being right or wrong," she said.

EDUCATION

Grade School and High School

McNutt attended Northrup Collegiate School (now the Blake Schools), a private, all-girls school in Minneapolis. When she graduated in 1970, she was named valedictorian of her class, an honor given to the top student in a graduating class. McNutt noted that growing up with sisters and being in all-female classes boosted her confidence to study science. "All the people around me were women—teachers, classmates. Until I got to Colorado College, I never had the experience of walking into a classroom and seeing that I was the only girl," she said. "And by that time, my sense that this [science] is something that I wanted to do was well established."

Later in her career, McNutt went to a meeting of distinguished women scientists and discovered that more than half had gone to either an all-female high school or college. "Clearly, there was something about those educational experiences that meant that these women chose science far out of proportion to women in the general population," McNutt said.

Colorado College and the Path to Marine Geophysics

McNutt entered Colorado College in Colorado Springs in autumn 1970, planning to study physics. When an adviser told her the subject was not suited for women, she simply switched advisers. She also gained another scientific interest when she enrolled in an introductory class in geology.

Colorado College followed a non-traditional "block schedule" that allowed students to take one class at a time and thus devote several weeks to a single subject. McNutt's geology professor asked the students to pack up their sleeping bags and head to the wilds of Colorado for about two months. The group then was challenged to trace the landscape's history, without using text books. "I saw more Colorado geography than most people see in their entire lives," McNutt recalled.

After only three years, McNutt became one of the first women to receive a Bachelor of Arts (BA) degree in physics from Colorado College. Her degree was awarded in 1973 *summa cum laude* (Latin for "with highest honors"). McNutt planned to take a year off and work as a housekeeper in a ski resort. But a professor, Richard Hilt, urged her to apply to graduate school instead. "Students tell themselves these days, 'Oh, I'm so burned out, I need to take a year off,'" Hilt said. "Marcia was never burned out. She was too busy burning up the track."

Hilt gave McNutt a list of reading on geophysics—the study of how the Earth's energy and matter interact. McNutt was especially struck by the relatively new theory of "plate tectonics"—or the movement of the relatively rigid upper layer of Earth's crust and upper mantle, called the "lithosphere." According to the theory, the lithosphere is approximately 100 kilometers thick and is divided into a series of large plates. Over time, the position and size of the plates change. The boundaries of the plates, where they move against each other, are areas of major geologic activity, including volcanoes, earthquakes, and mountain building.

Uniting her interest in plate tectonics with her love of the ocean, McNutt decided to become a marine geophysicist—a scientist who studies the movement of the plates that lie beneath the Earth's oceans. She was guided in this direction partly by her college professors. "They showed me that the era of big discoveries in nuclear physics was coming to an end," she said. "But they identified ocean science as an up-and-coming area."

Graduate School

McNutt returned to her grandmother's vacation spot, La Jolla, California, to attend graduate school at the Scripps Institute of Oceanography. Partly supported by a fellowship from the National Science Foundation, McNutt earned her doctoral degree (PhD) in Earth Sciences in 1978.

—————— " ——————

McNutt's decision to become a marine geophysicist—a scientist who studies the movement of the plates that lie beneath the Earth's oceans—was guided by her college professors. "They showed me that the era of big discoveries in nuclear physics was coming to an end," she said. "But they identified ocean science as an up-and-coming area."

—————— " ——————

As a graduate student, McNutt became interested in the underwater areas of Earth that can't be explained by the normal rules of plate tectonics. One of these areas is French Polynesia, a series of more than 100 volcanic islands in the South Pacific. It includes the islands of Tahiti and Bora Bora. The area has volcanoes located in the middle of the Earth's plates—not at the plates' edges, which would be the usual location. The source of the volcanic activity that creates islands in the middle of the plates is thought to be "hot spots" beneath the ocean. In geological terms, a hot spot is a plume of molten rock (called magma) that rises from within the Earth and reaches the surface. These plumes form underwater volcanoes, or may rise above sea level and form islands. McNutt saw that French Polynesia was an area ripe for study.

CAREER HIGHLIGHTS

Throughout her career, McNutt has studied underwater plate tectonics. This work has made her one of the leading ocean scientists in the world. In order to measure the physical properties of the Earth beneath the oceans, she uses the underwater technique of echo-sounding. She also uses data collected by satellites in outer space. In her current job as head of the Monterey Bay Aquarium Research Institute in California, she helps scientists and engineers work together to create new technology to advance ocean research.

Academic Success

After earning her doctorate in 1978, McNutt started her career at the University of Minnesota, working there for a year as a visiting assistant professor. In 1979, she joined the United States Geological Survey in Menlo Park,

One of MBARI's robot submarines, otherwise known as "Remotely Operated Vehicle," which McNutt and her team use for ocean exploration.

California, as a geophysicist researcher. Her job was to study the Earth's plates to help to predict when earthquakes would occur.

In 1982, McNutt left her job as an earthquake researcher to become an assistant professor in geophysics at the Massachusetts Institute of Technology (MIT) in Cambridge, Massachusetts, one of the nation's most prestigious universities. She quickly made her way through the ranks in the department of Earth, Atmospheric, and Planetary Sciences. She became an associate professor in 1986 and a full professor three years later. At MIT, McNutt became known among students as a lively and effective instructor. In 1985, she was honored with a Graduate Student Council Award for teaching.

In 1991, McNutt became the Earl A. Griswold Professor of Geophysics at MIT. Four years later, she was named to a key role in the world of ocean science. She became director of the Joint Program in Oceanography and Applied Ocean Science and Engineering. This graduate-education program is a collaboration between MIT and the Woods Hole Oceanographic Institution, a world-famous ocean-science center located in Woods Hole, Massachusetts.

Exploration and Discovery

While she was building her academic career, McNutt was also busy with field research in the oceans of the world. To date, she has taken part in at least 24 oceanographic expeditions. She has served as chief scientist on several major voyages. "I love going to sea," she said.

French Polynesia was the site of some of McNutt's most exciting and important trips. Few researchers had studied the area because it wasn't on a commercial sea route or in a strategic military zone. McNutt found much to discover there. She gathered evidence to prove that the region had been the center of intense volcanic ability for more than 100 million years. She called French Polynesia the Earth's "stovepipe," pointing out that major updrafts of heat from the mantle far beneath the region keep the Earth's upper mantle partly molten (or liquid). As a result, many volcanic islands were allowed to form. McNutt also discovered that the Earth's lithosphere is only about two-thirds of its usual thickness in French Polynesia.

McNutt has also studied the North American continent, theorizing that it eventually will break in two pieces—a Western North America and an Eastern North America. While such a shift is millions of years away, she said, "in terms of earthquake activity, it's already started." In addition, she has focused her attention on the central plateau of Tibet in Asia.

In order to collect data, McNutt needed one unusual job qualification: underwater-demolition expert. "Some of the work we do in the oceans requires using sound waves to image structures beneath the sea floor. One of the best ways to get a large volume of sound energy in the ocean is to set off an explosive charge," McNutt said. She explained that a certain number of scientists had to earn a license to build a charge and light an underwater fuse. She received her license after an intensive two months of training with the U.S. Navy Seals.

> *Sea voyages are like summer camp, according to McNutt, because they involve a small group of people in a closed environment with no access to television, radio, or newspapers. "You all have to get along, and you all have a common mission," she said. "Twenty-four hours a day, you are trying to make maximum use of time: just like at camp."*

McNutt said sea voyages are like summer camp, because they involve a small group of people in a closed environment with no access to television, radio, or newspapers. "You all have to get along, and you all have a common mission," she said. "Twenty-four hours a day, you are trying to make maximum use of time: just like at camp."

McNutt shown with other institute staffers on a small boat heading out to the MBARI research ship, R/V Western Flyer, *in Carmel Bay, California.*

Moving to Monterey Bay Aquarium Research Institute

In 1997, McNutt left her posts at MIT and Woods Hole to become President and Chief Executive Officer of the Monterey Bay Aquarium Research Institute (MBARI). It is a sister institution to the nearby Monterey Bay Aquarium, a well-known tourist destination. Both are located in Monterey County, in northern California. At the time she left MIT, McNutt was considered a sure bet to become head of her department. People wondered how she could leave her high-profile job for a research institute that was not as well known. But McNutt felt the institute was "poised to make a huge impact."

The institute was launched by the late billionaire David Packard, the co-founder of Hewlett-Packard. Funded by the Packard Foundation, MBARI is devoted to developing and exploiting new technologies in order to explore the oceans. It addresses both general research questions, such as how marine microbes mediate important chemical cycles, as well as very practical problems, such as how oceans will cope with the massive amounts of carbon dioxide they currently have to absorb. It's also devoted to the design and construction of underwater vehicles. These vehicles, either connected to a boat or free ranging, are designed to take samples from or to observe the ocean, its creatures, and the ocean floor.

*The Monterey Bay Aquarium Research Institute, on the coast
of the Pacific Ocean.*

In her job, McNutt oversees engineers and scientists, as well as support staff. The scientists propose ways to get information about the ocean. The engineers come up with the technology to make the studies happen, whether by building new technologies or adapting old ones. According to McNutt, MBARI works "to break down the disciplinary and cultural boundaries between science and engineering. We want to put our effort where there is the biggest chance of new technology leading to fundamental discovery," she said. "But what we have to do is go that extra step of making high-tech devices developed elsewhere for other purposes work autonomously under water."

Observers say the institute has an advantage over government-funded organizations because there is no clumsy bureaucracy that prevents scientists from moving quickly on ideas. They also have the freedom to carry out high-risk, long-term projects that are difficult for government agencies. In addition, MBARI has its own fleet of vessels, unlike federally-funded groups that have to share ships. Because she commands such rich resources, McNutt has a lot of power in her field. *Scientific American* magazine called her "one of the world's most influential ocean scientists."

McNutt is keenly aware that about 95 percent of the world's oceans—and the endless activities beneath them—remain unexplored. "Plankton bloom. Volcanoes erupt. Plates slip in earthquakes. Fish spawn," she said. "The chance of being in the right time and in the right place to catch such events in action is very small." She is committed to developing technology to help scientists capture more data—and to use the information to solve critical problems like over-fished seas, global warming, and depleted energy supplies.

McNutt enjoys the creative aspects of her job. "What's nice about geophysics is that it's not always apparent what needs to be done next, and you often find that talking a circuitous route is the quickest way to get from A to B."

A Leader in Geophysics

—— " ——

McNutt is a distinguished leader in her field. In 1999, she became president of the American Geophysical Union, made up of 35,000 Earth science professionals. Her duties include testifying before Congress.

McNutt was appointed the chair of President Bill Clinton's panel on Ocean Exploration. She also has served at the National Science Foundation as vice-chair of the Advisory Committee for Geosciences. In 2005, McNutt was named to the National Academy of Sciences, one of the highest honors a scientist can receive.

About 95 percent of the world's oceans—and the endless activities beneath them—remain unexplored, according to McNutt. "Plankton bloom. Volcanoes erupt. Plates slip in earthquakes. Fish spawn," she said. "The chance of being in the right time and in the right place to catch such events in action is very small."

MARRIAGE AND FAMILY

—— " ——

McNutt married Marcel Edward Hoffman in 1978, the same year she received her PhD. The couple had three daughters: older sister Meredith and identical twins Ashley and Dana. In 1990, McNutt's husband died unexpectedly, leaving her a widow with three young children to care for. In 1995, McNutt was featured on a PBS TV program about female scientists called "Discovering Women." The show portrayed McNutt at work as a distinguished academician and researcher who also managed to juggle such day-to-day children's activities as birthday parties and piano lessons.

McNutt said that her children gave her the best experience to prepare her for running MBARI, where she often must mediate between people who disagree. "So many times my twins get into an argument. Both are absolutely firm in their convictions," she said. "And if you say to either one of them they're wrong, then they start tuning you out."

In 1996, McNutt married Ian Wallace Young, a sea captain. They met when she was on an expedition to French Polynesia. McNutt and Young married in Tahiti, in "a Tahitian ceremony, with a Tahitian priest, war canoes, and native dancers and fire walkers," she said. McNutt and her family live in Salinas, California.

HOBBIES AND OTHER INTERESTS

In spite of her busy career, McNutt has many activities and interests outside of work. "I do have a life," she said. "I have a wonderful husband, three daughters, six horses, two dogs, two cats, and a rabbit. I ski, go on vacations, visit my mother, etc. I think there hasn't been anything I've had to forego." For many years, she rode a motorcycle. But she recently gave up bike-riding for horse-riding.

McNutt enjoys eating good food and in another life would like to be a gourmet chef. "I don't have time now to do really inventive cooking," she said. "Shopping is the activity I hate more than anything." She said her luxury is to go to bed early with a cup of hot tea and a good book.

HONORS AND AWARDS

Teaching Award (Graduate Student Council): 1985
James B. Macelwane Award for Outstanding Research by a Young
    Scientist (American Geophysical Union): 1988
Inducted into the National Academy of Sciences: 2005

FURTHER READING

Books

Notable Women Scientists, 1999
Oakes, Elizabeth. *International Encyclopedia of Women Scientists,* 2002

Periodicals

Boston Globe Magazine, Dec. 15, 1996, p.14
Monterey County Herald, June 30, 2002, p.E3
Scientific American, June 2001, p.38

Online Articles

http://www.coloradocollege.edu/success/success01/McNutt.htm
    (Colorado College Stories, "Success: Marcia McNutt," undated)
http://www.geotimes.org/july05/profiles.html
    (Geotimes, "Profiles: Marcia McNutt, Oceangoing Geophysicist," July
    2005)

http://www.radcliffe.edu/about/news/quarterly/200301/explorations4.
html
(Radcliffe Institute for Advanced Study, "Fellow Update: Marcia
McNutt B '86," Winter 2003)

Online Databases

Biography Resource Center Online, 2005, article from *Notable Women
Scientists*, 1999

ADDRESS

Marcia McNutt
Monterey Bay Aquarium Research Institute
7700 Sandholt Road
Moss Landing, CA 95039-9644

WORLD WIDE WEB SITES

http://www.mbari.org/staff/Marcia
http://www.coloradocollege.edu/success/success01/McNutt.asp

Lee Ann Newsom 1956-

Moroccan-Born American Paleoethnobotanist
and Educator
Recipient of a John D. and Catherine T. MacArthur
Foundation Fellowship, or "Genius Grant"

BIRTH

Lee Ann Newsom was born on October 26, 1956, in Morocco.
Her family was living there while her father worked as a pilot and
intelligence officer with the United States Navy in North Africa.
His job was to fly high-altitude spy missions over the Soviet
Union in order to photograph Soviet military installations.

YOUTH

Newsom's family returned to the United States when she was about four years old, and she grew up in northern Florida. Her early school years were spent in the city of Jacksonville, but when she was in the fifth grade her family moved to the town of Keystone Heights, which is located between Jacksonville and Gainesville. Her interest in the past began at a young age. "As long as I can remember, I used to pour over *National Geographics*," she told *Biography Today*. "I was interested in human evolution ... and archaeology in general and also the natural world—plants, animals, and how they came to be."

These interests would later lead Newsom to her career as a paleoethnobotanist—an archaeologist who studies the remains of plant matter so that she can better understand the people of the past. Her job requires her to intensely analyze small fragments of wood and plant matter that may be hundreds or even thousands of years old. Her ability to focus on tiny details was already evident in her childhood. "I was happiest if I was by myself out in the woods," Newsom remembered, "watching things, ... really studying the vegetation [and] studying ants for hours."

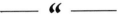

"As long as I can remember, I used to pour over **National Geographics,***" Newsom said. "I was interested in human evolution ... and archaeology in general and also the natural world—plants, animals, and how they came to be."*

FIRST JOBS

Despite her early love of archaeology, Newsom spent several years working in an entirely different field. This happened, in part, because few people encouraged her to pursue her interests in anthropology and nature. "When I first got out of high school and mentioned to anyone about wanting to be an archaeologist ... they would say 'there are no jobs,'" she remembered. "One person even told me it was not something for girls or women." Instead, when Newsom finished high school she became a paralegal—a person who assists lawyers—and spent several years working in law offices. She enjoyed the part of the job where she got to conduct detailed research, but eventually decided to make a change. "It wasn't what I wanted," she said of legal work. "I just dropped all that and went back to school to pursue my dream."

EDUCATION

Newsom enrolled in the anthropology program at the University of Florida in Gainesville. She had been a good student while in primary school, and she continued to do well in her university studies. She earned her Bachelor of Arts (BA) degree in 1982, then went on to receive two graduate degrees: a Master of Arts (MA) degree in 1986 and a PhD (doctorate) in 1993. While still an undergraduate, she became a volunteer at the Florida Museum of Natural History, which is located at the university, and later took a job as a secretary in the Anthropology Department. In the beginning, this job involved a lot of unexciting tasks such as typing, but it got better with time. "Finally they started giving me artifacts to sort out," she explained, which introduced her to real archaeological work.

—— " ——

"When I first got out of high school and mentioned to anyone about wanting to be an archaeologist . . . they would say 'there are no jobs.' One person even told me it was not something for girls or women."

—— " ——

One of the keys to Newsom's success is that she enrolled in a number of classes that were outside the field of anthropology. Because of her interest in plants, she studied botany, forestry, tropical ecology, and the properties of wood. "I took a background in botany," she explained, "and adapted it to archaeology." All this knowledge helps her to better understand the plant remains she uncovers, which in turn helps her understand the people who used those materials centuries ago. Mixing botany and archaeology has made her part of a very specialized group of scientists: there are fewer than 100 paleoethnobotanists in the entire world.

CAREER HIGHLIGHTS

Newsom's first major project began while she was still in college. In the mid-1980s, construction workers unearthed human bones near Titusville, Florida, and it was soon determined that the site was an ancient burial ground. Construction was halted, and archeologists went to work. Newsom was one of them. What they found was a cemetery that was 7,000 to 8,000 years old, where bodies had been buried beneath wooden teepee-style structures. Known as the Windover Archaeological Site, it contained the remains of 169 people. This made it one of the most extensive cemeteries ever discovered in North America from the Archaic period—the time just after the glaciers of the Ice Age had retreated.

But even more significant than the size of the burial site was the fact that it was located in a muddy pond bottom. Such "wetsites" are the best places for Newsom to search for artifacts because ancient plant materials will survive for long periods in still water, while those exposed to the oxygen in

Newsom in her lab at Penn State University.

the open air decay quickly. "If it's still and in muddy sediment, the normal agents of decay and the insects are not there," she explained. At Windover, the mud-encased artifacts were extremely well preserved. Brain tissue was even found in some of the skulls. "That kind of condition tells us that the people had to be placed down in the muddy, oxygen-poor pond bottom . . . within 36 hours of death," Newsom explained. These types of water burials, which have been found in other Florida sites, seem to have served a ceremonial or spiritual purpose for the ancient people of the area.

By carefully sifting the mud through fine mesh screens, Newsom and her colleagues were able to find some extremely tiny pieces of evidence. Among them was a collection of seeds that were found along with the bones of a woman. With just this small bit of evidence, Newsom was able to do some shrewd detective work. Because the seeds were near the woman's lower abdominal cavity—where her stomach had once been—Newsom decided that they had probably been swallowed as the woman's last meal. Strangely, most of the seeds were not broken, as they would be if the woman had chewed them. Because of this, she theorized that they had been swallowed as part of a tea. She identified more than 2,000 elderberry seeds, along with seeds from several other plants: grapes, black nightshade, holly, and a prickly pear cactus. Conducting further research, Newsom found that such fruits were used in medicinal teas by Native Americans in later centuries. She also found evidence that the woman was suffering from bone cancer.

Putting these clues together, Newsom came to some very precise conclusions: "It's likely this woman was in great pain when she died," she concluded. "Probably she took or was given the fruits, brewed as a medical infusion, to relieve the pain." Newsom has also wondered if the tea may have been used as a way to end the woman's life and put an end to her suffering. "In that quantity [the tea] could have been toxic," she said. "Maybe it was euthanasia." This analysis provided new insight into medical practices in ancient America, a subject that anthropologists know very little about.

―――― " ――――

"It's likely this woman was in great pain when she died," Newsom concluded about one body, found in a burial site near a collection of seeds. "Probably she took or was given the fruits, brewed as a medical infusion, to relieve the pain.… In that quantity [the tea] could have been toxic. Maybe it was euthanasia."

―――― " ――――

Ancient Clothing and Containers

The Windover site was also very important because it yielded woven fabrics that had been used for clothing, showing that the people hadn't relied on animal skins for protection, as had been previously thought. "We didn't even know people did any weaving, much less wore clothing back then," Newsom said. Also, the burial practices were quite elaborate, which suggests that the people had developed a relatively advanced society. "These were hunter-gatherers, not brutish people," Newsom said. "They cared enough about their people to bury them with respect."

In studying the ancient Floridians, Newsom often focused on a particular type of plant—the bottle gourd. These fruits can be hollowed out and used to hold food and water, so they were valuable items in the Archaic period. "This is long before pottery was manufactured," she explained, "so they recognized them as a useful container-type fruit." One of the gourds found at the Windover site was 7,000 years old, showing that the Archaic people of Florida were using them very early on. The bottle gourd originated in Africa, and Newsom believes that the fruit floated over to North America on ocean currents. The inhabitants of Florida found them and used them, but more importantly, they seem to have begun cultivating the plants themselves. "We're not looking at random 'hey there's a gourd on the beach,' kind of thing," Newsom said. "People were probably growing them. They recognized it as a useful fruit, saved the seeds, and planted the seeds." Previously, most anthropologists thought that plant cultivation didn't take place in Florida until much later and that the practice had been learned from the Native Americans who

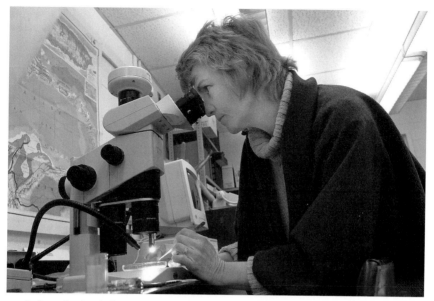

Lab analysis of plant materials is a key part of Newsom's work. She uses the microscope to help her identify plant samples through their cell structure.

lived farther west. But Newsom's analysis of the gourds suggests that the ancient people of Florida may have been important pioneers in the practice of farming. "This is pointing to that middle ground when people were recognizing the utility of plants and the lifecycle of plants and maybe were starting to do things that ultimately led to agriculture," she explained.

Finding and Organizing Artifacts

After receiving her doctoral degree (PhD) in 1993, Newsom became a curator at the Center for Archaeological Investigations at Southern Illinois University at Carbondale. She spent a lot of her time making an inventory of the center's collection, which included sacred objects and human remains of Native Americans. Newsom was also responsible for contacting various tribes around the country to let them know that the center had items in its collection related to their ancestors. These activities were required by a federal law that helps protect gravesites that are uncovered by archaeologists, and it gave Newsom a chance to make use of her paralegal skills. "That legal background gave me the ability to read all the legal documents and interpret them," she explained. Newsom also taught college courses in archaeology and botany while at Southern Illinois University.

Meanwhile, Newsom continued to conduct archaeological investigations. In addition to sites in Florida, she specializes in studying the inhabitants of the Caribbean Islands in the centuries before Christopher Columbus and other Europeans arrived in the New World. She has worked in Grenada, Cuba, Puerto Rico, the Bahamas, and many other islands. She drew on her first-hand knowledge of the region to create the book *On Land and Sea: Native American Uses of Biological Resources in the West Indies*, which was co-written by Elizabeth S. Wing.

——— **"** ———

"Sometimes you are digging and get into a layer, maybe you come upon a human burial. And you know you're seeing someone that was laid to rest hundreds, if not thousands, of years ago and at that moment you start to think about who they were.... They were a real person, a real part of the community. And that never ceases to amaze me. It feels like a real privilege."

——— **"** ———

An archaeological field investigation or "dig" demands a great deal of detail work—mapping the area, carefully removing and sifting the dirt or mud, and precisely recording where each item is found. Despite the exacting methods, Newsom finds fieldwork extremely rewarding. "I always enjoy it, and it's always something different," she said. "Sometimes you are digging and get into a layer, maybe you come upon a human burial. And you know you're seeing someone that was laid to rest hundreds, if not thousands, of years ago and at that moment you start to think about who they were.... You see the things buried with them and realize that somebody really cared about the person.... They were a real person, a real part of the community. And that never ceases to amaze me. It feels like a real privilege."

Old Wood and Prehistoric Poop

Newsom also spends a lot of time working in the laboratory, where she analyzes plant materials, often using a microscope to identify the sample through its cell structure. In addition to working on artifacts she has found on her own digs, she sometimes works with items found by other archaeologists. Frequently, she is called on to lend her expertise about a particular type of plant life—trees. By looking at the vascular structure of ancient wood samples under a microscope, Newsom is able to identify the type of tree it came from and to discover other important clues. In the case of the wood samples taken from the Windover site, for instance, she analyzed the channels cut into the wood by bark beetles and figured out that the trees used for the burial structures were always cut in late summer. This provided strong evidence that the people were migrational and only inhabited that area for part of the year.

Newsom has studied wood taken from several important shipwrecks, including boats sailed by the 17th-century explorer René-Robert Cavelier, Sieur de La Salle and by the pirate Edward Teach—better known as Blackbeard. "I have a thing about ships," Newsom said. "One of my grandfathers was a carpenter and joiner in the Belfast Naval Shipyard." Another project involves an even more famous sailor—Christopher Columbus. It's known that in 1492 Columbus and his crew established La Navidad, the first European settlement in the New World, on the north shore of Haiti on the island of Hispaniola. Historians had been unsure of the exact location, but a recent dig seems to have revealed the site. One of the clues comes from wooden artifacts examined by Newsom. It's known that Columbus's crew used timber from their ship that had run aground to construct one of the buildings at La Navidad. After examining pieces of wood found at the site, Newsom has identified them as pine. Because pine is common in Europe but not in Haiti, she believes that the wood came from Columbus's Spanish ship.

———— **"** ————

"It's funny how when people see [mastodon dung] in the lab and they don't know what it is, it looks like a bunch of chopped-up woody vegetation, and it's kind of interesting, even kind of pretty," Newsom says. "And then you tell them what it is, . . . suddenly it smells, and it's gross."

———— **"** ————

Newsom also learns about the ancient past by studying a rather unusual substance—mastodon dung. The large elephant-like creatures roamed North America tens of thousands of years ago, and in some cases their droppings have been preserved. The dung contains a lot of information about the mastodons and about the forests where they roamed. Newsom is able to identify the type of material they ate, which gives her a better idea of the types of plants that grew at that time. "It's really cool to be able to think about these long-extinct elephants and how they browsed through Florida forests, or any ancient forest, and just had a good day—eating hickory nuts and acorns and hazel nuts and beech nuts and walnuts and wild grapes."

Newsom has sometimes used middle school students to help her investigate the dung. "It's funny how when people see it in the lab and they don't know what it is, it looks like a bunch of chopped-up woody vegetation, and it's kind of interesting, even kind of pretty," Newsom says. "And then you tell them what it is, . . . suddenly it smells, and it's gross." Most of the students turned out to be first-rate dung-sorters, however. "The kids in that age group were very good and very careful and very interested," she said, and after helping out in the laboratory, "a lot of them say they want to be archaeologists." Newsom tries to encourage young students to pursue their interest in science, partly because she remembers the discouraging advice she once received about becoming an anthropologist. "I would urge all the kids to follow their hearts," she said, "to feel free to take science and math, especially girls. Don't let people talk you out of it. And pursue your dream, because it's worth it."

―――― " ――――

Newsom tries to encourage young students to pursue their interest in science, partly because she remembers the discouraging advice she once received about becoming an anthropologist. "I would urge all the kids to follow their hearts," she said, "to feel free to take science and math, especially girls. Don't let people talk you out of it. And pursue your dream, because it's worth it."

―――― " ――――

Winning the "Genius Grant"

Newsom joined the faculty at Pennsylvania State University in early 2002, where she is an associate professor of anthropology. Less than a year later, in September 2002, she received a phone call that shocked and delighted her. The caller told Newsom that she had been awarded one of the esteemed fellowships from the John D. and Catherine T. MacArthur Foundation. Often known as a "genius grant," a MacArthur Fellowship gives the recipient $500,000 over five years to use in any way they wish. "I still feel like I might be dreaming," Newsom said shortly after receiving the news. The award was especially surprising because the MacArthur Foundation does its work in secret. "The nominations are anonymous, so I still don't know how I was chosen," she said. "For a while I was in a daze. They just give you this money and say 'this is our vote of confidence in you, and your colleagues say you're worthy,' which is really humbling."

Newsom plans to use the MacArthur funds to support work on some of the research projects she is conducting, as well as those by graduate students with whom she works. She is especially interested in continuing to excavate artifacts from a mountain site in Puerto Rico where the residents were growing crops on terraced fields approximately 1,000 years ago. Whatever projects she chooses to pursue, Newsom will focus on the ways that the people of the past made use of the plant life around them. She sees their decisions and adaptations as being a key element in understanding ancient America. "It goes beyond food and technology," she explained. "How did those people perceive and think about where they lived? Maybe plants will reveal those things."

HOME AND FAMILY

Newsom has a son named Woodrow, better known as Woody, who was born in the early 1980s. Woody is an accomplished baseball player and recently attended college on a sports scholarship.

WRITINGS

Under Name Lee A. Newsom

Case Studies in Environmental Archaeology, 1996 (editor, with Elizabeth J. Reitz and Sylvia J. Scudder)
On Land and Sea: Native American Uses of Biological Resources in the West Indies, 2004 (with Elizabeth S. Wing)

HONORS AND AWARDS

Barbara Lawrence Award: 1992
John D. and Catherine T. MacArthur Foundation Fellowship: 2002

FURTHER READING

Periodicals

Archaeology, Sep./Oct. 2003, p.18
Current Biography Yearbook, 2004
Pittsburgh Post-Gazette, Sep. 25, 2002, p.D5
Tampa Tribune, Nov. 3, 2003, Nation/World section, p.1

Online Articles

http://www.psu.edu/ur/archives/intercom_2003/Feb20/research.html
   (*Penn State Intercom*, "Focus on Research: Seeds of Wisdom," Feb. 20, 2003)
http://www.rps.psu.edu/0305/planted.html
   (*Research Penn State*, "Profiles: Planted in the Past," May 2003)

Other

Information for this profile was also taken from an interview with *Biography Today* conducted in Aug. 2005.

ADDRESS

Lee Ann Newsom
Department of Anthropology
Pennsylvania State University
316 Carpenter Building
University Park, PA 16802

WORLD WIDE WEB SITES

http://www.anthro.psu.edu/newsom.html

Charlie Russell 1941?-
Canadian Naturalist, Author, and Photographer
Controversial Researcher of Bear Behavior

BIRTH

Charles Russell was born in about 1941 in a rural part of south-
western Alberta, near what is now Waterton Lakes National Park.
His father is Andy Russell, who was then a wilderness outfitter
and guide and later became a well-known naturalist, filmmaker,
and author. His mother is Kay (Riggall) Russell. Charles—often
known as Charlie—was the second of five children. He has three
brothers, Dick, John, and Gordon, and a sister named Anne.

YOUTH

Russell's interest in nature began at a young age, and the area where he grew up had plenty of nature to explore. His family owned a ranch that sat at the foot of the Rocky Mountains in Alberta. "I'd bet there are not more than a half dozen private dwellings in North America with a more splendid view from the front doorstep," he wrote in his book *Spirit Bear*. "The view is spectacularly beautiful because it is here that the prairies sweep right up to the base of the Rockies." The ranch had been established by his grandparents in the first decade of the 1900s, and they had also started a business where they guided visiting tourists through the mountains on horseback. Russell's father took over the guide service in the 1940s, and Charles began taking part in the mountain trips when he was just six years old.

> "I was riding close behind my father when Dad's horse stopped all of a sudden. A grizzly and two small cubs bounded up over the ledge, pausing right in front of us," Russell wrote. "[That night, the group told stories] about how dangerous and unpredictable grizzlies are. Still, I came away from that experience with more curiosity about bears than fear."

On his first outing, Russell was introduced to the animal that would become the focus of his adult life. "I was riding close behind my father when Dad's horse stopped all of a sudden," Russell wrote. "A grizzly and two small cubs bounded up over the ledge, pausing right in front of us." A jolt of fear went through both the horses and riders. In this case, the bears chose to flee, but the encounter made the members of the trip spend that evening telling scary tales about the bears. "The stories were about how dangerous and unpredictable grizzlies are," Russell recalled "Still, I came away from that experience with more curiosity about bears than fear."

Russell had several other bear encounters during his childhood, including some very close to the family's home. In addition to learning about wildlife, he was also picking up other skills that would later play a part in his professional career. His grandfather, Bert Riggall, was an avid photographer and showed the young boy how to take and develop photos. "I spent many exciting hours with him in his darkroom," Russell remembered. "The magic of watching by the red glow of the safelight as images appeared in the wash of chemicals got me interested in photography at a very young age." Bert Riggall was also very interested in natural history and conservation, and he passed this enthusiasm along to his grandson.

EDUCATION

Russell has made few comments about his schooling, but it is known that his only formal degree is a high school diploma. He has gained his expertise in the field rather than the classroom, which is somewhat unusual in an era when many naturalists have graduate degrees from universities. "I don't try to pretend I'm a scientist," Russell said in an article in *Backpacker*. "I do serious research on serious issues that scientists are afraid to tackle."

CAREER HIGHLIGHTS

Russell began his professional work with animals alongside his father, Andy Russell, who was then working as a wilderness guide. By the late 1950s his father had decided to get out of the guide business, partly because the mountain areas where he had conducted trips were being increasingly used by timber, mining, and energy companies. Andy was not ready to give up the wilderness that he loved, however. He began writing about the natural world and publishing tales about the rugged characters of the Canadian West. He also took up filmmaking, which allowed him to showcase Canada's natural beauty and helped him to convince others that greater environmental protection was needed. In 1958 Charlie, then 17, and his older brother Dick assisted their father on a film about bighorn sheep. Three years later, the family began work on a film about grizzly bears. Entitled *Grizzly Country*, the film project stretched over three years and took the Russells from Montana through the mountain provinces and territories of Canada and north to Alaska. "There was no precedent for filming grizzlies," Russell wrote, "much less anything on how to get the close shots we needed. . . . We knew we were on our own, and that our judgments and decisions might mean life or death."

"I don't try to pretend I'm a scientist," Russell said in an article in Backpacker *magazine. "I do serious research on serious issues that scientists are afraid to tackle."*

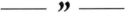

Grizzly bears, also known as brown bears, are considered one of the most dangerous bear species in North America. They are large (males can top 1,000 pounds, though those living in inland areas are smaller) and fast (running speeds can reach 40 miles per hour). Most importantly, they are considered much more likely to attack humans than such species as the black bear, and grizzlies will also kill cattle and wild game. These characteristics are part of the reason that the bears have been widely hunted.

Russell looking for grizzly bears in 1964, in southeastern British Columbia.

Because of this, and because human development is steadily taking over many of the wilderness areas where they live, grizzlies are now an endangered species. Despite their fierce reputation, many wildlife experts note that grizzlies aren't the killing machines that they're often made out to be. Much of their diet comes from wild berries, pine nuts, and fish, and when they do eat land animals it's usually ones that have already died from other causes. Still, filming the bears at close range was dangerous work for the Russells. In the beginning, the family carried guns for protection but they later opted to give them up. They learned to read the attitude of the animals and to keep their heads during "bluff" charges where the bears ran toward them but didn't attack. "Dad, Dick, and I probably worked with more than 300 grizzlies in those three years of filming *Grizzly Country*," Russell recalled. "We stood our ground in many full-blown charges and were not harmed."

Russell got more exposure to grizzlies in the following decades. In 1970 he began raising cattle on his family's Alberta ranch and frequently observed bears. Having never lost any cattle to the grizzlies, he began to believe that they posed little threat to livestock. This opinion was the opposite of the one held by most ranchers, who will hunt down bears that they believe are a threat to their animals. Once Russell even watched a bear walk directly through a herd of cows without harming them. "The grizzly seemed to make a deliberate attempt to be courteous as he selected his travel route through the resting cattle. To my amazement, virtually all the cows and their calves remained lying down, even when the bear passed by within 10 feet (3 m) of them!" Russell had observed similar occurrences with other wild creatures and began to believe that animals could sense danger according to the actions and "body language" of others. In this case, the cattle sensed that the bear posed no threat and so they were not alarmed by its presence.

New Ideas

Over time, Russell began to apply these ideas to the interactions between humans and bears. He came to believe that many bear attacks take place because the animals can sense the fear and agitation of the humans, and so they also become afraid. "A fearful bear is a dangerous animal," he explained. "And aggression in people will make a bear aggressive." The situation is made worse because humans hunt the bears, which creates more fear and aggression on the part of the animals. Rather than seeing the grizzlies as dangerous predators or unreasoning beasts, Russell began to sense a logic to their actions. "Bears are not unpredictable," he argued. "If they are treated well, they respond in kind."

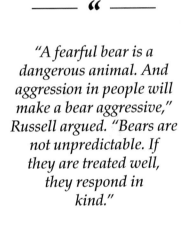

"A fearful bear is a dangerous animal. And aggression in people will make a bear aggressive," Russell argued. *"Bears are not unpredictable. If they are treated well, they respond in kind."*

This idea was quite different from the conventional logic regarding bears—grizzlies, in particular. Most wildlife experts and park managers believe that bears that lose their fear of humans are more dangerous than those that do not. According to this theory, the bears will become aggressive once accustomed to humans. This leads to attacks, so the bears that harm humans are hunted and killed. To reduce the danger, wildlife managers try to keep bears separated from people, but this has become increasingly difficult as more wilderness areas are developed and larger numbers of people visit national parks. Russell feels that it may be possible to create a friendlier relationship between humans and bears, which will allow them to live close together without as much bloodshed.

While he generally views bears as being good-natured around humans, Russell has also seen the animal's more dangerous side. In 1984 he and his son Anthony, who was then just ten years old, were attacked by a black bear while walking on the family's ranch in Alberta. "The bear plowed into me in a leap with her front feet extended, catching me squarely in the chest," Russell revealed. "Then she was on top of me—all teeth and claws." He was saved by Anthony, who distracted the bear by hitting it with an elk antler he had found along the trail. Together, father and son were able to drive off the bear. "Both of us got hurt," Russell later recalled, "but not seriously. If my son hadn't intervened, I would have been killed." Russell did not blame the bear for the attack, however. Instead, he attributed it to his own actions, because he had acted aggressively toward the bear to shoo it off the trail. As scary as the fight had been, it didn't make Russell fear the animals. He continued to observe them whenever he had the chance, and in 1991 he got the chance to take part in a project that brought him incredibly close to bears and allowed him to put some of his theories to the test.

Meeting the Spirit Bear

Collaborating with respected nature filmmakers Sue and Jeff Turner, Russell traveled to Princess Royal Island, a remote wilderness area along Canada's west coast, in British Columbia. Their quest was to make a film about the rare Kermode bears that are native to the island. These animals have white fur and look like a smaller version of the polar bear. They are actually a type of black bear, but their snowy appearance comes from a genetic variation. There are less than 20 of the Kermode bears living on Princess Royal, and they were often hidden away in the island's rugged and remote interior. Russell and the Turners spent two summers on the island to make the film. As related in Russell's book *Spirit Bear*, they were eventually able to locate some of the Kermodes, and one, in particular, was eager to become a movie star.

While filming along a river one day, Russell and Turner were approached by a young white bear that seemed to have no fear of people. "I ran out of slide film and headed downstream to my pack," Russell said about this first encounter. "The white bear scrambled down over the ledges in the stream toward me. I quickly lifted the back of my camera but before I could change the film, he stood on his hind legs and looked down into the camera. His nose was only inches from it! . . . Here was a wild bear, of fearsome lore, examining me and my trappings as though I were a novelty, a cousin from the big city come to visit—an object of curiosity, but definitely not something to fear, or to eat for that matter."

Russell came to call the animal the Spirit Bear, and their encounters grew even more friendly in the following weeks. The bear would dine on salmon alongside the filmmakers, confident that their presence would keep other

The Spirit Bear on Princess Royal Island in British Columbia.

bears from trying to steal the fish he had caught. The Spirit Bear allowed Russell and Jeff Turner to follow it into the backcountry, waiting for the slower humans to catch up when necessary. Humans and bear would occasionally settle down side by side for a rest and even engaged in friendly games of tug-of-war with a stick. Russell notes that all of this took place without using food to "tame" the bear. Instead, he believes that the animal had never had contact with humans before. Because it had not learned to fear people, the bear was curious and friendly. "From what I learned during my experiences in the rainforest," Russell concluded, "sharing the land with bears is not only possible, but safe as well."

Russell does not want people treating bears as playmates, however: "I am very reluctant ... to suggest to others that it is safe to be close to these powerful creatures. So much depends on a person's understanding of them; for example, it takes a lot of experience to discern their changing emotions." He is also convinced that human-bear relationships become unsafe once the animals associate the humans with food, whether it's handouts or garbage that has not been properly disposed of. "I cannot emphasize too strongly my fervent belief that keeping human food away from bears is vital in avoiding problems. A bear that expects a handout in a wilderness setting is 'Trouble with a capital T.'" Russell has found that one of the keys to developing a good relationship with bears was to speak to them in a calm manner. "They recognize in your voice very quickly what your intents are," he explained. "I just try to be calm about it and say things that are kind of sincere. They don't understand, of course, but they recognize [your intentions] in your tone." This approach has earned him the nickname "The Bear Whisperer."

The film that Russell and the Turners made on Princess Royal was released in 1994 as *Island of the Ghost Bear*. Russell's book about their experiences, entitled *Spirit Bear: Encounters with the White Bear of the Western Rainforest*, was published the same year. *Spirit Bear* allowed Russell to present some of his ideas on the relationship between humans and bears, but it was only a beginning. Soon he undertook an even more ambitious project that would teach him more about the animals.

Russian Adventure

In the early 1990s, Russell met Maureen Enns, an artist, photographer, and filmmaker, and they became personal and professional partners. Enns shared Russell's interest in bears and his belief that they were friendlier and more predictable than was widely believed. "It's no exaggeration," Enns once said, "to say that bears brought us together." In the mid-1990s the two decided to begin a study in Kamchatka, a remote peninsula in eastern Russia. They chose the area because it has more than 10,000 bears inhabiting a space the size of California. Russell and Enns believed that many of these bears had never been in contact with humans. This might allow the naturalists to complete a study proving that bears had no natural aggression against humans.

> "I cannot emphasize too strongly my fervent belief that keeping human food away from bears is vital in avoiding problems. A bear that expects a handout in a wilderness setting is 'Trouble with a capital T.'"

Undertaking a scientific study in Kamchatka was not easy. First, the weather was extreme: even in summer, when Russell and Enns would do most of their work, the temperatures were cool, and the area was buffeted by high winds, heavy rain, and even snow. Second, getting official permission from the Russian government for their activities was slow and frustrating. Finally, the bears themselves were larger and more intimidating than the black bears Russell had dealt with on Princess Royal Island. These were brown bears— the same species as the grizzly bear, though the term "grizzly" is mostly used in North America. Thanks to their steady diet of fish, the Kamchatka bears were even bigger than most of their American cousins. The larger males can stand eight feet tall and weigh as much as 1,400 pounds.

Despite the difficulties, Russell and Enns began their work in the South Kamchatka Sanctuary in 1996. For the next eight years, they spent their summers

Russell and Maureen Enns near his ultralight airplane.

in a tiny cabin that was very far away from other humans. To reach the nearest town, they had to travel 90 minutes by helicopter or plane (a trip that could cost as much as $1,600). Kambalnoye Lake, where their cabin was located, was a very lonely place—unless you wanted to spend time with bears. "It's hard to go for a pail of water without seeing a bear," Russell explained, but in the beginning the animals were not interested in meeting their new human neighbors. "We spent the first summer scaring bears," Russell said. "Everywhere we went we bumped into bears, and they were very fearful of us. It was kind of depressing; we didn't want to be so intrusive."

The second year, Russell and Enns turned their study in a new direction. They became aware of three cubs that were being held in a Kamchatka zoo because their mother had been killed by hunters. The zoo was unable to keep the cubs, so Russell and Enns volunteered to take them, planning to reintroduce them to the wild. After getting the okay from Russian authorities, they brought the bears—named Rosie, Chico, and Biscuit—to their remote cabin. In the beginning they fed the bears porridge and sunflower seeds, but they were careful not to give them the food directly—bowls would be set out when the bears were away, and the bears were allowed to find them later, on their own. The idea was to avoid having the cubs associate humans with food. Soon Russell and Enns began to teach the bears to find their own food, primarily fish, which were plentiful in the waters near the cabin. For part of the summer, the cubs were kept in an enclosure near the cabin that was surrounded by an electric fence. This was done to protect them from adult male bears, which will kill unprotected cubs if given the chance. In time, the bears were allowed to roam on their own, and as cold weather approached, the bears created their own dens to spend the winter in, just as wild bears do.

The cubs quickly adopted the friendly behavior that Russell had experienced with the Spirit Bear. They would accompany Russell and Enns on walks and engage in playful antics. "I did everything [including] going swimming with them," Russell said. "I would travel with them at night. I would do anything that would push the idea of whether we could trust them or not. . . . When they decided to have a nap, I would lay down beside them and have a nap too." Several wild bears in the area also became close to the Canadian researchers. "Some of the bears would come and sort of invite us on a walk," he explained. "They'd come to the cabin, and if we made a move to get our pack ready, they would kind of wait for us." One female bear in the area would even leave her cubs close to Russell and Enns for safekeeping while she fished. The couple's early experiences were documented in the television program "Walking with Giants: The Grizzlies of Siberia," which aired in 1999 on the PBS series "Nature." The couple has also published two books on their Kamchatka study: *Grizzly Heart: Living without Fear among the Brown Bears of Kamchatka* in 2002 and *Grizzly Seasons: Life with the Brown Bears of Kamchatka* in 2003. Of the two, *Grizzly Heart* contains a more detailed description of their experiences while *Grizzly Seasons* focuses on Enns's photographs.

———— " ————

"It's hard to go for a pail of water without seeing a bear," Russell said about working in the South Kamchatka Sanctuary in Russia. "We spent the first summer scaring bears. Everywhere we went we bumped into bears, and they were very fearful of us. It was kind of depressing; we didn't want to be so intrusive."

———— " ————

Controversial Research

Though Russell and Enns had some incredible experiences with the bears, their activities have also created controversy. Certain wildlife experts feel that the Canadian couple has set a dangerous example that will encourage untrained people to approach wild animals. Others think that Russell's theories about the essentially friendly nature of bears are simply wrong. They suggest that he "anthropomorphizes" the animals: that he claims that they have certain human-like characteristics that they don't actually possess. Another criti-

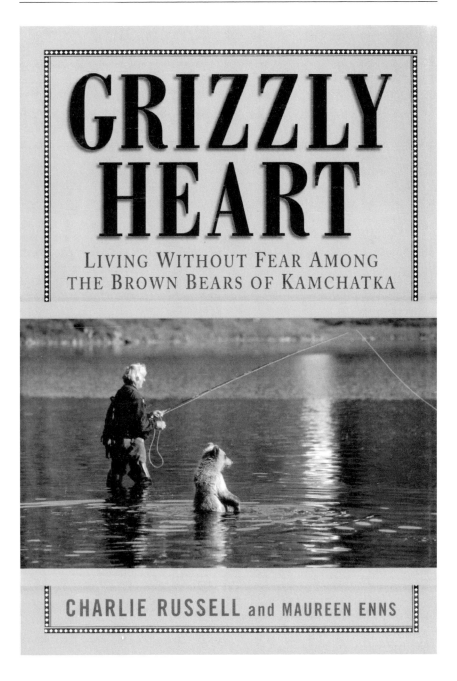

GRIZZLY HEART

LIVING WITHOUT FEAR AMONG
THE BROWN BEARS OF KAMCHATKA

CHARLIE RUSSELL and MAUREEN ENNS

cism is that their approach to the bears is only practical in certain areas and isn't appropriate in such places as the heavily populated national parks of North America. Charles Jonkel, a biologist with the Great Bear Foundation, argues that the grizzlies in Montana are far different than the coastal bears Charlie works with. "There, they get used to contact. Try that stuff around here, and they'll knock your block off." For his part, Russell generally agrees with such critics. "I'm not advocating anyone try this in Yellowstone," he said. "That would be foolish. I am simply trying to show that peace is possible."

One of the most common complaints about the Kamchatka research is that the bear cubs raised by Russell and Enns were essentially pets. In other words, because these cubs had been fed by humans and conditioned to human presence from a young age, their behavior was not the same as wild animals. One of the first people to voice this criticism was Vitaly Nikaelaenko (also spelled Nikolaenko and Nikolayenko), a Russian wildlife ranger and bear researcher who worked in Kamchatka for 25 years. Nikaelaenko strongly discouraged the feeding program begun by Russell and Enns because he felt that it made their research worthless.

> "I did everything [including] going swimming with them," Russell said about the three bear cubs named Rosie, Chico, and Biscuit. "I would travel with them at night. I would do anything that would push the idea of whether we could trust them or not.... When they decided to have a nap, I would lay down beside them and have a nap too."

Some of the experts who find fault with the conclusions made by Russell and Enns still see their work as being worthwhile in other ways. "What Charlie does is not science," said Charles Jonkel. "It's got value, though. Over the years he's taught even the most diehard so-called experts to take another look at how we think about bears." Kevin Van Tighem, manager of the ecosystems secretariat in Jasper National Park, made a similar point. "Charlie and Maureen have shown us the ideal and what could be possible if we were as good as we like to think we are. . . . In the parks we've done so much communication around bears based on negative messages. People hear about people who get chewed up and attacked by bears, so I think it's important it be balanced with this positive message."

Trouble in Kamchatka

In the first few years of their research, Russell and Enns learned that Kamchatka was not as much of a bear paradise as they had originally thought.

While there were many bears and few people, the animals were frequently killed by poachers seeking to collect the bile from their gall bladders. This substance is used in traditional Asian medicines and can earn the poachers a fair amount of money. The Canadian researchers were based in an area that had been declared a wildlife sanctuary, but in reality it afforded the bears little protection. Because Kamchatka is a very poor area, the government has little money to hire rangers to patrol the reserve. The poachers were able to operate freely and were killing an estimated 500 bears a year throughout the peninsula. In addition, the bears are also hunted legally— by hunters with official permits—which accounts for about the same number of bear deaths annually.

Russell and Enns took an active role in trying to stop the poaching. They began using some of their funds to hire a small force of well-armed rangers to patrol the sanctuary. They also kept an eye out for bear and salmon poachers from the air: Russell pilots his own ultralight aircraft and used it to patrol the region around their cabin.

——— **"** ———

"What Charlie does is not science," said Charles Jonkel, a biologist with the Great Bear Foundation. "It's got value, though. Over the years he's taught even the most diehard so-called experts to take another look at how we think about bears."

——— **"** ———

While dealing with these issues, Russell and Enns were saddened by the loss of two of their adopted bears. Rosie was killed by an aggressive male bear. Chico, as he became more mature, migrated away to another part of the peninsula. Biscuit remained in the area for several years, however, and grew into an adult bear. When Russell and Enns were wrapping up their work in the fall of 2002, they believed that Biscuit was pregnant, and they expected to find her with cubs when they returned the following spring.

Instead, Russell and Enns arrived in May 2003 to find an ominous clue: a bear gall bladder was nailed to the wall of their cabin. They began to notice other signs that made them uneasy: spent shotgun shells and bootprints around the cabin. Eventually they concluded that as many as 20 bears in the area had been slaughtered by poachers. "Our bears were murdered in cold blood," Russell said. "The bear population has been decimated and the ones that are left run away in fear." Russell and Enns never again saw Biscuit. "I am certain she is dead," Russell said. Authorities have had little success in finding those responsible for the slaughter.

Carrying On

Russell and Enns both found it difficult to deal with the killings. "Do I have guilt?" Russell pondered. "Yes, in so much that I taught these bears to trust humans and it backfired. I am haunted by the image of Biscuit not running when the hunters appeared." After returning to Canada, Maureen Enns decided she could no longer continue to work in Kamchatka, and she and Russell decided to split up.

More bad news soon followed. In October 2003 a bear researcher named Timothy Treadwell and his friend Amie Huguenard were killed by a grizzly in Alaska; a film about their experiences, *Grizzly Man*, was released in 2005. A few months later, Vitaly Nikaelaenko, Russell's colleague and rival in Kamchatka, was likewise killed by a bear. Treadwell's death was especially sad for Russell. The two men had been good friends, and Treadwell shared some of Russell's beliefs about the friendly nature of bears. Some people saw his death as proof that these theories were wrong, but Russell didn't agree. He felt that Treadwell took unnecessary risks. "Timothy would be alive today if he used electric fencing around his camp," Russell said. The electric fence is a safety precaution that Russell insists upon in his bear work because it keeps the animals out of human food supplies and living quarters. It can also shield humans from aggressive bears such as the one that attacked Treadwell and Huguenard.

> "There's always a reason bears attack. I still don't believe there is anything in a grizzly's nature to make it turn on a man for no reason," Russell explained. "The grizzly is an endangered species. I believe that the only way for them to survive is for humans and bears to coexist in an atmosphere of mutual respect."

During the winter of 2003-2004, Russell continued to struggle with an important question about the bear slaughter in Kamchatka. "I wanted to figure out whether our bears were killed as a result of poachers just poaching or was there a message that said leave and don't come back," Russell wrote in a letter posted on his web site. In other words, there was a possibility that poachers had carried out the slaughter near the cabin because they were trying to warn Russell and Enns not to interfere with their illegal hunting. Valery Komarov, who oversees the South Kamchatka Sanctuary, noted that "Russell's activities were in the way of this criminal structure," meaning the poachers. "Maybe they just did it for revenge. . . . It was a very cruel revenge."

Russell with the three bear cubs, Rosie, Chico, and Biscuit.

Initially, Russell agreed that the poachers wanted to send him a message, and he wondered if he would be putting his life in jeopardy by returning to Russia. After talking with other friends in Kamchatka, however, he decided that perhaps the killing of the bears near his cabin had simply been an unfortunate coincidence. When spring returned in 2004, he once again made his way to Russia. "I cannot give up on this place, these bears," he said. "I will not give in, no matter what happens."

Russell's latest focus is to make a film about his experiences with Enns in Kamchatka. After turning down offers from Hollywood studios, he is once again collaborating with his friends Jeff and Sue Turner. To make the film, Russell needs bears, so he has obtained several more brown bear cubs and once more set about teaching the bears how to fend for themselves in the wild. In 2004 he brought five cubs to the cabin. One was killed by a male bear, but the other four settled into their winter den in November. When Russell returned to Kamchatka in the spring of 2005, the bears were gone, but he believes they survived the winter and set off on their own. He has since obtained two more cubs, named Andy and Mallesh, and is working with them. Location filming for the movie is set to begin in 2006.

Despite the difficulties he has encountered in recent years, Russell's attitude toward bears has remained essentially the same. "These are magnificent and noble animals who want to live in peace," he said. In his opinion, the bears have no natural aggression against humans and that instead "it is man who changes the bears' behaviour" through hunting and other actions that threaten the animals. "There's always a reason bears attack," he explained. "I still don't believe there is anything in a grizzly's nature to make it turn on a man for no reason." His mission is to protect the bears and to help bring about a new, more peaceful attitude toward the animals. "The grizzly is an endangered species. I believe that the only way for them to survive is for humans and bears to coexist in an atmosphere of mutual respect."

MARRIAGE AND FAMILY

Russell was once married to a women named Margaret, who he has referred to as his "first wife," but he has made few public comments about her or subsequent spouses. His son Anthony was born in 1973 and later assisted Russell with his work on Princess Royal Island. Russell began his relationship with Maureen Enns in the mid-1990s. The two were usually referred to as "partners," so it's unclear if they ever married. They separated in 2003 or 2004. When not conducting his work in Russia, Russell lives in Cochrane, Alberta.

HOBBIES AND OTHER INTERESTS

Russell built and flies his own ultralight aircraft, which he has used in his work. The plane was initially used to obtain aerial film footage on Princess Royal Island, and Russell has also used it in Kamchatka, though authorities recently prohibited him from flying the craft in Russian airspace.

SELECTED WRITINGS

Spirit Bear: Encounters with the White Bear of the Western Rainforest, 1994
Grizzly Heart: Living without Fear among the Brown Bears of Kamchatka, 2002 (with Maureen Enns and Fred Stenson)
Grizzly Seasons: Life with the Brown Bears of Kamchatka, 2003 (with Maureen Enns)

FURTHER READING

Periodicals

Alberta Views, July-Aug. 2002, p.34

Backpacker, May 2003, p.58
Calgary (AL) Herald, Nov. 16, 2002, p.ES11
Los Angeles Times, Nov. 8, 2003, Foreign Desk, p.A1
Maclean's, Nov. 25, 2002, p.58
Mail on Sunday (London), Aug. 3, 2003, sec. FB, p.45
Outside, Dec. 2004, pp.151 and 172
Sierra, Mar.-Apr. 1999, p.50

Online Databases

Biography Resource Center Online, 2005, article from *Contemporary Authors*, 2004

Online Articles

http://www.pbs.org/wnet/nature/giants/living.html
(PBS, "Nature: Walking with Giants: The Grizzlies of Siberia," undated)
http://umanitoba.fitdv.com/new/articles/article.html?artid=319
(University of Manitoba Recreation Services, "Wild Things," Dec. 2004)

Other

"Dateline NBC," NBC News Transcripts, "Studying Grizzly Bears in Russia," July 3, 2000

ADDRESS

Charlie Russell
Author Mail, Random House of Canada
One Toronto St., Unit 300
Toronto, ON M5C 2V6, Canada

WORLD WIDE WEB SITES

http://www.cloudline.org

Linus Torvalds 1969-

Finnish Computer Programmer
Created the Linux Computer Operating System

BIRTH

Linus Benedict Torvalds was born on December 28, 1969, in Helsinki, Finland. He is named after both the chemist Linus Pauling and the cartoonist Charles Schulz's *Peanuts* character Linus. His father Nils (known as Nicke) was a television and radio journalist. His mother Anna (known as Mikke) was also a journalist and an editor with the Finnish News Agency. Linus has one sister named Sara.

YOUTH

When Torvalds was growing up, his family was different from most others in Finland. They spoke Swedish instead of Finnish, part of a minority group of Swedish-speaking Finns making up only about five percent of the country's population. Torvalds's father was a Communist who periodically lived in Moscow, the capital city of the former Soviet Union. It was hard for Torvalds to make friends because of the language difference, and even harder because of his father's unpopular political associations. Some of his schoolmates weren't allowed to play with him or visit his house because of his father's Communist affiliation. "Growing up, I was terribly embarrassed by him," Torvalds recalls.

As a child, Torvalds was a loner who devoted himself to intellectual challenges. When the family went on vacation together, he read math or computer books while the others went hiking or swimming. He had a focused intensity even while playing games like Monopoly or chess. "Linus put himself into each game and went at it again and again, regardless of how many times he lost," his sister Sara recalled. His mother described him as "a person whose eyes glaze over when a problem presents itself or continues to bug him, who does not hear you talking, who fails to answer any simple question, who is ready to forego food and sleep in the process of working out a solution and who does not give up. Ever."

> "
>
> *His mother described Torvalds as "a person whose eyes glaze over when a problem presents itself or continues to bug him, who does not hear you talking, who fails to answer any simple question, who is ready to forego food and sleep in the process of working out a solution and who does not give up. Ever."*
>
> "

Torvalds's first experience with computers came when he was about 11 years old. His maternal grandfather Leo Waldemar Törnqvist, a professor of statistics at Helsinki University, bought a Commodore computer, one of the first computers available for home use. At that time there wasn't much software available, so computer owners had to write their own programs. Torvalds worked with his grandfather to create computer programs for the Commodore. "I would sit on his lap and he would have me type in his programs, which he had carefully written out on paper because he wasn't comfortable with computers. I don't know how many other preteen boys sat in their grandfather's room, being taught how to simplify arithmetic expressions and type them correctly into a computer, but I remember doing that."

*Torvalds first worked on a Commodore computer (on the left),
shown here at the Computer Museum of America. Commodores
were very popular in the early days of home computers.*

With his grandfather's encouragement, Torvalds became fascinated with the computer and what it could do.

Torvalds began to read computer manuals written in English, which was not easy for a young Swedish-speaking boy. He pored over computer magazines containing sample programs for readers to try out. He soon realized that computers can only interpret the special sequences of ones and zeros called binary code, and that computer programs written in human-readable languages (such as BASIC) must be translated into the machine-readable language of binary code. Although there were computer programs to perform the binary translation automatically, at age 12 Torvalds began writing his own computer programs in machine language. He wrote his programs in number form and then translated the numbers into binary code.

Around this time, Torvalds's parents divorced. He and his sister Sara began to divide their time between their mother's and father's separate homes. For a while Sara lived with their father and Linus stayed with their mother. After his grandfather died, Linus and Sara moved with their mother into their grandparents' apartment. Linus took the smallest bedroom as his own, putting up black curtains on the windows to prevent light from coming in. He inherited his grandfather's computer, which he placed on a tiny desk against the window about two feet from his bed. Torvalds spent almost all of his time in this small, dark room working on computer programs.

EDUCATION

Torvalds attended schools for Swedish-speaking children in Helsinki. He was always very good at math and physics, and every year he won special cash awards for being the best in those subjects. He also enjoyed any subject that explained how things worked. "It was far easier for me not to daydream about my computer when we were learning about something more engaging than statistics, like the monsoons, for example, or the reasons for the monsoons."

During his years at Norssen High School, he spent a lot of time hanging out at a coffee shop near the school. This was a gathering place for boys who liked science and math. They would go there during free periods between classes or while skipping physical education class. "Let's face it, I was a nerd. A geek. From fairly early on. I didn't duct-tape my glasses together, but I might as well have, because I had all the other traits. Good at math, good at physics, and with no social graces whatsoever. And this was before being a nerd was considered a good thing. Everybody has probably known someone in school like me. The boy who is known as being best at math— not because he studies hard, but just because he is. I was that person in my class. . . . On the whole, school was good. I got good grades without having to work at it—never truly great grades, exactly because I didn't work at it."

In Finland, college tuition is almost free. Torvalds paid only about $50 per year to attend Helsinki University. After his first year, he took a break from attending classes in order to perform the mandatory Army duty required of all Finnish young men. He was a second lieutenant in the Finnish Army reserves. He returned to the university after completing his 11 months of service.

He attended university for eight years, eventually earning the equivalent of a master's degree. Most university students in Finland complete their degrees in less time than that, but Torvalds couldn't decide what he wanted to study. All he was really interested in was computer programming. But at that time, computer degrees were not yet offered. He tried taking the few computer programming classes the university offered and quickly found that he knew more about the subject than the teachers did. So he continued to spend most of his time working on his own, teaching himself how to write programs.

"Everybody has a book that changed his or her life," Torvalds said about that time. "For some it is the Bible or *Das Kapital* [by Karl Marx]. But the book

———— " ————

*"Let's face it, I was a nerd.
A geek. From fairly
early on. I didn't duct-tape
my glasses together, but I
might as well have, because
I had all the other traits.
Good at math, good at
physics, and with no
social graces whatsoever.
And this was before being
a nerd was considered a
good thing...."*

———— " ————

that launched me to new heights was *Operating Systems: Design and Implementation* by Andrew Tanenbaum." The author was a university professor in Amsterdam who had created an operating system called Minix. (An operating system is the series of commands, written in a symbolic computer language, that controls the basic functions of the computer. The operating system runs the applications software, the supplementary programs that allow the computer to perform such tasks as word processing, financial analysis, and surfing the web. Today, the best-known and most widely used operating system is Microsoft Windows.)

Tanenbaum used Minix as a teaching tool, and so he wrote errors into the programming on purpose. Students were supposed to fix the errors and by doing so, they would learn how operating systems worked. As Torvalds explored Minix, he began to get the idea that he could write his own operating system, exactly to his own specifications, and that it could be better than any of the current alternatives. So in 1991 he set the goal of creating Linux.

CAREER HIGHLIGHTS

Creating Linux

Torvalds didn't know at the time just how difficult writing an operating system would be. He was only a casual programmer working on a Sinclair QL, one of the first 32-bit, four megabyte personal computers. He started the project because "playing on a computer was fun, and also because the alternatives [for operating systems] weren't that attractive." Looking back, Torvalds said that many people told him that only a really good programmer would attempt to create their own operating system. This is true, because operating systems are complicated programs that require a lot of special knowledge to create. However, he admitted that "You also need to be bad enough because if you knew beforehand how much work it would have been to do, nobody sane would have even started it."

Torvalds started working on his operating system and became totally engrossed in the project. He stayed in his cramped and darkened room in his mother's apartment for many hours at a time. He wasn't aware of whether anyone else was at home, or if it was day or night. His mother joked that he was such a low maintenance son that she could leave him "in a closet, throw some dry pasta in, and he'd be happy." When Torvalds finally had his operating system functional enough to show it to other people, he decided to post it on an Internet newsgroup. He wrote, "Are you without a nice program and just dying to cut your teeth on an [operating system] you can try to modify for your own needs? Then this post might be just for you." The announcement included instructions to download Torvalds's program, which a friend had named Linux as a combination of Minix and Torvalds's first name, Linus.

"When I released Linux, I thought maybe one other person would be interested in it. . . . What happened almost immediately was that people started commenting on the missing features." Interest grew as more and more people downloaded Linux and tried to use it. Torvalds began to get email from all over the world. Someone asked if he would change Linux to make it work on computers with very little memory. The challenge was interesting enough that he worked all through the Christmas holiday to write a compression program. This one improvement greatly increased the usefulness of Linux and it quickly gained several hundred users. Some of the people who suggested changes also provided the computer programs to make the changes work. Torvalds took the best suggestions and added those new programs to Linux as well.

——— " ———

As Linux grew in popularity and word spread across the Internet newsgroups, people began asking Torvalds if he wanted any money for their use of his operating system. Shareware (computer software programs that are distributed online for a very small fee) was becoming common and people were used to sending $10 or $20 to programmers who released their work on the Internet. Torvalds told people not to send money, but to send him a postcard from wherever they lived instead. He began to receive postcards from all over the world, including New Zealand, Japan, and the United States. Many people also donated to an informal fund to pay off his computer, for which he still owed three years of monthly payments. Torvalds

"Everybody has probably known someone in school like me. The boy who is known as being best at math—not because he studies hard, but just because he is. I was that person in my class.... On the whole, school was good. I got good grades without having to work at it—never truly great grades, exactly because I didn't work at it."

——— " ———

Torvalds with some of his equipment in about 1999.

was grateful for the donations, but still not interested in making money from Linux. Instead, he wanted to make Linux an open source program.

Open Source

Computer software is usually distributed in one of two ways. Programs that are sold for a fee are normally "closed source," which means that users cannot change or even see the computer programs that make the software run. The Microsoft Windows operating system is an example of a closed source program. By contrast, computer programs that are given away for free are often "open source." These open source programs make their software programming accessible to users, showing the most basic, step-by-step inner workings of the program. The open source programming movement centers on the idea that software is not a proprietary product that inventors should protect, but rather something that others should be able to use, improve, and modify to fit their own needs. Thus anyone who downloads an open source program has access to the programming and can make changes to suit their own needs. Changes can be included in their personal version of the software or shared with friends.

Torvalds intended Linux to be an open source program. His goal was to create the best computer operating system possible, and he thought the best way to do that would be to allow others to help him improve his programming. By posting Linux on the Internet, he could get feedback from other programmers all over the world. "Linux is what I do for fun. It's what I do because I think it's important. It's what I do because I just love working on computers. When I do something for fun, I thnk it's important to share with others and make that part of the fun. . . . I think open source is a very good medium for doing certain things."

Within a few years of its release, Linux was generating so much interest and activity that Torvalds issued a modified open source licensing agreement. Now people were allowed to make money selling products and services for Linux as long as they continued to share the source code for any new features or solutions to problems. By 1993, new companies like Red Hat had sprung up around Linux. These companies began to create the support materials that Torvalds didn't provide: training manuals, installation instructions, and telephone support for Linux users. Looking back on this decision, Torvalds says that making Linux an open source program was the single best decision he made. "There are lots of advantages in a free system, the obvious one being that it allows more developers to work on it, and extend it." The community of Linux users and contributors continued to grow by leaps and bounds, with Torvalds as its leader.

"When I released Linux, I thought maybe one other person would be interested in it.... What happened almost immediately was that people started commenting on the missing features."

Leading the Worldwide Collaboration

Linux can be downloaded from the Internet, for free, by anyone in any part of the world. If a person discovers a problem with Linux, they can fix the problem on their own computer, instead of submitting a request to Torvalds and waiting for him to fix it. If someone wants Linux to do something new, they can write a new program to do it. So many people began sending Torvalds pieces of computer programs to be added to Linux that it became almost a full time job. "On average I almost have to read email for two hours a day just to keep up. On top of those two hours for just reading email, two or three hours to actually do something about it."

In 1996, Torvalds moved from Finland to the United States with his wife Tove and their newborn daughter. They relocated to California's Silicon Valley, where he accepted a job at Transmeta Corporation working on computer chip development. Although he had been offered many positions at various companies involved with Linux, he chose Transmeta specifically because it was not associated with Linux and would allow him to stay neutral.

In 2001, Torvalds published *Just for Fun: The Story of an Accidental Revolutionary*, co-written with journalist David Diamonds. This memoir covers his early life and details how he came to create Linux. The book was widely praised by critics as a fascinating look into the creative mind. According to a review in *Publishers Weekly*, "This breezy account of the life of Linux inventor Torvalds not only lives up to its insouciant title, it provides an incisive look into the still-raging debate over open source code. In his own words (interspersed with co-writer Diamond's tongue-in-cheek accounts of his interviews with the absentminded Torvalds), the programmer relates how it all started.... Even though Torvalds is now a bigger star in the computer world than Bill Gates, and companies like IBM are running Linux on their servers, he has retained his innocence: the book is full of statements like 'Open source makes sense' and 'Greed is never good' that seem sincere. Leavened with an appealing, self-deprecating sense of humor and a generous perspective that few hardcore coders have, this is a refreshing read."

———— " ————

"Linux is what I do for fun. It's what I do because I think it's important. It's what I do because I just love working on computers. When I do something for fun, I think it's important to share with others and make that part of the fun.... I think open source is a very good medium for doing certain things."

———— " ————

By 2003, Torvalds was still working at Transmeta, but Linux was demanding more and more of his time. It was becoming difficult for him to focus on his work at Transmeta, and he was beginning to feel guilty for neglecting his responsibilities. Then he was offered a job at Open Source Development Labs (OSDL), a nonprofit group dedicated to the development of software for Linux. The new position would give him the time and freedom he needed to concentrate on Linux. In 2003, the family moved to Portland, Oregon. "I was originally planning on just taking a year of unpaid leave from Transmeta because I felt I had to concentrate on getting [the next Linux release] out the door with no distractions," Torvalds explained. "The OSDL turned out to be a great way to do that without losing health coverage or pay and still remaining neutral."

Torvalds is at the center of all Linux activity, although there is far more development going on than one person can handle alone. Today a team of software developers helps him manage Linux. He says these team members "get picked—but not by me. Somebody who gets things done, and shows good taste—people just start sending them suggestions and patches. I didn't design it this way. It happens because this is the way people work naturally."

Torvalds's leadership style has contributed to the success of Linux. Torvalds describes his approach to leadership as lazy. "I try to manage by not making decisions and letting things occur naturally," he admitted. "That's when you get the best results." This approach seems to work especially well during times of conflict, when Torvalds often refuses to issue direct orders. "Eventually, some obvious solution will come to the fore or the issue will just fade away," Lin-

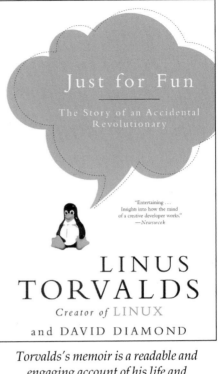

Torvalds's memoir is a readable and engaging account of his life and the creation of Linux.

ux contributor Andrew Morton told *Wired*. According to Cliff Miller, an early Linux contributor, "He is a great leader, which he may not even realize."

Torvalds is described as fair, open to the opinions of others, and willing to change his mind. He has a talent for making the right technical decisions and is known for getting people with different opinions to agree. He is also known for making sure that proper credit is given to all Linux contributors, saying that he directly created only the smallest fraction of Linux programming. "I think the most important part is that I got it started. Then people had something to concentrate on."

Dealing with Fame

Torvalds believes that his success can be attributed to a good combination of laziness and boredom. "I don't want to do something I don't have to do, but on the other hand, just sitting around and flipping channels is really, really, really boring. So that's where I think most of my motivation comes from, is finding something really interesting to be involved in."

135

As a product of his success, the Linux community has grown from a small, disorganized group of casual computer hobbyists to an international collaboration that is supported by both individuals and major corporations. Because the program is freely available to anyone, there is no way to count the exact number of users. Recent estimates are more than 18 million people in almost every country. Linux runs cell phones, robots, and the computers used to create animations and special effects for the movies *Shrek, A Shark's Tale*, and *Titanic*. Linux runs Internet servers for the eBay and Google web sites, as well as the supercomputers used in NASA's space shuttle simulations. Automobile navigation systems, digital cable television boxes, and military aircraft all use computers running Linux. Linux is used by the U.S. Postal Service, the Chinese postal service, and Japan's biggest grocery store chain.

—— " ——

"I don't want to do something I don't have to do, but on the other hand, just sitting around and flipping channels is really, really, really boring. So that's where I think most of my motivation comes from, is finding something really interesting to be involved in."

—— " ——

In the midst of all this, Torvalds has become the superstar of the open source movement. At one point in time, Internet search engines returned more hits on the name Linus Torvalds than on the names of some movie stars. He is invited to speak at conferences all over the world, and when he gives a talk, hundreds of people line up hours in advance to see him. According to Dirk Hohndel, a close friend of Torvalds's since 1993, "He was just overwhelmed by the fact that people would want to listen to him. He's still, to this day, surprised about his fame. He's developed very good skills in avoiding the attention that he doesn't want. I think he's pretty good in separating his real life and his family from the fame that he has."

Torvalds manages his celebrity status on his own. He doesn't have a personal assistant or even a secretary. He doesn't listen to voicemail messages and rarely answers email from strangers. Most of the email correspondence related to Linux is now handled by other developers. Torvalds spends his days working at home in his basement office, surrounded by computers and books. At home near Portland, he says the only time he's recognized in public is when he goes shopping at Fry's Electronics.

In the Internet community, many people idolize Torvalds because he gave Linux away instead of selling it. He has tried to correct the idea that he's against capitalism and making money. Torvalds says instead that it's not about money at all. "[Open source is] just a wonderful way of doing things, and I think it's a lot more fun to do it this way than to be at a company and do programming the old-fashioned way. . . . My personal belief system is more one of personal honor, and I don't care what anybody else does. . . . People have grown used to thinking of computers as unreliable, and it doesn't have to be that way. I don't mind Microsoft making money. I mind them having a bad operating system."

While many companies have profited from his creation, Torvalds has never been interested in making Linux into a business. "Some of the early Linux vendors actually sent me some checks just to show their gratitude and some-one calculated that I had an hourly wage of about 5 cents an hour. Even though I didn't benefit financially from Linux itself, the kind of indirect bene-fits were good. I mean how many peo-ple fresh out of school can basically select what place they go to work? In the end, I've been programming for more than half my life. I was the tradi-tional geekish person who easily sat in front of a computer for eight hours a day. [Developing Linux] was a little harder than I thought. It was hard, but it was hard in the challenging sense."

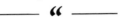

"People have grown used to thinking of computers as unreliable, and it doesn't have to be that way. I don't mind Microsoft making money. I mind them having a bad operating system."

Legal Troubles

Despite its success and growing user community, not everyone is happy about Linux being an open source program. Linux is currently involved in a lawsuit filed by the SCO Group, the company that owns the rights to the Unix operating system. SCO accused Linux contributors who were working for IBM of including thousands of lines of Unix programming in Linux without permission. SCO says that by including computer programs written by con-tributors without first verifying that the work was original, Torvalds has en-couraged Linux contributors and users to break copyright laws.

SCO executives criticize the open source development model because they feel that it does not provide any protection for companies who use the closed source model. Torvalds has denied the charges and continues to defend the development of Linux and the open source movement. He remains proud of his life's work and is adopting a wait-and-see attitude towards the lawsuit. "With the U.S. legal system, it's always hard to tell what . . . is going to happen. I can't just dismiss the lawsuit. . . . The fact is, I don't think in the end this is going to mean a whole lot."

Because of the lawsuit, Torvalds has changed the process used to add contributed software code in Linux. All contributors are now required to sign a Developer's Certificate of Origin. With this document, software developers identify the code they are submitting to Linux and state that the work is their own. "Does it guarantee that everybody is honest? No. But it, fundamentally, makes it much more likely that people are honest, and the transparency in the [open source] process also means that if dishonesty happens, you can go back and see what went on."

"What started out in my messy bedroom," Torvalds declared, "has grown to be the largest collaborative project in the history of the world."

When Torvalds started out as a curious university student in Finland, he never intended to revolutionize the way computer software is developed. He never imagined that his work might potentially change copyright laws in the United States and elsewhere in the world. "What started out in my messy bedroom has grown to be the largest collaborative project in the history of the world."

HOBBIES AND OTHER INTERESTS

When he's not working, Torvalds spends time with his family. He enjoys playing snooker, a form of billiards, and reading science fiction, thrillers, mystery, fantasy, and detective stories. He is fluent in Swedish (his native lanuage), Finnish, and English. He says his dream job is to be a beach bum.

Torvalds likes to visit the local zoo wherever he travels, particularly in Singapore, his favorite zoo. The penguin was chosen as the Linux mascot in part because of an experience he had at an Australian zoo. "I was bitten by a penguin. It was an open zoo. I made my finger look like a herring and the penguin fell for it. It was a very timid bite."

Every year Torvalds and the International Data Group present the IDG/Linus Torvalds Community Award. The $25,000 prize honors an association that actively supports the Linux community.

MARRIAGE AND FAMILY

Torvalds is married to Tove, a former kindergarten teacher and six-time Finnish karate champion. They met while he was teaching an introductory computer course at Helsinki University. The first homework assignment he gave the students was to send him an email message. Tove used the assignment to ask him out on a date. Linus and Tove have three daughters: Patricia, Daniela, and Celeste.

SELECTED WRITINGS

Just for Fun: The Story of an Accidental Revolutionary, 2001

HONORS AND AWARDS

Person of the Year (*PC Magazine*): 1999
Most Influential Executive of the Year (*Computer Reseller News*): 2004
Named One of the World's 100 Most Influential People (*Time*): 2004

FURTHER READING

Books

Brashares, Ann. *Linus Torvalds, Software Rebel,* 2001
Business Leader Profiles for Students, Vol. 2, 2002
Torvalds, Linus. *Just for Fun: The Story of an Accidental Revolutionary,* 2001
Who's Who in America, 2006
World of Compter Science, 2002

Periodicals

Business Week, Jan. 31, 2005, p.60
Computer Reseller News, Nov. 9, 1998, p.129; Nov. 15, 2004, pp.22 and 28; Nov. 22, 2004, p.27
Current Biography Yearbook, 1999
Investor's Business Daily, May 30, 2001, p.4
Los Angeles Times, Dec. 6, 1999, p.C1
New York Times, Feb. 21, 1999, sec. 6, p.34; June 17, 2003, p.C4
Oregonian, June 27, 2005, p.A1
Ottawa (ON) Citizen, July 23, 2001, p.D2
PC Magazine, Dec. 14, 1999, p.101

Online Articles

http://www.wired.com/wired/archive/11.11/linus.html?pg=1&topic=
&topic_set
(*Wired,* "Leader of the Free World," Nov. 2003)

Online Databases

Biography Resource Center Online, 2005, articles from *Business Leader Profiles for Students,* 2002; *Contemporary Authors Online,* 2005; *World of Computer Science,* 2002

ADDRESS

Linus Torvalds
OSDL Headquarters
12725 SW Millikan Way, Suite 400
Beaverton, OR 97005

WORLD WIDE WEB SITES

http://www.linux.org/info/linus.html
http://www.cs.helsinki.fi/u/torvalds

Neil deGrasse Tyson 1958-
American Astrophysicist, Author, and Television Host
Director of the Hayden Planetarium in New York City

BIRTH

Neil deGrasse Tyson was born on October 5, 1958, in the Bronx, a borough of New York City. He grew up in the Riverdale section, in one of a set of three buildings called Skyview Apartments. (Tyson said the name was "prophetic.") His father, Cyril deGrasse Tyson, is a retired sociologist who taught at Bronx Community College. He served for several years as a New York City commissioner, working mainly on youth employment. His mother, Sunchita Feliciano Tyson, was a homemaker when her children were young. Later, she earned a master's degree in gerontology (the study of aging and of elderly people). She had a job evaluating senior-citizen programs for the U.S. Public Health Service. Tyson has an older brother, Stephen, and a younger sister, Lynn.

Tyson shares he unusual middle name, deGrasse, with his father. It was his grandmother's maiden name and is believed to be French in origin. Tyson said it can be loosely traced to a French admiral who fought on the American side in the U.S. Revolutionary War. The admiral later was captured and held in the Caribbean Islands—the region where Tyson's grandmother was born and raised.

YOUTH

When he was nine, Tyson made his first visit to the Hayden Planetarium. The Hayden Planetarium, the world-famous center of astronomy that he now runs, is part of the American Museum of Natural History in New York City. "I looked through the planetarium telescope and I reacted the way every kid did and still does," he said. "I gasped." His passion for astronomy was confirmed when he was 11. One day he borrowed a friend's binoculars and happened to point them at the moon. He was fascinated to be able to see its surface. It was a "rich moonscape of mountains and valleys and craters and hills and plains," he recalled in his autobiography, *The Sky Is Not the Limit*. "The moon was no longer just a thing in the sky—it was another world."

> "A telescope was a window to another place—a whole other way of thinking about the world in which I lived," Tyson said. "Some people get it by reading novels. I got that by looking up at the universe."

Tyson began to read every book he could find on astronomy. His sixth-grade teacher noticed that this was the subject of most of his book reports, and she gave him a notice from the local paper of after-school classes for junior high and high school students at the Hayden Planetarium. Even though Tyson was a little young for the classes, his teacher thought he could handle them. "From then onward, the Hayden Planetarium became a much broader and deeper resource [than the classroom] for the growth of my life's interests," he recalled.

When he was in seventh grade, Tyson moved temporarily with his family to Lexington, Massachusetts. His father had a one-year appointment at Harvard University. While he was there, Tyson received his first telescope as a birthday gift from his parents. "A telescope was a window to another place—a whole other way of thinking about the world in which I lived,"

Tyson as a boy, assembling his first telescope with his dad, 1970.

Tyson said. "Some people get it by reading novels. I got that by looking up at the universe." He spent hours in the backyard studying the heavens. It was much easier to see the stars and planets in suburban Lexington than in New York, with the distracting glare of city lights. "My interest in the universe was in the fast lane," he said. The trouble was, his telescope wasn't strong enough to keep up with him.

Tyson decided to earn the money to buy a bigger, better one. When he returned to New York, he started a business walking dogs for the residents of Skyview Apartments. Pocketing 50 cents a walk, he soon earned enough money to purchase a Newtonian telescope with a nine-inch mirror. This he would haul to the roof of his 22-story apartment building. There was no electrical outlet there, but luckily a family friend lived in a 19th-floor apartment. He let Tyson run his 100-foot, heavy-duty extension cord from his bedroom window, across some safety railing, up to the roof. Neighbors who saw these activities often became alarmed—and three out of four times Tyson set up his telescope, someone called the police. When an officer arrived, Tyson would offer a peek at the heavens. "Whatever has been said of urban police officers, I have yet to meet one who was not impressed by the sight of the moon, planets, or stars through a telescope," Tyson said. "Saturn alone bailed me out a half dozen times."

Tyson has had to deal with prejudice against African Americans throughout his life. He has found that because he is black, people have often suspected him of being a criminal. As he grew up, he also found that teachers and other students expected him to be better at sports than at studies. For instance, teachers often would suggest he join after-school athletic activities, but they rarely guided him toward academic pursuits. "Being smart growing up in New York does not get the respect on the street, but athletics does, so I was athletic," he said. Tyson practiced until he was the fastest runner in his class and the first in his grade to slam-dunk in basketball. "But I stayed with astronomy," he said.

———— **"** ————

"Being smart growing up in New York does not get the respect on the street, but athletics does, so I was athletic," Tyson said. He practiced until he was the fastest runner in his class and the first in his grade to slam-dunk in basketball. "But I stayed with astronomy."

———— **"** ————

Tyson's parents did everything they could to encourage what he calls his "astrohabit." They combed bookstores for bargain books on the subject, took him to museums, and ushered him around the city for special classes. During junior high and high school, he attended at least six courses at the Hayden Planetarium. He found inspiring teachers there who confirmed for him "the simple joys of just looking up." An important role model was Mark Chartrand III, the head of the planetarium at the time. "Dr. Chartrand's command of astrophysics mixed with his sense of humor was a combination I had never dreamed possible," Tyson said. "If the universe is anything, it should be fun." Tyson had found a role model who showed that it was possible to unlock many mysteries of the universe—and to communicate them to others in a lively, understandable style.

Thanks to his planetarium classes, Tyson met Vernon Grey, the director of education at the New York Explorers' Club. Tyson's lively scientific curiosity impressed Grey. With his encouragement, Tyson took part in programs that the club sponsored. In the summer of 1973, he won an Explorers' Club scholarship to sail to Africa to view a total eclipse of the sun. At age 14, he was the youngest person with no parent or guardian aboard the ship. They traveled on a luxury liner that had been converted to a floating laboratory. Neil Armstrong, the first man to walk on the moon, and science writer Isaac Asimov were among the 2,000 scientists and observers on the expedition.

Later that summer, Tyson attended an astronomy camp in the Mojave Desert, in California. The director of the camp, Joe Patterson, remembered that even at age 14, Tyson had a dramatic flair that made him stand out from other students. "Neil arrived dressed in a big white shirt like a British explorer from the 19th century," Patterson recalled. Far from interfering lights, the desert skies displayed more stars than Tyson had ever seen before. What's more, he was able to use sophisticated telescopes and computers to study them. During the day, he and the other campers strengthened their scientific skills with advanced classes in math and physics.

The following year, Tyson had another thrilling opportunity when he traveled to Scotland on a grant from the U.S. Department of Education. He joined a scientific team that investigated connections between astronomy and groups of massive standing stones called megaliths. The oldest of the groups date from several thousand years before Christ. The most famous example, Stonehenge, is located in southern England. These standing stones are often thought to be the primitive astronomy laboratories of early people.

EDUCATION

Tyson attended the Bronx High School of Science, after passing a difficult exam to win a place at the specialized public school. Tyson thrived in high school as a student and an athlete. A talented wrestler, he was named the team captain in his senior year. In his final season, he achieved an individual match record of ten wins and no losses. As a senior, he also served as the editor-in-chief of the school's *Physical Science Journal*. He graduated in 1976. "A lot of guys were chasing girls," Tyson said of his high-school years. "But I was part of the crowd that wondered how it would feel to have an equation named for us."

Not long after Tyson started high school, a family friend at the City College of New York recommended him to a teacher there. Just two months past his 15th birthday, he gave his first paid scientific lecture. He spoke to 50 adults for an hour about a comet that was expected to soon pass over New York City. (Comets are masses made of ice and gravel that travel quickly through space, trailing tails of light. When they pass close to Earth, they can be seen with the unaided eye.) Tyson illustrated his points with photos he had taken in the Mojave Desert. Two days later he was shocked to receive a check in

Tyson in 1974.

the mail for $50—the equivalent of 100 dog walks. He felt uneasy at first about taking the money for sharing something that came so naturally to him. He was struck with the lesson that "knowledge and intelligence were no less a commodity than sweat and blood."

College Years

An excellent student, Tyson had his pick of top universities. At Cornell University, the famous astrophysicist and professor Carl Sagan wrote him a letter urging him to attend. Sagan personally drove him across campus to the bus station at the end of his visit. But ever the scientist, Tyson decided to make his choice based on hard data. He calculated which school had educated most of the contributors to the magazine *Scientific American*. The answer was Harvard University in Cambridge, Massachusetts. So that's where Tyson went to study physics, with an emphasis on astrophysics. In 1980 he earned his Bachelor of Arts (BA) degree in physics.

While at Harvard, Tyson joined the university's rowing team for a short time. He then returned to wrestling as a member of the school squad. He also explored his more creative side as a dancer in two troupes, performing ballet, jazz, and Afro-Caribbean dances. Viewers were often amazed that Tyson—at 6 feet, two inches tall and nearly 200 hundred pounds—was flexible enough to perform side-to-side splits. He could put his foot behind his head while seated, and do many other moves.

After Cambridge, Tyson went to the University of Texas in Austin, where he earned a Master of Arts (MA) degree in astronomy in 1983. For several years, he remained in Austin. He earned a living as a speaker and writer on scientific subjects, mostly for a general audience. In addition, he launched a question-and-answer column for *Star Date* magazine. Tyson chose the pen name Merlin (after King Arthur's wise magician) and offered easy-to-understand answers to readers' questions about astronomy and the universe. Later, when he became a graduate student at Columbia University, the university press published *Merlin's Tour of the Universe*, a collection of his columns. It since has been translated into seven languages.

> "
>
> *"A lot of guys were chasing girls," Tyson said of his high-school years. "But I was part of the crowd that wondered how it would feel to have an equation named for us."*
>
> "

From Texas, Tyson then moved to College Park, Maryland, where he worked as an astronomy instructor at the University of Maryland for one year. After that, he returned to New York City and began work at Columbia University on a doctorate, or PhD degree, in astrophysics. A PhD is the highest-level degree that a student can earn. At around the same time, Tyson made his first trip to Chile, in South America. He went there to study the heavens from the Cerro Tololo Inter-American Observatory, the home of a very powerful telescope. The observatory is located 7,000 feet above sea level in the Andes Mountains. He calls it the place "closest to my scientific soul" and has returned there many times to carry on his research.

With the information collected in Chile, Tyson completed his doctoral dissertation—the book-length research paper that students must write to earn a PhD. His subject was the "galactic bulge" of the Milky Way, the galaxy of stars and planets that is home to our solar system. He describes the bulge as "a slightly flattened spherical region that is packed with over ten billion stars—about ten percent of the galaxy's total." Tyson studied individual stars within the bulge to uncover important information about how the galaxy formed. As a top student in his class, he was chosen to give a commencement speech to the graduates from many departments of Columbia University. He had dreamed from the age of nine of earning a doctorate in astrophysics. Upon earning his doctorate in 1991, Tyson became one of only seven African-American astrophysicists of about 4,000 in the country. In his speech, he was able to share the difficulties he, as an African American, often faced while working toward his goal.

CAREER HIGHLIGHTS

Today, Tyson is respected as an accomplished scientist. But he is well known for taking a serious and complicated subject and making it seem simple and fun. For instance, to explain how much a neutron star weighs, he says, "a mere thimble of its material would weigh as much as a herd of 50 million elephants." In contrast to the stereotype of a nerdy, shy scientist, he often wears a flashy vest or ties decorated with the sun and stars. He jokes a lot and laughs often. A measure of his popular recognition and appeal was the special award that *People* magazine gave him in 2001: "Sexiest Astrophysicist Alive." He may be tall, handsome, and athletic, but most important, as journalist Patrick Rogers wrote, is Tyson's ability to "penetrate the secrets of the spheres and bring them down to earth."

Hayden Planetarium

After he earned his PhD from Columbia, Tyson began working as a researcher and teacher at Princeton University in Princeton, New Jersey. Joining the Princeton faculty in 1991, he quickly became known for his lively and inspiring teaching style.

In 1994, while he was working at Princeton, Tyson accepted the job of assistant astronomer at the place that had inspired him as a boy—the Hayden Planetarium at the American Museum of Natural History. In 1996, he was named its director—the youngest director in the planetarium's history, and also the first African American to hold the job. Tyson loves the Hayden and wanted to help educate people as its leader. But he was worried that he might lose his scientific

*Tyson at the Rose Center for Earth and Space, where the
Hayden Planetarium is located.*

edge. So he accepted the job only on the condition that he could build a re-search department within the planetarium. Tyson also kept a job at Princeton, as a visiting research scientist in astrophysics. He said, "To be both a research scientist and an educator, that mixture to me, is potent."

149

For Tyson, the education program at Hayden is one of its most exciting features. "Becoming the director put me in a position to influence a next generation of students as an educator and a scientist, as the previous generation influenced me," he said. "I feel an especially urgent sense of duty in this." He loves to make time to spend with young visitors to the Hayden Planetarium. "That's part of the payback of my career," he said. When he was a boy taking classes at the planetarium, Tyson was proud of the certificates he earned when he completed each one. Later, the planetarium discontinued the certificates. But when Tyson took over as director, he brought them back. A favorite part of his job is to sign these certificates personally "with an overpriced fountain pen," he noted.

——— " ———

"Becoming the director [of Hayden Planetarium] put me in a position to influence a next generation of students as an educator and a scientist, as the previous generation influenced me," Tyson said. "I feel an especially urgent sense of duty in this."

——— " ———

When Tyson joined the Hayden Planetarium, the facility was undergoing a massive $210-million reconstruction project. Tyson helped to guide the project to its completion. In 2001 the planetarium reopened to worldwide attention and rave reviews. Its state-of-the-art "sky theater" is contained in a sphere 87 feet in diameter. The shining, aluminum-covered sphere quickly became an architectural landmark in New York: it sits inside a 10-story glass cube, called the Rose Center for Earth and Science. In addition to the planetarium, the Rose Center includes halls devoted to planet Earth and to the universe.

Much time, effort, and creativity have gone into making a visit to the planetarium thrilling and informative. The custom-built machine that projects the stars and planets in the sky theater is state-of-the-art. A supercomputer can project three-dimensional cosmic maps that are equal to the ones used by the National Aeronautics and Space Administration (NASA). Even stars from Hollywood add to the pizzazz: The recorded voice of movie star Tom Hanks accompanies the show. The curving rampway, where visitors leave the building, is a good example of how Tyson and his staff bring information vividly to life. Displayed on the ramp is a timeline that shows the universe's 13-billion-year history. Each inch-long bit of the timeline represents more than three-and-a-half million years. According to this scale, the time of the dinosaurs is represented by 10 feet of ramp. All of human history, in comparison, takes up a single human hair. (Tyson says he knows whose hair it is, but he's not telling.)

Writings and Television Appearances

Most people who read Tyson's books or see him on TV are struck by his talent for making complicated things seem simple and striking. His colleague Sylvester James Gates compared him to the late Carl Sagan, the astrophysicist who brought the subject to millions of people through books and television: "In each of their cases, their potential is in the popularization of science, the ability to reach the general public and tell stories, introduce the personalities and issues that are currently topical in the field of science."

Tyson loves to share his passion for astronomy with people of all interests and all ages. He reaches out to general readers as a columnist and author. Besides his "Ask Merlin" column in *Star Date* magazine, he

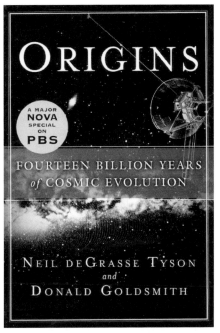

Tyson's book was a companion to the 2004 Nova TV series "Origins" on PBS.

contributes a monthly column, "Universe," to *Natural History* magazine. When a journalist asked him how he gets ideas for his column, he said, "I look up." Tyson also has written or co-written six books to date, including the original collection of "Merlin" columns, *Merlin's Tour of the Universe* (1989), and a later companion collection, *Just Visiting This Planet* (1998). In 1994 he published *The Universe Down to Earth*, a lively explanation of astronomy for nonscientists. In *One Universe: At Home in the Cosmos* (2000), he collaborated with Charles Liu, an astrophysicist, and Robert Irion, a science journalist. The book offers lively and accessible reading on four key areas of astrophysics: motion, matter, energy, and frontiers. His 2000 autobiography and memoir, *The Sky Is Not the Limit: Adventures of an Urban Astrophysicist*, is an engaging account of his life and passions. He followed that with *Origins: Fourteen Billion Years of Cosmic Evolution*, co-authored with Donald Goldsmith, a companion to the NOVA series "Origins" on PBS television that Tyson hosted in 2004.

In addition to hosting "Origins," Tyson has appeared frequently as a science commentator on such television programs as "ABC World News Tonight," "Good Morning America," and "The Today Show." He got a lot of media attention—and "hate mail" from third graders, he claims—when the Hayden planetarium dropped Pluto from its display of the solar system's planets. Tyson is

outgoing, and she is quiet and more serious. Their daughter, Miranda, was born in 1997. They named her after one of the 18 known moons of the planet Uranus. Their son, Travis, was born four years later.

Tyson and his family live near City Hall in lower Manhattan in New York City. They suffered a trauma during the terrorist attacks on New York City in September 2001. They had to flee their home, located not far from the site of the World Trade Center. When they returned after two weeks, it took six people four days to clean the thick dust from the explosion, which coated everything.

HOBBIES AND INTERESTS

A dancer, Tyson has been a member of troupes devoted to modern, jazz, ballet, African, and Latin dance. Wrestling remains a passion, and he has been known to spar with members of the Princeton team. Martial arts are another athletic interest.

Tyson enjoys blues music—the guitarist Buddy Guy is a favorite—and Broadway musical plays. He also loves gourmet cooking and fine wines, which he collects. At a dinner party with friends and family celebrating New Year's Day in 2000, he uncorked a 100-year-old bottle to mark the occasion. Tyson likes to feel connected to the past. He has been known to write poetry by candlelight, using an old-fashioned quill pen, made from a bird's feather, dipped into a pot of ink. The English physicist Isaac Newton, who lived about 500 years ago, is one of his heroes. Tyson owns a leather-bound volume of Newton's writings in Latin, published in 1706. He uses a Latin dictionary to pore over Newton's words.

SELECTED WRITINGS

Merlin's Tour of the Universe, 1989
Universe Down to Earth, 1994
Just Visiting This Planet, 1998
One Universe: At Home in the Cosmos, 2000 (with Charles Liu and Robert Irion)
The Sky Is Not the Limit: Adventures of an Urban Astrophysicist, 2000
Origins: Fourteen Billion Years of Cosmic Evolution, 2004 (with Donald Goldsmith)

HONORS AND AWARDS

Scientists' Writing Award (American Institute of Physics): 2001
Asteroid "13123 Tyson" Named in Tyson's Honor (International Astronomical Union): 2004

FURTHER READING

Books

Contemporary Black Biography, Vol. 15, 1997
Notable Black American Scientists, 1998
Who's Who in America, 2005

Periodicals

Current Biography Yearbook, 2000
Ebony, Aug. 2000, p.58
New Scientist, Apr. 10, 2004, p.46
New York Daily News, Mar. 23, 1996, p.13
New York Times, Dec. 31, 1999, p.B2
People, Feb. 28, 2000, p.77

Online Articles

http://www.americanscientist.org/template/InterviewTypeDetail/assetid/
39524
(*American Scientist Online*, "The Bookshelf Talks with Neil deGrasse
Tyson," Dec. 7, 2004)
http://www.pbs.org/wgbh/nova/origins/tyson.html
(Nova: Origins, "A Conversation with Neil deGrasse Tyson," June 29, 2004)
http://teacher.scholastic.com/scholasticnews/indepth/space/
latest%20news/index.asp?article
(*Scholastic News*, "Life, the Universe, and Everything: An Interview
with 'Origins' Host Neil deGrasse Tyson," Sep. 27, 2004)

Online Databases

Biography Resource Center Online, 2005, articles from *Contemporary Black
Biography*, 1997, and *Notable Black American Scientists*, 1998
H.W. Wilson Company/Wilson Web, 2005, article from *Current Biography
Yearbook*, 2000

ADDRESS

Neil Tyson
Department of Astrophysics
American Museum of Natural History
Central Park West at 79th Street
New York, NY 10024

WORLD WIDE WEB SITES

http://research.amnh.org/users/tyson

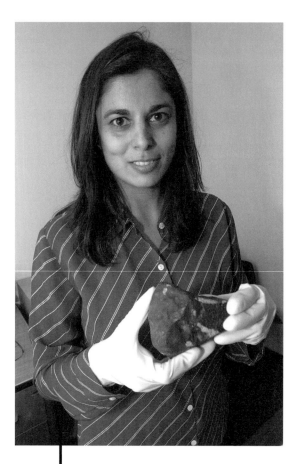

BRIEF ENTRY

Meenakshi Wadhwa 1967-
Indian-American Geologist and Planetary Scientist
Studies Meteorites at the Field Museum of Natural
History

EARLY YEARS

Meenakshi Wadhwa was born in India in 1967. Her father was
a logistics officer in the Indian Air Force, and the family moved
around the country many times when she was young.

As a child, Wadhwa showed an active interest in rocks, minerals,
and natural history. She recalls being eight years old and hearing
from a teacher that everyone breathes in oxygen and breathes
out carbon dioxide. Alarmed that this process would soon

deplete the world of oxygen, she spoke to her mother about the problem. Fortunately, her mother was able to explain the natural cycles that keep the Earth's atmosphere in balance. "So I learned at a young age," Wadhwa remarked, "that we don't understand how much we don't understand."

When Wadhwa was 15, her mother passed away. "I had to step into a motherly role with my younger sister," she explained. "I also felt I had to take care of my dad. It was a big responsibility, and I had to learn to deal with the world from a completely different perspective. I realized I couldn't always get things my way. I had to take other people into consideration."

EDUCATION

It was in college that Wadhwa realized she could make a career out of her interest in science. One reason she chose to study geology is that it combines a number of the sciences. "I could do physics, I could do chemistry, even biology," she explained. In addition, her family encouraged her to pursue a scientific career. In an interview posted at the Field Museum web site, she commented: "My parents encouraged my sister and me to do what we wanted to do. In India that's a big thing. Even in very educated families there is an expectation that once you graduate from college you get married and have kids.... My parents were not that way and I think that made a difference."

> "My parents encouraged my sister and me to do what we wanted to do. In India that's a big thing. Even in very educated families there is an expectation that once you graduate from college you get married and have kids.... My parents were not that way and I think that made a difference."

Attending India's Panjab University, Wadhwa earned a Bachelor of Science (BS) degree in geology in 1988, then a Master of Science (MS) degree in geology in 1989. "There were hardly any women undergraduates in the department," she remembered. "It was completely male dominated." Although she faced some sexist attitudes from her professors and fellow students, she enjoyed the work itself. "What particularly interested me about the science of geology is that it is interdisciplinary, in the sense of trying to understand the workings of the Earth and other planets through applying other sciences. I enjoyed the field work, too. Being able to travel all over is definitely one of the things that first drew me to geology."

Indeed, studying geology in India had advantages. The country has a diverse environment. Wadhwa was able to go on field trips to the country's

Wadhwa meeting with someone who found a meteorite piece in 2003 in Park Forest, Illinois.

western deserts and to the Himalayan Mountains in the north. After graduation, she was offered a job with the Oil and Natural Gas Commission in India, but decided instead to pursue further studies in the United States.

Wadhwa enrolled at Washington University in St. Louis, Missouri. There she had Ghislaine Crozaz, a professor of geochemistry, as her academic advisor. "I saw a woman doing exactly the sort of things I could be doing, and being incredibly successful. It was great to be able to see that," Wadhwa commented. "She was a rarity in her generation, and I was lucky to have her as my advisor. She made sure that everything that came out of the lab was of the highest quality. She was always rigorous about that. She played a big role in shaping my scientific approach to things."

Wadhwa became interested in the geology of other planets as well as Earth when a colleague showed her a meteorite in the college's collection that came from Mars. Meteorites are objects from space that hit the Earth. When the object is above the atmosphere, in space, it's called a meteoroid; when the object passes through the atmosphere and creates a flash of light, it's called a meteor.

In 1994, Wadhwa earned a doctorate degree (PhD) from Washington University in earth and planetary sciences. She then went on to the Scripps Institution of Oceanography at the University of California at San Diego for postdoctoral studies in geochemistry.

MAJOR ACCOMPLISHMENTS

In 1992, while still a student at Washington University, Wadhwa was given a special opportunity: she was selected to be one of the geologists in the U.S. Antarctic Search for Meteorites Expedition. Antarctica has been one of the most productive places for scientists to look for meteorites. Devoid of vegetation, the continent has been covered in a thick layer of ice for hundreds of thousands of years, which makes it easy to spot the dark rocks that are meteorites. In the past 20 years, Wadhwa explained in the Field Museum interview, over 15,000 meteorites have been found in Antarctica. For more than two months she participated in the meteorite search, enduring the extremely cold temperatures and the loneliness.

In 1995, Wadhwa joined the Field Museum of Natural History in Chicago, later becoming the associate curator of meteoritics. She studies how and when the meteorites in the museum's collection were originally formed. Much of the research involves determining the age of meteorites, which are considered to be among the oldest objects in the solar system. Age can be determined by examining the trapped gases within the rock by using a mass spectrometer in a time-consuming process. It may take months to find the age of one meteorite. From this work, it is hoped that scientists can get a better understanding of how planets and asteroids are formed. "The goals of my research program," Wadhwa commented, "are to gain a better understanding of the formation histories of asteroids and planets in our solar system through geochemical and isotopic means, and in particular, to resolve the chronology of events in early solar system history."

—— " ——

"The goals of my research program," Wadhwa commented, "are to gain a better understanding of the formation histories of asteroids and planets in our solar system through geochemical and isotopic means, and in particular, to resolve the chronology of events in early solar system history."

—— " ——

Wadhwa runs the museum's Isotope Geochemistry Laboratory, a joint project sponsored by NASA, the National Science Foundation, and the Field Museum. With the acquisition of a Micromass IsoProbe mass spectrometer in 2001—a 5,000-pound state-of-the-art instrument able to analyze and date meteorites—the Isotope Geochemistry Laboratory is now one of the nation's leading research centers for studying the origins of the solar system.

Some 99 percent of all meteorites that enter the Earth's atmosphere are actually debris that has broken off from an asteroid. A very small portion of meteorites is debris thrown up from the surface of Mars when an asteroid has struck the planet's surface. From these Martian meteorites, Wadhwa has been able to determine several important facts about the geologic evolution of Mars. In 2001 she announced that her research showed strong evidence that the surface of Mars once had water. Six meteorites she studied had signs of oxidation, or rusting, which had been caused by water. Furthermore, there was also evidence that Mars does not have tectonic plate shifts, which cause earthquakes and continental drift on Earth. The surface of the planet has remained stable for many thousands of years.

Recent Work

In the spring of 2003, Wadhwa had the unique opportunity to gather meteorites in Park Forest, Illinois, a suburb of Chicago. For the first time since 1938, a shower of meteorites fell from the sky and landed in Illinois. "There's never been a fall in such a densely populated area before," she commented. The Field Museum quickly found itself competing with collectors and rival natural history institutions to acquire the meteorites. Forming a consortium with the Adler Planetarium, the University of Chicago, the American Museum of Natural History, the Smithsonian Institution, and the Planetary Studies Foundation, the Field Museum was able to raise enough money to buy five of the meteorites. One of the meteorites was the size of a baseball. It had crashed through the roof of a suburban fire department. Wadhwa served as curator of an exhibition, titled "It Came from Outer Space," in which the meteorites were displayed to the public at the Field Museum. "This is such a great opportunity while you have the attention of people to educate them about meteorites," Wadhwa stated.

> "[My advice to young scientists] would be to not worry about looking 'geeky' or get distracted by people who think it's uncool in some way. It's not uncool.... There are going to be great opportunities in the future, and proficiency in science and math will be key...."

In 2004 Wadhwa was among the scientists who examined solar particles brought back by NASA's Genesis spacecraft. These particles were swept off the sun by solar wind and provided clues about the composition not only of the sun itself, but also of the types of gas and dust that formed our solar system. "The sun has basically more than 99 percent of the mass of the solar system in it," Wadhwa explained. "So if we know the composition very well of the sun, we basically understand the starting composition of the initial solar nebula." Her work on this project earned her a Guggenheim fellowship.

Since the mid 1990s, Wadhwa has published several research papers with colleagues in such publications as *Science, Meteoritics and Planetary Science,* and *Antarctic Meteorite Research,* and in the book *Protostars and Planets IV,* edited by A. P. Boss, V. M. Manning, and S. S. Russell. She also serves on NASA's Solar System Exploration Subcommittee and the Curation and Analysis Planning Team.

Wadhwa is currently involved with fellow scientists Andrew Davis and Michael Pellin in the creation of a center for cosmochemistry in Chicago. Such a center would increase Chicago's prominence in space research. "We are hoping to attract many more research scientists to come here from all over the world," Wadhwa explained.

> *There will hopefully be manned missions to other planetary bodies in the not-too-distant future; I'm envious of somebody who's in their teens now and may some day have the opportunity of exploring other planets firsthand."*

In addition to working as an associate curator of meteoritics at Chicago's Field Museum of Natural History, Wadhwa is a lecturer at the University of Chicago and an adjunct associate professor at the University of Illinois at Chicago. Her husband, Mark, is a planetary geologist at Northwestern University. The couple lives in Evanston, Illinois.

Advice to Young Scientists

Wadhwa had this advice for young scientists: "Just follow through on your interests and try not to care about peer pressure and things like that that usually distract kids," she said. "Try to keep up with the math and science. Math is definitely very important. A lot of kids hate it, but if you honestly apply even a moderate amount of effort, it's not very difficult at all.

"I'm a case in point. Through 4th or 5th grade I was awful in math. I was really scared of it and I hated it. My dad, who majored in math in college, said, 'Let me sit down and spend some time with you.' And we started from the very basic things and worked our way up. All it took was somebody that I wasn't afraid to ask questions for fear of looking stupid and who helped me do it right. That's what took care of it. It wasn't that difficult.

"So my advice would be to not worry about looking 'geeky' or get distracted by people who think it's uncool in some way. It's not uncool. There are lots of neat

Wadhwa in her office with one of the meteorites that fell in the Chicago area.

things going on, and there are going to be great opportunities in the future, and proficiency in science and math will be key. There will hopefully be manned missions to other planetary bodies in the not-too-distant future; I'm envious of somebody who's in their teens now and may some day have the opportunity of exploring other planets firsthand."

HONORS AND AWARDS

Asteroid 8356 Renamed Asteroid Wadhwa (International Astronomical Union): 1999
Nier Prize (Meteoritical Society): 2000, for outstanding research in meteoritics by a young scientist
Women of Discovery Award (Wings Trust): 2003, for air and space research
Guggenheim Fellow (Guggenheim Foundation): 2005, for work on solar particles

FURTHER READING

Books

Polk, Milbry, and Mary Tiegreen. *Women of Discovery: A Celebration of Intrepid Women Who Explored the World*, 2001

Periodicals

Chicago Sun-Times, Jan. 5, 2003, p.11; May 5, 2004, p.84
Chicago Tribune, Aug. 18, 1996, p. C1; Apr. 15, 2003, p.3
Discover, Mar. 2004, p.60
Meteoritical Society Newsletter, Nov. 2000
New York Sun, Mar. 18, 2003, p.13
Science, Feb. 23, 2001, p.1527
Springfield (IL) State Journal-Register, Mar. 11, 2001, p.56
Washington Post, July 30, 2001, p.A7

ADDRESS

Meenakshi Wadhwa
Field Museum of Natural History
1400 South Lake Shore Drive
Chicago, IL 60605–2496

WORLD WIDE WEB SITES

http://www.fieldmuseum.org/research_collections/geology/
  wadhwa_interview.htm

Photo and Illustration Credits

George Aldrich/Photos: George Aldrich (pp. 9, 12); Odor-Eaters (p. 16).

Paul Farmer/Photos: Jim Harrison Photography (pp. 18, 26, front cover); Dr. Mark L. Rosenburg (p. 30).

Donna House/Photos: Leonda Levchuk/NMAI (p. 34, 41, front cover); Katherine Fogden/NMAI (p. 37); R.A. Whiteside copyright © Smithsonian Institution/NMAI (p. 39).

Dean Kamen/Photos: Henny Ray Abrams/AFP/Getty Images (p. 43, front cover); U.S. Patent and Trademark Office (pp. 46, 52); Susan Lapsides/Getty Images (p. 48); Newscom.com (p. 51); Segway Inc. (pp. 54, 58).

Cynthia Kenyon/Photos: Courtesy of the University of California, San Francisco (p. 61); AP Images (pp. 64, 67, 71).

Clea Koff/Photos: Samantha Brown (p. 77); Physicians for Human Rights (pp. 80, 82). Cover: THE BONE WOMAN (Random House) copyright © 2004 by Clea Koff. Front jacket photographs copyright © Alex Majoli/Magnum Photos.

Marcia McNutt/Photos: Greg Pio for MBARI copyright © 1997 (p. 87); MBARI (pp. 91, 94); copyright © 2000 MBARI (p. 93).

Lee Ann Newsom/Photos: Greg Greico/Pennsylvania State University (pp. 98, 101, 103).

Charlie Russell/Photos: from GRIZZLY SEASONS (Firefly Books, 2003) photography copyright © Charlie Russell Photography/copyright © Maureen Enns Studio Ltd. (pp. 109, 123); from SPIRIT BEAR (Key Porter Books) copyright © 1994, 2002 by Charlie Russell (pp. 112, 115); Igor Revenko (p. 117). Cover: GRIZZLY HEART (Random House Canada) copyright © 2002 Charlie Russell. Jacket photography copyright © Maureen Enns Studio Ltd.

Linus Torvalds/Photos: AP Images (pp. 126, 128); copyright © Jim Sugar/CORBIS (p. 132). Cover: JUST FOR FUN (HarperBusiness/HarperCollins) copyright © 2001 by Linus Torvalds and David Diamond.

Cumulative General Index

This cumulative index includes names, occupations, nationalities, and ethnic and minority origins that pertain to all individuals profiled in *Biography Today* since the debut of the series in 1992.

Aaliyah . . . . Jan 02
Aaron, Hank . . . . Sport V.1
Abbey, Edward . . . . WorLdr V.1
Abdul, Paula . . . . Jan 92; Update 02
Abdul-Jabbar, Kareem . . . . Sport V.1
Aboriginal
  Freeman, Cathy . . . . Jan 01
Abzug, Bella . . . . Sep 98
activists
  Abzug, Bella . . . . Sep 98
  Arafat, Yasir . . . . Sep 94; Update 94;
    Update 95; Update 96; Update 97; Update
    98; Update 00; Update 01; Update 02
  Ashe, Arthur . . . . Sep 93
  Askins, Renee . . . . WorLdr V.1
  Aung San Suu Kyi . . . . . Apr 96; Update 98;
    Update 01; Update 02
  Banda, Hastings Kamuzu . . . . WorLdr V.2
  Bates, Daisy . . . . Apr 00
  Bellamy, Carol . . . . Jan 06
  Benjamin, Regina . . . . Science V.9
  Brower, David . . . . . WorLdr V.1; Update 01
  Burnside, Aubyn . . . . Sep 02
  Calderone, Mary S. . . . . Science V.3
  Chavez, Cesar . . . . Sep 93
  Chavis, Benjamin . . . . Jan 94; Update 94
  Cronin, John . . . . WorLdr V.3
  Dai Qing . . . . WorLdr V.3
  Dalai Lama . . . . Sep 98
  Douglas, Marjory Stoneman . . WorLdr V.1;
    Update 98
  Ebadi, Shirin . . . . Apr 04
  Edelman, Marian Wright . . . . Apr 93
  Fay, Michael . . . . Science V.9
  Foreman, Dave . . . . WorLdr V.1
  Forman, James . . . . Apr 05
  Fuller, Millard . . . . Apr 03
  Gibbs, Lois . . . . WorLdr V.1
  Haddock, Doris (Granny D) . . . . Sep 00

Huerta, Dolores . . . . Sep 03
Jackson, Jesse . . . . Sep 95; Update 01
Ka Hsaw Wa . . . . WorLdr V.3
Kaunda, Kenneth . . . . WorLdr V.2
Kenyatta, Jomo . . . . WorLdr V.2
Kielburger, Craig . . . . Jan 00
Kim Dae-jung . . . . Sep 01
LaDuke, Winona . . WorLdr V.3; Update 00
Lewis, John . . . . Jan 03
Love, Susan . . . . Science V.3
Maathai, Wangari . . . . . WorLdr V.1; Sep 05
Mandela, Nelson . . . . Jan 92; Update 94;
  Update 01
Mandela, Winnie . . . . WorLdr V.2
Mankiller, Wilma . . . . Apr 94
Martin, Bernard . . . . WorLdr V.3
Masih, Iqbal . . . . Jan 96
Menchu, Rigoberta . . . . Jan 93
Mendes, Chico . . . . WorLdr V.1
Mugabe, Robert . . . . WorLdr V.2
Marshall, Thurgood . . . . . Jan 92; Update 93
Nakamura, Leanne . . . . Apr 02
Nhat Hanh (Thich) . . . . Jan 04
Nkrumah, Kwame . . . . WorLdr V.2
Nyerere, Julius Kambarage . . . WorLdr V.2;
  Update 99
Oliver, Patsy Ruth . . . . WorLdr V.1
Parks, Rosa . . . . Apr 92; Update 94
Pauling, Linus . . . . Jan 95
Poussaint, Alvin . . . . Science V.9
Saro-Wiwa, Ken . . . . WorLdr V.1
Savimbi, Jonas . . . . WorLdr V.2
Spock, Benjamin . . . . Sep 95; Update 98
Steinem, Gloria . . . . Oct 92
Steingraber, Sandra . . . . Science V.9
Teresa, Mother . . . . Apr 98
Watson, Paul . . . . WorLdr V.1
Werbach, Adam . . . . WorLdr V.1
Wolf, Hazel . . . . WorLdr V.3
Zamora, Pedro . . . . Apr 95

For cumulative places of birth and birthday indexes, please see biographytoday.com.

For cumulative places of birth and birthday indexes, please see biographytoday.com.

169

For cumulative places of birth and birthday indexes, please see biographytoday.com.

171

For cumulative places of birth and birthday indexes, please see biographytoday.com.

For cumulative places of birth and birthday indexes, please see biographytoday.com.

For cumulative places of birth and birthday indexes, please see biographytoday.com.

For cumulative places of birth and birthday indexes, please see biographytoday.com.

175

For cumulative places of birth and birthday indexes, please see biographytoday.com.

For cumulative places of birth and birthday indexes, please see biographytoday.com.

177

For cumulative places of birth and birthday indexes, please see biographytoday.com.

    For cumulative places of birth and birthday indexes, please see biographytoday.com.

Douglas, Marjory Stoneman . . WorLdr V.1; Update 98
Dove, Rita . . . . Jan 94
Dragila, Stacy . . . . Sport V.6
Draper, Sharon . . . . Apr 99
Driscoll, Jean . . . . Sep 97
Duchovny, David . . . . Apr 96
Duff, Hilary . . . . Sep 02
Duke, David . . . . Apr 92
Dumars, Joe . . . . Sport V.3; Update 99
Dumitriu, Ioana . . . . Science V.3
Dunbar, Paul Lawrence . . . . Author V.8
Duncan, Lois . . . . Sep 93
Duncan, Tim . . . . Apr 04
Dunlap, Alison . . . . Sport V.7
Dunst, Kirsten . . . . PerfArt V.1
Dutch
  Lionni, Leo . . . . Author V.6
Earle, Sylvia . . . . Science V.1
Earnhardt, Dale . . . . Apr 01
Earnhardt, Dale, Jr, ... Sport V.12
Ebadi, Shirin . . . . Apr 04
Edelman, Marian Wright . . . . Apr 93
educators
  Armstrong, William H. . . . . Author V.7
  Arnesen, Liv. . . . . Author V.15
  Calderone, Mary S. . . . . Science V.3
  Córdova, France . . . . Science V.7
  Delany, Sadie . . . . Sep 99
  Draper, Sharon . . . . Apr 99
  Forman, Michele . . . . Jan 03
  Gates, Henry Louis, Jr. . . . . Apr 00
  Giff, Patricia Reilly . . . . Author V.7
  Jiménez, Francisco . . . . Author V.13
  Napoli, Donna Jo . . . . Author V.16
  Poussaint, Alvin . . . . Science V.9
  Rodriguez, Gloria . . . . Apr 05
  Simmons, Ruth . . . . Sep 02
  Stanford, John . . . . Sep 99
  Suzuki, Shinichi . . . . Sep 98
Egyptians
  Boutros-Ghali, Boutros . . . . Apr 93; Update 98
  Sadat, Anwar . . . . WorLdr V.2
Elion, Getrude . . . . Science V.6
Ellerbee, Linda . . . . Apr 94
Elliott, Missy . . . . PerfArt V.3
Ellison, Ralph . . . . Author V.3
Elway, John . . . . Sport V.2; Update 99
Eminem . . . . Apr 03
Engelbart, Douglas . . . . Science V.5

English
  Almond, David . . . . Author V.10
  Amanpour, Christiane . . . . Jan 01
  Attenborough, David . . . . Science V.4
  Barton, Hazel . . . . Science V.6
  Beckham, David . . . . Jan 04
  Berners-Lee, Tim . . . . Science V.7
  Blair, Tony . . . . Apr 04
  Bloom, Orlando . . . . Sep 04
  Cooper, Susan . . . . Author V.17
  Dahl, Roald . . . . Author V.1
  Diana, Princess of Wales . . . . Jul 92; Update 96; Update 97; Jan 98
  Goodall, Jane . . . . . . Science V.1; Update 02
  Handford, Martin . . . . Jan 92
  Hargreaves, Alison . . . . Jan 96
  Hawking, Stephen . . . . Apr 92
  Herriot, James . . . . Author V.1
  Jacques, Brian . . . . Author V.5
  Jones, Diana Wynne . . . . Author V.15
  Koff, Clea . . . . Science V.11
  Leakey, Louis . . . . Science V.1
  Leakey, Mary . . . . Science V.1
  Lewis, C. S. . . . . Author V.3
  MacArthur, Ellen . . . . Sport V.11
  Macaulay, David . . . . Author V.2
  Moore, Henry . . . . Artist V.1
  Potter, Beatrix . . . . Author V.8
  Pullman, Philip . . . . Author V.9
  Radcliffe, Daniel . . . . Jan 02
  Reid Banks, Lynne . . . . Author V.2
  Rennison, Louise . . . . Author V.10
  Rowling, J. K. . . . . Sep 99; Update 00; Update 01; Update 02
  Sacks, Oliver . . . . Science V.3
  Stewart, Patrick . . . . Jan 94
  Stone, Joss . . . . Jan 06
  Streeter, Tanya . . . . Sport V.11
  Tolkien, J.R.R. . . . . Jan 02
  Watson, Emma . . . . Apr 03
  Winslet, Kate . . . . Sep 98
environmentalists
  Abbey, Edward . . . . WorLdr V.1
  Adams, Ansel . . . . Artist V.1
  Askins, Renee . . . . WorLdr V.1
  Babbitt, Bruce . . . . Jan 94
  Brower, David . . . . . WorLdr V.1; Update 01
  Brundtland, Gro Harlem . . . . . . Science V.3
  Carson, Rachel . . . . WorLdr V.1
  Cousteau, Jacques . . . . Jan 93
  Cronin, John . . . . WorLdr V.3

For cumulative places of birth and birthday indexes, please see biographytoday.com.

183

For cumulative places of birth and birthday indexes, please see biographytoday.com.

For cumulative places of birth and birthday indexes, please see biographytoday.com.

Hanson, Zac
see Hanson . . . . Jan 98
Harbaugh, Jim . . . . Sport V.3
Hardaway, Anfernee "Penny" . . . Sport V.2
Harding, Tonya . . . . Sep 94
Hargreaves, Alison . . . . Jan 96
Harris, Bernard . . . . Science V.3
Hart, Melissa Joan . . . . Jan 94
Hartnett, Josh . . . . Sep 03
Hasek, Dominik . . . . Sport V.3
Hassan II . . . . WorLdr V.2; Update 99
Hathaway, Anne . . . . Apr 05
Haughton, Aaliyah Dana
see Aaliyah . . . . Jan 02
Hawk, Tony . . . . Apr 01
Hawking, Stephen . . . . Apr 92
Hayden, Carla . . . . Sep 04
Hayes, Tyrone . . . . Science V.10
Haynes, Cornell, Jr.
see Nelly . . . . Sep 03
Healy, Bernadine . . . . Science V.1; Update 01
Heimlich, Henry . . . . Science V.6
Heinlein, Robert . . . . Author V.4
Hendrickson, Sue . . . . Science V.7
Henry, Marguerite . . . . Author V.4
Hernandez, Livan . . . . Apr 98
Herriot, James . . . . Author V.1
Hesse, Karen . . . . Author V.5; Update 02
Hewitt, Jennifer Love . . . . Sep 00
Hill, Anita . . . . Jan 93
Hill, Faith . . . . Sep 01
Hill, Grant . . . . Sport V.1
Hill, Lauryn . . . . Sep 99
Hillary, Sir Edmund . . . . Sep 96
Hillenbrand, Laura . . . . Author V.14
Hillenburg, Stephen . . . . Author V.14
Hingis, Martina . . . . Sport V.2
Hinton, S.E. . . . . Author V.1
Hispanics
Aguilera, Christina . . . . Apr 00
Alba, Jessica . . . . Sep 01
Alvarez, Julia . . . . Author V.17
Alvarez, Luis W. . . . . Science V.3
Bledel, Alexis . . . . Jan 03
Carmona, Richard . . . . Science V.8
Castro, Fidel . . . . Jul 92; Update 94
Chambers, Veronica . . . . Author V.15
Chavez, Cesar . . . . Sep 93
Chavez, Julz . . . . Sep 02
Cisneros, Henry . . . . Sep 93
Córdova, France . . . . Science V.7
Cruz, Celia . . . . Apr 04
Diaz, Cameron . . . . PerfArt V.3
Domingo, Placido . . . . Sep 95
Estefan, Gloria . . . . Jul 92
Fernandez, Lisa . . . . Sport V.5
Fox, Vicente . . . . Apr 03
Fuentes, Daisy . . . . Jan 94
Garcia, Sergio . . . . Sport V.7
Gonzalez, Tony . . . . Sport V.11
Greer, Pedro José, Jr. . . . . Science V.10
Hernandez, Livan . . . . Sep 93
Huerta, Dolores . . . . Sep 03
Iglesias, Enrique . . . . Jan 03
Jiménez, Francisco . . . . Author V.13
Lopez, Charlotte . . . . Apr 94
Lopez, Jennifer . . . . Jan 02
López, George . . . . PerfArt V.2
Martin, Ricky . . . . Jan 00
Martinez, Pedro . . . . Sport V.5
Martinez, Victor . . . . Author V.15
Mendes, Chico . . . . WorLdr V.1
Moreno, Arturo R. . . . . Business V.1
Muniz, Frankie . . . . Jan 01
Novello, Antonia . . . . Apr 92
Ocampo, Adriana C. . . . . Science V.8
Ochoa, Ellen . . . . Apr 01; Update 02
Ochoa, Severo . . . . Jan 94
Pele . . . . Sport V.1
Prinze, Freddie, Jr. . . . . Apr 00
Pujols, Albert . . . . Sport V.12
Ramirez, Manny . . . . Sport V.13
Rivera, Diego . . . . Artist V.1
Rodriguez, Alex . . . . Sport V.6
Rodriguez, Eloy . . . . Science V.2
Rodriguez, Gloria . . . . Apr 05
Ryan, Pam Muñoz . . . . Author V.12
Sanchez, Ricardo . . . . Sep 04
Sanchez Vicario, Arantxa . . . . Sport V.1
Selena . . . . Jan 96
Shakira . . . . PerfArt V.1
Soriano, Alfonso . . . . Sport V.10
Soto, Gary . . . . Author V.5
Toro, Natalia . . . . Sep 99
Vega, Alexa . . . . Jan 04
Vidal, Christina . . . . PerfArt V.1
Villa, Brenda . . . . Jan 06
Villa-Komaroff, Lydia . . . . Science V.6
Zamora, Pedro . . . . Apr 95
Ho, David . . . . Science V.6

For cumulative places of birth and birthday indexes, please see biographytoday.com.

187

For cumulative places of birth and birthday indexes, please see biographytoday.com.

    For cumulative places of birth and birthday indexes, please see biographytoday.com.

For cumulative places of birth and birthday indexes, please see biographytoday.com.

For cumulative places of birth and birthday indexes, please see biographytoday.com.

193

For cumulative places of birth and birthday indexes, please see biographytoday.com.

For cumulative places of birth and birthday indexes, please see biographytoday.com.

199

For cumulative places of birth and birthday indexes, please see biographytoday.com.

For cumulative places of birth and birthday indexes, please see biographytoday.com.

For cumulative places of birth and birthday indexes, please see biographytoday.com.

   For cumulative places of birth and birthday indexes, please see biographytoday.com.

For cumulative places of birth and birthday indexes, please see biographytoday.com.

For cumulative places of birth and birthday indexes, please see biographytoday.com.

Biography Today

General Series

B iography Today **General Series** includes a unique combination of current biographical profiles that teachers and librarians — and the readers themselves — tell us are most appealing. The **General Series** is available as a 3-issue subscription; hardcover annual cumulation; or subscription plus cumulation.

Within the **General Series**, your readers will find a variety of sketches about:

- Authors
- Musicians
- Political leaders
- Sports figures
- Movie actresses & actors
- Cartoonists
- Scientists
- Astronauts
- TV personalities
- and the movers & shakers in many other fields!

"*Biography Today* will be useful in elementary and middle school libraries and in public library children's collections where there is a need for biographies of current personalities. High schools serving reluctant readers may also want to consider a subscription."
— *Booklist*, American Library Association

"Highly recommended for the young adult audience. Readers will delight in the accessible, energetic, tell-all style; teachers, librarians, and parents will welcome the clever format [and] intelligent and informative text. It should prove especially useful in motivating 'reluctant' readers or literate nonreaders."
— *MultiCultural Review*

"Written in a friendly, almost chatty tone, the profiles offer quick, objective information. While coverage of current figures makes *Biography Today* a useful reference tool, an appealing format and wide scope make it a fun resource to browse." — *School Library Journal*

"The best source for current information at a level kids can understand."
— Kelly Bryant, School Librarian, Carlton, OR

"Easy for kids to read. We love it! Don't want to be without it."
— Lynn McWhirter, School Librarian, Rockford, IL

ONE-YEAR SUBSCRIPTION

- 3 softcover issues, 6" x 9"
- Published in January, April, and September
- 1-year subscription, list price $62.
  School and library price $60
- 150 pages per issue
- 10 profiles per issue
- Contact sources for additional information
- Cumulative Names Index

HARDBOUND ANNUAL CUMULATION

- Sturdy 6" x 9" hardbound volume
- Published in December
- List price $69. **School and library price $62 per volume**
- 450 pages per volume
- 30 profiles — includes all profiles found in softcover issues for that calendar year
- Cumulative General Index

SUBSCRIPTION AND CUMULATION COMBINATION

- $99 for 3 softcover issues plus the hardbound volume

For Cumulative General, Places of Birth, and Birthday Indexes, please see www.biographytoday.com.

Biography Today

Subject Series

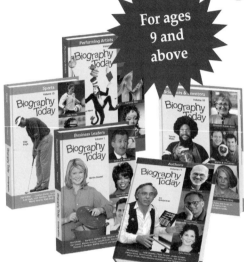

For ages 9 and above

Expands and complements the General Series and targets specific subject areas . . .

Our readers asked for it! They wanted more biographies, and the *Biography Today* **Subject Series** is our response to that demand. Now your readers can choose their special areas of interest and go on to read about their favorites in those fields. The following specific volumes are included in the *Biography Today* **Subject Series:**

- **Authors**
- **Business Leaders**
- **Performing Artists**
- **Scientists & Inventors**
- **Sports**

FEATURES AND FORMAT

- Sturdy 6" x 9" hardbound volumes
- Individual volumes, list price $44 each. **School and library price $39 each**
- 200 pages per volume
- 10 profiles per volume — targets individuals within a specific subject area
- Contact sources for additional information
- Cumulative General Index

For Cumulative General, Places of Birth, and Birthday Indexes, please see www.biographytoday.com.

NOTE: There is *no duplication of entries* between the **General Series** of *Biography Today* and the **Subject Series.**

AUTHORS

"A useful tool for children's assignment needs." — *School Library Journal*

"The prose is workmanlike: report writers will find enough detail to begin sound investigations, and browsers are likely to find someone of interest." — *School Library Journal*

SCIENTISTS & INVENTORS

"The articles are readable, attractively laid out, and touch on important points that will suit assignment needs. Browsers will note the clear writing and interesting details." — *School Library Journal*

"The book is excellent for demonstrating that scientists are real people with widely diverse backgrounds and personal interests. The biographies are fascinating to read." — *The Science Teacher*

SPORTS

"This series should become a standard resource in libraries that serve intermediate students." — *School Library Journal*

Methods in Enzymology

Volume 268
NITRIC OXIDE
Part A
Sources and Detection of NO;
NO Synthase

METHODS IN ENZYMOLOGY

EDITORS-IN-CHIEF

John N. Abelson   Melvin I. Simon

DIVISION OF BIOLOGY
CALIFORNIA INSTITUTE OF TECHNOLOGY
PASADENA, CALIFORNIA

FOUNDING EDITORS

Sidney P. Colowick and Nathan O. Kaplan

Methods in Enzymology

Volume 268

Nitric Oxide

Part A
Sources and Detection of NO; NO Synthase

EDITED BY

Lester Packer

DEPARTMENT OF MOLECULAR AND CELL BIOLOGY
UNIVERSITY OF CALIFORNIA
BERKELEY, CALIFORNIA

Editorial Advisory Board

ACADEMIC PRESS

San Diego   New York   Boston   London   Sydney   Tokyo   Toronto

Copyright © 1996 by ACADEMIC PRESS, INC.

Academic Press, Inc.
A Division of Harcourt Brace & Company
525 B Street, Suite 1900, San Diego, California 92101-4495

United Kingdom Edition published by
Academic Press Limited
24-28 Oval Road, London NW1 7DX

International Standard Serial Number: 0076-6879

International Standard Book Number: 0-12-182169-2

PRINTED IN THE UNITED STATES OF AMERICA
96 97 98 99 00 01 EB 9 8 7 6 5 4 3 2 1

Table of Contents

Section I. Generation, Detection, and Characterization of Biological and Chemical Sources of Nitric Oxide
A. Nitric Oxide Chemistry and Biology

B. Methods for Detection of Nitric Oxide

v

D. Molecular Cloning and Expression

E. Nitric Oxide Synthase and Hemoprotein Homology

F. Tissue Distribution of Nitric Oxide Synthase

Contributors to Volume 268

Article numbers are in parentheses following the names of contributors.
Affiliations listed are current.

TAKAAKI AKAIKE (20), *Department of Microbiology, Kimamoto University School of Medicine, Kumamoto 860, Japan*

CARMEN M. ARROYO (19), *Research Service (151), Veterans Administration Medical Center, Baltimore, Maryland 21218*

SALLY A. BAYLIS (44), *Biology Division, Wellcome Research Laboratories, Bechenham, Kent BR3 3BS, United Kingdom*

NADIR BETTACHE (26), *CNRS-URA 1856, Université Montpellier II, 34095 Montpellier, France*

ANNA BINI (22), *Department of Biomedical Sciences, University of Modena, 41100 Modena, Italy*

PHILIP A. BLAND-WARD (38), *Pharmacology Group, Biomedical Sciences Division, King's College, University of London, London SW3 6LX, United Kingdom*

FRANCIS T. BONNER (5), *Department of Chemistry, State University of New York at Stonybrook, Stony Brook, New York 11794*

KENNETH S. BOOCKVAR (13), *Department of Medicine, Columbia University School of Medicine, New York, New York 10027*

DAVID S. BREDT (42, 47), *Departments of Physiology and Pharmaceutical Chemistry, School of Medicine, University of California, San Francisco, California 94143*

JAMES E. BRIEN (8), *Department of Pharmacology and Toxicology, Faculty of Medicine, Queen's University, Kingston, Ontario K7L 3N6, Canada*

GARRY R. BUETTNER (17), *Free Radical Research Institute/EMRB 68, College of Medicine, The University of Iowa, Iowa City, Iowa 52242*

TOM CARTER (26), *Department of Neurophysiology and Neuropharmacology, National Institute for Medical Research, Mill Hill, London NW7 1AA, United Kingdom*

DANIEL S. CHAO (47), *Department of Physiology, School of Medicine, University of California, San Francisco, California 94143*

IAN G. CHARLES (44), *Biology Division, Wellcome Research Laboratories, Beckenham, Kent BR3 3BS, United Kingdom*

DANAE CHRISTODOULOU (7, 9), *Chemistry Section, Laboratory of Comparative Carcinogenesis, National Cancer Institute, Frederick Cancer Research and Development Center, Frederick, Maryland 21702*

ANN CHUBB (44), *Biology Division, Wellcome Research Laboratories, Bechenham, Kent BR3 3BS, United Kingdom*

JOHN A. COOK (7, 9, 10, 11), *Radiation Biology Section, Radiation Biology Branch, National Cancer Institute, Bethesda, Maryland 20892*

JOHN A. CORBETT (39), *Department of Biochemistry and Molecular Biology, Health Sciences Center, Saint Louis University, St. Louis, Missouri 63104*

JOHN E. T. CORRIE (26), *Department of Physical Biochemistry, National Institute for Medical Research, Mill Hill, London NW7 1AA, United Kingdom*

KEITH M. DAVIES (27), *Department of Chemistry, George Mason University, Fairfax, Virginia 22030*

JOHN DAWSON (44), *Department of Chemistry and Biochemistry, University of South Carolina, Columbia, South Carolina 29208*

TED M. DAWSON (34), *Departments of Neurology and Neuroscience, Johns Hopkins University School of Medicine, Baltimore, Maryland 21287*

VALINA L. DAWSON (34), *Departments of Neurology, Neuroscience, and Physiology, Johns Hopkins University School of Medicine, Baltimore, Maryland 21287*

BILLY W. DAY (18), *Departments of Environmental and Occupational Health, and Pharmaceutical Sciences, University of Pittsburgh Cancer Institute, University of Pittsburgh, Pittsburgh, Pennsylvania 15238*

WILLIAM M. DEEN (24), *Department of Chemical Engineering, Massachusetts Institute of Technology, Cambridge, Massachusetts 02139*

NAE J. DUN (50), *Department of Anatomy and Neurobiology, Medical College of Ohio, Toledo, Ohio 43614*

NABIL M. ELSAYED (18), *Department of Respiratory Research, Division of Medicine, Walter Reed Army Institute of Research, Washington, District of Columbia 20307; and Department of Environmental and Occupational Health, University of California, Los Angeles, California 90024*

CONCHITA FERNÀNDEZ (44), *Biology Division, Wellcome Research Laboratories, Bechenham, Kent BR3 3BS, United Kingdom*

PETER C. FORD (3, 7, 11), *Department of Chemistry, University of California, Santa Barbara, California 93106*

ULRICH FÖRSTERMANN (32, 50), *Department of Pharmacology, Johannes Gutenberg University, D-55101 Mainz, Germany*

NEALE FOXWELL (44), *Biology Division, Wellcome Research Laboratories, Bechenham, Kent BR3 3BS, United Kingdom*

JON M. FUKUTO (36), *Department of Pharmacology, Center for Health Sciences, University of California School of Medicine, Los Angeles, California 90024*

HO-LEUNG FUNG (25), *Department of Pharmaceutics, School of Pharmacy, State University of New York at Buffalo, Buffalo, New York 14260*

ERIC S. FURFINE (33), *Division of Biochemistry, Glaxo Wellcome, Inc., Research Triangle Park, North Carolina 27709*

EDWARD P. GARVEY (33), *Division of Biochemistry, Glaxo Wellcome, Inc., Research Triangle Park, North Carolina 27709*

INGOLF GATH (32), *Department of Pharmacology, Johannes Gutenberg University, D-55101 Mainz, Germany*

PEJMAN GHANOUNI (43), *Cardiovascular Division, Brigham and Women's Hospital, Harvard Medical School, Boston, Massachusetts 02115*

JOSEPH A. GLOGOWSKI (12), *Division of Toxicology, Massachusetts Institute of Technology, Cambridge, Massachusetts 02139*

NICOLAI V. GORBUNOV (18), *Department of Respiratory Research, Division of Medicine, Walter Reed Army Institute of Research, Washington, District of Columbia 20307*

DONALD L. GRANGER (13), *Division of Infectious Diseases, Department of Medicine, University of Utah School of Medicine, Salt Lake City, Utah 84132; and Veterans Affairs Medical Center, Salt Lake City, Utah 84145*

OWEN W. GRIFFITH (37), *Department of Biochemistry, Medical College of Wisconsin, Milwaukee, Wisconsin 53226*

MATTHEW B. GRISHAM (3, 7, 9, 10, 11, 23), *Department of Physiology, Louisiana State University Medical Center, Shreveport, Louisiana 71130*

STEVEN S. GROSS (15, 30), *Department of Pharmacology, Cornell University Medical College, New York, New York 10021*

HITOSHI HABU (14), *Department of Neuroscience, Institute of Molecular and Cellular Medicine, Okayama University Medical School, Okayama 700, Japan*

DAVID M. HALL (17), *Free Radical Research Institute/EMRB 68, College of Medicine, The University of Iowa, Iowa City, Iowa 52242*

CHRISTIAN HARTENECK (41), *Department of Pharmacology, Free University of Berlin, D-14195 Berlin, Germany*

JOHN B. HIBBS, JR. (13), *Division of Infectious Diseases, Department of Medicine, University of Utah School of Medicine, Salt Lake City, Utah 84132; and Veterans Affairs Medical Center, Salt Lake City, Utah 84145*

FRED HUANG (47), *Department of Physiology, School of Medicine, University of California, San Francisco, California 94143*

PAUL M. HWANG (47), *Department of Physiology, School of Medicine, University of California, San Francisco, California 94143*

ANNA IANNONE (22), *Department of Biomedical Sciences, University of Modena, 41100 Modena, Italy*

KOHJI ICHIMORI (19), *Department of Physiology 2, Tokai University School of Medicine, Bohseidai, Isehara, Kanagawa 259-11, Japan*

MASAYASU INOUE (49), *Department of Biochemistry, Osaka City University Medical School, Abeno, Osaka 545, Japan*

GLENDA G. JOHNSON (23), *Department of Physiology, Louisiana State University Medical Center, Shreveport, Louisiana 71130*

HIDEAKI KABUTO (14), *Department of Neuroscience, Institute of Molecular and Cellular Medicine, Okayama University Medical School, Okayama 700, Japan*

VALERIAN E. KAGAN (18), *Department of Environmental and Occupational Health, University of Pittsburgh Cancer Institute, University of Pittsburgh, Pittsburgh, Pennsylvania 15238*

B. KALYANARAMAN (16), *Biophysics Research Institute, Medical College of Wisconsin, Milwaukee, Wisconsin 53226*

LARRY K. KEEFER (27), *Chemistry Section, Laboratory of Comparative Carcinogenesis, National Cancer Insitute, Frederick Cancer Research and Development Center, Frederick, Maryland 21702*

ROBERT G. KILBOURN (37), *Section of Hematology, Rush-Presbyterian, St. Luke's Medical Center, Chicago, Illinois 60612*

NARENDRA S. KISHNANI (25), *Department of Pharmaceutics, School of Pharmacy, State University of New York at Buffalo, Buffalo, New York 14260*

PETER KLATT (35, 41), *Institut für Pharmakologie und Toxikologie, Karl-Franzens-Universität Graz, A-8010 Graz, Austria*

RICHARD G. KNOWLES (44), *Biology Division, Wellcome Research Laboratories, Bechenham, Kent BR3 3BS, United Kingdom*

WILLEM H. KOPPENOL (1, 2), *Laboratorium für Anorganische Chemie, Eidgenössische Technische Hochschule Zürich, CH-8092 Zürich, Switzerland*

YASHIGE KOTAKE (21), *Free Radical Biology and Aging Research Program, National Center for Spin Trapping and Free Radicals, Oklahoma Medical Research Foundation, Oklahoma City, Oklahoma 73104*

ANDREY V. KOZLOV (22), *Department of Biomedical Sciences, University of Modena, 41100 Modena, Italy*

MURALI C. KRISHNA (7, 9, 11), *Radiation Biology Section, Radiation Biology Branch, National Cancer Institute, Bethesda, Maryland 20892*

SETSUKI KUDO (7), *Department of Chemistry, University of California, Santa Barbara, California 93106*

JACK R. LANCASTER (4, 23), *Departments of Physiology and Medicine, Louisiana State University Medical Center, New Orleans, Louisiana 70112*

RANDY S. LEWIS (24), *School of Chemical Engineering, Oklahoma State University, Stillwater, Oklahoma 74078*

BARBARA M. LIST (41), *Institut für Pharmakologie und Toxikologie, Karl-Franzens-Universität Graz, A-8010 Graz, Austria*

QING LIU (30), *Department of Pharmacology, Cornell University Medical College, New York, New York 10021*

JOSEPH LOSCALZO (28), *Departments of Medicine and Biochemistry, Whitaker Cardiovascular Institute, Boston University School of Medicine, Boston, Massachusetts 02118*

HIROSHI MAEDA (20), *Department of Microbiology, Kumamoto University School of Medicine, Kumamoto 860, Japan*

MAHIN D. MAINES (46), *Departments of Biophysics and Environmental Medicine, University of Rochester School of Medicine, Rochester, New York 14642*

TADEUSZ MALINSKI (6), *Department of Chemistry and Institute of Biotechnology, Oakland University, Rochester, Michigan 48309*

GERALD S. MARKS (8), *Department of Pharmacology and Toxicology, Faculty of Medicine, Queen's University, Kingston, Ontario K7L 3N6, Canada*

BETTIE SUE SILER MASTERS (45), *Department of Biochemistry, The University of Texas*

Health Science Center at San Antonio, San Antonio, Texas 78284

BERND MAYER (35, 41), Institut für Pharmakologie und Toxikologie, Karl-Franzens-Universität Graz, A-8010 Graz, Austria

MICHAEL L. MCDANIEL (39), Department of Pathology, Washington University School of Medicine, St. Louis, Missouri 63110

BRIAN E. MCLAUGHLIN (8), Department of Pharmacology and Toxicology, Faculty of Medicine, Queen's University, Kingston, Ontario K7L 3N6, Canada

KIRK MCMILLAN (45), Pharmacopeia, Cranbury, New Jersey 08512

STEFAN MESAROS (6), Department of Chemistry and Institute of Biotechnology, Oakland University, Rochester, Michigan 48309

THOMAS MICHEL (43), Cardiovascular Division, Brigham and Women's Hospital, Harvard Medical School, Boston, Massachusetts 02115

ALLEN M. MILES (7, 9, 10, 11), Department of Physiology, Louisiana State University Medical Center, Shreveport, Louisiana 71130

JAMES B. MITCHELL (3), Radiation Biology Branch, National Cancer Institute, Bethesda, Maryland 20892

PHILIP K. MOORE (38), Pharmacology Group, Biomedical Sciences Division, Kings College, University of London, London SW3 6LX, United Kingdom

AKITANE MORI (14), Department of Neuroscience, Institute of Molecular and Cellular Medicine, Okayama University Medical School, 2-5-1 Shikatacho, Okayama 700, Japan

MARÍA ÁNGELES MORO (44), Department of Anatomy and Developmental Biology, University College, London, United Kingdom

RAMACHANDRAN MURUGESAN (7), Radiation Biology Section, Radiation Biology Branch, National Cancer Institute, Bethesda, Maryland 20892; and School of Chemistry, Madurai Kamaraj University, Madurai 625021, India

KANJI NAKATSU (8), Department of Pharmacology and Toxicology, Faculty of Medi-

cine, Queen's University, Kingston, Ontario K7L 3N6, Canada

HIROE NAKAZAWA (19), Department of Physiology 2, Tokai University School of Medicine, Bohseidai, Isehara, Kanagawa, 259-11, Japan

RAYMOND W. NIMS (9, 11, 27), Chemistry Section, Laboratory of Comparative Carcinogenesis, National Cancer Institute, Frederick Cancer Research and Development Center, Frederick, Maryland 21702

DAVID OGDEN (26), Department of Neurophysiology and Neuropharmacology, National Institute for Medical Research, Mill Hill, London NW7 1AA, United Kingdom

ANATOLY N. OSIPOV (18), Department of Environmental and Occupational Health, University of Pittsburgh Cancer Institute, University of Pittsburgh, Pittsburgh, Pennsylvania 15238

ROBERTO PACELLI (11), Radiation Biology Section, Radiation Biology Branch, National Cancer Institute, Bethesda, Maryland 20892

CHARLES M. B. POORE (9, 11), Quality Control, Chemical Synthesis Analysis Laboratory, SAIC Frederick, Frederick Cancer Research and Development Center, Frederick, Maryland 21702

LISA J. ROBINSON (43), Cardiovascular Division, Brigham and Women's Hospital, Harvard Medical School, Boston, Massachusetts 02115

JOHN C. SALERNO (45), Rensselaer Polytechnic Institute, Troy, New York 12181

EISUKE F. SATO (49), Department of Biochemistry, Osaka City University Medical School, Abeno, Osaka 545, Japan

KURT SCHMIDT (35, 41), Institut für Pharmakologie und Toxikologie, Karl-Franzens-Universität Graz, A-8010 Graz, Austria

CAROL A. SCORER (44), Biology Division, Wellcome Research Laboratories, Bechenham, Kent BR3 3BS, United Kingdom

PAULA A. SHERMAN (33), Division of Cell Biology, Glaxo Wellcome, Inc., Research Triangle Park, North Carolina 27709

DENNIS J. STUEHR (31), *Department of Immunology, Cleveland Clinic Research Institute, Cleveland, Ohio 44195; and Case Western Reserve University, Cleveland, Ohio 44106*

READ R. TAINTOR (13), *Division of Infectious Diseases, Department of Medicine, University of Utah School of Medicine, Salt Lake City, Utah 84132; and Veterans Affairs Medical Center, Salt Lake City, Utah 84145*

STEVEN R. TANNENBAUM (12), *Department of Chemistry and Division of Toxicology, Massachusetts Institute of Technology, Cambridge, Massachusetts 02139*

DIANE TEAGUE (11), *Radiation Biology Section, Radiation Biology Branch, National Cancer Institute, Bethesda, Maryland 20892*

CHRISTOPH THIEMERMANN (40), *The William Harvey Research Institute, St. Bartholomew's Hospital Medical College, London EC1M 6BQ, United Kingdom*

ALDO TOMASI (22), *Department of Biomedical Sciences, University of Modena, 41100 Modena, Italy*

PAUL TOMBOULIAN (6), *Department of Chemistry and Institute of Biotechnology, Oakland University, Rochester, Michigan 48309*

J. G. TRAYNHAM (1), *Department of Chemistry, Louisiana State University, Baton Rouge, Louisiana 70803*

DAVID R. TRENTHAM (26), *Department of Physical Biochemistry, National Institute for Medical Research, Mill Hill, London NW7 1AA, United Kingdom*

GILBERT R. UPCHURCH, JR. (28), *Evans Department of Medicine and Department of Biochemistry, Whitaker Cardiovascular Institute, Boston University School of Medicine, Boston, Massachusetts 02118*

KOZO UTSUMI (49), *Center for Adult Diseases, Kurashiki 710, Japan*

MARK N. WALLACE (48), *Department of Biomedical Sciences, Marischal College, University of Aberdeen, Aberdeen AB9 1AS, United Kingdom*

GEORGE N. WELCH (28), *Evans Department of Medicine and Department of Biochemistry, Whitaker Cardiovascular Institute, Boston University School of Medicine, Boston, Massachusetts 02118*

ERNST R. WERNER (35), *Department of Medicinal Chemistry and Biochemistry, University of Innsbruck, A-6020 Innsbruck, Austria*

D. LYN H. WILLIAMS (29), *Department of Chemistry, Science Laboratories, University of Durham, Durham DH1 3LE, United Kingdom*

DAVID A. WINK (3, 7, 9, 10, 11, 27), *Chemistry Section, Laboratory of Comparative Carcinogenesis, National Cancer Institute, Frederick Cancer Research and Development Center, Frederick, Maryland 21702; and Radiation Biology Section, Radiation Biology Branch, National Cancer Institute, Bethesda, Maryland 20892*

JOHN S. WISHNOK (12), *Division of Toxicology, Massachusetts Institute of Technology, Cambridge, Massachusetts 02139*

CHIN-CHEN WU (40), *Department of Pharmacology, National Defense Medical Center, Taipei, Taiwan, Republic of China*

HOUHUI XIA (42), *Departments of Physiology and Pharmaceutical Chemistry, School of Medicine, University of California, San Francisco, California 94143*

ISAO YOKOI (14), *Department of Neuroscience, Institute of Molecular and Cellular Medicine, Okayama University Medical School, Okayama 700, Japan*

ISABELLA ZINI (22), *Department of Biomedical Sciences, University of Modena, 41100 Modena, Italy*

Preface

The realization that nitric oxide (NO·), a free radical that is generated in biological systems, plays a pivotal role in physiology, pathology, and pharmacology has led to an explosion of new research. The recognition that the endothelial relaxing factor (ERDF) is actually NO· has been important in revolutionizing our thinking about how the vasculature is regulated. The physiological functions of NO· in signaling by the activation of guanylate cyclase and the existence of a multitude of other targets have now been identified for NO· in biological systems.

NO· is a free radical species, and therefore reactive as such. However, it reacts with the superoxide anion with a rate constant of about 6.7×10^9 $M^{-1} \sec^{-1}$, forming peroxynitrite ($ONOO^-$), a species more reactive toward lipids, DNA, and proteins, leading to their chemical modification and to pathological effects.

Overcoming difficulties in accurately assessing its generation, detection, and characterization in biological systems was the impetus for seeking contributions to these two *Methods in Enzymology* volumes on nitric oxide (268 and 269). They provide a comprehensive and detailed account of the methodology relating to four areas. This volume covers methods relating to the generation of NO·. In Section I the chemistry and biology of NO·, methods for its detection, and NO· donors are covered. Section II covers NO· synthase—its purification, assay of the activity of endogenous and inducible forms of NO· synthase, its hemoprotein homology, the tissue distribution of NO· synthase, and its molecular cloning and expression. In Volume 269 methods and assays relevant to the effects of NO· in cells and tissues and the pathological and clinical aspects of NO· are included. The articles in Section I focus on the reactivity of NO· and tissue-specific effects of NO· as well as on its effects in cell signaling mechanisms. The emphasis of Section II is on the pathological action of NO· recognized by reactions of nitrosylation and nitration and on the interaction of NO· with membranes, proteins, and nucleic acids. Methods for detecting the action of peroxynitrite, tissue and cell toxicity, and clinical aspects of NO· inhalation therapy are included.

In bringing these volumes to fruition, credit must be given to experts in various specialized fields of NO· research who provided contributions and to those who helped select the authors to provide the state of the art methodology. The topics and methods included in these volumes were chosen on the excellent advice of the volume advisors, Bruce N.

Ames, Joseph Beckman, Enrique Cadenas, Victor Darley–Usmar, Bruce Freeman, Barry Halliwell, Louis J. Ignarro, Hiroe Nakazawa, William Pryor, and Helmut Sies, to whom I extend my sincere thanks and most grateful appreciation.

LESTER PACKER

METHODS IN ENZYMOLOGY

VOLUME XVII. Metabolism of Amino Acids and Amines (Parts A and B)
Edited by HERBERT TABOR AND CELIA WHITE TABOR

VOLUME XVIII. Vitamins and Coenzymes (Parts A, B, and C)
Edited by DONALD B. MCCORMICK AND LEMUEL D. WRIGHT

VOLUME XIX. Proteolytic Enzymes
Edited by GERTRUDE E. PERLMANN AND LASZLO LORAND

VOLUME XX. Nucleic Acids and Protein Synthesis (Part C)
Edited by KIVIE MOLDAVE AND LAWRENCE GROSSMAN

VOLUME XXI. Nucleic Acids (Part D)
Edited by LAWRENCE GROSSMAN AND KIVIE MOLDAVE

VOLUME XXII. Enzyme Purification and Related Techniques
Edited by WILLIAM B. JAKOBY

VOLUME XXIII. Photosynthesis (Part A)
Edited by ANTHONY SAN PIETRO

VOLUME XXIV. Photosynthesis and Nitrogen Fixation (Part B)
Edited by ANTHONY SAN PIETRO

VOLUME XXV. Enzyme Structure (Part B)
Edited by C. H. W. HIRS AND SERGE N. TIMASHEFF

VOLUME XXVI. Enzyme Structure (Part C)
Edited by C. H. W. HIRS AND SERGE N. TIMASHEFF

VOLUME XXVII. Enzyme Structure (Part D)
Edited by C. H. W. HIRS AND SERGE N. TIMASHEFF

VOLUME XXVIII. Complex Carbohydrates (Part B)
Edited by VICTOR GINSBURG

VOLUME XXIX. Nucleic Acids and Protein Synthesis (Part E)
Edited by LAWRENCE GROSSMAN AND KIVIE MOLDAVE

VOLUME XXX. Nucleic Acids and Protein Synthesis (Part F)
Edited by KIVIE MOLDAVE AND LAWRENCE GROSSMAN

VOLUME XXXI. Biomembranes (Part A)
Edited by SIDNEY FLEISCHER AND LESTER PACKER

VOLUME XXXII. Biomembranes (Part B)
Edited by SIDNEY FLEISCHER AND LESTER PACKER

VOLUME XXXIII. Cumulative Subject Index Volumes I–XXX
Edited by MARTHA G. DENNIS AND EDWARD A. DENNIS

VOLUME XXXIV. Affinity Techniques (Enzyme Purification: Part B)
Edited by WILLIAM B. JAKOBY AND MEIR WILCHEK

VOLUME XXXV. Lipids (Part B)
Edited by JOHN M. LOWENSTEIN

VOLUME 74. Immunochemical Techniques (Part C)
Edited by JOHN J. LANGONE AND HELEN VAN VUNAKIS

VOLUME 75. Cumulative Subject Index Volumes XXXI, XXXII, XXXIV–LX
Edited by EDWARD A. DENNIS AND MARTHA G. DENNIS

VOLUME 76. Hemoglobins
Edited by ERALDO ANTONINI, LUIGI ROSSI-BERNARDI, AND EMILIA CHIANCONE

VOLUME 77. Detoxication and Drug Metabolism
Edited by WILLIAM B. JAKOBY

VOLUME 78. Interferons (Part A)
Edited by SIDNEY PESTKA

VOLUME 79. Interferons (Part B)
Edited by SIDNEY PESTKA

VOLUME 80. Proteolytic Enzymes (Part C)
Edited by LASZLO LORAND

VOLUME 81. Biomembranes (Part H: Visual Pigments and Purple Membranes, I)
Edited by LESTER PACKER

VOLUME 82. Structural and Contractile Proteins (Part A: Extracellular Matrix)
Edited by LEON W. CUNNINGHAM AND DIXIE W. FREDERIKSEN

VOLUME 83. Complex Carbohydrates (Part D)
Edited by VICTOR GINSBURG

VOLUME 84. Immunochemical Techniques (Part D: Selected Immunoassays)
Edited by JOHN J. LANGONE AND HELEN VAN VUNAKIS

VOLUME 85. Structural and Contractile Proteins (Part B: The Contractile Apparatus and the Cytoskeleton)
Edited by DIXIE W. FREDERIKSEN AND LEON W. CUNNINGHAM

VOLUME 86. Prostaglandins and Arachidonate Metabolites
Edited by WILLIAM E. M. LANDS AND WILLIAM L. SMITH

VOLUME 87. Enzyme Kinetics and Mechanism (Part C: Intermediates, Stereochemistry, and Rate Studies)
Edited by DANIEL L. PURICH

VOLUME 88. Biomembranes (Part I: Visual Pigments and Purple Membranes, II)
Edited by LESTER PACKER

VOLUME 89. Carbohydrate Metabolism (Part D)
Edited by WILLIS A. WOOD

VOLUME 90. Carbohydrate Metabolism (Part E)
Edited by WILLIS A. WOOD

VOLUME 91. Enzyme Structure (Part I)
Edited by C. H. W. HIRS AND SERGE N. TIMASHEFF

VOLUME 127. Biomembranes (Part O: Protons and Water: Structure and Translocation)
Edited by LESTER PACKER

VOLUME 128. Plasma Lipoproteins (Part A: Preparation, Structure, and Molecular Biology)
Edited by JERE P. SEGREST AND JOHN J. ALBERS

VOLUME 129. Plasma Lipoproteins (Part B: Characterization, Cell Biology, and Metabolism)
Edited by JOHN J. ALBERS AND JERE P. SEGREST

VOLUME 130. Enzyme Structure (Part K)
Edited by C. H. W. HIRS AND SERGE N. TIMASHEFF

VOLUME 131. Enzyme Structure (Part L)
Edited by C. H. W. HIRS AND SERGE N. TIMASHEFF

VOLUME 132. Immunochemical Techniques (Part J: Phagocytosis and Cell-Mediated Cytotoxicity)
Edited by GIOVANNI DI SABATO AND JOHANNES EVERSE

VOLUME 133. Bioluminescence and Chemiluminescence (Part B)
Edited by MARLENE DELUCA AND WILLIAM D. MCELROY

VOLUME 134. Structural and Contractile Proteins (Part C: The Contractile Apparatus and the Cytoskeleton)
Edited by RICHARD B. VALLEE

VOLUME 135. Immobilized Enzymes and Cells (Part B)
Edited by KLAUS MOSBACH

VOLUME 136. Immobilized Enzymes and Cells (Part C)
Edited by KLAUS MOSBACH

VOLUME 137. Immobilized Enzymes and Cells (Part D)
Edited by KLAUS MOSBACH

VOLUME 138. Complex Carbohydrates (Part E)
Edited by VICTOR GINSBURG

VOLUME 139. Cellular Regulators (Part A: Calcium- and Calmodulin-Binding Proteins)
Edited by ANTHONY R. MEANS AND P. MICHAEL CONN

VOLUME 140. Cumulative Subject Index Volumes 102–119, 121–134

VOLUME 141. Cellular Regulators (Part B: Calcium and Lipids)
Edited by P. MICHAEL CONN AND ANTHONY R. MEANS

VOLUME 142. Metabolism of Aromatic Amino Acids and Amines
Edited by SEYMOUR KAUFMAN

VOLUME 143. Sulfur and Sulfur Amino Acids
Edited by WILLIAM B. JAKOBY AND OWEN GRIFFITH

VOLUME 144. Structural and Contractile Proteins (Part D: Extracellular Matrix)
Edited by LEON W. CUNNINGHAM

VOLUME 269. Nitric Oxide (Part B: Physiological and Pathological Processes) (in preparation)
Edited by LESTER PACKER

VOLUME 270. High Resolution Separation and Analysis of Biological Macromolecules (Part A: Fundamentals) (in preparation)
Edited by BARRY L. KARGER AND WILLIAM S. HANCOCK

VOLUME 271. High Resolution Separation and Analysis of Biological Macromolecules (Part B: Applications) (in preparation)
Edited by BARRY L. KARGER AND WILLIAM S. HANCOCK

VOLUME 272. Cytochrome P450 (Part B) (in preparation)
Edited by ERIC F. JOHNSON AND MICHAEL R. WATERMAN

VOLUME 273. RNA Polymerase and Associated Factors (Part A) (in preparation)
Edited by SANKAR ADHYA

VOLUME 274. RNA Polymerase and Associated Factors (Part B) (in preparation)
Edited by SANKAR ADHYA

VOLUME 275. Viral Polymerases and Related Proteins (in preparation)
Edited by LAWRENCE C. KUO, DAVID B. OLSEN, AND STEVEN S. CARROLL

VOLUME 276. Macromolecular Crystallography, Part A (in preparation)
Edited by CHARLES W. CARTER, JR. AND ROBERT M. SWEET

Section I

Generation, Detection, and Characterization of Biological and Chemical Sources of Nitric Oxide

A. Nitric Oxide Chemistry and Biology
Articles 1 through 5

B. Methods for Detection of Nitric Oxide
Articles 6 through 24

C. Nitric Oxide Donors, Nitric Oxide Deactivation, and Nitric Oxide Gas
Articles 25 through 29

[1] Say NO to Nitric Oxide: Nomenclature for Nitrogen- and Oxygen-Containing Compounds

By W. H. KOPPENOL and J. G. TRAYNHAM

The molecule NO˙ is commonly named nitric oxide in the biochemical literature.* Names ending in "-ic" and "-ous" were introduced by Lavoisier for oxo acids, and these suffixes are supposed to indicate the relative content of oxygen. Thus, nitric oxide has a higher oxygen content (per nitrogen) than nitrous oxide. Nowadays the oxygen content is related to the oxidation state of the element, and it does not make sense that the same suffix -ic, as in nitric oxide and nitric acid, is used for different oxidation states, namely, $2+$ and $5+$. Thus, in order to make nomenclature more systematic, it was decided by the Commission on the Nomenclature of Inorganic Chemistry of the International Union of Pure and Applied Chemistry to abandon these suffixes. The systematic names were published as early as 1959. Yet, when it was found in the late 1980s that NO˙ was formed *in vivo*, it became known as nitric oxide, and the enzyme that made it as nitric oxide synthase (EC 1.14.13.39).

There are essentially two ways of naming compounds.[1] One is called additive, and the other substitutive nomenclature. The first is mainly used for inorganic, and the other for organic compounds. Additive nomenclature is simpler: one gives the composition, as in nitrogen dioxide for NO_2˙. Substitutive nomenclature is based on the names like methane, azane, oxidane, and silane for CH_4, NH_3, H_2O, and SiH_4, respectively. Thus, $SiCl_4$ is named tetrachlorosilane. The additive name is silicon tetrachloride. For coordination complexes a variation on additive nomenclature is used, according to which the name is tetrachlorosilicon (ligands first, then the central atom, ending "-ate", or "-ide" if anion; see examples in Table I). In Table I additive and/or coordination nomenclature is used, and venerable names are mentioned if still acceptable. In the near future the prefix "oxo" may be replaced by "oxido," and, to stress the fact that some of these compounds are radicals, the suffix "-yl" may be added. While one might not always find the official name palatable, one should bear in mind that is a decade from now, as the electronic literature retrieval becomes more routine, the use of systematic names may be more widespread. Therefore, to facilitate retrieval in the future, one

---

* This chapter follows the guidelines of the IUPAC for nomenclature.
[1] G. J. Leigh (ed.), "Nomenclature of Inorganic Chemistry." Blackwell, Oxford, 1990.

METHODS IN ENZYMOLOGY, VOL. 268

TABLE I

NAMES FOR INORGANIC NITROGEN- AND OXYGEN-CONTAINING SPECIES

Formula	Systematic name	Allowed name
$CO_2^{\cdot-}$	dioxocarbonate$(1-)$	
$ClO_2^{\cdot}$ $(OClO^{\cdot})$	dioxochlorine	
$HO^{\cdot}$	hydrogen monoxide	hydroxyl, oxidanyl[a]
$HO_2^{\cdot}$	hydrogen dioxide	dioxidanyl[a]
$HO_3^{\cdot}$	hydrogen trioxide	trioxidanyl[a]
$NO^{\cdot}$	nitrogen monoxide	
NO^+	nitrosyl	
NO^-	oxonitrate$(1-)$	
$NO_2^{\cdot}$	nitrogen dioxide	
NO_2^+	nitryl	
NO_2^-	dioxonitrate$(1-)$	nitrite
$NO_3^{\cdot}$	nitrogen trioxide	
NO_3^-	trioxonitrate$(1-)$	nitrate
N_2O	dinitrogen monoxide	
$N_2O_2^{\cdot-}$	dioxodinitrate$(N\text{-}N)(1-)$	
$N_3^{\cdot}$	trinitrogen	
N_3^-	trinitride$(1-)$	azide
$O^{\cdot-}$	oxide$(1-)$	oxidanidyl[a]
$O_2^{\cdot-}$	dioxide$(1-)$	superoxide, dioxidanidyl[a]
$O_3^{\cdot-}$	trioxide$(1-)$	trioxidanidyl[a]
$ONOO^{\cdot}$	(dioxo)oxonitrogen	nitrosoperoxyl
$ONOO^-$	oxoperoxonitrate$(1-)$[b]	
$SO_2^{\cdot-}$	dioxosulfate$(1-)$	
$SO_3^{\cdot-}$	trioxosulfate$(1-)$	
$SO_4^{\cdot-}$	tetraoxosulfate$(1-)$	

[a] Nomenclature approved by the Commission on the Nomenclature of Organic Chemistry. These names are derived from the systematic names of oxidane for water and dioxidane for hydrogen peroxide. The suffix "-id" indicates that the compound is an anion, and "-yl" means that a hydrogen atom has been removed. The Commission on the Nomenclature of Organic Chemistry also allows hydroperoxyl for $HO_2^{\cdot}$.[2]

[b] One finds both peroxynitrite and peroxonitrite for this compound. The latter name is not recommended.[1] For this reason the systematic name is preferred.

should include these names as key words in publications. The names of a few nonradical nitrogen- and oxygen-containing species have also been included in Table I.[2]

A radical is an atom or group of atoms with one or more unpaired electrons. It may have positive, negative, or zero charge. In the past the

[2] W. H. Powell, *Pure Appl. Chem.* **65**, 1357 (1993).

word "radical" was used to indicate a group or substituent like "methyl" in 2-methylpropane. To indicate a methyl radical by itself, the word "free" was added. Because a radical is an unattached particle, the word "free" in front of "radical" is now considered unnecessary and obsolete: all radicals are free. According to the IUPAC system of nomenclature, a radical is indicated by a superscripted dot, which precedes a charge, if present: superoxide is written as $O_2{}^{\cdot-}$, not $O_2{}^{-\cdot}$. Note that this dot is not a center dot; such dots are used to indicate, for instance, waters of crystallization. Superoxide is not a systematic name, but it has found widespread use. In contrast to the name nitric oxide, it is not burdened by an "outlawed" suffix, and therefore it is still an allowed name. The systematic name for $O_2{}^{\cdot-}$ is dioxide(1−), analogous to dichloride(1−) for $Cl_2{}^{\cdot-}$.

The result of the reaction of an inorganic radical with an organic compound is the creation of an organic radical, which may undergo subsequent reactions to form a more stable compound. The names of organic radicals are conveniently derived with the help of the rules of substitutive nomenclature.[2,3] However, there is a problem with the strict application of these rules, in that it leads to a change in the name of the "parent" compound. This is best illustrated with an example from the area of lipid peroxidation. A fatty acid that loses an allylic hydrogen and then reacts with dioxygen would ideally be named as a radical, not as an acid, because radicals rank highest in order of priority for choosing and naming a principal characteristic group: *cis,cis,trans*-9,12,14-octadecatrienoic acid becomes the 17-carboxy-*trans,cis,cis*-4,6,9-heptadecatrien-8-yldioxidanyl radical. This is likely to lead to confusion. However, organic nomenclature rules allow us to retain the original name, and to treat the −OO· group as substituent if the prefix "ylo-" is used. Thus, one can name the same radical: 8-yloperoxy-*cis,cis,trans*-9,12,14-octadecatrienoic acid, or, more systematically, 8-ylodioxidanyl, etc.

Nitrogen monoxide reacts at nearly diffusion-controlled rates with organic radicals; such reactions result in various nitrogen-containing compounds. In Table II names are given that would apply to substituents found as a result of such reactions. The substituents are given in alphabetical order and are preceded by the proper locants, as illustrated above.

NONOates are compounds that slowly release nitrogen monoxide in water. The systematic name for the group -N(O)=NO⁻ is best derived with the help of substitutive nomenclature. One starts with azane for NH_3, then diazene for NH=NH, diazenolate for HN=N−O⁻, and (*Z*)-diazen-

[3] J. G. Traynham, *Adv. Free Radical Biol. Med.* **2**, 191 (1986).

TABLE II
Names for Substituents

Substituent	Name
-C(O)O⁻	carboxylato
-C(O)OH	carboxy
-NO	nitroso
-N(O)=NO⁻	(Z)-diazen-1-ium-1,2-diolato[a]
-NO₂	nitro
-O˙	ylooxy or ylooxidanyl
-O⁻	oxido
-OH	hydroxy
-ONO	nitrito
-OO˙	yloperoxy or ylodioxidanyl
-OOH	hydroperoxy
-OONO	nitrosoperoxy
-S˙	ylosulfanyl
-SH	sulfanyl
-S⁻	sulfido

[a] The Z changes to E if a group with a higher priority than oxygen is attached to the first nitrogen.

TABLE III
Names of Nonoates

Formula	Name
⁻ON(O)=NO⁻	diazen-1-ium−1,2,3-triolate
⁻O₃SN(O)=NO⁻	(E)-1,2-dioxidodiazen-1-ium−1-sulfonate
(C₂H₅)₂NN(O)=NO⁻	(Z)-1-diethylaminodiazen-1-ium−1,2-diolate
(C₂H₅)₂NN(O)=NOCH₂OCH₃	(Z)-1-diethylamino-2-(methoxymethoxy)diazen-1-ium−1-olate
Cu[(C₂H₅)₂NN(O)=NO]₂CH₃OH	bis[(Z)-1-diethylaminodiazen-1-ium−1,2-diolato-O^1-O^2)] methanolcopper(II)[a]

[a] In this square pyrimidal complex the (C₂H₅)₂NN(O)=NO⁻ ligands are in the plane and the two -N(C₂H₅)₂ groups are on the same side [D. Christodoulou, D. A. Wink, C. F. George, J. E. Saavedra, and L. K. Keefer, in "Nitrosamines and Related N-Nitroso Compounds" (R. N. Loeppky and C. J. Michejda, eds.), p. 307. American Chemical Society, Washington, D.C., 1994], i.e., the only symmetry element present is a mirror plane. To indicate the relative position of the ligands, the name and structure can be preceded by [SPY-5-32].[1] This system is based on an abbreviation for the type of complex (SPY-5), the Cahn–Ingold–Prelog system for assigning priority to the ligands, and two numbers, the first of which (3) indicates that the lowest priority ligand (assigned the number 3, methanol) is at the top of the pyramid. The second number (2) indicates that in the plane a lower priority ligand (assigned the number 2, ^{2}O) is trans to the highest priority ligand (assigned the number 1, ^{1}O). For further details, see Ref. 1.

1-ium-1,2-diolate for -N(O)=NO⁻.* Then, the known NONOates are named as shown in Table III. The name of the N(O)=NO⁻ group as a substituent is given in Table II.

Acknowledgment

W. H. K. thanks Dr. L. K. Keefer for many constructive discussions.

---

* Z and E indicate the positions of the substituents in relation to the N=N bond. The oxygens are always *cis* relative to this bond.

[2] Thermodynamics of Reactions Involving Nitrogen–Oxygen Compounds

By W. H. KOPPENOL

Introduction

Thermodynamic considerations are used to determine whether a reaction is possible. Thermodynamics does not tell us whether a reaction with a negative Gibbs energy actually occurs; however, a large positive Gibbs energy allows us to exclude this reaction, which may be helpful if more than one mechanism is being considered.

There are enough reliable data available on nitrogen–oxygen compounds to calculate Gibbs energy changes. In this chapter a number of examples are given that show the reader how to calculate the energetics of reactions. Gibbs energies of formation[1–4] are given in Table I. The standard state refers to 25° and 1 molal concentrations for all compounds, including gases. As such, the Gibbs energies of gases are not standard

[1] D. D. Wagman, W. H. Evans, V. B. Parker, R. H. Schumm, I. Halow, S. M. Bailey, K. L. Churney, and R. L. Nuttal, *J. Phys. Chem. Ref. Data Suppl.* **11**(2), 37 (1982).
[2] D. M. Stanbury, *Adv. Inorg. Chem.* **33,** 69 (1989).
[3] W. H. Koppenol, *in* "Focus on Membrane Lipid Oxidation" (C. Vigo-Pelfrey, ed.), Vol. 1, p. 1. CRC Press, Boca Raton, Florida, 1989.
[4] W. H. Koppenol, J. J. Moreno, W. A. Pryor, H. Ischiropoulos, and J. S. Beckman, *Chem. Res. Toxicol.* **5,** 834 (1992).

METHODS IN ENZYMOLOGY, VOL. 268

TABLE I

GIBBS ENERGIES OF FORMATION OF RELEVANT
NITROGEN- AND OXYGEN-CONTAINING SPECIES

Compound	$\Delta_f G^{\circ\prime}$ (kJ/mol)[a]
HO$^\cdot$	65.7
H_2O	−157.3
H_2O_2	−59.0
NO$^\cdot$	102
NO$^+$	219
NO$^-$ (singlet)	136
NO$^-$ (triplet)	64
NO$_2^\cdot$	63
NO$_2^+$	218
NO$_2^-$	−32.2
NO$_3^\cdot$	131
NO$_3^-$	−108.7
N_2	17.5
N_2O	113.6
$N_2O_2^{\cdot-}$	141[b]
N_2O_3	147[c]
ONOO$^\cdot$	84
ONOO$^-$	42
O_2	16.4
$O_2^{\cdot-}$	31.8

[a] The Gibbs energies of formation apply to 1 molal concentrations, and to pH 7 in the case of hydrogen-containing compounds. Data were obtained from the literature.[1–4]

[b] Calculated from rate data [W. A. Seddon, J. W. Fletcher, and F. C. Sopchyshyn, *Can. J. Chem.* **51**, 1123 (1973)].

[c] Based on an estimated hydration energy of 8 kJ/mol.

values, which is indicated by a prime, as in $\Delta G^{\circ\prime}$. A list of reduction potentials is given in Table II.

Examples

Formation of NO$^+$ at pH 7.0

In principle, there are two possibilities for forming NO$^+$ at pH 7: (1) oxidation of nitrogen monoxide* and (2) equilibrium with nitrite. The first

---

* For the names used, please see W. H. Koppenol and J. G. Traynham, *Methods Enzymol.* **268**, Chap. 1, 1996 (this volume).

TABLE II

RELEVANT REDUCTION POTENTIALS OF NITROGEN-
AND OXYGEN-CONTAINING SPECIES

Couple	$E^{\circ\prime}$ (V)[a]
$HO^{\cdot}/H_2O$	2.31
$NO^{+}/NO^{\cdot}$	1.21
$NO^{\cdot}/NO^{-}$ (triplet)	0.39
$NO^{\cdot}/NO^{-}$ (singlet)	-0.35
$NO_2^{+}/NO_2^{\cdot}$	1.6
$NO_2^{\cdot}/NO_2^{-}$	0.99
$N_2O_3/NO^{\cdot},NO_2^{-}$	0.80[b]
$ONOO^{\cdot}/ONOO^{-}$	0.4
$ONOO^{-}/NO_2^{\cdot}$	1.4
$O_2/O_2^{\cdot-}$	-0.16
O_2/H_2O_2	0.305
O_2/H_2O	0.816
H_2O_2/H_2O	1.32
$H_2O_2/HO^{\cdot},H_2O$	0.32

[a] The reduction potentials apply to 1 molal concentrations at pH 7 (see Table I). Except as noted, data were obtained from the literature.[2–4]

[b] Value derived in this chapter.

possibility requires an oxidant with a reduction potential in excess of 1.21 V (see Table II). Considering that reduction potentials *in vivo* span the range of -0.3 V ($NAD^{+}/NADH$) to 0.82 V (O_2/H_2O), nitrogen monoxide cannot be oxidized to the nitrosyl cation. Even in the unlikely case that a hydroxyl radical reacts with nitrogen monoxide, nitrite is formed, not the nitrosyl cation. For the second possibility we consider the following reaction:

$$NO_2^{-} + 2H^{+} \rightarrow NO^{+} + H_2O \qquad \Delta_{rxn}G^{\circ\prime} = +94\ kJ \qquad (1)$$

Via $\Delta_{rxn}G^{\circ\prime} = -RT \ln K$ we calculate that $K = [NO^{+}]/[NO_2^{-}] = 3.7 \times 10^{-17}$. Note that the expression for K does not contain hydrogen ion, because the Gibbs energy of formation of water at pH 7 was used and water itself is not present, because of its constant concentration. Thus, in a 1 mM nitrite solution the concentration of the nitrosyl cation is an undetectable 3.7×10^{-20} M. Clearly, this pathway cannot yield NO^{+} either. Thus, the notion that the nitrosyl cation plays a role in some of the biochemistry of nitrogen monoxide[5] is not supported by thermodynamic considerations. Even if it were to be formed, it would react rapidly with water to form nitrite.

[5] J. S. Stamler, D. J. Singel, and J. Loscalzo, *Science* **258**, 1898 (1992).

Formation of NO^- at pH 7.0

The formation and the reactivity of oxonitrate(1−) has been studied by pulse radiolysis.[6–8] This anion is formed by reduction of nitrogen monoxide, but it is not clear how such a reduction would occur *in vivo*. If formed, it reacts fast with additional nitrogen monoxide to yield $(NO)_2^-$ and $(NO)_3^-$.[8] *In vivo* the concentration of nitrogen monoxide is not high enough to form $(NO)_3^-$, but $(NO)_2^-$ may be formed, which is believed to decay to dinitrogen monoxide, N_2O, and the hydroxyl radical[8]:

$$N_2O_2^{\cdot-} + H^+ \rightarrow HO^\cdot + N_2O \qquad \Delta_{rxn}G^{\circ\prime} = +38 \text{ kJ} \qquad (2)$$

This reaction has a positive Gibbs energy, but since one of the products disappears rapidly, it may be feasible. Energetically, $(NO)_3^-$ disproportionates more favorably to dinitrogen monoxide and nitrite.† In addition, oxonitrate(1−) reacts with dioxygen to form peroxynitrite [$O=NOO^-$, oxoperoxonitrate(1−)].[9] Thus, its lifetime is expected to be short. The reaction of two oxonitrate(1−) ions to form dinitrogen monoxide and water is kinetically an unlikely event. Since NO^- would disappear rapidly if it were formed, it is not likely to play a significant role in the functions ascribed to nitrogen monoxide.[5]

ONOOH as a Source of Hydroxyl Radicals

Frequently, one finds in the literature that hydrogen oxoperoxonitrate ($O=NOOH$) undergoes homolysis and yields hydroxyl and nitrogen dioxide radicals. The Gibbs energy change of this reaction is +88 kJ/mol.[4] Before going further, the basis of this value must be examined.

The calculated Gibbs energy change of 88 kJ/mol is based on the enthalpy of formation of oxoperoxonitrate(1−) of −45 kJ/mol determined in 1962 by Ray[10] in an experiment where both the enthalpy of peroxynitrite

[6] W. A. Seddon and H. C. Sutton, *Trans. Faraday Soc.* **59**, 2323 (1963).
[7] W. A. Seddon and M. J. Young, *Can. J. Chem.* **48**, 393 (1970).
[8] W. A. Seddon, J. W. Fletcher, and F. C. Sopchyshyn, *Can. J. Chem.* **51**, 1123 (1973).
† Why is it safe to make this statement, although one does not know the Gibbs energy of formation of $N_3O_3^{\cdot-}$? To answer this question, consider the hypothetical reaction $N_2O_2^{\cdot-}$ + $NO^\cdot \rightarrow N_2O + NO_2^-$. This reaction is favorable by 162 kJ. We add to this reaction the following one: $N_3O_3^{\cdot-} \rightarrow N_2O_2^{\cdot-} + NO^\cdot$, for which the Gibbs energy is not known. The sum of the two reactions is the desired reaction, and the sum of the Gibbs energies should be negative. This requires that the Gibbs energy of the second reaction is much smaller than + 162 kJ, which seems reasonable, when compared to the +25 kJ of the comparable reaction $N_2O_2^{\cdot-} \rightarrow NO^\cdot + NO^-$.
[9] C. E. Donald, M. N. Hughes, J. M. Thompson, and F. T. Bonner, *Inorg. Chem.* **25**, 2676 (1986).
[10] J. D. Ray, *J. Inorg. Nucl. Chem.* **24**, 1159 (1962).

formation from hydrogen peroxide and acidified nitrite and the isomerization to nitrate were measured. According to this enthalpy of formation, the enthalpy of isomerization of $O=NOO^-$ to NO_3^- is -160 ± 8 kJ. We have mixed alkaline solutions of oxoperoxonitrate$(1-)$ with hydrochloric acid, and measured the heat of this reaction. After correction for the considerable heat of the neutralization of hydroxide ions we find -159 ± 4 kJ [M. Manuszak and W. H. Koppenol, *Thermochim. Acta* **273**, 11 (1996)], a result identical to that obtained by Ray.[10]

Now that the enthalpy of formation of oxoperoxonitrate$(1-)$ has been confirmed, one can return to the question of whether homolysis is possible. We have argued[4] that this reaction is not feasible. Specifically, on the basis of the known rate constant for the reaction of the hydroxyl radical with nitrogen dioxide and the Gibbs energy change of 88 kJ/mol, one calculates that the rate constant for homolysis would be between 10^{-6} and 10^{-8} sec^{-1},[11] much slower than the rate of isomerization of 1.3 sec^{-1}.[4] In addition, the hydroxyl and nitrogen dioxide radical cannot be intermediates in the isomerization reaction because pulse radiolysis and flash photolysis studies[12–14] have shown that the hydroxyl radical reacts with nitrogen dioxide to form $O=NOOH$, not HNO_3. In summary, ONOOH stands for O, NO OH!

Reaction of NO· with ONOO⁻ and Hydrogen Peroxide

When nitrogen gas is passed over solid potassium, superoxide peroxynitrite is formed first.[15] Subsequently, a brown gas evolves and potassium nitrite is formed. In water this reaction is also possible:

$$ONOO^- + NO^\cdot \rightarrow NO_2^\cdot + NO_2^- \qquad \Delta_{rxn}G^{\circ\prime} = -113 \text{ kJ} \qquad (3)$$

The analogous reaction of nitrogen monoxide with hydrogen peroxide to form nitrite and water is energetically also favorable (exercise!), but there is no evidence that it actually occurs.

Decay of ONOO⁻ in Alkaline Solution

According to Edwards and Plumb[16] oxoperoxonitrate$(1-)$ can decay in alkaline solution according to Eq. (4):

[11] D. Bartlett, D. F. Church, P. L. Bounds, and W. H. Koppenol, *Free Radical Biol. Med.* **18**, 85 (1995).
[12] M. Grätzel, A. Henglein, and S. Taniguchi, *Ber. Bunsen–Ges. Phys. Chem.* **94**, 292 (1970).
[13] F. Barat, L. Gilles, B. Hickel, and J. Sutton, *J. Chem. Soc. (A),* 1982 (1970).
[14] T. Logager and K. Sehested, *J. Phys. Chem.* **97**, 6664 (1993).
[15] W. H. Koppenol, R. Kissner, and J. S. Beckman, *Methods Enzymol.* **269**, Chap. 27, (1996).
[16] J. O. Edwards and R. C. Plumb, *Prog. Inorg. Chem.* **41**, 599 (1993).

$$2 \, ONOO^- \rightarrow 2NO_2^- + O_2 \qquad \Delta_{rxn}G^{\circ\prime} = -132 \, kJ \qquad (4)$$

Earlier an incorrect value of 0 kJ had been reported.[4]

Oxidizing Properties of N_2O_3

The reduction potential of the couple $N_2O_3/NO^\cdot,NO_2^-$ is calculated from the Gibbs energy of reaction(5):

$$N_2O_3 + \tfrac{1}{2}H_2 \rightarrow NO^\cdot + NO_2^- + H^+ \qquad \Delta_{rxn}G^{\circ\prime} = -77 \, kJ \qquad (5)$$

Via $\Delta G^{\circ\prime} = -nF\Delta E^{\circ\prime}$ one finds 0.80 V versus the normal hydrogen electrode for the half-reaction:

$$N_2O_3(aq) + e^- \rightarrow NO^\cdot(aq) + NO_2^- \qquad (6)$$

This is sufficient to initiate lipid peroxidation. For the couple allylic$^\cdot$/allylic-H, a reduction potential of 0.6 V at neutral pH has been derived,[17] which would make oxidation favorable by 20 kJ.

Acknowledgments

This work was supported by grants from the National Institutes of Health (GM48829) and the Council for Tobacco Research—USA, Inc., and by the Eidgenössische Technische Hochschule Zürich.

[17] W. H. Koppenol, *FEBS Lett.* **264,** 165 (1990).

[3] Direct and Indirect Effects of Nitric Oxide in Chemical Reactions Relevant to Biology

By DAVID A. WINK, MATTHEW B. GRISHAM, JAMES B. MITCHELL, and PETER C. FORD

Introduction

The biology of nitric oxide (NO, nitrogen monoxide) has been the subject of vigorous investigation. This diatomic molecule, previously associated primarily with its toxic effects, is formed endogenously and participates in numerous physiological functions. The contrasting regulatory and toxic properties of NO have led to some confusion regarding its biological role.

A discussion of the chemical biology of NO will shed light on this dichotomy. The chemical biology of NO will be defined as the specific chemistry of NO involving biological targets, and this will be categorized into direct and indirect effects. Direct effects are defined as resulting from reactions between NO and specific biological molecules. Indirect effects are defined as those resulting from the reactions of reactive nitrogen oxide species (RNOS), which are derived from NO autoxidation with various biological targets. Chemistry associated with peroxynitrite might also fall into this category. The advantage of separating the chemical biology of NO into such categories is that the kinetics of NO autoxidation limit such indirect effects to higher NO concentrations, while the direct reactions are likely to dominate at lower concentrations of NO such as those that might be derived from constitutive nitric oxide synthase (cNOS) activity. At higher NO concentrations, such as those derived from inducible nitric oxide synthase (iNOS), indirect effects are likely to predominate. The chemical biology provides insight into the role NO plays in regulatory or toxicological mechanisms as well as development of therapeutic uses involving nitric oxide.

Nitric oxide plays key regulatory roles ranging from blood pressure control to neurotransmission.[1-4] NO is also a toxic constituent of air pollution and cigarette smoke,[5] reacting with oxygen in an aerobic environment to generate a number of RNOS that can exert deleterious effects on biological systems. So how can NO be critical to regulatory function and yet poisonous?

Part of the answer to this ambiguity lies in a discussion of the relevant chemical reactions that may occur under specific biological conditions. The advantage of separating the chemistry of NO into the categories of direct and indirect effects is that the kinetics of NO autoxidation has a major influence on determining at which NO concentration and which type of biological targets are likely to be affected. For example, biologically relevant direct effects of NO generally require low concentrations (locally <5 μM). For instance, NO will bind to the heme cofactor of guanylate cyclase, forming a metal–nitrosyl adduct. This adduct is activated to catalyze the conversion of GTP to cGMP which is the basis for controlling several physiological functions.[2-4] The rapid interaction between the heme metal

[1] E. Culotta and D. E. Koshland, *Science* **258**, 1862 (1992).
[2] L. J. Ignarro, *Annu. Rev. Pharmacol. Toxicol.* **30**, 535 (1990).
[3] S. Moncada, R. M. J. Palmer, and E. A. Higgs, *Pharmacol. Rev.* **43**, 109 (1991).
[4] R. F. Furchgott and P. M. Vanhoute, *FASEB J.* **3**, 2007 (1989).
[5] S. E. Schwartz and W. H. White, *in* "Trace Atmospheric Constituents: Properties, Transformation and Fates" (S. E. Schwartz, ed.), p. 1. Wiley, New York, 1983.

center and NO[6] makes this reaction ideal for regulating various physiological functions.

Indirect effects involve initial reactions of NO with either oxygen or superoxide to form various RNOS. These RNOS chemically damage proteins and DNA, resulting in potentially toxic consequences. As discussed below, rate equations for the formation of RNOS from O_2 require NO concentrations higher than those expected for direct effects. Because *in vivo* concentrations of NO are reduced by mitochondrial consumption[7] and scavenging by oxyhemoglobin,[8] reactions leading to RNOS formation require specific conditions where high local NO concentrations are present.

NO is formed endogenously via the conversion of arginine to citrulline[2,3] mediated by two categories of the enzyme nitric oxide synthase, constitutive (cNOS) and inducible (iNOS).[9,10] cNOS is associated with the formation of low NO concentrations for short periods of time. In contrast, the presence of some cytokines can result in the induction of iNOS in cells, generating high NO concentrations for prolonged periods of time. NO derived from cNOS would be in the domain of reactions classified as direct effects, but, since NO derived from iNOS would be at considerably higher concentration, both direct and indirect effects must be considered. Understanding such roles of NO in various physiological and toxicological mechanisms can provide insight into the development of potential therapeutic strategies utilizing this biologically important molecule.

Chemical Properties of Nitric Oxide

One of the principal reasons that the chemical biology can be categorized into direct and indirect effects is due to the fundamental chemical properties of NO. NO has an odd number of electrons with the unpaired electron in a pi (π) antibonding orbital; hence, it is a stable radical.[11] However, unlike many radicals, NO does not rapidly react with most biological substances in contrast to oxygen radicals such as ·OH. Since the lifetime of NO *in vivo* is relatively short, less than 10 sec,[3] only the faster direct reaction of NO, such as with metal centers or other radicals, is likely to prove important.

Physical properties of NO are also very important to understanding the fate of NO and its effect on biological systems. The solubility of NO is 1.9

[6] M. Hoshino, K. Ozawa, H. Seki, and P. C. Ford, *J. Am. Chem. Soc.* **115**, 9568 (1993).

[7] R. B. Clarkson, S. W. Norby, S. Boyer, N. Vahdi, A. Smirnov, R. W. Nims, and D. A. Wink, *Biochim. Biophys. Acta* **1243**, 496 (1995).

[8] J. Lancaster, *Proc. Natl. Acad. Sci. U.S.A.* **91**, 8137 (1994).

[9] M. A. Marletta, *J. Biol. Chem.* **268**, 12231 (1993).

[10] C. Nathan and Q. Xie, *J. Biol. Chem.* **269**, 13725 (1994).

[11] F. A. Cotton and G. Wilkinson, "Advanced Inorganic Chemistry," p. 331. Wiley, New York, 1989.

mM/atm in aqueous solution,[12,13] and NO has been reported to diffuse at a rate of 50 μm per sec in a single direction in biological systems.[14] A simple rule of thumb for the solubility and transport of NO is that these properties are similar to those of dioxygen.

The richness of the biological chemistry of NO can be attributed to the variety of nitrogen oxide species.[15] Nitric oxide can undergo either oxidation or reduction by one electron to nitroxyl anion (NO$^-$) or nitrosyl cation (NO$^+$),[16] respectively:

$$NO + e^- \rightarrow NO \qquad\qquad E_{1/2} = -0.33 \text{ V} \qquad\qquad (1)$$
$$NO \rightarrow NO^+ + e^- \qquad\qquad E_{1/2} = -1.2 \text{ V} \qquad\qquad (2)$$

where the $E_{1/2}$ values are the estimated half-cell potentials in aqueous solution. Nitroxyl is isoelectronic to O_2 and, like dioxygen, can exist in either a singlet and triplet electronic state. The triplet is likely to be lower in energy.[16] The direct reduction either at an electrode surface or via reduced methyl viologen reveals that reduction of oxygen is more facile (D. A. Wink, unpublished results). Thus, in a biological environment the formation of superoxide is far more likely than the formation of NO$^-$ by direct electron reduction. The NO$^+$ cation is isoelectronic to carbon monoxide. This species is unlikely to be a major direct participant in any biological phenomenon because the direct one-electron redox potential of NO is higher than would be expected to be generated endogenously. Furthermore, NO$^+$ reacts rapidly with water or other nucleophiles.

Despite the unlikely direct oxidation of NO to form nitrosonium ion, RNOS can be formed which can serve as NO$^+$ donors.[17] One of the most important sources of these species is via the autoxidation of NO. This reaction was shown, even at micromolar concentrations of NO, to proceed via a third-order rate equation: $d[NO]/dt = k[NO]^2[O_2]$, $k = 7 \times 10^6 \, M^{-2}$ sec^{-1}.[18-23] One of the fascinating aspects of this reaction is that the rate

[12] J. A. Dean, "Lange's Handbook of Chemistry," p. 10–7. McGraw-Hill, New York, 1985.
[13] J. N. Armor, *J. Chem. Eng. Data* **19**, 82 (1974).
[14] J. A. Gally, P. R. Montague, G. N. Reeke, and G. M. Edelman, *Proc. Natl. Acad. Sci. U.S.A.* **87**, 3547 (1990).
[15] J. S. Stamler, D. J. Singel, and J. Loscalzo, *Science* **258**, 1898 (1992).
[16] D. M. Stanbury, *Adv. Inorg. Chem.* **33**, 69 (1989).
[17] D. L. H. Williams, "Nitrosation." Cambridge Univ. Press, Cambridge, 1988.
[18] P. C. Ford, D. A. Wink, and D. M. Stanbury, *FEBS Lett.* **326**, 1 (1993).
[19] D. A. Wink, J. F. Darbyshire, R. W. Nims, J. E. Saveedra, and P. C. Ford, *Chem. Res. Toxicol.* **6**, 23 (1993).
[20] H. H. Awad and D. M. Stanbury, *Int. J. Chem. Kinet.* **25**, 375 (1993).
[21] V. G. Kharitonov, A. R. Sundquist, and V. S. Sharma, *J. Biol. Chem.* **309**, 5881 (1994).
[22] R. S. Lewis and W. M. Deen, *Chem. Res. Toxicol.* **7**, 568 (1994).
[23] M. Pires, D. S. Ross, and M. J. Rossi, *Int. J. Chem. Kinet.* **26**, 1207 (1994).

constant is little affected by pH, temperatures between 20° and 37°, and solvent, suggesting that this rate constant does not vary between different biological media.[18,20,22,23]

The third-order nature of this reaction is important because the second-order dependence on NO makes the half-life or longevity of this molecule in aqueous solution proportional to its concentration.[18] For instance, if the NO concentration is 1 μM the first half-life would be 13 min, yet as the NO concentration increases to 1 mM the half-life would be less than 1 sec. Under biological conditions, NO is formed and then diffuses from the cell. As it migrates from the cell, it dilutes thereby slowing the autoxidation and increasing its lifetime. This allows NO to find its biological target without the interference of the NO/O_2 reaction. Yet, as the NO concentration increases, autoxidation also increases exponentially generating higher fluxes of NO_x. These intermediates may be responsible for mediating some of the deleterious effects of NO *in vivo*.

It is the second-order nature of the autoxidation that allows the partitioning between direct and indirect effects. The selectivity of this molecule limits the possible chemical reactions and the concentration dependence of NO for formation of RNOS limits the conditions where these reactions might occur.

Direct Effects

Nitric Oxide Reactivity with Metals

Reactions with metal centers are crucial to understanding the bioregulatory behavior of NO and why this molecule can serve as a signaling agent. The reaction of NO with some transition metal complexes (not all) results in the formation of metal–nitrosyl adducts. The rate of these reactions, as well as the stability of the resultant metal–nitrosyl depends on the nature of the metal and ligands in the coordination sphere. For example, the reaction between ferrous ion and NO in acidic solution forms a simple iron nitrosyl with a formation constant of 4.1×10^2 M^{-1} [Eq. (3)][24]:

$$\text{Fe}^{2+} + \text{NO} \underset{k_{-1}}{\overset{k_1}{\rightleftharpoons}} \text{Fe}(\text{H}_2\text{O})_5\text{NO}^{2+} \tag{3}$$

where $k_1 = 6.2 \times 10^5$ M^{-1} sec^{-1} and $k_{-1} = 1.4 \times 10^3$ sec^{-1}. In contrast, the ferric aqueous ion does not form a stable nitrosyl species. Addition of EDTA to a ferrous solution not only increases the rate of NO reaction

[24] I. R. Epstien, K. Kustin, and L. J. Warshaw, *J. Am. Chem. Soc.* **102**, 3751 (1980).

with the metal center but also increases the stability of the Fe–nitrosyl complex [Eq. (4)][25]:

$$EDTA[Fe(II)] + NO \underset{k_{-2}}{\overset{k_2}{\rightleftharpoons}} EDTA[Fe(II)]\text{–}NO \tag{4}$$

where $k_2 = 6 \times 10^7 \ M^{-1} \ sec^{-1}$, $k_{-2} = 60 \ sec^{-1}$, and $K_2 = 10^6 \ M^{-1}$. Other biologically relevant complexes, such as ferric and ferrous hemes, also react with NO to give metal nitrosyl complexes[6]:

$$Fe(II)(TPPS) + NO \underset{k_{-3}}{\overset{k_3}{\rightleftharpoons}} Fe(II)(TPPS)NO \tag{5}$$

$$Fe(III)(TPPS) + NO \underset{k_{-4}}{\overset{k_4}{\rightleftharpoons}} Fe(III)(TPPS)NO \tag{6}$$

where $k_3 = 1.8 \times 10^9 \ M^{-1} \ sec^{-1}$, $k_{-3} \sim 0 \ sec^{-1}$, $K_3 \gg 10^9 \ M^{-1}$, $k_4 = 7.2 \times 10^6 \ M^{-1} \ sec^{-1}$, $k_{-4} = 6.8 \times 10^2 \ sec^{-1}$, and $K_4 = 1.1 \times 10^4 \ M^{-1}$. In general, iron complexes with porphyrin ligands have a higher affinity for NO than ones with nitrogen or oxygen ligands that lack available π orbital characteristics. Also, ferrous complexes have a greater affinity for NO than ferric ions.

Heme-containing proteins are important to the biology of NO. For instance, the reaction between NO and heme cofactors within the protein is important in the regulation of guanylate cyclase activity.[26] NO has been shown to bind to the heme moiety of this protein thereby stimulating the conversion of GTP to cGMP.

Another important direct reaction of NO is its interaction with cytochrome P450. Several studies[27–29] have shown that NO inhibits mammalian P450, which is thought to regulate hormone metabolism and under infectious conditions decrease drug metabolism in the liver. The proposed inhibitory mechanism relies on the formation of an Fe–NO which prevents the binding of oxygen, similar to mechanism for CO inhibition.[27] This nitrosyl formation was termed reversible inhibition. NO can react in both the ferrous state and the ferric state and is 100 times more potent an inhibitor than CO.

[25] V. Zang, M. Kotowski, and R. van Eldik, *Inorg. Chem.* **27,** 3279 (1988).

[26] L. J. Ignarro, B. K. Barry, D. Y. Gruetter, J. C. Edwards, E. H. Ohlstein, C. A. Gruetter, and W. H. Baricos, *Biochem. Biophys. Res. Commun.* **94,** 93 (1980).

[27] D. A. Wink, Y. Osawa, J. F. Darbyshire, C. R. Jones, S. C. Eshenaur, and R. W. Nims, *Arch. Biochem. Biophys.* **300,** 115 (1993).

[28] O. G. Khatsenko, S. S. Gross, A. B. Rifkind, and J. R. Vane, *Proc. Natl. Acad. Sci. U.S.A.* **90,** 11147 (1993).

[29] J. Stadler, J. Trockfeld, W. A. Shmalix, T. Brill, J. R. Siewert, H. Greim, and J. Doehmer, *Proc. Natl. Acad. Sci. U.S.A.* **91,** 3559 (1994).

where $k = 6.7 \times 10^9\ M^{-1}\ \sec^{-1}$. Indeed, the facile reaction of O_2^- with NO is 5 times faster than the decomposition of superoxide by superoxide dismutase.[47] Peroxynitrite is relatively unreactive in basic solution and slowly dismutates to nitrite and oxygen.[48] It reacts with sulfhydryl compounds resulting in the formation of disulfides at a rate constant of $10^3\ M^{-1}\ \sec^{-1}$.[49] Protonation of peroxynitrite gives the neutral HOONO species which can oxidize various biological substrates in competition with isomerization to nitrate[50]:

$$OONO^- \rightleftharpoons HOONO \qquad (15)$$
$$HOONO \rightarrow \text{oxidation} \qquad (16)$$
$$HOONO \rightarrow NO_3^- \qquad (17)$$

The reactive intermediates formed following protonation were first thought to be NO_2 and $\cdot$ OH in aqueous solution; however, a review of peroxynitrite chemistry suggests that the intermediate responsible for oxidation of various biological molecules is the isomer of peroxynitrous acid.[50] Peroxynitrite can oxidize substrates by either one or two electrons[51] and displays a distinctly different reactivity pattern from those of either OH or NO_2. It appears that this intermediate is considerably less reactive than the ROS formed in the Fenton reaction. Another reaction of potential biological importance is peroxynitrite nitriation of tyrosine in the presence of metal ions,[52] which may contribute to the inhibition and alteration of key cellular proteins.

Despite the facile reactions discussed above, NO does not react with all radicals. The nitroxide radical TEMPOL is unreactive with NO, although, line broadening in the ESR (electron spin resonance) spectrum of this compound is observed (D. A. Wink and M. C. Krishna, unpublished observation). In fact, the line broadening of stable radicals such as those found in fusinite has provided a technique to examine the intracellular pathways of NO.[7]

Indirect Effects

Although nitric oxide does not react directly with most biological molecules, RNOS formed in an aerobic environment can result in modification

[47] R. E. Huie and S. Padmaja, *Free Radical. Res. Commun.* **18,** 195 (1993).
[48] R. C. Plum and J. O. Edwards, *Prog. Inorg. Chem.* **41,** 599 (1994).
[49] R. Radi, J. S. Beckman, K. M. Bush, and B. A. Freeman, *J. Biol. Chem.* **266,** 4244 (1991).
[50] W. A. Pryor, *Am. J. Phys.* **268,** L699–721 (1995).
[51] W. A. Pryor, X. Jin, and G. Squadrito, *Proc. Natl. Acad. Sci.* **92,** 11173 (1994).
[52] H. Ischiropoulos, L. Zhu, J. Chen, M. Tsai, J. C. Martin, C. D. Smith, and J. S. Beckman, *Arch. Biochem. Biophys.* **298,** 431 (1992).

of important biomacromolecules, leading to potentially deleterious effects on biological systems. The RNOS formed from the NO/O_2 reaction in hydrophobic media are NO_2, N_2O_3, and N_2O_4,[5,53] species commonly associated with air pollution. These intermediates can nitrosate sulfhydryl and tyrosine groups[50–52,54–56] as well as oxidize various substrates. The intermediates formed in the gas phase autoxidation were originally assumed to be the same as those formed in aqueous solution. However, it has been suggested that the intermediates formed from the NO/O_2 reaction in aqueous solution are distinctly different from those in the gas phase.[19] In aqueous solution, there appears to be one primary intermediate (NO_X), whose empirical formula is N_2O_3.[57] Reactivity studies suggest that this may be a different isomer (possible ONONO) from that formed in the gas phase autoxidation of NO or from the acidification of nitrite in aqueous solution ($OH-NO_2$)[23] (Fig. 1). Nitrogen dioxide, which is a key intermediate in the autoxidation of NO in the gas phase and hydrophobic media, was not detected in NO autoxidation in aqueous solution.[19,58] Although the exact structure of this reactive nitrogen oxide species (NO_X) has not yet been clearly defined, its chemistry with various bioorganic molecules has been characterized.

NO_x rapidly hydrolyzes in aqueous media to nitrite. This intermediate is capable of oxidation of redox–active complexes,[19,59] and nitrosation of amine–[19,59] and thiol-containing substrates.[56] The oxidation chemistry of NO_x has been investigated using various immunosuppressive agents. 5-Aminosalicylic acid undergoes oxidation in the presence of NO_x.[59] It was concluded that the oxidation potentials of these immunosuppressive agents were low enough to afford efficient scavenging of the intermediate. Compounds with higher oxidation potentials such as 4-aminosalicylic acid were not as efficient and did not undergo one-electron oxidation but rather nitrosation of the exocyclic amine group. Furthermore, it was concluded that the effective oxidation potential of NO_x was less than 0.7 V.[59]

The hydrolysis to nitrite as well as oxidation, and nitrosation, of substrates by NO_x appears to be competitive, giving an opportunity to assess the relative selectivity of various biologically important substances. This has provided information as to the potential biological targets of NO_x.

[53] A. R. Butler and D. L. Williams, *Chem. Soc. Rev.*, 233 (1993).
[54] W. A. Pryor, D. F. Church, C. K. Govindan, and G. Crank, *J. Org. Chem.* **47**, 156 (1982).
[55] W. A. Prutz, H. Monig, J. L. Butler, and E. Land, *Arch. Biochem. Biophys.* **243**, 125 (1985).
[56] D. A. Wink, R. W. Nims, J. F. Darbyshire, D. Christodoulou, I. Hanbauer, G. W. Cox, F. Laval, J. Laval, J. A. Cook, M. C. Krishna, W. DeGraff, and J. B. Mitchell, *Chem. Res. Toxicol.* **7**, 519 (1994).
[57] D. A. Wink and P. C. Ford, *Methods (San Diego)* **7**, 14–20 (1995).
[58] M. N. Routledge, D. A. Wink, L. K. Keefer, and A. Dipple, *Chem. Res. Toxicol.* **7**, 628 (1994).
[59] M. B. Grisham and A. M. Miles, *Biochem. Pharmacol.* **47**, 1897 (1994).

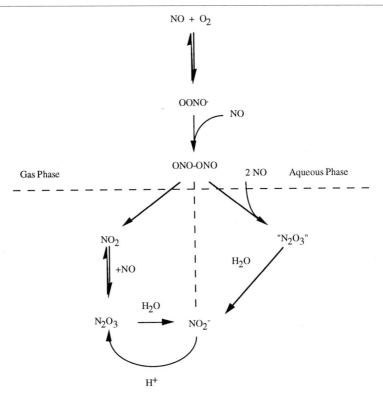

FIG. 1. Mechanistic aspects of the autoxidation of NO.

Sulfhydryl-containing proteins such as glutathione have a high affinity for this intermediate, forming S-nitrosothiol adducts [Eq. (18)][56]:

$$RSH + NO_x \rightarrow RSNO + NO_2^-$$ (18)

These adducts have been shown to form endogenously in the cardiovascular and pulmonary system.[60,61] These S-nitrosothiol adducts release NO over a period of time and activate guanylate cyclase *in vivo* and have even been proposed as an alternative chemical species to NO as EDRF (endothelium-

[60] J. S. Stamler, O. Jaraki, J. Osbourne, D. I. Simon, J. Keaney, J. Vita, D. Singel, R. Valeri, and J. Loscalzo, *Proc. Natl. Acad. Sci. U.S.A.* **89,** 7674 (1992).
[61] B. Gaston, J. Reilly, J. M. Drazen, J. Fackler, P. Ramdev, D. Arnelle, M. E. Mullins, D. J. Sugarbaker, C. Chee, D. J. Singel, J. Loscalzo, and J. S. Stamler, *Proc. Natl. Acad. Sci. U.S.A.* **90,** 10957 (1993).

derived relaxing factor).[62] The reactivity of sulfhydryls toward NO_x is 10^6 times greater than toward nucleic acids and 10^3 times greater than toward other amino acids except tyrosine.[56] In this context, it has been proposed that glutathione can serve as a scavenger of NO_x, playing a critical role in detoxification of RNOS,[56,63] and that proteins containing thiol residues critical to their function might be adversely effected.[56,61]

Biochemical Effects of Reactive Nitrogen Oxide Species

A number of different enzymes are inhibited by NO-derived RNOS. As discussed above, NO can reversibly inhibit cytochrome P450 activity via NO coordination to heme cofactor and by NO_x.[27] NO-mediated inhibition of ribonucleotide reductase is thought to play a role in cytotoxic mechanisms.[64] NO and NO donor compounds have been shown to affect the enzymatic activity of protein kinase C.[65] It has been proposed that NO-mediated ADP-ribosylation of glyceraldehyde-3-phosphate dehydrogenase (GAPDH) (or more correctly covalent modification with NAD) is mediated via the formation of an S-nitrosyl adduct.[66] Because NO does not react directly with thiol residues to form S-NO and NO_x does,[56] it appears that ribosylation is mediated by indirect effects.

Two DNA repair proteins have been shown to be inhibited by intermediates in the autoxidation of NO (NO_x).[67,68] The affinity of NO_x to form S-nitrosothiol complexes suggests that proteins which contain thiol-rich environments would be susceptible. One such DNA repair protein which contains a thiol group in its active site is DNA alkyltransferase, which repairs O^6-methylguanine and O^4-methylthymine residues.[67] This protein repairs by transferring the alkyl group on the modified guanine residue to a cysteine, the active site of the protein (Fig. 2). This protein is thought to prevent mutation and toxicity mediated by alkylating agents such as nitrosoureas.[69] Exposure of DNA alkyltransferase to an aerobic solution of NO results in inhibition of its DNA repair activity, both with the purified protein and in intact cells.[67] Following NO exposures, the activity slowly returns with the kinetics of the decomposition of S-nitroso–peptide com-

[62] P. R. Myers, R. L. Minor, R. Guerra, J. N. Bates, and D. G. Harrison, *Nature (London)* **345**, 161 (1990).

[63] M. W. Walker, M. T. Kinter, R. J. Roberts, and D. R. Spitz, *Pediatr. Res.* **37**, 41 (1995).

[64] N. S. Kwon, D. J. Stuehr, and C. F. Nathan, *J. Exp. Med.* **174**, 761 (1991).

[65] R. Gopalakrishna, Z. H. Chen, and U. Gundimeda, *J. Biol. Chem.* **268**, 27180 (1993).

[66] L. Molina y Vedia, B. McDonald, B. Reep, B. Brune, M. DiSilvio, T. R. Billiar, and E. G. Lapetina, *J. Biol. Chem.* **267**, 24929 (1992).

[67] F. Laval and D. A. Wink, *Carcinogenesis (London)* **15**, 443 (1994).

[68] D. A. Wink and J. Laval, *Carcinogenesis (London)* **15**, 2125 (1994).

[69] Y. Habraken and F. Laval, *Cancer Res.* **51**, 1217 (1991).

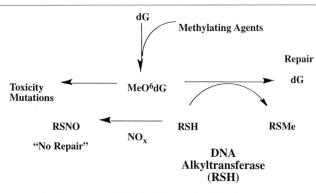

FIG. 2. Mechanism of NO inhibition of DNA alkyltransferase.

plexes. Furthermore, NO-treated cells showed marked enhancement in toxicity of BCNU, supporting the conclusion that NO can inhibit DNA alkyltransferase. It was proposed that reactive intermediates from the NO/ O_2 reaction nitrosated the thiol residues within the active site to form a protein–S-nitrosothiol adduct. The nitrosation of these residues inhibited the repair.

Another important class of DNA interacting proteins that contain thiol-rich environments are those with zinc finger motifs.[70] It has been shown that under aerobic conditions NO results in degradation of proteins containing a zinc finger motif.[68,71] In the case of the Fpg protein which repairs oxidative damage to DNA, the presence of NO irreversibly inhibits the activity.[68] It was concluded that the RNOS formed in the NO/O_2 reaction attack the sulfur residues within the zinc finger motif. This would result in labilization of the zinc ion and would compromise the protein structure (Fig. 3). Kroncke et al. were able to show that thiol-rich metal environments such as zinc finger motifs and those in metallothionein formed S-nitrosothiol adducts.[71] This suggests that these types of proteins are particularly susceptible to degradation mediated by NO_x (Figs. 2 and 3). Conversely, a marked increase in intracellular metallothionein (a protein that provides storage for various metals including toxic metals such as Cd) dramatically enhances the protection against the toxicity of NO_x in a manner analogous to glutathi-

[70] M. Schmeidescramp and R. E. Klevit, Curr. Opin. Struct. Biol. **4**, 3 (1994).
[71] K.-D. Kroncke, K. Fechsel, T. Schmidt, F. T. Zenke, I. Dasting, J. R. Wesener, H. Bettermann, K. D. Breunig, and V. Kolb-Bachofen, Biochem. Biophys. Res. Commun. **200**, 1105 (1994).

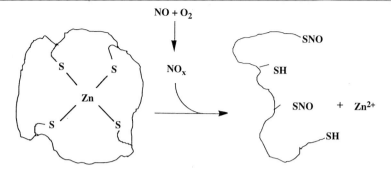

FIG. 3. Effect of NO on zinc finger-containing proteins.

one.[72] It should be noted that not all proteins and enzymes are subject to damage by NO_x. Several other DNA repair proteins including endonuclease III and IV as well as uracil glycosylase are unaffected by NO_x.[68]

The activity of some enzymes can be unaffected by the presence of NO and NO_x but the resultant products of their activity are affected. For instance, NO does not alter the oxidation of xanthine by xanthine oxidase but does effect the production of superoxide.[42,45,73,74] Xanthine oxidase is considered a model of oxidative stress and generates the reactive oxygen species superoxide and hydrogen peroxide (Fig. 4). In the presence of an NO-releasing agent, the amount of hydrogen peroxide produced by xanthine oxidase is unaffected. However, the amount of superoxide formed was dramatically reduced. It has been proposed that NO reacts with the produced superoxide formed from xanthine oxidase to form peroxynitrite which then isomerizes to nitrate[42,45,73,74]:

$$NO + O_2^- \rightarrow OONO^- \qquad (19)$$
$$OONO^- + DHR \rightarrow oxidation \qquad (20)$$
$$OONO^- \rightarrow NO_3^- \qquad (21)$$

If the same conditions were used in the presence of dihydrorhodamine (DHR), an increase in oxidation is observed in the presence of NO/xanthine

[72] M. A. Schwarz, J. S. Lazo, J. C. Yalowich, W. P. Allen, M. Whitmore, H. A. Bergonia, E. Tzeng, T. R. Billiar, P. D. Robbins, J. R. Lancaster, and B. R. Pitt, *Proc. Natl. Acad. Sci. U.S.A.* in press (1995).

[73] R. M. Clancy, J. Leszczynska-Piziak, and S. B. Abramson, *J. Clin. Invest.* **90**, 1116 (1992).

[74] A. M. Miles, M. Gibson, M. Krishna, J. C. Cook, R. Pacelli, D. A. Wink, and M. B. Grisham, *Free Radical Res.* **23**, 379–390 (1995).

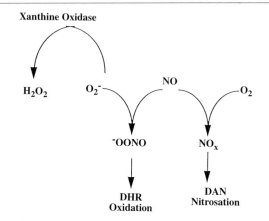

FIG. 4. Chemical aspects of the interaction between xanthine oxidase and NO.

oxidase. Peroxynitrite oxidizes DHR,[75] further supporting the hypothesis that peroxynitrite is an RNOS generated from NO/xanthine oxidase.

Conversely, the nitrosation chemistry of the NO/O_2 reaction can be inhibited by the presence of superoxide generated from xathine oxidase:

$$4NO + O_2 \rightarrow NO_x \qquad (22)$$
$$NO_x + \text{substrate} \rightarrow \text{nitrosation} \qquad (23)$$

Diaminonaphthylene when exposed to NO in an aerobic environment, is nitrosated by NO_x to the corresponding triazole.[74] When an NO donor compound was exposed to a solution containing 2,3-diaminonaphthylene (DAN), triazole formation was detected. However, in the presence of xanthine oxidase, the fluorescence was dramatically reduced (Fig. 4). It was concluded that NO was rapidly intercepted by superoxide to form peroxynitrite which then rapidly isomerizes to nitrate, hence, limiting the NO/O_2 reaction. It was also shown in this same report that peroxynitrite did not nitrosate substrate.[74] The small amount of nitrosation reported for peroxynitrite is probably due to the contaminating nitrite often found in the preparation of anion. The interplay between the formation of RNOS either by the NO/O_2 reaction or by NO/O_2^- reaction is crucial in understanding the toxicology of nitric oxide.

[75] N. W. Kooy, J. A. Royall, H. Ischiropoulos, and J. S. Beckman, *Free Radical Biol. Med.* **16,** 149 (1994).

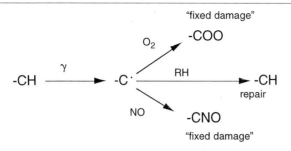

FIG. 5. Mechanism of radiosensitization by NO of hypoxic cells.

Biology of Direct and Indirect Effects of Nitric Oxide

As shown above, the chemistry of NO is diverse, resulting in a plethora of reactions that must be considered in determining the mechanism in biological systems. The categorizing of these reactions into direct and indirect effects can aid in determining the importance of each reaction under specific biological conditions. These classifications may serve as a guide in understanding different toxicological mechanisms or give insight into the development of new therapeutic strategies.

As discussed above, direct effects involve the interaction of NO with the chemical or biological target. For instance, radicals can be formed on DNA by ionizing radiation. In the absence of NO or oxygen, these reactive radical species abstract a hydrogen from neighboring proteins, resulting in repair to DNA (Fig. 5). In the presence of NO, these DNA radicals are postulated to react with NO, forming C-nitroso adducts. These resultant chemical species are unable to abstract neighboring hydrogens, and hence the damage to DNA is fixed. This increases the number of lesions per photon, thereby enhancing the radiosensitization of hypoxic cells[33,43,70,76] (Fig. 5). The population of hypoxic cells that are radioresistant within a tumor is thought to be responsible in part for limiting radiation therapy in cancer treatment. The direct interactions of these DNA radicals with NO may offer some insights into new radiotherapeutic strategies.

Indirect effects involve the chemistry of RNOS formed in an aerobic environment which includes nitrosation, nitration, and oxidation. Indirect effects generally are considered deleterious, leading to alterations of biomacromolecules, and are often invoked as causative agents in various toxicological mechanisms. For instance, NO_x derived from NO can damage DNA repair enzymes including those that repair alkylated lesions mediated by nitrosamines.[67] It been shown that with chronic hepatitis infection there

---

[76] P. Howard-Flanders, *Nature* (*London*) **180,** 1191 (1957).

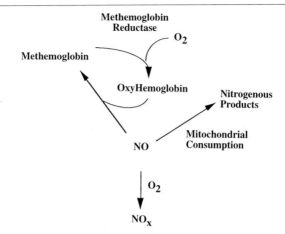

FIG. 6. *In vivo* control of NO concentrations, which influences the NO/O_2 reaction.

is a significant increase in nitrosamine formation due to nitrosation of dialkylamines by RNOS formed from endogenously formed NO.[77,78] These nitrosamines when metabolized by cytochrome P450 result in a product which then alkylates DNA. Because the presence of NO also inhibits the repair enzyme, alkylated lesions may be enhanced.

The likelihood that direct or indirect effects will predominate is partially based on NO concentrations. At lower NO concentrations direct effects will dominate, but at higher NO concentrations indirect effects would become important. As discussed above, the formation of intermediates from the NO/O_2 reaction increase exponentially with NO concentration. Because oxygen is generally in excess *in vivo*, NO is the limiting substance in the autoxidation reaction. Because NO is limiting, the consumption of NO by pathways associated with direct effects limit the production of NO_x. Oxyhemoglobin reacts with NO with a rate constant of $3 \times 10^7 \, M^{-1} \, sec^{-1}$ and can exist at 0.2–2 mM effective concentration *in vivo*.[8,30] Thus, the formation of NO_x *in vivo* at NO concentrations of nanomolar to micromolar, expected to be involved with bioregulatory mechanisms, would be limited (Fig. 6). Besides the hemoglobin reaction, the mitochondrion limits the intracellular formation of NO_x. A mathematical model predicts that little to no NO_x is generated from the NO/O_2 intracellularly at NO concentrations greater than 10 μM.[7] However, higher NO concentration conditions can exist where NO_x might be formed. The endogenous products resulting from nitrosation chemistry (*S*-nitrosothiols and nitrosamines) may repre-

[77] R. H. Liu, B. Baldwin, B. C. Tennant, and J. H. Hotchkiss, *Cancer Res* **51**, 3925 (1991).
[78] R. H. Liu, J. R. Jacob, B. D. Tennant, and J. H. Hotchkiss, *Cancer Res.* **52**, 4139 (1992).

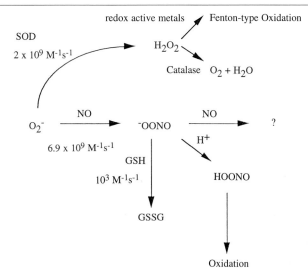

FIG. 7. Factors that influence the formation and reactivity of peroxynitrite.

sent the presence of the NO/O_2 and are found only in conjunction with the activated immune system. This suggests that there might be localized areas *in vivo* where the NO concentrations could be high enough to facilate the NO/O_2 reaction.

Another RNOS that must be considered in any toxicological mechanism is peroxynitrite. Formation of this RNOS is via the near diffusion-controlled reaction between superoxide and NO [Eq. (19)]. At first glance, the high rate constant suggests that chemistry of this intermediate may occur frequently *in vivo*. Careful consideration of the kinetics of formation and subsequent reactivity of peroxynitrite reveal that its formation and oxidation of biological critical molecules *in vivo* is tightly controlled. It has been reported that the flux of superoxide is never less than 66 nM.[79] NO has been estimated to be produced at the cellular environment at 1–10 μM[44]; therefore, superoxide is limiting, and the pathways associated with superoxide limit peroxynitrite formation. Since superoxide dismutase (SOD) and NO react with superoxide with similar rate constants, the flux of NO would have to rise to give NO levels comparable to those of SOD in order for peroxynitrite formation to be competitive. The intracellular SOD concentration has been estimated in some cells to be 10–40 μM. Therefore, in order to achieve appreciable intracellular peroxynitrite levels, the NO concentration would have to be as high as 10 μM (Fig. 7). In addition to

[79] D. D. Tyler, *Biochem. J.* **147**, 493 (1975).

limiting the formation of peroxynitrite, this intermediate can be efficiently scavenged directly by intracellular glutathione prior to the formation of the oxidant.[49] Therefore, damage to intracellular components by peroxynitrite is limited by SOD and glutathione.

It is interesting that the intracellular formation of both NO_x and peroxynitrite are predicted to occur significantly only when NO concentrations are greater than 10 μM. This suggests that the indirect effects of NO which are mediated by RNOS do not occur until significant local NO concentrations are achieved. In the case of both peroxynitrite and NO_x, thiol-containing peptides are critical to detoxication of these intermediates and are important when considering toxicological mechanisms.

One of the most important aspects of the NO chemistry in determining different toxicological mechanisms is the interaction between NO with ROS. ROS formed from Fenton-type reactions have been invoked as causative agents in diseases ranging from cancer to autoimmune diseases.[80] Many of the reactions involve the interaction of redox metals with peroxide to form powerful oxidants that can oxidize various biological macromolecules. As discussed above, NO reacts with hypervalent iron complexes formed from interactions between peroxide and iron complexes [Eq. (9)]. NO possesses antioxidant properties. The mechanism is believed to occur by the prevention of formation and scavenging of these reactive oxygen species implying a beneficial role in abating damage due to oxidative stress. Several studies have shown that NO abates the cytotoxicity of both hydrogen, xanthine oxidase, and alkyl hydroperoxides.[39,45,81] The flux of NO required to do this was determined to be as low as 1 μM. Because intracellular RNOS formation is predicted to be considerably higher, the antioxidant effects can be categorized as direct effects of NO.

There appear to be two distinct isoforms of nitric oxide synthase.[9,10] The constitutive form (cNOS) presumably releases NO at micromolar levels in the microenvironment of the cell. The other form is inducible (iNOS) and generates larger fluxes of NO. It is in the presence of iNOS that both nitrosation and nitration chemistry occur. It is the interaction of the various ROS and RNOS which is controlled by the different cytokines that appears to orchestrate the pathological response. In addition to consideration of NO production, distance from the NO source must be considered. NO diffuses at the rate of 50 μm per second. Like a smokestack, the concentration of NO near the point source is high and hence more likely to generate RNOS and indirect effects. However, as the NO moves away from the

[80] B. Halliwell and J. M. C. Gutteridge, *Biochem. J.* **219,** 1 (1984).
[81] D. A. Wink, J. A. Cook, M. C. Krichna, I. Hanbauer, W. DeGraff, J. Gamson, and J. B. Mitchell, *Arch. Biochem. Biophys.* in press (1995).

source, there is an exponential drop in concentrations. This implies that the indirect effects occur in a relatively localized area.

Summary

Categorization of the chemical reactions of NO into direct and indirect effects provides a framework to evaluate the role of NO in different biological situations. The diverse behavior of NO protecting against ROS toxicity yet potentiating the toxicity of other agents implies that the role of NO in each condition must be carefully evaluated. The chemical biology of NO can aid in the mechanistic questions with respect to this unique molecule.

[4] Diffusion of Free Nitric Oxide

By JACK R. LANCASTER, JR.

Introduction

Nitric oxide (·NO) is uncharged and is approximately 70 times more soluble in hydrophobic solvents than in aqueous solution.[1] This makes ·NO able to transmit information and inflict cellular damage without the necessity of specific export mechanisms such as vesicular secretion. Its ready diffusibility means that it will spread isotropically in all directions from a source cell, moving by random motion. It reacts with oxygen species (dioxygen, superoxide) and as a consequence possesses a finite half-life, which has been reported to be in the range of 5–15 sec.[2] This means that there will be a declining concentration profile of ·NO in all directions away from a cellular ·NO source. Two papers have appeared that apply diffusion calculations to simulate the profiles of cellular ·NO synthesis.[3,4] This chapter presents methods and results for some of these calculations. One important conclusion of these calculations is that ·NO is rapidly diffusible on a cellular scale, and this diffusivity is likely to play an important role in its biological actions where differences in cell types (targets of ·NO), scavenging mechanisms, sources of superoxide, and oxygen tension are heterogeneously distributed.

[1] J. F. Kerwin, Jr., J. R. Lancaster, Jr., and P. L. Feldman, *J. Med. Chem.* in press (1995).
[2] L. J. Ignarro, *Biochem. Pharmacol.* **41,** 485 (1991).
[3] J. R. Lancaster, Jr., *Proc. Natl. Acad. Sci. U.S.A.* **91,** 8137 (1994).
[4] J. Wood and J. Garthwaite, *Neuropharmacology* **33,** 1235 (1994).

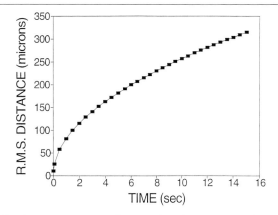

FIG. 1. Calculated root-mean-square distance of random movement for ·NO using Eq. (1) with $D = 3300 \ \mu m^2$.

Movement of Individual Nitric Oxide Molecules

For random motion, at any instant the direction of movement of a molecule is equally likely in any direction. Thus the probability of movement in a positive direction (with respect to a defined x axis) is identical to movement in the negative direction, and so the average value for net displacement ($\langle \Delta x \rangle$) is zero. We can, however, speak of the average of the square of the distance, $\langle (\Delta x)^2 \rangle$, which is defined by the Einstein–Smoluchowski equation:

$$\langle (\Delta x)^2 \rangle = 2Dt \tag{1}$$

where D is the diffusion coefficient and t is time. The value for D is characteristic for any molecule and is inversely proportional to the frictional forces that oppose the kinetic motion. Neglecting dipole effects, for nonelectrolytes D is inversely proportional to the molecular radius and so for small molecules will be quite large. For electrolytes in aqueous solution additional frictional drag occurs due to electrostatic interaction with the water solvent cage surrounding the molecule. It is therefore clear that small, uncharged molecules such as ·NO will possess very high values of D.

For nitric oxide, a value for D of 3300 μm^2/sec has been reported using microsensor measurements under physiological conditions.[5] Figure 1 presents a plot of the root-mean-square (r.m.s.) net displacement of ·NO

[5] T. Malinski, Z. Taha, S. Grunfeld, S. Patton, M. Kapturczak, and P. Tomboulian, *Biochem. Biophys. Res. Commun.* **193**, 1076 (1993).

$([\langle(\Delta x)^2\rangle]^{1/2})$ as a function of time, over the range of its reported half-life under physiological conditions. It is clear that ·NO is very widely diffusible, with a range of approximately 150–300 μm for a time of 4–15 sec. It is important to realize that this distance does not correspond to a straight line trajectory (since the process is random), but rather the radius of a sphere. Thus, when ·NO is produced in the cytosol of a cell, for example, it does not simply zoom directly out but randomly zigzags through the cell before crossing the plasma membrane. In addition, once a molecule has diffused any distance away from a point of origin, it is just as likely to reverse its direction and begin moving in a direction returning to the origin as it is to move directly away from it. Thus, once exited from a cell an individual ·NO molecule is equally likely to move away as to reenter the cell. As shown in Fig. 1, however, the average time it takes for the ·NO to make this circuitous journey within the cell is remarkably fast, on the order of 2–30 msec (for a cell of radius 4–15 μm).

Net Movement of Collections of Nitric Oxide Molecules

Even though diffusional direction of individual molecules is random, it is possible to have net movement of a collection of molecules from a region of higher concentration to one of lower concentration. Consider two adjacent compartments (A and B) with an imaginary plane between. At any instant in time the total probability that molecules will cross the plane from A to B will be directly proportional to the concentration of molecules in A (a first-order process). The converse is true for net movement from B to A. Thus, if the concentrations are the same, so will be these probabilities and there will be no net movement; the molecules will simply "change places." However, a concentration difference will un-equalize these probabilities, and net movement will occur from the higher to the lower concentration compartment. It is important to emphasize that this will be the only condition in which net movement will occur, and it will always be directed from higher to lower concentration. In the example cited above, for example, although it will be true that an individual molecule of ·NO situated adjacent to (or dissolved within) the plasma membrane is equally likely to move in as out, for a collection of molecules net diffusion outward always occurs if (and only if) the concentration is lower extracellularly than intracellularly.

Relative Rates of Reactions versus Diffusion of Nitric Oxide

In addition to autoxidation (reactions with O_2), ·NO reacts with two other major cellular species, metal ions and superoxide.[1] If the rates of

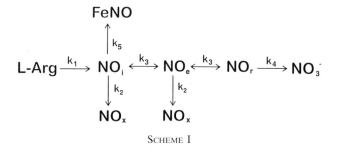

SCHEME I

reaction with these targets are rapid with respect to diffusion, the ·NO will exert an effect in the immediate vicinity of its production. If, in addition to a rapid intrinsic reaction rate, these species are present at high enough concentrations or generated (or regenerated) rapidly enough, ·NO will disappear more quickly, thus decreasing its effective half-life and consequently its distance of diffusion. These effects would clearly limit the distance of actions of ·NO.

Are there experimental data to indicate the relative rates of reaction of ·NO versus its rate of diffusion? There are several reports that extracellular addition of the ·NO scavenger hemoglobin or of intact red blood cells will dramatically decrease the reaction of intracellularly produced ·NO with metal-containing targets within the cell which produces it, specifically, guanylyl cyclase (guanylate cyclase) and nonheme iron (as cited in Ref. 3). The following kinetic model was developed[3] to quantitatively interpret this result, in specific terms of the prevention by red blood cells of the reaction of endogenously produced ·NO within the isolated rat hepatocyte with intracellular nonheme iron[6] (see Scheme I).

The production of ·NO within the cell is given by the rate constant k_1, and its reaction with an intracellular target at the source by k_5 (in this case, to form FeNO). The bidirectional rates of diffusion of ·NO are given by the rate constant k_3 for the symmetrical first-order diffusion between the internal cell compartment (NO_i) and the external compartment (NO_e) and between the external compartment and the erythrocyte internal compartment (NO_r). At every location the rate constant for autoxidation is given by k_2, and the reaction of NO_r with oxyhemoglobin within the erythrocyte is given by k_4. Using the standard steady-state assumption, it is possible to solve exactly for the rates of formation of products in terms of only the rate constants k_1 through k_5.

[6] J. Stadler, H. A. Bergonia, M. Di Silvio, M. A. Sweetland, T. R. Billiar, R. L. Simmons, and J. R. Lancaster, Jr., *Arch. Biochem. Biophys.* **302,** 4 (1993).

What relationships between the magnitudes of these constants must exist in order to result in a decrease in reaction of ·NO with intracellular target when the value of k_4 is increased? To answer this, each of the five rate constants was varied independently between 1 and 1000 in 10-fold increments and the values for the rates of steady-state FeNO formation computed. In this way, every possible combination of the relative rate constants will be considered over a 3-order magnitude range. Table I presents a compilation of the 20 conditions under which increasing the rate of reaction of ·NO with oxyhemoglobin (k_4) from 0 to 1000 decreases the rate of formation of FeNO by at least 90%, out of the 256 (4^4) possible combinations. The general result is that any condition in which the rate of diffusion (k_3) is greater than the rate of autocrine reaction (k_5) will result in the experimentally observed result, decrease in FeNO formation. An interesting result is that the prevention of reaction of ·NO with a target at the source of its production (intracellularly) by rapid extracellular scavenging

TABLE I
COMPILATION OF TWENTY CONDITIONS
USING SCHEME I[a]

k_1	k_2	k_3	k_5
1	1	100	1
1	1	1000	1
1	1	1000	10
1	10	1000	1
1	10	1000	10
10	1	100	1
10	1	1000	1
10	1	1000	10
10	10	1000	1
10	10	1000	10
100	1	100	1
100	1	1000	1
100	1	1000	10
100	10	1000	1
100	10	1000	10
1000	1	100	1
1000	1	1000	1
1000	1	1000	10
1000	10	1000	1
1000	10	1000	10

[a] Conditions are given for which increasing scavenging results in at least 90% decrease in reaction of ·NO with Fe to form FeNO complexes.

occurs independently of the rate of ·NO formation, that is, FeNO formation is prevented at all values of k_1 (Table I).

What is the mechanistic basis of this effect? On a molecular level, it can be envisaged that rapid consumption of ·NO by reaction within the erythrocyte establishes a diffusion gradient for ·NO, which will result in a net movement in this direction, that is, out of the ·NO-producing cell, through the external medium, and into the erythrocyte. If the rate of this diffusion is more rapid than the rates of reaction of ·NO with Fe, this means that this rapid external consumption will result in a decrease in the steady-state concentration of ·NO at all points along its diffusion path, including the source of its production (intracellularly). This is verified in Fig. 2, where the steady-state concentrations of ·NO in each of the three compartments is computed for increasing values of diffusion (k_3). For this calculation, the values of the other rate constants were $k_1 =$ 1000, $k_2 = 10$, $k_4 = 100$, and $k_5 = 10$. Thus, the rate of production of ·NO (k_1) is relatively high. Even under these conditions, where it might seem that rapid intracellular production of ·NO at the site of its reaction with Fe (intracellularly) would not be affected by scavenging two compartments away, it is clear that increasing diffusion to relatively modest values (less than or equal to production) significantly decreases the concentration of ·NO intracellularly ([NO]$_i$). Since the rate of formation of FeNO is directly proportional to this concentration, this results in a decline in FeNO formation. Figure 2 also illustrates the effects of increasing diffusion

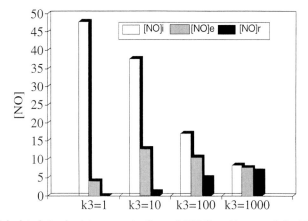

Fig. 2. Calculated steady-state concentrations of ·NO (in arbitrary units) within the three compartments described in Scheme I for increasing values of the rate constant for diffusion (k_3). Values for the other rate constants are given in the text.

rate on the relative concentrations of ·NO in each compartment. At low diffusion ($k_3 = 1$) the consumption of ·NO at NO_r results in a significant steady-state concentration gradient between the three compartments; as k_3 increases, the concentrations become more and more equalized, because the diffusion rate becomes more and more significant compared to the rates of reaction.

In summary, this analysis demonstrates that the extent to which addition of an external scavenger prevents reaction (and thus biological effect) of ·NO with a target within the cell producing it is actually a function of the relative rate of intracellular reaction compared to the rates of diffusion and scavenging. As pointed out previously,[3] prevention of the effects of ·NO in experimental systems by the addition of an external scavenger does not necessarily indicate that the actions of ·NO are mediated solely by intercellular movement; a similar effect would be observed if ·NO acts in strictly an autocrine manner but the rates of scavenging and diffusion are more rapid than the rate of intracellular reaction.

Overlap of Nitric Oxide Profiles from More than One Cell

On initiation of ·NO synthesis within a cell, the concentration will begin to rise within the cytosol and in the immediate vicinity of the cell, and spread out in a decreasing fashion. Soon, however, the concentrations at all points will reach a steady-state, where the rates of appearance (synthesis and diffusion) and disappearance (autoxidation) will exactly counterbalance one another. In the case of a single endothelial cell, this steady state is achieved in approximately 20 sec.[5] At this point, using Fick's law it can be shown that the concentration (C) at a distance Δx from the cell, where the concentration is $C(0)$, is given by the following expression[4,7]:

$$C = C(0) \exp\{-\Delta x[\ln 2/(Dt_{1/2})]^{1/2}\} \qquad (2)$$

where D is the diffusion constant and $t_{1/2}$ is the half-life for ·NO. Using ·NO-selective microsensors, Malinski et al.[5] have shown that under these steady-state conditions the ratio of the concentration at a distance of 100 μm from the source cell $[C/C(0)]$ is approximately 0.65 (0.85 μM/1.30 μM). Assuming a diffusion constant of 3300 μm^2/sec (Ref. 5), it can be calculated from Eq. (2) that the effective half-life of the ·NO is approximately 12 sec, within the range of that measured experimentally.

[7] J. Crank, "The Mathematics of Diffusion." Oxford Science Publ., Oxford, 1975.

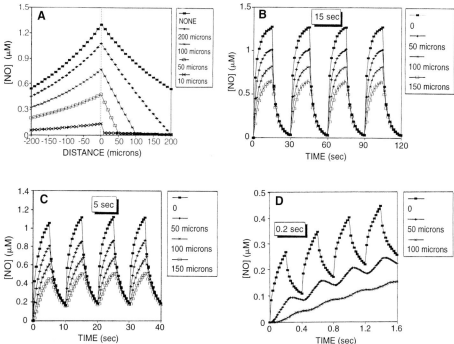

Fig. 4. Steady-state ·NO concentration profiles using the algorithm described in the text (the program used to generate the data in A is given in the Appendix). For A, one ·NO-producing cell is located at the origin, with either no scavenging (filled squares) or scavenger positioned at the distances away from the ·NO-producing cell indicated in the key. For B–D, oscillatory ·NO synthesis occurs at the indicated frequencies, and the concentrations at the distances away from the source indicated in the keys are plotted as a function of time.

·NO and products can be computed for any given values of the rate constants.

Figure 4A presents the results of one calculation utilizing this method, and the BASIC program that computed the data is included in the Appendix at the end of this chapter. The uppermost profile is a simulation of the steady-state concentration of ·NO when a single ·NO-producing cell is located at the origin and with no scavenging. For this calculation, the values for the various rate constants in Scheme II were chosen which mimic the data reported by Malinski et al.,[5] namely, that the concentration at the source reaches a steady-state in 10–20 sec and a ratio of 0.65 at a distance of 100 μm. This profile is virtually superimposable with that calculated using Fick's law (Fig., 3). Also shown in Fig. 4A is the effect of placing a site of scavenging (e.g., blood vessel or superoxide) at various distances away from the source. When this site is moved from 200 to 10 μm away, there is a virtually complete elimination of ·NO on the distal side of this site with respect to the source, and in addition there is a dramatic decrease in the concentration of ·NO at all positions, consistent with the conclusions utilizing the kinetic derivation above (Scheme I). This result shows that if the endothelium-derived relaxing factor is free ·NO, it will be scavenged very effectively by the luminal blood, even on the abluminal side.[3] In addition, locations of extensive superoxide formation (e.g., during infection or inflammation) will also scavenge ·NO in the vicinity, which could contribute to increased vascular tone and neutrophil adherence and aggregation.

Finally, Fig. 4B–D presents examples of the utility of this program in predicting ·NO concentration profiles throughout the time course, in addition to the steady state. For this example, pulsatile ·NO synthesis is initiated at the origin with different frequencies, and the rise and then fall in [NO] is predicted at various distances from the source. For a frequency of 15 sec (15 sec of synthesis followed by 15 sec without synthesis), the ·NO rises and falls in parallel at each distance from the source (50, 100, and 150 μm), and the time between synthesis phases is sufficient so that the ·NO disappears virtually completely (Fig. 4B). For a frequency of 5 sec (Fig. 4C), disappearance is also in parallel in all locations, but synthesis is reinitiated before the ·NO concentration returns to zero. For a frequency of 0.2 sec (Fig. 4D), the ·NO concentration during each synthetic phase is appreciably below steady state, but also declines only partially during the phase when ·NO is not synthesized. In addition, reinitiation of synthesis adds to this residual ·NO, making the amount higher than the previous phase. This effect occurs at each location, but an additional interesting phenomenon occurs at distances away from the source; the ·NO synthesis "waves" are significantly dampened. At a distance of 100 μm, for example, the ·NO rises more or less steadily, even though the synthesis at the source is occurring in bursts 0.2 sec apart. This is most likely due to the fact that the wave of ·NO will broaden by diffusion as it moves out away from the source. If the distance between the waves is short (i.e., the frequency is high) this broadening will result in increased overlap of the waves at progressively longer distances from the source. This phenomenon may have important consequences if ·NO is synthesized in an oscillatory manner.[8]

[8] H. Tsukahara, D. V. Gordienko, and M. S. Goligorsky, *Biochem. Biophys. Res. Commun.* **193,** 722 (1993).

Appendix

The BASIC program for generating the simulations in Fig. 4A is presented here.

```
REM PROGRAM NOSIM37.BAS

OPEN "C:\DOCS\CURRSRCH\NOSIM2\NOSIM37.DAT" FOR OUTPUT AS #3

DEFDBL D, F, H, K, N, T

DIM N(-40 TO 40), N2(-40 TO 40), N3(-40 TO 40), DN(-40 TO 40), DN2(-40 TO 40)

DIM DN3(-40 TO 40), NP(-41 TO 41), N2P(-40 TO 40), N3P(-40 TO 40)

DIM A1(10), F(5, -40 TO 40), C1(5), T3(5), N0(0 TO 41), NOR(20), NAV(20)

DIM N10(0 TO 41), T4(0 TO 41), T5(4), P(20), HB(2), B(5)

REM TU IS UPPER TIME CUTOFF

WRITE #3, "DATE IS", DATE$

WRITE #3, "PROGRAM NOSIM37.BAS;"

WRITE #3, "DATAFILE NOSIM37.DAT"

WRITE #3,

WRITE #3, "GENERATE TIME COURSE, STEADY-STATE PROFILE"

WRITE #3, "A2 IS POSITION (IN 10 MICRON INCREMENTS)"

WRITE #3, "FOR ONE N0-PRODUCING CELL"

WRITE #3, "AT 10 TO 200 MICRONS"

WRITE #3, "AWAY FROM A SITE OF SCAVENGING"

WRITE #3,

WRITE #3,

WRITE #3, "DOUBLE PRECISION"
```

```
WRITE #3, "K1=1.03D-5"

WRITE #3, "K2=0.73"

WRITE #3, "K3=91"

WRITE #3, "ASSUMING K4=6.93 FOR 4 uM Hb;"

WRITE #3, "(KELM ET AL. BBRC)"

WRITE #3,

WRITE #3, "TU=40"

TU = 40

K1 = .0000103

K2 = .173

K3 = 91

K4 = 1.7325 * 200

REM C1() ARE THE 3 VALUES OF THE EQUALLY-SPACED 20 TIME"

REM INTERVALS THAT (IN ADDITION TO THE 20th) WILL BE"

REM PRINTED IN PROFILE; Y IS THE INDEX FOR THESE"

C1(1) = 8

C1(2) = 12

C1(3) = 16

REM SET UP INITIAL VALUES

REM DT IS TIME STEP

REM NT IS AVE NO (ALL 21 POSITIONS)
```

```
REM N2T IS AVE NOX (ALL 21 POSITIONS)

REM N3T IS AVE NO3 (ALL 21 POSITIONS)

REM N(A2) IS NO AT POSITION A2

REM NP(A2) IS PRIOR NO AT POSITION A2

REM N2(A2) IS NOX AT POSITION A2

REM N3(A2) IS NO3 AT POSITION A2

REM N2P(A2) IS PRIOR NOX AT POSITION A2

REM N3P(A2) IS PRIOR NO3 AT POSITION A2

B(1) = 50

B(2) = 20

B(3) = 10

B(4) = 5

B(5) = 1

FOR M = 1 TO 5

Y = 1

WRITE #3,

WRITE #3, "TIME IS", TIME$

DT = .00001

T = 0

NT = 0

N2T = 0
```

```
N3T = 0

FOR A2 = -40 TO 40

N(A2) = .000000001#

N2(A2) = .000000001#

N3(A2) = .000000001#

NP(A2) = .000000001#

N2P(A2) = .000000001#

N3P(A2) = .000000001#

IF ABS(A2) > 20 GOTO 1010

NT = NT + N(A2)

N2T = N2T + N2(A2)

N3T = N3T + N3(A2)

1010 NEXT A2

WRITE #3,

WRITE #3, "FOR SCAVENGING AT POSITION", B(M) * 10, " MICRONS:"

WRITE #3,

WRITE #3, "T", "NT", "N2T", "N3T"

WRITE #3, T, NT * 1000000! / 41, N2T * 1000000! / 41, N3T * 1000000! / 41

REM C IS THE INDEX USED TO EQUALLY SPACE 20 TIME POINTS

C = 1

1020 IF C = 21 GOTO 1110
```

```
FOR A2 = -40 TO 40

1030 IF A2 = 0 THEN 1040

K1A = 0

IF A2 = B(M) THEN 1050

K4A = 0

GOTO 1060

1040 K1A = K1

K4A = 0

GOTO 1060

1050 K4A = K4

1060 NP(-41) = NP(-40) * NP(-40) / NP(-39)

NP(41) = NP(40) * NP(40) / NP(39)

DN(A2) = K1A + K3 * (NP(A2 - 1) + NP(A2 + 1)) - (2 * K3 + K4A) * NP(A2) - K2 * (NP

DN2(A2) = K2 * NP(A2)

DN3(A2) = K4A * NP(A2)

N(A2) = NP(A2) + DT * DN(A2)

REM FOLLOWING STATEMENTS TEST IF MORE THAN 1% CHANGE

IF (.99 > N(A2) / NP(A2)) OR (1.01 < N(A2) / NP(A2)) THEN 1090

N2(A2) = N2P(A2) + DT * DN2(A2)

N3(A2) = N3P(A2) + DT * DN3(A2)

NEXT A2
```

```
PRINT

PRINT "SCAVENGER POSITION="; B(M) * 10; " MICRONS"; " ("; M; " OF 5)"

PRINT "C="; C; "OF 20"

PRINT "DT="; DT

PRINT "T = "; T, "TOTAL TIME ="; TU

PRINT "N(ORIGIN)="; N(0) * 1000000#; " uM"

PRINT

REM FOLLOWING STATEMENTS CHECK IF TIME POINT SHOULD BE WRITTEN

C1 = C * .05

IF T + DT < C1 * TU GOTO 1080

C2 = (C + 1) * .05

IF T + DT > C2 * TU GOTO 1070

IF C <> C1(Y) GOTO 1065

FOR A4 = -20 TO 20

F(Y, A4) = N(A4) * 1000000#

NEXT A4

T3(Y) = T

Y = Y + 1

1065 C = C + 1

WRITE #3, T, NT * 1000000! / 41, N2T * 1000000! / 41, N3T * 1000000! / 41

PRINT
```

```
PRINT "TIME="; TIME$

PRINT "T", "NT", "N2T", "N3T"

PRINT T, NT * 1000000! / 41, N2T * 1000000! / 41, N3T * 1000000! / 41

PRINT

GOTO 1080

1070 DT = DT / 2

GOTO 1020

1080 T = DT + T

NT = 0

N2T = 0

N3T = 0

FOR A2 = -40 TO 40

NP(A2) = N(A2)

N2P(A2) = N2(A2)

N3P(A2) = N3(A2)

IF ABS(A2) > 20 GOTO 1085

NT = N(A2) + NT

N2T = N2(A2) + N2T

N3T = N3(A2) + N3T

1085 NEXT A2

GOTO 1100
```

```
1090 DT = DT / 1.3

GOTO 1020

1100 DT = DT * 1.2

GOTO 1020

1110 NOR(M) = N(0) * 1000000#

NAV(M) = NT * 1000000# / 41

WRITE #3,

WRITE #3,

WRITE #3, "FOR SCAVENGER POSITION=", B(M) * 10, " MICRONS"

WRITE #3,

WRITE #3, "", "T=", "T=", "T=", "T="

WRITE #3, "D", T3(1), T3(2), T3(3), T

FOR D = -20 TO 20

WRITE #3, D * 10, F(1, D), F(2, D), F(3, D), N(D) * 1000000!

NEXT D

NEXT M

WRITE #3,

WRITE #3, "SCAVENGER POSITION", "ORIGIN", "AVE"

FOR M = 1 TO 5

WRITE #3, B(M) * 10, NOR(M), NAV(M)

NEXT M
```

WRITE #3,

WRITE #3,

WRITE #3, "FINAL TIME IS", TIME$

CLOSE #3

END

Acknowledgments

This work was supported by research grants from the American Cancer Society (BE-128) and the National Institute of Diabetes and Digestive and Kidney Diseases (DK46935).

[5] Nitric Oxide Gas

By Francis T. Bonner

Purification and Handling of Nitric Oxide Gas

Because the nitric oxide molecule[1] has a large positive Gibbs energy of formation ($\Delta_f G°_{298}$ = 86.32 kJ mol^{-1}) it cannot be conveniently prepared in high yield by combination of its constituent elements N_2 and O_2, and most commercial NO production is carried out via the catalytic oxidation of ammonia. Several convenient laboratory-scale syntheses, for example, the reduction of aqueous nitrite by iodide ion [Eq. (1)], are available.

$$2 \, HNO_2(aq) + 2 \, I^-(aq) + 2 \, H^+(aq) \rightarrow 2 \, NO(g) + I_2(s) + 2 \, H_2O \quad (1)$$

Because NO gas reacts rapidly with O_2 in the gas phase to form NO_2, any synthesis employed must be carried out under anaerobic conditions, and the product must be carefully purified. The large positive value of $\Delta_f G°$ indicates that NO is intrinsically unstable against decomposition to N_2 and

---

[1] Background reading on NO and related nitrogen inorganic chemistry may be found in W. L. Jolly, "The Inorganic Chemistry of Nitrogen." Benjamin, New York, 1964; R. O. Ragsdale, in "Developments in Inorganic Nitrogen Chemistry" (C. B. Colburn, ed.), p. 1. Elsevier, Amsterdam, 1973; "Mellor's Comprehensive Treatise on Inorganic and Theoretical Chemistry," Vol. 8, Suppl. 2 (Nitrogen, Part 2). Wiley, New York, 1967; F. A. Cotton, and G. Wilkinson, "Advanced Inorganic Chemistry," 5th Ed. Wiley, New York, 1988; F. T. Bonner and M. N. Hughes, *Comments Inorg. Chem.* **7**, 215 (1988).

O_2 under ordinary conditions. However, the decomposition reaction is kinetically hindered, and NO can be stored indefinitely at 1 atm pressure and room temperature without detectable loss. It should be noted that thermodynamic instability is a general characteristic of the nitrogen oxides and their related molecules and ions (e.g., NO^+, NO^-), so that a majority of the reactions of interest here are kinetically rather than energetically driven.

Commercial NO, which is of course stored under compression, invariably contains impurities. Principally, these are N_2O and NO_2, but lesser amounts of N_2, O_2, and N_2O_3 are usually present as well. Formation of the two main contaminants is due to a disproportionation reaction [Eq. (2)], whose rate is vanishingly slow at 1 atm and below but becomes appre-

$$3 \ NO(g) \rightarrow N_2O(g) + NO_2(g) \qquad (2)$$

ciable at elevated pressures.[2] For this reason, purification of commercial NO, most particularly for removal of NO_2, is essential to its use in either research or clinical contexts. Once purified, NO can be safely stored in glass vessels at 1 atm pressure, employing vacuum line and/or septum and syringe methodology for access.[3a,b] Since the normal (1 atm) melting and boiling temperatures for NO are 109.5 and 121.4 K, respectively, purification is facilitated by the fact that NO can be readily transported within a high vacuum system by distillation from and condensation to 77 K (liquid N_2 temperature). Although NO gas is colorless, the solid and liquid forms exhibit a pale blue color. Appearance of the very slightest degree of greenish cast in condensed NO is a sure sign of NO_2 contamination. Bright blue droplets of N_2O_3 may also appear during distillation of NO_2-contaminated NO, since NO and NO_2 readily combine to form this oxide.

Removal of NO_2 from a large excess of NO can be accomplished by passage through aqueous alkali, but a more satisfactory product can be prepared by repeated passage over 5 Å molecular sieve at 113 K, the temperature of a 2-methylbutane–liquid N_2 slush bath (Ref. 3a, p. 157). Noncondensables such as N_2 can be removed by pumping on condensed NO, but prolonged periods of pumping may result in significant loss of product, since the vapor pressure of NO is still a few millitorr at 77 K, and must be avoided.

In preparation for the study of aqueous NO systems it is important that the solvent be thoroughly deoxygenated, since NO_2, the N_2O_3 it forms in

[2] T. P. Melia, *J. Inorg. Nucl. Chem.* **27**, 95 (1965).
[3a] H. Melville and B. G. Gowenlock, "Experimental Methods in Gas Reactions." St. Martin's Press, New York, 1964.
[3b] D. F. Shriver, "The Manipulation of Air-Sensitive Compounds." McGraw-Hill, New York, 1969.

combination with NO, and the nitrite that both of these species form on interaction with water may cause side reactions, some of them catalytic. In vacuum line methodology this can be accomplished by successive freeze–pump–thaw cycles. Otherwise, sparging with N_2 or argon can be effective as long as the sparging gas is sufficiently pure, a condition best assured by passage through an O_2-absorbing solution [e.g., a Cr(II) salt] or over an appropriate catalyst (e.g., BASF R3-11).

Status of Nitric Oxide in Aqueous Media

Each of the oxides N_2O_3 and N_2O_5 produces a corresponding oxyacid on contact and direct reaction with water. These are HNO_2 (nitrous acid, nitrogen oxidation state +3), and HNO_3 (nitric acid, nitrogen oxidation state +5), respectively. Their formation occurs in simple, nonredox, hydrolytic reactions [Eqs. (3) and (4)], and these oxides are chemical anhy-

$$N_2O_3 + H_2O \rightleftharpoons 2\,HNO_2 \tag{3}$$
$$N_2O_5 + H_2O \rightleftharpoons 2\,H^+ + 2\,NO_3^- \tag{4}$$

drides, in the same sense that CO_2 is the anhydride of diprotic carbonic acid, H_2CO_3. The dianion of a diprotic oxyacid containing two nitrogen atoms in average oxidation state +2 (that of NO) is well known in the compound sodium trioxodinitrate ($Na_2N_2O_3$, Angeli's salt). Aqueous trioxodinitrate decomposes to yield nitrous oxide and nitrite [Eq. (5)], in the

$$2\,HN_2O_3^-(aq) \rightarrow N_2O(g) + 2\,NO_2^-(aq) + H_2O \tag{5}$$

range about pH 4.0–8.0 in which the monoanion $HN_2O_3^-$ predominates. However, at higher acidity (pH $\leq$ 3) the principal decomposition product is NO [Eq. (6)],[4] and because of this relationship NO was at one time

$$H_2N_2O_3(aq) \rightarrow 2\,NO(g) + H_2O \tag{6}$$

widely believed to be the chemical anhydride of $H_2N_2O_3$. In other words, Eq. (6) was thought to be reversible, and aqueous solutions of NO were assumed to contain that species and its conjugate anions $HN_2O_3^-$ and $N_2O_3^{2-}$. Traces of this view of NO still occasionally appear in the literature, although it is now known that Eq. (6) occurs via an essentially irreversible chain process, that the NO molecule is seen by UV spectroscopy to be nearly completely unaffected by the presence of H_2O solvent, and that no oxygen isotope exchange occurs between NO and H_2O in the absence of

[4] F. T. Bonner and B. Ravid, *Inorg. Chem.* **14**, 558 (1975); M. N. Hughes and P. E. Wimbledon, *J. Chem. Soc., Dalton Trans.* 703 (1976).

NO_2.[5] The low water solubility of NO (1.7×10^{-3} M at $25°$ and P_{NO} of 1 atm) is comparable to that of other nonhydrolyzable molecules such as N_2 and CO. This hydrophobic property of NO enables the small diatomic molecule to cross cell boundaries freely and efficiently, and it is without doubt an important factor in the extraordinary range of its physiological functions.

Radical Character of Nitric Oxide

Because the NO molecule contains an odd number (11) of valence shell electrons it is a radical. In molecular orbital terminology, combination of the single $2s$ and three $2p$ atomic orbitals of N and O forms four bonding $[\sigma_{2s}, \pi_{2p} (2), \text{ and } \sigma_{2p}]$ and four antibonding $[\sigma^*_{2s}, \pi^*_{2p} (2), \text{ and } \sigma^*_{2p}]$ molecular orbitals. The energy level occupancy sequence for these orbitals is $\sigma_{2s} < \sigma^*_{2s} < \pi_{2p} < \sigma_{2p} < \pi^*_{2p} < \sigma^*_{2p}$, and hence the ground state configuration for NO is $\sigma_{2s}^2 \sigma^*_{2s}^2 \pi_{2p}^4 \sigma_{2p}^2 \pi^*_{2p}^1$, giving the molecule a bond order of 2 1/2. Unlike the NO_2 molecule and most other single electron radicals, NO has little tendency to combine with itself in the gas phase. The dimer molecule N_2O_2 is nearly undetectable in NO gas, in contrast to the ease of formation of N_2O_4 by NO_2 radicals. Liquid NO, on the other hand, contains a significant concentration of the dimer, and the solid is known to consist almost entirely of N_2O_2 molecules.

The reaction of NO with NO_2 to form N_2O_3 is an example of bimolecular radical combination, in which electron spin pairing occurs to yield a nonradical product. Most such reactions exhibit zero or near-zero activation energy, and they occur at rates close to the rates of bimolecular encounter. Both the NO + NO_2 and NO_2 + NO_2 reactions fit that description in aqueous solution. A second important example of NO radical recombination is its reaction with superoxide to form peroxonitrite [Eq. (7)], a product

$$NO + O_2^- \rightarrow {}^-OONO \qquad (7)$$

that disappears rapidly at physiological pH, largely because it undergoes rapid isomerization to form nitrate (NO_3^-). Aside from these and a small number of additional examples, free radical character is not a prominent feature of the reported aqueous chemistry of NO. This may be due in part to the fact that, unlike the case for most other radicals, the electron spin resonance (ESR) signal of NO is severely broadened by spin delocalization, rendering this powerful radical detection and characterization method essentially unavailable for use in aqueous NO studies.

[5] F. T. Bonner, *Inorg. Chem.* **9**, 190 (1970).

One-Step Oxidation of Nitric Oxide: NO^+ and Nitrosation

Removal of the lone π^* (antibonding) electron from the ground state NO molecule yields a diamagnetic cation of bond order 3. The nitrosonium ion NO^+ is a well-characterized species that occurs in numerous compounds, is isoelectronic with N_2, and exhibits the special stability associated with the presence of a triple covalent bond. The nitrogen in NO^+ is in the same (+3) oxidation state as that of nitrite (NO_2^-), nitrous acid (HNO_2), and its anhydride N_2O_3. Addition of an NO^+-containing compound (e.g., $NOBF_4$) to water results in a prompt hydrolysis reaction that proceeds nearly to completion [Eq. (8)]. However, the NO^+ ion is readily detectable

$$NO^+ + H_2O \rightarrow H^+ + HNO_2 \qquad (8)$$

in solutions of nitrite under conditions of very high acidity.[6]

The antibonding electron of ground state NO is relatively easily removed (ionization potential 9.25 eV), and much of the characteristic oxidation chemistry of NO is determined by this circumstance. Even in covalent compounds containing +3 nitrogen the NO^+ group can assert a significant presence, for example, in the nitrosyl halides XNO, which form in direct reaction between NO and elemental halogens X_2 [Eq. (9)]. These molecules

$$X_2 + 2\,NO \rightarrow 2\,XNO \qquad (X = F, Cl, Br) \qquad (9)$$

have a bent structure ($\sphericalangle$X–NO 120°), possess a high degree of polarity, and yield HNO_2 on hydrolysis.

The compounds ClNO and BrNO are well known to act as NO^+ carriers in nitrosation, a class of reactions characterized by attack of NO^+ or an NO^+ carrier at a nucleophilic center. A prominent example is found in the formation of N-nitrosamines from secondary amines [Eq. (10)].

$$R^1R^2NH + HNO_2 \rightarrow R^1R^2N-NO + H_2O \qquad (10)$$

Other nitrosating agents include N_2O_3 and nitrosyl thiocyanate (ONSCN). The N_2O_3 molecule is known to occur in two isomeric forms, the more stable of which is asymmetric ($ON-NO_2$) and the other linear: $O^{\diagdown}{}^{N}{}^{\diagdown}O^{\diagdown}{}^{N}{}^{\diagdown}O$. There is evidence that the latter species is a much more reactive reagent than its isomer, that it forms initially on recombination of NO and NO_2 from the gas phase to solution, and that it can act as a nitrosation agent at neutral and alkaline pH.[7]

[6] G. K. S. Prakash, L. Heiliger, and G. H. Olah, *Inorg. Chem.* **29**, 4965 (1990); Y. Ko, F. T. Bonner, G. B. Crull, and G. S. Harbison, *Inorg. Chem.* **32**, 3316 (1993).

[7] B. C. Challis and S. A. Kyrtopoulos, *J. Chem. Soc., Perkin Trans. 1*, 299 (1979); B. C. Challis and S. A. Kyrtopoulos, *J. Chem. Soc., Perkin Trans. 2*, 1296 (1978).

Nitric oxide itself is not counted among the nitrosation agents. It can be seen from Eq. (10) that for NO to form nitrosamines by reacting with secondary amines it would be required to detach a nitrogen-bound hydrogen atom, but NO reactions with amines lead preferentially to the formation of adducts containing an -N_2O_2 group.[8] In some cases these compounds (Drago adducts), which are generally prepared under nonaqueous conditions, can be employed for controlled release of NO gas.[9] Another example of a compound containing the -N_2O_2 group is nitrosohydroxylamine sulfonate, formed by reaction of NO with sulfite under alkaline aqueous conditions [Eq. (11)].[10] The -N_2O_2 group in this compound has been shown

$$2 \, NO + SO_3^{2-} \rightarrow [SO_3 \cdot N_2O_2]^{2-} \tag{11}$$

crystallographically to incorporate bonding between NO groups[10]:

$$\left[O_3S-N \begin{array}{c} O \\ \diagdown NO \end{array} \right]^{2-}$$

One-Step Reduction of Nitric Oxide: HNO and NO⁻

Nitric oxide is readily reduced by a variety of reducing agents, and in the case of single electron reagents such as Fe(II) a product containing nitrogen in the +1 oxidation state must be anticipated. The principal known species in that category are nitrous oxide (N_2O) and *trans*-hyponitrous acid ($H_2N_2O_2$). (As in the case of the relationship between NO and $H_2N_2O_3$, N_2O is not the chemical anhydride of *trans*-hyponitrous acid.)

Single electron reduction of NO is known to yield the reactive transient species HNO ("nitroxyl") or, more prominently at physiological pH, its conjugate anion NO⁻ (pK_a for HNO is 4.7). It has been established, for example, that in the reduction of NO by aqueous Fe(II), HNO/NO⁻ is the primary (but transient) product, in a process that is predominantly second order in a dinitrosyl complex $[Fe(NO)_2(aq)]^{2+}$.[11] The final nitrogenous reac-

[8] R. S. Drago and F. E. Paulik, *J. Am. Chem. Soc.* **82**, 96 (1960); R. S. Drago and B. R. Karstetter, *J. Am. Chem. Soc.* **83**, 1819 (1961); R. Longhi, R. O. Ragsdale, and R. S. Drago, *Inorg. Chem.* **1**, 768 (1962).

[9] R. O. Ragsdale, B. R. Karstetter, and R. S. Drago, *Inorg. Chem.* **4**, 420 (1965).

[10] R. S. Nyholm and L. Rannitt, *Inorg. Synth.* **5**, 117 (1957); G. A. Jeffrey and H. P. Stadler, *J. Chem. Soc.*, 146 (1951).

[11] F. T. Bonner and K. A. Pearsall, *Inorg. Chem.* **21**, 1973 (1982); K. A. Pearsall and F. T. Bonner, *Inorg. Chem.* **31**, 1978 (1982).

tion product is N_2O, rapidly formed by an essentially diffusion-controlled dehydrative dimerization process [Eq. (12)]. Additional known solution

$$HNO + HNO \rightarrow N_2O + H_2O \tag{12}$$

reactions of HNO/NO^- include reduction to N_2 by hydroxylamine [Eq. (13)],[12] nitrosylation of $Ni(CN)_4{}^{2-}$ [Eq. (14)][13] and of Fe(III) heme proteins [Eq. (15)],[14] reaction with NO to form N_2O and nitrite [Eq. (16)],[15] reaction with sulfhydryl groups to form disulfides [Eq. (17)],[16] and nitrosylation of the Fe(III) center in cytochrome d.[17]

$$HNO + NH_2OH \rightarrow N_2 + 2\,H_2O \tag{13}$$
$$Ni(CN)_4{}^{2-} + NO^- \rightarrow [Ni(NO)(CN)_3]^{2-} + CN^- \tag{14}$$
$$Hb^+ + NO^- \rightarrow HbNO \tag{15}$$
$$2\,NO + NO^- \rightarrow N_2O + NO_2{}^- \tag{16}$$

$$HNO + C_6H_5SH \rightarrow C_6H_5SNHOH \xrightarrow{C_6H_5SH} C_6H_5SSC_6H_5 + NH_2OH \tag{17}$$

The spontaneous thermal decomposition of trioxodinitrate (Angeli's salt) [Eq. (5)] has been thoroughly studied as a source of HNO in aqueous solution. It has been shown to occur, in the range around pH 4.0–8.0 in which the monoanion $HN_2O_3{}^-$ predominates, via the reversible dissociation step [Eq. (18)], followed by rapid dimerization to release N_2O [Eq. (11)].[4]

$$HN_2O_3{}^- \rightleftharpoons HNO + NO_2{}^- \tag{18}$$

A similarly well-established HNO source reaction is the self-decomposition of N-hydroxybenzenesulfonamide (Piloty's acid) [Eq. (19)].[18] As in the case

$$C_6H_5SO_2NHO^- \rightleftharpoons HNO + C_6H_5SO_2{}^- \tag{19}$$

of trioxodinitrate monoanion, the initial dissociation step that releases the transient intermediate has been shown to occur reversibly.

The reduction of NO by hydroxylamine is another thoroughly studied reaction in which HNO/NO^- is known to appear as a primary intermediate product [Eq. (20)]. In this case the active reducing agent is the O-depro-

$$2\,NO + 2\,NH_2OH \rightarrow N_2 + N_2O + 3\,H_2O \tag{20}$$

[12] F. T. Bonner, L. S. Dzelzkalns, and J. A. Bonucci, *Inorg. Chem.* **17**, 2487 (1978).

[13] F. T. Bonner and M. J. Akhtar, *Inorg. Chem.* **20**, 3155 (1981).

[14] D. A. Bazylinski and T. C. Hollocher, *J. Am. Chem. Soc.* **107**, 7982 (1985).

[15] M. Grätzel, S. Taniguchi, and A. Henglein, *Ber. Bunsen–Ges. Phys. Chem.* **74**, 1003 (1970).

[16] M. P. Doyle, S. N. Mahapatro, R. D. Broene, and J. K. Guy, *J. Am. Chem. Soc.* **110**, 593 (1988).

[17] F. T. Bonner, M. N. Hughes, R. K. Poole, and R. I. Scott, *Biochim. Biophys. Acta* **1056**, 133 (1991).

[18] F. T. Bonner and Y. Ko, *Inorg. Chem.* **31**, 2514 (1992).

tonated hydroxylamine anion NH_2O^-, and the overall reaction proceeds via a three-step mechanism [Eqs. (21)–(23)].[19] The first step in the mechanism

$$NH_2O^- + NO \rightarrow HNO + HNO^- \tag{21}$$
$$HNO^- + NO \rightarrow N_2O + OH^- \tag{22}$$
$$NH_2O^- + HNO \rightarrow N_2 + OH^- + H_2O \tag{23}$$

[Eq. (21)] consists of hydrogen atom abstraction to NO. As previously mentioned, the NO molecule has essentially zero power of nitrosation, and for that reason there has been some tendency to regard NO as having zero H-atom abstraction capacity as well. However, Eq. (21) provides a well-established counterexample. In studies of NO reduction by N-alkylated hydroxylamine compounds it has also been found that NO can and does abstract an H atom from nitrogen in the monoalkylated species $RNHO^-$. Surprisingly, NO also abstracts hydrogen from an α-carbon atom in its reaction with dialkylated hydroxylamines R_2NO^-.[20] H-atom abstraction by NO from hyponitrous acid has also been observed under conditions of very high acidity.

The anion NO^- has two antibonding electrons, giving it a bond order of 2, and it is isoelectronic with O_2. In their ground states, both NO^- and O_2 contain a single electron in each of two π^* antibonding orbitals, with their spins aligned. This configuration is characteristic of a triplet state. The first excited state in both cases is known to be singlet, in which the two antibonding electrons occupy a single π^* orbital, with spins opposed. The reactivity of singlet O_2 is well known to be greater than that of triplet O_2 by several orders of magnitude. The known reversibility of Eq. (18) strongly suggests that, in the trioxodinitrate decomposition reaction, the HNO/NO^- intermediate product must appear in the singlet state. The HNO/NO^- product of the NO–hydroxylamine reduction reaction [Eq. (21)] has been shown to be substantially less reactive than that of the trioxodinitrate intermediate [Eq. (18)], suggesting that the NO^- in this case is released in its triplet ground state.[19,20]

[19] F. T. Bonner and N.-Y. Wang, *Inorg. Chem.* **25**, 1858 (1986).
[20] N.-Y. Wang and F. T. Bonner, *Inorg. Chem.* **25**, 1863 (1986).

[6] Nitric Oxide Measurement Using Electrochemical Methods

By Tadeusz Malinski, Stefan Mesaros, and Paul Tomboulian

Introduction

In this chapter, electrochemical methods are described for the measurement of nitric oxide in a single cell and in tissue. These newer methods for nitric oxide determination offer several features that are not available using analytical spectroscopic methods. Most important is the capability afforded by the use of ultramicroelectrodes for direct *in situ* measurements of NO in single cells near the source of NO synthesis.

Electrochemical methods currently available for nitric oxide detection are based on the electrochemical oxidation of NO on solid electrodes.[1,2] If the current generated during NO oxidation is linearly proportional to the concentration, the oxidation current can be used as an analytical signal. The current can be measured in either an amperometric or a voltammetric mode, both methods providing a quantitative signal. In the amperometric mode, current is measured while the potential at which nitric oxide is oxidized is applied and kept constant. In the voltammetric mode, the current is measured while the potential is linearly scanned through the region that includes nitric oxide oxidation. Although the amperometric method is faster than the voltammetric method, voltammetry provides not only quantitative but also qualitative information that can prove that the current measured is in fact due to NO oxidation.

Generally, the oxidation of nitric oxide on solid electrodes proceeds via a two-step EC mechanism with step (1), an electrochemical reaction, being followed by step (2), a chemical reaction. The first electrochemical step is a one-electron transfer from an NO molecule to the electrode resulting in the formation of a nitrosonium ion:

$$NO - e^- \rightarrow NO^+ \tag{1}$$

NO^+ is a relatively strong Lewis acid and in the presence of OH^- is converted to nitrite (NO_2^-):

$$NO^+ + OH^- \rightarrow HNO_2 \tag{2}$$

[1] F. Kiechle and T. Malinski, *Am. J. Clin. Pathol.* **100,** 567 (1993).
[2] S. Archer, *FASEB J.* **1,** 349 (1993).

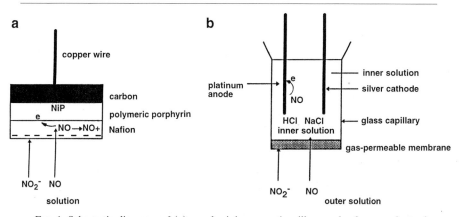

FIG. 1. Schematic diagrams of (a) porphyrinic sensor (auxillary and reference electrodes are not shown) and (b) Clark-type probe for determination of nitric oxide.

The rate of the chemical reaction [Eq. (2)] increases with increasing pH. Because the oxidation potential of nitrite in aqueous solution is only 60–80 mV more positive than that of NO, oxidation of NO on solid electrodes with scanned potential results in the transfer of two additional electrons. Thus nitrite is ultimately oxidized to nitrate, NO_3^-, the final product of electrochemical oxidation of NO.

Figure 1 shows sensors that have been developed for the electrochemical measurement of nitric oxide. One is based on the electrochemical oxidation of nitric oxide on a conductive polymeric porphyrin (porphyrinic sensor).[3] The other is based on an oxygen probe (Clark electrode) and operates in the amperometric mode.[4,5] In the porphyrinic sensor, nitric oxide is oxidized on a polymeric metalloporphyrin (n-type semiconductor) on which the oxidation reaction occurs at 630 mV [versus saturated calomel electrode (SCE)], 270 mV lower than the potential required for the comparable metal or carbon electrodes. The current efficiency (analytical signal) for the reaction is high, even at the physiological pH of 7.4.

The Clark probe consists of platinum wire as a working electrode (anode) and silver wire as the counter electrode (cathode). The electrodes are mounted in a capillary tube filled with a sodium chloride/hydrochloric acid solution separated from the analytic solution by a gas-permeable membrane. A constant potential of 0.9 V is applied, and current (analytical

[3] T. Malinski and Z. Taha, Nature (London) 358, 676 (1992).
[4] J. Janata, in "Principles of Chemical Sensors." Plenum, New York and London, 1989.
[5] K. Shibuki, Neurosci. Res. 9, 69 (1990).

signal) is measured from the electrochemical oxidation of nitric oxide on the platinum anode.

Methods

Porphyrinic Sensor

Microsensors are produced by threading a carbon fiber (diameter 7 μm, Amoco) through the pulled end of a capillary tube with about 1 cm left protruding. Nonconductive epoxy is put at the glass/fiber interface. After the epoxy cement drawn into the tip of the capillary has cured, the carbon fiber is sealed in place. The carbon fiber is then sharpened by gradual burning (propane–air microburner, 1300–1400°). The sharpened fiber is immersed in melted wax–rosin (5:1) at a controlled temperature for 5–15 sec, and after cooling is sharpened again. The flame temperature and the distance of the fiber from the flame need to be carefully controlled. The resulting electrode is a slim cylinder with a small diameter (0.5–2 μm) rather than a short taper, a geometry that aids in implantation and increases the active surface area. The tip (length 2–6 μm) is the only part of the carbon fiber where electrochemical processes can occur. For the sensor to be implanted into a cell, this length must be less than the cell thickness. The unsharpened end of the fiber is attached to a copper wire lead with silver epoxy cement.

Monomeric nickel(II) tetrakis(3-methoxy-4-hydroxyphenyl)porphyrin [Ni(II) TMHPP] is synthesized according to a procedure described previously.[6] The polymeric film of Ni(II) TMHPP is deposited on a single carbon fiber electrode from a solution of 5×10^{-4} M monomeric Ni(II) TMHPP using cyclic scanning of potential between 0.2 to 1.0 V (versus SCE) with a scan rate of 100 mV/sec for 10–15 scans. Dip coating the dried polymeric porphyrin/carbon fiber tip (3 times for 5 sec) in 1% Nafion in alcohol (Aldrich, Milwaukee, WI) produces a thin anionic film that repels or retards charged ionic species while allowing the small neutral and hydrophobic NO molecule access to the underlying catalytic surface. The sensor is interference-free from the following readily oxidizable secretory products at concentrations of at least two orders of magnitude greater than their expected physiological concentrations: epinephrine, norepinephrine, serotonin, dopamine, ascorbate, acetylcholine, glutamate, glucose, the NO-decay produced NO_2^-, and peptides containing tryptophan, tyrosine, and

---

[6] T. Malinski, B. Ciszewski, J. Bennett, J. R. Fish, and L. Czuchajowski, *J. Electrochem. Soc.* **138**, 2008 (1991).

cystine. The porphyrinic sensor has a response time of 0.1 msec at micromolar NO concentrations and 10 msec at the detection limit of 5 nM.

For *in vivo* and *in vitro* measurements of NO in tissue and blood, a catheter-protected porphyrinic NO sensor is constructed from the needle of a 22-gauge, 1-inch-long intravenous catheter/needle unit (Angiocath, Becton Dickinson, Lincoln Park, NJ) truncated and polished flat to be 5 mm shorter than a 20-gauge catheter.[7-9] A bundle of seven carbon fibers (each 7 μm in diameter, protruding 5 mm, 12 Ω cm, Amoco) is mounted inside the hollow truncated 22-gauge needle with conducting epoxy cement. After curing, the exterior of the truncated needle is coated with nonconductive epoxy (2-TON, Devcon) and allowed to cure again. The protruding 5-mm carbon fiber bundle is made more sensitive and selective for NO by covering it with polymeric porphyrin and Nafion, before calibration with NO. To implant the porphyrinic NO sensor, ventricular tissue is pierced with a standard 20-gauge angiocatheter needle (clad with its catheter containing four 400-μm ventilation holes near the tip), and subsequently advanced to the desired location. After intracavitary contact of the catheter, the tip is withdrawn 2–4 mm. The position of the catheter is secured, and the placement needle is removed and quickly replaced with the truncated 22-gauge porphyrinic NO sensor.

At an operational potential of 0.63–0.65 V, the sensor does not respond to other gases such as oxygen, carbon dioxide, and carbon monoxide. The sensor is too slow to respond to superoxide, which in the biological environment is scavenged in fast reactions with other molecules including nitric oxide ($K = 3 \times 10^9 M^{-1} \sec^{-1}$).

The quality of the fine structure of the conductive polymeric film is related to the selectivity and sensitivity of the porphyrinic sensor.[10] The film must exhibit a large catalytic effect on the oxidation of nitric oxide as well as sufficient electronic (metallic) conductivity. Both of these features depend on an organization of porphyrinic molecules in the polymeric film. The current efficiency depends on the central metal (iron $\geq$ nickel > cobalt $\geq$ zinc, copper). If the current efficiency of a given polymeric porphy-

---

[7] T. Malinski, S. Patton, B. Pierchala, E. Kubaszewski, S. Grunfeld, and K. V. S. Rao, in "Frontiers of Reactive Oxygen Species in Biology and Medicine" (K. Asada and T. Yoshikawa, eds.), p. 207. Elsevier, Amsterdam, 1994.

[8] D. J. Pinsky, M. C. Oz, S. Koga, Z. Taha, M. J. Broekman, A. J. Marcus, H. Liao, Y. Naka, J. Brett, P. J. Cannon, R. Nowygrod, T. Malinski, and D. M. Stern, *J. Clin. Invest.* **93,** 2291 (1994).

[9] D. J. Pinsky, N. Yoshifumi, N. C. Chowdhury, H. Liao, M. C. Oz, R. E. Michler, E. Kubaszewski, T. Malinski, and D. M. Stern, *Proc. Natl. Acad. Sci. U.S.A.* **91,** 12086 (1994).

[10] T. Malinski, Z. Taha, S. Grunfeld, A. Burewicz, P. Tomboulian, and F. Kiechle, *Anal. Chim. Acta* **279,** 135 (1993).

rin is not affected by changing the central metal, the film probably does not have the optimum properties for nitric oxide oxidation. The desirable properties of the film depend not only on the structure of monomeric porphyrins, but also on the amount of impurities, method of polymerization, supporting electrolyte concentration, range of potential scanned, properties of the solid support surface on which the film is plated, distribution of the electrical field (orientation of solid electrode versus counter electrode), shape of the solid electrode, thickness, and structural homogeneity of the porphyrinic film.

Response and Calibration of the Porphyrinic Sensor

Differential pulse voltammetry (DPV) and differential pulse amperometry (DPA) can be used to monitor analytical signals, where current is linearly proportional to NO concentration. In DPV, a potential modulated with rectangular pulses (amplitude 1–40 mV) is linearly scanned from 0.4 to 0.8 V. The resulting voltammogram (alternating current versus voltage plot) contains a peak due to NO oxidation. The maximum current of the peak should be observed at a potential of 0.63 to 0.67 V (at 40 mV pulse amplitude), the characteristic potential for NO oxidation on the porphyrinic/Nafion sensor. Differential pulse voltammetry is used primarily to verify that the current measured is due to NO oxidation. In DPA measurements, a potential of 0.63 to 0.67 V modulated with rectangular pulses is kept constant, and a plot of an alternating current versus time is recorded. The amperometric method (with a response time better than 10 msec) provides rapid quantitative measurement of minute changes of NO concentration. Differential pulse voltammetry also provides quantitative information but requires approximately 5–40 sec for the voltammogram to be recorded, and DPV is therefore used mainly for qualitative analysis.

Many other electroanalytical techniques including normal pulse voltammetry, square wave voltammetry, fast scan voltammetry, and coulometry can be used to measure nitric oxide with a porphyrinic sensor. Amperograms and voltammograms can be recorded with two- or three-electrode systems. However, differential pulse voltammograms should always be recorded in the three-electrode systems in order to obtain accurate and reproducible values of peak potentials. The three-electrode systems consist of a NO sensor working electrode, a platinum wire (0.25 mm) counter electrode, and a silver/silver chloride electrode or SCE as the reference electrode. The reference electrode is omitted from the two-electrode system. The porphyrinic sensor can be connected to any fast response potentiostat for amperometric or coulometric measurements, or to a voltammetric analyzer (a potentiostat and waveform generator) for voltammetric measurements. An instrumental current sensitivity of 100 pA/inch of recorder display will be sufficient for most of the measurements using a multifiber sensor. For single fiber experiments, at least 10 times more sensitivity is required, which is readily achieved by adding a low noise current-sensitive preamplifier to the potentiostat. The sensor can be calibrated with saturated NO solution at 2 mM as a standard, by preparing a calibration curve or using the standard addition method.

A typical amperometric response of the sensor under different flow conditions is shown in Fig. 2. In static solutions where mass transport of NO to the electrode is due only to a diffusion process, a linear increase in current reaching a plateau is followed by a slow decrease in current due to NO oxidation (Fig. 2a). In a flowing or stirred homogeneous NO solution, a rapid increase in current reaching a plateau occurs after release of NO (Fig. 2b). In heterogeneous flowing solutions with high localized concentrations of NO such as blood, the amperometric signal is observed in the form of a peak (Fig. 2c).

Clark Probe for Nitric Oxide Detection

The Clark probe, originally designed for the detection of oxygen, is a glass pipette with the opening sealed by a gas-permeable membrane of thick rubber. Only a low molecular weight gas can readily diffuse into the glass pipette through the membrane, and be oxidized or reduced at the

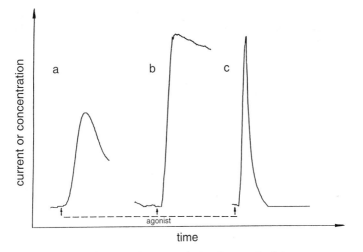

Fig. 2. Amperograms (current–time curves) showing porphyrinic sensor responses for nitric oxide in (a) homogeneous static solution, (b) homogeneous laminar flow solution, and (c) heterogeneous laminar flow solution.

surface of the metal electrode (working electrode). In the Clark probe for oxygen detection, a working electrode (platinum) is polarized with a potential -0.8 V (versus silver counter/reference electrode), and current due to the reduction of oxygen is observed. For the detection of nitric oxide with the Clark probe, only the polarization of the electrodes must be changed. To oxidize nitric oxide on the platinum electrode, the polarization has to be reversed to 0.8 V (versus the silver electrode) instead of -0.8 V for oxygen detection. As electrolyte in the Clark probe for NO detection, a mixture of NaCl and HCl (1 M) can be used.

The Clark probe operates in the amperometric mode with direct current measured using a simple electronic potentiostat (current–voltage converter). As an analytical signal, current is measured at a constant potential of 0.8–0.9 V. For a Clark probe made with a glass pipette diameter of 300 μm, 50-μm platinum anode, and 200-μm silver cathode, the current developed is between 3 and 100 pA/μM. This relatively low current is due to several factors, of which the most important is a low net NO concentration in the glass pipette as compared with the concentration at the source of NO release. The detection limit of the electrode, about 10^{-8} M, can be achieved by measuring NO in a homogeneous synthetic solution where a constant NO concentration can be established on both sides of the gas-permeable membrane.

When the probe is used for measurements of NO concentrations in biological materials with heterogeneous environments, however, several limitations affect the utility of the Clark probe. The electrode response is slow, 1.4 to 3.2 sec for 50% rise time and 2.2–3.5 sec for 75% rise time at an NO concentration of 1 μM. This response time is about 1000 times slower than a porphyrinic sensor and results not only from the long distance NO must diffuse to the electrode, but also the significant consumption of NO by redox reactions outside as well as inside the probe. In addition, because of its larger size, the electrode cannot be placed exactly at the site of high NO concentration, the membrane of the cell. NO that is supplied to the probe by diffusion is consumed not only in fast reactions such as with superoxide but also in much slower reactions with oxygen and sulfhydryl groups. The fraction of the NO which finally reaches the capillary probe chamber can be oxidized by oxygen, which diffuses easily through the membrane and is present in the capillary at concentrations much higher than those of nitric oxide.

The Clark probe also has a very high temperature coefficient (10 times higher than the porphyrinic sensor) due to the change of NO diffusion rate through the membrane with temperature. The temperature coefficient of the Clark probe is 14–18% per degree Celsius, which may be viewed as a significant change of current (baseline drift) equivalent to changes of NO concentration of 65–80 nM per degree Celsius. Therefore, the temperature during NO measurement has to be carefully controlled (within ±0.1°) to avoid small fluctuations of temperature that can lead to serious errors. The Clark probe is sensitive not only to O_2 and NO but also to N_2O and CO. Significant changes in the baseline will also be observed due to fluctuations of CO_2 concentration in the inner solution of the probe. This effect is more noticeable at lower pH where the electrode is most sensitive to NO.

Most of the commercially available miniaturized oxygen probes (Clark electrodes, Clark probes) can be used for detection of nitric oxide. A low cost probe can be relatively easily prepared as follows, using a glass pipette, silver and platinum wires, and a gas-permeable membrane. The pipette tip (1–3 cm length) with a diameter of 150–350 μm is flame polished. The pipette is then filed with an acidic solution of electrolyte to provide sufficient conductivity and environment for NO oxidation; usually 30 mM NaCl and 0.13 mM HCl are used. The optimal pH is about pH 3.5; at higher pH, electrode sensitivity will be significantly reduced, and in basic solution the probe shows high noise levels and is not sensitive to NO. A soft wax (beeswax), melted or dissolved in turpentine, is painted on the outer surface of the pipette, and the tip is then sealed with a gas-permeable membrane. Several different materials can be used as gas-permeable membranes: Teflon, polyethylene, silicon rubber, and chloroprene rubber; the chloroprene rubber membrane is easiest to prepare. Common rubber cement can also be used as a material for simple preparation of the gas-permeable membrane. The electrode tip can be placed on the surface of a blob of rubber cement or in a solution of chloroprene rubber. The sealing procedure has to be repeated two to three times to obtain sufficient membrane strength. The membrane thickness will vary depending on the material used for membrane preparation. Teflon membranes will usually have a thickness of 6–8 μm, and the chloroprene rubber membrane will be 1–5 μm.

A Teflon-coated platinum wire (diameter 50–100 μm) is then inserted into the pipette. The Teflon coating is removed by gradual burning from the wire tip. About 100–200 μm of bare platinum wire must be exposed to the solution and closely positioned at the membrane at the orifice. As a counter/reference electrode, a silver wire (diameter 100–200 μm) is inserted into the pipette. The Clark probe can be connected to any commercially available potentiostat with the capability of measuring small currents (pA). The platinum electrode must have a positive potential of 0.9–0.8 V relative to the silver electrode. Any current change can be continuously monitored with a chart recorder or storage oscilloscope. The Clark probe can also be connected to a simple and inexpensive current–voltage converter made of an FET operational amplifier.[2]

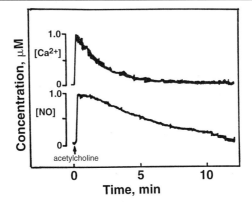

FIG. 3. Time course of nitric oxide production and calcium flux measured simultaneously in a single endothelial cell.

Single Cell Measurements with a Porphyrinic Sensor

By use of a manual or motorized computer-controlled micromanipulator with 0.2-μm x–y–z resolution, the porphyrinic sensor can be implanted into a single cell, or placed on the surface of the cell membrane, or kept at a controlled distance (0.2–0.5 μm) from a cell membrane surface.[11,12] The highest concentration of NO released from a cell containing constitutive nitric oxide synthase (cNOS) is on the cell membrane. For measurements of NO on the cell membrane, a bundle of 2–5 carbon fibers mounted on an L-shaped capillary is effective. The cell can be growing on any type of solid support such as a glass or plastic plate. An injection of the agonist near the cell to stimulate NO release requires application by a picopipette or femtopipette. Depending on the forces applied during the injection, an initial release of NO may be due to a shear stress.

Figure 3 shows a typical amperometric response of the porphyrinic sensor to NO released from a single endothelial cell. In this experiment with rabbit aortic endothelium exposed to acetylcholine, the sensor detected NO at the cell membrane surface within 5 sec. The surface NO concentration reached a maximum of 950 ± 70 nM within 9 sec. Simultaneous with NO measurements, intracellular calcium ion ($[Ca^{2+}]_i$) measurements were performed with fura-2-acetoxymethyl ester (Fura2-AM) and a fluorescence

---

[11] T. Malinski, Z. Taha, S. Grunfeld, S. Patton, M. Kapturczak, and P. Tomboulian, *Biochem. Biophys. Res. Commun.* **193**, 1076 (1993).

[12] J. Balligand, D. Ungureanu-Longrois, W. Simmons, D. Pimental, T. Malinski, M. Kapturczak, Z. Taha, C. Lowestein, A. Davidoff, R. Kelly, T. Smith, and T. Michel, *J. Biol. Chem.* **269**, 27580 (1994).

imaging system. The intracellular calcium increased at a rate of 130 ± 10 nM/sec within 3 sec after the addition of acetylcholine.

Intracellular calcium remained near maximum levels (0.90 ± 0.07 μM) for 10–45 sec after application of bradykinin, followed by a decline and return to basal levels within 360 sec. Because cell surface NO levels represent NO synthase activation as well as subsequent diffusion within both the cytosol and cell membrane, NO detected at the cellular surface would be expected to outlast the calcium transient. The rapid release of NO was observed after injection of 10 nmol of acetylcholine with a nanoinjector. This maximum NO concentration will be the same if the measurement of NO is performed on the membrane of a single isolated cell, or on the membrane of single cells in the group of similar cells, or cells in a tissue. However, the duration of the plateau will be much different and will depend on the number of neighboring cells. For an isolated cell, the duration of plateau time will be shorter due to the rapid depletion of NO and the higher concentration gradient. The membrane of the cell is a storage reservoir for NO, and a small membrane volume can develop a relatively high concentration within a short period when NO is released by the NO-producing enzyme. From an analytical viewpoint, the detection of NO at the site of highest concentration, the surface of the cell membrane, is a most convenient and accurate method of measurement of endogenous NO.

Measurements in Tissue with a Porphyrinic Sensor

Figure 4a shows a typical amperogram of nitric oxide in rat mesenteric resistance artery of a 15-week-old rat. A multifiber porphyrinic sensor (20

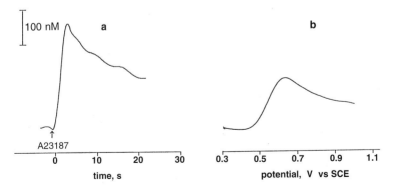

FIG. 4. Amperogram (a) and differential pulse voltammogram (b) of nitric oxide release from endothelial cells of rabbit mesenteric resistance artery in response to acetylcholine (a); the differential pulse voltammogram was recorded after 10 sec from time of injection of acetylcholine. The potential scan rate was 25 mV/sec and the pulse amplitude 40 mV.

fibers, diameter 35 μm) was inserted in the lumen of the resistance artery. Twenty microliters of a 1 mM solution of the calcium ionophore A23187 was then injected to reach a final concentration of 10 μM in the organ chamber. Immediately after injection of the calcium ionophore, a rapid increase of NO concentration was observed. The rate of concentration increase was 160 nM/sec, and peak concentration was reached 2.2 sec after injection of calcium ionophore. Figure 4b shows a differential pulse voltammogram recorded 10 sec after injection of calcium ionophore with the potential scanned from 0.30 to 1.00 V, using a scan rate of 25 mV/sec. A peak potential at 650 mV indicates that the electrochemical process is due to oxidation of nitric oxide, and the peak current indicates that the average NO concentration during the time of voltammogram measurement is 130 nM.

Measurement in Vivo with Porphyrinic Sensor

Figure 5 presents a typical amperometric curve obtained for *in vivo* measurements of NO after the administration of acetylcholine. The porphyrinic sensor was stored in a physiological saline solution spiked with 1000 U/ml of heparin for 15 min before the implantation in the left ear auricular vein of the rabbit. About 13 sec after intravenous injection of acetylcholine (1 ml, 10 pM), a peak due to NO release was observed, reaching a maximum concentration of 320 nM. This response represents a significant increase

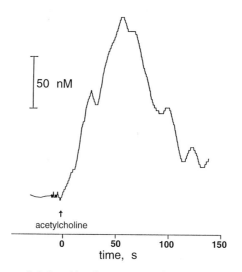

Fig. 5. Amperogram of nitric oxide release measured *in vivo* in rabbit ear (auricular vein) with a porphyrinic sensor protected by an intravenous catheter.

of NO concentration from its basal level in blood of 3–5 nM. For *in vivo* measurements, this sensor was calibrated using flow system and a dextran (molecular weight 70,000)/saline solution with viscosity similar to that of blood (3.5 cP).

Conclusion

Although considerable effort may be required to establish conditions for obtaining a stable, high sensitivity, miniature porphyrinic sensor, the electrochemical approach can lead to the detection of low NO concentrations (10^{-8}–10^{-9} M) in biological environments with short (millisecond) response times to nitric oxide. A wide spectrum of information about kinetics and the dynamics of nitric oxide release can be obtained that are not available by other methods. The sensor permits an extensive exploration of the reactivities of NO with redox molecules, as well as analysis of NO propagation *in vitro* or *in vivo*. The method is ideally suited for the characterization of labile systems for which conditions must be met for preparation of spectroscopic samples.

The Clark probe can be used for measurement of NO in synthetic homogeneous solutions containing high concentrations of nitric oxide, for example, for studies of NO release from drugs. However, the Clark probe has very limited application for measurement of NO from biological samples due to the high temperature coefficient, slow response time, interferences, baseline drift, and relatively large size.

[7] Electrochemical Methods for Detection of Nitric Oxide

By DANAE CHRISTODOULOU, SETSUKO KUDO, JOHN A. COOK, MURALI C. KRISHNA, ALLEN MILES, MATTHEW B. GRISHAM, RAMACHANDRAN MURUGESAN, PETER C. FORD, and DAVID A. WINK

Introduction

Nitric oxide (NO) has been shown to be an important bioregulator molecule involved in physiological functions such as blood pressure control, neurotransmission, and immune surveillance.[1–3] This diatomic molecular

---

[1] S. Moncada, R. M. J. Palmer, and E. A. Higgs, *Pharmacol. Rev.* **43,** 109 (1991).
[2] P. L. Feldman, O. W. Griffith, and D. J. Stuehr, *Chem. Eng. News* December 20, 26 (1992).
[3] L. J. Ignarro, *Annu. Rev. Pharmacol. Toxicol.* **30,** 535 (1990).

METHODS IN ENZYMOLOGY, VOL. 268

radical is only transiently stable under biological conditions, making detection of this species challenging. Detection of NO has required either techniques that extract NO from tissues or the analysis of oxidation products such as nitrite and nitrate (for review see Ref. 4). As such, these methods make spatial specificity and real-time analysis difficult. Electrochemical techniques for monitoring NO concentrations *in vivo* as well as *in vitro* present an attractive alternative possibly useful for real-time measurement. This chapter discusses some currently used electrochemical techniques for the measurement of NO.

Electrochemical detection of oxygen has utilized an electrode called a Clark electrode[5] which consists of a capillary tube with a gas-permeable membrane and a platinum (Pt) electrode in acidic solutions. This style of electrode provides an amperometric technique that monitors the reduction of O_2 at $E = -0.9$ V versus SSCE (standard saturated calomel electrode):

$$O_2 + 2e^- \rightarrow H_2O_2 \tag{1}$$

Nitric oxide has a similar reduction potential as oxygen (-0.9 V versus SSCE), and under anaerobic conditions, the Clark-style electrode can also be used for the detection of NO. However, under aerobic conditions, oxygen and nitric oxide cannot be differentiated using this method.

Shibuki described an electrochemical method to detect NO using a miniature oxygen electrode.[6,7] However, instead of monitoring reduction, the potential was maintained at $+0.9$ V[8] where oxygen would not interfere. This NO-sensitive device consisted of a capillary tube sealed with gas-permeable membrane (chloroprene rubber) and equipped with a Pt working electrode and a Pt counter electrode in a 30 mM NaCl/0.3 mM HCl solution. The gas-permeable membrane permitted passage or low molecular weight gases only. This method is based on the following reaction:

$$2\,NO + 4\,OH^- \rightarrow 2HNO_3 + 6\,e^- + 2\,H^+ \tag{2}$$

Shibuki and Okada demonstrated the use of this electrode for the measurement of NO in brain slices.[8,9] This electrochemical technique is very sensitive: NO concentrations as low as 10 nM can be measured, and current versus NO concentration plots are linear up to 400 nM. This approach provided the first electrochemical method for virtual real-time analysis of NO.[9] Despite the sensitivity of the electrode, there are a few drawbacks

[4] S. Archer, *FASEB J.* **7**, 349 (1993).
[5] L. C. Clark, *Trans. Am. Soc. Artif. Intern. Organs* **2**, 41 (1956).
[6] K. Shibuki, *Brain Res.* **487**, 96 (1989).
[7] K. Shibuki, *J. Physiol. (London)* **422**, 321 (1990).
[8] K. Shibuki, *Neurosci. Res.* **9**, 69 (1990).
[9] K. Shibuki, and D. Okada, *Nature (London)* **349**, 326 (1991).

that can limit its use in biological and chemical experiments. One is that the current is not linear with NO concentrations above 1 μM.[8] The second is that of rupturing of the membrane and current saturation effects, which are observed when the electrode is exposed in a single experiment to NO at concentrations over 1 μM over any given period of time.

These points result, in part, from the fact that an acidic solution of nitrate and nitrite is formed during NO oxidation, either at the electrode or by oxygen. A variety of nitrogen oxide species can be generated in acidic solution under these conditions. NO can be formed in these reactions and/or consumed via these reactions, accounting for the instability that is sometimes observed with this style of electrode and the deviation from linearity between current and NO concentrations above 1–5 μM. Therefore, the Shibuki electrochemical technique is generally limited to measuring low NO concentrations over short periods of time. However, one of the ideal aspects of this electrode is that currently available oxygen electrodes used for measuring gas *in vivo* can readily be converted to monitoring NO.

Several reports have described the use of porphyrin-coated electrodes for detection of NO.[10,11] These electrodes can be used to measure NO at the cellular level in several tissues.[10] This technique, like the Shibuki design, utilizes electrochemical oxidation of NO. Malinski and Taha described nickel 3-methoxy-4-hydroxphenyl porphyrin coated on the surface of a carbon fiber for detection of NO at +0.8–0.7 V versus SSCE.[10] The use of porphyrin-coated electrodes provides a stable response to NO for a wide range of concentrations from 10 nM to 200 μM. Although the electrode is stable to high concentrations of NO, there are some drawbacks with this method. Because the surface of the electrode is in direct contact with the medium, a variety of biological substances can interfere with NO detection. This presents severe limitations when using this style of electrode to detect endogenously formed NO *in vivo*.[12] This chapter addresses the fabrication procedures of these electrodes, their potential uses, and limitations.

Materials and Methods

Nickel tetra-N-methylpyridiniumporphyrin chloride [Ni(TMPP)] and tetra-N-methylpyridiniumporphyrin chloride (TMPP) are purchased from MidCentury Chemicals (Posen, IL) and used without further purification.

[10] T. Malinski and Z. Taha, *Nature (London)* **358**, 676 (1992).
[11] D. A. Wink, R. W. Nims, J. F. Darbyshire, D. Christodoulou, I. Hanbauer, G. W. Cox, F. Laval, J. Laval, J. A. Cook, M. C. Krishna, W. DeGraff, and J. B. Mitchell, *Chem. Res. Toxicol.* **7**, 519 (1994).
[12] D. A. Wink, D. Christodoulou, M. Ho, M. C. Krishna, J. A. Cook, H. Haut, J. K. Randolph, M. Sullivan, G. Coia, R. Murray, and T. Meyer, *Methods (San Diego)* **7**, 71 (1995).

This series of porphyrins is readily dissolved (2 mM) in 0.1 M NaOH. Four percent Nafion solutions are purchased from Aldrich (Milwaukee, WI). Ascorbic acid, sodium nitrate, and dopamine are purchased from Sigma (St. Louis, MO) and made up as stock solutions in phosphate-buffered saline (PBS), pH 7.4 (BioWhittaker, Walkersville, MD). S-Nitroso-N-acetylpenicillamine (SNAP) and 3-morpholinosydnonium (SIN-1) are purchased from Alexis (San Diego, CA). Aliquots of the stock solution are added to the PBS solution giving the final concentrations indicated. (Dopamine solutions must be prepared fresh daily and protected from light.) All experiments are carried out at room temperature in PBS unless otherwise indicated.

Electrochemical experiments are conducted with either an EG&G Princeton Applied Research potentiostat/galvanostat Model 273 with PAR 270 software (EG&G Princeton Applied Research, Princeton, NJ), a Model 100B/W electrochemical analyzer (Bioanalytical System, Inc., Lafayette, IN) or a WPI Isolated-Nitric Oxide Meter and Sensor [World Precision Instrument (WPI), Sarasota, FL]. Single and multifiber carbon fiber electrodes (Medical Systems, Greenvale, NY) used in this study have dimensions of 35 μm in diameter and 100 to 200 μm in length. The response to NO (nA/μM) is proportional to the length of the carbon fiber (CF) electrode. Therefore, each fabricated electrode must be individually calibrated. Linear sweep voltammograms are recorded as the current response on sweeping the potential in a single direction. [Note: Cyclic voltammetry (CV) is a reversible technique that scans the changes in current with respect to potential in two directions, whereas linear sweep scans only in a single direction. Amperometry monitors current as a function of time at a constant potential.] Constant stirring is necessary to ensure uniformity of concentration of added substances. In controlled potential electrolysis, the current that passes at a fixed potential is measured. Typically, electrochemical experiments are conducted in 10 ml of solution.

Calibration of the electrodes is done under both anaerobic and aerobic conditions. Under aerobic conditions, NO stock solutions are added via an air-tight syringe to a PBS solution. Under anaerobic conditions, an electrolytic cell is a septum-sealed cylindrical type with 10 ml of solution and 13.5 ml of head space.

Nitric oxide stock solutions are prepared as previously described.[13] Briefly, 50 ml PBS in a septum-sealed vial is degassed by sonication under vacuum for 30 min. The head space is replaced with an argon atmosphere. Nitric oxide is then bubbled through the deoxygenated solution for 20

[13] D. A. Wink, J. F. Darbyshire, R. W. Nims, J. E. Saveedra, and P. C. Ford, *Chem. Res. Toxicol.* **6**, 23 (1993).

min. The NO concentration from the stock solutions is determined by colorimetric methods (see [9] in this volume[13a]). Aliquots of the NO stock solution are delivered to the experimental solution using air-tight syringes.

Fabrication of Nitric Oxide-Sensitive Carbon Fiber Electrodes

Reports of modification of electrodes with porphyrin materials have appeared over a number of years.[14-17] The fabrication of an NO-sensitive electrode coated with Ni(TMPP) is done by electrochemical oxidation (anodization), which enhances sensitivity of these carbon fiber electrodes to NO. Furthermore, by application of a second material, Nafion, to the electrode, a greater selectivity for NO is obtained.

A Ni(TMPP)-coated carbon fiber (0.5 μm in diameter and 25 μm in length) was previously described for the detection of NO.[10] In this procedure, a larger, commercially available carbon fiber (35 μm in diameter and 100–200 μm in length) is used. A carbon fiber electrode, a Pt wire counter electrode, and a standard saturated calomel electrode (SSCE) are placed in a solution containing 2 mM Ni(TMPP) dissolved in 0.1 M NaOH. There are two methods for electrochemical oxidation, repetitive cyclic voltametry and controlled potential electrolysis. With cyclic voltametry, the potential is varied between 0 and 1.0 V versus SSCE at 0.1 V/sec until no voltammetric changes are observed. The electrode is then taken out of the solution and rinsed with water.

The electrode also can be modified to give a Ni-porphyrin film by controlled potential electrolysis. A cyclic voltammogram (CV) is initially recorded between 0 and +1.0 V with a scan rate of 0.2 V/sec. The potential is held at +0.8 V versus SSCE for 1.5–2 min. After the electrolysis period, another CV is recorded (Fig. 1). Comparison with the initial CV shows a significant increase in the current at 0.45 V, which is representative of the Ni(II)/Ni(III) couple of polymerized Ni-porphyrin on the surface (Fig. 1). After completion of the coating process, the electrode is washed with water.

Oxidation of Ni(TMPP) results in a film on the surface of the carbon fiber. The extent of the deposit can be determined by the current from the Ni(II)/Ni(III) couple at 0.45 V versus SSCE (Fig. 1), which is present only in basic solution. Amperometric techniques are used to detect NO with respect to time. While the potential is held at either 0.7 or 0.8 V versus

[13a] R. W. Nims, J. C. Cook, M. C. Krishna, D. Christodoulou, C. M. B. Poore, A. M. Miles, M. B. Grisham, and D. A. Wink, *Methods Enzymol.* **268**, Chap. 9, 1996 (this volume).
[14] J. N. Younthan, K. S. Wood, and T. J. Meyer, *Inorg. Chem.* **15**, 3280 (1992).
[15] K. A. Macor and T. G. Spiro, *J. Am. Chem. Soc.* **105**, 5601 (1983).
[16] S. Dong and R. Jiang, *J. Inorg. Biochem.* **30**, 189 (1987).
[17] R. H. Felton, *Porphyrins, Part C*, 53 (1978).

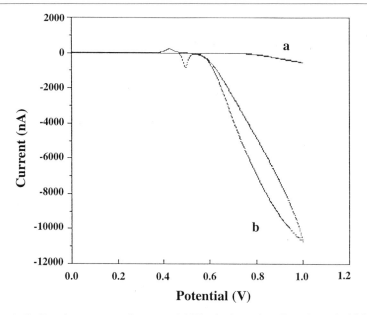

Fig. 1. Cyclic voltammograms (scan rate 0.1 V/sec) of a carbon fiber electrode (a) before and (b) after anodization via controlled potential electrolysis at 0.8 V versus SSCE in 0.1 *M* NaOH containing 2 m*M* Ni(TMPP). An EG&G Princeton Applied Research potentiostat/galvanostat Model 273 with PAR 270 software was used.

SSCE, current changes are recorded with respect to time. Introduction of NO to an aerobic solution results in an increase in current followed by a decay (Fig. 2A). Aliquots of NO at concentrations from 1 to 10 μM are added to 10 ml PBS solution under aerobic conditions. The observed current changes are recorded. The change in current versus NO concentrations is determined by measuring the current before and after NO introduction (Fig. 2A). A plot of NO concentration versus current is linear (Fig. 2B). The same experiments can be done but under anaerobic conditions. Introduction of an aliquot of NO to the solution under argon results in a peak which decays to equilibrium with the headspace (Fig. 3A). A plot of the NO concentration at equilibrium and current is linear over 4 logs (Fig. 3B).

Further studies have shown that simply oxidizing a carbon fiber electrode can lower the potential for oxidation of various substrates such as dihydroquinones and catechol,[18] owing to the modification of the carbon surface of the electrodes. The oxidation potential of NO on a carbon fiber

[18] G. E. Cabaniss, A. A. Diamantis, W. R. Murphy, R. W. Linton, and T. J. Meyer, *J. Am. Chem. Soc.* **107**, 1845 (1985).

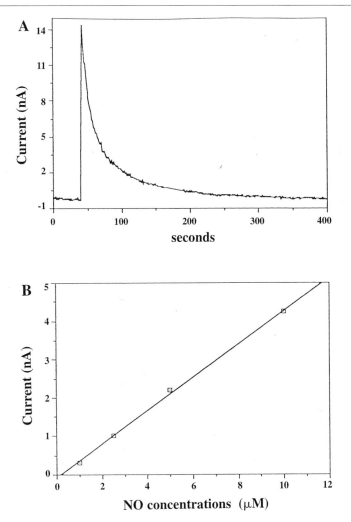

FIG. 2. (A) Amperometry experiment when an aliquot of the NO stock solution was added at time 20 sec to give an NO concentration of 30 μM in PBS using a Ni(TMPP)/Nafion-coated carbon fiber electrode at 0.7 V versus SSCE (time increments of 0.1 sec). (B) Plot of NO concentration with current change under aerobic conditions. The change in current was measured 2 sec after introduction of the NO stock solution and subtracted from the prior current measurement. An EG&G Princeton Applied Research potentiostat/galvanostat Model 273 was used.

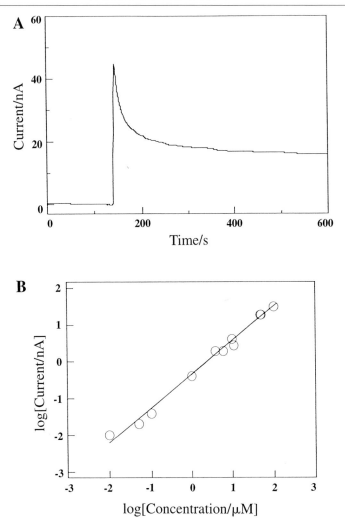

FIG. 3. (A) Current–time curve at +0.80 V versus SSCE (sample interval 0.5 sec) when an aliquot of the NO stock solution was added at time 2.3 min to give an NO concentration of 45 μM in phosphate buffer solution (pH 7.4). A carbon multifiber electrode was used. (B) Calibration curve for NO in a pH 7.4 buffered solution obtained with three carbon multifiber electrodes. Amperometric steady-state currents at +0.80 V versus SSCE are plotted against instantaneous initial NO concentrations estimated. Background corrections were made on all measurements. A BAS Model 100B/W electrochemical analyzer was used.

surface exceeds 0.9 V versus SSCE. The lowering of this potential, observed with the Ni-modified electrode, to 0.7 V has little to do with the porphyrin surface but rather the modification of the carbon material on the surface of the electrode.[12] When a CF electrode is anodized via oxidation in base at 0.1 V, a similar potential for oxidation is observed. Hence, it is postulated that the modification of the electrode surface is the cause for lowering the oxidation potential of NO by providing oxygen-based binding sites for the NO^+ that is generated by oxidation.[12] However, the benefit of the Ni or other porphyrin material is to increase the signal-to-noise ratio, and the electrode provides more reliable electrochemical response.

Nafion-Coated Electrodes

A second coating of a Nafion membrane to reduce interferences (discussed below) can be done as follows. To coat either a Ni(TMPP) electrode or a bare carbon fiber electrode, the following procedure is used. The porphyrin-coated electrode is placed in an oven at 85° for 5 min to dry. The tip of the electrode is then dipped in Nafion solution for 1–3 sec and placed in the oven at 85° for 5 min. The coating cycle was repeated 5–10 times. The electrode can be stored dry with no special precautions. The best method is to store in water or PBS. This will assure that the Nafion coat is hydrated properly and enhances signal-to-noise ratio.

Interferences

The Shibuki-style NO electrode utilizes a gas-permeable membrane that allows the exclusion of solutes in the measured solution, thereby giving tremendous advantages for *in vivo* measurements. Nevertheless, stability of the electrode can be a problem. The CF electrode, on the other hand, is more stable, but other substances can also be detected with this style of electrode, which lacks specificity for NO. For example, nitrite ion (which is the resultant product from the autoxidation of NO) can interfere with the electrochemical detection of NO with this porphyrin-coated electrode.[10,12] The current–response ratio of NO to nitrite varies from 20:1 to 100:1 in this study. In addition to nitrite, common biological substances such as ascorbate and catecholamines can also interfere with this style of electrode (Fig. 4). As shown in Fig. 4, the linear voltammogram of solutions containing 1 mM nitrite, ascorbate, or dopamine reveals significant current response between 0.7 and 1.0 V with a Ni(TMPP) modified electrode without Nafion. As previously described, a coating of Nafion can be placed on the porphyrin-coated electrode to exclude anions.[10,12] The Nafion coat enhances the NO selectivity by acting as a membrane barrier to anion interference.

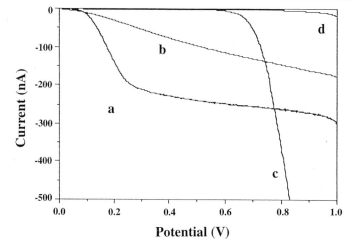

Potential (V)

Fig. 4. Linear sweep voltammograms of dopamine, nitrite, and ascorbate. Voltammograms were done between 0 and 1.0 V versus Ag/AgCl in the presence of 1 mM (a) dopamine, (b) nitrite, or (c) asorbate (d is baseline with no analyte) dissolved in PBS at 25°. An EG&G Princeton Applied Research potentiostat/galvanostat Model 273 with PAR 270 software was used.

Nafion is a polyfluorinated polyacid with cation-exchange properties and rejects anions when coated on an electrode surface. In our previous report, the effectiveness of the Nafion coat with several different analytes were examined.[12] The rejection of nitrite is increased by 100 times with Nafion coating, thereby increasing the NO/NO$_2^-$ sensitivity ratio to 5000.[12] Nafion coating also reduces interference by ascorbate by increasing the ascorbate : NO response from 1 : 1 to 1 : 5000.[12] Therefore, if NO concentrations are 0.1–10 μM, concentrations as high as 1–10 mM nitrite and ascorbate might be tolerated. The Nafion coating can be checked by introducing 1 mM ascorbate into the solution. If the coating integrity is good, no current change should be observed. If current response is observed, the electrode should be rinsed with distilled water and allowed to dry. This procedure should be repeated for 2 to 3 more coats.

The Nafion coating does not appreciably affect the NO response.[12] Yet, the ratio of the response to NO versus that to nitrate or ascorbate is significantly increased. Electrodes with Nafion coating are stable in PBS (pH 7.4) for a week and can be air stored for several weeks. (Note: Hydration of Nafion is important to obtain a good signal-to-noise ratio, therefore, leaving the coating in buffer is a preferred method of storage.) Although the stability of the electrode is fairly good, when the electrode is used repeatedly in a variety of experiments, it should be periodically tested for coating integrity.

Even the best Nafion-coated electrode can have potential interferences. For instance, the catecholamines, norepinephrine, and dopamine can be detected at the same potential as NO despite the Nafion coating. In fact, several commercially available electrochemical techniques utilize Nafion-coated electrodes to determine catecholamine *in vivo*.[19] The selectivity ratio is about 30:1 to 50:1 (NO/catecholamine), suggesting that when NO concentrations are 0.1–1 μM, catecholamine concentrations of 1–10 μM might present a problem.[12] *In vivo*, catecholamines in extracellular tissue exist at concentrations far below 1 μM,[20] but this may or may not be the case when measuring localized concentrations at the cellular level. Fortunately, a comparison of responses at different oxidation potentials can be used to differentiate between NO and catecholamines. Dopamine is oxidized at 0.2 V (Fig. 4), whereas NO is electrochemically inactive at this potential. As shown in Fig. 4, dopamine gives a dose-dependent increase at both 0.2 and 0.7 V versus SSCE. If interferences from catecholamines are a problem *in vivo*, monitoring at two potentials, +0.7 and +0.2 V versus SSCE, can be useful. In biological experiments, the interferences must be taken into account.

Use of Nafion-Coated Carbon Fiber (NO-Porphyrin) for Nitric Oxide Detection

Because modification of the CF electrode by the porphyrin coat simply reduces oxidation potential of NO,[12] a carbon-fiber electrode with a Nafion coating should be equally effective for the detection of NO simply by monitoring at a higher potential than the Ni(TMPP)-modified CF electrode. Because a bare carbon fiber electrode detects NO at 0.9 V, this electrode should be equally effective (Fig. 5A). Examination of the current response to various NO concentrations with a Nafion coated unanodized CF electrode resulted in a dose-dependent increase in current. A plot of NO versus current reveals a linear relationship (Fig. 5B). This type of electrode is currently used in the detection of dopamine and other neurotransmitters; therefore, care must be taken when using this style of electrode in biological experiments. The Ni(TMPP) style electrode does have advantages with respect to the detection of oxygen. A Nafion-coated untreated electrode will detect oxygen above −0.7 V versus SSCE but will also detect NO. However, the Ni(TMPP)/Nafion electrode detects oxygen at −0.5 V SSCE

[19] M. T. Su, T. V. Dunwiddie, M. Mynlieff, and G. A. Gerhardt, *Neurosci. Lett.* **110**, 186 (1990).
[20] R. C. Engstrom, R. M. Wightman, and E. W. Kristen, *Anal. Chem.* **60**, 651 (1988).

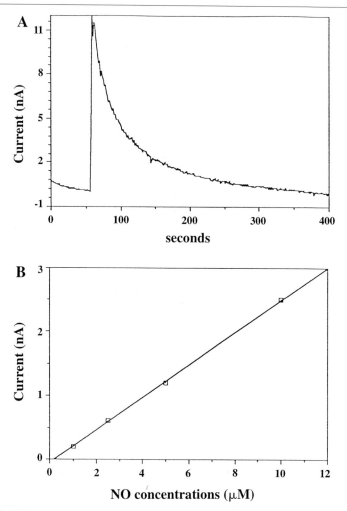

Fig. 5. (A) Amperometry experiment when an aliquot of the NO stock solution was added at time 20 sec to give an NO concentration of 30 μM in PBS using a Nafion-coated carbon fiber electrode (no porphyrin) at 0.9 V versus SSCE (time increments of 0.1 sec). (B) Plot of NO concentration with current change under aerobic conditions. The change in current was measured 2 sec after introduction of the NO stock solution and subtracted from the prior current measurement. An EG&G Princeton Applied Research potentiostat/galvanostat Model 273 with PAR 270 software was used.

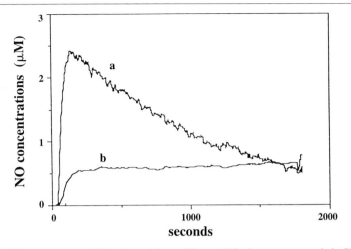

FIG. 6. Measurement of NO released from different NO–donor compounds in PBS, pH 7.4, at 25° using a Ni(TMPP)/Nafion electrode with (a) 0.1 mM DEA/NO or (b) 1 mM SNAP. An EG&G Princeton Applied Research potentiostat/galvanostat Model 273 with PAR 270 software was used.

with no appreciable interference with NO.[12] The advantage of the porphyrin-coated electrode is not its ability to detect NO, but its ability to separate out various analytes by changing redox potential.

Measurement of Nitric Oxide in Real Time

One of the advantages that electrochemical techniques provide is a real-time evaluation of NO under a variety of conditions. Various NO–donor complexes have provided valuable tools for studying the effects of NO on various biological assays.[21–24] The time–release profile of the NO–donor compounds can dramatically differ and possibly give different biological results. Using a Ni(TMPP)/Nafion CF, the NO time–release profiles are determined in PBS solution containing 0.1 mM DEA/NO (Fig. 6). This complex has been shown to release NO in a predictable manner.[24] As seen in aerobic solution, NO is released but is then consumed by the NO/O_2 reaction and dissipates by diffusion from the solutions as well, yielding a

[21] M. Feelisch, *J. Cardiovasc. Pharmacol.* **17**, S25 (1991).
[22] M. Feelisch, M. te Pool, R. Zamora, A. Deussen, and S. Moncada, *Nature (London)* **368**, 62 (1994).
[23] M. Feelisch, J. Ostrowski, and E. Noack, *J. Cardiovasc. Pharmacol.* **14**, S13 (1989).
[24] C. M. Maragos, D. Morley, D. A. Wink, T. M. Dunams, J. E. Saavedra, A. Hoffman, A. A. Bove, L. Isaac, J. A. Hrabie, and L. K. Keefer, *J. Med. Chem.* **34**, 3242 (1991).

peak at 2 μM (Fig. 6). Using the same technique, SNAP (*S*-nitroso-*N*-acetylpenicillamine), a *S*-nitroso complex which generates NO, also showed NO formation (Fig. 7). Using the WPI NO sensor, NO release profiles can also be detected (Fig. 7). The DEA/NO at 0.02 mM yields a peak NO concentration of 1.5 μM. The NO donor compound SIN-1 (3-morpholino-sydnonium), which releases NO via the formation of O_2^-, shows no appreciable NO. This is presumed to be because NO/O_2^- reaction occurs so rapidly that NO is consumed. Yet, when 3 mg/ml superoxide dismutase is present NO formation is observed. Thus, these electrode techniques do provide a valuable tool for studying the NO release profiles for various NO–donor compounds.

Conclusion

Both oxidation and reduction of NO can be used in electrochemical detection of NO. The Shibuki-style electrode offers sensitivity without interferences by substances such as ascorbate and catecholamines and can

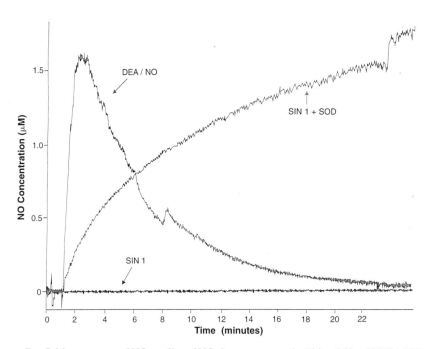

FIG. 7. Measurement of NO profiles of NO donor compounds. Either 0.02 mM DEA/NO, 1 mM SIN-1, or 1 mM SIN-1 plus 3 mg/ml superoxide dismutase (SOD) were dissolved in PBS, pH 7.4, at 37°. A WPI Isolated-Nitric Oxide Meter and Sensor was used.

be used selectively nanomolar NO concentrations. Existing oxygen electrode techniques can be easily adapted for measuring NO. However, its lack of stability to prolonged NO exposure and its lack of design flexibility can pose problems. The oxidatively modified carbon fiber electrodes described in this chapter are useful, sensitive, and provide flexibility in design and long-term stability; however, other biological substances can interfere with NO detection. It is recommended that the two electrochemical methods be used in tandem to verify and check the authentic NO under various conditions.

[8] Chemiluminescence Headspace-Gas Analysis for Determination of Nitric Oxide Formation in Biological Systems

By James F. Brien, Brian E. McLaughlin, Kanji Nakatsu, and Gerald S. Marks

Introduction

Nitric oxide (NO) is a gaseous radical that readily diffuses from its site of formation to its site(s) of action in various organ systems, where it is involved in physiological, pharmacological, or pathological processes.[1–7] As such, it is an intercellular messenger involved in the regulation of vascular smooth muscle tone, synaptic plasticity, excitatory amino acid-induced neurotoxicity, and antimicrobial action of macrophages. Nitric oxide is synthesized during the oxidation of L-arginine to L-citrulline in the endothelium, neurons, and macrophages in a reaction catalyzed by different isoforms of nitric-oxide synthase (NOS; EC 1.14.13.39), which have been purified, cloned, and expressed.[8,9] Furthermore, NO is the apparent active metabolite produced in the metabolic activation of nitrovasodilator agents (e.g., glyc-

[1] R. F. Furchgott and P. M. Vanhoutte, *FASEB J.* **3,** 2007 (1989).
[2] S. Moncada, R. M. J. Palmer, and E. A. Higgs, *Pharmacol. Rev.* **43,** 109 (1991).
[3] C. Nathan, *FASEB J.* **6,** 3051 (1992).
[4] D. S. Bredt and S. H. Snyder, *Neuron* **8,** 3 (1992).
[5] L. J. Ignarro, *FASEB J.* **3,** 31 (1989).
[6] M. A. Marletta, *Trends Biochem. Sci.* **14,** 488 (1989).
[7] J. Garthwaite, *Trends Neurosci.* **14,** 60 (1991).
[8] U. Förstermann, J. S. Pollock, W. R. Tracey, and M. Nakane, *Methods Enzymol.* **233,** 258 (1994).
[9] C. J. Lowenstein and S. H. Snyder, *Methods Enzymol.* **233,** 264 (1994).

eryl trinitrate),[10-13] and it is considered to be responsible for the vasorelaxant and antiplatelet action of these prodrugs.

In view of the exponential increase in scientific interest in the biology of NO since the mid 1980s, it has become increasingly important to provide direct evidence for the formation and/or action of NO in its myriad biological effects. Hence, there has been a corresponding increase in the development of analytical methods for the quantitation of NO per se in biological systems. These methods are based on the physicochemical and biochemical properties of NO.[14] Quantitation of NO can be achieved with one of the following analytical approaches: (1) reaction of NO with oxyhemoglobin to yield nitrate anion (NO_3^-) and methemoglobin (metHb), the latter of which can be measured spectrophotometrically[15]:

$$\cdot NO + O_2Hb \rightarrow NO_3^- + metHb$$

(2) reaction of NO with deoxyhemoglobin to form nitrosylhemoglobin (NOHb), a stable adduct, which can be measured by electron paramagnetic resonance spectrometry[16-19]:

$$\cdot NO + Hb \rightarrow \cdot NOHb$$

(3) an amperometric method involving the oxidation of NO at the surface of an electrode, followed by measurement of the electrical current that is formed[20]:

$$\cdot NO \rightarrow NO^+ + e^-$$

(4) an amperometric method involving a metalloporphyrin coating on an electrode to catalyze the oxidation of NO, which enhances the sensitivity

[10] L. J. Ignarro, H. Lippton, J. C. Edwards, W. H. Baricos, A. L. Hyman, P. J. Kadowitz, and C. A. Gruetter, *J. Pharmacol. Exp. Ther.* **218,** 739 (1981).

[11] J. F. Brien, B. E. McLaughlin, S. M. Kobus, J. H. Kawamoto, K. Nakatsu, and G. S. Marks, *J. Pharmacol. Exp. Ther.* **244,** 322 (1988).

[12] L. J. Ignarro, *Circ. Res.* **65,** 1 (1989).

[13] G. S. Marks, B. E. McLaughlin, K. Nakatsu, and J. F. Brien, *Can. J. Physiol. Pharmacol.* **70,** 308 (1992).

[14] S. Archer, *FASEB J.* **7,** 349 (1993).

[15] M. E. Murphy and E. Noack, *Methods Enzymol.* **233,** 240 (1994).

[16] Å. Wennmalm, B. Lanne, and A.-S. Petersson, *Anal. Biochem.* **187,** 359 (1990).

[17] H. Kruszyna, R. Kruszyna, R. P. Smith, and D. E. Wilcox, *Toxicol. Appl. Pharmacol.* **91,** 429 (1987).

[18] Q. Wang, J. Jacobs, J. DeLeo, H. Kruszyna, R. Kruszyna, R. Smith, and D. Wilcox, *Life Sci.* **49,** PL55 (1991).

[19] L. R. Cantilena, Jr., R. P. Smith, S. Frasur, H. Kruszyna, R. Kruszyna, and D. E. Wilcox, *J. Lab. Clin. Med.* **120,** 902 (1992).

[20] K. Shibuki, *Neurosci. Res.* **9,** 69 (1990).

of the assay[21]; (5) measurement of nitrite anion (NO_2^-) and NO_3^- as decomposition products of NO using a diazotization assay in which NO_2^- is reacted with the Griess reagent to form a colored reaction product that is quantitated spectrophotometrically (NO_3^- must be reduced to NO_2^- either enzymatically or chemically, which then is quantitated by the colorimetric assay[14,22]), with this method being an indirect assay of NO and having been used in this capacity[23]; (6) reaction of NO with ozone (O_3) to form nitrogen dioxide (excited state, $\cdot NO_2^*$), which then emits a photon during conversion to $\cdot NO_2$ (ground state), with the photon emission being quantitated (chemiluminescence)[14]:

$$\cdot NO + O_3 \rightarrow \cdot NO_2^* + O_2$$
excited state

$\vdash hv$ (quantitation)

$\cdot NO_2$
ground state

Chemiluminescence Method for Quantitation of Nitric Oxide

The chemiluminescence-based assay for the direct measurement of NO is rapid and reliable. Chemiluminescence methods have been utilized to measure NO formation and release by endothelial cells,[24] NO formation in the determination of NO synthase activity,[25,26] NO production during the biotransformation of nitrovasodilator agents including glyceryl trinitrate[13,27] and sodium nitroprusside,[28] and NO production during photochemical-induced degradation of sodium nitroprusside and streptozotocin.[29] The chemiluminescence assay is also being used to ensure that the desired NO dosage regimen is given by inhalation in the treatment of persistent pulmonary hypertension of the newborn and the adult respiratory distress syndrome.

[21] T. Malinski and Z. Taha, *Nature* (*London*) **358**, 676 (1992).

[22] J. M. Hevel and M. A. Marletta, *Methods Enzymol.* **233**, 250 (1994).

[23] L. J. Ignarro, G. M. Buga, K. S. Wood, R. E. Byrns, and G. Chaudhuri, *Proc. Natl. Acad. Sci. U.S.A.* **84**, 9265 (1987).

[24] R. M. J. Palmer, A. G. Ferrige, and S. Moncada, *Nature* (*London*) **327**, 524 (1987).

[25] M. A. Marletta, P. S. Yoon, R. Iyengar, C. D. Leaf, and J. S. Wishnok, *Biochemistry* **27**, 8706 (1988).

[26] A. J. Hobbs, J. M. Fukuto, and L. J. Ignarro, *Proc. Natl. Acad. Sci. U.S.A.* **91**, 10992 (1994).

[27] S.-J. Chung and H.-L. Fung, *J. Pharmacol. Exp. Ther.* **253**, 614 (1990).

[28] J. N. Bates, M. T. Baker, R. Guerra, Jr., and D. G. Harrison, *Biochem. Pharmacol.* **42**, S157 (1991).

[29] S. K. O'Neill, S. Dutta, and C. R. Triggle, *J. Pharmacol. Toxicol. Methods* **29**, 217 (1993).

In the original chemiluminescence method that was utilized in the identification of endothelium-derived relaxing factor as NO,[24] the biological sample is refluxed in a sodium iodide/glacial acetic acid solution prior to instrumental analysis; this procedure reduces chemical compounds containing nitrogen oxide substituents to NO.[30,31] This chemical reduction has been avoided in other chemiluminescence-based assays by transferring the biologically formed NO from the sample into the gas phase and then into the chemiluminescence detector by using a stream of inert gas.[31,32]

Chemiluminescence Headspace-Gas Method for the Quantitation of Nitric Oxide

The method that we have used and refined since the late 1980s was originally developed at a time when there was a paucity of reliable procedures for the quantitation of NO formation from the nitrovasodilator drugs in a biological milieu. The procedure is based on the chemiluminescence quantitation of NO in a headspace-gas sample obtained during incubation of a biological system in a sealed environment.[33] The unique aspect of our method is the technique of analyzing headspace gas collected above the biological sample. Only substances that are gaseous at the experimental temperature will be present in the headspace, be sampled, and ultimately drawn via vacuum into the reaction chamber. This approach decreases the potential for interference with the chemiluminescence signal when the NO_2 product, formed from the gas-phase reaction of NO with O_3, changes from excited state to ground state; it also decreases potential contamination of the chemiluminescence detector.

Chemicals and Solutions

Routine chemicals for our chemiluminescence headspace-gas method are obtained from a variety of commercial suppliers and are at least reagent-grade quality. Drugs and other specialty pharmacological agents are obtained from various pharmaceutical companies or are custom synthesized, and they meet criteria for purity required for experimentation (usually $\geq 99\%$ purity). The drug/agent solutions are prepared on the day of experimentation, and the solvents used to prepare these solutions are utilized as

[30] N. K. Menon, A. Wolf, M. Zehetgruber, and R. J. Bing, *Proc. Soc. Exp. Biol. Med.* **191,** 316 (1989).
[31] P. R. Myers, R. Guerra, Jr., and D. G. Harrison, *Am. J. Physiol.* **256,** H1030 (1989).
[32] M. Feelisch and E. A. Noack, *Eur. J. Pharmacol.* **139,** 19 (1987).
[33] J. F. Brien, B. E. McLaughlin, K. Nakatsu, and G. S. Marks, *J. Pharmacol. Methods* **25,** 19 (1991).

the respective blank samples. For studies involving glyceryl trinitrate, all glassware used in the assay is treated with a siliconizing agent (Surfasil, Chromatographic Specialties, Brockville, ON). Compressed gases, prepurified or medical grade, are obtained from Union Carbide Canada, Praxair Division (Mississauga, ON). Nitric oxide calibration gases (Scott Specialty Gases, Troy, MI) are obtained as mixtures in nitrogen (1.0, 5.0, 10, 30, 75, and 200 ppm). The regulator outlets on the NO compressed-gas cylinders have septa (GC general-purpose septum ST531, Chromatographic Specialties); select volumes of the calibration gas are taken with a gas-tight syringe (Pressure-Lok, series A-2 syringe with side-port needle, Supelco Canada, Oakville, ON).

Equipment

Incubation of the biological system in a sealed environment involves a micro-Fernbach flask (7.1-ml volume, Ace Glass, Vineland, NJ) that is sealed with a rubber sleeve-septum (Aldrich, Milwaukee, WI). Before initiating incubation of the biological system under anaerobic conditions, the contents of the flask are deoxygenated with 95% argon (Ar)/5% CO_2. The buffer used in our studies is Krebs solution; thus, 5% CO_2 is part of the gas mixture used to treat the samples so that pH 7.4 is maintained. Stainless steel, Teflon-lined tubing (Chromatographic Specialties), with a 7.5-cm stainless steel needle (Hamilton 22-gauge with CTFE hub, Chromatographic Specialties) attached to the end of the tubing, is used to deliver the gas into the sealed flask, which is vented with a 26-gauge needle. The 95% Ar/5% CO_2 gas is bubbled into the biological system at a flow rate of 15 ml/min for 5 min. Before adding a drug (or drug vehicle) solution to the biological system using a gas-tight syringe (Pressure-Lok, series A-2 syringe with side-port needle, Supelco Canada), the flow of gas is stopped by simultaneously removing the two needles from the septum of the flask. Throughout the gassing and incubation of the biological system, the flask contents are maintained at 37° using water-jacketed beakers attached to a circulating water bath (Haake D1-L, Fisher Scientific, Toronto, ON). To facilitate equilibration of NO between the aqueous and gaseous phases in the sealed system, the contents of the flask are stirred rapidly using microstir bars and a six-place stirrer (Labline Multi-Magnestir, Model 1278; Fisher Scientific). All solutions added to the biological system are deoxygenated with 95% Ar/5% CO_2. After adding a solution, the syringe is rinsed with water followed by acetone and then dried with nitrogen (N_2) gas. For incubation under aerobic conditions, the contents of the flask and solutions added to the biological system are gassed with 20% O_2/5% CO_2/ balance N_2.

Headspace gas from the sealed biological system is analyzed for NO using a nitric oxide analyzer (NOA Model 270B, Sievers Research, Boulder, CO). The inport of the reaction chamber of the NOA is fitted with a septum (GC general-purpose septum ST531, Chromatographic Specialties). The headspace-gas sample injected through the septum, and the O_3 generated elsewhere in the NOA, are drawn into the reaction chamber by vacuum. Photon emission from the chemiluminescence reaction of NO with O_3 is detected using a photomultiplier tube, and the resultant signal is amplified and presented on a strip-chart recorder.

The equipment that we are currently using is a second-generation instrument with electronic upgrading compared with the first-generation Redox Chemiluminescence Detector (RCD Model 207B, Sievers Research). The electronics of the NOA Model 270B instrument include two amplifier output filters, with fast and slow output. The slow-output filter is used in our instrumental analysis to ensure reliable recording of the detector output, especially large chemiluminescence signals. These modified electronics improve the lower limit of quantitative sensitivity of the method.

Calibration of Method

The assay is calibrated using aqueous NO standards that are meticulously prepared as follows. For each standard, a 3.0-ml aliquot of deionized water is added to a micro-Fernbach flask, which is heated in a water bath at 37° for 10 min and then sealed with a rubber sleeve-septum. The contents of the flask are gassed with 95% Ar/5% CO_2 (anaerobic conditions) or 20% O_2/5% CO_2/balance N_2 (aerobic conditions) as described above. The time for stirring the standard normally is the same as the incubation period for the biological sample. Also, if biochemical agents (e.g., enzymes such as superoxide dismutase) are added to the biological system, they should be present in the aqueous NO standards. To mimic the addition of a small volume of drug/pharmacological agent solution to a biological system in a sealed environment, a 0.1-ml aliquot of deionized water, previously gassed with 95% Ar/5% CO_2 or 20% O_2/5% CO_2/balance N_2, is added to the flask using a gas-tight syringe. An aliquot of NO calibration gas to give a known amount of NO is calculated by the ideal gas law, $PV = nRT$, using standard laboratory conditions, and is added using a gas-tight syringe by bubbling it through the flask contents. Rapid stirring of the flask contents with a microstir bar is maintained throughout preparation and analysis of each standard. A 400-μl aliquot of headspace gas, obtained with a gas-tight syringe, is injected into the NOA. To ensure accurate quantitation of NO, residual sample in the dead volume of the syringe needle has to be removed as the NOA draws the sample into the instrument by vacuum. Hence, the syringe needle is replaced with a needle previously flushed with N_2 gas, and the hub of the syringe is flushed with N_2. A blank aqueous standard is prepared by using N_2 in a volume of 200 μl to mimic the largest aliquot of authentic NO calibration gas used to prepare an aqueous standard. The gas-tight syringe is flushed with N_2 before use to inject a sample into the NOA. After use, the needle (only) used to sample the headspace gas is rinsed with acetone to remove moisture and then is dried exhaustively with N_2 gas to remove residual acetone.

The NOA chemiluminescence signal for each aqueous NO standard is corrected by subtracting the peak height value for the blank. The slope and y-intercept of the aqueous NO standard curve, established on each experimental day, are calculated by determining the line of best fit via least-squares linear regression analysis. Representative aqueous NO standard curves for anaerobic and aerobic conditions are presented in Fig. 1. Note the lower slope of the NO standard curve for aerobic conditions, which is consistent with the reaction of NO with O_2. For both conditions, the lower limit of quantitative sensitivity is 8 pmol NO.

Recovery and Precision of the Method

Samples containing known amounts of NO are analyzed for each type of biological system studied in order to determine NO recovery for that

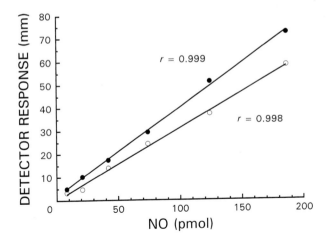

FIG. 1. Aqueous NO standard curve for 8 to 186 pmol NO in 3.0 ml of deionized water contained in a 7.1-ml sealed flask under anaerobic [95% Ar/5% CO_2] ($\bullet$) or aerobic [20% O_2/5% CO_2/balance N_2] ($\bigcirc$) conditions. r is the correlation coefficient of the line of best fit as determined by least-squares regression analysis.

particular incubation system, including the solvent used for the drug/ pharmacological agent solution and the buffer used as the incubation medium. The sample blank contains the biological system and N_2 gas in a volume equivalent to that of the NO calibration gas. After incubation at 37° for 5 min, a 400-μl aliquot of headspace gas is removed from each sample and injected into the NOA. The peak height of the chemiluminescence detector response for each NO sample is corrected with the sample blank, and the amount of NO measured is calculated by interpolation on the aqueous NO standard curve:

$$\% \text{ NO recovery} = (\text{amount NO measured/amount NO added}) \times 100$$

The precision of the method is evaluated by the interday coefficient of variation (CV), which is determined by analyzing NO samples containing the same amount of analyte on 3 days. The interday CV for a particular amount of NO in a sample is calculated from the NOA peak height, determined in triplicate:

$$CV = (\text{SD/mean peak height}) \times 100$$

The recovery of NO is dependent on the matrix of the biological system under investigation. For example, NO recovery from samples of bovine pulmonary artery incubated for 20 min under aerobic conditions [20% O_2/5% CO_2/balance N_2] was 76 ± 8% ($n = 3$), whereas NO recovery from buffer incubated for 20 min under aerobic conditions was 100 ± 9% ($n = 3$). With these biological systems, the interday CV was 10 and 9%, respectively, for samples containing 124 pmol NO.

Measurement of Nitric Oxide in Representative Biological Systems

This chemiluminescence headspace-gas method has been applied to several research projects in our laboratory. First, the role of biotransformation in the mechanism of action of nitrovasodilator drugs has been the subject of intense research activity for the last 10 years, with focus on glyceryl trinitrate (GTN) as a prodrug that undergoes metabolic activation by vascular tissue to the vasorelaxant metabolite, NO.[13]

Second, there is no known radioligand method to quantitate NO binding by biological systems. Thus, we applied the chemiluminescence headspace-gas method to measure NO sequestration by subcellular fractions of vascular tissue as a novel technique to determine NO binding sites.[34,35]

[34] E. D. Beaton, Z. Liu, B. E. McLaughlin, J. F. Brien, K. Nakatsu, and G. S. Marks, *J. Pharmacol. Toxicol. Methods* **30,** 217 (1993).
[35] Z. Liu, K. Nakatsu, J. F. Brien, E. D. Beaton, G. S. Marks, and D. H. Maurice, *Can. J. Physiol. Pharmacol.* **71,** 938 (1993).

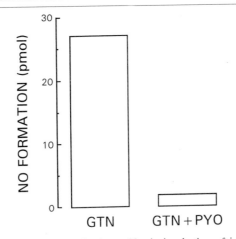

F<small>IG</small>. 2. Nitric oxide formation following a 20-min incubation of intact isolated bovine pulmonary artery ($n = 1$) with 100 μM GTN plus 10 μM pyocyanin (PYO) or 100 μM GTN plus PYO vehicle (0.1 ml of Krebs solution) under aerobic conditions [20% O_2/5% CO_2/ balance N_2].

Third, the action of pyocyanin, formed by *Pseudomonas aeruginosa*, as an antagonist of GTN-induced vasodilation appears to involve, at least in part, pyocyanin-induced inhibition of NO formation from GTN. As shown in Fig. 2, incubation of vascular tissue with GTN plus pyocyanin resulted in less NO measured in the headspace gas compared with GTN alone. The experimental protocol utilized in this study is a modification of a previously described method.[13] To a micro-Fernbach flask (7.1-ml volume) are added 3.0 ml of 30 mM K^+-depolarizing solution (Krebs solution with isomolar replacement of Na^+ with K^+ to produce submaximal contraction of vascular tissue[36]), 0.1 ml of 3000 U/ml superoxide dismutase (SOD) to yield a final concentration of 100 U/ml, and a longitudinal strip (40 × 10 mm) of bovine pulmonary artery, which is mechanically denuded of endothelium and weighs about 300 mg. The flask is sealed and then gassed with a stream of 20% O_2/5% CO_2/balance N_2 directed above the flask contents for 5 min. A 100-μl aliquot of 3 mM GTN and a 100-μl aliquot of 300 μM pyocyanin (or pyocyanin vehicle) are added to give final concentrations of 100 μM GTN and 10 μM pyocyanin, a concentration that has been shown to antago-nize GTN-induced vasodilation.[37] The sealed system is incubated at 37° for

[36] J. H. Kawamoto, J. F. Brien, G. S. Marks, and K. Nakatsu, *Can. J. Physiol. Pharmacol.* **65,** 1146 (1987).
[37] J. Bozinovski, J. F. Brien, G. S. Marks, and K. Nakatsu, *Can. J. Physiol. Pharmacol.* **72,** 746 (1994).

20 min, during which time the aqueous solution is stirred rapidly with a microstir bar; then, a 400-μl aliquot of the headspace gas is analyzed for NO by the NOA. Control samples consist of 3.0 ml of 30 mM K$^+$-depolarizing solution and 100 U/ml SOD with 100 μM GTN and 10 μM pyocyanin (or pyocyanin vehicle) and are incubated for 20 min at 37°. Sample blanks are prepared by adding 100 μl of GTN vehicle and 100 μl of pyocyanin vehicle to the control sample or the sample containing bovine pulmonary artery, and then incubated at 37° for 20 min. The chemiluminescence signal for NO measured in the samples is corrected with the appropriate blank before interpolation of the peak height value on the aqueous NO standard curve.

Finally, study of NO formation by hippocampal brain slices exposed aerobically to various stimuli is being conducted using the conventional method of analyzing headspace gas above the brain slices incubated in artificial cerebrospinal fluid in a sealed system. Furthermore, a modified headspace-gas technique is being used to measure NO in enriched incubation medium rather than in the headspace gas above the incubate. An aliquot of the enriched medium is removed from the sealed system, placed in a second sealed system previously deoxygenated with 95% Ar/5% CO$_2$, heated at 37° for 5 min, and then analyzed by taking a 400-μl aliquot of the headspace gas and injecting it into the NOA for the quantitation of NO. This constitutes the first concerted effort to measure NO formation in an intact brain-slice preparation, in which receptors and signal transduction mechanisms, including constitutive NO synthase, are functionally linked.

In conclusion, chemiluminescence coupled with headspace-gas analysis provides a selective and sensitive analytical procedure for the quantitation of NO. The major challenge is applying this physicochemical technique in individual research projects that require direct quantitation of NO in a biological system. Commitment of time to optimize the chemiluminescence headspace-gas method in order to meet the analytical requirements of a particular project is time well spent, as it will yield a direct quantitative assay for NO that is rapid and reliable.

Acknowledgments

The research from our laboratory that is presented in this chapter was supported by operating grants from the Heart and Stroke Foundation of Ontario (G. S. M., J. F. B., and K. N.) and the Medical Research Council of Canada (J. F. B., K. N., J. F. B., and G. S. M.).

[9] Colorimetric Assays for Nitric Oxide and Nitrogen Oxide Species Formed from Nitric Oxide Stock Solutions and Donor Compounds

By Raymond W. Nims, John C. Cook, Murali C. Krishna,
Danae Christodoulou, Charles M. B. Poore, Allen M. Miles,
Matthew B. Grisham, and David A. Wink

Introduction

The discovery of the endogenous formation of nitric oxide (NO) in a variety of tissues has led to a proliferation of literature addressing its biological roles.[1–3] This molecular radical has been shown to play many key physiological roles. Despite this, NO is unstable in an aerobic environment, making the accurate evaluation of its presence and concentration in neutral aqueous solutions challenging. The most commonly employed methods for the analysis of NO in aqueous solution have included (1) nitrite analysis by the Griess reagent [sulfanilamide (SULF) and N-(1-naphthyl)ethylenediamine dihydrochloride (NEDD)]; (2) chemiluminescence; and (3) reactions with oxymyoglobin or oxyhemoglobin.[4]

Quantification of NO concentrations in stock solutions and the determination of the amounts and rates of NO release from various donor agents with such techniques can be cumbersome. For example, determination of NO concentrations by nitrite analysis of an oxidized NO solution can lead to erroneous measurements, owing to the presence of excess nitrite from contaminating nitrogen oxides formed during preparation of the stock solutions. This analytical method, therefore, generally indicates a higher concentration of NO than is actually present in the stock solution.[5] Chemiluminescence is an exquisitely sensitive method for NO detection, yet for routine laboratory measurements this method can be expensive and time consuming.[6] The technique employing oxyhemoglobin or oxymyoglobin has been one of the standard methods for the detection of NO.[7] This method can

[1] S. Moncada, R. M. J. Palmer, and E. A. Higgs, *Pharmacol. Rev.* **43**, 109 (1991).
[2] C. J. Nathan, *J. Biol. Chem.* **269**, 13725 (1994).
[3] Feldman *et al.*, *Chem. Eng. News* **71**, 26, (1992).
[4] S. Archer, *FASEB J.* **7**, 349 (1993).
[5] H. H. Awad and D. M. Stanbury, *Int. J. Chem. Kinet.* **25**, 375 (1993).
[6] L. C. Green, D. A. Wagner, J. Glogowski, P. L. Skipper, J. S. Wishnok, and S. R. Tannenbaum, *Anal. Biochem.* **126**, 131 (1982).
[7] M. J. Feelisch, *J. Cardiovasc. Pharmacol.* **17**(Suppl.), S25 (1991).

be complicated by reactions of interfering agents with the porphyrin metal center, such as oxidation by nitrite.[8,9] Neither oxyhemoglobin nor oxymyoglobin can be purchased in pure form. Therefore, each time an assay is to be performed with this methodology, it is necessary to prepare one or the other of the globins via reduction with dithionite or ascorbate reduction, followed by desalting, either by passage through a sizing column or by overnight dialysis. These assays can therefore be awkward for the simple determination of NO concentration in stock solutions or for determining the rate or extent of NO release from various donor compounds.

This chapter presents three colorimetric assays for evaluating NO concentration in neutral aqueous solution. The methods each take advantage of the fact that free NO, in an aerobic aqueous solution, will react with oxygen as shown in Eq. (1) to yield reactive nitrogen oxide intermediates (RNOS) that can subsequently oxidize or nitrosate various substrates.

$$NO + O_2 \rightarrow NO_x \tag{1}$$

The first two methodologies discussed utilize the oxidative nature of the intermediates (NO_x). One method is based on the fact that NO, in the presence of oxygen, will convert ferrocyanide to ferricyanide. The second method involves the conversion, by NO and oxygen, of the colorless 2,2′-azinobis(3-ethylbenzthiazoline-6-sulfonic acid) (ABTS) to the intense green $ABTS^+$ complex.[10] Both of the substrates described above undergo one-electron oxidation.

The third methodology depends on the nitrosative properties of NO_x. The nitrosation of SULF by acidic nitrite solutions in the presence of NEDD results in an azo dye with an absorption maximum at 540 nm[11] which shifts to 496 nm.[10] In this chapter, we report that the same chemistry can be monitored at neutral pH for the determination of NO concentration in aqueous solution.

Materials and Methods

Sulfanilamide, NEDD, sodium nitroprusside (SNP), and sodium ferrocyanide are purchased from Aldrich (Milwaukee, WI) and used without

---

[8] M. P. Doyle and J. W. Hoekstra, *J. Inorg. Biochem.* **14**, 351 (1981).

[9] M. P. Doyle, R. A. Pickering, T. M. Deweert, J. W. Hoekstra, and D. Peter, *J. Biol. Chem.* **256**, 12393 (1981).

[10] R. W. Nims, J. F. Darbyshire, J. E. Saavedra, D. Christodoulou, I. Hanbauer, G. W. Cox, M. B. Grisham, J. Laval, J. A. Cook, M. C. Krishna, and D. A. Wink, *Methods (San Diego)* **7**, 48–54.

[11] J. Joseph, B. Kalyanaraman, and J. S. Hyde, *Biochem. Biophys. Res. Commun.* **192**, 926 (1993).

further purification. 2,2'-Azinobis(3-ethylbenzthiazoline-6-sulfonic acid) and superoxide dismutase (SOD) are purchased from Sigma (St. Louis, MO). Phosphate-buffered saline (PBS) is purchased from Whittaker (Walkersville, MD). $(C_2H_5)_2N[N(O)NO]Na$ (DEA/NO) is prepared as described previously.[12] S-Nitrosoglutathione (GSNO), S-nitroso-N-acetylpenicillamine (SNAP), and 3-morpholinosydnonimine (SIN-1) are purchased from Alexis (San Diego, CA). Absorbance values are determined with a Hewlett-Packard 8451 UV–visible diode-array spectrophotometer. It is critical to zero the spectrophotometer for each assay. All experiments are carried out at room temperature.

Nitric oxide stock solutions are prepared as described previously.[13] Nitric oxide gas is purified by passage through a 1 M NaOH solution. Phosphate-buffered saline is placed in a vial with a rubber septum. The buffer is degassed with argon for 2 min per milliliter of buffer. This is followed by passing NO through the solution for 20 min.

Preparation of Colorimetric Solutions

A 25 mM sodium ferrocyanide solution is prepared by dissolving 1 g of ferrocyanide in 100 ml of PBS, pH 7.4. Aliquots of NO stock solutions are added to the resulting solution. The absorbance changes at 420 nm are measured immediately.

A 5 mM ABTS solution is prepared by dissolving 340 mg ABTS in 200 ml of PBS, pH 7.4. Aliquots of nitric oxide stock solution are added to the resulting solution. The absorbance changes at 660 nm are monitored.

The SULF/NEDD solutions are made as follows: 0.5 g of SULF and 10 mg of NEDD are placed in 100 ml of PBS, pH 7.4. The solution is stirred and gently heated for 15–30 min or until all the solid has dissolved. Aliquots of NO stock solution are added to this SULF/NEDD/PBS, pH 7.4, solution. The resulting absorbance changes at 496 nm are measured.

Results and Discussion

Oxidative Methods

Ferrocyanide Method. The method involving the oxidation of ferrocyanide by the intermediates in the NO/O_2 reaction has been instrumental for

---

[12] C. M. Maragos, D. Morley, D. A. Wink, T. M. Dunams, J. E. Saavedra, A. Hoffman, A. A. Bove, L. Issac, J. A. Hrabie, and L. K. Keefer, *J. Med. Chem.* **34,** 3242 (1991).

[13] D. A. Wink, J. F. Darbyshire, R. W. Nims, J. E. Saavedra, and P. C. Ford, *Chem. Res. Toxicol.* **6,** 23 (1993).

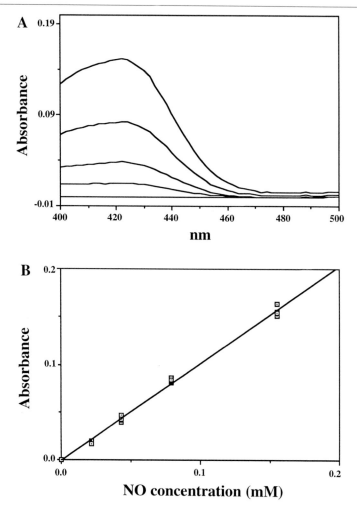

FIG. 1. (A) The UV–Vis spectral changes of a PBS solution, pH 7.4, containing 25 mM ferrocyanide on exposure to 22, 43, 78, or 155 μM NO. (B) Plot of absorbance changes at 420 nm versus various NO concentrations with a slope of 1.02 mM^{-1} ($r^2 = 0.995$).

determining some of the mechanistic aspects of this reaction.[13,14] Addition of various amounts of NO from a stock solution to a 25 mM ferrocyanide solution (1 g/100 ml) results in an increase in absorption at 420 nm, indicative of ferricyanide formation (Fig. 1A). A plot of NO concentration versus A_{420} is linear from 20 to 200 μM NO, with a slope of 1018 ± 90 M^{-1} cm^{-1}

[14] M. N. Routledge, *et al.*, *Chem. Res. Toxicol.* **7,** 628 (1994).

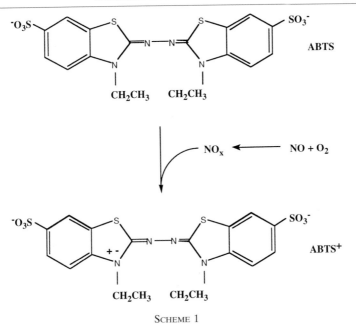

SCHEME 1

(Fig. 1B). Because the change in the extinction coefficient is 1000 M^{-1} cm^{-1}, a 1 : 1 ratio exists between NO and ferrocyanide, assuming the reaction has gone to completion. As reported previously, ferrocyanide at neutral pH will not react with anaerobic solutions of NO. Ferrocyanide in the presence of 10 mM nitrite does not form appreciable ferricyanide at neutral pH in less than 1 hr. However, at lower pH values, ferrocyanide is readily oxidized in the presence of nitrite, and care must therefore be taken when evaluating NO concentration under acidic conditions with this metal complex.

ABTS Method. The conversion of ABTS to ABTS$^+$ (Scheme 1) results in a strongly absorbing green complex, making this substrate ideal for evaluation of solutions with low NO concentrations. In fact, several studies have been based on this reaction for following oxidation mediated by various peroxidases.[15] When incremental amounts of an NO stock solution are added to an aerobic PBS, pH 7.4, containing 5 mM ABTS, an absorbance increase is observed in the spectral region between 420 and 800 nm. Since several groups have reported the value of the extinction coefficient at 660

[15] D. P. Barr and S. D. Aust, *Arch. Biochem. Biophys.* **303,** 377 (1993).

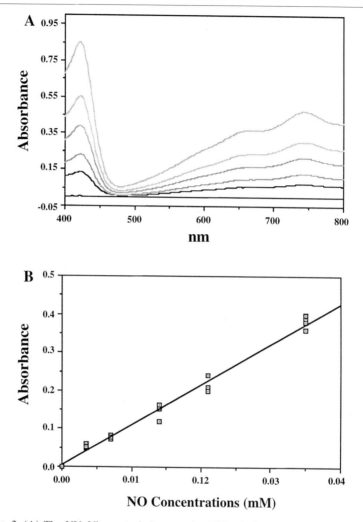

FIG. 2. (A) The UV–Vis spectral changes of a PBS solution, pH 7.4, containing 5 mM ABTS on exposure to 4, 8, 16, 24, or 40 μM NO. (B) Plot of absorbance changes at 420 nm versus various NO concentrations with a slope of 10.6 mM^{-1} ($r^2 = 0.985$).

nm,[15] this wavelength is monitored (Fig. 2A). A plot of NO concentration versus A_{660} is linear, with a slope of 10,600 $\pm$ 1500 M^{-1} cm^{-1} (Fig. 2B). Comparison of this value with the reported[15] extinction coefficient for ABTS$^+$ of 12,000 M^{-1} cm^{-1} clearly shows a 1:1 relationship of NO to ABTS$^+$ formation, again assuming that the reaction has gone to completion.[10,15]

ABTS$^+$ is stable for 24 hr in the absence of a reductant. As previously reported,[10] anaerobic solutions of NO do not oxidize ABTS to ABTS$^+$. However, excess NO (>100 μM) will cause a decrease in the absorption of ABTS$^+$, suggesting that NO concentrations no greater than 100 μM should be assayed directly with this technique. It should be noted that nitrite, at neutral pH, will not oxidize ABTS; however, under acidic conditions in the presence of nitrite, ABTS is readily converted to ABTS.$^+$

Nitrosative Method

SULF/NEDD Method. The Griess reagent is used to detect nitrite, taking advantage of a nitrosating agent formed by nitrite under acidic conditions. Nitrosation of SULF results in a diazonium salt which then couples with an aromatic amine (NEDD) to form an azo dye complex (Scheme 2). The intermediates of the NO/O$_2$ reaction result in the nitrosation of amines and thiol-containing complexes.[10,13] When aliquots of NO stock solutions are added to PBS, pH 7.4, containing 17 mM SULF (500 mg/100 ml) and 0.4 mM NEDD (10 mg/100 ml), an orange color (λ_{max} 496 nm) is imparted to the solution. A plot of NO concentration versus A_{496} is linear with a slope of 12,000 $\pm$ 1500 M^{-1} cm^{-1}. To determine if this new product is the same azo complex that is formed in acidic nitrite solutions, acid may be added to the orange solution resulting from NO$_x$. The λ_{max} then is observed to shift from 496 nm to the characteristic chromophore of the azo dye at 540 nm. This 540-nm maximum is indicative of the azo complex formed from acidic nitrite solution. Comparison of the extinction coefficients in neutral versus acidic solutions reveals that the coefficient at 496 nm is one-half that of the coefficient at 540 nm. Because the extinction coefficient at 540 nm is 53,000 M^{-1} cm^{-1}, the 496-nm peak in neutral solution is 26,500 M^{-1} cm^{-1}.[10,11] The slope in Fig. 3B is 13,000 M^{-1} cm^{-1} with respect to NO, suggesting that 2 mol of NO is required to form 1 mol of the azo complex.

The formation of the azo complex does not occur in the presence of anaerobic solutions of NO, nor in the presence of 10 mM nitrite. The final product is unaffected by the presence of reducing agents. It is critical to note that the ratio of SULF to NEDD should always be greater than 1:20. Because of the affinity of NO$_x$ for NEDD, no azo complex will form at lower SULF/NEDD ratios. The real advantage of the SULF/NEDD method is that the stability of the azo complex, once formed, is not affected by redox active complexes. This can be a problem when attempting to use this method to measure NO in media containing reducing species such as dithiothreitol, or when attempting to measure NO release from NO-releasing compounds in cases where the parent compound may be redox active.

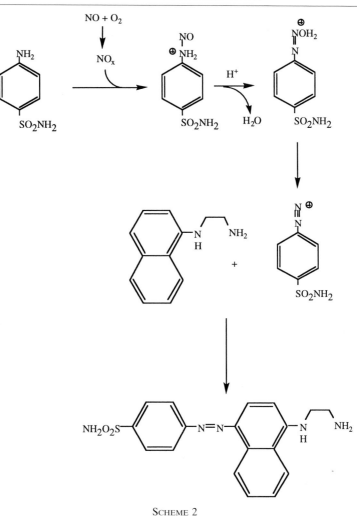

SCHEME 2

Quantification of Free Nitric Oxide Released from Nitric Oxide Donor Complexes

The standardization of the amount of NO released from NO-donating agents over a give time under a variety of conditions can be challenging. However, by using these colorimetric techniques, the release and subsequent oxidation of NO to RNOS can be followed. In Fig. 4, the rate of NO release from the NONOate DEA/NO is followed after the NO donor is introduced into a solution containing SULF/NEDD at room temperature.

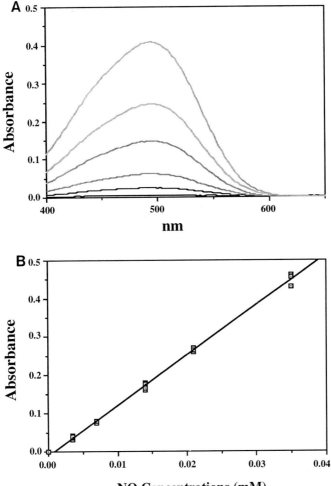

Fɪɢ. 3. (A) The UV–Vis spectral changes of a 17 mM SULF and 0.4 mM NEDD PBS solution, pH 7.4, on exposure to 0, 4, 8, 16, 24, or 40 μM NO. (B) Plot of absorbance at 496 nm versus various NO concentrations (slope = 13.1 mM^{-1}, r^2 = 0.997).

The absorbance at 496 nm versus time displays a steady increase. The first-order rate constant calculated for this effect matches that for the decay of the characteristic chromophore at 250 nm under the same conditions.

It has been shown that the NONOates release free NO in a first-order manner, generating up to 2 mol of NO per mole of starting material. However, evaluation of other NO-donating complexes reveals much less

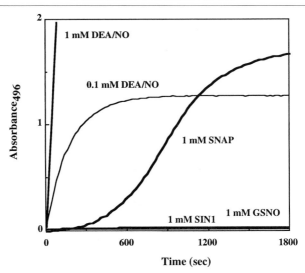

FIG. 4. Temporal absorbance changes of a 17 mM SULF and 0.4 mM NEDD PBS solution, pH 7.4, on exposure to NO donor compounds, 1 mM DEA/NO, 0.1 mM DEA/NO, 1 mM SNAP, 1 mM GSNO, and 1 mM SIN. (Note: The presence of 0.1 mg/ml SOD showed no difference.)

formation of the azo product with absorbance at 496 nm. SIN-1 has been used as an NO donor. This agent presumably generates NO via initial oxidation by oxygen, forming superoxide.[7] As seen in Fig. 4, little absorption indicative of NO generation by this agent is observed, even in the presence of copious amounts of superoxide dismutase. As presented in [7] in this volume,[15a] no appreciable NO release from this agent is detected via electrochemical techniques. Another class of NO-donating agents includes thiol–nitrosyl complexes. One compound from this class, SNAP, has been shown via electrochemical measurements to generate various amounts of NO.[7] As seen in Fig. 4, some nitrosation of SULF/NEDD occurs in solutions containing SNAP. S-Nitrosoglutathione (GSNO) can also release free NO. In this case, little or no nitrosation of SULF/NEDD is observed over the course of 1 hr.

The formation of nitrosating species in cell experiments as well as *in vivo* has been associated with arginine-derived NO.[16–18] Effects on cells

[15a] D. Christodoulou, S. Kudo, J. A. Cook, M. C. Krishna, A. Miles, M. B. Grisham, R. Murugesan, P. C. Ford, and D. A. Wink, *Methods Enzymol.* **268,** Chap. 7, 1996 (this volume).

[16] M. A. Marletta, *Chem. Res. Toxicol.* **1,** 249 (1988).

[17] Liu *et al., Cancer Res.* **51,** 3925 (1991).

[18] Liu *et al., Cancer Res.* **52,** 4139 (1992).

and biomacromolecules, such as enzyme inhibition[19] and deamination of DNA,[14,20,21] have been studied with various methods for delivering NO. As shown above and in this volume,[15a] NO may be released from NO-donating complexes in a manner that does not lead to substrate nitrosation. These colorimetric methods allow the determination of both nitrosation and oxidation and should therefore be more universally useful for monitoring release from NO donors.

Applications of Colorimetric Assays

Because of the dramatic color changes caused by NO in solutions of ABTS or SULF/NEDD, the assays based on these changes are useful for evaluating laboratory experiments involving NO dosing or administration.

Nitric Oxide Configuration

One of the most understated problems in delivering NO to biological systems is the design of the containment vessel. For instance, a petri dish has a significant surface to volume ratio. Therefore, gas exchange is rapid, and NO added as a bolus or generated *in situ* can escape rapidly, thus limiting the amount of NO_x formed in a solution contained within such a vessel. However, if the same amount of NO is added or generated within a solution contained in a narrow test tube, where the surface to volume ratio is dramatically reduced, then less NO escapes and the amount of the intermediates from the NO/O_2 reaction increases. This can be a problem when comparing experimental results from different laboratories. In the case of studying enzyme inhibition[19] mediated by NO_x, or comparing the ability of NO donor compounds to confer radiosensitization of hypoxic cells,[22] dramatically different results can be obtained if the experiments are carried out in a petri dish or in a syringe (Table I). If we compare the degree of SULF/NEDD released from DEA/NO in a syringe, test tube, microcentrifuge tube, or a petri dish, a dramatic loss of NO is observed in the petri dish, relative to the other vessels.

[19] D. A. Wink, Y. Osawa, J. F. Darbyshire, C. R. Jones, S. C. Eshenaur, and R. W. Nims, *Arch. Biochem. Biophys.* **300**, 115 (1993).
[20] D. A. Wink, K. S. Kasprzak, C. M. Maragos, R. K. Elespuru, M. Misra, T. M. Dunams, T. A. Cebula, W. H. Koch, A. W. Andrews, J. S. Allen, and L. K. Keefer, *Science* **254**, 1001 (1991).
[21] M. N. Routledge, D. A. Wink, L. K. Keefer, and A. Dipple, *Carcinogenesis* (*London*) **14**, 1251 (1993).
[22] D. A. Wink, I. Hanbauer, M. C. Krishna, W. DeGraff, J. Gamson, and J. B. Mitchell, *Proc. Natl. Acad. Sci. U.S.A.* **90**, 9813 (1993).

TABLE I
COMPARISON OF NITRIC OXIDE DELIVERED TO PETRI
DISH, TEST TUBE, OR SYRINGE

Vessel	$A_{510}{}^a$
Petri dish	0.11 ± 0.01
Test tube	0.28 ± 0.02
Syringe	0.33 ± 0.01

^{a} Values shown are means ± SD for three repli-
cates.

Examination of Heterogeneity of Nitric Oxide Delivery

Nitric oxide donors, NO gas, and sparging NO through a frit or through Silastic tubing can lead to different intermediates in the oxidation of NO as well as different areas of homogeneity.[14]

Nitric Oxide Litmus Paper

One of the most convenient aspects of these methods is that the concentration of NO can be monitored throughout a given experiment. By setting up a series of test tubes, NO stock solutions can be periodically monitored to see if loss of NO concentration has occurred and to ensure that NO is delivered in equal amounts throughout a given experiment. Using the SULF/NEDD reagent, a litmus paper can be constructed to rapidly test if NO is present in a given stock solution. Opening of vessels containing NO solutions might result in an unwanted and potentially harmful exposure to nitrogen oxides. To test whether NO is present in a solution, a litmus paper can be quite useful. This paper can also be useful for qualitatively checking NO preparations.

An NO-sensitive litmus paper may be prepared as follows: 0.5 g of SULF and 20 mg of NEDD are dissolved in methanol. The solution is transferred to a 12.5-cm diameter petri dish. A 10-cm diameter filter paper is then dipped into the solution for 30 sec. The paper is removed from the solution and allowed to dry. The paper can then be cut to the desired size and shape. To test a solution suspected of containing NO, one merely has to add a drop to the litmus paper via an air-tight syringe. An orange spot will be observed if NO is present in the solution.

The NO litmus paper can also be useful in determining when a solution of an NO-donating compound has been exhausted of NO. For example, consider the following case. A reaction involving an NO-donating solution occurs in an experiment. As the experiment proceeds, samples of the solution can be placed on the litmus paper. As the NO is released and is subsequently oxidized, the amount of remaining starting material will progressively decrease. Using the litmus paper, one can tell when no further release of NO will occur. The NO litmus paper might also be useful for the detection of NO_x in the gas phase. By passing gases containing aerobic mixtures of NO over such a paper that has been moistened with water, the paper will turn orange to purple. This can be convenient when working with biological experiments in which NO gas is being delivered to the test system.

Summary

Colorimetric analysis methods can be useful when delivering NO to biological systems or when studying the chemical properties of NO. Ferrocyanide can be used with NO concentrations higher than 25 μM, whereas ABTS can be used at NO concentrations as low as 2 μM. These oxidative methods are useful; however, interference from reductants may in some cases limit their use. The SULF/NEDD method is not subject to this problem and is accurate to greater than 5 μM NO. These techniques are relatively simple and require only a UV–visible spectrophotometer.

Acknowledgments

By acceptance of this article, the publisher or recipient acknowledges the right of the U.S. government to retain a nonexclusive, royalty-free license and to any copyright covering the article. The content of this publication does not necessarily reflect views or policies of the Department of Health and Human Services, nor does mention of trade names, commercial products, or organizations imply endorsement by the U.S. government.

[10] Determination of Nitric Oxide Using Fluorescence Spectroscopy

By ALLEN M. MILES, DAVID A. WINK, JOHN C. COOK, and MATTHEW B. GRISHAM

Introduction

The discovery of nitric oxide (NO) as a biomolecule with important physiological function has lead to the development of various analytical methods for its detection and quantification. Fundamental to the development of specific and sensitive analytical methods for the detection of NO is an understanding of the interaction between NO and molecular oxygen (O_2) in aqueous solutions. For example, it is well appreciated that NO will rapidly and spontaneously interact with O_2 in the gas phase to yield a variety of nitrogen oxides:

$$2NO + O_2 \rightarrow 2NO_2 \tag{1}$$
$$2NO + 2NO_2 \rightarrow 2N_2O_3 \tag{2}$$
$$2N_2O_3 + 2H_2O \rightarrow 4NO_2^- + 4H^+ \tag{3}$$

where NO_2, N_2O_3, and NO_2^- represent nitrogen dioxide, dinitrogen trioxide, and nitrite, respectively.[1] Dinitrogen trioxide and possibly NO_2 are potent oxidizing and N-nitrosating agents.[1] The overall stoichiometry for solution decomposition of NO has been determined to be:

$$4NO + O_2 + 2H_2O \rightarrow 4NO_2^- + 4H^+ \tag{4}$$

The rate law obtained from the oxidation of NO is given by Eq. (5):

$$-d[NO]/dt = 4k_{aq}[NO]^2[O_2] \tag{5}$$

with $k_{aq} = 2 \times 10^6 \ M^{-2} \ sec^{-1}$.[2] These data demonstrate that the rate law for NO autoxidation is second order with respect to NO. Although NO_2^- is the only stable nitrogen oxide formed following decomposition in an aqueous solution *in vitro*, predominantly nitrate (NO_3^-) is found in extracellular fluids such as plasma or urine.[1]

Compounds such as N_2O_3 have been suggested as possible oxidation intermediates with the ability to promote the N-nitrosation of amino compounds in aqueous solution,[2–5] although the exact chemical nature of the specific NO-derived N-nitrosating agent(s) NO_X, remains to be definitely defined.[5] In fact, the determination of NO_2^- by the Griess reaction is based on the two-step diazotization reaction in which acidified NO_2^- produces a nitrosating agent which reacts with sulfanilic acid to produce the diazonium

[1] L. J. Ignarro, J. M. Fukuto, J. M. Griscavage, and N. E. Rogers, *Proc. Natl. Acad. Sci. U.S.A.* **90,** 8103 (1993).

[2] P. C. Ford, D. A. Wink, and D. M. Stanbury, *FEBS Lett.* **326,** 1 (1993).

[3] M. Marletta, *Chem. Res. Toxicol.* **1,** 249 (1988).

[4] D. L. H. Williams, *in* "Nitrosation" (D. L. H. Williams, ed.), p. 113. Cambridge Univ. Press, Cambridge, 1988.

[5] D. A. Wink, J. F. Darbyshire, R. W. Nims, J. E. Saavedra, and P. C. Ford, *Chem. Res. Toxicol.* **6,** 23 (1992).

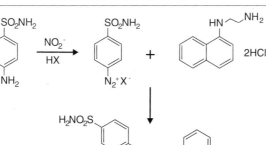

λmax = 543 nm

Fig. 1. Proposed reaction pathway for the Griess reaction.

ion (Fig. 1[5a]). This ion is then coupled to N-(1-naphthyl)ethylenediamine to form the chromophoric azo derivative (Fig. 1).

In attempts to enhance the sensitivity of measuring NO generated under physiological conditions or NO_2^- under acidic conditions, several different fluorimetric methods have been developed that exploit the ability of NO to produce N-nitrosating agents.[6–16] A number of these methods have employed the use of the aromatic diamino compound 2,3-diaminonaphthalene (DAN) as an indicator of NO formation.[9–16] The relatively nonfluorescent DAN reacts rapidly with the NO-derived N-nitrosating agent(s) to yield the highly fluorescent product 2,3-naphthotriazole (NAT; Fig. 2).

Sensitive analytical methods that rely on the fluorescent characteristics of NAT were originally developed for determination of NO_2^- and NO_3^-.[9–11]

[5a] A. M. Miles, Y. Chen, M. W. Owens, and M. B. Grisham, *Methods (San Diego)* **7**, 40 (1995).

[6] A. M. Hartley and R. I. Asa, *Anal. Chem.* **35**, 1207 (1963).

[7] A. M. Hartley and R. I. Asa, *Anal. Chem.* **35**, 1214 (1963).

[8] T. Ohta, Y. Arai, and S. Takitani, *Anal. Chem.* **58**, 3132 (1986).

[9] J. H. Wiersma, *Anal. Lett.* **3**, 123 (1970).

[10] C. R. Sawicki, *Anal. Lett.* **4**, 761 (1971).

[11] P. Damiani and G. Burini, *Talanta* **33**, 649 (1986).

[12] R. Ralt, J. S. Wishnok, R. Fitts, and S. T. Tannenbaum, *J. Bacteriol.* **170**, 359 (1988).

[13] X. Ji and T. C. Hollocher, *Appl. Environ. Microbiol.* **54**, 1791 (1988).

[14] H. Kosaka, J. S. Wishnok, M. Miwa, C. D. Leaf, and S. R. Tannenbaum, *Carcinogenesis* **10**, 563 (1989).

[15] T. P. Misko, W. M. Moore, T. P. Kasten, G. A. Nickols, J. A. Corbett, R. G. Tilton, M. L. McDaniel, J. R. Williamson, and M. G. Currie, *Eur. J. Pharmacol.* **223**, 119 (1993).

[16] T. P. Misko, R. J. Schilling, D. Salvenmini, W. M. Moore, and M. G. Currie, *Anal. Biochem.* **214**, 11 (1993).

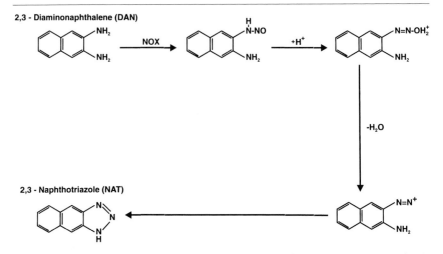

FIG. 2. N-Nitrosation of 2,3-diaminonaphthalene (DAN) to yield 2,3-naphthotriazole (NAT) by NO-derived N-nitrosating agent (NOX). From Ref. 5a with permission.

Analysis for nitrate requires reduction of NO_3^- to NO_2^-, which then decomposes in an acidic environment to produce N-nitrosating species. Earlier methods required multiple organic phase extractions of NAT and produced detection limits for NO_2^- and NO_3^- in the low nanomolar range (i.e., 150 nM).[9,10] Modifications of these earlier methods have eliminated the tedious solvent extraction steps and significantly improved sensitivity (detection limits now approach 10 nM).[11,16] Sawicki[10] observed that increasing the alkalinity of NAT solutions considerably improved both fluorescence intensity and stability. Extension of this study lead to the observation that pH 11.7 is optimal for quantifying triazole at levels as low as 9 nM.[11] Further modifications of procedures for detection of NO_2^- in buffered solutions, tissue culture media, and extracellular fluids (i.e., plasma, and urine) has lead to further increases in sensitivity by allowing for substantial decreases in the volume of sample required for analysis (e.g., 100 μl) with sensitivity for NO_2^- ranging from 10 nM (10 pmol/ml) to 10 μM (10 nmol/ml).

This chapter outlines the spectrofluorometric methods used in our laboratory to quantify NO generated by NO-releasing compounds and cultured cells as well as methods to quantify NO_2^- and NO_3^-.

Preparation of 2,3-Diaminonaphthalene and
2,3-Naphthotriazole Solutions

2,3-Diaminonaphthalene (DAN; Sigma, St. Louis, MO) is prepared fresh as 10 mM stock solution in dimethylformamide (DMF) and kept on

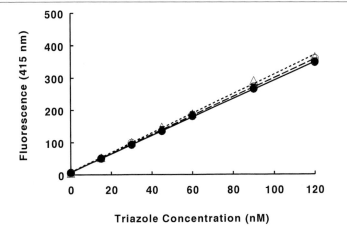

FIG. 3. 2,3-Naphthotriazole (NAT) fluorescence in the presence of different buffers. Reaction volumes (500 μl) containing 20 mM buffer and varying concentrations of NAT were diluted 6-fold by the addition of 2.5 ml of 10 mM NaOH and the fluorescence determined at 415 nm using 375 nm as the excitation wavelength. Fluorescence measurements were made in 1-cm path length cuvettes at 25° on a SLM Model SPC500 fluorometer. Filled circles represent no buffer (distilled water), open circles represent phosphate buffer, filled squares represent Tris buffer, and open triangles represent HEPES buffer. From Ref. 5a with permission.

ice in the dark until used. We have found that recrystallization of DAN removes contaminants and/or oxidation products that may interfere with the ability to interact with a NO-derived N-nitrosating agent.

Pure 2,3-naphthotriazole (NAT) is synthesized according to the method described by Wheeler et al.[17] Standard NAT solutions are prepared by appropriate dilution of an aqueous solution with 10 mM NaOH such that the final pH is maintained between pH 11.0 and pH 12.0. The presence of different buffers in the initial NAT solution does not appear to affect the magnitude of standard curve regression values of NAT diluted with 10 mM NaOH (Fig. 3). The UV–Vis spectrum for NAT in 10 mM NaOH is presented in Fig. 4. The absorption maxima of 365 and 375 nm for NAT agree well with previously published values.[16,17]

Emission spectra (excitation at 365 or 375 nm) for equimolar concentrations of DAN and NAT are illustrated in Fig. 5. A number of earlier reports recommended use of excitation wavelengths between 360 and 365 nm.[12,14–16] However, we have found that excitation at these particular wavelengths

---

[17] G. L. Wheeler, J. Andrejack, J. H. Wiersma, and P. Lott, *Anal. Chim. Acta* **46,** 239 (1969).

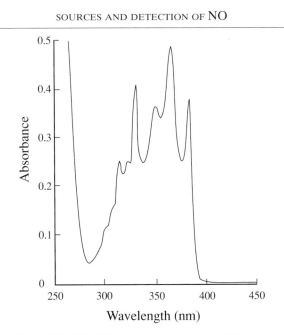

Wavelength (nm)

Fig. 4. Ultraviolet–visible (UV–Vis) absorption spectrum of 2,3-naphthotriazole (NAT). The UV–Vis absorption spectrum of NAT (10 μg/ml) in 10 mM NaOH was determined at 25°. From Ref. 5a with permission.

tends to reduce slightly the sensitivity of NAT detection owing to the small but significant increase in fluorescence of DAN under these conditions. The emission spectrum of DAN exhibits a broad emission band center at 390 nm, whereas the NAT spectrum possesses four major emission bands centered at 395, 415, 435, and 455 nm. Fluorescence intensity for NAT is at least 90- to 100-fold higher than that observed for an equimolar concentration of DAN when the solution is excited at 375 nm and emission is monitored at the emission maximum for NAT of 415 nm (Fig. 5). The quantitative limit of detection of NAT is less than 10–30 nM (10–30 pmol/ml), with linearity of fluorescence increase extending to greater than 6 μM (Fig. 6). Figure 7 shows the difference spectrum recorded for 30 nM NAT in the presence of 30 μM DAN in phosphate-buffered saline (PBS), pH 7.4. Although the fluorescence of NAT at other emission wavelengths (e.g., 450 nm) is less intense, the linearity of response with increasing NAT concentration is conserved (Fig. 6).

Reaction of 2,3-Diaminonaphthalene with Authentic Nitric Oxide

Solutions saturated with NO are prepared at 25° in a 500-ml gas sampling flask (Fisher Scientific, Pittsburgh, PA) containing 100 ml of argon-deaer-

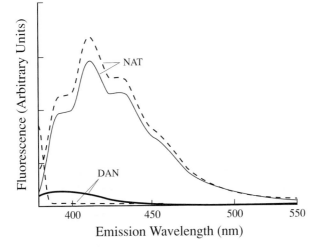

FIG. 5. Comparison of fluorescence emission spectra of 2,3-diaminonaphthalene (DAN) and 2,3-naphthotriazole (NAT). Emission spectra were recorded for separate 1.0 μM solutions (10 mM NaOH; pH 11.6) of DAN and NAT in 1-cm path length cuvettes at 25° with excitation wavelengths of either 365 nm (dashed lines) or 375 nm (solid lines). From Ref. 5a with permission.

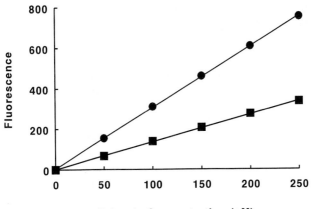

FIG. 6. Fluorescence of various concentrations of 2,3-naphthotriazole (NAT). The fluorescence of varying concentrations of NAT (in 10 mM NaOH) were determined at 25° and emission wavelengths of 415 nm (●) or 450 nm (■) (excitation wavelength 375 nm). From Ref. 5a with permission.

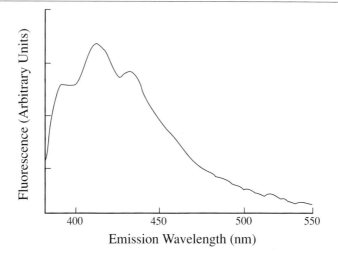

Emission Wavelength (nm)

Fig. 7. Difference fluorescence emission spectrum of 2,3-naphthotriazole (NAT). The emission spectrum represents the difference between separately recorded fluorescence spectra (excitation at 375 nm; 25°) of 30 μM DAN only and 30 μM DAN plus 30 nM NAT in 10 mM NaOH. From Ref. 5a with permission.

ated doubly deionized water. The NO gas (99.9%) is first passed through a solution of 1 M NaOH to remove traces of gaseous contaminants (e.g., NO_2) before being bubbled through the 100 ml of liquid contained in the gas sampling flask. Collection of NO gas is continued for 10 to 20 min after which flask outlets are sealed with 7 × 13 mm rubber septa (Rusch, Duluth, GA) to prevent subsequent exposure to air and to facilitate later removal of aliquots with argon-flushed Hamilton gas-tight syringes. The concentration of "authentic" NO is determined by its reaction with oxyhemoglobin (HbO_2). It has been demonstrated that NO reacts stoichiometrically with oxyhemoglobin (or oxymyoglobin) to yield methemoglobin (metHb).[18] Calculation of NO concentration is based on absorbance measurements made at 560, 576, and 630 nm according to the method of Benesch et al.[19] Saturated solutions of NO range in concentration between 1.3 and 2.0 mM and are stable for several weeks.

A 5- to 10-μl aliquot of NO-saturated stock solution is extracted from the gas sampling flask using a deaerated gas-tight syringe and injected into 0.5 ml of a solution containing 200 μM DAN in PBS, pH 7.4. After 5 to 10 min of incubation at 25°, the 0.5 ml solution is diluted 6-fold by the addition of 2.5 ml of 10 mM NaOH. Triazole production is determined

[18] M. Feelisch, J. Cardiovasc. Pharmacol. 17(Suppl. 3), S25 (1991).
[19] R. E. Benesch, R. Benesch, and S. Yung, Anal. Biochem. 55, 245 (1973).

TABLE I
PRODUCTION OF 2,3-NAPHTHOTRIAZOLE BY
REACTION OF NITRIC OXIDE WITH
2,3-DIAMINONAPHTHALENE[a]

	NAT formation (nmol)	
NO added (nmol)	pH 7.4	pH 11.6
9.8	4.1	2.6
19.5	7.9	4.6
29.4	12.3	6.5

[a] Aliquots of 1.0 mM deoxygenated NO solutions were added to 0.5 ml of 0.1 mM DAN dissolved in PBS, pH 7.4, or in 10 mM NaOH at 37°. Following 6-fold dilution with 10 mM NaOH, the NAT concentration was determined by fluorescence spectroscopy.

fluorometrically as described above. We have calculated the trapping efficiency of NO by DAN at 25° or 37° and pH 7.4 to be approximately 80% (Table I). This trapping efficiency decreases substantially at alkaline pH (Table I). A limitation for reduced efficiency of trapping of NO may be the limited solubility of DAN. DAN is only slightly soluble in aqueous media, thereby limiting the amount that can be used to effectively trap all nitrosating agents generated by the decomposition of NO.

Reaction of 2,3-Diaminonaphthalene with Nitric Oxide-Releasing Compounds

Certain nitrovasodilators such as nitroglycerin and sodium nitroprusside are examples of drugs that decompose directly or are metabolized to generate NO.[20,21] A number of newly synthesized NO adducts of the general chemical structure XN(O$^-$)N=O, where X is a nucleophilic compound, have been suggested for use as possible NO generators in biological systems.[22] These so-called NONOates spontaneously decompose at 37° at known and predictable rates to yield NO.[22] These NO adducts have been

[20] M. Feelisch and M. Kelm, *Biochem. Biophys. Res. Commun.* **180,** 286 (1991).
[21] J. N. Bates, M. T. Baker, R. Guerra, D. G. Harrison, *Biochem. Pharmacol.* **42**(Suppl.), S157 (1991).
[22] C. M. Maragos, D. Morley, D. A. Wink, T. M. Dunams, J. E. Saavedra, A. Hoffman, A. A. Bove, L. Isaac, J. A. Hrabie, and L. Keefer, *J. Med. Chem.* **34,** 3242 (1991).

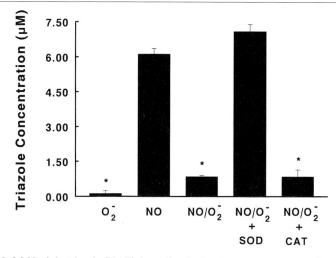

FIG. 8. 2,3-Naphthotriazole (NAT) formation in the absence or presence of a superoxide generator. Reaction volumes of 500 μl containing 20 mM phosphate buffer, 0.2 mM DAN, and 50 μM spermine–NO adduct (NO-releasing compound) were incubated for 60 min at 37°. For some experiments 0.5 mM hypoxanthine and 0.01 U/ml xanthine oxidase were added to generate superoxide (O_2^-). Following the incubation period, samples were diluted 6-fold by the addition of 2.5 ml of 10 mM NaOH, and NAT formation was determined as described above using 375 nm for excitation and monitoring the emission at 415 nm. From Ref. 5a with permission. *$P < 0.05$ compared to NO alone. SOD and CAT represent superoxide dismustase and catalase, respectively.

shown to function effectively as potent vasodilators *in vivo*.[23] Spermine–NO (Sp/NO) $\{H_2N(CH_2)_3NH_2^+(CH_2)_4N[N(N=O)O^-](CH_2)_3NH_2\}$, for example, is a bis adduct of the polyamine spermine and NO which spontaneously decomposes ($t_{1/2}$ 39 min) under physiological conditions to produce 1 mol of spermine and 2 mol of NO.[22]

The quantity of NO produced by compounds such as Sp/NO may be easily determined via N-nitrosation of DAN. For example, 0.5-ml reaction volumes containing PBS (pH 7.4), 200 μM DAN, and 50 μM of spermine–NO adduct (supplied by Dr. Larry Keefer, National Cancer Institute, Frederick, MD) are incubated for 60 min at 37°. Following the incubation period, 2.5 ml of 10 mM NaOH is added, and NAT is determined by fluorescence spectroscopy as described prevoiusly. Using this type of system we can demonstrate significant NAT production (Fig. 8).[24] Addition of a superoxide generator such as hypoxanthine/xanthine oxidase virtually

[23] J. G. Diodati, A. A. Quyyumi, and L. K. Keefer, *J. Cardiovasc. Pharmacol.* **22,** 287 (1993).
[24] A. M. Miles, M. F. Gibson, M. Kirshna, J. C. Cook, R. Pacelli, D. Wink, and M. B. Grisham, *Free Radical Res.* **23,** 379 (1995).

eliminates N-nitrosation of DAN, indicating an interaction between NO and O_2^- to yield one or more compounds with limited ability to mediate N-nitrosation reactions.[24]

The slow and spontaneous liberation of NO by nitrite at neutral pH represents another mechanism for the continuous generation of NO *in vitro*. It is well known that NO_2^- exists in equilibrium with its conjugate acid, nitrous acid (HNO_2; pK_a 3.22)[25]:

$$NO_2^- + H^+ \rightleftharpoons HNO_2 \qquad (6)$$

Because of this equilibrium, a small but significant amount of HNO_2 will be present at any one time, even at physiological pH. Once formed, HNO_2 may then transnitrosate another molecule of HNO_2 via the transfer of the NO^+ group:

$$HNO_2 + HNO_2 \rightarrow N_2O_3 + H_2O \qquad (7)$$

Dinitrogen trioxide may also decompose to yield NO_2 and NO; however, that reaction occurs relatively slowly. The formation and disproportionation of nitrous acid to yield N_2O_3 is enhanced dramatically in an acid environment. Continuous interaction of the NO-derived nitrosating agent with DAN would effectively shift the equilibrium of Eq. (7) to the right toward the formation of more nitric oxide. Thus, although nitrite is considered to be relatively innocuous and unreactive at neutral pH, it may in fact serve as a reservoir for the formation of more reactive nitrogen oxides using extended incubation times. Indeed, large amounts of nitrite incubated at neutral or slightly acidic pH have been shown to cause dose-dependent transformation of cultured cells as well as inhibit *Escherichia coli* growth *in vitro*.[26]

In an attempt to determine the rate of NO production in solutions containing nitrite at physiological pH, varying concentrations of $NaNO_2$ were incubated in PBS (pH 7.4) containing 200 μM DAN for varying lengths of time at 37°. Five hundred-microliter aliquots of each reaction mixture were removed at various times and diluted 6-fold by the addition of 2.5 ml of 10 mM NaOH, and NO production was determined via NAT production (Fig. 9). We found that the rate of production of NO was judged to be approximately 600 pmol/hr or 10 pmol/min using 20 mM $NaNO_2$. The presence of trace ferrous iron (Fe^{2+}) may also produce NO from NO_2^- by the following reaction:

$$NO_2^- + Fe^{2+} + 2H^+ \rightarrow NO + Fe^{3+} + H_2O \qquad (8)$$

[25] T. Moeller, *in* "Inorganic Chemistry," p. 615. Wiley, New York, 1965.
[26] H. Tsuda and M. Hasegawa, *Carcinogenesis (London)* **11**, 595 (1990).

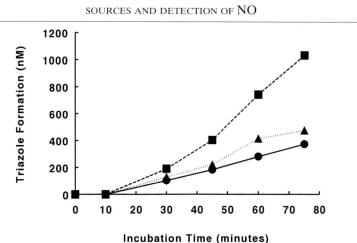

FIG. 9. 2,3-Naphthotriazole (NAT) formation by sodium nitrite. Varying concentrations of NaNO₂ were incubated for different lengths of time in 0.5-ml reaction volumes containing PBS and 200 μM DAN at 37°. Following incubation samples were diluted 6-fold by the addition of 2.5 ml of 10 mM NaOH. The concentration of NAT was determined by fluorescence emission spectroscopy at 415 nm with excitation at 375 nm. Circles represent 10 mM NaNO₂, triangles represent 15 mM NaNO₂, and squares represent 20 mM NaNO₂. From Ref. 5a with permission.

Formation of NO by reaction (8) appears unlikely, since all iron will exist as Fe^{3+} in phosphate buffer at neutral pH in the absence of a reducing agent.[27]

Reaction of 2,3-Diaminonaphthalene with Nitric Oxide Generated by Cultured Cells

The use of DAN to quantify NO generation by bacteria and macrophages has been reported.[28,29] We have modified previously published reports to characterize the L-arginine-dependent formation of nitrogen oxides by extravasated (elicited) rat neutrophils *in vitro*. We found, using NAT formation as an indicator of nitric oxide synthase (NOS) induction and NO production in extravasated neutrophils, a time- and cell-dependent increase in NOX production *in vitro* (Fig. 10).[30]

Briefly, elicited polymorphonuclear leukocytes (PMNs) are obtained

---

[27] G. Cohen, *in* "Handbook of Methods for Oxygen Radical Research," (R. A. Greenwald, ed.), p. 57. CRC Press, Boca Raton, Florida, 1985.

[28] R. Ralt, J. S. Wishnok, R. Fitts, and S. T. Tannenbaum, *J. Bacteriol.* **170,** 359 (1988).

[29] X. Ji and T. C. Hollocher, *Appl. Environ. Microbiol.* **54,** 1791 (1988).

[30] M. B. Grisham, K. Ware, H. E. Gilleland, Jr., L. B. Gilleland, C. L. Abell, and T. Yamada, *Gastroenterology* **103,** 1260 (1992).

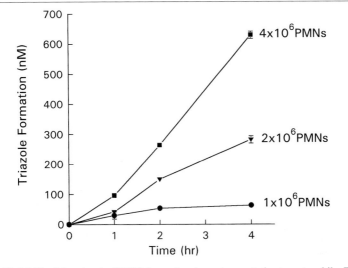

FIG. 10. 2,3-Naphthotriazole (NAT) formation by extravasated rat neutrophils. Extravasated (elicited) rat neutrophils (PMNs) were incubated for varying lengths of time at 37° in a DMEM salt solution containing 20 mM HEPES (pH 7.4), 20 mM glucose, 4 mM glutamine, 1 mM L-arginine, 0.2 mM DAN, and 50 U/ml each of penicillin and streptomycin. NAT formation was quantified by fluorescence spectroscopy as described in Fig. 8. From Ref. 5a with permission (data from Ref. 25).

from male Sprague-Dawley rats (300–400 g) following an intraperitoneal injection of 20 ml of 1% (w/v) oyster glycogen in PBS, pH 7.4.[30] Cells are harvested 5–6 hr after injection by peritoneal lavage using 50 ml heparinized PBS. Cells are washed twice with cold PBS, and contaminating erythrocytes are removed by hypotonic lysis. The neutrophil-rich pellet is then washed three times with cold PBS, counted, and placed on ice. Cells are routinely found to be over 95% pure with viability exceeding 95% as judged by trypan blue exclusion. The PMNs are suspended in a balanced salt medium containing all electrolytes and salts present in Dulbecco's modified Eagle's medium (DMEM) supplemented with 20 mM HEPES (pH 7.4), 20 mM glucose, 0.2 mM DAN, 4 mM glutamine, 1 mM L-arginine, and 50 U/ml each of penicillin and streptomycin. Cell suspensions (0.5-ml containing varying numbers of PMNs) are added to fetal bovine serum (FBS)-coated microtiter wells (1 cm^2) and incubated 4 hr at 37°. Coating tissue culture plastic with FBS has been shown to minimize the nonspecific metabolic activation of PMNs by the plastic and presents a surface more closely related to the tissue interstitium.[31] Following the incubation period, the

[31] C. F. Nathan, *J. Clin. Invest.* **80**, 1550 (1987).

microtiter plates are centrifuged at 400 g for 5 min at 4°C, and the supernatants (0.5 ml) are removed and placed into glass tubes for triazole determinations. To 0.5 ml of supernatant is added 2.5 ml of 10 mM NaOH, and the fluorescence of each sample is determined using an excitation wavelength of 375 nm and an emission wavelength of 415 nm. Concentrations of the triazole are calculated from a standard curve derived using known concentrations of the purified triazole.

Nitric oxide-dependent N-nitrosating activity may also be mediated by cells other than phagocytic leukocytes. For example, we have demonstrated that rat pleural mesothelial cells derived from the visceral pleura of female rats and incubated with 0.2 mM DAN and triple combinations of lipopolysaccharide, γ-interferon, tumor necrosis factor α, or interleukin-1β for 72 hr show enhanced NO and NAT formation from normally undetectable levels to 1.5 nmol NAT/10^6 cells.[32]

Nitrate and Nitrite Determinations Using 2,3-Diaminonaphthalene

An assay for the detection of very small amounts of NO_2^- and NO_3^-, based on the previously published methods cited above, has been reported by Misko and co-workers.[16] The assay is based on acid-catalyzed, NO_2^--dependent formation of N-nitrosating agents and subsequent N-nitrosation of DAN to yield NAT.[16] Quantification of total NO_2^- and NO_3^- formation requires the reduction of NO_3^- to NO_2^- using a variety of inorganic or enzymatic methods. Misko and co-workers found that they could measure as little as 10 nM (10 pmol/ml) NO_2^-, a quantity similar to that reported in this chapter.

On the basis of these studies we have modified this method further to measure total NO_2^- and NO_3^- formed by the inducible NOS associated with extravasated PMNs. Extravasated (elicited) rat PMNs are isolated as described above, centrifuged into a pellet containing 10^8 cells, and homogenized in 1–3 ml of 20 mM HEPES buffer (pH 7.4) containing 0.1 mM EDTA, 1 mM glutathione (GSH), 1 $\mu$$M$ tetrahydrobiopterin (BH$_4$), and 0.2 mM phenylmethylsulfonyl fluoride (PMSF). The homogenate is centrifuged at 20,000 g for 20 min at 4° and the supernatant saved on ice. Each reaction volume (0.5 ml) contains 20 mM HEPES buffer (pH 7.4), 1 mM MgCl$_2$, 1 mM CaCl$_2$, 1 $\mu$$M$ FAD$^+$, 50 mM L-valine (to inhibit arginase), 2 mM L-arginine, and 2 mM NADPH. One hundred microliters of homogenate is added to each tube to initiate the reaction. Each reaction is incubated at 37° for 1–4 hr depending on the amount of enzyme activity in the homogenate. For some samples, 1 mM L-NMMA is included to inhibit all

[32] M. W. Owens and M. B. Grisham, *Free Radical Res.* **23**, 371 (1995).

NOS activity. For other samples, $CaCl_2$ is omitted and 1 mM EGTA is included to inhibit the Ca^{2+}-dependent NOS activity. Following incubation, residual NADPH is oxidized by the addition of 5 μl of lactate dehydrogenase (diluted 10-fold with PBS; Sigma) and 50 μl of 100 mM pyruvic acid and incubated for an additional 10 min at 37°. Any residual GSH is oxidized by the addition of 5 μl of 20 mM H_2O_2 and 5 μl of GSH peroxidase (Sigma) and incubated an additional 10 min at 37°. Both NADPH and GSH interfere with the nitrosation of DAN. Finally, 50 μl of an acidic DAN solution (50 μg/ml in 6 N HCl) is added to all tubes and vortexed immediately. Tubes are allowed to incubate for an additional 10 min at room temperature. Seventy-five microliters of 10 N NaOH is then added to each tube to alkalinize the sample, and the fluorescence of each tube is determined using excitation and emission wavelengths of 375 and 415 nm, respectively.

We have found that PMN-inducible iNOS produces substantial amounts of NO_2^- using this method. In contrast to the method described by Misko et al.,[16] we substitute GSH for dithiothreitol (DTT) in the homogenization buffer because we have found that as little as 0.1 mM DTT completely inhibits the acid-catalyzed N-nitrosation of DAN. The reason for this difference is not apparent.

Conclusions

A variety of different spectrophotometric methods have been developed to measure NO directly as in the case of the reaction of NO with hemoglobin to produce methemoglobin or indirectly via the Griess reaction. The lower limit of detection of NO via the hemoglobin method is approximately 1 nmol; however, the assay suffers from lack of specificity in that other oxidizing agents (e.g., O_2^-, H_2O_2) may also react with oxyhemoglobin to produce methemoglobin. The Griess reaction is a well-known two-step diazotization reaction in which NO-derived nitrosating agents, generated from the acid-catalyzed formation of nitrous acid from nitrite, reacts with sulfanilic acid to produce a diazonium ion which is then coupled to N-(1-naphthyl)ethylenediamine to form a chromophoric azo derivative. Although the diazotization assay is more specific than the hemoglobin method, its sensitivity limit is only 0.1–1.0 μM. The N-nitrosation of 2,3-diaminonaphthalene to yield the highly fluorescent 2,3-naphthotriazole offers the additional advantages of specificity, sensitivity, and versatility. This assay is capable of detecting as little as 10–30 nM naphthotriazole (10–30 pmol/ml) and may be used to quantify NO generated under biologically relevant conditions (e.g., neutral pH) with minimal interference by nitrite decomposition. Although the trapping efficiency of DAN for NO is less than for the Griess reaction, the enhanced sensitivity of this assay provides a valuable assay for the determination of small amounts of NO.

Acknowledgments

Some of the work reported in this chapter was supported by grants from the National Institutes of Health (CA63641 and DK47663; MBG). Much of the work reported in this chapter was originally published in *Methods (San Diego)* **7**, 40–47 (1995).

[11] Determination of Selectivity of Reactive Nitrogen Oxide Species for Various Substrates

By DAVID A. WINK, MATTHEW B. GRISHAM, ALLEN M. MILES,
RAYMOND W. NIMS, MURALI C. KRISHNA, ROBERTO PACELLI,
DIANE TEAGUE, CHARLES M. B. POORE, JOHN A. COOK,
and PETER C. FORD

Introduction

Understanding the chemistry of reactive nitrogen oxide species (RNOS) has provided a description of potential biological targets lending insights into the role NO might play in various toxicological mechanisms. The NO/O_2 reaction forms a variety of nitrogen oxide species that have been shown to have potentially deleterious effects on biological systems[1]:

$$2 \text{ NO} + O_2 \rightarrow NO_x \tag{1}$$

These RNOS have been shown to deaminate nucleic acids, to induce strand breaks,[2-5] to inhibit some enzymes,[6-12] and to mobilize intracellular toxic

[1] S. E. Schwartz and W. H. White, *in* "Trace Atmospheric Constituents: Properties, Transformation and Fates" (S. E. Schwartz, ed.), p. 1. Wiley, New York, 1983.

[2] S. Gorsdorf, K. E. Appel, C. Engeholm, and O. Gunter, *Carcinogenesis (London)* **11**, 37 (1990).

[3] D. A. Wink, K. S. Kasprzak, C. M. Maragos, R. K. Elespuru, M. Misra, T. M. Dunams, T. A. Cebula, W. H. Koch, A. W. Andrews, J. S. Allen, and L. K. Keefer, *Science* **254**, 1001 (1991).

[4] T. Nguyen, D. Brunson, C. L. Crespi, B. W. Penman, J. S. Wishnok, and S. R. Tannenbaum, *Proc. Natl. Acad. Sci. U.S.A.* **89**, 3030 (1992).

[5] W. A. Pryor, *in* "Lipid Peroxides in Biology and Medicine," p. 1. Academic Press, New York, 1982.

[6] D. A. Wink and J. Laval, *Carcinogenesis (London)* **15**, 2125 (1994).

[7] F. Laval and D. A. Wink, *Carcinogenesis (London)* **15**, 443 (1994).

[8] D. A. Wink, Y. Osawa, J. F. Darbyshire, C. R. Jones, S. C. Eshenaur, and R. W. Nims, *Arch. Biochem. Biophys.* **300**, 115 (1993).

metals.[13] As in investigating the role of antioxidants as scavengers of the toxic reactive oxygen species, there is a need to find scavengers of RNOS.[14] This chapter describes a method for determining the effectiveness of different compounds in scavenging these intermediates in the NO/O_2 reaction.

The RNOS formed from the NO/O_2 reaction in nonaqueous media are NO_2, N_2O_3, and N_2O_4.[15] These are commonly associated with air pollution, and their deleterious effects on biological systems are well characterized. These intermediates nitrosate sulfhydryl groups and tyrosine.[16-18] However, it has been suggested that NO_2, the quintessential intermediate formed in the gas-phase autoxidation of NO, does not significantly participate in oxidation of substrates in aqueous NO solutions.[19,20] Subsequent examination of the reactive intermediates in aqueous solution reveals that there appears to be an intermediate, with the empirical formula N_2O_3,[21] which can nitrosate or oxidize some substrates. A comparison of phenol nitrosation by the nitrosating species in the aqueous NO/O_2 reaction with those formed in acidic nitrite led Pires *et al.* to conclude that the RNOS formed under these two circumstances are different.[22]

Although the reactive nitrogen oxide species, NO_x, derived from the aqueous NO/O_2 reaction is not fully characterized, its chemistry with various bioorganic molecules has been examined. This intermediate is capable of bimolecular reactions involving the oxidation of redox-active complexes [$E_{effective} < 0.7$ V versus saturated calomel electrode (SCE)], though considerably less than oxygen radical species,[14] as well as nitrosation of amines and thiol-containing complexes.[18,19] The hydrolysis to nitrite, oxidation, and nitrosation appear to be competitive, providing an opportunity to assess the relative selectivity of the NO_x intermediate for various biologically

[9] N. S. Kwon, D. J. Stuehr, and C. F. Nathan, *J. Exp. Med.* **174,** 761 (1991).
[10] A. Hausladen and I. Fridovich, *J. Biol. Chem.* **269,** 29405 (1994).
[11] L. Castro, M. Rodrigue, and R. Radi, *J. Biol. Chem.* **269,** 29409 (1994).
[12] R. Gopalakrishna, Z. H. Chen, and U. Gundimeda, *J. Biol. Chem.* **268,** 27180 (1993).
[13] J. C. Drapier, H. Hirling, J. Wietzerbin, P. Kaldy, and L. C. Kuhn, *EMBO J.* **12,** 3643 (1993).
[14] M. B. Grisham and A. M. Miles, *Biochem. Pharmacol.* **47,** 1897 (1994).
[15] W. C. Nottingham and J. R. Sutter, *Int. J. Chem. Kinet.* **25,** 375 (1989).
[16] W. A. Pryor, D. F. Church, C. K. Govindan, and G. Crank, *J. Org. Chem.* **47,** 156 (1982).
[17] W. A. Prutz, H. Monig, J. L. Butler, and E. Land, *Arch. Biochem. Biophys.* **243,** 125 (1985).
[18] D. A. Wink, R. W. Nims, J. F. Darbyshire, D. Christodoulou, I. Hanbauer, G. W. Cox, F. Laval, J. Laval, J. A. Cook, M. C. Krishna, W. DeGraff, and J. B. Mitchell, *Chem. Res. Toxicol.* **7,** 519 (1994).
[19] D. A. Wink, J. F. Darbyshire, R. W. Nims, J. E. Saveedra, and P. C. Ford, *Chem. Res. Toxicol.* **6,** 23 (1993).
[20] M. N. Routledge, D. A. Wink, L. K. Keefer, and A. Dipple, *Chem. Res. Toxicol.* **7,** 628 (1994).
[21] D. A. Wink and P. C. Ford, *Methods (San Diego)* **7,** 14–20 (1995).
[22] M. Pires, D. S. Ross, and M. J. Rossi, *Int. J. Chem. Kinet.* **26,** 1207 (1994).

important substances. A report has shown that sulfhydryl-containing peptides such as glutathione have a high affinity for this intermediate, forming S-nitrosothiol adducts[18]:

$$NO_x + RSH \rightarrow RSNO \qquad (2)$$

These adducts have been shown by Stamler *et al.* to form endogenously in the cardiovascular and pulmonary system.[23,24] The affinity of sulfhydryl groups for NO_x is 10^6-fold greater than that for nucleic acids and 10^3-fold greater than that for other amino acids, except tyrosine.[18] It has been shown that glutathione may serve as scavenger of NO_x, playing a critical role in detoxication.[18,25] On the other hand, enzymes containing thiol groups critical to their catalytic functions are inhibited or inactivated by these intermediates whereas other enzymes are not.[6,7]

Competitive kinetic investigations of the selectivity of NO_x versus other known RNOS toward different substrates have been employed as a means of characterizing the intermediate generated in aqueous NO/O_2 reactions. Kinetics of oxidation of ferrocyanide indicated that NO_x is not NO_2.[19] Azide, which is a good scavenger of nitrosating agents, was used to determine the selectivity between nitrite formation, ferrocyanide oxidation, and nitrosation of azide.[20] Addition of various concentrations of azide to a fixed amount of ferrocyanide showed quenching of the ferricyanide formed. A comparison of the azide quenching of ferricyanide formation between the intermediate formed in the NO/O_2 reaction to the expected pattern for NO^+ and peroxynitrite anion clearly ruled out the participation of both of the latter species.[19] Furthermore, there was a distinct difference in selectivity between the N_2O_3 thought to form in the gas-phase NO/O_2 reaction, as well as in weakly acidic nitrite solution, and that of NO_x.[22]

Experimental studies of this type can be useful in characterizing not only the nature of the reactive intermediate but the selectivities of other substrates. Spectroscopic tools can be used to probe the reactivity of NO_x toward various substrates.[19,20] Competitive studies can be informative for accessing the relative affinities of NO_x for different substrates. Described here are two methods that can be employed for determining the selectivity of NO_x for various substances: (1) double-reciprocal plots of product formation versus substrate concentration and (2) quenching of product formation from one substrate by a second substrate.

[23] J. S. Stamler, O. Jaraki, J. Osbourne, D. I. Simon, J. Keaney, J. Vita, D. Singel, R. Valeri, and J. Loscalzo, *Proc. Natl. Acad. Sci. U.S.A.* **89**, 7674 (1992).

[24] B. Gaston, J. Reilly, J. M. Drazen, J. Fackler, P. Ramdev, D. Arnelle, M. E. Mullins, D. J. Sugarbaker, C. Chee, D. J. Singel, J. Loscalzo, and J. S. Stamler, *Proc. Natl. Acad. Sci. U.S.A.* **90**, 10957 (1993).

[25] M. W. Walker, M. T. Kinter, R. J. Roberts, and D. R. Spitz, *Pediatr. Res.* **37**, 1002 (1995).

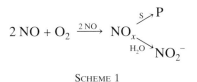

Materials

Azide, glutathione, cysteine, ascorbate, and 2,3-diaminonaphthylene (DAN) are purchased from Aldrich (Milwaukee, WI). DAN is recrystallized from hot dichloromethane, followed by addition of methanol. The solid is filtered and washed with diethyl ether before being predissolved in acetonitrile as a 100 mM stock solution. DAN is then diluted in the aqueous buffer to the desired concentration. Nitric oxide stock solutions are prepared as previously described and the concentration determined by colorimetric methods.[26] Fluorescence measurements are done on a Perkin-Elmer (Norwalk, CT) fluorometer; excitation is at 350 nm and emission is monitored at 450 nm.

Methods

Product Formation Analysis

The rate at which NO_x undergoes hydrolysis in aqueous solutions will limit the reactions this molecule can undergo with various substrates (Scheme 1). From these equations, we can derive an expression that will provide the ratio of rate constants for a variety of reactions. Such information should provide a better understanding of the selectivity of NO_x.

One example is the nitrosation of DAN to form a fluorescent triazole (TRI). Exposure of DAN to the NO/O_2 reaction yields a production of fluorescence corresponding to TRI[14]:

$$NO_x + H_2O \rightarrow NO_2^- \qquad (3)$$
$$NO_x + DAN \rightarrow \text{triazole (TRI)} \qquad (4)$$

The formation of TRI is directly proportional to the initial DAN concentration such that a plot of (fluorescence)$^{-1}$ versus $[DAN]^{-1}$ is linear. From the slope and the y-intercept, a ratio between the rate constant for the reaction of NO_x with DAN [Eq. (4)] and that for the hydrolysis to nitrite [Eq. (3)]

[26] R. W. Nims, J. F. Darbyshire, J. E. Saavedra, D. Christodoulou, I. Hanbauer, G. W. Cox, M. B. Grisham, J. Laval, J. A. Cook, M. C. Krishna, and D. A. Wink, *Methods (San Diego)* **7**, 48–54 (1995).

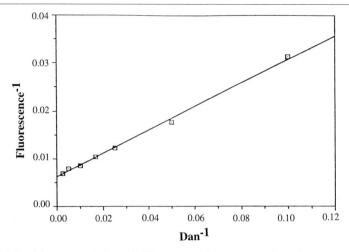

FIG. 1. Double-reciprocal plot of DAN concentration versus resultant fluorescence. A 100 mM stock solution of DAN in acetonitrile was diluted to the specified concentration. A 10 μM solution was added via air-tight syringe to the stirring solution in a cuvette. A final reading was taken after 5 min. Fluorescence measurements were done on a Perkin-Elmer Model 846 fluorometer where the excitation was 350 nm and the emission was monitored at 450 nm. The slope of the line was 16.87 μM with a y-intercept of 0.006.

may be determined. From Fig. 1, the ratio (Eqs. 3 and 4, $k_s : k_H$) is $1 : 20,000$ M^{-1}. This is an example of the type of information that can help to create a chemical interpretation of the potential biological targets.

A mathematical model can be used to determine the relative affinities of various substrates for NO_x. The ratio of rate constants $k_s : k_H$ establishes the relative affinity of substrate (S) and the amount of product (P) that will be formed at specific substrate concentrations or, in other words, the fraction of total NO_x that is scavenged by S. The ratio between k_s and k_H can be assessed by analyzing the product formation as a function of substrate concentration. This is analogous to the Lineweaver–Burke plots commonly employed in the study of enzyme kinetics. The following mathematical derivation for Scheme 1 will aid in the determination of the selectivity.

The ratio of product formed versus nitrite formed is proportional to the rates of formation for each reaction pathway such that

$$(d[P]/dt)/(d[N]/dt) = \text{ratio of product formation to nitrite formation} \quad (5)$$

since

$$d[P]/dt = k_s[NO_x][S] \quad (6)$$

and nitrite formation is unimolecular, since water is the solvent. Therefore,

$$d[N]/dt = k_H[NO_x] \quad (7)$$

and

$$d[P]/d[N] = (k_s[NO_x][S]/(k_H[NO_x])) \quad (8)$$

Simplifying Eq. (8) gives

$$[P]/[N] = k_s[S]/k_H \quad (9)$$

The amount of P as it relates to amount of nitrite formed via hydrolysis is

$$[P]_0 = [P] + [N] \quad (10)$$

where $[P]_0$ is equal to the total amount of P formed at infinite S concentration or, in other words, the total NO_x formed.

If one solves for [N], $[N] = [P]_0 - [P]$, which then can be substituted into Eq. (9):

$$[P]/([P]_0 - [P]) = k_s[S]/k_H \quad (11)$$

This can then be solved algebraically in terms of $1/[P]$ to yield

$$1/[P] = k_H/(k_s[S])[P]_0^{-1} + ([P]_0)^{-1} \quad (12)$$

A plot of $1/[P]$ versus $1/[S]$ will give a line with slope $= k_H/(k_s)$ $(1/[P]_0)$ and y-intercept $1/[P]_0$. Therefore,

$$k_s/k_H = (y\text{-intercept})/\text{slope} \quad \text{or} \quad -(x\text{-intercept}) \quad (13)$$

Using this methodology, the negative reciprocal of the x-intercept represents the concentration of substrate required to scavenge 50% of the available NO_x, that is, the concentration of substrate required such that the rate of product formation is equal to the rate hydrolysis of NO_x. Hence, $k_H = k_s[S]_{0.5}$ which can be solved as follows:

$$k_H/k_s = [S]_{0.5} = -1/x\text{-intercept} \quad (14)$$

Product Quenching

Another approach is to design a study of the competition between two different substrates S and Q (quencher) for NO_x (Scheme 2). As mentioned

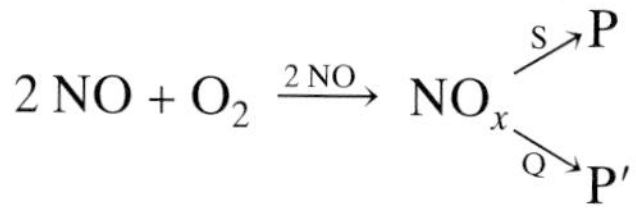

$$2\,NO + O_2 \xrightarrow{2\,NO} NO_x \begin{array}{c} \overset{S}{\nearrow} P \\ \underset{Q}{\searrow} P' \end{array}$$

SCHEME 2

earlier, 2,3-diaminonaphthylene (DAN) reacts with NO_x to form a fluorescent triazole complex. Using the product formation method described above, a selectivity was determined. From Fig. 1, the ratio $k_s : k_H$ is 1 : 20,000 M^{-1}. Azide is a very good scavenger of nitrosating agents such as NO_x and has been shown to quench the oxidation of ferrocyanide and the nitrosation in S-nitrosothiol formation in a concentration-dependent manner.[18,19] When the DAN concentration is held constant and the azide concentration is increased, a concentration-dependent reduction in the amount of triazole is observed (Fig. 2). A plot of azide concentration versus absorbance at 340 nm is linear, indicating a value of 1 : 20 for $k_s : k_Q$. The advantage of this method is that, if product formation from a particular substrate is difficult to quantify, then the competitive technique allows one to determine the quantitative reactivity of the substrate. This allows the evaluation of rates for a large number of substrates, including those for which product analysis cannot be performed.

A mathematical expression can be derived for Scheme 2 which yields the ratio of rate constants for k_s and k_Q for reactions of NO_x with the respective substrates S and Q. As above, the ratio [P]/[P'] is proportional to the ratio of their rates of formation:

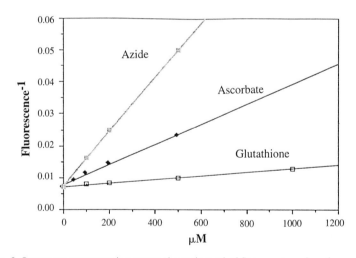

FIG. 2. Scavenger concentration versus the reciprocal of fluorescence when the scavenger is ascorbate, azide, and glutathione. Various concentrations of azide, glutathione, and ascorbate were added to 500 μM DAN in phosphate-buffered saline (PBS). To these solutions was added 10 μM NO. Fluorescence was measured as described in Fig. 1. A plot of [scavenger] versus fluorescence^{-1} was linear, yielding the following slopes: azide, 8×10^{-5} M^{-1} ($r^2 = 0.999$); ascorbate, 3.1×10^{-5} M^{-1} ($r^2 = 0.995$); and glutathione, 5.5×10^{-6} M^{-1} ($r^2 = 1.0$). The y-intercept was 0.0075 ± 0.03 for all three plots. Each point represents four measurements all within less than 10% error.

$$(d[P]/dt)/d[P']/dt) = d[P]/d[P']$$ (15)

Since

$$d[P]/dt = k_s[NO_x][S]$$ (16)
$$d[P']/dt = k_Q[NO_x][Q]$$ (17)

then

$$[P]/[P'] = (k_s[NO_x][S])/(k_Q[NO_x][Q])$$ (18)

Often it is inconvenient to quantify product P'; it can be expressed in terms of P. In the absence of Q, P is the only product, and $[P]_T$ is the total scavengable NO_x found under these conditions (when $k_s[S] \gg k_H$) when both P and Q are present. Then,

$$[P]_T = [P] + [P']$$ (19)

and therefore

$$[P'] = [P]_T - [P]$$ (20)

Thus,

$$[P]/([P]_T - [P]) = (k_s[S])/(k_Q[Q])$$ (21)

Solving Eq. (21) for 1/[P] gives

$$1/[P] = (k_Q[Q])/(k_s[S]) \times (1/[P]_T - 1/[P])$$ (22)

In this type of experiment, the substrate concentration remains constant while the amount of quencher Q is varied. A plot of 1/[P] versus [Q] yields a linear graph with slope $(k_Q)/(k_s[S]) \times (1/[P]_T)$ and y-intercept $1/[P]_T$. If [S] is known, then

$$k_Q/k_s = [S](\text{slope}/y\text{-intercept})   \text{or}   [S](x\text{-intercept})$$ (23)

It is important to note that with this type of experiment, the substrate concentration should be such that over 90% of the NO_x is scavenged by S in the absence of Q. UV–visible absorbance spectroscopy is often employed, owing to its convenience. The Beer–Lambert law states that

$$\text{Absorbance} = \Delta\varepsilon\, Cb$$ (24)

where $\Delta\varepsilon$ is the change in molar absorbance at a specific wavelength, C is the concentration of the product, b is the path length of the cell in centimeters (commonly, $b = 1$ cm). Therefore, when solving any equation whether using the product formation or quenching methods, 1/A can be substituted

TABLE I
SELECTIVITY OF NO_x TO REACTION WITH VARIOUS SUBSTRATES IN
AQUEOUS SOLUTION

Substrate	$k_s/k_H \ (M^{-1})^a$	Concentration required to scavenge 90% of NO_x (mM)
Ferrocyanide	5×10^2	20
Cysteine	5×10^3	2
Glutathione	10^4	1
Tyrosine	25	400
DAN	$3 \times 10^4 \ ^b$	0.3
Ascorbate	$3 \times 10^4 \ ^b$	0.3
Azide ion	10^5	0.1
Amino acids	<5	2000
Cytosine	<0.005	2×10^5
5-Aminosalicylic acid	$2 \times 10^3 \ ^b$	5
Dopamine	$1 \times 10^3 \ ^b$	10
Phosphate	25	400

^{a} Obtained by monitoring of the resultant product with absorbance at 400 nm.
^{b} Obtained by monitoring the formation of the resultant oxidized product with absorbance 475 nm.

for 1/[P]. Table I lists some relative rate constants for NO_x with various biological substrates as summarized from several reports and experiments of this type.[3,18,19]

Reactive Nitrogen Oxide Species Scavenging by Various Biological Solutions

When trying to compare the chemical, biochemical, or toxicological mechanisms under a variety of conditions, different media or solutions which could contain elements that might scavenge RNOS may lead to different experimental results. For instance, dithiothreitol (DTT) and ascorbate are often found in various biochemical preparations. We have found that these compounds are good scavengers of NO_x. One experiment may result in modification of a protein by RNOS; yet when this same experiment is repeated with a different preparation of the protein, no modification is observed. Often ascorbate and DTT are present in biological preparations to provide stability. By comparing DAN fluorescence with the fluorescence in regular buffered solution, one can determine if RNOS scavengers are present. This knowledge will aid the experimentalist in mechanistic interpretations.

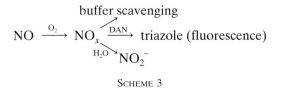

SCHEME 3

Another potential problem is the presence of nucleophiles in buffered solutions. It was pointed out that phosphate might scavenge nitrosating species in the NO/O_2 reaction. This may present a problem in some experimental interpretations. By adjusting the DAN concentration such that 50% of NO_x resulted in triazole formation, a comparison of various solvents can be done (see Scheme 3).

In Fig. 3, a comparison of some commonly used solutions is shown. HEPES, Tris, carbonate, and phosphate-buffered saline (PBS) showed little attenuation. However, when the phosphate concentration approached 0.1 M there was a decrease in fluorescence. This suggests that phosphate

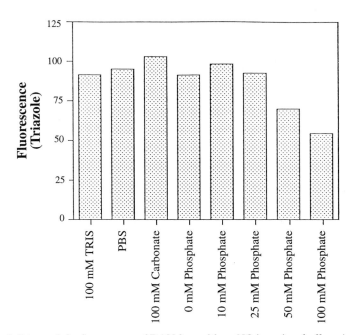

FIG. 3. Bar graph for fluorescence of DAN formed from NO in various buffers. A solution of 50 μM DAN was present in the various buffered solutions. Then 10 μM NO was added via a gas-tight syringe and the fluorescence measured after 5 min.

has a selectivity of $1:25\ M^{-1}$. Although in most experiments buffer scavenging may not present a problem, it might need to be considered.

Acknowledgments

By acceptance of this article, the publisher or recipient acknowledges the right of the U.S. government to retain a nonexclusive, royalty-free license and to any copyright covering the article. The content of this publication does not necessarily reflect views or policies of the Department of Health and Human Services, nor does mention of trade names, commercial products, or organizations imply endorsement by the U.S. government.

[12] Quantitation of Nitrate, Nitrite, and Nitrosating Agents

By John S. Wishnok, Joseph A. Glogowski, and Steven R. Tannenbaum

Introduction

The explosive growth in nitric oxide research since about 1987 has been accompanied by an active effort to develop reliable and sensitive analytical methods for this substance and its reaction products. Detection of nitric oxide itself in physiological systems has been difficult because of the short lifetimes and low concentrations of this compound under such conditions. Several advances, including the development of electrochemical nitric oxide detectors[1] and membrane inlets for mass spectrometers and thermal energy analyzers (TEA),[2] now allow direct quantitation of nitric oxide in solution. Measurement of nitrite and nitrate, the final products of the chemical oxidation pathways of nitric oxide, and of the nitrosation products arising from active intermediate compounds can nonetheless yield important information concerning the total amount of nitric oxide formed, the apportioning of the nitric oxide into potentially toxic and detoxified products, and the mechanisms of the related chemical and biochemical processes. These measurements are the subject of this chapter.

The cascade of reactions just mentioned begins when nitric oxide reacts with oxygen to form N_2O_3 and ends with reaction with nucleophilic substances, among the most significant being amine nitrogens from N-nitroso

[1] T. Malinski and Z. Taha, *Nature* (*London*) **358**, 676 (1992).
[2] R. S. Lewis, W. M. Deen, S. R. Tannenbaum, and J. S. Wishnok, *Biological Mass Spectrometry* **22**, 45 (1992).

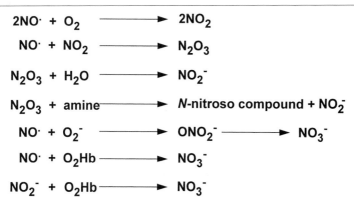

SCHEME 1. Reactions arising from the interaction of nitric oxide with oxygen.

compounds and water to form nitrite (Scheme 1; a more complete discussion of this chemistry and the associated kinetics can be found in Lewis and Deen[3]). Reaction of nitric oxide with superoxide or oxyhemoglobin, or reaction of nitrite with oxyhemoglobin, can result in the formation of nitrate.[4–6]

Early research concerning the origin of the nitrogen in urinary nitrate, and subsequent research concerning the biochemical pathways leading to nitric oxide, required quantitation of [^{15}N]nitrate.[7–10] The relationship of these pathways to endogenous nitrosation of amines can be studied by quantitating ^{15}N incorporation into N-nitroso compounds. Measurement of this relatively simple set of end points, namely, nitrate and nitrite in physiological fluids and ^{15}N incorporation into nitrate and nitrosamines, has provided major insight into nitric oxide biochemistry and physiology and into some potentially important toxicological and epidemiological consequences of nitric oxide production.

[3] R. S. Lewis and W. M. Deen, *Chem. Res. Toxicol.* **7,** 568 (1994).

[4] R. C. Plumb and J. O. Edwards, *J. Phys. Chem.* **96,** 3245 (1992).

[5] W. H. Koppenol, W. A. Pryor, J. J. Moreno, H. Ischiropoulos, and J. S. Beckman, *Chem. Res. Toxicol.* **6,** 834 (1992).

[6] J. P. Crow, C. Spruell, J. Chen, C. Gunn, H. Ischiropoulos, M. Tsai, C. D. Smith, R. Radi, W. H. Koppenol, and J. S. Beckman, *Free Radical Biol. Med.* **16,** 331 (1994).

[7] D. A. Wagner, D. S. Schultz, W. M. Deen, V. R. Young, and S. R. Tannenbaum, *Cancer Res.* **43,** 1921 (1983).

[8] M. A. Marletta, P. S. Yoon, R. Iyengar, C. D. Leaf, and J. S. Wishnok, *Biochemistry* **27,** 8706 (1988).

[9] D. A. Wagner, V. R. Young, and S. R. Tannenbaum, *Proc. Natl. Acad. Sci. U.S.A.* **80,** 4518 (1983).

[10] R. Iyengar, D. J. Stuehr, and M. A. Marletta, *Proc. Natl. Acad. Sci. U.S.A.* **84,** 6369 (1987).

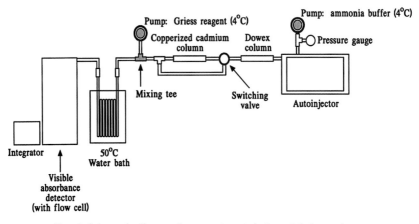

FIG. 1. Schematic diagram for an automated nitrate/nitrite analyzer.

Quantitation of Nitrate/Nitrite by the Griess Reaction

Quantitation of nitrate and nitrite in our laboratory is based on the Griess reaction, in which a chromophore with a strong absorbance at 540 nm is formed by reaction of nitrite with a mixture of naphthylethylenediamine and sulfanilamide.[11,12] Following cleanup, an aliquot of the sample is mixed with fresh reagent and the absorbance is measured in a spectrophotometer to give the nitrite concentration. If nitrate concentrations are desired, a second aliquot is treated with copperized cadmium to reduce nitrate to nitrite. The concentration of nitrite in this aliquot now represents the total of nitrate plus nitrite. The nitrate concentration in the sample is thus given by the difference between the two aliquots. The analysis can be done manually for occasional small numbers of samples, but it is well-suited to automation for frequent measurements of larger numbers of samples (see below and Fig. 1).

Materials

Buffer: 1% (w/v) ammonium chloride, adjusted to pH 8.0 with sodium borate; store at 4°

Griess reagent: 1:1 solution of 0.1% (w/v) N-(1-naphthyl)ethylenediamine dihydrochloride and 1% (w/v) sulfanilamide, in 5% (v/v) phosphoric acid; store at 4°

[11] P. Griess, *Ber. Deutsch. Chem. Ges.* **12**, 426 (1879).

[12] L. C. Green, D. A. Wagner, J. Glogowski, P. L. Skipper, J. S. Wishnok, and S. R. Tannenbaum, *Anal. Biochem.* **126**, 131 (1982).

SSA solution: 35% (w/v) sulfosalicylic acid
Cupric sulfate: 5% (w/v) cupric sulfate
Copperized cadmium: −100, +325 mesh; store in 5% (v/v) HCl
Dowex: Dowex 50W-X12 200–400 mesh, spheres, ionic form H⁺

Sample Preparation

Protein-Containing Solutions

Place 500 μl of the sample in a small tabletop centrifuge tube and add 200 μl of 35% sulfosalicylic acid. Begin vortexing immediately to prevent clumping, taking care that the acid reaches the tip of the tube, and continue to vortex for 1 min. Let the solution stand for 30 min, mixing at 5-min intervals. The protein particles should be very fine. Centrifuge in a tabletop centrifuge for 5 min, or until a firm pellet is formed. Remove 200 μl of the supernatant, place it in a sample tube, add 300 μl buffer, mix well, and analyze. Further dilution may be required. This procedure can be used for all proteinacious samples, for example, plasma, blood, or milk.

Nonprotein Samples

Nonprotein samples are simply diluted with distilled water to the point where the nitrate–nitrite levels fall within the range of the standards. Acidic samples must be adjusted to a pH near neutrality, so as not to interfere with the reduction of nitrate by the cadmium.

Copperized Cadmium

The cadmium metal is washed three times with 5% (v/v) HCl in a 250-ml Erlenmeyer flask, inverting the flask several times during each washing. The metal is then rinsed with distilled water until it is free from acid. At this stage the metal should be light in color. After the final rinse, as much of the water as possible is removed. The cadmium is then copperized with 200 ml of 5% cupric sulfate. Gently invert the flask several times. Decant the liquid after about 15 sec, but before the solution becomes colorless. Depending on the amount of cadmium used (i.e., more than about 10 g), a second copperization may be necessary. Do not copperize to the point that copper particles can be seen. At this stage the cadmium should look dark. Wash with water to remove excess fines. Gently invert the flask several times, allow the bulk of the material to settle, and decant the upper layer. Repeat until the most of the particles settle within 8 sec. Store in 5% HCl until needed. At this stage the cadmium is ready to use in batch or automated analysis.

Automated Analysis

Off-the-shelf components can be assembled to permit analysis with little human intervention. The required parts (Fig. 1) include an automatic sample injector, a column-switching valve, a mixing tee, two standard tees, two high-performance liquid chromatography (HPLC) pumps, a water bath, an absorbance detector set to 540 nm, and an integrator. Standard Swageloc fittings and 1/16-inch Teflon tubing will also be needed. A 10-foot coil of tubing is placed in a 50° water bath to delay passage into the detector and thus allow complete color development. Two columns, one packed with Dowex and the other with copperized cadmium, are made from 6-inch pieces of 1/8-inch Teflon tubing. The column-switching valve is arranged so that the sample always flows through the Dowex column; the cadmium column is selected when total nitrate is desired. The Dowex column removes contaminants that might affect the reduction efficiency of the cadmium. This arrangement is shown schematically in Fig. 1.

Batch Analysis

A small amount of copperized cadmium is placed in a small tabletop centrifuge tube and washed with distilled water. As much of the water as possible is removed with a Pasteur pipette. Five hundred microliters of diluted sample is added to each tube and mixed well. Allow about 5 min, with intermittent mixing, for the reduction to go to completion. Centrifuge if necessary to obtain a clear supernatant. Add 300 μl of the sample to a new tube, add 150 μl Griess reagent, mix well, and allow the color to develop for 2–5 min in a 50° water bath. Read the absorbance on a spectrophotometer at 540 nm.

Standards

Nitrate and nitrite standards are prepared at concentrations of 6, 12, 24, and 60 μM. A pooled urine sample is used as a control sample to check the efficiency of the analysis from day to day.

Calculations

Linear regression is done using the peak areas from the nitrate or nitrite standards. The resulting equation is then used to calculate the unknown sample concentrations.

Quantitation of [^{15}N]Nitrate by Gas Chromatography–Mass Spectrometry

Nitric oxide can be measured in real time in a mass spectrometer with a membrane inlet,[2] and this technique can therefore be used in principle to measure incorporation of ^{15}N into nitric oxide arising from labeled precursors. Although efficient and effective, this requires that the instrumentation be assembled and tuned for high sensitivity and that the reactions be carried out in the same room as the mass spectrometer. Measurement of label in [^{15}N]nitrate, on the other hand, can be done on stored aliquots using standard gas chromatography–mass spectrometry (GC–MS) instruments. [^{15}N]Nitrate, in addition, reflects the total production of nitric oxide and thus requires less sensitivity than membrane measurements that reflect the much lower instantaneous or steady-state concentrations of nitric oxide.

The method of choice for this analysis involves the conversion of nitrate to nitrobenzene by reaction with benzene, under strongly acidic conditions.[12–14] The nitrobenzene can then be analyzed by GC–MS using fused-silica capillary columns coated with moderately polar to polar stationary phases such as HP-5, DB-17, or Supelcowax. If this technique is also being used to quantitate total nitrate, the sample volumes must be accurately measured and an internal standard should be added.[15] If the incorporation of ^{15}N is the only quantity of interest then neither of these is necessary, because the [^{14}N]nitrate serves as the standard for determining the ratio ^{15}N/[14]N.

Equipment

Screw-cap test tubes
Ice bucket with ice
Tabletop centrifuge
Vortex mixer
Heating block at 70°
Pipetman (1000 and 200 or 100)
Pasteur pipettes and bulb

Chemicals

Ag_2SO_4 (solid)
Zn_2SO_4 (saturated solution)
Benzene
Concentrated H_2SO_4
5 N NaOH (on ice)
Ethyl acetate
Na_2SO_4 (anhydrous)

[13] L. Castillo, T. C. deRojas, T. E. Chapman, J. Vogt, J. F. Burke, S. R. Tannenbaum, and V. R. Young, *Proc. Natl. Acad. Sci. U.S.A.* **90,** 193 (1993).
[14] B. J. Dull and J. H. Hotchkiss, *Toxicol. Lett.* **23,** 79 (1984).
[15] B. J. Dull and J. H. Hotchkiss, *Food Chem. Toxicol.* **22,** 105 (1984).

Sample Preparation

Samples are prepared as described earlier for nitrate/nitrite analysis. To 1 ml urine in a screw-cap test tube add aproximately 20 mg Ag_2SO_4 and 0.5 ml saturated Zn_2SO_4 solution and heat for 5 min at 70°. Vortex for 30 sec and then centrifuge for 5 min at medium speed in a tabletop centrifuge. Transfer 0.5 ml of the supernatant to another screw-cap test tube. Put the test tube in an ice bucket, and, while working in a fume hood, add 50 μl benzene and 1 ml concentrated H_2SO_4. Vortex for 30 sec and then heat for 15 min at 70°, vortexing every 5 min. Cool the reaction mixture on ice. Slowly add 0.5 ml ice-cold 5 N NaOH, while gently vortexing and keeping the mixture cool with ice. Repeat three times (add a total of 2.0 ml of 5 N NaOH). Add 0.5 ml ethyl acetate and vortex for 2 min. Centrifuge for 5 min at medium speed in a tabletop centrifuge to separate the layers. Remove the ethyl acetate layer (top layer) and transfer to a small vial. Add approximately 25 mg Na_2SO_4 to remove residual water. This solution can now be injected directly into the GC–MS.

General Considerations for Gas Chromatography–Mass Spectrometry

For GC–MS quantitation the mass spectrometer is usually operated in the selected ion-monitoring (SIM) mode using characteristic high-abundance ions if possible. The dwell times should be sufficiently short that 7–12 cycles can be obtained during the elution of the peak. For analyses of extracts of biological fluids, for example, urine or cell culture medium, the temperature program should continue well above the elution temperature of the analyte in order to clear the column of components that may have coextracted with the compounds of interest (compare Fig. 4A with Fig. 4B,C).

The major ions monitored for nitrobenzene are m/z 123 and m/z 124, that is, the respective molecular ions for [14N]- and [15N]nitrobenzene. If significant amounts of $M - 1$ ions are generated in the mass spectrometer (see below), then m/z 122 should also be monitored. The mass chromatograms shown in Fig. 2 were obtained on a fused-silica capillary column coated with Supelcowax 10 (15 m × 0.25 mm, 0.25 μm film thickness). The head pressure was 5 psi (35 kPa). The injector temperature was 240°. The oven temperature was held at 80° during the splitless time of 0.5 min and was then programmed at 20°/min to a final temperature of 220°. The dwell times were 50 msec for each ion. The mass spectrometer was tuned with the standard autotune routine included in the software. The individual mass chromatograms were integrated with the automatic integration routines in the data analysis software.

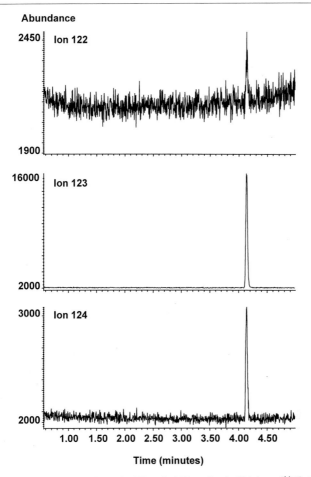

FIG. 2. Mass chromatograms for m/z 122, m/z 123, and m/z 124 from [^{14}N]nitrobenzene. Chromatography was done with a Supelcowax 10 column under the conditions described in the text.

Data Analysis

In our experience, the electron ionization (EI) mass spectra for [^{14}N]- and [^{15}N]nitrobenzene are instrument dependent. Note that even though the full mass spectrum of nitrobenzene (threshold of 50) shows no signal at m/z 122 (Fig. 3), a small peak can nonetheless be observed in the mass chromatogram of m/z 122 (Fig. 2). In our initial experiments,[12] in addition to the $M + 1$ (m/z 124) ion that arises from natural abundance ^{13}C, there was a peak at $M - 1$ (m/z 122). At high enrichment, then, the $M - 1$

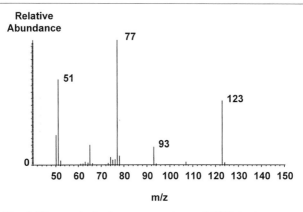

FIG. 3. Electron ionization mass spectrum of [^{14}N]nitrobenzene.

peak from [^{15}N]nitrobenzene could contribute significantly to the nominal molecular ion for [^{14}N]nitrobenzene, leading in turn to incorrect (lowered) values for ^{15}N because of incorrectly high values of ^{14}N. In more recent experiments,[13] with a different mass spectrometer, no $M - 1$ peak was observed, but the $M + 1$ peak was persistently 6.4% of the molecular ion as opposed to the expected value of just over 6.6%. In each of these cases, the integrated areas were corrected by an algorithm based on data obtained from standard mixtures of [^{15}N]- and [^{14}N]nitrobenzene. If a high degree of accuracy is needed, then similar algorithms should probably be developed specifically for the mass spectrometer that is being used for the measurements. For measurements of low incorporation of ^{15}N (e.g., atom-percent excess of less than 1% of the natural abundance of ^{13}C), better results can probably be obtained with an isotope-ratio mass spectrometer.[16–18]

Quantitation of Nitrosating Agents

Nitric oxide-related nitrosations arise from either N_2O_3 or N_2O_4, although N_2O_3 predominates in physiological systems.[10,19,20] Both N_2O_3 and N_2O_4 react rapidly with water, amines, and other nucleophiles that might be present in the system, and the steady-state concentrations of these intermediates are therefore low. Their net nitrosating potential, however,

[16] J. H. Cherney and J. M. Duxbury, *J. Plant Nutr.* **17**, 2053 (1994).
[17] E. Deleeens, J.-B. Cliquet, and J.-L. Prioul, *Aust. J. Plant Physiol.* **21**, 133 (1994).
[18] E. M. Postlethwaite and A. Bidani, *Toxicol. Appl. Pharmacol.* **98**, 303 (1989).
[19] M. A. Marletta, *Chem. Res. Toxicol.* **1**, 249 (1988).
[20] D. J. Stuehr and M. A. Marletta, *Cancer Res.* **47**, 5590 (1987).

can be readily estimated by quantitating the nitrosation products. Morpholine is often used as the nitrosatable amine because its high pK_a assures a significant concentration of free amine at physiological pH.[21] Quantitation is by GC–TEA or by GC–MS. If GC–MS is available, this method can also be used to quantitate incorporation of ^{15}N into the nitrosamine.[10] If there are no confounding factors such as hydrophobicity,[22–24] the rates of nitrosation of other secondary amines relative to morpholine can be estimated on the basis of their pK_a values.[21,25] 2,3-Diaminonaphthalene has also been used to assess nitrosation potential because it can be conveniently quantitated via the fluorescence of the resulting triazene.[26–28]

Sample Preparation of N-Nitrosomorpholine

N-Nitrosomorpholine can be extracted directly from most aqueous systems with dichloromethane. Media that contain cells, cellular debris, or high concentrations of protein may be cleaned up prior to extraction by deproteinization and/or centrifugation. In a typical experiment, centrifuge tubes are prepared with 250 μl of dichloromethane containing an internal standard and 250 μl of NaOH (1–5 N) or NaN$_3$ (4 N). If detection is by GC–TEA, the internal standard should also be an N-nitrosamine, for example, N-nitrosodimethylmorpholine or N-nitrosopyrrolidine. For GC–MS detection, the internal standard should chromatograph well, elute in the vicinity of N-nitrosomorpholine, and have a good mass spectral response; nitrobenzene, for example, is well suited for analyses on Supelcowax or Carbowax columns (see Fig. 2). Aliquots (250 μl) of the sample are added to the tubes which are vortexed for several seconds and then centrifuged in a tabletop centrifuge to separate the layers. In most cases the dichloromethane solutions can be injected directly onto the GC–MS or GC–TEA. If the GC columns are sensitive to water (e.g., Carbowax or Supelcowax), then the dichloromethane layer can be dried with an agent such as anhydrous Na$_2$SO$_4$ prior to injection.

[21] S. S. Mirvish, *Toxicol. Appl. Pharmacol.* **31,** 325 (1975).
[22] H. S. Yang, J. D. Okun, and M. C. Archer, *J. Agric. Food Chem.* **25,** 1181 (1977).
[23] J. D. Okun and M. C. Archer, *in* "Environmental N-Nitroso Compounds Analysis and Formation" (E. A. Walker, P. Bogovski, and L. Griciute, eds.), p. 147, IARC 14. International Agency for Research on Cancer, Lyon, 1976.
[24] J. D. Okun and M. C. Archer, *J. Org. Chem.* **42,** 391 (1977).
[25] M. Miwa, D. J. Stuehr, M. A. Marletta, J. S. Wishnok, and S. R. Tannenbaum, *Carcinogenesis* (*London*) **8,** 955 (1987).
[26] D. Ralt, J. S. Wishnok, R. Fitts, and S. R. Tannenbaum, *J. Bacteriol.* **170,** 359 (1988).
[27] X.-B. Ji and T. C. Hollocher, *Appl. Environ. Microbiol.* **54,** 1791 (1988).
[28] J. H. Wiersma, *Anal. Lett.* **3,** 123 (1970).

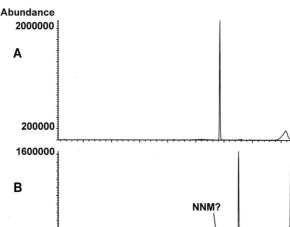

FIG. 4. (A) Mass chromatogram for m/z 116, the molecular ion of N-nitrosomorpholine. The sample was an N-nitrosomorpholine standard. (B) Total-ion chromatogram for an extract of cell culture medium from activated macrophages. Ions were monitored at m/z 116, m/z 86, m/z 56, and m/z 128. The first three ions are characteristic of N-nitrosomorpholine, and the last is the molecular ion for the internal standard naphthalene. (C) Expanded views of the mass chromatograms at m/z 116, m/z 86, and m/z 56 from the same experiment as in (B). The analyses were done on a Supelcowax 10 column under the conditions described in the text.

Gas Chromatography–Mass Spectrometry of N-Nitrosomorpholine

The electron ionization mass spectrum of N-nitrosomorpholine contains several characteristic ions including the molecular ion at m/z 116 (39%)

and fragment ions at m/z 86 (26%) and m/z 56 (base peak),[29] all of which are useful for GC–MS analysis. The internal standard in the analyses shown below was naphthalene; the molecular ion at m/z 128 was monitored. The mass chromatograms shown in Fig. 4 were obtained on a fused-silica capillary column coated with Supelcowax 10 (15 m × 0.25 mm, 0.25 μm film thickness). The head pressure was 3 psi (~20 kPa). The injector temperature was 240°. The oven temperature was held at 40° during the splitless time of 0.5 min and was then programmed at 20°/min to a temperature of 115° and then at 30°/min to a final temperature of 220°. The dwell times were 40 msec for each ion. The mass spectrometer was tuned with the standard autotune routine included in the software. The individual mass chromatograms were integrated with the automatic integration routines in the data analysis software.

Figure 4A shows the mass chromatogram at m/z 116 for an N-nitrosomorpholine standard; Fig. 4B shows the total-ion chromatogram (m/z 116, 86, 56, 128) for an extract of the culture medium from activated macrophages; Fig. 4C shows an expanded view, covering the expected retention time of N-nitrosomorpholine (about 5.9 min), of the mass chromatograms at m/z 116, m/z 86, and m/z 56 from the culture medium extract. The observation that all three ions elute at the expected retention time with the appropriate relative intensities confers additional confidence that the correct peak is being analyzed (note that other components of the mixture, eluting between 6.2 and 6.4 min, also show peaks for all three ions, but with different relative intensities, and at different retention times, than would be expected for N-nitrosomorpholine).

Data Analysis

To correct for extraction efficiency, standard solutions of N-nitrosomorpholine are prepared in the reaction medium at concentrations in the range expected for the experiments being conducted. These are then extracted with dichloromethane and analyzed as described above. The individual mass chromatograms are integrated, and one is generally selected for quantitation. In the example given above, for example, the ions at m/z 56 and m/z 116, while not the most intense ions in the N-nitrosomorpholine mass spectrum, give the cleanest mass chromatograms under the conditions of this particular experiment (Fig. 4C).

Acknowledgments

This work was supported by National Institutes of Health Grants CA26731 and ES02109. The contents of this chapter are based solely on the opinions of the authors and do not necessarily represent the official views of the National Cancer Institute.

[29] W. T. Rainey, W. H. Christie, and W. Lijinsky, *Biomed. Mass Spectrom.* **5**, 395 (1978).

Comments

Cole and Wimpenney, in 1968, showed that high concentrations of nitrate in *E. coli* growth medium resulted in the induction of high levels of nitrate reductase but very low levels of nitrite reductase activity.[24] The 12-hr incubation in preparation of the bacteria should be adhered to in order to induce nitrate reductase selectively. Our laboratory (J. B. Hibbs and R. R. Taintor) has used *E. coli* as a source of nitrate reductase without detectable nitrite reductase activity,[6,14] similar to the observation of Bartholomew.[22]

The *E. coli* nitrate reductase uses formate ion as an exogenous electron donor for enzymatic nitrate reduction. Formate, at the concentration used, has a moderate inhibitory effect on the associated Griess reaction. It is therefore necessary to incubate standards and samples with an equivalent amount of formate. Even though there is no interfering nitrite reductase activity detectable in our *E. coli* preparations, we incubate both samples and the nitrate standards with the complete *E. coli* preparations, we incubate both samples and the nitrate standards with the complete *E. coli*/formate/HEPES mixture. This also will internally correct for any nitrite reductase activity present.

The standards should be prepared in the same medium as the samples whenever possible. This will internally correct the values. This may become important when the samples contain protein and/or color. Culture medium containing 10% or less serum is not a problem as long as the same sample/standard environment is adhered to. Phenol red is an example of a chromophore that is commonly contained in medium but is not a significant problem because it is yellow at the assay pH. The increase in absorbance at A_{540} amounts to 2 μM nitrite equivalents above the blank when phenol red is not added to the standards. Other chromophores may pose a greater problem. Therefore, it is best to follow our recommendation to use standards prepared in the same medium as the sample or, if the sample is a biological fluid, to approximate the sample composition as closely as possible. Standards contain nitrite when measuring nitrite only and nitrate when measuring nitrite plus nitrate. Standards are prepared in PBS for urine samples or for ultrafiltered plasma and serum.

Bacteria prepared and stored as stated are stable for at least 1 year. We have not attempted to quantitate the amount of *E. coli* other than by weight. However, all the batches that we have prepared show remarkable similarity in terms of nitrate reductase activity per volume of cell suspension.

---

[24] J. A. Cole and J. W. T. Wimpenny, *Biochim. Biophys. Acta* **162**, 39 (1968).

Method 2: *Pseudomonas oleovorans* Nitrate Reductase

Reagents

YMA⁻: Dulbecco's modified Eagle's medium without bicarbonate with the following additives: (a) NaMOPS buffer, pH 7.4, to a concentration of 25 mM; (b) NaHCO$_3$ to a concentration of 25 mM; (c) D-glucose to a final concentration 15.5 mM; (d) gentamicin to a concentration of 10 μg/ml; (e) penicillin G to a concentration of 100 U/ml

Griess reagent A: 1% sulfanilamide in 2.5% phosphoric acid (bring up 5 g sulfanilamide and 14.7 ml concentrated phosphoric acid to 500 ml with deionized, distilled water; store in refrigerator)

Greiss reagent B: 0.5% N-(1-naphthyl)ethylenediamine (NEDA) in 2.5% phosphoric acid (bring up 2.5 g NEDA and 14.7 ml concentrated phosphoric acid to 500 ml using deionized, distilled water; store in a tinted bottle in refrigerator not longer than 2 months, and if color develops, discard the reagent)

Preparation of Nitrate Reductase-Containing Bacteria

1. Obtain *Pseudomonas oleovorans*[15,23] from the American Type Culture Collection (ATCC 8062). Streak for isolation on nutrient agar.

2. Pick a colony, inoculate into 50 ml nutrient broth, and grow overnight at 37° with shaking in an air atmosphere.

3. Repeat step 2, taking a loop of the broth culture, inoculating 50 ml fresh nutrient broth, and incubating overnight with shaking. Repeat this step three times.

4. Inoculate 1 liter of nutrient broth with 0.5 ml of the last overnight culture. Incubate overnight at room temperature, with shaking, until the culture is cloudy.

5. Weigh an empty 250-ml centrifuge tube.

6. Divide the overnight 1-liter broth culture and centrifuge at 6000 rpm (4300 g) for 15 min in a Sorvall SS-35 fixed-angle rotor at 4°. Remove supernatants, resuspend pellets in PBS, and transfer to the weighted centrifuge tube.

7. Centrifuge at 6000 rpm for 15 min at 4°C. Wash with PBS. Repeat three times.

8. Remove supernatant. Weigh tube plus pellet. Calculate wet pellet weight. Resuspend, adding 10 ml YMA⁻ medium per gram wet pellet.

9. Place 0.5- or 1.0-ml volumes of bacterial suspension into polypropylene freezer vials. Store at −85°.

Preparation and Assay of Samples

1. Collect urine samples in 2-propanol to prevent growth of bacteria (~1 ml 2-propanol/5 ml urine).
2. Microcentrifuge samples to remove debris.
3. Dilute samples at least 1/10 in NaHEPES buffer (0.2 M; pH 7.4).
4. Thaw an aliquot of *P. oleovorans* as prepared above. Dilute 1/20 in YMA$^-$ medium.
5. To a 1.5-ml microfuge tube add 300 μl diluted urine sample, 150 μl of 0.2 M NaHEPES buffer, and 150 μl diluted bacteria.
6. Cap the tubes, vortex the mixtures, and incubate at 37° for 90 min.
7. Microcentrifuge the tubes (about 15,000 rpm) for 2 min.
8. Transfer 400 μl of supernatant to a 4.5-ml cuvette.
9. To the cuvette add 800 μl of Griess reagent A followed by 800 μl of Griess reagent B. Vortex. Let stand for 15 min.
10. Measure absorbance at 543 nm. The presence of nitrite is indicated by a pink color. Calculation of total nitrite plus nitrate concentration in unknown samples is made after generating a standard curve relating absorbancies to known nitrate concentrations. Standards should range between 0 and 100 μM final concentration sodium nitrate.

Comments

We have not observed any nitrite reductase activity in *P. oleovorans* prepared as above. However, a sodium nitrite control (100 μM) is always included in each assay to check for any activity that could deplete nitrite as it is formed from nitrate enzymatically.

Bacteria prepared and stored as stated are stable for at least 1 year. Quantitative plate counts on several lots have shown approximately 5 × 10^{10} colony-forming units (cfu)/ml. A 1/1000 dilution of stored bacteria in PBS gives an optical density of approximately 0.190 at 520 nm for a 1-cm light path. Thawed, diluted bacteria should be prepared just before use and kept on ice. The bacteria are susceptible to penicillin/gentamicin present in YMA$^-$.

Unlike the *E. coli* nitrate reductase, the *P. oleovorans* nitrate reductase cannot use the formate ion as an exogenous electron donor for enzymatic nitrate reduction. As a result, the use of YMA$^-$ in this assay is critical for obtaining full reduction of nitrate in the unknown sample. YMA$^-$ is a complex mixture of cell culture ingredients, several of which are required for efficient nitrate reductase activity. In a series of experiments obligate constituents were found to be D-glucose, nicotinamide, calcium, and magnesium. The most complete reduction of nitrate, however, occurred with the complete medium, and hence we recommend using this mixture.

For urine samples (human, mouse, and rat) initial dilutions of less than 1/5 are inhibitory to the bacterial nitrate reductase. Initial dilutions of 1/10 are usually satisfactory to give nitrate concentrations equal to or greater than 10 μM. For concentrations greater than 75 μM at a 1/10 dilution, serial twofold dilutions beginning at 1/10 are run to achieve a concentration greater than 10 μM but less than 75 μM nitrate. The sensitivity of the assay was found to extend to approximately 5–10 μM.

For analysis of serum or plasma samples an ultrafiltrate should be prepared. This is accomplished by centrifugation–ultrafiltration in a microcentrifuge using Millipore ultrapore filter units. For analysis of serum-containing [up to 10% (v/v)] cell culture medium, ultrafiltration is not necessary.

For the most accurate results, standards should be run by spiking the type of sample being analyzed (e.g., urine) containing zero nitrate/nitrite. For urine we use a pool of mouse urine obtained from uninfected animals ingesting a nitrate/nitrite-free defined diet[15] and receiving 150 μmol N^{ω}-monomethyl-L-arginine per day by gastric gavage to inhibit constitutive NO syntheses.[25] Standard curves developed using nitrate/nitrite-free urine, cell culture medium, or deionized, distilled water have different slopes and different y-intercepts. RPMI cell culture medium should not be used because calcium (1.2 mM) is added as the nitrate salt.

Conclusion

The Griess reaction[20] has proved to be an extremely durable experimental tool. When used in conjunction with a nitrate reductase assay, it is sensitive, accurate, inexpensive, and accessible to all laboratories for measuring nitrite and nitrate in tissue culture systems and in biological fluids. When properly prepared and used, nitrate reductases from both E. coli and P. oleovorans are highly effective analytical tools. This simple assay employing nitrate reductase and the Griess reaction has made an important contribution in elucidating the role of iNOS as an effector component of the cell-mediated immune response.

Acknowledgments

This work was supported by National Institutes of Health Grant AI26188 (D. L. G.), the Department of Veterans Affairs, Washington, D.C., and National Institutes of Health Grant CA58248 (J.B.H.). We are grateful to Ms. Janet Welsh for assistance in preparation of the manuscript. This chapter was adapted from a manuscript submitted to Methods: A Companion to Methods in Enzymology 7, 78 (1995).

[25] K. Boockvar, D. L. Granger, R. M. Poston, M. Maybodi, M. D. Washington, J. B. Hibbs, Jr., and R. L. Kurlander, Infect. Immun. 62, 1089 (1994).

[14] Analysis of Nitrite, Nitrate, and Nitric Oxide Synthase Activity in Brain Tissue by Automated Flow Injection Technique

By ISAO YOKOI, HITOSHI HABU, HIDEAKI KABUTO, and AKITANE MORI

Introduction

In the brain, nitric oxide (NO), which is synthesized from L-arginine by nitric oxide synthase (NOS), is assumed to act as both an intra- and intercellular second messenger.[1,2] Nitric oxide is relatively unstable in the presence of molecular oxygen, with an apparent half-life of approximately 3–5 sec,[3] and it is oxidized to nitrite and nitrate so rapidly that it is difficult to determine NO directly. Many methods for the estimation of NO by analyzing its metabolites or activated substances, such as citrulline and cyclic guanosine 3',5'-monophosphate, *in vivo* and *in vitro* have been reported, and each method has its own advantages and disadvantages. Some methods have higher sensitivity, but the instruments used for those methods seem to be complex and are not easy to operate.[4]

Automated flow injection analyzers of nitrite and nitrate (NO_x)[5] are widely used in the detection of environmental pollution.[6] The principle of this method is dependent on Griess reaction for diazonium ion.[7] This chapter describes an automated flow injection technique for nitrite and nitrate analysis in the brain and its application for determination of NOS activity in the brain.[8,9]

Materials and Procedure for Nitrite–Nitrate Assay

Principle. In an oxygenized solution NO decomposes to form nitrite and nitrate. Nitrite directly reacts with the Griess reagent to form a purple

[1] J. Garthwaite, S. L. Charles, and R. Chess-Williams, *Nature* **336,** 385 (1988).
[2] R. G. Knowles, M. Palacios, M. J. Palmer, and S. Moncada, *Proc. Natl. Acad. Sci. U.S.A.* **86,** 5159 (1989).
[3] R. M. J. Palmer, A. G. Ferrige, and S. Moncade, *Nature (London)* **327,** 524 (1987).
[4] C. Garside, *Mar. Chem.* **11,** 159 (1982).
[5] A. Termin, M. Hoffmann, and R. J. Bing, *Life Sci.* **51,** 1621 (1992).
[6] J. Ruzicka and E. H. Hansen, "Flow Injection Analysis." Wiley, New York, 1981.
[7] Y. Higuchi, K. Hirano, H. Maeda, and K. Matsuda, *Jpn. Laid Open Patent Publication* **03-115974,** 535 (1991).
[8] H. Habu, I. Yokoi, H. Kabuto, and A. Mori, *Neuroreport* **5,** 1571 (1994).
[9] I. Yokoi, H. Kabuto, H. Habu, and A. Mori, *J. Neurochem.* **63,** 1565 (1994).

azo compound, and its absorbance at 540 nm is measured with a spectropho-tometer connected to a chart recorder. Nitrate, on the other hand, must first be reduced to nitrite with a cadmium–copper column, and then the nitrite is measured as above.

Brain Preparation. The mice or rats are sacrificed by decapitation or by microwave irradiation of the head at 3 kW (0.2 sec) for mice or 5 kW (1.2 sec) for rats using a Metabostat NJE 2601 (New Japan Radio Co., Ltd., Tokyo). The whole brain is removed immediately and blood vessels and arachnoidea are removed from the brain, which is placed in ice-cold buffer (2 mM EDTA, 300 mM sucrose, and 20 mM Tris-HCl, pH 7.4) and rinsed with 10 ml of ice-cold buffer (20 mM Tris-HCl and 2 mM EDTA, pH 7.4). Then the brain is separated into eight regions (cortex, striatum, hippocampus, midbrain, hypothalamus, medulla oblongata, cerebellum, and olfactory bulb) according to the method of Glowinski and Iversen.[10]

Deproteinization. As nitrite is known to be more stable in alkali solution than in acidic solution, deproteinization is performed under alkali condi-tions. The methods of Somogyi[11] and Nelson,[12] for the determination of blood glucose, are applied to the deproteinization of the brain. Each tissue of the brain region is added to 10 times its weight of ice-cold buffer (20 mM Tris-HCl and 2 mM EDTA, pH 7.4). The tissue is then homogenized and centrifuged at 400 g for 10 min at 4°. The supernatant (100 μl) is added to a mixture of 400 μl of distilled water and 300 μl of 0.3 N NaOH solution. The solution is kept for 5 min at room temperature; then 300 μl of 5% (w/v) ZnSO$_4$ is added. The mixture is allowed to stand for another 5 min after shaking and is then centrifuged at 10,000 g for 20 min at 4°C ~ room temperature. The nitrite and nitrate contents in 100 μl of the supernatant are determined using the automated NO$_x$ analyzer.

Chemicals. The flow injection analysis carrier solution (1.9 mM EDTA in 56 mM NH$_4$Cl) and Griess reagent (29 mM sulfanilamide and 1.9 mM N-1-naphthylethylenediamine dihydrochoride in 0.6 N HCl) are obtained from Tokyo Kasei Kogyo (Tokyo, Japan, and Portland, OR). All reagents should be prepared with high-purity water and analytical-grade chemicals. The accuracy of the 5% ZnSO$_4$ solution is less important than the require-ment that 0.3 N NaOH must neutralize the ZnSO$_4$ solution precisely, vol-ume for volume. One must determine the nitrite and/or nitrate in each chemical (Tris, EDTA, sucrose, Griess reagent, ZnSO$_4$, NaOH, HCl, water, etc.). All experimental utensils, even new test tubes and pipette tips, should be washed carefully to avoid contamination so that they do not contain significant concentrations of nitrate and/or nitrite.

[10] J. Glowinski and L. L. Iversen, *J. Neurochem.* **13**, 655 (1966).
[11] M. Somogyi, *J. Biol. Chem.* **160**, 69 (1945).
[12] N. Nelson, *J. Biol. Chem.* **153**, 375 (1944).

Procedure. Nitrite and nitrate are determined using an autoanalyzer (Model TIC-NOX1000; Tokyo Kasei Kogyo), which employs the technique of automated flow injection analysis (Fig. 1). Nitrite reacts with the Griess reagent to form a purple azo compound, and its absorbance at 540 nm is measured with a spectrophotometer (Model S/3250; Somakogaku, Tokyo) connected to a chart recorder (Model RC-225, Jasco, Tokyo). Nitrate is determined by reducing it to nitrite using an A7200 Cd–Cu reduction column (Tokyo Kasei Kogyo), and then measuring the nitrite as above. Samples are loaded onto the sample injector (Model SVI-6U7; Tokyo Kasei Kogyo). Both the carrier solution and the Griess reagent are prepared daily, warmed at 30°, and made to flow at a rate of 1.5 ml/min. Both sodium nitrite and nitrate solution (NOX standard solution, Tokyo Kasei Kogyo) are used as standards.

Using this method, the content of nitrite in the sample is measured directly from the peak height on the chart. After passing the solution through a reduction column for the determination of nitrate, the peak height recorded in the chart represents the content of nitrate and nitrite, so that the actual nitrate content is obtained after subtraction of nitrite content. The limit of detection of nitrite/nitrate is 500 nM, that is, 50 pmol/injection (99% confidence limit); interassay and intrassay coefficients of variation are 1.6 and 0.7%, respectively.[9] By means of the autoanalyzer, 40 samples of nitrite and 25 of nitrate can be analyzed per hour.

Figure 2 shows the analytical curves generated by the addition of nitrate to brain homogenates, and these curves indicate a linear relation. The overall recoveries of nitrite added to decapitated and microwave-irradiated brain homogenates are 105.5 and 102.5%, respectively. The data indicate

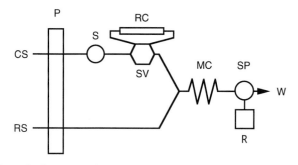

Fɪɢ. 1. Schematic diagram of nitrite and nitrate determination by the flow injection technique. CS, Carrier solution; RS, reagent solution; P, double-plunger pump; S, sample injector; RC, copperized cadmium reduction column; SV, column switching valve; MC, mixing coil; SP, spectrophotometer; R, recorder; and W, waste.

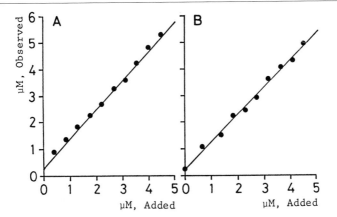

FIG. 2. Analytical recovery of nitrate added to brain homogenates derived from animals sacrificed by (A) Decapitation ($r = 0.99$, $y = 1.103x + 0.317$) and (B) Microwave irradiation ($r = 0.99$, $y = 1.047x + 0.235$). Abscissa, Nitrate in brain homogenate, added; ordinate, nitrate in brain homogenate, observed. Reprinted from H. Habu, I. Yokoi, H. Kabuto, and A. Mori, (1994). *Neuroreport* **5,** 1571.

that there are no substances in the brain that interfere with or enhance the quantitative reduction of nitrite and nitrate.

Comments. We have not observed any statistical differences between the two methods of sacrifice. Inactivation of NOS in the brain by microwave irradiation of the head may prevent NO postmortem synthesis; therefore, microwave irradiation may be the more appropriate method for determination. We have also observed that nitrite and nitrate content in the brain decrease after freezing at −80° for 24 hr (Fig. 3). The extraction and deproteinization must be performed immediately without cryopreservation.

Flow Injection Technique to Measure Activity of Nitric Oxide Synthase

Principle. Activity of NOS is determined by measuring nitrite and nitrate, which are stable end products of the NO produced during the reaction.

Crude Enzyme Preparation. Rats are sacrificed by decapitation. After removing blood vessels and arachnoidea from the brain and rinsing, the brain is homogenized with 3.5 ml of ice-cold buffer (20 mM Tris-HCl and 2 mM EDTA, pH 7.4). The homogenate is centrifuged for 20 min at 21,000 g, and the supernatant is used as a crude enzyme solution after passing it over a 3-ml column of Dowex 50W-X8 (Na$^+$ form) at 4° to remove endogenous L-arginine.

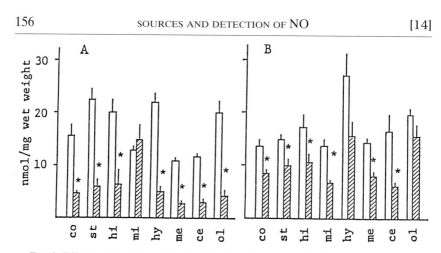

FIG. 3. Effects of freezing on levels of nitrite and nitrate in brain homogenates derived from animals sacrificed by (A) Decapitation and (B) microwave irradiation. Open columns denote the day of sacrifice without freezing, whereas hatched columns represent samples after 24 hr of freezing. Each column shows the mean ± SEM ($n = 5$). An asterisk (*) signifies $p < 0.05$ by paired t-test. co, Cortex; st, striatum; hi, hippocampus; mi, midbrain; hy, hypothalamus; me, medulla oblongata; ce, cerebellum; ol, olfactory bulb. Reprinted from H. Habu, I. Yokoi, H. Kabuto, and A. Mori, (1994) *Neuroreport* **5**, 1571.

Procedure. Incubations are initiated by the addition of 60 μl of the crude enzyme solution to a buffer containing (final concentrations) 1 mM NADPH, 750 μM CaCl$_2$, and L-arginine (concentration is varied from 2.5 to 40 μM) in a total volume of 190 μl. After 15 min of incubation at 37°, the reaction is stopped by the addition of 180 μl of 0.3 N NaOH, and then 180 μl of 5% (w/w) ZnSO$_4$ solution is added. After 20 min of centrifugation at 10,000 g (4°C ~ room temperature), the content of NO$_x$ in the incubates is determined using an NO$_x$ analyzer (TCI-NOX1000). The values obtained are corrected for the background content of NO$_x$ after incubation with NADPH-free incubation medium without L-arginine addition.

Data are analyzed by nonlinear least-squares regression[13] using equations according to Segel.[14] The Michaelis constant (K_m) value and maximum velocity (V_{max}) of NOS in the brain homogenate are 5.64 ± 0.87 μM and 210 ± 11 pmol NO$_x$ formation/mg protein/min (mean ± SEM, $N = 12$), respectively (Fig. 4). This K_m of the rat brain NOS is similar to that of previous observations (8.4 μM; Knowles *et al.*[15]).

Comments. When we measure total activity of NOS in brain, we use the supernatant of the homogenate without passing it over a column of

[13] D. W. Marquardt, *J. Soc. Ind. Appl. Math.* **11**, 431 (1963).
[14] I. H. Segel, "Biochemical Calculations," 2nd Ed. Wiley, New York, 1976.
[15] R. G. Knowles, M. Palacios, R. M. Palmer, and S. Moncada, *Biochem. J.* **269**, 207 (1990).

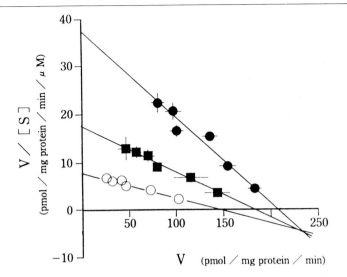

FIG. 4. Effect of α-guanidinoglutaric acid (GGA) on NOS activity. Incubations of brain homogenates were carried out without GGA ($\bullet$, $n = 12$) or with 5 μM ($\blacksquare$, $n = 6$) or 10 μM GGA ($\bigcirc$, n = 8). An Eadie–Hofstee plot was constructed; data are means ± SEM (bars). The apparent K_m and V_{max} values are 5.64 ± 0.87 μM and 210 ± 11 pmol NO$_x$ formation/ mg protein/min (mean ± SEM, $N = 12$), respectively. GGA inhibited NOS activity in a linear mixed manner, and the apparent K_i value and α factor[14] are 2.69 ± 0.34 μM and 9.10 ± 1.68 (mean ± SEM), respectively. Reprinted from I. Yokoi, H. Kabuto, H. Habu, and A. Mori, (1994) *J. Neurochem.* **63**, 1565.

Dowex 50W-X8. Then 100 μM of L-arginine is added to the incubation medium (final concentration).

Inhibition of Nitric Oxide Synthase by α-Guanidinoglutaric Acid, an Endogenous Nitric Oxide Synthase Inhibitor

Crude Enzyme Preparation. Crude enzyme is prepared from rat brain as mentioned above.

Chemicals. α-Guanidinoglutaric acid (GGA) is synthesized as described.[16]

Procedure. Incubations are initiated by the addition of 60 μl of crude enzyme solution to buffer containing (final concentrations) 1 mM NADPH, 750 μM CaCl$_2$, and L-arginine (concentration is varied from 2.5 to 40 μM) in a total volume of 190 μl with or without GGA (5 or 10 μM). After 15 min of incubation at 37°, the reaction is stopped by the addition of 180 μl

[16] A. Mori, M. Akagi, Y. Katayama, and Y. Watanabe, *J. Neurochem.* **35**, 603 (1980).

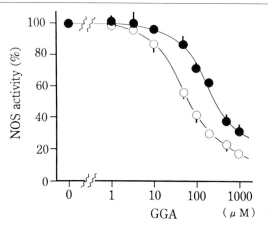

Fig. 5. Dose-dependent inhibition of NOS by GGA. Incubations of brain homogenate were carried out at physiological (○) and at high (●) concentrations of L-arginine. The apparent IC$_{50}$ values at physiological (120 μM) and at high (520 μM) L-arginine concentrations are 64 and 283 μM, respectively. Data are means ± SEM (bars) from four determinations. Reprinted from I. Yokoi, H. Kabuto, H. Habu, and A. Mori, (1994). *J. Neurochem.* **63**, 1565.

of 0.3 N NaOH, and thereafter 180 μl of 5% (w/w) ZnSO$_4$ solution is supplemented. After 20 min of centrifugation at 10,000 g, the content of NO$_x$ in the incubates is determined using an NO$_x$ analyzer (TCI-NOX1000). In another experiment, incubations are carried out with a constant L-arginine concentration (120 or 520 μM) with a varied GGA concentration (0–1 mM) to predict the IC$_{50}$.

Data are analyzed by nonlinear least-squares regression[13] using the equations according to Segel.[14] The inhibition model that gives the lowest sum of the squared residuals (SSR) is chosen as the type of inhibition, because lower SSRs better fit the model for inhibition kinetics.[17]

The endogenous non-N^G-substituted guanidino compound GGA[16] inhibits NOS activity in the linear mixed manner as shown in Fig. 4. Linear mixed-type inhibition is a form of noncompetitive inhibition. The dissociation constant of the inhibitor–enzyme–substrate complex changes by a factor α to reach equilibrium.[14] The calculated K_i value and the α factor are 2.69 ± 0.34 μM and 9.10 ± 1.68 μM (mean ± SEM, $N = 8$), respectively. The K_i values of N^G-methyl-L-arginine, a well-known NOS competitive inhibitor,[15] and GGA for L-arginine are almost equal. The IC$_{50}$ values at physiological and high L-arginine concentrations (120 and 520 μM, respectively) are calculated to be 64 and 283 μM, respectively (Fig. 5).

[17] Y. Watanabe, I. Yokoi, S. Watanabe, H. Sugi, and A. Mori, *Life Sci.* **43**, 295 (1988).

Conclusions

The NO_x autoanalyzer with automated flow injection analysis offers many advantages. (1) Many samples (25–40 samples per hour) can be determined, (2) the autoanalyzer is simple to operate, and highly sensitive (the limit of detection is 500 nM), with a low rate of mechanical failure, and (3) the operating cost is low. The NO content, NOS activity, and NOS inhibition of the brain are successfully estimated by determination of nitrite and nitrate using the analyzer after deproteinization employing the $ZnSO_4$– NaOH method, and this appears to be promising for applications in neuroscience or in other areas of bioscience.

Acknowledgments

This work was supported by Grants-in-Aid from the Ministry of Education, Science and Culture of Japan (No. 04454362 and No. 05671164). We thank Professor Emeritus Kyoji Tôei (Okayama University) for invaluable advice.

[15] Microtiter Plate Assay for Determining Kinetics of Nitric Oxide Synthesis

By Steven S. Gross

Introduction

It has long been appreciated that nitric oxide (NO) binds to iron in ferrous hemoproteins with extremely high avidity. This phenomenon has been utilized in a spectrophotometric assay for detection of NO release from biological systems.[1] In this chapter I describe a 96-well microtiter plate adaptation of this assay that we have used to quantify the rate of NO production by enzymes, NO donor compounds, and immunostimulant-activated cells in culture.[2,3] In our hands, the limit of NO detection by this assay is approximately 5 pmol/min in a 100-μl reaction volume.

By this technique NO production is deduced from the rate of oxidation of ferroheme by NO, resulting in a progressive increase in A_{405}. Advantages over alternative techniques for NO determination are compelling: (a) high

[1] M. Kelm, et al., Biochem. Biophys. Res. Commun. **154**, 236 (1988).
[2] S. S. Gross, E. A. Jaffe, R. Levi, and R. G. Kilbourn, Biochem. Biophys. Res. Commun. **178**, 823 (1991).
[3] S. S. Gross and R. Levi, J. Biol. Chem. **267**, 25722 (1992).

data throughput—NO synthesis rates are measured in 96 samples simultaneously, (b) speed—high-quality data collection can be completed in less than 15 min, (c) precision—results are based on 50–150 data points collected for each sample, (d) parsimony—incubation volumes can be as small as 60 μl and often require less than 5 μl of NOS-containing cell extract or NO-donor compound, (e) high information yield—kinetic data superior to end point determinations in that they reveal the progress of NO generation, and (f) automation—sample preparation can utilize microtiter plate technology (e.g., multichannel pipettors, repeating dispensers, robotics) and computer-assisted data analysis.

The technique requires a specialized spectrophotometer that measures the change in absorption over time, rather than the more conventional end point determination of optical density. The microplate reader also requires computer-assisted data analysis to handle the large number of data points accumulated in a typical assay. Although many suitable instruments are commercially available and will suffice for the method described herein, the instrument used in this laboratory is from Molecular Devices (THERMOMAX; Menlo Park, CA). This particular kinetic microplate reader provides added benefits of intelligent software for instrument control and data analysis, thermostatic regulation of sample temperature, shaking of microplates between readings, and use of 96 fiber-optic conduits for illuminating samples from a single source (signal-to-noise ratios are thus improved since neither the microplate nor the light source moves during the course of repeated sample assay).

Dithionite-reduced myoglobin is used to capture NO on ferroheme, leading to ferriheme generation which is monitored as an increase in A_{405}. We routinely prepare ferroheme myoglobin as described below in quantities sufficient for 1000–2000 assays and store aliquots at $-20°$ for use within 3 months. Although NO synthesis can be effectively assayed with a variety of ferroheme proteins, including hemoglobin, myoglobin offers several advantages for the microplate assay. First, wavelength selection in most 96-well spectrophotometers uses standard 5–10 nm band-pass filters. The 405-nm filter which comes with almost every instrument [provided for alkaline phosphatase-based enzyme-linked immunosorbent assay (ELISA)] provides near-optimal detection of the progressive increase in the heme Soret band absorption arising from NO-dependent oxidation of ferro- to ferriheme myoglobin. In contrast, ferroheme oxidation with oxyhemoglobin is optimally detected at 401 nm and is best monitored using a custom filter. Moreover, the fact that myoglobin exists as a monomer precludes any possibility of allosteric interactions which can occur between heme moieties in multimeric hemoproteins, such as tetrameric hemoglobins.

Preparation of Ferroheme Myoglobin

A PD-10 column (Pharmacia, Uppsala, Sweden) is equilibrated with 50 mM Tris (pH 7.6) by two successive 10-ml washes. A solution of 2 mM horse heart myoglobin (Sigma, St. Louis, MO) is prepared in 2.5 ml of 50 mM Tris buffer, and approximately 0.5–1.0 mg of fresh sodium hydrosulfite (dithionite) is added to reduce ferri- to ferroheme. The change in heme–iron status is reflected by an instant change in solution color from muddy brown to blood red. As dithionite must be rapidly removed from the reduced hemoprotein to prevent secondary reactions that result in protein degradation, the sample is immediately applied to the PD-10 column. After sample permeation into the gel, ferroheme myoglobin in over 97% yield is eluted by the addition of 3.5 ml of 50 mM Tris. The 3.5 ml volume of eluate is diluted with an additional 9.0 ml of 50 mM Tris; this results in a final ferroheme myoglobin concentration of approximately 400 μM. Precise determination of concentration can be calculated from A_{434}, based on a published extinction coefficient ε for ferrous myoglobin[4] of 114×10^3 cm^{-1} M^{-1}. Aliquots of ferroheme myoglobin are frozen at $-20°$ and thawed no more than twice before use.

The NO binding to ferroheme proteins occurs at a near diffusion-limited rate, precluding direct measurement of the rate constant by present methods. Nonetheless, equilibrium displacement studies reveal that NO binding is over 1500 times that of CO.[5] Thus, the capture efficiency of NO by ferroheme myoglobin is essentially 100% in the present assay. Accordingly, the amount of ferroheme myoglobin that must be added to samples for measurement of NO production is dictated by the anticipated range of NO synthetic rates in the samples under investigation, rather than a particular constraint of the assay method per se. Too little myoglobin addition will result in its full oxidation before completion of the assay (providing a reduced number of data points that can be used to determine the maximum rate of ferroheme oxidation); too much myoglobin will diminish assay sensitivity by elevating the background absorption and effectively increase the noise. Myoglobin oxidation from ferro- to ferriheme is monitored as an increase in A_{405} versus time; linear kinetics are observed until all myoglobin is oxidized. The slope of the line describing the increase in A_{405} per minute is used to calculate nanomoles NO generated per minute. This is accomplished by dividing the slope, measured in optical density units (OD) per minute, by an experimentally determined value having units of OD

[4] S. Schuder, J. B. Whittenberg, B. Haseltine, and B. A. Whittenberg, *Anal. Biochem.* **136,** 473 (1979).
[5] Q. H. Gibson and F. J. W. Roughton, *J. Physiol. (London)* **136,** 507 (1957).

per nanomole NO produced. Although the published extinction coefficient of any molecule is a constant and can be applied to all conventional spectrophotometric assays that use standard 1-cm light path cuvettes, the nonstandard geometry of microtiter plates, band-pass filters, and assay volumes requires that the constant be experimentally determined for each microplate assay system. Nonetheless, as this value is fixed, it must be determined only once for a given experimental configuration.

Determination of Conversion Factor Relating Increase in A_{405} to Nitric Oxide Production

In a 96-well plate, prepare two sets of sample wells, each with identically increasing concentrations of ferroheme myoglobin (prepared as above). One set of sample wells will contain ferroheme, whereas the second set will be oxidized to ferriheme. Typically, two groups of triplicate samples are prepared in which 10-μl volumes containing 0, 2.5, 5.0, and 10.0 nmol of ferroheme myoglobin are added to 40 μl of 200 mM Tris (pH 7.6). In one set of triplicate wells, ferroheme is oxidized to completion by adding 10 μl of 1.2 mM potassium ferricyanide. Volumes in all wells are then adjusted with distilled water to 100 μl, plates are mixed, and absorbances are read at 405 nm. Blank values are subtracted from each sample set ("0" myoglobin values, respectively) and differences in A_{405} between ferri- and ferroheme myoglobin are plotted for each myoglobin concentration tested. Linear regression analysis is performed to calculate the slope of the resulting line. While the slope in OD per nanomole should approximate 100, the precise value will depend on the particular microtiter plate used and characteristics of the filter used for wavelength selection in the microplate reader.

Assuming that in the NO–heme capture assay every mole of NO which is produced results in the oxidation of 1 mol of ferriheme to ferroheme, division by this value converts the measured increase in OD per minute to nanomoles NO produced per minute. The validity of the assumption of 100% NO capture efficiency by ferroheme is supported by the finding that reducing or increasing the myoglobin concentration over a 16-fold range (from 5 to 80 μM, not shown) does not alter the maximal rate of heme oxidation observed with a constant source of NO. As the net increase in A_{405} obtained after oxidation of ferroheme myoglobin by ferricyanide is identical to that obtained after exposure to an NO donor compound [e.g., 3-morpholinosydnonimine (SIN-1), not shown], ferriheme appears to be the sole accumulating product that accounts for the NO-mediated increase in A_{405}. Thus, although nitrosoheme is an intermediate, and stable under anerobic conditions, its lifetime is probably too brief in the context of the present assay method to justify its consideration. On the other hand, it should be appreciated that peroxynitrite, produced by the reaction of NO and superoxide anion, also oxidizes ferroheme and cannot be discriminated from NO per se in this assay. In studies employing an NO-selective electrode we have determined that inducible nitric oxide synthase (iNOS) generates substantial quantities of peroxynitrite (Sussman and S. S. Gross, unpublished) consistent with prior findings that NADPH consumption by NOS is partially uncoupled and produces superoxide anion concomitantly with NO.[6] Thus, peroxynitrite may contribute significantly to the oxidation of ferroheme by NOS-derived NO.

Nitric Oxide Synthase Assay

Although NO assay by ferroheme capture can be used to quantify NO production from any source, a useful application is in the determination of NOS activity in crude and purified enzyme preparations. This allows rapid and precise determination of V_{max} and K_m values for substrates and K_i values for inhibitors. For NOS assay, we employ a 100-μl final reaction volume (so that the above determined conversion factor can be employed) and perform all assays in triplicate. Reagents are typically prepared as 10× stock solutions to facilitate the use of repeating dispensers and 12-channel multipipettors for sample preparation. For determining NOS activity in cell extracts, 10-μl volumes of each of the following agents are added to sample wells: Tris (200 mM, pH 7.6), NADPH (10 mM), L-arginine (10 mM), dithiothreitol (DTT) (10 mM), 5,6,7,8-tetrahydrobiopterin (BH$_4$; 100 μM), and dithionite-reduced myoglobin (200–500 μM). Sample volume is adjusted to 90 μl by further addition of distilled water, calcium/calmodulin [for constitutive NOS (cNOS) assays], or desired test compounds. Whereas the indicated additions allow for determination of maximal NOS activity in the preparation, determination of K_m and K_i values for compounds under investigation require appropriate modification of incubation mixture constituents.

Formation of NO is initiated by addition of 10 μl of NOS enzyme (preferably with a repeating dispenser for speed and reproducibility); microplates are then mixed by gentle rocking and rapidly transferred to the spectrophotometer for data acquisition. The rate of change in A_{405}, reflecting ferroheme oxidation, is continually measured in all samples at 15-sec intervals, for 15 min. In samples where linearity is maintained throughout the duration of assay, all points are used to calculate the slope of the line, reflecting ΔOD per minute. In samples where ferroheme is consumed before completion of the assay period (resulting in a curve having the form of a "hockey stick"), the maximum increase in ΔOD per minute

---

[6] B. Mayer, *et al.*, *J. Cardiovasc. Pharmacol.* **20**(Suppl. 12), S54 (1992).

is calculated by considering only the linear phase. The capacity to shake the plate between readings is a feature of many microplate readers and is needed for maximum sensitivity of the assay and perhaps to maintain oxygen saturation of samples. Experiments requiring longer periods of data collection (i.e., samples with low NOS activity) are accommodated by extending the read duration. The rate of ferroheme oxidation in OD per minute is converted to nanomoles NO per minute using the conversion factor as calculated above.

Figure 1 provides an example of raw and calculated data obtained from a kinetic microplate assay of iNOS activity in crude cytosol from

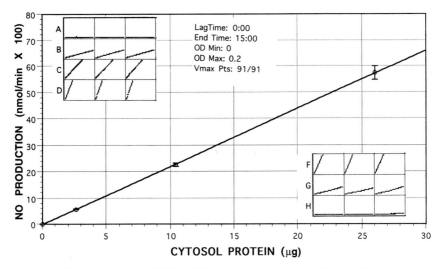

FIG. 1. Microplate assay of NOS activity in cytosol from rat aortic smooth muscle cells grown in culture, showing linearity with protein concentration and dependence on BH$_4$, NADPH, and L-arginine. BH$_4$-depleted iNOS was induced in cells by a 16-hr pretreatment with a combination of lipopolysaccharide (LPS, serotype 0111B$_4$, 30 μg/ml), rat γ-interferon (IFN-γ) (50 ng/ml), and inhibitors of BH$_4$ synthesis: methotrexate (10 μM) and 2,4-diamino-6-hydroxypyrimidine (3 mM). Cells were harvested and crude cytosol was prepared as previously described.[3] *Inset:* Raw data from triplicate assays of iNOS activity, performed by monitoring the increase in A_{405} over a 15-min period in the presence of 40 μM ferroheme myoglobin. Incubation mixtures were as described in the text, with modification as follows: (A–D) added cytosolic protein was increased from 0 to 2.6, 10.4, and 26.0 μg, respectively; (F–H) the complete reaction containing 26.0 μg protein (F) was deprived of BH$_4$ (G) or NADPH and L-arginine (H). The graph confirms that the rate of NO production, calculated from the slopes of data sets A–D, is a linear function of the amount of cytosolic protein added. A quantity of cytosolic protein from untreated aortic smooth muscle cells equivalent to that in H above causes an increase in A_{405} which is only about 0.5% of that obtained from immunostimulant-activated cells (as above); notably, this background activity is unaffected by removal of BH$_4$, NADPH, and L-arginine.

immunostimulant-activated vascular smooth muscle cells. This particular cytosol was harvested from cells that were grown in the presence of inhibitors of BH synthesis; hence, enzyme activity is dependent in large measure on added BH_4. The rate of increase in A_{405}, and hence NO generation, is shown to rise as a linear function of the quantity of cytosolic protein added per well (see raw data for triplicate samples A–D in Fig. 1 and linear plot of mean values after conversion to units of NO production). That NO production is responsible for the increase in A_{405} during this 15-min assay is indicated by elimination of NO when arginine and NADPH are omitted from the incubates (sample H) and 10-fold reduction when BH_4 is omitted (sample G). The small background increase in A_{405}, which may be detected with cell cytosol when NOS activity is prevented, is the summation of many processes, perhaps including the generation of superoxide anion[7] and peroxide[6] by NOS itself when deprived of substrates.

A bonus of the microplate technique for measuring NO formation is that one can also measure the rate of NADPH consumption by NOS, in the same microplate, without significant additional effort. This is accomplished by simply replacing the microplate in the spectrophotometer (no further reagents are required) and recording the rate of decline in A_{340}. Although NADPH exhibits a large extinction coefficient at 340 nm, NADP is without appreciable absorption. This allows measurement of rates of both substrate consumption (NADPH) and product generation (NO) in the same samples, offering a means to confirm NOS activity determinations and to obtain potentially important additional information, such as, reaction stoichiometry. An example of the utility of such dual measurements of NOS activity is provided in Fig. 2.

Measuring Kinetics of Nitric Oxide Generation by Cells

A notable limitation of spectrophotometry-based assays is the need for optically "clear" samples, making assay of NO generation by membrane-bound enzymes difficult. Nonetheless, if NO production is sufficiently high, a large background OD (due to light scatter) is tolerable. An example of this is provided by the quantitation of high-output NO production spectrophotometrically, using a light beam that passes through a living cell monolayer in culture medium (Fig. 3). Measurement of the increase in A_{405} which arises specifically from ferroheme oxidation, can be improved by subtracting the component due to the light scatter by cells. This is accomplished by subtracting A_{650}, a wavelength at which light scatter will be comparable to A_{405}, while heme absorption is negligible. As the lid to the cell culture

---

[7] S. Pou, W. S. Pou, D. S. Bredt, S. H. Snyder, and G. M. Rosen, *J. Biol. Chem.* **267**, 24173 (1992).

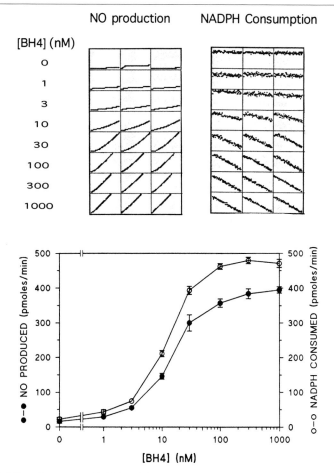

FIG. 2. Microplate assay of iNOS activity from cytosol of BH_4-depleted rat aortic smooth muscle cells grown in culture, showing BH_4-dependence of ferromyoglobin oxidation and NADPH consumption rates. BH_4-depleted iNOS-containing cytosol was prepared as described in Fig. 1. Reaction mixtures contained a constant amount of cytosolic protein in complete reaction mix (analogous to set D in Fig. 1), except that the concentration of BH_4 was varied as indicated. *Top:* Raw data, obtained from triplicate sample wells, depict the kinetics of ferrous myoglobin oxidation (ΔA_{405}; full scale, 0.40 OD) and NADPH consumption (ΔA_{340}; full scale, −0.10 OD), assessed during sequential 15-min intervals from the same samples. *Bottom:* Plotted rates of NO production and NADPH consumption (means ± SD) calculated from the above data, based on an increase in 1 mOD at A_{405} of 10.05 pmol/min NO produced and a decrease in 1 mOD/min at A_{340} of 67.2 pmol NADPH consumed, under the conditions employed. In the absence of added BH_4, NO production and NADPH consumption were 4.02 and 4.06%, respectively, of that obtained with a maximally active concentration of BH_4 (1000 nM). The ratio of NADPH consumed to NO produced, considering all concentrations of BH_4 tested, was 1.327 ± 0.106 (mean ± SEM).

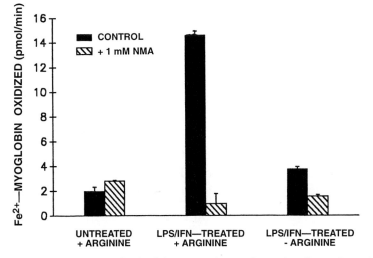

Fig. 3. Assay of NO production by living rat aortic smooth muscle cell monolayers in 96-well culture plates. Cell monolayers were grown to confluence in 96-well plates and either untreated or pretreated for 24 hr with a combination of 50 μg/ml LPS and 50 ng/ml IFN-γ (LPS/IFN). After this time the cell culture medium was replaced with 200 μl of fresh medium either containing or free of L-arginine (1.24 mM), in the absence or presence of the NOS inhibitor N^{ω}-methyl-L-arginine (NMA, 1 mM). Ferromyoglobin (5 μM) was added to each well, and the rate of increase in $A_{405-650}$ was monitored at 16-sec intervals for 30 min at 37°. Reprinted with permission from Gross and Levi.[3]

plate does not interfere with spectrophotometric determinations, cells can be maintained sterile throughout the procedure (assuming the ferrous myoglobin has been filter sterilized) and therefore the same plate may be repeatedly removed from the incubator to assay NO synthesis at various times. Fogging of the plate can be a problem when assays are to be performed at elevated temperature in the microplate reader (e.g., at 37°) for periods longer than 20 min. Prior treatment of the microplate lid with a commercially available antifogging agent is usefully effective.

Measuring Kinetics of Nitric Oxide Generation from Nitric Oxide Donor Compounds

When assessing NO generation from NO donors, the protocol is identical to that described for NOS, except, of course, that substrates and cofactors of NOS can be eliminated. An amount of ferromyoglobin should be added to each reaction well that will accommodate all of the NO produced during the assay period. Results of a small trial run are useful to confirm that reaction conditions are appropriate before setting up an extensive experiment. Solution pH in excess of pH 8.0 (and probably below pH 6.0 as well) interfere with the assay, and such solutions should be used with caution, if at all.

[16] Detection of Nitric Oxide by Electron Spin Resonance in Chemical, Photochemical, Cellular, Physiological, and Pathophysiological Systems

By B. KALYANARAMAN

Introduction

Electron spin resonance (ESR) spectoscopists have been using nitric oxide (·NO) to probe the structural environment of metals in heme and nonheme proteins for many years.[1] In the 1960s, Commoner and others observed ESR signals of iron-nitrosyl complexes in neoplastic tissues from animals treated with carcinogens.[2-4] Unfortunately, the mechanism leading to formation of such complexes could not be determined, and consequently the connection between ·NO and tumor formation was not realized. Nevertheless, a great deal of knowledge about the interactions of ·NO in biological systems has since been gained through pioneering ESR investigations.[5,6] Several new and innovative ESR-active ·NO traps have been developed. These compounds may have therapeutic potential in diseases characterized by overproduction of ·NO and may also afford ESR-imaging possibilities of ·NO production in whole organs. Excellent reviews on this subject already exist in the literature.[5,6] This chapter deals with the methodological aspects of detecting ·NO by ESR in chemical, photochemical, cellular, and physiological systems.

[1] W. A. Blumberg, *Methods Enzymol.* **76,** 312 (1981).
[2] A. J. Vithayathil, J. L. Ternberg, and B. Commoner, *Nature (London)* **207,** 1246 (1965).
[3] M. J. Brennan, T. Cole, and J. A. Singley, *Proc. Soc. Exp. Biol. Med.* **123,** 715 (1966).
[4] N. M. Emanuel, A. W. Saprin, V. A. Shabalkin, L. E. Kozlova, and K. E. Krvgijakova, *Nature (London)* **222,** 165 (1969).
[5] Y. Henry, M. Lepoivre, J.-C. Drapier, C. Ducrocq, J.-L. Boucher, and A. Guissani, *FASEB J.* **7,** 1124 (1993).
[6] Y. Henry, C. Ducrocq, J.-C. Drapier, D. Servent, C. Pellat, and A. Guissani, *Eur. Biophys. J.* **20,** 1 (1991).

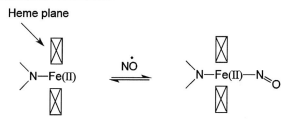

FIG. 1. Trapping of ·NO by heme protein complex to form a nitrosyl-heme protein complex.

Nitric Oxide Complexes of Heme Proteins

Background

Iron and iron-containing enzymes are ubiquitous in nature. Evidence exists for the presence of small molecular weight iron pools in cells.[7] Nitric oxide binds strongly to iron to form iron-nitrosyl complexes, such as heme-nitrosyl and/or nonheme-dinitrosyl complexes. These complexes exhibit distinctly different ESR spectra.[5,6] Some relevant heme-nitrosyl complexes include nitrosylhemoglobin (HbNO), nitrosylmyoglobin (MbNO), nitrosyl cytochrome P450, nitrosyl cytochrome P420, nitrosyl catalase, nitrosyl cytochrome-c oxidase, and nitrosylguanylate cyclase. Nitric oxide binds reversibly to ferrous heme proteins under anaerobic conditions to form nitrosyl heme proteins (Fig. 1). Nitrosyl heme proteins are paramagnetic ($S = \frac{1}{2}$), and their ESR spectra can be observed at room temperature[8] and at low temperatures (77 K).[1,9,10] Interpretation of ESR spectra of nitrosyl heme proteins at room temperature can be complex because of a dynamic equilibrium between conformers[1,11]; in addition, the signal-to-noise ratio, in most cases, can be greatly improved at low temperatures. In the frozen state, the ESR spectra of NO–heme protein complexes usually exhibit a powder pattern due to overlapping g anisotropies. Both the g value and the nitrogen hyperfine coupling of ·NO are sensitive to the nature of the attached ligand[12] *trans* to ·NO (Fig. 1).

In biological systems, nitrosyl complexes of several heme proteins are likely to be formed, namely, HbNO, MbNO, nitrosyl cytochrome P450 (P450–NO), nitrosyl cytochrome P420, nitrosyl catalase, nitrosyl cyto-

[7] A. F. Vanin, L. A. Blyumenfel'd, and A. G. Chetverikov, *Biofizika* **12**, 829 (1967).

[8] L. E. Göran Eriksson, *Biochem. Biophys. Res. Commun.* **203**, 176 (1994).

[9] H. Kon, *J. Biol. Chem.* **243**, 4350 (1968).

[10] H. Kon, *Biochim. Biophys. Acta* **379**, 103 (1975).

[11] M. E. John and M. R. Waterman, *FEBS Lett.* **106**, 219 (1979).

[12] K. Kobayashi, M. Tamura, and K. Hayashi, *Biochim. Biophys. Acta* **702**, 23 (1982).

chromes, nitrosylguanylate cyclase, nitrosyl cytochrome-c oxidase, and nitrosyl peroxidase. Also refer to the reviews by Henry *et al.*[5,6]

Nitrosylhemoglobin

The ESR spectrum of HbNO in the frozen state is generally characterized by three absorptions corresponding to g_x = 2.07–2.08, g_y = 1.98–2.01, and g_z = 2.003.[9,10,12] Both g_x and g_y correspond to the orientation of the HbNO with the external magnetic field in the heme plane, and g_z corresponds to a direction perpendicular to the heme plane. This absorption band is the strongest and is always split into three lines (a_{NO} = 18–20 G) from ^{14}N of [14]NO or into two lines from ^{15}N of [15]NO. The spectral resolution is greatly influenced by added reagents such as detergent.[9] The smaller hyperfine coupling from ^{14}N of the histidine nitrogen is usually not resolved except under special detection conditions.[1] *In vivo,* this hyperfine structure reflects the arteriovenous difference of oxygen saturation in hemoglobin.[13]

ESR Spectroscopy. The spectra of HbNO are measured at liquid nitrogen temperature (77 K) using 10 mW microwave power, 2–5 G modulation amplitude, 9.1–9.2 GHz microwave frequency, 400 G scan range, and 3250 G field set. A blood sample (200 μl) is transferred to a 3-mm ESR quartz tube and immediately frozen in liquid nitrogen. The frozen sample is then placed in a finger Dewar inside the ESR cavity.[8,14] Red blood cells are usually packed gently in a 3-mm quartz tube by centrifugation before ESR analysis.[8]

Spectra of HbNO from red blood cells can be recorded at room temperature.[8] The shape of the ESR spectrum has been reported to change with time, depending on the internal arrangement of the NO ligand between the subunits of hemoglobin.[1,13] The concentration of HbNO can be determined by double integration and comparison with Cu–EDTA standard.

Applications. (1) The postoperative formation of HbNO can be monitored directly in blood samples from recipients of allogenic and syngeneic heart transplants[15–19] and from naive animals. During allograft rejection,

[13] H. Kosaka, Y. Sawai, H. Sakaguchi, E. Kumura, N. Harada, M. Watanabe, and T. Shiga, *Am. J. Physiol.* **1400,** C1403 (1994).

[14] W. Chamulitrat, S. J. Jordon, R. P. Mason, K. Saito, and R. G. Cutler, *J. Biol. Chem.* **268,** 11520 (1993).

[15] J. R. Lancaster, Jr., J. M. Langrehr, H. A. Bergonia, N. Murase, R. L. Simmons, and R. A. Hoffman, *J. Biol. Chem.* **267,** 10994 (1992).

[16] N. R. Bastian, S. Xu, X. L. Shao, J. Shelby, D. L. Granger, and J. B. Hibbs, Jr., *Biochim. Biophys. Acta* **1226,** 225 (1994).

[17] N. K. Worrall, W. D. Lazenby, T. P. Misko, T.-S. Lin, C. R. Rodi, P. T. Manning, R. G. Tilton, J. R. Williamson, and T. B. Ferguson, Jr., *J. Exp. Med.* **181,** 63 (1995).

[18] P. Plonka, B. Plonka, and S. J. Lukiewicz, *Curr. Top. Biophys.* **18,** 46 (1994).

[19] J. M. Langrehr, A. R. Müller, H. A. Bergonia, T. D. Jacob, T. K. Lee, W. H. Schraut, J. R. Lancaster, Jr., and R. H. Hoffman, *Surgery* **112,** 395 (1992).

there is increased production of HbNO complex, which can be used as an indicator of ·NO formation. Formation of HbNO at the site of allograft rejection was completely quenched by prior administration of the immuno-suppressant FK506. Increased formation of HbNO has also been observed during the course of small bowel allograft rejection in the rat. However, the connection between increased ·NO production and allograft rejection is not fully understood.[16] (2) In the blood-perfused rabbit model, HbNO formation was found to be increased during ischemia.[20] Formation of HbNO has been used as an *in vivo* indicator of ·NO formation in whole organs and tissues subjected to ischemia. (3) Electron spin resonance has been used to detect HbNO complex[21–25] in blood specimens of human subjects and animals during treatment with ·NO donors and cytokines. (4) Nitric oxide production during endotoxic shock in carbon tetrachloride-treated rats was monitored using HbNO as a diagnostic marker.[26,27] A synergistic increase in HbNO formation was noted in animals treated with the hepato-toxin and lipopolysaccharide (LPS). This may provide a novel animal model for investigating the combined effect of hepatotoxins, cytokines, and ·NO.

Nitrosomyoglobin

The ESR spectrum of MbNO at low temperature (30–70 K) is character-ized by three absorptions corresponding to $g_x = 2.08$, $g_y = 1.98$, $g_z = 2.0$.[28] In single-crystal studies, the existence of a triplet of triplets feature for g_z has been reported.[29,30] This is due to electron coupling to ^{14}N of ·NO and to a nitrogen atom of the ligand-bound *trans* to ·NO. At liquid nitrogen temperatures, MbNO does not usually display the triplet hyperfine features.

[20] A. Wennmalm and A. S. Petersson, *J. Cardiovasc. Pharmacol.* **17**(Suppl. 3), 534 (1991).
[21] R. Kruszyna, H. Kruszyna, R. P. Smith, C. D. Thron, and D. E. Wilcox, *J. Pharmacol. Exp. Ther.* **241**, 307 (1987).
[22] H. Kruszyna, R. Kruszyna, R. P. Smith, and D. E. Wilcox, *Toxicol. Appl. Pharmacol.* **91**, 429 (1987).
[23] R. Kruszyna, H. Kruszyna, R. P. Smith, and D. E. Wilcox, *Toxicol. Appl. Pharmacol.* **94**, 458 (1988).
[24] H. Kosaka, N. Harada, M. Watanabe, H. Yoshihara, Y. Katsuki, and T. Shiga, *Biochem. Biophys. Res. Commun.* **189**, 392 (1992).
[25] L. R. Cantilena, Jr., R. P. Smith, S. Frasur, H. Kruszyna, R. Kruszyna, and D. E. Wilcox, *J. Lab. Clin. Med.* **120**, 902 (1992).
[26] W. Chamulitrat, S. J. Jordon, R. P. Mason, A. L. Litton, J. G. Wilson, E. R. Wood, G. Wolberg, and L. Molina y Vedia, *Arch. Biochem. Biophys.* **316**, 30 (1995).
[27] W. Chamulitrat, S. J. Jordon, and R. P. Mason, *Mol. Pharmacol.* **46**, 391 (1994).
[28] R. H. Morse and S. I. Chan, *J. Biol. Chem.* **255**, 7876 (1980).
[29] L. C. Dickinson and J. C. W. Chien, *J. Am. Chem. Soc.* **93**, 5036 (1971).
[30] D. H. O'Keeffe, R. E. Ebel, and J. A. Peterson, *J. Biol. Chem.* **253**, 3509 (1978).

Typically, a broad absorption at $g = 2.08$ is the characteristic feature evident for MbNO in biological systems.

ESR Spectroscopy. Spectra of MbNO are measured at low temperatures (30–77 K) using nonsaturating microwave powers (<1 mW), 2–5 G modulation amplitude, 9.0–9.2 GHz microwave frequency, and 400 G scan range. Tissue samples are minced (not pulverized), thawed, and homogenized with an equal volume of buffer, immediately transferred to 3-mm quartz ESR tube, and kept frozen at 77 K.

Application. Formation of MbNO was detected in rat heart allograft tissue specimens. This signal was detected from heart tissue but not from other tissues such as liver, lung, and spleen.[15]

Nitrosyl Cytochrome P450 and Cytochrome P420

Nitric oxide has been used as a spin probe to investigate the structural environment of the oxygen-binding site of cytochrome P450.[30,31] The ferrous-NO complex of cytochrome P450 (P450–NO) exhibits an ESR signal centered around $g = 2$ having a rhombic symmetry with $g_x = 2.062$, $g_y = 1.97$, and $g_z = 2.002$. The absorption at g_z is split into a triplet with a 20 G hyperfine coupling for ^{14}N from ^{14}NO attached to the heme. The second-derivative ESR spectrum of P450–NO also shows hyperfine couplings for g_x and g_y. The ferrous–NO complex of P420 (P420–NO) is formed from denaturation of the P450–NO complex. The ESR spectrum of P420–NO has a broad absorption at $g_x = 2.089$ and $g_z = 2.009$. The g_z absorption is split by a nitrogen coupling ($a_N = 16$ G). The spectrum of P420–NO resembles that of a pentacoordinate heme–NO species.

ESR Spectroscopy. The ESR spectra of P450–NO and P420–NO are measured at 77 K using 10 mW microwave power, 1–5 G modulation amplitude, 9–9.2 GHz microwave frequency, and 400 G scan range.

Limitations. (1) The P450–NO complex is unstable and degrades to P420–NO. (2) In cellular systems, the ESR spectra generally consist of a mixture of pentacoordinate heme–NO species with similar spectral characteristics.

Applications. (1) During liver inflammation in a mouse model, P420–NO complex has been detected *in vivo*.[26,27] (2) A P420–NO complex, presumably formed from P450–NO, has been observed during hepatic injury.[26] (3) Both P450–NO and P420–NO complexes could be used as indicators of *in vivo* ·NO production in animals exposed to hepatotoxicants.[26,27]

---

[31] R. E. Ebel, D. H. O'Keefe, and J. A. Peterson, *FEBS Lett.* **55**, 198 (1975).

Ferrous-Nitrosyl Complex of Prostaglandin H Synthase

Prostaglandin H (PGH) synthase has both cyclooxygenase and peroxidase activities that are responsible for stereospecific oxygenation of arachidonic acid to PGH_2.[32] The ferrous enzyme reacts with ·NO to form the nitrosyl complex.[33] Depending on the time and temperature of incubation, both 5-coordinate and 6-coordinate ferrous-nitrosyl complexes are formed. The 6-coordinate ferrous-nitrosyl complex exhibits a rhombic ESR signal at g_x = 2.07, g_z = 2.01, and g_y = 1.97. The 5-coordinate signal shows an axial symmetry with $g_\parallel$ = 2.12 and $g_\perp$ = 2.001. Both complexes exhibit a ^{14}N hyperfine coupling from the attached NO (a_N = 17 G) in the g_z or $g_\perp$ signal. However, in contrast to the horseradish peroxidase–NO complex, there is no superhyperfine coupling from a histidine ligand. It is speculated that tyrosine might be the endogenous ligand of the heme in PGH synthase.

ESR Spectroscopy. Measurements of the PGH synthase–NO complex are obtained at 90 K using 9.2 GHz microwave frequency, 2 mW microwave power, 2 G modulation amplitude and 400 G scan range.

Application. Nitric oxide has been shown to activate PGH synthase. It will be important to determine whether ·NO selectively inhibits the peroxidase or the cyclooxygenase activity of this enzyme.

Nitrosyl–Soluble Guanylate Complex

It has been hypothesized that ·NO activates soluble guanylate cyclase (SGC) by binding to the heme of the ferrous enzyme.[34] The resulting ferrous-nitrosyl complex of SGC is paramagnetic. The ESR spectra of the ferrous ($^{14}N/^{15}N$) nitrosyl complexes of the purified enzyme have been obtained. The spectrum exhibits a close resemblance to the 5-coordinate heme–NO complex. The g value, hyperfine coupling parameters, and line widths obtained by computer simulations are given by Stone *et al.*[35]

ESR Spectroscopy. Spectra of NO–SGC are obtained by signal averaging at 25 K using a 4 G modulation amplitude, 2 mW microwave power, and 400 G scan range.

Application. The addition of several NO–heme proteins such as nitrosyl catalase and P420–NO has been shown to cause the activation of guanylate cyclase.[34] Whether this occurs through a transfer of ·NO between the heme

[32] B. Samuelson, M. Goldyne, E. Grandström, M. Hamberg, S. Hammerström, and C. Malmsten, *Annu. Rev. Biochem.* **47**, 997 (1978).

[33] R. Karthein, W. Nastainczyk, and H. H. Ruf, *Eur. J. Biochem.* **166**, 173 (1987).

[34] P. A. Craven, F. R. DeRubertis, and D. W. Pratt, *J. Biol. Chem.* **254**, 8213 (1979).

[35] J. R. Stone, R. H. Sands, W. R. Dunham, and M. A. Marletta, *Biochem. Biophys. Res. Commun.* **207**, 572 (1995).

proteins is not known. With the ESR spectrum of ·NO–SGC characterized, it may be possible to investigate such possibilities.

Limitation. In microsomal preparations, interference from other 5-coordinate heme–NO complexes such as P420–NO may complicate spectral interpretations.[26,27]

Other Heme–Nitrosyl Complexes

In addition to the above-mentioned heme proteins, ·NO will react with other heme protein targets in cells, such as catalase, cytochrome-*c* oxidase, and cytochrome-*c* peroxidase. The ESR parameters of ferrous-nitrosyl complexes of these heme proteins are discussed elsewhere.[5,6,36]

Nitrosyl Complex of Nonheme Protein Lipoxygenase

Soybean lipoxygenase is a nonheme iron enzyme that catalyzes the hydroperoxidation of unsaturated fatty acids by oxygen.[37] Both ferric and ferrous states of the enzyme are believed to be mechanistically important in this oxidation. Nitric oxide has been used to probe the environment of iron. Exposure of ferrous lipoxygenase to ·NO results in the formation of a nitrosyl-iron complex, which exhibits a ESR spectrum characteristic of a nearly axial $S = \frac{3}{2}$ system.[38] The ferrous lipoxygenase–·NO complex is inactive and, thus, unable to catalyze the oxidation of unsaturated fatty acid.

The ESR spectrum of the ferrous lipoxygenase–NO complex is characterized by a strong absorption band at $g_x' = g_y' = 4.0$ and a relatively weaker absorption at $g_z' = 2.0$. The binding of ·NO to ferrous lipoxygenase is reversible. The ESR absorption at $g = 4.0$ is dependent on the pH, added solvent, and other variables.[38] In the presence of ethanol, the g values correspond to a species with rhombic symmetry. With spermine NONOate, an ·NO donor that releases ·NO slowly and spontaneously, two different absorption peaks at $g = 4$ with differing microwave power saturation characteristics have been observed.[39]

ESR Spectroscopy. Measurements are usually performed at liquid helium temperatures (5–20 K) using 8–10 G modulation amplitude, 20–100 mW microwave power, and 2000 G scan range. The field is set at 2000 G such that absorptions at $g = 4.0$ are detected at 1600 G.

[36] T. Yonetani, H. Yamomoto, J. E. Erman, J. S. Leigh, Jr., and G. H. Reed, *J. Biol. Chem.* **247**, 2447 (1992).

[37] J. J. M. C. DeGroot, G. J. Garssen, J. F. G. Vilegenthart, and J. Boldingh, *Biochim. Biophys. Acta* **326**, 279 (1973).

[38] M. J. Nelson, *J. Biol. Chem.* **262**, 12137 (1987).

[39] H. Rubbo, S. Parthasarthy, S. Barnes, M. Kirk, B. Kalyanaraman, and B. A. Freeman, *J. Biol. Chem.* **269**, 26066 (1994).

Applications. (1) Nitric oxide has been shown to inhibit lipoxygenase activity. However, it is not clear whether this inhibition arises from inhibiting the enzymatic activity or scavenging the radicals produced from the oxidation of linoleic acid. ESR measurements show that $\cdot$NO at physiologically relevant concentrations does not inhibit the lipoxygenase activity.[39] (2) Murine fibroblasts, which express high levels of human lipoxygenase, were shown to mediate enhanced modification of low-density lipoprotein.[40] Further investigations on the formation of ferrous lipoxygenase–NO complex in these cells will be of interest.

Iron-Nitrosyl Complexes from Ferritins

Ferritin is the major reservoir for nonheme iron in cells. It is believed that "free" nonheme iron is in a dynamic equilibrium with ferritin. Nitric oxide has been reported to release iron from ferritin. Lee *et al.* have observed three types of ESR signals from the interaction between $\cdot$NO and ferritin.[41] The rhombic $S = \frac{1}{2}$ A-type complex has features at $g_x' = 2.055$, $g_y' = 2.033$, and $g_z' = 2.015$, corresponding to an iron-nitrosylhistidine complex. The $S = \frac{1}{2}$ axial B-type has features at $g_\perp = 2.033$ and $g_\parallel = 2.014$ that are attributed to an iron-dinitrosylcysteine complex. The $S = \frac{3}{2}$ axial C-type spectrum has absorptions at $g_\perp' = 4$ and $g_\parallel' = 2$ that are characteristic of a paramagnetic Fe^{3+}–NO^- complex with nonspecific binding to the carboxylate groups.

ESR Spectroscopy. Spectra of A- and B-type spectra are obtained at 77 K using 10 mW microwave power, 1 G modulation amplitude, 9.3 GHz microwave frequency, and 400 G field scan. A scan range of 4000 G is used to obtain the C-type signal.

Iron-Nitrosyl Complexes or $g = 2.03$ Complexes

Nitric oxide and ferrous ion in the presence of ligands form complexes of the type $Fe(NO)_2L_2$, which are either neutral, monopositive, or mononegative depending on the charge of the attached ligand. For example, the overall charge of the $Fe(NO)_2(RS)_2$ complex is mononegative. These complexes exhibit an intense ESR signal in the region $g = 2.03$–2.04.[42,43] The structures of several iron-nitrosylthiol and iron-nitrosylhistidine complexes

[40] D. J. Benz, M. Mol. M. Ezaki, N. Mori-ito, I. Zelán, A. Miyanohara, T. Friedmann, S. Parthasarathy, D. Steinberg, and J. L. Witztum, *J. Biol. Chem.* **270**, 5191 (1995).
[41] M. Lee, P. Arosio, A. Cozzi, and N. D. Chasteen, *Biochemistry* **33**, 3679 (1994).
[42] D. R. Eaton and T. R. Bryar, *in* "Electronic Magnetic Resonance of the Solid State" (J. A. Weil, ed.), p. 309. Canadian Society of Chemistry, Ottawa, 1987.
[43] A. R. Butler, C. Glidewell, and M.-H. Li, *Adv. Inorg. Chem.* **32**, 335 (1988).

have been elegantly characterized using ^{15}N and ^{57}Fe substitution.[44,45] At low temperatures (i.e., 77 K), these complexes exhibit an axial feature with $g_\perp = 2.042$ and $g_\parallel = 2.012$.[44-50] The (NO-Fe-S)-type signal with similar g values has also been observed in a variety of experimental systems such as cytokine-activated macrophages,[51-53] pancreatic islets,[54,55] vascular smooth muscle cells,[56] tumor target cells cocultured with activated macrophages,[57] transfected L1210-R2 cells overexpressing the R2 subunit of ribonucleotide reductase,[58] and hepatocytes exposed to inflammatory stimuli.[59]

The source of iron and thiolate ligand in the $g = 2.03$ complexes is under investigation. Although the iron–sulfur center has been shown to be responsible for the production of these iron-nitrosyl complexes in microbial systems,[60] the situation is far from clear in macrophages and other cells. Although this signal is causally related to the production of ·NO, it is not clear whether cell toxicity is related to the formation of a dinitrosyl-iron complex. Vanin et al.[61] have suggested that the line width of the signals could be used to indicate whether the thiolate ligand is derived from a small molecular weight thiol or a protein thiol. Despite the structural ambi-

[44] C. C. McDonald, W. D. Phillips, and H. F. Mower, J. Am. Chem. Soc. **87**, 3319 (1965).

[45] J. C. Woolum, E. Tiezzi, and B. Commoner, Biochim. Biophys. Acta **160**, 311 (1968).

[46] J. C. Salerno, T. Ohnishi, J. Lim, and T. E. King, Biochem. Biophys. Res. Commun. **73**, 833 (1976).

[47] A. Mülsch, A. Vanin, P. Mordvintcev, S. Hauschildt, and R. Busse, Biochem. J. **2881**, 597 (1992).

[48] P. Mordvintcev, A. Mülsch, R. Busse, and A. Vanin, Anal. Biochem. **199**, 142 (1991).

[49] N. V. Voevodskaya and A. F. Vanin, Biochem. Biophys. Res. Commun. **186**, 1423 (1992).

[50] A. Mülsch, P. I. Mordvintcev, A. F. Vanin, and R. Bussi, Biochem. Biophys. Res. Commun. **196**, 1303 (1993).

[51] J. R. Lancaster, Jr., and J. B. Hibbs, Jr., Proc. Natl. Acad. Sci. U.S.A. **87**, 1223 (1990).

[52] C. Pellat, Y. Henry, and J. C. Drapier, Biochim. Biophys. Res. Commun. **166**, 119 (1990).

[53] A. F. Vanin, C. B. Men'shikov, I. A. Moriz, P. I. Mordvintcev, V. A. Serezhenkov, and D. Sh. Burbaev, Biochim. Biophys. Acta **1135**, 275 (1992).

[54] J. A. Corbett, J. R. Lancaster, Jr., M. A. Sweetland, and M. L. McDaniel, J. Biol. Chem. **266**, 21351 (1991).

[55] J. A. Corbett, J. L. Wang, J. H. Hughes, B. A. Wolf, M. A. Sweetland, J. R. Lancaster, Jr., and M. L. McDaniel, Biochem. J. **287**, 229 (1992).

[56] Y.-J. Geng, A. S. Petersson, A. Wennmalm, and G. K. Hansson, Exp. Cell Res. **214**, 418 (1994).

[57] J. C. Drapier, C. Pellat, and Y. Henry, J. Biol. Chem. **266**, 10162 (1991).

[58] M. Lepoivre, J. M. Flaman, P. Bobé, G. Lemaire, and Y. Henry, J. Biol. Chem. **269**, 21891 (1994).

[59] J. Stadler, H. A. Bergonia, M. DiSilvio, M. A. Sweetland, T. R. Billiar, R. L. Simmons, and J. R. Lancaster, Jr., Arch. Biochem. Biophys. **302**, 4 (1993).

[60] D. Reddy, J. R. Lancaster, Jr., and D. P. Cornforth, Science **221**, 769 (1983).

[61] A. F. Vanin, S. V. Kiladze, and L. N. Kubrina, Biophysics (Engl. Trans.) **20**, 1089 (1975); Biofizika **20**, 1068 (1975).

guities of these iron-dinitrosyl complexes, the ESR spectrum could be used as a qualitative diagnostic marker of $\cdot$NO production in tissues. Apometallothionen and Zn-metallothionen have been shown to form an ESR spectrum similar to that of $[Fe(NO)_2(RS)_2]^{-1}$ complex in the presence of $\cdot$NO and Fe^{2+}.[62]

ESR Spectroscopy. Spectra of iron-dinitrosyl complexes are usually obtained at 77 K using a 5 G modulation amplitude, 1 mW microwave power, and 400 G scan range.

Limitations. (1) Absorptions due to other paramagnetic species often appear in this region ($g = 2.04$–2.0). To identify the absorption due to iron-dinitrosyl complexes, microwave power saturation experiments should be carried out. The iron-dinitrosyl complex will saturate less readily than organic radicals absorbing in this region. (2) Although the iron-nitrosyl complex has been recovered exclusively in the cytosolic fraction, the possibility of exchange reaction between nitrosylated complexes makes it difficult to pinpoint their origin.

Iron-Nitrosyl Dithiol Complexes

Nitric oxide binds Fe^{2+} to form an iron-nitrosyl complex. Depending on the nature of the attached ligand, both mononitrosyl- and dinitrosyl-iron complexes are formed. With sulfhydryl ligands, complexes of the type $Fe^{2+}(NO)_2(monothiol)_2$ (4-coordinate) and $Fe^{2+}(NO)(dithiol)_2$ (5-coordinate) were characterized years ago using ESR.[63] One of the most frequently used dithiol ligands is dithiocarbamate (DETC) (Fig. 2). The complex $Fe^{2+}(NO)(DETC)_2$ (Fig. 3, $R = R' = C_2H_5$) is relatively stable in the presence of oxygen and exhibits a distinct three-line ESR spectrum at room temperature ($a_N = 12.7$ G, $g_{iso} = 2.04$ G) and at 100 K ($a_N = 13.4$ G, $g_\perp = 2.039$ G, $g_\parallel = 2.02$ G).[63] In the presence of $^{15}\cdot$NO, a two-line spectrum ($a_N = 17.6$ G) is formed. Although DETC is water soluble, $Fe^{2+}(DETC)_2$ and $Fe^{2+}NO(DETC)_2$ are hydrophobic and thus form precipitates in physiological buffers.[48] Therefore, DETC or $Fe^{2+}(DETC)_2$ have to be incorporated into yeast cell membranes or other hydrophobic membranes. Using a water-soluble derivative of DETC, N-methyl-D-glucamine dithiocarbamate $(MGD)^{64-66}$ (Fig. 2), a stable water-soluble $Fe^{2+}(NO)(MGD)_2$ complex with

[62] M. C. Kennedy, T. Gau, W. E. Antholine, and D. H. Petering, *Biochem. Biophys. Res. Commun.* **29**, 632 (1993).

[63] B. A. Goodman, J. B. Raynor, and M. C. R. Symons, *J. Am. Chem. Soc.* 2572 (1969).

[64] L. A. Shinobu, S. C. Jones, and M. M. Jones, *Acta Pharmacol. Toxicol.* **54**, 189 (1984).

[65] A. M. Komarov, D. Mattson, M. M. Jones, P. K. Singh, and C.-C. Lai, *Biochem. Biophys. Res. Commun.* **195**, 1191 (1993).

[66] C.-S. Lai and A. M. Komarov, *FEBS Lett.* **345**, 120 (1994).

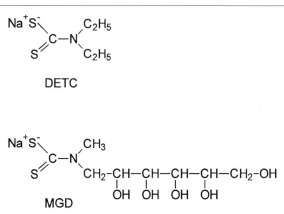

FIG. 2. Structures of dithiocarbamate ligands.

a characteristic ESR spectrum at room temperature was observed (a_N = 12.6 G, g_{iso} = 2.04). An ESR spectrum with an anisotropic g value has been obtained at 77 K. The Fe^{2+}(NO)(MGD)$_2$ complex is persistent in the presence of oxygen for several hours.

Synthesis of Iron–Dithiocarbamate Complex. Dithiocarbamate is available from Aldrich (Milwaukee, WI). Cells are generally loaded with DETC by incubating with DETC (1 mg/ml) for 10–15 min at 37°. Alternatively, Fe^{2+}(DETC)$_2$ complex can be solubilized in yeast membranes and added to cells. The iron bound to DETC is derived from intracellular iron. In animal experiments, DETC is administered intraperitoneally.

The water-soluble ligand MGD is synthesized according to Shinobu *et al.*[64] and purified by recrystallization. The precursor chemicals, namely, *N*-methyl-D-glucamine and carbon disulfide, are commercially available (Aldrich). Stock solutions of Fe^{2+}(MGD)$_2$ complex are prepared by adding ferrous ammonium sulfate or ferrous sulfate to MGD at a ratio of 1:5 or 1:10 and used immediately. The Fe^{2+}MGD)$_2$ complex does undergo autoxidation with time.

ESR Spectroscopy. Spectrometer conditions to detect Fe^{2+}(NO)(dithiol)$_2$ complexes *in vitro* are the following: 9.3 GHz microwave frequency,

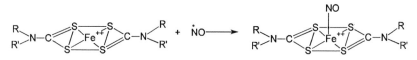

FIG. 3. Trapping of ·NO by ferrous dithiocarbamate to form a mononitrosyl iron-dithiocarbamate complex.

20 mW microwave power, 5–10 G modulation amplitude, and 200 G field scan. Either a flat cell or Pasteur pipette is used as a sample holder. When using cells in a flat cell, it is preferable to place the flat cell in a horizontal position as described by Kotake *et al.*[67] to avoid sedimentation of cells. *In vivo* measurements of ·NO using an $Fe^{2+}(MGD)_2$ complex are performed using an ESR spectrometer equipped with an S-band (1–2 GHz) bridge and a low frequency loop–gap resonator operating at 3.5 GHz.

Applications. (1) Nitric oxide generation can be monitored continuously from ·NO donors and from enzymatic generation.[68] Kinetics of production of ·NO can be measured by this technique, and stoichiometric accumulation of ·NO with respect to L-citrulline has been demonstrated. (2) *In vivo* formation of ·NO during ischemia in brain, gut, etc., has been demonstrated.[69–75] (3) In the isolated heart model, production of ·NO during ischemia was shown using an $Fe^{2+}(MGD)_2$ complex.[76] (4) Electron spin resonance imaging of ·NO in ischemic organs is potentially feasible.

Advantages. (1) The $Fe^{2+}(NO)(MGD)_2$ complex can be quantitated using a standard $Fe^{2+}(NO)(S_2O_3)^{2-}$, which has similar relaxation characteristics. (2) The $Fe^{2+}(NO)(dithiol)_2$ complexes are stable in the presence of oxygen. (3) The $Fe^{2+}(dithiol)_2$ complexes have a higher affinity for ·NO relative to oxygen. (4) *In vivo* measurement of ·NO in real time is feasible.

Limitations. (1) The dithiolate ligands, especially the lipid-soluble complexes, are toxic. (2) The water-soluble MGD ligand has been shown to be toxic at high concentrations.[76] (3) Dithiols have been reported to inhibit NO synthase[77] and superoxide dismutase (SOD) activities. Inhibition of SOD may enhance ·NO levels in tissues. (4) Low-temperature ESR spectroscopy of $Fe^{2+}(NO)(dithiol)_2$ complexes is often complicated by the endogenous $Cu(DETC)_2$ signal.

[67] Y. Kotake, L. A. Reinke, T. Tanigawa, and H. Koshida, *Free Radical Biol. Med.* **17**, 215 (1994).
[68] A. Mülsch, M. Hecker, P. I. Mordvintcev, A. F. Vanin, and R. Busse, *Nauyn-Schmiedeberg's Arch. Pharmacol.* **347**, 92 (1993).
[69] S. Sato, T. Tominaga, T. Ohnishi, and S. T. Ohnishi, *Biochim. Biophys. Acta* **1181**, 195 (1993).
[70] A. F. Vanin, P. I. Mordvintcev, S. Hauschildt, and A. Mülsch, *Biochim. Biophys. Acta* **1177**, 37 (1993).
[71] L. N. Kubrina, W. S. Caldwell, P. I. Mordvintcev, I. V. Malenkova, and A. F. Vanin, *Biochim. Biophys. Acta* **1099**, 233 (1992).
[72] A. Mülsch, P. Mordvintcev, A. F. Vanin, and R. Busse, *FEBS Lett.* **294**, 252 (1991).
[73] V. D. Mikoyan, L. N. Kubrina, and A. F. Vanin, *Biochem. Mol. Biol. Int.* **32**, 157 (1994).
[74] T. Tominaga, S. Sato, T. Ohnishi, and S. T. Ohnishi, *Brain Res.* **614**, 342 (1993).
[75] S. Sato, T. Tominaga, T. Ohnishi, and S. T. Ohnishi, *Brain Res.* **647**, 91 (1994).
[76] J. L. Zweier, P. Wang, and P. Kuppusamy, *J. Biol. Chem.* **270**, 304 (1995).
[77] A. Mülsch, B. Schray-Utz, P. I. Mordvintcev, S. Hauschildt, and R. Busse, *FEBS Lett.* **321**, 215 (1993).

Nitronyl Nitroxides as Nitric Oxide Probes

Nitronyl nitroxides (NNO) are a group of organic compounds containing both nitrone ($>N^+-O^-$) and nitroxide ($>N-\cdot O$) functional groups.[78-82] These compounds can be either hydrophilic or hydrophobic, depending on the R group (Fig. 4). Nitronyl nitroxides, first synthesized in the 1960s by Ulmann and co-workers,[79] have been used to detect $\cdot NO$ present in atmospheric air. Nitronyl nitroxide reacts with $\cdot NO$ to form an imino nitroxide (INO) (Fig. 5). This reaction is unique to NNO and does not occur with other nitroxides.

The NNO reaction can be monitored continuously by ESR. Nitronyl nitroxide has a five-line ESR spectrum with an intensity ratio of $1:2:3:2:1$, due to the interaction of two equivalent nitrogen nuclei with the unpaired electron ($a_N = 8.0$ G). The INO exhibits a distinctly different ESR spectrum; typically, either a seven-line or nine-line spectrum is observed as a result of the electron interacting with the two inequivalent nitrogen atoms ($a_N^1 = 4-5$ G, $a_N^2 = 9-10$ G). Because the low field lines of NNO and INO are well separated, the transformation of NNO to INO is best observed by monitoring the low field line of each spectrum. The height of the peaks is proportional to the nitroxide concentration. However, owing to the decrease in the line width of the imino nitroxide as compared with that of nitronyl nitroxide, the spectral amplitude of the imino nitroxide is greater than that of nitronyl nitroxide at the same concentration.

Using ESR, Hogg et al.[83] have demonstrated that the stoichiometry between NNO and $\cdot NO$ is dependent on the rate of generation of $\cdot NO$ and is $1:1$ only at low rates of $\cdot NO$ generation ($\sim 10^{-13}$ M/sec). However, the stoichiometry approaches 0.5-1.0 at higher rates of $\cdot NO$ production or when NNO is added as a bolus. This is contrary to an earlier study, suggesting a $1:1$ stoichiometry.[81]

Nitric oxide reacts with NNO to yield INO and $\cdot NO_2$ with a rate constant of 10^4 M^{-1} sec^{-1}.[63] The reaction between $\cdot NO$ and O_2 is second order with respect to $\cdot NO$ ($k \approx 6 \times 10^6$ M^{-2} sec^{-1}). Therefore, the reaction between

[78] J. S. Nadeau and D. G. B. Boocock, *Anal. Chem.* **49**, 1672 (1977).

[79] E. F. Ulmann, J. H. Osiecki, D. G. B. Boocock, and R. Darcy, *J. Am. Chem. Soc.* **94**, 7049 (1972).

[80] J. Joseph, B. Kalyanaraman, and J. S. Hyde, *Biochem. Biophys. Res. Commun.* **192**, 926 (1993).

[81] T. Akaike, M. Yoshida, Y. Miyamoto, K. Sato, M. Kohno, K. Sasamoto, K. Miyazaki, and H. Maeda, *Biochemistry* **32**, 827 (1993).

[82] R. J. Singh, N. Hogg, H. S. Mchaourab, and B. Kalyanaraman, *Biochim. Biophys. Acta* **1201**, 437 (1994).

[83] N. Hogg, R. J. Singh, J. Joseph, F. Neese, and B. Kalyanaraman, *Free Radical Res.* **22**, 47 (1995).

Nitronyl nitroxide

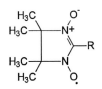

Hydrophilic R	Hydrophobic R

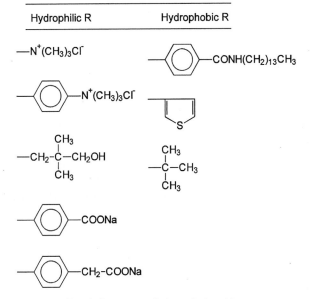

FIG. 4. Structures of nitronyl nitroxides.

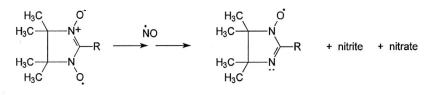

Nitronyl nitroxide (NNO)   Imino nitroxide (INO)

FIG. 5. Reaction between nitric oxide and nitronyl nitroxide to form an imino nitroxide.

·NO and NNO will outcompete the reaction of ·NO with oxygen. Kinetic simulations of the reaction between ·NO, NNO, and O_2 have been obtained.[84,85]

Synthesis of Nitronyl Nitroxides. Nitronyl nitroxide containing various R groups can be synthesized following the procedure of Ullman and co-workers or by a slight modification. Nitronyl nitroxide containing the 4-carboxyphenyl group (also known as carboxy-PTIO) can be purchased from Alexis Corporation (San Diego, CA) or Caymen Chemicals (Ann Arbor, MI).

ESR Spectroscopy. The room temperature spectrometer conditions are similar to those used for detecting stable nitroxides. Samples can be taken in either a pipette, microcapillary, flat cell, or 3-mm quartz tube, depending on the solvent (not applicable for solvents with high dielectric constants). The ESR conditions are as follows: 9.5 GHz microwave frequency, 0.5–1 G modulation amplitude, 1–20 mW microwave power, and 100 G scan range (full spectrum) or 10 G (low field absorptions of NNO and INO). To monitor the kinetics of the decay of NNO and formation of NNO, the magnetic field can be set to the maximum of NNO or INO, respectively.

Applications in Physiology. (1) Nitronyl nitroxides have been used as probes to investigate the mechanism of vasodilatory action of nitrovasodilators and spin traps in isolated rat heart. Nitronyl nitroxides inhibited vasodilation and cGMP release elicited by sodium nitroprusside (SNP) and *S*-nitroso-*N*-acetylpenicillamine (SNAP), implicating ·NO as a causal vasodilatory agent. However, NNO did not inhibit nitroxide- or nitrone-induced vasodilation, suggesting that ·NO is not involved in spin trap- or spin label-induced vasodilation.[86] (2) It has been shown that supplementation of cardioplegic solutions with nitrosoglutathione improved postischemic functional recovery.[87] Nitronyl nitroxide reversed this protective effect, implicating the intermediacy of ·NO. Therefore, NNO can be used as an ·NO antagonist in perfused organs. (3) Nitronyl nitroxide was reportedly more effective than ·NO synthase inhibitors in inhibiting acetylcholine- and ATP-induced relaxation of the smooth muscle of rabbit aorta.[81] (4) Nitronyl nitroxide suppressed ·NO-induced extravasation in tumors.[88] Un-

[84] R. J. Singh, N. Hogg, F. Neese, J. Joseph, and B. Kalyanaraman, *Photochem. Photobiol.* **61**, 325 (1995).

[85] Y. Y. Woldman, V. V. Khramtsov, I. A. Grigor'ev, I. A. Kiriejuk, and D. I. Utepbergenov, *Biochem. Biophys. Res. Commun.* **202**, 195 (1994).

[86] E. A. Konorev, M. M. Tarpey, J. Joseph, J. E. Baker, and B. Kalyanaraman, *Free Radical Biol. Med.* **18**, 169 (1995).

[87] E. A. Konorev, M. M. Tarpey, J. Joseph, J. E. Baker, and B. Kalyanaraman, *J. Pharmacol. Exp. Ther.* **274**, 200 (1995).

[88] M. Maeda, Y. Nogushi, K. Sato, and T. Akaike, *Jpn. J. Cancer Res.* **85**, 331 (1994).

like the case for EDRF (endothelial derived relaxing factor), the unregulated overproduction of ·NO has been implicated in various diseases and pathologies including septic shock and multiorgan failure. Suggested therapeutic approaches include drugs to decrease ·NO levels. Nitronyl nitroxides such as carboxynitronyl nitroxide showed a beneficial effect in endotoxic shock.[89] The imino nitroxide was detected in the urine. Yoshida *et al.*, using NNO, reported that NNO enhanced rather than decreased the antimicrobial action of ·NO.[90] Nitronyl nitroxide has also been used as a tool to probe antimicrobial mechanisms of ·NO.

Applications in Photochemistry. It has been shown that nitronyl nitroxides can be used to continuously monitor photoproduction of ·NO from nitrovasodilators and to measure the action spectrum and quantum yield for ·NO production.[84,91] Nitronyl nitroxides have weak absorption bands in the visible region; therefore, light absorption by the probes does not pose a major problem. The quantum yield for ·NO production (ϕ_{NO}) can be calculated by knowing $-d[NNO]/dt$ and the intensity of light. The initial rate of decay of NNO, due to reaction with ·NO generated from photochemical decomposition of GSNO, was greatly enhanced in the presence of sensitizers.

Advantages. (1) The ESR assay is continuous and quantitative. Hogg *et al.*[83] have reinvestigated the actual stoichiometry between ·NO and NNO. (2) The ability to synthesize both hydrophobic and hydrophilic nitronyl nitroxides makes it possible to monitor ·NO production in biological membranes. (3) Nitronyl nitroxides can be used as antagonistic inhibitors of ·NO.

Limitations. (1) Reduction of NNO and INO to inactive hydroxylamines in the presence of reductants such as ascorbic acid and glutathione poses a major problem in biological systems. (2) However, hydroxylamines of INO can be reoxidized to INO by $K_3Fe(CN)_6$. (3) ·NO_2, and N_2O_3 are products of the reaction between NNO and ·NO. These species can be potentially toxic.

Trapping of Nitric Oxide by Nitric Oxide Chelotropes

Nitric oxide chelotropes (NOCTs) are compounds containing the 7,7,8,8-tetraalkyl-*o*-quinodimethane type moiety (Fig. 6). These compounds (i.e., **1, 2,** and **3**) react with ·NO or ·NO_2 to form either a single nitroxide or a

[89] A. Yoshida, T. Akaike, Y. Wada, K. Sato, K. Ikeda, S. Ueda, and H. Maeda, *Biochem. Biophys. Res. Commun.* **202,** 923 (1994).
[90] K. Yoshida, T. Akaiki, T. Doi, K. Sato, S. Uiri, M. Suga, M. Ando, and H. Maeda, *Infect. Immunol.* **61,** 3552 (1993).
[91] R. J. Singh, N. Hogg, J. Joseph, and B. Kalyanaraman, *FEBS Lett.* **360,** 47 (1995).

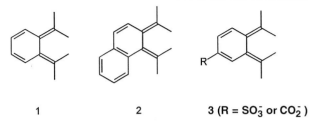

1   2   3 (R = SO$_3^-$ or CO$_2^-$)

FIG. 6. Structure of nitric oxide chelotropes (NOCT).

mixture of such compounds.[91-93] Reaction with ·NO produces a persistent nitroxide of the type 1,1,3,3-tetramethylisoindolin-2-oxyl (**1NO, 2NO**, and **3NO** in Fig. 7) that can be detected by steady-state ESR spectroscopy at ambient temperature. These ·NO adducts typically exhibit a characteristic three-line ESR signal (a_N = 13–15 G) with g values around 2.005. The NOCTs also react with ·NO$_2$ to produce species similar to an alkoxy nitroxide radical (**1NO$_2$** and **2NO$_2$** in Fig. 7). The ESR spectra of these species are characterized by a large nitrogen hyperfine coupling constant (a_N = 28 G). Compound **3** is more suitable for detecting ·NO$_2$, and the resulting **3NO$_2$** is more persistent.

Synthesis of Nitric Oxide Chelotropes. The NOCTs are fairly unstable; depending on the structure, the half-life varies from minutes to hours. Therefore, these compounds must be synthesized either *in situ* or immediately prior to the experiment. They are typically synthesized by photodecomposition of 1,1,3,3-tetramethyl-2-indanone type compounds (Fig. 8).

ESR Spectroscopy. The spectrometer conditions are similar to those used to detect TEMPONE or CTPO. Depending on solvent and spin concentration, either a 50- to 100-mm capillary, 3-mm quartz tube, or a flat cell can be used. Spectrometer conditions are as follows: 0.5–1 G modulation amplitude, 1–10 mW microwave power, 100 G scan range, 3390 G field set, and 9.5 GHz microwave frequency. Note that some adducts, such as **3NO**, do not saturate even at 100 mW. Under these conditions, one can use a loop–gap resonator in the dispersion mode.

Applications. (1) The NOCTs have been used to monitor ·NO formation by cultured liver macrophages, the Kupffer cells. Using the spin trap, about 6% of the ·NO produced by Kupffer cells was trapped. ·NO$_2$ was also detected in this system. After incubation, the medium was extracted with

[92] H. G. Korth, K. U. Ingold, R. Sustmann, H. DeGroot, and H. Sies, *Angew Chem. Int. Ed. Engl.* **31,** 891 (1992).
[93] H. G. Korth, R. Sustmann, P. Lommes, T. Paul, A. Ernst, H. DeGroot, L. Hughes, and K. U. Ingold, *J. Am. Chem. Soc.* **116,** 2767 (1994).

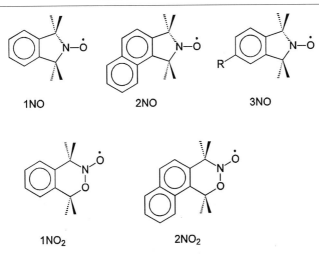

FIG. 7. Trapping of ·NO and ·NO$_2$ by NOCT to form a nitroxide adduct.

n-hexane, and oxygen was removed by bubbling with argon and the sample taken up in a 3-mm quartz tube. With newer traps, the yield of ·NO measured by ESR was 3–4 times greater than that observed by other methods. (2) Using **2,** SNAP was reported to produce primarily 2NO while 3-morpholinosydnonimine (SIN-1), which forms both $O_2^{·-}$ on ·NO and ultimately peroxynitrite, produced 2NO$_2$ at higher concentrations. It is likely that peroxynitrite produces ·NO$_2$ under these conditions. (3) Compound **3** trapped ·NO$_2$ and formed a very persistent **3NO$_2$**.

Advantages. (1) The rate of formation of ·NO can be measured. (2) Spin concentrations can be determined by double integration of the nitroxide and comparison with the spin standard. (3) Both ·NO and ·NO$_2$ can be measured. (4) The method is ideally suited for measurement of ·NO in the lipid phase. (5) Electron spin resonance imaging of ·NO in tissues is likely.

Limitations. (1) These compounds are not commercially available. (2) The active trap needs to be generated every time by photolysis. (3) The reduction of nitroxide in cellular systems is a common problem. This may

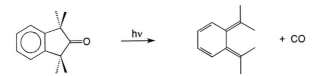

FIG. 8. Photolytic formation of NOCT.

be overcome by the use of $K_3Fe(CN)_6$ to reoxidize the hydroxylamines to the parent nitroxide. A report has appeared on trapping of ·NO by open-chain dienes.[94,95] The adduct, however, has not been completely characterized.

Nitrosyl Complexes of Iron-Sulfur Centers

Reddy et al.[60] have demonstrated nitrosylation of [4Fe–4S] center in microbial systems. At present, there is great interest in the mechanism of interaction between ·NO and the mitochondrial aconitases. Interested readers are referred to excellent articles by Kroneck and Zumft,[96] Cammack and co-workers,[97] and Butler et al.[43] for the ESR parameters of iron–thiol-nitrosyl complexes derived from the interaction between ·NO and iron-sulfur centers.

Other Nitric Oxide Traps

The ferrous iron bleomycin has been shown to bind ·NO avidly and to form an iron–bleomycin–NO complex with a characteristic ESR spectrum.[98] Spin trapping of ·NO with conventional nitrone spin traps appears to be controversial.[99]

Nitric Oxide Donor Compounds

Both organic nitrates (sodium nitroprusside, nitroglycerin) or organic/inorganic nitrosothiols (nitrosoglutathione, nitrosocysteine, S-nitroso-N-acetylpenicillamine, etc.) can release ·NO photolytically or in the presence of metal ions. Some new generation ·NO donors include SIN-1 and NONOates (spermine NONOate). The donor SIN-1 also forms the superoxide anion, which reacts with ·NO to form peroxynitrite. Most ·NO donors are photolabile. Nitrosothiols can be synthesized according to the published procedure.[79,80,100] Most nitric oxide donors are commercially available (Cay-

[94] I. M. Gabr, U. S. Rai, and M. C. R. Symons, J. Chem. Soc. Chem. Commun. 1099 (1993).
[95] A. Rockenbauer and L. Korecz, J. Chem. Soc. Chem. Commun. 145 (1994).
[96] P. M. H. Kroneck and W. G. Zumft, in "Dentrification in Soil and Sediment" (N. P. Revsbech and J. Sørensen, eds.), p. 1. Plenum, New York, 1990.
[97] M. J. Payne, C. Glidewell, and R. Cammack, J. Gen. Microbiol. 136, 2077 (1990).
[98] W. E. Antholine and D. H. Petering, Biochem. Biophys. Res. Commun. 91, 528 (1979).
[99] S. Pou, L. Keaton, W. Surichamorn, P. Frigillana, and G. M. Rosen, Biochim. Biophys. Acta 1201, 118 (1994).
[100] B. Roy, A. M. d'Hardemare, and M. Fontecave, J. Org. Chem. 59, 7019 (1994).

men Chemicals and Alexis Corporation). These compounds are used increasingly to mimic the effects of ·NO in *in vitro* and *in vivo* systems.

Conclusions

(1) Nitric oxide will react with a number of intracellular heme- and nonheme targets to form ESR-active nitrosyl complexes. These complexes have characteristic ESR spectra that can be detected at ambient and low temperatures. (2) Iron dithiocarbamates can be added as exogenous traps to detect intracellular and extracellular formation of ·NO. (3) Nitronyl nitroxides react with ·NO to form imino nitroxides. This transformation can be monitored continuously by ESR. Nitronyl nitroxides can, therefore, be used to antagonize ·NO formation in biological systems. (4) The chelotropic traps will react with ·NO and ·NO$_2$ to form stable nitroxides, and they can be used to detect ·NO in hydrophilic and hydrophobic compartments of cells. (5) Nitric oxide causes physical broadening of stable lipid-soluble nitroxides,[82] and ESR can be used to calculate the diffusion coefficients of ·NO in biological membranes. (6) In simple systems, ESR will provide quantitative measurements of ·NO production. (7) Finally, it has been proposed that ·NO inhibits the ·NO-synthase activity by binding directly to the heme moiety of the enzyme.[101,102] ESR will undoubtedly be a useful structural tool to help delineate this negative feedback mechanism.

Acknowledgments

This research was supported by National Institutes of Health Grants HL45048, HL47250, CA49089, GM22923, and RR01008. The author expresses gratitude to Drs. E. A. Konorev, N. Hogg, R. J. Singh, J. Joseph, and Mr. Steve Gross for scientific contributions, and thanks to Margaret Wold for preparing the manuscript. The author extends thanks to Drs. M. Claire Kennedy, Jimmy Feix, and Neil Hogg as well as Lillian Kalyanaraman for helpful comments and to D. Karen Hyde for preparing the figures.

[101] J. Assreuy, F. Q. Cunha, F. Y. Liew, and S. Moncada, *Br. J. Pharmacol.* **108**, 833 (1993).
[102] G. M. Buga, J. M. Griscavage, N. E. Rogers, and L. J. Ignarro, *Circ. Res.* **73**, 808 (1993).

[17] *In Vivo* Spin Trapping of Nitric Oxide by Heme: Electron Paramagnetic Resonance Detection *ex Vivo*

By DAVID M. HALL and GARRY R. BUETTNER

Introduction

Nitrogen monoxide (nitric oxide, ·NO) is one of the 10 smallest molecules found in nature. Nitric oxide is a stable, neutrally charged, paramagnetic gas, with moderate water solubility (2 mM at 1 atm and 20°). The unpaired electron resides in its π^*_{2p} antibonding orbital and is thought to be localized on the N–O triple bond.[1,2] Unlike most radicals, ·NO does not dismute nor covalently dimerize; it readily diffuses through cell membranes.[3]

Nitric oxide can act as either an oxidant or a reductant. The reactivity of ·NO evolves from the interrelated redox couples it forms with the nitrosonium cation (NO$^+$) and the nitroxyl anion (NO$^-$), its conjugate acid being HNO (pK_a 4.7).[1,2] There are several important chemical properties of ·NO: (i) it forms adducts with nucleophiles such as amines, sulfite, and thiols, which in turn can slowly and spontaneously release ·NO by first-order kinetics, and (ii) it coordinates with transition metals such as manganese, copper, and iron [both Fe(II) and Fe(III)] in complexes. These general properties endow ·NO with tremendous versatility in biological systems, enabling it to act as either a toxic molecule or as a regulator molecule, the key factors being concentration and duration of release.

Nitric oxide has been used since the late 1960s as an electron paramagnetic resonance (EPR) probe to study oxygen binding sites in oxygen carriers and oxygen-metabolizing metalloenzymes; consequently, a considerable literature exists detailing its EPR spectral characteristics as a ligand in transition metal complexes. An excellent review by Henry includes data on the nitrosylated heme proteins, iron–sulfur proteins, nonheme and non-Fe-S iron proteins, multicopper proteins, and hemerythrin.[4]

Nitric oxide readily complexes with heme proteins, forming paramagnetic species (·NO–heme, $S = \frac{1}{2}$) that are observable at low temperatures

[1] Y. Henry, M. Lepoivre, J. Drapier, C. Ducrocq, J. Boucher, and A. Guissani, *FASEB J.* **7,** 1124 (1993).

[2] J. S. Stamler, D. J. Singel, and J. Loscalzo, *Science* **258,** 1898 (1992).

[3] H. Galla, *Angew. Chem., Int. Ed. Engl.* **32,** 378 (1993).

[4] Y. Henry, C. Ducrocq, J.-C. Drapier, D. Servent, C. Pellat, and A. Guissani, *Eur. Biophys. J.* **20,** 1 (1991).

by EPR. In red blood cells, ·NO will (1) form hemoglobin (Hb) complexes, HbNO·, or (2) be oxidized to nitrite and nitrate with formation of methemoglobin, Fe(III)-Hb. Under these conditions, the hemoglobin tetramer forms a mixture of nitrosylated valency hybrids that can be precisely characterized by EPR spectroscopy.[1,4] In arterial blood (O_2 saturation 94–99%), ·NO is almost quantitatively converted to Fe(III)-Hb and nitrate with little HbNO· formation.[5] In venous blood (O_2 saturation 36–85%) there is more HbNO· and less nitrate formed.[5] This allows blood to be sampled across a vascular bed to assess localized tissue ·NO release. Arterial samples serve as controls, and changes in HbNO· and nitrite concentration in venous samples can serve as indicators of changes in ·NO release. The purpose of this chapter is to detail a method by which ·NO release can be assessed *in vivo* by quantifying HbNO· and plasma nitrite concentrations in whole blood.

Methods

The purpose of our experiments is to assess ·NO release within the splanchnic region of the heat-stressed rat. We collect femoral artery and portal venous blood from hyperthermic rats so that it can be examined by EPR for the presence of HbNO·. Male Sprague-Dawley rats weighing 320–350 g are anesthetized with sodium pentobarbital (Nembutal). In these experiments it is essential to avoid anesthetics that generate ·NO as part of their mechanism of action. A midline laparotomy is performed, the portal vein isolated, and a catheter (silastic tubing over PE 10, Clay Adams, Parsippany, NJ), filled with heparinized saline (100 U/ml), is placed in the portal vein through a tributary vessel. Rats are also fitted with a femoral artery catheter for collecting arterial blood samples. Placing a length of Silastic tubing at the end of these catheters is extremely important for collecting blood samples *in vivo*. The more flexible Silastic tubing allows the catheter to accommodate animal movement. A stiffer form of tubing has a tendency to lay against the vessel, precluding blood collection. The distal end of each catheter is tunneled subcutaneously to the dorsal neck, exteriorized between the scapula, and capped with a stainless steel stylette. The midline incision is closed, and the animals are allowed to recover from surgery. On recovery, rats are heated, and blood samples are collected in sterile, 1-ml Monoject syringes[6] and immediately delivered into quartz EPR tubes (3 mm inner diameter). For selected samples the pH is lowered by

[5] A. Wennmalm, G. Benthin, and A.-S. Persson, *Br. J. Pharmacol.* **106**, 507 (1992).
[6] G. R. Buettner, B. D. Scott, R. E. Kerber, and A. Mügge, *Free Radical. Biol. Med.* **11**, 69 (1991).

catalase by NO· contributed to increased amounts of oxidative stress in hepatocytes. Kanner et al.[7] demonstrated that NO· was able to prevent the prooxidant effects of hemoglobin and nonheme iron compounds by formation of stable complexes.

Ferrylhemoglobin (ferrylHb) and ferrylmyoglobin (ferrylMb), the high oxidation states of the hemoproteins and analogs of compound II of peroxidases formed by interactions of methemoproteins with hydroperoxides, are known to promote peroxidative reactions[8] (e.g., lipid peroxidation). We have reported that NO· inhibited these oxidations by reducing ferrylhemoproteins.[9] This chapter focuses on methodological approaches to study interactions of NO· with ferrylhemoproteins using electron spin resonance (ESR) and liquid chromatography-mass spectrometry (LC–MS).

Materials and Methods

Human methemoglobin (metHb), horse heart metmyoglobin (metMb), tert-butyl hydroperoxide (t-BuOOH), 5,5'-dimethyl-1-pyrroline N-oxide (DMPO), luminol, and deferoxamine mesylate are available from Sigma (St. Louis, MO). High-purity gaseous NO· and N_2 are available from many vendors (e.g., Valley Welding Supply, Cranberry, PA). 4,4,5,5-Tetramethyl-2-(4-trimethylammoniophenyl)-2-imidazoline-3-oxide-1-yloxyl methyl sulfate [nitronyl nitroxyl radical (NNR)] was a gift from Dr. I. A. Grigor'ev (Institute of Organic Chemistry, Novosibirsk, Russia). Gas-permeable Teflon tubing (0.8 mm internal diameter, 0.013 mm wall thickness) is available from Alpha Wire (Elizabeth, NJ).

All buffers should be prepared free of metals with deionized water double-distilled from quartz glassware that has been stirred overnight in the presence of Chelex 100 ion-exchange resin (Bio-Rad, Richmond, CA). Solutions of NO· are prepared by saturating previously deoxygenated (with N_2 gas) 100 mM phosphate buffer, pH 7.5, with NO· gas. The concentration of NO· in solution is determined by means of the NNR assay.[10,11] To measure NO· concentration in solution, aliquots of the nitric oxide-containing phosphate buffer are added to a deoxygenated NNR solution (250 mM), and ESR spectra are immediately recorded. On the basis of the

[7] J. Kanner, S. Harel, and R. Granit, Arch. Biochem. Biophys. **289**, 130 (1991).

[8] M. Maiorino, F. Ursini, and E. Cadenas, Free Radical Biol. Med. **16**, 661 (1994).

[9] N. V. Gorbunov, A. N. Osipov, B. W. Day, B. Zayas-Rivera, V. E. Kagan, and N. M. Elsayed, Biochemistry in press (1995).

[10] T. Akaike, M. Yoshida, Y. Miyamoto, K. Sato, M. Kohno, K. Sasamoto, K. Miyazaki, S. Ueda, and H. Maeda, Biochemistry **32**, 827 (1993).

[11] J. Joseph, B. Kalyanaraman, and J. S. Hyde, Biochem. Biophys. Res. Commun. **192**, 926 (1993).

spectral parameter $(b/a + b)$, NO· concentration can be obtained from a calibration plot (Fig. 1B).

Electron Spin Resonance Measurements

Sample solutions (50 μl) are transferred to gas-permeable Teflon tubing under an N_2 atmosphere, folded into quarters, then placed in the quartz tube of the spectrometer. Spectra are obtained at room temperature. We use a JEOL JES-RE1X (X-band) spectrometer (JEOL, Tokyo, Japan) equipped with 100 kHz magnetic field modulation. Useful ESR settings are as follows: magnetic field magnitude 335.5 mT, microwave power 10 mW and microwave frequency of 9.44 GHz, modulation amplitude 1.6 mT, time constant 0.01 sec. The g factor and ESR signal intensity can be determined relative to external standards containing Mn^{2+} (in MgO). We also simulated spectra using a computer program created by David R. Duling (Laboratory of Molecular Biophysics, National Institute of Environmental Health Sciences, Research Triangle Park, NC).

Mass Spectral Measurements

Pneumatically assisted electrospray (IonSpray) mass spectra can be obtained using a Perkin-Elmer/Sciex (Toronto, Ontario, Canada) API *I* mass spectrometer equipped with an atmospheric pressure ionization source and an articulated IonSpray interface. By linking the mass spectrometer in tandem (with glass capillary tubing) to a high-performance liquid chromatograph (LC), for example, a Hewlett Packard 1090 series II liquid chromatograph equipped with a Hewlett Packard 1040 diode array UV detector, effluent can be monitored both with a diode array UV detector (e.g., using a primary monitoring wavelength of 214 nm) and by mass spectrometry. We typically maintain the IonSpray interface at 5 kV.

High-purity air or nitrogen may be used as the nebulizing gas at a typical operating pressure of 40 psi. Analytes are introduced into the ionization source directly from the LC system at 40 μl/min without splitting using 1 : 1 H_2O–CH_3OH (v/v) containing 0.05% CH_3COOH and, in some cases, 2 mM NH_4OOCCH_3, as the mobile phase. The presence or absence of NH_4^+ in the mobile phase does not affect results in this case. The orifice voltage is generally set at 90 V to detect covalent modifications, and at 40 V to detect coordinate covalently bound analytes. High purity N_2 is used as the curtain gas, flowing at 0.6 liter/min. The quadrupole is scanned in the appropriate m/z range in 8–11 sec/scan at a resolution of m/z 0.1. Protein masses are reconstructed from multiply charged envelopes of quasi-molecular ions by the Fenn algorithm as implemented by the mass spectrom-

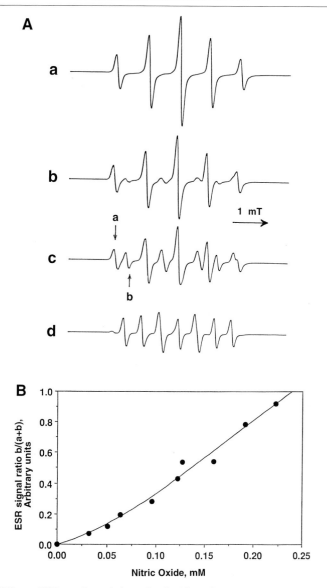

FIG. 1. Effects of NO· on nitronyl nitroxyl radical (NNR) as measured by ESR spectroscopy. (A) Spectra of NNR and imino nitroxide radical (INR) in the absence (a) and presence (b–d) of different NO· concentrations. The incubation medium contained NNR (0.25 mM) in 100 mM phosphate buffer, pH 7.4. (a) NNR without NO·; (b–d) NNR plus NO· at 0.02, 0.12, and 0.22 mM, respectively. Arrows a and b show the low-field components of ESR signals of NNR and INR, respectively. (B) Dependence of the ratio of the ESR signal intensities of INR (arrow b) to the sum of the signals of NNR plus INR (a + b) on the concentration of NO· in the incubation medium.

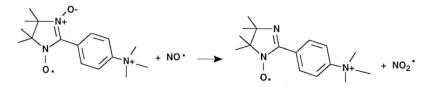

Nitronyl Nitroxyl Radical   Imino Nitroxyl Radical

Scheme 1

eter manufacturer,[12] resulting in a resolution of ±1.5–3 atomic mass units (amu) in the reconstructed mass ranges studied.

In the experiments discussed below, the concentrations of reagents are as follows: metMb, 1 mM, in purified H_2O; t-BuOOH, 4 mM. Solutions of metMb are treated with t-BuOOH for 3 min under an N_2 atmosphere, then exposed to NO· (bubbled into the solution at 1 cm^3/min). The completed reaction mixture can either be frozen in liquid N_2 or filtered through Sephadex G-25 prior to preparation of apomyoglobin. Control solutions should be studied for interfering or unexpected signals (i.e., metMb alone, metMb treated with t-BuOOH only, and metMb treated with NO· only).

Results

Measurements of Nitric Oxide by Nitronyl Nitroxyl Radical Assay

Concentrations of NO· in the incubation medium can be measured by an assay based on the reaction of NNR with NO· that yields a stable, ESR-detectable imino nitroxide radical (INR) (Scheme 1). Spectral characteristics of the INR radical ESR signal are measurably different from those of NNR.[10,11,13] On completion of reaction with NO·, the NNR, which has a five-line spectrum with the ratio of line intensities of 1:2:3:2:1 (Fig. 1A, spectrum a), is converted to INR, which has a seven-line spectrum (Fig. 1A, spectrum d). The reaction rate constant is sufficiently high[13] for quantitation [for 4,4,5,5-tetramethyl-2-(4-trimethylammoniophenyl)-2-imidazoline-3-oxide-1-yloxyl it was reported to be 0.6 × 10^{-4} M^{-1} sec^{-1}]. Thus, at concentrations of NO· lower than that of NNR, the superposition of the ESR spectra of both NNR and INR is observable (Fig. 1A, spectra band

[12] T. R. Covey, R. F. Bonner, B. I. Shushan, and J. Henion, *Rapid Commun. Mass Spectrom.* **2**, 249 (1988).
[13] Y. Y. Woldman, V. V. Khramtsov, I. A. Grigor'ev, I. A. Kiriljuk, and D. I. Utepbergenov, *Biochem. Biophys. Res. Commun.* **202**, 195 (1994).

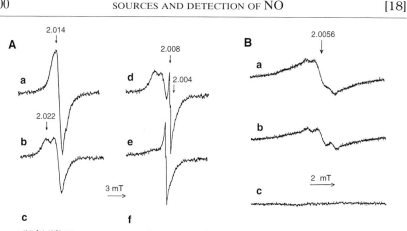

FIG. 3. The ESR spectra produced by incubations of metmyoglobin with t-BuOOH under aerobic (A) or anaerobic (B) conditions. (A) Spectra of metMb (3 mM) and t-BuOOH (12 mM) in the presence (c, f) and absence (a, b, d, e) of NO·; t-butylperoxyl radical ($g = 2.014$) is detectable after 1 min of incubation (a). Spectra of the same sample after incubations for 3 (b), 5 (d), and 15 min (e). Addition of NO· gas immediately after mixing metMb and t-BuOOH (c) or after a 5-min incubation of metMb and t-BuOOH eliminates ESR signals. (B) Spectra of metMb (3 mM) and t-BuOOH (12 mM) incubated in an N_2 atmosphere for 5 min (a) or 10 min (b), or 10 min after substitution of N_2 for NO· (c).

the t-BuO·/DMPO spin adduct (as can be seen by the lack of its effect on the ESR signal of the adduct). Since NO· does not affect Fe(II)-induced t-BuO·/DMPO spin adducts, we conclude that interaction of NO· with ferrylHb prevents generation of t-BuOOH-derived radicals.

Direct Electron Spin Resonance Measurements of Interactions of Metmyoglobin with tert-Butylhydroperoxide and Nitric Oxide

Exposure of heme proteins such as metMb and metHb to peroxides (ROOH) has been reported to form both oxoferryl protein radicals and a number of ROOH-derived radical species (ROO·, RO·, R·).[16–19] In accord with this observation, the mixing of air-saturated solutions of metMb (3 mM) with t-BuOOH (12 mM) leads to the initial observation of a broad singlet signal with a g value of 2.014 (denoted by the arrow in Fig. 3A, spectrum a, 1 min after mixing). This signal is characteristic of peroxyl

[16] B. Kalyanaraman, C. Mottley, and R. P. Mason, *J. Biol. Chem.* **258,** 3855 (1983).
[17] M. J. Davies, *Free Radical Biol. Med.* **15,** 257 (1989).
[18] H. Nohl and K. Stolze, *Free Radical Biol. Med.* **15,** 257 (1993).
[19] D. J. Kelman, J. A. DeGray, and R. P. Mason, *J. Biol. Chem.* **269,** 7458 (1994).

radicals and is similar to that observed in the reaction of t-BuOOH with free heme.[16,17] The low-field part of this signal is asymmetrical, suggesting the presence of additional radical species. Indeed, this signal decays rapidly and a second radical signal appears 3 min after mixing of metMb with t-BuOOH as a low-field shoulder (arrow at $g = 2.022$ in Fig. 3A, spectrum b). This second species ($g = 2.022$) may be tentatively assigned to a protein-derived transitional radical.[17,18] Both of these signals decay over time, and a new two-line anisotropic signal at $g = 2.008$ and $g = 2.004$ appears approximately 5 min after mixing the reagents (Fig. 3A, spectrum d). The anisotropic signal grows over time and plateaus at approximately the 15-min time point in the incubation (Fig. 3A, spectrum e). This doublet signal could be assigned to a protein-derived peroxyl radical produced in the presence of oxygen.[19]

Application of NO· immediately after mixing metMb and t-BuOOH prevents detection of ESR signals that are characteristic of the presence of metMb/t-BuOOH (Fig. 3A, spectrum c). Similarly, NO· eliminated all the ESR signals if added at any point during the incubation of metMb/t-BuOOH when the signals were observable in the spectra. This holds true for both aerobic (Fig. 3A, spectrum f) and anaerobic incubations (Fig. 3B, spectrum c).

Indeed, forcing the system to anoxic conditions by purging the reaction system with nitrogen gas for 5 min results in the formation of a completely different signal (Fig. 3B, spectrum a). This signal (g value at the zero-crossing point calculated to be 2.0056)[9] contains a partially resolved hyperfine structure and broad low- and high-field shoulders and could be assigned to a protein-derived radical.[18] The magnitude of the protein radical ESR signal increases within 5 min of mixing of metHb with t-BuOOH, after which decay of the signal is observed. This is accompanied by both a decrease in the intensity of the central-field component of the spectrum and a shift in the g factor from 2.0056 to 2.0044 (Fig. 3B, spectrum b). Omission of either of the two reagents results in complete loss of any ESR response both in aerobic and anaerobic conditions.

Mass Spectrometric Analysis of Reaction of Metmyoglobin with tert-Butylhydroperoxide and Nitric Oxide

The spectroscopic data suggest that the redox interaction of metMb with t-BuOOH is accompanied by generation of ferrylMb as well as radical products containing fragments of t-BuOOH that are quenched by NO·. The apparent antiradical effect of NO· can be further elucidated by mass spectrometric analyses of metMb, its reaction products with t-BuOOH and NO· singly, and the sequential treatment of the protein with t-BuOOH and

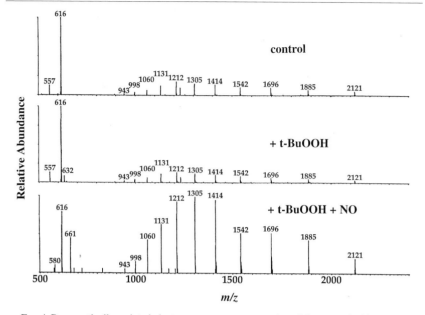

FIG. 4. Pneumatically assisted electrospray mass spectra of metMb, treated with t-BuOOH. From top to bottom, spectra were obtained in an N_2 atmosphere, then subsequently with NO· gas by displacement of the N_2 atmosphere. Note that the presence of oxoferryl heme (m/z 632) in the t-BuOOH-treated spectrum of the protein is evident, as well as its disappearance on subsequent treatment with NO·. Ion signals present between m/z 650 and m/z 900 in the bottom spectrum are not reproducible, and appear to be due to unsubtracted solvent and/or electronic noise.

NO·. In these determinations, the crude reaction mixtures as well as the apoprotein and corresponding heme fractions, prepared by precipitation/ separation in cold, acidic acetone, can be analyzed. Reconstructed mass spectra of metMb obtained at high orifice voltage (90 eV in this case) show the presence of the apoprotein (16,951 Da in reconstructed spectra) and very low or undetectable amounts of heme-retaining protein (~17,567 Da). When spectra are recorded at a lower orifice voltage (e.g., 40 eV), the heme remains attached to the protein, resulting in a significant amount of signal in the 17,567 Da (apoprotein + heme) and 17,600 Da (apoprotein + heme + O_2) regions of reconstructed spectra.[20] Close analysis of the raw spectrum in the heme region (m/z 616) additionally reveals the presence of O_2 bound to heme (m/z 648) when a low orifice voltage is used. The presence of molecular oxygen in such a sample is likely a result

[20] Y. Konishi and R. Feng, *Biochemistry* **33**, 9706 (1994).

of mass spectrometer-induced reduction of Fe(III) to Fe(II) and subsequent attachment of atmospheric O_2 abundant in the ionization source.

Reactions of metmb with t-BuOOH result in the loss of heme, as can easily be detected visually (precipitation of heme in the reaction mixture), by UV analysis, and by mass spectrometry. Evident in mass spectral determinations at high orifice voltage of myoglobin treated with t-BuOOH is formation of ferrylMb, consistently detectable as the heme adduct (m/z 632) (Fig. 4). When the native protein is treated with NO·, a ferrylMb signal is not observed, nor are any covalent modifications. When the t-BuOOH-treated protein is treated with NO·, the ferrylMb signal disappears, and the resulting spectra are equivalent to those from the untreated and NO·-treated protein (Fig. 4).

Additionally, no evidence for covalent modification of the protein by NO· is detectable. The potential modifications, either nitrosylation of heme (e.g., m/z 646 that would be detectable in the heme region), nitrosylation of tyrosyl or thiyl radicals (e.g., 16,980 Da in the reconstructed spectra of myoglobin or apomyoglobin) or nitrosylation of tyrosine (e.g., 16,996 Da in reconstructed spectra), are not found in the mass spectra, regardless of the orifice voltage employed in the determinations.

[19] Electron Spin Resonance for Spin Trapping of 3,5-Dibromo-4-nitrosobenzene Sulfonate

By Kohji Ichimori, Carmen M. Arroyo, and Hiroe Nakazawa

Introduction

3,5-Dibromo-4-nitrosobenzene sulfonate (DBNBS) was first developed by Perkins and co-workers in 1981 as a trap for C-centered radicals.[1] Although application of DBNBS in biological systems started only relatively recently,[2–4] several works demonstrated that DBNBS traps radicals derived from the reaction related to nitric oxide (NO) in neuroblastoma cells[3] and platelets.[4] In this chapter, we describe the method to assess NO-dependent radical formation with DBNBS in the human platelet system and some basic reactions between DBNBS and various NO-related compounds to

[1] H. Kaur, K. H. W. Leung, and M. J. Perkins, *J. Chem. Soc. Chem. Commun.* 142 (1981).
[2] A. Samuni, A. Samuni, and H. M. Swartz, *Free Radical Biol. Med.* **7,** 37 (1989).
[3] C. M. Arroyo and C. Forray, *Eur. J. Pharmacol.* **208,** 157 (1991).
[4] L. Pronai, K. Ichimori, H. Nozaki, H. Nakazawa, H. Okino, A. Charmichael, and C. M. Arroyo, *Eur. J. Pharmacol.* **202,** 923 (1991).

identify DBNBS spin adducts.[5] Cautions in applying DBNBS to biological samples are also detailed.

Isolation of Platelets

Platelets are isolated according to the method of Blackwell et al.[6] with slight modifications. Blood (60 ml) from healthy adult volunteers who have not taken any drugs for at least 14 days is collected by venipuncture into a plastic flask containing 3.15% sodium citrate (1:9, v/v). Platelet-rich plasma (PRP) is prepared by centrifuging the citrated blood (800 g, 8 min) immediately after blood collection. To prepare washed platelets (WP, 1.5–3.5 × 10^5/μl), prostacyclin (300 ng/ml) is added to platelet-rich plasma and the mixture is centrifuged for 18 min. The supernatant is removed and the platelet pellet is washed once in 20 ml calcium-free oxygenated buffer A (0.32 M sucrose, 10 mM HEPES, and 1 mM DL-dithiothreitol, pH 7.4) containing 300 ng/ml of prostacyclin. The cells are then resuspended in buffer A (5 ml) without prostacyclin. Indomethacin (10 μM) and CaCl$_2$ (1 μM) are added to the final platelet suspension.

Preparation of Platelet Cytosol

Washed platelets are centrifuged (150,000 g, 30 min) and resuspended in buffer A (5 ml). Cell membranes are then disrupted by sonicating twice for 5 sec with a Branson B-12 sonicator (Danbury, CT). The supernatant is passed through a 3-ml column of AG 50W-X8 cation-exchange resin (Bio-Rad Laboratories, Richmond, CA) to remove endogenous L-arginine.

Electron Paramagnetic Resonance Detection of DBNBS Spin Adducts

All experiments should be performed in the dark to prevent any photolytic degradation of DBNBS. Aqueous DBNBS solutions are prepared by dissolving sodium DBNBS (100 mM, Sigma, St. Louis, MO) in double-deionized double-distilled water. The PRP, WP, and platelet cytosol (PC) are mixed with 40 mM (final concentration) of DBNBS and incubated at 37° for 2 min in the presence of Ca^{2+} (1–3 μM). Activation of platelets is initiated by collagen (17 μg/ml, Horman-Chemie, Munich, Germany), and the resultant solution (140 μl) is pipetted into a quartz flat cell (Labotec

---

[5] K. Ichimori, C. M. Arroyo, L. Pronai, M. Fukahori, and H. Nakazawa, *Free Radical Res. Commun.* **19,** S129 (1993).

[6] G. J. Blackwell, M. Radomsky, J. R. Vargas, and S. Moncada, *Biochim. Biophys. Acta* **718,** 60 (1982).

LLC04A, Tokyo) for EPR measurement, which is started at 1 min after the activation. EPR spectra are recorded at room temperature on a JEOL JES-FE2XG X-band spectrometer (JEOL Akishima, Tokyo) with 100 kHz magnetic field modulation. The usual instrumental conditions are as follows: field intensity, 335.5 ± 5 mT; field modulation width, 0.1 mT; gain, 6.3 × 10^3; sweep time, 4 or 8 min/10 mT; microwave power, 8 mW. The spectra are analyzed by computer simulation according to the method of Oehler and Janzen.[7]

Electron Spin Resonance Spectra Obtained from Platelet-Related Reaction

Figure 1a shows the EPR spectrum obtained from the PRP fraction activated by collagen. Figure 1b is the computer simulation of Fig. 1a. The broad background signal that may be originating from a radical adduct immobilized by a large molecule such as a protein is not considered in the process of computer simulation. The simulated spectrum consists of three components as shown in Fig. 1c–e. To simplify the identification process of spin adducts, we arbitrarily designate the small triplet as S_T, the small sextet S_S, and the large triplet L_T. These spin adducts are stable for more than 10 min.

The washed platelets are activated in the same way. Figure 2a shows the spectrum obtained and Fig. 2b shows the computer stimulation of Fig. 2a, consistent with two components as shown in Fig. 2c, d. They are also arbitrarily designated as the small triplet (S_T) and the large sextet (L_S). The S_T is identical to the spectral feature obtained from the PRP fraction. The L_S represents a newly obtained stable adduct, and its hyperfine splitting constants (hfsc) are 1.40 mT for one nitrogen and 0.78 mT for one hydrogen. Therefore, activated human platelets yielded four adducts in total, S_T, L_T, S_S, and L_S. To ascertain that these spectra are dependent on the generation of nitric oxide, experiments should be repeated in the presence of a specific NO synthase inhibitor such as L-N^G-monomethylarginine (L-NMMA, Sigma). No DBNBS spin adducts should result.

Platelet cytosol also produces DBNBS spin adducts observed in the experiments with washed platelets when the same stimulation procedures are performed in the presence of NADPH (1 mM), Ca^{2+} (1 μM), and 40 mM DBNBS. To ascertain that no spin adducts are observed in the absence of Ca^{2+}, L-arginine, or NADPH, additional experiments should be performed with the substitution of L-arginine for D-arginine. No spin adducts should form, confirming the origin of spin adducts as the NO-related reac-

[7] U. M. Oehler and E. G. Janzen, *Can. J. Chem.* **60,** 1542 (1982).

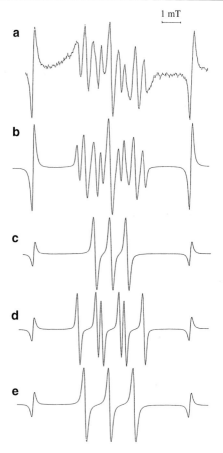

FIG. 1. (a) The EPR spectrum obtained from the platelet-rich plasma fraction of human platelets activated by collagen (17 μg/ml) in the presence of DBNBS (40 mM). (b) Overall computer simulation of (a) [the addition of (c), (d), and (e) (3:3:5 intensity ratio)]. (c) Small triplet (S_T: a_N = 0.92 mT, line width 0.20 mT). (d) Small sextet (S_S: a_N = 1.33 mT, a_H = 1.02 mT, and line width 0.16 mT). (e) Large triplet (L_T: a_N = 1.39 mT, linewidth 0.20 mT). The signals on both sides of the central EPR spectra correspond to a Mn^{2+} internal instrumental standard.

tions. It should be noted that the addition of superoxide dismutase enhances spin adduct formation in all experiments, although the underlying mechanism is not understood. Oxyhemoglobin (10 μM) partially inhibits spin adduct formation.

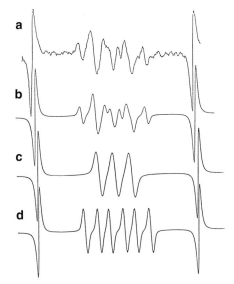

FIG. 2. (a) The EPR spectrum obtained from the WP fraction of human platelets activated by collagen (17 μg/ml) in the presence of DBNBS (40 mM). (b) Overall computer simulation of (a) [the addition of (c) and (d) (0.53:0.36 intensity ratio)]. (c) Small triplet S_T which has the same a_N as Fig. 1c. (d) Large sextet (S_S: a_N = 1.40 mT, a_H = 0.78 mT, and line width 0.21 mT).

Identification of Spin Adducts

To identify radicals obtained from unknown biological samples, the EPR parameters of their DBNBS spin adducts should be compared with those of previously reported DBNBS spin adducts with definite assignments. Table I summarizes the EPR parameters of DBNBS spin adducts. Because DBNBS spin adducts observed in the activation of human platelets are eliminated by NO synthase inhibitor, all of these adducts should originate from NO itself and/or NO-related molecules. The addition of 50 mM DBNBS to an NO-saturated solution results in the formation of two kinds of spin adducts. One is identical to S_T, and the EPR parameters of the other are identical to the reported parameters of the DBNBS–SO$_3^-$ adduct obtained by SO$_3^{2-}$ oxidation with water and horseradish peroxidase,[8] confirming that S_T is a spin adduct generated by the reaction between NO or NO-related molecules and DBNBS.

[8] K. Stolze and R. P. Mason, *Biochem. Biophys. Res. Commun.* **143**, 941 (1987).

TABLE I
HYPERFINE COUPLING CONSTANTS OF DBNBS SPIN ADDUCTS

Radical	a_N (mT)	a_H (mT)	Ref.
From human platelets			
S_T	0.92	—	4
S_S	1.33	1.02(1H)	4
L_S	1.40	0.78(1H)	4
L_T	1.39	—	4
Carbon-centered			
$H_3C\cdot$	1.45	1.35(3H)[a]	1
$HOCH_2\cdot$	1.37	0.92(2H)[a]	1
$HOCH_2CH_2\cdot$	1.41	1.13(2H)[a]	1
CH_3CHOH	1.40	0.92(1H)[a]	1
$CH_3CHOC_2H_5$	1.25	0.71(1H)[a]	1
$(CH_3)_2CH\cdot$	1.42	0.93(1H)[a]	1
$H_5C_6\cdot$	1.142	0.310(3H)[b]	5
$2,4,6\text{-}Cl_3H_5C_6\cdot$	0.95	—	5
Sulfur-centered			
SO_3^-	1.26	0.06(2H)[c]	8
NAP·[d]	1.40	—	5
GS·[e]	1.43	—	5

[a] β-Hydrogen.
[b] Ortho and para protons of phenyl radical.
[c] Two protons on DBNBS.
[d] NAP·, N-Acetyl-DL-penicillamine thiyl radical.
[e] GS·, Glutathionyl radical.

However, S_T does not belong to the DBNBS–NO adduct between S_T does not have the hyperfine splitting arising from the β-nitrogen. The characteristics of a previously identified nitrosobenzene–NO adduct should be similar to the DBNBS–NO adduct and show β-nitrogen hyperfine splitting. This adduct is very unstable in the presence of trace water or acid and can easily dimerize to the diphenylaminoxyl radical. In addition, the hfsc of DBNBS-2,4,6-trichlorophenyl adduct is almost the same as that of S_T. When this evidence is taken together, S_T is assigned as the dimerized product of DBNBS.

The L_T adduct is assigned as an S-centered radical adduct because only a nitrogen hyperfine splitting (hfs) and no additional hydrogen hfs, which is essential for primary and secondary C-centered radical adducts, is observed. S-Nitrosothiol is one of the species proposed as EDRF (endothelial derived relaxing factor) and easily decomposes into an S-centered radical and NO. Support for this comes from a study in which S-nitroso-N-acetyl-

DL-penicillamine (SNAP),[9] a relatively stable S-nitrosothiol, yielded a stable triplet signal with the nitrogen hfs close to that of L_T adduct. The glutathionyl radical adduct also shows similar nitrogen hfsc.

For the assignment of the two sextets, S_S and L_S, C-centered radicals provide the most plausible explanations because these contain one hydrogen, possibly a β-hydrogen. The hfsc of S_S and L_S adducts fall into the range of reported C-centered radicals (Table I). The origin of these radicals has not yet been determined.

DBNBS traps four radical species in the activated human platelet system, and these species are related to biological NO synthesis. The S_T adduct is derived from the reaction with NO. However, it is not an NO adduct itself, but a secondary dimerized product. The L_T signal arises from an S-centered radical, which may be generated through the reaction of NO with a sulfhydryl group. The S_S and L_S signals are from C-centered radicals. Further investigations are necessary to determine the underlying mechanisms for the generation of these radicals in activated cells.

Cautions for Applications of DBNBS to Biological Media

Because several radicals can be trapped by applying DBNBS to biological systems, the spectrum of DBNBS radical adducts should be separated into its components with the aid of computer simulation or liquid column chromatography. After the separation, the origin of the individual spin adduct can be postulated. It is known that the DBNBS spin adduct can also be formed through several nonradical/nonspecific reactions. Although S_T in the human platelet system is detected only when the platelets are activated by collagen and S_T can be eliminated by inhibitors of NO synthase, ultraviolet light-induced decomposition of DBNBS also shows both S_T and DBNBS–SO_3^- as summarized in Fig. 3. The NADH reduction of concentrated DBNBS (100 mM) yields a mixture of S_T and another adduct.

The DBNBS–SO_3^- adduct is the most common adduct and has been observed in the following systems: (1) the horseradish peroxidase-catalyzed oxidation of sulfite by H_2O_2,[8,10] (2) the xanthine–xanthine oxidase system containing dimethyl sulfoxide (DMSO),[11,12] (3) the Fenton reaction system

[9] L. Field, R. V. Dilts, R. Ravichandran, P. G. Lenhert, and G. E. Carnahan, *J. Chem. Soc. Chem. Commun.*, 249 (1978).

[10] T. Ozawa and A. Hanaki, *Biochem. Biophys. Res. Commun.* **142**, 410 (1987).

[11] T. Ozawa and A. Hanaki, *Biochem. Biophys. Res. Commun.* **136**, 657 (1987).

[12] N. B. Nazhat, G. Yang, R. E. Allen, D. R. Blake, and P. Jones, *Biochem. Biophys. Res. Commun.* **166**, 817 (1990).

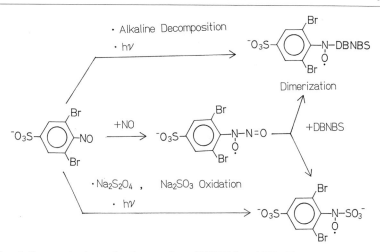

FIG. 3. Proposed scheme for the reaction of DBNBS and NO. The reaction of DBNBS and NO results in the generation of a labile DBNBS–NO adduct, which decomposes into the dimerized product of DBNBS and DBNBS–SO$_3^-$. These decomposed products can be also generated by the nonspecific reactions noted.

including H_2O_2 and Fe^{2+},[13] and (4) Ce^{4+} oxidation of selenite.[14] Although an identical signal is obtained in all of these systems and the different assignments have been made according to the reaction medium, detailed analysis using [33]S satellite hfs[8] clearly demonstrates that the spectrum should be assigned to DBNBS–SO$_3^-$ adduct. The DBNBS spin adduct is susceptible to both oxidation and reduction, which result in the formation of other stable nitroxyl radicals such as DBNBS–SO$_3^-$.

Although the reaction between nitroso-type spin traps such as DBNBS or 2-methyl-2-nitrosopropane and O-centered radicals such as ·OH and ROO· seems to be fast, resultant spin adducts are not stable and decompose into secondary radical and nonradical products. However, the DBNBS spin adduct of C-centered radicals is so stable that main radical reactions may be concealed behind C-centered radical adducts. Prolonged incubation of DBNBS with unsaturated fatty acids[15] and some amino acids[16] such as tryptophan causes the formation of C-centered radical adducts through

[13] M. Kohno, M. Yamada, K. Mitsuta, Y. Mizuta, and T. Yoshikawa, *Bull. Chem. Soc. Jpn.* **64,** 1447 (1991).

[14] T. Ozawa and A. Hanaki, *Bull. Chem. Soc. Jpn.* **64,** 1976 (1991).

[15] B. Kalyanaraman, J. Joseph, N. Kondratenko, and S. Parthasarathy, *Biochim. Biophys. Acta* **1126,** 309 (1992).

[16] K. Hiramoto, Y. Hasegawa, and K. Kikugawa, *Free Radical Res.* **21,** 341 (1994).

nonradical reactions. Therefore, care should be taken in the interpretation of the DBNBS adducts generated in biological systems, and artifactually produced adducts should be excluded.

It is clear that there are several pitfalls in the DBNBS system, and caution is necessary to exclude nonspecific reactions of DBNBS, such as dimerization and SO_3^- formation by oxidation, reduction, or decomposition of labile adducts.

[20] Quantitation of Nitric Oxide Using 2-Phenyl-4,4,5,5-tetramethylimidazoline-1-oxyl 3-Oxide (PTIO)

By TAKAAKI AKAIKE and HIROSHI MAEDA

Introduction

To date increasing attention in diverse research fields has been paid to the multiple functions of nitric oxide (NO).[1,2] A number of analytical methods are available for detection and quantitation of NO generated in biological systems.[3-6] However, very few methods are recommended for quantitation of NO in biological systems due to a lack of specificity, quantitativeness, and sensitivity.

A series of investigations suggest that complicated electron-transferring reactions are involved in the enzymatic reaction of nitric oxide synthase (NOS)[7] to produce NO from L-arginine. A perplexing transcriptional regulation of NOS appears to occur at the molecular level in the cells expressing NOS.[8,9] Therefore, it is critically important to quantify accurately NO being formed in biological systems for the better understanding of the pathophysiological role of NO and the molecular mechanism of the regulation of NOS activity.

It was previously reported that stable organic radical nitronyl nitroxide

[1] S. Monchada and A. Higgs, *N. Engl. J. Med.* **329,** 2002 (1993).
[2] H. Maeda, T. Akaike, M. Yoshida, and M. Suga, *J. Leukocyte Biol.* **56,** 588 (1994).
[3] K. Shibuki, *Neurosci. Res.* **9,** 69 (1990).
[4] P. Mordvintcev, A. Mülsch, R. Busse, and A. Vanin, *Anal. Biochem.* **199,** 142 (1991).
[5] H. Kosaka, Y. Sawai, H. Sakaguchi, E. Kimura, N. Harada, M. Watanabe, and T. Shiga, *Am. J. Physiol.* **266,** C1400 (1994).
[6] S. L. Archer, *FASEB J.* **7,** 349 (1993).
[7] D. J. Stuehr and O. W. Griffith, *Adv. Enzymol. Relat. Areas Mol. Biol.* **65,** 287 (1992).
[8] C. Nathan, *FASEB J.* **6,** 3051 (1992).
[9] T. Akaike, E. Weihe, M. Schaefer, Z. F. Fu, Y. M. Zheng, W. Vogel, H. Schmidt, H. Koprowski, and B. Dietzschold, *J. NeuroVirol.* **1,** 118 (1995).

A

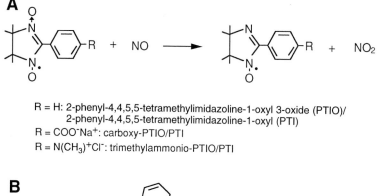

R = H: 2-phenyl-4,4,5,5-tetramethylimidazoline-1-oxyl 3-oxide (PTIO)/
2-phenyl-4,4,5,5-tetramethylimidazoline-1-oxyl (PTI)
R = COO⁻Na⁺: carboxy-PTIO/PTI
R = N(CH₃)⁺Cl⁻: trimethylammonio-PTIO/PTI

B

4-phenyl-2,2,5,5-tetramethylimidazoline-1-oxyl

FIG. 1. (A) Chemical structures of nitronyl nitroxide (PTIO) derivatives and the chemical reaction with NO. (B) Structure of 4-phenyl-2,2,5,5-tetramethylimidazoline-1-oxyl used as a standard nitroxide radical for quantitation of PTIs in ESR spectroscopy.

derivatives, namely, 2-phenyl-4,4,5,5-tetramethylimidazoline-1-oxyl 3-oxide (PTIO) derivatives (PTIOs), possess a specific scavenging action against NO released in *ex vivo* and *in vivo* systems.[10–12] More importantly, the reaction of PTIOs with NO gives a clear change in electron spin resonance (ESR) signals, yielding nitroxide radicals such as 2-phenyl-4,4,5,5-tetramethylimidazoline-1-oxyl (PTI) or PTI derivatives (PTIs) in a stoichiometric manner[10] (Figs. 1 and 2). The apparent second-order rate constant is approximately $10^4\ M^{-1}\ \sec^{-1}$ according to Eq. (1).[10,13]

$$\text{PTIOs} + \text{NO} \rightarrow \text{PTIs} + \text{NO}_2 \tag{1}$$

Based on the stoichiometric reaction, it is possible to quantitate the amount of NO by measuring the change in electron spin resonance (ESR) signal. In

[10] T. Akaike, M. Yoshida, Y. Miyamoto, K. Sato, M. Kohno, K. Sasamoto, K. Miyazaki, S. Ueda, and H. Maeda, *Biochemistry* **32**, 827 (1993).
[11] M. Yoshida, T. Akaike, Y. Wada, K. Sato, K. Ikeda, S. Ueda, and H. Maeda, *Biochem. Biophys. Res. Commun.* **202**, 923 (1994).
[12] T. Az-ma, K. Fujii and O. Yuge, *Life Sci.* **54**, PL 185 (1994).
[13] Y. Y. Woldman, V. V. Khramtsov, I. A. Grigor'ev, I. A. Kiriljuk, and D. I. Utepbergenov, *Biochem. Biophys. Res. Commun.* **202**, 195 (1994).

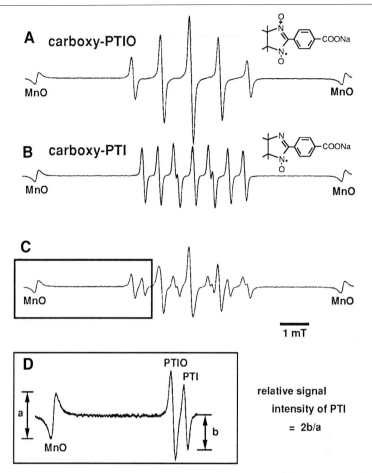

Fig. 2. Electron spin resonance spectra of PTIO derivatives. (A) Carboxy-PTIO, (B) carboxy-PTI, and (C) mixture of carboxy-PTIO and PTI produced by the reaction of carboxy-PTIO with NO. (D) A part of spectrum (C) is enlarged to show the method of calculating the relative signal intensities of PTIs.

this chapter, quantitative assay procedure using PTIOs including liposome PTIO for NO produced in biological systems is described.

Reagent: Nitronyl Nitroxides

A series of nitronyl nitroxides have been synthesized as described previously.[10] Among nitronyl nitroxide derivatives, for the assay of NO we test three types of imidazolineoxyl *N*-oxides, namely, PTIO (the prototype compound), 2-[4-carboxyphenyl]-4,4,5,5-tetramethylimidazoline-1-oxyl 3-oxide (abbreviated carboxy-PTIO), and 2-[4-trimethylammonio]-4,4,5,5-tetramethylimidazoline-1-oxyl 3-oxide (abbreviated TMA–PTIO) (Fig. 1A). All these PTIO derivatives are available from Dojindo Laboratory (Mashiki-machi, Kumamoto 861-22, Japan). Some other commercially available PTIOs are not satisfactory for quantitative work due to impurities.

Electron Spin Resonance Spectroscopy for Measurement of PTIOs and PTIs

The ESR spectra of carboxy-PTIO/-PTI are representative for all other PTIO derivatives (Fig. 2). Each ESR spectrum is obtained at room temperature with an X-band JES-RE1X ESR spectrometer (JEOL Akishima, Tokyo, Japan) by using a quartz flat cell with an effective volume of 180 μl. Typical conditions for the ESR measurement are as follows: modulation frequency, 100 kHz; modulation amplitude, 0.05 mT; response time, 0.03 sec; sweep time, 1 min; and microwave power, 10 mW. Hyperfine splitting constants (hfc) of PTIO and PTI are $a_N^{1,3} = 0.82$ mM and $a_N^1 = 0.98$ mT and $a_N^3 = 0.44$ mT, respectively, and g values ($g = 2.007$) as well as hfc of the prototype PTIO/PTI are almost the same as those for other PTIO/PTI derivatives. These radicals are very stable in solution except that free forms of PTIOs/PTIs, but not liposome PTIO, are susceptible to various reducing compounds that form N-hydroxy derivatives of PTIOs or PTIs as described below (cf. Fig. 3). The exact amount of PTIOs and PTIs can be readily quantitated by ESR spectroscopy at room temperature.

We usually measure the absolute amount of each nitroxide radical by double integration of experimental signals after normalization with the manganese (MnO) ESR signal recorded simultaneously. 4-Phenyl-2,2,5,5-tetramethylimidazoline-1-oxyl (98% purity; Aldrich, Milwaukee, WI) (Fig. 1B) is used as a standard nitroxide radical for the quantitation of PTIOs or PTIs; a simple and stable three-line hyperfine structure, the line width of which is similar to those of both PTIOs and PTIs, is obtained by this standard nitroxide radical.

More specifically, even when the reaction mixture of PTIOs and NO yields a complicated mixture of ESR spectra of unreacted PTIOs and reacted PTIs, the ESR signals of PTIOs and PTIs are quite different from one another, as demonstrated in Fig. 2C. Thus, the relative signal intensity of PTIs generated by the reaction of PTIOs with NO can be simply calculated by measuring the signal heights of MnO and PTIs (a and b in Fig. 2D, respectively). Because a very good linear correlation is observed between the values of the double integration of the signals for PTIOs or PTIs and that of the ESR signal height of each compound, for instance, height

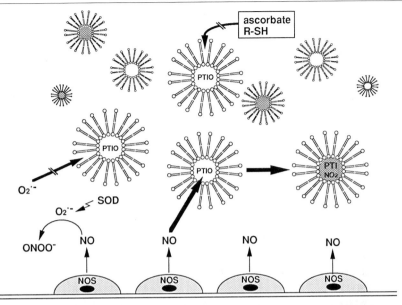

FIG. 3. Schematic drawing of the reaction of liposome PTIO with NO. Only hydrophobic NO is accessible to the PTIO compartment in the liposome vesicle.

b for PTI in Fig. 2, the concentration of PTIs (carboxy-PTI) can be quantified from the experimental value of $2b/a$ (relative signal intensity of PTIs against MnO); the concentration of PTIs is determined by comparing its double integration value with that of known concentrations of a standard nitroxide radical (4-phenyl-2,2,5,5-tetramethylimidazoline-1-oxyl) (Fig. 1B).

Preparation of Liposome-Encapsulated PTIO

We have observed that the nitronyl nitroxides (PTIOs) per se have a limitation for the assay of NO in biological systems because PTIOs are susceptible to nonspecific reduction by various reducing agents such as ascorbate, thiol compounds, and even superoxide anion radical (Fig. 3). Woldman et al.[13] report that encapsulation in a liposome vesicle made nitronyl nitroxide remarkably stable. We have also successfully prepared a much more stable liposome PTIO than that reported earlier.

Liposome PTIO is prepared by a reversed-phase evaporation method as described previously[14] by using L-α-phosphatidylcholine (PC) (Sigma,

[14] F. Szoka, Jr., and D. Papahadjopoulos, *Proc. Natl. Acad. Sci. U.S.A.* **75**, 4194 (1978).

St. Louis, MO), dimyristoylamido-1,2-deoxyphosphatidylcholine (DDPC) (Dojindo Laboratory), a derivative of phosphatidylcholine, and TMA–PTIO (Dojindo Laboratory). Briefly, 40 mg PC and 10 mg DDPC are dissolved in 4 ml of $CHCl_3$, and the solution is placed in a rotary evaporator to remove solvent and to form a thin-layer film in a 100-ml flask. The PC/DDPC film is then dissolved in 4 ml diethyl ether, to which 1.5 ml of 2.0 mM TMA–PTIO in 10 mM sodium phosphate-buffered saline (0.15 M NaCl) (PBS, pH 7.4) is added, followed by sonication of the flask in a bath-type sonicator (Tocho, Tokyo) for 30 min until a homogeneous one-phase dispersion is obtained. Subsequently, the organic solvent (ether) in the mixture is removed completely in a rotary evaporator; at this step a viscous gel is formed as the organic solvent is removed. The residual nonencapsulated materials (TMA–PTIO) and organic solvent are further removed by washing the preparation with PBS by centrifuging four times at 10,000 g at 4° for 10 min. Using this procedure for liposome PTIO preparation, 500 μl of 800 μM to 1 mM liposome PTIO is usually obtained.

A derivative of PC, DDPC, is added so that the unilamellar membrane of the liposome becomes more stable in a biological system and TMA–PTIO can retain stability in this liposome vesicle[15]; more than 80% of TMA–PTIO remains in the vesicle even in an aqueous environment for as long as 1 month at 4°. It should be noted that this liposome formulation can prevent nonspecific reduction of PTIO by various reducing agents present in a biologic system as shown in Fig. 3.

In addition, we have found that PTIO derivatives showed some cytotoxicity against cells in culture; cultivation of HeLa cells at more than 100 μM concentration of PTIO or carboxy-PTIO resulted in significant growth inhibition of the cells. In contrast, liposome PTIO prepared in our laboratory does not have any toxic effect, at least under the conditions of NO measurement as described below, suggesting another benefit of liposome encapsulation of PTIO in NO measurements.

Although the line widths of ESR signals of both PTIO and PTI are somewhat broadened by the liposome encapsulation of TMA–PTIO as shown in Figs. 4 and 6, other ESR parameters such as g value and hfc are not changed at all. Thus, PTI generated in liposome is clearly discriminated by ESR spectroscopy, and the amount of liposome PTI can be determined as described above (Fig. 2). Accordingly, the absolute amount of NO reacted with liposome PTIO can be quantitated from the signal intensity of liposome PTI.

---

[15] J. Sunamoto, M. Goto, K. Iwamoto, H. Kondo, and T. Sato, *Biochim. Biophys. Acta* **1024**, 209 (1990).

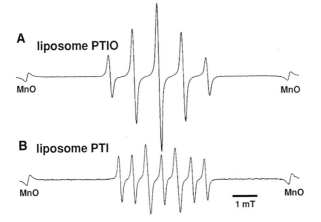

FIG. 4. The ESR spectra of liposome PTIO (A) and liposome PTI (B).

Stoichiometric Conversion of PTIOs to PTIs during Reaction of PTIOs with Nitric Oxide: Quantitation of Nitric Oxide Release from Nitric Oxide-Releasing Agents

Stoichiometric conversion of PTIOs to PTIs via the reaction with NO is clearly shown in Fig. 5. In this experiment, propylamine NONOate [1-hydroxy-2-oxo-3-(*N*-methyl-3-aminopropyl)-3-methyl-1-triazene] (Dojindo Laboratory) (see structure in Fig. 5A), originally described by Hrabie *et al.*[16] as a spontaneous NO-releasing compound in neutral solution (half-life of 7.5 min in neutral solution at 37°), is used as a source of NO generation. Because the compound contains two molecules of NO, it is expected that the amount of NO released from propylamine NONOate would be 2 mol per NONOate under effective NO-releasing conditions in neutral solution. In fact this is substantiated by measuring the amount of carboxy-PTI/liposome PTI produced from carboxy-PTIO/liposome PTI in the reaction system containing NONOate (Fig. 5). Specifically, when the concentration of PTIs generated is plotted against that of propylamine NONOate added to the system, the slope of the curve is close to 1.0 : 2.0 for NONOate to PTI (Fig. 5). However, as the concentration of NONOate increases, the slope of the curve gradually changes (Fig. 5A). The decrease in reaction efficacy of carboxy-PTIO/liposome PTIO with NO in a higher concentration range of NONOate relative to the concentration of PTIO might be

---

[16] J. A. Hrabie, J. R. Klose, D. A. Wink, and L. K. Keefer, *J. Org. Chem.* **58,** 1472 (1993).

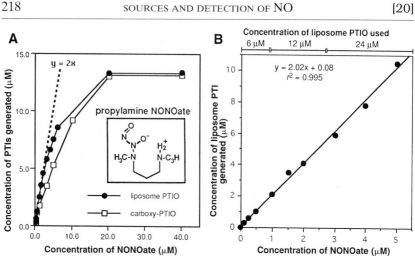

FIG. 5. (A) Generation of NO quantified by PTIs being formed in the reaction of PTIOs plus NO released from the NONOate. The reaction is initiated by the addition of various concentrations of NONOate (structure given in the inset) to PTIO (13.5 μM) solution in PBS (pH 7.4), and the mixture is incubated for 30 min at 37°. (B) Correlation of the concentration of liposome PTI formed and NONOate added to the reaction as in (A). Three different concentrations of liposome PTIO are used for the reaction with NO. All data are means of three different experiments.

due to the interference of NO_2, a product of NO and PTIO [Eq. (1)], which reacts as in Eq. (2):

$$NO + NO_2 \rightarrow N_2O_3 \tag{2}$$

Interestingly, it appears that the slope showing the concentration of carboxy-PTI being formed tends to be lower than that of the liposome PTI (Fig. 5A). This indicates that liposome PTIO captures NO more effectively than carboxy-PTIO. Furthermore, when different concentrations of liposome PTIO are added to the system with NO-releasing NONOate, a linear generation of PTI in liposome is observed, which is strictly dependent on concentration of NONOate added to the system (Fig. 5B); r^2 is 0.995 and the slope is 2.02. We estimate that at least 3 molar excess concentrations of PTIOs to NO are needed to capture NO completely with the use of liposome PTIO. These results indicate that 2 mol of NO is released from 1 mol of NONOate and that PTIOs react with NO in a completely stoichiometric manner. Furthermore, use of liposome PTIO to quantitate NO accurately in the NO-generating system is warranted as follows.

Quantitation of Nitric Oxide Released from Cells by Using
Liposome PTIO

To examine whether liposome PTIO can react with NO generated in
biological systems, liposome PTIO is incubated with a murine macrophage
cell line (RAW264) in culture with and without stimulation by both lipopolysaccharide (LPS; *Escherichia coli* 026B) (Difco Laboratories, Detroit,
MI) and recombinant murine γ-interferon (IFN-γ) (Genzyme, Cambridge,
MA). The RAW264 cells are cultured in Dulbecco's modified Eagle's medium (DMEM) (GIBCO, Grand Island, NY) supplemented with nonessential amino acids (GIBCO) and 10% (v/v) fetal bovine serum (FBS) on a
24-well polystyrene plate (Falcon, Becton Dickinson Labware, Lincoln
Park, NJ; diameter, 1 cm). The cells at saturation density (1×10^6 cells/
well) are stimulated with 10 μg/ml of LPS and 200 U/ml of IFN-γ. After
various incubation periods with and without LPS and IFN-γ at 37° in a
CO_2 incubator (5% CO_2/95% air, v/v), DMEM is removed and the cells
are washed three times with Krebs–Ringer–phosphate buffer (KRP) supplemented with 0.2% bovine serum albumin (BSA). Liposome PTIO is
then added to each culture well to give 10 to 20 μM PTIO concentration
in 0.2 ml of either KRP containing 0.2% BSA or DMEM supplemented
with 10% FBS with or without either Cu,Zn-superoxide dismutase (SOD)
or L-arginine, followed by incubation in a CO_2 incubator. After a 30-min
incubation period, the solution containing liposome PTIO is transferred to
the ESR quartz cell, and ESR measurement is performed to quantitate the
amount of liposome PTI produced in the cell culture as described above.

The ESR signals are very stable for several hours of incubation with
RAW264 cells even in the presence of FBS and reducing agents such as
ascorbate and thiol compounds. As demonstrated in Fig. 6A, the generation
of liposome PTI can be readily identified and quantitated. Intriguingly,
addition of Cu,Zn-SOD to the liposome solution resulted in an increase
in the generation of liposome PTI (data not shown) owing to the removal
of the superoxide generated in the culture system. It is expected that superoxide reacts very rapidly with NO, yielding ONOO$^-$; thus, NO becomes
unavailable to be captured by PTIO (see Fig. 3). Deletion of L-arginine or
addition of an NOS inhibitor such as N^ω-monomethyl-L-arginine (L-
NMMA) to the mixture gives no appreciable production of liposome PTI
(Fig. 6A), indicating that liposome PTIO indeed trapped NO generated
from NOS and from the cells. NO is accessible to liposome PTIO outside
the cells. The time profile of NO production determined by the liposome
PTIO/ESR method is demonstrated in Fig. 6B, which correlates well with
that of the mRNA expression of inducible NOS examined by Northern
blot analysis (data not shown). To assess NO production accurately, the

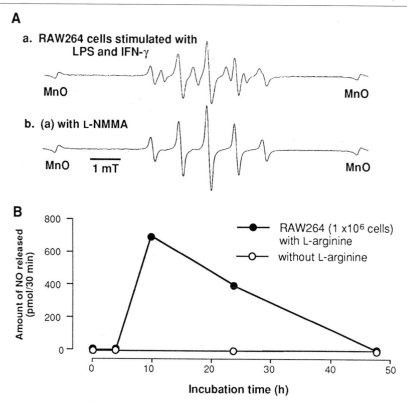

FIG. 6. Quantitation of NO produced by RAW264 cells (a murine macrophage cell line) by using liposome PTIO with ESR spectroscopy. (A) Spectra observed with liposome PTIO incubated with RAW264. Note the effect of an NOS inhibitor (L-NMMA) in (b), which leads to almost complete inhibition of NO. (B) Time profile of NO production by RAW264 cells stimulated with LPS and IFN-γ, both added at time zero.

amount of liposome PTIO added to the assay mixture must be adequate to cover the range of NO generated in the test systems, because an excess amount of NO compared with that of PTIOs will result in inefficient capturing of NO by the liposome PTIO.

Sensitivity and Specificity of Nitric Oxide Measurement Using PTIOs and Liposome PTIO

When ESR spectroscopy with liposome PTIO is applied for quantitation of NO, the limit of detection is entirely dependent on the sensitivity of each ESR spectrometer used. The signal-to-noise ratios (S/N) of ESR signals can be greatly improved by repeated sweeps in the magnetic field for PTIOs and PTIs signals combined with the computer data analyzing system. When we measure the ESR spectrum of PTIs in ESR quartz flat cell with 180 μl volume by using X-band JEOL ESR spectrometer and data analyzing system (Labotec, Tokyo), the minimal detectable limit of the PTIs generated in the reaction of either PTIOs or liposome PTIO with NO is above 0.05 μM (absolute amount, >9 pmol). Thus, the PTIOs/ESR method appears to be almost 20 times more sensitive than the spectrophotometric method for the NO_2^- assay with the Griess reagent.[17]

In our assay system the liposomal membrane functions as a barrier to prevent various polar or water-soluble reducing compounds from reaching the PTIO, and it will permit only diffusion of hydrophobic small molecules, especially NO, into the PTIO compartment of the liposome. The chemical reaction forming PTIs from PTIOs is essentially specific for NO because no other substances that react with PTIOs to form PTIs have been found so far. In addition, PTIOs directly react with NO but not with other NO-related molecular species such as nitrosothiols (RS–NO), iron-nitrosyl complexes, and nitrites (NO_2^-). Therefore, a specific, sensitive, and quantitative measurement of NO produced in biological systems has become possible by application of PTIOs and liposome PTIO in ESR spectroscopy.

Conclusion

On the basis of the unique reaction of PTIOs and NO, we have described here a method to quantify the amount of NO generated from the cultured cells that can be measured by using ESR spectroscopy and various PTIO derivatives. The specificity and sensitivity of this method are much improved by using the liposome formulation of PTIO. The shelf-life of liposome PTIO is more than 1 month, it has no cytotoxic effects, and it is more stable than free PTIOs in cell culture systems. In addition, these PTIO derivatives can be applied as specific NO scavengers in studies on the pathophysiology of NO.[2,10,11,18]

Acknowledgments

Helpful discussion with Dr. Y. Katayama, Dojindo Laboratory, is gratefully acknowledged. Thanks are also due to Ms. R. Yoshimoto and Dr. T. Okamoto for help in preparing the manuscript.

[17] D. L. Green, D. A. Wagner, J. Glogowski, P. L. Skipper, J. S. Wishnok, and S. R. Tannenbaum, *Anal. Biochem.* **126,** 131 (1982).
[18] K. Yoshida, T. Akaike, T. Doi, K. Sato, S. Ijiri, M. Suga, M. Ando, and H. Maeda, *Infect. Immun.* **61,** 3552 (1993).

in L-arginine-containing medium.[8] This spectrum is assigned to the mononi-trosyl complex of iron–MGD in which one NO molecule has a coordination bond with iron. The EPR spectrum shown in Fig. 1A has hyperfine structure originating from the ^{14}N nucleus in the NO complex. When L-arginine contained in the incubation medium was replaced with L-[^{15}N]arginine, an EPR spectrum with a two-line pattern (Fig. 1B) was obtained, indicating that the ^{15}NO complex was produced. The origin of the oxygen atom in NO is also verified using a spin trap solution in which ^{17}O is dissolved. Presence of the $N^{17}O$ complex is seen as a broad wing in both ends of the EPR spectrum (Fig. 1C).

In Situ Spin Trapping of Macrophage Nitric Oxide Generation

Experimental procedures to continuously and quantitatively detect NO generation in suspensions of mouse peritoneal macrophages are described. As a spin trap, the iron complex of MGD dissolved in the RMPI 1640 medium is used.

Experimental Procedures

Materials. The MGD sodium salt reagent is available from OMRF Spin Trap Source (Oklahoma City, OK). L-Arginine-free RPMI medium can be prepared using Select-Amine kit (GIBCO, Grand Island, NY). L-[^{15}N]Ar-ginine may be purchased from Isotec (Miamisburg, OH). Sources of other chemicals and media used in these experiments are specified in the pro-cedure.

Macrophage Preparation. Peritoneal macrophages are obtained from adult BALB/c mice (or any common strain) 5 days after intraperitoneal injection of 2 ml of sterile 4% (w/w) brewer's thioglycollate medium (Sigma, St. Louis, MO). After injection of thioglycollate, greater than 95% of the cells in the peritoneal cavity are macrophages. After the mouse is eutha-nized, the macrophages are collected by infusing the peritoneal cavity with ice-cold RPMI 1640 medium (Sigma) which is subsequently removed. The collected cell suspension is centrifuged at 1200 g for 10 min, and the cell pellet is washed twice and then resuspended in RPMI 1640 with 5% (v/v) fetal calf serum (FCS, Sigma) to make a cell suspension of a final concentra-tion of 6 × 10^6 cells/ml.

Activation and Incubation. The cell suspension is drawn into a flat EPR sample cell (quartz, inside thickness 0.3 mm, 200 μl in volume, Wilmad, Buena, NJ, WG803) that has been washed with detergent. With rubber

---

[8] Y. Kotake, T. Tanigawa, M. Tanigawa, and I. Ueno, *Free Radical Res.* **23**, 287 (1995).

septa at both ends the sample cell is kept in a horizontal position at 37° for 20 min to promote cell adhesion to the inner surface of the tube. The quartz tube is then turned so that the other face of the tube faces down, and a second aliquot of cell suspension is introduced for 20 min to allow cells to attach to the other inner surface of the EPR sample cell. The total number of attached cells in the sample cell should be approximately 3×10^6.

Using a syringe, the medium in the EPR sample cell is gently replaced with RPMI which contains LPS (from *Escherichia coli* 0111.B4, Sigma, 100 ng/ml) and INF-γ (mouse recombinant, 500 U/ml Boeringer-Mannheim, Indianapolis, IN) to induce activation. The cells are incubated for 3 hr in this medium during which time the activation medium is replaced three times to avoid oxygen deficiency. Then the activation medium is replaced with RPMI 1640 with 5% FCS but without LPS and INF-γ for additional incubation. To avoid hypoxia during this incubation, the medium is continuously infused to the sample cell at the rate of 0.4 ml/hr using a syringe infusion pump (Harvard Apparatus, South Natick, MA; Model 942) for up to 18 hr. If an infusion pump is not available, the medium may be manually replaced every half an hour. These procedures are carried out at 37° ± 1° in a warm room. Determining the dependence of NO generation rate on the length of incubation following stimulation requires several EPR sample cells containing cells that were harvested at the same time and then incubated simultaneously.

After various incubation times, the sample cells are infused with spin trap solution. Because the iron–MGD spin trap is not cytotoxic, macrophages in a single EPR sample cell can be repeatedly monitored for their rate of NO generation. In such a case, after the first EPR measurement the spin trap solution is drained and replaced with incubation medium. The macrophages in the sample cell are then incubated for an additional period in a warm room. The sample cell is then returned to the EPR cavity and new spin trap solution is again infused for a second EPR measurement.

Preparation of Spin Trap Solution. Spin trap solution is prepared in RPMI 1640 medium that contains HEPES (Sigma, 20 m*M*), sodium MGD (10 m*M*), and FeSO$_4$ (Sigma, 1 m*M*) under a nitrogen atmosphere. First MGD and HEPES are added to the RPMI 1640 medium and bubbled with nitrogen gas, and then the mixture is added to nitrogen-bubbled FeSO$_4$–RPMI 1640 solution. After preparation of the spin trap solution under nitrogen, it is briefly aerated by exposure to room air. The solution turns brown because of the oxidation of iron ion. When the medium with a specific ingredient is required such as L-arginine-free RPMI 1640 medium, the Select-Amine kit (GIBCO) is used.

Electron Paramagnetic Resonance Measurement. After incubation, the EPR sample cell is sealed at both ends using rubber septa and set in an

EPR cavity equipped with flat-cell holders. An EPR cavity with the sample insertion holes horizontally arranged is ideal for cellular spin trapping,[9] because in a vertically held sample cell the cells tend to sediment out of the region of signal acquisition in the EPR cavity. However, in the case of macrophages or any other cells that tightly attach to the glass surface, sedimentation will not occur even with the vertical setting found in most cavities. The ideal temperature for macrophage function is 37° in the EPR cavity; however, NO spin trapping from macrophages can also be successfully performed at room temperature. To control the temperature of cells in the EPR sample cell, soft copper tubing (5 mm o.d.) can be wound around the cavity, maintaining good contact with the cavity wall, so that when the tubing is connected to a temperature-controlled water pump there will be efficient heat exchange between the cavity and the circulating heated water. The temperature of circulating water may be adjusted to obtain the desired temperature as measured at the center of the EPR cavity. If the cavity is additionally wrapped with polystyrene foam sheets one can achieve better control of the temperature.

Through the bottom septum, the spin trap solution is slowly injected into the EPR sample cell using a syringe to replace the incubation medium. A needle with thin plastic tubing punctured through the top rubber septum is used to discard the expelled medium. An EPR spectrometer (X-band) with 100 kHz field modulation is employed for the recording of EPR spectra. Signal intensity at every 2 min after infusion of spin trap solution is recorded. Typical spectrometer settings are as follows: modulation amplitude, 2.0 gauss; microwave power, 20 mW; time constant, 0.1 sec. Because the g value of the NO complex (spin adduct) is 2.04, the signal is centered at about 60 gauss lower than the field region where the common radical is found.

The amount of spin adduct can be calibrated using aqueous solutions of a stable nitroxide, 2,2,5,5-tetramethylpiperidine-1-oxyl (TEMPO, Sigma) as a concentration standard. An aqueous solution of TEMPO (10^{-5} or $10^{-6}\ M$) is loaded to the same EPR sample cell used for spin trapping. The EPR spectra of the spin adduct solution and the TEMPO solution should be recorded at spectrometer settings (cavity Q value, modulation amplitude, time constant, field scan rate, and microwave power) as similar as possible. Different spectrometer sensitivity settings may be used for the sample and standard and calibrated later. Both of the first-derivative EPR spectra are double-integrated (by computer or manually) to obtain a number propor-

[9] Y. Kotake, L. A. Reinke, T. Tanigawa, and H. Koshida, *Free Radical Biol. Med.* **17**, 215 (1994).

tional to the concentration, and then the concentration of spin adduct is calculated using the ratio of these two numbers.

Results of Testing Experiments Following Described Procedures

Introduction of the spin trap solution to the EPR sample cell containing activated macrophages produces a three-line EPR spectrum (Fig. 1B). The spectral parameters of this EPR signal (g = 2.04, a_N = 12.6 gauss) are identical to those observed when an aqueous solution of authentic NO is added to a solution containing the spin trap. In control experiments, no decrease in the EPR signal intensity was observed when the spin adduct solution was drained to a vial and exposed to air for at least 1 day. No EPR signal was obtained from nonactivated macrophages even after incubation for up to 10 hr. The generation of the NO spin adduct in these systems was dependent on the presence of intact macrophages as evidenced by the fact that neither the spin trap solution alone nor the spin trap solution with heat-killed macrophages produced an EPR signal after exposure to the activating agents with subsequent incubation.

Rate of Nitric Oxide Generation. Figure 2 shows typical time courses for the increase of the NO spin adduct recorded from activated macrophages concurrently incubated for various periods. The EPR signal of the NO adduct of iron–MGD was visible within 2 min after replacement of the medium with spin trap solution. This signal continued to increase for about 10 min. The increase of EPR signal intensity usually terminates within 10 min because of oxygen deficiency. The rate of macrophage NO generation thus can be calculated using the slope of the increase in the NO spin adduct. Initial rates should be the most representative of NO production since the oxygen concentration in the quartz cells eventually declines as the macrophages metabolize it.

Usually, the concentration of the NO complex spin adduct (Fig. 1A) obtained 2 min (required for tuning of the spectrometer) after infusion of spin trap solution is less than 10^{-6} M; therefore, the intial EPR signal has a low signal-to-noise ratio. One is able to improve the signal quality by increasing the number of cells in the EPR sample cell, however crowded cells consume more oxygen during incubation, thus requiring more frequent replacement of incubation medium to ensure oxygenation. The signal-to-noise ratio of the EPR signal may also be increased by applying a faster magnet-field scan over a single EPR line. For example, one can set the center field at the middle line of the triplet and scan the field for 10 gauss for 10 sec and accumulate the signal for 10 times. To record the time course

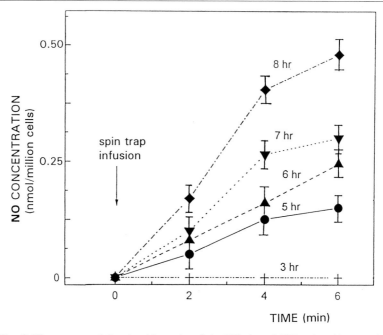

FIG. 2. Time course of the signal intensity of the NO–iron–MGD spin adduct produced by activated macrophages. Cells were activated by incubation with RPMI 1640 containing LPS (100 ng/ml) and INF-γ (500 U/ml) in an EPR sample cell for 3 hr and then incubated for various times ranging from 3 to 8 hr. The EPR spectra were recorded immediately after the spin trap solution was infused. The EPR intensity was recorded every 2 min after infusion. The NO concentration indicated on the vertical axis was calculated using the EPR intensity by assuming the 100% trapping efficiency.

directly, the magnet field may be set on the peak of the middle line and the x axis of the recorder switched to time scan. In such a case, the time constant can be set higher to reduce noise.

As a result of a series of measurements of NO generation rates from macrophages as a function of incubation time, an activation profile of macrophage NO generation has been obtained. The NO generation rate reaches a maximum level with incubation for 8 hr after activation (3 hr) is finished and then levels off.[10] Finally, because the present method can monitor real-time NO generation, it is applicable to the dynamic measure-

[10] Y. Kotake, T. Tanigawa, M. Tanigawa, I. Ueno, D. R. Allen, and C.-S. Lai, *Biochim. Biophys. Acta,* in press (1996).

ment of inhibition or priming of NO generation rate by manipulations of the enzymatic pathways that converge on cellular NO synthase.

Acknowledgments

The contributions of Drs. Toru Tanigawa, Mari Tanigawa, Ikuko Ueno, and Randel Allen at various stages in developing the described method are gratefully acknowledged.

[22] Electron Paramagnetic Resonance Characterization of Rat Neuronal Nitric Oxide Production *ex Vivo*

By Andrey V. Kozlov, Anna Bini, Anna Iannone, Isabella Zini, and Aldo Tomasi

Introduction

Nitric oxide (NO) has been suggested to be a vasorelaxant in the cardiovascular system and a neurotransmitter in the central nervous system. Evidence indicates that NO serves not only as an intra- and interneuronal messenger, but also mediates neurotoxicity.[1]

Hemoglobin (Hb) and related hemoproteins can be used for the detection of NO. The reaction forming nitrosyl hemoglobin (HbNO),

$$Hb-Fe^{2+} + NO \rightarrow Hb-Fe^{2+}-NO \qquad (1)$$

is diffusion limited and is as fast as the reaction between NO and oxygenated Hb,

$$Hb-Fe^{2+}-O_2 + NO \rightarrow Hb-Fe^{3+} + NO_3^- \qquad (2)$$

which yields methemoglobin and nitrate.[2] These reactions are conceivably physiologically relevant, and an NO regulatory role for hemoglobin has been envisioned *in vivo*.[3]

A fast and specific reaction also takes place between NO and iron complexes different from heme, such as diethyl dithiocarbamate (DETC) and iron–citrate complexes.[4,5] Direct measurement of NO is extremely

[1] E. Anggard, *Lancet* **343**, 1199 (1994).
[2] M. P. Doyle and J. W. Hoekstra, *J. Inorg. Chem.* **14**, 351 (1981).
[3] E. Noack and M. Murphy, *in* "Oxidative Stress: Oxidants and Antioxidants" (H. Sies, ed.), p. 445. Academic Press, London, 1991.
[4] L. N. Kubrina, W. S. Caldwell, P. I. Mordvintcev, I. V. Malenkova, and A. F. Vanin, *Biochim. Biophys. Acta* **1099**, 233 (1992).
[5] C. S. Lai and A. M. Komarov, *FEBS Lett.* **345**, 120 (1994).

difficult under physiological conditions, and various methods for NO measurement are discussed in this volume. The high specificity and high rate constant of the reaction give the best credentials to heme- or metal-based NO assays. The possibility of HbNO formation *in vivo* has been reported in various papers.[6,7] Murphy and Noack[8] have proposed a spectrophotometric assay of nitric oxide based on reaction (2). Here, reaction (1) and its detection by electron paramagnetic resonance (EPR) spectroscopy are discussed.

Procedures

Preparation of Hemoglobin

We found that freshly prepared Hb from concentrated hemolysates serves better than commercially available Hb, which in any case has to be treated because of the presence of methemoglobin. Blood (7–9 ml) is withdrawn from the right auricola of an anesthetized rat (Ketalar, 100 mg/kg; Parke-Davis) and collected into a heparinized tube (30 U of heparin). The erythrocytes are washed three times with isotonic saline, lysed with an equal volume of ice-cold distilled water, and allowed to stand at $0°$ for 20–30 min. The lysate is centrifuged for 45 min at 16,000 rpm to remove cell membranes. The resulting solution is dialyzed overnight in Ringer's solution, kept at $4°$, and used within 2 days. The Hb concentration is estimated using a molar extinction (ε) of 125,000 M^{-1} cm^{-1} at 415 nm[9]; under these conditions no methemoglobin is observed. The final concentration of Hb used in the experiments is adjusted to 3 mM.

In Vitro Nitrosyl Hemoglobin Complex Formation and Preparation of Calibration Curve

At $2°$ and 760 mm Hg, 6.18 mg of NO dissolves in 100 g of water, so the calculation of the NO concentration in a saturated solution is easily performed. First, oxygen is completely removed from water by flowing oxygen-free nitrogen. The solution is then bubbled with NO gas for 10 min.

[6] L. R. Cantilena, R. P. Smith, S. Frasur, H. Kruszyna, R. Kruszyna, and D. E. Wilcox, *J. Lab. Clin. Med.* **120,** 902 (1992).

[7] H. Kosaka, Y. Sawai, H. Sakaguchi, E. Kumura, N. Harada, M. Watanabe, and T. Shiga, *Am. J. Physiol.* **266,** C1400 (1994).

[8] M. E. Murphy and E. Noack, *in* "Oxygen Radicals in Biological Systems" (L. Packer, ed.), p. 240. Academic Press, San Diego, 1994.

[9] E. Antonini and M. Brunori, "Hemoglobin and Myoglobin in Their Reactions with Ligands." North-Holland Publ., Amsterdam, 1971.

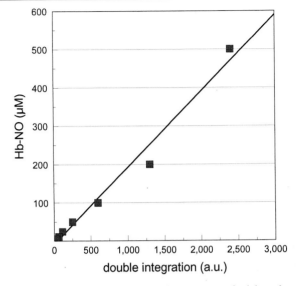

FIG. 1. Calibration curve for HbNO. The HbNO was prepared mixing a known concentration of NO in water and Hb in Ringer's phosphate, pH 6. The EPR spectrum was double integrated and expressed in arbitrary units (au).

The NO-saturated water is taken into a syringe, from which oxygen is removed, and diluted, to obtain the desired NO concentration, by mixing in a second syringe filled with oxygen-free water. The NO solution is eventually added to a third syringe filled with 3 mM hemoglobin in Ringer's phosphate, pH 6. This solution also is oxygen-free. A calibration curve is built between 5 and 500 μM; the curve obtained is shown in Fig. 1.

Hemoglobin Injection in Selected Area of Rat Brain

Adult male Sprague-Dawley rats are anesthetized by halothane (5%, reduced promptly to 1.0% after stabilization) and fixed in a stereotaxic frame. Two small injection cannulae (27 gauge) are implanted into both the right and left caudate-putamen to a depth of 4.3 mm from the dura mater, 0.9 mm anterior, and 2.5 mm lateral to the bregma, in accordance to the Paxinos and Watson atlas[10]; 5 μl of Hb is slowly injected through the cannulae (0.2 μl/min). Control animals are treated in the same way, but Ringer's solution is injected instead.

Hemoglobin has a relatively high molecular weight. Once Hb is injected,

[10] G. Paxinos and C. Watson, "The Rat Brain in Stereotaxic Coordinates." Academic Press, New York, 1986.

its diffusion is limited to the extracellular space; it distributes quickly in the striatum following the infusion. The Hb diffusion border coincides with the striatum border, providing evidence that most of the Hb does not leave the brain region. Under the conditions described, the concentration of Hb in the striatum (which weighs 30–40 mg) is about 500 μM.

Striata Preparation for Electron Paramagnetic Resonance Detection of Nitrosyl Hemoglobin

Animals are sacrificed by decapitation 30 min after Hb injection. The brain is quickly removed and dissected to obtain the neostriata. Usually two neostriata are used to form a single sample. The striata are inserted in a Teflon tube (3 mm i.d.) and immediately stored in liquid nitrogen until use.

Nitrosyl hemoglobin gives a characteristic EPR signal, which has been well described in the literature.[11,12] The spectrum depicted in Fig. 2e shows a characteristic triplet whose hyperfine structure is well evident in the high-field feature of the signal. The best instrumental conditions for maximum sensitivity in an X-band spectrometer (Klystron frequency 9.52205 GHz) are as follows: microwave power, 2.5 mW; modulation amplitude, 0.32 mT; scan width, 20 mT; sample at liquid nitrogen temperature. It is advisable to accumulate the spectra electronically in order to obtain a low noise-to-signal ratio and to perform double integration for the quantitative estimation of the species.

Results

Nitric Oxide Detectable in Brain Neostriatum under Basal Conditions

When saline is injected in the neostriatum, three EPR absorptions become evident in control brain: a $g = 2.00$ signal, assigned to ubiquinone and flavoproteins, a $g = 1.94$ signal due to Fe–S centers of the respiratory chain, and a very weak signal at $g = 2.25$, which can be assigned to cytochrome P450 (Fig. 2b). In the presence of hemolysate, the magnitudes of the listed signals do not change significantly; however, a new large signal is evident at $g = 2.03$ (Fig. 2a). This spectrum, once subtracted from the control spectrum (saline only injection) evidently shows the typical hyperfine structure of the HbNO spectrum (Fig. 2c). The signal is not present in the hemolysate used for the injection (Fig. 2d). The same signal observed

---

[11] J. Bennet, D. J. E. Ingram, P. George, and J. S. Grifith, *Nature* (*London*) **176**, 394 (1955).
[12] H. Rein, O. Ristau, and W. Scheller, *FEBS Lett.* **24**, 24 (1972).

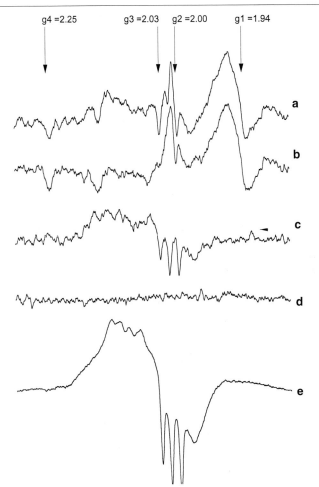

FIG. 2. Nitric oxide detection in brain striatum. The $g_1 = 1.94$ signal is due to Fe–S centers of the respiratory chain; $g_2 = 2.00$ is assigned to ubiquinone and flavoproteins; $g_4 = 2.25$ can be tentatively assigned to cytochrome P450. Spectrum (b) is obtained from sham-injected striatum and spectrum (a) from hemoglobin-injected striatum. Spectrum (c) is obtained by subtracting spectrum (a) from spectrum (b); the triplet has the typical hyperfine structure of the HbNO spectrum. (d) The signal is not present in hemolysate used for the injection. (e) The signal is obtained after incubation of hemolysate at pH 6.00 in an NO atmosphere.

in the striatum after Hb injection can be seen after incubation of hemolysate at pH 6.00 in an NO atmosphere (Fig. 2e). Above pH 7.4 the hyperfine structure does not appear. It is easy to see that the shape and g value of the signals are equal.

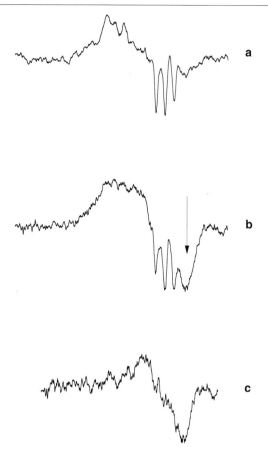

Fig. 3. Two different spectra contribute to the HbNO spectrum. Spectrum (a) is mainly due to HbNO, where Hb is in the low-affinity, T state quaternary structure (hyperfine coupling constant of 1.6 mT). The spectrum was obtained after Hb injection in the striatum under basal conditions. Spectrum (b) was obtained from spectrum (a), but adjusting to pH 7.2. The arrow indicates the component of the spectrum due to Hb in the high-affinity, R state conformation. This component is evident in spectrum (c), obtained after subtraction of spectrum (a) from (b).

Nitrosyl Hemoglobin Spectrum Showing Two Components

The HbNO spectrum is a composite spectrum, and the NO binding to hemoglobin causes a very complex series of spectral transitions.[13,14] The

[13] R. Hille, J. S. Olson, and G. Palmer, *J. Biol. Chem.* **254**, 12110 (1979).
[14] M. Chevion, A. Stern, J. Peisach, W. E. Blumberg, and S. Simon, *Biochemistry* **17**, 1745 (1978).

TABLE I
EFFECT OF HEMOGLOBIN INJECTION ON
CONCENTRATION OF THIOBARBITURIC-REACTIVE
SUBSTANCES IN RAT STRIATUM[a]

Time	TBARS (nmol/mg protein)	
	Control	Hemoglobin treated
1 hr	0.405 ± 0.042	0.429 ± 0.022
24 hr	0.411 ± 0.018	0.430 ± 0.032

[a] Data represent the mean ± SD of five experiments.

HbNO EPR spectrum associated with α-hemes in the low-affinity, T state quaternary structure is characterized by three well-evident lines with a hyperfine coupling constant of 1.6 mT (Fig. 3a). This feature is due to a five-coordinated HbNO and has been described by Tajima[15]; it depends on the fractional NO saturation of Hb and on pH. The second feature of the HbNO spectrum (Fig. 3c) is associated with a six-coordinated HbNO. The loss of the three-line hyperfine signal is associated with the transition of the heme quaternary structure to the high-affinity R state conformation.[14] There is a strong pH dependency of the equilibrium between the two forms, and it is possible to calculate roughly the pH at which the HbNO adduct has been formed when freezing the striatum.

Problems and Interferences

Storage of Nitrosyl Hemoglobin Complexes without Significant Decomposition

The procedure of Hb injection and brain preparation takes longer than 30 min. The question of how stable is the NOHb complex under the experimental conditions has been answered by the following experiment. The HbNO complex is prepared *in vitro* incubating hemolysate under an NO atmosphere. The complex is added to brain homogenate, under an air or nitrogen atmosphere, and the intensity of the EPR spectrum recorded up to 5 hr. Under air, the signal decreases to about 50% of the original intensity after 5 hr. In the absence of oxygen, no significant difference in signal intensity is found within the initial 2 hr; a 10% decrease is recorded at 5-hr incubation time.

[15] K. Tajima, *Inorg. Chim. Acta* **169**, 211 (1990).

Endogenous Hemoglobin to Form Complexes with Nitric Oxide under Experimental Conditions

To estimate if endogenous hemoglobin is able to trap NO in brain tissue, brain is prepared as above, without perfusion of Hb. No EPR signals have been detected under this condition.

Possible Injury Caused by Hemoglobin Injection

Injection of Hb may cause a tissue injury. In general this damage is associated with the prooxidant properties of Hb. This point has been addressed by studying thiobarbituric-reactive substance (TBAR) accumulation after Hb injection in the striatum. Hemolysate is injected in the striatum, while saline is injected in the control group. The striata are removed 1 and 24 hr after the injections and homogenized. The TBARs are determined in the homogenate as described.[16] Table I shows TBAR concentrations in the striatum in control and hemoglobin-treated rats. Clearly, no difference was noted between groups.

Signal Intensity to Reflect Nitric Oxide Production of Striatum

The quantification is difficult to interpret, since, as noted above, reactions (1) and (2) are equally fast and so the proportion of NO trapped by binding to Hb is strictly dependent on the proportion of Hb that is oxygenated as it is exposed to NO. The oxygenation state at the site of NO production is difficult to estimate. Concurrent determination of methemoglobin formation could also give an indication as to how relevant reaction (2) is. However, we are not able to determine any methemoglobin variation in our model system. A report[17] stating that HbNO has been detected *in vivo* in the blood after nitroglycerin administration also could not determine any relationship between methemoglobin and HbNO formation *in vivo*.

Acknowledgments

A.K. was on a visiting grant generously given by the European Science Foundation. The work has been supported by a grant from the Italian National Research Council (CNR), Project "Aging."

---

[16] A. V. Kozlov, D. Y. Yegorov, Y. A. Vladimirov, and O. A. Azizova, *Free Radical Biol. Med.* **13,** 9 (1992).
[17] M. Kohno, T. Masumizu, and A. Mori, *Free Radical Biol. Med.* **18,** 451 (1995).

[23] Quantitation of Nitrate and Nitrite in Extracellular Fluids

By Matthew B. Grisham, Glenda G. Johnson,
and Jack R. Lancaster, Jr.

Introduction

Approximately 56% of the human body is fluid. Although most of the fluid is localized within the intracellular compartment (intracellular fluid), approximately 30% of the total body water is found in the spaces outside the cells and is termed extracellular fluid. Examples of some extracellular fluids include plasma, lymph, urine, cerebrospinal fluid (CSF), intraocular fluid, sweat, and tears as well as a variety of gastrointestinal fluids including salivary, gastric, intestinal, pancreatic, and biliary secretions. Extracellular fluids such as plasma, lymph, and CSF are continuously being transported via the circulation to all parts of the body. This rapid transport and subsequent mixing between the plasma and extracellular fluid via diffusion through the capillary endothelial cells allows all cells in the body to be exposed to essentially the same extracellular environment. Thus, the presence of certain metabolites in extracellular fluid provides a good indicator for those metabolic processes that occur at the cellular and tissue level. Furthermore, because some extracellular fluids (e.g., urine, saliva, tears) are normally excreted, these fluids may be collected and metabolites analyzed in a noninvasive manner, thereby allowing the continuous determination of systemic levels of various metabolites.

One metabolite that has been known to be present in plasma and urine is nitrate (NO_3^-).[1] Because saliva and lymph also contain substantial amounts of nitrite (NO_2^-) and NO_3^-, one would predict that other fluids such as CSF, bile, tears, sweat, and intraocular fluid also contain this low molecular weight metabolite.[2,3] In 1981 it was demonstrated that rodents and humans excrete much larger amounts of NO_3^- than could be accounted for by ingestion of food.[4] Subsequent studies revealed that germfree rats also excreted significantly more NO_3^- than could be accounted for by dietary ingestion, suggesting that mammalian cells have the biochemical

---

[1] H. H. Mitchell, H. A. Shonle, and H. S. Grindley, *J. Biol. Chem.* **24,** 461 (1916).
[2] J. Tenovuo, *Oral Pathol.* **15,** 303 (1986).
[3] S. Bodis and A. Haregewoin, *Biochem. Biophys. Res. Commun.* **194,** 347 (1993).
[4] L. C. Green, K. Ruiz de Luzuriaga, D. A. Wagner, and W. Rand, *Proc. Natl. Acad. Sci. U.S.A.* **78,** 7764 (1981).

machinery necessary to synthesize oxidized metabolites of nitrogen.[5] Subsequent studies from several disciplines converged to identify NO as the precursor of NO_3^- and an important secretory molecule involved in regulation of the immune, cardiovascular, and nervous systems.[6,7]

It has been known for many years that NO is relatively unstable in the presence of molecular oxygen (O_2) and will rapidly and spontaneously autoxidize in the gas phase to yield a variety of nitrogen oxides:

$$2NO + O_2 \rightarrow 2NO_2$$
$$2NO + 2NO_2 \rightarrow 2N_2O_3$$
$$2N_2O_3 + 2H_2O \rightarrow 4NO_2^- + 4H^+$$

where NO_2 and N_2O_3 represent nitrogen dioxide and dinitrogen trioxide, respectively.[8,9] Although this reaction pathway has been proposed to occur in aqueous (i.e., physiological) solutions, there is some controversy as to whether N_2O_3 is formed as an intermediate.[10,11] There is no doubt the only stable product formed by the spontaneous autoxidation of NO in oxygenated solutions is NO_2^-.[9] However, when one analyzes urine or plasma, predominantly NO_3^- is found in these extracellular fluids.[9] Although the mechanisms by which NO is converted to NO_3^- *in vivo* are not entirely clear, there are at least two possibilities. One mechanism, proposed by Ignarro *et al.*,[9] suggests that the NO_2^- derived from NO autoxidation is rapidly converted to NO_3^- via its oxidation by certain oxyhemoproteins ($P-Fe^{2+}O_2$) such as oxyhemoglobin or oxymyoglobin:

$$2P-Fe^{2+}O_2 + 3NO_2^- + 2H^+ \rightarrow 2P-Fe^{3+} + 3NO_3^- + H_2O$$

or

$$4P-Fe^{2+}O_2 + 4NO_2^- + 4H^+ \rightarrow 4P-Fe^{3+} + 4NO_3^- + O_2 + 2H_2O$$

It should be noted however, that these investigators used large concentrations of NO (300 μM) which will rapidly autoxidize to NO_2^-. Although the authors suggested that the NO_2^- would in turn react with the hemoproteins, this reaction is quite slow, requiring 2–3 hr.[9] A second, possibly more

[5] L. C. Green, S. R. Tannenbaum, and P. Goldman, *Science* **212**, 56 (1981).
[6] C. Nathan, *FASEB J.* **6**, 3051 (1992).
[7] S. Moncada and A. Higgs, *N. Engl. J. Med.* **329**, 2002 (1993).
[8] M. A. Marletta, *Chem. Res. Toxicol.* **1**, 249 (1988).
[9] L. J. Ignarro, J. M. Fukuto, J. M. Griscavage, N. E. Rogers, and R. E. Byrns, *Proc. Natl. Acad. Sci. U.S.A.* **90**, 8103 (1993).
[10] R. S. Lewis and D. M. Deen, *Chem. Res. Toxicol.* **7**, 568 (1994).
[11] D. A. Wink, J. F. Darbyshire, R. W. Nims, J. E. Saaverdra, and P. C. Ford, *Chem. Res. Toxicol.* **6**, 23 (1993).

reasonable explanation for the presence of predominately NO_3^- *in vivo* may have to do with the fact that the levels of NO produced by nitric oxide synthase (NOS) *in vivo* would be much smaller and thus the half-life of NO would be much longer. In this case, NO would react directly and very rapidly with oxyhemoproteins to yield NO_3^- before it has an opportunity to autoxidize to NO_2^-.[12] It should be noted that saliva does contain relatively high concentrations of NO_2^- which many investigators suggest is synthesized by the oral bacteria.[2,13]

There is a growing body of both clinical and experimental data which demonstrates that activation of the immune system, whether locally or systemically, is associated with an overproduction of NO. For example, it has been shown in experimental animals and humans that arthritis,[14,15] glomerular nephritis,[16] sepsis,[17] endotoxemia,[18,19] hepatitis,[20] colitis,[21–24] cytokine therapy,[25] graft versus host disease,[26] pulmonary inflammation,[27] and certain forms of chemotherapy[28] are associated with the upregulation of inducible NOS (iNOS) and the overproduction of NO as measured by increases in plasma and/or urinary levels of NO_2^- and NO_3^-.

Enhanced release of NO by inflammatory phagocytes and/or parenchymal cells may injure surrounding tissue by promoting intracellular iron

---

[12] M. P. Doyle and J. W. Hoekstra, *J. Inorg. Biochem.* **14**, 351 (1981).

[13] W. G. Zumft, *Arch. Microbiol.* **160**, 253 (1993).

[14] N. McCartney-Francis, J. B. Allen, D. E. Mizel, *et al., J. Exp. Med.* **178**, 749 (1993).

[15] A. J. Farrell, D. R. Blake, R. M. J. Palmer, and S. Moncada, *Ann. Rheum. Dis.* **51**, 1219 (1992).

[16] R. Sever, T. Cook, and V. Cattell, *Clin Exp. Immunol.* **90**, 326 (1992).

[17] J. B. Ochoa, A. O. Udekwu, T. R. Billiar, *et al., Ann. Surg.* **214**, 621 (1991).

[18] J. A. Mitchell, K. L. Kohlhaas, R. Sorrentino, T. D. Warner, F. Murad, and J. R. Vane, *Br. J. Pharmacol.* **109**, 265 (1993).

[19] C. Thiemermann, C. C. Wu, C. Szabo, M. Perretti, and J. R. Vane, *Br. J. Pharmacol.* **110**, 177 (1993).

[20] T. R. Billiar, R. D. Curran, B. G. Harbrecht, D. J. Stuehr, A. J. Demetris, and R. L. Simmons, *J. Leukocyte Biol.* **48**, 565 (1990).

[21] W. E. W. Roediger, M. J. Lawson, and B. C. Radcliffe, *Dis. Colon Rectum* **33**, 1034 (1990).

[22] S. J. Middleton, M. Shorthouse, and J. O. Hunter, *Lancet* **341**, 465 (1993).

[23] T. Yamada, R. B. Sartor, S. Marshall, R. D. Specian, and M. B. Grisham, *Gastroenterology* **104**, 759 (1993).

[24] N. K. Boughton-Smith, S. M. Evans, C. J. Hawkey, A. T. Cole, M. Balsitis, B. J. R. Whittle, and S. Moncado, *Lancet* **342**, 338 (1993).

[25] J. B. Hibbs, C. Westenfelder, R. Taintor, Z. Vavrin, C. Kablitz, R. L. Baranowski, J. H. Ward, R. L. Menlove, M. P. McMurry, J. P. Kushner, and W. E. Samlowski, *J. Clin. Invest.* **89**, 867 (1992).

[26] J. M. Langrehr, N. Murase, P. M. Markus, X. Cai, P. Neuhaus, W. Schraut, R. L. Simmons, and R. A. Hoffman, *J. Clin. Invest.* **90**, 679 (1992).

[27] M. S. Mulligan, J. M. Hevel, M. A. Marletta, and P. A. Ward, *Proc. Natl. Acad. Sci. U.S.A.* **88**, 6338 (1991).

[28] L. L. Thomsen, L. M. Ching, and B. C. Baguley, *Cancer Res.* **50**, 6966 (1990).

release, inhibition of mitochondrial function, and inhibition of DNA synthesis. It is known that NO production results in inhibition of three mitochondrial enzymes including aconitase (tricarboxylic acid cycle), NADH-ubiquinone oxidoreductase [NADH dehydrogenase (ubiquinone)], and succinate-ubiquinone oxidoreductase [succinate dehydrogenase (ubiquinone)] (complex I and complex II of the mitochondrial respiratory chain).[29–31] The inhibition is a result of the NO-mediated degradation of the iron–sulfur clusters associated with these three enzymes. This interaction may also account for the NO-mediated release of nonheme iron from certain target cells.[32,33] In addition, NO has been shown to inactivate ribonucleotide reductase, which is consistent with its ability to inhibit DNA synthesis.[34] Beckman and co-workers have suggested that the apparent toxicity of NO may be due to its ability to interact with superoxide (O_2^-) to yield the potent, cytotoxic oxidant peroxynitrite ($ONOO^-$).[35] Because many different pathophysiological conditions are associated with enhanced NO metabolism, a simple, sensitive, and inexpensive method to measure the stable NO-derived metabolites may provide an important tool for monitoring NO production and possibly disease activity *in vivo*.

This chapter outlines the methods used in our laboratory to quantify NO_2^- and NO_3^- in extracellular fluids such as plasma, urine, and/or lymph. The same methods may also be used for other extracellular fluids including saliva, tears, sweat, and possibly bile.

Preparation of Extracellular Fluids: Complications and Considerations

Determination of urinary or plasma levels of NO_3^- and NO_2^- provides a useful method to quantify systemic NO production. Although little is known regarding the ability of the kidneys to excrete, absorb, and/or synthesize NO_3^-, analysis of urine for the presence of nitrogen oxides remains one of the easiest methods to assess noninvasively systemic NO metabolism. It should be remembered that urinary (or plasma) NO_3^- levels reflect not only endogenous NO production but also total NO_3^- ingestion from the diet as well as the minor contribution made by bacterial metabolism of

[29] D. L. Granger, R. R. Taintor, J. L. Cook, and J. B. Hibbs, *J. Clin. Invest.* **65,** 357 (1980).
[30] J. C. Drapier and J. B. Hibbs, *J. Clin. Invest.* **78,** 790 (1986).
[31] J. C. Drapier and J. B. Hibbs, *J. Immunol.* **140,** 2829 (1988).
[32] J. B. Hibbs, R. R. Taintor, and Z. Vavrin, *Biochem. Biophys. Res. Commun.* **123,** 716 (1984).
[33] J. B. Hibbs, R. R. Taintor, and Z. Vavrin, *Biochem. Biophys. Res. Commun.* **123,** 716 (1984).
[34] N. S. Kwon, D. J. Stuehr, and C. F. Nathan, *J. Exp. Med.* **174,** 761 (1991).
[35] J. S. Beckman, J. Beckman, J. Chen, P. A. Marshall, and B. A. Freeman, *Proc. Natl. Acad. Sci. U.S.A.* **87,** 1620 (1990).

amino compounds in the gut. Thus, animals should either be fasted or allowed to ingest an NO_3^--/NO_2^--free diet in order to minimize dietary contributions of nitrogen oxides. It has been our experience that a 24-hr fast will reduce plasma NO_3^- levels by 60–80%, demonstrating that the majority of the circulating nitrate in rats is contributed by the diet. One also needs to be careful with long periods of fasting, however, since it is quite possible that extended fasting periods (36–48 hr) may downregulate or inhibit normal NO metabolism (M. B. Grisham and H. D. Battarbee, unpublished observations, 1995).

There are a few problems associated with the measurement of urinary NO_3^- that can be present significant interpretational difficulties and need to be addressed. First, state-of-the-art metabolic cages are very effective at sorting urine from formed fecal pellets. However, none of these cages prevent the introduction of fine food particles into the urine collection tubes. We have found that as rodents eat food pellets, small particle shavings or dust from the chow fall onto the collection tray below the wire bottom floor and are eventually washed into the urine collection tube by the flow of urine down this slanted surface. Obviously, this represents a significant problem in that these food particles contain substantial amounts of NO_3^- and NO_2^-.[36] We have found that using NO_3^--/NO_2^--free chow or fasting the animals during urine collection alleviates much of this problem.

Another potential problem arises when one is collecting urine from animals exhibiting moderate or severe diarrhea. The loose (and in some cases liquid) stools adhere to the collecting tray below the wire mesh floor and may be washed into the urine tubes by the flow of urine. We have found that certain water-soluble substances associated with the fecal material strongly inhibit the Griess reaction (M. B. Grisham and T. Yamada; unpublished data, 1993). Furthermore, it is important to include antibiotics in the collection tubes, for example, penicillin/streptomycin (100 U/ml each), to prevent bacterial growth during collection.

Finally, little is known regarding the ability of the kidneys to handle NO_3^-. It has been assumed that plasma NO_3^- is freely filterable and thus urinary levels of NO_3^- are an accurate reflection of systemic (i.e., plasma) levels. If, however, the kidney synthesizes and releases or concentrates filterable NO_3^-, then urinary NO_3^- levels would not accurately reflect blood levels of this nitrogen oxide. Wennmalm *et al.* suggest that plasma NO_3^- derived from inhaled NO is in fact freely filterable by the kidneys in humans.[37] More studies are needed to characterize physiological processing

[36] D. L. Granger, J. B. Hibbs, and L. M. Broadnax, *J. Immunol.* **146,** 1294 (1991).
[37] A. Wennmalm, G. Benthin, A. Edlund, L. Jungersten, N. Keiler-Jensen, S. Lundin, U. N. Westfelt, A. Petersson, and F. Waagstein, *Circ. Res.* **73,** 1121 (1993).

of nitrogen oxides by the kidneys. Nevertheless, urine can be frozen at $-70°$ and analyzed at a future time.

The collection and processing of plasma and lymph also require some precaution. We have found that heparinized plasma or lymph may form a precipitate on addition of the highly acidic Griess reagent, rendering these samples unusable for analysis. Interestingly, the precipitation does not occur in all samples and will occasionally occur even when protein is first removed by addition of $ZnSO_4$ or ultrafiltration (M. B. Grisham, G. G. Johnson, and R. L. Lancaster, Jr., unpublished data, 1994). Because of these inconsistent results it has been difficult to determine the mechanism of this precipitation reaction. We have discovered that the presence of heparin may promote precipitation of the plasma or lymph samples when acidified by the Griess reagent. We propose that the inability to produce consistent precipitation in all samples may be a result of the small but significantly different amounts of heparin used for each sample, as the volume of heparin is never accurately measured when using this anticoagulant. We have found that the use of citrate as an anticoagulant or allowing plasma to clot to yield serum completely prevents this problem. We have also determined that when the need arises to assess plasma or lymph NO_3^- and NO_2^- levels in heparinized fluid, we can do so if the heparin is removed using protamine sulfate precipitation prior to addition of the Griess reagent. Details of the methods for this procedure are outlined below.

Determination of Nitrate and Nitrite

One method for the indirect determination of NO involves the spectrophotometric measurement of its stable decomposition products. This method requires that NO_3^- first be reduced to NO_2^- and then NO_2^- determined by the Griess reaction. We have found enzymatic reduction of NO_3^- to NO_2^- using a commercially available preparation of nitrate reductase to be the most satisfactory method. *Aspergillus* nitrate reductase (NADPH: nitrate oxidoreductase, EC 1.6.6.2; Boehringer Mannheim, Indianapolis, IN) is commercially available and highly efficient at reducing very small amounts of NO_3^- to NO_2^-.[38] For convenience, stock solutions of nitrate reductase (10 U/ml) are prepared by dissolving the lyophilized powder in distilled water via stirring for 30 min at room temperature to ensure complete dissolution of the enzyme. Small aliquots (100 μl) are frozen at $-70°$ for future use. We have found no noticeable change in activity over several weeks or months when the enzyme prepared and stored in this manner.

[38] H. H. H. W. Schmidt, T. D. Warner, M. Nakane, U. Forstermann, and F. Murad, *Mol. Pharmacol.* **41,** 615 (1992).

The following solutions are recommended for the assay:

10 U/ml *Aspergillus* nitrate reductase (kept on ice until use)
1 *M* HEPES buffer (pH 7.4) (Sigma, St. Louis, MO) (may be kept at 4°)
0.1 m*M* Flavin adenine dinucleotide, disodium salt (FAD; Sigma)
1 m*M* Nicotinamide adenine dinucleotide phosphate, reduced form, tetrasodium salt (NADPH; Sigma)
1500 U/ml Lactate dehydrogenase (LDH; bovine muscle, Sigma)
100 m*M* Pyruvic acid, sodium salt, type II (Sigma)
Griess reagent (equal volumes of 0.2% (w/v) naphthyleneethylenediamine and 2% (w/v) sulfanilamide in 5% (v/v) phosphoric acid)

When the nitrate reductase, FAD, NADPH, and LDH are placed on ice, they may be used during the entire day. These solutions should, however, be made fresh each day.

The following protocol is used to determine total NO_3^- and NO_2^-:

1. A 100-μl aliquot of the sample (urine, citrated plasma, lymph, or serum) is incubated 30 min at 37° in the presence of 0.2 U/ml *Aspergillus* nitrate reductase, 50 m*M* HEPES buffer, 5 μ*M* FAD, and 0.1 m*M* NADPH in a total volume of 500 μl as outlined in Table I (sample 1 serves as the blank)

2. Following the incubation, 5 μl of lactate dehydrogenase (1500 U/ml) and 50 μl of 100 m*M* pyruvic acid are added to each tube to oxidize any unreacted NADPH. This LDH-catalyzed oxidation of NADPH is essential

TABLE I
EXPERIMENTAL DESIGN USING *Aspergillus* NITRATE REDUCTASE[a]

Tube	Water	1 *M* HEPES (pH 7.4)	Sample	0.1 m*M* FAD	1 m*M* NADPH	10 U/ml Nitrate reductase
1	390 μl	25 μl	0	25 μl	50 μl	10 μl
2	290 μl	25 μl	100 μl	25 μl	50 μl	10 μl

[a] Either borosilicate culture or polypropylene microcentrifuge tubes may be used for the assay. To determine the concentration of nitrite and nitrate in each sample, the following formula is used:

$$\text{Total nitrate and nitrite } (\mu M) = \frac{(A_{543} \text{ sample} - A \text{ blank})(\text{dilution factor})}{\text{slope}}$$

The dilution factor used in our protocol is 5, because the 100-μl sample is diluted to a total volume of 500 μl. The slope is determined experimentally using known concentrations of nitrite and nitrate (Fig. 1).

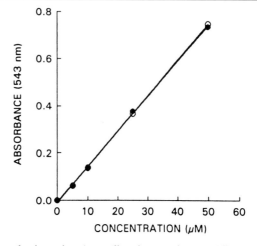

Fig. 1. Nitrate reduction using *Aspergillus* nitrate reductase. All assays were performed in the presence of 100 μl of 24-hr fasted plasma as described in the text. Nitrite standards were included for comparison. Basal levels of nitrate and nitrite in the fasted plasma were subtracted from all samples. Each symbol represents the mean value obtained from six different determinations. Open circles represent nitrate values, whereas filled circles represent the nitrite standards. Data derived from Ref. 42 with permission.

because reduced pyridine nucleotides (NADPH, NADH) strongly inhibit the Griess reaction.[39]

3. Samples are then incubated for an additional 10 min at 37°. An alternative method for oxidizing any unreacted NADPH is to replace the LDH/pyruvate system with 1 mM potassium ferricyanide. Samples are incubated for 10 min at 25° and then processed as described in Step 4. It is important to maintain the temperature at 25° to ensure optimal enzymatic activity. Nitrate reductase is known to catalyze the NADPH-dependent reduction of ferricyanide such that all NADPH is consumed and eliminated from the reaction volume.[40,41]

4. One milliliter of premixed Griess reagent is then added to each tube. After a 10-min incubation at room temperature, the absorbance of each sample is determined at 543 nm.

5. If nitrate or nitrite levels are to be determined individually, then two sets of samples must be analyzed with nitrate reductase omitted from one

[39] A. Medina and D. J. D. Nicholas, *Biochim. Biophys. Acta* **23,** 440 (1957).
[40] J. R. Lancaster, Jr., C. J. Batie, H. Kamin, and D. B. Knaff, *in* "Methods in Chloroplast Molecular Biology" (M. Edelman, R. B. Hallick, and N.-H. Chua, eds.), p. 723. Elsevier, Amsterdam, 1982.
[41] C. J. Kay and M. J. Barber, *J. Biol. Chem.* **261,** 14125 (1986).

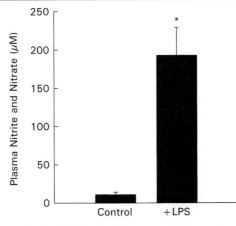

FIG. 2. Lipopolysaccharide (LPS)-induced increases in plasma nitrate and nitrite. Fasted (24 hr) rats were injected intraperitoneally with either saline (control; $n = 3$) or LPS (4 mg/kg; $n = 3$) and plasma NO_3^- and NO_2^- determined at 12 hr postinjection. Data derived from Ref. 42 with permission. *$P < 0.05$ compared to control.

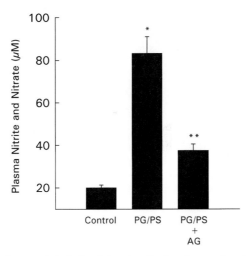

FIG. 3. Plasma nitrate and nitrite levels in rats with chronic granulomatous colitis. Chronic granulomatous colitis with liver and spleen inflammation was induced in rats via the intramural (subserosal) injection of sterile, endotoxin-free peptidoglycan/polysaccharide (PG/PS) into the distal colon ($n = 10$). Controls received injections of sterile saline ($n = 7$). One group of animals received the nitric oxide synthase inhibitor aminoguanidine (2 μmol/kg/day) beginning 2 days before PG/PS injection and continuing for the entire 3-week period (PG/PS + AG; $n = 7$). Fasted (24 hr) plasma was obtained from all animals at 3 weeks following the induction of colitis. Data derived from Ref. 42 with permission. *$P < 0.05$ compared to control and **$P < 0.05$ compared to PG/PS group.

set of samples. Griess-positive reactions in these samples will indicate the presence of nitrite only. Nitrate concentrations may then be calculated from the difference between values obtained in the presence and absence of nitrate reductase (see Figs. 1, 2, and 3).[42]

We have found that the presence of heparin in plasma or lymph samples may produce precipitation on addition of the Griess reagent. Therefore, heparin must be removed prior to the addition of the Griess reagent. Following the incubation with LDH and pyruvic acid (Step 3), 10–100 μl of a 10 mg/ml solution of protamine sulfate (Sigma) should be added to each tube; the tubes are then vortexed and incubated 5 min at room temperature. The tubes are centrifuged for 10 min at 10,000 rpm at 25° to remove the insoluble heparin–protamine complex. The supernatants are then transferred to glass culture tubes. One milliliter of Griess reagent is added to each supernatant, and the samples are incubated 10 min at room temperature. The absorbance of each sample is then determined at 543 nm. The volume and concentration of protamine sulfate are based on the fact that 1 mg of protamine sulfate will neutralize approximately 90 USP units of heparin derived from beef lung or about 115 USP units of heparin derived from porcine intestinal mucosa. Knowing the exact amount of heparin present in each sample is not essential to determine the amount of protamine sulfate to use. We have found that an approximation of the amount of heparin present is sufficient to estimate the amount of protamine sulfate to be used.

Acknowledgments

This work was supported by grants from the National Institutes of Health: CA63641 (M. B. G.), DK47663 (M. B. G.), and DK46935 (J. R. L.), and by the American Cancer Society (BE-128; J. R. L.). We would also like to acknowledge the excellent technical assistance of John Bovastro. Much of the work reported in this chapter was originally published in the journal *Methods: A Companion to Methods in Enzymology* **7**, 84–90 (1995).

---

[42] M. B. Grisham, G. G. Johnson, M. D. Gautreaux, and R. D. Berg, *Methods (San Diego)* **7**, 84 (1995).

[24] Stirred Reactor with Continuous Nitric Oxide Sampling for Use in Kinetic Studies

By RANDY S. LEWIS and WILLIAM M. DEEN

Introduction

The multifaceted role of nitric oxide (NO) as both a biological messenger and a cytotoxic or carcinogenic agent[1] has made it important to measure the kinetics of various reactions involving NO. We describe here a novel reactor that has proved useful in studying the kinetics of several such reactions in oxygenated solutions.[2,3] A key feature of the apparatus is the ability to monitor continuously the aqueous NO concentration. The system for sampling and analysis of NO has a response time of only a few seconds, making it possible to obtain real-time measurements when studying rate processes that have characteristic times exceeding about 1 min. The approach is versatile, in that it has been shown that the same system can be used to study the rate of formation of NO and several of its reaction products in suspension cultures of macrophages.[4]

Systems of this type can be constructed in a variety of sizes and configurations, depending on their intended application. In this chapter we focus on the factors that affect apparatus design and data interpretation. A systematic review of what is known about the kinetics of NO reactions in aqueous solutions is beyond the scope of the present discussion. Kinetic results are mentioned only briefly at the end, as examples of the utilty of this experimental approach.

Apparatus

General Considerations

The basic concept we have used for sampling of aqueous NO, which may be implemented in a variety of ways, is to allow NO to enter a detector via diffusion across a gas-permeable membrane.[5] Mass spectrometers and

[1] S. Moncada, R. M. J. Palmer, and E. A. Higgs, *Pharmacol. Rev.* **43,** 109 (1991).
[2] R. S. Lewis and W. M. Deen, *Chem. Res. Toxicol.* **7,** 568 (1994).
[3] R. S. Lewis, S. R. Tannenbaum, and W. M. Deen, *J. Am. Chem. Soc.* **117,** 3933 (1995).
[4] R. S. Lewis, S. Tamir, S. R. Tannenbaum, and W. M. Deen, *J. Biol. Chem.* **270,** 29350 (1995).
[5] R. S. Lewis, W. M. Deen, S. R. Tannenbaum, and J. S. Wishnok, *Biol. Mass Spectrom.* **22,** 45 (1992).

chemiluminescence instruments are both suitable detectors for NO; we have preferred chemiluminescence on the basis of cost, selectivity, and convenience. The type of chemiluminescence instrument needed for this application is one in which a stable vacuum can be maintained with the inlet line closed (i.e., blocked by a membrane); some instruments designed specifically for ambient air monitoring will not operate properly in this configuration. Whether mass spectrometry or chemiluminescence is employed, it is not necessary that the membrane be selective for NO relative to O_2 or other gases, because other gases do not ordinarily interfere with the NO signal. An exception is that if NO_2 is present at a concentration comparable to that of NO, formation of NO^+ in a mass spectrometer due to fragmentation of NO_2^+ can lead to artificially high NO readings.[5] This is unlikely to be a problem with most physiological solutions, because the ratio of the NO_2 to the NO concentration is predicted to be quite small.[2,3] Because the membrane does not have to be highly selective, a wide variety of materials should be adequate, including polymeric membranes designed for gas separations and various microporous membranes. The main requirement is that the membrane be sufficiently permeable to NO to give the desired sensitivity and time response; the relationship between membrane properties and detector response is discussed in the section on measurement of NO concentration. We have employed polydimethylsiloxane (Silastic) because it exhibits a high NO permeability[6] and is available in several forms (sheet or tubing in various dimensions).

For kinetic studies of the type described here the reactor is a small vessel containing a fixed amount of liquid that is stirred at a carefully controlled rate. Provision is made for membrane sampling of NO and for continuous flow of O_2 or other desired gases through the head space. Because the reactor is an open system with respect to NO and other dissolved gases, it is important to determine the rates of mass transfer through the membrane inlet and across the gas–liquid interface. As described later (see section on reactor modeling and data interpretation), this is done using a series of measurements made in the absence of chemical reactions. The reactor size and shape, the rate of stirring, and the positioning and surface area of the membrane inlet are all factors that must be taken into account in the design.

Reactor Design

We employ as a reactor a modified ultrafiltration cell with a capacity of 200 ml (Amicon, Danvers, MA, Model 8200), as shown in Fig. 1. To

[6] W. L. Robb, *Ann. N.Y. Acad. Sci.* **46,** 119 (1968).

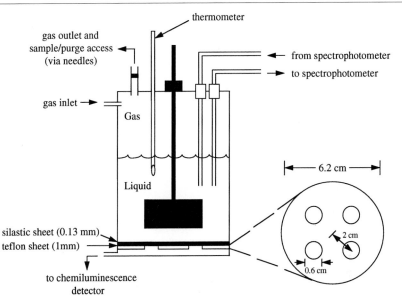

FIG. 1. Schematic of apparatus used to study the kinetics of NO reactions in aqueous solutions. A composite membrane at the base of the reactor allowed continuous entry of NO into a chemiluminescence detector. A flow loop connected to a spectrophotometer made it possible to continuously monitor the concentrations of certain other species, such as NO_2^-. (Reprinted with permission from Ref. 2, © 1994 American Chemical Society.)

make the reactor more suitable for studies with cell suspensions, the stirrer is replaced with that from a CYTOSTIR bioreactor (Kontes, Vineland, NJ). The base of the ultrafiltration cell is fitted with a composite membrane of 6.2 cm diameter consisting of a 0.13 mm thick sheet of Silastic (Membrane Products, Albany, NY; MEM-100) attached with silicone adhesive to a 1 mm thick sheet of polytetrafluoroethylene (Teflon). The Teflon sheet, which contains four symmetrically positioned holes of 0.6 cm diameter, is used to limit the amount of NO entering the chemiluminescence detector (Thermedics Detection, Woburn, MA; Model TEA-502). The composite membrane is seated on a stainless steel mesh within the base of the stirred cell. This provides space for a vacuum to develop below the membrane when the base of the cell is connected to the detector. The connection is made via a 1/8 inch stainless steel tube soldered to the base of the cell (also made of stainless steel). The vacuum developed in the detector provides the partial-pressure driving force for NO diffusion across the base of the reactor, from the aqueous solution to the chemiluminescence instrument.

The stock ultrafiltration cell includes a gas inlet port. As shown in Fig. 1, we add a septum port, a thermometer, and two ports for a 1/8 inch diameter flow loop which can be connected to a spectrophotometer. A 20-gauge hypodermic needle inserted in the septum port is used as a gas outlet. Flow through the external loop is maintained with a pulseless pump (Cole-Parmer Instrument, Chicago, IL; Models 000-305 and 184-000) at approximately 50 ml/min through a 10-mm spectrophotometer flow cell. To ensure that the flow loop does not significantly impede mixing in the reactor, the volume of the flow loop is made much smaller than that of the reactor contents.

Measurement of Nitric Oxide Concentration

Calibration

To calibrate the chemiluminescence detector, a mixture of nitric oxide and argon is prepared by mixing the two gases at a tee junction using controlled gas flowmeters (Porter Instrument, Hatfield, PA). Prior to mixing, argon is passed through an oxygen trap. Following mixing, the calibration gas is passed through a column (1.7 cm o.d., 50 cm length) packed with 4–8 mesh soda lime for removal of possible NO_x impurities.

The solution to be used (typically 150 ml of 10 mM phosphate buffer at pH 7.4) is added to the reactor, and stirring is initiated at the desired rate (usually 100 rpm for cell-free systems). To provide more rapid gas exchange than could be achieved using the regular gas inlet, a hypodermic needle (20-gauge) is connected to the calibration gas supply and inserted into the solution via the septum port. Initially, argon is bubbled into the solution for at least 40 min to remove O_2, after which NO is added to the argon to achieve the desired NO concentration in the calibration gas. The steady-state detector response (~10–20 min after NO introduction) corresponds to the saturated aqueous NO concentration as calculated from the solubility of NO in water, which is 0.019 and 0.016 M/MPa for NO at 23° and 37°, respectively.[7] Using a buffer of low ionic strength is desirable because it limits the effects of various anions on the NO solubility.[8] The calibration is valid only for experiments performed at the same stirring speed, for the reasons discussed below.

The response of the detector is found to be linear up to NO concentrations of at least 40 μM. The minimum detectable concentration at a stirring rate of 100 rpm is estimated to be around 0.01 μM (at a signal-to-noise ratio of 3).[2]

[7] N. A. Lange, "Lange's Handbook of Chemistry," 10th Ed., McGraw-Hill, New York, 1967.
[8] A. Schumpe, *Chem. Eng. Sci.* **48**, 153 (1993).

Factors That Affect Nitric Oxide Sensitivity

The sensitivity that can be achieved in NO concentration measurements by this method depends not only on the intrinsic properties of the chemiluminescence detector but also on the design of the reactor and sampling system. The signal from the detector is proportional to the rate at which NO enters the instrument, denoted here as m_{NO} (e.g., in mol/sec). In addition to the aqueous NO concentration, the factors that control m_{NO} are the dimensions (thickness and exposed area) and physical properties (NO diffusivity and solubility) of the membrane inlet, and the rate of mass transfer from the bulk contents of the reactor to the membrane surface. For a reactor of the type shown in Fig. 1, these factors are related according to

$$m_{NO} = k_B A_B C_{NO} \qquad (1)$$

where k_B is the overall mass transfer coefficient for NO at the base of the reactor and A_B is the exposed area of membrane. Thus, the detector signal is proportional to the aqueous concentration of nitric oxide, C_{NO}, but the proportionality factor depends on the mass transfer resistance exhibited by the membrane inlet. Increases in the mass transfer coefficient and/or membrane area will lower the NO concentration at which one will achieve a given value of m_{NO}, thereby increasing sensitivity. Decreases in the mass transfer coefficient and/or area will have the opposite effect, reducing sensitivity.

The membrane area can be increased, of course, by employing a stirred reactor of larger diameter. For a given diameter, the exposed area can be decreased by covering part of the membrane, as done in our design. The overall mass transfer coefficient at the base of the stirred reactor is determined by the membrane permeability coefficient (k_M) and the aqueous-phase mass transfer coefficient at the base (k_A). The mass transfer resistances in the membrane and solution are in series, so that

$$1/k_B = 1/k_M + 1/k_A \qquad (2)$$

The membrane permeability coefficient equals the effective diffusivity (based on aqueous concentrations) divided by the membrane thickness. The aqueous-phase mass transfer coefficient depends in part on the effectiveness of the mixing; for small reactors and moderate stirring rates, such that the flow is laminar (as in our system), k_A varies inversely with the square root of the stirring speed.[9] Accordingly, k_B can be increased by employing a thinner membrane and/or a higher stirring speed, depending on which of the two terms on the right-hand side of Eq. (2) is most important.

[9] C. K. Colton and K. A. Smith, *AIChE J.* **18**, 958 (1972).

When using any concentration sensor which works by removing some of the substance it measures, the need for sensitivity must be weighed against the extent to which it is permissible to perturb the system under study. Thus, when employing chemiluminescence to monitor NO continuously, the rate processes that one seeks to study will impose upper bounds on m_{NO}, and therefore also on $k_B A_B$. Ideally, m_{NO} should be a small fraction of the rate at which NO is being formed or consumed in the experimental system.

The fact that only small amounts of NO need to be withdrawn for chemiluminescence detection is illustrated by calculations for the system shown in Fig. 1. On the basis of the solubility and diffusivity of NO in Silastic,[6] we calculate that k_M was 7×10^{-3} and 9×10^{-3} cm/sec at 23° and 37°, respectively. At a stirring rate of 100 rpm, the corresponding values of k_A were found to be 6×10^{-3} and 8×10^{-3} cm/sec (for the methods used, see section on reactor modeling and data interpretation). Thus, the membrane and aqueous-phase resistances were roughly equal. Based on Eq. (2), k_B was 3×10^{-3} and 4×10^{-3} cm/sec at 23° and 37°, respectively. With $A_B = 1.1$ cm^2 (the total area of the four holes in the Teflon sheet) and $C_{NO} = 0.01$ μM, we estimate from Eq. (1) that the minimum detectable flow of NO through the instrument was approximately 0.04 pmol/sec.

Factors That Affect Nitric Oxide Time Response

When using either mass spectrometry or chemiluminescence, we have found that the response when measuring NO is approximately exponential in time, with a time constant τ. That is, if the final (steady-state) detector response is unity, the transient signal is of the form $[1 - \exp(-t/\tau)]$, where t is time. We have found that the value of τ, which is on the order of a few seconds, is governed mainly by the time delay for diffusion through the membrane inlet. A theoretical model for transient diffusion through a membrane in contact with a flowing solution has been shown to yield reliable predictions for the response time.[5] For a membrane inlet contacting a liquid solution, as in Fig. 1, the theoretical value of τ is given by

$$\tau \cong \delta^2/D_{NO}\beta_1^2 \tag{3}$$

where δ is the thickness of the membrane and D_{NO} is the diffusivity of NO in the membrane material. The quantity β_1 is the smallest positive root of the equation

$$\beta \cot \beta + Bi = 0 \tag{4}$$

where Bi, the Biot number, is a dimensionless group defined as

$$Bi \equiv k_A/k_M \tag{5}$$

Thus, Bi is the mass transfer resistance in the membrane divided by that in the aqueous solution. When Bi is small compared to unity, the dominant resistance is that in the solution; when Bi is large, the dominant resistance to diffusion is in the membrane.

Equation (3) indicates that thin membranes with large diffusivities for NO will give the fastest responses (i.e., the smallest values of τ). For membrane inlets in contact with stirred gases, Bi is effectively infinite,[5] and Eq. (4) gives $\beta_1 = \pi$. In such cases τ is simply proportional to the square of the membrane thickness. For membrane inlets used to sample aqueous solutions, the mass transfer resistance in the solution is not ordinarily negligible and Bi is finite. Because Bi is inversely related to the membrane permeability coefficient [Eq. (5)], it is directly proportional to the membrane thickness. Accordingly, the value of β_1 will depend on the membrane thickness, and the relationship between δ and τ will be more complicated than for gas sampling. For a given membrane, as the diffusional resistance in the liquid increases, β_1 because smaller and τ becomes larger. The use of very thin and/or highly permeable membranes for aqueous sampling can decrease the response time, but only to a limited extent, because τ eventually will be controlled entirely by the aqueous mass transfer resistance. In other words, the inability to achieve perfect mixing in the liquid limits the improvements that can be made in response time.

For the system in Fig. 1, $Bi \cong 0.9$ at 100 rpm. With this value of Bi, the smallest root from Eq. (4) is $\beta_1 = 2$. With $\delta = 0.013$ cm and $D_{NO} = 1 \times 10^{-5}$ cm^2/sec (an estimate for Silastic material that has not been subjected to heating[5]), the value of τ predicted by Eq. (3) is 4 sec.

Reactor Modeling and Data Interpretation

Mass Balance Equations

In an open system such as that depicted in Fig. 1, the concentrations of NO and other relevant chemical species are affected not only by their rates of reaction, but also by transport in and out of the reactor. To interpret time-dependent concentration data in terms of specific rate processes, it is necessary to employ mass balance equations for each of the chemical species involved. In a well-mixed reactor of the type shown in Fig. 1, changes in the concentration C_i of species i are described by

$$dC_i/dt = R_i + S_i - (k_B A_B/V)_i C_i - (k_G A_G/V)_i (C_i - C_i^*) \qquad (6)$$

The volumetric rate of formation of species i by chemical reactions (e.g., in M/sec) is represented by R_i. For a complex chemical system, such as an oxygenated NO solution, R_i may depend on the kinetics of multiple reactions, and it may be a function not only of C_i but also the concentrations of several other species.[2,3] According to whether there is net formation or net loss of i by all chemical reactions, R_i will turn out to be positive or negative, respectively.

In modeling stirred suspensions of cells one may need an additional source term in Eq. (6), written as S_i, that represents the rate at which i enters the extracellular solution as a result of cellular metabolism. Again, S_i may be positive or negative. Release of NO synthesized by suspended macrophages[4] is an example where $S_{NO} > 0$. The reason that cellular metabolism is accounted for in this way is because the mass balance in Eq. (6) is based on the volume of extracellular fluid, denoted as V. Thus, suspended cells act as sources or sinks distributed throughout the reactor volume.

The last two terms in Eq. (6) account for species i leaving the solution by either of two physical pathways, namely, mass transfer into the detector and through the gas–liquid interface. The term $(k_B A_B / V)_i$ is the volumetric mass transfer coefficient for movement of species i through the base of the reactor and into the NO detector. The small rates of NO transport into the chemiluminescence detector have already been discussed (see section on measurement of NO concentration); other dissolved gases, such as O_2, are also removed slowly in this manner. The remaining term in Eq. (6) represents transport across the gas–liquid interface at the top of the reactor, which for our apparatus was very important.[2] It is assumed here that the gas-phase resistance to mass transfer is negligible, so that the mass transfer coefficient k_G refers only to the liquid side of the gas–liquid interface. The surface area A_G is that based on the full diameter of the reactor ($A_G = 30$ cm^2 for the reactor in Fig. 1). The aqueous concentration that would be in equilibrium with the gas-phase concentration for species i is denoted as C_i^*. Thus, the rate of loss to the headspace is proportional to $C_i - C_i^*$. At high rates of gas flow through the headspace (we typically used 300–350 std. cm^3/min), C_i^* is affected very little by transport into or out of the liquid; rather, it is controlled by the partial pressures in the inlet gas and by the solubility of each gas component in water.

Computer simulations of the various time-dependent concentrations are needed for fitting rate constants to measured concentrations, or for predicting the concentrations of species which could not be measured. Such simulations are performed by solving the set of mass balance equations obtained by applying Eq. (6) to all of the key chemical species. For species that are of interest but are present only in trace amounts, pseudo-steady-state approximations can be used to convert the corresponding differential equations to algebraic equations,[2,3] thereby reducing the number of differential equations that must be solved simultaneously. There are several methods for solving sets of first-order, ordinary differential equations of the type given by Eq. (6), subject to specified concentrations at $t = 0$. A discussion of the practical aspects of various methods, including FORTRAN source codes, is given by Press *et al.*[10] We have employed a semi-implicit Runge–Kutta algorithm.[11]

Experimental Evaluation of Mass Transfer Coefficients

To calculate the physical losses of NO (or other species) from the reactor, experimental values are needed for the volumetric mass transfer coefficients in Eq. (6), namely, $(k_B A_B / V)$ and $(k_G A_G / V)$. It has been seen already in Eq. (2) that the factors that determine k_B are k_M and k_A, and the evaluation of k_M for NO has been discussed. Liquid-phase mass transfer coefficients for a given vessel operated at a specified stirring rate differ in predictable ways among various solutes, according to their diffusivities. An effective strategy for determining k_A and k_G for NO and other species of interest is to measure each coefficient under a single set of conditions, and then to use laminar boundary layer theory[12] to extrapolate those results to other solutes and temperatures.

Benzoic acid was chosen as a convenient solute for the measurement of k_A in the reactor of Fig. 1. The Teflon sheet (without the Silastic layer) is first placed on a metal surface in a freezer for at least 10 min. Benzoic acid pellets are melted in a beaker and immediately poured into the four holes of the Teflon sheet. (The cold surface helps to achieve a uniform crystal structure.) After crystallization, the benzoic acid is sanded smooth, and the reactor is assembled with the Teflon–benzoic acid sheet at the base. Deionized water in the usual volume (150 ml) is added, and stirring is begun at the desired rate (100 rpm). The reactor and a saturated solution of benzoic acid are placed in the same water bath (at ambient temperature) to ensure that both are at the same temperature throughout the experiment. The solution in the reactor is sampled several times with a syringe (at 10- to 20-min intervals), and the saturated solution is sampled at the end of the experiment. Each sample is assayed with a spectrophotometer at 271 nm.

[10] W. H. Press, B. P. Flannery, S. A. Teukolsky, and W. T. Vetterling, "Numerical Recipes." Cambridge Univ. Press, Cambridge, 1986.
[11] M. L. Michelsen, *AIChE J.* **22,** 594 (1976).
[12] T. K. Sherwood, R. L. Pigford, and C. R. Wilke, "Mass Transfer." McGraw-Hill, New York, 1975.

The differential mass balance equation for benzoic acid, analogous to Eq. (6), is

$$dC_{ben}/dt = (k_A A_B/V)_{ben}(C^*_{ben} - C_{ben}) \tag{7}$$

where C_{ben} and C^*_{ben} are the concentrations of benzoic acid in the bulk of the reactor and in a saturated solution, respectively. Integration of Eq. (7) leads to

$$\ln[1 - C_{ben}(t)/C^*_{ben}] = (k_A A_B/V)_{ben} t \tag{8}$$

Thus, plotting the benzoic acid data versus time in the manner suggested by Eq. (8) yields a straight line with a slope equivalent to $k_A A_B/V$ for benzoic acid.

The value of k_A for any other solute i is calculated according to

$$(k_A)_i/(k_A)_{ben} = (D_i/D_{ben})^{2/3} \tag{9}$$

where D_i and D_{ben} are the respective diffusivities in water. Equation (9) is appropriate for concentration boundary layers adjacent to solid–liquid interfaces.[12] The aqueous diffusivities (10^{-5} cm^2/sec) are 2.7 and 5.1 for NO at 23° and 37°, respectively.[13] The benzoic acid diffusivity is approximately 1.1 at 23°.[14] Thus, for example, the value of k_A given earlier for NO at 37° is 2.8 times the value measured for benzoic acid at 23°. The same approach was used to calculate k_A for oxygen.[2]

The determination of $k_G A_G/V$ is based on measurements of NO disappearance from the reactor in the absence of oxygen, which eliminated the effects of chemical reactions. Removal of O$_2$ and addition of NO follow the same protocol outlined in the section on the calibration of NO concentration measurements. When the desired steady-state concentration for NO is observed with the detector, the hypodermic needle used for adding NO is removed from the septum, and the residual NO in the headspace is continuously flushed out for the remainder of the experiment by admitting inert gas (at approximately 300 std. cm^3/min) through the gas inlet. This ensures that $C^*_{NO} \cong 0$. With no reaction or source terms and no NO in the headspace, integration of Eq. (6) for NO gives

$$\ln[C_{NO}(t)/C_{NO}(0)] = -(k_G A_G/V + k_B A_B/V)_{NO} t \tag{10}$$

Linear regression based on Eq. (10) is used to determine the sum of the volumetric mass transfer coefficients. This allows $k_G A_G/V$ to be calculated by difference, using the value of $k_B A_B/V$ obtained from the membrane

[13] D. L. Wise and G. Houghton, *Chem. Eng. Sci.* **23**, 1211 (1968).
[14] S. Y. Chang. S. M. Thesis, Massachusetts Institute of Technology, Cambridge, MA (1949).

properties and benzoic acid data. It was found that 97% of the physical losses of NO were through the gas–liquid interface, with only 3% entering the detector. For example, the values of $(k_G A_G/V)_{NO}$ and $(k_B A_B/V)_{NO}$ at 37° were 9.9×10^{-4} and 0.3×10^{-4} sec^{-1}, respectively.

The calculation of k_G for other species (e.g., O_2) at the gas–liquid interface is again based on laminar boundary layer theory. For the liquid side of a gas–liquid interface, the appropriate relation is[12]

$$(k_G)_i/(k_G)_{NO} = (D_i/D_{NO})^{1/2} \tag{11}$$

The values of k_B for O_2 are almost the same as those for NO, whereas the values of k_G for O_2 are 8–20% lower than those for NO. The relatively fast mass transfer at the gas–liquid interface helps to maintain the supply of O_2 from the gas phase, whereas the restricted area at the base of the reactor minimizes the loss of O_2 as well as NO.

Applications in Studies of Nitric Oxide Reaction Kinetics

Kinetics of Nitric Oxide Oxidation

Perhaps the most fundamental reaction of NO in biological fluids is its reaction with molecular oxygen. The stirred reactor has been used to study the kinetics of the reaction of NO with O_2 in buffer solutions, as reported previously.[2] In these experiments O_2 is purged and NO is added to 150 ml of 10 mM phosphate buffer solution at pH 7.4, following the protocol described in the section on the calibration of NO concentration measurements. After removal of the hypodermic needle used to bubble in the NO, the gas phase is purged via the gas inlet at 300 std. cm^3/min for 1 min to remove NO from the headspace. After that, a gas mixture with the desired O_2 concentration is flowed continuously through the headspace (via the gas inlet) for the remainder of the experiment. Oxidation of the dissolved NO is initiated by diffusion of O_2 into the aqueous solution. The principal end product of this reaction is nitrite (NO_2^-). Accordingly, in addition to monitoring the aqueous concentration of NO, continuous measurements of the NO_2^- concentration are obtained by recirculating fluid through a spectrophotometer and determining the absorbance at 209 nm.

At initial NO concentrations of 10–30 μM, the reaction is complete within about 30 min. When physical losses (primarily into the headspace) are taken into account, virtually all of the initial NO could be accounted for as NO or NO_2^-, confirming that other NO_x species are present only in trace amounts. The rate constant for the reaction of NO with O_2 is determined by choosing the value in the kinetic model[2] that minimizes the difference between the measured NO concentrations and the numerical

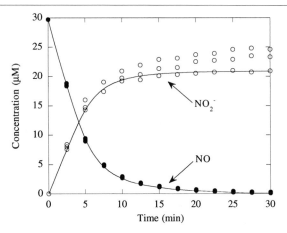

FIG. 2. Change in NO and NO_2^- concentrations with time during the reaction of NO with O_2 at 37° and pH 7.4. An initial NO concentration of 30 μM was present in the liquid when O_2 was introduced into the gas phase (time 0); thereafter, the gas was maintained at 21% O_2. Selected data points obtained from the continuous concentration measurements are shown by the symbols. The curves are from computer simulations based on a kinetic model for the oxidation of NO.[2]

solution of Eq. (6) for NO. Representative concentration data are given in Fig. 2, which shows the close correspondence between the measured NO concentrations and the NO curve computed with the kinetic model. Also shown in Fig. 2 is the very satisfactory agreement obtained between the NO_2^- concentration data and the model, using the same rate constants.

Kinetics of N-Nitrosation of Morpholine

The aqueous reaction of NO with O_2 generates a trace intermediate, most likely N_2O_3, that nitrosates secondary amines to form N-nitrosamines.[3,15,16] A variety of N-nitrosamines lead to DNA damage,[17] so that the kinetics of N-nitrosation at physiological pH are important for assessing the carcinogenic potential of NO. The stirred reactor has been used to study the N-nitrosation of a model amine, morpholine.[3] The procedure used is similar to that already described, except that various amounts of morpholine are added to the initial buffer solution. The quantities of mor-

[15] S. S. Mirvish, *Toxicol. Appl. Pharmacol.* **31,** 325 (1975).
[16] T. Y. Fan and S. R. Tannenbaum, *J. Agric. Food Chem.* **21,** 237 (1975).
[17] S. R. Tannenbaum, S. Tamir, T. deRojas-Walker, and J. S. Wishnok, *in* "Nitrosamines and Related N-Nitroso Compounds" (R. N. Loeppky and C. J. Michejda, eds.), p. 120. American Chemical Society, Washington, D.C., 1993.

pholine are chosen so that the concentration of the reactive (uncharged) form does not vary significantly during a given experiment. In addition to the concentrations of NO and NO_2^-, the concentration of the nitrosation product, N-nitrosomorpholine (Nmor), is also measured continuously, by absorbance at 250 nm. The additional absorbance of Nmor observed at 209 nm necessitates a correction in the calculated NO_2^- concentration.[3]

It was found that phosphate and (to a lesser extent) chloride inhibited the formation of Nmor at physiological pH, whereas several other anions had little or no effect. A scheme in which phosphate and chloride react with N_2O_3 to form nitrosyl compounds, which are then rapidly hydrolyzed to NO_2^-, explains the inhibitory effects of these anions. Rate constants for the reactions of morpholine, phosphate, and chloride with N_2O_3 were determined at 25° and 37°. The values of the various rate constants needed to model NO oxidation and nitrosation reactions were discussed.[3]

Summary

We have described a novel apparatus for studying the rates of certain reactions of NO in aqueous solutions. A principal feature of this system is the ability to continuously measure NO concentrations, by employing a membrane inlet in conjunction with a chemiluminescence detector. The design variables that influence the performance of such systems have been discussed in some detail. This apparatus has already proved useful for determining the rate constants of several reactions in oxygenated NO solutions, and it is also well suited for quantitative studies using suspension cell cultures.

Acknowledgment

This work was supported by a grant from the National Cancer Institute (P01-CA26731).

[25] Nitric Oxide Generation from Pharmacological Nitric Oxide Donors

By NARENDRA S. KISHNANI and HO-LEUNG FUNG

Introduction

Although the classic nitrovasodilators, namely, nitroglycerin and iso-amyl nitrite, have been used therapeutically since the late 1800s, their biochemical mechanism of action has been elucidated only relatively recently. These compounds are believed to exert their hemodynamic effects by *in vivo* generation of nitric oxide (NO), which activates soluble guanylate cyclase, increases intracellular cyclic GMP, and produces vasorelaxation. More recently, other pharmacological agents such as *S*-nitrosothiols, sydnonimines, and nucleophilic NO adducts, have also been shown to produce their pharmacological action through the production of NO. These agents constitute a new class of pharmacological compounds termed NO donors.

Until a few years ago, NO donors were essentially considered only for their action on the cardiovascular system. However, with the increasing awareness of the involvement of NO in various pathophysiological states, these agents may now find therapeutic applications for the treatment of diseases associated with diverse organ systems such as the immune system, lungs, brain, sexual organs, and gastrointestinal system.

Release of Nitric Oxide from Nitric Oxide Donors

The mechanism of NO release from NO donors can be either chemical or enzymatic. The nucleophile–NO adducts liberate NO primarily through a chemical reaction, whereas the organic nitrates rely principally on enzymatic breakdown to form NO. Other NO donors such as organic nitrites, *S*-nitrosothiols, sodium nitroprusside, and the sydnonimines utilize both chemical and enzymatic mechanisms to generate NO *in vivo*.

Chemical liberation of NO from most NO donors can be readily brought about by reaction with thiols or other reducing agents such as NADPH or ascorbic acid. The exact enzymes that catalyze the biochemical activation of NO donors, however, have not been fully characterized. For example, at least three discrete enzymes have been proposed to mediate the metabolic formation of NO from nitroglycerin, namely, glutathione *S*-transferases, cytochrome P450, and a microsomal enzyme in vascular smooth muscle cells. The biochemical pharmacology and therapeutics of NO donors have been reviewed.[1,2]

The biochemical generation of NO from its donors can be studied in intact animals, isolated tissues, cultured tissues, or subcellular fractions of specific tissues, or in the presence of purified proteins. To date, much of the NO generation data available involve vascular cellular preparations, which is the focus of this chapter.

[1] J. A. Bauer, B. P. Booth, and H.-L. Fung, *in* "Nitric Oxide: Biochemistry, Molecular Biology and Therapeutic Implications" (L. Ignarro and F. Murad, eds.), p. 361. Academic Press, San Diego, 1995.
[2] J. A. Bauer and H.-L. Fung, *J. Myocard. Ischemia* **7**, 17 (1995).

Methods

Preparation of Vascular Microsomes and Cytosol

Studies of the metabolism of NO donors with subcellular fractions of specific tissues such as the liver or vascular smooth muscle have yielded important information about the localization of the responsible proteins. The protocol for preparing the microsomal and cytosolic fractions from vascular tissue such as the aorta and the coronary artery is essentially as follows.[3] All procedures are performed at 4°. First, the adjoining fat and connective tissue is carefully trimmed off, and the tissue is soaked and thoroughly washed in a homogenization buffer such as one consisting of 250 mM sucrose, 50 mM Tris, pH 7.4, and 1 mM phenylmethylsulfonyl fluoride (PMSF) (added from a 100 mM stock in ethanol). The tissue is then cut longitudinally, and the outer adventitious layer is carefully stripped off from the medial smooth muscle layer by clipping at the junction of the two layers (the medial layer is usually pale yellow in color while the adventitious layer is pinkish). The tissue is weighed, cut into small pieces (2–4 mm), mixed with 4 volumes of homogenization buffer, and homogenized in either a Waring-type blender, a Polytron homogenizer, or a Teflon–glass Potter–Elvehjem tissue grinder. The homogenate is then centrifuged at 10,000 g for 30 min. The supernatant is collected and centrifuged at 100,000 g for 1 hr to yield the cytosolic fraction (supernatant) and the microsomal fraction (pellet), which is resuspended in the homogenization buffer or a resuspension buffer (250 mM sucrose, 700 mM KCl) to a final concentration of 1–2 mg/ml, divided into aliquots, and stored at −70° for up to 4 weeks. Additional protease inhibitors of various types and antioxidants may be added during this protocol. Commonly, dithiotheritol (0.1–5 mM), 2-mercaptoethanol (14 mM), sodium ascorbate (0.1–0.25 M), EDTA and EGTA (0.1–5 mM), ε-aminocaproic acid (0.1%, w/v), benzamide (1 mM), benzamidine hydrochloride (1 mM), leupeptin (2 μg/ml), aprotinin (5 μg/ml), pepstatin A (2 μg/ml), antipain (1 μg/ml), and trypsin inhibitor (10 μg/ml) are used.

Preparation of Vascular Cellular Subfractions

Identification of subcellular site(s) of enzymatic activity not only permit understanding of the processes involved in *in vivo* activation, but may also facilitate purification of the responsible enzyme. Subcellular fractionation is often accomplished by using differential sedimentation and sucrose or glycerol density gradient centrifugation, as discussed in several previous

---

[3] S.-J. Chung and H.-L. Fung, *J. Pharmacol. Exp. Ther.* **253**, 614 (1990).

TABLE I
METHODS OF NITRIC OXIDE QUANTIFICATION

Method	Principle	Reported sensitivity/linearity	Specificity/interferences	Key precautions/comments	Refs.[a]
Direct methods					
Spectroscopic					
Chemiluminescence	$NO + O_3 \rightarrow NO_2 + O_2 + h\nu$; emitted photons measured by photomultiplier tube (λ between 660 and 900 nm)	Typically 20–50 pmol, but can be as low as 0.5 pmol; linear 0.5–5 pmol; also linear 20–200 and 300–3000 pmol	$DMSO,^b$ NH_3, H_2S, olefins may elicit artifactual signals	Exclusion of O_2 is imperative; elimination of H_2O preferred	1, 2
Visible spectroscopy	$HbO_2 + NO \rightarrow MetHb$ (Fe^{2+}) $\quad\quad (Fe^{3+})$	Threshold, 1 nM, 1 pmol	Although NOHb is formed, assay is not affected	NO formed monitored by λ_{max} shift from 433 to 406 nm or extinction difference between 401 and 411 nm	3, 4
Electron spin resonance or electron paramagnetic resonance (EPR)	NO trapped in spin trap in excited state; exhibits characteristic spectrum on relaxation	Threshold, 500 mM, 1 nmol, probably the least sensitive of all direct NO assays	Nitroso and Hb traps more accurate than nitrone traps	Samples may need to be frozen for assay	5
Mass spectroscopy	NO trapped by thioproline to form nitrosothioproline which is derivatized for mass spectroscopic detection	10–20 pmol detected, similar in sensitivity to chemiluminescence	None reported	Tedious, involves extraction, derivatization before assay	6
Amperometric					
Porphyrin-based electrode	Electrochemical oxidation of NO at 0.63 V resulting in increase in current proportional to NO concentration: $NO \cdot - e^- \rightarrow NO^+$	Threshold, 10–20 nM, 10^{-2} attomol detected within a single cell; sensitive due to small volume (1 pl) and proximity to NO formation; linear to 300 μM	Catecholamines detected by similar principle, but sensitivity is 3 orders of magnitude lower; interferences when concentrations exceed 10 μM	NO_2^- interference reduced by polymeric coating of Nafion	7
Pt/Ag electrode	Potential difference of 0.9 V applied	Threshold, 500 nM, but potential for variability; better suited for >5 μM	Similar interferences as for porphyrin electrode; NO_2^- also can be oxidized at 0.9 V	Fragile glass electrode; response time slower than porphyrin electrode	8

Pt/Ir alloy coated with NO-selective resin	0.5–0.8 V required	5 nM; linear to 1 mM	PTIO[b] and L-NAME[b] cause nonspecific current	NO$_2^-$ and NO$_3^-$ not detected	9
Indirect methods					
Measurement of denitrated metabolites	HPLC[b] or GC[b]	150 pg/ml, 1 nM, 1 pmol	None	Does not necessarily indicate NO production	10–12
Measurement of nitrite ion by				Does not necessarily indicate NO production	
Griess reaction	Diazotization of NO (more commonly NO$_2^-$) with sulfanilic acid or sulfacetamide and subsequent coupling with N-(1-naphthyl) ethylenediamine	Threshold = 2 nM, 2 pmol; typically linear 5–100 μM	Indiscrimatory toward NO and NO$_2^-$	Total NO and NO$_2^-$ determined by reduction with NaI and Cl$_3$CCOOH or vanadium(III)	13–15
Fluorescence	Acid-catalyzed ring closure of 2,3-diaminonaphthane to form fluorescent 2,3-diaminonaphthatriazole	Linear 3–1000 pmol; lower limit = 3 pmol; λ_{ex} = 365 nm and λ_{em} = 450 nm	Fluorescence attenuated by hemoglobin, phenol red, albumin (1%), dithiothreitol (100 μM), serum (1%)	Specific assay for nitrite; nitrate not detected	16

[a] *Key to References*: (1) O. C. Zafiriou and M. McFarland, *Anal. Chem.* **52**, 1662 (1980); (2) S.-J. Chung and H.-L. Fung, *Anal. Lett.* **25**, 2021 (1992); (3) M. Feelisch and E. A. Noack, *Eur. J. Pharmacol.* **139**, 19 (1987); (4) M. Kelm, M. Feelisch, R. Sphar, H. M. Piper, E. Noack, and J. Schrader, *Biochem. Biophys. Res. Commun.* **154**, 237 (1988); (5) Y. Henry, M. Lepoivre, J.-C. Drapier, C. Ducrocq, J.-L. Boucher, and A. Guissani, *FASEB J.* **7**, 1124 (1993); (6) L. Gustafsson, A. Leone, M. Persson, N. Wiklund, and S. Moncada, *Biochem. Biophys. Res. Commun.* **181**, 852 (1991); (7) T. Malinski and Z. Taha, *Nature (London)* **358**, 676 (1992); (8) K. Shibuki, *Neurosci. Res.* **9**, 69 (1990); (9) K. Ichimori, H. Ishida, T. Yamashita, H. Nakazawa, and E. Murakami, Third International Meeting of Biology of Nitric Oxide (Abstract), 1993; (10) S.-J. Chung, S. Chong, P. Seth, C. Y. Jung and H.-L. Fung, *J. Pharmacol. Exp. Ther.* **260**, 652 (1992); (11) B. P. Booth, B. M. Bennett, J. F. Brien, D. A. Ellicott, G. S. Marks, J. L. McCans, and K. Nakatsu, *Biopharm. Drug Dispos.* **11**, 663 (1990); (12) C. Han, M. Gumbleton, D. T. W. Lau, and L. Z. Benet, *J. Chromatogr.* **579**, 237 (1992); (13) J. P. Griess, *Ber. Deutsch. Chem. Ges.* **12**, 426 (1879); (14) L. C. Green, D. A. Wagner, J. Glogowski, P. L. Skipper, J. S. Wishnok, and S. R. Tannenbaum, *Anal. Biochem.* **126**, 131 (1982); (15) R. S. Braman and S. A. Hendrix, *Anal. Chem.* **61**, 2715 (1989); (16) T. P. Misko, R. J. Schilling, D. Salvemini, W. M. Moore, and M. G. Currie, *Anal. Biochem.* **214**, 11 (1993).

[b] DMSO, Dimethyl sulfoxide; PTIO, 2-phenyl-4,4,5,5-tetramethylimidazoline-1-oxyl-3-oxide; L-NAME, N^G-nitro-L-arginine methyl ester; HPLC, high-performance liquid chromatography; GC, gas chromatography.

volumes in this series.[4-6] Vascular homogenates have been subjected sequentially to differential sedimentation and sucrose gradient centrifugation to provide various subcellular fractions: nuclear, mitochondrial, and microsomal fractions and cytosol, plasma membrane, endoplasmic reticulum, and inner mitochondria.[3] Briefly, the vascular homogenate is subjected to sequential centrifugation at 1000, 10,000, and 210,000 g to provide postnuclear supernatant (nuclei and unbroken cells pellet), postmitochondrial supernatant (mitochondria pellet), and postmicrosomal supernatant (cytosol) and microsomal pellet, respectively. The microsomal pellet is then resuspended in the homogenization or resuspension buffer and overlayed on a discontinuous sucrose gradient comprising of layers of 18, 28, 40, and 60% (w/v) sucrose and centrifuged at 250,000 g for 2 hr. The subcellular fractions are then collected at the interfaces (plasma membrane, 18/28%; endoplasmic reticulum, 28/40%; and inner mitochondria, 40/60%) and assayed for specific enzyme markers to determine their relative purities.

Reaction Conditions and Cofactors

Nitric oxide is reactive with many components of the *in vitro* assay, for example, radicals in the aqueous medium, oxygen, and superoxide anions. The surface of the container, especially glass, can also adsorb low concentrations of nonpolar NO donors, for example, nitroglycerin.[7] Thus, it is advisable in these experiments to utilize silanized glassware, Teflon-coated septa and stir bars, and superoxide anion scavengers. A typical incubation mixture consists of the following: cellular fraction (100–800 μg protein) in a 50 mM phosphate buffer, pH 7.4, 100 U/ml superoxide dismutase, and 12 μg/ml NADPH in a 5-ml microreaction vial (final volume 1.5–3 ml). The vials are sealed tightly and equilibrated at 37° for 10–30 min before addition of the NO donor through the septum via a gas-tight syringe. Alternatively, following sealing, the contents of the vials are thoroughly degassed by vacuum until a partial pressure of 1–2 torr is achieved and is maintained for several minutes. The vials are then purged with argon, typically for 3–5 min, and the NO donor is then added. The incubation time chosen will depend on the rate of NO formation under the conditions of the specific experiment and can range from a few minutes to several hours. A NADPH-regenerating system consisting of 1.4 mM NADP$^+$, 4.2 mM D-glucose 6-phosphate, and 0.25 U glucose-6-phosphate dehydrogenase may be added,

[4] G. Hoogeboom, *Methods Enzymol.* **1**, 16 (1955).
[5] S. Fleischer and L. Packer (eds.), *Methods Enzymol.* **31** (1974).
[6] M. P. Deutscher (ed.), *Methods Enzymol.* **182** (1990).
[7] R. A. Morrison and H.-L. Fung, *J. Chromatogr.* **308**, 153 (1984).

especially for more prolonged incubations.[8] Glutathione (13 μM) and flavin adenine dinucleotide (FAD; 2.5 μM) are other cofactors that appear to enhance NO formation and may be used.

Nitric Oxide Detection

Direct measurement of NO formed from biological samples is difficult because the concentration is low, and NO is highly reactive with physiological agents such as hemoglobin, thiols, and oxygen radicals. Indeed, some of the spectroscopic and electrochemical methods developed for direct measurement of NO are based on these reactions. The concentrations of the reaction products, such as those of nitrite ion or citrulline (which is formed when arginine is converted to NO), are also used to provide indirect estimates of NO production. Other indirect methods of NO quantitation utilize its biological and pharmacological properties, including those of vasorelaxation, inhibition of platelet aggregation, and increase in accumulation of cyclic GMP. In intact animals and isolated tissues, NO is typically measured by indirect methods, although a porphyrin-based microsensor has been used to measure NO levels directly within a single cell and at the surface of cells.[9] Table I summarizes the major characteristics of current methods of measurement of NO from biological samples. It is evident that the choice of NO detection method would depend on the focus of the experiment. For example, the kinetics of NO may be more readily assessed by direct NO measurement via methods such as chemiluminescence rather than electron paramagnetic resonance (EPR) or mass spectroscopy, which involve time delays in sample manipulation. In terms of sensitivity and ease of sample handling, the chemiluminescence method may be the preferred method for NO measurement, in both *in vitro* experiments and in some *in vivo* experiments, such as analyses of exhaled air.[10,11] However, in the presence of proteins, the recovery of NO from incubations may not be complete, and suitable control experiments will need to be conducted.[7]

Acknowledgment

This work was supported in part by NIH Grant HL22273.

[8] K. M. Boje and H.-L. Fung, *J. Pharmacol. Exp. Ther.* **253,** 20 (1990).
[9] T. Malinski and Z. Taha, *Nature (London)* **358,** 676 (1992).
[10] L. E. Gustafsson, A. M. Leone, M. G. Persson, N. P. Wilklund, and S. Moncada, *Biochem. Biophys. Res. Commun.* **181,** 852 (1991).
[11] J. A. Bauer, J. A. Wald, S. Doran, and D. Soda, *Life Sci.* **55,** 1903 (1994).

[26] Photolabile Donors of Nitric Oxide: Ruthenium Nitrosyl Chlorides as Caged Nitric Oxide

By NADIR BETTACHE, TOM CARTER, JOHN E. T. CORRIE, DAVID OGDEN, and DAVID R. TRENTHAM

Introduction

Nitric oxide (NO) is an important bioregulatory molecule that is generated by specific enzymes present in many different cell types in response to vascular, neural, and inflammatory stimuli.[1] It is formed in small amounts in biological systems,[2] and because of its high chemical reactivity (e.g., with oxygen, superoxide, hemoproteins) it has a short half-life (0.1–6.0 sec).[3,4] This lability has made it difficult when using solutions of NO applied by perfusion to quantify the action of NO in complex biological systems. The technique of flash photolysis of thermally and hydrolytically stable, but biologically inert, photolabile "caged" precursors affords a means of making rapid and precise changes in concentration of substrate or ligand at or near the site of action.[5–9] This technique is most usefully applied at sites within a cell or preparation that are only slowly accessible by diffusion, where uptake by conventional perfusion techniques distorts both the time course and steady-state concentration of the physiological ligand. In the case of nitric oxide there are additional considerations. Besides its instability, NO is soluble at millimolar concentrations in aqueous solution and is able to permeate across cell membranes from extracellular to intracellular domains. Indeed, these are properties relating to its mechanism of action. Thus, there is potential value in being able to generate NO rapidly at known

[1] S. Moncada, R. M. J. Palmer, and E. A. Higgs, *Pharmacol. Rev.* **43**, 109 (1991).
[2] R. M. J. Palmer, A. G. Ferridge, and S. Moncada, *Nature (London)* **327**, 524 (1987).
[3] T. M. Griffith, D. H. Edwards, M. J. Lewis, A. C. Newby, and A. H. Henderson, *Nature (London)* **308**, 645 (1984).
[4] M. Kelm, M. Feelish, R. Spahr, H. M. Piper, E. Noake, and J. Schrader, *Biochem. Biophys. Res. Commun.* **154**, 236 (1988).
[5] J. A. McCray and D. R. Trentham, *Annu. Rev. Biophys. Biophys. Chem.* **18**, 239 (1989).
[6] J. E. T. Corrie and D. R. Trentham, *in* "Biological Applications of Photochemical Switches" (H. Morrison, ed.), p. 243, Wiley, New York, 1993.
[7] A. M. Gurney, *in* "Microelectrode Techniques for Cell Physiology" (D. Ogden, ed.), 2nd Ed., p. 389. Company of Biologists, Cambridge, 1994.
[8] J. H. Kaplan, *Annu. Rev. Physiol.* **52**, 897 (1990).
[9] S. R. Adams and R. Y. Tsien, *Annu. Rev. Physiol.* **55**, 755 (1993).

concentration within a biological preparation at specific locations, such as the extracellular space.

Nitrosyl derivatives of ruthenium have been shown to be thermally stable but photolabile, releasing NO on exposure to near-UV light,[10,11] which is the characteristic property of caged compounds. We describe here the biophysical characterization of two caged NO compounds, trichloronitrosylruthenium ($RuNOCl_3$) and dipotassium pentachloronitrosylruthenate ($K_2RuNOCl_5$), and their use in quantitative study of the action of NO in biological preparations. In addition to the smooth muscle relaxation described here as a test system, these caged NO compounds have been applied in hippocampal slices to study long-term potentiation of synaptic transmission,[12,13] depression of N-methyl-D-aspartate receptor-mediated transmission at hippocampal synapses,[13] and interneuronal activity in molluscs.[14] It is noteworthy that these ruthenium nitrosyl compounds are water-soluble salts and so are unlikely to cross biological membranes. Alternative caged NO compounds that have been synthesized may also allow control of the site of NO release, but their NO release kinetics have been less well defined (≤ 5 msec).[15] Preliminary details of the work described here have previously been presented as an abstract.[16]

To assay the extent and rate of NO release from caged NO on photolysis we measure the spectral changes produced by the interaction of NO with deoxyhemoglobin (deoxyHb). Unlike many commonly used assays, this method measures NO directly rather than as nitrite produced by oxidation of NO. To validate our deoxyHb assay by comparison with earlier literature, aqueous NO solutions prepared by equilibration with gaseous NO obtained from a gas cylinder are used. These aqueous NO solutions typically contain nitrite that may interfere in chemical and biological assays of NO. To clarify these issues we describe: (1) the preparation of aqueous solutions with NO obtained from a gas cylinder, (2) methods to assay both NO and nitrite in such solutions, and (3) how nitrite can be removed from solutions containing

[10] A. B. Cox and R. M. Wallace, *Inorg. Nucl. Chem. Lett.* **7**, 1191 (1971).
[11] P. N. Komozin, V. M. Kazakova, I. V. Miroshnichenko, and N. M. Snitsyn, *Russ. J. Inorg. Chem.* **28**, 1806 (1983).
[12] J. H. Williams, N. Bettache, D. R. Trentham, and T. V. P. Bliss, *J. Physiol. (London)* **467**, 166P (1993).
[13] K. P. S. J. Murphy, J. H. Williams, N. Bettache, and T. V. P. Bliss, *Neuropharmacology* **33**, 1375 (1994).
[14] A. Gelperin, *Nature (London)* **369**, 61 (1994).
[15] L. R. Makings and R. Y. Tsien, *J. Biol. Chem.* **269**, 6282 (1994).
[16] N. Bettache, J. E. T. Corrie, T. Carter, J. Williams, D. Ogden, T. V. P. Bliss, and D. R. Trentham, *Biophys. J.* **64**, A190 (1993).

NO. Finally the photolysis of caged NO to induce relaxation of smooth muscle in rabbit aortic rings[17] is described to show how caged NO can be used in a biological preparation.

Methods

Properties of Caged Nitric Oxide Compounds $RuNOCl_3$ and $K_2RuNOCl_5$

Both $RuNOCl_3$ and $K_2RuNOCl_5$ are available commercially as laboratory reagents (e.g., Alfa, Ward Hill, MA). The structure of $(NH_4)_2RuNOCl_5$ has been determined by X-ray diffraction.[18] The salt used here, $K_2Ru NOCl_5$, is also a crystalline substance with well-defined spectroscopic properties, whereas $RuNOCl_3$ is more heterogeneous, possibly containing water of hydration. Although both compounds liberate NO on photolysis, $K_2Ru NOCl_5$ is the better characterized and more useful reagent, as is borne out by the data below. In what follows the concentration of each compound is based on weighed amounts of reagent as supplied.

For photochemical studies of a caged compound it is important to characterize the absorption band used to effect the photolysis and to show how the absorbance changes during photolysis. Spectra recorded in the 280–500 nm range before and after sequential irradiations of $K_2RuNOCl_2$ are shown in Fig. 1 and exhibit an isosbestic point at 303 nm. Further features of the $K_2RuNOCl_5$ spectrum are a maximum at 253 nm (ε 11,000 $M^{-1} cm^{-1}$) and a shoulder at 335 nm. No change in the near-UV absorption spectrum of $K_2RuNOCl_5$ occurs after stirring the solution for several days in the dark, indicating the thermal stability of $K_2RuNOCl_5$.

Nitric Oxide Assay with Deoxyhemoglobin or Oxyhemoglobin

The preparation of bovine deoxyHb for spectroscopic assay of caged NO photolysis is taken from a procedure described by Antonini and Brunori.[19] Bovine Hb (Sigma, St. Louis, MO) in 3.5 ml of 100 mM sodium ascorbate and 100 mM potassium phosphate at pH 7.0 and 20° is placed in a quartz cuvette (path length 1 cm) sealed with a rubber septum, in which two

[17] T. D. Carter, N. Bettache, D. C. Ogden, and D. R. Trentham, *J. Physiol. (London)* **467**, 165P (1993).

[18] J. T. Veal and D. J. Hodgson, *Inorg. Chem.* **11**, 1420 (1972).

[19] E. Antonini and M. Brunori, in "Hemoglobin and Myoglobin in Their Reactions with Ligands" (A. Neuberger and E. L. Tatum, eds.), Vol. 21 in the monograph series "Frontiers in Biology," pp. 13 and 43. North-Holland Publ., Amsterdam, 1971.

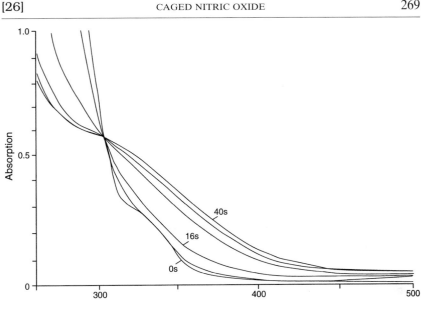

FIG. 1. Spectral changes on irradiation of $K_2RuNOCl_5$. A solution of 200 μM $K_2RuNOCl_5$ in 100 mM potassium phosphate at pH 7.0 and 20° in a 1-cm path quartz cuvette was subjected to successive 8-sec irradiations. Irradiation was effected by a xenon arc lamp mounted in a PRA lamp housing at the focus of a parabolic mirror. The light was transmitted through a water heat filter and a Hoya U 340 band-pass filter (300–360 nm) and condensed down to a 4 cm diameter beam onto the cuvette placed 25 cm from the lamp.

syringe needles are inserted to permit exit and entry of gaseous N_2. Caged NO is included at an appropriate concentration. The solution is purged with N_2, and conversion of oxyhemoglobin (oxyHb) to deoxyHb (Fe^{II}) is established by observation of its characteristic spectrum (Fig. 2).[19] Photolysis of caged NO by near-UV irradiation produces spectral changes characteristic of the conversion of deoxyHb to nitrosylhemoglobin (nitrosylHb) (Fig. 2). The extinction coefficient at 560 nm is reduced on going from deoxyHb to nitrosylHb by a $\Delta\varepsilon$ (per heme group) of -2000 M^{-1} cm^{-1} (estimated error ± 200 M^{-1} cm^{-1}).

Oxyhemoglobin is frequently used in biological experiments to trap NO, and so inhibit processes mediated by NO (e.g., as in Fig. 7b). The spectral changes that accompany this reaction[20,21] are an alternate assay of

[20] M. E. Murphy and E. Noack, *Methods Enzymol.* **233,** 240 (1994).
[21] J. M. Hevel and M. A. Marletta, *Methods Enzymol.* **233,** 250 (1994).

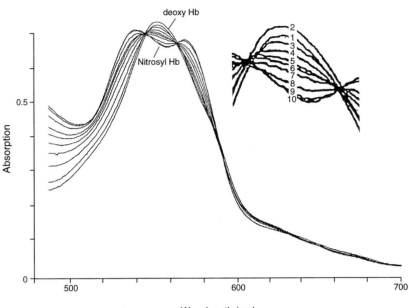

FIG. 2. Spectral changes when a solution of RuNOCl$_3$ (250 μM nominal concentration by weight) was irradiated in the presence of deoxyHb (60 μM in heme groups, for which ε = 12,500 M^{-1} cm^{-1} at 555 nm[19]) under conditions described in the text. Irradiation was from a xenon arc lamp as described for Fig. 1. Spectral changes in the range 540–570 nm are shown with expanded scale. Records 1 and 2 are spectra of the solution before and after RuNOCl$_3$ addition. Records 3–10 are spectra after successive 8-sec irradiations. The observed 0.066 absorbance change at 560 nm indicates release of 33 μM NO.

NO release by caged NO photolysis. The reaction involves formation of methemoglobin [metHb (Fe^{III})] as follows:

$$\text{oxyHb (Fe}^{II}) + \text{NO} \rightarrow \text{metHb (Fe}^{III}) + \text{NO}_3^- \qquad (1)$$

To prepare oxyHb (Fe^{II}), a solution of bovine hemoglobin in 100 mM potassium phosphate at pH 7.0, with 1 mM sodium dithionite present to reduce any metHb (Fe^{III}), is dialyzed overnight at 4° in 100 mM potassium phosphate, pH 7.0, to remove residual dithionite. Following addition of excess (200 μM) K$_2$RuNOCl$_5$, the solution is irradiated and spectral changes characteristic of metHb (Fe^{III}) formation are observed (Fig. 3).

The reaction [Eq. (1)] is described in more detail elsewhere.[20,21] It is accompanied by large absorption changes in the Soret band as well as in the 560-nm region which we prefer to use for assays of concentration changes. However, one should be aware of the pH dependence of the

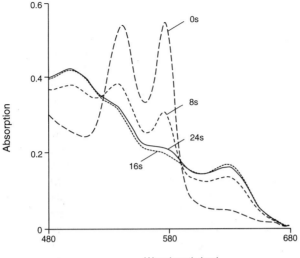

FIG. 3. Spectral changes on irradiation of $K_2RuNOCl_5$ in the presence of oxyHb. A solution of 200 μM $K_2RuNOCl_5$ together with oxyHb (40 μM in heme groups for which $\varepsilon = 14{,}600$ M^{-1} cm^{-1} at 577 nm[19]) dissolved in aqueous 100 mM potassium phosphate at pH 7.0 and 20° in a 10-mm quartz cuvette was subjected to successive 8-sec irradiations from a xenon arc lamp as described for Fig. 1.

metHb spectrum.[19] It is our experience that assays based on absorption changes in the Soret band region (410 nm) are critically instrument dependent because of the steep dependence of absorption change on wavelength. This necessitates careful calibration because of variation in quality of spectrophotometer monochromators (cf. spectral analyses in Refs. 20 and 21).

Product Quantum Yield of Photolysis of Caged Nitric Oxide

The product quantum yield, Q_p, is the ratio of the molecules of NO formed from caged NO on irradiation to the number of photons absorbed. Accurate estimates of Q_p are generally done with a chemical actinometer, but an alternative approach relies on comparing the extent of photolysis of two compounds, one of which has known Q_p. The evaluation of Q_p for caged NO described here uses the latter approach by comparison of photolysis with caged ADP, the P^2-1-(2-nitrophenyl)ethyl ester of ADP, which has $Q_p = 0.63$. The Q_p value of 0.63 is assumed equal to the corresponding caged ATP.[22] It is equally appropriate to use caged ATP in this

[22] J. W. Walker, G. P. Reid, J. A. McCray, and D. R. Trentham, *J. Am. Chem. Soc.* **110**, 7170 (1988).

assay, and may well be more convenient because caged ATP is commercially available (e.g., Calbiochem, La Jolla, CA). Laser flash photolysis (see legend to Fig. 4) as opposed to use of the xenon arc lamp is the preferred mode of irradiation because, by using a single wavelength, differences in the absorption spectra of the two types of chromophore can be neglected, and also because submillisecond time resolution is needed (see below). The shape of the caged NO absorption band in the 300–350 nm region is similar to that of caged ADP (or caged ATP). This means that estimates of NO release from caged NO in physiological experiments can be made using a xenon arc flash lamp and caged ADP (or caged ATP) as the standard (see Fig. 7 and associated text).

A typical protocol is as follows. Solutions of $RuNOCl_3$ and caged ADP are each prepared in 100 mM potassium phosphate at pH 7.0 so that they have the same absorption at 320 nm. The assay for NO release requires deoxyHb which also absorbs at 320 nm. Accordingly both solutions contain deoxyHb and are kept anaerobic. This means that, when the solutions are irradiated, approximately the same fraction of light is absorbed by each. The experimental setup is the same as for the time-resolved experiment (Fig. 4). The extent of conversion to ADP can be estimated from the

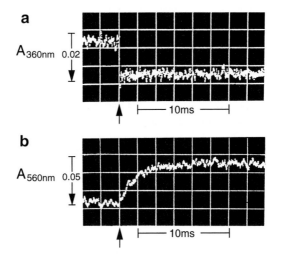

Fig. 4. Kinetic records at (a) 360 nm and (b) 560 nm of laser flash photolysis (irradiation at 320 nm) of $K_2RuNOCl_5$ at 19° in an aqueous solution containing (a) 2.5 mM $K_2RuNOCl_5$, 50 mM K_2HPO_4 adjusted to pH 7.0 with HCl, and (b) as in (a) with the addition of deoxyHb (72 μM in heme groups). Arrows on the abscissa of the oscilloscope traces mark the time of the laser pulse. The flash spectrophotometer, which has previously been described,[22] uses a Candela Model 1050 dye laser, and the solution is placed in a square 4-mm path-length quartz cuvette.

absorption of a transient *aci*-nitro anion intermediate (ε = 9100 M^{-1} cm^{-1} at 406 nm[22]), which forms and then decays during photolysis.[22] Even though in principle no time resolution is needed for the NO assay, in practice it is important so that random and systematic noise can be quantified and minimized. Moreover, for the caged ADP photolysis, a time-resolved spectrometer is essential because of the transient nature of the intermediate.

The Q_p for caged NO can then be measured from the ratio of NO concentration formed when caged NO is photolyzed to that of the *aci*-nitro anion intermediate formed on caged ADP photolysis. The absorption change on photolysis at 320 nm of 2.5 mM RuNOCl$_3$ in the presence of deoxyHb (100 μM in heme groups) is 0.0017 cm^{-1} at 560 nm, which corresponds to formation of 0.85 μM NO (cf. Fig. 2). The absorption change on photolysis of 0.88 mM caged ADP is 0.148 cm^{-1} at 406 nm which corresponds to 16.3 μM *aci*-nitro anion intermediate. From these data the quantum yield for NO formation from RuNOCl$_3$ is given by

$$Q_p = 0.85[\text{caged ADP}] \times Q_p \text{ (for caged ADP)}/16.3[\text{RuNOCl}_3] = 0.012$$

For K$_2$RuNOCl$_5$, Q_p = 0.060, which is derived from comparative assay between K$_2$RuNOCl$_5$ and RuNOCl$_3$ based on the spectral change when photoreleased NO interacts with deoxyHb. Thus conversion of K$_2$RuNOCl$_5$ is 5-fold more efficient than for RuNOCl$_3$.

Photolysis Kinetics of Caged Nitric Oxide

The rate of NO release on photolysis of caged NO can be measured either from the rate of the absorption change at 360 nm associated with photolysis (Fig. 1) or from the rate of the absorption change at 560 nm when photolysis is done in the presence of deoxyHb (Fig. 2). Figure 4 shows such absorption changes when K$_2$RuNOCl$_5$ is exposed to a 1-μsec pulse of 320-nm light from a dye laser. The change at 360 nm on photolysis of K$_2$RuNOCl$_5$ alone occurs within the time resolution of the spectrophotometer. On the other hand, when the flash photolysis of K$_2$RuNOCl$_5$ is carried out in the presence of deoxyHb, a process is observed at 560 nm that is rate-limited by the association of photoreleased NO with deoxyHb. This is because the rate constant of the exponential process, 570 sec^{-1}, divided by 72 μM (the heme group concentration), gives a calculated second-order rate constant of 8 $\times$ 10^6 M^{-1} sec^{-1}. This value correlates well with the directly measured[23] overall rate constant of 1.5 $\times$ 10^7 M^{-1} sec^{-1} at 21°, since the reaction is cooperative, with the intrinsic rate constant of NO binding to the first heme in deoxyHb being less than one-third that of

[23] Q. H. Gibson and F. J. W. Roughton, *J. Physiol. (London)* **136,** 507 (1957).

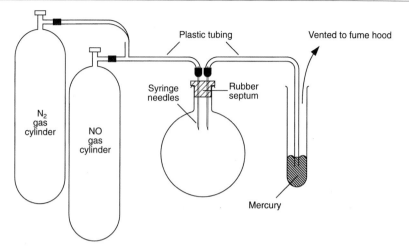

FIG. 5. Schematic drawing of apparatus for handling NO gas. A separate nitrogen gas line (not shown) is required to flush the syringe prior to withdrawal of NO gas via the rubber septum.

NO binding to triply NO-liganded Hb.[23] Thus from Fig. 4a the rate of release of NO on photolysis is greater than 10^5 sec^{-1}.

Handling and Assay of Nitric Oxide

Because NO reacts rapidly with oxygen, all handling of NO gas and solutions is conducted, as far as practicable, under an atmosphere of nitrogen. The precautions taken correspond to the types of apparatus readily available in a biochemical laboratory. It should be remembered that NO and its oxidation products are highly toxic and irritant.[24] All work with NO gas should therefore be conducted in a well-ventilated hood. Figure 5 shows a typical setup for handling NO gas, which is adaptable to the various manipulations described here. In essence, a flow of oxygen-free nitrogen or argon is used to flush oxygen from the system, which is maintained under a small (≤ 1 cm Hg) positive pressure by having the gas exit tube located below a mercury surface. The slight positive pressure ensures that no atmospheric oxygen can penetrate the apparatus.

To prepare aqueous solutions of NO, the apparatus is purged with nitrogen for 45 min, and then the nitrogen flow is stopped and the apparatus flushed with NO for several minutes. A disposable plastic syringe is flushed with nitrogen by filling and emptying it several times from a nitrogen gas line and then filled with NO by withdrawal through the rubber septum.

[24] S. Archer, *FASEB J.* **7,** 349 (1993).

The syringe and needle are rapidly transferred to a second septum-capped flask containing an aqueous solution (3 ml; distilled water or buffered solutions) which has also been nitrogen flushed for 45 min. The NO gas is then injected slowly into the solution. Dilutions from this stock solution are made similarly by transfers of the aqueous solution with nitrogen-flushed syringes. This simple procedure inevitably involves exposure to atmospheric oxygen of the contents at the tip of the syringe needle, but as the time of exposure to oxygen is only about 1 sec and the tip volume is an extremely small proportion of the total syringe contents, it is considered adequate for the purpose. Similar protocols have been described elsewhere.[24,25]

Solutions prepared as described above are expected to be virtually saturated with NO; however, the water solubility of the gas is temperature-dependent (3.2 mM at 0° and 1 mM at 60°),[26] and a convenient, accurate assay is required. One such method is titration of the conversion of deoxy-hemoglobin to nitrosylhemoglobin along the lines described in Fig. 2. Dilutions of the stock solutions to give a range of concentrations can be made using deoxygenated distilled water or buffered solutions. Another and superficially more attractive approach is the colorimetric assay introduced by Ignarro et al.[27] as a modification of an earlier method.[28] The assay is claimed to be specific for NO (and substances that generate NO under acidic conditions) and to be 100-fold more sensitive for NO than for nitrite. Unfortunately, no evidence to support these claims has been presented, nor was an explanation given for the chemistry leading to the color development. The assay is supposedly based on the diazotization of sulfanilic acid (by NO in acidic medium) followed by coupling with N-(1-naphthyl)ethylenedi-amine to generate a chromophore. While the second step is unexceptional, the supposed diazotization is remarkable. Diazotization of aromatic amines such as sulfanilic acid normally involves the nitrosonium ion (NO^+) or a related species,[29] and it is unclear that NO, in the absence of oxygen, could perform the same chemistry. It has been suggested[25] that contamination by nitrite was responsible for the color development, which would be chemically rational. Protocols for detecting the putative nitrite contamination are now described.

[25] W. R. Tracey, J. Linden, M. J. Peach, and R. A. Johns, J. Pharmacol. Exp. Ther. **252,** 922 (1990).

[26] R. C. West (ed.), "CRC Handbook of Chemistry and Physics," 70th Ed., p. B-111. CRC Press, Boca Raton, Florida, 1989.

[27] L. J. Ignarro, G. M. Buga, K. S. Wood, R. E. Byrnes, and G. Chaudhuri, Proc. Natl. Acad. Sci. U.S.A. **84,** 9265 (1987).

[28] F. K. Bell, J. J. O'Neill, and R. M. Burgison, J. Pharm. Sci. **52,** 637 (1963).

[29] J. March, "Advanced Ogranic Chemistry," 3rd Ed., p. 570. Wiley, New York, 1985.

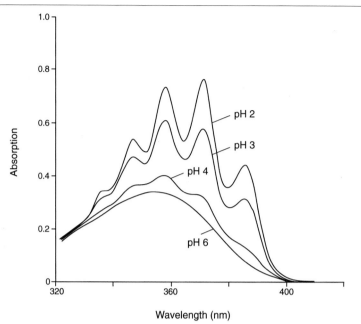

Wavelength (nm)

FIG. 6. Near-UV absorption spectra in a 10-mm path length quartz cuvette for solutions of 15 mM NaNO$_2$ in 100 mM citric acid adjusted to pH 2.0 with HCl or to pH 3.0–6.0 with NaOH. The spectra of solutions of NO gas, sampled from the apparatus shown in Fig. 5 and equilibrated with the same buffers, are not shown but were identical in shape to the spectra of NaNO$_2$.

Nitric oxide solutions, when prepared as above in distilled water, are strongly acidic (pH ~2.0). When the solutions are prepared instead in buffers at pH 2.0, 4.0, and 6.0, their near-UV spectra are markedly pH dependent (see legend to Fig. 6). Thus the spectrum at pH 2.0 is essentially identical to that prepared in distilled water and shows strong vibrational fine structure in the range 330–390 nm. The fine structure diminishes as the pH is raised, to be replaced at pH 6.0 by a smooth absorption band (λ_{max} 354 nm). Nitric oxide does not absorb in this region. These spectra are consistent with the presence of nitrite, which at low pH would be present as nitrous acid (HNO$_2$), for which the published gas-phase spectrum[30] closely matches that of the NO solution in distilled water. The pK_a of nitrous acid is 3.37, which fits well with the observed pH dependence; that is, at pH 4.0 only 18% of the total nitrate is still protonated, and hence

[30] G. W. King and D. Moule, *Can. J. Chem.* **40**, 2057 (1962).

the vibrational fine structure is greatly reduced and disappears by pH 6.0 when the nitrite is fully ionized.

With the nature of the contaminant identified, it is possible to reproduce the NO solution spectra with solutions of sodium nitrite at various pH values (Fig. 6). In particular, the extinction coefficient for the low pH spectrum is 50 M^{-1} cm^{-1} at 371 nm, and hence the concentration of contaminating nitrite in acidic NO solutions can be assayed directly. Typical values are 2–5 mM, although values as high as 15 mM have been observed. The latter value corresponds to approximately 2% of the total NO present in the volume of gas used to prepare these samples. Using the equipment and protocols described here, one cannot be certain whether the nitrite arises from contaminants present in the NO gas as supplied or by reaction with remaining traces of oxygen in the system.

In summary, solutions prepared by passing commercial NO gas into distilled water are likely to be strongly acidic and may be contaminated by nitrite at levels at least equal to the saturating concentration of NO. The acidity can be controlled by adequate buffering, but the nitrite contamination is more problematic, since nitrite itself may elicit physiological responses.[25] Nitrite (as nitrous acid) can be destroyed in strongly acidic solution (pH ≤ 1.0) by treatment with urea [Eq. (2)].

$$NH_2CONH_2 + H^+ + HNO_2 \rightarrow NH_4^+ + N_2 + CO_2 + H_2O \qquad (2)$$

Destruction of nitrite is demonstrated using the sulfanilic acid diazotization assay.[27,28] Preincubation of nitrite solutions (range 0–0.15 mM) with an equal volume of 10 mM urea in 4 M hydrochloric acid for 30 min at 25° prior to sequential addition of sulfanilic acid and N-(1-naphthyl)ethylenediamine gives a 19-fold reduction of the color development read at 548 nm when compared to controls without urea preincubation. Incubations for shorter times or with lesser amounts of urea result in less quenching of the color development, which shows that the destruction of nitrite by urea is a kinetically slow process. At higher pH values there is no reaction between urea and nitrite. When solutions prepared by equilibrating NO gas with distilled water as described above are incubated with urea hydrochloride, the characteristic nitrous acid spectrum is abolished. Although this protocol is therefore an effective means to remove nitrite from NO solutions, the requirement for highly acidic solutions means that the method is unlikely to be applicable for NO solutions to be used for biological assays.

Relaxation of Isolated Rabbit Aortic Rings on Photolysis of Caged Nitric Oxide

Endothelium-derived relaxing factor, now identified as nitric oxide,[2] was first identified in experiments using the isolated rabbit aortic ring preparation.[31] This preparation is relatively simple to prepare and use and is extremely sensitive to nitric oxide.[2] In a physiological context, NO released from endothelial cells in response to vasodilators such as acetylcholine produces relaxation of the adjacent smooth muscle. The system is sensitive to NO applied in solution in the nanomolar range,[2] but questions remain concerning the precise concentrations and rate of action of NO and acetylcholine in vascular smooth muscle and endothelia.

Figure 7a shows the experimental apparatus.[32] One part comprises a temperature-controlled tissue bath and an isotonic tension transducer. The other is a xenon arc flash lamp from which 1-msec pulses of near-UV light are focused via a quartz window onto aortic rings suspended in the chamber.

Near-UV light ($\sim$300–350 nm) with sufficient intensity for photolysis ($>$50 mJ cm^{-2} at 300–350 nm) can be produced by xenon arc flash lamps as in Fig. 7, continuous mercury or xenon arc lamps with a shutter, or certain lasers with lines in the near-UV. Details of light sources and their utilization have been reviewed.[5] Xenon arc flash lamps[32] with either an elliptical mirror (producing a large area of illumination suitable for experiments described here) or quartz refractive optics (focusing to a smaller spot) generate brief pulses (0.5–1 msec duration) and energies up to 250 mJ at 300–350 nm with Schott UG11 or Hoya U350 filters (suppliers Hi-Tech, Salisbury, Hants, UK; Cairn Research, Faversham, Kent, UK).

Quantification of the extent of photorelease of NO is required. This can be determined by measuring the extent of photolysis of a solution of caged ATP, the P^3-1-(2-nitrophenyl)ethyl ester of ATP, in a cuvette sited at the position occupied by the aortic ring in the experiment. The conversion of caged NO is calculated from the Q_p values of caged ATP and caged NO given above. As noted earlier it is reasonable to do this because the shape of the caged ATP spectrum closely matches that of caged NO in the 300–350 nm region. To illustrate the protocol, the caged ATP trial may be performed in a quartz cuvette of optical path length 4 mm and 2 mm width filled to a depth of 5 mm with a solution of 100 μM caged ATP. The extent of photolysis of caged ATP is then determined from the relative amounts of caged ATP remaining and of photoreleased ATP, which can be assayed using anion-exchange HPLC.[33] One must also take into account the fraction of light absorbed by the caged ATP sample compared to that absorbed by the solution containing the caged NO. In the simplest case, if the caged ATP test solution in the 4 mm path length of the cuvette absorbs the same fraction of light as the caged NO solution over the total distance from the

[31] R. F. Furchgott and J. V. Zawadzki, *Nature (London)* **288,** 373 (1980).
[32] G. Rapp and K. Güth, *Pfluegers Arch.* **411,** 200 (1988).
[33] J. W. Walker, G. P. Reid, and D. R. Trentham, *Methods Enzymol.* **172,** 288 (1989).

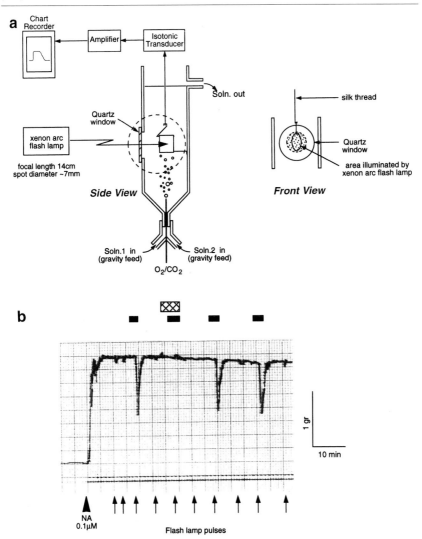

FIG. 7. Experimental arrangement for recording photoreleased NO-mediated relaxation of isolated rabbit aortic rings precontracted with noradrenaline (NA). The tissue ring is suspended in an organ bath filled with physiological saline and placed at the focal point of the xenon arc flash lamp directed into the bath through a quartz window. In these experiments a Rapp–Güth[32] xenon flash lamp with ellipsoidal mirror (focal length 14 cm, spot size 7 mm; Hi-Tech, Salisbury, Hants, UK) and a UG11 filter was used. Vasoconstriction and relaxation are recorded by means of an isotonic transducer and amplifier and displayed on a chart recorder. (b) Record of relaxations of the noradrenaline-contracted rabbit aortic ring by NO photoreleased by photolysis of 2 μM $K_2RuNOCl_5$. Brief exposure of the preparation to near-UV light (arrows) in the presence of caged NO (solid bars) produced relaxations of the tissue ring. These are blocked in the presence of 1 μM oxyhemoglobin (cross-hatched bar).

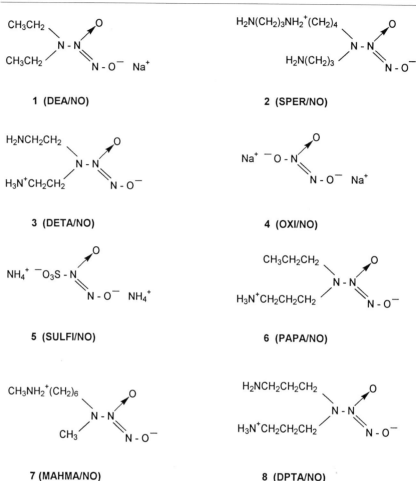

FIG. 1. Structures of selected diazeniumdiolates. See Table II for systematic names of compounds.

cal properties of NO are shown in Fig. 1. They are generally easy to synthesize according to Eq. (1) by exposing solutions of suitable nucleophilic species (X^-) to 5 atmospheres of NO under anaerobic conditions, adding base as necessary to keep the $[N(O)NO]^-$ group thus formed in its stable, anionic form, and collecting the product by suction filtration.[2-7] Many mem-

[2] R. S. Drago and F. E. Paulik, *J. Am. Chem. Soc.* **82**, 96 (1960).
[3] R. S. Drago and B. R. Karstetter, *J. Am. Chem. Soc.* **83**, 1819 (1961).

bers of this series have been isolated as white powders that can be stored indefinitely in the refrigerator under appropriate conditions. When dissolved in blood, cell culture medium, or buffer, however, many diazeniumdiolates dissociate according to Eq. (2) to regenerate NO, leaving the nucleophilic starting material of Eq. (1) as a by-product.

$$X^- + 2\,NO \rightarrow \underset{\substack{\text{a NONOate (1-substituted} \\ \text{diazen-1-ium-1,2-diolate)}}}{X-[N(O)NO]^-} \tag{1}$$

$$X-[N(O)NO]^- \xrightarrow{H^+} X^- + 2\,NO \tag{2}$$

Choosing a Diazeniumdiolate

Generally, the two most important criteria to bear in mind when deciding which diazeniumdiolate to use for a given biomedical application are the rate of its dissociation to NO and the properties of the other products generated in its decomposition.

Kinetics

The half-lives of the compounds whose structures are shown in Fig. 1 range from 1 min to 1 day in physiological buffer at 37°, making them suitable for a variety of applications in which controlled generation of NO is required. If a rapid but brief infusion of NO is desired, for example, to produce a perceptible, transient drop in blood pressure within seconds of administering an intravenous bolus of a few nanomoles per kilogram,[8] a short-lived diazeniumdiolate such as DEA/NO would be suitable. If, on the other hand, a relatively constant flux of NO is required over many hours or days, as in experiments designed to study the effects of prolonged cytostasis on vascular smooth muscle cells in culture,[9] the 20-hr half-life for DETA/NO would be preferable.

The rates of NO release for all of these compounds have so far proved to be cleanly first order under a given set of conditions, but they can vary, sometimes dramatically, as the conditions are changed. For example, some

[4] R. S. Drago, in "Free Radicals in Inorganic Chemistry" (C. B. Colburn, ed.), p. 143. American Chemical Society (Advances in Chemistry Series Number 36), Washington, D.C. 1962.
[5] R. Longhi, R. O. Ragsdale, and R. S. Drago, Inorg. Chem. 1, 768 (1962).
[6] C. M. Maragos, D. Morley, D. A. Wink, T. M. Dunams, J. E. Saavedra, A. Hoffman, A. A. Bove, L. Isaac, J. A. Hrabie, and L. K. Keefer, J. Med. Chem. 34, 3242 (1991).
[7] J. A. Hrabie, J. R. Klose, D. A. Wink, and L. K. Keefer, J. Org. Chem. 58, 1472 (1993).
[8] J. G. Diodati, A. A. Quyyumi, and L. K. Keefer, J. Cardiovasc. Pharmacol. 22, 287 (1993).
[9] D. L. Mooradian, T. C. Hutsell, and L. K. Keefer, J. Cardiovasc. Pharmacol. 25, 674 (1995).

of the rates show unusual temperature dependence, with increases of up to 9-fold on going from 22° to 37° having been documented.[7] Additionally, because dissociation to NO is acid catalyzed, as indicated in Eq. (2), the rate decreases as the pH is raised; we have noted that, if the pH of the medium is close to the pK_a for the protonation step responsible for the catalysis, even a small change in pH can lead to a large variation in the rate. The identity of the buffer employed may also affect the results. The decomposition of SULFI/NO is specifically catalyzed by boric acid,[10] and nitrite ion can markedly affect the rate of NO production from OXI/NO.[11,12] Previously unrecognized medium effects may also be operative.

Table I lists not only the published half-lives for the eight diazeniumdiolates shown in Fig. 1 but also the full range of half-life determinations known to us as of mid 1995, including several reported by colleagues working elsewhere. Note that the range can be substantial, with the results for SPER/NO reflecting a 9-fold difference between the shortest and longest values seen to date. Although the possibility of even order-of-magnitude rate variations might not be of concern in most applications, it should be borne in mind when close control of NO release kinetics is required. If desired, the rate of NO generation under the exact (or simulated) experimental conditions to be employed can usually be checked, for example, by using the spectrophotometric and/or chemiluminescence techniques described below. Further studies aimed at fully elucidating the origins of this variability are currently in progress.

By-products of Nitric Oxide Generation

For most diazeniumdiolates, decomposition in solution involves the straightforward production of NO (2 mol) and the nucleophile with which it was originally reacted (1 mol),[6] as in Eq. (2). Thus, if the accumulating nucleophile residue (X^-) develops significant pharmacological or toxicological activity during the course of the experiment, this activity will be superimposed on that of the NO. For instance, dissociation of SPER/NO produces the physiologically important polyamine spermine, a fact that must be taken into account when interpreting the results.[13] This may be of particular concern at millimolar concentrations, where even simple amines can have cytotoxic effects.

Some diazeniumdiolates decompose to N_2O as well as nitric oxide. The

[10] E. G. Switkes, G. A. Dasch, and M. N. Ackermann, *Inorg. Chem.* **12,** 1120 (1973).
[11] M. N. Hughes and P. E. Wimbledon, *J. Chem. Soc., Dalton Trans.,* 1650 (1977).
[12] M. J. Akhtar, C. A. Lutz, and F. T. Bonner, *Inorg. Chem.* **18,** 2369 (1979).
[13] C. M. Maragos, J. M. Wang, J. A. Hrabie, J. J. Oppenheim, and L. K. Keefer, *Cancer Res.* **53,** 564 (1993).

TABLE I
PHYSICOCHEMICAL DATA FOR SELECTED DIAZENIUMDIOLATES

Property	DEA/NO (1)	SPER/NO (2)	DETA/NO (3)	OXI/NO (4)	SULFI/NO (5)	PAPA/NO (6)	MAHMA/NO (7)	DPTA/NO (8)
Half-life ($t_{1/2}$) for NO release at $37°$[a,b]	2 (2–4) min[c]	39 (10–90) min[c]	20 (20–23) hr[d]	2 (2–4) min[c]	7 (2–15) min[c]	15 (8–30) min[d]	1 (1–2) min[e]	3 (1–4) hr[d]
Half-life ($t_{1/2}$) for NO release at $22°$–$25°$[a]	16 min[f]	230 min[f]	57 hr[f]	17 min,[g] 25 min[h]	24 min,[i] 32 min[i]	77 min[f]	3 min[f]	5 hr[f]
Efficiency of NO release (E_{NO}, in moles of NO per mole that dissociates)	1.5	2	2	≤0.5	0	2	2	2
Known by-products of NO release	NO_2^-, $(C_2H_5)_2NH_2^+$, $(C_2H_5)_2NNO$	NO_2^-, spermine	NO_2^-, $(H_2NCH_2CH_2)_2NH_2^+$	NO_2^-, N_2O	SO_4^{2-}, N_2O	NO_2^-, C_3H_7NH $(CH_2)_3NH_3^+$	NO_2^-, $CH_3NH_2^+$ $(CH_2)_6NHCH_3$	NO_2^-, $[H_2N(CH_2)_3]_2$ NH_2^+
Ultraviolet absorbance maximum (λ_{max}) (nm)[a]	250	252	252	237	259	252	250	252
Extinction coefficient ($\in_{max}$) (mM^{-1} cm^{-1})[a]	6.5	8.5	7.6	6.1	7.1	8.1	7.3	7.9

[a] Data are for the solution in buffer at pH 7.4.

[b] Published values are given without parentheses. Numbers in parentheses represent the smallest and largest values, respectively, among the several determinations of which we have been informed as of mid 1995 (including those reported to us by colleagues at other institutions).

[c] C. M. Maragos, D. Morley, D. A. Wink, T. M. Dunams, J. E. Saavedra, A. Hoffman, A. A. Bove, L. Isaac, J. A. Hrabie, and L. K. Keefer, J. Med. Chem. 34, 3242 (1991).

[d] D. L. Mooradian, T. C. Hutsell, and L. K. Keefer, J. Cardiovasc. Pharmacol. 25, 674 (1995).

[e] S. R. Hanson, T. C. Hutsell, L. K. Keefer, D. L. Mooradian, and D. J. Smith, Adv. Pharmacol. 34, 383 (1995).

[f] J. A. Hrabie, J. R. Klose, D. A. Wink, and L. K. Keefer, J. Org. Chem. 58, 1472 (1993).

[g] M. N. Hughes and P. E. Wimbledon, J. Chem. Soc., Dalton Trans. 703 (1976).

[h] F. T. Bonner and B. Ravid, Inorg. Chem. 14, 558 (1975).

[i] F. Seel and R. Winkler, Z. Naturforsch. 18A, 155 (1963).

[j] E. G. Switkes, G. A. Dasch, and M. N. Ackermann, Inorg. Chem. 12, 1120 (1973).

ability of SULFI/NO to produce only N_2O has been exploited as a type of negative control, in that this compound contains the $[N(O)NO]^-$ moiety but generates negligible NO at physiological pH; its absence of potent vasodilatory activity contrasts with the micromolar EC_{50} values of other short-lived diazeniumdiolates, suggesting that the $[N(O)NO]^-$ functional group itself makes little or no contribution to the observed vasoactivity, which must therefore be dominated by NO release alone.[6] Compounds in which the $[N(O)NO]^-$ group is attached to nitrogen can decompose to the corresponding N-nitroso derivatives, of importance as possible toxic species. Thus, the potent carcinogen, N-nitrosodiethylamine, can often be detected in at least trace quantities after the decomposition of DEA/NO,[14] and the fact that the isopropylamine-derived analog, $(CH_3)_2CHNH-[N(O)NO]^-Na^+$, elevates lung tumor incidence in mice may originate mechanistically in its tendency to produce a potentially DNA-alkylating diazonium ion (via the primary nitrosamine) during decomposition in aqueous media.[15]

Quality Control and Preparation of Dosing Solutions

The propensity of the compounds to decompose to NO is essential to their utility in pharmacological research, but care must be taken to ensure that this does not occur prematurely. Fortunately, this can be accomplished with confidence for all the compounds of Fig. 1 by following a series of simple rules.

Storing Reagents

Many of the diazeniumdiolates show remarkable stability in the solid phase. Their survival as pure materials can usually be assured with careful handling. We recommend storing them in a 4° refrigerator with protection from moisture and acids. In addition, we routinely flush the reagent bottle with dry nitrogen or argon before each closing, then seal the junction between bottle and cap with plastic wrap before returning to cold storage.

Visual Inspection

All the compounds of Fig. 1 are free-flowing white powders or granules when pure. Any discoloration or tendency to congeal is an indication that

---

[14] R. O. Ragsdale, B. R. Karstetter, and R. S. Drago, *Inorg. Chem.* **4**, 420 (1965).
[15] L. K. Keefer, L. M. Anderson, B. A. Diwan, C. L. Driver, D. C. Haines, C. M. Maragos, D. A. Wink, and J. M. Rice, *Methods (San Diego)* **7**, 121 (1995).

the purity of the sample should be checked (see below) and/or that the sample should be replaced.

Quality Control

To supplement the visual criteria mentioned above, it may on occasion be desirable to confirm the purity of solid diazeniumdiolates. This can best be accomplished by elemental analysis. Melting points for the compounds of Fig. 1 reflect decomposition rather than reversible phase changes and are thus not very reliable indicators of purity. Identity can in most cases best be confirmed by nuclear magnetic resonance techniques and/or combustion analysis.

Diazeniumdiolate concentrations in solution are conveniently determined by ultraviolet spectrophotometry.[6] Thus, an alternate means of establishing the purity of a solid sample involves dissolving it in dilute alkali, reading the absorbance of the resulting solution immediately after mixing it with a large excess of pH 7.4 phosphate buffer, and comparing the observed value to the extinction coefficient for a pure reference standard. Similarly, the concentration of diazeniumdiolate in a given stock or dosing solution can be confirmed, and the rate of its decomposition can be conveniently followed, by spectrophotometric methods. The extinction coefficients and wavelengths corresponding to the characteristic absorbance maxima for the compounds of Fig. 1 are given in Table I.

To measure the amount of NO generated in the decomposition of a given diazeniumdiolate, the following chemiluminescence method can be used. A freshly prepared solution in 10 mM sodium hydroxide is placed in a three-neck flask equipped with a septum on one sidearm and a fritted glass gas bubbling tube directed to the bottom through the other. Argon or another inert gas is passed through the bubbler such that the liquid is continuously purged, with the effluent being piped via a condenser attached to the middle neck into a pair of cold traps (the first at around 0° to remove the bulk of the water vapor, the second at less than or equal to −78°) and thence into the inlet of a chemiluminescence detector. Purging is continued until a steady baseline is established on the associated chart recorder, usually within 1–5 min, whereon a large excess of degassed buffer is injected through the septum to lower the pH and start the reaction. The integral of the resulting chemiluminescence trace is compared to that found when a known number of moles of an authentic NO gas standard is injected just before and/or just after observing the diazeniumdiolate decomposition, allowing calculation of the amount of NO released from the sample under study. If the chemiluminescence signal is too large or too small to be integrated properly, appropriate adjustments in the sample size should allow satisfactory results in subsequent runs.

For compounds whose half-lives are so long that the integration must be interrupted before the chemiluminescence trace returns to baseline, an alternative procedure can be used in which the rate of NO generation is measured as a function of time. The run is initiated as in the previous paragraph, but integration is not begun until the chemiluminescence signal achieves a relatively constant value. The area under the curve for the next 5–10 min is computed, divided by the number of integral units per mole of NO seen for the separately injected gas standard, and divided in turn by the length of time the integration was conducted. This gives a value for the mean rate at which NO was being generated over that time interval. The natural logarithm of this measured rate is then plotted (as the ordinate) against the time, t (as the abscissa), where t is the total time elapsed between initiation of the reaction and the midpoint of the time interval during which the integral was accumulated. Periodic repetition of this procedure leads to a graph representing the rate of NO generation as a function of time under the experimental conditions employed.

If the dissociation is a first-order reaction (as is the case for all the compounds of Fig. 1), it follows that the rate of NO generation will also show a first-order exponential decay with time. Linear regression analysis of the ln(rate) versus time plot therefore yields the initial rate of NO generation (R_0) from the y-intercept and the first-order rate constant, k, from the slope (slope $= -k$). The abscissa value corresponding to half the initial rate is the half-life $(t_{1/2})$; alternatively, the half-life can be calculated by dividing the rate constant, k, into 0.693. If the rate data are expressed as the rate of NO generated per mole of diazeniumdiolate added at the beginning of the experiment, the total amount of NO released per mole of diazeniumdiolate that dissociates (E_{NO}) can be computed via Eq. (3). The E_{NO} values we have found for the compounds of Fig. 1 are given in Table I.

$$E_{NO} = R_0/k = R_0 t_{1/2}/0.693 \tag{3}$$

Preparation of Solutions

The compounds of Fig. 1, being ionic or zwitterionic, are all highly soluble in aqueous media. They also increase in stability as the pH is raised. Capitalizing on these facts, the following two-step approach can be used to prepare dosing solutions.

First, prepare a concentrated stock solution by dissolving a weighed amount of diazeniumdiolate powder in dilute alkali. In this way, a compound such as MAHMA/NO, which has a half-life of about 1 min at pH 7.4 and 37°, can be prepared as a 10 mM to 1 M stock solution in 1–10 mM sodium hydroxide having a half-life of many hours. As an extra precaution, the stock solution should be kept cold (stability increases as the temperature is lowered) and should be used as soon as possible after dissolution of the powder.

To dose the animal, the culture dish, the enzyme/substrate mixture, etc., a small aliquot of stock solution is mixed immediately before use with such a large excess of buffer in the saline, culture medium, or other dosing vehicle that the tiny amount of sodium hydroxide does not change the pH of the vehicle. To reach the desired diazeniumdiolate concentration conveniently, it may be desirable to perform the dilution in two steps, for example, to bring a 100 mM stock solution to 10 μM by successive 100-fold dilutions for intravenous injection; in this case, the first dilution may be effected by adding the concentrated stock to 100 volumes of 1–10 mM sodium hydroxide to keep the pH high, with the second being made into buffered administration vehicle immediately prior to dosage.

Sometimes a decision will be made to avoid dissolution in alkali altogether, for example, so that a highly concentrated solution or one of minimal ionic strength can be administered. It may also be necessary to sterilize the ultimate dosing solution by ultrafiltration before use. Under these circumstances, we recommend keeping the temperature as low as possible, consistent with the requirements of the experiment, and minimizing the length of time the diazeniumdiolate is in solution before administration is accomplished. With a bit of practice and teamwork, we have routinely been able to complete such ultrafiltration and other predosage manipulations within 10–45 sec after dissolution at the pH desired for administration.

Adherence to these rules regarding preparation of dosing solutions increases in importance as the half-life of the diazeniumdiolate under the conditions of the predosage regimen decreases; conversely, the rules may be entirely unnecessary if the total time the diazeniumdiolate is in solution is short relative to its half-life under those conditions. If desired, the fraction (F) of the diazeniumdiolate that decomposes prior to administration can be estimated by way of Eq. (4), where k is the first-order dissociation rate constant of the compound and t is the length of time it is allowed to dissociate under those conditions. The k values for the diazeniumdiolates of Fig. 1 at pH 7.4 can be calculated by dividing the half-life (Table I) into 0.693.

$$F = 1 - e^{-kt} \tag{4}$$

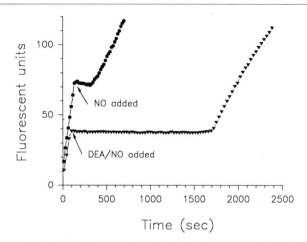

FIG. 2. Inhibition of cytochrome P450 activity in phenobarbital-induced rat liver microsomes by two nitric oxide sources: (●) aqueous solution of molecular NO at an initial concentration of 100 μM; (▼) 50 μM DEA/NO (structure **1** of Fig. 1). (Reprinted from Ref. 16.)

Application in Enzymology: Inhibition of Cytochrome P450

In an experiment illustrating the use of diazeniumdiolates in enzymological research, the effect of DEA/NO on the activity of cytochrome P450 was compared to that of molecular NO.[16] When spectrophotofluorimetry was used to follow the rate of 7-benzyloxyphenoxazone dealkylation by phenobarbital-induced rat liver microsomes, the steady generation of a fluorescent product (excitation at 522 nm, emission at 586 nm) was seen in 2-ml reaction volumes, each of which initially contained 0.1 mg of microsomal protein, 50 mM Tris (pH 7.5), 25 mM MgCl$_2$, 0.1 mM dicumarol, 0.6 mM NADPH, and 5 μM substrate. This reaction is known to be catalyzed by enzymes of the cytochrome P450 family. Boluses of either NO (100 μM) or DEA/NO (50 μM) added after the reaction was underway provided complete but transient inhibition of substrate turnover.[16] The results of a typical experiment are shown in Fig. 2.

The data illustrate a key difference between the diazeniumdiolates and solutions of molecular NO itself as tools for studying the effects of nitric oxide on an enzyme. Aqueous NO at an initial concentration of 100 μM completely inhibited the cytochrome P450 for only a few minutes in this experiment, presumably because the NO rapidly disappeared from the solution by autoxidation or escape into the atmosphere. By contrast, the

[16] D. A. Wink, Y. Osawa, J. F. Darbyshire, C. R. Jones, S. C. Eshenaur, and R. W. Nims, *Arch. Biochem. Biophys.* **300**, 115 (1993).

diazeniumdiolate at half that molar concentration continued the reversible inhibition for a considerably longer period by releasing approximately the same total amount of NO steadily into solution such that it compensated for NO lost from the system, keeping the NO concentration above an apparent threshold value through many DEA/NO half-lives.

Reporting Results

There are two features of the diazeniumdiolates that merit special attention when experiments in which they have been used are publicly described. One concerns the nomenclature issue.

Clearly Identifying the Compound Employed

To provide an unambiguous designation of a given diazeniumdiolate, we strongly recommend using its systematic name at least once in any publication describing its use, preferably with a drawing of the structure as well, to erase any possible uncertainty about the identity of the compound under study. Koppenol and Traynham have suggested a nomenclature system in [1] in this volume[17] that is based on rules promulgated by the International Union of Pure and Applied Chemistry (IUPAC). We prefer a slight variant of this system in which the IUPAC rules on group priority are relaxed as necessary to allow all compounds containing the $[N(O)NO]^-$ group to be named with the same root, that is, as 1-substituted diazen-1-ium-1,2-diolates (rather than "NONOates," as we had previously suggested). The systematic names we propose are given in Table II. The Chemical Abstracts Service registry numbers can also be given as unambiguous identifiers. However, some compounds have more than one registry number; previously undescribed compounds have none; and they cannot be translated to a name or a structure without access to the Chemical Abstracts database. The registry numbers for the compounds of Fig. 1 are given in Table II. The Chemical Abstracts names are also systematic, but they employ several entirely different roots for the diazeniumdiolates and are often difficult to formulate and decipher. It may also be convenient to identify a diazeniumdiolate in terms of the starting materials for its synthesis according to Eq. (1), for example, as "the spermine/NO adduct." However, we strongly recommend against using such names (including the acronyms of Fig. 1 and Table II) without clearly identifying them in terms of a structure, an unambiguous systematic name, and/or the registry number.

---

[17] W. H. Koppenol and J. G. Traynham, *Methods Enzymol.* **268,** Chap. 1, 1996 (this volume).

TABLE II
1-SUBSTITUTED DIAZEN-1-IUM-1,2-DIOLATES: ALTERNATIVE IDENTIFICATION SYSTEMS

Structure[a]	Acronym[a]	Chemical Abstracts Service registry number	Systematic name
1	DEA/NO	92382-74-6	Sodium (Z)-1-(N,N-diethylamino) diazen-1-ium-1,2-diolate
2	SPER/NO	136587-13-8	(Z)-1-{N-[3-Aminopropyl]-N-[4-(3-aminopropylammonio)butyl]-amino}diazen-1-ium-1,2-diolate
3	DETA/NO	146724-94-9	(Z)-1-[N-(2-Aminoethyl)-N-(2-ammonioethyl)amino]diazen-1-ium-1,2-diolate
4	OXI/NO (Angeli's salt)	13826-64-7 (37035-81-7 as the monohydrate)	Disodium diazen-1-ium-1,2,2-triolate
5	SULFI/NO	61142-90-3	Bis(ammonium) (E)-1-sulfonatodiazen-1-ium-1,2-diolate
6	PAPA/NO	146672-58-4	(Z)-1-[N-(3-Ammoniopropyl)-N-(n-propyl)amino]diazen-1-ium-1,2-diolate
7	MAHMA/NO	146724-86-9	(Z)-1-{N-Methyl-N-[6-(N-methylammoniohexyl)amino]}diazen-1-ium-1,2-diolate
8	DPTA/NO	146724-95-0	(Z)-1-[N-(3-Aminopropyl)-N-(3-ammoniopropyl)amino]diazen-1-ium-1,2-diolate

[a] From Fig. 1.

Selection of Control Experiments

It is also critical to choose the proper controls for a given diazeniumdiolate experiment, but it is not always obvious how to do so. Several approaches have been used. One is to allow the compound to decompose through many half-lives before injecting it or adding it to the medium; the resulting "spent" diazeniumdiolate by definition contains all the ultimate by-products of the decomposition. One of these is the nitrite ion (the autoxidation product of NO in aqueous solution[18]), which is bioactive in some experiments. Another approach is to use authentic samples of these by-products as controls, alone or in combination. The known decomposition products of the compounds of Fig. 1 are listed in Table I.

[18] L. J. Ignarro, J. M. Fukuto, J. M. Griscavage, N. E. Rogers, and R. E. Byrns, *Proc. Natl. Acad. Sci. U.S.A.* **90,** 8103 (1993).

Summary

1-Substituted diazen-1-ium-1,2-diolates have proved useful as tools in enzymology and other pharmacological research applications in which spontaneous generation of nitric oxide according to a reasonably well-defined time course is required. This chapter summarizes relevant physicochemical data, including the NO release rates and product profiles, for a selection of these compounds. Guidelines for quality control and a systematic nomenclature scheme are also presented. It is hoped that, in summarizing this information here, our chapter will help those contemplating new applications of diazeniumdiolate technology as they seek to capitalize on what we believe are the inherent advantages of this compound type in research on the pharmacological properties of nitric oxide.

Acknowledgment

We thank Professors W. H. Koppenol and J. G. Traynham for invaluable advice on nomenclature.

[28] S-Nitrosothiol Detection

By George N. Welch, Gilbert R. Upchurch, Jr.,
and Joseph Loscalzo

Introduction

Low molecular weight S-nitrosothiols (RSNO) are believed to play an integral role in a variety of different NO-dependent physiological processes, particularly in the vasculature. The physiological relevance of S-nitrosothiols has been confirmed by the demonstration that the predominant redox form of NO in mammalian plasma is S-nitroso serum albumin, a substituted derivative of NO and serum albumin.[1] Total plasma RSNO concentration is approximately 1 μM; in contrast, the concentration of free NO in plasma is approximately 3 nM.[1] S-Nitroso serum albumin accounts for greater than 85% of the plasma RSNO pool. These observations underscore the need for analytic techniques capable of separating and detecting S-nitrosothiols in plasma and other biological fluids.

---

[1] J. S. Stamler, O. Jaraki, J. Osborne, D. I. Simon, J. F. Keaney, J. A. Vita, D. Singel, C. R. Valeri, and J. Loscalzo, *Proc. Natl. Acad. Sci. U.S.A.* **89,** 7674 (1992).

High-Performance Liquid Chromatography
with Electrochemical Detection

In 1977, Rubenstein and Saetre described an application of high-performance liquid chromatography (HPLC) with electrochemical detection (ECD) for the measurement of picomole quantities of low molecular weight thiols in biological fluids.[2] The detection process identified thiols based on their relative redox state and affinity for a mercury electrode.[2] Slivka and colleagues subsequently modified this methodology to permit detection of S-nitrosothiols as well.[3] Using hydrodynamic voltammetry, the optimal reductive potential for S-nitrosothiols was found to be -0.15 V. A C_{18} reversed-phase HPLC column is coupled to an electrochemical detector with a dual Au|Hg electrode set in series at both oxidizing ($+0.15$ V) and reducing (-0.15 V) potentials versus an Ag|AgCl reference electrode. Using this configuration, S-nitrosothiols were reliably separated and detected in the nanomolar concentration range.[4]

Principle

S-Nitrosoglutathione, S-nitroso-L-cysteine, and S-nitrosohomocysteine are initially separated by HPLC using a C_{18} reversed-phase column. The working electrodes are configured in series with the reducing (upstream) electrode set at -0.15 V and the oxidizing (downstream) electrode set at $+0.15$ V. S-Nitrosothiols are detected by both electrodes, first as S-nitrosothiols at the upstream electrode during a reduction step that generates a thiol, which in turn is detected downstream at the oxidizing electrode. The half-reaction that occurs at the reducing electrode is

$$2RSNO + 2H^+ + 2e^- \rightarrow 2RSH + 2NO$$

The half-reaction that occurs at the oxidizing electrode is[5]

$$2RSH + Hg \rightarrow Hg(SR)_2 + 2H^+ + 2e^-$$

Reagents

Citrate–phosphate–dextrose (CPD) anticoagulant (15.6 mM citric acid, 90 mM sodium citrate, 16 mM NaH$_2$PO$_4 \cdot$ H$_2$O, and 142 mM dextrose, pH 7.35) is needed for plasma measurements; 2 mM diethylenetriaminepenta-

[2] D. L. Rubenstein and R. Saetre, *Anal. Chem.* **49,** 1036 (1977).
[3] A. Slivka, J. S. Scharfstein, C. Duda, J. S. Stamler, and J. Loscalzo, *Circulation* **88,** I-523 (1993).
[4] J. S. Scharfstein, J. F. Keaney, A. Slivka, G. N. Welch, J. A. Vita, J. S. Stamler, and J. Loscalzo, *J. Clin. Invest.* **94,** 1432 (1994).
[5] L. A. Allison and R. E. Stroup, *Anal. Chem.* **55,** 12 (1982).

acetic acid (DTPA) is required to minimize metal ion-induced redox reactions. The mobile phase for HPLC is 0.1 M monochloroacetic acid, 0.125 mM disodium ethylenediaminetetraacetic acid (EDTA), 1.25 mM sodium octyl sulfate, and 1% (v/v) acetonitrile, pH 2.8. The mobile phase should be prepared using high purity buffers and deionized, HPLC-grade water. The prepared mobile phase should be filtered through a 0.2-μm filter before use. Wash all glassware beforehand with 0.1 N HCl.

Assay Procedure

The HPLC–ECD system can be assembled using commercially available components. The HPLC column used is a C_{18} (octadecylsilane) column [Bioanalytical Systems (BAS), West Lafayette, IN] and the electrochemical detector consists of a dual Au|Hg electrode (BAS) and an Ag|AgCl reference electrode (BAS). A Rheodyne 20-μl sample injector (Model 712S, Berkeley, CA) and a Model 200A Chromatographic Analyzer (BAS) linked to an IBM computer supplied with chromatographic analysis software (BAS) are incorporated in this system.

The mobile phase is placed in a 1-liter glass flask connected to the C_{18} column. During operation, the mobile phase must be thoroughly deoxygenated by constantly bubbling helium through it (an option built into this particular chromatographic setup). Deoxygenation of the mobile phase prevents two significant problems: (1) dissolved oxygen oxidizes thiols and S-nitrosothiols during elution, leading to poor reproducibility of measurement; and (2) reduction of oxygen at the upstream electrode causes a high negative current at both electrodes. Individual samples should also be deoxygenated with helium to reduce the oxygen content prior to injection. The column flow rate is set at 0.7 ml/min. The mobile phase effluent should be discarded after analysis and not recycled to the mobile phase reservoir.

Electrodes

The dual electrode consists of two circular gold electrodes, each 3.2 mm in diameter. The mercury/gold amalgam is prepared according to the methodology described by Allison and Stroup.[5] A drop of mercury is applied to each electrode surface (enough to cover the entire surface). After 2–3 min, the excess mercury is removed with the edge of a thin plastic card and the electrode surface is wiped with tissue. A well-prepared electrode should have a dull sheen. Reflective areas are indicative of excess mercury, which should be removed with a tissue. The electrode may then be installed and a potential applied; however, an equilibration period of approximately 1 hr is required before using the electrode.

Sample Preparation and Chromatography

The stability of *S*-nitrosothiols is greatly influenced by ambient conditions including pH, oxygen tension, and contaminant metals. The half-life of RSNO under physiological conditions (pH 7.4, 10 mM sodium phosphate) varies widely for biologically relevant RSNOs and is 120 sec for *S*-nitroso-L-cysteine, 70 min for *S*-nitrosohomocysteine, and 5.5 hr for *S*-nitroso-glutathione.[6] To minimize oxidation of RSNOs during sample preparation, the metal chelator DTPA should be added to all samples (final concentration 2 mM). Overnight storage of some biological samples at $-70°$ often results in loss of signal, and, thus, all samples should be analyzed as soon as possible after acquisition until the stability of a given RSNO under the specific conditions of measurement is determined.

Plasma samples are prepared by adding 1 ml of CPD anticoagulant containing 20 mM DTPA to every 9 ml of blood drawn, and the sample should then be immediately centrifuged at 1000 g for 10 min at 4°. The plasma is microfiltered using a Centrifree micropartition system (Amicon, Beverly, MA) with a molecular weight cutoff of 30,000 at 1500 g.[4] The resulting filtrate is then gently deoxygenated by bubbling a stream of helium gas through it for 3–5 min. An aliquot of 30 μl (20-μl injection loop) is then injected into the HPLC–ECD device. All samples should be kept on ice during preparation.

Standard Curves and Recoveries

S-Nitrosothiols are identified and quantified by comparison with authentic standards. The current generated (peak height) is linear over a range of 50 nM to 50 μM ($r = 0.99$).[3] Intra- and interassay variability are both less than 5%. When *S*-nitroso-L-cysteine is added to plasma and immediately subjected to sample preparation, the typical recovery for the RSNO is 93%.

Photolysis–Chemiluminescence

Principle

Detection of NO with the chemiluminescence method is based on the observation that the chemical oxidation of nitric oxide by ozone generates electronically excited NO_2^*, which manifests chemiluminescence on decay to the ground state that is directly proportional to NO concentration. Standard chemiluminescence devices rely on a pyrolyzer to release the nitrosyl radical (NO·). In this modification, we replace the pyrolyzer with a photoly-

[6] P. Ramdev, J. Loscalzo, M. Feelisch, and J. S. Stamler, *Circulation* **88,** I-523 (1993).

sis cell (Nitrolite, Thermedix, Woburn, MA) linked to the reaction chamber and detector portion of a chemiluminescence device (Model 543 Thermal Energy Analyzer, Thermedix).[1]

Assay Procedure

Samples of interest (10- to 100-μl sample volume) are introduced via HPLC pump under a pressure of 350–1000 psi (Model 2350, Isco, Lincoln, NB) into a photolysis cell that consists of a borosilicate glass coil (15 loops each of 8.8 cm external diameter with a total height of 12.0 cm and a total length of 414.6 cm) with a 200-W high-pressure mercury vapor lamp vertically mounted in its center.[1] Irradiation of the sample with UV light (300–400 nm bandwidth) results in complete homolytic photolysis of the S–N bond of RSNOs, thereby allowing measurement of total NO content (free and bound NO). Operating the device with the UV light off measures free NO in any sample. A carrier stream of helium (5 liters/min) transports the effluent through the photolysis cell with a total exposure time to UV light of 5 sec. After exiting the photolysis cell, the sample is carried into two cold traps in series with progressively colder temperatures (0° and −75°) where liquid and gaseous fractions of the mobile phase are removed. Nitric oxide is then transported by the helium stream into the chemiluminescence spectrophotometer where free NO is detected by its reaction with ozone yielding chemiluminescence on return of NO_2^* to the ground state. Signals are recorded with an integrator (Model 3393A, Hewlett-Packard).

Standard Curves and Limits of Detection

Standard curves are determined for S-nitroso-L-cysteine, S-nitrosoglutathione, and S-nitrosoalbumin and are linear with correlation coefficients r of ≥0.98 for all standards.[1] The limit of detection is approximately 10 nM,[1] and the intra- and interassay variability are less than 2%.

Capillary Zone Electrophoresis

Capillary zone electrophoresis (CZE) has been demonstrated to separate compounds reliably on the basis of molecular mass and charge. However, standard CZE frequently involves alkaline conditions under which RSNOs are extremely unstable, decomposing rapidly to yield nitric oxide.[7] Our group, therefore, developed alternate (acidic) electrophoretic conditions for detecting RSNOs. Electrophoretic mobility [cm²/(sec/V)] can be

[7] L. J. Ignarro, H. Lipton, J. C. Edwards, W. H. Baricos, A. L. Hyman, P. J. Kadowitz, and C. A. Gruetter, *J. Pharmacol. Exp. Ther.* **218**, 739 (1981).

related to migration time, t_m, by the relationship $\mu_e = L^2/tV = 5.39 \times 10^{-4}/t_m$, substituting $L_d L_t$ for L^2 where L_d is the length of the capillary from sample injection site to detector and L_t is the full length of the capillary.

Apparatus

A Bio-Rad (Richmond, CA) HPC-100 capillary electrophoresis system is fitted with a silica-coated capillary (20 cm $\times$ 25 μm). Electrophoretic separations are recorded with a Model 1321 single-pen strip-chart recorder (Bio-Rad) with a chart speed of 1.0 cm/min.

Sample Preparation

Samples should be immediately diluted prior to use in 10 mM electrophoresis buffer, which consists of 0.01 N HCl, 10 mM sodium phosphate, pH 2.3.[8] Concentrations of the stock solutions are determined by the Saville reaction.[9]

Assay Procedure

The sample (10 μl) is loaded for 9 sec at 11 kV. After each run, the capillary is flushed with electrophoresis buffer. The power supply is set for positive polarity, thereby resulting in migration of cations toward the detector. Eluted volumes are initially monitored at 200 nm for optimal sensitivity, and then S-nitrosothiol detection is confirmed at 320 nm.

Standard Curves and Limits of Detection

The relationship between peak height and concentration is linear, with a correlation coefficient of 0.99 and intra- and interassay variability of less than 2%. The major drawback of the technique is a lack of sensitivity, with the concentration limits of detection being in the micromolar range.[8]

[8] J. S. Stamler and J. Loscalzo, *Anal. Chem.* **64,** 779 (1992).
[9] B. Saville, *Analyst* **83,** 670 (1958).

[29] S-Nitrosothiols and Role of Metal Ions in Decomposition to Nitric Oxide

By D. Lyn H. Williams

Introduction

S-Nitrosothiols (RSNO), sometimes called thionitrites, are the sulfur analogs of the alkyl nitrites RONO. They are by no means as well-known as are the alkyl nitrites, mainly because many of them are unstable in the pure state at room temperature. Nitrosothiols have come to prominence as part of the nitric oxide story, since they are believed to decompose nonenzymatically to give nitric oxide and could in principle be used therapeutically as NO-producing drugs, for example, in place of the much used glyceryl trinitrate, which is subject to a tolerance problem in some patients. Additionally, nitrosothiols have been detected *in vivo,* and they may play a part in the mechanisms of the well-documented physiological processes that have been attributed to nitric oxide. Indeed, there have been suggestions that nitrosothiols rather than nitric oxide itself constitute the so-called endothelium-derived relaxing factor (EDRF), but this is not the current majority view. Because of these possibilities much more attention has been paid to the chemistry (and pharmacology) of nitrosothiols. Studies have concentrated on their synthesis, reactions that lead to nitric oxide formation, and reactions whereby the NO group can be transferred to other thiol groups. This chapter attempts to bring together aspects of synthesis, properties, and reactions of nitrosothiols with particular emphasis on the decomposition pathway leading to nitric oxide formation brought about in aqueous solution by catalytic quantities of metal ions, most notably Cu^{2+}.

Synthesis of Nitrosothiols

Nitrosothiols are readily formed[1] from thiols and any electrophilic nitrosating agent XNO which acts as a reagent capable of delivering NO^+ as outlined in Eq. (1). The most commonly used reagent is an aqueous solution

$$RSH + XNO \rightarrow RSNO + X^- + H^+ \tag{1}$$

of nitrous acid generated from sodium nitrite and mineral acid and the nitrosothiol separated by filtration or by solvent extraction. It is equally

---

[1] D. L. H. Williams, *Chem. Soc. Rev.* **14,** 171 (1985).

METHODS IN ENZYMOLOGY, VOL. 268

possible to form nitrosothiols from thiols and alkyl nitrites in aqueous acid or alkaline solution and also in a number of nonaqueous solvents such as acetone and chloroform. The reaction is the sulfur analog of the reaction whereby alkyl nitrites are generated from alcohols and a source of NO^+. One difference between the two reactions is that although alkyl nitrite formation is a significantly reversible process (and the reaction driven to completion by removal of the alkyl nitrite by distillation), the reaction of thiols is essentially irreversible, which makes separation of the product easier. The difference can readily be explained in terms of the difference in nucleophilicities and basicities of the sulfur and oxygen atoms in these systems.

In general nitrosothiols are not as stable in the pure state as are the alkyl nitrites. A number, however, have been successfully purified and characterized; some have been known for a number of years.[2] These include the nitrosothiols derived from *tert*-butyl thiol [$(CH_3)_3CSNO$] and triphenyl-methylthiol [$(C_6H_5)_3CSNO$]. Nitrosothiols from *N*-acetyl-DL-penicillamine[3] (SNAP) and glutathione[4] (GSNO) can be isolated and kept as solids at room temperature indefinitely. A detailed X-ray crystal structure determination has been carried out for the former. Similarly, some nitrosothiols from proteins containing the -SH group are quite stable[5] as is *S*-nitrosocysteine within a polypeptide chain[6] (even though *S*-nitrosocysteine itself is quite unstable) and also the dinitroso derivative of a penicillamine dipeptide.[7] A range of nitrosothiols based on cysteamine and its derivatives has been described.[8] Most of the successful syntheses and isolation of stable products were carried out with nitrous acid or *tert*-butyl nitrite. Quite often attempted syntheses have resulted in decomposition at the last moment with the evolution of brown fumes of nitrogen dioxide.

It is possible to generate aqueous solutions of all nitrosothiols readily by treatment of a thiol solution with one of sodium nitrite under acid conditions. These solutions are generally sufficiently stable to enable experiments to be carried out usually after appropriate adjustment of the solution pH, particularly if light is excluded. Nitrosothiol formation from thiols is

[2] H. Rheinboldt, *Chem. Ber.* **59,** 1311 (1926); G. Kresze and U. Uhlich, *Chem. Ber.* **92,** 1048 (1959).

[3] L. Field, R. V. Dilts, R. Ravichandran, P. G. Lenhert, and G. E. Carnahan, *J. Chem. Soc., Chem. Commun.,* 249 (1978).

[4] T. W. Hart, *Tetrahedron Lett.* **26,** 2013 (1985).

[5] J. S. Stamler, D. I. Simon, J. A. Osborne, M. E. Mullins, O. Joraki, T. Michael, D. J. Singel, and J. Loscalzo, *Proc. Natl. Acad. Sci. U.S.A.* **89,** 444 (1992).

[6] P. R. Myers, R. L. Minor, R. Guerra, J. N. Bates, and D. G. Harrison, *Nature* (*London*) **345,** 161 (1990).

[7] H. A. Moynihan and S. M. Roberts, *J. Chem. Soc., Perkin Trans. 1,* 797 (1994).

[8] B. Roy, A. du Moulinet d'Hardemare, and M. Fontecave, *J. Org. Chem.* **59,** 7019 (1994).

usually a very rapid process, so that, in practical terms, when thiol and sodium nitrite solutions (both at a concentration of, say, $1 \times 10^{-2} M$) are mixed in acid solution (say, 50 mM) the nitrosothiol is formed quantitatively within a minute. The reaction mechanism has been established[9] for the nitrous acid reaction; as expected, it is one of electrophilic attack at sulfur and shows the same characteristics as nitrosation of amines, alcohols, and a range of aliphatic and aromatic systems. The reaction is acid catalyzed and also catalyzed by nucleophiles such as halide and thiocyanate ions (when the corresponding nitrosyl halides and thiocyanate are involved). Since thiols are not protonated in dilute acid solution the reactions are generally much faster than the corresponding amine nitrosations.

Physical and Chemical Properties

The stable nitrosothiols are green or red solids or liquids.[10] Generally tertiary structures (such as SNAP) are green and primary ones (such as GSNO) are pink or red. There are characteristic infrared frequencies at 1480–1530 cm^{-1} (N$=$O stretch) and 600–730 cm^{-1} (C–S stretch). In the UV–visible region there are two bands in the 330–350 nm and 550–600 nm regions. The former has the larger extinction coefficient (typically 10^3 dm^3 mol^{-1} cm^{-1}) and is the one usually used to monitor the disappearance of nitrosothiols in quantitative studies such as kinetic measurements. Both ^{1}H and ^{13}C nuclear magnetic resonance (NMR) spectroscopy have been used to characterize nitrosothiols. The shift due to both α protons and α carbons on S-nitrosation is quite diagnostic.[8]

It has long been known that nitrosothiols can decompose to yield the corresponding disulfide and initially nitric oxide as in Eq. (2). Both a

$$2RSNO \rightarrow RSSR + 2NO \qquad (2)$$

photochemical[11] and a thermal[3,12] pathway has been established. In solution at room temperature in the absence of light, decomposition also occurs, and the reaction has been much studied, particularly in aqueous solution, given the intense interest in the development (since the late 1980s) of alternative NO-releasing compounds. The quantitative results reported in the literature are, however, extremely erratic, and there are major differences in rate form (i.e., in the kinetic order of reactions) and in reactivities

[9] P. A. Morris and D. L. H. Williams, *J. Chem. Soc., Perkin Trans. 2*, 513 (1988).

[10] S. Oae and K. Shinhama, *Org. Prep. Proc. Int.* **15**, 165 (1983).

[11] J. Barrett, L. J. Fitygibbones, J. Glauser, R. H. Still, and P. N. W. Young, *Nature (London)* **211**, 848 (1966); J. Barrett, D. F. Debenham, and J. Glauser, *J. Chem. Soc., Chem. Commun.*, 248 (1965).

[12] H. Rheinbolt and F. Mott, *J. Prakt. Chem.* **133**, 328 (1932).

(e.g., as measured in half-lives) between measurements made on the same or similar compounds in different laboratories. Consequently, until 1993 when the importance of the presence of catalytic quantities of Cu^{2+} was realized,[13] not even a qualitative mechanistic picture was available for these reactions. The current position is discussed in the next section.

Another important reaction of nitrosothiols is that in which the nitroso group is transferred to another molecule. There are a number of literature reports referring to transfer to amines and thiols. In principle, such a reaction could occur directly, where the nitrosothiols act as carriers of NO^+ as do alkyl nitrites, or indirectly by initial NO loss [Eq. (2)], which is then oxidized to a higher oxidation state of nitrogen which will allow nitrosation of amines, etc., to occur. If this oxidation is not possible (e.g., if the reaction is carried out anaerobically) then the reaction will not occur, as nitric oxide itself will not act as a nitrosating agent.

The NO group exchange between a nitrosothiol and a thiol has been demonstrated,[14] although under certain circumstances the nitrosothiols will also decompose leading to mixtures of disulfides. It has been shown[15] that the reaction actually involves the attack of the thiolate anion, since the pH–rate profile follows the thiol ionization. Reaction occurs quite generally [Eq. (3)] for a wide range of R and R' structures. The reaction rate is much

$$RSNO + R'S^- \rightleftharpoons RS^- + R'SNO$$
$$\begin{array}{ccc} \updownarrow & & \updownarrow \\ R'SH & & RSH \end{array} \tag{3}$$

faster than that of the decomposition of RSNO and occurs quite readily at physiological pH, depending on the pK_a of the thiol. Rate[15] and equilibrium[16] constants have been reported.

Reactions with Cu^{2+}

The presence of Cu^{2+} in solution has a profound effect on the rate of decomposition of SNAP in water at pH 7.4.[13] The Cu^{2+} is catalytic, and even concentrations as low as 10^{-6} M can be sufficient to bring about the reaction. Indeed, in many samples of distilled water the [Cu^{2+}] is sufficient to bring about decomposition. This accounts for the wide variety of rate data that have been presented in the literature since the adventitious [Cu^{2+}] was not monitored and would be a major variable from one laboratory to

[13] J. McAninly, D. L. H. Williams, S. C. Askew, A. R. Butler, and C. Russell, *J. Chem. Soc., Chem. Commun.*, 1758 (1993); S. C. Askew, D. J. Barnett, J. McAninly, and D. L. H. Williams, *J. Chem. Soc., Perkin Trans.* **2,** 741 (1995).

[14] J. W. Park, *Biochem. Biophys. Res. Commun.* **152,** 916 (1988).

[15] D. J. Barnett, J. McAninly, and D. L. H. Williams, *J. Chem. Soc., Perkin Trans. 2,* 1131 (1994).

[16] D. J. Meyer, H. Kramer, N. Ozer, B. Coles, and B. Kettever, *FEBS Lett.* **345,** 177 (1994).

the next. Reaction can be completely stopped, even for the most reactive of nitrosothiols (e.g., S-nitrosocysteine), by the addition of EDTA which complexes out Cu^{2+}. Thus, if solutions are kept in the dark at room temperature, they are quite stable, so long as the Cu^{2+} level is reduced to a very low level indeed.

The initial products are the disulfide and nitric oxide, that is, the same as for the photochemical and thermal reactions [Eq. (2)]. We have detected nitric oxide from the decomposition of SNAP and other nitrosothiols using the NO-probe electrode system when the reaction is carried out anaerobically. Yields exceeding 70% have been noted for the more reactive nitrosothiols, but as yet we have not taken steps to minimize the loss of NO to the headspace, so that for the slower reacting compounds this loss is a major competitor. In the presence of oxygen, however, the final detected product is nitrite ion, which is formed quantitatively. Separate experiments using only nitric oxide solutions under aerobic conditions have confirmed[17] that nitrite ion is the only product. The rationalization, given in Eqs. (4)–(6),

$$2NO + O_2 \rightleftharpoons 2NO_2 \tag{4}$$
$$NO_2 + NO \rightleftharpoons N_2O_3 \tag{5}$$
$$N_2O_3 + 2OH^- \rightleftharpoons 2NO_2^- + H_2O \tag{6}$$

is that nitric oxide is oxidized to nitrogen dioxide that in turn reacts with more nitric oxide to give dinitrogen trioxide which in aqueous solution, pH 7.4, will be converted to nitrite anion.

We have studied kinetically the reaction of a range of nitrosothiols, many of which are derivatives of S-nitrosocysteine. Reactions are followed spectrophotometrically, noting the disappearance of the absorbance in the 350-nm region due to the reactant, and are carried out at pH 7.4 at 25° over a range of added $[Cu^{2+}]$. Within a given range for each substrate, the reaction shows quite good first-order behavior. Outside this range we find more complex behavior including autocatalysis at low $[Cu^{2+}]$ and a tendency toward zero-order behavior at high $[Cu^{2+}]$. To date we have concentrated on the first-order range in an attempt to establish a structure–reactivity relationship as a probe into the reaction mechanism. Through quite a reasonable $[Cu^{2+}]$ range, the reaction is also first-order in $[Cu^{2+}]$ because plots of the first-order rate constant versus $[Cu^{2+}]$ are linear. There is always a relatively small positive intercept at added $[Cu^{2+}] = 0$, which we take to be the component of the reaction brought about by the adventitious Cu^{2+} present in the water and buffer components. Thus we have established Eq. (7) and determined values of k for a large range of RSNO species. Values

[17] D. A. Wink, J. F. Darbyshire, R. W. Nims, J. E. Saavedra, and P. C. Ford, *Chem. Res. Toxicol.* **6,** 23 (1993).

$$\text{Rate} = k[\text{RSNO}][\text{Cu}^{2+}] \qquad (7)$$

of k vary hugely from approximately 0 for S-nitroso-N-acetylcysteine, S-nitroso-N-acetylcysteamine, and S-nitroso-$tert$-butyl thiol to 67,000, 65,000, and 24,500 mol^{-1} dm^3 sec^{-1} for S-nitrosopenicillamine, S-nitrosocysteamine, and S-nitrosocysteine, respectively, with a number of intermediate reactivity. The results suggest strongly that for rapid reaction to occur, the copper needs to be bidentately bound within an intermediate, probably with the nitrogen atoms of the nitroso group and of the free amine group in the three very reactive nitrosothiols listed above. All of the nitrosothiols fit the general pattern outlined.

A more detailed kinetic and mechanistic study has recently been published.[18a] The full analysis is a little complex and not appropriate within this chapter; however, it is clear that we can explain the unusual kinetic behavior qualitatively, if we assume that Cu^{2+} is reduced during the reaction and that Cu^+ is the true catalyst, which regenerates Cu^{2+} at a later stage of the reaction. It is well-known[18] that thiolate ion can bring about such a reduction [Eq. (8)]. It is likely that RSNO samples contain enough thiol

$$\text{RS}^- + \text{Cu}^{2+} \rightleftharpoons \text{RS}\cdot + \text{Cu}^+ \qquad (8)$$

impurity to bring about such a reduction at the low concentration levels required, but maybe such a reduction could be brought about by RSNO itself. We have tested this theory by attempting the reaction in the presence of a well-known chelating agent for Cu^+, neocuproine.[19] The complex is shown as structure (**1**). Using SNAP at 1×10^{-3} M and added Cu^{2+} at

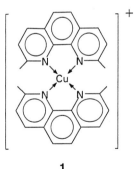

1

2×10^{-5} M we have examined the effect of added neocuproine. The effect is quite dramatic; the rate constant is reduced 10-fold by the addition of

[18a] A. P. Dicks, H. R. Swift, D. L. H. Williams, A. R. Butler, H. H. Al-Sadoni, and B. G. Cox, *J. Chem. Soc., Perkin Trans.* **2**, 481 (1996).

[18] I. M. Klotz, G. H. Czerlinski, and H. A. Fiess, *J. Am. Chem. Soc.* **80**, 2920 (1958).

[19] G. F. Smith and W. H. McCurdy, *Anal. Chem.* **24**, 371 (1952); Y. Yoshida, J. Tsuchiya, and E. Niki, *Biochim. Biophys. Acta* **1200**, 85 (1994).

8×10^{-5} M neocuproine, and reaction is effectively stopped when a large excess $(1 \times 10^{-3}$ M$)$ is added. Further, the characteristic spectrum[19] of the Cu^+ adduct is obtained with an absorption maximum at 456 nm. Similar results are obtained with the nitrosothiol derived from N-(2-mercaptopropionyl)glycine.

Further evidence in favor of involvement of Cu^+ in these reactions comes from an investigation of the effect of adding Cu^+ instead of Cu^{2+}. Again using SNAP as the nitrosothiol, we detect a much faster reaction (as measured by the disappearance of SNAP spectrophotometrically) than for the added Cu^{2+} reaction. The Cu^+ is generated by reduction of Cu^{2+} with dithionite and the SNAP decomposition examined under anaerobic conditions. High yields of nitric oxide are also detected using the NO-probe electrode. The rate equation rate $= k[RSNO][Cu^+]$ is established and the value of k is approximately 50 times greater than for the corresponding reaction using added Cu^{2+}.

On the basis of the results obtained to date we propose the reaction sequence given in Eqs. (9)–(11) as the likely outline mechanism for NO

$$RS^- + Cu^{2+} \rightleftharpoons X^1 \rightarrow RS\cdot + Cu^+ \qquad (9)$$
$$RSNO + Cu^+ \rightleftharpoons X^2 \rightarrow RS^- + Cu^{2+} + NO \qquad (10)$$
$$RSNO + RS\cdot \rightarrow RSSR + NO \qquad (11)$$

or

$$2RS\cdot \rightarrow RSSR$$

formation from nitrosothiols brought about by added Cu^{2+}. Intermediate X^1 is likely to be a structure based on $RSCu^+$, and intermediate X^2 is that given in structure (2). The exact details of the breakup of X^2 are not clear

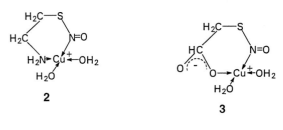

2   **3**

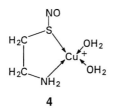

4

at this stage, but the reaction could occur in one step or in several involving a copper–NO complex of some kind. There are still some experimental results that do not fit this picture which will have to be modified; notably, we sometimes find (for the less reactive substrates such as GSNO) reproducibly an induction period for reaction which can be as great as 1 hr. This may be due to the presence of dissolved oxygen which is used up to reoxidize Cu^+ to Cu^{2+}, until all has been removed. However, we are confident that the main mechanistic elements have been put into place.

Our structure–reactivity results fit in well. N-Acetylation of the amine group in **2** would be expected to make the nitrogen atom less nucleophilic and to reduce coordination with Cu^+. The introduction of a further CH_2 into the ring (i.e., going from nitrosocysteine to nitrosohomocysteine) causes a large rate reduction, which can be rationalized in terms of the lower stability of a seven- rather than a six-membered ring intermediate. We also find high reactivity when one of the oxygen atoms of a carboxylate group can bind with the copper as in the *S*-nitroso derivative of thioglycolic acid (or mercaptoacetic acid); the proposed intermediate is shown in **3**. Esterification of the carboxylic group reduces the reactivity greatly, as does the addition of a further CH_2 group to give *S*-nitrosolactic acid. Both of these results fit in with the general picture presented.

An alternative structure for X_2 could reasonably be that given in **4** where Cu^+ is coordinated to the NH_2 group and the sulfur atom of the nitrosothiol. Certainly binding to sulfur is well established for Cu^+. At the present time we prefer our earlier interpretation which involves binding to the nitroso group nitrogen atom. Our reasons are based on the fact that decomposition of nitrosothiols can occur in an acid-catalyzed reaction (at very high acidities) to give initially NO^+, where protonation of sulfur probably occurs.[20] Similarly, as outlined in the next section, very rapid denitrosation of nitrosothiols can be brought about by mercuric ion[21] to give NO^+, again where it is believed that reaction occurs at the sulfur atom. This suggests that coordination at sulfur leads to NO^+ loss while NO is formed from coordination at nitrogen.

Reactions with Other Metal Ions

The discovery of Cu^{2+} catalysis of nitrosothiol decomposition was made during a systematic investigation of possible metal ion catalysis. Our approach was to complex all metal ions naturally present in our solutions

[20] S. S. Al-Kaabi, D. L. H. Williams, R. Bonnett, and S. L. Ooi, *J. Chem. Soc., Perkin Trans. 2*, 227 (1982).
[21] B. Saville, *Analyst* **83**, 670 (1958).

with EDTA and then to examine the effect of any one metal ion by addition of a slight excess over and above the [EDTA]. Thus the Cu^{2+} catalysis came to light. We found no measurable catalysis by added Zn^{2+}, Ca^{2+}, Mg^{2+}, Ni^{2+}, Co^{2+}, Mn^{2+}, Cr^{3+}, or Fe^{3+}. There was catalysis by Cu^+ as indicated in the previous section and also by Fe^{2+} generated by reduction of Fe^{3+} under anaerobic conditions, but this reaction has not yet been further studied.

There was also marked catalysis by Hg^{2+} and to a lesser extent by Ag^+. The former is a well-known reaction[21] and has been used as the basis of an analytical procedure for thiol determination. We examined the reaction kinetically along the same lines as for the Cu^{2+}/Cu^+-catalyzed reactions. There were marked differences: (a) the Hg^{2+} reactions were much faster than the copper reactions; (b) the reactions with Hg^{2+} were stoichiometric rather than catalytic; (c) no trace of nitric oxide was detected with the electrode, when the system was examined anaerobically; and (d) there was very little structure–reactivity dependence as, for example, the rate constants for the reactions of SNAP and S-nitrosopenicallamine differed only by a factor of two whereas for the Cu^{2+} reactions the rate constant ratio was at least 10^5. Consequently Hg^{2+} catalysis may occur by monodentate coordination of Hg^{2+} to the sulfur atom (well known in Hg^{2+} chemistry) of the nitrosothiol, followed by loss of NO^+ either unimolecularly or, more probably, by attack of a water molecule to give finally nitrous acid, as outlined in Eqs. (12) and (13). A similar sequence is proposed for the Ag^+

$$RSNO + Hg^{2+} \rightleftharpoons [RS(Hg)NO]^{2+} \qquad (12)$$
$$[RS(Hg)NO]^{2+} + H_2O \rightarrow RSHg^+ + HNO_2 + H^+ \qquad (13)$$

reaction, which shows the same experimental characteristics as does the Hg^{2+} reaction; the Ag^+ reactions are slower as expected since Ag^+ is known to coordinate less strongly to sulfur sites than does Hg^{2+}. Neither of these reactions appears to have any particular biological significance.

Nitrosothiols in Vivo

Nitrosothiols have been detected and quantified in vivo. Most occur naturally in human plasma as the S-nitrosoalbumins.[22] Further, S-nitroso-glutathione (GSNO) has been measured in up to micromolar concentrations in human bronchial fluid.[23] A number of nitrosothiols including GSNO

[22] J. S. Stamler, O. Jaraki, J. Osborne, D. I. Simon, J. Keaney, J. Vita, D. Singel, C. R. Valeri, and J. Loscalzo, Proc. Natl. Acad. Sci. U.S.A. **89**, 7674 (1992).
[23] B. Gaston, J. Reilly, J. M. Drazen, J. Fackler, P. Ramdev, D. Arnelle, M. E. Mullins, D. J. Sugarbaker, C. Chee, D. J. Singel, J. Loscalzo, and J. Stamler, Proc. Natl. Acad. Sci. U.S.A. **90**, 10957 (1993).

have been shown to possess vasodilatory activity[24] as well as the ability to inhibit platelet aggregation.[25] They are also implicated in a number of other biological processes. An earlier suggestion[6] that the EDRF is not free nitric oxide but a nitrosothiol is now not a view which is widely held, but nitrosothiols may well play an important role in nitric oxide storage within the body, given the ready pathway for NO group transfer to a thiolate ion. Already nitrosothiols, specifically GSNO, are being used therapeutically (a) to inhibit platelet aggregation during coronary angioplasty[26] and (b) to treat a form of preeclampsia in pregnant women.[27] Its activity may be associated with its ability to inhibit platelet aggregation at dose levels that do not lower blood pressure, in contrast to other available NO donors.

Acknowledgments

I thank Dr. A. R. Butler (University of St. Andrews, Scotland) and Dr. V. Darley-Usmar (Wellcome Research Laboratories) for many stimulating discussions of nitrosothiol chemistry. I acknowledge also the contribution of members of my research group in Durham University to parts of the work described in this chapter, particularly Dr. D. J. Barnett, Dr. J. McAninly, Mr. A. P. Dicks, and Miss H. R. Swift.

[24] T. B. Mellion, L. J. Ignarro, L. B. Myers, E. H. Ohlstein, B. A. Ballot, A. L. Hyman, and P. J. Kadowitz, *Mol. Pharmacol.* **23,** 653 (1983).
[25] L. J. Ignarro, H. Lippton, J. C. Edwards, W. H. Baricos, A. L. Hyman, J. Kadowitz, and C. A. Gruetter, *J. Pharmacol. Exp. Ther.* **218,** 739 (1981).
[26] E. J. Langford, A. S. Brown, R. J. Wainwright, A. J. de Belder, M. R. Thomas, R. E. A. Smith, M. W. Radomski, J. F. Martin, and S. Moncada, *Lancet* **344,** 1458 (1994).
[27] A. de Belder, C. Lees, J. Martin, S. Moncada, and S. Campbell, *Lancet* **345,** 124 (1995).

Section II

Biochemistry and Molecular Biology of Enzymes and Proteins Associated with Nitric Oxide Metabolism

A. Nitric Oxide Synthase: Reaction Mechanism, Purification, and Activity Assays
Articles 30 through 35

B. Inhibitors of Nitric Oxide Synthase Isozymes
Articles 36 through 39

C. Induction of Nitric Oxide Synthase
Articles 40 and 41

D. Molecular Cloning and Expression
Articles 42 through 44

E. Nitric Oxide Synthase and Hemoprotein Homology
Articles 45 and 46

F. Tissue Distribution of Nitric Oxide Synthase
Articles 47 through 50

[30] Binding Sites of Nitric Oxide Synthases

By QING LIU and STEVEN S. GROSS

Introduction

Consideration of nitric oxide synthase (NOS; EC 1.14.13.39) structure reveals a classic strategy in protein evolution: complex structure–function relationships emerging from the assembly of discrete polypeptide modules subserving distinct ligand-binding and functional roles. On the basis of amino acid consensus sequences shared between NOSs, putative ancestral bacterial proteins, and mammalian homologs, it is apparent that NOSs have evolved from preexisting genes by duplication, rearrangement, and fusion. Although the selective advantage conferred to the first NO-producing cells is unclear, the ubiquity of NO synthesis throughout phylogenetic kingdoms attests to its broad utility. Indeed, arginine-derived NO synthesis has been identified in mammals,[1] fish,[2] birds,[3] invertebrates,[4] plants, and bacteria.[5] Best studied are mammals, where arginine-derived NO synthesis arises from three distinct genes that encode isoforms of NOS. These NOS genes are composed of either 26 exons (inducible NOS[6] and endothelial NOS[7]; iNOS and eNOS) or 29 exons (neuronal NOS[8]; nNOS) which are telling with regard to their domain structure and evolutionary ancestry. This chapter summarizes our knowledge of domains and sites on mammalian NOS isoforms that have been implicated in the binding of substrates, cofactors, and prosthetic groups. We also provide a simple protocol that can be used to assess radioligand binding to NOS. To date this method has been useful for characterization and localization of arginine and tetrahydrobiopterin (BH₄) sites, and their interaction. Nonetheless, it should have general utility in the evaluation of ligand-binding domains of NOS.

---

[1] C. Nathan, *FASEB J.* **6**, 3051 (1992).
[2] P. Hylland and G. E. Nilsson, *J. Cereb. Blood Flow Metab.* **15**, 519 (1995).
[3] K. H. Lee, *et al.*, *J. Biol. Chem.* **269**, 14371 (1994).
[4] U. Muller and G. Bicker, *J. Neurosci.* **14**, 7521 (1994).
[5] Y. Chen and J. P. Rosazza, *Biochem. Biophys. Res. Commun.* **203**, 1251 (1994).
[6] D. A. Geller, *et al.*, *Proc. Natl. Acad. Sci. U.S.A.* **90**, 3491 (1993).
[7] K. Miyahara, *et al.*, *Eur. J. Biochem.* **223**, 719 (1994).
[8] A. V. Hall, *et al.*, *J. Biol. Chem.* **269**, 33082 (1994).

General Features of Catalysis by Nitric Oxide Synthase as Revealed
by Substrates, Cofactors, Prosthetic Groups, and Homologies

Nitric oxide synthases are homodimeric proteins that produce NO by
catalyzing a five-electron oxidation of one of the equivalent guanidino
nitrogen atoms of L-arginine (L-Arg). Although the arginine-binding site
in NOS has not been precisely identified, its localization in nNOS may be
limited to a 170-amino acid sequence in the N-terminal oxygenase domain[9]
(see below). Arginine oxidation by NOS occurs via two successive monooxygenation reactions producing N^ω-hydroxyl-L-arginine as an isolatable intermediate; 2 mol of O_2 and 1.5 mol of NADPH are consumed per mole of
NO formed.[10] Thus, for catalysis to occur, NOS must twice bind and activate
O_2 in tight proximity to the L-Arg-binding active site, using electrons derived
from NADPH. This task is achieved and regulated using five bound cofactors and prosthetic groups: flavin adenine dinucleotide (FAD), flavin mononucleotide (FMN), iron-protoporphyrin IX (heme), tetrahydrobiopterin
(BH_4), and calmodulin (CaM). Although these factors are widely found in
nature, NOSs are the only enzymes to simultaneously require all five. An
appreciation of how and where these factors act lies at the heart of our
understanding of NOS catalytic function.

Important insight into NOS structure and function was revealed with
the molecular cloning of rat nNOS and deduction of its amino acid sequence.[11] The C-terminal half of the protein was shown to be remarkable
in its homology to only one mammalian protein, cytochrome P450 reductase
(CPR). The enzyme CPR is itself composed of an N-terminal hydrophobic
sequence that serves as an anchor to the endoplasmic reticulum, followed
by two polypeptide subdomains that display marked homology with FMN-
containing electron transferases (e.g., bacterial flavodoxins) and FAD/
NADPH-containing transhydrogenases (e.g., ferredoxin-NADP$^+$ reductase; FNR).[12] Before the discovery of NOS, CPR was singular among mammalian proteins in its content of an electron transferase domain and a
transhydrogenase domain, fused in a single polypeptide. Flavin- and
NADPH-binding sites on NOS, as well as CPR, are predicted from striking
sequence homologies with bacterial and mammalian flavoproteins that
uniquely contain either FMN or FAD and whose three-dimensional cofac-
tor-containing structures have been revealed at high resolution (see below).
By analogy with CPR and its ancestral protein "building blocks," it is
apparent that the overall function of the reductase domain in NOS is 2-

[9] J. S. Nishimura, et al., Biochem. Biophys. Res. Commun. 210, 288 (1995).
[10] D. J. Stuehr and O. W. Griffith, Adv. Enzymol. Relat. Areas Mol. Biol. 65, 287 (1992).
[11] D. S. Bredt, et al., Nature (London) 351, 714 (1991).
[12] T. D. Porter, T. W. Beck, and C. B. Kasper, Biochemistry 29, 9814 (1990).

fold: (a) to serve as a conduit for delivering single electrons to molecular oxygen from NADPH, an obligate two-electron donor (electrons flow from NADPH through FAD to FMN, in that order[13]), and (b) to operate as an electron reservoir (with an electron capacity of four, corresponding to fully reduced FAD and FMN), enabling delivery of an odd number of electrons required for production of one molecule of NO, despite the capacity of NADPH to provide only an even number of electrons. As for CPR, "leak" of electrons from either of the flavins can contribute to the uncoupling of NADPH consumption and substrate oxidation.

All NOS isoforms are catalytically self-sufficient, contrasting with the P450 reductase/monooxygenase system in which CPR serves as a ubiquitous reductase needed for function of all members of the extensive cytochrome P450 monooxygenase gene family. Catalytic sufficiency of NOS is explained in its structure; the CPR-homologous C-terminal reductase domain is bridged to an N-terminal heme-containing oxygenase domain that displays characteristics of a cytochrome P450 monooxygenase. The interdomain "bridge" between the oxygenase and reductase domains of NOS is provided by a prototypic calmodulin-binding sequence which, in the case of iNOS, has such high avidity that calmodulin binds even at levels of Ca^{2+} which are far lower than basal in mammalian cells.[14] All three mammalian NOS isoforms share this bidomain structure and calmodulin-binding sequence, displaying 50–60% homology with one another at the amino acid level.

Precedent for the linkage on a single polypeptide of P450-like reductase and oxygenase functionalities is provided in $P450_{BM-3}$, a catalytically self-sufficient fatty acid monooxygenase from *Bacillis megaterium* that is 33% homologous with mammalian CPR in its C-terminal domain and 25% homologous with a mammalian microsomal type IV cytochrome P450 monooxygenase at its N terminus.[15] Just as limited trypsin proteolysis has been shown to bisect $P450_{BM-3}$ into its two functional domains,[15] nNOS[16] and iNOS[17] can be similarly cleaved, enabling study of the domains in isolation.

Calmodulin binding to nNOS has been demonstrated to regulate catalytic activity by triggering electron flux from FMN to heme, thereby effectively coupling the oxygenase and reductase domains.[18] Whereas calmodulin is presumed to achieve this effect by an allosteric mechanism involving the realignment of bound FMN and heme within NOS, it is notable that calmodulin also facilitates NADPH-mediated reduction of cytochrome *c*

[13] J. L. Vermilion, D. P. Ballou, V. Massey, and M. J. Coon, *J. Biol. Chem.* **256,** 266 (1981).
[14] H. J. Cho, *et al., J. Exp. Med.* **176,** 599 (1992).
[15] R. T. Ruettinger, L. P. Wen, and A. J. Fulco, *J. Biol. Chem.* **264,** 10987 (1989).
[16] E. A. Sheta, K. McMillan, and B. S. Masters, *J. Biol. Chem.* **269,** 15147 (1994).
[17] D. K. Ghosh and D. J. Stuehr, *Biochemistry* **34,** 801 (1995).
[18] H. M. Abu-Soud and D. J. Stuehr, *Proc. Natl. Acad. Sci. U.S.A.* **90,** 10769 (1993).

and ferricyanide in heme- and BH_4-depleted nNOS.[19] This suggests that calmodulin may activate nNOS by facilitating electron transfer both from FMN to heme and between the flavins. The perpetual activity of iNOS is explained by a remarkably high avidity for calmodulin, such that calmodulin dissociation is incomplete even after such drastic procedures as boiling in sodium dodecyl sulfate (SDS) and 8 M urea.[14]

Perhaps the least understood aspect of NOS enzymology concerns the role of its reduced pterin cofactor. The initial discovery of BH_4 as a component of purified iNOS led to the prediction that BH_4 would function as a redox-active cofactor,[20,21] serving to activate O_2 for catalysis, analogous to its function in catalysis by the aromatic amino-acid hydroxylases.[22] This view, however, was opposed by subsequent findings that BH_4 is required in catalytic rather than stoichiometric quantities[23] and knowledge that an accessory dihydropteridine reductase is not needed by NOS to regenerate BH_4 from BH_2. Thus, direct evidence for redox cycling of BH_4 is lacking. Nonetheless, the observation that numerous tetrahydropterin analogs can substitute for BH_4 in supporting NOS catalysis, while such support has never been seen with a homologous dihydropterin analog (S. Gross, unpublished), suggests that BH_4 may be redox active in NOS catalysis. Indeed, we hypothesize that redox cycling of BH_4 takes place *in situ*, while bound to NOS; such an event would not be detected by techniques that have been applied. Notwithstanding, NOSs are heme-containing and heme-dependent, and they exhibit a CO difference spectrum prototypic of cytochrome P450. Thus, it is appropriate that present mechanisms to explain NOS catalysis have arisen based on analogy to cytochromes P450 function. Nonetheless, the critical function of BH_4 in NOS catalysis remains to be accommodated. As described below, analysis of BH_4-binding to NOS has offered some insight into BH_4 function.

Traversing Nitric Oxide Synthase from Amino Terminus to Carboxyl Terminus in Search of Binding Domains

Syntrophin-Homology Domain

Alignment of the three mammalian NOS gene products reveals that nNOS from rat and humans contains an N-terminal leader sequence of

[19] H. M. Abu-Soud, L. L. Yoho and D. J. Stuehr, *J. Biol. Chem.* **269**, 32047 (1994).
[20] N. S. Kwon, C. F. Nathan, and D. J. Stuehr, *J. Biol. Chem.* **264**, 20496 (1989).
[21] M. A. Tayeh and M. A. Marletta, *J. Biol. Chem.* **264**, 19654 (1989).
[22] S. Kaufman, *Annu. Rev. Nutr.* **13**, 261 (1993).
[23] J. Giovanelli, K. L. Campos, and S. Kaufman, *Proc. Natl. Acad. Sci U.S.A.* **88**, 7091 (1991).

about 290 amino acids which is absent from iNOS and eNOS. This is reflected in an initial three exons that are present in the human nNOS gene but conspicuously missing from human iNOS and eNOS genes. As first noted by Ponting and Phillips,[24] a search of this sequence against the nonredundant protein database reveals significant homology to syntrophins, a multigene family of proteins that are predominantly localized to sarcolemma.[25] Notably, syntrophins are enriched at the neuromuscular junction via binding to C-terminal domains of dystrophin, utrophin, and homologs. Binding to dystrophin in skeletal muscle[26] may explain the unusual membrane localization of nNOS in this tissue and loss of membrane localization in the dystropin-deficient *mdx* mouse.[26a] Direct binding of nNOS to dystrophin and homologs is predictable but has not yet been demonstrated. Moreover, the relevance of a syntrophin homology domain in nNOS to NO function and dysfunction of skeletal muscle awaits investigation.

Heme-Binding Site

Stoichiometric quantities of heme cofactor are present in nNOS and are required for full catalytic activity.[27–29] Moreover, NOS activity is disrupted by heme-binding ligands such as CO in the presence of NADPH,[28] imidazoles,[30] and certain arginine analogs which additionally ligand heme.[31] The interaction of arginine with heme in nNOS is revealed by the ability of arginine to elicit a "type I" difference spectrum,[32] indicative of a shift in the iron from a low-spin to high-spin state. Resonance Raman spectra demonstrate that heme coordination is pentavalent and that thiolate serves as a fifth axial ligand.[33] Identification of the specific cysteine residue involved in heme coordination was tentatively distinguished in rat nNOS on the basis of homology with cytochromes P450 to be Cys-415 and confirmed by site-directed mutagenesis.[34] A similar mutational analysis supports the view that the homologous cysteine in eNOS also provides the fifth ligand to

[24] C. P. Ponting and C. Phillips, *Trends Biochem. Sci.* **20**, 102 (1995).
[25] M. F. Peters, N. R. Kramarcy, R. Sealock, and S. C. Froehner, *Neuroreport* **5**, 1577 (1994).
[26] L. Kobzick, M. Reid, D. Bredt, and J. Stamler, *Nature* (*London*) **372**, 504 (1994).
[26a] J. E. Brenman, D. S. Chao, H. Xia, K. Aldape, and D. S. Bredt, *Cell* **82**, 743 (1995).
[27] D. J. Stuehr and M. Ikeda-Saito, *J. Biol. Chem.* **267**, 20547 (1992).
[28] K. A. White and M. A. Marletta, *Biochemistry* **31**, 6627 (1992).
[29] K. McMillan, *et al.*, *Proc. Natl. Acad. Sci. U.S.A.* **89**, 11141 (1992).
[30] D. J. Wolff, G. A. Datto, and R. A. Samatovicz, *J. Biol. Chem.* **268**, 9430 (1993).
[31] C. Frey, *et al.*, *J. Biol. Chem.* **269**, 26083 (1994).
[32] K. McMillan and B. S. Masters, *Biochemistry* **32**, 9875 (1993).
[33] J. Wang, D. J. Stuehr, M. Ikeda-Saito, and D. L. Rousseau, *J. Biol. Chem.* **268**, 22255 (1993).
[34] K. McMillan and B. S. Masters, *Biochemistry* **34**, 3686 (1995).

heme.[35] Indeed, this cysteine is conserved in all isoforms of NOS from every species examined and corresponds to Cys-200 in human iNOS and Cys-184 in human eNOS. Exons encoding the heme–thiolate-containing sequence of NoSs are also highly conserved; each encodes a 54-amino acid sequence corresponding to exon 6 (nNOS and iNOS) or exon 4 (eNOS).

Arginine- and Tetrahydrobiopterin-Binding Domains

Although it has been assumed that arginine and BH_4 each bind to sites on the oxygenase domain of NoSs (residues 1–724 of rat nNOS and iNOS[1–501]), this was formally demonstrated in studies of the isolated domains. Taking advantage of a single trypsin-sensitive site at the N-terminal end of the calmodulin domain in rat nNOS at Ala-728, Sheta *et al.* cleaved nNOS and purified its N-terminal heme-containing fragment.[16] Notably, it was deduced that this fragment bound L-arginine. Spectral characterization of this oxygenase domain (rat nNOS[1–714]), following expression in bacteria, revealed a type 1 difference spectrum on addition of either arginine or BH4,[34] thus confirming the presence of cognate binding sites. A study of tryptic fragments of iNOS similarly demonstrated by spectral analyses that the oxygenase domain could bind arginine, CO, and imidazole and additionally contains BH_4 and a site(s) involved in protein dimerization.[17]

Radioligand binding studies with ^{3}H-labeled N^ω-nitro-L-arginine (NNA), a selective NOS inhibitor, have been used to probe the arginine site of rat nNOS.[36,37] Since BH_4 is largely retained in NOS after its purification, the importance of BH_4 for modulation of the arginine binding site was not appreciated in these initial reports. As shown in Fig. 1, studies of NNA binding to BH_4-depleted iNOS reveals that BH_4 is essential for specific NNA binding to occur. In the presence of BH_4 a single class of high-affinity NNA site is observed (K_D 200–300 nM). The concentration of BH_4 required for a half-maximal "appearance" of NNA binding is approximately 20 nM, consistent with the K_D which we have observed for binding of ^{14}C]BH_4 to iNOS (Fig. 2) and activation of iNOS catalysis by BH_4 (not shown). It is significant that the potency of tetrahydropterin analogs for eliciting NNA binding correlates with their relative abilities to support catalysis by iNOS. A truncated oxygenase domain comprising nNOS[220–721] was expressed in *Escherichia coli* and found to bind NNA with a high affinity similar to that observed with holo-nNOS ($\sim$50 nM), and

[35] P. F. Chen, A. L. Tsai, and K. K. Wu, *J. Biol. Chem.* **269**, 25062 (1994).

[36] A. D. Michel, R. K. Phul, T. L. Stewart, and P. P. Humphrey, *Br. J. Pharmacol.* **109**, 287 (1993).

[37] P. Klatt, K. Schmidt, F. Brunner, and B. Mayer, *J. Biol. Chem.* **269**, 1674 (1994).

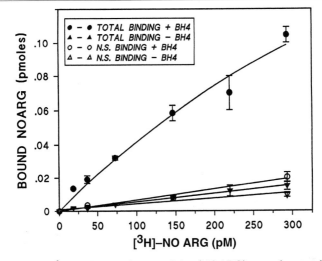

FIG. 1. Binding of ^{3}H-labeled N^ω-nitro-L-arginine (NOARG) to crude cytosol from BH$_4$-depleted rat aortic smooth muscle cells grown in culture. Cells were grown in the presence of BH$_4$ synthesis inhibitors, and iNOS was induced by 16 hr of treatment with a combination of lipopolysaccharide LPS; 0111:B4, 30 μg/ml) and rat γ-interferon (100 ng/ml). Cells were harvested and cytosol prepared as previously described [S. S. Gross and R. Levi, *J. Biol. Chem.* **267**, 25722 (1992)]. Binding of NOARG was evaluated in the absence and presence of 10 μM BH$_4$, following filtration through Whatman (Clifton, NJ) GF/B paper.

again BH$_4$ was essential for binding to occur.[9] It is notable that *E. coli* does not produce BH$_4$, and hence bacterial expressed nnos is pterin-free unlike that from mammalian sources. This confirms by direct measurement that BH$_4$ and arginine sites are contained within nNOS[220–721]. Moreover, it indicates that an important function of BH$_4$ in NOS catalysis may be to serve as an allosteric effector of the arginine binding site, allowing arginine to bind and correctly orient with heme.

Appreciation of the presence of a 160-amino acid sequence within the oxygenase domain of nNOS with apparent homology to dihydrofolate reductase (J. Salerno, unpublished), a pterin-binding enzyme, raised the possibility that this site could contribute to the BH$_4$-binding subsite. Interestingly, this putative DHFR module (nNOS[558–721]) was expressed in *E. coli* and found to bind NNA, albeit with lower affinity than the intact oxygenase domain (nNOS[220–721]).[9] However, BH$_4$ dependence of NNA binding to nNOS[558–721] was not observed. In contrast, nNOS[220–558] was found to be incapable of binding either BH$_4$ or NNA. We interpret these findings to indicate that nNOS[558–721] contains sufficient sequence for arginine binding, but extension N-terminally of up to 338 amino acids is needed for high-affinity binding and regulation by BH$_4$.

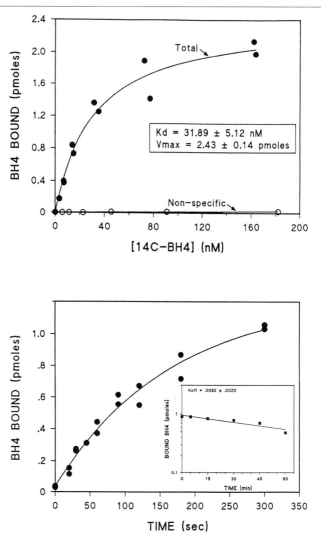

Fig. 2. Binding of [^{14}C]BH$_4$ to crude cytosol from BH$_4$-depleted rat aortic smooth muscle cells grown in culture. The iNOS-containing cytosol was prepared and binding reactions were performed essentially as described for Fig. 1, except that [^{14}C]BH$_4$ was used as the radioligand and assay included 1 mM L-arginine. *Top*: Saturation binding analysis; *bottom*: kinetics of association and dissociation.

Studies of the BH_4 site of nNOS and iNOS suggest isoform differences. Direct binding of [^{3}H]BH_4 to purified nNOS from pig brain indicated a K_D of 250 nM and a 6-fold increase in affinity with arginine.[38] Interestingly, binding was inhibited by 7-nitroindazole, an agent thought to inhibit NOS by binding to heme. Thus, interactions between the heme and arginine sites could be detected at the BH_4 site of nNOS. In contrast, studies of [^{14}C]BH_4 binding to iNOS suggest a K_D of 30 nM (Fig. 2, top) and no significant increase in affinity on addition of L-arginine (S. Gross, unpublished, 1993). Nonetheless, arginine is found to increase the number of sites available for binding BH_4. The rate of BH_4 association with iNOS is rapid and dissociation is slow; a $t_{1/2}$ of about 70 min for dissociation from iNOS at 25° is observed (Fig. 2, bottom), which is markedly greater than that reported for nNOS. Although BH_2 is an exceedingly weak compatititor for BH_4 binding to iNOS (K_D >300 μM; S. Gross, unpublished, 1993), it potently inhibits binding to nNOS (K_D 2.2 μM).[38] From these disparities significant differences in BH_4 binding sites of NOS isoforms may be anticipated.

Calmodulin-Binding Site

The appreciation that nNOS requires calmodulin for activity enabled the first purification of an NOS isoform.[39] As discussed above, calmodulin (CaM) binding serves to gate the flux of electrons between reductase and oxygenase domains of NOSs, and is the principal means for regulation of eNOS and nNOS. Rat iNOS possesses extremely high CaM avidity even in the presence of Ca^{2+} chelators; although CaM-binding to human iNOS may display a somewhat greater Ca^{2+} dependence,[6] for practical purposes it may still be considered Ca^{2+} independent. Putative CaM-binding domains in NOSs have been defined by their canonical content of basic and lipophillic amino acids. They span 20–25 amino acids and arise from two exons in each of the mammalian NOS genes. It is notable that the calmodulin-binding domain of eNOS contains a 4-amino acid deletion in its N-terminal aspect, perhaps giving a lower affinity for calmodulin. The only direct measurement of calmodulin binding affinity has been performed with nNOS, where calmodulin was found by flurorescence quenching to bind with a K_D of 1 nM in the presence of calcium.[16] Study of a 23-amino acid peptide comprising the putative calmodulin domain of nNOS revealed that calmodulin binds 1 : 1 to this fragment, with a 2.2 nM affinity in the presence of calcium.[40] Circular dichroism and two-dimensional (2D) nuclear magnetic resonance (NMR) measurements suggest that the peptide assumes

---

[38] P. Klatt, *et al.*, *J. Biol. Chem.* **269**, 13861 (1994).
[39] D. S. Bredt and S. H. Snyder, *Proc. Natl. Acad. Sci. U.S.A.* **87**, 682 (1990).
[40] M. Zhang and H. J. Vogel, *J. Biol. Chem.* **269**, 981 (1994).

an α-helical conformation on interaction with CaM, analogous to the conformation of the CaM-bound domain of myosin light chain kinase.

FMN-Binding Domain

On the basis of homology with ancestral flavoproteins such as flavodoxins, which contain only FMN, the FMN domain of NOS can be considered to extend from the calmodulin site toward the C terminus including about 200 amino acids (corresponding to nNOS$^{736-936}$). This sequence is encoded by three exons of CPR, which correspond to exons 13–16 of iNOS, 14–18 of nNOS, and 12–16 of eNOS. It is notable that exon 17 of nNOS and exon 15 of eNOS are unique and not represented in either iNOS or CPR, resulting in an insert of approximately 30 amino acids with unknown function. Homology between NOSs and CPR commences approximately 10 amino acids from the C-terminal end of the CaM domain, beginning with Ile-80 of CPR. Crystallographic studies of flavodoxin strongly suggest that this initial segment, which is conserved in CPR, cytochrome P450$_{BM-3}$, and sulfite reductase, serves to bind the phosphate group of FMN.[41] Additionally, in flavodoxins and CPR the isoalloxazine ring of FMN is known to be shielded on either side by aromatic amino acid residues. CPR ring-shielding residues are Tyr-140 and Tyr-178 which maintain a hydrophobic environment for the flavin ring and may participate in π–π stacking.[42] Mutation of Tyr-178, the exterior ring-shielding group that has been shown to lie coplanar with the flavin ring in flavodoxin, abolishes CPR activity and causes a loss of FMN.[43] On the other hand, mutation of Tyr-140, which lies interiorly and at a 45° angle to the flavin ring, causes a modest decrease in CPR activity, but no loss of FMN. It is notable that 100% conservation of homologous tyrosine residues (Tyr-791 and Tyr-889 in rat nNOS) are observed in NOS isoforms from all species sequenced to date. Moreover, the amino acids surrounding the exterior Tyr have been demonstrated in flavodoxin to engage in hydrogen bonding with the pyrimidine moiety of the FMN isoalloxazine ring.[41] This sequence is highly conserved in NOSs, CPR, cytochrome P450$_{BM-3}$, and sulfite reductase and corresponds to rat nNOS$^{878-895}$

FAD-Binding Domain

For approximately 50 amino acids from the end of the FMN domain, sequence homology is well conserved between NOSs, but not with CPR.

[41] K. D. Watenpaugh, L. C. Sieker, and L. H. Jensen, *Proc. Natl. Acad. Sci. U.S.A.* **70**, 3857 (1973).

[42] T. D. Porter and C. B. Kasper, *Biochemistry* **25**, 1682 (1986).

[43] A. L. Shen, T. D. Porter, T. E. Wilson, and C. B. Kasper, *J. Biol. Chem.* **264**, 7584 (1989).

This sequence is encoded within two exons of CPR and the NOSs. The remaining C-terminal sequence of NOSs and CPR comprises the FAD domain, which contains binding sites for both FAD and NADPH and is encoded by the terminal eight exons (eNOS and iNOS) or nine exons (nNOS) in the NOS genes. The extreme C-terminal sequence of NOSs (21 and 33 amino acids in rat iNOS and nNOS, respectively) extends beyond the C terminus of CPR and, at least in the case of iNOS, is not required for catalysis.[44] However, deletion from iNOS of a further two or three C-terminal amino acids results in a 71 and 95% loss of activity, respectively.[44]

Homology with ferredoxin-NADP$^+$ reductase (FNR; an FAD-containing transhydrogenase[45]) begins approximately 40 amino acids from the end of the FMN domain of CPR and extends for 60 amino acids before being disrupted by a 117-residue insert.[46] Sequence homology between CPR and FNR resumes following this insert and is sustained thereafter. This overall structural relationship is maintained in the FAD domain of the NOSs. Comparison with the crystal structure of FAD-protein glutathione reductase[47] indicates that the initial (N-terminal) sequence which is conserved with FNR represents the FAD pyrophosphate-binding site in CPR[43] and, by analogy, the NOSs. This apparent FAD pyrophosphate-binding site, appreciated by Bredt and Synder in their seminal nNOS cloning report,[11] corresponds to nNOS$^{1029-1040}$. The large insert which follows, and which is not found in flavoproteins possessing a single flavin, is likely to provide orientation for interflavin electron transport.[46] Sequence alignment resumes following the insert with a sequence corresponding to nNOS$^{1174-1181}$ that is highly conserved among all FAD proteins and that is thought to function as the FAD isoalloxazine ring-binding region.[42]

The NADPH pyrophosphate-binding site in NOS is ascribed to a conserved consensus motif, GXGXGX, which has been established to engage in hydrogen bonding to pyrophosphate in glutathione reductase.[48] This sequence is conserved in all NOSs (rat nNOS$^{1249-1254}$) and aligns perfectly with that in CPR and FNR. Following this glycine-rich sequence by 30 amino acids is a cysteine residue that is conserved in CPR, cytochrome P450$_{BM-3}$, and all NOSs (nNOS^{1282}) and contributes to the NADPH site as deduced from the ability of NADPH to protect against reaction with sulfhydryl reagents.[49] A highly conserved lysine (corresponding to

[44] Q. W. Xie, et al., J. Biol. Chem. **269**, 28500 (1994).
[45] Y. Yao, T. Tamura, K. Wada, H. Matsubara, and K. Kodo, J. Biochem. (Tokyo) **95**, 1513 (1984).
[46] T. D. Porter, Trends Biochem. Sci. **16**, 154 (1991).
[47] G. E. Schulz, R. H. Schirmer, and E. F. Pai, J. Mol. Biol. **160**, 287 (1982).
[48] M. Rescigno and R. N. Perham, Biochemistry **33**, 5721 (1994).
[49] M. Haniu, T. Iyanagi, K. Legesse, and J. E. Shively, J. Biol. Chem. **259**, 13703 (1984).

nNOS[1320]) is also thought to contribute to the NADPH binding site by interacting with the 2′-phosphate group on the adenosine ribose; accordingly NADPH protects against covalent reaction with this lysine.[50] NADPH adenine binding to CPR further involves a final stretch of highly conserved C-terminal sequence, which is homologous to nNOS[1346–1358]. Thus, although there has been little investigation of NOS binding sites for flavins and reduced pyridine nucleotides, the wealth of knowledge from homologous proteins makes it likely that these tentative assignments will prove correct. Ligand binding studies in conjunction with site-directed mutagenesis of NOSs should allow direct testing.

Protocol for Determination of Radioligand Binding to Nitric Oxide Synthases

The following is a simple protocol that can be used to quantitate number, affinity, and modulation of [³H]NNA and [¹⁴C]BH4 binding sites on NOS. In our hands it has proved effective with both crude NOS-containing cell extracts and purified enzymes. As the method is merely an effective means for separating NOS-bound and free radioligand, we anticipate its use for binding studies involving other nonprotein radioligands that bind NOS with high affinity. For simplicity, we describe only the protocol we use for NNA binding. An example of an NNA-binding experiment performed using this protocol is provided in Fig. 3, including raw data and plotted results (see Ref. 51). The NNA reagent (³H-labeled N^ω-nitro-L-arginine) is available from DuPont New England Nuclear (Beverly, MA) with a specific activity of about 34 mCi/mmol in quantities of 250 and 1000 μCi.

Binding assays are performed in 96-well microfiltration plates [opaque, polyvinyldifluoride (PVDF) membrane-bottom; Millipore, Bedford, MA]. This has the advantage that 96-well technology can be applied (multichannel pipettors, repeating pipettors, etc.) and a single microfiltration plate can be used for incubation, filtration, and scintillation counting. In addition to advantages of speed, throughput, and precision, the quantities of scintillant consumed (25 μl) and radioactive waste produced (700 μl) per sample are minimal.

The PVDF membrane must be wet before use; thus, all wells of a microfiltration plate are preincubated with 100 μl of 50% (v/v) ethanol for 2–3 min (or until the membrane changes color to off-white). Ethanol is removed using two washes with 200 μl of 50 mM Tris-HCl, pH 7.6, under vacuum filtration. Binding assays are routinely performed in triplicate and

[50] R. L. Chan, N. Carrillo, and R. H. Vallejos, *Arch. Biochem. Biophys.* **240**, 172 (1985).
[51] L. J. Roman, E. A. Sheta, P. Martasek, S. S. Gross, Q. Liu, and B. S. S. Masters, *Proc. Natl. Acad. Sci. U.S.A.* **92**, 8428 (1995).

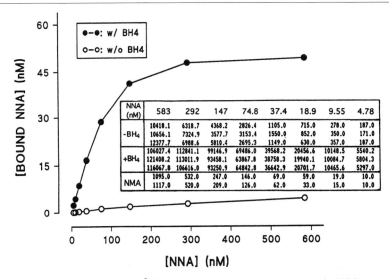

NNA (nM)	583	292	147	74.8	37.4	18.9	9.55	4.78
-BH₄	10418.1	6318.7	4368.2	2826.4	1105.0	715.0	278.0	187.0
	10656.1	7324.9	3577.7	3153.4	1550.0	852.0	350.0	171.0
	12377.7	6988.6	5810.4	2695.3	1149.0	630.0	357.0	187.0
+BH₄	106027.4	112841.1	99146.9	69486.0	39568.2	20456.6	10148.5	5540.2
	121408.2	113011.9	93458.1	63867.8	38758.3	19940.1	10084.7	5804.3
	116067.8	106616.0	93250.9	64842.8	36642.9	20701.7	10465.6	5297.0
NMA	1095.0	532.0	247.0	146.0	69.0	59.0	19.0	10.0
	1117.0	520.0	209.0	126.0	62.0	33.0	15.0	10.0

FIG. 3. Total and nonspecific [³H]NNA binding to bacterial expressed nNOS measured as a function of NNA concentration. Binding assays were performed in triplicate in the absence and presence of 10 μM BH₄, using the 96-well PVDF microfiltration plate method as detailed in the text. Raw data (inset) and plotted results are given.

employ a total reaction volume of 100 μl. For simplicity, all stock solutions are 10× with respect to their desired final concentrations in the incubation mixture; an exception is the binding buffer, which is at 2× concentration. The 2× binding buffer contains 100 mM Tris-HCl, pH 7.6, and 2 mM dithiothreitol (DTT). For a typical assay, we add to each well the following: 50 μl of binding buffer, 10 μl of 100 μM BH₄ (except when investigating BH₄ dependency), 10 μl of [³H]NNA (at 10× of the desired final concentration), and an additional 20 μl to include test agents or distilled water. For determination of nonspecific binding, 10 μl of 1 mM N^{ω}-methyl-L-arginine (NMA) is substituted for distilled water. Finally, we add 10 μl NOS protein (~10 pmol) to all wells and mix by gentle rotation. The plate is then incubated at room temperature (25°, or as desired) for 15 min. Binding reactions are terminated by vacuum filtration, using a Millipore MultiScreen vacuum manifold, leaving NOS protein bound to the membrane by hydrophobic interactions. If desirable, "hot" filtrate can be collected in a clean plate and used for further analysis or specialized disposal. Wells are then rapidly washed under vacuum, three times with 200 μl of 50 mM Tris-HCl, pH 7.6, and left to air dry for an additional 10 min. Then 25 μl of a high-capacity scintillation cocktail (e.g., OptiPhase SuperMix; Wallac, Gaithersburg, MD) is added to each well for counting in a microplate scintillation counter (e.g., Wallac MicroBeta, Packard Topcount). When such a microplate counter is not accessible, the microplate filter bottoms can be punched out and assayed using a conventional scintillation counter.

Binding Assay Notes

In lieu of the microfiltration plate assay described above, it is possible to use a conventional cell harvester (e.g., from Brandel Instruments, Gaithersburg, MD) for vacuum filtration of samples in test tubes or 96-well microtiter plates. In this setting, we have obtained good results using Whatman GF/B filter paper.

The appropriate concentration of radiolabeled NNA depends on experimental intent. For competition studies it is customary to include about 1 K_D. To determine the K_D of NNA by saturation binding, experiments are generally performed that include NNA concentrations ranging from 0.05 to 20 times the anticipated K_D.

Solutions of BH_4 are unstable, especially at low concentrations and neutral pH (even when kept on ice). To offset this problem, we store small aliquots of a 10 mM BH_4 stock prepared in 10 mM HCl at $-80°$. A vial of stock solution is removed the morning of an experiment and used to prepare dilutions prior to each assay. Dilute BH_4 solutions at neutral pH should be maintained on ice and discarded within 1–2 hr.

Washing is a key step for accurate binding assays. Insufficient washing results in a high background, whereas prolonged washing can cause false low binding. An optimal washing protocol depends on the off-rate of the ligand from the protein (k_{off}). For rat brain nNOS and rat aortic smooth muscle cell iNOS, we find that washing with 200 μl 50 mM Tris-HCl, pH 7.6, three times at room temperature (it takes several seconds per wash) is suitable. Nonetheless, optimization of washing conditions should be performed when dealing with a new radioligand–NOS pair, especially if erratic triplicates are observed in preliminary measurements. In cases where radioligand dissociation is deemed to be significant during the period of wash, use of ice-cold buffer may offer a simple fix.

[31] Purification and Properties of Nitric Oxide Synthases

By Dennis J. Stuehr

Introduction

The nitric oxide synthases (NOSs; EC1.14.13.39) are dimeric enzymes that catalyze the stepwise conversion of L-arginine to NO and L-citrulline,

METHODS IN ENZYMOLOGY, VOL. 268

with NADPH and O_2 acting as cosubstrates in the reaction (for reviews, see Refs. 1 and 2). Two isoforms (inducible iNOS and neuronal nNOS) are soluble and found predominantly in the cell cytosol, while the endothelial NOS (eNOS) is membrane associated.[3] Early work with lysates from cytokine-treated cells that express iNOS showed that NO generation required only NADPH and L-arginine to be added to the assay. However, as the iNOS was purified, a requirement for additional cytosolic factors that enabled the enzyme to express and maintain its NO synthesis activity became apparent. These factors were identified as tetrahydrobiopterin, thiol [glutathione or dithiothreitol (DTT)], FAD, and FMN.[4–7] The purification of nNOS and eNOS revealed similar requirements for NADPH, L-arginine, tetrahydrobiopterin, thiol, and flavins.[8,9] In addition, exogenous Ca^{2+} and calmodulin (CaM) needed to be added in order for the eNOS and nNOS isoforms to generate NO.[10]

Subsequent work from several groups has shown that the NOS are dual-flavin heme proteins that optimally contain per subunit 1 mol each of FAD, FMN, iron protoporphyrin IX (heme), and tetrahydrobiopterin.[1,2] All four prosthetic groups are thought to have roles in the electron transfer and/or oxygen activation steps that lead to NO synthesis. Thus, the requirement for added tetrahydrobiopterin, FAD, and FMN in the assay buffers presumably reflects a loss of these prosthetic groups from the enzyme during its purification. In addition to their catalytic roles, tetrahydrabiopterin and L-arginine also appear to be involved in forming and stabilizing the dimeric structure of iNOS.[11] Because dissociated iNOS subunits are unable to generate NO, tetrahydrobiopterin and/or L-arginine have also been included in buffers to help prevent dissociation of dimeric iNOS during purification.[7,11]

Each NOS isoform has a CaM-binding consensus sequence located near the center of its polypeptide chain. As noted, CaM binding to nNOS or eNOS activates NO synthesis. The mechanism for nNOS appears to involve a CaM-induced conformational change that causes electrons to transfer

[1] O. W. Griffith and D. J. Stuehr, *Annu. Rev. Physiol.* **57,** 707 (1995).

[2] M. A. Marletta, *J. Biol. Chem.* **268,** 12231 (1993).

[3] L. Busconi and T. Michel, *J. Biol. Chem.* **268,** 8410 (1993).

[4] N. S. Kwon, C. F. Nathan, and D. J. Stuehr, *J. Biol. Chem.* **264,** 20496 (1989).

[5] M. A. Tayeh and M. A. Marletta, *J. Biol. Chem.* **264,** 19654 (1989).

[6] D. J. Stuehr, N. S. Kwon, and C. F. Nathan, *Biochem. Biophys. Res. Commun.* **168,** 558 (1990).

[7] D. J. Stuehr, H. J. Cho, N. S. Kwon, M. F. Weise, and C. F. Nathan, *Proc. Natl. Acad. Sci. U.S.A.* **88,** 7773 (1991).

[8] B. Mayer, M. John, and E. Bohme, *FEBS Lett.* **277,** 215 (1990).

[9] H. H. H. W. Schmidt, R. M. Smith, M. Nakane, and F. Murad, *Biochemistry* **31,** 3243 (1992).

[10] D. S. Bredt and S. H. Snyder, *Proc. Natl. Acad. Sci. U.S.A.* **87,** 682 (1990).

[11] K. J. Baek, B. A. Thiel, S. Lucas, and D. J. Stuehr, *J. Biol. Chem.* **268,** 21120 (1993).

onto the heme iron, enabling oxygen activation to occur.[12] The CaM binding also stimulates cytochrome c reduction by nNOS,[13] apparently by increasing the rate of electron transfer into the nNOS flavins.[14] Sequence differences within the CaM-binding sites of the three NOS isoforms result in their displaying different affinities for CaM. For example, the moderate affinity exhibited by nNOS and eNOS allow for CaM binding and release at physiological (and experimentally obtainable) Ca^{2+} concentrations. Thus, in the absence of added Ca^{2+}, nNOS and eNOS purify as their CaM-free forms and require that Ca^{2+} and CaM be added back to activate NO synthesis. In contrast, iNOS has such high affinity for CaM that CaM remains tightly bound to the enzyme at any given Ca^{2+} concentration,[15] and therefore iNOS generates NO independent of added Ca^{2+} or CaM.

This chapter summarizes a general procedure for purifying and assaying soluble NOS isoforms (iNOS and nNOS). The few methodological differences that arise during purification of these isoforms are noted in each section. A procedure to isolate the membrane-associated eNOS can be obtained from published literature.[16]

Cell Culture and Lysis

Inducible Nitric Oxide Synthases

Mouse inducible NOS (iNOS) can be expressed in a wide variety of cells, including several cultured macrophage-like cell lines available from the American Tissue Type Culture Collection (Rockville, MD). Of these, the RAW 264.7 cell line was judged the best on the basis of its ease of growth and level of enzyme induction.[17] Although RAW 264.7 cells are adherent, they can also be grown in spinner cultures, which is the preferred method for generating milligram quantities of iNOS.

Cell Culture. The RAW 264.7 cells are grown under standard conditions in CO_2 incubators using RPMI medium supplemented with 7% (v/v) calf serum (serum endotoxin level $\leq$ 10 μg/liter), 1.7 mM L-glutamine, 83 units/ml penicillin, and 83 μg/ml streptomycin. Two confluent culture plates of

[12] H. M. Abu-Soud and D. J. Stuehr, *Proc. Natl. Acad. Sci. U.S.A.* **90**, 10769 (1993).
[13] P. Klatt, B. Heinzel, M. John, M. Kastner, E. Böhme, and B. Mayer, *J. Biol. Chem.* **267**, 11374 (1992).
[14] H. M. Abu-Soud, L. L. Yoho, and D. J. Stuehr, *J. Biol. Chem.* **269**, 32047 (1994).
[15] H. J. Cho, Q.-W. Xie, J. Calaycay, R. A. Mumford, K. M. Swiderek, T. D. Lee, and C. Nathan, *J. Exp. Med.* **176**, 599 (1992).
[16] J. S. Pollock, U. Forstermann, J. A. Mitchell, T. D. Warner, H. H. H. W. Schmidt, and F. Murad, *Proc. Natl. Acad. Sci. U.S.A.* **88**, 10480 (1991).
[17] D. J. Stuehr and M. A. Marletta, *Cancer Res.* **47**, 5590 (1987).

RAW 264.7 cells (100 mm diameter, ~2 × 10^7 cells) are seeded into a 500-ml spinner flask containing 500 ml of cell culture medium at 37°. Once the cells reach a density of approximately 1 × 10^6 cells/ml (3 days of spinner culture), they are used to seed two 3-liter spinner flasks each containing 2.5 liters of cell culture medium at 37°. After reaching approximately 1 × 10^6 cells/ml (3–4 days of spinner culture), the cells are induced to express iNOS by adding to each flask 9 ml of cell culture medium containing 1 × 10^5 units mouse γ-interferon and 3 mg *Escherichia coli* lipopolysaccharide (serotype 0.127:B8). The spinner culture is continued for an additional 8 hr, at which point the cells are harvested as detailed below.

Cell Harvest and Preparation of Cell Supernatant. Harvest cells by centrifugation at 700 rpm for 7 min at 4° in 250-ml conical tubes. Aspirate the medium and resuspend each pellet in approximately 2 ml of the remaining cell culture medium. Pool the cell suspensions into 50-ml conical tubes kept on ice. Centrifuge the 50-ml conical tubes as before, and pool the cell pellets into two 50-ml conical tubes by resuspending each pellet in cold saline containing 25 mM glucose. Add additional saline plus glucose to each tube to give 40 ml, recentrifuge, and resuspend the pellets in cold lysis buffer [40 mM Tris, pH 7.9, containing 5 μg/ml aproteinin, 1 μg/ml leupeptin, 1 μg/ml pepstatin A, 0.1 mM phenylmethylsulfonyl fluoride (PMSF), 3 mM DTT, 4 μM FAD, 4 μM tetrahydrobiopterin, and 1 mM L-arginine] added at a ratio of 8 ml lysis buffer to 5 ml of packed cells. Freeze the cell suspensions in liquid N_2 or a dry ice–acetone bath, and thaw at 37° just until the ice has melted in each tube. Repeat the freeze-thaw procedure twice more. Prepare the soluble fraction of the cell lysate by centrifugation in an ultracentrifuge at 30,000 rpm for 2 hr at 4°. The soluble fraction can be removed and stored in aliquots at −70°.

Neuronal Nitric Oxide Synthase

Neuronal NOS (nNOS) was first isolated from rat cerebellum.[10] Submilligram to milligram quantities can be isolated from pig cerebellum.[8,9] However, it is most convenient to isolate nNOS from cells that have been transfected to stably express nNOS, such as transfected R293 cells.[18] Although R293 cells are adherent, they can be grown in spinner culture under conditions similar to those noted for the macrophage cell line RAW 264.7.

Cell Culture, Harvest, and Preparation of Cell Supernatant. Spinner cultures are seeded and grown as for the macrophage cell line RAW 264.7, except that the culture medium is a mixture of 50% high-glucose Dulbecco's modified Eagle's medium (DMEM) plus 50% Ham's F12 medium supple-

[18] D. S. Bredt, C. D. Ferris, and S. H. Snyder, *J. Biol. Chem.* **267**, 10976 (1992).

mented with serum, L-glutamine, and penicillin–streptomycin as noted above. Also, the transfected cells express nNOS continuously and therefore do not need to be activated with lipopolysaccharide or γ-interferon. After the two 3-liter spinner flasks reach a density of approximately 2×10^6 cells/ml, the cells are harvested as for macrophage iNOS. Lysis buffer in this case is 40 mM Bis–Tris propane, pH 7.4, containing protease inhibitors as above, 3 mM DTT, 4 μM FAD, 4 μM tetrahydrobiopterin, 5 mM L-arginine, 150 mM NaCl, and 1 mM EDTA. Cells are lysed and the soluble fraction is prepared as for macrophage iNOS.

Chromatographic Purification of Nitric Oxide Synthases

Various groups have succeeded in purifying NOSs to homogeneity using a procedure that involves 2′,5′-ADP Sepharose affinity and anion exchange chromatography.[7,10,11,19–21] The procedure detailed below can be used to purify either mouse macrophage iNOS or rat brain nNOS. The points in the purification where methods differ between the two isoforms are noted in the nNOS section.

2′,5′-ADP Sepharose

The crude supernatant from two iNOS harvests (i.e., four 3-liter cultures) are pooled at 4° and passed through a 1.2-μm syringe filter. Approximately 30–40 ml of cell supernatant at 20–50 mg protein/ml is loaded at 0.7 ml/min onto a 10 mm × 10 cm column containing 2′,5′-ADP Sepharose resin (Pharmacia, Piscataway, NJ) previously equilibrated with loading buffer (40 mM Bis–Tris propane, pH 7.4, containing 10% glycerol, 3 mM DTT, 2 μM FAD, 2 μM tetrahydrobiopterin, and 1 mM L-arginine). The column effluent is monitored at 280 nm. After the sample has run onto the column, loading buffer is run at 1 ml/min until the protein absorbance approaches background (an additional 30–40 ml). The column is then washed at 1 ml/min with 40–50 ml of loading column buffer containing 0.5 M NaCl to remove nonspecifically bound protein. The column is next eluted sequentially with 5 ml of loading buffer, 5 ml loading buffer containing 0.7 mM NADP$^+$ at 0.5 ml/min, 5 ml of loading buffer, and 7 ml of 10 mM NADPH at 0.5 ml/min to elute the bound iNOS. Aliquots (10 μl) from the fractions containing the NADPH eluate are assayed for iNOS activity in duplicate using a microplate assay that is described below. Column

[19] K. A. White and M. A. Marletta, *Biochemistry* **31**, 6627 (1992).
[20] D. J. Stuehr and M. Ikeda-Saito, *J. Biol. Chem.* **267**, 20547 (1992).
[21] K. McMillan, D. S. Bredt, D. J. Hirsch, S. H. Snyder, J. E. Clark, and B. S. S. Masters, *Proc. Natl. Acad. Sci. U.S.A.* **89**, 11141 (1992).

performance is routinely checked by also assaying for iNOS activity in the flow-through, salt wash, and NADP$^+$ elution. The column is cleaned after each run by injecting 3 ml of 5 M NaCl in loading buffer to remove tightly bound material that does not elute with NADPH. Fractions can be stored at $-70°$ overnight before concentrating them if desired. The NADPH fractions that contain iNOS activity are pooled and concentrated in a Centricon-30 microconcentrator (Amicon, Danvers, MA) at 4° according to the manufacturer's directions to a final volume of approximately 500 μl.

Anion-Exchange Chromatography

Dimeric macrophage iNOS can be further purified (and separated from dissociated iNOS subunits if they are present) by anion-exchange chromatography on Mono Q resin (Pharmacia)[11] or on conventional Dowex anion-exchange resins.[22] An FPLC (fast protein liquid chromatography)-based Mono Q purification that utilizes a flow-through detector set at 280 nm is described here. The concentrated, partially purified iNOS sample (~500 μl) from 2′,5′-ADP Sepharose chromatography is loaded at 0.4 ml/min onto a 5 mm × 5 cm Mono Q column previously equilibrated with 40 mM Bis–Tris propane, pH 7.4, containing 3 mM DTT, 4 μM tetrahydrobiopterin, 10% (v/v) glycerol, and 100 mM NaCl. After the sample has been loaded, approximately 15 ml of column buffer is run through the column to elute nonbound protein. Residual NADPH and NADP$^+$ usually elute from the solution at this point. A linear gradient of NaCl from 100 to 210 mM is then run to elute iNOS subunits and dimeric iNOS, which elute separately at approximately 125 and 175 mM NaCl, respectively.[11] Following elution of the iNOS peaks, the column is cleaned by running column buffer containing 1 M NaCl. Column fractions (0.5 ml) are assigned to contain either iNOS subunits or dimeric iNOS on the basis of their NO synthesis activity (only dimeric iNOS can generate NO) and their position within the two chromatographic peaks. The fractions collected between the two peaks contain mixtures of dissociated subunits and dimeric iNOS and can be pooled, concentrated, and rechromatographed. The fractions that contain either pure iNOS subunits or dimeric iNOS are pooled separately and concentrated in two Centricon-30 microconcentrators to about 300 μl.

The NOS at this stage should be approximately 80–95% pure as judged by sodium dodecyl sulfate–polyacrylamide gel electrophoresis (SDS–PAGE) and have a specific activity between 600 and 1000 nmol NO/min/mg. Typical purification factors and yields obtained in the two-column procedure for iNOS and nNOS are shown in Table I.

---

[22] J. M. Hevel and M. A. Marletta, *Biochemistry* **31**, 7160 (1992).

TABLE I
TWO-COLUMN PURIFICATION OF DIMERIC INDUCIBLE AND NEURONAL
NITRIC OXIDE SYNTHASE

Fraction	Protein (mg)	Total activity[a]	Specific activity[b]	Yield (%)	Purification factor
iNOS					
Lysate supernatant[c]	1620	5022	3.1	100	1
2′,5′-ADP	11	2090	190	42	61
Mono Q[d]	2.1	1380	650	27	210
nNOS					
Lysate supernatant[c]	2656	6640	2.5	100	1
2′,5′-ADP	20	4300	215	65	86
Mono Q	4.1	2710	661	41	264

[a] Activities are given as nmol nitrite/min (lysate supernatants) or nmol NO/min (2′,5′-ADP and Mono Q).
[b] Specific activities are given as nmol nitrite (or NO for the column concentrates)/min/mg.
[c] Supernatant of 100,000 g centrifugation of cell lysate.
[d] This preparation also yielded 1.3 mg of purified monomeric iNOS subunits.

Modifications for Neuronal Nitric Oxide Synthase Purification

All column buffers are reduced to pH 7.4 for purification of nNOS. The Mono Q loading buffer NaCl concentration is reduced to 50 mM. The nNOS is eluted from the Mono Q column by running a salt gradient from 50 to 250 mM.

Additional Purification Methods

Several additional methods are briefly noted here. The reader should consult the literature for details.

Ammonium Sulfate Precipitation. Natural sources of nNOS such as cerebellum express nNOS at relatively low levels.[8–10] To concentrate nNOS prior to chromatography, an ammonium sulfate precipitation step is carried out on the soluble fraction of the tissue homogenate. The nNOS can be precipitated with 176 g/liter ammonium sulfate.[8,13]

Calmodulin Agarose. Calmodulin agarose has been used as an alternative to anion-exchange resin in the purification of nNOS.[23] It relies on the capacity of nNOS to undergo reversible, Ca^{2+} dependent binding to calmodulin. The partially purified NOS is bound to the resin in the presence

[23] H. H. H. W. Schmidt, J. S. Pollock, M. Nakane, L. D. Gorsky, and F. Murad, *Proc. Natl. Acad. Sci. U.S.A.* **88,** 365 (1991).

of Ca^{2+} and then eluted with buffer containing a Ca^{2+} chelator such as EGTA.

Gel Filtration. Gel filtration has been used as a final step in purifying iNOS[7] and nNOS.[23] It has also been used to estimate molecular mass[7,19,21,23] and the relative amounts of dimeric iNOS and dissociated iNOS subunits present in a preparation.[11] Gel-filtration chromatography of iNOS can be carried out using either a 60-cm TSK-G4000 SW column (Pharmacia) or a 60-cm Superdex 200 column (Pharmacia) equilibrated with 40 mM Bis–Tris propane buffer, pH 7.7, containing 3 mM DTT, 1 mM L-arginine, 4 μM tetrahydrobiopterin, 10% glycerol, and 200 mM NaCl. The injected sample ($\leq$200 μl) is run at 0.2 ml/min (TSK column) or 0.5 ml/min (Superdex column). Under these conditions, or in cases where either L-arginine or tetrahydrobiopterin is omitted from the buffer, dimeric iNOS will not dissociate into its subunits.[7,11]

Assays for Catalytic Function

Crude Supernatant and Column Fractions

Microplate Assay for Nitrite. The microplate nitrite assay is a convenient endpoint assay for NOS activity based on the Griess reaction which requires a microplate reader that can read between 530 and 550 nm.[24] It can be used to estimate NOS activity in crude material or to monitor the location of NOS in column fractions during purification. The following describes the assay procedure for iNOS.

Aliquots (1–20 μl) from cell lysate supernatants, column fractions, or pooled concentrates are transferred to microwells containing 40 mM Tris buffer, pH 7.8, supplemented with 3 mM DTT, 1 mM arginine, 1 mM NADPH, and 4 μM each of FAD, FMN, and tetrahydrobiopterin, to give a final volume of 0.1 ml. Reactions are initiated by adding NADPH and are run at 37° for 90 min. Remaining NADPH, which interferes with the colorimetric assay described below, is removed at the end of the incubation by adding 50 mM pyruvate and 40 units/ml lactate dehydrogenase and incubating further for 15 min at 37°[13]

To assay nNOS, the assay buffer is Bis–Tris propane, pH 7.4. The nNOS assay also includes 15 μg/ml calmodulin, 0.9 mM EDTA, and 1.2 mM Ca^{2+} in the reaction, for a final volume of 150 μl. In general, 50× stock solutions of DTT, FAD, FMN, and tetrahydrabiopterin can be prepared and stored frozen in small aliquots. The 50× tetrahydrobiopterin stock solution also contains 3 mM DTT to prevent oxidation of the tetrahydrobiopterin during

[24] A. Ding, C. F. Nathan, and D. J. Stuehr, *J. Immunol.* **141,** 2407 (1988).

storage. Prior to assay, aliquots of the stock solutions are diluted to 10× (or 15× for nnos) in reaction buffer for addition to the microplate wells. The 10× NADPH solution (or 15× for nnos) is prepared fresh daily for use in the plate assay.

Colorimetric Griess Assay for Nitrite. The nitrite that has accumulated in the microplate wells during NO synthesis (nitrite is one stable oxidation product of NO) can be quantitated by a colorimetric method based on the Griess reaction (see Ref. 24 and references therein). This is done by adding 100 μl of Griess reagent to each well (the Griess reagent is prepared by mixing equal amounts of 0.1% (w/v) naphthylethylenediamine dihydrochloride solution with a 1% (w/v) sulfanilamide solution containing 4.25% (v/v) phosphoric acid), waiting 10 min at room temperature for color development, and reading on a plate reader at approximately 550 nm. The experimental absorbance values are compared to the absorbance values of standard wells that contain known concentrations of sodium nitrite.

Purified Nitric Oxide Synthase

Below are described methods to assay NO synthesis, NADPH oxidation, and electron transfer to dyes by purified iNOS. For nNOS, the conditions are similar except that the assay buffer is Bis–Tris propane, pH 7.4, and the nNOS assay also includes 15 μg/ml CaM, 0.9 mM EDTA, and 1.2 mM Ca^{2+} in the reactions.

Nitric Oxide Synthesis. Synthesis of NO by purified NOS can be assayed using the oxyhemoglobin (HbO_2) spectrophotometric assay.[11,19,20,25] The technique measures the initial rate of NO synthesis in cuvettes and uses a conventional double-beam UV–visible spectrophotometer.

An aliquot of purified iNOS (to give a final [NOS] of ~0.01 to 0.1 μM) is transferred to a cuvette containing 40 mM Tris buffer, pH 7.8, supplemented with 5–10 μM HbO_2, 0.3 mM DTT, L-arginine, 0.1 mM NADPH, 4 μM each of FAD, FMN, and tetrahydrabiopterin, 100 units/ml catalase, 10 units/ml superoxide dismutase (SOD), and 0.1 mg/ml bovine serum albumin, to give a final volume of 0.7 ml. The control cuvette contains everything except iNOS. The NO-mediated conversion of oxyhemoglobin to methemoglobin is monitored at 37° over time as an increase in absorbance at 401 nm, and quantitated using an extinction coefficient of 38 mM^{-1} cm^{-1}. The reaction is initiated by adding iNOS.

In general, it is useful to start recording the scan at 401 nm prior to the addition of enzyme to ensure that a flat baseline is present. The control

[25] M. Kelm, M. Feelisch, R. Spahr, H. M. Piper, E. A. Noack, and J. Schrader, *Biochem. Biophys. Res. Commun.* **154**, 236 (1988).

cuvette prevents a negative baseline drift that occurs as a consequence of including thiol (DTT) in the assay. The SOD is added to prevent destruction of NO by superoxide, which may also be generated during the assay. If desired, the total reaction volume can be scaled down to 300 μl for use in microcuvettes. The HbO_2 assay for NO often does not work well for crude lysate supernatants, possibly owing to their variable ability to reduce methemoglobin. The HbO_2 can be prepared from commercially available hemoglobin, which is sold in its oxidized (methemoglobin) state, by dissolving 3–5 mg hemoglobin in 200 μl of Bis–Tris propane buffer and adding a few grains of sodium dithionite. The solution is vortexed until it turns bright red (5–15 sec) at which time it is immediately loaded onto a small Sephadex G-25 column that has been preequilibrated with Bis–Tris propane buffer. The column is eluted with the same buffer, and the red HbO_2 is collected as it elutes from the column.

NADPH Oxidation. The rate of iNOS NADPH oxidation is determined spectrophotometrically by monitoring the decrease in absorbance at 340 nm over time, using an extinction coefficient of 6.22 mM^{-1} cm^{-1}. Assays can be carried out at 37° in 1 ml of 40 mM Tris buffer, pH 7.8, containing 3 mM DTT, 1 mM L-arginine, 4 μM each of FAD, FMN, and tetrahydrobiopterin, 10 units/ml catalase, and 0.1 mM NADPH. Reactions are initiated by adding approximately 1–10 μg iNOS.

Reduction of Electron Acceptors. All NO synthases can transfer electrons derived from NADPH to various electron acceptors at rates that are 2–30 times faster than their rate of NO synthesis.[11,13,14,21] The NOS-catalyzed reduction of cytochrome c, dichlorophenolindophenol (DCPIP), and ferricyanide can be measured by spectroscopic assay. Wavelengths and extinction coefficients used to quantitate the NADPH-dependent reduction of cytochrome c, DCPIP, and ferricyanide are 550 nm (21 mM^{-1} cm^{-1}), 600 nm (20.6 mM^{-1} cm^{-1}), and 420 nm (1.2 mM^{-1} cm^{-1}), respectively. The initial concentrations of the three acceptors in the incubations are 100 μM, 100 μM, and 1 mM, respectively. Reactions are run in cuvettes containing 40 mM Tris buffer, pH 7.8, 0.2 mM NADPH, 4 μM each of FAD and FMN, 10 units/ml catalase, 0.1 mg/ml bovine serum albumin, 100 units/ml superoxide dismutase, 0.1–1 μg NOS, and no DTT or tetrahydrobiopterin, which will reduce the acceptors nonenzymatically. Reactions are initiated by adding NADPH after a 5-min incubation period that allows for oxidation of residual tetrahydrobiopterin and DTT present in the diluted enzyme preparations.

[32] Purification of Isoforms of Nitric Oxide Synthase

By ULRICH FÖRSTERMANN and INGOLF GATH

Introduction

Many cell types can synthesize nitric oxide (NO). Three isoforms of NO synthase (NOS; EC 1.14.13.39) have been characterized, purified, and their cDNAs isolated.[1] All NOSs catalyze a five-electron oxidation of one guanidino nitrogen of L-arginine to the nitric oxide radical (·NO) and L-citrulline; molecular oxygen and reduced nicotinamide adenine dinucleotide phosphate (NADPH) are cosubstrates of this reaction.[2] All NOSs are homo-dimers of subunits with molecular masses between 130 and 160 kDa. The C-terminal portion of the molecules contains a cytochrome P450 reductase-like domain with binding sites for flavin adenine dinucleotide (FAD), flavin mononucleotide (FMN), and NADPH. This reductase domain is also re-sponsible for the NADPH diaphorase activity of the NOSs. The N-terminal portion of all three NOSs contains a heme-binding oxygenase domain. All NOSs require $(6R)$-5,6,7,8-tetrahydrobiopterin (BH_4) as an additional cofactor that is bound with high affinity and is necessary for dimerization of the NOS.[3] In the center of the NOS molecule, between the oxygenase and reductase domains, all three isozymes exhibit a recognition site for calmodulin, suggesting a role for calmodulin in modulating a spatial orienta-tion of these domains that is required for catalytic activity.[4]

The activities of the NOS are found distributed between the soluble and particulate fractions of cells. The NOS I (or ncNOS; initially isolated from brain) and NOS II (or iNOS, initially isolated from cytokine-induced macrophages) are mostly soluble proteins[5-9]; NOS III (or ecNOS, mainly

[1] U. Förstermann, E. I. Closs, J. S. Pollock, M. Nakane, P. Schwarz, I. Gath, and H. Kleinert, *Hypertension (Dallas)* **23,** 1121 (1994).
[2] M. A. Marletta, *Cell (Cambridge, Mass.)* **78,** 927 (1994).
[3] K. J. Baek, B. A. Thiel, S. Lucas, and D. J. Stuehr, *J. Biol. Chem.* **268,** 21120 (1993).
[4] E. A. Sheta, K. McMillan, and B. Masters, *J. Biol. Chem.* **269,** 15147 (1994).
[5] D. S. Bredt and S. H. Snyder, *Proc. Natl. Acad. Sci. U.S.A.* **87,** 682 (1990).
[6] B. Mayer, M. John, B. Heinzel, E. R. Werner, H. Wachter, G. Schultz, and E. Böhme, *FEBS Lett.* **288,** 187 (1991).
[7] H. H. H. W. Schmidt, J. S. Pollock, M. Nakane, L. D. Gorsky, U. Förstermann, and F. Murad, *Proc. Natl. Acad. Sci. U.S.A.* **88,** 365 (1991).
[8] D. J. Stuehr, H. J. Cho, N. S. Kwon, M. F. Weise, and C. F. Nathan, *Proc. Natl. Acad. Sci. U.S.A.* **88,** 7773 (1991).
[9] J. M. Hevel, K. A. White, and M. A. Marletta, *J. Biol. Chem.* **266,** 22789 (1991).

present in endothelial cells) is myristylated and found predominantly in the particulate fraction.[10,11] The activities of NOSs I and III are Ca^{2+}/calmodulin-regulated with $[Ca^{2+}]$ in the nanomolar range (no activity at $[Ca^{2+}] \leq 100$ nM, full activity at $[Ca^{2+}] \geq 500$ nM). The activity of NOS II is largely (human) or completely (murine) independent of $[Ca^{2+}]$; calmodulin seems to be tightly bound, even in the absence of Ca^{2+}. The cDNA-deduced amino acid sequences of the human enzymes show less than 59% identity. Across species, amino acid sequences for each NOS are well conserved (>90% for NOSs I and III, >80% for NOS II). On the basis of sequence information, there is no evidence for more than one inducible isoform of NOS. Similar but not identical procedures are used to purify the different isozymes.

Purification of Nitric Oxide Synthase I from Rat Brain

Nitric oxide synthase I was first purified from rat brain on DEAE cellulose followed by 2′,5′-ADP agarose.[5] Later, modified methods of purification including ammonium sulfate precipitation and calmodulin-agarose chromatography were established.[7,12] We have developed a procedure that is somewhat simpler and more reproducible.[13] All purification steps are performed at 4° or on ice. Rat brains or cerebella (about 200 g) are homogenized on ice with a Polytron homogenizer in 5 volumes of ice-cold buffer A [50 mM Tris-HCl, pH 7.5, containing 0.5 mM EDTA and 0.5 mM EGTA, 2 mM dithiothreitol (DTT), 7 mM glutathione (GSH), 10% (v/v) glycerol, 10 μg/ml pepstatin, 10 μg/ml aprotinin, 10 μg/ml leupeptin, and 0.2 mM phenylmethylsulfonyl fluoride (PMSF)] and centrifuged for 20 min at 10,000 g. Subsequently, the supernatant is centrifuged at 100,000 g for 1 hr.

The supernatant of the second centrifugation step (cytosolic fraction) is directly loaded onto a 2-ml column of 2′,5′-ADP Sepharose (Pharmacia, Piscataway, NJ) equilibrated with buffer A, and the flow-through is recirculated several times. The column is washed with 50 ml of buffer A containing 0.5 M NaCl and then with 10 ml of buffer A. The NOS is eluted with 8 ml of buffer A containing 20 mM NADPH. The eluted fraction is concentrated to 500 μl by ultrafiltration using a Centricon-50 cartridge (Amicon, Danvers, MA) and applied to an FPLC (fast protein liquid chromatography) Su-

[10] U. Förstermann, J. S. Pollock, H. H. H. W. Schmidt, M. Heller, and F. Murad, *Proc. Natl. Acad. Sci. U.S.A.* **88**, 1788 (1991).
[11] J. S. Pollock, U. Förstermann, J. A. Mitchell, T. D. Warner, H. H. H. W. Schmidt, M. Nakane, and F. Murad, *Proc. Natl. Acad. Sci. U.S.A.* **88**, 10480 (1991).
[12] B. Mayer, M. John, and E. Böhme, *FEBS Lett.* **277**, 215 (1990).
[13] M. Nakane, J. Mitchell, U. Förstermann, and F. Murad, *Biochem. Biophys. Res. Commun.* **180**, 1396 (1991).

perose 6 gel-permeation column (HR 10/30, Pharmacia) equilibrated with buffer B [10 mM Tris-HCl, pH 7.5, containing 0.1 M NaCl, 0.5 mM EDTA or 0.5 mM EGTA, 2 mM DTT, and 10% (v/v) glycerol] at a flow rate of 0.4 ml/min. The NOS I elutes at approximately 13.6 ml. The eluted fractions that show NOS activity and migrate as a single band of 160 kDa on sodium dodecyl sulfate–polyacrylamide gel electrophoresis (SDS–PAGE) are pooled (protein concentration should be more than 100 μg/ml to improve stability), divided into small aliquots, frozen immediately in liquid nitrogen, and stored at $-80°$. Under these conditions, the enzyme activity is about 200 to 300 nmol L-citrulline/min/mg protein and is stable for at least 1 year.

Purification of Nitric Oxide Synthase II from Induced RAW 264.7 Macrophages

The soluble and particulate NOS II activities found in induced macrophages represent the same protein; the majority of the activity is found in the soluble fraction (approximately 70% soluble, 30% particulate).[14,15] The soluble NOS II is purified from induced macrophages using a three step purification scheme modified from previously described procedures.[9,16] Murine RAW 264.7 macrophages are cultured in roller bottles (passages 5–11) and, once confluent, are induced with 1 μg/ml lipopolysaccharide (*Escherichia coli*, serotype 055 : B5, Sigma, St. Louis, MO) for 10 hr. Cells are scraped and rinsed with ice-cold phosphate-buffered saline (PBS). The cells are resuspended in ice-cold buffer C (10 mM K_2HPO_4, pH 7.5, containing 0.5 mM L-arginine, 0.5 mM EDTA and 0.5 mM EGTA, 2 mM DTT, 7 mM GSH, 0.2 mM PMSF, 10 μg/ml leupeptin, 10 μg/ml pepstatin A, and 10 μg/ml aprotinin) and homogenized. The crude homogenate is subjected to three cycles of rapid freeze–thawing and then centrifuged at 10,000 g for 20 min; the supernatant is recentrifuged at 100,000 g for 1 hr.

The resulting supernatant (cytosolic fraction) is filtered through glass wool and preequilibrated with 2 μM tetrahydrobiopterin. The soluble material is then applied to a column containing 5 ml (~1 g of desiccated gel) of 2',5'-ADP Sepharose (Pharmacia) that has been preequilibrated with buffer C. The column is washed with 7 ml of buffer C, 30 ml of buffer C containing 0.5 M NaCl, 3 mM L-malic acid, 0.2 mM NADP$^+$, and 2 μM tetrahydrobiopterin, and 15 ml of buffer C containing 2 μM tetrahydrobi-

[14] U. Förstermann, H. H. H. W. Schmidt, K. L. Kohlhaas, and F. Murad, *Eur. J. Pharmacol. Mol. Pharmacol.* **225**, 161 (1992).

[15] W. R. Tracey, C. Xue, V. Klinghofer, J. Barlow, J. S. Pollock, U. Förstermann, and R. A. Johns, *Am. J. Physiol.* **266**, L722 (1994).

[16] J. M. Hevel and M. A. Marletta, *Biochemistry* **31**, 7160 (1992).

opterin. Enzyme activity is eluted with 10 ml of buffer C containing 3 mM NADPH, 0.75 mM NADP$^+$, 15 mM NaCl, and 2 μM tetrahydrobiopterin. The eluate is directly applied to a 1.5-ml column of DEAE-Bio-Gel A (Bio-Rad, Richmond, CA) that has been preequilibrated with buffer D (buffer C without L-arginine). The DEAE agarose is washed with 15 ml of buffer D containing 2 μM tetrahydrobiopterin, followed by 15 ml of buffer D containing 80 mM NaCl and 2 μM tetrahydrobiopterin. Nitric oxide synthase activity is eluted with 6 ml of buffer D containing 120 mM NaCl and 2 μM tetrahydrobiopterin. The volume of the DEAE eluate is reduced to less than 500 μl by ultrafiltration using 50-kDa cutoff Microsep concentrators (Filtron Technology, Northborough, MA). The concentrate is then washed three times with 3 ml of 15 mM HEPES (pH 7.5) containing 10% (v/v) glycerol. This concentration/washing step also removes a smaller protein ($\sim$55 kDa) that is often present in the DEAE eluate. Purified fractions that show NOS activity and migrate as a single band (or occasionally as a doublet) of approximately 130 kDa on SDS–PAGE are divided into aliquots and stored at $-80°$.

Purification of Nitric Oxide Synthase III from Bovine Aortic Endothelial Cells

Endothelial NOS III is found mainly in the particulate fraction of endothelial cells.[10] This NOS III can be purified from cultured and native bovine aortic endothelial cells (BAEC) by a simple two-step purification scheme.[11] The scheme is a modification of the above protocol for NOS I and includes a solubilization step of the particulate NOS III with the detergent 3-[(3-cholamidopropyl)dimethylammonio]-1-propane sulfonate (CHAPS). The cells are cultured to confluence in roller bottles, washed with PBS, scraped, washed again, and homogenized by sonication with 10–12 pulses in ice-cold buffer A (see above). Alternatively, native BAEC scraped from 50–60 bovine aortas (freshly obtained from the slaughterhouse) can be used. Scrapings have to be washed at least twice with PBS before being homogenized in ice-cold buffer A. The crude homogenate is then centrifuged at 100,000 g for 60 min. The supernatant usually contains no more than 5% of the total NO synthase activity and may be discarded. It is, however, possible to purify small amounts of NOS III from this fraction using the procedure described below.

The particulate fraction is washed for 10 min with buffer A containing 1 M KCl and recentrifuged at 100,000 g for 30 min. The resulting pellet is resuspended by homogenization and solubilized with 20 mM CHAPS in buffer A (rotating shaker, 20 min at 4°). The mixture is centrifuged again at 100,000 g for 1 hr, and the supernatant (CHAPS extract) is purified by

TABLE I

NITRIC OXIDE SYNTHASE ISOFORMS

Isoform	Major source	Subcellular location	Denatured molecular mass	Substrates	Prosthetic groups	Number of amino acids	mRNA	Refs.
NOS I (ncNOS)	Brain[a]	Soluble > particulate (in brain)[b]	160 kDa	L-Arginine, O_2, NADPH	Equimolar FAD/FMN, BH_4,[e] heme	1429 (rat), 1433 (human)	10.5 kb (rat), 10.0 kb (human)	5, 7, 12 (purification, characterization) 17, 18 (cDNA isolation)
NOS II (iNOS)	Cytokine-induced macrophages[c]	Soluble > particulate	130 kDa	L-Arginine, O_2, NADPH	Equimolar FAD/FMN, BH_4, heme	1144 (mouse), 1153 (human)	4.4–5.0 kb (mouse), 4.5 kb (human)	8, 9, 16, 19 (purification, characterization) 19–22 (cDNA isolation)
NOS III (ecNOS)	Endothelial cells[d]	Particulate > soluble	133 kDa	L-Arginine, O_2, NADPH	Equimolar FAD/FMN, BH_4, heme	1205 (bovine), 1203 (human)	4.4–4.8 kb (bovine), 4052 bases (human)	11 (purification, characterization) 23–26 (cDNA isolation)

[a] NOS I is also present in peripheral nitrergic nerves, skeletal muscle, and certain epithelial cells.[1]

[b] In skeletal muscle, most of the NOS I protein is found in the particulate fraction. The posttranslational modification mediating this membrane association is not known.

[c] NOS II can be induced in almost any cell type.[1]

[d] NOS III has also been identified in LLC-PK_1 kidney tubular epithelial cells and in syncytiotrophoblasts of human placenta.[1]

[e] BH_4, Tetrahydrobiopterin.

$2',5'$-ADP Sepharose chromatography followed by FPLC Superose 6 gel-permeation chromatography (Pharmacia) as described for NOS I (see above). To preserve enzyme solubility, 10 mM CHAPS is included in all buffers used in these purification steps. The NOS III elutes anomalously from the Superose 6 column near the total included volume (at ~19 ml) owing to nonspecific interactions with the column materials.[11] Eluted fractions that show NOS activity and migrate as a single band of approximately 135 kDa on SDS–PAGE are pooled, divided into aliquots, and stored at $-80°$. Table I summarizes the properties of the three isoforms of NOS.

[17] D. S. Bredt, P. M. Hwang, C. E. Glatt, C. Lowenstein, R. R. Reed, and S. H. Snyder, *Nature* (*London*) **351**, 714 (1991).

[18] M. Nakane, H. H. H. W. Schmidt, J. S. Pollock, U. Förstermann, and F. Murad, *FEBS Lett.* **316**, 175 (1993).

[19] P. A. Sherman, V. E. Laubach, B. R. Reep, and E. R. Wood, *Biochemistry* **32**, 11600 (1993).

[20] Q. W. Xie, H. J. Cho, J. Calaycay, R. A. Mumford, K. M. Swiderek, T. D. Lee, A. Ding, T. Troso, and C. F. Nathan, *Science* **256**, 225 (1992).

[21] C. R. Lyons, G. J. Orloff, and J. M. Cunningham, *J. Biol. Chem.* **267**, 6370 (1992).

[22] D. A. Geller, C. J. Lowenstein, R. A. Shapiro, A. K. Nussler, S. M. Di, S. C. Wang, D. K. Nakayama, R. L. Simmons, S. H. Snyder, and T. R. Billiar, *Proc. Natl. Acad. Sci. U.S.A.* **90**, 3491 (1993).

[23] K. Nishida, D. G. Harrison, J. P. Navas, A. A. Fisher, S. P. Dockery, M. Uematsu, R. M. Nerem, R. W. Alexander, and T. J. Murphy, *J. Clin. Invest.* **90**, 2092 (1992).

[24] W. C. Sessa, J. K. Harrison, C. M. Barber, D. Zeng, M. E. Durieux, D. D. D'Angelo, K. R. Lynch, and M. J. Peach, *J. Biol. Chem.* **267**, 15274 (1992).

[25] P. A. Marsden, K. T. Schappert, H. S. Chen, M. Flowers, C. L. Sundell, J. N. Wilcox, S. Lamas, and T. Michel, *FEBS Lett.* **307**, 287 (1992).

[26] P. A. Marsden, H. H. Q. Heng, S. W. Scherer, R. J. Stewart, A. V. Hall, X. M. Shi, L. C. Tsui, and K. T. Schappert, *J. Biol. Chem.* **268**, 17478 (1993).

[33] Purification and Inhibitor Screening of Human Nitric Oxide Synthase Isozymes

By EDWARD P. GARVEY, ERIC S. FURFINE, and PAULA A. SHERMAN

Introduction

Nitric oxide (NO) and L-citrulline are produced in the two-step oxidation of L-arginine by the three isozymes of nitric oxide synthase (NOS; EC 1.14.13.39): inducible NOS (iNOS), endothelial NOS (eNOS), and neuronal

NOS (nNOS).[1,2] Because the three isozymes produce NO in separate tissues for different purposes in both normal and diseases states,[3,4] selective inhibition of the appropriate isozyme could avoid complications in the treatment of a diseased state. One example is the need for selective inhibition of nNOS to treat cerebral ischemia. Because inhibition of eNOS would cause vasoconstriction, a high selectivity for nNOS versus eNOS could avoid further loss of blood flow to the impaired region of the brain.

As a necessary step in developing selective inhibitors of NOS, we sought a plentiful, easily obtainable source for all the human NOS isozymes. Initially, we isolated human iNOS from the colon carcinoma cell line DLD-1,[5] human eNOS from placenta,[6] and human nNOS from brain. Such preparations resulted in authentic purified human NOS isozymes for use in inhibitor screens. We present here the methods for purifying the three human isozymes to homogeneity and highlight a potential problem that might be encountered in screening inhibitors of NOS by exemplifying the steady-state kinetics of isothioureas (ITUs) and isothiocitrullines (ITCs).

Materials

The DLD-1 cell line (ATCC, Rockville, MD, No. CCL 221) is derived from a human colorectal adenocarcinoma. Human placenta is obtained from the birth center at a local hospital. Human brain samples are provided by the Cooperative Human Tissue Network (Birmingham, AL). 2',5'-ADP affinity resin linked to agarose or to Sepharose is purchased from Sigma (St. Louis, MO) or Pharmacia LKB (Piscataway, NJ), respectively; no differences are observed. Calmodulin agarose is from Sigma, L-[^{14}C-U]arginine from DuPont New England Nuclear (Beverly, MA), and L-N^G-nitroarginine (L-NA), S-methyl- and ethylisothiourea (ITU), and aminoguanidine are from Aldrich (Milwaukee, WI). S-Methyl- and S-ethyl-L-isothiocitrulline (ITC) are synthesized by J. Oplinger (Wellcome Research Lab, Research Triangle Park, NC). L-N^G-Methylarginine (L-MA) and N-iminoethyl-L-ornithine (L-NIO) are synthesized by H. Hodson (Wellcome Research Lab, Beckenham, England).

[1] U. Forstermann, H. H. H. W. Schmidt, J. S. Pollock, H. Sheng, J. A. Mitchell, T. D. Warner, M. Nakane, and F. Murad, *Biochem. Pharmacol.* **42,** 1849 (1991).
[2] D. J. Stuehr and O. W. Griffith, *Adv. Enzymol.* **65,** 287 (1992).
[3] S. Moncada, R. M. Palmer, and E. A. Higgs, *Pharmacol. Rev.* **43,** 109 (1991).
[4] C. Nathan, *FASEB J.* **6,** 3051 (1992).
[5] P. A. Sherman, V. E. Laubach, B. R. Reep, and E. R. Wood, *Biochemistry* **32,** 11600 (1993).
[6] E. P. Garvey, J. V. Tuttle, K. Covington, B. M. Merrill, E. R. Wood, S. A. Baylis, and I. G. Charles, *Arch. Biochem. Biophys.* **311,** 235 (1994).

Methods and Results

Nitric Oxide Synthase Assay

The oxidation of L-arginine is monitored by the conversion of L-[^{14}C]arginine to L-[^{14}C]citrulline as described by Schmidt *et al.*[7] Reaction mixtures contain 20 mM HEPES, pH 7.4, 2.5 mM dithiothreitol (DTT), 125 μM NADPH, 10 μM tetrahydrobiopterin, 10 μM FAD, and 0.2 to 10 μM L-[^{14}C]arginine. When eNOS or nNOS is assayed, 10 μg/ml calmodulin and 2.5 mM CaCl$_2$ are included. Reactions are performed at 37°. [To increase NOS stability when long time courses (>30 min) are examined, reactions are conducted at 30°.]

General Purification Comments

These preparations are variations of the procedures of Bredt and Synder,[8] Hevel *et al.*,[9] and Schmidt *et al.*[7] In initial studies, each of the human NOS isozymes displayed varying stability during purification and storage. Each of the preparations have therefore evolved to contain stabilizers (e.g., glycerol, sucrose, Tween 20) and to have a high (>0.5 mg/ml) concentration of protein [either by rapid concentration of NOS itself or by addition of bovine serum albumin (BSA)] at the final step. Purified NOS under these conditions can be quick frozen and stored at −70° for at least 1 year without loss of activity. Each purified NOS is judged to be greater than 90% pure by sodium dodecyl sulfate–polyacrylamide gel electrophoresis (SDS–PAGE). All preparations are done at 4° and as rapidly as possible. Results of the purifications are summarized in Table I.

Purification of Human Inducible Nitric Oxide Synthase from DLD-1 Cells After Induction with Cytokines

Cells are grown at 37°, 5% (v/v) CO$_2$, in RPMI 1640 medium (GIBCO BRL, Gaithersburg, MD) supplemented with L-glutamine, penicillin, streptomycin, and 10% heat-inactivated fetal bovine serum. Cells are plated into ten 150-cm^2 flasks (20 ml of medium per flask), grown to confluence, and treated with 100 U/ml γ-interferon, 200 U/ml interleukin-6, 10 ng/ml tumor necrosis factor α (TNFα) and 0.5 ng/ml 1β-interleukin. At 18–24 hr postinduction, cells are harvested by scraping and washed with phosphate-buffered saline (PBS). A typical cell pellet weighs 2 g and can be stored at −70°.

[7] H. H. H. W. Schmidt, J. S. Pollock, M. Nakane, L. D. Gorsky, U. Forstermann, and F. Murad, *Proc. Natl. Acad. Sci. U.S.A.* **88,** 365 (1991).
[8] D. S. Bredt and S. H. Synder, *Proc. Natl. Acad. Sci. U.S.A.* **87,** 682 (1990).
[9] J. M. Hevel, K. A. White, and M. A. Marletta, *J. Biol. Chem.* **266,** 22789 (1991).

TABLE I
PURIFICATION OF HUMAN NITRIC OXIDE SYNTHASE ISOZYMES

Isozyme and step	Volume (ml)	Protein (mg)	Units[a] (nmol/min)	Specific activity (units/mg)	Yield (%)
iNOS[b]					
Extract	5	20	3.4	0.24	—
2',5'-ADP agarose	3	0.5	1.4	27	41
DEAE Bio-Gel A	1	0.002	0.5	288	15
eNOS[c]					
Extract	1180	43,700	113	0.0026	—
2',5'-ADP agarose	92	33	51	1.5	45
Calmodulin agarose	4.4	2.4	24	7.6	22
Mono Q	0.6	0.3	11	10.0	11
nNOS					
Extract	3000	—	—	—	—
Ammonium sulfate	400	—	70	—	100
2',5'-ADP agarose	60	11	190	17	270
Calmodulin agarose	4	2	120	60	170

[a] Nitric oxide synthase activity measured at 10 μM L-arginine.
[b] Data from P. A. Sherman, V. E. Laubach, B. R. Reep, and E. R. Wood, *Biochemistry* **32,** 11600 (1993).
[c] Data from E. P. Garvey, J. V. Tuttle, K. Covington, B. M. Merrill, E. R. Wood, S. A. Baylis, and I. G. Charles, Arch. Biochem. Biophys. **311,** 235 (1994).

Cell extract is prepared by resuspending the cell pellet in 2.5 volumes of TDGB [20 mM Tris-HCl, pH 7.4 (pH at 25°), 1 mM DTT, 10% (v/v) glycerol, and 2 μM tetrahydrobiopterin] and lysing by three cycles of rapid freeze–thawing. Because a significant amount (~25%) of iNOS remained in the pellet after high-speed centrifugation, CHAPS {(3-[(3-cholamidopropyl)dimethylammonio]-1-propane sulfonate} is added to a concentration of 5 mM and the extract is slowly rotated for 20 min. The extract is centrifuged for 1 hr at 100,000 g.

The supernatant is applied by gravity to a 200-μl column of 2',5'-ADP Sepharose that has been equilibrated in TDGB. The resin is washed sequentially with 3 ml each of TDGB, 500 mM NaCl in TDGB, 3 mM malic acid plus 0.15 mM NADP$^+$ in TDGB, 1 mM 2'-AMP in TDGB, 1 mM NADH in TDGB, and TDGB. The NOS is then eluted with 3 ml of 3 mM NADPH in TDGB. The preparation is applied to a 1-ml column of DEAE Bio-Gel A agarose (Bio-Rad, Richmond, CA) that has been equilibrated with TDGB at a flow of 0.2 ml/min. The resin is washed with 5 ml each of TDGB and 50 mM NaCl in TDGB. The NOS is eluted with a linear gradient (10 ml, 50 to 500 mM) of NaCl in TDGB. The NOS is eluted at about 200 mM NaCl. The NADPH that is present from the 2',5'-ADP chromatography step partially coelutes during the salt gradient of the ion-exchange step. If NADPH needs to be completely removed, the iNOS preparation is desalted using PD-10 Sephadex G-25 columns (Pharmacia LKB).

Purification of Human Endothelial Nitric Oxide Synthase from Placenta

Amnion and chorion are removed ($\leq$1 hr after delivery) from fresh placenta (typically, ~600 g), which is then rinsed with 0.9% NaCl and homogenized in a Waring blender in 3 volumes of HEDS buffer [20 mM HEPES, pH 7.8 (pH at 25°), 0.1 mM EDTA, 5 mM DTT, and 0.2 M sucrose] plus 0.1 mM phenylmethylsulfonyl fluoride (PMSF). The CHAPS is added to a concentration of 5 mM. The homogenate is slowly stirred for 30 min and then centrifuged at 27,500 g for 30 min.

The 2′,5′-ADP agarose (10 ml) is added to the supernatant. The slurry is mixed slowly overnight and then packed into a column. The resin is sequentially washed with 50 ml each of HEDS, 500 mM NaCl in HEDS, and HEDS. The NOS is then eluted with 100 ml of 2 mM NADPH in HEDS. (Note: A 0–10 mM NADPH gradient shows that NOS begins to elute at <0.5 mM NADPH and provides no greater purification than batch elution.)

Next, CaCl$_2$ is added to the pooled fractions to a concentration of 1 mM; this solution is loaded onto a 0.5-ml column of calmodulin agarose that has been equilibrated with HEDS containing 1 mM CaCl$_2$. The resin is washed with HEDS, 1 mM CaCl$_2$, 1% (v/v) Nonidet P-40 (NP-40) (10 ml) and then reequilibrated with HEDS, 1 mM CaCl$_2$ (5 ml). The NP-40 wash is to remove residual cytochrome P450 reductase that is nonspecifically bound to NOS. The NOS is then eluted with HEDS, containing 5 mM EDTA and 1 M NaCl.

Pooled fractions are made 0.1% (v/v) with Tween 20. The pool is concentrated using a Centricon-30 microconcentrator and then desalted using Sephadex G-25. Enzyme is then applied to a Mono Q HR 5/5 column (5 × 50 mm), which has been equilibrated with HEDS containing 0.1% Tween 20. After washing with 5 ml of equilibration buffer, the column is developed with a gradient (14 ml, 0–500 mM) of NaCl in equilibration buffer. The NOS is then eluted at about 300 mM NaCl. Pooled fractions are desalted in HEDS containing 0.1% Tween 20 and then concentrated to a protein concentration of about 0.5 mg/ml.

Purification of Human Neuronal Nitric Oxide Synthase from Brain

Samples of human brain are collected until 1000 g or more has been accumulated and then homogenized in a Waring blender for 1 min in 2.5 volumes HED [50 mM HEPES, pH 7.5 (pH at 25°), 0.5 mM EDTA, 10 mM

DTT]. The mixture is centrifuged at 13,000 g for 1 hr and the supernatant is removed. Solid ammonium sulfate is added to 30% of saturation, and the mixture is stirred slowly for a total of 30 min. The precipitate is collected by centrifugation at 13,000 g for 30 min and is resuspended in approximately one-fifth of the original volume with HED that includes 4 μM tetrahydrobiopterin, 1 μM FAD, and 1 μM FMN. The solution is centrifuged at 41,000 g for 60 min and the supernatant is removed, frozen in liquid nitrogen, and stored at $-70°$.

After thawing, the supernatant is applied to a 5-ml column of ADP-agarose (equilibrated in HED) at 4 ml/min. The column is washed with 100 ml HED, 200 ml of 500 mM NaCl in HED, and 100 ml HED. The NOS is then eluted with 10 mM NADPH in 40 ml HED. The enzyme solution is made 15% (v/v) glycerol, 1 mM CaCl$_2$, 10 μM tetrahydrobiopterin, 0.1% (v/v) Tween 20, 1 μM FAD, and 1 μM FMN. The enzyme is applied to a 1-ml column of calmodulin agarose (equilibrated with 15% glycerol, 1 mM CaCl$_2$ in HED). The column is washed with 15 ml each of 15% glycerol, 1 mM CaCl$_2$ in HED, and 15% glycerol, 5 mM EDTA in HED. The NOS is eluted with 3 ml of 15% glycerol, 5 mM EDTA, and 1 M NaCl in HED. The enzyme solution is made 10 μM tetrahydrobiopterin, 1 μM FAD and FMN, and 0.1% Tween 20. This solution is concentrated to reach a protein concentration of about 0.5 mg/ml.

Kinetic Parameters of Purified Human Nitric Oxide Synthase Isozymes

The specific activities of the purified human NOS isozymes and the kinetic constants for L-arginine and some common NOS inhibitors are given in Tables I and II. These values were all within the typical range that have been observed for NOS isozymes.[1,2] As previously described[10] for isozymes from other sources, inhibition by L-NA occurred on a relatively slow time scale for the two human constitutive NOS enzymes (eNOS and nNOS) compared to iNOS. The potential for NOS inhibitors to display a slow onset of action and a suggested procedure to measure this interaction are addressed below.

Another distinction between the constitutive and inducible isozymes was the instabilities of their catalytic activities when incubated at 37°, and the dependence of this instability on the concentration of L-arginine. Reaction curves at various concentrations of L-arginine and appropriate amounts of eNOS that would avoid substrate depletion are shown in Fig. 1. At 0.5 μM substrate, the reaction catalyzed by eNOS was linear only for 10 min. At higher concentrations (10 μM), the reaction was linear for 60 min.

[10] E. S. Furfine, M. F. Harmon, J. E. Paith, and E. P. Garvey, *Biochemistry* **32,** 8512 (1993).

TABLE II
KINETIC CONSTANTS FOR HUMAN NITRIC OXIDE SYNTHASE ISOZYMES

Kinetic constant	iNOS	eNOS	nNOS
V_{max} (nmol/min/mg)	290	10	90
K_m, L-arginine (μM)	2.2	0.90	1.6
K_i, L-MA (μM)	0.86	0.41	0.84
K_i, L-NIO (μM)	0.34	0.81	0.23
K_i or K_d, L-NA (μM)	0.67 (K_i)	0.039 (K_d)	0.015 (K_d)
k_{on}, L-NA (M^{-1} sec^{-1})	Rapid	1.4×10^4	4.4×10^4
k_{off}, L-NA (sec^{-1})	Rapid	5.7×10^{-4}	6.5×10^{-4}
K_i, S-methyisothiourea (μM)	0.12	0.20	0.16
K_i, S-ethyisothiourea (μM)	0.019	0.039	0.029
K_i or K_d, S-methylITC (μM)	0.040 (K_i)	0.011 (K_i)	0.0012 (K_d)
k_{on}, S-methylITC (M^{-1} sec^{-1})	1×10^5	1.1×10^5	2.6×10^5
k_{off}, S-methylITC (sec^{-1})	4×10^{-3}	1.2×10^{-3}	3×10^{-4}

Similar results were observed with human nNOS. In contrast, human iNOS was linear up to 60 min at 0.5 μM L-arginine.

Rapid versus Slow Onset Inhibition of Human Nitric Oxide Synthase Isozymes

A disadvantage of using a single time-point enzyme assay for an inhibitor screen is that the true potency of a compound might not be observed if its binding is relatively slow (i.e., $t_{1/2}$ for the slow binding approximates the time point of assay). In our initial screening of compounds, we chose to use a low concentration of L-arginine (0.5 μM) in order to maximize potential binding of the inhibitor. Because of the instability of eNOS and nNOS, the length of assay was limited to 10 min. Therefore, we have been cautious that novel inhibitors might display time dependence, and that our initial screen might not measure the full potency of inhibition. Therefore, whenever deemed of interest, we examine the complete time course of that new inhibitor. Pertinent examples are the isothiourea[11] (ITU) and isothiocitrulline[12] (ITC) inhibitors.

An immediate question that arose on finding that simple alkyl ITUs were nanomolar inhibitors of NOS was the structural mechanism for such tight binding. One possible mechanism would be that the ITU reacted

[11] E. P. Garvey, J. A. Oplinger, G. J. Tanoury, P. A. Sherman, M. Fowler, S. Marshall, M. F. Harmon, J. E. Paith, and E. S. Furfine, *J. Biol. Chem.* **269**, 26669 (1994).

[12] E. S. Furfine, M. F. Harmon, J. E. Paith, R. G. Knowles, M. Salter, R. J. Kiff, C. Duffy, R. Hazelwood, J. A. Oplinger, and E. P. Garvey, *J. Biol. Chem.* **269**, 26677 (1994).

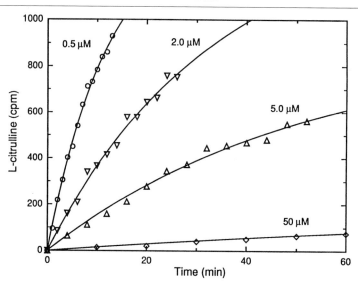

FIG. 1. Effect of concentration of L-arginine on linearity of rate catalyzed by eNOS. L-[^{14}C]Arginine was held constant at 0.5 μM (~9000 total counts/min), and unlabeled L-arginine was added to give the final concentration indicated. Progress curves for L-citrulline formation are shown as counts/minute of citrulline formed versus time. The initial rate of citrulline formation and the apparent first-order rate constants for inactivation were as follows: 1.9 pmol/min and 0.084 min^{-1} at 0.5 μM L-arginine (○), 2.7 pmol/min and 0.030 min^{-1} at 2.0 μM L-arginine (▽), 3.1 pmol/min and 0.019 min^{-1} at 5.0 μM L-arginine (△), and 3.0 pmol/min and 0.0075 min^{-1} at 50 μM L-arginine (◇). From E. P. Garvey, J. V. Tuttle, K. Covington, B. M. Merrill, E. R. Wood, S. A. Baylis, and I. G. Charles, *Arch. Biochem. Biophys.* **311**, 235 (1994).

chemically with NOS. If this did occur, inhibition might be progressive. However, when a time course of 60 min was examined with human iNOS and *S*-ethyl-ITU, a linear inhibited rate was observed. In addition, when human iNOS was preincubated with a relatively high concentration of *S*-ethyl-ITU (10 times the K_i value) and was then highly diluted (1/100) into a reaction at 10 μM L-arginine, the rate was the same as iNOS preincubated in the absence of inhibitor. Therefore, inhibition by ITUs was rapid and reversible.

In contrast, the amino acid analogs *S*-methyl- and *S*-ethyl-ITC inhibited NOS slowly. The progress curve for inhibition of human nNOS by *S*-methyl-ITC is shown in Fig. 2. The inset shows that the dependence of the first-order rate constant (k_{obs}) on inhibitor concentration was linear. Thus from Eq. (1), the apparent association rate constant (apparent k_{on}) was calculated

$$k_{obs} = k_{on}[I] + k_{off} \tag{1}$$

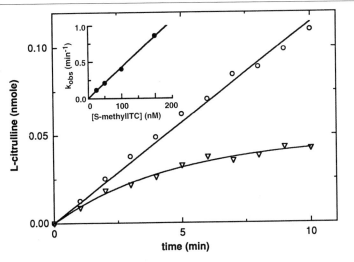

FIG. 2. Time dependence of nNOS inhibition by S-methyl-ITC. Progress curves for
L-citrulline formation with $6~\mu M$ L-[^{14}C]arginine, $100~\mu M$ NADPH, and $0~\mu M$ (circles) or
$0.05~\mu M$ (triangles) S-methyl-ITC, in a 100-μl reaction. *Inset:* Dependence of k_{obs} for S-
methyl-ITC inhibition on the concentration of S-methyl-ITC. The solid line was calculated
from the best fit of the parameters in Eq. (1) to the data. From E. S. Furfine, M. F. Harmon,
J. E. Paith, R. G. Knowles, M. Salter, R. J. Kiff, C. Duffy, R. Hazelwood, J. A. Oplinger,
and E. P. Garvey, *J. Biol. Chem.* **269**, 26677 (1994).

($7.1 \times 10^4~M^{-1}~\text{sec}^{-1}$ at $6~\mu M$ L-arginine). If L-arginine and S-methyl-ITC
bound to the same site on nNOS, then L-arginine should competitively
inhibit binding of S-methyl-ITC with a K_s value equal to its K_m value as a
substrate. L-Arginine reduced k_{obs} with a K_s value [Eq. (2)] of $2.3~\mu M$. The

$$k_{obs} = \frac{k'_{obs}}{1 + [S]/K_s} \qquad (2)$$

association rate constant (k_{on}) for S-methyl-ITC was calculated (2.6×10^4
$M^{-1}~\text{sec}^{-1}$) by Eq. (3) using the apparent association rate constant at $6~\mu M$

$$k_{on} = k_{on\text{-app}}(1 + [S]/K_s) \qquad (3)$$

L-arginine and the K_s for L-arginine.

S-Methyl-ITC inhibition was slowly reversible. The normalized rate of
nNOS-catalyzed formation of product L-citrulline in the absence of inhibitor
was linear (Fig. 3). However, when nNOS was preincubated with S-methyl-
ITC, NADPH, and calcium/calmodulin and was then used to initiate a
reaction with saturating ($50~\mu M$) L-arginine, the rate of product formation
was initially zero, but accelerated to the final steady-state rate of the unin-
hibited reaction (Fig. 3). The apparent first-order rate constant (3.0×10^4

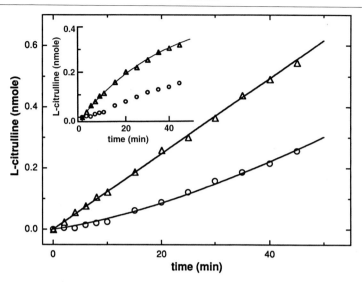

FIG. 3. Dissociation rate constant for S-methyl-ITC and nNOS. Progress curves for L-citrulline formation in a 100-μl reaction containing 50 μM L-[¹⁴C]arginine and 200 μM NADPH were constructed. The nNOS (0.12 μM S-methyl-ITC binding sites) was incubated with 160 μM NADPH and 0.016 mg/ml calcium/calmodulin, in the absence (triangles) or presence (circles) of 0.23 μM S-methyl-ITC for 10 min at room temperature then diluted 1:21 into an assay mixture with 50 μM L-arginine. The acquired data (inset) were normalized to account for the exponential decay of enzyme activity. From E. S. Furfine, M. F. Harmon, J. E. Paith, R. G. Knowles, M. Salter, R. J. Kiff, C. Duffy, R. Hazelwood, J. A. Oplinger, and E. P. Garvey, *J. Biol. Chem.* **269**, 26677 (1994).

$M^{-1} \sec^{-1}$) for the acceleration to the steady-state rate was the dissociation rate constant (k_{off}) for S-methyl-ITC from the S-methyl-ITC–nNOS complex [Eq. (4)],

$$P(t) = A[e^{-k_{\mathrm{off}}(t)} - 1] + Bt \qquad (4)$$

where $P(t)$ is the amount of product formed at time t, A is the amplitude of the lag in product formation, and B is the final (steady-state) rate. Finally, the K_d value calculated from $k_{\mathrm{off}}/k_{\mathrm{on}}$ was 1.2 nM. It is important to note that this full description of inhibition not only measured the true potency of these compounds but also allowed us to define the ITCs as highly selective for human nNOS.[12]

It is unclear what the structural requirements are for slow binding to NOS. In comparing the ITUs and ITCs, the obvious difference is the presence of the amino acid functionality in the ITCs. To date, there is only one example of non-amino acid analogs of L-arginine that show progressive inhibition.[13] In addition, so far all slow-binding inhibitors possess modifications of the guanidine moiety. Therefore, although all novel inhibitors should be examined for time dependence, special attention should be given to amino acid analogs that have novel modifications of the guanidine functionality.

Acknowledgments

We thank Jeff Oplinger who heads the chemistry effort at Wellcome Research Laboratories, Research Triangle Park. Kemp Covington, William Rutledge, Siegfried Shyu, Marilyn Harmon, and Jerilin Paith were students who purified enzymes and performed the inhibitor screens. We thank all of our colleagues at WRL in Beckenham, U.K., Tom Spector for initiating the enzymology effort at WRL, RTP, and Tom Zimmerman and Tom Krenitsky for their support.

[13] D. J. Wolff and A. Lubeskie, *Arch. Biochem. Biophys.* **316**, 290 (1995).

[34] Generation of Isoform-Specific Antibodies to Nitric Oxide Synthases

By TED M. DAWSON and VALINA L. DAWSON

Introduction

Nitric oxide (NO) is a prominent vascular and neuronal messenger molecule first identified as having endothelium-derived relaxing factor (EDRF) activity.[1,2] Nitric oxide is also formed in macrophages and other peripheral blood cells and mediates immune responses.[3,4] Nitric oxide is formed from arginine by NO synthase (NOS; EC 1.14.13.39) which oxidizes the guanidino nitrogen of arginine, releasing NO and citrulline. Several distinct NOS enzymes have been purified and molecularly cloned (Table I). Once it was recognized that NOS is a calmodulin-dependent enzyme, the first isoform to be purified was the neuronal isoform, nNOS.[5] Soon thereafter NOS was purified from macrophages and endothelial tissue.[6] Following the purification of nNOS, peptide sequences from tryptic diges-

[1] T. M. Dawson and S. H. Snyder, *J. Neurosci.* **14**, 5147 (1994).
[2] S. Moncada and A. Higgs, *N. Engl. J. Med.* **329**, 2002 (1993).
[3] C. Nathan, *FASEB J.* **6**, 3051 (1992).
[4] M. A. Marletta, *J. Biol. Chem.* **268**, 12231 (1993).
[5] D. S. Bredt and S. H. Snyder, *Proc. Natl. Acad. Sci. U.S.A.* **87**, 682 (1990).
[6] U. Forstermann, J. S. Pollock, W. R. Tracey, and M. Nakane, *Methods Enzymol.* **233**, 258 (1994).

TABLE I
Properties of Nitric Oxide Synthase Isoforms

First identified	Isoform	Name	Subcellular location	Denatured molecular mass (Da)	Regulation	Cofactors	Number of amino acids	mRNA (kb)
Brain	I	Neuronal NOS (nNOS)	Soluble > particulate	160,000	Ca^{2+}/calmodulin	NADPH, FAD/FMN, tetrahydrobiopterin, hemoprotein	1429 (rat)	10.5 (rat)
Macrophage	II	Immunological or macrophage NOS (iNOS)	Soluble > particulate	130,000	Inducible by cytokines, Ca^{2+} independent	Calmodulin, NADPH, FAD/FMN, tetrahydrobiopterin, hemoprotein	1144 (mouse)	4.4–5.0 (mouse)
Endothelium	III	Endothelial NOS (eNOS)	Particulate > soluble	135,000	Ca^{2+}/calmodulin	NADPH, FAD/FMN, tetrahydrobiopterin, hemoprotein	1203 (human)	4.3 (human)

tion enabled the molecular cloning of the complementary DNA (cDNA) for nNOS.[7] The molecular cloning for endothelial and the macrophages NOS isoforms shortly followed the cloning of nNOS. The structure and function of the various NOS isoforms have been clarified by the molecular cloning and biochemical studies.

Insight into the action of a variety of proteins has come from information about their localization. In a similar manner, the function of NO in biological systems has been greatly clarified by the localization of the various isoforms of NOS. In this chapter, we detail how isoform-specific antibodies to the NOS isoforms were made and describe the localization of neuronal, endothelial, and macrophage NOS using these isoform-specific antibodies.

Generation of Isoform-Specific Antibodies

The production of isoform-specific antibodies can be accomplished through a variety of approaches, including the production of monoclonal antibodies against purified protein, fusion protein, or synthesized peptides from the deduced amino acid sequence. Polyclonal antibodies directed against regions of the NOS isoforms with low homology can also be used to generate isoform-selective antibodies. Selection of peptides has been made easier by the development of computer programs that can assist in the design of peptides. Important considerations to keep in mind are the following. The peptide should be unique to the protein or at the very least have a low homology to the known isoforms. In addition it should have a high antigenic index, and it is extremely helpful if it is water soluble. The methods, techniques, and theory behind production of both monoclonal and polyclonal antibodies as well as the potential pitfalls that may arise in making antibodies is beyond the scope of this chapter. However, we routinely follow the protocols for making antibodies as described in the laboratory manual by Harlow and Lane[8] and we refer readers to that manual for a description of the methodologies.

Several different approaches could be utilized to generate isoform-selective antibodies to the isoforms of NOS. The N-terminal portions of the NOS isoforms provide the most diverse sequences. One could simply make fusion proteins or peptides to the N-terminal portions of all three isoforms to generate isoform-selective antibodies. In addition, there is diver-

---

[7] D. S. Bredt, P. M. Hwang, C. E. Glatt, C. Lowenstein, R. R. Reed, and S. H. Snyder, *Nature* (*London*) **351**, 714 (1991).

[8] E. Harlow and D. Lane "Antibodies: A Laboratory Manual." Cold Spring Harbor Laboratory, Cold Spring Harbor, New York, 1988.

gence in the sequence of all three isoforms at the C terminus. However, in contrast to the N-terminal portion of the NOS isoforms in which there are long stretches of low homology, the C terminus only has very short stretches of approximately 15–20 amino acids that are of low homology between the various isoforms. Antibody against nNOS was first made against the purified protein.[9] Because this antibody was raised against the purified protein, it also had some cross-reactivity with the endothelial isoform owing to the close homology of the two isoforms. Despite the cross-reactivity, antibodies raised against the intact nNOS protein are quite good for most immunohistochemical or biochemical studies. The initial immunohistochemical studies of nNOS in the brain revealed discrete localization to limited populations of cells in the cerebral cortex and corpus striatum, to basket and granule cells of the cerebellum, and to other select sites.[9] On the basis of molecular cloning studies, we subsequently generated an isoform-specific antibody to nNOS by generating a glutathione S-transferase (GST) fusion protein containing the first 181 amino acids of nNOS.[10,11] The GST–nNOS fusion protein was purified using a glutathione-Sepharose column. The GST–nNOS was cleaved with thrombin while on the glutathione-Sepharose column, and the N-terminal 181 amino acids of nNOS were thus separated from the GST. The first 181 amino acids of neuronal NOS were then injected in rabbits to raise antiserum. Antibodies were then affinity purified on an affinity column containing the N-terminal 181 amino acids of nNOS immobilized on cyanogen bromide-activated Sepharose.

We chose to make an endothelial NOS (eNOS)-selective antibody based on a peptide that was synthesized from amino acids 1185–1208 of bovine eNOS.[10] This peptide was conjugated to bovine serum albumin and injected into rabbits to raise antiserum. Antibodies were affinity purified on a column consisting of ovalbumin–eNOS peptide conjugate immobilized on cyanogen bromide-activated Sepharose.

A variety of approaches have been used to generate macrophage NOS antibodies. These include fusion protein approaches, generation of antibodies raised against peptides, as well as the generation of monoclonal antibodies against the purified protein.

[9] D. S. Bredt, P. M. Hwang, and S. H. Snyder, *Nature* (*London*) **347,** 768 (1991).

[10] J. L. Dinerman, T. M. Dawson, M. J. Schell, A. Snowman, and S. H. Snyder, *Proc. Natl. Acad. Sci. U.S.A.* **91,** 4214 (1990).

[11] A. J. Roskams, D. S. Bredt, T. M. Dawson, and G. V. Ronnett, *Neuron* **13,** 289 (1994).

Immunostaining

Rats or mice are anesthetized with pentobarbital (100 mg/kg intraperi-toneal injection) and perfused with 200 to 300 ml of 50 mM phosphate-buffered saline (PBS), pH 7.4 at 4°, followed by 200 to 300 ml of 4% freshly depolymerized paraformaldehyde (w/v) and 0.1% glutaraldehyde (v/v) in 0.1 M phosphate buffer (PB), pH 7.4. The brains are removed and postfixed for 2 hr in 4% paraformaldehyde (v/v) in PB before cryoprotection in 20% (v/v) glycerol in PB. Alternatively the brains can be cryoprotected in 30% (v/v) sucrose in PB by sequentially bathing the tissue in 10, 20, and 30% sucrose. Slide-mounted or free floating tissue sections are then permeabilized in 50 mM Tris-HCl-buffered saline (1.5% NaCl), pH 7.4 (TBS) containing 0.4% (v/v) Triton X-100 for 30 min at room temperature. They are then blocked for 1 hr in TBS containing 4% normal goat serum (NGS) (v/v), 0.2% Triton X-100 (v/v), and 0.02% NaN$_3$ (v/v) at room temperature. The sections are then incubated overnight at 4° in TBS con-taining 0.1% Triton X-100 (v/v), 2% NGS (v/v), and 0.02% NaN$_3$ (v/v) with an appropriate dilution of primary antibody. This is followed by rinsing the tissue section with TBS containing 1% NGS (v/v) for 10 min, three times. The sections are then incubated in TBS containing 1.5% NGS (v/v) with biotinylated goat anti-rabbit antibody (Vector Laboratories, Burl-ingame, CA) at a 1:200 dilution for 1 hr at room temperature. The sections are then washed two times for 10 min in TBS containing 1% NGS (v/v), then twice for 10 min in TBS followed by incubation with an avidin–biotin–peroxidase complex (Vector Elite, 1:50 dilution; Vector Laboratories) in TBS for 1 hr at room temperature. The sections are again washed three times for 10 min each time in TBS and developed with substrate solution consisting of 0.1% H$_2$O$_2$ (v/v) and 0.5 mg/ml diaminobenzidine in TBS. Sections are then rinsed with TBS and mounted on subbed glass slides. After dehydration, the sections receive coverslips with Permount (Fisher Scientific, Pittsburg, PA).

Localization of Neuronal Nitric Oxide Synthase

In the brain the highest density of nNOS is evident in the cerebellum and the olfactory bulb.[12,13] The accessory olfactory bulb has even more

[12] D. S. Bredt, C. E. Glatt, P. M. Hwang, M. Fotuhi, T. M. Dawson, and S. H. Snyder, *Neuron* **7**, 615 (1994).
[13] J. Rodrigo, D. R. Springall, O. Uttenthal, M. L. Bentura, F. Abadia-Molina, V. Riveros-Moreno, R. Martinez-Murillo, J. M. Polak, and S. Moncada, *Philos. Trans. R. Soc. London* **345**, 175 (1994).

prominent staining. Other areas of high-density staining include the pedunculopontine tegmental nucleus, the superior and inferior colliculi, the supraoptic nucleus, the islands of calleja, the caudate-putamen, and the dentate gyrus of the hippocampus. In the cerebellum, nNOS occurs in glutaminergic granule cells as well as GABAergic basket cells. In the cerebral cortex nNOS-staining neurons are colocalized with somatostatin-, neuropeptide Y (NPY), and γ-aminobutyric acid (GABA)-containing cells. In the corpus striatum, NOS neurons also stain for somatostatin and NPY. In the pedunculopontine tegmental nucleus of the brain stem, NOS neurons stain for choline acetyltransferase but do not stain for somatostatin and NPY. Even though there does not seem to be a single neurotransmitter that colocalizes with NOS, all NOS neurons identified colocalize with NADPH diaphorase (NDP)[14] (Fig. 1), a histochemical stain originally described by Thomas and Pearse.[15,16] Enzymes that possess diaphorase activity reduce tetrazolium dyes in the presence of NADPH, but not NADH, to a dark blue formazan precipitant. Nitric oxide synthase catalytic activity accounts for diaphorase staining because transfection of cultured human kidney 293 cells with nNOS cDNA produces cells that stain for both nNOS and NADPH diaphorase.[14] The coincidence of NOS immunoreactivity and NDP staining in neurons is only observed under appropriate paraformaldehyde fixation. Presumably, NOS is resistant to paraformaldehyde fixation, whereas all other NADPH-dependent oxidative enzymes are inactivated by fixatives.

Throughout the gastrointestinal tract, nNOS staining neurons are present in the myenteric plexus. The nNOS neurons are also prominent in penile tissue, specifically in the pelvic plexus and its axonal processes that form the cavernous nerve as well as the nerve plexus and the adventitia of the deep cavernosal sinusoids in the corpora cavernosa.[17] Neuronal NOS also occurs in the autonomic nerves in the outer adventitial layers of cerebral cortical and retinal blood vessels.[18] Neuronal NOS occurs in discrete ganglia cells and fibers in the adrenal medulla, where it may regulate blood flow. Neuronal NOS is also prominent within the posterior pituitary gland in fibers and terminals. In the spinal cord nNOS is localized in the substantia

[14] T. M. Dawson, D. S. Bredt, M. Fotuhi, P. M. Hwang, and S. H. Snyder, *Proc. Natl. Acad. Sci. U.S.A.* **88,** 7797 (1991).

[15] E. Thomas and A. G. E. Pearse, *Histochemistry* **2,** 266 (1961).

[16] E. Thomas and A. G. E. Pearse, *Acta Neuropathol.* **3,** 238 (1964).

[17] A. L. Burnett, C. J. Lowenstein, D. S. Bredt, T. S. K. Chang, and S. H. Snyder, *Science* **257,** 401 (1992).

[18] K. Nozaki, M. A. Moskowitz, K. I. Maynard, N. Koketsu, T. M. Dawson, D. S. Bredt, and S. H. Snyder, *J. Cereb. Blood Flow Metab.* **13,** 70 (1993).

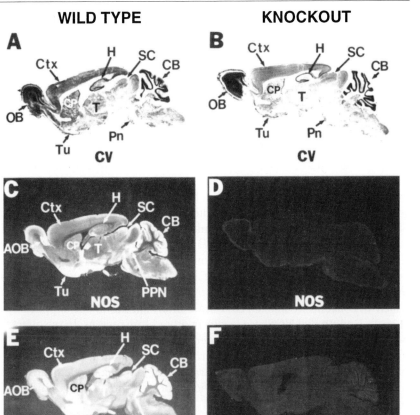

FIG. 1. Neuronal NOS null mice (KNOCKOUT) are devoid of NDP staining and nNOS immunostaining and have normal cytoarchitecture. Wild-type mice are shown in (A), (C), and (E), and nNOS knockout mice are shown in (B), (D), and (E). The absence of NDP in the nNOS null mice confirms that NOS catalytic activity accounts for NDP staining. CV, Cresyl violet; NOS, neuronal nitric-oxide synthase; NDP, NADPH diaphorase staining; AOB, accessory olfactory bulb; CP, caudate-putamen; Ctx, cortex; CB, cerebellum; H, hippocampus; OB, olfactory bulb; Pn, pontine nuclei; T, thalamus; Tu, olfactory tubercle; PPN, pedunculopontine tegmental nucleus; SC, superior colliculus. Bar: 2.5 mm. Reproduced with permission from Ref. 21.

gelatinosa and the intermediolateral cell column and neurons around the central canal.[19] Neuronal NOS may be constitutively expressed in

[19] S. Saito, G. J. Kidd, B. D. Trapp, T. M. Dawson, D. S. Bredt, D. A. Wilson, R. J. Traystman, S. H. Snyder, and D. R. Hanley, *Neuroscience (Oxford)* **59,** 447 (1994).

astrocytes.[20] It has also been localized to the macula densa of the kidney[21] and to the sarcolemna of skeletal muscle.[22]

Localization of Endothelial Nitric Oxide Synthase

Endothelial NOS has been localized to the endothelium of blood vessels in the periphery and the nervous system. Extensive mapping with antiserum selective for eNOS has not been recorded. Targeted disruption of neuronal NOS in mice produced greater than 90% depletion of NOS catalytic activity in the brain.[21] However the residual NOS activity displayed a discrete regional distribution, suggesting that neurons in some areas of the brain may express a form of NOS coded for by a different gene. Endothelial NOS was found to be selectively concentrated in the hippocampus.[10] Endothelial NOS staining was evident in pyramidal cells of the CA1 region and in granule cells of the dentate gyrus. Hippocampal pyramidal cells demonstrated eNOS immunoreactivity throughout their perikarya, with staining at the cell body surface, consistent with the localization to the plasma membrane. Staining for eNOS contrasts with the localization of nNOS which is concentrated in GABA-ergic interneurons in the hippocampus (Fig. 2). Endothelial NOS also occurs in other brain regions. In the olfactory bulb immunoreactivity is concentrated within neurons and neuropil of the internal granule cell layer and neuropil of the glomerular and external plexiform layers. Using high concentrations of glutaraldehyde fixatives, we found that NADPH diaphorase provided robust staining of pyramidal cells of the CA1 region.

Nitric oxide synthase has also been identified in neurtrophils, platelets, epithelial cells,and the large airway epithelium in lung, although the exact isoform that is localized in these cell types has not been clarified.[23]

Localization of Macrophage or Immunological Nitric Oxide Synthase

Immunological NOS (iNOS) was first localized to macrophages after immunological challenge with cytokines or lipopolysaccharide.[3,4] The iNOS isozyme has now been localized to a variety of cells, and under appropriate

[20] S. Murphy, M. L. Simmons, L. Agullo, A. Garcia, D. L. Feinstein, E. Galea, D. J. Reis, D. Minc-Golomb, and J. P. Schwartz, *Trends Neurosci.* **16**, 323 (1993).

[21] P. L. Huang, T. M. Dawson, D. S. Bredt, S. H. Snyder, and M. C. Fishman, *Cell* (*Cambridge, Mass.*) **75**, 1273 (1993).

[22] L. Kozik, M. B. Reid, D. S. Bredt, and S. H. Snyder, *Nature* (*London*) **372**, 546 (1994).

[23] B. Gaston, J. M. Drazen, J. Loscalzo, and J. S. Stamler, *Am. J. Respir. Crit. Care Med.* **149**, 538 (1994).

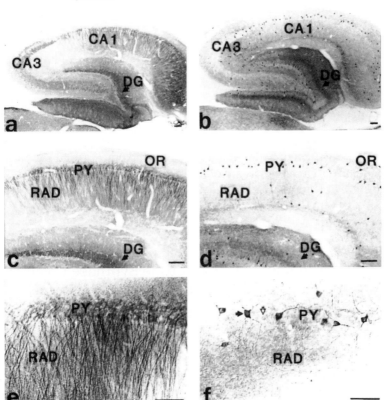

Fig. 2. CA1 hippocampal pyramidal neurons stain prominently for eNOS, as shown in (A), (C), and (E), but not nNOS, as shown in (B), (D), and (F). Cell bodies and dendrites of CA1 pyramidal neurons stain for eNOS. The nNOS immunoreactivity is limited to interneurons. DG, Dentate gyrus; OR, stratum oriens; PY, pyramidal cell layer of CA1; RAD, stratum radiatum. Bar: 100 μm (A–D) and 50 μ (E and F). Reproduced with permission from Ref. 10.

conditions it is likely that any eukaryotic cell can be induced to make iNOS.[3,4]

NADPH Diaphorase Staining

Under appropriate conditions of paraformaldehyde fixation NADPH diaphorase staining can be used to identify all NOS isoforms. For unknown reasons, NOS is resistant to paraformaldehyde fixation whereas all other NADPH-dependent oxidative enzymes are inactivated by fixatives. NADPH diaphorase staining is performed by incubating paraformalde-hyde-fixed tissue or cultures with 1 mM NADPH, 0.2 mM nitro blue tetrazo-lium in 0.1 M Tris-HCl buffer (pH 7.2) containing 0.2% Triton X-100 (v/v) and 0.015% NaN$_3$ (v/v).

Conclusion

The development of selective and specific antibodies for nNOS, eNOS, and iNOS has facilitated the characterization and function of these proteins. The identification of NO as a biological agent and the localization of NOS isoforms will lead to a better understanding of the physiology and patho-physiology of NOS.

[35] Determination of Nitric Oxide Synthase Cofactors: Heme, FAD, FMN, and Tetrahydrobiopterin

By PETER KLATT, KURT SCHMIDT, ERNST R. WERNER, and BERND MAYER

Introduction

The biological messenger molecule nitric oxide (NO) is synthesized from L-arginine by differently regulated isoforms of NO synthase (EC 1.14.13.39).[1-3] The Ca^{2+}/calmodulin-dependent isozymes are constitutively expressed in endothelial cells and neuronal tissues, whereas the expression of a Ca^{2+}-insensitive NO synthase in macrophages is regulated by induction of transcription. Nitric oxide synthases are homodimers with subunit molec-ular masses of 160 kDa (neuronal NO synthase) or 130 kDa (endothelial and macrophage NO synthase) that require NADPH and molecular oxygen for the five-electron oxidation of L-arginine to stoichiometric amounts of NO and L-citrulline.

The identification of the prosthetic groups bound to NO synthases has shed light on the unique complexity of these enzymes as they represent tetrahydrobiopterin-binding proteins with a flavin-containing reductase do-

[1] D. S. Bredt and S. H. Snyder, *Annu. Rev. Biochem.* **63**, 175 (1994).
[2] M. A. Marletta, *Cell (Cambridge, Mass.)* **78**, 927 (1994).
[3] B. Mayer, *Semin. Neurosci.* **5**, 197 (1993).

main and a heme moiety located on the same polypeptide. Analysis by high-performance liquid chromatography (HPLC)[4–7] and fluorescence spectroscopy[8,9] showed that FAD and FMN are noncovalently bound to NO synthase in a one to one stoichiometry. Treatment of the protein with I_2/ KI as previously described for the determination of biopterins in biological tissues[10] and subsequent analysis of the supernatant by HPLC[11] further demonstrated that NO synthases contain variable amounts of tightly associated tetrahydrobiopterin.[4,7,12,13] The identification of neuronal NO synthase as an iron protein by means of atomic absorption spectroscopy[4] and the evaluation of native, CO, and pyridine hemochrome spectra[6,14–16] showed that NO synthases represent cytochrome P450-like heme proteins, containing one ferroprotoporphyrin IX per subunit.

Here we describe reliable analytical procedures for the specific and sensitive quantitative determination of heme, FAD, FMN, and tetrahydrobiopterin in NO synthase preparations. The data were obtained with recombinant rat brain NOS purified from baculovirus-infected Sf9 (*Spodoptera fugiperda* full armyworm ovary) cells as described in detail in [41] in this volume.[17]

Determination of Heme

Reagents

Reagent A: 0.2 ml of 5 M NaOH, 2.5 ml pyridine, and H_2O to 5 ml
Reagent B: Sodium dithionite ($Na_2S_2O_4$)

[4] B. Mayer, M. John, B. Heinzel, R. Werner, H. Wachter, G. Schultz, and E. Böhme, *FEBS Lett.* **288**, 187 (1991).
[5] H. H. H. W. Schmidt, R. M. Smith, M. Nakane, and F. Murad, *Biochemistry* **31**, 3243 (1992).
[6] K. McMillan, D. S. Bredt, D. J. Hirsch, S. H. Snyder, J. E. Clark, and B. S. S. Masters, *Proc. Natl. Acad. Sci. U.S.A.* **89**, 11141 (1992).
[7] J. S. Pollock, E. R. Werner, J. S. Mitchell, and U. Förstermann, *Endothelium* **1**, 147 (1993).
[8] J. M. Hevel, K. A. White, and M. A. Marletta, *J. Biol. Chem.* **266**, 22789 (1991).
[9] D. S. Bredt, C. D. Ferris, and S. H. Snyder, *J. Biol. Chem.* **267**, 10976 (1992).
[10] T. Fukushima and J. C. Nixon, *Anal. Biochem.* **102**, 176 (1980).
[11] E. R. Werner, D. Fuchs, A. Hausen, G. Reibnegger, and H. Wachter, *Clin. Chem.* **33**, 2028 (1987).
[12] J. M. Hevel and M. A. Marletta, *Biochemistry* **31**, 7160 (1992).
[13] H. H. H. W. Schmidt, R. M. Smith, M. Nakane, and F. Murad, *Biochemistry* **31**, 3243 (1992).
[14] K. A. White and M. A. Marletta, *Biochemistry* **31**, 6627 (1992).
[15] D. J. Stuehr and M. Ikeda-Saito, *J. Biol. Chem.* **267**, 20547 (1992).
[16] P. Klatt, K. Schmidt, and B. Mayer, *Biochem J.* **288**, 15 (1992).
[17] B. Mayer, P. Klatt, B. M. List, C. Harteneck, and K. Schmidt, *Methods Enzymol.* **268**, Chap. 41, 1996 (this volume).

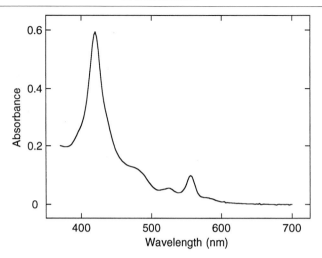

FIG. 1. Spectrum of the reduced pyridine hemochrome of recombinant rat brain NO synthase. The spectrum of NO synthase (0.80 mg/ml) was recorded after mixing 0.1 ml of the protein solution with 0.1 ml of 50% (v/v) pyridine in 0.2 M NaOH followed by the addition of a few grains of sodium dithionite.

Absorption Spectroscopy

A solution of NO synthase (0.2–1.6 mg/ml) is thoroughly mixed with an equal volume of freshly prepared reagent A, followed by the immediate addition of a few grains of solid sodium dithionite and mixing. Spectra of the reduced pyridine hemochrome are recorded in 0.2-ml cuvettes from 370 to 700 nm against blanks containing buffer and reagent A. Heme concentrations are calculated from the differences in absorbance at 556 versus 540 nm using an absorption coefficient of 22.1 mM^{-1} cm^{-1}.[18] Absorbance is linear in the range 1–10 μM ferroprotoporphyrin IX.

Figure 1 shows a representative pyridine hemochrome spectrum of recombinant rat brain NO synthase (0.80 mg/ml), purified from baculovirus-infected insect cells supplemented with hemin during infection. The relative intensities and positions of the α, β, and γ bands at 420, 524, and 556 nm are typical for ferroprotoporphyrin IX-containing proteins. Quantitative evaluation of spectra derived from different NO synthase samples gives a heme content of 0.9 $\pm$ 0.13 mol heme per mole NO synthase subunit (mean $\pm$ SEM, $n = 3$). These and the following calculations of cofactor/protein ratios are based on a molecular mass of 160 kDa per brain NO

[18] E. A. Berry and B. L. Trumpower, *Anal. Biochem.* **161,** 1 (1987).

synthase subunit[19,20] and determination of protein concentrations by the method of Bradford[21] with bovine serum albumin as standard.

Comments

(1) The appearance of the reduced pyridine hemochrome is time dependent. Maximal absorbance is obtained 1–3 min after addition of sodium dithionite. It is thus recommended to record several spectra following the addition of the reductant and to calculate heme concentrations from the spectrum displaying maximal difference in absorbance at 556 versus 540 nm. (2) The formation of the reduced pyridine hemochrome critically depends on the amount of sodium dithionite added to the sample. We routinely add a few additional grains of sodium dithionite after the absorbance at 556 nm has reached a plateau in order to ensure maximal chromogen formation. Addition of excess sodium dithionite may prevent detection of the α band, but it does not interfere with the absorption in the β and γ region. (3) NADPH present in NO synthase preparations at concentrations greater than 1 mM may lead to substantial underestimation of heme concentrations by interfering with detection of the γ band.

Determination of FAD and FMN

Solvents

Solvent A: 10 mM K_2HPO_4 adjusted to pH 6.0 with 85% (w/w) H_3PO_4
Solvent B: Methanol

Sample Preparation

The noncovalently bound flavins FAD and FMN are released from NO synthase into the supernatant by heat denaturation of the enzyme (95° for 5 min in the dark). It is essential to use well-sealed vials for this procedure in order to avoid uncontrolled reduction of sample volume. Subsequently, samples are cooled to 0°–4°, and to recover water, which may have condensed at the top of the vials, the vials are briefly spun down by centrifugation. Samples are kept at 4° in the dark until HPLC analysis.

[19] D. S. Bredt, P. M. Hwang, C. E. Glatt, C. Lowenstein, R. R. Reed, and S. H. Snyder, *Nature* (*London*) **351**, 714 (1991).
[20] C. Harteneck, P. Klatt, K. Schmidt, and B. Mayer, *Biochem. J.* **304**, 683 (1994).
[21] M. M. Bradford, *Anal. Biochem.* **72**, 248 (1976).

Chromatographic

Samples (30 μl) are injected into an HPLC system (LiChroGraph L-6200, Merck, Vienna, Austria) equipped with an autosampler (AS-4000, Merck) and a low-pressure gradient controller. FAD and FMN are separated on a 250 × 4 mm C_{18} reversed-phase column fitted with a 4 × 4 mm C_{18} guard column (LiChrospher 100 RP-18, 5 μm particle size, Merck) by means of gradient elution. A linear gradient from 80% solvent A and 20% solvent B ($t = 0$) to 50% solvent A and 50% solvent B ($t = 10$ min) is generated at a flow rate of 1 ml/min. Prior to injection of the next sample, the gradient is reversed within 10 min, followed by a further 10 min of column equilibration. FAD and FMN are detected by fluorescence (F-1050, Merck) at excitation and emission wavelengths of 450 and 520 nm, respectively. The method is calibrated with solutions of authentic FAD and FMN freshly prepared in the buffer used for dilution of NO synthase and subjected to heat treatment as described above. The FAD calibration curves are linear from 10 nM to 1 μM (0.3–30 pmol per 30 μl injection). The fluorescence of FMN is approximately 3.5-fold higher than that of FAD, allowing reliable detection of FMN down to 3 nM (0.1 pmol per 30 μl injection).

Figure 2 shows a representative HPLC chromatogram obtained with recombinant rat brain NO synthase (16 μg/ml), purified from baculovirus-

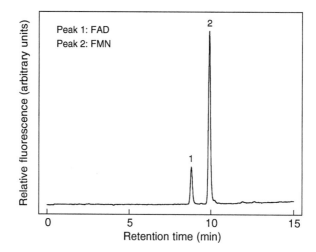

FIG. 2. Analysis by HPLC of flavins bound to recombinant rat brain NO synthase. NO synthase (16 μg/ml) was heat-denatured (95° for 5 min), and noncovalently bound FAD (Peak 1) and FMN (Peak 2) released from the enzyme were separated by reversed-phase HPLC and detected by fluorescence.

infected insect cells, which had been supplemented with 0.1 mM riboflavin during infection. FAD and FMN are well separated, with retention times of 8.8 and 9.9 min, respectively. Quantitative evaluation of the peak areas shows that the FAD and FMN content of purified NO synthase is 0.7 ± 0.03 and 0.8 ± 0.02 mol per mole NO synthase subunit (mean values ± SEM, n = 3), respectively.

Comments

(1) Analysis of FAD and FMN by HPLC can be simplified by using isocratic elution with 10 mM K$_2$HPO$_4$, pH 6.0, containing 25% (v/v) methanol. However, under these conditions, we observed substantial peak broadening and loss of baseline separation. (2) Because solutions of FAD and FMN are unstable and light-sensitive, samples should be kept in the dark and analyzed within a few hours.

Determination of Tetrahydrobiopterin

The reduced pteridines tetrahydro- and dihydrobiopterin can be oxidized to biopterin by treatment with KI/I$_2$ under acidic conditions. To determine the amount of tetrahydrobiopterin, a second series of samples is oxidized at alkaline pH. Under these conditions, dihydrobiopterin is converted to biopterin, whereas only the alkali-labile tetrahydrobiopterin loses the side chain at C-6 and is oxidized to pterin. Thus, the difference between the amount of biopterin formed by oxidation at acidic pH (i.e., total biopterin) versus biopterin formed at alkaline pH (i.e., total biopterin minus tetrahydrobiopterin) corresponds to the amount of tetrahydrobiopterin in the sample.

Solutions and Buffers

Solution A: 0.1 M I$_2$ dissolved in an aqueous solution of 0.5 M KI
1 M HCl
1 M NaOH
0.2 M ascorbic acid
Buffer E: 20 mM NaH$_2$PO$_4$ (pH 3.0 with 85% H$_3$PO$_4$) in 5% (v/v) methanol

Sample Preparation

Solution A is mixed with an equal volume of 1 M HCl, and 10 μl of this freshly prepared reagent is added to 50 μl of a solution containing 5–50 pmol NO synthase. A second series of samples is subjected to oxidation under alkaline conditions by treating 50-μl aliquots with 10 μl of a freshly prepared mixture of solution A and 1 M NaOH (1 : 1, v/v). Samples are kept at ambient temperature in the dark for 1 hr prior to neutralization of acidic and alkaline samples with 5 μl of 1 M NaOH and 5 μl of 1 M HCl, respectively. Subsequently, excess iodine is destroyed by the addition of 5 μl of 0.2 M ascorbic acid.

Chromatographic Analysis

Samples (30 μl) are injected by means of an autosampler (AS-4000, Merck) onto a 250 × 4 mm C_{18} reversed-phase column fitted with a 4 × 4 mm C_{18} guard column (LiChrospher 100 RP-18, 5 μm particle size, Merck) and analyzed for biopterin and pterin by HPLC (LiChroGraph L-6200, Merck). Pteridines are eluted isocratically with buffer E at a flow rate of 1 ml/min and detected by fluorescence (F-1050, Merck) at excitation and emission wavelengths of 350 and 440 nm, respectively. Run times are routinely set to 15 min without any additional column regeneration required for at least 50 samples. The method is calibrated by oxidizing known samples of tetrahydrobiopterin to biopterin (i.e., at acidic pH) under strictly identical conditions. Biopterin calibration curves are linear in the range from 10 nM to 1 μM (0.2–20 pmol per 30 μl injection).

Figure 3 shows HPLC chromatograms obtained on treatment of purified

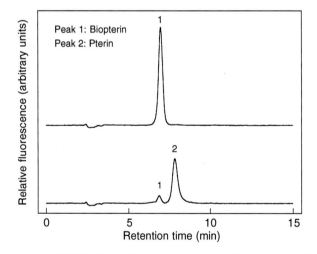

Fig. 3. Analysis by HPLC of pteridines bound to recombinant rat brain NO synthase. Reduced pteridines in NO synthase preparations (40 μg protein/ml) were oxidized under acidic (upper trace) or alkaline (lower trace) conditions and analyzed by reversed-phase HPLC and fluorescence detection. Biopterin (Peak 1) is formed from dihydro- and tetrahydrobiopterin by oxidation of acidic pH (top trace) as well as from dihydrobiopterin by oxidation at alkaline pH (lower trace). Tetrahydrobiopterin-derived pterin (Peak 2) is the major product formed on alkaline oxidation (lower trace).

recombinant rat brain NO synthase (40 μg/ml) with I_2/KI at acidic (top trace) and alkaline pH (lower trace). Under acidic conditions, biopterin is the sole reaction product (Peak 1, 6.9 min), and a total biopterin content of 0.44 ± 0.012 mol per mole protein subunit (mean ± SEM, $n = 3$) is calculated from the peak area. Under alkaline conditions, two peaks are observed, which correspond to biopterin (Peak 1, 6.9 min) and tetrahydro-biopterin-derived pterin (Peak 2, 7.9 min). The amount of alkali-stable bio-pterin is calculated as 0.03 ± 0.001 mol per mole NO synthase subunit (mean ± SEM, $n = 3$). Accordingly, this NO synthase preparation contains 0.41 ± 0.025 mol tetrahydrobiopterin per mole of protein subunit.

Comments

(1) The I_2/KI solutions are stable for at least 1 year if stored at ambient temperature in the dark. (2) The oxidizing reagent (i.e., the mixture of I_2/KI with HCl or NaOH) should be prepared immediately before use. (3) The amount of the I_2/KI solution required for complete oxidation of pteridines largely depends on the amount of reducing agents present in the samples. The present method has been worked out for NADPH-free NO synthase solutions containing 12 mM 2-mercaptoethanol. Sufficient I_2/KI has been added when a brownish-yellow color is still observable after the 1-hr oxida-tion period and neutralization of the samples. (4) Ascorbic acid solutions should be prepared freshly and used within 1 day, since oxidation products of ascorbic acid severely interfere with the fluorescence detection of pteri-dines. (5) The amount of ascorbic acid used to destroy excess iodine has to be increased when the sample does not become colorless after addition of the reductant. (6) Owing to the limited stability of biopterin, it is recom-mended that samples be analyzed within a few hours.

[36] Chemistry of N-Hydroxy-L-arginine

By JON M. FUKUTO

Introduction

Owing to the fairly recent discoveries of its diverse and ubiquitous physiological functions, nitric oxide (NO) has become a molecule of extreme interest. The biosynthesis of nitric oxide by the class of enzymes referred to as the nitric oxide synthases (NOS) requires a five-electron oxidation of one of the terminal nitrogen atoms of the guanidine function of L-arginine. This oxygen- and NADPH-dependent oxidation of L-arginine

METHODS IN ENZYMOLOGY, VOL. 268

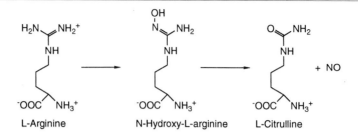

FIG. 1. Conversion of L-arginine to L-citrulline and NO by nitric oxide synthase via the biosynthetic intermediate N-hydroxy-L-arginine.

appears to be stepwise. The first step in the oxidative process involves the hydroxylation of L-arginine to generate N-hydroxy-L-arginine (Fig. 1). The intermediacy of N-hydroxy-L-arginine in NO biosynthesis has been demonstrated chemically, biochemically,[1,2] and pharmacologically.[3] Although it is possible that enzymatically generated N-hydroxy-L-arginine can be released from NOS, it is generally thought that the majority of it remains bound and undergoes further oxidation to eventually give citrulline and NO.[1,2] If N-hydroxy-L-arginine release from NOS results in significant physiological concentrations, it has been proposed that it may be able to regulate L-arginine levels by serving as an inhibitor of arginase.[4] Also, it has been reported that N-hydroxy-L-arginine can react with NO to produce a vasoactive species which has yet to be identified.[5]

    In spite of the discovery of the intermediacy of N-hydroxy-L-arginine in NO biosynthesis and the fact that it may even have some physiological functions of its own, the chemistry of N-hydroxy-L-arginine remains relatively unexplored. In fact, little is known of the chemistry of N-hydroxyguanidines in general. Certainly, an understanding of the chemical properties of N-hydroxyguanidines may serve as a basis for the eventual understanding of the mechanism by which NO is oxidatively released from N-hydroxy-L-arginine as well as provide some idea of its own potential physiological chemistry and fate. Thus, the purpose of this chapter is to first describe the synthesis of N-hydroxy-L-arginine (although the reagent is available commercially, a review of the synthetic methods may be useful for those

[1] D. J. Stuehr, N. S. Kim, C. F. Nathan, O. W. Griffith, P. L. Feldman, and J. Wiseman, J. Biol. Chem. 266, 6259 (1991).
[2] P. Klatt, K. Schmidt, G. Uray, and B. Mayer, J. Biol. Chem. 268, 14781 (1993).
[3] G. C. Wallace, P. Gulati, and J. M. Fukuto, Biochem. Biophys. Res. Commun. 176, 528 (1991).
[4] F. Daghigh, J. M. Fukuto, and D. E. Ash, Biochem. Biophys. Res. Commun. 202, 174 (1994).
[5] A. Zembowicz, M. Hecker, H. Macarthur, W. C. Sessa, and J. R. Vane, Proc. Natl. Acad. Sci. U.S.A. 88, 11172 (1991).

wishing to synthesize analogs or derivatives of N-hydroxy-L-arginine) followed by a brief discussion of the known chemical properties of N-hydroxy-L-arginine that may be of some physiological relevance. Because the chemical function of interest is the N-hydroxyguanidine moiety of N-hydroxy-L-arginine, the chemistry of N-hydroxyguanidine and related species is also included in the discussion of the possible chemistry.

Synthesis of N-Hydroxy-L-arginine

There are four reported syntheses of N-hydroxy-L-arginine.[6-9] The first reported synthesis of N-hydroxy-L-arginine by Feldman[6] consists of 10 steps and utilizes an isothiourea as a crucial intermediate (Fig. 2). This synthesis results in an overall 18% yield (based on the commercially available starting material, N^δ-benzyloxycarbonyl-L-ornithine) of enantiomerically pure N-hydroxy-L-arginine. Significantly, this synthetic strategy allowed for the facile incorporation of ^{15}N into either the free or hydroxylated terminal guanidinium nitrogen atom. The synthesis of N-hydroxy-L-arginine by Wallace and Fukuto[7] is based on the reaction of hydroxylamine with a diprotected N^δ-cyanoornithine derivative and consists of six steps that result in an overall yield of 28% (the enantiomeric purity has not, however, been determined) (Fig. 3). The synthetic strategy utilized by Pufahl and co-workers[8] and by Wagenaar and Kerwin[9] is also based on the chemistry of the cyanoornithine derivative from which other arginine derivatives can be synthesized along with N-hydroxy-L-arginine. A description of N-hydroxy-L-arginine synthesis[7] that utilizes the reaction of hydroxylamine with a diprotected cyanoornithine compound is described below. Alternative methods used by others for several of the steps are also noted and commented on.

Step 1: α-Carboxylate Protection (Fig. 3). Protection of the carboxylic acid via the formation of the *tert*-butyl ester is performed as described by Bodanszky and Bodanszky.[10] Thus, commercially available N^δ-(benzyloxycarbonyl)-L-ornithine is taken up in *tert*-butyl acetate (15 ml/mmol of amino acid) and perchloric acid (11 mEq in the form of a 60% solution, w/v). The solution is stirred for 2 days. Water is then added to the reaction mixture followed by the addition of NaOH until the solution is basic (litmus to

[6] P. L. Feldman, *Tetrahedron Lett.* **32**, 875 (1991).
[7] G. C. Wallace and J. M. Fukuto, *J. Med. Chem.* **34**, 1746 (1991).
[8] R. A. Pufahl, P. G. Nanjappan, R. W. Woodward, and M. A. Marletta, *Biochemistry* **31**, 6822 (1992).
[9] F. L. Wagenaar and J. F. Kerwin, Jr., *J. Org. Chem.* **58**, 4331 (1993).
[10] M. Bodanszky and A. Bodanszky, *in* "The Practice of Peptide Synthesis," p. 48. Springer-Verlag, New York, 1984.

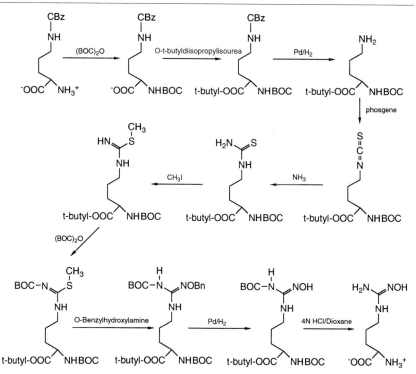

FIG. 2. Pathway for *N*-hydroxy-L-arginine synthesis utilized by Feldman.[6] (BOC)$_2$O, *tert*-Butyl pyrocarbonate; BOC, *tert*-butyloxycarbonyl; CBz, benzyloxycarbonyl.

blue) and subsequent extraction with ethyl acetate. Rotary evaporation of the organic extracts affords an oil in approximately 70% yield that can be used without further purification. Nuclear magnetic resonance (NMR) data (CDCl$_3$) are as follows: δ 1.44 (s, 9H), 1.5–1.9 (m, 4H), 3.23 (t, 2H), 3.31 (t, 1H), 5.09 (s 2H and s, 1H, broad), 7.35 (s, 5H). It should be noted that this compound is now commercially available, and this step can be omitted if desired.

Step 2: α-Amino Protection (Fig. 3). The α-amino group of the above product is then protected via the formation of the *tert*-butyloxycarbonyl (BOC) derivative. Thus, N^δ-(benzyloxycarbonyl)-L-ornithine *tert*-butyl ester from step 1 is taken up in dichloromethane (~1 ml/mmol) and cooled in an ice bath. Then 1.15 Eq of *tert*-butyl pyrocarbonate in dichloromethane is slowly added. The reaction mixture is stirred for 1 hr in the ice bath and 3 hr at room temperature. The solvent is removed by rotary evaporation and the product isolated by silica gel chromatography using hexane/ethyl

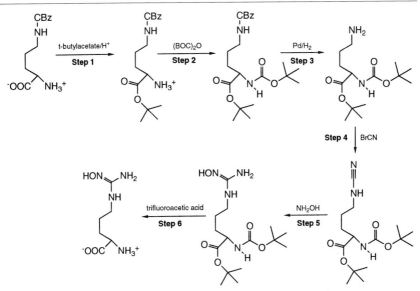

FIG. 3. Pathway for N-hydroxy-L-arginine synthesis based on the reaction of hydroxylamine with a cyanamide.[7–9] $(BOC)_2O$, *tert*-Butyl pyrocarbonate; CBz, benzyloxycarbonyl.

acetate, 3:1 (v/v). The product, N^α-(*tert*-butyloxycarbonyl)-N^δ-(benzyloxy-carbonyl)-L-ornithine *tert*-butyl ester, has an R_f of 0.33 on silica gel thin-layer chromatography (TLC) using the same eluting solvent. Rotary evaporation of the appropriate fractions affords a product oil in greater than 90% yield. The NMR data $(CDCl_3)$ are as follows: δ 1.44 (s, 9H), 1.46 (s, 9H), 1.5–1.9 (m, 4H), 3.23 (t, 2H), 4.17 (t, 1H), 4.88 (s, 1H broad), 5.09 (s, 2H and s, 1H broad), 7.35 (s, 5H).

N^α-(*tert*-Butyloxycarbonyl)-N^δ-(benzyloxycarbonyl)-L-ornithine *tert*-butyl ester can also be made from N^δ-(benzyloxycarbonyl)-L-ornithine *tert*-butyl ester by utilizing dicyclohexylcarbodiimide-*tert*-butanol in dichloromethane containing 4-(dimethylamino)pyridine.[8] The reported yield, however, is slightly lower (58%) than the above-described procedure.

Step 3: Removal of N^δ-Amino-Protecting Group (Fig. 3). Removal of the N^δ-benzyloxycarbonyl (CBz) protecting group is accomplished by hydrogenolysis.[11] Thus, N^α-(*tert*-butyloxycarbonyl)-N^δ-(benzyloxycarbonyl)-L-ornithine *tert*-butyl ester is taken up in methanol (~2.5 ml/mmol) and placed into a three-neck round-bottomed flask with a magnetic stirrer. The flask is then flushed with nitrogen and the catalyst added (10% Pd on

[11] M. Bodanszky and A. Bodanszky, *in* "The Practice of Peptide Synthesis," p. 153. Springer-Verlag, New York, 1984.

charcoal, ~0.25 g of catalyst/g of the compound). The flask is purged with a slow stream of H_2 while the solution is being vigorously stirred. The exiting gas is passed through a bubbler. The evolution of CO_2 is monitored by periodically passing the exiting gas through a solution of $Ba(OH)_2$, which forms a $BaCO_3$ precipitate. Once the evolution of CO_2 ceases (it could take several days), the solution is cooled with an ice bath and purged with N_2, and the solution is filtered through Celite. The filter pad is washed with methanol. Rotary evaporation of the combined methanolic solutions affords the product, N^α-(tert-butyloxycarbonyl)-L-ornithine tert-butyl ester (Fig. 3), in greater than 95% yield as an oil. The NMR data ($CDCl_3$) are as follows: δ 1.44 (s, 9H), 1.46 (s, 9H), 1.5–1.9 (m, 4H), 2.73 (t, 2H), 4.17 (t, 1H), 5.2 (s, 1H broad). On freezing, this oil will solidify. This material is then used in the next step without further purification.

The hydrogenolysis of N^α-(tert-butyloxycarbonyl)-N^δ-(benzyloxycarbo-nyl)-L-ornithine tert-butyl ester can also be accomplished under pressure using a Parr bottle.[8] This procedure also yields the product in high yield and can be accomplished in less time.

Step 4: Cyanamide Formation (Fig. 3). Utilizing the general method of Bailey et al.[12] for making cyanamides of amines, N^α-(tert-butyloxycarbonyl)-L-ornithine tert-butyl ester is taken up in methanol (~2.5 ml/mmol) along with sodium acetate (2.4 Eq). The solution is then cooled in an ice bath, and 1.1 Eq of cyanogen bromide in methanol is added slowly. After the addition is complete, the reaction mixture is stirred for 2.5 hr in the ice bath and 3 hr at room temperature. The solvent is then removed by rotary evaporation. The residue is taken up in water (~2 ml/mmol of starting compound) and extracted three times with an equivalent amount of ethyl ether. The ether extracts are combined and dried with magnesium sulfate, and the solvent is removed by rotary evaporation. The residue is then purified by flash chromatography on 230–400 mesh silica using hexane/ethyl acetate (2:1, v/v). The product, N^α-(tert-butyloxycarbonyl)-N^δ-cyano-L-ornithine tert-butyl ester, has an R_f of 0.6 on silica TLC using the same solvent mixture. The NMR data ($CDCl_3$) are as follows: δ 1.44 (s, 9H), 1.46 (s, 9H), 1.5–1.9 (m, 4H), 3.17 (t, 2H), 4.17 (t, 2H and s, 1H broad), 5.19 (s, 1H broad).

The synthesis of N^α-(tert-butyloxycarbonyl)-N^δ-cyano-L-ornithine tert-butyl ester from N^α-(tert-butyloxycarbonyl)-L-ornithine tert-butyl ester can also be accomplished using cold ethyl ether as solvent.[8]

Step 5: N-Hydroxyguanidine Formation (Fig. 3). Using a slightly modi-fied procedure of Bailey et al.,[12] the N-cyanoderivative is converted to the

[12] D. M. Bailey, C. G. DeGrazia, H. E. Lape, R. Frering, D. Fort, and T. Skulan, J. Med. Chem. 16, 151 (1973).

N-hydroxyguanidine function via reaction with hydroxylamine. Thus, N^α-(*tert*-butyloxycarbonyl)-N^δ-cyano-L-ornithine *tert*-butyl ester and a 4-fold equivalent of hydroxylamine hydrochloride and sodium carbonate (both dried under vacuum prior to use) are added to dry dioxane (~3 ml/mmol, dried by distillation from sodium metal). The mixture is refluxed for 1 hr. The reaction mixture is then filtered and the solvent removed by rotary evaporation. The crude residue is dissolved in dichloromethane and extracted three times with water, pH 5.5 (acetic acid). The aqueous extracts are combined and washed with dichloromethane and the water removed by rotary evaporation. This procedure gives crude material that contains approximately 70% of the desired compound, N^α-(*tert*-butyloxycarbonyl)-N^ω-hydroxy-L-arginine *tert*-butyl ester. The NMR data (CDCl$_3$) are as follows: δ 1.44 (s, 9H), 1.46 (s, 9H), 1.5–1.9 (m, 4H), 3.17 (t, 2H), 4.19 (t, 2H), 4.29 (s, 1H broad), 5.19 (s, 1H broad). This residue can be used directly in the following step (however, see the note below).

The above reaction can also be carried out in methanol or ethanol using triethylamine as the base. Purification of N^α-(*tert*-butyloxycarbonyl)-N^ω-hydroxy-L-arginine *tert*-butyl ester can be accomplished using a combination of silica gel [6:1 (v/v) dichloromethane/ethanol[9] or 9:1 (v/v) chloroform/methanol[8]] and semipreparative reversed-phase (C$_{18}$) chromatography[8] [42:58 (v/v) acetonitrile with 1% trifluoroacetic acid/water, isocratic].

Note: N-Hydroxy-L-arginine is unstable under basic conditions. Thus, once the N-hydroxyguanidine function is made, it is advisable to keep all solutions either neutral or acidic. Therefore, it may be appropriate to purify N^α-(*tert*-butyloxycarbonyl)-N^ω-hydroxy-L-arginine *tert*-butyl ester in order to avoid a final cation-exchange purification step (below) which requires slightly basic conditions during product elution. Separation of N-hydroxy-L-arginine from the base-catalyzed decomposition products is extremely difficult.

Step 6: Deprotection of α-Amino and α-Carboxylate (Fig. 3). Deprotection of N^α-(*tert*-butyloxycarbonyl)-N^ω-hydroxy-L-arginine *tert*-butyl ester to generate the desired product can be accomplished by the method of Bodanszky and Bodanszky.[13] Thus, N^α-(*tert*-butyloxycarbonyl)-N^ω-hydroxy-L-arginine *tert*-butyl ester is taken up in trifluoroacetic acid (~8.5 ml/mmol) and stirred at room temperature for 1 hr. If the compound was purified prior to deprotection, rotary evaporation of the trifluoroacetic acid yields pure N-hydroxy-L-arginine as the trifluoroacetate salt.[8] If crude N^α-(*tert*-butyloxycarbonyl)-N^ω-hydroxy-L-arginine *tert*-butyl ester was used, the residue remaining after removal of the trifluoroacetic acid is purified by cation-

[13] M. Bodanszky and A. Bodanszky, *in* "The Practice of Peptide Synthesis," p. 170. Springer-Verlag, New York, 1984.

exchange chromatography (Dowex-50W, 4% cross-linked, dry mesh 200–400) using 50 mM ammonium hydroxide as the eluting solvent. The basic fractions are quickly freeze-dried and analyzed for product by ^{1}H NMR. The NMR data (D$_2$O) show δ 4.06 (t, 1H), 3.25 (t, 2H), and 1.5–2.05 (m, 4H).

Deprotection can also be accomplished by treating purified N^α-(tert-butyloxycarbonyl)-N^ω-hydroxy-L-arginine tert-butyl ester with 4 N HCl in dioxane for 23 hr.[9] Under these conditions, N-hydroxy-L-arginine precipitates from solution as the dihydrochloride salt, which is rinsed with ethyl ether.

As mentioned earlier, it is wise to try to avoid the cation-exchange purification step because N-hydroxy-L-arginine may decompose under the basic conditions required to elute it from the column. It is, therefore, essential to get N^α-(tert-butyloxycarbonyl)-N^ω-hydroxy-L-arginine tert-butyl ester as pure as possible before final deprotection. The final deprotection step is an extremely clean reaction, and the resulting N-hydroxy-L-arginine will typically maintain the state of purity of the diprotected precursor.

Physiologically Relevant Chemistry of N-Hydroxy-L-arginine

Because of the guanidine function of L-arginine, it is the most basic of all amino acids. N-Hydroxylation of the guanidine function, however, significantly decreases its basicity (the pK_a of guanidine is 13.6 and the pK_a of N-hydroxyguanidine is 8.1).[12] As mentioned earlier, N-hydroxy-L-arginine is unstable with respect to base. However, it is acid stable and is typically isolated as the salt of a strong acid.

N-Hydroxy-L-arginine and related N-hydroxyguanidines can be oxidized with a variety of agents such as PbO$_2$, Pb(OAc)$_4$, K$_3$Fe(CN)$_6$, Ag$_2$CO$_3$, or peracids,[14,15] and although NO can be generated under certain circumstances, the major nitrogen oxide product is typically HNO (Fig. 4). This is not really unexpected since HNO would be the predicted two-electron oxidation product, whereas NO requires an overall three-electron oxidation and the majority of the chemical oxidants utilized in the previous studies were two-electron oxidants. Also, it has been demonstrated that peroxidatic oxidation of N-hydroxy-L-arginine by nitric oxide synthase results in the generation of HNO.[16] Direct detection of HNO is normally difficult owing to the fact that it is a metastable species which can react

[14] J. M. Fukuto, G. C. Wallace, R. Hszieh, and G. Chaudhuri, *Biochem. Pharmacol.* **43,** 607 (1992).

[15] J. M. Fukuto, D. J. Stuehr, P. L. Feldman, M. P. Bova, and P. Wong, *J. Med. Chem.* **36,** 2666 (1993).

[16] R. A. Pufahl, J. S. Wishnok, and M. A. Marletta, *Biochemistry* **34,** 1930 (1995).

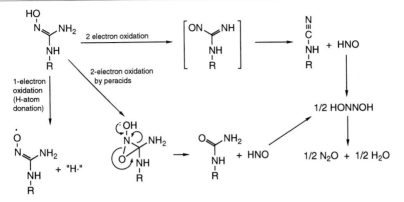

FIG. 4. One- and two-electron oxidation of an N-hydroxyguanidine. Formation of HNO from two-electron oxidation and a radical species from a single-electron oxidation is possible.

with itself to generate nitrous oxide (N_2O). Therefore, evidence for the production of HNO can be obtained indirectly by detection of N_2O. Thus, gas chromatographic analysis of reaction headspace samples using a Porapak Q column running at low temperatures (50°–70°) and utilizing a thermoconductivity detector will allow N_2O formation to be monitored. The organic product from the oxidation of N-hydroxyguanidines can be either the urea, the citrulline equivalent product, or the cyanamide, depending on the oxidant (Fig. 4). Detection of NO from N-hydroxyguanidine oxidation is easily accomplished by purging the reaction solutions with nitrogen into a chemiluminescence detector equipped with an ozone source. Inside the chemiluminescence detector, ozone oxidizes NO to excited state NO_2 which releases a photon of light when it relaxes to the ground state. This method is extremely sensitive and, although indirect, extremely specific for NO.

N-Hydroxyguanidines can also be oxidized by a single electron (i.e., they can serve as one-electron reducing agents, with E°_{ox1} being estimated to be $+0.1 \pm 0.04$ V versus normal hydrogen electrode).[17] For example, it has been proposed that N-hydroxyguanidine inhibits ribonucleotide reductase, in a manner analogous to hydroxyurea, by quenching the active site tyrosyl radical via hydrogen atom donation.[18] In an analogous chemical reaction, N-hydroxyguanidine is capable of reducing potassium nitrosodisulfonate, $(KO_3S)_2NO\cdot$ (which is blue in color), by hydrogen atom donation to give the colorless $(KO_3S)_2NOH$. The ability of the N-hydroxyguanidine function to quench the tyrosyl radical and inhibit ribonucleotide reductase

[17] H.-G. Korth, R. Sustmann, C. Thater, A. R. Butler, and K. U. Ingold, *J. Biol. Chem.* **269,** 17776 (1994).
[18] K. Larson, B.-M. Sjoberg, and L. Thelander, *Eur. J. Pharmacol.* **125,** 75 (1982).

may be the reason N-hydroxyguanidine, and derivatives of N-hydroxygua-
nidines, possess significant anticancer activity.[19,20] Also, it has been proposed that hydrogen atom donation by N-hydroxy-L-arginine to heme-
bound molecular oxygen is a crucial step in NO biosynthesis.[17] Thus, one
of the dominant chemical properties of N-hydroxy-L-arginine and N-hy-
droxyguanidines, in general, is their ability to act as reducing agents by
both one- and two-electron pathways. Two-electron oxidation will result
in the release of HNO, whereas single electron oxidation would generate,
as the initial product, a radical species (Fig. 4).

In microsomal systems, it has been demonstrated that N-hydroxyguani-
dines can be reduced to the corresponding guanidine via an NADH-depen-
dent process.[21] Thus, it appears that N-hydroxyguanidines are capable of
serving as both an electron source, as described above, and an electron
acceptor, in the case of the reduction to the guanidine. Interestingly, the
same study also indicates that N-hydroxyguanidines are able to uncouple
microsomal monooxygenase activity to generate superoxide (O_2^-), which
can further oxidize the N-hydroxyguanidine to the corresponding urea.

Pharmacological evidence indicates that N-hydroxy-L-arginine or N-
hydroxyguanidine can react with NO to form either an adduct or a separate
species that possesses biological activity.[5] The possible chemical interaction
between N-hydroxy-L-arginine and NO has yet to be elucidated, and thus
the identification or nature of the reaction product remains a mystery. This
interaction may, however, represent a novel and important physiological
process.

Finally, N-hydroxyguanidines, when deprotonated, have been proposed
to possess significant nucleophilic character and may therefore bind electrophilic centers.[22] In fact, under basic conditions they can react with esters to
form novel aminooxadiazoles (which are central nervous system-penetrable
muscarinic agents).[23]

Summary

The synthesis of N-hydroxy-L-arginine can be accomplished by a relatively simple and straightforward procedure. Also, a variety of arginine
derivatives can be synthesized using minor modifications of this procedure.
N-Hydroxy-L-arginine is subject to decomposition under either basic or

[19] R. H. Adamson, *Nature (London)* **236**, 400 (1974).
[20] A. W. Tai, E. J. Lien, M. M. Lai, and T. A. Khwaja, *J. Med. Chem.* **27**, 236 (1984).
[21] B. Clement, M.-H. Schultze-Mosgau, and H. Wohlers, *Biochem. Pharmacol.* **46**, 2249 (1993).
[22] A. M. Sapse, L. Herzig, and G. Snyder, *Cancer Res.* **41**, 1824 (1981).
[23] J. Saunders, A. M. MacLeod, K. Merchant, G. A. Showell, R. J. Snow, L. J. Street, and R. Baker, *J. Chem. Soc., Chem. Commun.*, 1618 (1988).

oxidizing conditions. In fact, one of the dominant chemical features of *N*-hydroxy-L-arginine (or *N*-hydroxyguanidines), which would be significant to those interested in exploring its role either as a biosynthetic intermediate in NO generation or as an independently acting species, is its ability to act as a reducing agent. Even a cursory inspection of *N*-hydroxy-L-arginine indicates that the *N*-hydroxyguanidine function is electron rich and could be easily oxidized. Oxidation of *N*-hydroxy-L-arginine is, indeed, facile and can lead to either the release of HNO (from a two-electron oxidation) or the formation of an apparent radical species (from one-electron oxidation). The ability of *N*-hydroxy-L-arginine to act as a one-electron reducing agent (or hydrogen atom-donor) may be important in the biosynthesis of the NO radical since an odd-electron step is required.[17] Regardless, it is likely that *N*-hydroxyguanidines can act as electron sources and may participate in redox reactions with biological oxidants. The physiological relevance of such processes, however, remains to be determined.

[37] Nitric Oxide Synthase Inhibitors: Amino Acids

By Owen W. Griffith and Robert G. Kilbourn

Introduction

Nitric oxide synthase (NOS; EC 1.14.13.39) catalyzes the NADPH- and O_2-dependent oxidation of L-arginine to citrulline and nitric oxide (NO). Three distinct isoforms of NOS have been identified in mammals, and each is thought to serve specific functions. The neuronal isoform (nNOS) plays a role in neurotransmission, whereas the isoform in vascular endothelium (eNOS) produces NO that acts as a vasodilator in the normal regulation of blood pressure and organ perfusion. Both nNOS and eNOS are constitutive, Ca^{2+}/calmodulin-dependent enzymes and are tightly controlled by mechanisms regulating intracellular Ca^{2+} levels; they normally produce small (nanomolar) amounts of NO. The third NOS isoform is not present constitutively (at least in most cells) but is induced as part of an immune response in many cell types by endotoxin or combinations of inflammatory cytokines [e.g., γ-interferon plus interleukin (IL-1) or tumor necrosis factor (TNF)]. This inducible isoform (iNOS) contains calmodulin but is not regulated by intracellular changes in Ca^{2+} levels.[1-4]

[1] O. W. Griffith and D. J. Stuehr, *Annu. Rev. Physiol.* **57,** 707 (1995).
[2] D. S. Bredt and S. H. Snyder, *Annu. Rev. Biochem.* **63,** 175 (1994).

Because NOS activity and NO are difficult to characterize in complex systems (e.g., vascular rings or intact animals), many studies of NO biology have relied on the use of NOS inhibitors. A biological phenomenon is taken to be NOS-dependent and NO-mediated if it is reduced or eliminated by addition of a NOS inhibitor. Although lack of inhibitor specificity is always a concern in such studies, remarkably few difficulties have attended *in vitro* and *in vivo* use of the NOS-inhibiting amino acids discussed here; the few known caveats are mentioned as they apply to specific inhibitors. Other important and useful NOS inhibitors including aminoguanidine,[5] imidazole, and substituted imidazoles[6] are discussed elsewhere.

The NOS-inhibiting amino acids discussed here all are recognized by and associate with the substrate binding site for L-arginine. As such, they have been used to investigate the NOS reaction mechanism and to probe interactions between the L-arginine binding site and the binding sites for heme and tetrahydrobiopterin, the NOS oxygenase domain cofactors.[1,3] The NOS-inhibiting amino acids have also been used extensively *in vivo* to control both physiological and pathophysiological NO formation.[7] With respect to the latter, there is now good evidence that the unregulated Ca^{2+} influx occurring in cerebral ischemia (stroke) causes nNOS to overproduce NO with toxic consequences.[2] In certain anaphylactic reactions, inappropriate release of histamine and possibly other autocoids may cause eNOS-mediated overproduction of vasoactive NO.[8,9] More commonly, overproduction of NO is due to iNOS because that isoform is typically expressed at high levels and is essentially unregulated once expressed.[10] The high NO concentrations attained (10–100 μM) are potentially cytotoxic both to iNOS-containing cells and to adjacent cells and can be disruptive to the delicate signal transduction mechanisms normally served by nNOS and eNOS. Studies with inhibitors show that formation of cytotoxic levels of NO is beneficial to the organism if it contributes to macrophage attack on tumor cells[11,12] or leads to the destruction of intracellular viruses or

---

[3] B. S. S. Masters, *Annu. Rev. Nutr.* **14**, 131 (1994).

[4] W. C. Sessa, *J. Vasc. Res.* **31**, 131 (1994).

[5] J. A. Corbett and M. L. McDaniel, *Methods Enzymol.* **268**, Chap. 39, 1996 (this volume).

[6] D. J. Wolff, G. A. Datto, R. A. Samatovicz, and R. A. Tempsick, *J. Biol. Chem.* **268**, 9425 (1993).

[7] C. Szabo and C. Thiemermann, *Curr. Opin. Invest. Drugs* **2**, 1165 (1993).

[8] C. Szabo, C. C. Wu, C. Thiemermann, and J. R. Vane, *Br. J. Pharmacol.* **110**, 31P (1993).

[9] C. Thiemermann, *Adv. Pharmacol.* **28**, 45 (1994).

[10] R. G. Kilbourn and O. W. Griffith, *J. Natl. Cancer Inst.* **84**, 827 (1992).

[11] J. B. Hibbs, Jr., Z. Vavrin, and R. R. Taintor, *J. Immunol.* **138**, 550 (1987).

[12] J. B. Hibbs, Jr., R. R. Taintor, Z. Vavrin, and E. M. Rachlin, *Biochem. Biophys. Res. Commun.* **157**, 87 (1988).

microorganisms.[13] On the other hand, high levels of iNOS-derived NO cause vascular leak and severe hypotension in septic shock[10] and contribute importantly to the tissue destruction seen in diabetes mellitus, rheumatoid arthritis, and other inflammatory and autoimmune disorders.[14,15]

It will be appreciated from the foregoing discussion that isoform-selective inhibitors would be of considerable research and clinical interest, and the search for such compounds is a major focus of work in many laboratories.[16-20] As summarized below, the currently known NOS-inhibiting amino acids in some cases show moderate selectivity for different isoforms, but, in our view, none is adequately specific to achieve the pharmacological ideal of specific isoform inhibition in isolated tissues or whole animals. Nevertheless, factors other than isoform selectivity per se may favor the use of one inhibitor over another for some purposes, and those factors are discussed. The structures and K_i values of the most useful NOS-inhibiting amino acids are shown in Table I.

N^ω-Methyl-L-arginine

N^ω-Methyl-L-arginine (L-NMA) was shown to antagonize the L-arginine-dependent cytotoxicity of activated macrophages even before NOS-mediated formation of NO was characterized.[11] Since then, L-NMA has proved to be one of the most useful NOS inhibitors due to its commercial availability, chemical stability (unaffected by extremes of pH at room temperature; stable at 100° at acidic or neutral pH), water solubility, very low toxicity, and apparent specificity for NOS. Because arginase neither degrades nor is inhibited by L-NMA, administration of L-NMA does not interfere with the urea cycle, and metabolic loss of drug is slow. There is no evidence from intact cell or *in vivo* studies that L-NMA interferes with other L-arginine-dependent processes such as protein synthesis (direct studies remain to be done, however). The system y^+ and $B^{0,+}$ arginine transporters do recognize L-NMA with an affinity comparable to that shown L-arginine,[21,22] and tissue uptake of L-NMA is thus not a problem.

[13] C. F. Nathan and J. B. Hibbs, Jr., *Curr. Opin. Immunol.* **3**, 65 (1991).
[14] M. Stefanovic-Racic, J. Stadler, and C. H. Evans, *Arthritis Rheum.* **36**, 1036 (1993).
[15] H. Kolb and V. Kolb-Bachofen, *Immunol. Today* **13**, 157 (1992).
[16] O. W. Griffith and S. S. Gross, in "Methods in Nitric Oxide Research" (M. Feelish and J. Stamler, eds.), p. 187. Wiley, New York, 1996.
[17] J. F. Kerwin, Jr. and M. Heller, *Med. Res. Rev.* **14**, 23 (1994).
[18] J. M. Fukuto and Y. Komori, *Annu. Rep. Med. Chem.* **29**, 83 (1994).
[19] M. A. Marletta, *J. Med. Chem.* **37**, 1899 (1994).
[20] J. M. Fukuto and G. Chaudhuri, *Annu. Rev. Pharmacol. Toxicol.* **35**, 165 (1995).
[21] K. Schmidt, P. Klatt, and B. Mayer, *Mol. Pharmacol.* **44**, 615 (1993).
[22] O. W. Griffith, R. D. Allison, R. Rouhani, M. Handlgten, and M. S. Kilberg, *FASEB J.* **6**, A1255 (1992).

TABLE I
STRUCTURES AND KINETIC PROPERTIES OF ARGININE AND AMINO ACID NITRIC OXIDE
SYNTHASE INHIBITORS
$R-NH(CH_2)_3CH(NH_2)COOH$

Compound	R	K_i values nNOS	eNOS	iNOS
L-Arg[a]	$^+NH_2$ $\|\|$ NH_2C-	1.6 μM (rat)[b] 1.2 μM (cow)[e]	1 μM (human)[c] 5 μM (cow)[f] 3 μM (cow)[g]	2.3 μM (mouse)[d] 10 μM (mouse)[e] 19 μM (rat)[b]
L-NMA	$^+NH_2$ $\|\|$ CH_3NHC-	0.2 μM (rat)[b] 1.4 μM (rat)[g]	0.4 μM (human)[c] 0.9 μM (cow)[h]	6 μM (rat)[b] 13 μM (mouse)[i]
L-NNA[j]	NH $\|\|$ O_2NNHC-	15 nM (cow)[e] 170 nM (pig)[k]	39 nM (human)[c]	4.4 μM (mouse)[e]
L-NIO[l]	$^+NH_2$ $\|\|$ CH_3C-	0.6 μM (rat)[m]	~0.2 μM (pig)[n]	2.0 μM (rat)[m]
L-NAA[l]	$^+NH_2$ $\|\|$ NH_2NHC-	~0.2 μM (rat)[o]	<0.1 μM (cow)[p]	~2.0 μM (mouse)[p]
L-TC	S $\|\|$ NH_2C-	0.06 μM (rat)[b]	Not determined	3.6 μM (rat)[b]
L-SMTC[q]	$^+NH_2$ $\|\|$ CH_3SC-	1.2 nM (human)[r] 0.5 μM (rat)[s]	11 nM (human)[r]	40 nM (human)[r] 0.8 μM (rat)[s]

[a] K_m values shown.
[b] C. Frey, K. Narayanan, K. McMillan, L. Spack, S. S. Gross, B. S. Masters, and O. W. Griffith, *J. Biol. Chem.* **269**, 26083 (1994).
[c] E. P. Garvey, J. V. Tuttle, K. Covington, B. M. Merrill, E. R. Wood, S. A. Baylis, and I. G. Charles, *Arch. Biochem. Biophys.* **311**, 235 (1994).
[d] D. J. Stuehr, N. S. Kwon, C. F. Nathan, O. W. Griffith, P. L. Feldman, and J. Wiseman, *J. Biol. Chem.* **266**, 6259 (1991).
[e] E. S. Furfine, M. F. Harmon, J. E. Paith, and E. P. Garvey, *Biochemistry* **32**, 8512 (1993).
[f] D. J. Wolff, A. Lubeski, and S. C. Umansky, *Arch. Biochem. Biophys.* **314**, 360 (1994).
[g] D. S. Bredt and S. H. Snyder, *Proc. Natl. Acad. Sci. U.S.A.* **87**, 682 (1990).
[h] J. S. Pollock, U. Föstermann, J. A. Mitchell, T. D. Warner, H. H. H. W. Schmidt, M. Nakane, and F. Murad, *Proc. Natl. Acad. Sci. U.S.A.* **88**, 10480 (1991).
[i] N. M. Olken and M. A. Marletta, *Biochemistry* **32**, 9677 (1993).
[j] K_D values for nNOS and eNOS; K_i value for iNOS (see text).
[k] P. Klatt, K. Schmidt, F. Brunner, and B. Mayer, *J. Biol. Chem.* **269**, 1674 (1994).
[l] K_i values estimated from IC_{50} values by comparison with other inhibitors or by calculation assuming competitive inhibition.
[m] M. A. Hayward, T. Sander, and O. W. Griffith, unpublished (1994).
[n] D. D. Rees, R. M. J. Palmer, R. Schulz, H. F. Hudson, and S. Moncada, *Br. J. Pharmacol.* **101**, 746 (1990).
[o] L. Lambert, J. P. Whitten, B. M. Baron, H. C. Cheng, N. S. Doherty, and I. McDonald, *Life Sci.* **48**, 69 (1991).

N^{ω}-Methyl-D-arginine (D-NMA) does not inhibit NOS, consistent with the fact that all NOS isoforms are enantiomer specific for their amino acid substrate. For this reason D-NMA, which is commercially available or readily synthesized for D-ornithine,[23] is often used as a noninhibiting control in studies employing L-NMA. N^{ω}-Alkyl-L-arginine analogs of L-NMA with ethyl and propyl alkyl groups are comparable to L-NMA as NOS inhibitors; the N^{ω}-butyl analog is less effective.[24,25] N^{ω},N^{ω}-Dimethyl-L-arginine is an effective inhibitor, but the isomer in which the methyl groups are on separate guanidinium nitrogens (i.e., $N^{\omega},N^{\omega\prime}$-dimethyl-L-arginine) is not a good inhibitor.[24,25] N^{ω}-Allyl- and N^{ω}-cyclopropyl-L-arginine, analogs which easily form reactive radical intermediates, are also potent inhibitors.[26] To date, none of these analogs has shown sufficient advantage over L-NMA to warrant more than occasional use.

Use of N^{ω}-Methyl-L-arginine with Tissue Homogenates or Purified Enzymes

In initial rate, steady-state kinetic studies, NOS inhibition by L-NMA is competitive with L-arginine; its K_i is typically one-third to one-tenth the K_m of L-arginine when the comparison is made with the same NOS isoform under similar reaction conditions (Table I). Inhibition is initially fully reversible by removal of L-NMA or by addition of excess L-arginine. In longer studies (>5 min), the nonlinearity of product versus time graphs and other data demonstrate that inhibition by L-NMA has an irreversible component. Studies from several groups have shown that L-NMA is processed as a pseudosubstrate by NOS. Such processing requires NADPH and O_2 and

---

[23] J. L. Corbin and M. Reporter, *Anal. Biochem.* **57**, 310 (1974).
[24] D. J. Stuehr and O. W. Griffith, *Adv. Enzymol. Relat. Areas Mol. Biol.* **65**, 287 (1992).
[25] O. Fasehun, S. S. Gross, E. Pipili, E. Jaffe, O. W. Griffith, and R. Levi, *FASEB J.* **4**, 309 (1990).
[26] N. M. Olken and M. A. Marletta, *J. Med. Chem.* **35**, 1137 (1992).

---

[p] S. S. Gross, D. J. Stuehr, K. Aisaka, E. A. Jaffe, R. Levi, and O. W. Griffith, *Biochem. Biophys. Res. Commun.* **170**, 96 (1990).
[q] K_D values for human nNOS; other values are K_i.
[r] E. S. Furfine, M. F. Harmon, J. E. Paith, R. G. Knowles, M. Salter, R. J. Kiff, C. Duffy, R. Hazelwood, J. A. Oplinger, and E. P. Garvey, *J. Biol. Chem.* **269**, 26677 (1994).
[s] K. Narayanan, L. Spack, K. McMillan, R. G. Kilbourn, M. A. Hayward, B. S. S. Masters, and O. W. Griffith, *J. Biol. Chem.* **270**, 11103 (1995).

is accompanied by irreversible loss of NOS activity, possibly due to attack on the heme cofactor.[27-29]

As a practical matter, L-NMA is most useful *in vitro* as a reversible, competitive inhibitor; irreversible inhibition requires incubating the enzyme with NADPH under conditions where much activity is also lost by mechanisms not involving L-NMA.[27] If the K_i for L-NMA and the K_m for L-arginine are known for the animal species and NOS isoform of interest, the amount of L-NMA needed for any desired initial level of inhibition in mixtures containing known concentrations of L-arginine can be predicted[30]:

$$\% \text{ Inhibition} = \frac{100[I]}{[I] + K_i (1 + [Arg]/K_m^{Arg})}$$

Where % inhibition is greater than calculated, irreversible inhibition is probably occurring. If the kinetic constants are not known for the species studied, L-NMA is typically added at a concentration that is about 10-fold higher than L-arginine to effect greater than 90% inhibition (see Segel[30] for a more complete discussion). It may be noted that it is generally not possible to reach true 100% inhibition with L-NMA in short-term studies both because it is only competitive with L-arginine and because L-NMA is itself a substrate that yields citrulline and NO at 0.5 to 2% of the rate seen with L-arginine.[27-29]

For *in vitro* studies not confined to initial rate measurements, inhibition will be mixed reversible–competitive and irreversible; kinetic analysis becomes challenging. Fortunately, irreversible inhibition can often be minimized because L-NMA does not cause such inhibition in the absence of NADPH. If the reaction mixture contains NOS and L-NMA, then the reaction should be initiated by adding NADPH; if the mixture contains L-NMA and NADPH, then reaction should be initiated by adding NOS. If premature irreversible inhibition is to be avoided, one should not prepare reaction mixtures containing NOS, L-NMA, and NADPH and then initiate the reaction by adding L-arginine.

Use of N^{ω}-Methyl-L-arginine with Intact Cells or Isolated Tissues

The considerations summarized above also apply to studies with intact cells and tissues. However, because there is an endogenous and generally unknown intracellular level of L-arginine, it is not possible to calculate

---

[27] P. L. Feldman, O. W. Griffith, H. Hong, and D. J. Stuehr, *J. Med. Chem.* **36,** 491 (1993).
[28] N. M. Olken and M. A. Marletta, *Biochemistry* **32,** 9677 (1993).
[29] N. M. Olken, Y. Osawa, and M. A. Marletta, *Biochemistry* **33,** 14784 (1994).
[30] I. H. Segel, *in* "Enzyme Kinetics," p. 105. Wiley, New York, 1975.

precisely or to predict levels of inhibition. With intact cells and tissues, one must also allow time for transport equilibrium to be attained; these phenomena can be quite complex because the system y^+ transporter can also exchange endogenous intracellular L-arginine for extracellular L-NMA. In many cases, true transport equilibrium may not occur during the time of the experiment. With many (perhaps most) cell types, there is also the confounding fact that the NOS product L-citrulline will be recycled through L-argininosuccinate to L-arginine.[31] The capacity of different cell types to effect citrulline recycling varies but can be significant; accurate assay of the NOS reaction by quantitating citrulline formation is often not possible. It has also been suggested that recycling of citrulline derived from NOS-mediated metabolism of L-NMA may produce L-arginine which then partially overcomes inhibition by L-NMA,[32] but we think this is unlikely to occur often (or at all) given the slow metabolism of L-NMA seen with isolated NOS.

In L-arginine-free cell culture or tissue bath media, all NOS isoforms should be substantially but incompletely ($>50\%$; usually $>90\%$) inhibited by 0.1–1.0 mM L-NMA. Concentrations as high as 10 mM L-NMA can be used with little concern for nonspecific effects (D-NMA becomes an appropriate control). Where the medium contains L-arginine, the L-NMA concentration should be 5- to 10-fold higher than that of L-arginine; it is obviously preferable to keep the L-arginine concentration low (0.1–0.5 mM) where it is possible to do so. Note that for cell types able to convert L-citrulline to L-arginine, L-citrulline in the media may also reduce inhibition by L-NMA. Liver, but not other cells, will convert L-ornithine to L-arginine, possibly causing a similar problem.

Use of N^ω-Methyl-L-arginine in Animals

A number of studies have been carried out in which L-NMA is administered to experimental animals by oral or intravenous (i.v.) routes; other parenteral routes (e.g., intraperitoneal or subcutaneous) are effective but less commonly used. Selection of L-NMA dose is obviously dependent on the effect intended (see below), but a few generalizations are possible. For bolus i.v. injection, doses lower than 1 mg/kg generally have little or no effect, whereas doses of approximately 20 mg/kg often achieve the maximal degree of short-term eNOS or iNOS inhibition possible. Doses higher than 20 mg/kg typically have longer lived effects but cause no greater inhibition than 20 mg/kg. Bolus injection, typically completed in less than 30 sec, can

---

[31] M. Hecker, W. C. Sessa, H. J. Harris, E. E. Änggard, and J. R. Vane, *Proc. Natl. Acad. Sci. U.S.A.* **87**, 8612 (1990).

[32] S. L. Archer and V. Hampl, *Biochem. Biophys. Res. Commun.* **188**, 590 (1990).

be repeated at intervals of several minutes to several hours depending on the duration of effect desired.[33-35]

Oral doses of L-NMA have been explored mainly in small rodents. Granger and co-workers found that inclusion of 50 mM of L-NMA in the drinking water of mice yielded a daily dose of approximately 2000 mg/kg and caused substantial iNOS inhibition over several days as judged by urinary nitrate excretion.[36,37] To our knowledge, absorption of orally administered L-NMA from the gut has not been systematically examined, but it would be expected to be good. The circadian eating and drinking behavior of rodents can, however, present a problem with oral L-NMA administration; if an animal does not eat or drink for several hours, inhibition may be lost because L-NMA is cleared fairly rapidly from plasma ($t_{1/2}$ = 4.5 hr in dogs).[38] Oral administration may also cause local effects such as decreased gut perfusion.

For studies with L-NMA (and other inhibitors), the results obtained are generally dependent in considerable degree on the species selected. Most experimental species (rat, guinea pig, rabbit, dog, monkey, pig, sheep) are useful for studies of the role of NO in normal blood pressure homeostasis, where it is consistently observed that administration of L-NMA causes vasoconstriction and an increase in pressure as eNOS-mediated formation of vasoactive NO is blocked. Typically, the animals (anesthetized or awake) are instrumented to monitor systemic blood pressure (and perhaps other parameters), and L-NMA is given by bolus or continuous i.v. infusion. With bolus injection, blood pressure increases 10–60% for 5–90 min (depending on dose and species) and then returns to baseline.[33-35,39,40] Repeat injection causes a renewed increase in pressure, but in rats and at least some other species a profound tachyphylaxis is evident after 3–4 doses.[35] The basis of this effect is not yet determined, but, as a practical matter, it cannot be assumed that naive animals and animals previously given L-NMA will show equivalent responses to the drug. Similar concerns apply to the other inhibitors discussed here.

[33] R. G. Kilbourn, S. S. Gross, A. Jubran, J. Adams, O. W. Griffith, R. Levi, and R. F. Lodato, *Proc. Natl. Acad. Sci. U.S.A.* **87**, 3629 (1990).

[34] R. G. Kilbourn, A. Jubran, S. S. Gross, O. W. Griffith, R. Levi, J. Adams, and R. F. Lodato, *Biochem. Biophys. Res. Commun.* **172**, 1132 (1990).

[35] L. Spack and O. W. Griffith, unpublished observation (1994).

[36] D. L. Granger, J. B. Hibbs, Jr., and L. M. Broadnax, *J. Immunol.* **146**, 1294 (1991).

[37] T. G. Evans, L. Thai, D. L. Granger, and J. B. Hibbs, Jr., *J. Immunol.* **151**, 907 (1993).

[38] R. G. Kilbourn, L. Owen-Schaub, D. M. Cromeens, S. S. Gross, M. Flaherty, S. M. Santee, A. M. Alak, and O. W. Griffith, *J. Appl. Physiol.* **76**, 1130 (1994).

[39] K. Aisaka, S. S. Gross, O. W. Griffith, and R. Levi, *Biochem. Biophys. Res. Commun.* **160**, 881 (1989).

[40] D. D. Rees, R. M. J. Palmer, and S. Moncada, *Proc. Natl. Acad. Sci. U.S.A.* **86**, 3375 (1989).

For studies of septic shock or cytokine-induced shock, selection of an appropriate species and proper induction of shock are crucial if the results are to be clinically relevant.[41] For such studies, rodents are not ideal because they are extremely insensitive to the effects of endotoxin and cytokines, and the physiological changes in rodents (hypoglycemia, bowel necrosis, pulmonary hemorrhage) are often different than those observed in septic shock patients. Other species such as dogs, sheep, or monkeys display similar sensitivity to endotoxin and bacteria as humans and manifest some of the same hemodynamic and physiological changes observed in clinical septic shock. We also note that anesthetized animals should be avoided where possible since anesthetic agents affect blood pressure and can alter NO levels.[42–44]

The procedures used to cause iNOS expression and shock are also important. Rapid infusion of high doses (mg/kg of endotoxin) cause an immediate hypotension due to stimulation of eNOS rather than induction of iNOS.[45] Ideally, a low dose of endotoxin (10 to 50 μg/kg)[34] or a slow infusion of bacteria should be administered over a prolonged period (hours) to avoid immediate effects on blood pressure and to allow for the induction of endogenous cytokine biosynthesis. Evidence for vasodilation, which is an important characteristic of septic shock, should occur after, not during, the infusion of the inflammatory agent or cytokine.[34] That is, there should be a delay consistent with iNOS induction.

All animals should have hemodynamic monitoring with an arterial catheter attached to a transducer. In large animals, a balloon-tipped pulmonary artery catheter can be used to measure cardiac output and pulmonary capillary wedge pressure, which reflect the myocardial function and the volume status, respectively. It is crucial to avoid hypovolemia-induced hypotension or severe myocardial depression, which can be observed in models using high doses of endotoxin. Hypovolemia can be avoided by using the pulmonary catheter wedge pressure to guide volume replacement. The use of a pulmonary catheter also permits the calculation of vascular resistance, a reflection of vascular tone and the parameter most directly affected by nitric oxide.

Once hypotension occurs, the interventional agent should be administered. It is important to wait until evidence of vasodilation is obtained

[41] R. G. Kilbourn and T. Billiar, in "Methods in Nitric Oxide Research" (M. Feelish and J. Stamler, eds.), p. 619. Wiley, New York, 1996.

[42] J. R. Tobin, L. D. Martin, M. J. Breslow, and R. J. Traystman, Anesthesiology 81, 1264 (1994).

[43] M. F. Doursout, R. G. Kilbourn, and J. E. Chelly, Anesthesiology 81, A768 (1994).

[44] T. Lechevalier, M. F. Doursout, R. G. Kilbourn, and J. E. Chelly, Anesthesiology 81, A647 (1994).

[45] C. Thiemermann and J. Vane, Eur. J. Pharmacol. 182, 591 (1990).

because this is the crucial clinical change in patients that defines septic shock. Furthermore, evidence suggests that early intervention with NOS inhibitors before vasodilation occurs may be detrimental.[46] These factors may account for the failure of NOS inhibitors to improve survival in some models. Finally, the dose of inhibitor selected should restore vascular tone but not cause overconstriction leading to compromised organ blood flows. In the case of L-NMA, an initial bolus dose of 20 mg/kg given over 5 min followed by a continuous infusion of 5 mg/kg/hr will result in the immediate restoration of vascular tone and will maintain the blood pressure in a normal range for 3 days in dogs receiving high continuous interleukin-2 infusions.[38]

N^{ω}-Nitro-L-arginine and N^{ω}-Nitro-L-arginine Methyl Ester

N^{ω}-Nitro-L-arginine (L-NNA) and its far more soluble methyl ester (L-NAME) are commercially available, inexpensive, and widely used NOS inhibitors. L-NNA is a particularly effective inhibitor of the constitutive NOS (nNOS and eNOS) to which it binds tightly but noncovalently. Although inhibition was initially reported to be irreversible,[47] detailed kinetic studies show slow reversal with a $t_{1/2}$ of 10–30 min.[48,49] Initial binding is competitive with L-arginine, but inhibition increases with time. In contrast, L-NNA acts as a freely reversible inhibitor of iNOS, competitive with L-arginine. Because L-NNA does not show tight binding to iNOS, it is a less effective inhibitor of this isoform than of eNOS and nNOS in studies lasting more than a few minutes (i.e., in studies lasting long enough for tight binding to nNOS or eNOS to occur). Furfine et al. report, for example, that at equilibrium L-NNA is a 300-fold more potent inhibitor of nNOS than of iNOS.[48] Klatt et al. point out that L-NNA is a much more potent inhibitor of nNOS than is L-NMA (confirming earlier work[50]), but they note that initial binding affinities for the two inhibitors are similar (0.61 μM for L-NMA versus 0.53 μM for L-NNA).[49] L-NNA is the more potent inhibitor in noninitial rate studies because its dissociation is very slow ($k_{off} = 7.4 \times 10^{-2}$ min^{-1} [49] or 3.9×10^{-2} min^{-1} [48]). In contrast to L-NMA, both L-NNA and L-NAME inhibit the superoxide or hydrogen peroxide

[46] C. E. Wright, D. D. Rees, and S. Moncada, Cardiovasc. Res. **26,** 48 (1992).
[47] M. A. Dwyer, D. S. Bredt, and S. H. Snyder, Biochem. Biophys. Res. Commun. **176,** 1136 (1993).
[48] E. S. Furfine, M. F. Harmon, J. E. Paith, and E. P. Garvey, Biochemistry **32,** 8512 (1993).
[49] P. Klatt, K. Schmidt, F. Brunner, and B. Mayer, J. Biol. Chem. **269,** 1674 (1994).
[50] S. S. Gross, D. J. Stuehr, K. Aisaka, E. A. Jaffe, R. Levi, and O. W. Griffith, Biochem. Biophys. Res. Commun. **170,** 96 (1990).

formation catalyzed by pig nNOS[48] in the absence of L-arginine.[51] L-NNA is not metabolized by NOS, and D-NNA does not inhibit.

Inhibition of NOS by L-NAME is not yet fully characterized. Because other studies show that the carboxylate of L-arginine is important to binding, it is expected that affinity for L-NAME will be much lower than for L-NNA. Consistent with this view, in reaction mixtures with 0.1 mM L-arginine pig nNOS exhibited IC_{50} values for L-NNA and L-NAME of 0.7 μM and 2.8 μM, respectively.[51] In the presence of esterases L-NAME is, in fact, hydrolyzed to L-NNA, and this is likely to be the main route by which it inhibits in studies with crude homogenates, intact cells, isolated tissues, or whole animals.[52] Although the solubility of L-NAME makes it easier to use than L-NNA, it should be appreciated that the intervention of a hydrolytic step in (fully) activating the compound as a NOS inhibitor contributes to the complexity of the experiment (i.e., the concentration of L-NNA, the more potent inhibitor, increases as L-NAME hydrolyzes).

Use of N^{ω}-Nitro-L-arginine or N^{ω}-Nitro-L-arginine Methyl Ester with Tissue Homogenates or Purified Enzymes

At neutral pH and 37°, the solubility of L-NNA is about 4 mM. Refrigerating or freezing solutions of that concentration will generally induce crystallization, and they will require resolubilization before reuse. These considerations have perhaps discouraged use of L-NNA in studies with isolated NOS, but the difficulties are easily overcome. L-NNA is quite stable at neutral pH, and its solutions can be stored for several days at room temperature, thus avoiding crystallization during cooling. Solutions containing precipitate can be warmed to 50°–60° to more quickly effect full solubilization. It is also possible to prepare acidified stock solutions (pH 1–2) in which the solubility of L-NNA is much greater (~50 mM). If this approach is taken, it is necessary to assure that the reaction mixtures receiving the acidified L-NNA stock solution are adequately buffered.

For studies with iNOS, L-NNA acts as a rapidly reversible inhibitor, competitive with L-arginine.[48] Although it has less affinity than L-NMA and is thus less potent, appropriate concentrations for any desired degree of inhibition can be calculated or estimated as described for L-NMA. With nNOS or eNOS, tight binding of L-NNA causes inhibition by L-NNA to appear to be irreversible [e.g., if nNOS or eNOS is preincubated with L-NNA and the enzyme is then assayed for a short time (<5 min) in the

---

[51] B. Heinzel, M. John, P. Klatt, E. Böhme, and B. Mayer, *Biochem. J.* **281**, 627 (1992).
[52] G. J. Southan, S. S. Gross, and J. R. Vane, *in* "The Biology of Nitric Oxide" (S. Moncada, M. Feelish, R. Busse, and E. A. Higgs, eds.), Vol. 4, p. 4. Portland Press, London and Chapel Hill, North Carolina, 1994.

presence of relatively low (10–30 μM) concentrations of L-arginine]. The difficulty with such studies is, of course, that the NOS reaction rate is not truly constant but is (perhaps subtly) increasing with time as L-NNA dissociates; meaningful comparison of results between experiments carried out under even slightly different conditions of incubation time or L-NNA and L-arginine concentration can be impossible.

Studies in which L-NNA is not preincubated with nNOS or eNOS (e.g., NOS is added to reaction mixtures containing NADPH, L-NNA, and L-arginine) are somewhat less troublesome because full inhibition is developed within 1–4 min when [L-NNA] ≥ [L-arginine] (e.g., see Ref. 48). Nevertheless, inhibition will not be strong in the initial minutes of such studies, and it would be inaccurate to conclude that there was a constant level of inhibition based on a single time point or even on several time points taken later in the reaction course (e.g., at 10–30 min). Unless one is prepared to carry out a full kinetic analysis, it is best to add nNOS and eNOS to otherwise complete reaction mixtures where [L-NNA] ≥ [L-arginine] and to interpret the results only semiquantitatively.

Because of its variable and confounding hydrolysis to L-NNA, L-NAME should not be used in studies with crude homogenates where quantitative analysis of the results is intended. In other words, L-NAME is a relatively weak inhibitor, but in cell or tissue homogenates endogenous esterases will convert a variable and unknown fraction of L-NAME to L-NNA, a much more potent inhibitor. Such studies will be difficult to interpret or reproduce. L-NAME can be used with highly purified NOS that is esterase free, but L-NAME is, of course, not so strong an inhibitor as L-NNA in such studies.

Use of N^{ω}-Nitro-L-arginine or N^{ω}-Nitro-L-arginine Methyl Ester with Intact Cells or Isolated Tissues

Although the concerns regarding solubility still apply, L-NNA is in some respects a more useful inhibitor for cell and tissue studies than it is for studies with isolated NOS. Thus, time is required to transport L-NNA (or any inhibitor) into cells before inhibition is maximal; the delay due to transport masks at least in part the slow binding of L-NNA to nNOS or eNOS. L-NNA has, in fact, two advantages: (1) the slow dissociation of L-NNA means that once inhibition is established, the extent of inhibition is relatively constant and is not easily altered by modest fluctuations in the intracellular L-NNA concentration, and (2) L-NNA, in contrast to L-arginine and L-NMA, is a neutral amino acid and is transported as such.[53,54]

[53] R. G. Bogle, S. B. Coade, S. Moncada, J. D. Pearson, and G. E. Mann, *Biochem. Biophys. Res. Commun.* **180,** 926 (1991).
[54] K. Schmidt, P. Klatt, and B. Mayer, *Biochem J.* **301,** 313 (1994).

L-Arginine in the medium does not interfere with L-NNA uptake (L-arginine does interfere with initial L-NNA binding to NOS, however). Note that large neutral amino acids (e.g., L-leucine, L-phenylalanine) will interfere with L-NNA transport; if the concentration of L-NNA added to the medium is not comparable to or greater than the concentration of such amino acids, onset of inhibition may be slow.

L-NAME is more useful inhibitor in cell and tissue studies than it is with isolated NOS. Its solubility in media constitutes a significant advantage, and one can be reasonably confident that intracellular esterases will convert it to L-NNA. There are, of course, likely to be variations in the rate of L-NAME hydrolysis among cell types and perhaps even variations within one cell type grown under different conditions. The mechanism of L-NAME transport is unknown, but studies with other amino acid esters show that they are readily taken up and that the free amino acid is in some cases "trapped" or concentrated in the cytosol following ester hydrolysis. In the presence of constant extracellular L-NAME concentration, the L-NNA concentration in the cell may thus continue to increase for many minutes with consequent increase in NOS inhibition. These considerations suggest that it will be difficult to reproducibly establish a constant but partial NOS inhibition with L-NAME; one should try to use L-NAME in high enough concentration and with sufficient preincubation to cause as near complete NOS inhibition as possible. Especially for nNOS and eNOS it should be possible to reproducibly achieve greater than 90% inhibition.

Use of N^ω-Nitro-L-arginine or N^ω-Nitro-L-arginine Methyl Ester in Animals

The considerations summarized for L-NMA apply also to L-NNA and L-NAME. L-NNA has been administered to mice by twice daily intraperitoneal injection for 7 days; the daily dose was 75 mg/kg.[55] Intravenous administration of L-NNA must allow for its poor solubility at physiological pH, but it has been used. L-NAME can be given i.v. with good expectation of *in vivo* hydrolysis to L-NNA. It is particularly notable that L-NNA can effect very prolonged inhibition of brain nNOS. Dwyer *et al.* found that rat cerebellar nNOS remained significantly inhibited 5 days after giving L-NNA at a dose of 50 mg/kg.[47]

N^δ-(Iminoethyl)-L-ornithine

N^δ-(Iminoethyl)-L-ornithine (L-NIO), an arginine antimetabolite produced by a streptomycete,[56] was identified by Rees *et al.* as an eNOS

---

[55] M. Bansinath, B. Arbabha, H. Turndorf, and U. C. Garg, *Neurochem. Res.* **18**, 1063 (1993).
[56] J. P. Scannell, H. A. Ax, D. L. Preuss, T. Williams, T. C. Demny, and A. Stempel, *J. Antibiot.* **25**, 179 (1972).

inhibitor in 1990.[57] L-NIO is now commercially available but is also easily synthesized; it is reportedly hydrolyzed by arginase and hot alkali but is stable to acid and cold alkali.[56] A wide variety of L-NIO analogs have been synthesized by reaction of alkylimidates with L-ornithine or L-lysine; alkyl groups as large as *n*-butyl yield good inhibitors.[16] L-NIO and its short-chain alkyl homologs are readily soluble in water and physiological solutions.

Use of N^δ-(Iminoethyl)-L-ornithine with Tissue Homogenates or Purified Enzymes

Initial inhibition of NOS by L-NIO is competitive with L-arginine, but prolonged inhibition is reported to cause irreversible inhibition of rat iNOS.[58] The mechanism accounting for irreversibility has not yet been established. Inhibition of eNOS is reportedly reversible.[57,59] Practical use of L-NIO should follow the guidelines outlined for L-NMA; relevant K_i values are given in Table I.

Use of N^δ-(Iminoethyl)-L-arginine with Intact Cells or Isolated Tissues

Only limited studies with L-NIO have been reported. Rees *et al.* found that L-NIO was more potent than L-NMA in blocking basal NO formation by eNOS in rat aortic rings; L-NIO was effective at lower doses ($ED_{50} = 2.1 \pm 0.6 \ \mu M$ versus $ED_{50} = 12.5 \pm 1.3 \ \mu M$ for L-NMA) and caused greater maximal contraction (92 versus 40%).[59] This result, if general, suggests that L-NIO can be used at somewhat lower doses than L-NMA. L-NIO is transported as an L-arginine analog, and uptake will thus be affected by the concentration of L-arginine in the media.[22]

Use of N^δ-(Iminoethyl)-L-arginine in Animals

There are relatively few reports of studies in which L-NIO was given to animals. In general the considerations outlined for L-NMA apply to L-NIO. In view of its greater potency with aortic rings, it is interesting that L-NIO was not more effective than L-NMA in raising the blood pressure of rats. The EC_{50} values for both L-NIO and L-NMA were approximately 18 mg/kg, and maximal effects required doses of 300 mg/kg.[58] It should be

---

[57] D. D. Rees, R. Schulz, H. F. Hodson, R. M. J. Palmer, and S. Moncada, *in* "Nitric Oxide from L-Arginine: A Bioregulatory System" (S. Moncada and E. A. Higgs, eds.), p. 485. Elsevier, Amsterdam, 1990.

[58] T. B. McCall, M. Feelisch, R. M. J. Palmer, and S. Moncada, *Br. J. Pharmacol.* **102,** 234 (1991).

[59] D. D. Rees, R. M. J. Palmer, R. Schulz, H. F. Hodson, and S. Moncada, *Br. J. Pharmacol.* **101,** 746 (1990).

noted, however, that we find that L-NMA causes its maximal pressor effect in rats at a dose of about 20 mg/kg rather than 300 mg/kg.[35]

N^ε-(Iminoethyl)-L-lysine (L-NIL or L-homo-NIO) is a relatively selective iNOS inhibitor and therefore of particular value in the treatment of septic shock.[60] It remains to be determined if the modest *in vitro* selectivity (~28-fold) is sufficient to give pharmacologically significant selectivity in animals.

N^ω-Amino-L-arginine

Inhibition of NOS by N^ω-amino-L-arginine (L-NAA) was reported by both Fukuto *et al.*[61] and Gross *et al.*[50] in 1990; structural similarity between L-NAA and N^ω-hydroxy-L-arginine, the NOS reaction intermediate, may account for the potent inhibition of all isoforms seen with this analog.[50] L-NAA is now commercially available but can also be synthesized by partial reduction of L-NNA.[62,63] L-NAA is a basic amino acid (pK_a values of 2.45, 9.32, 11.8[16]) and is therefore readily soluble in water and physiological solutions; it is stable to acid but is less stable in base.

Use of N^ω-Amino-L-arginine with Tissue Homogenates or Purified Enzymes

Few studies using L-NAA with isolated NOS isoforms have been reported. In general the same considerations outlined for L-NMA apply except that L-NAA is somewhat more potent. Although initial inhibition is clearly competitive with L-arginine and reversible, the extent to which inhibition becomes irreversible with longer incubation has not been established.

Use of N^ω-Amino-L-arginine with Intact Cells or Isolated Tissues

With bovine aortic endothelial cells, L-NAA is a potent inhibitor, showing an ED_{50} of approximately 1 μM versus about 100 μM for L-NMA.[50] With isolated rabbit aortic rings, L-NAA blocked acetylcholine-induced relaxation about 30-fold more effectively than L-NMA.[50] With bovine intrapulmonary arterial rings, L-NAA was 10- to 100-fold more potent than L-NMA.[64] L-NAA was also more potent than L-NMA as an inhibitor of

[60] W. M. Moore, R. K. Webber, G. M. Jerome, F. S. Tjoeng, T. P. Misko, and M. G. Currie, *J. Med. Chem.* **37**, 3886 (1994).
[61] J. M. Fukuto, K. S. Woods, R. E. Byrns, and L. J. Ignarro, *Biochem. Biophys. Res. Commun.* **168**, 458 (1990).
[62] A. Turan, A. Patthy, and S. Bajusz, *Acta Chim. Acad. Sci. Hung.* **85**, 327 (1975).
[63] O. W. Griffith, U.S. Patent 5,059,712 (1991).
[64] L. Lambert, J. P. Whitten, B. M. Baron, H. C. Cheng, N. S. Doherty, and I. McDonald, *Life Sci.* **48**, 69 (1991).

NO release by rat aortic endothelial cells.[65] With nNOS and iNOS, the greater potency of L-NAA over L-NMA is less evident; IC_{50} values for L-NAA are one-fourth to one-third those for L-NMA.[50,64]

Use of N^{ω}-Amino-L-arginine in Animals

At i.v. doses of 0.1 to 10 mg/kg, L-NAA causes an immediate (<2 min) 60% increase in the blood pressure of anesthetized guinea pigs. The potency was about 10-fold higher than that of L-NMA, but the maximal pressor effects obtained were comparable.[50] In anesthetized dogs, L-NAA (20 mg/kg i.v. bolus) caused a 72% increase in systemic vascular resistance and a 19% increase in mean arterial pressure. These changes were easily reversed by administration of excess L-arginine. L-NAA also reversed the hypotension seen in anesthetized dogs given interleukin-1, a cytokine that induces iNOS, and in awake dogs given endotoxin, a model of septic shock in which iNOS is also overexpressed.[66]

Although its potency suggested L-NAA would be an attractive drug, studies show L-NAA is a convulsant[66,67] and thus a poor inhibitor for studies with intact animals. Toxicity was not seen in early studies with rodents (LD_{50} > 600 mg/kg[38]) but was seen in studies with awake control and iNOS-expressing dogs. The mechanism accounting for this toxicity has not been elucidated but is apparently independent of NOS inhibition per se since it is neither reversed nor prevented by excess L-arginine, administration of which overcomes NOS inhibition.[66]

L-Thiocitrulline

L-Citrulline, the NOS amino acid product, is not a useful inhibitor (K_i > 100 μM). In contrast, L-thiocitrulline (L-TC), the citrulline analog in which the ureido oxygen is replaced by sulfur, is a very strong inhibitor; K_i values are given in Table I. L-TC is available commercially, and a method of synthesis has been reported.[68] The compound is soluble in water and physiological solutions, and it is stable to acid.

Use of L-Thiocitrulline with Tissue Homogenates or Purified Enzymes

Inhibition of NOS by L-TC is reversible and competitive with L-arginine; D-TC is not an inhibitor. In contrast to L-NMA, NOS does not metabolize

[65] H. M. Vargas, J. M. Cuevas, L. J. Ignarro, and G. Chaudhuri, *J. Pharmacol. Exp. Ther.* **257,** 1208 (1991).
[66] R. G. Kilbourn, S. S. Gross, R. F. Lodato, J. Adams, R. Levi, L. L. Miller, L. B. Lachman, and O. W. Griffith, *J. Natl. Cancer Inst.* **84,** 1008 (1992).
[67] J. P. Cobb, C. Nathanson, W. D. Hoffman, R. F. Lodato, S. Banks, C. A. Koev, M. A. Solomon, R. J. Elin, J. M. Hosseini, and R. L. Danner, *J. Exp. Med.* **176,** 1175 (1992).
[68] K. Narayanan and O. W. Griffith, *J. Med. Chem.* **37,** 885 (1994).

L-TC; there is, in particular, no formation of citrulline or ornithine from L-TC.[69] Both optical and electron paramagnetic resonance (EPR) spectroscopy establish that the sulfur of L-TC can interact as a sixth axial ligand with the heme iron of NOS, although in its predominant binding mode L-TC perturbs the heme iron without forming a direct bond.[69,70] L-Homothiocitrulline inhibits less strongly than L-TC and does not act as an effective heme iron ligand.[69]

Where K_m and K_i values are known, the concentration of L-TC needed for any desired degree of inhibition can be calculated as shown for L-NMA. Higher concentrations of L-arginine require higher levels of L-TC.

Use of L-Thiocitrulline with Intact Cells or Isolated Tissues

Acetylcholine-mediated relaxation of epinephrine-contracted isolated rabbit or rat aortic rings is strongly inhibited by L-TC; the potency is similar to that seen with comparable concentrations of L-NMA.[69,71] Transport of L-TC into cells and tissue has not been directly examined but is expected to be by neutral amino acid transport systems rather than by the system y^+ and system $B^{0,+}$ transporters used by L-arginine and L-NMA.

Use of L-Thiocitrulline with Intact Animals

L-TC is a potent pressor in both control and endotoxemic rats when given by i.v. bolus injection.[69] The maximum pressor response is achieved at a dose of approximately 20 mg/kg, comparable to L-NMA, but the maximum pressor effect is about 20% greater than that achieved with L-NMA.[35] As with L-NMA, repeated doses of L-TC cause a tachyphylaxis.[35]

S-Methyl-L-thiocitrulline

S-Methyl-L-thiocitrulline (L-SMTC) and the related S-ethyl and S-propyl compounds are very potent NOS inhibitors.[68,72,73] The structure of L-SMTC and the K_i values for the NOS isoforms are given in Table I. L-SMTC is available commercially, and a method of synthesis has been published.[68]

[69] C. Frey, K. Narayanan, K. McMillan, L. Spack, S. S. Gross, B. S. Masters, and O. W. Griffith, *J. Biol. Chem.* **269**, 26083 (1994).

[70] J. C. Salerno, C. Frey, K. McMillan, R. F. Williams, B. S. S. Masters, and O. W. Griffith, *J. Biol. Chem.* **270**, 27423 (1995).

[71] G. A. Joly, K. Narayanan, O. W. Griffith, and R. G. Kilbourn, *Br. J. Pharmacol.* **115**, 491 (1995).

[72] K. Narayanan, L. Spack, K. McMillan, R. G. Kilbourn, M. A. Hayward, B. S. S. Masters, and O. W. Griffith, *J. Biol. Chem.* **270**, 11103 (1995).

[73] E. S. Furfine, M. F. Harmon, J. E. Paith, R. G. Knowles, M. Salter, R. J. Kiff, C. Duffy, R. Hazelwood, J. A. Oplinger, and E. P. Garvey, *J. Biol. Chem.* **269**, 26677 (1994).

Use of S-Methyl-L-thiocitrulline with Tissue Homogenates or Purified Enzymes

Initial binding of L-SMTC to NOS is competitive with L-arginine. Although the methylthio group of L-SMTC is potentially displaceable by active site nucleophiles, no evidence of irreversible covalent inhibition has been found.[72,73] There is also no indication from optical spectroscopy studies that L-SMTC directly ligates with the heme iron.[72] Detailed kinetic studies do show that dissociation of L-SMTC from nNOS is slow.[72,73] The $t_{1/2}$ for reactivation of human nNOS is about 40 min,[73] but the reactivation of rat nNOS is more rapid, with $t_{1/2}$ around 5 min.[72]

No special precautions are needed in using L-SMTC as a NOS inhibitor other than avoidance of media with high pH in which the compound is expected to be less stable.

Use of S-Methyl-L-thiocitrulline with Intact Cells or Tissues

Joly et al. have carried out extensive studies comparing the ability of L-NMA, L-TC, and L-SMTC to prevent acetylcholine-mediated relaxation of aortic rings from normal and endotoxemic rats.[71] These studies show that the three inhibitors are comparably effective with control rings and that L-SMTC is somewhat more effective than L-NMA or L-TC with rings from endotoxemic rats.

Use of S-Methyl-L-thiocitrulline with Intact Animals

L-SMTC causes an immediate pressor response when given to normal anesthetized rats as an i.v. bolus. The maximum pressor effect is evident within 10 min, persists for 20–30 min, and is achieved at a dose of 10–20 mg/kg.[35,72] In endotoxemic rats or dogs, i.v. L-SMTC restores blood pressure within a few minutes; the magnitude and duration of the effect are somewhat greater but generally comparable to that achieved with L-NMA.[72]

[38] 7-Nitroindazole: An Inhibitor of Nitric Oxide Synthase

By PHILIP K. MOORE and PHILIP A. BLAND-WARD

Introduction

Nitric oxide (NO) is synthesized from the semiessential amino acid L-arginine by the enzyme nitric oxide synthase (NOS; EC 1.14.13.39). The widespread distribution of NOS in mammalian species coupled with its ability to alter a range of cellular and tissue functions via activation of soluble guanylate cyclase (GC) has created considerable interest in the identification of NOS inhibitors with potential clinical use in humans.[1,2] Early studies revealed that classic substrate-based inhibitors of this enzyme, for example, N^G-nitro-L-arginine methyl ester (L-NAME) and N^G-mono-methyl-L-arginine (L-NMMA), exhibited a number of potentially useful clinical effects (e.g., neuroprotection for the treatment of conditions such as cerebral stroke, AIDS dementia, and Parkinson's disease,[3] and analgesia[4]). However, early enthusiasm was tempered by reports in the literature testifying to the widespread vasoconstriction induced by these agents when administered to both animals and humans.[5,6] The hypertensive effect of L-NAME and L-NMMA coupled with their ability to restrict blood flow in sensitive vascular beds (e.g., coronary and cerebral circulations) effectively preclude their widespread clinical application.

Nitric oxide synthase has been purified and cloned and is now known to exist as at least three structurally distinct isoforms termed endothelial (eNOS), neuronal (nNOS), and inducible (iNOS).[7] This discovery has sparked a search for isoform-selective NOS inhibitors. We have described a series of indazole derivatives with potent NOS inhibitory activity both *in vitro* and *in vivo* but devoid of hypertensive activity.[8-10] Within the

[1] E. Anggard, *Lancet* **343**, 1199 (1994).
[2] S. Moncada and E. A. Higgs, *N. Engl. J. Med.* **239**, 2002 (1993).
[3] S. R. Vincent, *Neurobiology* **42**, 129 (1994).
[4] P. K. Moore, A. O. Olyuomi, R. C. Babbedge, P. Wallace, and S. L. Hart, *Br. J. Pharmacol.* **102**, 198 (1991).
[5] A. Petros, D. Bennett, and P. Vallance, *Lancet* **338**, 1557 (1991).
[6] D. D. Rees, R. M. J. Palmer, and S. Moncada, *Proc. Natl. Acad. Sci. U.S.A.* **86**, 3375 (1989).
[7] R. G. Knowles and S. Moncada, *Biochem. J.* **298**, 249 (1994).
[8] R. C. Babbedge, P. A. Bland-Ward, S. L. Hart, and P. K. Moore, *Br. J. Pharmacol.* **110**, 225 (1993).

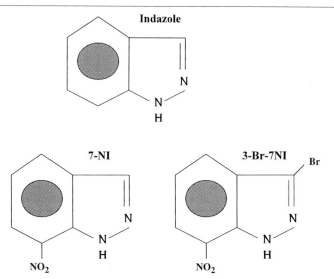

FIG. 1. Structure of some indazole-based NOS inhibitors.

indazole series 7-nitroindazole (7-NI) and 3-bromo-7-nitroindazole (3-Br-7NI) have proved to be the most potent NOS inhibitors (see Fig. 1 for structures).

Inhibition of Nitric Oxide Synthase by Indazoles

Effect on Broken Cell Preparations in Vitro

Indazole derivatives inhibit NOS enzyme activity in organ homogenates from a variety of different sources and species. For *in vitro* experiments of this type 7-NI is best dissolved by sonication in 0.5% (w/v) sodium carbonate solution (solubility about 2 mg/ml) because organic solvents such as ethanol and dimethyl sulfoxide (in which 7-NI is more soluble, about 5 mg/ml) considerably reduce NOS activity in these assays. In our laboratory primary screening of compounds for NOS inhibitory activity is undertaken in crude (10,000 g) homogenates of rat cerebellum (for nNOS), bovine aortic endo-thelial cells (for eNOS), and lungs removed 6 hr following intraperitoneal

---

[9] P. K. Moore, P. Wallace, Z. A. Gaffen, S. L. Hart, and R. C. Babbedge, *Br. J. Pharmacol.* **108,** 296 (1993).

[10] P. K. Moore, P. Wallace, Z. A. Gaffen, S. L. Hart, and R. C. Babbedge, *Br. J. Pharmacol.* **110,** 219 (1993).

injection into anaesthetized rats of bacterial lipopolysaccharide (for iNOS) utilizing an assay which measures the conversion of L-[^{3}H]arginine to L-[^{3}H]citrulline. This procedure is sensitive (limit of detection of citrulline in the picomole range), is applicable both to crude tissue and purified enzyme preparations, and is relatively simple to perform and suitable for large numbers of compounds (100 samples per assay is quite feasible). However, care should be taken to ensure that arginase enzyme activity does not contribute to the citrulline production either by demonstrating dose-related inhibition of citrulline formation with established NOS inhibitors or by including valine (5 mM) to inhibit arginase activity.

Organ homogenates (1 : 10 in 20 mM Tris-HCl buffer, pH 7.4, containing 2 mM EDTA; 25 μl) are incubated (15 min, 37°) with L-[^{3}H]arginine (120 nM, 0.5 μCi), NADPH (0.5 mM), and 0.75 mM CaCl$_2$ as cofactors. For iNOS determination CaCl$_2$ is omitted. Under these experimental conditions 7-NI and related indazoles are found to cause potent inhibition of all three NOS isoforms *in vitro* with IC$_{50}$ values in the low micromolar range, that is, approximately five times more potent that L-NAME and L-NMMA (Table I).

Effect on Intact Cerebellar Slices and Aortic Rings in Vitro

Because NO exerts the majority (although most probably not all) of its biological effects by activating soluble guanylate cyclase, the effect of NOS inhibitors may also be evaluated by monitoring cGMP concentration in

TABLE I

INHIBITION OF NITRIC OXIDE SYNTHASE ISOFORMS
BY INDAZOLES AND RELATED COMPOUNDS[a]

	IC$_{50}$ (μM)		
Compound	nNOS	eNOS	iNOS
Indazole	177.0	ND	ND
7-Nitroindazole (7-IN)	0.71	0.78	5.8
3-Bromo-7-nitroindazole (3-Br-7NI)	0.17	0.86	0.29
2,7-Dinitroindazole	0.62	0.47	1.56
6-Nitroindazole	31.6	ND	ND
5-Nitroindazole	47.3	ND	ND
7-Aminoindazole	>1000	ND	ND

[a] nNOS (rat cerebellum), eNOS (bovine aortic endothelial cell), and iNOS (lungs from lipopolysaccharide-pretreated rats) were assayed for NOS activity as described. Each inhibitor was assayed over a range of concentrations (0.01–1000 μM). Results are means of at least five separate experiments. ND, Not determined.

intact cell preparations. The effect of 7-IN on nNOS in cross-chopped (400 × 400 μm, ~25 mg) slices from 8- to 12-day-old neonatal rats (either sex) and eNOS activity from rabbit aortic rings (2–3 mm, ~10 mg) has been evaluated. In each case cerebellar slices or aortic rings are preincubated [37°, aerated with 95% O_2 : 5% CO_2 (v/v)] in physiological Krebs solution for 90–120 min and thereafter challenged (2 min) either with the L-glutamate agonist N-methyl-D-aspartate (NMDA, 100 μM; cerebellum) or with the muscarinic cholinoceptor agonist carbachol (10 μM; aorta). At the end of the stimulation period cerebellar slices are rapidly plunged into 1 ml of boiling 50 mM Tris-HCl buffer (containing 4 mM EDTA) for 5 min, homogenized, and centrifuged (10,000 g, 2 min, 4°). The intracellular concentration of cGMP is determined by radioimmunoassay using ^{125}I-labeled cGMP as ligand. For aortic ring experiments, extracellular cGMP released into the Krebs incubate following activation of eNOS by carbachol is assayed.

The agonist NMDA elevated basal levels of cGMP in neonatal rat cerebellar slices by 594 ± 55% (n = 20), whereas carbachol stimulated aortic ring cGMP formation by 97 ± 14% (n = 20). Both 7-NI and L-NAME inhibited NMDA-induced cerebellar cGMP accumulation with IC_{50} values of 155 and 205 μM, respectively. In contrast, 7-NI (up to 100 μM) failed to influence extracellular cGMP concentration in the medium of carbachol-stimulated rabbit aortic rings, whereas L-NAME (100 μM) totally abolished the response to carbachol.

Although both L-NAME and 7-NI are potent inhibitors of nNOS and eNOS in broken cell preparations *in vitro* and of nNOS activity in intact cerebellar slices, it is perhaps remarkable that 7-NI (unlike L-NAME) appears to have no effect on eNOS in intact blood vessels. Whether this lack of effect reflects the inability to access the eNOS isoform across the endothelial cell membrane or perhaps a rapid destruction of 7-NI by an enzyme(s) in endothelial (but clearly not neuronal) cytosol is unknown. The lack of effect of 7-NI on eNOS in these experiments is paralleled by functional experiments using isolated blood vessels and intact animals.

Time Course of Brain Nitric Oxide Synthase Inhibition following Parenteral Administration of 7-Nitroindazole in Vivo

Parenteral administration of 7-NI (30 mg/kg, intraperitoneal or oral) to conscious rats produces within 30 min a significant (>80%) inhibition of NOS enzyme activity in homogenates prepared from cerebellum, corpus striatum, hippocampus, olfactory bulb, and cerebral cortex.[11] In these exper-

[11] G. M. Mackenzie, S. Rose, P. A. Bland-Ward, P. K. Moore, P. Jenner, and C. D. Marsden, *NeuroReport* **5,** 1993 (1994).

iments control animals received an appropriate volume of vehicle (arachis oil). Other solvents that may be employed for this purpose include propylene oxide–ethanol–water (40 : 10 : 50, v/v). This effect of 7-NI in the intact animal is relatively transient, with a half-life for NOS inhibition of 4 hr and no inhibition apparent at 24 hr. Interestingly, greater and more prolonged inhibition of brain NOS is observed after intraperitoneal administration of 7-NI in the rat, which suggests either reduced absorption after oral administration or perhaps accelerated catabolism by this route.[11] Further experiments are needed to examine the pharmacokinetic profile of 7-NI after parenteral administration in experimental animals. It should be stressed that no information is available concerning the catabolism of 7-NI either *in vitro* or *in vivo*. Clearly, the transient nature of NOS inhibition by 7-NI should be borne in mind by researchers when designing experiments utilizing 7-NI *in vivo*.

Mechanism of Nitric Oxide Synthase Inhibition by 7-Nitroindazole

Preliminary experiments in our laboratory based on competition studies with L-arginine suggested that 7-NI interacted competitively with the substrate binding site on the NOS enzyme.[8] This conclusion was supported by the report that 7-NI displaces binding of L-[^{3}H]NAME to rat brain cytosolic NOS.[12] More stringent analysis has revealed that eNOS and nNOS inhibition by 7-NI and related indazoles is indeed competitive with respect to L-arginine but, in addition, is also competitive with respect to tetrahydrobiopterin.[13] The precise manner in which 7-NI interacts with NOS has also received attention. The possibility that 7-NI binds to the heme prosthetic site of the enzyme in such a way as to impede access of both L-arginine and tetrahydrobiopterin has been suggested.[13]

Pharmacological Effects of 7-Nitroindazole

A number of reports of the pharmacological effects of 7-NI have appeared in the literature. Such studies have concentrated on the central nervous and cardiovascular systems. Thus, 7-NI exhibits potent antinociceptive (analgesic) activity in the mouse assessed as either inhibition of formalin-induced hind-paw licking or acetic acid-induced abdominal constrictions.[9,10] In each case the site of action of 7-NI would appear to be nNOS-containing neurons in the dorsal horn of the spinal cord. 7-Nitroindazole

[12] A. Michel, R. K. Phul, T. L. Stewart, and P. P. A. Humphrey, *Br. J. Pharmacol.* **109**, 287 (1993).
[13] B. Mayer, P. Klatt, E. R. Werner, and K. Schmidt, *Neuropharmacology* **33**, 1253 (1994).

has also been reported both to augment nigrostriatal dopamine neuron death elicited by NMDA in the rat[14] and to reduce infarct size following occlusion of the middle cerebral artery (an experimental model of cerebral stroke) in the same species.[15] In the cardiovascular system 7-NI injected either intravenously or intraperitoneally does not affect mean arterial blood pressure in the anesthetized mouse, rat, or cat.[8–10,15,16]

Conclusion

7-Nitroindazole exhibits a novel biochemical and pharmacological profile as an inhibitor of NOS. Although 7-NI is an isoform-nonselective NOS inhibitor *in vitro,* administration of 7-NI to the intact animal leads to a range of biological effects attributed to nNOS inhibition in the central nervous system without the expected cardiovascular effects due to eNOS inhibition. These experiments raise the possibility that isoform-selective NOS inhibition may be achieved in intact cells/animals with compounds which show little or no isoform selectivity *in vitro.*

[14] B. P. Connop, N. G. Rolfe, R. J. Boegman, K. Jhamandas, and R. J. Beninger, *Neuropharmacology* **33,** 1439 (1994).
[15] T. Dalkara, T. Yoshida, K. Irikura, and M. A. Moskowitz, *Neuropharmacology* **33,** 1447 (1994).
[16] A. G. B. Kovach, Z. Lohinai, I. Balla, J. Marczis, Z. Dombovary, M. Reivich, T. M. Dawson, and S. H. Snyder, *Endothelium* **1**(Suppl. 1), 211 (1993).

[39] Selective Inhibition of Inducible Nitric Oxide Synthase by Aminoguanidine

By John A. Corbett and Michael L. McDaniel

Introduction

Since the discovery that mammalian cells produce nitric oxide, an intense research effort has been initiated to determine the cellular sources, physiological functions, and regulatory mechanisms of nitric oxide production. Nitric oxide is a small, uncharged, inorganic secretory product of cells that displays minimal specificity in its actions because of its high chemical reactivity and short-lived stability. Nitric oxide functions in neuronal transmission, regulation vascular tone, inhibition of tumor cell proliferation, destruction of host cells during the development of autoimmune disease conditions, and as a primary effector molecule in host defense against invading pathogens.[1-3] The physiological functions of nitric oxide appear to be determined primarily by the quantity produced and the site of production. Nitric oxide synthase (NOS, EC 1.14.13.39) catalyzes the oxidation of one of the guanidino nitrogens of L-arginine to form the product nitric oxide. There are three distinct isoforms of NOS, brain NOS (bNOS, NOS I), endothelial NOS (eNOS, NOS III), and cytokine-inducible NOS (iNOS, NOS II), that have been cloned and extensively characterized.[4-7] These isoforms fall into two general categories on the basis of regulation of enzymatic activity. The first category of NOS comprises the constitutively expressed eNOS and bNOS isoforms, whose production of nitric oxide is regulated by Ca^{2+} and calmodulin activation.[1,4] Nitric oxide is produced in low levels by these isoforms and functions as a signaling molecule.[8] The second category of NOS, inducible NOS, is regulated at the level of expression. Cytokines and endotoxin stimulate its mRNA transcription and translation. Nitric oxide is produced in high levels by this isoform, and it functions as a cytostatic and cytotoxic molecule.[1,4]

Intense effort has been directed at the identification of selective inhibitors of the individual isoforms of NOS. Primary focus has been on inhibitors of the inducible isoform of NOS because nitric oxide produced by iNOS has been implicated in the development of a number of clinical disease conditions including sepsis, autoimmune diabetes, transplantation rejection, and multiple sclerosis. It is believed that selective inhibition of iNOS may prevent or retard the development of pathologies associated with the production of nitric oxide by iNOS, without impairing normal physiological processes under the control of eNOS or bNOS. Aminoguanidine has been identified as one of the first selective inhibitors of iNOS.[9,10] This chapter outlines methods used to characterize this inhibitor of iNOS, with the

[1] C. Nathan, *FASEB J.* **6,** 3051 (1992).

[2] J. R. Lancaster, Jr., *Am. Sci.* **80,** 248 (1992).

[3] L. J. Ignarro, *Annu. Rev. Pharmacol. Toxicol.* **30,** 535 (1990).

[4] M. A. Marletta, *J. Biol. Chem.* **268,** 12231 (1993).

[5] D. S. Bredt, P. M. Hwang, C. E. Glatt, C. Lowenstein, R. R. Reed, and S. H. Snyder, *Nature* (*London*) **351,** 714 (1991).

[6] D. J. Stuehr, H. J. Cho, N. S. Kwon, M. F. Weise, and C. F. Nathan, *Proc. Natl. Acad. Sci. U.S.A.* **88,** 7773 (1991).

[7] D. A. Geller, C. J. Lowenstein, R. A. Shapiro, A. K. Nussler, M. DiSilvio, S. C. Wang, D. D. Nakayama, R. L. Simmons, S. H. Snyder, and T. R. Billiar, *Proc. Natl. Acad. Sci. U.S.A.* **90,** 3491 (1993).

[8] S. Moncada, R. M. J. Palmer, and E. A. Higgs, *Pharmacol. Rev.* **43,** 109 (1991).

[9] J. A. Corbett, R. G. Tilton, K. Chang, K. S. Hasan, Y. Ido, J. L. Wang, M. A. Sweetland, J. R. Lancaster, Jr., J. R. Williamson, and M. L. McDaniel, *Diabetes* **41,** 552 (1991).

[10] T. P. Misko, W. M. Moore, T. P. Kasten, G. A. Nickols, J. A. Corbett, R. G. Tilton, M. L. McDaniel, J. R. Williamson, and M. G. Currie, *Eur. J. Pharmacol.* **233,** 119 (1993).

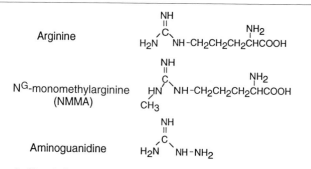

FIG. 1. Chemical structures of arginine, NMMA, and aminoguanidine.

primary focus on how to use this inhibitor for both *in vitro* and *in vivo* studies. The inhibitory effects of aminoguanidine on NOS activity are compared with those of N^G-monomethyl-L-arginine (NMMA), which inhibits the three isoforms of NOS with nearly identical kinetics.

Aminoguanidine

Aminoguanidine is a nucleophilic hydrazine compound that contains two chemically equivalent guanidino nitrogens (Fig. 1). It was initially identified as an inhibitor of nonenzymatic formation of advanced glycation end products (AGE).[11] AGE products are formed by glycosylation of extracellular or cellular protein constituents, and their accumulation has been associated with the development of diabetic complications. Aminoguanidine prevents the formation of AGE products by blocking reactive carbonyls on early glycosylation products,[11] and it attenuates the development of several diabetes-induced vascular, neuronal, and collagen changes.[12] It is believed that the hydrazine moiety of aminoguanidine is essential for its selectivity for iNOS. Methylation of this hydrazine (methylguanidine) results in the loss of both potency and selectivity for iNOS.[13]

Two chemical forms of aminoguanidine, the hemisulfate and bicarbonate salts, are commercially available (Sigma, St. Louis, MO, and LC Laboratories, Woburn, MA). The hemisulfate salt of aminoguanidine is freely soluble in aqueous solution. We routinely prepare stock solutions of 0.1 to 1 M of this salt form in either tissue culture medium or 0.1 M phosphate-buffered saline (PBS). The bicarbonate salt of aminoguanidine is much less

[11] M. Brownlee, H. Vlassara, A. Kooney, P. Ulrich, and A. Cerami, *Science* **232**, 1629 (1986).
[12] J. W. Baynes, *Diabetes* **40**, 405 (1990).
[13] K. Hasen, B.-J. Heesen, J. A. Corbett, M. L. McDaniel, K. Chang, W. Allison, B. H. R. Wolffenbuttel, J. R. Williamson, and R. G. Tilton, *Eur. J. Pharmacol.* **249**, 101 (1993).

soluble than the hemisulfate salt in aqueous solution. The bicarbonate salt of aminoguanidine is soluble at concentrations of $1-10$ mM in tissue culture medium or PBS. We have used a third salt form of aminoguanidine, the HCl (hydrochloride) salt, that performs in a manner very similar to the hemisulfate salt of aminoguanidine. Aminoguanidine tends to precipitate out of solution when stored at 4° for prolonged periods (3–7 days); therefore, we routinely prepare fresh solutions of aminoguanidine for each experiment.

Inhibition of Inducible Nitric Oxide Synthase by Aminoguanidine

We have used a whole cell assay system to assess the inhibitory effects of aminoguanidine on iNOS activity. The use of this whole cell assay system allows for the assessment of both cellular uptake and inhibition of iNOS enzymatic activity. It is based on the accumulation of the stable oxidation product of nitric oxide, nitrite, produced following the induction of iNOS. This method allows for the identification of inhibitors of cytokine-induced nitric oxide accumulation, and it can be modified for use with any cell line that expresses iNOS.

Inhibition of iNOS activity has been evaluated by examining the effects of aminoguanidine on the accumulation of nitrite by the rat insulinoma cell line RINm5F stimulated with interleukin-1 (IL-1). IL-1-induced nitrite formation by RINm5F cells is first detectable following an 8-hr incubation with IL-1, and production is linear for the next 24–48 hr. In this assay RINm5F cells are removed from T-75 tissue culture flasks by treatment with 5 ml of 0.05% trypsin–0.02% EDTA for 5 min at 37°. The cells are then plated in 96-well microtiter plates at a concentration of 200,000 cells per 0.2 ml of complete CMRL-1066 tissue culture medium [CMRL-1066 (GIBCO-BRL, Grand Island, NY) containing 10% heat-inactivated fetal bovine serum (Hyclone, Logan, UT), 2 mM L-glutamine, 50 units/ml penicillin, and 50 μg/ml streptomycin], and cultured overnight under an atmosphere of 95% air and 5% CO_2 at 37°. The medium is replaced with 0.2 ml of fresh CRML-1066, and the experiments are initiated by the addition of 5 units/ml IL-1β (Cistron Biotechnology, Pine Brook, NJ) in the presence or absence of aminoguanidine. Following an 18-hr incubation, media nitrite concentrations are determined by mixing 50 μl of culture supernatant with 50 μl of the Griess reagent (a 1:1 mixture of 1.32% (w/v) sulfanilamide in 60% (v/v) acetic acid and 0.1% (w/v) N-1-naphthylethylenediamine hydrochloride and measuring the absorbance at 540 nm using a Titertek Multiskan MCC/340 plate reader. Nitrite concentrations are then calculated from a nitrite standard curve.

The inhibitory effects of aminoguanidine and the classic NOS inhibitor

NMMA in this whole cell assay system are shown in Fig. 2a. Aminoguanidine and NMMA inhibit IL-1-induced nitrite accumulation by RINm5F cells in a concentration-dependent fashion, with half-maximal inhibition observed at approximately 10 μM for both aminoguanidine and NMMA.

Caution should be exercised when evaluating inhibitors of NOS by the accumulation of nitrite. Interleukin-1 requires a 6- to 8-hr incubation period to induce the transcription and translation of iNOS, and then another 1–2 hr to produce levels of nitrite that are detectable by the Griess reagent. Inhibitors of mRNA transcription (actinomycin D) and protein synthesis (cycloheximide) also will completely prevent IL-1-induced nitrite formation by RINm5F cells. In addition, compounds with poor cellular permeability may diffuse into cells during the long incubation period. Thus, it is important to examine the effects of potential inhibitors of NOS on the enzymatic activity of iNOS and on the cellular permeability.

To determine the effects of aminoguanidine on the inhibition of iNOS

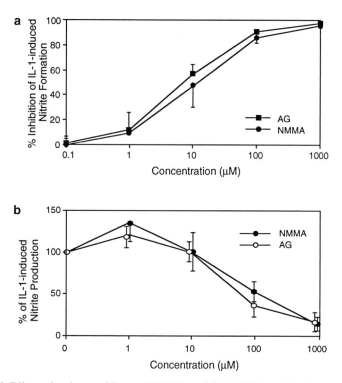

FIG. 2. Effects of aminoguanidine and NMMA on (a) IL-1β-induced nitrite accumulation and (b) iNOS activity in RINm5F cells. [Data reprinted from J. A. Corbett *et al.*, *Diabetes* **41,** 552–556 (1992), from the American Diabetes Association.]

enzymatic activity and to examine the cellular uptake of this NOS inhibitor, a modified version of the method previously described has been employed. The RINm5F cells are plated at a density of 800,000 cells per 0.2 ml of complete CRML-1066 as described above and then preincubated for 18 hr in the presence of 5 units/ml IL-1 under an atmosphere of 95% air and 5% CO_2 (v/v) at 37°. The cells are then washed three times with 0.2 ml per wash of complete CMRL-1066 tissue culture medium and cultured for 4 hr in 0.2 ml of complete CRML-1066 containing the NOS inhibitors. The washing step removes nitrite produced during the 18-hr incubation with IL-1. Following the 4-hr incubation, the medium is removed and nitrite formation is determined as described above. As shown in Fig. 2b, aminoguanidine and NMMA display nearly identical inhibitory effects on iNOS activity, with half-maximal inhibition of nitrite formation observed at concentration of approximately 100 μM for both NMMA and aminoguanidine. This method also demonstrates that aminoguanidine and NMMA are readily taken up by whole cells and inhibit the enzymatic activity of iNOS induced by IL-1 pretreatment.

Inhibitory Effects of Aminoguanidine on Endothelial Nitric Oxide Synthase Activity

Nitric oxide, produced by endothelial cells, mediates the relaxation of blood vessels by stimulating the activity of smooth muscle cell guanylate cyclase, resulting in the accumulation of cGMP.[3,8] Inhibition of nitric oxide production prevents the activation of guanylate cyclase in smooth muscle cells, thereby preventing vasorelaxation and stimulating an increase in blood pressure. The inhibitory effects of aminoguanidine on the enzymatic activity of eNOS have been evaluated by examining changes in the mean arterial blood pressure of anesthetized rats. The effects of aminoguanidine were compared to NMMA, which inhibits both eNOS and iNOS with nearly identical inhibitory kinetics.

In these experiments male Sprague-Dawley rats are anesthetized at 100 mg/kg body weight with Inactin. The right iliac artery is cannulated with polyethylene (PE) tubing filled with heparinized saline, and the trachea is cannulated and connected to a small-rodent respirator for continuous ventilator support. After arterial pressure stabilizes, increasing amounts of aminoguanidine or NMMA (μmol/kg body weight) are injected in a constant volume and the peak arterial pressure increase recorded. As shown in Fig. 3, both aminoguanidine and NMMA increase the mean arterial blood pressure in a dose-dependent fashion. However, aminoguanidine is over 40-fold less effective at stimulating this increase in blood pressure as compared to NMMA. These findings indicate that aminoguanidine has

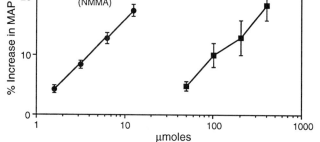

FIG. 3. Effects of aminoguanidine and NMMA on mean arterial blood pressure (MAP). [Data reprinted from J. A. Corbett *et al.*, *Diabetes* **41**, 552–556 (1992), from the American Diabetes Association.]

minimal effects on vasoregulation in rats at concentrations that inhibit iNOS activity. Examination of the effects of potential iNOS inhibitors on changes in mean arterial blood pressure provides a direct evaluation of potential hemodynamic changes that may develop when using iNOS inhibitors under *in vivo* conditions.

Selectivity of Aminoguanidine for Partially Purified Inducible Nitric Oxide Synthase as Compared to Brain Nitric Oxide Synthase

It is also essential to characterize the effects of inhibitors directly on the enzymatic activity of the individual isoforms of NOS. The inhibitory effects of aminoguanidine on the enzymatic activity of iNOS and bNOS have been evaluated in collaboration with Thomas Misko and co-workers at Monsanto Corporate Research. We have used the conversion of L-[^{14}C]arginine to L-[^{14}C]citrulline and a cGMP reporter system[10] that are extensively detailed in [13, 31, and 32] of this volume and will not be described further. The iNOS is isolated from LPS-treated RAW 264.7 cells and bNOS is isolated from rat brain by standard protocols that are outlined in [31] and [32] in this volume, respectively. The IC$_{50}$ values for aminoguanidine and NMMA on the activity of iNOS and bNOS are shown in Table I. Consistent with the RINm5F cell data, aminoguanidine is 20- to 30-fold more effective at inhibiting the enzymatic activity of iNOS compared to bNOS. Also, aminoguanidine is slightly more effective at inhibiting iNOS activity when directly compared to NMMA.

Ex Vivo Approach to Demonstrate Nitric Oxide Production during Development of Autoimmune Diabetes

Nitric oxide has been implicated in the development in a number of disease conditions. We have developed an *ex vivo* model system to demon-

TABLE I

IC$_{50}$ VALUES FOR AMINOGUANIDINE (AG) AND N^G-MONOMETHYL-L-ARGININE (NMMA) ON INHIBITION OF PARTIALLY PURIFIED INDUCIBLE^a AND BRAIN NITRIC OXIDE SYNTHASE^{b,c}

NOS Assay	iNOS (μM)		bNOS (μM)	
	AG	NMMA	AG	NMMA
Citrulline	5.4 ± 5.8	11 ± 3.2	160 ± 0.0	5.5 ± 3.5
cGMP	45 ± 6.6	52 ± 7.6	750 ± 76	5 ± 0.8

^{a} From LPS treated RAW 264.7 cells.
^{b} From rat brain.
^{c} Data reprinted with permission from T. P. Misko, W. M. Moore, T. P. Kasten, G. A. Nickols, J. A. Corbett, R. G. Tilton, M. L. McDaniel, J. R. Williamson, and M. G. Currie, Eur. J. Pharmacol. **233**, 119–125 (1993).

strate directly *in vivo* induction of iNOS and the production of nitric oxide by tissues targeted for destruction. We have used this *ex vivo* model to demonstrate the production of nitric oxide by islets of Langerhans undergoing autoimmune destruction.[14] Nonobese spontaneously diabetic mice (NOD) develop diabetes by 9 months after birth. Diabetes in this animal model is characterized by autoimmune destruction of insulin-secreting β cells. Using an adoptive transfer protocol, the time required for the development of diabetes in these mice can be reduced to 11–13 days. Spleen cells are harvested from diabetic female mice and transferred (2×10^7 cells/transfer) into irradiated nondiabetic male mice by tail vein injection. Methods of adoptive transfer of diabetes in the NOD mouse have been described previously.[15]

Islets are isolated from both male NOD mice receiving the spleen cell transfer and from irradiated control male NOD mice. Islet isolation has been described in detail previously in this series.[16] Following isolation, islets (100 per 200 μl of complete CRML-1066) are immediately cultured in 96-well microtiter plates in the presence or absence of aminoguanidine for 24 hr. The medium is then removed, and the nitrite production is determined on the cultured medium as outlined previously. As shown in Fig. 4 the transfer of spleen cells from a diabetic female to a nondiabetic male induces the time-dependent production of nitric oxide by islets isolated from the recipient male mice at days 6, 9, and 13 after spleen cell transfer. This *ex vivo* approach shows that is is possible to demonstrate the *in vivo* induction

[14] J. A. Corbett, A. Mikhael, J. Shimizu, K. Frederick, T. P. Misko, M. L. McDaniel, O. Kanagawa, and E. R. Unanue, *Proc. Natl. Acad. Sci. U.S.A.* **90**, 8992 (1993).
[15] L. S. Wicker, B. J. Miller, and Y. Mullen, *Diabetes* **35**, 855 (1986).
[16] M. L. McDaniel, J. R. Colca, N. Kotagal, and P. E. Lacy, *Methods Enzymol.* **98**, 182 (1983).

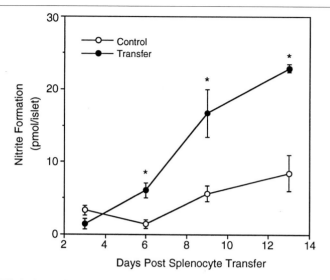

FIG. 4. Nitrite formation by isolated NOD mouse islets after spleen cell transfer. [Reprinted from J. A. Corbett *et al.*, *Proc. Natl. Acad. Sci. USA* **90**, 8992–8995 (1993) with permission from the National Academy of Sciences (USA).]

of iNOS and the production of nitric oxide by tissues targeted for destruction. This system can be modified for other animal models of diseases in which iNOS expression and nitric oxide have been implicated in the progression of the condition.

In Vivo Inhibition of Inducible Nitric Oxide Synthase by Aminoguanidine

To fully implicate nitric oxide as an effector molecule that participates in the development of pathological disease conditions, it is important to demonstrate the attenuation of symptoms of these ailments by the *in vivo* inhibition of NOS. This section focuses on concentrations and methods of administration of aminoguanidine that have proved most effective at delaying the onset of diabetes in the NOD mouse and preventing the development of experimental autoimmune encephalomyelitis in mice. The expression of iNOS and production of nitric oxide have been implicated in the development of these diseases.

To delay the onset of diabetes induced by the transfer of spleen cells from a diabetic female into an irradiated nondiabetic male NOD mice, we have achieved the best results by administering aminoguanidine in two daily intraperitoneal injections of 2 mg/mouse (300–400 mg of aminoguanidine/kg body weight) per injection. Aminoguanidine administered to recipient mice using this dosage regime delays the development of diabetes by 7–10 days. Lower doses of aminoguanidine (50–200 mg/kg body weight) or single daily injections were less effective at delaying the development of diabetes induced by adoptive transfer. Single injections of aminoguanidine are less effective probably because of the relatively short half-life of the inhibitor. Preliminary experiments indicate that aminoguanidine has a half-life of between 6 and 8 hr *in vivo* (J. A. Corbett and M. L. McDaniel, unpublished observation, 1992).

Similar results have been obtained by Cross and co-workers, who showed that aminoguanidine prevents the development of experimental autoimmune encephalomyelitis (EAE) in SJL mice.[17] In this mouse model of EAE, three daily intraperitoneal injections of aminoguanidine totaling 400 mg/kg body weight per day prevented the development of clinical symptoms of EAE. At lower doses (100 and 200 mg/kg per day by three daily injections) aminoguanidine was less effective at preventing the clinical symptoms of EAE.

The route of administration of aminoguanidine is also important. Aminoguanidine is not effective at preventing the development of diabetes in the NOD mouse when administered in the drinking water at a concentration of 1% (w/v). At concentrations of aminoguanidine above 1% mice do not drink the water, presumably because of the extreme bitter taste. Intraperitoneal injections have proved to be the most effective route of administration of aminoguanidine.

These studies demonstrate that *in vivo* administration of aminoguanidine can prevent or delay the development of EAE and diabetes, autoimmune diseases in which nitric oxide has been implicated as a mediator of tissue destruction. Aminoguanidine has also been shown to prevent blood pressure changes and death induced by endotoxin,[18] and to prevent the clinical symptoms of uveitis.[19] These studies demonstrate the usefulness of aminoguanidine as a pharmacological tool for the investigation of pathophysiological conditions associated with the production of nitric oxide.

Comments

This chapter outlines methods that we have used for the identification of aminoguanidine as a selective inhibitor of iNOS, and it provides technical information for the *in vivo* use of aminoguanidine. Aminoguanidine is a

[17] A. H. Cross, T. P. Misko, R. F. Lin, W. F. Hickey, J. L. Trotter, and R. G. Tilton, *J. Clin. Invest.* **93**, 2684 (1994).

[18] C.-C. Wu, S.-J. Chen, C. Szabo, C. Thiemermann, and J. R. Vane, *Br. J. Pharmacol.* **114**, 1666 (1995).

[19] R.G. Tilton, K. Chang, J. A. Corbett, T. P. Misko, M. G. Currie, N. S. Sora, H. J. Kaplan, and J. R. Williamson, *Invest. Ophthalmol. Visual Sci.* **35**, 3278 (1994).

potent and selective inhibitor of iNOS. In many cases the use of iNOS inhibitors is prohibitive because of cost of reagents and effects of these reagents on the activity of eNOS and bNOS. Aminoguanidine is a cost-effective inhibitor of iNOS that does not suffer from the drawbacks of other NOS inhibitors. It is inexpensive and effective at inhibiting iNOS activity under both *in vitro* and *in vivo* conditions without modulating the activity of eNOS or bNOS. Aminoguanidine is most effective *in vivo* by multiple intraperitoneal injections ranging from two to three times daily at concentration of 200–400 mg/kg body weight per injection. Selective inhibition of iNOS has proved to be a successful strategy for attenuation of a number of disease conditions associated with the production of nitric oxide by iNOS in animal models. Aminoguanidine represents a useful, cost-effective reagent for studies directed at determining the role of nitric oxide under physiological and pathophysiological conditions.

[40] Biological Control and Inhibition of Induction of Nitric Oxide Synthase

By Chin-Chen Wu and Christoph Thiemermann

Introduction

Nitric oxide (NO), an inorganic radical, is a vasodilator autacoid that is produced by NO synthase (NOS; EC 1.14.13.39) from L-arginine in many mammalian cells. Nitric oxide has many diverse biological functions in the cardiovascular, nervous, and immune systems. Once formed, NO diffuses to adjacent cells where it activates soluble guanylate cyclase, resulting in the formation of cGMP, which in turn mediates many, but not all, of the biological effects of NO. At least three isoforms of NOS have been cloned. The NOS in endothelial cells (eNOS) and neuronal cells (bNOS) are expressed constitutively, whereas activation of macrophages and other cells with proinflammatory cytokines, lipopolysaccharide (LPS; endotoxin), lipoteichoic acid (LTA; a cell-wall component from the gram-positive bacterium *Staphylococcus aureus*), or some exotoxins (e.g., toxic shock syndrome toxin; TSST-1) results in the expression of a "calcium-independent" or inducible NOS (iNOS) activity. In contrast to the case for eNOS or bNOS, the availability of L-arginine can become rate-limiting for maximal generation of NO by iNOS. Formation of NO due to activation of eNOS (shear stress) causes vasodilatation (regulation of blood flow and pressure) and

inhibits adhesion of platelets and neutrophils to the endothelium. Generation of large amounts of NO by iNOS in cytokine-activated macrophages
contributes to the bactericidal and tumoricidal effects of these cells (host defense).[1,2]

In 1990, several groups independently discovered that an enhanced
formation of endogenous NO contributes to (1) hypotension[3] and vascular
hyporesponsiveness to vasoconstrictor agents[4,5] in rodents with endotoxic
shock; (2) hypotension caused by cytokines and endotoxin in dogs;[6] (3)
reduction in liver protein synthesis;[7] and (4) protection of the liver in
rodents with sepsis and septic shock.[8] We know that circulatory shock of
various etiologies (e.g., endotoxemia, hemorrhage, and trauma) is associated with enhanced formation of NO due to the early activation of eNOS
and the delayed induction of iNOS activity (e.g., macrophages, vascular
smooth muscle, hepatocytes, and cardiac myocytes). Prolonged periods of
shock also result in an impairment of eNOS and (in some models) bNOS
activity. Enhanced formation of NO in septic shock may contribute to
circulatory failure (hypotension, vascular hyporeactivity to vasoconstrictor
agents, increase in shunts, maldistribution of blood flow), myocardial dysfunction, organ injury (due to inhibition of mitochondrial respiration or
direct cytotoxic effects), and ultimately multiple organ dysfunction syndrome (reduced oxygen delivery, reduced oxygen extraction, etc.). Thus,
it has been argued that inhibition of NO formation may have therapeutic
benefit in patients with septic shock. Enhanced formation of NO in septic
shock, on the other hand, may also exert beneficial effects including vasodilation, prevention of platelet and leukocyte adhesion, improvement of mi-
crocirculatory blood flow and tissue oxygen extraction, and augmentation
of host defense.[2,9] Thus, it is not entirely surprising that many colleagues
have advocated the use of contrasting therapeutic strategies in septic shock
to (1) reduce NO formation, (22) enhance NO formation, or (3) combine

[1] S. Moncada and A. Higgs, *N. Engl. J. Med.* **329**, 2002 (1993).
[2] C. Thiemermann, *Adv. Pharmacol.* **28**, 45 (1994).
[3] C. Thiemermann and J. R. Vane, *Eur. J. Pharmacol.* **182**, 591 (1990).
[4] G. Julou-Schaeffer, G. A. Gray, I. Fleming, C. Schott, J. R. Parratt, and J. C. Stoclet, *Am. J. Physiol.* **259**, H1038 (1990).
[5] D. D. Rees, S. Cellek, R. M. J. Palmer, and S. Moncada, *Biochem. Biophys. Res. Commun.* **173**, 541 (1990).
[6] R. G. Kilbourn, S. S. Gross, A. Jubran, J. Adams, O. W. Griffith, R. Levi, and R. F. Lodato, *Proc. Natl. Acad. Sci. U.S.A.* **87**, 3629 (1990).
[7] R. D. Curran, T. R. Billiar, D. J. Stuehr, J. B. Ochoa, B. G. Harbrecht, S. G. Flint, and R. L. Simmons, *Ann. Surg.* **212**, 462 (1990).
[8] T. R. Billiar, R. D. Curran, B. G. Habrecht, D. J. Stuehr, A. J. Demetris, and R. L. Simmons, *J. Leukocyte Biol.* **48**, 565 (1990).
[9] C. Szabo and C. Thiemermann, *Shock* **2**, 145 (1994).

both approaches. Although a consensus as to which strategy should be used in clinical care of patients with sepsis has yet to be reached, a clinical (phase II) trial evaluating the use of a non-isoenzyme-selective inhibitor of NOS activity has already started.

In addition to shock, an enhanced formation of NO following the induction of iNOS also occurs in local (e.g., polyarthritis, osteoarthritis) or systemic inflammatory disorders, diabetes, arteriosclerosis, transplant rejection, and other diseases. It is, however, less clear whether the formation of NO in these disorders is a surrogate marker or a cause of the underlying pathology.

This chapter describes some of the methods that have been helpful in elucidating (1) the regulation and biological control and (2) the physiological and particularly pathophysiological role of NO generated by iNOS. The selected methods are described in detail to allow reproduction without referring to the literature. Whenever possible, reference is made to the original description of a particular method, and examples of key discoveries made since 1990 by means of the particular technology in question are given throughout the review.

Measurement of Nitrite Formation as Indicator of Nitric Oxide Formation by Inducible Nitric Oxide Synthase

The formation of NO (by iNOS) can easily be assessed by measuring the accumulation of nitrite in the culture medium of cells activated with LPS, LTA, or a mixture of proinflammatory cytokines [e.g., tumor necrosis factor-α (TNFα), interleukin-1 (IL-1), γ-interferon (INF$_\gamma$)] by the Griess reaction.[10] In our laboratory, the mouse macrophage cell line J774.2 (or any other primary cell culture or cell line known to express iNOS activity) is cultured in Dulbecco's modified Eagle's medium (DMEM; Sigma, St. Louis, MO). The medium is supplemented with 3.5 mM L-glutamine and 10% fetal calf serum (FCS; GIBCO, Grand Island, NY). Cells are cultured in T75 flasks (Marathan) and then further subcultured in 96-well plates until they reach confluence ($\sim$60,000 cells per well). To induce iNOS, fresh culture medium containing LPS (1 μg/ml) or LTA (10 μg/ml) is added. Nitrite accumulation in the medium is measured at 24 hr after the application of LPS or LTA. To assess their effects on nitrite production, drugs (expected to prevent or enhance the induction of iNOS protein and activity) are added at 1 hr prior to LPS or LTA to cells. In addition, the effect of drugs alone on nitrite production should be assessed.

[10] L. C. Green, D. A. Wangner, K. Glogowski, P. L. Skipper, J. S. Wishnok, and S. R. Tannenbaum, *Ana. Biochem.* **126**, 131 (1982).

Nitrite is measured by adding 100 μl of Griess reagent (1% sulfanilamide and 0.1% naphthylethylenediamide in 5% phosphoric acid) to 100-μl samples of medium. The optical density at 550 nm (OD_{550}) is measured by using a Molecular Devices microplate reader (Richmond, CA). Nitrite concentrations are calculated by comparison with OD_{550} values of standard solutions of sodium nitrite prepared in culture medium.

Control experiments are necessary to ensure that any potential reduction in nitrite formation is due to reduced formation of NO, rather than a reduced cell viability arising from toxic effects of any of the drugs or procedures used. Thus, it is essential to assess cell respiration, an indicator of cell viability, for example, by assessing the release of LDH (lactate dehydrogenase, a cytosolic marker enzyme) or by measureing the mitochondrial-dependent reduction of MTT [3-(4,5-dimethylthiazol-2-yl)-2,5-diphenyltetrazolium bromide] to formazan. Cells in 96-well plates are incubated with MTT (0.2 mg/ml for 60 min) at 37°. Culture medium is removed by aspiration, and the cells are solubilized in 100 μl dimethyl sulfoxide (DMSO). The extent of reduction of MTT to formazan within cells is quantitated by measurement of OD_{550}. The MTT assay used in our laboratory was first introduced by Mossman in 1983.[11]

Measurement of iNOS protein expression by Western blot analysis can be performed in the same cells in the following manner: J774.2 cells are cultured in T75 flasks to confluence and activated with vehicle or LPS (1 μg/ml) in the absence (control) and presence of drugs. The cells are subsequently lysed in 3 ml phosphate buffer solution containing 10 mM EDTA, 1% Triton X-100, 1 mM phenylmethylsulfonyl fluoride (PMSF), and 0.01% leupeptin, and iNOS protein is measured by Western blot analysis (see below and Fig. 1).

This technique (particularly when combined with Western blot analysis for iNOS protein expression and/or Northern blot analysis for iNOS mRNA, see below) has been extremely helpful in elucidating the signal transduction mechanisms leading to the expression of the iNOS gene as well as the regulation of iNOS expression. For instance, we know today that LPS (from gram-negative bacteria) or LTA (from gram-positive bacteria) activates cells to release proinflammatory cytokines (e.g., TNFα, IL-1, IFNγ) or platelet-activating factor (PAF) which either alone or in concert initiate a signal transduction event that includes (1) activation of tyrosine kinase; (2) activation and nuclear binding of the transcription factor NF-κB; and ultimately (3) transcription and translocation of the iNOS gene. Gene expression of iNOS is tonically inhibited (*in vivo*) by endogenous glucocorticoids, interleukin-4, and possibly polyamines and interleukin-10.

[11] T. Mossman, *J. Immunol. Methods* **65**, 55 (1983).

The inhibition of iNOS gene expression afforded by dexamethasone[12] is mediated by endogenous lipocortin-1, whereas the prevention of the expression of cyclooxygenase-2 (COS-2) caused by this steroid is due to a direct effect of dexamethasone on a "glucocorticoid-response element" on the promoter region of the COX-2 gene (independent of lipocortin-1).[13] The endogenous polyamines spermine and spermidine (and to a lesser extent putrescine and cadaverine) inhibit iNOS expression possibly by being metabolized (*in vivo*) by polyamine oxidase to spermine dialdehyde (or another yet unidentified aldehyde metabolite of spermine).[14]

Although the measurement of nitrite (or even nitrate) has been extensively used as an indicator of NO formation/accumulation *in vitro* (e.g., in tissue culture medium) or *in vivo* (biological samples), one has to be aware of the limitation of this assay. Clearly, NO is a reactive molecule which can be oxidized to nitrosonium ion (NO^+) equivalents and can also react with superoxide anion ($O_2^{\cdot-}$) to form peroxinitrite ($ONOO^-$) which in turn induces lipid peroxidation as well as the indiscriminant oxidation of thiol groups. The biological chemistry of NO is further complicated by its high reactivity with porphyrin iron ions present in hemoglobin, forming nitrosyl-hemoglobin adducts. Moreover, the NO present in mammalian plasma may circulate as thermodynamically stabler *S*-nitrosothiols (RSNO), predominantly *S*-nitrosoproteins such as *S*-nitrosoalbumin. Thus, nitrite is just one of many potential reactive metabolites formed by NO in biological fluids. It is, hence, conceivable that a reduction by a certain drug in the amounts of nitrite produced by cytokine-activated cells is due to the reaction of the test compound with the NO radical yielding a metabolite or adduct which cannot be determined by the Griess reaction.

Determination of Inducible Nitric Oxide Synthase Expression by Western Blot Analysis

The determination of iNOS protein expression by Western blot analysis in cultured cells activated with LPS or cytokines has been extremely useful in evaluating whether certain drugs or mediators attenuate the formation of nitrite caused by LPS by inhibiting the activity of iNOS or by preventing the expression of the iNOS protein. Western blotting is also useful in

---

[12] M. W. Radomski, R. M. J. Palmer, and S. Moncada, *Proc. Natl. Acad. Sci. U.S.A.* **87**, 10043 (1990).

[13] C. C. Wu, J. D. Croxtall, M. Perretti, C. E. Bryant, C. Thiemermann, R. J. Flower, and J. R. Vane, *Proc. Natl. Acad. Sci. U.S.A.* **92**, 3473 (1995).

[14] C. Szabo, G. J. Southan, E. Wood, C. Thiemermann, and J. R. Vane, *Br. J. Pharmacol.* **112**, 355 (1994).

elucidating the signal transduction events leading to the expression of the iNOS gene.

Cell homogenates or lysates (see above) are boiled (3 min) with gel loading buffer [50 mM Tris/10% sodium dodecyl sulfate (SDS)/10% glycerol/ 10% 2-mercaptoethanol/2 mg/ml bromphenol blue] in a ratio of 1:1 (v/v) and centrifuged at 10,000 g for 10 min. Protein concentrations of the supernatants are determined according to Bradford,[15] and total protein equivalents for each sample are separated on 10% SDS–polyacrylamide minigels (Hoefer, Scientific Instruments, San Francisco, CA) using the Laemmli buffer system and transferred to poly(vinylidene difluoride) membranes (Millipore, Bedford, MA). Nonspecific immunoglobulin G (IgG) binding sites are blocked with 5% dried milk protein, and the samples are then incubated with the antibody to iNOS (1:2000). Bands are detected with a horseradish peroxidase-conjugated secondary antibody and developed with diaminobenzidine tetrahydrochloride. Rainbow (Amersham, Bucks, UK) and prestained blue (Sigma) protein markers are used for molecular weight determinations.

The evaluation of the degree of iNOS protein expression (measured by Western blot analysis) caused by LPS in macrophages or vascular smooth muscle cells has been used to demonstrate that the inhibition of nitrite formation caused by dihydropyridine-type calcium-channel antagonists,[16] glibenclamide,[17] or even N-acetylserotonin (an agent known to inhibit sepiapterin reductase)[18] and, hence, the formation of tetrahydrobiopterin (a cofactor of iNOS) inhibit the expression of iNOS protein, rather than inhibiting iNOS enzyme activity.

Northern Blot Analysis

Transcription of iNOS mRNA can be determined by Northern blot analysis independent of or in conjunction with determination of iNOS protein expression (Western blot analysis). For example, J774.2 cells are stimulated for 24 hr with either medium alone, medium plus LPS (1 μg/ ml), or medium plus LPS in the presence of drugs. Total RNA is extracted using RNAzol reagent according to the manufacturer's instructions (Biogenesis, Bournemouth, UK). The RNA samples (10 μg quantified from the OD_{260}) are electrophoresed on a formaldehyde–agarose gel and transferred

[15] M. M. Bradford, *Anal. Biochem.* **72**, 248 (1976).
[16] C. Szabo, C. Thiemermann, and J. R. Vane, *Biochem. Biophys. Res. Commun.* **196**, 825 (1993).
[17] C. C. Wu, C. Thiemermann, and J. R. Vane, *Br. J. Pharmacol.* **114**, 1273 (1995).
[18] P. Klemm, M. Hecker, H. Stockhausen, C. C. Wu, and C. Thiemermann, *Br. J. Pharmacol.* **114**, 363 (1995).

using 20× SSPE buffer (sodium chloride 3.6 M, sodium phosphate 0.2 M, pH 7.7; disodium EDTA mM) onto a nylon membrane (Hybond N⁺, Amersham) and fixed by exposure to UV radiation. The cDNA probe for iNOS is labeled with [α-³²P]dCTP (3000 Ci/mm, ICN Flow, High Wycombe, UK) using a multiprime DNA labeling system (Amersham) according to the manufacturer's instructions.

Prehybridization is performed as follows: nylon membranes are incubated at 42° for 1 hr with 5× SSPE, formamide (50%, v/v), 5× Denhardt's solution [bovine serum albumin 0.1% (w/v), Ficoll 0.1% (w/v), polyvinylpyrrolidone 0.1% (w/v), and SDS 0.5% (w/v) supplemented with 20 μg/ml denatured herring sperm DNA] (Promega, Southampton, UK). Following this, membranes are incubated with the ³²P-labeled NOS probe for 18 hr at 42° in the above buffer minus herring sperm DNA. Buffer is removed and membranes washed twice with 50 ml of 1× SSPE/0.1% SDS for 15 min at 42°, then with 50 ml of 1× SSPE/0.1% SDS for 30 min at 65°. Finally, a high stringency wash is performed with 0.1% SSPE/0.1% SDS for 15 min at 65°. The membranes are then sealed in plastic wrap and autoradiographed at −70° using an intensifying screen (DuPont, Herts, UK). As a control for consistency of loading, robosomal RNA (18 S) is quantified by ethidium bromide fluorescence and photography of the formaldehyde–agarose gel before transfer and quantitation by Northern blot analysis.

Northern blot analysis has been used to demonstrate that dexamethasone (presummably via lipocortin-1) attenuates the expression of iNOS mRNA in J774.2 macrophages activated with LPS. Interestingly, antifungal imidazoles (e.g., clotrimazole, econazole, miconazole) inhibit the formation of nitrite caused by LPS in these cells without affecting the transcription of the iNOS gene, suggesting that Northern blot analysis, at least when used in isolation, does not necessarily provide a decisive answer to the question as to whether a certain drug or procedure affects the formation of NO by iNOS.[19]

Measurement of Nitric Oxide Synthase Activity by Determination of Formation of Tritiated Citrulline from Tritiated L-Arginine (Citrulline Assay)

Both calcium-dependent (eNOS or bNOS) and functionally calcium-independent NOS activities (iNOS) can be determined in tissue or cell

---

[19] R. G. Bogle, G. St. J. Whiteley, S.-C. Soo, A. P. Johnstone, and P. Vallance, *Br. J. Pharmacol.* **111**, 1257 (1994).

homogenates by means of measuring the conversion (in the presence or absence of calcium) of tritiated L-arginine to tritiated citrulline, a technique first described by Bredt and Snyder in 1990.[20] This technique has been used to determine the time course as well as the tissue distribution of the expression of iNOS activity in rodents with endotoxic or hemorrhagic shock.[21,22]

For instance, at 180 min after the injection of LPS to anesthetized rats, organs such as the lungs are removed to measure iNOS activity (i.e., organ with the highest iNOS activity after endotoxemia or hemorrhage in rats). Organs or tissues are obtained from different groups of rats treated with LPS in the absence (LPS controls) or presence of drug pretreatment and frozen in liquid nitrogen. Organs from sham-operated rats are also prepared for determination of baseline NOS activity. Organs are stored for no more than 2 weeks at $-80°$ before assay. Frozen lungs are homogenized on ice with an Ultra-Turrax T 25 homogenizer (Janke & Kunkel, IKA Labortechnik, Staufen im Breisgau, Germany) in a buffer composed of 50 mM Tris-HCl, 0.1 mM EDTA, 0.1 mM EGTA, 12 mM 2-mercaptoethanol, and 1 mM phenylmethylsulfonyl fluoride (pH 7.4). Conversion of L-[^{3}H]arginine to L-[^{3}H]citrulline is measured in the homogenates. Tissue homogenates (30 μl, $\sim$60 μg protein) are incubated in the presence of L-[^{3}H]arginine (10 μM, 5 kBq/tube), NADPH (1 mM), calmodulin (30 nM), tetrahydrobiopterin (5 μM), and calcium (2 mM) for 25 min at 25° in HEPES buffer (pH 7.5). Reactions are stopped by dilution with 1 ml of ice-cold HEPES buffer (pH 5.5) containing EGTA (2 mM) and EDTA (2 mM). Reaction mixtures are applied to Dowex 50W (Na$^+$ form) columns and the eluted L-[^{3}H]citrulline activity is measured by scintillation counting (Beckman, LS3801; Fullerton, CA). Experiments performed in the absence of NADPH determine the extent of L-[^{3}H]citrulline formation independent of a specific NOS activity. Experiments in the presence of NADPH, without calcium and with EGTA (5 mM), determine the calcium-independent NOS activity, which is taken to represent iNOS activity. The presence of iNOS protein can be verified (if necessary) by Western blot analysis (see below). The iNOS activity is expressed as picomoles citrulline formed in a given time (e.g., 25 min) per milligram protein present in the homogenate. The respective protein concentration is measured spectrophotometrically in 96-well plates with Bradford reagent,[15] using bovine serum albumin as standard.

[20] D. S. Bredt and S. H. Snyder, *Proc. Natl. Acad. Sci. U.S.A.* **87,** 69 (1990).
[21] M. Salter, R. G. Knowles, and S. Moncada, *Fed. Am. Soc. Exp. Biol. Soc. J.* **291,** 145 (1991).
[22] C. Thiemermann, C. Szabo, J. A. Mitchell, and J. R. Vane, *Proc. Natl. Acad. Sci. U.S.A.* **90,** 267 (1993).

Determination of Vascular Hyporeactivity to Vasoconstrictor Agents as Indicator of the Induction of Inducible Nitric Oxide Synthase in Vascular Smooth Muscle

Following the discovery that the hyporesponsiveness to vasoconstrictor agents (vascular hyporeactivity, vasoplegia) caused by endotoxin *in vivo*[4,23] or by exposure of isolated vascular rings (e.g., rat aortic rings) to endotoxin and/or cytokines is due to an enhanced formation of NO following induction of iNOS activity in vascular smooth muscle,[5] numerous investigators have used this technique to evaluate the mechanisms involved in the expression and regulation of iNOS activity in vascular smooth muscle cells. The following paragraphs describe the methodology used in our laboratory to evaluate the NO-mediated hyporeactivity to vasoconstrictor agents *in vivo* (rat) or *ex vivo* (rat aortic rings):

Male Wistar rats (240–300 g) are anesthetized with thiopentone sodium (Trapanal; 120 mg/kg, intraperiotoneally). The trachea is cannulated to facilitate respiration, and rectal temperature is maintained at 37° with a homeothermic blanket (BioSciences, Sheerness, Kent, UK). The right carotid artery is cannulated and connected to a pressure transducer (P23XL, Statham, Oxnard, CA) for the measurement of phasic and mean arterial blood pressure and heart rate, which are displayed on a Grass Model 7D polygraph recorder (Grass Instruments, Quincy, MA). The left femoral vein is cannulated for the administration of drugs. On completion of the surgical procedure, cardiovascular parameters are allowed to stabilize for 15–20 min. After recording baseline hemodynamic parameters, the pressor response to norepinephrine (NE; 1 μg/kg, intravenously) is recorded. At 10 min after injection of NE, animals receive LPS (10 mg/kg, intravenously) as a slow injection over 10 min, and pressor responses to NE are reassessed at 60, 120, and 180 min after LPS injection. The evaluation of the effects of a drug or intervention on vascular hyporeactivity of rat aortic rings to NE or other vasoconstrictor agents can be done in the same experiment in the following manner:

At 180 min after the injection of LPS, thoracic aortas are removed to measure vascular reactivity. Thoracic aortas are obtained from different groups of rats treated with LPS in the absence (LPS controls) or presence of drug pretreatment (intervention aimed to attenuate or enhance the expression of iNOS activity) or from sham-operated rats (baseline control). The vessels are cleared of adhering periadventitial fat, and the thoracic aortas are cut into rings of 3–4 mm width. The endothelium is removed

[23] I. Fleming, G. A. Gray, G. Julou-Schaeffer, J. R. Parratt, and J. C. Stoclet, *Biochem. Biophys. Res. Commun.* **171,** 562 (1990).

by gently rubbing the intimal surface. The lack of a relaxation to acetylcholine (1 μM) following precontraction of rings with NE (1 μM) is considered as evidence that the endothelium had been removed. The rings are mounted in 10-ml organ baths filled with warmed (37°), oxygenated (95% O_2/5% CO_2 v/v) Krebs solution (pH 7.4) consisting of 118 mM NaCl, 4.7 mM KCl, 1.2 mM, KH_2PO_4, 1.17 mM $MgSO_4$, 2.5 mM $CaCl_2$, 25 mM $NaHCO_3$, and 5.6 mM glucose. Indomethacin (5.6 μM) is added to prevent the production of prostanoids. Isometric force is measured with Grass FT03 type transducers and recorded on a Grass Model 7D polygraph recorder (Grass Instruments). A tension of 2 g is applied, and the rings are equilibrated for 60 min, changing the Krebs' solution every 15 min. In every experimental group, dose–response curves to NE (10^{-9} to 10^{-6} M) are obtained before and after treatment with N^ω-nitro-L-arginine (NO_2Arg) methyl ester, an inhibitor of NOS[24] (3 × 10^{-4} M for 20 min), to elucidate whether (1) endotoxemia causes vascular hyporeactivity to NE (or potentially other vasoconstrictors), (2) this vascular hyporeactivity is due to an enhanced formation of NO by iNOS in the vascular smooth muscle (eNOS is not involved as the endothelium is removed), and (3) any of the drugs or procedures used to prevent the development of vascular hyporeactivity act by preventing the induction of iNOS. Although there is now good evidence that the vascular hyporeactivity to vasoconstrictor agents is due to an enhanced formation of NO secondary to the induction of iNOS in vascular smooth muscle cells, it should be borne in mind that there is also evidence that at least a part of this hyporeactivity appears to be due to a rise in cGMP which is mediated by a factor other than NO.[25]

Concluding Remarks

This chapter outlines some of the key techniques and methods that have been instrumental (and hence widely used) in elucidating the mechanisms leading to the induction of iNOS caused by endotoxin (LPS), lipoteichoic acid (LTA), or cytokines *in vitro* and *in vivo*. Figure 1 summarizes in schematic form the mechanisms leading to the induction of iNOS caused by LPS, the key methods used to assess either iNOS expression or activity, and the pharmacological tools that have been used to interfere with the cascade of events leading to the formation of NO generated by iNOS. There is now good evidence that the activation of cells (e.g., macro-

[24] P. K. Moore, O. A. al-Swaych, N. W. S. Chong, R. A. Evans, and A. Gilson, *Br. J. Pharmacol.* **99**, 408 (1990).
[25] C. C. Wu, C. Szabo, S. J. Chen, C. Thiemermann, and J. R. Vane, *Biochem. Biophys. Res. Commun.* **201**, 436 (1994).

Pharmacological tools   Signal transduction of iNOS expression   Methodology

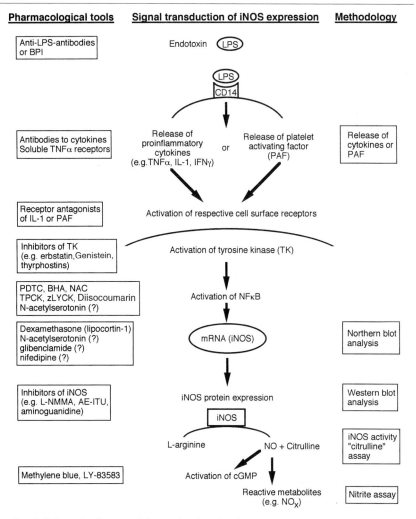

FIG. 1. Schematic diagram of the mechanisms leading to the induction of iNOS caused by LPS, the key methods used to assess either iNOS expression or activity, and the pharmacological tools used to interfere with the cascade of events leading to the formation of NO generated by iNOS. BPI, Bacterial/permeability increasing protein; PDTC, pyrrolidine dithiocarbamate; BHA, butylated hydroxyanisole; NAC, *N*-acetylcysteine; TPCK, tosyl phenyl chloromethyl ketone; zLYCK, benzyloxycarbonyl-Leu-Tyr-chloromethyl ketone; AE-ITU, aminoethylisothiourea; LY-83583, inhibitor of soluble guanylate cyclase.

phages) by LPS (following the binding of LPS to the CD14 receptor on the surface of these cells) leads to the generation of numerous proinflammatory cytokines (e.g., IL-1, TNFα, INFγ) or PAF, which either alone or in concert cause the activation of a variety of cells. The signal transduction events leading to the expression of iNOS protein by these cytokines involve (1) binding of the respective cytokines to their surface receptors, (2) activation of tyrosine kinase, and (3) activation and nuclear binding of the transcription factor NF-κB to the promoter region of the iNOS gene. Transcription and translation subsequently lead to a rise in iNOS protein and activity which, in turn, results in the formation of large amounts of NO from L-arginine (with the formation of L-citrulline as a by-product). The formation of NO by iNOS is functionally calcium-independent (as calmodulin is already tightly bound to iNOS), and the availability of L-arginine can become rate-limiting for a maximal formation of NO by iNOS.

Numerous pharmacological tools have been useful to interfere with the above-mentioned steps leading to the induction of iNOS activity by LPS. For instance, the activation of cells by LPS can be prevented by agents which (1) bind and inactivate endotoxin (monoclonal or polyclonal antibodies to core structures of the LPS molecule), (2) prevent the effects of proinflammatory cytokines or PAF (antibodies to TNFα or INFγ, PAF or IL-1 receptor antagonists, soluble TNFα receptors), and (3) prevent the activation of tyrosine kinase (e.g., erbstatin, Genistein, thyrphostins) or nuclear transcription factor NE-κB (e.g., antioxidants, inhibitors of I-κB-protease); all of these agents prevent the transcription of the iNOS gene. Translation and hence the formation of iNOS protein can be prevented by dexamethasone, and this effect of glucocorticosteroids is mediated by lipocortin-1. In addition, there is some evidence that the expression of the iNOS gene can be prevented by glibenclamide, N-acetylserotonin, or dihydropyridine-type calcium-channel antagonists (e.g., nifedipine). The formation of NO by iNOS can be prevented by inhibitors of NOS activity such as the L-arginine analog N^G-monomethyl-L-arginine (L-NMMA), isothiourea derivatives (e.g., S-methylisothiourea, amino-ethylisothiourea),[26,27] or aminoguanidine. As many, but not all, of the effects of NO are due to activation of soluble guanylate cyclase resulting in a rise in intracellular cyclic GMP, agents that prevent the activation of cyclic GMP (e.g., methylene blue or LY-83583) may be instrumental in elucidating some of the biological effects of NO.

It is hoped that the advances made in our understanding of the mechanisms leading to the expression of iNOS protein and activity as

[26] C. Szabo, G. J. Southan, and C. Thiemermann, *Proc. Natl. Acad. Sci. U.S.A.* **91,** 12472 (1994).
[27] G. J. Southan, C. Szabo, and C. Thiemermann, *Br. J. Pharmacol.* **114,** 510 (1995).

well as the biological control mechanisms involved may translate into a better understanding of the pathophysiology and, ultimately, therapy of disorders associated with an enhanced formation of NO due to expression of iNOS.

[41] Large-Scale Purification of Rat Brain Nitric Oxide Synthase from Baculovirus Overexpression System

By Bernd Mayer, Peter Klatt, Barbara M. List, Christian Harteneck, and Kurt Schmidt

Introduction

Oxidation of L-arginine to L-citrulline and nitric oxide (NO) is catalyzed by at least three different NO synthase (NOS; EC 1.14.13.39) isozymes: the constitutively expressed neuronal and endothelial isoforms, which require Ca^{2+} calmodulin for activity, and a Ca^{2+}-independent form, which is expressed in most mammalian cells in response to cytokines and endotoxin.[1–3] Albeit regulated in a different manner, the NOS isoforms identified so far are biochemically similar. They exist as homodimers under native conditions, with subunit molecular masses ranging from 130 kDa (endothelial and inducible NOSs) to 160 kDa (neuronal NOS). L-Arginine oxidation and reductive activation of molecular oxygen is catalyzed by a cysteine thiol-ligated P450-like prosthetic heme group localized in the N-terminal half of the protein.[4,5] This part of the enzyme is thus referred to as the oxygenase domain of NOS. The C-terminal half of the enzyme, separated from the oxygenase domain by a binding site for calmodulin, contains the flavins FAD and FMN that serve to shuttle reducing equivalents from the cofactor NADPH to the heme. This reductase domain of NOS shows pronounced sequence similarities to cytochrome P450 reductase[6] and exhibits similar catalytic activities.[7] These results suggest that NOSs represent

[1] M. A. Marletta, *J. Biol. Chem.* **268**, 12231 (1993).
[2] R. G. Knowles and S. Moncada, *Biochem. J.* **298**, 249 (1994).
[3] B. Mayer, *Cell Biochem. Funct.* **12**, 167 (1994).
[4] P. F. Chen, A. L. Tsai, and K. K. Wu, *J. Biol. Chem.* **269**, 25062 (1994).
[5] M. K. Richards and M. A. Marletta, *Biochemistry* **33**, 14723 (1994).
[6] D. S. Bredt, P. M. Hwang, C. E. Glatt, C. Lowenstein, R. R. Reed, and S. H. Snyder, *Nature* (*London*) **351**, 714 (1991).
[7] P. Klatt, B. Heinzel, M. John, M. Kastner, E. Böhme, and B. Mayer, *J. Biol. Chem.* **267**, 11374 (1992).

self-sufficient cytochrome P450s with both reductase and oxygenase activities associated with one single protein. In contrast to the classic microsomal cytochrome P450 systems, however, NOSs require the pteridine tetrahydrobiopterin as an additional cofactor with as yet unknown function.[8-10]

We have worked out a method for purification of rat brain NOS overexpressed in a baculovirus/insect cell system.[11] Here we describe an upscaled version of this protocol yielding about 100 mg of the pure enzyme from 3000-ml Sf9 (*Spodoptera frugiperda* fall armyworm ovary) cell cultures.

Plasmid Construction

The cDNA encoding for rat brain NOS (Genbank accession No. X59949),[6] a generous gift from Drs. D. S. Bredt and S. H. Snyder, was cloned in the baculovirus expression vector pVL 1393. Cloning was performed according to standard laboratory protocols and is only briefly described here.[12] To reduce the 5' noncoding region of the original cDNA, a *Sse*8387I fragment of NOS (bp 308–4241) was cloned in the *Pst*I site of pBluescript SK(−) (Stratagene, La Jolla, CA). A clone with the C-terminal part next to the *Not*I site of the multiple cloning site of pBluescript was selected and cut with *Ehe*I (position 1560) and *Not*I (multiple cloning site of pBluescript). The 3139-bp *Ehe*I (position 1560) and *Not*I (position 4699) fragment of the original cDNA encoding the C-terminal part was then ligated in the cloning intermediate. The resulting cDNA was cloned in the transfer vector pVL 1393 using *Eco*RI/*Not*I.

Infection of Sf9 Cells with Recombinant Baculovirus

Fall armyworm ovary cells (*Spodoptera frugiperda;* Sf9) are obtained from the ATCC (Rockville, MD; CRL 1711). Cells are grown in TC-100 medium (Sigma, St. Louis, MO) supplemented with 10% fetal calf serum (SEBAK GmbH, Suben, Austria), amphotericin B (1.25 mg/liter), penicillin (100,000 U/liter), streptomycin (100 mg/liter), and 0.2% Pluronic F-68 (Sigma) under continuous shaking (60–70 rpm) using an orbital shaker. Optimal growth (doubling time of ~24 hr) is achieved at cell densities ranging from 5×10^5 to 2×10^6 cells/ml and a temperature of $27° \pm 1°$.

[8] P. Klatt, M. Schmid, E. Leopold, K. Schmidt, E. R. Werner, and B. Mayer, *J. Biol. Chem.* **269**, 13861 (1994).

[9] B. Mayer, P. Klatt, E. R. Werner, and K. Schmidt, *J. Biol. Chem.* **270**, 655 (1995).

[10] B. Mayer and E. R. Werner, *Naunyn-Schmiedeberg's Arch. Pharmacol.* **351**, 453 (1995).

[11] C. Harteneck, P. Klatt, K. Schmidt, and B. Mayer, *Biochem. J.* **304**, 683 (1994).

[12] J. Sambrook, E. F. Fritsch, and T. Maniatis, "Molecular Cloning: A Laboratory Manual." Cold Spring Harbor Laboratory, Cold Spring Harbor, New York, 1989.

The recombinant virus is generated by cotransfection of Sf9 cells with the expression vector (see section on plasmid construction) and BaculoGOLD baculovirus DNA (Dianova, Hamburg, Germany) using the lipofection method.[13] Positive viral clones are isolated by plaque assay and identified by the ability to direct the expression of NOS as revealed by appearance of a 150- to 160-kDa band in immunoblots of the cell extracts using a polyclonal antibody against brain NOS (ALEXIS, Läufelfingen, Switzerland) for detection. The purified virus is then amplified and the titer estimated by plaque assay. For expression of NOS, the culture medium is supplemented with 20% (w/v) fetal calf serum, and Sf9 cells (4.5×10^9 cells/3000 ml) are infected with the recombinant baculovirus at a ratio of 5 pfu (plaque-forming units) per cell in the presence of 4 mg/liters hemin (Sigma). Stock solutions (2 mg/ml) of hemin are prepared in 0.4 M NaOH/ethanol (1:1, v/v). After 48 hr, cells are harvested by centrifugation for 3 min at 1000 g and washed with 500 ml of serum-free TC-100 medium. Finally, cells are resuspended in buffer A (see section on solutions and buffers) to give a final volume of 100 ml and used for enzyme preparation as described below.

Comments

(1) For preparation of NOS as described in this chapter, we have used three 1800-ml Fernbach flasks, each containing not more than 1000 ml of cell suspension to ensure sufficient oxygenation of the cells. (2) In initial experiments we found that culture of Sf9 cells at ambient temperature not only slowed down cell growth but also markedly reduced NOS expression levels. It is strongly recommended, therefore, to use an incubator with a built-in cooling system to keep the cells at 27°. (3) Addition of hemin during infection turned out to be crucial to obtain functionally intact NOS. Interestingly, we observed even higher expression levels in cells infected in the absence of hemin; however, a large part (>90%) of the enzyme remained insoluble under these conditions, and the remaining soluble part was only poorly active, apparently due to low heme content (~0.2 mol per mole 160-kDa subunit). (4) As previously observed by others,[14,15] we found that hemin cytotoxicity was prevented by infecting cells in the presence of 20% (w/v) fetal calf serum. (5) Supplementation of the culture medium with either riboflavin (0.1 mM) or FAD and FMN (0.1 mM each) increased the amount of flavins bound to the purified enzyme from 0.2 to 0.7–0.9 mol per mole 160-kDa subunit. This is not essential, however, because

[13] D. R. Groebe, A. E. Chung, and C. Ho, *Nucleic Acids Res.* **18**, 4033 (1990).

[14] A. Asseffa, S. J. Smith, K. Nagata, J. Gillette, H. V. Gelboin, and F. J. Gonzalez, *Arch. Biochem. Biophys.* **274**, 481 (1989).

[15] F. J. Gonzalez, S. Kimura, S. Tamura, and H. V. Gelboin, *Methods Enzymol.* **206**, 93 (1991).

flavin-deficient NOS is readily reconstituted by addition of FAD and FMN during incubation.[11] (6) It should be considered that specific NOS activities in crude preparations of Sf9 cells decrease at increasing concentrations of total protein. (7) Occasionally and without any obvious reason, infection of Sf9 cells did not yield satisfactory NOS expression levels. It is recommended, therefore, to determine NOS activity in homogenates or supernatants prepared from a small aliquot of the infected cells prior to enzyme purification.

Enzyme Purification

The protocol for purification of rat brain NOS involves two sequential affinity chromatography steps. First the enzyme is bound to 2',5'-ADP–Sepharose 4B (Pharmacia, Piscataway, NJ) and eluted with excess NADPH or 2'-AMP (see comments below). Subsequently it is chromatographed in the presence of Ca^{2+} over calmodulin–Sepharose 4B (Pharmacia) and eluted by chelating Ca^{2+} with excess EGTA. The following buffers and solutions should be prepared 1 day before enzyme preparation in double-distilled water and be adjusted to pH 7.4 at ambient temperature (20°–25°). The buffers are passed through a 0.22-μm filter and kept overnight at 4°–6°.

Solutions and Buffers

2-Mercaptoethanol should be added to buffers A–E immediately before use.

1.5 ml of 0.5 M EDTA (298 mg Na_4EDTA · H_2O)
10 ml of 200 mM $CaCl_2$ (296 mg $CaCl_2$ · $2H_2O$)
Buffer A (500 ml): 20 mM triethanolamine hydrochloride (TEA; 1.86 g), adjusted to pH 7.4 with 5 M NaOH; 0.5 mM EDTA (0.5 ml EDTA stock); 12 mM 2-mercaptoethanol (0.5 ml)
Buffer B (250 ml): 50 mM TEA (2.32 g) and 0.5 M NaCl (7.31 g) adjusted to pH 7.4 with 5 M NaOH; 0.5 mM EDTA (0.25 ml EDTA stock); 12 mM 2-mercaptoethanol (0.25 ml)
Buffer C (250 ml): 50 mM TEA (2.32 g) and 150 mM NaCl (2.19 g) adjusted to pH 7.4 with 5 M NaOH; 0.5 mM EDTA (0.25 ml EDTA stock); 12 mM 2-mercaptoethanol (0.25 ml)
Buffer D (500 ml): 20 mM Tris-HCl (1.21 g Tris base) and 150 mM NaCl (4.38 g) adjusted to pH 7.4 with 6 M HCl; 2 mM $CaCl_2$ (5 ml $CaCl_2$ stock); 12 mM 2-mercaptoethanol (0.5 ml)
Buffer E (250 ml): 20 mM Tris-HCl (0.61 g Tris base), 150 mM NaCl (2.19 g), and 4 mM EGTA (0.38 g) adjusted to pH 7.4 with 6 M HCl; 12 mM 2-mercaptoethanol (0.25 ml)

Column Chromatography

Geometry of the columns is probably not critical, but bed volumes should be adapted to the scale of the enzyme preparations to avoid dilution of the protein or overloading of the columns. We have used two 20 × 2.5 cm Econo-Columns (Bio-Rad, Richmond, CA) equipped with flow adaptors and filled with the affinity resins to give bed volumes of 35 ml each. Flow rates are 2 ml/min throughout enzyme preparation. Columns are equilibrated with 4 bed volumes (140 ml) of buffer A (2',5'-ADP–Sepharose) or buffer D (calmodulin–Sepharose) prior to enzyme purification.

Regeneration of the columns is performed at flow rates of 1 ml/min. The 2',5'-ADP–Sepharose is washed with 100 ml of alkaline buffer (0.1 M Tris, 0.5 M NaCl, 0.1% (w/v) NaN$_3$, pH 8.5) followed by 100 ml of acidic buffer (0.1 M sodium acetate, 0.5 M NaCl, 0.1% (w/v) NaN$_3$, pH 4.5). This cycle is repeated three times, and finally the column is washed with 100 ml of double-distilled water containing 0.1% (w/v) NaN$_3$ for storage. Calmodulin–Sepharose is regenerated with 200 ml of 50 mM Tris, 2 mM EGTA, 1 M NaCl, 0.1% NaN$_3$, pH 7.5, and finally equilibrated with 100 ml of 50 mM Tris, 2 mM CaCl$_2$, 150 mM NaCl, 0.1% NaN$_3$, pH 7.5, for storage.

Purification Procedure

Infected cells suspended in buffer A and kept on ice are sonicated four times for 10 sec each time at 150 W, homogenates are centrifuged for 15 min at 30,000 g (Sorvall SS-34 rotor; 17,000 rpm), and the supernatant is collected. To increase recovery of NOS by about 50%, the pellet is washed once with buffer A (final volume 50 ml). The combined supernatant is loaded onto the equilibrated 2',5'-ADP–Sepharose column, which is subsequently washed with 70 ml of buffer B followed by 35 ml of buffer C. Elution of bound enzyme is performed with 90 ml of 10 mM NADPH in buffer C, and fractions (3 ml) containing NOS (visible as red-brown color) are pooled to give about 60 ml of 2',5'-ADP–Sepharose eluate.

The 2',5'-ADP–Sepharose eluate is adjusted to 2 mM CaCl$_2$ by addition of CaCl$_2$ stock solution (1%, v/v) and passed over the calmodulin–agarose column. The column is washed with 105 ml of buffer D, and the enzyme is eluted with 105 ml of buffer E. Fractions (3 ml) containing NOS (visible as red-brown color) are pooled to give about 30 ml of eluate, containing approximately 4 mg of purified NOS per milliliter. If required, the final eluate can be further concentrated up to 20 mg/ml using Centricon-30 microconcentrators (Amicon, Danvers, MA). The enzyme should be stored at $-70°$.

Comments

(1) The method described is rather insensitive to downscaling, albeit the relative amounts of recovered enzyme may be lower at smaller scales. Initially, we have purified the enzyme from 400-ml cultures of infected cells and obtained results similar to those described here,[11] and sometimes we perform minipreparations from 150-ml cultures yielding approximately 1 mg of pure NOS. If required, several of these minipreparations can be done simultaneously, using small disposable plastic columns with a bed volume of 0.5 ml for affinity chromatography. (2) Yasukochi and Masters[16] have described elution of cytochrome P450 reductase from $2',5'$-ADP–Sepharose with $2'$-AMP, which is considerably less expensive than NADPH. In accordance with this previous report, we found that recombinant rat brain NOS was efficiently eluted from the affinity resin in the presence of 20 mM $2'$-AMP (Sigma, containing ~50% of inactive $3'$-AMP) and 0.5 M NaCl without interference with subsequent binding of the enzyme to calmodulin–Sepharose. (3) Purified NOS is sensitive to repeated freezing and thawing. Thus, the final eluate should be frozen in small aliquots at reasonable protein concentrations. (4) The enzyme is unstable if diluted or assayed in the absence of either serum albumin (2–10 mg/ml) or certain detergents. Routinely we dilute the enzyme in the presence of 1 mM 3-[(3-cholamidopropyl)dimethylammonio]-1-propanesulfonate (CHAPS), giving final concentrations of 0.2 mM CHAPS in enzyme assays.

Results of Representative Purification

We now describe the results of a typical purification of NOS from 3000-ml cultures of Sf9 cells. Protein is determined with the method of Bradford[17] using bovine serum albumin (BSA) as standard. Unless otherwise indicated, NOS activity is assayed as conversion of [^{3}H]arginine to [^{3}H]citrulline as described in detail by Mayer *et al.*[18]

Figure 1 shows a Coomassie blue-stained sodium dodecyl sulfate (SDS)–polyacrylamide gel of Sf9 cell supernatant (lane B), $2',5'$-ADP–Sepharose eluate (lane C), and the final calmodulin–Sepharose eluate (lane D). Nitric oxide synthase appears as a 155-kDa band on the gels, which is in good accordance with the molecular mass calculated from the amino acid sequence (160 kDa).[6] Densitometric analysis of the gel indicated that NOS accounted for approximately 6% of total soluble cell protein. Data on

---

[16] Y. Yasukochi and B. S. S. Masters, *J. Biol. Chem.* **251**, 5337 (1976).
[17] M. M. Bradford, *Anal. Biochem.* **72**, 248 (1976).
[18] B. Mayer, P. Klatt, E. R. Werner, and K. Schmidt, *Neuropharmacology* **33**, 1253 (1994).

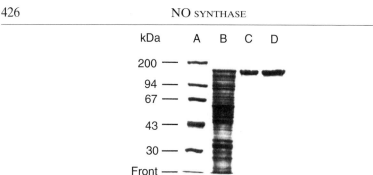

FIG. 1. Coomassie blue-stained SDS–polyacrylamide gel (10%) of marker proteins (lane A), supernatant of rat brain NOS-recombinant baculovirus-infected Sf9 cells (lane B), 2',5'-ADP–Sepharose eluate (lane C), and calmodulin–Sepharose eluate (lane D). Occasionally, the 2',5'-ADP–Sepharose eluates contained some additional bands in the range of 40–90 kDa, accounting for 2–5% of total stained protein. These minor bands were never observed, however, in the calmodulin–Sepharose eluates.

enzyme activities and protein recovery during purification are summarized in Table I. About 3 g of soluble protein was obtained from 4.5 × 10⁹ cells, and NOS activity was 0.051 μmol citrulline/mg/min in the cell supernatant. Chromatography over 2',5'-ADP–Sepharose yielded about 150 mg of protein with a specific activity of 0.9 μmol citrulline/mg/min, which is similar to the activities previously described for NOS purified from rat and porcine

TABLE I
PURIFICATION OF RECOMBINANT RAT BRAIN NITRIC OXIDE SYNTHASE[a]

Fraction	Volume (ml)	Protein (mg)	Total activity (μmol/min)	Specific activity (μmol/mg/min)	Purification (-fold)	Yield (%)
30,000 g supernatant	85	3080	157	0.051	1	100
2',5'-ADP–Sepharose	60	156	141	0.90	18	90
Calmodulin–Sepharose	30	123	117	0.95[b]	19	75
Centricon concentrate	4.6	83	91	1.10[b]	21	58

[a] Nitric oxide synthase was purified from 4.5 × 10⁹ Sf9 cells that had been infected with rat brain NOS-recombinant baculovirus for 48 hr in 3000 ml culture medium supplemented with 4 mg/liter hemin. Enzyme activity was measured at 37° for 10 min as conversion of [³H]arginine (0.1 mM) to [³H]citrulline. Results from a representative purification are shown.

[b] Differences in specific activities of NOS prior and after protein concentration are not statistically significant when different purifications are compared (n = 3; p > 0.20).

brain.[19,20] Further purification over calmodulin–Sepharose resulted in about 2-fold concentration of the protein and sometimes slightly enhanced its specific activity. Loss of enzyme was about 20% in this step, giving an overall yield of 75% of NOS activity over crude supernatants. In the calmodulin–Sepharose eluate, the NOS concentration was 4 mg/ml corresponding to a 25 μM solution of the subunits. For biophysical characterization, the enzyme was further concentrated by centrifugation in Centricon-30 microconcentrator devices. Typically, concentration of NOS to 15–20 mg/ml results in 20–30% loss of enzyme without significant change in specific activity.

Purified NOS exhibited a K_m for L-arginine of 5 μM and a V_{max} of 1.2–1.5 μmol L-citrulline/mg/min, indicating that recombinant rat brain NOS is kinetically similar to the enzyme purified from porcine brain.[21] Determination of bound prosthetic groups[22] showed almost stoichiometric presence of heme (molar ratio 0.90–0.95 per subunit), but the flavins and tetrahydrobiopterin were present at substoichiometrical amounts (0.2 and 0.4 mol per mole of subunit, respectively).[11] As indicated in the comments for cell infection (see above), the flavin content of purified NOS can be increased to a molar ratio of 0.7–0.9 per subunit when cells are infected in the presence of 0.1 mM riboflavin or FAD/FMN, whereas the amount of bound tetrahydrobiopterin is not increased by infection of cells in the presence of various pteridines or sepiapterin, a precursor of tetrahydrobiopterin biosynthesis.

[19] D. S. Bredt and S. H. Snyder, *Proc. Natl. Acad. Sci. U.S.A.* **87,** 682 (1990).
[20] B. Mayer, M. John, and E. Böhme, *FEBS Lett.* **277,** 215 (1990).
[21] P. Klatt, K. Schmidt, G. Uray, and B. Mayer, *J. Biol. Chem.* **268,** 14781 (1993).
[22] P. Klatt, K. Schmidt, E. R. Werner, and B. Mayer, *Methods Enzymol.* **268,** Chap. 35, 1996 (this volume).

[42] Cloned and Expressed Nitric Oxide Synthase Proteins

By Houhui Xia and David S. Bredt

Cloning of Nitric Oxide Synthase Genes

Initial biochemical characterization of nitric oxide synthase (NOS; EC 1.14.13.39) activities in mammalian tissues suggested the existence of at least two distinct enzymes. Blood vessel endothelial cells were first shown to generate NO by a constitutive NOS activity physiologically regulated by calcium.[1,2] In this pathway, neurotransmitters such as bradykinin and acetylcholine bind to extracellular receptors on endothelial cells and cause mobilization of intracellular calcium, and this transiently activates endothelial NOS. Nanomolar concentrations of NO formed serve as the endothelial-derived relaxing factor that augments guanylate cyclase activity in smooth muscle cells and affords vasorelaxation. In unrelated studies, researchers found that macrophages produce NO by a calcium-insensitive enzyme. However, NO formation by this calcium-independent pathway only occurred in immunologically activated cells.[3] This inducible NOS continuously produces much larger amounts of NO, which serve as a toxic mediator for eliminating tumor cells and intracellular pathogens.[4]

Following the characterization of physiological functions for NO in vascular and immune cells, a constitutive NOS was also described in brain tissue.[5] Like the NOS in endothelium, this enzyme was noted to be transiently activated by neurotransmitters and entirely dependent on elevated levels of intracellular calcium.[6,7] All three NOS activities were found to produce NO and L-citrulline from L-arginine with NADPH serving as a cosubstrate. Pharmacological studies with arginine analogs readily differentiated the inducible NOS in macrophages from the constitutive NOS activities in endothelium and brain, which themselves were essentially indistinguishable.

Isolation of NOS proteins and cDNA cloning allowed definitive characterization of the molecular isoforms. Purification of NOS was facilitated by a simple, sensitive, and specific enzyme assay, monitoring the conversion of [^{3}H]arginine to [^{3}H]citrulline.[8] It was also noted that partially purified enzyme preparations from brain tissue required a soluble cofactor for activity. This cofactor was identified as calmodulin, which explained the calcium requirement for constitutive NOS activities.[8] Homogeneous purification was achieved by affinity chromatography using 2′,5′-ADP–agarose. The purified NOS from brain was identified as a 160-kDa protein on sodium

[1] R. M. Palmer, D. S. Ashton, and S. Moncada, *Nature (London)* **333,** 664 (1988).
[2] R. M. Palmer, and S. Moncada, *Biochem. Biophys. Res. Commun.* **158,** 348 (1989).
[3] M. A. Marletta, P. S. Yoon, R. Iyengar, C. D. Leaf, and J. S. Wishnok, *Biochemistry* **27,** 8706 (1988).
[4] J. B. Hibbs, Jr., R. R. Taintor, and Z. Vavrin, *Science* **235,** 473 (1987).
[5] J. Garthwaite, S. L. Charles, and R. Chess-Williams, *Nature (London)* **336,** 385 (1988).
[6] R. G. Knowles, M. Palacios, R. M. Palmer, and S. Moncada, *Proc. Natl. Acad. Sci. U.S.A.* **86,** 5159 (1989).
[7] D. S. Bredt and S. H. Snyder, *Proc. Natl. Acad. Sci. U.S.A.* **86,** 9030 (1989).
[8] D. S. Bredt and S. H. Snyder, *Proc. Natl. Acad. Sci. U.S.A.* **87,** 682 (1990).

dodecyl sulfate–polyacrylamide gel electrophoresis (SDS–PAGE). Two tryptic peptides sequenced from the purified NOS were used to design degenerate PCR (polymerase chain reaction) probes, which amplified a 600-base pair (bp) probe. This larger probe was used to obtain the full coding cDNA from a rat brain library.[9] The sequence of neuronal NOS was later used to isolate unique NOS cDNAs from endothelial cells and activated macrophages (for review, see Refs. 10 and 11). These three genes are now commonly referred to as neuronal NOS (nNOS), endothelial NOS (eNOS), and inducible NOS (iNOS). The historical nomenclature of NOS genes can be misleading. We now appreciate that the gene cloned from neurons (nNOS) is expressed in numerous cell types including epithelial cells and skeletal muscle,[12,13] while the gene cloned from endothelial cells (eNOS) occurs in certain neurons.[14] No other NOS cDNAs have been isolated despite extensive searches in numerous laboratories. This may suggest that these three genes represent the complete family of NOS forms in mammals.

Catalytic Domains of Nitric Oxide Synthase Gene Products

Sequence analysis of the predicted protein sequences of NOS isoforms indicates several important functional motifs (Fig. 1A). The protein can be conceptually divided into an amino-terminal heme domain and a carboxyl-terminal oxidase domain. A calmodulin-binding motif functionally links the two domains. The carboxyl-terminal reductase domain shares approximately 35% identity with cytochrome P450 reductase (CPR). The NOS and CPR enzymes share consensus binding sites for NADPH as well as flavin adenine dinucleotide (FAD) and flavin adenine mononucleotide (FMN). These redox-active cofactors serve as a path for electron flow in CPR such that NADPH transfers its pair of electrons to FAD and these electrons are transferred one at a time to FMN.[15] Electrons from the FMN cofactor of CPR are shuttled to the heme active site of cytochrome P450 enzymes, which are distinct integral membrane proteins. Nitric oxide synthase repre-

[9] D. S. Bredt, P. M. Hwang, C. E. Glatt, C. Lowenstein, R. R. Reed, and S. H. Snyder, *Nature* (*London*) **351,** 714 (1991).

[10] D. S. Bredt and S. H. Snyder, *Annu. Rev. Biochem.* **63,** 175 (1994).

[11] C. Nathan and Q. W. Xie, *J. Biol. Chem.* **269,** 13725 (1994).

[12] H. H. Schmidt, G. D. Gagne, M. Nakane, J. S. Pollock, M. F. Miller, and F. Murad, *J. Histochem. Cytochem.* **40,** 1439 (1992).

[13] L. Kobzik, M. B. Reid, D. S. Bredt, and J. S. Stamler, *Nature* (*London*) **372,** 546 (1994).

[14] J. L. Dinerman, T. M. Dawson, M. J. Schell, A. Snowman, and S. H. Snyder, *Proc. Natl. Acad. Sci. U.S.A.* **91,** 4214 (1994).

[15] T. D. Porter and C. B. Kasper, *Biochemistry* **25,** 1682 (1986).

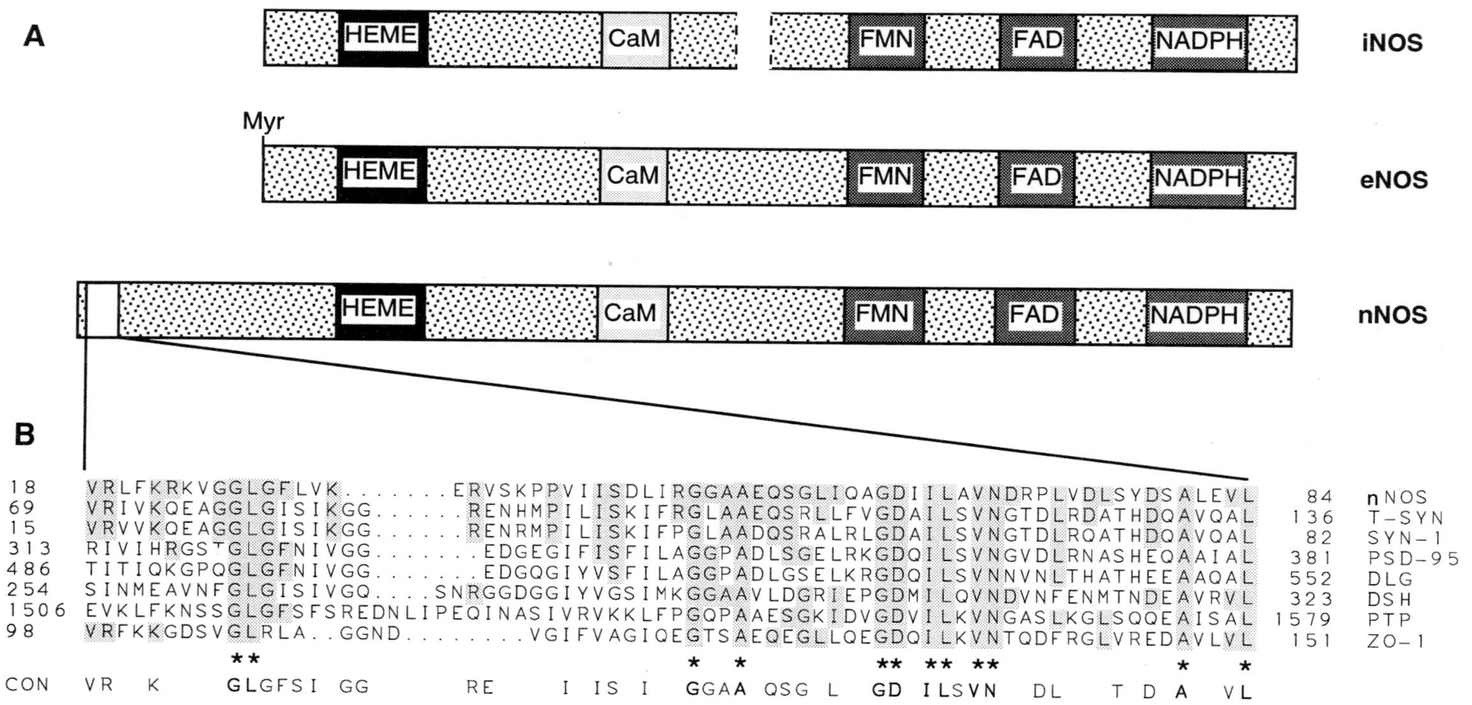

A

iNOS

HEME | CaM | FMN | FAD | NADPH

eNOS

Myr

HEME | CaM | FMN | FAD | NADPH

nNOS

HEME | CaM | FMN | FAD | NADPH

B

```
18     VRLFKRKVGGLGFLVK.......    ERVSKPPVIISDLIRGGAAEQSGLIQAGDIILAVNDRPLVDLSYDSALEVL    84    nNOS
69     VRIVKQEAGGLGISIKGG.....    RENHMPILISKIFRGLAAEQSRLLFVGDAILSVNGTDLRDATHDQAVQAL   136    T-SYN
15     VRVVKQEAGGLGISIKGG.....    RENRMPILISKIFPGLAADQSRALRLGDAILSVNGTDLRQATHDQAVQAL    82    SYN-1
313    RIVIHRGSTGLGFNIVGG.....    .EDGEGIFISFILAGGPADLSGELRKGDQILSVNGVDLRNASHEQAAIAL   381    PSD-95
486    TITIQKGPQGLGFNIVGG.....    .EDGQGIYVSFILAGGPADLGSELKRGDQILSVNNVLTHATHEEAAQAL    552    DLG
254    SINMEAVNFGLGISIVGQ.....    SNRGGDGGIYVGSIMKGGAAVLDGRIEPGDMILQVNDVNFENMTNDEAVRVL   323    DSH
1506   EVKLFKNSSGLGFSREDNLIPEQINASIVRVKKLFPGQPAAESGKIDVGDVILKVNGASLKGLSQQEAISAL  1579   PTP
98     VRFKKGDSVGLRLA..GGND......VGIFVAGIQEGTSAEQEGLLQEGDQILKVNTQDFRGLVREDAVLVL   151    ZO-1
```

```
       **               **                                   *  **  ** **    *
CON    VR    K   GLGFSI GG    RE    I IS I    GGAA QSG L    GD ILSVN    DL   T DA   VL
```

FIG. 1. (A) Schematic alignment of cofactor binding domains of iNOS, eNOS, and nNOS. Note the N-terminal myristoylation of eNOS and extended N terminus of nNOS. (B) Alignment of the GLGC/dystrophin-binding domain of nNOS with syntrophins and a family of other cytoskeletal associated proteins. See text for abbreviations.

sents a unique eukaryotic cytochrome P450 pathway because the heme active site is present in the amino terminus of NOS, rather than a distinct polypeptide.[16] Transfer of electrons between the reductase and heme domains of NOS is regulated by calmodulin, which occupies a site between the two halves of the protein.[17]

Nitric oxide synthase gene products display significant heterogeneity only at their amino-terminal domains. This region of the proteins is involved in the unique subcellular distribution of NOS proteins. Tight regulation of NOS localization within cells is critical for restricting NOS actions to specific targets within a defined microenvironment, while also minimizing toxic actions of NO at inappropriate sites. Endothelial NOS localization to endothelial membranes is mediated by two fatty acid modifications.[18] Cotranslational N-terminal myristoylation of eNOS is necessary for membrane association. In addition, eNOS is posttranslationally palmitoylated by a dynamic process regulated by a specific agonist, bradykinin. Depalmitoylation of eNOS following bradykinin treatment of endothelial cells results in cytosolic translocation, phosphorylation, and downregulation of eNOS activity.

Neuronal NOS, which lacks consensus sequences for fatty acid modification, also occurs largely in particulate fractions.[19] The majority of nNOS immunoreactivity in neurons is associated with rough endoplasmic reticulum and specialized electron-dense synaptic membrane structures,[20] whereas in skeletal muscle nNOS is associated with the sarcolemma. It appears that determinant within the N terminus of nNOS, which are not present in the other NOS isoforms, likely account for selective sarcolemmal–cytoskeletal association. Within this N-terminal domain, nNOS contains a 66-amino acid motif that bears homology to a heterogeneous family of signaling enzymes which share the property of being localized to specialized cell–cell junctions (Fig. 1B). Proteins containing this motif, which was previously named GLGF for a conserved tetrapeptide, include the following: *dlg-1,* the product of the lethal discs–large tumor suppressor gene that localizes to the undercoat of the septate junction in *Drosophila;* disheveled (*dsh*), a gene required for planar cell polarity in *Drosophila;* PSD-95, a brain-specific protein that localizes to the postsynaptic density in mammals; ZO-1 and ZO-2, peripheral membrane proteins that localize to tight junctions (zona occludens) of epithelial and endothelial cells; and

[16] M. A. Marletta, *J. Biol. Chem.* **268,** 12231 (1993).
[17] H. M. Abu-Soud and D. J. Stuehr, *Proc. Natl. Acad. Sci. U.S.A.* **90,** 10769 (1993).
[18] L. J. Robinson, L. Busconi, and T. Michel, *J. Biol. Chem.* **270,** 995 (1995).
[19] M. Hecker, A. Mulsch, and R. Busse, *J. Neurochem.* **62,** 1524 (1994).
[20] C. Aoki, S. Fenstemaker, M. Lubin, and C. G. Go, *Brain Res.* **620,** 97 (1993).

certain protein tyrosine phosphatases, such as PTP1E, which are thought to localize at the junction between the plasma membrane and the cytoskeleton.[21–24]

The N-terminal domain shows highest homology to syntrophins (syn), a family of cloned dystrophin-binding proteins, that colocalize with nNOS beneath the sarcolemmal membrane of skeletal muscle.[25,26] The subcellular localization of nNOS in skeletal muscle is mediated by anchoring of nNOS to dystrophin,[27] the protein product of the gene mutated in Duchenne and Becker muscular dystrophy.[28,29] Skeletal muscle from patients with Duchenne muscular dystrophy and *mdx* mice, which lack skeletal muscle dystrophin, evince a selective loss of nNOS protein and catalytic activity from membrane and cytoskeletal fractions and an accumulation of nNOS in muscle cytosol.[27] Deregulation of nNOS disposition in dystrophic skeletal muscle may contribute to the pathophysiology of this disease. Interestingly, the subcellular distribution of nNOS in brain of dystrophic mice is unaltered, suggesting that proteins other than dystrophin anchor nNOS to neuronal membranes.[27]

Heterologous Expression of Nitric Oxide Synthase

Efficient methods for heterologous expression of NOS proteins are now being developed for overexpression and mutagenesis studies. All three NOS isoforms have been successfully transfected into mammalian cells, such as human embryonic kidney 293 cells and COS cells. These cell lines apparently make sufficient cofactors including tetrahydrobiopterin to support NOS activity. For reasons that remain unclear, the nNOS gene is expressed much more efficiently than eNOS or iNOS in mammalian cells (H. Xia and D. S. Bredt, personal observations). The following detailed protocol is used to express nNOS transiently in cultured cells. The expression vector, pcDNA III (Invitrogen, San Diego, CA), uses a high-efficiency

[21] D. F. Woods and P. J. Bryant, *Cell* (*Cambridge, Mass.*) **66,** 451 (1991).
[22] K. O. Cho, C. A. Hunt, and M. B. Kennedy, *Neuron* **9,** 929 (1992).
[23] L. A. Jesaitis and D. A. Goodenough, *J. Cell Biol.* **124,** 949 (1994).
[24] D. Banville, S. Ahmad, R. Stocco, and S. H. Shen, *J. Biol. Chem.* **269,** 22320 (1994).
[25] A. H. Ahn, M. Yoshida, M. S. Anderson, C. A. Feener, S. Selig, Y. Hagiwara, E. Ozawa, and L. M. Kunkel, *Proc. Natl. Acad. Sci. U.S.A.* **91,** 4446 (1994).
[26] M. E. Adams, M. H. Butler, T. M. Dwyer, M. F. Peters, A. A. Murnane, and S. C. Froehner, *Neuron* **11,** 531 (1993).
[27] J. E. Brenman, D. S. Chao, H. Xia, K. Aldape, and D. S. Bredt, *Cell* **82** (1995).
[28] K. Ohlendieck and K. P. Campbell, *J. Cell Biol.* **115,** 1685 (1991).
[29] J. M. Ervasti, K. Ohlendieck, S. D. Kahl, M. G. Gaver, and K. P. Campbell, *Nature* (*London*) **345,** 315 (1990).

cytomegalovirus promoter to drive transcription of rat nNOS.[9] Plasmid DNA must be of high purity for efficient transfection. DNA can be either banded with CsCl or purified by ion-exchange chromatography (Qiagen, Chatsworth, CA).

Calcium Phosphate-Mediated Transfection of Neuronal Nitric Oxide Synthase in Human Embryonic Kidney Cells

Reagents. HEPES-buffered saline (HBS) is prepared by dissolving NaCl (8.2 g), Na_2HPO_4 (0.20 g), and HEPES (5.94 g) into 800 ml of distilled water; the pH is adjusted to 7.1 with NaOH, the volume is brought to 1 liter, and the solution is sterilized through a 0.22-μm filter. The 2× HBS reagent is prepared identically except that the final volume is 0.5 liter. Glycerol (15%)/HBS is prepared by combining 30 ml of glycerol, 100 ml of 2× HBS, 70 ml of distilled water and sterilizing by filtration. Phosphate-buffered saline (PBS) is prepared by dissolving 8.0 g NaCl, 0.2 g KCl, 1.44 g Na_2PO_4, and 0.24 g KH_2PO_4 in 800 ml of distilled water. The pH is adjusted to 7.2, the volume is brought to 1 liter, and the solution is sterilized. Finally, 2 M $CaCl_2$ is prepared by adding 29.4 g $CaCl_2$ to 100 ml of distilled water followed by sterilization.

Procedure. Human embryonic kidney (HEK) 293 cells (American Type Culture Collection, Rockville, MD) are grown in Dulbecco's modified Eagle's medium (DMEM)/low glucose medium (GIBCO, Grand Island, NY) containing 10% fetal calf serum. The day prior to transfection cells are plated on 10-cm culture dishes at 10^6 cells/dish. Calcium phosphate precipitation of plasmid DNA is performed immediately prior to transfection. For each 10-cm dish to be transfected, combine 10 μg pcDNAIII/ nNOS DNA with 219 μl of sterile water and 31 μl of 2 M $CaCl_2$. To this mixture slowly add 250 μl of 2× HBS. This solution should become opalescent and should be allowed to form a precipitate for 5 min at room temperature. Drop the solution (0.5 ml/plate) onto HEK 293 cells containing 10 ml of medium and incubate at 37°. After 3–5 hr remove the medium and replace with 1 ml of 15% glycerol/HBS. After 1 min of glycerol shock, 9 ml of PBS should be added to each plate. The PBS is then aspirated, fresh medium is added, and cells are returned to the incubator.

Cells are harvested 48–72 hr after transfection. This protocol provides a convenient method for expressing moderate amounts of NOS protein (2–10 μg/dish) for biochemical and enzymatic assays. The HEK 293 cells serve as an appropriate host for transfection as these cells do not contain detectable NOS activity or immunoreactivity for known NOS proteins. Therefore, enzymatic assays of specific NOS isoforms can be conducted in crude transfected cell homogenates.

Assay of Nitric Oxide Synthase Activity in Transfected HEK 293 Cells

The NOS activity in transfected cells can be conveniently assayed by monitoring the conversion of [^{3}H]arginine to [^{3}H]citrulline, as this occurs stoichiometrically with the enzymatic formation of NO.

Reagents. Homogenization buffer contains 25 mM Tris, pH 7.4, 1 mM ethylenediaminetetraacetic acid (EDTA), and 1 mM ethylene glycol bis(β-aminoethyl ether)tetraacetic acid (EGTA). Radiolabeled arginine is also required. Prior to initiating enzyme assays it is essential to verify that the Dowex resin effectively retains the radioactive arginine substrate; otherwise, a high blank value will greatly reduce the sensitivity of the assay. To assess the blank value, 100 μl of reaction cocktail [25 mM Tris, pH 7.4, 1 μCi/ml of 10 μM [^{3}H]arginine (Amersham, Arlington Heights, IL) or [^{14}C]arginine, 3 μM tetrahydrobiopterin, 1 μM flavin adenine dinucleotide, 1 μM flavin adenine mononucleotide, 100 nM calmodulin, 1 mM NADPH (NADPH cannot be stored in solution for more than 24 hr] is applied to an equilibrated column of Dowex (see below). Nonadherent radioactivity is eluted with 4 ml of stop buffer [50 mM N-(2-hydroxyethylpiperazine-N'-(2-ethanesulfonic acid) (HEPES), pH 5.5, 5 mM EDTA], the flow-through is collected, and radioactivity is quantitated by scintillation counting. Greater than 99% of the applied radioactivity should be retained by the column, which represents a relatively low blank. If more than 1% of the counts flow through the column, it is important to purify the arginine prior to conducting assays. We find that [^{3}H]arginine is prone to radiolytic decay and must be purified every 2 months; [^{14}C]arginine is stable but much more expensive.

The strongly acidic cation exchanger Dowex 50X8-400 (Sigma, St. Louis, MO) is sold as the acidic (H$^+$) form and must be converted to the basic (Na$^+$) form before use. To exchange to the Na$^+$ form, resin is suspended in water stirred with a magnetic vortex mixer. Pellets of NaOH are added slowly until the pH of the resin exceeds pH 12.0. This basic mixture is stirred for 1 hr at room temperature. After this equilibration, the resin is neutralized by extensive washing with water. Washing can be carried out by transferring the resin to a large flask filled with water. After the beads settle, the water is decanted and fresh water is added. This procedure is repeated until the pH of the suspension is less than pH 8.0.

Separation of radiolabeled arginine from citrulline is done using disposable, polystyrene ion-exchange chromatography columns (Evergreen Scientific, Los Angeles, CA). For routine assays a 0.5-ml bed volume of Dowex (Na$^+$ form) is added to the column which is then equilibrated with 5 ml of stop buffer.

Tissue Preparation and Assay. Between 48 and 72 hr after transfection, cells are harvested in PBS (10 ml/plate), pelleted by centrifugation (1000 g

for 5 min), and resuspended in homogenization buffer (2 ml/plate). Tissue homogenates are disrupted with a Polytron (Brinkmann Instruments, Westbury, NY). For routine assays 25 μl of homogenate is added to 100 μl of reaction cocktail in a 12 × 75 mm borosilicate disposable culture tube. As nNOS requires calcium for enzyme activity, it is essential to add this ion. A 10-μl addition of 6 mM calcium yields a final free calcium concentration of approximately 75 μM which is optimal for NOS activity. Reaction incubations may be carried out for 10 min at 22°. Following this incubation, 4 ml of stop buffer is added to the reaction test tube, and the mixture is applied to 0.5-ml columns of Dowex equilibrated with stop buffer. The flow-through is collected into 20-ml scintillation vials that are filled with 16 ml biodegradable scintillation cocktail (Amersham) and counted.

Nitric oxide synthase activity in the citrulline assay is defined as counts per minute (cpm) in a test incubate as compared to an appropriate blank. Several control reactions can serve as a blank, including inclusion of a competitive NOS inhibitor (e.g., 1 mM nitro-L-arginine methyl ester), boiling of the extract prior to assay, omission of either NADPH or calcium from the reaction, and incubation of the reaction on ice. We usually define the blank in incubations in the presence of a competitive NOS inhibitor. As for any quantitative enzyme assay it is important to verify that reaction conditions are such that the assay is linear with respect to time and tissue concentration. We find that NOS activity in transfected HEK cell homogenates is linear for at least a 30-min reaction. Specific enzyme activity and substrate affinity of NOS can be assessed by carrying out replicate reactions in the presence of varying amounts of unlabeled arginine. As the K_m of nNOS is in the range of 2–5 μM, appropriate concentrations of arginine for kinetic studies are 0.1–30 μM.

Expression of Nitric Oxide Synthase Isoforms Using Baculovirus System

Baculovirus has been used to express larger quantities of active NOS. Functional expression of NOS proteins in this system require supplementation of the medium with hemin, riboflavin, nicotinic acid, and sepiapterin. Using this method to infect *Spodoptera frugiperda* cells in culture, NOS proteins have been expressed at levels up to 10% of the total soluble protein at 48 hr postinfection.[30-32] Thus far, full-length mammalian NOS proteins

---

[30] I. G. Charles, A. Chubb, R. Gill, J. Clare, P. N. Lowe, L. S. Holmes, M. Page, J. G. Keeling, S. Moncada, and V. Riveros-Moreno, *Biochem. Biophys. Res. Commun.* **196**, 1481 (1993).
[31] P. F. Chen, A. L. Tsai, and K. K. Wu, *J. Biol. Chem.* **269**, 25062 (1994).
[32] M. K. Richards and M. A. Marletta, *Biochemistry* **33**, 14723 (1994).

have not been functionally expressed in bacterial cells. Heterologous expression using a variety of methods in bacteria yields inactive insoluble NOS protein (H. Xia and D. S. Bredt, unpublished observations).

Mutagenesis and heterologous expression of NOS are also being used to dissect the specific residues important for cofactor interaction and catalysis. Whereas the reductase domain of NOS shows strong homology to cytochrome P450 reductase, the N-terminal half of NOS, the heme domain, is not broadly similar to any cloned gene. An important question relates to the region involved in heme coordination and arginine binding. Although the classic P450 heme-binding cysteinyl peptide sequence is absent in NOS, the amino acids surrounding Cys-415 of nNOS show some of the expected homology. Site-directed mutagenesis has been used to construct a C415H mutant. Expression of this mutant in a baculovirus system yields an nNOS protein that is devoid of heme and is catalytically inactive.[32] Mutation of the corresponding cysteine in eNOS, to form a C184A mutant, similarly resulted in loss of heme binding, indicating that this residue functions as a critical heme ligand in multiple NOS isoforms.[31] Future functional and structural studies of cloned and expressed NOS proteins should further elucidate the unique free radical enzymology involved in NO biosynthesis.

[43] Posttranslational Modifications of Endothelial Nitric Oxide Synthase

By Lisa J. Robinson, Pejman Ghanouni, and Thomas Michel

Introduction

The endothelial nitric oxide synthase (ecNOS) is regulated by a complex pattern of covalent modifications, including phosphorylation,[1] myristoylation,[2] and palmitoylation.[3] The dynamic regulation of ecNOS posttranslational modifications may be an important control point for NO-dependent signaling in the vascular wall. This chapter describes experimental protocols for the study of ecNOS modifications in cultured cells. These approaches may also be applicable in investigations of the posttranslational processing of other NOS isoforms. Both the neural (n) and inducible (i) NOS isoforms

[1] T. Michel, G. K. Li, and L. Busconi, *Proc. Natl. Acad. Sci. U.S.A.* **90,** 6252 (1993).
[2] L. Busconi and T. Michel, *J. Biol. Chem.* **268,** 8410 (1993).
[3] L. J. Robinson, L. Busconi, and T. Michel, *J. Biol. Chem.* **270,** 995 (1995).

METHODS IN ENZYMOLOGY, VOL. 268

have been shown to be phosphorylated in cell culture.[4] However, N-terminal myristoylation of these isoforms is highly unlikely, as they lack the obligate amino acid consensus sequence. Consensus sequences for protein palmitoylation are less well characterized, but no studies to date have reported palmitoylation of the other NOS isoforms. The possibility that the NO synthases undergo other covalent posttranslational modifications remains to be investigated.

Phosphorylation of Endothelial Nitric Oxide Synthase

Because many inter- and intracellular signaling pathways are modulated by reversible phosphorylation, we explored the possibility of regulated phosphorylation of ecNOS in endothelial cells. We found that ecNOS phosphorylation is stimulated by enzyme agonists, and by NO donors, suggesting that phosphorylation might play a role in product regulation of NOS.[1] In addition, phosphorylation of ecNOS is associated with translocation of this predominantly membrane-associated isoform to the cytosol.[1] Phosphorylation of all three NOS isoforms has now been demonstrated in cell culture.[4] Even the inducible isoform, which is importantly regulated at the transcriptional level, appears to undergo phosphorylation in cultured cells.[4] Phosphorylation of the neural NOS (nNOS) has been described in several reports,[5–8] although it has not yet been explicitly demonstrated in native cell types.

The functional consequences of NOS phosphorylation remain less well determined. Phosphorylation of nNOS has been hypothesized to inhibit enzyme activity.[7] For example, phorbol ester treatment, either of cultured cells stably transfected with nNOS or of endothelial cells, has been shown to decrease NO production and to increase NOS phosphorylation.[1,7,9] Furthermore, NOS activity in cultured gastric smooth muscle cells increases following treatment with the protein kinase C (PKC) inhibitor calphostin C.[10] These observations suggest that PKC phosphorylation causes NOS inhibition. However, the effects of both phorbol esters and

---

[4] C. Nathan and Q.-W. Xie, *J. Biol. Chem.* **269**, 13725 (1994).
[5] M. Nakane, J. Mitchell, U. Forstermann, and F. Murad, *Biochem. Biophys. Res. Commun.* **180**, 1396 (1991).
[6] B. Brune and E. G. Lapetina, *Biochem. Biophys. Res. Commun.* **181**, 921 (1991).
[7] D. S. Bredt, C. D. Ferris, and S. H. Snyder, *J. Biol. Chem.* **267**, 10976 (1992).
[8] T. M. Dawson, J. P. Steiner, V. L. Dawson, J. L. Dinerman, G. R. Uhl, and S. H. Snyder, *Proc. Natl. Acad. Sci. U.S.A.* **90**, 9808 (1993).
[9] H. Tsukahara, D. V. Gordienko, and M. S. Goligorsky, *Biochem. Biophys. Res. Commun.* **193**, 722 (1993).
[10] K. S. Murthy, J.-G. Jin, and G. M. Makhlouf, *Am. J. Physiol.* **266**, G161 (1994).

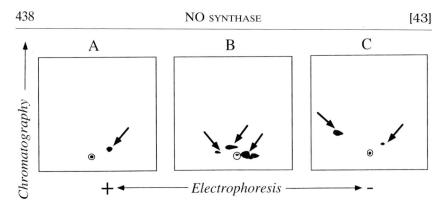

FIG. 1. Two-dimensional (2D) phosphopeptide mapping of ecNOS, phosphorylated (A) in bradykinin-treated bovine aortic endothelial cells,[1] (B) in phorbol ester-treated COS-7 cells transiently transfected with ecNOS cDNA,[2] or (C) *in vitro* using purified protein kinase C (Upstate Biotechnology, Lake Placid, NY) with recombinant ecNOS[11] as substrate. Cells were biosynthetically labeled with ortho[^{32}P]phosphoate, and ecNOS was processed for peptide mapping according to the protocols described in the text; *in vitro* phosphorylation with [γ-^{32}P]ATP was performed as described.[7] Samples were resolved by electrophoresis in the horizontal direction (anode at left) and then by ascending chromatography, as described in the text. The origin of sample application is circled; phosphopeptides are indicated with arrows.

PKC inhibitors on intact cells are pleiotropic: the change in NO production, and even the increase in NOS phosphorylation, may not reflect direct effects of PKC on NO synthase. Indeed, studies using purified PKC to phosphorylate nNOS *in vitro* have yielded variable results.[5,7] In part this may reflect the occurrence, *in vitro,* of additional phosphorylation reactions not occurring *in vivo.*

We have found that the phosphorylation of ecNOS *in vitro,* and even in heterologous cell types, may not accurately model the phosphorylation reactions occurring in endothelial cells. Figure 1 shows the differing tryptic phosphopeptide maps obtained from ecNOS phosphorylated in endothelial cells, in transiently transfected COS cells, and *in vitro* using purified PKC.[11] The results indicate that the sites of ecNOS phosphorylation under these various conditions are not identical, and that the characterization of ecNOS phosphorylation using these heterologous systems may be problematic. Such results underscore the importance of analyzing the pattern of NOS phosphorylation in native host cells. The following sections describe methods we have found useful in the characterization of ecNOS phosphorylation sites.

[11] L. Busconi and T. Michel, *Mol. Pharmacol.* **47**, 655 (1995).

Metabolic Labeling of Endothelial Nitric Oxide Synthase with Ortho[^{32}P]phosphate in Cell Culture

Although optimal labeling conditions may vary with the NOS isoform and host cell being studied, we have found the following method satisfactory for ^{32}P-labeling of ecNOS not only in bovine aortic endothelial cells (BAEC) but also in a variety of transfected [COS-7, CHO (Chinese hamster ovary)] cell types. Cultures of endothelial cells, or stably transfected heterologous cell lines, are labeled when confluent; transiently transfected cells are labeled 48 to 72 hr after transfection.

For labeling, cultures are washed twice with phosphate-free Dulbecco's modified Eagle's medium) (DMEM) (GIBCO–BRL, Gaithersburg, MD) then incubated at 37°, 5% (v/v) CO_2, and 100% humidity with ortho[^{32}P]phosphate. For 35-mm culture dishes we add 0.125 mCi of ortho[^{32}P]phosphate in 1 ml phosphate-free DMEM plus 10% dialyzed fetal calf serum and incubate for 4 hr. Effects of enzyme agonists or other drugs may be tested by addition, in small volumes, directly to the labeling medium (e.g., 10 μl of 1 mM bradykinin). Labeling is stopped by transferring the cultures to ice and removing the labeling medium. The cells are then washed twice with ice-cold phosphate-buffered saline (PBS), scraped into 1 ml PBS, and collected by low-speed centrifugation (1000 rpm for 5 min at 4° in a tabletop microcentrifuge). After removal of the supernatant, the cells are resuspended in buffer. When subcellular fractionation is to be performed, the cells are resuspended in 500 μl of a hypotonic, detergent-free buffer containing 10 mM Tris (pH 7.6 at 25°), 1 mM dithiothreitol (DTT), 0.1 mM EDTA, 0.1 mM EGTA, phosphatase inhibitors (50 mM NaF, 40 mM β-glycerophosphate), and protease inhibitors (10 μg/ml each of soybean trypsin inhibitor, lima bean trypsin inhibitor, antipain, and leupeptin); otherwise, the cells are resuspended directly in 1 ml of buffer B, which is 10 mM Tris (pH 7.6 at 25°), 1 mM EDTA, 0.1% sodium dodecyl sulfate (SDS), 1% sodium deoxycholate, 1% Triton X-100, phosphatase inhibitors (50 mM NaF, 500 μM sodium orthovanadate, 10 mM β-glycerophosphate), and protease inhibitors (10 μg/ml each of soybean trypsin inhibitor, lima bean trypsin inhibitor, antipain, and leupeptin).

The cells are incubated in these buffers on ice for 20 min and then, to complete cell lysis, are sonicated using a Branson Sonifier 450 (Branson Ultrasonic, Danbury, CT) for three 10-sec pulses. Following sonication, unbroken cells are removed by centrifugation at 1000 rpm for 5 min at 4°. The cleared cell lysate may then be analyzed further by subcellular fractionation and/or immunoprecipitation. Ultracentrifugation at 100,000 g for 60 min at 4° separates the cell lysate into soluble (cytosol) and particulate (membrane) fractions. The pelleted membrane fraction is solubilized in buffer B, and the soluble cytosolic fraction diluted 5-fold with buffer B, prior to immunoprecipitation.

Immunoprecipitation of ^{32}P-labeled Endothelial Nitric Oxide Synthase

For immunoprecipitation of ecNOS, our laboratory uses antisera directed against epitopes based on peptide sequences that are identical in human and bovine ecNOS, but significantly different from the homologous regions of nNOS and iNOS. We raise antipeptide antisera in rabbits, by standard techniques, against the keyhole limpet hemocyanin (KLH)-coupled oligopeptide epitopes PYNSSPRPEQHKSYK (amino acids 598–612) and VTSRIRTQSFSLQER (amino acids 1171–1185). Polyclonal and monoclonal antibodies to ecNOS are now commercially available and have also been reported to be effective for immunoprecipitation of the enzyme (Transduction Laboratories, Lexington, KY), but the optimal conditions for immunoprecipitation may differ from those described here.

Antisera is added to cleared cell lysates at a dilution of 1 : 100 (10 μl per 1 ml lysate from a 35-mm culture) and incubated overnight (12–16 hr) at 4° with continuous gentle agitation. Following this incubation, aggregated material is removed by centrifugation at 12,000 g for 10 min at 4°. To collect the immune complexes from 1 ml of supernatant, 50 μl of a 1 : 1 slurry of preswollen protein A–Sepharose in PBS is added. Protein A–Sepharose (Sigma, St. Louis, MO) is prepared as follows: 250 mg protein A–Sepharose is washed twice for 20 min in approximately 15 ml PBS at 4° with continuous agitation. It is then incubated in about 15 ml 2% (w/v) bovine serum albumin (BSA) in PBS overnight at 4°, again with continuous agitation, followed by three further 20-min washes in PBS at 4°. If the protein A–Sepharose is not adequately preswollen, there may be a marked increase in nonspecific binding with a consequent increase in background. Washing protein A–Sepharose in BSA also appears to help reduce background.

After addition of protein A–Sepharose, the lysates are incubated for a further 1.5 hr at 4° with gentle agitation, then centrifuged at 12,000 g for 20 sec at 4° to collect the protein A–Sepharose and bound immune complexes. The supernatant is removed, and the protein A–Sepharose/immune complexes are washed three times with buffer B, by incubating in 1 ml buffer B at 4° for 10 min with continuous agitation then collecting by centrifugation at 12,000 g, 4°, for 20 sec. This is followed by a fourth wash in 1 ml of 150 mM NaCl, 10 mM Tris (pH 7.6 at 25°), plus protease and phosphatase inhibitors as for buffer B.

After collecting the protein A–Sepharose plus immune complexes by centrifugation as before, ecNOS is released by boiling for 5 min in 50 μl SDS–polyacrylamide gel electrophoresis (SDS–PAGE) sample buffer [62.5

mM Tris-HCl (pH 6.8), 2% SDS, 10% glycerol, 5% 2-mercaptoethanol, and 0.003% bromphenol blue]. The ^{32}P-labeled, immunoprecipitated ecNOS can then be analyzed by SDS–PAGE and autoradiography, according to standard protocols, or it may be processed for phosphoamino acid analysis or phosphopeptide mapping as described in the following section.

Phosphopeptide and Phosphoamino Acid Analysis

Immunoprecipitated ^{32}P-labeled ecNOS may be prepared for phosphopeptide or phosphoamino acid analysis by precipitation with trichloroacetic acid (TCA) or by electrophoretic transfer to nitrocellulose or polyvinyldifluoride (PVDF) membranes (Millipore, Bedford, MA). For TCA precipitation, the immunoprecipitated, ^{32}P-labeled NOS in sample buffer is incubated on ice for 1 hr in 0.5 ml of ice-cold 25% (w/v) trichloroacetic acid, plus 25 μl of 1 mg/ml BSA (to serve as a carrier). The TCA-precipitated protein is collected by centrifugation at 12,000 g for 15 min at 4°. To remove residual TCA, the pellet is washed by addition of 0.5 ml of ice-cold 100% ethanol, followed by centrifugation at 12,000 g for 10 min at 4°. The precipitated protein is air dried and may then be processed for phosphoamino acid analysis or two-dimensional (2D) peptide mapping as previously described.[12]

Briefly, for phosphoamino acid analysis, the protein is incubated in 0.1 ml of 6 N HCl at 100° for 1 hr to effect partial acid hydrolysis. The products of acid hydrolysis are lyophilized using a SpeedVac (Savant, Hicksville, NY) and then resuspended in 5 μl of buffer containing 15 parts pH 1.9 buffer [for 1 liter, mix 25 ml formic acid (88%), 78 ml glacial acetic acid, and 897 ml distilled water] and 1 part phosphoamino acid standards (1.0 mg/ml each of phosphoserine, phosphothreonine, and phosphotyrosine). The samples are then analyzed by 2D high-voltage thin-layer electrophoresis at pH 1.9 and then at pH 3.5 using the Hunter thin-layer electrophoresis system (HTLE-7000, CBS Scientific, Del Mar, CA) as described in detail by Boyle et al.[12]

For phosphopeptide mapping, the TCA-precipitated protein is first treated with performic acid to oxidize methionine and cysteine residues to methionine sulfone and cysteic acid, respectively. Without performic acid oxidation, these amino acids may be variably oxidized during peptide mapping, thus creating oxidation isomers with differing mobilities on 2D mapping.[12] Performic acid is prepared fresh by combining 900 μl concentrated formic acid and 100 μl of 30% hydrogen peroxide and then chilling on ice. The protein sample is incubated on ice for 1 hr with 0.1 ml ice-cold performic

---

[12] W. J. Boyle, P. van der Geer, and T. Hunter, *Methods Enzymol.* **201**, 110 (1991).

acid. These conditions need to be carefully observed as prolonged exposure to performic acid or incubation at higher temperatures may result in cleavage of peptide bonds. After treatment with performic acid, the sample is frozen on dry ice, lyophilized to dryness (typically overnight), and then resuspended in 50 μl of 50 mM ammonium bicarbonate (pH 8–8.3). The sample may then be treated with proteases. For trypsin digestion, we add 10 μl of 1 mg/ml L-1-p-tosylamino-2-phenylethyl chloromethyl ketone (TPCK)-treated trypsin (Worthington Biochemical, Freehold, NJ). Following incubation at 37° for 4 hr, a second 10 μl of 1 mg/ml TPCK–trypsin is added, and the sample is incubated at 37° overnight (~16 hr). After trypsin digestion, the sample is diluted with 0.4 ml water, frozen on dry ice, and then lyophilized. The peptides are then washed with 0.3 ml water, vortexed for 1 min, and lyophilized. This is repeated twice, following which the lyophilized peptides are resuspended in 5 μl of pH 8.9 buffer (10 g/liter ammonium carbonate in water). The sample is then applied to cellulose thin-layer chromatography plates (EM Science, Gibbstown, NJ), and the peptides are separated by thin-layer electrophoresis, followed by ascending chromatography, as described in detail by Boyle et al.[12] For ecNOS, we have obtained the best resolution of phosphopeptides using chromatography buffer containing 785 ml n-butanol, 607 ml pyridine, 122 ml glacial acetic acid, and 486 ml deionized water, and, for electrophoresis, pH 8.9 buffer.

As an alternative to TCA precipitation, phosphorylated ecNOS may be prepared for phosphopeptide and phosphoamino acid analysis by electrophoretic transfer to nitrocellulose membranes, according to standard protocols for immunoblotting. The ^{32}P-labeled ecNOS is isolated by SDS–PAGE on a 7% gel, then electrophoretically transferred in a Bio-Rad (Richmond, CA) Trans-Blot apparatus. For ecNOS, we obtain the best efficiency of transfer using transfer buffer containing 25 mM CAPSO (pH 7.0) plus 20% (v/v) methanol at 30 V for approximately 16 hr at 4°. Following transfer, the phosphoprotein can be identified either by autoradiography or by standard Ponceau S protein staining, if the quantities of protein are sufficient. The filter is then washed with water, and the phosphoprotein band is excised and cut into small fragments (~2 mm^2) to facilitate digestion.

Phosphoamino acid analysis then proceeds as for TCA-precipitated proteins with addition of 100 μl of 6 N HCl to the membrane fragments and incubation at 100° for 1 hr. After brief centrifugation to pellet the filter fragments, the released phosphoamino acids are transferred to a fresh tube and then lyophilized, resuspended in 5 μl pH 1.9 buffer with phosphoamino acid standards, and analyzed by 2D thin-layer electrophoresis as described above.

The protocol for protease digestion of electroblotted rather than TCA-precipitated phosphoproteins differs in that the immobilized protein is treated with proteases first, and the resulting peptides are eluted from the filter prior to performic acid oxidation. This is necessary as oxidation of the protein on the filter may inhibit the elution of phosphopeptides. Release of peptides may also be enhanced by soaking the filter in 0.5% polyvinylpyrrolidone (PVP)-360 in 100 mM acetic acid at 37° for 30 min before protease digestion.[13] For trypsin digestion, the filter fragments containing the immobilized protein are treated with 10 μg TPCK–trypsin in 100 μl of 50 mM ammonium bicarbonate (pH 8.0) at 37° for 4 hr, followed by addition of another 10 μl of 1 mg/ml TPCK–trypsin and further incubation at 37° overnight (~16 hr). The trypsin digest is then diluted by addition of 0.4 ml of water and centrifuged briefly in a microcentrifuge to collect the filter fragments, and the supernatant containing the released peptides is transferred to a new tube. After lyophilization, the peptides are oxidized by addition of 100 μl ice-cold performic acid and incubated for 1 hr on ice. The oxidized peptides are then lyophilized, washed three times as described above with 0.3 ml water (to remove residual performic acid), and resuspended in 5 μl of pH 8.9 buffer for 2D mapping.

We have found the quantities of ecNOS protein obtained from 35-mm culture dishes adequate for 2D phosphopeptide mapping. Characterization of tryptic phosphopeptides by other chromatographic methods, for example, by reversed-phase high-performance liquid chromatography (HPLC), also appears feasible. However, it is difficult to obtain from BAEC cultures the quantities of phosphorylated ecNOS required for preparative HPLC and amino acid sequence determination (detailed protocols for these methods may be found in Stone et al.,[14] Aebersold,[15] and Wettenhall et al.[16]).

Phosphorylation of NOS may also be analyzed by chemical digestion of ^{32}P-labeled protein using cyanogen bromide.[17] Cyanogen bromide, which cleaves proteins at methionine residues, typically generates larger peptides that may be analyzed by SDS–PAGE. For cyanogen bromide digestion we obtain significantly better results by transferring the phosphorylated ecNOS to PVDF membranes, rather than using the TCA-precipitated protein. After electrophoretic transfer, using the conditions described above, the

[13] K. Luo, T. R. Hurley, and B. M. Sefton, Methods Enzymol. 201, 149 (1991).
[14] K. L. Stone, M. B. LoPresti, J. M. Crawford, R. DeAngelis, and K. R. Williams, in "A Practical Guide to Protein and Peptide Purification for Microsequencing" (P. T. Matsudaira, ed.), p. 33. Academic Press, San Diego, 1989.
[15] R. Aebersold, in "A Practical Guide to Protein and Peptide Purification for Microsequencing" (P. T. Matsudaira, ed.), p. 73. Academic Press, San Diego, 1989.
[16] R. E. H. Wettenhall, R. H. Aebersold, and L. E. Hood, Methods Enzymol. 201 (Part B), 186 (1991).
[17] N. LeGendre and P. Matsudaira, in "A Practical Guide to Protein and Peptide Purification for Microsequencing" (P. T. Matsudaira, ed.), p. 52. Academic Press, San Diego, 1989.

phosphoprotein band is excised and cut into small fragments that are then incubated overnight (~16 hr) at room temperature and protected from light in 250 μl of freshly prepared 0.15 M cyanogen bromide in 70% formic acid. Following digestion, the filter fragments are lyophilized, washed once by addition of 50 μl water, and lyophilized again. The dried filter fragments are then incubated at room temperature for 90 min in 50 μl of 2% SDS, 1% Triton-X100 in 50 mM Tris (pH 9.2–9.5) to elute the peptides. A pH of 9.0 or higher appears to be necessary for complete release of peptides. The sample is then centrifuged briefly to pellet the filter fragments, and the supernatant containing the peptides is transferred to a new tube. After addition of 25 μl of 87.5 mM Tris-HCl (pH 6.8), 2% SDS, 30% glycerol, 15% 2-mercaptoethanol, and 0.009% bromphenol blue, the sample is boiled for 5 min and then analyzed by SDS–PAGE (15% acrylamide gel) and autoradiography.

Acylation of Endothelial Nitric Oxide Synthase

In addition to phosphorylation, the endothelial NOS is modified by two distinct acylation reactions: N-myristoylation and palmitoyl thioester formation.[2,3] Myristoylation is a cotranslational modification catalyzed by N-myristoyltransferase, whereby myristic acid is linked to the N terminus of proteins via amide formation (for a review, see Resh[18]). This bond is highly stable and generally irreversible under physiological conditions. Myristoylation has been suggested to play a role in the membrane association of a variety of proteins, including some G-protein α subunits and *src*-related tyrosine kinases. Endothelial NOS is myristoylated at glycine-2 (after removal of the initial methionine residue), within a consensus sequence for protein N-myristoylation: MGXXXS.[2] Analysis of a myristoylation-deficient mutant of ecNOS revealed that this modification is also critical for targeting ecNOS to cell membranes. However, a fraction of wild-type ecNOS, although also myristoylated, is found in the cytosol of endothelial cells, and the proportion of cytosolic enzyme increases on treatment with enzyme agonists, without concomitant loss of myristate. These results suggest that factors other than myristoylation are involved in regulating the subcellular distribution of the enzyme. Furthermore, thermodynamic studies of myristoylated peptides and proteins have indicated that their interactions with lipid bilayers are readily reversible; other hydrophobic or electrostatic interactions with membrane phospholipids appear to be necessary for stabilizing the membrane association of myristoylated proteins.[18]

---

[18] M. D. Resh, *Cell (Cambridge, Mass.)* **76,** 411 (1994).

It has been shown that ecNOS is also modified by addition of palmitic acid, which may provide additional hydrophobic interactions with membranes.[3] Palmitic acid is linked to cysteine residues via postranslational fatty acid thioester formation, which is catalyzed by as yet uncharacterized palmitoylthiotransferases. Unlike the amide bond of myristolyation, the thioester linkage of palmitoylation is reversible; its cleavage is catalyzed by an unknown palmitoylthioesterase.[18] Thus, protein palmitoylation is potentially subject to dynamic regulation. It has been shown that agonists regulate palmitoylation of some receptors and G-protein α subunits.[19,20] Palmitoylation of ecNOS is also regulated: specifically, depalmitoylation of ecNOS is stimulated by enzyme agonists known to promote dissociation of ecNOS from cell membranes.[3] This second acylation may thus underlie the ability of the enzyme to form stable, but dynamically regulated, associations with cell membranes. The next sections describe methods useful in the identification and analysis of lipid modifications of NOS.

Metabolic Labeling of Endothelial Nitric Oxide Synthase with Tritiated Fatty Acids

Protein acylation may be demonstrated by metabolic labeling with tritiated fatty acids. Labeling with tritiated fatty acids can be more difficult to detect not only because of the lower energy of tritium radiation but also because of the relatively large pool of unlabeled fatty acids in cells. To obtain an adequate signal we generally use 60-mm culture dishes of BAEC at confluency or COS-7 cells 48–72 hr after transfection. Cultures are washed twice in 3 ml of DMEM plus 5% dialyzed fetal calf serum (FCS) before addition of labeling medium. To prepare [³H]myristate labeling medium, tritiated myristic acid in ethanol (Amersham, Arlington Heights, IL; 50 Ci/mmol, 1 mCi/ml) is concentrated by drying under a stream of air to about 5% of the original volume and then added to DMEM plus 5% dialyzed FCS at a final concentration of 0.2 mCi/ml. Because myristoylation is a cotranslational modification, only newly synthesized protein will be labeled. Thus, a relatively long labeling period is required for an adequate signal. Cultures are therefore incubated in 2 ml of [³H]myristate labeling medium at 37°, 5% (v/v) CO_2, and 100% humidity overnight (~16 hr). For labeling with tritiated palmitic acid, we use [³H]palmitic acid from NEN–DuPont (Boston, MA; 40–60 Ci/mmol, 5 mCi/ml in ethanol). This is concentrated by drying under a stream of air to about 5% of the original volume and then added to DMEM plus 5% dialyzed fetal calf serum at a

---

[19] B. Mouillac, M. Caron, H. Bonin, M. Dennis, and M. Bouvier, *J. Biol. Chem.* **267**, 21733 (1992).
[20] P. B. Wedegaertner, P. T. Wilson, and H. R. Bourne, *J. Biol. Chem.* **270**, 503 (1995).

final concentration of 1 mCi/ml. A higher concentration of tritiated palmitic acid is used because of the larger cellular pool of palmitate compared to myristate. However, the turnover of ecNOS-associated palmitate is rapid enough to permit a relatively short incubation time of about 2 hr. Labeling is stopped by transfer of the cultures onto ice and removal of labeling medium.

Pharmacological agents can be tested for their effects on acylation of ecNOS by addition, in small volumes, directly to the labeling medium. Short-term effects of agonists and other drugs on protein palmitate turnover may be difficult to detect if these compounds are added after [³H]palmitate labeling of ecNOS has reached steady state (~2 hr). Although drug effects on [³H]palmitate incorporation into NOS may be more easily discerned prior to steady state, the concurrent changes in specific activity of the labeled intracellular palmitate pool may complicate the interpretation of results. On the other hand, pulse–chase experiments can be designed more selectively to quantitate protein depalmitoylation, using the following protocol.

For pulse–chase experiments, cultures are labeled as above with 2 ml of [³H]palmitate labeling medium (1 mCi/ml [³H]palmitic acid in DMEM plus 5% dialyzed FCS) for 2 hr at 37°. Following this incubation, the labeling medium is removed, and the cultures are washed and then incubated in DMEM plus 10% FCS supplemented with 100 μM unlabeled palmitic acid. Drugs potentially influencing depalmitoylation may be added to this washing medium. The incubation is stopped by placing the cultures on ice and harvesting the cells.

The cells containing ³H-labeled fatty acids are then washed, collected, and lysed, as described above for ³²P-labeled cultures (except that the buffers need not contain phosphatase inhibitors). Immunoprecipitation of ecNOS is also performed as described above except for one modification: [³H]palmitate-labeled ecNOS is eluted from protein A–Sepharose in SDS–PAGE sample buffer containing 5 mM dithiothreitol rather than 5% 2-mercaptoethanol. Use of higher concentrations of reducing agents at any point in the processing of [³H]palmitate-labeled proteins may result in significant loss of label due to cleavage of the labile thioester bond. Complete omission of reducing agents from sample buffer is also not desirable, however, as it may result in anomalous migration of proteins on SDS–PAGE. Following staining and fixation, the gels are soaked in fluor (EN³HANCE, NEN–DuPont) for 20 min at room temperature (for 0.75-mm, 7% acrylamide gels), then washed and exposed to high-speed X-ray film with intensifier screens at −70°.

Analysis of the results of these labeling experiments is complicated by the possibility of cellular metabolism of the added ³H-labeled fatty acid, which may create other radioactive species that could be incorporated into proteins. In particular, myristic and palmitic acids are readily intercon-verted; metabolism to amino acids is also possible. Thus, it is important to confirm the identity of the protein-bound label, for example, by acid hydro-lysis and thin-layer chromatography, as described in the next section. Using the labeling protocols described above, we have never detected incorpora-tion of any species other than the ^{3}H-labeled fatty acid originally added. If metabolism to amino acids causes spurious labeling, it may be helpful to increase the concentration of nonessential amino acids in the labeling medium.[21]

Analysis of Protein-Bound Fatty Acids

Amide- and ester-linked fatty acid modifications of proteins may be readily distinguished by their differing susceptibility to hydroxylamine cleavage. Amide bonds, characteristic of protein N-myristoylation, are resis-tant to hydroxylamine, whereas thioester-linked fatty acids, such as palmi-tate, are released by hydroxylamine treatment at neutral pH.[22] Hydroxyl-amine treatment of ^{3}H-fatty acid labeled proteins may be performed following SDS–PAGE analysis of the immunoprecipitated proteins. When testing the hydroxylamine sensitivity of ^{3}H-fatty acid labeled NOS, two aliquots of the labeled, immunoprecipitated protein are subjected to SDS–PAGE 0.75 mm, 7% gel). The replicate lanes are cut apart and incubated, at room temperature for 4 hr with continuous agitation, in either 1 M hy-droxylamine hydrochloride (pH 7.0) or 1 M Tris (pH 7.0). The hydroxyl-amine solution should be prepared fresh as it is unstable at pH 7.0. The gels are then processed for fluorography as before. Labeling will be observed on both gels when amide-linked tritiated fatty acids are present; when there are only thioester-linked tritiated fatty acids, labeling will be observed after incubation in Tris but not after exposure to hydroxylamine.

To determine the identity of the bound tritiated fatty acid we use a protocol modified from Paiges *et al.*[23] The ecNOS immunoprecipitated from lysates of 100-mm cultures, following metabolic labeling with tritiated myristic or palmitic acid, is isolated by SDS–PAGE then electrophoretically transferred to PVDF as described above for ^{32}P-labeled protein. The protein band is excised from the filter, cut into small fragments, and transferred to a glass tube. The membrane fragments are then subjected to vapor-phase acid hydrolysis with 6 N HCl at 110° for 16 hr *in vacuo*, which will

---

[21] W. J. Masterson and A. I. Magee, *in* "Protein Targeting: A Practical Approach" (A. I. Magee and T. Wileman, eds.), p. 233. Oxford Univ. Press, Oxford, 1992.

[22] D. A. Towler and J. I. Gordon, *Annu. Rev. Biochem.* **57**, 69 (1988).

[23] L. A. Paiges, M. J. S. Nadler, M. L. Harrison, J. M. Cassady, and R. L. Geahlen, *J. Biol. Chem.* **268**, 8669 (1993).

cleave both amide and ester bonds.[22] To recover the released fatty acids, toluene (0.3 ml) is added to the acid-treated fragments. The tube is vortexed for 1 min, and then the toluene is transferred to a fresh tube. This is repeated twice. The toluene washes are pooled and dried under nitrogen. Then 100 μl of 100% ethanol is added, and the tube is vortexed to redissolve the fatty acids. After drying under nitrogen to reduce the volume to approximately 10 μl, the sample is applied to a C_{18} reversed-phase thin-layer chromatography plate (Whatman, Clifton, NJ). Samples of authentic ^{3}H-labeled fatty acids (~0.01 μCi each) are run in parallel as standards. The plate is developed with 1:1 (v/v) acetonitrile/acetic acid, then dried, sprayed with EN^{3}HANCE, and exposed to high-speed X-ray film at $-70°$ with intensifier screens. The identity of the labeled species released from the protein can then be determined by comparing its mobility to that of the known standards.

Conclusion

In this chapter, we have described techniques useful in the analysis of ecNOS phosphorylation, myristoylation, and palmitoylation. As discussed above, it is critical to correlate the pattern of enzyme modifications seen *in vitro,* or in heterologous cell systems, with those observed in native cell types. Biosynthetic labeling and immunoprecipitation are powerful experimental approaches in the analysis of ecNOS posttranslational modifications and methods similar to the ones described above may prove useful in the investigation of other NOS isoforms, as well as in further studies of ecNOS regulation both in endothelial and nonendothelial cells.

Acknowledgments

These studies were supported by grants from the National Institutes of Health (HL46457 and HL09172) and from the American Heart Association. T. M. is a Wyeth-Ayerst Established Investigator of the American Heart Association.

[44] Expression of Human Nitric Oxide Synthase Isozymes

By Ian G. Charles, Carol A. Scorer, María Ángeles Moro,
Conchita Fernàndez, Ann Chubb, John Dawson, Neale Foxwell,
Richard G. Knowles, and Sally A. Baylis

Introduction

Nitric oxide (NO), a relatively recently identified messenger molecule, has been found to play diverse roles in biology including neurotransmission, mediation of vasodilation, and host defense.[1] Nitric oxide is generated from L-arginine by a family of enzymes known as NO synthases (NOS; EC 1.14.13.39). To date, the analysis of NOS cDNAs has indicated the existence of three different isoforms which map to three distinct chromosomal locations[2,3]: the three isozymes have been described as the neuronal (nNOS; NOS1) and endothelial (eNOS; NOS3) forms, which are usually expressed constitutively, and the cytokine-inducible form (iNOS; NOS2).[4] The nNOS and eNOS isozymes are highly regulated by Ca^{2+} and calmodulin, whereas the iNOS has calmodulin tightly bound. Nitric oxide synthases are heme proteins that also contain tightly bound FAD and FMN and require tetrahydrobiopterin for activity, while NADPH is utilized as a substrate.

The isolation of cDNAs encoding all three forms has led to the generation of mammalian cell lines expressing the proteins.[5–7] The levels of NOS protein obtained from such cell lines has, however, been quite low. To obtain higher amounts of recombinant NOS for biochemical studies we have previously expressed both the rat nNOS cDNA and the murine iNOS

---

[1] S. Moncada, R. M. J. Palmer, and E. A. Higgs, *Pharmacol. Rev.* **43,** 109 (1991).
[2] W. Xu, P. Gorman, D. Sheer, G. Bates, J. Kishimoto, L. Lizhi, and P. Emson, *Cytogenet. Cell Genet.* **64,** 62 (1993).
[3] W. Xu, I. G. Charles, S. Moncada, P. Gorman, D. Sheer, L. Liu, and P. Emson, *in* "The Biology of Nitric Oxide" (S. Moncada *et al.,* eds.), p. 121. Portland Press, London and Chapel Hill, North Carolina, 1995.
[4] R. G. Knowles and S. Moncada, *Biochem. J.* **298,** 249 (1994).
[5] I. G. Charles, R. M. J. Palmer, M. Hickory, M. T. Bayliss, A. P. Chubb, V. S. Hall, D. W. Moss, and S. Moncada, *Proc. Natl. Acad. Sci. U.S.A.* **90,** 11419 (1993).
[6] S. P. Janssens, A. Shimouchi, T. Quertermous, D. B. Bloch, and K. D. Bloch, *J. Biol. Chem.* **267,** 14519 (1992).
[7] M. Nakane, H. H. H. W. Schmidt, J. S. Pollock, U. Förstermann, and F. Murad, *FEBS Lett.* **316,** 175 (1993).

cDNA in a baculovirus-directed insect cell expression system.[8,9] The purified nNOS and iNOS recombinant proteins have been found to have properties highly similar to those of the native enzymes,[9,10] with the advantage of producing higher levels of protein (e.g., 30 mg of soluble nNOS per liter of culture).

This chapter describes how the human family of NO synthases can be isolated, cloned, and expressed in insect cell lines. The ready availability of NOS enzyme generated by this system will aid in the biochemical characterization of NOS and will assist in the screening of compounds with inhibitory activity against the NOS family that may have significant therapuetic value.

cDNA Library Screening, and Construction of Expression Vectors for Human Nitric Oxide Synthases

Inducible Nitric Oxide Synthase

A cDNA encoding human iNOS has been isolated from a λZAP II library prepared from poly(A)⁺ mRNA isolated from interleukin-1β-treated human chondrocytes.[5] An iNOS-containing fragment has been conveniently excised as an *Xba*I fragment (Fig. 1a) and ligated into the baculovirus transfer vector pVL1393 (Invitrogen, San Diego, CA) as reported previously.[11] All DNA manipulations are as previously described.[5]

Endothelial Nitric Oxide Synthase

The full-length eNOS cDNA is constructed from two overlapping clones isolated from human placenta and endothelial cell cDNA libraries with the 5' end isolated as a PCR (polymerase chain reaction) product from human umbilical vein endothelial cells (HUVECs). A probe is derived from a human placenta cDNA library using PCR with eNOS-specific primers: 5'-CAGTGTCCAACATGCTGCTGGAAATTG (sense) and 5'-TAAAGG-TCTTCTTCCTGGTGATGCC (antisense). The primers are based on the

[8] I. G. Charles, A. Chubb, R. Gill, J. Clare, P. N. Lowe, L. S. Holmes, M. Page, J. G. Keeling, S. Moncada, and V. Riveros-Moreno, *Biochem. Biophys. Res. Commun.* **196,** 1481 (1993).

[9] D. W. Moss, X. Wei, F. Y. Liew, S. Moncada, and I. G. Charles, *Eur. J. Pharmacol.* **289,** 41 (1995).

[10] V. Riveros-Moreno, B. Heffernan, A. Chubb, B. Torres, I. Charles, and S. Moncada, *Eur. J. Biochem.* **230,** 52 (1995).

[11] I. G. Charles, M. Page, C. Scorer, R. Knowles, N. Foxwell, L. S. Holmes, A. Chubb, R. J. M. Palmer, and S. Moncada, in "The Biology of Nitric Oxide" (S. Moncada *et al.*, eds.), p. 316. Portland Press, London and Chapel Hill, North Carolina, 1995.

[12] J. L. Marsh, M. Erfle, and E. J. Wyles, *Gene* **32,** 481 (1984).

published eNOS sequence.[6] A 485-bp product is amplified by 35 cycles of the following sequential steps: 96° for 35 sec, 56° for 2 min, and 72° for 2 min. The PCR product is cloned into pT7Blue (Novagen, Madison, WI), and a BamHI/NdeI fragment is used to screen a human placenta λgt11 cDNA library. A 3555-bp fragment of eNOS is isolated, the 5′ end of which maps to base 470 of the published protein sequence.[6] The 3555-bp band is excised as an EcoRI fragment and cloned into the EcoRI site of pUC18 to generate the plasmid pUCeNOS1.

Further clones are isolated by screening a human endothelial cell λgt11 cDNA library using a second PCR fragment generated using the following eNOS-specific primers: 5′-CAAGTTCCCTCGTGTGAAGAACTG (sense) and 5′-GGAGCTGTAGTACTGGTTGATGAAGTC (antisense). A 214-bp product is amplified by 35 cycles of the same sequential steps described above. The product is cloned into pT7Blue as before, and a BamHI/NdeI fragment is used to screen a human endothelial λgt11 cDNA library. A 1988-bp fragment of eNOS is isolated as an EcoRI fragment, the 5′ end of which maps to base 162 of the coding sequence.[6] This EcoRI fragment is subcloned into the EcoRI site of pUC18, and a HindIII/BsmI fragment of approximately 700 bp is isolated and cloned into HindIII/BsmI cut pUCeNOS1 to create the plasmid pUCeNOS2, which contains 3863 bp of the eNOS cDNA with the 5′ end mapping to nucleotide 162 of the eNOS coding sequence.[6]

The 5′ end of the eNOS cDNA is obtained by RNA-PCR using mRNA isolated from HUVECs. The primers 5′-GTAACATGGGCAACTTGAA-GAGCGTG (sense) and 5′-GGAGCTGTAGTACTGGTTGAT-GAAGTC (antisense) are used in a PCR to amplify reverse-transcribed HUVEC mRNA. Amplification by PCR is performed as above. The 415-bp PCR fragment is subcloned into pT7Blue to create the plasmid pT7eN-OS3WT. The 5′ end of eNOS is excised from pT7eNOS3WT as an EcoRI/ScaI fragment; this is ligated together with a 3.6-kb eNOS EcoRI/ScaI fragment from pUCeNOS2 into EcoRI-cut pBluescript II SK (+). The fully assembled eNOS cDNA has been sequenced and found to be identical to the original published sequence[6] except for two nucleotides: a nucleotide substitution at position 1997 (G for C, not affecting the amino acid encoded) and a deletion of a C residue 278 bp beyond the translational stop codon in the 3′ untranslated region.

For expression, the full-length eNOS coding region is excised from pBluescript II SK (+) as a 4-kb EcoRI fragment and cloned into the EcoRI site of the baculovirus transfer vector pVL1393 to create the plasmid pVLeNOSWT (Fig. 1b). The PCR is used to abolish the eNOS myristoyla-tion site and convert the glycine residue at position 2 in the coding sequence to an alanine by the use of a mutagenic primer where the glycine codon

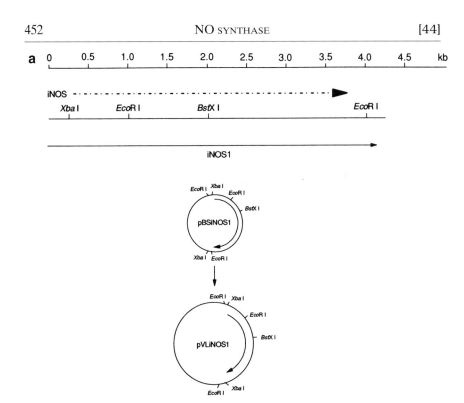

Fig. 1. Cloning of full-length human NO synthase cDNAs and their ligation into the baculovirus transfer vector pVL1393 for subsequent expression studies. (a) Cloning of the human iNOS cDNA. A clone encompassing the entire open reading frame (ORF) for iNOS was obtained from a human chondrocyte cDNA library as previously described[5] and ligated as an XbaI fragment into the baculovirus transfer vector pVL1393 (Invitrogen). Recombinant baculovirus expressing iNOS was generated using Baculogold transfection reagents (Pharmingen) in accordance with the manufacturer's instructions. (b) Cloning of full-length native and mutant forms of human eNOS. The full-length eNOS cDNA was constructed as described in the text. Wild-type eNOS and a mutant form of eNOS with the myristoylation site abolished were transferred into the vector pVL1393 (pVLeNOSWT and pVLeNOSΔ, respectively) for expression studies. (c) Cloning of full-length human nNOS into the baculovirus expression vector pVL1393. Four positive clones from a human cerebellum cDNA library (pBSnNOS1, pBSnNOS2, pBSnNOS3, and pBSnNOS4) were ligated together with the PCR cloned 5′ fragment (pT78nNOS5) to generate the full-length ORF (pVLnNOS1) that was used to generate an nNOS-expressing recombinant baculovirus.

GGC is altered to alanine G<u>CC</u>. An XbaI site is introduced at the 5′ end of the coding sequence to facilitate subsequent cloning of the fragment. The plasmid pT7eNOSWT is used as a template, and the following primers are used in the PCR: 5′-CCC<u>TCTAGA</u>ACATGGC<u>C</u>AACTTGAA-GAGCGTG (sense) and 5′-GGAGCTGTAGTACTGGTTGAT-

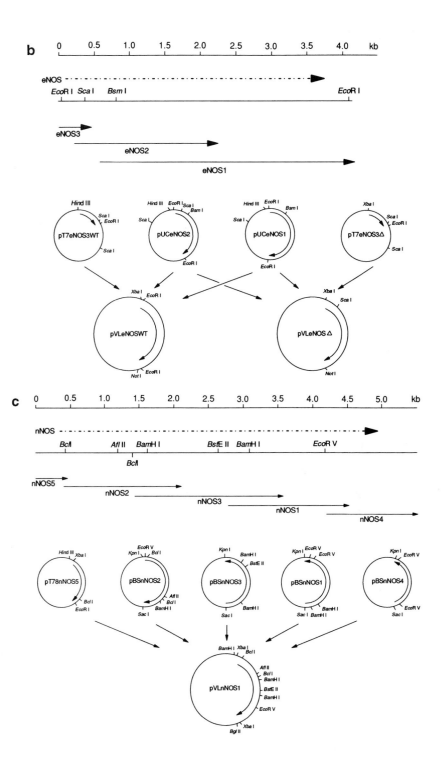

GAAGTC (antisense). The underlined regions represent the *Xba*I site, the initiation codon, and the site-directed change. The PCR is performed as before, and the 423-bp product is cloned into pT7Blue to create the plasmid pT7eNOS3Δ, and sequenced. The mutated 5' end of the eNOS cDNA is excised from pT7eNOS3Δ as an approximately 400-bp *Xba*I/*Sca*I fragment and ligated together with a *Sca*I/*Not*I fragment of approximately 3.5-kb from the full-length eNOS cDNA from pBluescript II SK (+) and cloned into *Xba*I/*Not*I digested pVL1393. The final plasmid pVLeNOSΔ with the myristoylation site abolished is used in subsequent expression studies.

Neuronal Nitric Oxide Synthase

Four clones isolated from a human brain cDNA library (nNOS1 to nNOS4, spanning most of the coding region of nNOS; see Fig. 1c) are cloned into pBluescript II SK (+) at the *Eco*RI site of the polylinker, yielding pBSnNOS1 to pBSnNOS4 respectively. The extreme 5' region, which is isolated by PCR using primers based on the published sequence,[7] is cloned directly into pT7Blue, yielding pT78nNOS5 (Fig. 1c). The full-length nNOS cDNA is then constructed in pT7Blue using restriction sites in overlapping regions of the clones. These sites, and the sites at the ends of the polylinkers [*Sac*I and *Kpn*I for pBlueScript II SK (+) and *Hin*dIII and *Eco*RI for pT7Blue] are shown for orientation. The full-length clone in pT7Blue is transferred to pIC20H[11] as an *Xba*I–*Kpn*I fragment using a *dam*+ host strain. The nNOS cDNA is then excised as an *Xba*I fragment using a *dam*- host strain. This is cloned into *Xba*I-cut pVL1393 to yield pVLnNOS1.

Cell and Virus Maintenance

Spodoptera frugiperda Sf21, fall armyworm ovary) cells are maintained as described previously.[8] Essentially, the cells are grown at 18° in TC-100 medium supplemented with 10% (v/v) heat-inactivated fetal calf serum, 2 m*M* glutamine, antibiotic–antimycotic solution, and 20 μg/ml gentamicin (all from GIBCO, Grand Island, NY). Cells are maintained in spinner flasks at 2×10^5 to 1×10^6 cells/ml by subculturing every 3–4 days. Virus stocks are maintained by infecting *Sf*21 cells in monolayers (5×10^7 cells per 150-cm² flask) with a multiplicity of infection (m.o.i) of 5–10. The flasks are incubated with virus at 28° for 1 hr before adding 50 ml of complete medium and continuing the incubation for 4 days. Medium is removed, centrifuged at 200 *g* for 5 min and the supernatant stored at 4°.

Expression

Optimum conditions for expression of active enzyme are determined to be as follows.

1. Neuronal NOS is expressed in $Sf21$ cells growing in suspension. The cell suspension is centrifuged at 200 g for 5 min, the medium removed, and the cells resuspended in virus stock at an m.o.i of 5–10. The cell suspension is incubated with virus for 1 hr at 28° and then diluted with fresh medium to give 10^6 cells/ml and incubation continued in spinner flasks for 48 hr.

2. Endothelial NOS is expressed in monolayers on 500-cm^2 plates. Cells are infected for 48 hr with the addition of 0.5 μg/ml hemin, 5 μM nicotinic acid, 1 μM riboflavin, and 10 μM sepiapterin to the medium.

3. Inducible NOS is expressed in monolayers on 500-cm^2 plates. Cells are infected for 24 hr with 2.5 μg/ml hemin in arginine-free TC-100 medium (plus dialyzed serum).

Extraction

Cells containing nNOS, from suspension cultures, are centrifuged at 200 g for 5 min and washed twice with Dulbecco's phosphate-buffered saline (PBS). The cell pellet is resuspended (10^8 cells/ml) in ice-cold extraction buffer containing 320 mM sucrose, 50 mM Tris, 1 mM EDTA, 1 mM DL-dithiothreitol (DTT), 100 μg/ml phenylmethylsulfonyl fluoride (PMSF), 10 μg/ml leupeptin, 10 μg/ml soybean trypsin inhibitor, and 2 μg/ml aprotinin (brought to pH 7.0 at 20° with HCl).

Cells containing iNOS and eNOS, from monolayer cultures, are scraped into the same extraction buffer as above with the flasks held on ice. The cells (expressing iNOS, eNOS, or nNOS) are lysed by sonication with three 10-sec bursts (amplitude 14 μm) using an MSE Soniprep 150 Ultrasonic Disintegrator. The lysed cells are then centrifuged at 40,000 g for 30 min at 4° to remove insoluble material. To the supernatant, 0.1 ml of 2′,5′-ADP–agarose (Sigma, St. Louis, MO) previously equilibrated in buffer A [50 mM HEPES, pH 7.5, 10 mM dithiothreitol, 10% (v/v) glycerol, 0.5 μM leupeptin, 0.5 μM pepstatin, 10 μM chymostatin, and 1 mM PMSF] is added per 50 ml of the original cell culture volume. The sample is mixed for 45 min at 4° and then poured into a column. The ADP-agarose is washed with at least 10 volumes of buffer A. Bound proteins are eluted with 10 mM NADPH in buffer A and fractions collected.

Some preparations are also purified on calmodulin–agarose (phosphodiesterase 3′,5′-cyclic nucleotide activator, Sigma) using a method based on

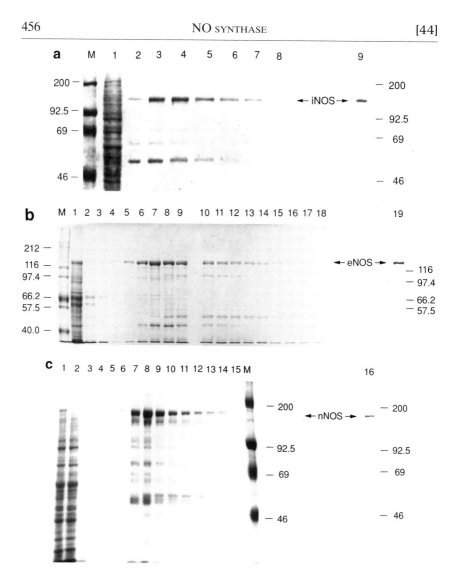

FIG. 2. Analysis by SDS–PAGE of recombinant NOS proteins expressed and purified from baculovirus-infected insect cells. (a) Extracts from recombinant baculovirus-infected Sf21 cells expressing iNOS were run on a 10% SDS–polyacrylamide gel. Track 1 corresponds to the infected cell supernatant loaded onto the ADP–Sepharose column. Tracks 2–8 correspond to fractions eluted from ADP–Sepharose with 10 mM NADPH. Track 9 shows Western blot analysis of the infected cell supernatant with an iNOS-specific antibody. The 131-kDa iNOS protein is indicated by the arrow. Protein molecular weight markers are indicated (M). (b) Extracts from recombinant baculovirus-infected Sf21 cells expressing eNOS were run on a 7.5% SDS–polyacrylamide gel. Track 1 shows the total cell lysate, track 2 shows the soluble supernatant applied to the ADP–Sepharose column, track 3 shows the flow-through from the

that of Furfine *et al.*[13] In these cases, fractions from ADP–agarose are pooled and adjusted to 1 mM CaCl$_2$, 10 μM tetrahydrobiopterin, 1 μM FAD, and 1 μM FMN before being applied to calmodulin–agarose (0.1 ml per 100-ml culture) preequilibrated in buffer B (1 mM CaCl$_2$, 10 μM tetrahydrobiopterin, 1 μM FAD, and 1 μM FMN in buffer A). The column is washed with 5 mM EGTA in buffer B, and bound NOS is eluted in 5 mM EGTA, 1 M NaCl in buffer B.

Proteins are analyzed by SDS–PAGE on 7.5–10% acrylamide gels according to the method of Laemmli.[14] Western blots are performed using a polyclonal antibody raised against baculovirus-derived rat nNOS and monoclonal antibodies against iNOS and eNOS (Transduction Laboratories, Lexington, KY) as described previously.[8]

Gel analysis of the ADP elution profiles for recombinant human iNOS, eNOS, and nNOS are shown in Fig. 2. Full-length protein may be isolated for all three NOS isoforms. Smaller molecular weight bands are also eluted from the ADP column that may represent protein degradation products. The expression of recombinant eNOS, using the myristoylation-minus mutant cDNA sequence, showed increased protein levels when compared with the native cDNA sequence (data not shown).

Assay of Nitric Oxide Synthase Activity and Determination of Cofactor Dependence

All three expression systems yield crude extracts with substantial NO synthase activity as determined by the dual-wavelength spectrophotometric assay of NO oxidation of oxyhemoglobin.[15,16] The activity from the nNOS and eNOS constructs (typically 40 and 80 nmol/min per 10^8 cells) is signifi-

---

[13] E. S. Furfine, M. F. Harmon, J. E. Paith, and E. P. Garvey, *Biochemistry* **32**, 8512 (1993).
[14] U. K. Laemmli, *Nature (London)* **227**, 680 (1970).
[15] M. Feelisch and E. Noack, *Eur. J. Pharmacol.* **139**, 19 (1987).
[16] R. G. Knowles, M. Salter, S. L. Brooks, and S. Moncada, *Biochem. Biophys. Res. Commun.* **172**, 1042 (1990).

---

column, and tracks 4–18 show the fractions eluted from the ADP–Sepharose with 10 mM NADPH. Track 19 shows Western blot analysis of the infected cell lysate with an eNOS-specific antibody. The 133-kDa eNOS protein is indicated by the arrow. Protein molecular weight markers are indicated (M). (c) Extracts from recombinant baculovirus-infected Sf21 cells expressing nNOS were run on an 8% SDS–polyacrylamide gel. Track 1 shows the total cell lysate, and track 2 is the column flow-through. Tracks 3–15 are fractions eluted from the ADP–Sepharose column with 10 mM NADPH. Track 16 shows Western blot analysis of the infected cell lysate with an nNOS-specific antibody. The 161-kDa nNOS protein is indicated by the arrow. Protein molecular weight markers are indicated (M).

cantly higher than that from the iNOS system (typically 0.6 nmol/min per 10^8 cells). This is consistent with the relative abundance of the NOS protein bands observed on electrophoretic analysis of the crude extracts (Fig. 2). No NO synthase activity is detected in the cytosol of uninfected Sf21 cells (data not shown).

For the cofactor dependence analysis of recombinant NO synthase, the iNOS, eNOS, or nNOS activities in extracts are measured spectrophotometrically in a microtiter plate assay based on that using the oxidation of oxyhemoglobin to methemoglobin by NO as described previously.[15,16] Prior to analysis, the enzyme extract is treated with Dowex to remove endogenous arginine, which is present at a high concentration in TC-100 medium. Briefly, 2 volumes of extract is mixed with 1 volume of Dowex 50X8-400 (Sigma, sodium form equilibrated in extraction buffer) on ice. The samples are centrifuged 10,000 g for 2 min and the supernatants removed. This extraction is repeated twice. The incubations, with all cofactors added, contain 3 μM oxyhemoglobin (monomer), 200 μM CaCl$_2$, 1 mM MgCl$_2$, 1 μM FAD, 1 μM FMN, 100 μM NADPH, 0.1 μM calmodulin (CaM), 10 μM tetrahydrobiopterin (BH$_4$), 30 μM L-arginine, 100 μM DTT in 100 mM HEPES buffer, pH 7.4, and extract containing NOS in a total volume of 250 μl. Incubations are started by the addition of enzyme extract. The change in the difference in absorbance at 405 and 420 nm is monitored over 15 min with a dual-wavelength microplate reader (Dynatech MR7000, Chantilly, VA) at 37°. Oxyhemoglobin oxidation is confirmed as resulting from NO synthase activity by inhibition with 1 mM N^G-monomethyl-L-arginine (L-NMMA). The Ca^{2+} dependence is assessed by adding EGTA to 1 mM to chelate free Ca^{2+}. Protein is measured using BCA reagent (Pierce, Rockford, IL) and bovine serum albumin as a standard.

Characterization of Recombinant Baculovirus–Insect Cell Derived Human Nitric Oxide Synthase

All three NO synthases are known to require FMN, FAD, BH$_4$, CaM, NADPH, and arginine for activity, and eNOS and nNOS are also calcium-dependent.[4] As part of the characterization of the three expressed human isoforms, we have determined the requirements for the addition of these factors (Fig. 3). All three isoforms require the addition of arginine and NADPH. This is an important prerequisite for studies of substrate and inhibitor effects on these enzymes. The activity of recombinant nNOS and eNOS is found to be highly dependent on Ca^{2+} and NADPH, and for eNOS calmodulin is also required. Inducible NOS is not dependent on calcium or on added calmodulin. Of the three enzymes, eNOS also has the highest requirement for tetrahydrobiopterin for activity. The observation that all

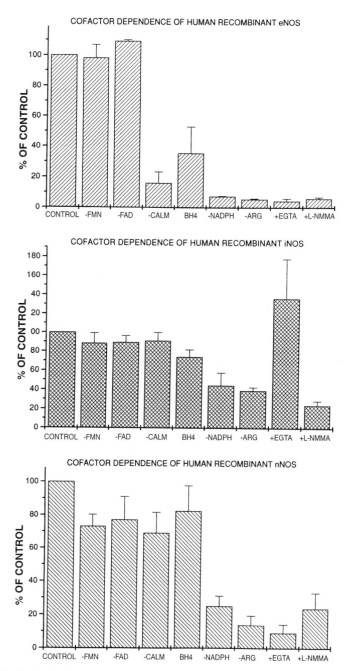

FIG. 3. Analysis of the cofactor dependence, calcium dependence, and sensitivity to L-NMMA of the three unpurified human recombinant NO synthases. Incubations were carried out in the presence or absence of $1 \mu M$ FMN, $1 \mu M$ FAD, $0.1 \mu M$ CaM, $10 \mu M$ BH$_4$, $100 \mu M$ NADPH, $30 \mu M$ L-arginine, 1 mM EGTA, and $300 \mu M$ L-NMMA.

three isoforms express significant activity in the absence of added FMN, FAD, or BH_4 is consistent with reports that even after purification to homogeneity at least some of these cofactors remains bound to the enzyme (reviewed in Ref. 4). In all cases, the activity of the enzyme preparations could be initiated by 300 μM L-NMMA.

While this work was in preparation, Nakane et al.[17] reported the baculovirus/insect cell-mediated expression of all three human NO synthases.

Summary

(1) High levels of human eNOS and nNOS can be produced using the Sf21/baculovirus expression system. (2) Recombinant iNOS, although produced at lower levels, provides significant amounts of enzyme that can be purified for further biochemical characterization. (3) Recombinant baculovirus-derived human NO synthase isozymes have biochemical properties that are highly similar to their native counterparts. (4) Large-scale production of recombinant NO synthase enzymes reduces the risk of batch-to-batch variation. (5) The production of recombinant human NO synthases obviates the need for a supply of tissue and also reduces the risks associated with handling human material.

[17] M. Nakane, J. S. Pollock, V. Klinghofer, F. Basha, P. A. Marsden, A. Hokari, T. Ogura, H. Esumi, and G. W. Carter, *Biochem. Biophys. Res. Commun.* **206**, 511 (1995).

[45] Nitric Oxide Synthases: Analogies to Cytochrome P450 Monooxygenases and Characterization of Recombinant Rat Neuronal Nitric Oxide Synthase Hemoprotein

By Kirk McMillan, John C. Salerno, and Bettie Sue Siler Masters

Introduction

Nitric oxide synthases (NOSs; EC 1.14.13.39) catalyze the NADPH-dependent[1,2] conversion of L-arginine to nitric oxide (NO) and citrulline

[1] R. Iyengar, D. J. Stuehr, and M. A. Marletta, *Proc. Natl. Acad. Sci. U.S.A.* **84**, 6369 (1987).
[2] D. J. Stuehr, N. S. Kwon, S. S. Gross, B. A. Thiel, R. Levi, and C. F. Nathan, *Biochem. Biophys. Res. Commun.* **161**, 420 (1989).

utilizing molecular oxygen.[3] Substrate metabolism occurs through two successive monooxygenations at the guanidino function of L-arginine, during which N^ω-hydroxy-L-arginine (NHA) is formed as an enzyme-bound reaction intermediate.[4] The NOSs are large polypeptides ($\geq$130 kDa) that contain iron–protoporphyrin IX,[5–8] flavin adenine dinucleotide (FAD) and flavin mononucleotide (FMN),[9–11] and tetrahydrobiopterin $(BH_4)^{9,12,13}$ prosthetic groups. Three isoforms that are the products of distinct genes and which share approximately 50% sequence identity have been identified in mammals: the constitutive neuronal (n)[14,15] and endothelial (e)[16,17] enzymes and the cytokine-responsive, inducible (i) NOS.[10,18,19] The enzymes have been characterized as functional homodimers.[14,18–21] The constitutive NOSs require calmodulin binding for activity in the presence of agonist-stimulated elevated calcium levels,[14,16] whereas the inducible NOS binds calmodulin as an integral subunit at basal intracellular calcium levels.[22]

[3] N. S. Kwon, C. F. Nathan, C. Gilker, O. W. Griffith, D. E. Matthews, and D. J. Stuehr, *J. Biol. Chem.* **265**, 13442 (1990).

[4] D. J. Stuehr, N. S. Kwon, C. F. Nathan, O. W. Griffith, P. L. Feldman, and J. Wiseman, *J. Biol. Chem.* **266**, 6259 (1991).

[5] K. A. White and M. A. Marletta, *Biochemistry* **31**, 6627 (1992).

[6] D. J. Stuehr and M. Ikeda-Saito, *J. Biol. Chem.* **267**, 20547 (1992).

[7] K. McMillan, D. S. Bredt, D. J. Hirsch, S. H. Snyder, J. E. Clark, and B. S. S. Masters, *Proc. Natl. Acad. Sci. U.S.A.* **89**, 11141 (1992).

[8] P. Klatt, K. Schmidt, and B. Mayer, *Biochem. J.* **288**, 15 (1992).

[9] B. Mayer, J. Mathias, B. Heinzel, E. R. Werner, H. Wachter, G. Schultz, and E. Böhme, *FEBS Lett.* **288**, 187 (1991).

[10] D. J. Stuehr, H. J. Cho, N. S. Kwon, M. F. Weise, and C. F. Nathan, *Proc. Natl. Acad. Sci. U.S.A.* **88**, 7773 (1991).

[11] D. S. Bredt, C. D. Ferris, and S. H. Snyder, *J. Biol. Chem.* **267**, 10976 (1992).

[12] M. A. Tayeh and M. A. Marletta, *J. Biol. Chem.* **264**, 19654 (1989).

[13] N. S. Kwon, C. F. Nathan, and D. J. Stuehr, *J. Biol. Chem.* **264**, 20496 (1989).

[14] D. S. Bredt and S. H. Snyder, *Proc. Natl. Acad. Sci. U.S.A.* **86**, 9030 (1990).

[15] D. S. Bredt, P. M. Hwang, C. E. Glatt, C. Lowenstein, R. R. Reed, and S. H. Snyder, *Nature (London)* **351**, 714 (1991).

[16] J. S. Pollock, U. Förstermann, J. A. Mitchell, T. D. Warner, H. H. H. W. Schmidt, M. Nakane, and F. Murad, *Proc. Natl. Acad. Sci. U.S.A.* **88**, 10480 (1991).

[17] S. Lamas, P. A. Marsden, G. K. Li, P. Tempst, and T. Michel, *Proc. Natl. Acad. Sci. U.S.A.* **89**, 6348 (1992).

[18] J. M. Hevel, K. A. White, and M. A. Marletta, *J. Biol. Chem.* **266**, 22789 (1991).

[19] Q. Xie, H. J. Cho, J. Calaycay, R. A. Mumford, K. M. Swiderek, T. D. Lee, A. Ding, T. Troso, and C. Nathan, *Science* **256**, 225 (1992).

[20] H. H. W. Schmidt, J. S. Pollock, M. Nakane, L. D. Gorsky, U. Förstermann, and F. Murad, *Proc. Natl. Acad. Sci. U.S.A.* **88**, 365 (1991).

[21] L. J. Robinson, L. Busconi, and T. Michel, *J. Biol. Chem.* **270**, 995 (1995).

[22] H. J. Cho, Q. Xie, J. Calaycay, R. A. Mumford, K. M. Swiderick, T. D. Lee, and C. Nathan, *J. Exp. Med.* **176**, 599 (1992).

Properties and Significance of Heme Prosthetic Group

The detection of a heme prosthetic group in NO synthases that elicited a 445-nm chromophore for the ferrous–carbonyl complex[5–7] provided the initial evidence for a proximal thiolate axial ligand to the heme iron. Nitric oxide synthases, as purified, exhibit a predominantly high spin ($\geq$85%), pentacoordinate ferriheme.[5–7] The addition of substrate (L-arginine or NHA) or N-guanidino-substituted L-arginine analogs, such as N^ω-methyl-L-arginine (NMA), which are inhibitors of NOS, favor the equilibrium toward the high spin form.[23,24] Inhibition of citrulline formation from L-arginine[5–7] and NHA[24] by the heme-directed inhibitor CO implicated the heme prosthetic group as the site of oxygen activation for substrate oxidation. These properties prompted the comparison of NO synthases to the cytochrome P450 monooxygenases, thiolate-liganded hemoproteins the nomenclature of which derive from the approximately 450 nm absorption maximum of the ferrous–CO complex. The thiolate axial heme ligand, which serves as a strong internal electron donor, is crucial in the process of oxygen bond scission during cytochrome P450 catalysis. Ligands bound *trans* to the proximal thiolate exhibit increased basicity in comparison to the parallel *trans*-imidazole adducts in myoglobin. X-Ray crystallographic data of cytochrome $P450_{cam}$ indicate that the distal and proximal sides of the heme-binding pocket are apolar, lacking residues that would hydrogen bond the proximal thiolate or distal oxygen.[25] In the activation of peroxide, catalyzed by peroxidases with a proximal imidazole ligand, a "push–pull" process is envisioned, in which hydrogen bonding of the *trans* proximal base and peroxide oxygens facilitates oxygen bond scission. Apparently, the electron density imposed by the proximal thiolate of cytochromes P450, and hence NO synthases, is sufficient to activate dioxygen bond scission and also stabilizes a high valence state, ferryloxo, hydroxylating species.[26]

The mechanism for the five-electron oxidation of L-arginine to NO and citrulline is proposed to occur through an initial N-hydroxylation by an electrophilic ferryloxo species, with the consumption of 1 mol of reduced nicotinamide adenine dinucleotide phosphate (NADPH), followed by nucleophilic attack at the guanidino carbon of the oxime tautomer of NHA by an iron–hydroperoxy species, with the consumption of 0.5 mol of NADPH.[27–29] Although the N-hydroxylation of L-arginine proceeds

[23] K. McMillan and B. S. S. Masters, *Biochemistry* **32**, 9875 (1993).
[24] R. A. Pufahl and M. A. Marletta, *Biochem. Biophys. Res. Commun.* **193**, 963 (1993).
[25] T. L. Poulos, B. C. Finzel, and A. J. Howard, *J. Mol. Biol.* **195**, 687 (1987).
[26] J. H. Dawson and M. Sono, *Chem. Rev.* **87**, 1255 (1987).
[27] M. A. Marletta, *J. Biol. Chem.* **268**, 12231 (1993).
[28] P. L. Feldman, O. W. Griffith, and D. J. Stuehr, *Chem. Eng. News* **71**, 26 (1994).

through a mechanism analogous to cytochromes P450, that is, mediated by a high-valence state $(FeO)^{3+}$ heme iron–oxygen complex, the mechanism of aromatase has been invoked as a precedence for the rationalization of the second monooxygenation at the guanidino carbon.[27]

In preliminary experiments, Stuehr and Ikeda-Saito[6] reported in electron paramagnetic resonance (EPR) spectroscopic studies that rat Nnos, in the absence of L-arginine, exhibited a predominantly high spin signal characterized by g values at 7.68, 4.12, and 1.81 and a minority low spin signal with $g = 2.44$, 2.29, and 1.89, consistent with the properties of cytochrome P450 hemoproteins.[26] In addition, a $g = 2.0$ signal that corresponded to an air-stable flavin semiquinone was present in the EPR spectrum of resting enzyme, which was abolished on oxidation of the enzyme with ferricyanide. The identity of the proximal axial heme ligand was subsequently confirmed by resonance Raman spectroscopy, which exhibited a low frequency line, $\nu_4 = 1347$ cm^{-1}, for the ferroheme enzyme and 562 cm^{-1} for the Fe–C–O bending mode of the ferrous–CO adduct.[30] EPR spectroscopy of nNOS in the presence of L-arginine and imidazole has been conducted by our laboratory.[31,32] The low temperature (10–12 K) EPR spectrum of the resting enzyme exhibited high-spin heme iron signals at g values around 7.5, 4, and 1.8. L-Arginine shifted the high spin g values at 7.65 to 7.59 and at 4.03 to 4.13, representing a single high spin component, and indicated differences in the heme environment between the high spin states of the resting (absence of L-arginine) and substrate-bound enzymes. A minority low spin species was detected at 20 K in the resting enzyme, $g = 2.42$, 2.28, and 1.9. These findings correlate with the observed spin-state equilibrium of NOS at room temperature, in which the high spin species is favored. The EPR spectrum, in the presence of imidazole, exhibited low spin signatures at 2.65, 2.28, and 1.75, with minority species at 2.54 and 2.49. The spectral inhomogeneity was interpreted as distortion of the heme-binding pocket due to steric constraints imposed by the relatively large heme ligand, imidazole.

The role of calmodulin in the activation of NOS enzymes is the modulation of electron transfer from NADPH via the flavoprotein to the heme iron reaction center.[33,34] Presumably, electron flow occurs as in the cytochrome

[29] H. Korth, R. Sustmann, C. Thater, A. R. Butler, and K. U. Ingold, *J. Biol. Chem.* **269,** 17776 (1994).
[30] J. Wang, D. J. Stuehr, M. Ikeda-Saito, and D. L. Rousseau, *J. Biol. Chem.* **268,** 22255 (1993).
[31] J. C. Salerno, C. Frey, K. McMillan, R. F. Williams, B. S. S. Masters, and O. W. Griffith, *J. Biol. Chem.* **270,** 27423 (1995).
[32] J. C. Salerno, K. McMillan, and B. S. S. Masters, unpublished observations (1994).
[33] H. M. Abu-Soud and D. J. Stuehr, *Proc. Natl. Acad. Sci. U.S.A.* **90,** 10769 (1993).
[34] H. M. Abu-Soud, L. L. Yoho, and D. J. Stuehr, *J. Biol. Chem.* **269,** 32047 (1994).

P450: NADPH cytochrome P450 reductase system located in the mammalian endoplasmic reticulum: NADPH → FAD → FMN → heme Fe. Based on the earliest mechanism studies of Masters et al.[35] and Yasukochi et al.[36] the transfer of electrons from NADPH, via FAD, which serves as the low-potential flavin, and FMN, which serves as the high-potential flavin, to the heme iron was originally described by Vermilion et al.[37] Guengerich elaborated this hypothesis to involve the oxidation of FADH·/FMNH$_2$ to FADH·/FMNH· by the ferric cytochrome P450 and subsequent equilibration to FAD/FMNH$_2$, which could donate a second electron to the oxygenated heme iron, forming FAD/FMNH·.[38] This species could then be reduced by NADPH to FADH$_2$/FMNH·, regenerating by internal electron transfer FADH·/FMNH$_2$, which is the reductant of (donor to) external electron acceptors.

Formation of an enzyme–substrate complex, characterized by a type I difference spectrum, is the initial event in catalysis with the various mammalian cytochromes P450 and the soluble, bacterial proteins P450$_{cam}$ and P450$_{BM-3}$.[39] This is in contrast to peroxidase reactions where the oxidant (H$_2$O$_2$) reacts first to form higher valency state heme iron complexes followed by discharge on addition of substrates. In the microsomal cytochrome P450-mediated reactions, the hemoprotein initially binds substrate followed by subsequent reduction of the ferric heme iron to Fe(II) by an electron derived from NADPH, via the flavins, and then binds molecular oxygen. Transfer of the second electron from NADPH through the flavoprotein oxidoreductase to the heme iron results in fission of the bound dioxygen and oxygenation of the substrate. The NADPH : substrate : O$_2$ stoichiometry of these reactions equals 1 : 1 : 1. The heme–substrate interaction of NO synthase, observed by optical difference spectrophotometry for L-arginine and NHA,[23,24] offers support for the analogy of the catalytic mechanisms of cytochromes P450 and NO synthase, at least in the primary substrate binding event(s). The stoichiometry of NO synthase reactions has been the subject of many publications and reviews.[4,24,27–29]

[35] B. S. S. Masters, H. Kamin, Q. H. Gibson, and C. H. Williams, Jr., J. Biol. Chem. 240, 921 (1965).

[36] Y. Yasukochi, J. A. Peterson, and B. S. S. Masters, J. Biol. Chem. 254, 7097 (1979).

[37] J. L. Vermilion, D. P. Ballou, V. Massey, and M. J. Coon, J. Biol. Chem. 256, 266 (1981).

[38] F. P. Guengerich, Biochemistry 22, 2811 (1983).

[39] S. G. Sligar and R. I. Murray, in "Cytochrome P450: Structure, Mechanism and Biochemistry" (P. R. Ortiz de Montellano, ed.), p. 429. Plenum, New York, 1986.

Sequence Homology of Nitric Oxide Synthases and Cytochromes P450

Hemoproteins that employ an axial thiolate ligand to the heme iron donated by a cysteine residue include, in addition to cytochromes P450, chloroperoxidase, thromboxane synthase, and prostacyclin synthase. Conserved peptide sequences termed cysteinyl peptides have been identified,[40] wherein FXXGXXXCXG represents the peptide motif in cytochromes P450. McMillan et al.[7] suggested putative cysteine thiolate donors in rat neuronal (Cys-415), bovine endothelial (Cys-186), and murine macrophage (Cys-194) NOSs, by sequence inspection, observing the presence of conserved dodecapeptide sequences within the three enzyme isoforms. Renaud et al.[41] concurred with these observations and assigned putative roles for residues within the peptide sequence on the basis of comparison to the analogous residue in cytochrome P450$_{cam}$: Trp-1, cysteinate protection; Ala-4, hairpin turn; Arg-6, interaction with heme propionate; and Gly-10, close contact to the heme. A comparison of these cysteinyl peptide sequences to those of other hemoproteins is shown in Table I.[42-47]

Site-directed mutagenesis has verified the position of the proposed thiolate donors in the human endothelial[48] and rat neuronal enzymes[49,50] as cysteines 184 and 415, respectively. The C184A mutation of human eNOS resulted in the abolishment of catalytic activity and the 445 nm ferrous–CO complex. Mutation of Cys-99 in human eNOS also resulted in loss of activity without affecting the 445 nm ferrous–CO complex formation. The C415H mutant nNOS, expressed in a baculoviral system, failed to incorporate heme.[49] Expression of the C415H mutant as a recombinant hemoprotein

[40] D. W. Nebert and F. J. Gonzalez, Annu. Rev. Biochem. **56**, 945 (1987).
[41] J.-P. Renaud, J.-L. Boucher, S. Vadon, M. Delaforge, and D. Mansuy, Biochem. Biophys. Res. Commun. **192**, 53 (1993).
[42] F. T. Gonzales, D. W. Nebert, J. P. Hardwick, and C. B. Kasper, J. Biol. Chem. **260**, 7435 (1985).
[43] R. T. Ruettinger, L. P. Wen, and A. J. Fulco, J. Biol. Chem. **264**, 10987 (1989).
[44] M. Haniu, L. G. Armes, K. T. Yasunobu, B. A. Shastry, and I. C. Gunsalus, J. Biol. Chem. **257**, 12657 (1982).
[45] C. Yokoyama, A. Miyata, K. Suzuki, Y. Nishikawa, T. Yoshimoto, S. Yamamoto, R. Nusing, V. Ullrich, and T. Tanabe, Biochem. Biophys. Res. Commun. **178**, 1479 (1991).
[46] S. Hara, A. Miyato, C. Yokoyama, H. Inoue, R. Brugger, F. Lottspeich, V. Ullrich, and T. Tanabe, J. Biol. Chem. **269**, 19897 (1994).
[47] G. H. Faug, P. Kenigsberg, M. J. Axley, M. Nuell, and L. P. Hager, Nucleic Acids Res. **14**, 8061 (1986).
[48] P. Chen, A. Tsai, and K. K. Wu, J. Biol. Chem. **269**, 25062 (1994).
[49] M. K. Richards and M. A. Marletta, Biochemistry **33**, 14723 (1994).
[50] K. McMillan and B. S. S. Masters, Biochemistry **34**, 3686 (1995).

TABLE I

COMPARISON OF PUTATIVE CYSTEINYL PEPTIDES IN VARIOUS ENZYMES

Enzyme	Peptide sequence	Ref.
Rat nNOS	W R N A S R — C V G R	15
Murine iNOS	W R N A P R — C I G R	19
Bovine eNOS	W R N A P R — C V G R	17
P4503A1	F G N G P R N C I G	42
P450BM3	F G N G Q R A C I G	43
P450cam	F G H G S H L C L G	44
Thromboxane synthase	F G A G P R A C I G	45
Prostacyclin synthase	W G A G H N Q C L G	46
Chloroperoxidase	Y V I G S D — C — G	47

in *Escherichia coli* produced a heme-containing protein for which the ferric–imidazole complex exhibited absorption maxima at 412, 530, and ~560 nm (shoulder) for the Soret, β-, and α-transition bands, respectively.[50] These optical properties were indicative of a bisimidazole heme iron complex, consistent with a histidine residue in the proximal site.[51] The ferrous–CO complex exhibited a markedly diminished absorptivity in the Soret region (~20% wild-type) with an absorption maximum at 420 nm, which coincides with the observed phenotype in the cysteine to histidine mutant of cytochrome $P450_d$.[52]

Nitric oxide synthases exhibit essentially no sequence homology to the cytochrome P450 enzyme superfamily[53] with the exception of a very modest similarity within the cysteinyl peptide motif, represented by the conserved aromatic residue at the N terminus of the motif, the cysteine thiolate donor, and conserved glycine and arginine residues. Attempts to align the amino acid sequence of the N-terminal heme-binding module of nNOS to those of the cytochrome $P450_{cam}$[44] and the $P450_{BM-3}$[43] hemoprotein, for which tertiary structural information are available, failed to demonstrate the presence of I and L helices that are considered to be structural determinants of the cytochromes P450. Thus, although the NO synthases are heme-containing monooxygenases, structurally these enzymes are at most distantly related to the cytochromes P450 and likely represent a convergence

[51] A. S. Brill and R. J. P. Williams, *Biochem. J.* **78**, 246 (1961).

[52] T. Shimizu, K. Hirano, M. Takahashi, M. Hatano, and Y. Fujii-Kuriyama, *Biochemistry* **27**, 4138 (1988).

[53] D. W. Nebert, D. R. Nelson, M. J. Coon, R. W. Estabrook, R. Feyereisen, Y. Fujii-Kuriyama, F. J. Gonzalez, F. P. Guengerich, I. C. Gunsalus, E. F. Johnson, J. C. Loper, R. Sato, M. R. Waterman, and D. J. Waxman, *DNA Cell Biol.* **10**, 1 (1991).

toward analogous chemistry at the heme iron reaction center. In consideration of the proclivity of cytochromes P450 toward hydrophobic substrates in contrast to the hydrophilic substrate, L-arginine, of NOSs, substantial differences in the substrate-binding sites and oxygenation center are not surprising.

Modular Structure of Nitric Oxide Synthases

Bredt and colleagues[15] reported binding sites for NADPH, FAD, FMN, and calmodulin within the deduced amino acid sequence of rat nNOS. The C-terminal 641 residues of rat nNOS exhibited significant sequence similarity (58%) to the FAD- and FMN-containing rat liver NADPH-cytochrome P450 reductase and E. coli sulfite reductase. Moreover, the presence of the pyridine nucleotide-binding site is exploited in the purification of NO synthases by 2',5'-adenosine diphosphate (2',5'-ADP)–Sepharose 4B affinity chromatography, a method that was first applied in the purification of NADPH-cytochrome P450 reductase.[54] Elution of NOSs from the affinity medium is obtained in the presence of millimolar concentrations of NADPH, but not by 2'-adenosine monophosphate (2'-AMP), which effectively elutes cytochrome P450 reductase. However, the addition of 0.4–0.5 M NaCl to a 5 mM 2'-AMP solution elicits the sharp elution of nNOS, without exposure of the enzyme to NADPH-derived redox equivalents and employing a less expensive ligand.[50]

Subsequent to the detection of the heme prosthetic group and tentative assignment to the N-terminal half of NOS, a bidomain structure for rat nNOS composed of an N-terminal heme- and L-arginine-binding domain and a C-terminal flavoprotein oxidoreductase was proposed by our laboratory and later demonstrated by limited trypsinolysis.[55] These findings led to an analogy of NOSs to the catalytically self-sufficient 119-kDa fatty acid hydroxylase cytochrome P450$_{BM-3}$ that is also composed of an N-terminal heme-binding oxygenase domain and a C-terminal flavoprotein oxidoreductase.[56,57] Molecular dissection was employed to resolve the functional modules into distinct proteins that could be reconstituted as a competent fatty acid hydroxylase system.[58,59] The availability of the cytochrome P450$_{BM-3}$ polypeptides has facilitated physical studies of the isolated prosthetic heme

[54] Y. Yasukochi and B. S. S. Masters, J. Biol. Chem. 251, 5337 (1976).
[55] E. Sheta, K. McMillan, and B. S. S. Masters, J. Biol. Chem. 269, 15147 (1994).
[56] L. O. Narhi and A. J. Fulco, J. Biol. Chem. 261, 7160 (1986).
[57] L. O. Narhi and A. J. Fulco, J. Biol. Chem. 262, 6683 (1987).
[58] H. Li, K. Darwish, and T. L. Poulos, J. Biol. Chem. 266, 11909 (1991).
[59] S. S. Boddupalli, T. Oster, R. W. Estabrook, and J. A. Peterson, J. Biol. Chem. 267, 10375 (1992).

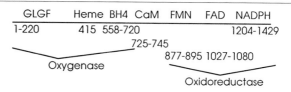

FIG. 1. Modular structure of rat neuronal NO synthase.

and flavin prosthetic groups, as well as providing a structure in the hemo-protein that proved amenable to crystallization and resolution of tertiary structure.[60]

Salerno and Morales employed homology-based modeling studies using various dihydrofolate reductases in the localization of the pterin-binding module to approximately residues 558–720.[61] This assertion places the binding site of the pterin cofactor between the heme cysteinyl peptide and calmodulin-binding motif. The neuronal NOS contains an additional 220 amino acids or so in comparison to other NOS isoforms, in which a GLGF motif has been detected beginning at residue 27.[62] The GLGF motif has been observed in rat postsynaptic density protein (psd95) and in the *Drosophila* homolog *dlg*. A putative role for this region is in the intracellular targeting of nNOS through protein–protein interactions. Figure 1 depicts the modular structure of rat nNOS as a linear array.[50] The NO synthases appear to be the result of evolutionary gene fusion that formed a series of functional modules aligned within the linear protein sequence, namely, the fusion of the heme-binding oxygenase with the flavoprotein oxidoreductase by a connecting modulatory sequence.

Expression and Purification of Neuronal Nitric Oxide
   Synthase Hemoprotein

The heme-binding oxygenase module of rat nNOS has been expressed in *Escherichia coli* using molecular cloning methods.[50] Polymerase chain reaction (PCR) amplification of the cDNA encoding residues 1–714 as an *Nde*I/*Hin*dIII fragment with the incorporation of a 5′ GCA[CAC]$_4$ sequence is employed to yield an N-terminal AlaHis$_4$ modification to facilitate

[60] K. G. Ravichandran, S. S. Boddupalli, C. A. Hasemann, J. A. Peterson, and J. Deisenhofer, *Science* **261**, 731 (1993).
[61] J. C. Salerno and A. J. Morales, *in* "Biochemistry and Molecular Biology of Nitric Oxide, First International Conference" (L. Ignarro and F. Murad, eds.), p. 72. UCLA, Los Angeles, California, 1994.
[62] K. Cho, C. A. Hunt, and M. A. Kennedy, *Neuron* **9**, 929 (1992).

protein purification.[63] The amplification product is restricted, ligated into the expression vector pCW,[64] and transformed in *E. coli* JM109. Expression of the His$_4$-tagged hemoprotein is significantly enhanced at 30°, which minimizes the formation of degradation products.

Recombinant *E. coli* transformed by the plasmid described above are cultured in Fernbach flasks containing 1 liter of modified TB medium (20 g/liter yeast extract, 10 g/liter tryptone, 19.5 mM KH$_2$PO$_4$, 30.5 mM Na$_2$HPO$_4$, 4 ml/liter glycerol, 50 mg/liter ampicillin) at 30° with shaking at 200 rpm. Induction of protein expression is obtained by addition of isopropylthiogalactoside (IPTG) to 0.5 mM and δ-aminolevulinate to 0.2 mM at an optical density of about 1 at 600 nm, followed by overnight incubation. Cells (8 liters) are harvested by centrifugation and stored at $-80°$ until processed further. Cells are lysed by thawing in 2 volumes of lysis medium [50 mM Tris-Cl, 0% (v/v) glycerol, 5 mM ethylenediaminetetraacetic acid (EDTA), 5 mM 2-mercaptoethanol (BME), 1 mM phenylmethylsulfonyl flouride (PMSF), 1 mM ethylene glycol bis(β-aminoethyl ether)-N,N,N',N'-tetraacetic acid (EGTA), 5 μg/ml leupeptin/pepstatin, 0.5 mg/ml lysozyme, pH 7.5] and sonicating for 60–90 sec. The lysate is clarified by centrifugation for 20 min at 17,000 g and 60 min at 100,000 g at 5°. Neutral saturated (NH$_4$)$_2$SO$_4$ solution is added to 55% saturation, and the mixture is stirred for 30 min. The precipitate is recovered by centrifugation for 30 min at 17,000 g and dissolved in 100 ml of sodium phosphate buffer (50 mM sodium phosphate, 10% glycerol, 0.2 M NaCl, 10 mM imidazole, 1 mM BME, 0.2 mM PMSF, pH 7.8). Following overnight dialysis against 4 liters of sodium phosphate buffer, the sample is applied to a 30-ml column of nickel-nitrilotriacetic acid agarose (Ni-NTA agarose; Qiagen, Chatsworth, CA) equilibrated in the same buffer. The column is washed with 300 ml of 10 mM imidazole in sodium phosphate buffer followed by 50 ml of 20 mM imidazole in sodium phosphate buffer. The hemoprotein is eluted with 100 mM imidazole in sodium phosphate buffer, and fractions are pooled on the basis of absorbance at 420 nm. The pooled fractions are concentrated by ultrafiltration (Centriprep-30). The yield of hemoprotein, estimated from the ferrous–CO complex absorption ($\varepsilon \approx 75$ mM^{-1}) which serves as a simple assay for the hemoprotein, is about 140 nmol/liter of induced cell culture. The concentrated hemoprotein is subjected to Sephacryl 200 chromatography in 50 mM TrisCl, 10% glycerol, 0.1 M NaCl, 0.1 mM EDTA, 1 mM BME, pH 7.5, using a 2.5 $\times$ 80 cm column, and fractions are pooled on the basis of an absorbance ratio of A_{280}/A_{418} of about 1.5–1.6.

[63] A. Hoffmann and R. G. Roder, *Nucleic Acids Res.* **19**, 6337 (1991).
[64] J. A. Gegner and F. W. Dahlquist, *Proc. Natl. Acad. Sci. U.S.A.* **88**, 750 (1991).

Characterization of Neuronal Nitric Oxide Synthase Hemoprotein

The 80-kDa hemoprotein, purified by Ni-chelate chromatography, formed the characteristic 445 nm ferrous–CO complex and bound L-arginine and BH_4, detected as the optically monitored low-to-high spin conversion of the heme iron, thus localizing the binding site of BH_4 to within the amino-terminal half of the NOS molecule and demonstrating a role for pterin in the modulation of the heme iron spin state equilibrium. Also, the binding of radiolabeled N^ω-nitro-L-arginine and BH_4 with affinities analogous to those of the intact enzyme was demonstrated. Distinct from the intact enzyme, Fig. 2 shows the optical properties of the ferric hemoprotein purified by Ni chelate and molecular exclusion chromatographic methods (curve A), which were indicative of predominantly low spin, hexacoordinate heme characterized by absorption maxima at 418, 537, and 565 nm representing the Soret, β, α transitions, respectively, and a charge-transfer band

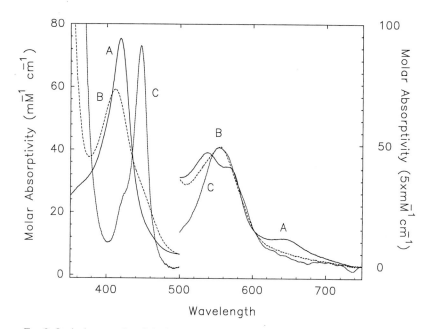

FIG. 2. Optical properties of the hemoprotein. The optical spectra of purified 18 μM nNOS hemoprotein were acquired using a Shimadzu 2101 UV–Vis spectrophotometer, and the spectra were normalized to display the absorption in terms of molar extinction. Curve A (solid line) was obtained with the resting ferrihemoprotein; curve B (dashed line) displays the ferrous hemoprotein produced by reduction with solid sodium dithionite immediately prior to recording of the spectrum; and curve C (dotted line) represents the ferrous–carbonyl complex, obtained by bubbling the sample with CO, followed by dithionite reduction. The visible molar absorptivities were multiplied by a factor of 5 for presentation.

at 647 nm. The ferrous (curve B in Fig. 2) and ferrous–carbonyl (curve C in Fig. 2) hemoproteins were spectroscopically identical to the holoenzyme, exhibiting wavelength maxima at 412 and 445 nm, respectively, for the Soret transitions and about 555 nm for the β/α bands. The ferric–imidazole complex displayed wavelength maxima at 428, 544, and 575 nm. Similar absorptivities are observed for the Soret band absorption of resting and low spin ferric NOS and its ferrous–CO complex. Various heme–ligand complexes, including the 2-mercaptoethanol and sulfide complexes, have been analyzed optically, and they exhibit spectral properties characterized by a split Soret band with wavelength maxima at 374 and 456 nm, indicative of bisthiolate axial ligation of the heme iron.[26] The split Soret bands of the ferric–cyanide hemoprotein complex at around 370 and 440 nm are typical of that observed in the intact enzyme. The splitting of the Soret transition is another property analogous to cytochromes P450 and has been attributed to hyperporphyrin absorption.[26]

Electron paramagnetic resonance spectroscopy of the hemoprotein, in the absence of added substrate or BH$_4$, demonstrated the presence of at least three low spin species characterized by g_z values at 2.47, 2.41, and 2.35.[65] The addition of L-arginine and BH$_4$ resulted in a significant increase in the high spin population and the abolishment of the $g_z = 2.35$ signal. The $g_z = 2.35$ signal was attributed to the formation of a bisthiolate complex with a cysteine thiolate located within the distal heme pocket that becomes available to a population of the hemoprotein through a collapse or deformation of the distal site in the absence of pterin. This suggests a requirement for the pterin cofactor for the integrity of the distal heme/substrate oxygenation site, as well as its effects on spin-state modulation and substrate binding.

The NADPH-dependent electron transfer to the hemoprotein catalyzed by a recombinant NOS flavoprotein (residues 750–1429) was monitored optically by the formation of the 445 nm ferrous–CO complex.[66] The experimental conditions involved conducting the measurements using CO-saturated samples, sealed under 1 atmosphere of CO, with either equivalent or 4-fold excess flavoprotein. Although the rates for reduction of the heme iron were relatively slow in comparison to the overall turnover for the intact enzyme, clearly the reconstitution of electron transfer to the heme oxygenation center was obtained. The absolute requirement and concentration dependence of the rate of heme iron reduction on the flavoprotein was demonstrated, and, interestingly, cytochrome P450 reductase was also

[65] K. McMillan, J. C. Salerno, and B. S. S. Masters, unpublished observations (1994).
[66] K. McMillan, Q. Liu, S. S. Gross, J. C. Salerno, and B. S. S. Masters, unpublished observations (1995).

shown to be a competent oxidoreductase in this system. Furthermore, the consumption of NADPH by the reconstituted NOS hemoprotein : flavoprotein system was highly uncoupled in the presence of CO, suggesting the potential for flavin-mediated oxygen activation. The addition of BH_4 to the reaction mixtures had no significant effect on the rate of electron transfer or coupling on NADPH consumption.

Oxidation of radiolabeled [^{14}C]arginine to both NHA and citrulline by the hemoprotein was analyzed by strong cation-exchange high-performance liquid chromatography (HPLC) and on-line radiometric detection.[66] Resolution of analytes was obtained using a water (A)–0.1 M sodium citrate, pH 3.0 (B), system, eluting with a linear gradient of 0–5% B over 0–5 min followed by 100% B over 5–20 min.[67] Product formation required the presence of NADPH, BH_4, and a flavoprotein catalyst and exhibited concentration dependence with respect to the hemoprotein oxygenase and flavoprotein oxidoreductase.

These studies have demonstrated the feasibility of dissecting neuronal NO synthase into functional modules encompassing the heme-/pterin-binding oxygenation center and flavoprotein oxidoreductase, which can be reconstituted to catalyze the oxidation of L-arginine. The resolved polypeptides, expressed in E. coli, provide a ready source of material for physical studies by various spectroscopic methods and, owing to their smaller molecular mass, may represent an advantage in protein crystallization and structural determination over the intact enzyme. A bidomain structure for murine macrophage NOS has been demonstrated by limited proteolysis,[68] indicating that the view of a modular structure is applicable to all NOS isoforms, which would be predicted on the basis of the sequence similarity of the various cofactor/substrate binding sites. The application of molecular cloning methods in the dissection of the NO synthases is also facilitating structure–function studies directed at the localization of cofactor and substrate-binding sites and reaction mechanism.

Acknowledgments

Research was supported by The Robert A. Welch Foundation (Grant AQ-1192) and, in part, by the National Institutes of Health (Grant HL30050). K.McM. is a Senior Scientist, Pharmacopeia, Inc., Cranbury, N.J.

[67] K. L. Campos, J. Giovanelli, and S. Kaufman, J. Biol. Chem. 270, 1721 (1995).
[68] D. K. Ghosh and D. J. Stuehr, Biochemistry 34, 801 (1995).

[46] Carbon Monoxide and Nitric Oxide Homology: Differential Modulation of Heme Oxygenases in Brain and Detection of Protein and Activity

By MAHIN D. MAINES

Introduction

Work on the function of carbon monoxide (CO) produced by the heme oxygenase (HO) system, as a signal molecule for production of cGMP in the brain, was stimulated by the intriguing observation that the specific activity of HO in the brain is nearly equivalent to that found in the spleen,[1] the main site of hemoglobin heme degradation, and also by the finding that HO-2 mRNA and protein are highly abundant in the brain.[2,3] These findings provoked the idea that "HO has function(s) in the brain aside from that of heme degradation."[3] Then, in analogy with nitric oxide (NO), the suggestion was made that one such function may be the generation of cGMP in the brain[4,5] and in the periphery.[6] Subsequently, it was shown that HO activity is indeed linked to the generation of cGMP,[7–9] not only in the brain, but also in the cardiovascular system.[10–13] Further, interest concerning the functions of cGMP in a wide range of cellular activities stimulated studies in comparative physiology of NO and CO generating systems.[13–16]

[1] M. D. Maines, *FASEB J.* **2**, 2557 (1988).

[2] G. M. Trakshel and M. D. Maines, *J. Biol. Chem.* **264**, 1323 (1989).

[3] Y. Sun, M. O. Rotenberg, and M. D. Maines, *J. Biol. Chem.* **265**, 8212 (1990).

[4] J. F. Ewing and M. D. Maines, *Mol. Cell. Neurosci.* **3**, 559 (1992).

[5] M. D. Maines, *Mol. Cell. Neurosci.* **4**, 389 (1993).

[6] G. S., Marks, J. F. Brien K. Nakatsu, and B. E. McLaughlin, *Trends Pharmacol. Sci.* **12**, 185 (1991).

[7] M. D. Maines, J. Mark, and J. F. Ewing, *Mol. Cell. Neurosci.* **4**, 398 (1993).

[8] A. Verma, D. J. Hirsch, C. E. Glatt, G. V. Ronnett, and S. H. Snyder, *Science* **259**, 381 (1993).

[9] C. M. Weber, B. C. Eke, and M. D. Maines, *J. Neurochem.* **63**, 953 (1994).

[10] J. F. Ewing, V. S. Raju, and M. D. Maines, *J. Pharmacol. Exp. Ther.* **271**, 408 (1994).

[11] T. Morita, M. A. Perrella, M. Lee, and S. Kourembanas, *Proc. Natl. Acad. Sci. U.S.A.* **92**, 1475 (1995).

[12] N. R. Prabhakar, J. L. Dinerman, F. H. Agani, and S. H. Snyder, *Neurobiology* **92**, 1994 (1995).

[13] V. S. Raju and M. D. Maines, *J. Pharmacol. Exp. Ther.* (1996).

[14] M. Zhuo, S. Small, E. A. Kandel, and R. D. Hawkins, *Science* **260**, 1946 (1993).

[15] S. Rattan and S. Chakder, *Am. Physiol. Soc.* **265**, G799 (1993).

Carbon monoxide (CO), like NO, is a gaseous ligand for heme (Fe protoporphyrin IX, FePP, heme b). Reportedly, the two gaseous molecules share a common mechanism for activation of soluble guanylate cyclase[17] and conversion of GTP to cGMP.[18] The activation is suspected to involve NO or CO breaking the bond that forms the fifth coordinate of heme Fe, presumed to be between the metal and the imidazole of the proximal histidine,[19] allowing the participation of the freed histidine in the conversion of GTP to cGMP. Activation of guanylate cyclase by CO is lower than that by NO because of the properties of the interaction between heme and its gaseous ligands.[5] This, however, can be compensated by the relative availability of the two ligands. The ability to generate CO, as reflected by HO activity, is considerably higher in the brain than NO, as indicated by NO synthase protein and transcript levels. The same consideration holds for the cardiovascular system.[10]

Beyond the common mechanism for activation of guanylate cyclase, CO and NO share homology in properties of the enzyme systems that generate them; in fact, this homology makes it difficult to discern the relative contribution of the two ligands for generation of cGMP. Heme oxygenase, like NO synthase, has inducible and constitutive forms,[20,21] with the inducible form (HO-1) responding to a great variety of stimuli,[22] including all known inducers of NO synthase, such as lipopolysaccharide (LPS) and cytokines.[23] The constitutive form, HO-2, is a member of the glucocorticoid-regulated gene family[24] and is upregulated by adrenal glucocorticoids.[9] Nitric oxide synthase is also regulated by the glucocorticoid;[23] in this instance, the constitutive form is downregulated.[9] In view of these similarities, it is impossible to make distinctions as to the relative contribution of CO and NO to baseline guanylate cyclase activation, unless the systems are differentially manipulated. This can be achieved by using specific inhibitors

---

[16] G. Pozzoli, C. Mancuso, A. Mirtella, P. Preziosi, A. P. Grossman, and P. Navarra, *Endocrinology (Baltimore)* **135**, 2314 (1994).

[17] V. G. Kharitonov, V. S. Sharma, R. B. Pilz, D. Magde, and D. Koesling, *Proc. Natl. Acad. Sci. U.S.A.* **92**, 2568 (1995).

[18] L. J. Ignarro, J. B. Adams, P. M. Horwitz, and K. S. Woods, *J. Biol. Chem.* **261**, 4997 (1986).

[19] J. R. Stone and M. A. Marletta, *Biochemistry* **33**, 5636 (1994).

[20] M. D. Maines, G. M. Trakshel, and R. K. Kutty, *J. Biol. Chem.* **261**, 411 (1986).

[21] I. Cruse and M. D. Maines, *J. Biol. Chem.* **263**, 3348 (1988).

[22] M. D. Maines, "Heme Oxygenase: Clinical Applications and Functions." CRC Press, Boca Raton, Florida, 1992.

[23] D. A. Geller, A. K. Nussler, M. DiSalvio, C. J. Lowenstein, R. A. Shapiro, S. C. Wang, R. L. Simmons, and T. R. Billar, *Proc. Natl. Acad. Sci USA* **90**, 522 (1993).

[24] W. K. McCoubrey, Jr., and M. D. Maines, *Gene* **139**, 155 (1994).

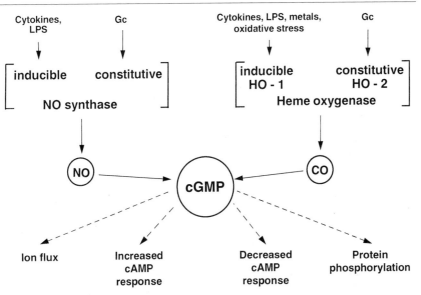

FIG. 1. Homology of CO- and NO-generating systems. Adapted from H. H. H. W. Schmid, S. M. Lohmann, and U. Walter, *Biochem. Biophys. Acta* **1178,** 153 (1993).

and/or inducers of the HO system. Homology between CO and NO generating systems is depicted in Fig. 1.

Modulation of Heme Oxygenase

To date, only one compound, Zn-protoporphyrin (ZnPP) has been identified as a potentially selective inhibitor of HO activity.[25] This selectivity, however, is best realized when ZnPP is used at concentrations of 1–10 μM *in vitro* and 40 μmol/kg *in vivo*, although a 100 μM concentration of ZnPP has been reported to have no effect on NO synthase activity *in vitro*.[26] At one concentration or another, a number of other metalloporphyrins inhibit HO activity and are assumed to be selective, but most of these compounds have been shown to lack the selectivity of HO inhibition; in fact, many of the compounds are photosensitizers of tissue destruction, and some, judging from their structure, cannot be selective. Indeed, ZnPP itself can affect macromolecules if not protected from intense lighting. The selectivity of ZnPP relates to the fact that all HO isozymes share a conserved

[25] M. D. Maines, *Biochim. Biophys. Acta* **673,** 339 (1981).
[26] D. Luo and S. R. Vincent, *Eur. J. Pharmacol.* **267,** 263 (1994).

region known as the "heme oxygenase signature" consisting of 24 amino acids.[21,27] This forms a pocket that holds the porphyrin ring of heme by hydrophobic contacts and allows formation of a five-coordinate heme Fe with histidine. This histidine in HO-2 is believed to be the residue in the signature motif, and it is essential for oxidation of FePP by HO-2.[28] The heme pocket does not differentiate between Fe and Zn chelated in the porphyrin ring as long as the ring can make contact with the pocket.[29,30]

Using this principle, ZnPP has been used to discriminate between the contribution of CO and NO to generation of cGMP, and to examine the comparative function of the gaseous molecules in neuronal signaling. At present, selective inhibition of the two different forms of HO is not feasible using ZnPP. Also, different forms of NO synthase cannot be selectively inhibited with present technology. The synthase enzymes can be inhibited utilizing the same principle used for inhibiting HO activity, that is, using substrate analogs (see [37] in this volume).[30a] The disadvantage of using ZnPP for *in vivo* studies of brain function is that it does not gain entry into the brain; however, it can be useful when injected intraventricularly. Induction of HO isozymes, however, can be manipulated individually. The activity of HO-1 can be increased in brain (also in systemic organs) by heat shock and glutathione (GSH) depletion.[31,32] Selective induction of HO-1 is achieved by depleting GSH using the selective inhibitor of its synthesis, buthionine (*S, R*)-sulfoximine (BSO).[7,33] Expression of HO-2 activity in the brain can be upregulated with glucocorticoids in normal animals (also in tissue culture) without changing HO-1.[9] Glucocorticoids, together with oxidative stress (e.g., heat shock), increase HO-1.[34] In such systems, the contributions of NO and CO to the generation of cGMP can be separated by using arginine analogs, inhibitors of NO synthase; these compounds do not affect HO activity. Experimental details for modulating HO-1/HO-2 are provided in the following.

To increase HO-1 in brain, inject 2-day-old newborn rats (when the blood–brain barrier is permeable) intraperitoneally (i.p.) with 3 mmol/kg BSO, in saline twice daily for 2 days. This results in a near doubling of HO-1 activity with a reduction in NO synthase activity by about 40%. Brain

---

[27] M. O. Rotenberg and M. D. Maines, *Arch. Biochem. Biophys.* **290**, 336 (1991).
[28] W. K. McCoubrey, Jr., and M. D. Maines, *Arch. Biochem. Biophys.* **302**, 402 (1993).
[29] M. D. Maines and A. Kappas, *Biochemistry* **16**, 419 (1977).
[30] I. N. Rublevskaya and M. D. Maines, *J. Biol. Chem.* **269**, 26390 (1994).
[30a] *Methods Enzymol.* **268**, Chap. 37, 1996 (this volume).
[31] J. F. Ewing and M. D. Maines, *Proc. Natl. Acad. Sci. U.S.A.* **88**, 5364 (1991).
[32] J. F. Ewing and M. D. Maines, *J. Neurochem.* **60**, 1512 (1993).
[33] A. Meister and M. Anderson, *Annu. Rev. Biochem.* **52**, 711 (1983).
[34] M. D. Maines, B. C. Eke, C. M. Weber, and J. F. Ewing, *J. Neurochem.* **64**, 1769 (1995).

HO-1 in adult rat glial cells can be increased by injecting subcutaneously (s.c.) diethylmaleate (DEM, 4 mmol/kg); within 10 hr after treatment, there is a severalfold increase in HO-1 transcript (~1.8 kb) in whole brain and an intense staining for HO-1, when visualized by immunocytochemistry (ICC).[32] The reagent DEM also can be utilized to increase HO-1 activity in cells in culture (10 μM final concentration). A more robust increase is obtained when DEM treatment is followed by addition of a metal salt ($CoCl_2$, $CdCl_2$, $NaAsO_2$) at a concentration of 25–50 μM.[35] To inhibit HO-1 (and HO-2) *in vivo*, inject rats intravenously (iv) or sc with 40 μmol/kg ZnPP; prepare the metalloporphyrin solution (ZnPP or others) immediately before use by dissolving in a minimum volume of NaOH (0.1 N), adjusting to pH 7.4 with 0.1 N HCl. The volume of injection should not exceed 1.0 ml/100 g body weight. This treatment will inhibit HO activity in systemic organs, but not in the brain. However, because HO-1 activity is present at a minimum level in normal brain, there is no obvious reason to attempt to inhibit this isozyme in the brain. To inhibit HO-1/HO-2 purified preparations, cells in culture, or microsomes, add 0.1–10 μM ZnPP to the assay system before the addition of FePP; the concentration of FePP should not exceed that of ZnPP because of kinetic considerations. A good source of information regarding kinetics of interactions of purified HO-2 with ZnPP (and CoPP) is available.[30]

To induce HO-2 activity and mRNA in cell culture systems, we have treated HeLa cells with dexamethasone (DX) as follows: HeLa cells are maintained at 37° in an incubator under 5% (v/v) CO_2 in Dulbecco's modified Eagle's medium (DMEM) containing 10% (v/v) bovine calf serum supplemented with 4.1 mM L-glutamine, 100 units/ml penicillin, and 100 μg/ml streptomycin sulfate. The cells are subcultured weekly in T25 flasks. Cells are grown in 225-cm^2 flasks for 2–3 days until 60–70% confluent. Thereafter, the cells are grown in the medium containing only the GMS-X (GIBCO/BRL, Gaithersburg, MD) serum supplement or GMS-X serum supplement plus DX, at 2–5 μM concentrations. The cells are harvested 24 hr after hormone administration. In studies involving immunohistochemical visualization of HO-2, HeLa cells are seeded at a density of 4 × 10^4 cells/chamber in a Nunc 4-well chamber slide in DMEM containing 10% (v/v) bovine calf serum and antibiotics for 24 hr. Subsequently, the cells are grown in DMEM containing GMS-X serum supplement for 24 hr, and are subjected to hormone treatment for 24 hr at the specified concentrations. Control cells are given DX vehicle, dimethyl sulfoxide (DMSO), only. Expression of HO-2 mRNA can be increased *in vivo* in the adult rat

[35] E. L. Saunders, M. D. Maines, M. J. Meredith, and M. L. Freeman, *Arch. Biochem. Biophys.* **288**, 368 (1991).

cerebellum by injecting (s.c.) daily 40 μg/g corticosterone dissolved in commercial corn oil for 20 days. This treatment decreases NO synthase activity and transcript levels by half that of normal, and causes atrophy of NO synthase expressing neurons.[9] In newborn rats, daily treatment with the steroid (5 μg/g, s.c.) on days 2–6 causes a marked increase in brain HO-2 when examined on day 14 after birth.[35a] Activity of NO synthase can be inhibited *in vitro* without affecting HO-1/HO-2 activity using either N^ω-nitro-L-arginine (L-NOArg) or N^G-monomethyl-L-arginine (L-NMMA). These compounds should be used at concentrations below 100 μM.

Quantitation of Brain Heme Oxygenase Activity

A variety of techniques have been developed to measure degradation products of HO activity as assessed by CO or bilirubin production.[22] Biliverdin is the immediate product of heme oxidation, but because of its low extinction it is more readily measured when it is reduced to bilirubin by biliverdin reductase. In our laboratory, HO activity is assessed on the basis of the rate of bilirubin formation. The source of the reductase is the tissue cytosol; for routine measurements a saline-perfused liver cytosol fraction (105,000 g, 1 hr, 4°) can be used as the enzyme source. It is important to note that the HO contribution reflects the total activity of both HO-1 and HO-2 isozymes present in a given sample. The following procedure allows for reliable measurement of HO activity in preparations from the whole organ, select brain regions, or cultured cells. It should also be noted that use of partially purified or homogeneous preparations of biliverdin reductase is more desirable than the cytosol because hemoglobin interference with spectral analysis is eliminated. These preparations can be obtained by further processing of the cytosol.[36] Purified preparation of biliverdin reductase is commercially available (StressGen, Victoria, BC, Canada). Also, when measuring HO activity in a reconstituted system or when the tissue has been frozen and thawed, the addition of exogenous NADPH-cytochrome P450 reductase is necessary. The reductase provides the reducing equivalents needed for oxidation of heme. As a precaution, the reductase should be routinely added to the assay system when measuring the HO activity of the brain or cultured cells. The reductase preparation used for this purpose does not need to be homogeneous. The NADPH-cytochrome P450 reductase can be readily purified,[37] partially or completely, from livers of rats treated with phenobarbital (three s.c. injections of 50 mg/kg/day).

[35a] M. D. Maines, B. C. Eke, and X-D. Zhao, *Brain Res.*, in press (1996).
[36] T. J. Huang, G. M. Trakshel, and M. D. Maines, *J. Biol. Chem.* **264,** 7844 (1989).
[37] M. Nishimoto, J. E. Clark, and B. S. Masters *Biochemistry* **32,** 8863 (1993).

Purified preparations of the reductase are also commercially available (StressGen). Microsomal preparations of optimum quality can be obtained by differential centrifugation of tissue homogenates obtained from saline-perfused organs. For the brain, transcardial perfusion of brain tissue with saline for about 2–3 min with a Cornwall syringe is adequate. Ten tissue volumes of 10 mM Tris containing 250 mM sucrose (pH 7.5) are used for homogenization. Homogenates are centrifuged at 9000 g (10 min). When a limited tissue source is available, such as is the case with cultured cells or isolated brain regions, the 9000 g supernatant fraction can be used as the HO enzyme source. The microsomal fraction is then sedimented from the 9000 g supernatant by ultracentrifugation at 105,000 g for 1 hr. The microsomal pellet can be "washed" by resuspension (on ice) in 10 tissue volumes of 20 mM potassium phosphate buffer containing 1 M KCl and 10 mM EDTA, pH 7.4, and the microsomes resedimented. The microsomal pellet is gently scraped from the tube and resuspended in 0.2 tissue volume of 20 mM Tris containing 1 mM EDTA and 20% (v/v) glycerol, pH 7.5. Microsomes are best stored on ice until assay. This preparation is suitable for activity measurement and Western blotting. Enzyme activity is stable for at least 24 hr when samples are handled in this manner. Once samples become frozen–thawed, a significant loss of enzyme activity is observed.

Protein is estimated in the brain microsomal sample using a modified form of the Lowry method.[38] An aliquot of microsomes is digested for 30 min at room temperature in 1 N NaOH. Because of the high lipid content of brain tissue, the digest is assayed for protein using 2% (w/v) Na_2CO_3, 1% (w/v) sodium dodecyl sulfate (SDS) in 0.1 M NaOH, and Folin solution. Protein in the microsomal preparation is typically adjusted to 2.5–5 mg protein/ml using the above resuspension buffer. Protein concentration in the HO incubation mixture can be as low as 0.3 up to 1.0 mg/ml assay volume. The same procedure can be used for microsomal preparation from other organs.

Notes. Access to a split-beam scanning spectrophotometer is essential. Bilirubin is rapidly destroyed by light, and heme, in solution, polymerizes with time.

Reagents. Required reagents include 0.1 M potassium phosphate buffer containing 1 mM EDTA, pH 7.4; 2.75 mM β-NADPH, in the same buffer, stored in the dark at $-20°$; 0.1 M HCl; and 10 mg/ml Trizma solution. A solution of 1 mM heme b is prepared by dissolving 0.652 mg heme b (molecular weight 652; Sigma, St. Louis, MO) in 0.25 ml of 0.1 M NaOH. To this, 0.1 ml of a solution of 10 mg/ml Trizma base is added and the

---

[38] O. H. Lowry, N. J. Rosebrough, A. L. Farr, and R. J. Randall, *J. Biol. Chem.* **193,** 265 (1957).

mixture vortexed until heme is fully dissolved. Add 0.25 ml distilled water and dissolve 13.2 mg bovine serum albumin (BSA) into solution with vortexing. Add dropwise 0.23–0.25 ml of 0.1 M HCl. Dilute to 1.0 ml with 0.1 M potassium phosphate buffer containing 1 mM EDTA, pH 7.4. Store in the dark. This solution may be kept for up to 12 hr at 4°. The same procedure is used to prepare ZnPP or other metalloporphyrins. The molecular weight for ZnPP is 626.05, and it can be purchased from Porphyrin Products (P.O. Box 31, 195 South 700 West, Logan, UT 84321). The source of biliverdin reductase enzyme is the supernatant (105,000 g) from saline-perfused rat liver (or kidney). As noted above, a more highly purified preparation of the enzyme may be used. Aliquots of cytosolic fraction may be stored frozen at −80° for several weeks. When liver is homogenized in 1/3 (w/v) of buffer and used for preparation of the cytosol, the biliverdin reductase activity of the preparation will be approximately 20–25 units/ml. One unit is the amount that produces 1 nmol bilirubin per minute.

Procedure. Perform the assay in dimmed lighting on ice. Use a 13 × 100 mm glass test tube holding 0.2 ml of microsomal preparation (2.5–5 mg protein/ml) in 0.1 M potassium phosphate buffer containing 1 mM EDTA, pH 7.4. To this, add 1.7 ml of a mixture comprising the same buffer with 20 µl heme solution (final concentration in incubation mixture 10 μM) and 50 µl cytosol preparation (the reductase is added in excess) or 0.5–1 unit of a purified reductase preparation. Mix the sample by gentle vortexing, and then divide into two equal halves by pipetting into two 13 × 100 mm tubes (each tube should now contain 0.95 ml of the reaction mix). One tube is designated as test and the other as reference. Pipette 50 µl of phosphate buffer into the reference tube, and 50 µl NADPH solution into the test mixture. Vortex the samples and incubate in a 37° water bath (shaking) for 8–15 min, depending on activity. Following incubation, terminate the reaction by placing samples on ice.

The bilirubin concentration can be determined by measurement of the difference spectrum (464–530 nm) between test and reference samples with the split-beam mode of a spectrophotometer (e.g., Aminco DW2C). It is best to scan between 410 and 600 nm; baseline is established using cuvettes containing buffer. Under these conditions bilirubin shows a characteristic absorbance at 465 nm. The amount of bilirubin formed during the incubation is calculated on the basis of an extinction coefficient of 40 mM^{-1} cm^{-1}.[39] The HO activity is expressed as nanomoles bilirubin formed per minute per milligram protein.

The activity of purified preparations of HO-1/HO-2[20] can be assessed in a reaction mixture (2 ml final volume) containing varying concentrations

---

[39] M. D. Maines and A. Kappas, *Proc. Natl. Acad. Sci. U.S.A.* **71**, 4293 (1974).

of heme (1–10 μM), excess purified biliverdin reductase (0.50 unit/ml), and purified NADPH-cytochrome P450 reductase (0.5 unit), each unit having the amount of protein that catalyzes reduction of 1 μmol cytochrome c per minute, in 0.1 M potassium phosphate buffer, pH 7.4, and varying amounts of purified HO-1 or HO-2 (obtained from tissue or from an expression clone). The reaction is initiated by the addition of 50 μl of 2.75 mM NADPH to the test reaction mixture. The HO-1 and HO-2 isozymes can be purified, respectively, from rat liver and testis.[20,40] To increase HO-1 protein in liver, rats are treated with $CoCl_2$ (50 mg/kg, s.c.) 24 hr before sacrifice. *Escherichia coli* expressed truncated HO-1 (28 kDa) can be purified as described by Wilks and Ortiz de Montellano,[41] and full-length HO-2 can be purified as described by Rublevskaya and Maines.[30]

Immunodetection of Heme Oxygenase Isozymes

The fact that HO isozymes are antigenically distinct[1,21,39] has allowed for the generation of monospecific polyclonal antiserum in New Zealand White rabbits. The antisera are selective for HO-1 and HO-2 proteins and can be used for HO isozyme protein visualization by ICC or Western blotting. Immunocytochemistry with these antibodies is capable of localizing HO-1 and HO-2 protein in brain tissue sections. This procedure[4,9,31,32,35a,42,43] has become a powerful technique for identifying the cellular sites of HO mRNA translation in tissue from both normal and stressed rats. Furthermore, the immunoperoxidase and immunofluorescence techniques can be combined to allow localization of HO-1- and HO-2-expressing cells in the same tissue section, or combined with NADPH diaphorase staining to identify neurons that express both HO isozymes and NO synthase.[44] For colocalization of HO isozymes and NO synthase, the sections are first processed for immunofluorescence after photography, the coverslip is removed, and sections are rinsed in buffer and then stained for NADPH diaphorase (NADPH dehydrogenase) (see [48] in this volume).[44a]

For analysis of cell types that express HO isozymes and NO synthase, NADPH diaphorase histochemistry is conducted, followed by immunoperoxidase labeling of HO isozymes. This results in brown staining of HO immunoreactive structures and dark blue staining of NO synthase-containing cells and processes. For this, free floating tissues slices are stained

[40] G. M. Trakshel, R. K. Kutty, and M. D. Maines, *J. Biol. Chem.* **261**, 11131 (1986).
[41] A. Wilks and P. R. Ortiz de Montellano, *J. Biol. Chem.* **268**, 22357 (1993).
[42] J. F. Ewing, S. N. Haber, and M. D. Maines, *J. Neurochem.* **58**, 1140 (1992).
[43] J. F. Ewing, C. M. Weber, and M. D. Maines, *J. Neurochem.* **61**, 1015 (1993).
[44] S. R. Vincent, S. Das, and M. D. Maines, *Neuroscience (Oxford)* **63**, 223 (1994).
[44a] *Methods Enzymol.* **268**, Chap. 48, 1996 (this volume).

for diaphorase; thereafter, they are washed in 0.1 M phosphate buffer, pH 7.4, containing 0.3% Triton X-100 (~20 ml) for 5 min at room temperature. The wash step is repeated three times. Slices are then processed for HO-1/HO-2 ICC by proceeding directly to the HO blocking step. To prepare systemic organs such as testes,[45] heart,[10,13] and blood vessels,[10] paraffin-embedded tissues are used. The tissue is fixed in 4% (v/v) paraformaldehyde for 6–8 hr at 25° before dehydration and paraffin embedding. Tissue sections 5 μm thick are cut and mounted on Superfrost Plus slides (Fisher Scientific, Pittsburgh, PA). Sections can be stored at 25° before use. Analysis of HO isozymes is carried out as follows.

Reagents and Procedure for Tissue Preparation. Prepare 0.2 M phosphate buffer (PB) by adding 10.6 g anhydrous monobasic sodium phosphate to 56 g anhydrous dibasic potassium phosphate and adjusting the volume to 2 liter with distilled water. The pH should be approximately pH 7.3. Prepare 0.1 M PB by diluting an equal volume of 0.2 M PB with distilled water. Prepare 0.9% (w/v) saline by adding 9 g NaCl to 1 liter distilled water. Also needed is 4% (w/v) paraformaldehyde in 0.1 M PB and containing 1.5% (w/v) sucrose (standard fixative). Heat 500 ml distilled water to 90°. Remove from heat and dissolve 40 g paraformaldehyde. Clarify the solution by dropwise addition of 1 N NaOH. Add 500 ml of 0.2 M PB containing 15 g sucrose. Filter the solution using general usage filter paper. Standard fixative is usually prepared within 48 hr of use. Graded sucrose solutions contain 0.1 M PB with 10, 20, and 30% (w/v) sucrose. Also prepare 50 mM PB, 30% (v/v) ethylene glycol containing 30% (w/v) sucrose (cryoprotectant).

For animals more than 14 days old, transcardial perfusion may be performed using a peristaltic pump. Depending on the individual perfusion setup, it may be necessary to adjust the tubing diameter, pump type, and intravenous catheter to give proper flow of solutions through the animals. For neonatal animals less than 14 days old, the transcardial perfusion may be performed manually using a 30 cm³ syringe fitted with a 25-gauge needle.

Anesthetize animals by intraperitoneal injection of pentobarbital (50 mg/kg), and begin the surgery when no toe-pinch reflex is observed. Open the abdominal cavity with a midline incision to the sternum. Access the heart by diagonal incisions through the rib cage to either side of the sternum and extending to each side of the neck. Clamp back the sternum, and occlude the descending aorta with hemostatic forceps to direct the flow of fluids to the upper body. Now make a small incision in the right atria. Insert an intravenous catheter (18 gauge for adult rats; 22 gauge for neonates) into the left ventricle so that the tip is positioned in the aortic arch; begin the perfusion process by clearing the adult tissue of blood with 250 ml of

[45] J. F. Ewing and M. D. Maines, *Endocrinology* (*Baltimore*) **136,** 2294 (1995).

0.9% saline delivered over 10–15 min. For neonate animals, 60–75 ml saline should be infused over 10 min. Following clearing, fixation of the adult brain is accomplished by perfusion with 500 ml of standard fixative delivered over 20–30 min. The neonatal brain is perfused with 100–200 ml of fixative. The brain should be removed from the skull and postfixed for 1 hr at room temperature, with the exception of neonatal tissue from rats less than 8 days of age which may be postfixed for 16 hr at 4° to improve the quality of the tissue. It is notable that we have not observed significant alteration in the pattern or intensity of HO immunostaining when fixation is extended from 1 hr (25°) to 16 hr at 4°. Following postfixation of tissue, sequentially immerse the organ for 1–2 days (4°) in 10, 20, and 30% (w/v) graded sucrose solutions to afford cryoprotection. Intact brains may be placed in cryoprotectant at −20° for storage prior to sectioning.

Brain equilibrated in 20 or 30% (w/v) sucrose may be sectioned using a freezing sliding microtome (Reichert-Jung, Division of Leica, Buffalo, NY). Frozen sectioning of tissues cut in a coronal orientation at 30 μm thickness affords both good resolution of brain structure and recovery of stained sections. Brain tissue from neonatal animals less than 14 days of age is best recovered when sectioned at 40 μm (or greater) thickness. Furthermore, we have found that the neonatal cerebellum is only reasonably recovered when sectioned in a sagittal orientation. Tissue sections may be stored at −20° in compartmentalized boxes containing cryoprotectant solution prior to staining. Tissue preserved in this state can be stored for several years without apparent effect on the observed pattern of HO staining.

Reagents and Procedure for Immunocytochemistry. The following reagents are needed for ICC: 0.1 M PB containing 0.3% (v/v) Triton X-100 (PB/TX); Cytoseal 60 mounting medium; 50 mM Tris, pH 7.5; graded ethanol solutions (50, 70, 80, 95, and 100%, v/v, ethanol/distilled H_2O); normal goat serum (NGS; GIBCO–BRL, Grand Island, NY); goat anti-rabbit γ-globulin (GAR; Organon Teknika Cappel, Durham, NC); rabbit peroxidase antiperoxidase (rPAP; Organon Teknika Cappel); HO-1/HO-2 polyclonal antiserum (StressGen, Victoria, BC, Canada); goat anti-rabbit γ-globulin conjugated to fluorescein isothiocyanate (Organon Teknika Cappel; required only for immunofluorescent detection); 30% (w/v) H_2O_2; 3,3′-Diaminobenzidine tetrahydrochloride dihydrate (Aldrich, Milwaukee, WI); PB/TX containing 10% (v/v) NGS (antibody buffer; the solution is passed through a 0.45-μm filter prior to use); and 0.5 M Tris, pH 7.5, containing 0.5% (w/v) diaminobenzidine (DAB/Tris). The last solution is prepared by dissolving 50 mg 3,3′-diaminobenzidine tetrahydrochloride dihydrate in 100 ml 50 mM Tris and then filtering using general usage filter paper. It is notable that DAB is a carcinogen. Accordingly, this solution should be prepared in a chemical hood using protective covering. Following use, all contaminated items and solution should be treated with bleach to inactivate the DAB. Waste should be disposed in accordance with institutional guidelines. Also needed are the following: DAB/Tris containing 0.001% (v/v) H_2O_2 (developer), prepared by adding to 100 ml DAB/Tris 33 μl of 3% (v/v) H_2O_2 immediately prior to use; and xylene (J.T. Baker, Phillipsburg, NJ).

Note: All washes are performed on a platform shaker at room temperature, unless otherwise specified.

Free floating frozen brain sections should be rinsed of cryoprotectant by soaking in PB overnight in a cold room. Transfer sections with a paintbrush into netted compartments (Brain Research, Boston, MA) that are immersed in staining dishes containing PB. Wash tissue three times for 5 min each. Equilibrate tissue with PB/TX by washing it three times for 5 min each. Block tissue in antibody buffer for 20 min at room temperature. Following blocking, transfer the tissue into small polystyrene culture dishes containing primary antibody, and incubate for 1–4 days on a platform shaker in a cold room. The optimal dilution and incubation time of the HO primary antibody may differ depending on the preparation and should be empirically determined. In our studies, we use 1/1000 or 1/2000 antibody dilution (v/v, in antibody buffer).

The tissue should be rinsed of primary antibody with eight washes of PB/TX over 1.5–3 hr. The tissue should again be reequilibrated in antibody buffer for 20 min immediately prior to transfer to dishes containing the GAR secondary antibody diluted 1/1000 (v/v) in antibody buffer. The tissue is now ready to be returned to the cold room for overnight incubation on a platform shaker.

Rinse tissue of excess secondary antibody with eight washes of PB/TX over 1.5–3 hr, equilibrate with antibody buffer for 20 min, and then transfer to dishes containing rPAP freshly diluted 1/500 (v/v) in antibody buffer. Following a room temperature incubation with tertiary antibody for 1 hr, wash tissue with repeated changes of PB over 1–2 hr. Equilibrate the tissue in 50 mM Tris, pH 7.5, with two washes, 10 min each, and then in DAB/Tris solution for 10 min. Visualization of antibody–antigen complexes is brought about by incubation of tissue in developer for up to 15 min. Cells containing HO protein will turn brown in color, and the degree of staining should be monitored by visually inspecting select sections under a microscope. Terminate the color reaction with two rapid rinses of 1 min each in 50 mM Tris, pH 7.5, followed by three 10 min washes in the same buffer. Wash tissue three times for 10 min each in PB and store, covered, at 4° prior to mounting. Should an extended storage period be required, a bacteriostatic agent such as sodium azide or thimersol should be added to the PB.

Mount tissue out of PB onto Superfrost Plus or gelatin-coated slides and dry overnight on a slide warmer at 37°–42°. Dehydrate tissue by immersion in Coplin jars containing distilled water (1 min), 50% (v/v) ethanol (3 min), 70% (v/v) ethanol (3 min), 80% (v/v) ethanol (3 min), twice for 3 min each in 95% (v/v) ethanol, and three times for 3 min each in 100% ethanol. Finally, clear the tissue by incubating in xylene 3 times for 15 min each prior to adding coverslips with Cytoseal 60 mounting medium.

Brain cells expressing HO may be visualized using immunofluorescence technique as follows. Prepare and process tissue through incubation with primary antibody as described above. Then rinse tissue of primary antibody with eight washes PB/TX over 1.5–3 hr. Equilibrate tissue in antibody buffer for 20 min. Transfer to culture dishes containing fluorescein isothiocyanate (FITC)-GAR secondary antibody freshly diluted to 1/1000 (v/v) in antibody buffer under dimmed lighting. To avoid photobleaching of the immunofluorescence signal, cover the dishes with aluminum foil. Incubate the tissue with secondary antibody on a platform shaker overnight in a cold room. Rinse tissue of secondary antibody with eight washes of PB/TX over 1.5–3 hr in dimmed lighting. Wash tissue three times with PB for 15 min each, prior to mounting and drying. Add coverslip to the slide with 70% (v/v) glycerol and keep slides wrapped in foil at 4° prior to visualization using a fluorescence microscope.

Heme oxygenase isozymes can also be localized in cell culture. After treatment with the desired agent, the medium is removed and the cells are washed with ice-cold phosphate-buffered saline (PBS) for 5 min. The process is repeated twice. The cells are fixed for 10 min with 95% ethanol (4°) and then washed twice with ice-cold PBS. Thereafter, cells are sequentially incubated with 3% H_2O_2 in PBS (5 min on ice), 5% normal goat serum (25°, 20 min), and anti-HO antiserum (1/1000 or 1/2000 dilution) or preimmune serum (1/1000 or 1/2000 dilution) at 4° for 15–18 hr. The antigen–antibody complex is detected by a peroxidase detection system. Essentially the same procedure can be used for ICC analysis of induced HO-1 or control HO-1/HO-2 in a variety of cells in culture.

Controls

The authenticity of antibody–antigen complexes may be validated by preadsorption of primary antiserum with an excess of antigen serving as a negative control. Staining of additional brain sections in preadsorbed antiserum should significantly diminish or abolish staining observed with primary antibody. Antisera to HO may be preadsorbed as follows. Place equal amounts of primary antiserum in 1.5-ml Eppendorf tubes. To the primary antiserum to be preadsorbed, pure HO-1 or HO-2 protein is added to give a final concentration greater than 1 mg/ml. To the control antibody, an equal amount of protein diluent without HO antigen is added. Incubate mixtures for 2 hr at room temperature and then dilute each to the final working concentration with antibody buffer. Continue incubation overnight at 4°. Alternatively, preimmune rabbit serum, diluted to the same concentration as the primary antibody, may be used as a negative control; however, it is notable that unless the preimmune serum is obtained from the same host in which the primary antibody is derived, this control is of limited value.

Endogenous Peroxidase Inhibitor

In tissue that has not been completely cleared of red blood cells, a nonspecific spotting occurs due to the presence of endogenous peroxidase. This may be abolished by preincubating tissue in endogenous peroxidase inhibitor (EPI) for 5–8 min and then rinsing the tissue six times with PB over 1 hr prior to initial equilibration in PB/TX and primary antibody incubation. The EPI reagent can be prepared fresh by mixing 80 ml PB, 10 ml 30% (w/v) H_2O_2, and 10 ml methanol. Tissue will usually foam as the endogenous enzyme activity is inactivated.

Western Blotting

Our laboratory has assessed a variety of immunoblotting procedures and detection methods in an effort to derive an optimal protocol for the visualization of both HO-1/HO-2 proteins in brain tissue. In particular, detection of the HO-1 form is challenging since it is expressed at very low levels in normal adult rat brain.[3] In contrast, brain HO-2 protein is abundantly expressed in the adult organ,[2] and there are a number of Western immunoblotting protocols suitable for its detection. The methodology described here may be applied to assess either brain HO-1 or HO-2 protein.

To detect HO-1/HO-2 in brain, microsomes are prepared as described earlier for quantitation of HO activity. For analysis of brain HO-2 protein, the sample (~100 μg microsomal protein) may be directly prepared for electrophoresis. For analysis of brain HO-1 protein, the microsomal preparation must be concentrated by acetone precipitation as follows. Place the microsomal sample (~250 μg total microsomal protein) in a microcentrifuge tube and bring to a total volume of 100 μl with 0.1 M Tris, pH 7.5, containing 1 mM EDTA and 20% (v/v) glycerol. To this add 30 μl ice-cold acetone, mix, and place the sample on dry ice for 5 min. The fluffy white precipitate that forms should be pelleted in a microcentrifuge in a cold room. Decant the supernatant and allow the pellet to air dry for 10 min. Dissolve the pellet in loading buffer prior to denaturation and electrophoresis.

Reagents and Procedures. A stock is prepared of 100 mM potassium phosphate buffer containing 0.75 M NaCl, pH 7.4 (5× PBS stock); 1× PBS is prepared by dilution of stock with the appropriate quantity of distilled water. Blocking solution contains 20 mM potassium phosphate buffer, pH 7.4, with 0.15 M NaCl, 3% (w/v) bovine serum albumin (BSA), 10% (v/v) normal goat serum, and 0.02% Thimerosol. Also prepare 1× PBS, pH 7.4, with 20% (v/v) glycerol and PBS containing 0.5% (w/v) sodium cholate (PBS–cholate). Antibody diluent is PBS–cholate containing 10% (v/v) normal goat serum and 3% (w/v) BSA (NGS, GIBCO–BRL). Also prepare the following Tris buffers: 25 mM Tris, pH 8.3, containing 192 mM glycine; 25 mM Tris, pH 8.3, containing 192 mM glycine and 0.1% (w/v) SDS; 25 mM Tris, pH 8.3, containing 192 mM glycine and 20% methanol (transfer buffer). The HO-1/HO-2 antibody is from StressGen. Goat anti-rabbit immunoglobulin conjugated to horseradish peroxidase (HRP–GAR) is from Organon Teknika Cappel. Antibodies are diluted to 0.2 mg/ml with 20 mM potassium phosphate buffer, pH 7.4, containing 150 mM NaCl, 10% (v/v) glycerol, and 0.01% (w/v) Thimersol and stored in aliquots at $-20°$ until use. The 30% (w/v) H_2O_2 is from Sigma. Development reagents are as follows: a fresh 4-chloro-3-naphthol (Sigma) stock solution (15 mg dissolved in 5 ml of methanol) is prepared and stored in the dark. Developer is prepared by dilution of 5 ml of 4-chloro-3-naphthol (3 mg/ml) and 6 ml of 5× PBS stock solution to 30 ml final volume with distilled water. Complete by adding 30 μl of 30% (w/v) H_2O_2 stock immediately prior to use.

Proteins are separated under denaturing conditions on a 10% running gel (13 cm × 1.5 mm) with a 4% stacking gel. The upper reservoir should hold 25 mM Tris, pH 8.3, containing 192 mM glycine and 0.1% (w/v) SDS. Fill the lower reservoir with the appropriate volume of 25 mM Tris, pH 8.3, containing 192 mM glycine. Following electrophoresis, rinse the gel briefly with distilled water, and then equilibrate in transfer buffer for 15 min prior to transblotting. Electroblot brain microsomal protein onto a 0.45-μm Immobilon P membrane (Millipore, Bedford, MA) presoaked in methanol and equilibrated in transfer buffer. Alternatively, a 0.2-μm nitrocellulose membrane (Schleicher and Schuell, Keene, NH) may be used. Carry out transfer at 0.5 mA current for 1.5 hr, after which the filter is blocked in blocking solution overnight at room temperature, or for 1 hr at 37°. Next, incubate the blot in primary antibody diluted to the appropriate concentration in antibody diluent for 2 hr at room temperature. It is important that the optimal dilution of primary serum be determined empirically, since it will depend on the source and the titer of the preparation. Wash the filter once for 5 min with PBS–cholate and then wash three times for 5 min each with PBS. Incubate the filter in HRP–GAR (100 μl HRP–GAR diluted in 10 ml antibody diluent) for 30 min. Following secondary antibody incubation, the filter should be rinsed once briefly with

PBS–cholate and then twice more in the same buffer for 5 min each. The filter should then be rinsed briefly with 1× PBS and then two more times in the same buffer for 5 min each. Now place the filter in developer under dimmed lighting until the desired band intensity is obtained. Terminate the development reaction by rinsing the filter several times in PBS. Filters may be incubated overnight in PBS containing 20% (v/v) glycerol prior to drying between sheets of filter paper. In our hands, this step improved the shelf life of the blot and the stability of band intensity. Filters are stored in darkness.

Acknowledgments

I thank Justin Thornton for preparation of the manuscript. I also express appreciation for support from the Burroughs Wellcome Fund, and National Institutes of Health Grants ES01247, ES03968, and R37ES04391.

[47] Localization of Neuronal Nitric Oxide Synthase

By Daniel S. Chao, Paul M. Hwang, Fred Huang, and David S. Bredt

Introduction

The discovery of nitric oxide (NO) as the endothelial-derived relaxation factor (EDRF) that regulates cyclic guanosine 3′,5′-monophosphate (cGMP) levels in the vascular system[1,2] prompted investigations of the possible role for NO in controlling cGMP levels in nervous tissue. Within the brain, the highest levels of cGMP are found in cerebellum, where excitatory transmitters rapidly elevate cGMP levels both *in vitro*[3] and *in vivo*.[4] In 1988 Garthwaite and co-workers found that cerebellar cells stimulated with the excitatory amino acid glutamate release a diffusible factor with physical and biological properties of EDRF.[5] Definitive evidence for a role for NO in controlling cGMP levels in brain derived from studies showing that NO synthase (NOS) inhibitors such as monomethylarginine

[1] R. F. Furchgott and J. V. Zawadzki, *Nature (London)* **288**, 373 (1980).
[2] R. M. Palmer, A. G. Ferrige, and S. Moncada, *Nature (London)* **327**, 524 (1987).
[3] J. A. Ferrendelli, M. M. Chang, and D. A. Kinscherf, *J. Neurochem.* **22**, 535 (1974).
[4] G. Biggio, B. B. Brodie, E. Costa, and A. Guidotti, *Proc. Natl. Acad. Sci. U.S.A.* **74**, 3592 (1977).
[5] J. Garthwaite, S. L. Charles, and R. Chess-Williams, *Nature (London)* **336**, 385 (1988).

block glutamate-linked enhancements of cGMP levels.[6,7] In addition to these biochemical studies of NO in the central nervous system (CNS), physiological experiments demonstrated a role for NO in autonomic neurotransmission.[8,9] However, in both brain and peripheral tissues it was not clear whether NO formed in association with neuronal activity derived from muscle, glia, endothelium, or blood cells, all of which occur in close association with neurons.

Functions of neurotransmitters are frequently elucidated by determining their cellular loci. Because of the inherent chemical instability of NO, our understanding of NO disposition largely derives from studies of NOS. The abundance of NOS in brain facilitated the initial isolation of an NOS enzyme from rat cerebellum.[10] Purification of NOS permitted the generation of polyclonal antibodies for immunohistochemical studies.[11] In both brain and peripheral tissues NOS is almost exclusively associated with neurons. For example, glutamate-linked enhancement of cerebellar cGMP levels appears to result from NO derived from cerebellar granule cells which are enriched with both glutamate receptors and NOS.[11] Similarly, NOS is abundantly expressed in inhibitory motor neurons of the myenteric plexus[11,12] that are responsible for NO-dependent relaxation of the gastrointestinal tract.[9]

Immunolocalization of Nitric Oxide Synthase in Brain

The recognition that NO functions as a major messenger molecule in diverse processes in the central and peripheral nervous systems has motivated intensive immunohistochemical studies to delineate the distribution of NOS. Both monoclonal and polyclonal sera have been successfully used for immunohistochemistry, and these reagents are now commercially available. Discrete localization of NOS in restricted populations of neurons allows for facile identification using a variety of immunohistochemical protocols. The methodology used in our laboratory for localization of NOS in rat brain and skeletal muscle is described here in detail.

Reagents. All immunohistochemical solutions are prepared in phosphate-buffered saline (PBS), which is made by dissolving 8.0 g NaCl, 0.2 g

[6] D. S. Bredt and S. H. Snyder, *Proc. Natl. Acad. Sci. U.S.A.* **86,** 9030 (1989).
[7] J. Garthwaite, G. Garthwaite, R. M. Palmer, and S. Moncada, *Eur. J. Pharmacol.* **172,** 413 (1989).
[8] J. S. Gillespie, X. R. Liu, and W. Martin, *Br. J. Pharmacol.* **98,** 1080 (1989).
[9] H. Bult, G. E. Boeckxstaens, P. A. Pelckmans, F. H. Jordaens, Y. M. Van Maercke, and A. G. Herman, *Nature (London)* **345,** 346 (1990).
[10] D. S. Bredt and S. H. Snyder, *Proc. Natl. Acad. Sci. U.S.A.* **87,** 682 (1990).
[11] D. S. Bredt, P. M. Hwang, and S. H. Snyder, *Nature (London)* **347,** 768 (1990).
[12] M. Costa, J. B. Furness, S. Pompolo, S. J. Brookes, J. C. Bornstein, D. S. Bredt, and S. H. Snyder, *Neurosci. Lett.* **148,** 121 (1992).

KCl, 1.44 g Na_2HPO_4, and 0.24 g KH_2PO_4 in 800 ml of distilled water. The solution is adjusted to pH 7.2, and the volume is brought to 1 liter. The 2× PBS reagent is prepared by an identical procedure except that the final volume is brought to only 0.5 liter. Tissue fixation uses 4% paraformaldehyde, prepared by adding 8 g of paraformaldehyde to 100 ml of water. Heat the suspension to 60° in a fume hood for 10 min and add a few drops of 1 M NaOH to help dissolve the paraformaldehyde. After the solid is fully dissolved, allow the solution to cool to room temperature, add 100 ml of 2× PBS, and store at 4°. This stock solution of paraformaldehyde should be prepared fresh daily.

Immunoperoxidase Staining of Rat Brain

Rats are anesthetized with pentobarbital (50 mg/kg intraperitoneally) and perfused through the heart with freshly depolymerized paraformaldehyde (4%) in PBS. The brain is dissected and postperfusion fixed in paraformaldehyde for 4 hr at 4°. Following postfixation, the brain is cryoprotected in 20% sucrose in PBS for 16 hr at 4° and then frozen rapidly in a bed of crushed dry ice. Tissue sections are then prepared using a cryostat (10–20 μm), or free floating sections can be cut on a freezing sliding microtome (40 μm). We find that floating sections retain more detailed morphology than cryostat sections.

The sections are then processed at room temperature in solutions of PBS containing 0.1% Triton X-100 (PBST). Tissues are first permeabilized in PBST for 20 min. Endogenous peroxidase is quenched by incubating sections in 1% H_2O_2 in PBS for 20 min. After being washed twice for 5 min, sections are incubated for 1 hr in blocking solution containing 2% goat serum in PBST. Tissues are then incubated in blocking solution supplemented with an appropriate dilution of primary antibody for 1–16 hr. High-quality antibodies are commercially available from numerous distributors. We have had success with antibodies from Transduction Laboratories (Lexington, KY). After incubation with primary antiserum, visualization of bound antibodies utilizes a commercially available avidin–biotin peroxidase kit (Elite, Vector Laboratories, Burlingame, CA), closely following the manufacturer's suggested protocol. Briefly, sections are washed twice for 5 min in PBST and incubated with a biotinylated goat anti-rabbit secondary antibody (1 : 200) for 1 hr. After being washed twice for 5 min in PBST, sections are incubated in Vectastain ABC reagent for 1 hr. Sections are then washed twice for 5 min in PBS and developed for 5 min with peroxidase solution containing 0.5 mg/ml diaminobenzidine (Sigma, St. Louis, MO) and 0.003% H_2O_2. Slides are dehydrated by sequential 1-min incubations in each of the following: 70% (v/v) ethanol; 95% (v/v) ethanol; two changes of 100% ethanol; and xylene. DPX medium (Fluka, Ronkonkoma, NY) is used to mount coverslips. Sections identically processed without incubation with primary antibody serve as valuable controls for nonspecific peroxidase labeling. Figure 1A represents the immunohistochemical distribution of NOS in a sagittal section of adult rat brain.

Localization of Nitric Oxide Synthase by NADPH Diaphorase Staining

Immunohistochemical mapping of NOS in forebrain revealed that NOS is discretely enriched in about 1% of neurons that have the morphology of medium aspiny neurons. These cells were all noted to contain somatostatin and neuropeptide Y, and all stain for NADPH diaphorase (NADPH-d; NADPH dehydrogenase).[13,14] NADPH-d is a histochemical stain that utilizes NADPH and a one-electron acceptor, such as nitro blue tetrazolium (NBT). Enzymatic reduction of NBT causes precipitation of this dye and blue staining of cells containing NADPH diaphorase.[15] Although all cells stain in unfixed brain tissues, only a defined subpopulation of cells are NADPH-d positive in paraformaldehyde-fixed sections. Because NOS colocalizes with NADPH-d cells, and NOS utilizes NADPH as a cofactor, it was suggested that NOS is responsible for NADPH diaphorase staining of neurons. Because NADPH-d is a histochemical stain used on paraformaldehyde-fixed tissue sections, it cannot be purified by biochemical extraction procedures. In fact, NOS accounts for only a minute fraction of NADPH-d activity in unfixed tissue homogenates.[14] Evidence that NOS accounts for NADPH-d staining of neurons derive from studies showing that cultured cells transfected with NOS cDNA display NADPH diaphorase staining following paraformaldehyde fixation.[16] This conclusion is further confirmed by the absence of NADPH-d staining in brain of mutant mice lacking NOS.[17]

Results with NADPH-d staining must be interpreted with caution. First, NADPH-d is a potentially nonspecific stain that may be a product of enzymes other than NOS. For example, the cortex of the adrenal gland and the adult olfactory neuroepithelium display strong NADPH-d staining

[13] D. S. Bredt, C. E. Glatt, P. M. Hwang, M. Fotuhi, T. M. Dawson, and S. H. Snyder, *Neuron* **7**, 615 (1991).

[14] B. T. Hope, G. J. Michael, K. M. Knigge, and S. R. Vincent, *Proc. Natl. Acad. Sci. U.S.A.* **88**, 2811 (1991).

[15] E. Thomas and A. G. E. Pearse, *Acta Neuropathol.* **3**, 238 (1964).

[16] T. M. Dawson, D. S. Bredt, M. Fotuhi, P. M. Hwang, and S. H. Snyder, *Proc. Natl. Acad. Sci. U.S.A.* **88**, 7797 (1991).

[17] P. L. Huang, T. M. Dawson, D. S. Bredt, S. H. Snyder, and M. C. Fishman, *Cell (Cambridge, Mass.)* **75**, 1273 (1993).

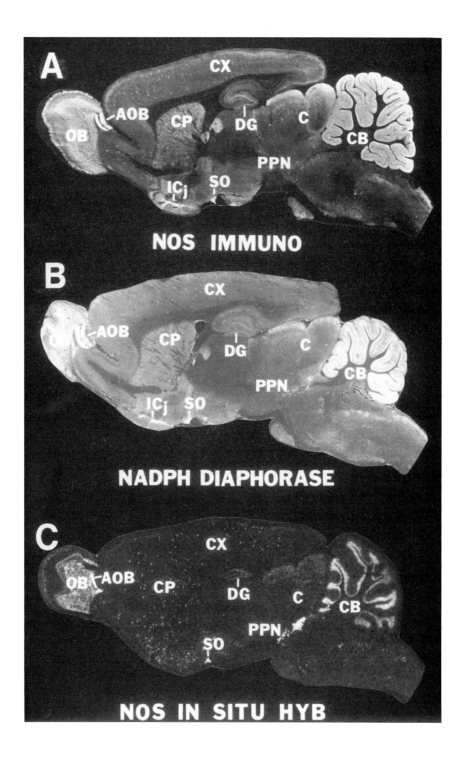

NOS IMMUNO

NADPH DIAPHORASE

NOS IN SITU HYB

but do not contain NOS.[16,18] Presumably, other NADPH-utilizing enzymes in these tissues account for staining. On the other hand, certain NOS-containing cells do not stain robustly for NADPH-d. In the developing rat brain, transient NOS neurons are ubiquitous in the cerebral cortical plate from embryonic day 14 to postnatal day 3.[19] However, the NOS in these cells do not stain robustly for NADPH-d.[19] This lack of staining may reflect a unique molecular environment for NOS in embryonic neurons which renders the enzyme more sensitive to paraformaldehyde fixation.

Despite these caveats, in the majority of cases NADPH-d allows for facile identification of NOS neurons in brain. The protocol used in our laboratory differs little from the original method described by Thomas and Pearce.[15] Tissues are harvested from paraformaldehyde-perfused animals, postfixed, and sectioned on a cryostat or a freezing microtome as described above. Tissue sections are rinsed once for 5 min in 100 mM Tris-HCl buffer, pH 8.0, and then stained at 37° for 30–60 min in the same Tris-HCl buffer solution supplemented with 1 mg/ml NADPH (Sigma), 0.3 mg/ml nitro blue tetrazolium (Sigma), and 0.2% Triton X-100. Slides are dehydrated with ethanol, and coverslips are added using DPX mountant as described earlier. Sections incubated in the same staining solution without added NADPH serve as a control. The distribution of NADPH-d in a sagittal section of rat brain is shown in Fig. 1B. Comparison with NOS immunohistochemical staining in Fig. 1A illustrates the coincidence of NOS and NADPH-d in all major brain structures.

Localization of Nitric Oxide Synthase by *in Situ* Hybridization

Nitric oxide synthase occurs both in neuronal soma and processes, so that it is often difficult to discern the cellular source of NOS immunoreactiv-

[18] J. Kishimoto, E. B. Keverne, J. Hardwick, and P. C. Emson, *Eur. J. Neurosci.* **5,** 1684 (1993).
[19] D. S. Bredt and S. H. Snyder, *Neuron* **13,** 301 (1994).

FIG. 1. Histologic localizations of neuronal NOS protein, NADPH diaphorase activity, and mRNA in brain. Adjacent sagittal brain sections were processed for (A) NOS immunohistochemistry, (B) NADPH diaphorase histochemistry, and (C) NOS *in situ* hybridization. All three methods show densest staining in the accessory olfactory bulb (AOB), pedunculopontine tegmental nucleus (PPN), and cerebellum (CB), with lesser staining in the dentate gyrus of the hippocampus (DG), main olfactory bulb (OB), superior and inferior colliculus (C), and supraoptic nucleus (SO). Intensely staining isolated cells are apparently scattered throughout the cerebral cortex (CX), caudate putamen, and basal forebrain. Some regions enriched in NOS protein and diaphorase staining are devoid of NOS mRNA, suggesting that in these regions the NOS protein has been transported in nerve fibers distant from its site of synthesis. These regions include the molecular layer of the cerebellum, the islands of Callejae (ICj), and the neuropil of the caudate putamen (CP) and cerebral cortex (CX).

ity in certain brain regions. *In situ* hybridization often can be used to resolve these questions, as NOS mRNA is largely restricted to neuronal cell bodies. For example, diffuse immunohistochemical staining for NOS in cerebellar cortex occurs together with strong *in situ* hybridization signal restricted to the granule cell layer.[13] This indicates that NOS in cerebellar cortex derives from parallel fibers of the granule cells rather than from Purkinje cells or glia which also have diffuse projections there. Another advantage of *in situ* hybridization is that it allows cellular quantitation of relative mRNA densities. A drawback to using *in situ* hybridization is that NOS mRNA levels are relatively low so that radioactive *in situ* hybridization techniques must be used and autoradiographic exposure times can extend to several weeks.

There are numerous excellent sources that describe applications of *in situ* hybridization to neurobiology,[20–22] and these methods will not be reiterated here. A unique aspect to NOS *in situ* hybridization is the possibility of double labeling sections with NADPH-d. This double labeling allows qualitative comparison of density and distribution of NOS mRNA and protein levels in a single tissue section. Because of the simplicity of NADPH-d staining we routinely double label all sections processed for *in situ* hybridization. NADPH-d staining of fixed cryostat sections prior to processing for NOS *in situ* hybridization is performed as described above except that a minimal volume of NADPH-d staining solution is used (~100 μl/slide) and all buffers are made strictly RNase free. Following NADPH-d staining, tissues are processed for *in situ* hybridization by standard procedures.[21,22] An example of *in situ* hybridization for NOS in a sagittal section of rat brain is shown in Fig. 1C.

Localization of Nitric Oxide Synthase in Skeletal Muscle

Studies have identified a major role for NOS in vertebrate skeletal muscle. The mRNA for NOS occurs at higher levels in human skeletal muscle than in human brain.[23] Studies of NO in cultured chick skeletal muscle indicate that NO participates in myoblast fusion.[24] Immunohistochemical studies indicate the NOS is present beneath the sarcolemma of

[20] C. A. Ross, M. W. MacCumber, C. E. Glatt, and S. H. Snyder, *Proc. Natl. Acad. Sci. U.S.A.* **86**, 2923 (1989).

[21] D. Sassoon and N. Rosenthal, *Methods Enzymol.* **225**, 384 (1993).

[22] D. G. Wilkinson and M. A. Nieto, *Methods Enzymol.* **225**, 361 (1993).

[23] M. Nakane, H. H. Schmidt, J. S. Pollock, U. Forstermann, and F. Murad, *FEBS Lett.* **316**, 175 (1993).

[24] K. H. Lee, M. Y. Baek, K. Y. Moon, W. K. Song, C. H. Chung, D. B. Ha, and M. S. Kang, *J. Biol. Chem.* **269**, 14371 (1994).

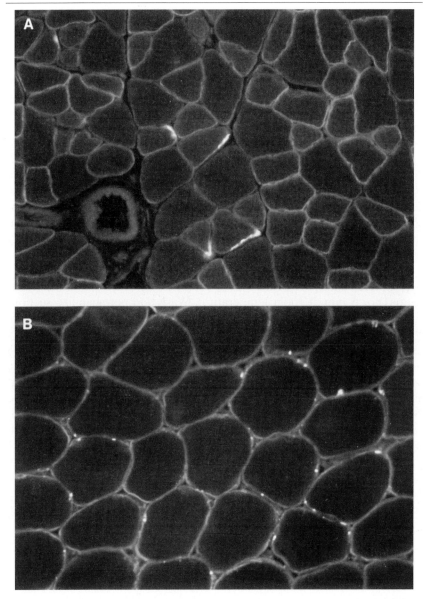

FIG. 2. Localization of nNOS in mammalian skeletal muscle. Cryostat sections of (A) rat and (B) human skeletal muscle were processed as described for immunofluorescence using a polyclonal antiserum to neuronal NOS purified from rat cerebellum. (A) Neuronal NOS is selectively enriched at the sarcolemmal membrane in a subset of muscle fibers in rat muscle. (B) The sarcolemma of essentially all fibers from human skeletal muscle are brightly stained. Magnification: ×200.

a subset of skeletal muscle fibers.[25] In addition, ATPase staining indicates that NOS positive fibers largely correspond to the type I or fast twitch fibers.[25]

Immunofluorescent Labeling of Nitric Oxide Synthase in Rodent Skeletal Muscle. Localization of NOS in skeletal muscle is most conveniently carried out using immunofluorescence. Rats are euthanized and appropriate muscle tissues are dissected without animal perfusion or fixation. Muscles are then mounted with gum tragacanth (Sigma) on a thin cross section of a No. 7 cork. Muscle fibers should be mounted perpendicular to the cork if muscle cross sections are desired and parallel if longitudinal sections are needed. Tissue is snap-frozen for 40 sec by dropping cork-mounted muscle in a bath of 2-methylbutane (isopentane) cooled with liquid nitrogen. Muscle sections (4–10 μm) are cut using a cryostat and collected on treated microscope slides (Plus, Fisher Scientific, Pittsburgh, PA). Snap-frozen skeletal muscle tissue and slide-mounted sections may be stored at $-80°$ indefinitely with no loss in histological quality.

For NOS immunofluorescent labeling, fix sections in a solution of freshly depolymerized 2% paraformaldehyde in PBS (see section on immunolocalization) for 5 min at room temperature. Wash and permeabilize sections twice with PBST for 5 min. Sections are incubated in blocking solution of PBS containing 3% goat serum for 30 min at room temperature. The NOS antibody is diluted in blocking solution (Transduction Laboratory bNOS antibody, dilution 1 : 200) and applied sparingly to completely cover muscle sections (50 μl/cm^{-2}). Sections are incubated with the NOS antibody at room temperature for 2 hr at 4° in a humid chamber. Slides are then washed twice with PBST for 5 min and incubated with FITC-conjugated goat anti-rabbit immunoglobulin G (IgG, 1 : 200 dilution; Jackson Labs, Bar Harbor, ME) for 60 min at room temperature. Sections are washed twice with PBST for 5 min each, and a fluorescent mountant (Fluoromount-G, Southern Biotechnology Associates, Birmingham, AL) is used to apply the glass coverslip. Sections identically treated without incubation with primary antibody serve as a control. Figure 2 demonstrates sarcolemmal staining of neuronal NOS in cross sections of rat and human skeletal muscle.

[25] L. Kobzik, M. B. Reid, D. S. Bredt, and J. S. Stamler, *Nature* (*London*) **372,** 546 (1994).

[48] NADPH Diaphorase Activity in Activated Astrocytes Representing Inducible Nitric Oxide Synthase

By MARK N. WALLACE

Introduction

Following activation, astrocytes normally become swollen and have a greatly increased metabolic rate. The levels of many enzymes are increased.[1] Other enzymes are synthesized that are not present at detectable levels in the resting state. One of these latter enzymes is the inducible form of nitric oxide synthase (iNOS).[2,3] The function of the nitric oxide released by the astrocytes is not known. It is possible that under some conditions it may be neuroprotective, while in the presence of free radicals it may be neurotoxic.[4] The function of the iNOS produced by the astrocytes will be difficult to elucidate because other cell types in the brain may also start synthesizing iNOS under pathological conditions. These include microglia,[5] invading macrophages, and even neurons.[6] Thus, in studying astrocytic iNOS it is not sufficient to perform standard biochemical assays on brain tissue. Even with cell culture it is usually not possible to obtain pure populations of astrocytes free from microglia.[2]

In assessing the contribution of specific cell types to nitric oxide (NO) production, it is necessary to identify microscopically the location of the synthesizing enzyme. This can be done, using antibodies against the macrophage form of iNOS, if a suitable antibody is available. However immunohistochemical methods are both time-consuming and relatively expensive. Histochemical detection of diaphorase activity that is dependent on the reduced form of nicotinamide adenine dinucleotide phosphate (NADPH) provides a simple, inexpensive method for studying the distribution of all three isoforms of NOS.[7] It is highly sensitive and can detect minute changes in NOS production associated with a few cells (Fig. 1A,B). By studying samples of brain taken before and after an experimental manipulation it

[1] K. A. Osterberg and L. W. Wattenberg, *Arch. Neurol.* **7,** 57 (1962).
[2] E. Galea, D. L. Feinstein, and D. J. Reis, *Proc. Natl. Acad. Sci. U.S.A.* **89,** 10945 (1992).
[3] S. Murphy, M. L. Simmons, L. Agullo, A. Garcia, D. L. Feinstein, E. Galea, D. J. Reis, D. Minc-Golomb, and J. P. Schwartz, *Trends Neurosci.* **16,** 323 (1993).
[4] S. A. Lipton, Y.-B. Choi, Z.-H. Pan, S. Z. Lei, H.-S. V. Chen, N. J. Sucher, J. Loscalzo, D. J. Singel, and J. S. Stamler, *Nature* (*London*) **364,** 626 (1993).
[5] M. L. Simmons and S. Murphy, *J. Neurochem.* **59,** 897 (1992).
[6] C. Nathan and Q.-W. Xie, *J. Biol. Chem.* **269,** 13725 (1994).
[7] M. N. Wallace and S. K. Bisland, *Neuroscience* (*Oxford*) **59,** 905 (1994).

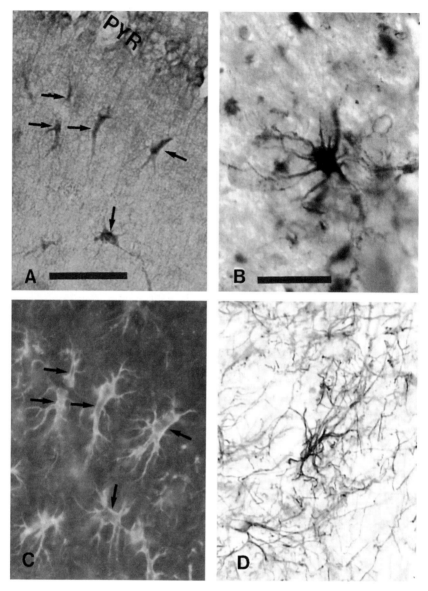

FIG. 1. (A) Coronal section through the CA1 field of the mouse showing NADPH diaphorase activity in activated astrocytes 5 days after a stab wound. The pyramidal cell layer is indicated (PYR), and the double-labeled cells that are also shown in (C) are indicated by arrows. (B) Coronal section through the stratum moleculare-lacunosum of the CA1 field of the human hippocampus showing intense NADPH diaphorase staining in activated astrocytes associated with crystalline deposits. The deposits appear to be perivascular accumulations of calcium and other metal salts. (C) Same section as that in (A) that had subsequently been stained for iNOS using an antibody against the NOS found in mouse macrophages and a fluorescent secondary antibody. Double-labeled cells are indicated by arrows. (D) Glial fibrillary acidic protein immunoreactivity in astrocytes of the same field and from a section near that shown in (B). The same magnification is used in A and C, and in B and D. In all cases, bar: 50 μm.

is possible to determine rapidly the presence of recently synthesized enzyme in new populations of cells. Thus, following kainic acid lesions,[8] ischemic damage,[9] or stab wounds,[7] iNOS is present in activated astrocytes and migrating endothelial cells[10] that had previously been unstained. If new populations of cells are being studied under different experimental parameters, it will also be necessary to confirm which type of NOS isoform is present, using a specific antibody or *in situ* hybridization.[11]

Rationale for NADPH Diaphorase Histochemistry

The diaphorases are a group of naturally occurring enzymes that in a histochemical medium are able to use an electron donor such as NADPH to reduce the soluble reagent nitro blue tetrazolium to produce insoluble diformazan dye. A number of enzymes with NADPH diaphorase activity exist in the brain, but independent studies have shown that only the different forms of NOS will withstand fixation with 4% (w/v) paraformaldehyde.[12,13] The diaphorase activity of NOS is thought to derive from the reduction by NADPH of a tightly bound flavin molecule which then directly reduces the nitro blue tetrazolium.[14] In the normal brain most NADPH diaphorase (NADPH dehydrogenase) is associated with the NOS found in neurons.[15,16] Lower levels of NADPH diaphorase are associated with the endothelium of blood vessels[17] and in some instances with glial cells,[12] but so far there does not seem to have been any conclusive evidence of specific NADPH diaphorase activity that is not associated with NOS following fixation in 4% paraformaldehyde. With mild fixation a general background level of NADPH diaphorase remains, but this forms a reddish monoformazan deposit that can be removed by dissolving it in acetone.

[8] M. N. Wallace and K. Fredens, *NeuroReport* **3**, 953 (1992).

[9] M. Endoh, K. Maiese, W. A. Pulsinelli, and J. A. Wagner, *Neurosci. Lett.* **154**, 125 (1993).

[10] P. D. Kitchener, J.-P. Bourreau, and J. Diamond, *Neuroscience (Oxford)* **53**, 613 (1993).

[11] E. Galea, D. J. Reis, and D. L. Feinstein, *J. Neurosci. Res.* **37**, 406 (1994).

[12] H. H. H. W. Schmidt, G. D. Gagne, M. Nakane, J. S. Pollock, M. F. Miller, and F. Murad, *J. Histochem. Cytochem.* **40**, 1439 (1992).

[13] T. Matsumoto, M. Nakane, J. S. Pollock, J. E. Kuk, and U. Förstermann, *Neurosci. Lett.* **155**, 61 (1993).

[14] D. S. Bredt, C. E. Glatt, P. M. Hwang, M. Fotuhi, T. M. Dawson, and S. H. Snyder, *Neuron* **7**, 615 (1991).

[15] B. T. Hope, G. J. Michael, K. M. Knigge, and S. R. Vincent, *Proc. Natl. Acad. Sci. U.S.A.* **88**, 2811 (1991).

[16] T. M. Dawson, D. S. Bredt, M. Fotuhi, P. M. Whang, and S. H. Snyder, *Proc. Natl. Acad. Sci. U.S.A.* **88**, 7797 (1991).

[17] B. T. Hope and S. R. Vincent, *J. Histochem. Cytochem.* **37**, 653 (1989).

Procedures

Transcardiac Perfusion of Animals

Following an overdose of pentobarbital sodium (administered intraperitoneally), the animal is watched until it just stops breathing. It is then laid supine on a metal rack over a dish and all four paws stretched out using drape hooks or masking tape. A midline incision is made with a scalpel, from the manubrium to the upper abdomen, and the skin is rapidly separated from the rib cage. Grasping the base of the sternum with toothed forceps, scissors are used to cut through the diaphragm and the pericardium. At this point the heart should start beating again because of the mechanical stimulation. The right atrium is cut to permit efflux of blood, and the blunted perfusion needle is inserted across the left ventricle until its tip comes to lie within the ascending aorta.

Perfusion is started immediately using a solution of 4% paraformaldehyde in 0.1 M phosphate buffer (pH 7.4). The outside diameter of the needle should be slightly smaller than the aorta (Luer size 0 for a rat) and in larger animals should be of rigid plastic or metal. The needle is connected to a perfusion flask placed about 1 m above the animal via wide-bore tubing (1 cm) to minimize resistance and ensure that the pressure at the needle tip is approximately 140 mm Hg. There is no rinse step before perfusion with the aldehyde so that ideally the tissue should go directly from being perfused with oxygenated blood by the heart, to 4% paraformaldehyde. Mixing the aldehyde with the blood directly prevents clotting, and the absence of any delay in perfusion means that the arterioles should be fixed in a distended position rather than constricted due to anoxia induced spasm. This in turn means that there is a minimal time for autolysis in the brain tissue before fixation. If these conditions are fulfilled then most blood should be washed out of the liver and the limbs should start to go stiff within 1 min. For small rodents the optimal perfusion time is 2 min. If longer perfusion times are used then the brain starts to shrink as water-soluble components are lost, and it starts to become hard and rubbery. The brain is removed, cut into blocks, and placed in cold 30% (w/v) sucrose, in phosphate buffer, overnight or until they sink. The sucrose solution acts both as a cryoprotectant and to wash out any excess fixative from the tissue.

Fixation of Postmortem Tissue

The brain should be perfused *in situ* with as short a postmortem delay as possible. For human tissue the brain is perfused bilaterally through the internal carotids and, if possible, the vertebral arteries by the insertion of cannulae. A total volume of 4 liters of 4% paraformaldehyde is perfused over a period of 6–15 hr depending on the flow rate. Reasonably good NADPH diaphorase staining of activated astrocytes was obtained in tissue with a postmortem delay of 28 hr that had been perfused for 15 hr (Fig. 1B). Alternatively, if the brain has already been removed, it can be perfused through large arteries such as the middle cerebral or basilar.

If perfusion is not possible, small blocks of tissue can be postfixed for 8–24 hr in 4% paraformaldehyde. However, fixation in this way tends to produce a gradient of fixation with the outside of the block overfixed and the inside, especially the white matter, only poorly fixed. This makes the interpretation of results difficult because overfixation abolishes the moderate levels of NADPH diaphorase present in astrocytes and underfixation permits the expression of general NADPH diaphorase activity that is not associated with NOS. Aldehyde fixation is partly reversible, and so overfixed tissue can be placed in a sodium borohydride solution (25 mg of sodium borohydride in 50 ml of phosphate buffer, pH 8) for 15 min. Although this procedure improves immunohistochemical staining it does not appear to be effective in improving NADPH diaphorase activity.

Blocks of brain are cut to have a thickness of no more than 1 cm and are placed in 30% sucrose in phosphate buffer for at least 24 hr, or until they sink. They are then frozen on a chuck, in a jet of solid carbon dioxide from a cylinder with liquid withdrawal, and stored in a $-70°$ freezer. Cultured cells can also be studied by fixation in 4% paraformaldehyde for 30 min followed by washing in phosphate buffer for 2 hr.

Histochemistry

Sections are cut on a cryostat at a thickness of 20–50 μm and mounted directly onto gelatin-subbed slides (slides are dipped in a solution of 1 liter of distilled water containing 12.5 g gelatin and 0.25 g of chromium potassium sulfate at 60° before being dried in the oven). Once the sections are completely dry they can be stored in a slide box containing desiccant in a $-20°$ freezer for a week. Longer storage seems to be associated with loss of enzyme activity, and most sections are incubated the same day as cutting. Sections are incubated to demonstrate NADPH diaphorase in the following medium: 10 ml of phosphate buffer (pH 7.4) containing 2 mg of nitro blue tetrazolium and 10 mg of β-NADPH for 15–30 min at 37°. If human postmortem tissue is used, longer incubation times are required (typically up to 1 hr) and this requires the application of freshly prepared incubation medium after 30 min. A higher concentration of nitro blue tetrazolium is also used, up to 10 mg per 10 ml of buffer. With the thicker human tissue the incubation medium also contains 0.2% Triton X-100 to aid penetration of the chemicals. After incubation, the sections are rinsed in buffer and dehydrated in a graded series of ethanol solutions. The final step, before mounting in synthetic resin, is the removal of nonspecific monoformazan deposits that provide a reddish background staining. These are partly removed by the ethanol but are most effectively removed by immersion in 95% acetone (2 min). Prolonged incubation in either ethanol or acetone does not remove the purple/blue diformazan deposits associated with the diaphorase.

NADPH diaphorase activity is associated with all three forms of NOS. If diaphorase histochemistry is being used in a new situation it will probably be necessary to confirm both the type of NOS isoform and the identity of the cell types involved. There is evidence that astrocytes contain low levels of the neuronal form of NOS in the resting state,[12] although iNOS seems to be the main form expressed in activated astrocytes.[11] The iNOS isoform can be confirmed by the use of specific antibodies (Fig. 1A,C) such as that synthesized by J. R. Weidner and R. A. Mumford at the Merck Research Laboratories.[7] This is a rabbit antibody raised against a synthetic peptide corresponding to the C terminus of the long form of mouse macrophage iNOS, Cys-Nle-Glu-Glu-Pro-Lys-Ala-Thr-Arg-Leu-COOH.

To demonstrate the presence of iNOS, cryostat sections mounted on slides are incubated as follows: (I) 5% normal goat serum containing 1% Triton X-100 for 60 min; (II) same solution containing primary antibody diluted 1:100 overnight; (III) three 10-min rinses; (IV) 5% normal goat serum containing goat anti-rabbit antibody conjugated to fluorescein isothiocyanate (Sigma, St. Louis, MO), diluted 1:75 for 60 min; and (V) three 10-min rinses. Finally, sections receive coverslips with a drop of glycerol and are immediately photographed under epiillumination in a fluorescent microscope. All solutions are made up in 0.1 M phosphate buffer (pH 7.4), and this is also used for the rinse solutions.

Other commercially produced antibodies against iNOS are available. However caution must be observed in their use. The monoclonal antimacrophage NOS antibody available from Transduction Laboratories (Lexington, KY) gives beautiful staining of neurons in the mouse brain but does not seem to recognize the presence of iNOS in activated astrocytes of fixed tissue. Their polyclonal antibody to macrophage NOS does not stain neurons, but it does not seem to be sensitive enough to stain activated astrocytes either. Part of the problem is that use of the sensitive avidin–biotin system for visualizing antibodies (Vector ABC Elite kit, Vector Laboratories, Burlingame, CA) gives nonspecific staining of activated astrocytes. Astrocytes are stained by the Vectastain kit even in the absence of any primary antibody. Use of the peroxidase–antiperoxidase method (Dako, Carpinteria, CA 93013) does not give nonspecific binding but is less sensitive. Activated cells can be identified as astrocytes by the presence of glial fibrillary acidic protein (GFAP), an intermediate filament protein that is specific to astrocytes and certain related glia. GFAP can be visualized using anti-GFAP antibodies (e.g., rabbit anti-GFAP from Sigma) using a protocol similar to that for iNOS (Fig. 1D).

In conclusion, NADPH diaphorase histochemistry provides a simple and highly sensitive method for detecting changes in NOS expression in the brain and is especially useful for studying activated astrocytes in both animal and human tissue.

Acknowledgments

I am grateful to Stuart K. Bisland and Anne M. MacIntyre for help with the histochemistry and to Duncan A. Farquhar for staining the sections shown in Fig. 1B,D. Financial support was provided by a grant from The Wellcome Trust VS/94/ABE/009.

[49] Human Oral Neutrophils: Isolation and Characterization

By Eisuke F. Sato, Kozo Utsumi, and Masayasu Inoue

Introduction

Circulating polymorphonuclear leukocytes (PMN) migrate into tissues and play crucial roles both in protecting hosts against infecting bacteria and in promoting inflammatory tissue injury.[1] Under physiological conditions, a large number of PMN also migrate into the gastrointestinal lumen and respiratory tract. Although the biochemical properties of human PMN in circulation have been well documented, those from other sources have not been well characterized. The oral cavity is a convenient source of PMN from healthy human subjects that have migrated from the circulation.[2,3] When migrated from the salivary gland and gingival crevice into oral cavity, PMN seem to be primed by various ligands, such as lipopolysaccharide and cytokines. Yamamoto et al.[4] reported that PMN isolated from the oral cavity spontaneously release active oxygen species. To study the biochemical properties and physiological functions of oral PMN, a fairly large number of the cells should be prepared with high purity.

[1] B. M. Babior, N. Engl. J. Med. 298, 659 (1978).
[2] R. Attström, J. Periodont. Res. 5, 42 (1970).
[3] H. Skapski and T. Lehner, J. Periodont. Res. 11, 19 (1976).
[4] M. Yamamoto, K. Saeki, and K. Utsumi, Arch. Biochem. Biophys. 289, 76 (1991).

Isolation of Oral Neutrophils

Oral PMN can be obtained from healthy human subjects by the following method (Fig. 1). One hour after subjects have brushed the teeth without toothpaste, the oral cavity is thoroughly washed for 30 sec with 15 ml of Krebs–Ringer–phosphate buffer solution (KRP) for 5 times. The combined solution (150–200 ml) is centrifuged at 250 *g* for 5 min at 4°. The precipitated

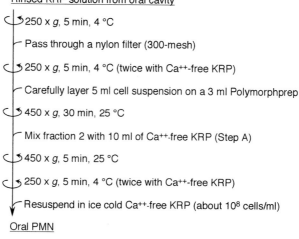

Rinsed KRP solution from oral cavity

250 x *g*, 5 min, 4 °C

Pass through a nylon filter (300-mesh)

250 x *g*, 5 min, 4 °C (twice with Ca++-free KRP)

Carefully layer 5 ml cell suspension on a 3 ml Polymorphprep

450 x *g*, 30 min, 25 °C

Mix fraction 2 with 10 ml of Ca++-free KRP (Step A)

450 x *g*, 5 min, 25 °C

250 x *g*, 5 min, 4 °C (twice with Ca++-free KRP)

Resuspend in ice cold Ca++-free KRP (about 10^8 cells/ml)

Oral PMN

20 ml of citrated fresh blood

Carefully layer 5 ml blood on a 3 ml Polymorphprep

450 x *g*, 30 min, 25 °C

same as for oral PMN (Step A)

Peripheral PMN

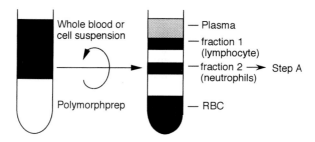

Whole blood or cell suspension — Plasma

— fraction 1 (lymphocyte)

— fraction 2 → Step A (neutrophils)

Polymorphprep — RBC

FIG. 1. Preparation of PMN.

cells are resuspended in 10 ml KRP and passed through a nylon filter (300 mesh) to separate oral PMN from oral epithelial cells and cell debris. The oral PMN-enriched filtrate is centrifuged at 250 g for 5 min at 4° and resuspended in KRP. The viability of cells is tested by the trypan blue exclusion method. The precipitated cells are resuspended in 10 ml KRP and subjected to centrifugation in a 15-ml centrifuge tube at 450 g for 30 min on a 3 ml cushion of Polymorphprep (Nycomed, Oslo, Norway) at 20°. The cells collected in the interface between KRP and Polymorphprep are washed with KRP (1 × 10^8 cells/ml) and kept on ice until used for the experiments. Plastic tubes should be used for the isolation of PMN to avoid surface activation of the cells.

To compare the biochemical properties of PMN from the oral cavity to those from peripheral blood, cells are also isolated from fresh blood of healthy volunteers. Briefly, 5-ml citrated blood samples are subjected to centrifugation at 450 g, on a 3 ml cushion of Polymorphprep as described for the isolation of oral PMN. The PMN obtained from venous blood are suspended in KRP (1 × 10^8 cells/ml) and stored on ice until use (Fig. 1).

Characterization of Oral Polymorphonuclear Leukocytes

Generation of superoxide radicals (O_2^-) by the two PMN samples is assayed by the cytochrome c reduction method[5] using a dual-beam spectrophotometer equipped with a water-jacketed cell holder and a magnetic stirrer. The reaction mixture contains a final volume of 2 ml KRP, 1 mM CaCl$_2$, 20 μM cytochrome c, 10 mM glucose, 5 mM NaN$_3$, and 1–4 × 10^6 cells. The reaction is started by adding the cells at 37°, and the change in absorbance at 550–540 nm (A550–540) is recorded. Stimulation-dependent generation is also determined by adding various ligands, such as opsonized zymosan (OZ) and formylmethionylleucylphenylalanine (FMLP, dissolved in ethanol). In the absence of ligands, oral PMN but not peripheral PMN reveal spontaneous generation of O_2^- (Fig. 2). When stimulated by receptor-mediated ligands, such as FMLP and OZ, oral PMN generate significantly larger amounts of O_2^- than do peripheral PMN. After priming by various agents, such as tumor necrosis factor α (TNF-α) and granulocyte colony-stimulating factor (G-CSF), peripheral PMN reveal ligand-dependent generation of O_2^- as potently as oral PMN.

To verify the reactive oxygen species generated by oral PMN, changes in luminol chemiluminescence (LCL) are determined in a Luminescence Reader (Aloka BRL-201, Tokyo, Japan) equipped with a thermostatically controlled cuvette holder. Reaction mixtures contain a final volume of

[5] B. M. Babior, Kipnes, and J. T. Curnutte, *J. Clin. Invest.* **52,** 741 (1973).

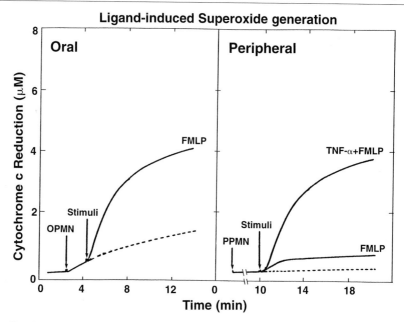

FIG. 2. Superoxide generation by oral and peripheral PMN. Cytochrome c reduction was monitored with a dual-beam spectrophotometer (Shimadzu UV300). The total reaction volume was 2 ml. The concentrations of TNF-α, FMLP, and OZ were 10 units/ml, $1.25 \times 10^{-8} M$, and 400 μg/ml, respectively. The dashed lines represent O_2^- generation without addition of any stimuli.

500 μl KRP, 0.1 μM luminol, 1 mM CaCl$_2$, 10 mM glucose, 5×10^5 cells, and other additions. The reaction is started by adding various ligands at 37°, and chemiluminescence intensity (counts per minute) is determined by measuring the peak height and area under the curve (integral chemiluminescence).[6,7] As observed with O_2^- generation, oral PMN but not peripheral PMN reveal spontaneous luminol chemiluminescence (Fig. 3). When stimulated by some ligands which selectively interact with surface receptors, such as FMLP and OZ, oral PMN exhibit a significantly potent luminol chemiluminescence relative to peripheral PMN.

Nitric Oxide Metabolism

Biochemical properties of oral PMN suggest that these cells are fully primed and continuously generating reactive oxygen species. Because nitric

[6] T. Matsuno, K. Orita, K. Edashige, H. Kobuchi, E. F. Sato, B. Inoue, M. Inoue, and K. Utsumi, *Biochem. Pharmacol.* **39**, 1255 (1990).
[7] R. C. Allen, *Methods Enzymol.* **133**, 449 (1986).

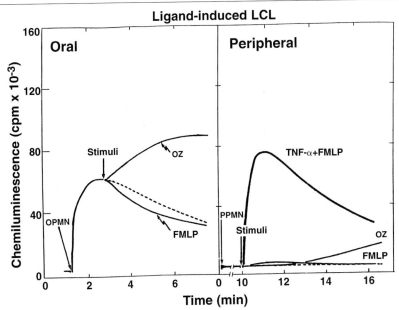

FIG. 3. Luminol chemiluminescence by oral and peripheral PMN. Luminol chemiluminescence was monitored with a calcium analyzer (Jasco CAF-100, mode for aequorin chemiluminescence). The total reaction volume was 1 ml. The concentrations of TNF-α, FMLP, and
OZ were the same as for Fig. 2. The dashed lines represent luminol chemiluminescence
without addition of any stimuli.

oxide (NO) plays important roles in host defense, cellular levels of nitric
oxide synthase (NOS) and its mRNA and the rate of NO generation are
determined with oral and peripheral PMN. The PMN are cultured in RPMI
medium in 24-well cell culture plates (1 $\times$ 10^6 cells/ml/well) in a CO_2
incubator. After incubation, amounts of $NO_2{}^-$ released into culture medium
are determined by the Griess method.[8] Briefly, 100 μl of culture medium
is mixed with 150 μl of Griess reagent (1% (w/v) sulfanilamide/0.1% (w/v)
naphthylethylenediamine dichloride/3% (w/v) H_3PO_4). After incubation at
25° for 10 min, absorbance at 555 nm is determined in a Hitachi U-2000
spectrophotometer. The amounts of $NO_2{}^-$ released in the medium are
significantly larger with oral PMN (9.97 pmol/10^6 cells/min) than with
peripheral PMN (0.11 pmol/10^6 cells/min), suggesting the enhanced generation of NO by the former.

[8] K. A. Rockett, M. M. Awburn, W. B. Cowden, and I. A. Clark, *Infect. Immun.* **59**, 3280 (1991).

Nitric Oxide Synthase Activity

For assay of NOS, PMN are homogenized at 4° in 5 volumes of ice-cold buffer solution containing 50 mM Tris-HCl (pH 7.4), 1 mM ethylenediaminetetraacetic acid (EDTA), 10 μg/ml each of antipain, leupeptin, pepstatin, and chymostatin, and 100 μg/ml of phenylmethylsulfonyl fluoride (PMSF). The homogenates are centrifuged at 100,000 g for 60 min at 4°, and NO synthase activity in the supernatant fractions is measured as previously described.[9] Briefly, the reaction mixture contains, in a final volume of 0.15 ml, 0.2 mM [H^3]arginine, 50 mM Tris-HCl (pH 7.4), 1 mM EDTA, 1.25 mM CaCl$_2$, 1 mM dithiothreitol (DTT), and 10 μg/ml calmodulin. The reaction is started by adding 25 μl of the supernatant fraction. After incubation for 15–30 min at 37°, the reaction is stopped by adding 2 ml of ice-cold 20 mM HEPES buffer (pH 5.5) containing 2 mM EDTA. The incubation mixture is subjected to column chromatography on a Dowex AG50W-X8 column (2 ml, Na$^+$ form) which has been equilibrated with water. After washing the column with 2 ml of deionized water, the eluted fractions are combined and the radioactivity determined in a liquid scintillation counter. Comparative analysis reveals that oral PMN contain significantly larger amounts of NO synthase than do peripheral PMN.

Western Blot Analysis of Nitric Oxide Synthase

To study the dynamic aspects of NO synthase in PMN, levels of NO synthase isozymes and their mRNAs are also determined. After washing three times with Ca^{2+}- and Mg^{2+}-free phosphate-buffered saline (PBS), 1 $\times$ 10^6 of PMN are lysed in 500 μl of radioimmunoprecipitation assay buffer [50 mM Tris-HCl buffer, pH 8.0, 150 mM NaCl, 1% (v/v) Triton X-100, 1% (w/v) deoxycholate, and 0.1% (w/v) sodium dodecyl sulfate (SDS)] containing 1 mM EGTA, 0.01% leupeptin, and 1 mM PMSF. The lysate is centrifuged at 10,000 g for 30 min at 4°. To the supernatant is added SDS to give a final concentration of 5%, and the mixture is boiled at 100° for 3 min. The samples are then subjected to SDS–polyacrylamide gel electrophoresis (7.5%). The electrophoresed proteins are transferred to a polyvinylidene difluoride filter.[10] Then, the filter is incubated with 5% nonfat dry milk in 20 mM Tris-HCl, pH 7.4, and 150 mM NaCl at 4° overnight and with the monoclonal antibody against either inducible (iNOS) or constitutive NO synthase (cNOS) (diluted 1:2000) in the same buffer containing 1% nonfat dry milk at 25° for 1 hr. The filter is washed with the

---

[9] J. F. Arnal, L. Warin, and J. B. Michel, *J. Clin. Invest.* **90,** 647 (1992).
[10] L. Towbin, T. Staehelin, and J. Gordon, *Proc. Natl. Acad. Sci. U.S.A.* **76,** 4350 (1979).

buffer containing 0.05% Tween 20 and incubated for 1 hr with peroxidase-conjugated anti-rabbit immunoglobulin antibody (diluted 1 : 2000). The filter is washed extensively with the buffer containing 0.05% Tween 20. Then, immunoreactive protein bands are visualized autoradiographically. The Western blot analysis reveals that oral PMN contain significantly large amounts of iNOS; cNOS is not detectable in either oral PMN and peripheral PMN.

Messenger RNA for Nitric Oxide Synthase

To investigate the dynamic aspects of iNOS in PMN, total RNA is isolated by using acid guanidine thiocyanate, phenol, and chloroform.[11] Briefly, 6×10^6 PMN are homogenized in 0.5 ml of the solution containing 4 M guanidine thiocyanate, 25 mM sodium citrate (pH 7.0), 0.5% N-lauroylsarcosine, and 100 mM 2-mercaptoethanol through a 18-gauge needle. To the homogenate is added 50 μl of 2 M sodium acetate (pH 4.0), 0.5 ml of water-saturated phenol, and 100 μl of a 24 : 1 mixture of chloroform and 3-methyl-1-butanol (v/v). The mixture is centrifuged at 10,000 g and 4° for 10 min. The aqueous phase is mixed with 0.5 ml of 2-propanol and incubated at −20° for 1 hr. After centrifugation of the mixture at 10,000 g and 4° for 10 min, the precipitated RNA is dissolved in 500 μl of guanidine thiocyanate solution and incubated with 1 volume of 2-propanol at −20° for 1 hr. After centrifugation at 10,000 g and 4° for 10 min, the pellet is suspended in 75% (v/v) ethanol, precipitated by centrifugation, and dried by evacuation. RNA samples thus obtained are dissolved in 100 μl of 0.5% SDS. Reverse transcriptase–polymerase chain reaction (RT-PCR) is performed with the RNA samples as previously described.[12] Briefly, 1 μg of RNA is reverse transcribed into cDNA using random hexamers. One-tenth of the cDNA is amplified by PCR for 35 cycles. Half of the reaction products are analyzed by 1.7% agarose gel electrophoresis, and bands are visualized by ethidium bromide staining. The iNOS primers (1) 5′ ACA GGG AAG TCT GAA GCA CTA G 3′ and (2) 5′ CAT GCA AGG AAG GGA ACT CTC C 3′ define an amplicon of 1033 bp. The RT-PCR analysis reveals that cellular levels of iNOS mRNA are significantly higher in oral PMN than in peripheral PMN. Thus, primed PMN from the oral cavity constantly express iNOS mRNA and maintain high levels of iNOS. Since the oral cavity is always exposed to arginine-containing food and proteins, the infiltrated PMN might continuously generate NO and related metabolites. Thus, NO and reactive oxygen species derived from oral PMN might play important roles in the defense mechanism within the oral cavity.

[11] P. Chomczynski and N. Sacchi, *Anal. Biochem.* **162,** 156 (1987).
[12] R. Makino, T. Sekiya, and K. Hayashi, *Technique* **2,** 295 (1990).

[50] Immunohistochemical Localization
of Nitric Oxide Synthases

By ULRICH FÖRSTERMANN and NAE J. DUN

Introduction

Nitric oxide (NO) is involved in the regulation of multiple physiological and pathophysiological processes in various cells and tissues. Three isoforms of NO synthase (NOS; L-arginine, NADPH : oxygen oxidoreductase, nitric oxide forming; EC 1.14.13.39) have been identified and characterized at the protein and cDNA level.[1] Two of the three known NOS are constitutively expressed in specific cell types (NOS I or neuronal NOS, and NOS III or endothelial NOS), whereas the expression of the third isoform (NOS II or inducible NOS) can be induced in many cell types with cytokines and other agents. The three NOS proteins show marked differences; for example, the amino acid identity of the three human enzymes is less than 59%. All NOS isoforms catalyze a five-electron oxidation of a guanidino nitrogen of L-arginine to NO and L-citrulline. Molecular oxygen and reduced nicotinamide adenine dinucleotide phosphate (NADPH) participate in the reaction as cosubstrates. All three NOS contain flavin adenine dinucleotide (FAD), flavin mononucleotide (FMN), and heme iron as prosthetic groups, and they also require the cofactor 6(R)-5,6,7,8-tetrahydrobiopterin (BH$_4$). Purification of native NOS proteins, as well as cDNA isolation and expression, has allowed the generation of antibodies to whole proteins or peptide sequences of the NOS. Using these antibodies, the presence of the NOS isoforms has been detected in cells and tissues throughout the organism. This chapter describes techniques and results of NOS immunohistochemistry.

Immunohistochemistry for Nitric Oxide Synthase

Immunohistochemical techniques have been described for the detection of immunoreactivity to (neuronal) NOS I.[2] The same or very similar procedures can be used to detect (inducible) NOS II or (endothelial) NOS III

---

[1] U. Förstermann, E. I. Closs, J. S. Pollock, M. Nakane, P. Schwarz, I. Gath, and H. Kleinert, *Hypertension* (*Dallas*) **23,** 1121 (1994).

[2] H. H. H. W. Schmidt, G. D. Gagne, M. Nakane, J. S. Pollock, M. F. Miller, and F. Murad, *J. Histochem. Cytochem.* **40,** 1439 (1992).

immunoreactivities.[3,4] The immunohistochemical procedure consists of the following major steps: (1) perfusion–fixation, (2) tissue sectioning, and (3) immunostaining. The procedure described below has mostly been used for adult rats but is applicable to most laboratory animals.[5,6]

Perfusion–Fixation. Rats (200–350 g) are deeply anesthetized with ketamine hydrochloride (70 mg/kg, injected intraperitoneally). After exposing the heart with a midline incision, a beveled 25-gauge needle connected to a motorized peristaltic pump via a polyethylene tube is inserted into the left ventricle. The right atrium or ventricle is opened to allow efflux of blood and perfusate. The vascular system is perfused at a rate of 50 ml/min with cold (4°) phosphate-buffered saline (PBS; 11.5 g Na_2HPO_4, 2.87 g NaH_2PO_4, and 9 g NaCl per liter water), pH 7.4, to which 400 units heparin are added. A total of 200 ml PBS is infused. This is followed immediately by 500 ml of freshly prepared 4% (w/v) paraformaldehyde in PBS. Thereafter, the tissue of interest is removed and placed in the same fixative for 1–2 hr at 4°. The tissue is then transferred to PBS and kept in the refrigerator until sectioned.

Tissue Sectioning. The tissue is embedded in 4% warm agar solution which is then cooled until it solidifies (at room temperature). The tissue–agar block is attached to the tissue chuck with cyanoacrylic adhesion glue and immersed in cold (4°) PBS. The block is sectioned to 50 μm thick slices (or other thickness as desired). Sections are stored in PBS (4°) prior to immunostaining.

Immunostaining. Avidin/biotin peroxidase staining is the preferred method for NOS I immunohistochemistry. The following description is for a primary polyclonal antibody generated in rabbits against purified rat cerebellar NOS I.[2] The same method can be used for other rabbit polyclonal antibodies (IgGs) and, with the appropriate choice of a secondary antibody, for anti-NOS antibodies from other species. First, the tissue is immersed in 3% (v/v) H_2O_2/PBS for 5 min to denature endogenous peroxidase. The slice is then washed three times with PBS (10 min each). To block nonspecific antigenic sites found in the tissue, the latter is incubated in 10% normal goat serum (diluted with 0.4%, v/v, Triton X-100 in PBS) for about 1 hr. Thereafter, the tissue is incubated in the primary NOS antibody (1:2000 to 1:3000 dilution) or negative control solution (0.4% Triton X-100 in PBS

[3] W. R. Tracey, C. Xue, V. Klinghofer, J. Barlow, J. S. Pollock, U. Förstermann, and R. A. Johns, *Am. J. Physiol.* **266,** L722 (1994).

[4] J. S. Pollock, M. Nakane, L. K. Buttery, A. Martinez, D. Springall, J. M. Polak, U. Förstermann, and F. Murad, *Am. J. Physiol.* **265,** C1379 (1993).

[5] N. J. Dun, S. L. Dun, S. Y. Wu, U. Förstermann, H. H. H. W. Schmidt, and L. F. Tseng, *Neuroscience (Oxford)* **54,** 845 (1993).

[6] N. J. Dun, S. L. Dun, and U. Förstermann, *Neuroscience (Oxford)* **59,** 429 (1994).

without the NOS antibody) for 24 to 48 hr at 4° (in a cold room) with gentle agitation. The section is washed 3 times with cold PBS (10 min each). The tissue is then incubated with biotinylated anti-rabbit IgG (diluted 1 : 150 with 0.4% Triton X-100 in PBS) at room temperature for 2 hr. After washing three times with PBS (10 min each), the tissue is incubated with ABC solution (1 : 100 with 0.4% Triton X-100 in PBS, Vector Laboratories, Burlingame, CA) for 1 hr at room temperature. The slice is then washed three times with 0.25 M Tris-HCl-buffered saline, pH 7.4 (10 min each). To develop the color reaction, tissue is incubated in diaminobenzidine/H_2O_2 solution. This is made fresh by dissolving a 10 mg diaminobenizidine tablet in 20 ml Tris–saline buffer and adding 7 μl of 30% (v/v) H_2O_2. The incubation time of the tissue in this solution is 5–10 min, until the color of the peroxidase reaction product appears dark brown. The reaction is terminated by washing three times with Tris-HCl-buffered saline, pH 7.4 (10 min each). The tissue is then mounted on gelatinized slides, air dried, dehydrated with increasing ethanol concentrations, cleared in xylene, and coverslipped with Permount.

Immunofluorescence. Alternatively, the indirect immunofluorescence method, which involves the use of a secondary antibody that binds the primary anti-NOS I antibody and is fluorescently tagged with a substance such as fluorescein isothiocyanate or Texas Red, can be successfully employed to visualize NOS I-positive cells. In this case, pretreatment of the tissue with H_2O_2 is not needed. Tissue is incubated with NOS I antibody (1 : 500 to 1 : 1000) at 4° with gentle agitation for 48 hr. After washing with PBS for 30 min, the tissue is incubated with biotinylated anti-rabbit IgG (1 : 50 with 0.4% Triton X-100 in PBS) for 2 hr. Tissue is then washed and incubated with fluorescein avidin D solution or Texas Red avidin D (1 : 50 in PBS, Vector Laboratories) for 3 hr. Finally, the tissue is washed for 30 min with PBS, mounted in Citilfluor (Ted Pella), and coverslipped.

NADPH Diaphorase Staining

NADPH diaphorase (NADPH-d) staining is being used by many laboratories to localize NOS I histochemically.[7] The technique is based on the ability of several enzymes including NOS to reduce soluble tetrazolium salts to an insoluble, dark blue formazan. The C-terminal portion of all three NOS isoforms conveys NADPH-d activity.[8] For unknown reasons, the

---

[7] B. T. Hope, G. I. Michael, K. M. Knigge, and S. R. Vincent, *Proc. Natl. Acad. Sci. U.S.A.* **88,** 2811 (1991).

[8] W. R. Tracey, M. Nakane, J. S. Pollock, and U. Förstermann, *Biochem. Biophys. Res. Commun.* **195,** 1035 (1993).

NADPH-d activity of non-NOS enzymes is rapidly destroyed by common fixatives such as paraformaldehyde. Also, NOS II and NOS III enzymes seem to be more vulnerable to paraformaldehyde than NOS I. This results in the frequent histochemical correlation between NOS I immunoreactivity and NADPH-d staining.[2,7,9,10] It is important, however, to note that the extent of NADPH-diaphorase staining depends on the pretreatment of the tissue (e.g., with fixative), is not specific for NOS, and does not prove that NOS enzymes are present in a given tissue.

Technique of NADPH Diaphorase Staining of Tissues. Staining with NADPH-d is performed by incubating the paraformaldehyde-fixed tissue slice with 1 mM β-NADPH, 0.25 mM nitro blue tetrazolium, and 0.1% Triton X-100 in 0.1 M Tris-HCl, pH 7.4, for 15 min to 2 hr at room temperature until the dark blue staining appears. The reaction is stopped by immersion in 0.1 M Tris-HCl buffer. The tissue is washed in PBS, mounted on gelatinized slides, air dried, dehydrated with increasing ethanol concentrations, cleared in xylene, and coverslipped.

Tissue Distribution of Neuronal Nitric Oxide Synthase Immunoreactivity

Constitutive expression of NOS I was first detected in neurons of the central nervous system.[11,12] In many neurons, NOS I seems to be colocalized with other neurotransmitters (or neurotransmitter-synthesizing enzymes). For example, in dentate hilar neurons of the rat hippocampus, NOS I immunoreactivity was colocalized with somatostatin.[13] Suggested functions of centrally released NO include long-term regulation of synaptic transmission in the central nervous system and (central) regulation of blood pressure. Pathophysiologically, NO has been implicated in neuronal death following cerebrovascular stroke.

However, the distribution of NOS I is not limited to neurons in the brain. Immunoreactivity has been found in certain areas of the spinal cord,[5,14] in

[9] T. Matsumoto, M. Nakane, J. S. Pollock, J. E. Kuk, and U. Förstermann, *Neurosci. Lett.* **155**, 61 (1993).

[10] M. J. Saffrey, C. J. Hassall, C. H. Hoyle, A. Belai, J. Moss, H. H. H. W. Schmidt, U. Förstermann, F. Murad, and G. Burnstock, *NeuroReport* **3**, 333 (1992).

[11] D. S. Bredt and S. H. Snyder, *Proc. Natl. Acad. Sci. U.S.A.* **87**, 682 (1990).

[12] H. H. H. W. Schmidt, J. S. Pollock, M. Nakane, L. D. Gorsky, U. Förstermann, and F. Murad, *Proc. Natl. Acad. Sci. U.S.A.* **88**, 365 (1991).

[13] N. J. Dun, S. L. Dun, R. K. S. Wong, and U. Förstermann, *Proc. Natl. Acad. Sci. U.S.A.* **91**, 2955 (1994).

[14] N. L. Dun, S. L. Dun, U. Förstermann, and L. F. Tseng, *Neurosci. Lett.* **147**, 217 (1992).

sympathetic ganglia and adrenal glands,[15,16] in peripheral nitrergic nerves,[10] in epithelial cells of lung, uterus, and stomach,[2] in kidney macula densa cells,[2] in pancreatic islet cells,[2] and in skeletal muscle.[17] In the peripheral autonomic nervous system, NOS I immunoreactivity has been detected in pre- and postganglionic sympathetic neurons together with choline acetyltransferase and dopamine β-hydroxylase, respectively.[15,16] Functions of NO generated in peripheral nitrergic nerves include smooth muscle relaxation in the gastrointestinal tract and vasodilatation.

Tissue Distribution of Inducible Nitric Oxide Synthase Immunoreactivity

The expression of NOS II can be induced in many cell types by cytokines, bacterial lipopolysaccharide (LPS), and some other agents. The enzyme produces large amounts of NO that has cytostatic effects on parasitic target cells and certain tumor cells. Induced NOS II may also be involved in the pathophysiology of autoimmune diseases and septic shock. Inducible NOS was first isolated from murine macrophages.[18,19] Immunohistochemical localization of NOS II in rats induced with *Propionibacterium acnes* and LPS demonstrated the presence of the enzyme, for example, in macrophages, some lymphocytes, neutrophils, and eosinophils in spleen; Kupffer cells, endothelial cells and hepatocytes in liver; alveolar macrophages in lung; and histiocytes, eosinophils, mast cells, and endothelial cells in colon.[20] Some NOS II immunoreactivity has also been reported in pancreatic islets of diabetic BB rats but not Wistar rats; the immunoreactivity was restricted to areas of islet infiltration by macrophages.[21] Immunohistochemistry with our NOS II-specific antibody demonstrated strong immunoreactivity in alveolar macrophages from a patient with acute bronchopneumonia, whereas no NOS II was detected in normal human lung tissue.[3]

[15] N. L. Dun, S. L. Dun, S. Y. Wu, and U. Förstermann, *Neurosci. Lett.* **158,** 51 (1993).
[16] H. Sheng, G. D. Gagne, T. Matsumoto, M. F. Miller, U. Förstermann, and F. Murad, *J. Neurochem.* **61,** 1120 (1993).
[17] L. Kobzik, M. B. Reid, D. S. Bredt, and J. S. Stamler, *Nature (London)* **372,** 546 (1994).
[18] J. M. Hevel, K. A. White, and M. A. Marletta, *J. Biol. Chem.* **266,** 22789 (1991).
[19] D. J. Stuehr, H. J. Cho, N. S. Kwon, M. F. Weise, and C. F. Nathan, *Proc. Natl. Acad. Sci. U.S.A.* **88,** 7773 (1991).
[20] T. Bandaletova, I. Brouet, H. Bartsch, T. Sugimura, H. Esumi, and H. Ohshima, *APMIS* **101,** 330 (1993).
[21] R. Kleemann, H. Rothe, V. Kolb-Bachofen, Q. W. Xie, C. Nathan, S. Martin, and H. Kolb, *FEBS Lett.* **328,** 9 (1993).

Tissue Distribution of Endothelial Nitric Oxide Synthase Immunoreactivity

Endothelial NOS is constitutively expressed in endothelial cells. Interestingly, expression can be regulated, for example, by shear stress, steroids, and cytokines. Nitric oxide from endothelial cells dilates blood vessels, prevents the adhesion of platelets and white cells, and probably inhibits vascular smooth muscle proliferation. Immunohistochemical studies using a specific antibody to NOS III indicated that this enzyme is relatively specific for endothelial cells. It is found in various types of endothelial cells (arterial and venous) in many tissues, including human tissues.[4] Endothelial nitric oxide synthase immunoreactivity has also been detected in syncytiotrophoblasts of human placenta,[22] LLC-PK$_1$ kidney tubular epithelial cells,[23] and interstitial cells of the canine colon.[24]

[22] L. Myatt, D. E. Brockman, A. Eis, and J. S. Pollock, *Placenta* **14,** 487 (1993).
[23] W. R. Tracey, J. S. Pollock, F. Murad, M. Nakane, and U. Förstermann, *Am. J. Physiol.* **266,** C22 (1994).
[24] C. Xue, J. S. Pollock, H. H. H. W. Schmidt, S. M. Ward, and K. M. Sanders, *J. Auton. Nerv. Syst.* **49,** 1 (1994).

Author Index

Numbers in parentheses are footnote reference numbers and indicate that an author's work is referred to although the name is not cited in the text.

Clement, B., 374
Cliquet, J.-B., 138
Closs, E. I., 334, 338(1), 510
Coade, S. B., 386
Cobb, J. P., 390
Cohen, G., 116
Coia, G., 71, 77(12), 78(12), 79(12), 81(12)
Colca, J. R., 405
Cole, A. T., 239
Cole, J. A., 148
Cole, T., 168
Coles, B., 302
Colton, C. K., 251
Commoner, B., 168, 176
Connop, B. P., 398
Cook, J. A., 18, 21, 22(56), 23(56), 30, 30(39), 69, 71, 77(12), 78(12), 79(12), 81(12), 94, 99(10), 102, 120–121, 122(18), 123, 126(18), 128(18)
Cook, J. C., 25, 26(74), 73, 93, 105, 114, 115(24)
Cook, J. L., 240
Cook, T., 239
Coon, M. J., 313, 464–466
Corbett, J. A., 107, 109(15), 176, 376, 398–400, 404(10), 405, 407
Corbin, J. L., 379
Cornforth, D. P., 176, 186(60)
Corrie, J. E. T., 266–267
Costa, E., 488
Costa, M., 489
Cotton, F. A., 14, 50
Covey, T. R., 197
Covington, K., 340, 342, 346, 378
Cowden, W. B., 507
Cox, A. B., 267
Cox, G. W., 21, 22(56), 23(56), 71, 94, 99(10), 121, 122(18), 123, 126(18), 128(18)
Cozzi, A., 175
Crank, G., 21, 121
Crank, J., 37
Crawford, J. M., 443
Crespi, C. L., 120
Cromeens, D. M., 382
Cross, A. H., 407
Crow, J. P., 131
Croxtall, J. D., 412
Cruse, I., 474, 476(21), 481(20)
Cuevas, J. M., 390
Culotta, E., 13

Cunha, F. Q., 187
Cunningham, J. M., 338(21), 339
Curnette, J. T., 505
Curran, R. D., 239, 409
Currie, M. G., 107, 108(16), 109(15, 16), 118(16), 119(16), 263, 389, 399, 404(10), 405, 407
Cutler, R. G., 170
Czerlinski, G. H., 304
Czuchajowski, L., 60

D

Daghigh, F., 366
Dahlquist, F. W., 469
Dalkara, T., 398
Damiani, P., 107, 108(11)
D'Angelo, D. D., 338(24), 339
Danner, R. L., 390
Darbyshire, J. F., 15, 17, 21, 21(19), 22(56), 23(27, 56), 71–72, 94–95, 96(13), 99(10, 13), 103, 106, 120–121, 122(18, 19), 123, 126(18, 19), 128(18, 19), 238, 290, 303
Darcy, R., 180, 186(79)
Darwish, K., 467
Das, S., 481
Dasch, G. A., 284–285
Dasting, I., 24
Datto, G. A., 315
Davidoff, A., 66
Davies, K. M., 281
Davies, M. J., 198, 200, 201(17)
Dawson, J. H., 449, 462, 463(26), 471(26)
Dawson, T. M., 349, 352–356, 356(10), 398, 429, 437, 491, 493(16), 494(13), 499
Dawson, V. L., 349, 437
Day, B. W., 193–194, 198(9), 201(9)
Dean, J. A., 15
DeAngelis, R., 443
de Belder, A. J., 308
Debenham, D. F., 301
Deen, A. M., 247
Deen, D. M., 238
Deen, W. M., 15, 16(22), 130–131, 134(2), 143, 247, 248(2, 3, 5), 250(2), 253(5), 254(2, 3), 256(2), 257(2), 258(2, 3), 259(3)
DeGraff, W., 19, 21, 22(56), 23(56), 25(45), 27(43), 30, 30(45), 71, 103, 121, 122(18), 126(18), 128(18)
DeGray, J. A., 200, 201(19)

X

Y

Z

Subject Index

A

B

C

the

UNEXPECTED SALE

the

UNEXPECTED SALE

guidance for the
EXECUTOR/ADMINISTRATOR OF AN ESTATE

ALEX LEHR

Advantage®

Published by Advantage, Charleston, South Carolina.
Member of Advantage Media Group.

ADVANTAGE is a registered trademark, and the Advantage colophon is a trademark of Advantage Media Group, Inc.

Printed in the United States of America.

10 9 8 7 6 5 4 3 2 1

ISBN: 978-1-59932-836-2
LCCN: 2017950344

Cover design by Katie Biondo.
Layout design by Megan Elger.

This publication is designed to provide accurate and authoritative information in regard to the subject matter covered. It is sold with the understanding that the publisher is not engaged in rendering legal, accounting, or other professional services. If legal advice or other expert assistance is required, the services of a competent professional person should be sought.

Advantage Media Group is proud to be a part of the Tree Neutral® program. Tree Neutral offsets the number of trees consumed in the production and printing of this book by taking proactive steps such as planting trees in direct proportion to the number of trees used to print books. To learn more about Tree Neutral, please visit **www.treeneutral.com.**

Advantage Media Group is a publisher of business, self-improvement, and professional development books. We help entrepreneurs, business leaders, and professionals share their Stories, Passion, and Knowledge to help others Learn & Grow. Do you have a manuscript or book idea that you would like us to consider for publishing? Please visit advantagefamily.com or call **1.866.775.1696.**

To the brave souls who have taken on the task of carrying out one's final wishes and have tried to do the right thing even when it's not spelled out ... I am eternally grateful for the lessons I have gleaned through your efforts!

TABLE OF CONTENTS

PART III: THE MARKETING PHASE

ACKNOWLEDGMENTS

I would like to acknowledge my wife, Denise, for encouraging me
to write this book and helping me remember a few of the standout
memories over the past thirty-plus years.

What to Do with Inherited Property

I was sitting in my real estate office when a potential new client called with a very unusual request. Her aunt had recently passed away, leaving her to dispose of a house in Daly City, California. The caller, Connie (not her real name), mentioned several times that when I would meet her there, I should dress in clothes that I didn't care about and would be comfortable throwing away.

Of course, I asked questions to better understand the physical condition of the property, a postwar row house in a blue-collar city just south of San Francisco. Connie explained that construction projects over the years at the home were never completed, leaving some rooms with no electricity and some parts of the house in total disrepair. I stressed to her it wouldn't be a problem, that I had dealt with similar situations.

My office is in San Carlos, California, a suburb midway between San Francisco and Silicon Valley. The technology industry has brought a lot of recent wealth to this San Francisco peninsula, but both the area's diverse history and my business focus on inherited properties expose me to a wide range of people and properties. I have been through many estates in all varieties of conditions and knew I could avoid expressing shock or surprise. I made an appointment to meet Connie, an administrative professional in her late forties, and she reminded me again to change into disposable clothes.

Wanting to make a good first impression with my new client, I showed up for our appointment in business-casual attire. When I stepped out of the car, Connie looked at me and said, "I don't think you understand what we're about to walk into. Please, if you can, I'll wait. Go get some clothes that you really don't care about." I looked at her face and her expression, and I understood that she really meant it. I immediately went and changed into cleaning-out-the-garage clothes. We then proceeded to tuck our pants into our socks to keep the fleas off our legs as we entered a property strewn with rats, both live and dead.

The sight and stench were a bit overwhelming, and Connie obviously had a real sense of concern, not just embarrassment, about dealing with this property. Walls had been stripped to the studs in many parts of the house, and there was old lath visible where plaster was missing. When we finally came to the kitchen, there was an old stove heavily coated in grease and the remnants of many years of cooking, along with a sink heavily stained by what looked like yellowish tar. The bathroom had only a claw-foot tub, a toilet, and an old pedestal sink sitting on a wooden floor from which the tile had been removed.

We formulated a plan on how to dispose of the contents of the property and eliminate the biohazards, including the hiring of an exterminator to fumigate and eradicate the fleas. As the cleanup process was going on over the next few weeks, a neighbor called me one day to say that water was cascading down the front steps! When I arrived at the scene, I quickly found the source of the water: The claw-foot tub had had both supply lines broken off, and a geyser of water was flooding the entire property. Once I turned off the water at the main shutoff, it became apparent that thieves had broken into the property to steal the claw-foot tub and never took the time to disconnect the water supply. When they broke the supply lines off, they obviously were startled and scared, and ran off without that extremely heavy tub. I immediately called Connie so we could hire a flooding-remediation contractor and begin drying out the property.

If you are wondering why anyone would spend the time and effort we were putting into this property, especially after the flooding, well, then you need to learn about handling a probate sale. And you have come to the right place. In chapter 8, I will go into greater detail about the probate process, which entails court supervision over administering the estate of someone who has died. However, the legal requirements surrounding probate affect *all* aspects of handling inherited property, and I'll be discussing these throughout this book.

All too often, an executor of an estate might want to throw his or her hands in the air and say, "Sell it for whatever we can get." But once someone has taken on the duty of an executor or trust administrator, that's not necessarily an option. That person has been charged with the duty of getting the highest value possible from the estate's assets. If, for example, a beneficiary or an heir to an estate found out that the property sold for less because a water leak was not remediated and mold started to form, the executor or administrator would face potential legal liability.

Connie's story is extreme but not trivial. It illustrates a few things for the people I hope are reading this book: the ones who are choosing or may be chosen as the executor of an estate or administrator of a trust, either as relatives, friends, or institutional administrators. The story's lessons:

🏠 An institutional administrator can be a bank's trust-department official, a probate paralegal, an attorney, or a professional fiduciary to look after someone else's assets.

1. No matter what you think of your friends or relatives, you may be surprised by the conditions in which they lived. I asked Connie how long the house had been that way. She said she didn't know, because her aunt had never let her inside. From the outside, it looked fine.

2. Once a property becomes vacant, it becomes an attractive nuisance, creating liability on the estate's behalf to make sure it's secured against people who might break in and potentially hurt themselves or burn down the surrounding houses.

3. It's difficult to get insurance on a vacant house, especially one that is in extremely poor condition, but the executor or administrator is still required to do so.

Because I specialize in selling properties for estates, I reach out to people like Connie whose names are on the public record when estates are filed in a county recorder's office or a county clerk's office. Some executors or administrators are very proactive and have already begun selling assets, but others are completely lost and overwhelmed. Along with my office staff and the vetted professionals we work with, I help them get the best outcome. In Connie's case, that outcome was the sale of her aunt's house to a contractor who fixed up and flipped houses.

Usually the biggest asset in an estate and the most difficult to resolve is a house. Since the late 1980s, I have been involved in property sales for more than five hundred estates and trusts. I have watched executors or administrators from all walks of life approach the estate process in a variety of ways. Some face situations like Connie's where they wonder, "How could my family members or friends ever live like that?" Others marvel at how organized their departed family members or friends were. Usually it runs somewhere in between—but there is no "normal." The death might have been expected or might have been a shock, but either way the executors are thrust into the spotlight, with everyone watching and wondering how they're going to handle the sale of assets.

Most executors come into the task with no training or experience, so it can be frightening. They may feel like they've suddenly been called down to the airport and asked to go to work in the air-traffic-control tower. The similarity is that they have to make quick decisions with significant consequences. Probate has difficult logistics; a lot of things will be up in the air, and someone has to decide when it's best for each to take off or land. The craziest part of this analogy is that while nobody ever hopes an air-traffic controller will fail, executors may actually have heirs or beneficiaries rooting or working against them.

Even with supportive family and friends, many executors find it reassuring to work with a probate specialist on the real estate front. Both private and professional administrators hire me through a listing agreement, with a rider outlining the extensive services we provide to estates.

My Background in Guardianship

I happened upon this specialty by accident when I began my real estate career. I was knocking on doors of homes, including some that seemed like the old haunted house on the block. As I did more research, I found out that the owners often had either died recently or were still alive but had no family members. Whether relatives or county appointees were overseeing the properties through estates, trusts, or conservatorships, I realized that in most cases, these properties could fall into further disrepair without some outside help.

I began to study the probate process and eventually was chosen to work with San Mateo County's Public-Guardian program, which helps conserve the assets of people in long-term care (for dementia or other impairments) who have no relatives to watch over them. The county has an interest in making sure that predatory characters don't deprive these people of their assets, leaving them penniless or even homeless. I became very familiar with the probate process and the way every sale under the Public Guardian's office required court confirmation. Once I realized how many sales were being confirmed by the courts, I began to explore how to help people avoid difficult probate. As a petition was filed to appoint an executor to an estate, I would contact that executor and offer my assistance. I found that people from all different socioeconomic and educational backgrounds had a common element: a family member, relative, or friend with assets that had to be dealt with.

Many times, the administrator or executor was from another part of the country and was struggling to handle personal or physical property and deal with financial institutions from afar. So, it became my job to develop local resources that anybody could plug in to no matter where they were physically. There also was a human element that I will be covering throughout this book. Some of the cases I'll be discussing involved cohesive and harmonious families; in other instances, highly combative family members made things difficult by dredging up old rivalries from their childhood. I learned that my first encounter with an executor or administrator of an estate would always be a delicate conversation because of the variety of emotional elements or undercurrents of family dynamics that come into play. Watching these elements unfold during the process can be endearing or—in far too many cases—chilling.

In real estate, we are typically coming in contact with people during a time of uncertainty. They're about to take on large financial obligations or, sometimes, relieve themselves of financial commitments, but either way, they're creating change in their lives with the ensuing uncertainty and anxiety. A real estate agent walks into people's lives when they're emotionally charged and, in many cases, physically taxed from getting a property ready to sell. Even in conventional home sales, I sometimes had to provide a good shoulder to cry on or be a sounding board during friction between spouses. I discovered I could similarly help people get through challenging times in probate, including times when their family's emotional or financial pillar was suddenly gone.

What You Can Learn Here

This book will explore the family dynamics, situations, and personalities that can result in conflicts over who's in control of the disposition of estate assets. Regardless of who's in control, the objective should be to help them get the best results for the estate.

Being an executor is a high-responsibility, time-consuming, and often thankless job that people often take on while grieving. If that is what's happening to you, realize that you need to heal yourself when the estate is settled. My goal in this book is to make that process easier by raising practical questions for you to ask yourself, your legal advisor, and your fellow beneficiaries as you maneuver through the bureaucratic maze. My hope is to deliver the answers that you need to many of the most puzzling questions—and help you find peace of mind.

To this end, I have devised a three-part system to walk you through the handling of an inherited property from beginning to end. The three parts are:

1. The ASSESSMENT Phase

2. The PLANNING and PREPARATION Phase

3. The MARKETING Phase

In the first several chapters, I'll discuss the role of an executor and how you need to initially assess the situation. I'll briefly explain what probate is and provide some advice about dealing with different personality types. I will also address the major questions: Sell the house or rent it? Renovate or repair, or do nothing to the property? Sell it and show it furnished or unfurnished? And, last but not least, we'll consider tax consequences.

In the middle of the book, I'll answer the who, what, where, when, why, and how questions that come up during planning and preparation of the estate's disposition. I'll outline the steps you should take in preparing to put a property on the market, including the need to document everything and keep all beneficiaries informed. I will also address the question of what disclosures are required and what inspections it makes sense to have performed. How are the assets valued and distributed? How do you clear out the home?

The final chapters, the marketing section, will focus on the sale of the property, from choosing the right agent to explaining how the probate process actually works and the type of probate that's preferred. I'll walk you through the "minefield" of marketing a probate property, including situations where a property is in foreclosure or there are tenants.

Throughout the book, I will address challenges and complications an executor faces. Heirs and beneficiaries impaired by use of alcohol, prescription drugs, or controlled substances are in many cases the loudest and most irrational voices in the process, and yet they still have to be heard. The deceased may have been taking care of family members with special needs or disabilities. Having a paid-off home may have been the pride and joy of a generation that saved money, but it's being passed on to a different generation with people who may not have the financial capacity to hold on to the property. In many cases, the property needs to be divided among a number of surviving relatives. People in the process are coming from different places in terms of emotional and physical distance. I have seen occasions where unscrupulous people have tried to take advantage of the bereaved.

A wealthy person who had the resources and foresight to create an elaborate trust to avoid probate may have failed to keep it up-to-date as assets were bought and sold. You'll see that this has happened to some of the most famous people in the world. Even when you have handlers taking care of your assets and your personal affairs, things still get missed.

In the United States, about 2.6 million people die each year, according to the National Center for Health Statistics. The Census Bureau reports that more than 60 percent of US households are homeowners, and homeownership rates rise to nearly 80 percent among elderly Americans. Taking into account all the heirs of each deceased homeowner, those figures show that millions of ordinary people are affected each year by the issues covered in this book.

No matter the size of the estate, executors need to learn and respect deadlines and legal requirements. These requirements vary by state and locality, and laws and regulations change over time. In any case, *no portion of this book should be construed as offering actual legal advice.* I am not a lawyer, and my direct personal experience is limited to California. Readers elsewhere may still find this book helpful, but all readers should consult a local attorney for legal advice.

Finally, you may have heard this truism:

Q. How do you eat an elephant?

A. One bite at a time.

The probate process may seem hard to digest, especially with regard to property matters, which is why I have broken it down into manageable bites. Drawing on my extensive experience in handling hundreds of probate sales—from the disastrous messes like the house Connie inherited, to the rarefied estates of the super-wealthy—I'll walk you through the process. It begins with understanding the role of the executor, which we'll address in chapter 1.

PART I
The Assessment Phase

CHAPTER 1

The Role of the Executor

Back in the 1990s, I contacted the head of a very successful east-coast manufacturing company who had been named executor of his sister's estate in Atherton, California. The area is called "Billionaire's Row" because some Silicon Valley corporate titans live there. The executor, whom I'll call Jack to protect his privacy, explained that he was frustrated by having to deal with his sister's estate. He was too busy with his own life and corporation. What's more, he was shocked to discover in the reading of his sister's will that she had given all her assets to the Reverend Jerry Falwell's ministry. Jack was not a fan of the television evangelist, to put it mildly.

I met Jack at the property in Lindenwood, a huge estate that had been broken into one-acre, brick-walled parcels with elegant homes and impeccably manicured lawns. But, when we pulled into his sister's section of the private enclave, we couldn't see a house. Eventually we realized we were not in someone's backyard woods;

we were on a concrete driveway so overgrown with grass and foliage that it was more like a tunnel. As we walked through, we began to see old cars that had become intertwined with the trees. We entered the house and found art on the walls—but furs and expensive personal effects were strewn about. The house had not been lived in for many years and was full of dust and cobwebs. I found out later that the owner had gone into a care facility.

The property was in what I call "Smithsonian condition"— physically sound but extremely dated. In the backyard, I saw ducks and thought there might be a beautiful pond overgrown by grass. When I got closer, the ducks flew off, and I realized it was actually a swimming pool, turned green from years of neglect. Once Jack hired me to begin working with the estate, we brought in arborists and landscape contractors to eliminate all the overgrowth. Then we could get a line of sight from the street to the property and show buyers how big it was. It took weeks of clearing and hauling before the property was ready to be marketed.

During the entire process, Jack maintained a disinterested tone because any value from the estate would not go to anyone he knew. He just wanted to get on with it as quickly as possible while ful-filling his legal duty as the executor of the estate. Ultimately, the property sold for a price beyond our expectations due to the location and wealthy neighbors, some of whom would have thought nothing of spending $1 million just to increase the size of their backyards. Instead, a developer bought the property, took down the house, and built himself a magnificent mansion. This was a lucky break for the estate because the brother was far from the ideal executor. He lived far away, had substantial assets, and this was just another burden on his list of things to do. With no one in the family receiving a benefit from the estate, the duty was performed but without any real gusto.

This story contains lessons for everyone involved throughout the probate process, from those making wills and trusts to those carrying them out, as well as all the friends and professionals those people turn to for help and advice. With better estate planning by his sister, Jack would not have found himself in such an unwelcome situation. Proper conservatorship would have kept the property in shape, and it could have passed to the beneficiary without surprising a relative with an undue burden. When choosing an executor, it's important to make sure he or she understands and respects the duties. At the time of this writing, though, the current trend seems to lean toward the use of more professional administrators/fiduciaries. Given that living trusts have become more prevalent, the actual number of probate cases are expected to trend lower over the next twenty years. But estate planning is beyond the scope of this book. Here we are explaining the process from the point where an executor or administrator of the estate must assess what's involved in the job ahead.

The primary job of the executor is to carry out the wishes of the decedent—that's the legal term for the person who died. But the job carries a load of responsibilities:

- Inform everyone necessary of the death.

- Secure the property and valuables.

- Act as liaison to the heirs and beneficiaries.

- Take inventory of all assets and possessions.

- Make arrangements with a funeral home.

- Get and distribute copies of the death certificate.

- File tax returns.

- Deal with the licensing and registration of motor vehicles.

- Collect any debts owed to the decedent.

- Pay any debts owed before making sure the beneficiaries receive their due inheritance.

And those are only some of the responsibilities leading up to dealing with a real estate sale. Does that sound like a lot of fun?

An executor must remain aware of family dynamics while being willing to make tough decisions that not everybody approves of. I will discuss the role of different personality types, starting in chapter 2. There are essentially four different personality types, and the way they respond to loss or tragedy can vary. I also will cover various circumstances that may make an estate easier or harder to settle, including how the death occurred. If it was a long illness and everybody had an opportunity to say goodbye and get their minds emotionally around it, they might be better equipped to complete the process than a family dealing with an unexpected death, such as in a car accident.

To help you understand some basics that shape the role of the executor, I'll explain to you in this chapter:

- *Fees and legal expenses*

- *Living trusts*

- *Emotional and practical considerations*

- *An institution as executor*

Fees and Legal Expenses

In exchange for all the work of being an executor, there is some pay. Executor fees are regulated by each state and can be paid out as a flat fee, a percentage of the value of the estate, or at an hourly rate. In California, it is often 6 percent of the estate's worth. Sometimes executors handling the estates of family members or friends don't feel right taking a fee, but they should not be afraid to do so. They sustain a real cost in lost time at work or lost productivity, not to mention the stress associated with the process.

An executor should hire an attorney to ensure that all legal documentation is properly filed and to guard against personal liability. An attorney is particularly necessary if the decedent's property is substantial or subject to taxation, or if the executor suspects that other parties besides the named beneficiaries might declare an interest.

Unless the estate is protected through a *living trust*, it must go through probate. And even when there's a trust, probate may be unavoidable if the trust was inadequate or out-of-date. The decedent may have refinanced a property, for instance, and then failed to put it back into the trust. So, that property would definitely have to go through probate. The complicated estates of many international celebrities were forced into the probate process, even though they had the best possible financial and legal advice—Roy Disney, Steve Jobs, J. P. Morgan, Michael Jackson, Whitney Houston, Princess Diana, Pablo Picasso, and Howard Hughes, to name a few.

WHAT IS A LIVING TRUST?

A living trust is a written legal document that partially substitutes for a will. With a living trust, your assets (e.g., your home, bank accounts, and stocks) are put into the trust, administered for your benefit during your lifetime, and then transferred to your beneficiaries when you die.

Most people name themselves as the trustee in charge of managing their trust's assets. This way, even though your assets have been put into the trust, you can remain in control of your assets during your lifetime. You can also name a successor trustee (a person or an institution) who will manage the trust's assets if you ever become unable or unwilling to do so yourself.

Source: State Bar of California

Estate planning lawyers in California often recommend a living trust for clients who have significant assets (more than $150,000 worth of property that is not passing directly to beneficiaries) that they want to avoid becoming subject to probate-court oversight when they die or if they become incapacitated.

If a living trust is regularly updated to include all assets, then the estate can avoid going through probate, thereby saving time and legal fees to the heirs. Court supervision of the administration of the estate delays the passing of the property and possessions on to the heirs. Executors may have to hire a probate lawyer or other professionals to help with the process, especially if an estate includes properties in multiple jurisdictions. Wills in probate are public records, so privacy-seeking celebrities create living trusts.

Emotional and Practical Considerations

The executor often has to deal with conflict among heirs over the disposition of assets. Some heirs want to hold on to a family home out of an emotional sense of duty—because their parents told them, "Never sell this property." On the other hand, financial obligations might not allow for keeping the home, and then friction occurs in the family between the more emotional and more practical factions. An executor may encounter family members who want to buy the property and live in it to maintain a legacy, even when they don't have the means to do so. An executor who gives in too easily and lets them try may cost the estate financially by missing the chance to sell in a good market.

There also are cases where the executor is so callous, cavalier, or rushed that he or she fails to account for anybody's emotional state during the probate process. In such cases, the emotionally connected sorts will feel like they have no say, and they may hire their own attorneys to halt the process and allow their wishes to be heard.

The assessment phase of being an executor is a balancing act in which one of the most important steps is taking an emotional inventory of the parties involved. Is their disposition more practical, or more emotional? If they have more of an emotional connection to the situation, do they have the financial capacity to carry out their emotional wishes?

An Institution as Executor

When a will names a third-party outsider (such as the trust department of a bank) to administer an estate or trust, relatives and friends often feel slighted. They may wonder why someone in the family wasn't entrusted with the job. But this decision may be the greatest gift of all. Even if it costs the estate a little extra financially, the decision eliminates some of the emotional conflict that can occur within the family. Instead of everybody ganging up on a family member making all the decisions, the family unites to deal with the outsider overseeing the estate. The old saying, "The enemy of my enemy is my friend" seems to apply, although the individual or institution has a fiduciary role, which means a *legal and ethical requirement* to act in the best interests of the estate.

If parents name the oldest child to administer the estate, the other siblings might say, "See? Mom and Dad liked you more. You were the oldest. You were always in control. You were always pushing all of us around. Nothing's changed. It just continues." The parents might choose a fiduciary for that reason alone. Many times, they'll choose a fiduciary if children have drug or alcohol dependencies or physical limitations, or if they just may not be good with money. Sometimes, a will or trust is created when children are young, and the intention is to set up a time frame for the beneficiaries to receive the assets over many years. A fiduciary oversees the estate to ensure transparency so all parties can see the annual disbursements and returns.

A third party that is not emotionally connected to the estate will execute the will based on the written document and not the stories or interpersonal dynamics that ensue. Eliminating the emotional sensitivity can resolve an estate more quickly, especially when there's a need to sell a property that a family member is still occupying.

To avoid misinterpretation, people writing a will or setting up a living trust that will be executed or administered by an institution should be very specific about their wishes. I've seen trust departments liquidate real estate assets over the objections of family members whose deceased loved ones had always told them real estate was the best asset to stay in. Trust-department officials have the duty to act on what they think are best interests, but they should also be careful to honor the wishes of the person who died and, more importantly, listen to what the heirs or beneficiaries are saying. Honoring as many wishes as possible creates less resistance.

The process must maintain a certain pace to meet legal deadlines. But, as discussed in the introduction of this book, before the marketing phase, there are steps to assess and plan. As an old saying goes, the time to have a map of the forest is before you enter the woods. Discussing the timeline with the heirs and the beneficiaries in advance prevents friction. Plans can change, but the people involved should have a general idea of what to expect. It is up to the executor to assess not only the physical assets of an estate but also the people and emotions involved, a subject covered in the next chapter.

CHAPTER 2

People Are People

A woman I'll call Linda became my client shortly after her mother died; her father had died a few years earlier. The parents had raised Linda in an almost stereotypically normal postwar life. She grew up in a three-bedroom, two-bath, ranch-style home on a tree-lined street, knew all the neighbors, and played hide-and-go-seek with her friends. Her two brothers, sister, and mom and dad celebrated the holidays and the special events of her childhood in this home. And as the most responsible child, Linda was the natural choice to be appointed as an executor.

When her father passed away, it came to light that he had been previously married. Linda asked a lot of questions about that long-ago marriage, but she never got many answers, and let it rest. When going through her parents' papers after her mom died, Linda found documents revealing a half-sister she never knew about. She didn't give it much thought and continued with her duties in administering the estate. This was before the internet, and finding people was not as easy as it is today.

Linda carefully interviewed real estate agents before picking me to sell her childhood home, which sold quickly for an amazing price. The buyers conducted inspections, obtained financing, and prepared to close escrow on time, so everything was going as planned—until the title company prepared the final closing documents. The questionnaire relating to the title history asked if the title had ever been transferred into Linda's mother's name after her dad died. Linda's parents had held title to the house as community property, and she assumed this clerical issue had been taken care of after her father died. In fact, if the parents had held the property as joint tenants, then the father's portion would have been transferred to Linda's mother with a simple form, an affidavit of death of joint tenants. But in reality, they held the property as tenants in common, the default form of property ownership in California, which does not automatically grant survivorship rights. That meant the home needed a separate probate, apart from the one Linda already was dealing with for her mother's estate. Probating Dad's portion of the estate could take an additional three to six months, and that was a real problem.

Linda's mother's estate had entered into a contract with the buyers, who had performed their part of the agreement. They were ready to take ownership, with their loan interest rate locked for a set period. If that time expired and the settlement of the home sale could not be completed before mortgage rates rose, the estate would face legal exposure. The estate might have to "buy-down" the buyers' higher interest rate or be liable for the difference of the potentially higher payments the buyers would face over the life of their loan.

So, what did we do? Clearly, the title company couldn't transfer the title, and the first-time buyers had already given notice to vacate their rental home. After consulting with two different attorneys, we came up with a highly unusual plan to let the buyers occupy the property for free prior to the close of escrow in exchange for their agreement not seeking any damages for interest rate differentials. The attorneys generated a pile of releases and "what if" documents that would cover all the parties before the buyers ultimately became owners nearly six months later.

In the meantime, the newly found sibling had to be located because she was entitled to one-fifth of Dad's probated estate. Naturally, she didn't turn down the money.

This expensive lesson for Linda demonstrates how an executor must assess not just the physical assets of an estate but also consider all the people who might be involved before a property goes to market. The number of people who come into play can be surprising, even if there were no unmentioned children of prior marriages.

As a crucial part of the assessment phase, I strongly urge executors to not only ask lots of questions, but also to obtain a title report long before a property hits the market, to make sure the estate has full authority to sell. I have seen executors get hung up on the fact that they couldn't find the deed for the property in the decedent's paperwork—although that's unnecessary once the title company has pulled the necessary documents from the county recorder's office.

To help you expect the unexpected, I'll explain to you in the pages ahead:

- *Dealing with emotions*

- *The live-in companions*

- *Looking out for the beneficiaries*

- *Assessing personalities*
- *Considering the payoff*

Dealing with Emotions

To avoid explosive situations, the executor must be a practical psychologist, assessing all the people involved and what drives their behavior. They may be driven by grief, money, power, respect, obligation, or advice from well-meaning or self-serving friends. As the clues emerge, the wise executor writes down the details. A time will come when the executor is facing a tough situation, feeling weary or underappreciated, and at risk of responding in an overly emotional way. Surprises like the ones Linda encountered can lead to stress, shock, disbelief, or even feelings of betrayal. Reviewing the notes can help the executor maintain a perspective to plan or stick with the best approach and defuse bad situations.

When growing up, family members took on certain roles that become ingrained. Most adults are just little kids in older skin, and they revert back to their old roles in the family pecking order, thereby creating the certainty of acceptance from the family, or at least attention—positive or negative. I have seen adults go through major public meltdowns to fit back into old behaviors, or just behave like bratty little kids among brothers and sisters. Heirs will throw up smoke screens and argue over frivolous points while carrying on this form of family ritual. The executor needs to work out emotionally charged decisions involving money in this precarious situation. The only way to succeed is to assess the personalities and their behaviors.

An executor, particularly one trying to settle an estate after a violent death, may still be grieving. It's possible for an executor to even become immobilized by grief when tasked with the duty to unwind somebody's life while simultaneously trying to unwind his or her own personal emotions. If you've been thrust into a scenario like this, it's not uncommon to feel conflicted about trying to set aside personal grief to focus on dealing with the estate. But you'll have to compartmentalize the emotional part to get through—then go back and grieve later. Talk to somebody, seek counseling, spend time with other friends or relatives who share the loss.

When I am around a family that has come together after a death, I often see them revert to a tribal way of speaking, using terminology familiar to them and picking up on each other's sentence structure, cadence, pace, volume, and other speaking inflections. That tribal-speak shows unity. In contrast, I was helping two brothers sell their parents' home, and their communication showed a completely disassociated relationship. One brother was well-read and articulate but had not accomplished much; the other was successful in a skilled trade but rough-spoken. All they did around me was try to display how the other had gone wrong. My job was to speak to their two different language patterns so both felt that "this guy gets me." It's not a form of manipulation but a way of creating rapport and trust.

As they tested my reactions to judge whose side I would be on, I told them, "I treat it as though the *house* hired me. The house called me and said, 'Are you the best person to get the most value for me?' So remember, gentlemen, I'm neutral. I'm working for the house." I knew they would continue to dredge up silly childhood rivalries, but I needed them to feel we were all working toward the one common goal of settling the estate.

Often the beneficiaries just want to keep the family peace, but their spouses behind the scenes are stirring the pot. That dynamic puts the heirs in a tight spot. They either avoid friction with their brothers and sisters, or they keep the family peace where they put their heads down on their pillow at night. Because more than one person is always weighing in on the decisions, I never assume that a family member questioning me is the true source of the question. If I have the opportunity, I ask, "Are you married?" And if so, I'll ask if the wife or husband has been through handling an estate. That often explains a question that comes out of nowhere. They were told to ask it.

The Live-In Companions

In selling homes for estates, I have found myself consoling family members who had to tell a brother or sister who had been living with Mom or Dad for many years as a caregiver that it was time for him or her to go. The caretaker felt slighted, mistaken for a freeloader by relatives who didn't understand the amount of work he or she had put in. My job became to help that person feel validated but also to help the executor or administrator feel confident that he or she was still doing the right thing on behalf of the estate. I had to learn to compartmentalize myself to give clear counsel to the people involved.

As the cost of housing and nursing homes has become so expensive, it has become more common to find someone living with the decedent as a caregiver. In some cases, they may have been hired but now have an emotional connection and feel entitled to be a beneficiary of the estate or to be compensated for moving out. Some will have planned for the death and their departure from the home, but others may resist it. Some are like grave robbers, and jewelry and cash turn up missing. When I initially come in contact with these caregivers, I have to use my expertise to help transition them from the property without their taking the assets. Immediately, suspicions increase. The sense of justice steps up dramatically. When things are missing, the heirs or the beneficiaries come out with pitchforks and torches looking for the caregiver.

Looking Out for the Beneficiaries

I recently handled the sale of a former tech titan's property with the proceeds donated to Stanford University's women's basketball program. He just loved to watch women's basketball and connected with that team.

Beneficiaries come in all shapes and sizes. They include charities, educational institutions, and people with mental or physical disabilities. Beneficiaries can be children, with or without special needs. They can be wealthy or destitute adult children. Or, they can be siblings, including those who are highly successful and others who never quite made it. These beneficiaries may put pressure on an executor for different reasons.

For example, the Stanford board of trustees looked on the women's basketball bequest of property as an investment asset. Taking a very businesslike and practical approach, the board put $50,000 into enhancing the property and netted $150,000 through its sale. Other beneficiaries are desperate to get cash as soon as possible.

The executor must assess, "Whom are we dealing with? What is their motivation? And what is their capacity?"

This assessment helps executors understand they are dealing with people who have different perspectives and realize they can't please everybody 100 percent during the process. If part of an estate is being donated to an institution, part to children, and part to grandchildren, there may be compromises in which not everyone wins. If nobody's completely happy, the executor has probably done a good job.

I worked with a family in which communication broke down over handling of the estate. One brother hired an attorney and constantly threatened to sue the executor, his sister. She was very methodical and followed the letter of the law, but ultimately—to find out what he really wanted—she had to knock on her brother's door to talk to him without the barrier of the attorney. Typically, the most demanding relative just wants to be heard out or needs the biggest hug.

🏠 Typically, the most demanding relative just wants to be heard out or needs the biggest hug.

Assessing Personalities

One executor I met with asked me to have a second meeting "with our attorney and a couple members of the family." I readily agreed but was surprised by the formal setting the executor chose, a conference meeting room in a hotel. Well, I walked into the room, and there was the executor's attorney, and then the estate's financial planner, and four or five different family members, each with an attorney. They all had questions about what I was going to do and how it would benefit the estate. Later, they would vote among themselves on whether I was the right candidate.

That story is unusual, but an executor does come into contact with a large number of professional people, including court officials, real estate agents, attorneys, accountants, and bankers. An executor addresses all manner of issues regarding the property with contractors and workers. The executor must choose to work with not the person he or she likes best but the one who will best serve the interests of all of the beneficiaries. The executor must maintain that same best-interests standard in handling the expectations of the heirs. What's that expression about sometimes needing the wisdom of Solomon and the patience of Job?

Right from the beginning in working as an executor, it is extremely useful to appreciate that the world is made up of different personality types. Quite often this can lead to some frustration and even serious head-butting. Take a moment to identify your own personality, and then if you are an executor, identify the personalities of those with whom you have to work. Understand that this is the way people are, and make adjustments when dealing with them so that your role as executor can be as painless as possible.

Here are the four main types I have encountered over the years:

Driver: This is the "let's make it happen" person. Get it done! If there's a group of you evaluating your grandmother's belongings, the driver is the one who will say, "Toss it! The value isn't worth the time. Quit looking at it. Let's keep moving."

Expressive: Some people feel the need, especially at this emotional time, to reminisce and tell stories about the decedent or the property. They wear their hearts on their sleeve. Selling the house and possessions takes second place to the memories.

Amiable: These good-natured people have a soft spot—for everything. They will say, "I can't part with it. It would be a sacrilege to let it go. It belonged to Mom." They won't want to sell it, give it to charity, or throw it away. Even down to the toothpicks!

Analytical. The analytical types have an entirely different approach to selling a property and its contents. They have the need to inventory everything onto a spreadsheet (and I do mean everything).

They will want to categorize all of the possessions into subcategories and then itemize by color, size, shape, and so forth.

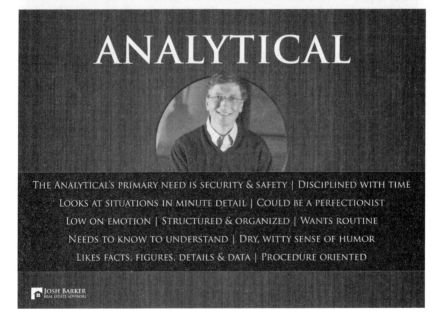

I ask people, "Just out of curiosity, what type of work do you do?" If they say they're an artist or a financial analyst, that provides a sense of their personality type. When I'm speaking to the "analytical" types, I talk facts, figures, numbers, and data points. I know they're slow to make a decision, and the data I give them will just lead to more questions, because analytical people don't want to appear foolish. My job is to give them the data that makes them comfortable knowing their decision was the right one.

I'll deliver the same message to the other personality types, but I deliver it in a context they can understand. For the "amiables," that means I have to explain it in the big picture, because once all the pieces of this amazing puzzle come together, they will feel everyone is connected. The "drivers" just want to know the bottom line. I have to answer the question on their minds, which is, "What do we have to do to get this stuff done?"

For the "expressives," I need to let them tell their stories. They're the ones who say, "You know, man, we used to have some amazing parties at this house." And they want to talk about the great times they had with their friends. To them, I say, "I know it's a daunting time, but it doesn't need to be a daunting process. This can be a time where everyone's here together, having a good time, getting through this, reliving some of the old memories, and ultimately, it lets you move on in your life to all the cool things you'll be doing in the future."

If you allow the people to speak in the terms that they need to, it really helps the process along.

There have been times when an institution, such as a bank trust department, was acting as executor, and the administrator was so analytical that his or her focus on the data left family members feeling disconnected. Most of the family fit the amiable personality type and considered the administrator sterile and uncaring. So, I would explain the family's resistance to the administrator this way: "There's an element here I think we're missing. If you can acknowledge their feelings during the course of this, we'll probably get the family to move along with the process easier."

Finally, there's *YOU*. It's just as important to identify your own personality type. For instance, if you're a "driver" and you're dealing with someone who's "amiable," you could really annoy each other. Remember: Know your respective types, and adjust your behavior accordingly. It will make for a smoother ride.

Considering the Payoff

In assessing how different personalities may affect the decision-making process in settling an estate, you've got to understand the payoff people are seeking. The issue may be money, but the payoff may be more emotional than financial. For example, consider an institutional executor who, when she grew up, was always the one who rescued others and saved the day. That's her self-identity, and that's the payoff she wants to see validated in her work. Those with the "amiable" personality have a tough time making decisions because of a fear of hurting others. If they are cleaning out Mom's house, they can't bring themselves to throw out or give away something they know Mom loved, even though she is gone.

I'm not saying that certain personality types should not be executors—but how individuals make decisions is something to think about. Parents who realize their child may have trouble making decisions could pre-designate items in a will to ease the process and set a time frame. I've found I also can move along the process by introducing executors to various contractors who work with physical assets. The executor may be from another part of the country and need resources to box up contents for shipment or help determine the value of cars, jewelry, and collectibles. In my case, the payoff is getting a home listing on the market without a potentially costly delay. An executor's failure to meet deadlines has consequences, which we'll discuss in chapters 8 and 9. But first, we will discuss how to assess and plan for timely decisions, the subject of the next chapter.

CHAPTER 3

Big Decisions on
the Home Front

An example of an executor who was in over his head in planning and decision-making involves a twenty-year-old I'll call Chad. Chad's alcoholic father, Ron, was a contractor who died at age forty-seven. Ron's estranged wife wanted nothing to do with him, and his three children had been out of his life for a while. Ron left no will, so it was up to Chad, the oldest child and next of kin, to deal with the estate, including a house in a coastal town south of San Francisco. The court required Chad to get bonded, or insured, to act on behalf of the estate as executor.

Unfortunately, Chad also inherited his father's chemical-dependency issues. So, while reeling from the death of his dad, Chad went to the house and discovered a considerable amount of cash there, close to $100,000. Plus, he was able to access any funds in the bank.

That led to a month-long binge with a bunch of bottom-feeders who joined him in turning the house into a drug den. That was the situation when Chad's grandfather got me involved.

Chad or the drug dealers he was consorting with had spray-painted the interior walls of the house and cut a hole in the kitchen floor so they could privately sell drugs between the main house and a garage down below. Ron's tools, his motorcycle, and various recreational items in the garage were stolen. The garage door was knocked off the tracks. The house was left in ramshackle condition, looking like a haunted house. And to make matters worse, the title had a lien from Ron's income-tax problems.

With the house heading into foreclosure, my best option to save it for the estate was to contact the next child in line, Katy, and ask her to become executor. She understood that the house was valuable if it could be fixed up and that if nothing were done, it would go to investors who had bought the bank loan, and they would make a handsome profit. We had to wait a few weeks for her to turn eighteen, at which time she immediately was forced to make decisions about the remaining assets and what would be best for her and her younger sister. We helped her hire an attorney and got the bank to postpone the foreclosure. Ultimately, we were able to sell the house—though not for the amount it would have fetched if the foreclosure had not created a deadline and if her brother had not mismanaged the estate. There were many anxious moments during the process when she thought she would lose the house.

The insurance company that bonded Chad was forced to reimburse the two daughters the money their brother stole. The insurer then filed criminal charges against Chad.

That's perhaps a worst-case scenario of what happens when someone leaves property and an abundance of cash but no will or trust. If someone becomes executor who is not emotionally, physically, and mentally prepared to do so, it can produce a complete unwinding for the entire family and the entire legacy.

Chad's story may seem extreme, but he and Katy were like many executors in feeling caught in unfamiliar territory and forced to make difficult decisions with a big impact on themselves and their family. The assessment phase sets up those decisions.

To help you understand the scope of the decisions and considerations involved, the pages ahead will explore:

- *Keep or sell the house?*
- *Can you manage a property investment?*
- *Establishing the value of a property*
- *To disclose or not?*
- *Furnished or unfurnished?*
- *Repair and renovate?*

Keep or Sell the House?

In Ron's case, he left a coastal California home with enough equity in it that in normal circumstances the family could have held it as a rental property with a nice cash flow, or they could have fixed it up and sold it at a profit. Keep or sell is often the first big decision that executors face. There are several considerations for the heirs. Some may want to sell the property for financial benefit; others for closure, to relieve their grief and memories. Some heirs can't bear to be around the house any longer, and others want to sell and divide the proceeds to distance themselves from their fellow heirs.

The most common final directive in a typical last will and testament is: "My estate shall be divided equally among my children." But the parent's attempt to treat the offspring in a fair and equitable manner often backfires. It may not be the blessing that it first appears to be. The family home is usually by far the largest asset of an estate, and determining the fate of a place filled with so many memories can be the thorniest issue for the executor. What if one sibling wants to sell it, while one wants to live in it, and another wants to rent it out? This conflict can break out over a vacation home, as well: One sibling who doesn't live far away suggests keeping it in the family so everyone can take an allotted time to vacation there, but there's a brother who lives in another state, desperately needs cash, and wants to sell it—now. A sister, on the other hand, was never crazy about the old getaway place and prefers the idea of rental income.

Not only are there competing interests, but also deep-seated resentments often emerge once Mom and Dad have left the scene. Death can provoke the worst side of family dynamics. The executor, caught in the middle, has to sit down with all the heirs, ask them to keep their emotions under control, and put the cold, rational facts on the table. It may well be that a sale is mandated by the terms of the will or is necessary to raise funds to pay off the estate's debts. Selling may be the best option if medical bills, alimony, child support, tax issues, or a host of other reasons require cashing out.

If there is a choice, the fair way to move forward is to try to make a decision based on what someone would do if he or she had no personal connection to the property. Selling is often the best decision. It produces a specific dollar amount, which can then be split equally. Any other "solution"—such as renting the property out or using it as a second home—only leads to further negotiations and challenges in terms of working out an equitable financial formula.

A plan to "time share" the property among the estate's beneficiaries or to rent it to others can result in petty squabbles or major disputes among the heirs for years to come. Finding and keeping tenants is a lot of work; handling maintenance and bookkeeping is a lot of work. Who gets paid what for that onerous burden? And what are the chances that everybody's going to be happy with the results?

Can You Manage a Property Investment?

If there are multiple heirs to the estate and keeping it in the family is under strong consideration, I always stress (especially to the executor) that everyone should stop and ask themselves: Would you choose the other beneficiaries to be your partners in any long-term investment? Because, by keeping the property, that's what you're doing. Let's take the questioning a stage further:

a. Is there a possibility any of the other beneficiaries could divorce each other?

b. Could they go bankrupt?

c. Could they be bringing any other entanglements into the partnership that you would never entertain in any business investment?

It may be uncomfortable, but it's important to step back mentally and analyze what could happen in the future.

Regardless of the amount of equity the estate has in the property or its potential rental income, some hard-dollar questions apply: Would you have bought that particular property as an investment? What is the demand for rentals in your area? Is it a rising or falling market? Is there a better way to generate returns on that money?

There also are emotional costs. Imagine someone else living in your parents' home and you're tasked with collecting rent and maintaining the property. How would you feel every time you got a call to fix something? Would you be constantly worried that the tenants were possibly damaging the place? If so, it's not the right investment for you.

Executors should be wary of getting into the position where they are representing the interests of a group of beneficiaries. They're not only managing a property—they're managing the group that owns the property! Once the property is distributed among heirs rather than having the estate's name on the title, everyone has to agree on a sale, rather than one executor making the decision. Emotional and family dynamics can take their toll.

A HELPING HAND SLAPPED

Another tough call is whether or not to help someone in the family buy the home. I personally know of a case in which three sisters inherited a property, and they decided it should go to the sister who had just been through a divorce and had four children. She was able to qualify for financing only when a relative reluctantly cosigned for the mortgage. Two years later, the house was in foreclosure, destroying the credit of the family member who agreed to help. The lesson? If you are asked to cosign or help, consider lending the equity that you would have received from the estate. Damaged credit can hurt you for a long time. If you don't feel comfortable lending your share, you definitely should not cosign!

Establishing the Value of a Property

If one heir or beneficiary wants to buy the house, the estate must determine the market value and get a fair price for the rest of the heirs and beneficiaries. One way is to get two appraisals, which can come from a bank or an independent certified appraiser—or for higher-end work, someone who has earned the MAI designation as a member of Appraiser's Institute. The executor may also look at estimates from a real estate website, such as Zillow, which uses public information about the home and comparable sales to set a value.

If the two estimates and the Zillow price are close, they can be used to set the value, but if they are more than 5 percent apart, the executor may need to get a third appraisal. The appraisals will cost about $500 apiece, but spending $1,000 to $1,500 to establish real values is cheap insurance when tens of thousands of dollars are at stake in setting the right price. Looking up the Zillow estimate is free, but it may be based on outdated or inaccurate information. For example, county records may not reflect an addition to the home in the square footage.

Alternatively, the executor can put the property on the market with the expressed provision that one of the heirs has the first right of refusal to match the highest offer. That way, the highest bid on the property really establishes its market value, and the heir can buy it from the estate for that amount. In a really hot housing market, the other beneficiaries can take comfort from this method. It also disabuses any heirs of the notion that they could buy the property for a lot less than it was worth in an open marketplace.

In California, we see a different situation, which you might call the HGTV effect: Heirs from other parts of the country overestimate our property values, thinking every home in the San Francisco Bay Area is worth over a million dollars. But many are worth half that, and those heirs need to be educated about the marketplace.

To Disclose or Not?

One benefit to selling during the probate is that the executor, who may be coming in from outside the area and not be that familiar with the property, is exempt from some disclosure requirements. A seller normally has to disclose any material facts that would affect a home's value. Regardless of any legal liability, we recommend sellers disclose anything the buyers are likely to learn soon anyway. Invariably, the buyer will meet a neighbor who asks, "Did they tell you about the problem with . . . ?" If there was a murder or suicide at the home, it is best to disclose that "a violent death" occurred there. Because superstitions can be powerful, giving the buyers an understanding of what happened can help them get their minds around what really took place.

Furnished or Unfurnished?

It's not unusual for a home in probate to be filled with a thirty-plus-year accumulation of stuff, which should not be left in place when the property goes on the market. In most cases, thinning out the furnishings or leaving the home unfurnished will help it show better. Nine out of ten buyers first see the home in online photographs where the home must look enticing enough to attract people to visit the property. For that reason, we often stage the property as part of our marketing plan. If a home has been recently furnished or renovated, it may be OK to leave it alone, so each case should be looked at based on the marketplace it's in, the type of property, and the demographic profile of likely buyers.

Repair and Renovate?

The executor must make sure the house is maintained in good condition, that necessary repairs are carried out, and that it is kept insured. Most houses in probate are not brand new; many are older and require some work. An executor can be personally liable for failure to maintain a property that results in losses for the heirs. But how much work is worthwhile before putting a home on the market? This is a big question that depends on the individual property and circumstances.

Letting a house sit empty can be costly, unless the time is spent on improvements that considerably increase the property value. Location used to be the major determining factor in that value calculation, but timing of the sale has become important too. More people than ever are invested in the stock market, and its ups and downs can affect the real estate market, as can interest rates.

If the house needs some "light lipstick"—painting, carpeting, landscaping, that kind of thing—it usually makes sense to proceed to put the best face on the property. But "heavy lifting"—such as kitchen and bathroom remodels—call for a deeper cost-benefit analysis. An older property may be in good condition but terribly dated, if everything is exactly the way Grandma has kept it since 1950. If a death occurred on the property, a brand-new look makes that factor less disturbing to buyers. The calculation is different for properties in complete disrepair, with the roof falling in and termites holding up the walls. Extensive renovations may be worthwhile if the estate has the money, the executor has the time, and the payoff is top dollar. But if the timing is off from the market standpoint, selling the house "as-is" may make more sense. A good real estate agent can help with these decisions.

A good example involves two neighboring 1950s ranch homes that were nearly identical. I was handling the sale of one for two brothers after their mother died. She had lived there for about thirty years. I had met with this family there a year before, when the father passed away, and we worked together on a complete remodeling— kitchen, bathrooms, new hardwood flooring, lighting, landscaping, and garage doors. Our agency has a project coordinator who not only provides referrals to contractors but also can help pick the trending materials and colors. In that marketplace, we knew there were young buyers working in technology who wanted to be at their jobs versus working on their homes. They wanted a modern home with no sweat equity. The calculation proved correct, as that property ultimately sold for the highest price in the neighborhood.

Meanwhile, next door there were brothers whose dad was in a care facility, and they knew he didn't have long to live. They planned to sell the property as-is until they saw our results. As soon as the father died, they hired us, and we replicated the next-door renovation with a few high-end additions. That home sold for $200,000 higher than the neighboring house. The market was up, but the unprecedented sale price was a compound effect of the work done on *both* houses. The sellers realized the profit that otherwise might have gone to buyers who could have fixed up and flipped the houses if they went to market without renovating it first.

On the other hand, I worked with two brothers and a sister who also inherited a home where their mother had lived for about thirty years. It was really outdated and needed repairs. The brothers wanted to do the repairs themselves but were busy doing other things, and time was slipping by, to the frustration of the sister, who was the executor. She was being patient, but I was concerned that further delays in a falling market could lead to a point where they would not realize the maximum potential value of the property. We met for a consultation, and I showed that it warranted spending just a small amount of money to make a good profit with a quick sale date, rather than investing time in a more extensive renovation.

This strategy resulted from assessing the marketplace, comparing the sale price of fixer-uppers with those homes that were in good condition. The family wound up getting multiple offers, with one beyond their wildest expectations. The brothers were also happier, because they were able to concentrate on their other responsibilities rather than a project they had felt obligated to do in their mother's memory.

We have covered many considerations that go into the strategic decisions for an estate that's left including a house. What they all have in common is that time was taken to assess the situation, including the value of the property, the market, and the family's needs. However, there's one more big player in this drama—the government—which we will address in the following chapter on tax considerations.

CHAPTER 4

The Taxman Cometh

Eddie, a young man in his twenties, was very close to his grandmother, who left him two properties in San Francisco when she passed away. Unfortunately, she had houses but no money. She was the helping-hand type who had let people live in her properties without paying, and she had not paid property taxes for many years. The houses were poorly maintained, and the city was on the verge of condemning and seizing them.

One house was completely decrepit. It had broken sewer pipes and raw sewage running through it. And it was not located in the best of neighborhoods. Eddie had his own financial obligations and very limited time and money to spend on repairs and renovations. Eddie and I assessed whether it was worth selling one of the properties and using the capital to fix the other. We had to balance timing, cost, and ultimately market price.

We put together a simple plan: With the aid of family members, we cleaned out the contents of the decrepit house, and we brought in specialists to take care of the sewage and some other unpleasant work. Within ninety days, we had the property ready to go to market and ended up getting top dollar, given the condition of the property.

Eight months later, after the tax issues were resolved and the estate had filed income taxes, Eddie fully inherited the second property. Even though it was out of probate, we went through the same repair and sale process.

Some tax issues, like Eddie's grandmother's unpaid property taxes, affect only a minority of estates. I'm not a tax expert, and readers should get expert tax advice from an accountant or lawyer. But every executor inevitably needs to consider taxes.

To help you begin to look at the tax issues that can affect an estate, this brief chapter will discuss:

- *Property taxes*

- *Estate taxes*

- *Capital gains taxes*

Property Taxes

As Eddie learned, it's a good idea for an executor to check right away on whether the property taxes on an inherited home are current. In California, the information is generally available online from county tax collectors. Each county also has a tax assessor who determines when a change in ownership has occurred, at which point the property is reassessed to its current fair-market value.

California law allows "a parent-child transfer" after a death, which allows the parent to pass a property to a child with no change in tax base. That benefit can make a big difference in property taxes, which usually go up substantially when a property changes hands, and its value is reassessed. In the case of the three sisters who inherited a home, when they decided one sister would buy out the other two, the property taxes went up, because that was not a parent-child transfer. Appropriate tax planning can preserve the benefit. If the family knows one sibling wants the house and there is enough cash in the estate, the house can be willed to the person who would have ended up buying it, and the cash willed to the other heirs.

Estate Taxes

Another tax that executors often worry about is the federal estate tax, even though it only affects large estates. The exemption, which changes annually, was $5.49 million in 2017. So, if someone died in 2017, any sum above $5.49 million that they gave away or left to heirs would be subject to the estate tax, which at this writing is 40 percent. The IRS website has the latest information about who has to file the estate tax return.

Capital Gains Taxes

Any size estate may have to pay capital gains taxes. When someone sells inherited property, its tax basis is its value on the date of death. If it's a home that subsequently sells for a higher amount, the difference between the tax basis and the sale price is subject to a capital gains tax. The larger the estate, the larger the tax implications are, but this tax can affect anyone in a rising market. If three siblings inherit equal shares, they share the gain and tax consequences equally.

The courts obtain the date-of-death value from somebody called "a probate referee" who never actually enters the property. The court-appointed referees do what's called a "drive-by" or "desktop" appraisal, meaning they may not have even seen the condition of the property. Unlike general appraisers, the referees in California are paid based on a percentage of the value they set. I'm not saying that they're dishonest or trying to mislead anybody, but it's worth checking their values.

If the estate is planning to sell the property soon and the date-of-death value is lower than market value, an unfair capital gains tax will result. If heirs are planning to keep the property for some years, they might want the date-of-death value to be as high as possible to reduce the potential capital gains tax if property values go up in the future. But a high value is not good for a property subject to estate taxes.

A real estate agent can provide information to help appeal a date-of-death value. We see the same data in comparable sales as the "drive-by" appraiser but may know with which sales the cost per square foot can be more accurately compared. We can help make a sensible, defensible argument for a different value based on a property being substandard or above standard, or the referee's value simply not reflecting actual sales. For instance, I sold two properties for a family, and the referee had overvalued these apartment buildings significantly, creating an estate-tax issue. I ended up testifying on behalf of the estate in tax court, and ultimately we were able to get the IRS to reduce estate taxes significantly. More typically, we go through an administrative process to appeal a value for the capital gains tax basis. Or, if we know there is going to be an issue, such as when a neighborhood has an eclectic mix of properties, we provide comparable sales data to the estate's probate attorney to submit to the referee before the valuation letter is even received.

Another tax consideration, which affects income properties, is depreciation. If the date-of-death value is high, the estate or trust gets a tax-savings benefit by being able to depreciate a more expensive asset over the years. If the decedent held the property for many years, it may have lost all of its depreciation value, but then it gets a new, higher date-of-death value in probate, and an heir who keeps the property gets a new deduction for depreciation.

It's most important for those involved with an estate to double-check that current and prior-year property taxes have been paid and to find out what value the probate referee has placed on the property. Many people don't even know that there is a third party issuing a value on the property that they're receiving—but if it's wrong, they need to get the value corrected as soon as possible to avoid long-term impact.

I promised to give you a three-part system for dealing with an inherited property: Assessment, Planning and Preparation, and Marketing. At this point, we have wrapped up the process of assessing the estate's situation and will move on in the next chapter to planning and preparation, which begins with a personal communications strategy.

PART II

The Planning and Preparation Stage

CHAPTER 5

Keeping Everyone Happy

I used to do work for the San Mateo County conservator's office, which protects the interests of people who need long-term care and have no family members looking after them. They may be elderly, disabled, or suffering from Alzheimer's disease, and if they own a home, it may be falling into disrepair. I was involved with selling those homes so the conservator could use the proceeds to pay for the long-term care. That work resulted in my being recommended for a very different task. One day, I got a call from the district attorney of Mendocino County, up on California's north coast, asking for help with an estate whose probate had run well past the time limit, which is usually one year.

Frustrated by the delay, the court had required the district attorney to step in and take over the estate, which is quite unusual. I came to understand that the estate had more than thirty properties. Some of the family members were personally involved in the development of a very successful rental-property business and wanted to preserve it, but others had different ideas for liquidating the assets. They had all lawyered up and were fighting one another. The dissension had kept the estate in probate for nearly two years. A lot of this property was in Ukiah, which is about 175 miles north of my office. So, my question was, "Why are you calling me?" It turned out the family had two large apartment buildings in Daly City, in my county south of San Francisco. The district attorney decided those buildings had to be sold to fund the legal fees and expenses needed to wrap up the estate.

That forced sale is an extreme example of how lack of trust among heirs can drain an estate's value, in this case by at least a million dollars. It was unnerving to the tenants to get the kind of cold, official communications that occur when court officers decide your home must be sold. I felt the lack of trust myself as I got random calls from the various heirs expressing interest in buying the properties at a discount. I sensed they were testing me to see if I would let one of their rivals get away with something. This family was large enough to have feuding factions, so the dynamics were complicated. But settling an estate can be extremely divisive, whether it is large or small, and no matter how many people are involved.

The lesson I took from the experience and have shared with many people over the years is that whatever assets you have, you need to take the time to plan what will happen to your legacy—and leave clear instructions.

A client of mine who really thought things through was a wrestling coach who invested wisely in real estate and bought many buildings over the years. By the time he was in his seventies, he had a plan to donate those buildings after his death in a way that would give his heirs a lifetime cash flow without their having to worry about managing or selling the buildings. Most people don't want to do that kind of planning, but if you have large assets, part of being a good steward of your wealth is taking the time to think of how it could unravel your family rather than tie your relatives closer together.

To help you anticipate the emotional ups and downs of an executor's planning and preparation work, this chapter will discuss:

- *The emotional backdrop*
- *Survivors with special needs*
- *Documenting everything*
- *Positive experiences*

The Emotional Backdrop

If you think about all of the variety of ways people die and the complexity of their relationships to survivors, you can start to appreciate the mix of emotions that compounds the decision-making of those who must execute an estate. Individual survivors won't necessarily see the others' perspectives or appreciate their grief, shock, anxiety, guilt, or other emotional state. For example, when older parents pass from natural causes after a full life, family members tend to be more at peace with the deaths. If one or the other parent survives, or if one of the children dies before the parents, there's a different dynamic. An accident, murder, or suicide can also change the emotions involved.

The death of a young person compounds the grief. A divorce adds to the tension of family communications. A suicide leaves everyone in shock with some associated anger and guilt. I dealt with a case of a man who set fire to his house before he locked himself in the bathroom to commit suicide. But he still left an estate, and the family had to deal with it, however they were feeling. They had to figure out whether the house was insured and what taxes might be owed—although all the documents had burned in the fire. What an overwhelming task!

Going through a relative's home after a death can be a shocking experience. I had a client who came upon her brother's written suicide plan while cleaning out his condo. Another had to clean out his uncle's creek-side house in an affluent town and found it infested with rats because the man was a hoarder with an affinity for extension cords and microwave ovens, which were stacked floor to ceiling. The shock affects how the executors are able to function.

Survivors with Special Needs

Physical, mental, and developmental issues often result in uncertainty about how to deal with a family member's special needs. If one heir is in an expensive care facility, adequate funds have to be set aside, but the other survivors may worry about whether they will receive their distribution properly once that special-needs person no longer needs care. I've seen cases where some heirs are very understanding, and others feel like they're being ripped off. Sometimes I'm shocked that people really just don't "get it," and other times I'm awed by the generosity I witness.

In some cases, heirs are eager to sell a house after the owner's death but have to figure out what to do about someone still there, such as a live-in caretaker or an elderly or dysfunctional dependent.

The executor has to seek some balance or compromise to keep everybody as happy as possible.

For example, I dealt with a woman who was handling the estate of her mother, whom she described as the breadwinner in her second marriage. My client wanted to sell her mother's house, which had no mortgage, to get the proceeds. However, the mother had left her second husband a "life estate," which meant he could live out his life in the home rent-free as long as he paid the property taxes and insurance premiums. He also had to meet a vague requirement to ensure the property was not falling into a state of disrepair. My client wanted to overturn the life estate by establishing that her stepdad had not been maintaining the house properly. I didn't think a court would look favorably on that kind of end run around what obviously was her mother's dying wish that her eighty-five-year-old husband be cared for and given a home.

My client even suggested selling the house as-is (occupied for life by a man paying no rent) so she could get her money sooner. If the actuarial tables said the stepdad could live to age ninety-five, the price would have to be discounted for ten years of lost rent—say $3,000 a month or $360,000 total discount—or else nobody would want to buy it. Even then, the buyer would be just parking cash to speculate, and betting against an old man's life. I explained to her the difficulty of quantifying the amount of discount that would attract a buyer to such an investment. My client took my advice to hold on to the house, carry out the mother's wishes, and just borrow money against the property if necessary.

Documenting Everything

Write this down: *Document everything!* Whenever I get involved with an estate, I urge the executors to buy a notebook or diary in which to document the days and time they're spending and all associated expenses. We'll discuss the financial issues in more detail later, but first let me explain what documentation means: They should note every conversation with each attorney, insurance agent, banker, or anyone they might talk with about the assets of the estate. If it's regarding a house, they should note even a routine call to a utility company. Each diary entry should contain detailed, contemporaneous notes about the conversation, because if somebody challenges the executors about moving too slowly or not fulfilling their duties, the courts will be favorably impressed by a journal full of handwritten notes in chronological order.

Electronic records are not as convincing because computers make it too easy to alter documents. But anything reliably date-stamped, such as an e-mail, a YouTube video, or an audio file dictated into a mobile phone, can supplement your documentation. Lists and photographs of the most important effects and a video of the entire property, room by room and even item by item, can be helpful.

If there's family friction, jot that down under the dates it occurred: "Today I had a call from so-and-so. They were upset about such-and-such." The executor may be the only family member who understands how much time he or she spent on chores related to settling the estate, and noting that time in the journal can help executors justify the fee they are entitled to. Too many executors simply waive that fee, but I think they are more comfortable taking it if they see in their own journal how many hours they worked. The less dissension there is, the more likely executors are to waive the fee they deserve for getting the job done smoothly.

When executors start using their own money to do things for the estate, they are asking for trouble getting that money back. This is so important: If they are going to be preparing a house for the market, they need to document all the money they spend and not mix up their personal funds and the estate funds. Disputes often arise later over how much estate money was spent.

🏠 **When executors start using their own money to do things for the estate, they are asking for trouble getting that money back.**

Positive Experiences

One of the smoothest estate settlements I worked on involved a mother who came up with a brilliant way to make sure the process didn't get difficult. She stipulated in her will that all assets had to be liquidated within six months and distributed immediately after, or the entire estate would go to charity. This encouraged the heirs to rally to the cause of clearing out the properties, and they worked as a team to beat that deadline. Even if they might not have gotten every last nickel out of selling possessions in their haste, everybody got along fine. It was amazing. I don't think the mother expected contentiousness, but she just wanted her children to be able to get back to their lives quickly.

I worked with three sisters whose father left a small estate with a very simple but clear trust document. They had no problem working harmoniously to handle it to the letter but then decided to pool some of their own cash to fix up the house he left to get a better price for it.

In another estate, a mother who collected curios knew her daughters all liked them, so on the bottom of each one, she had written which daughter it went to. She left clear notes about how all her possessions were to be divided. Distribution instructions like that mother's are found in a majority of estates where there is a properly constructed will or trust document. The more valuable or esoteric the collection (whether it is stamps, cameras, guns, or any collectibles, the more detailed the instructions should be.

Families tend to be scattered across the country these days, but they can use technology to communicate well. Some create private Facebook groups to display photos for each other of property they are distributing or selling. They use group e-mail lists to make sure everyone gets the same information, whether or not they have the time or money to travel to see what is happening with the estate. The point is to be transparent so everyone feels included and good about the process.

An executor can use positive emotions to ease the process of settling the estate, playing up the relief that comes from closure and the sense of belonging that comes from getting something done for the family.

I have been able to play a part in keeping everyone happy by facilitating communications. Often, an executor will get instructions from the court relayed by an attorney and be reluctant to ask a lot of questions about what the legal language means. ("I'm just calling to let you know we've gotten your letters testamentary.") I can help translate and explain what the executor needs to do and what the attorney may or may not be doing.

We've covered how contentious heirs can drain the value of an estate and how smart planning, meticulous documentation, and transparent communications can ease the process of wrapping up probate no matter the emotional backdrop. You may have gotten the impression that I am advocating speed and efficiency throughout the process, but when it comes to putting a property up for sale, I say "Not so fast!" The next chapter explains why.

CHAPTER 6

Don't Rush to Market

When a gentleman I'll call Lou died in San Francisco one November, his family members didn't know or care much about the official process of settling an estate. The heirs were a close bunch, and they figured the holidays provided them time to get together, clear out Lou's house, and put it up for sale. That's what they did, without waiting for any court papers. Having grown up in the Depression Era, Lou never threw any possessions away, so his house was full of stuff, neatly organized. By the fourth day, they had filled a large trash bin and had it hauled away to the dump.

A neighbor who had been away for the holidays came over and said, "Hey guys, good to see you. What are you up to?" They explained they were getting the house cleared out for sale. The neighbor asked, "Well, what did you guys do with all the paint cans?" They said, "Oh. We just threw all those away." The neighbor said, "Well, you opened them, right?" And they said, "Well, no. I mean, they were just old, dry paint cans, so we just threw them away." The neighbor said, "But that's where Lou kept all his money." Like I said, Lou was a Depression-era guy, so he didn't trust the banks. His savings were in old, empty paint cans in the garage.

To show how an executor should be systematic and deliberate in planning and preparing to take a home to market, the pages ahead will cover:

- *Making a timeline*
- *Checking the property title*
- *Valuing the assets*
- *Cleaning out the assets*
- *Don't rush to clean out a home*
- *Home seller disclosures*
- *Inspections*
- *Informal purchase offers*

Making a Timeline

If you're thrust into an estate, your instinct may be to take a running start at it. But before you swing into action, make sure all of the following is in place:

- You have been legally authorized to execute the estate. The court-issued paperwork in California is called the *letters testamentary*.

- You have assessed the situation, as explained in chapters 1-4.

- You have set up a system to keep yourself organized and on track.

An organizational system doesn't have to be sophisticated, but it must include a timeline of tasks and deadlines. A written checklist is extremely important in a job that involves so many dynamics and strong emotions. Write down everything you've been told you have to do, and all of the major assets you need to dispose of, whether they are financial assets, real estate, vehicles, or high-value possessions.

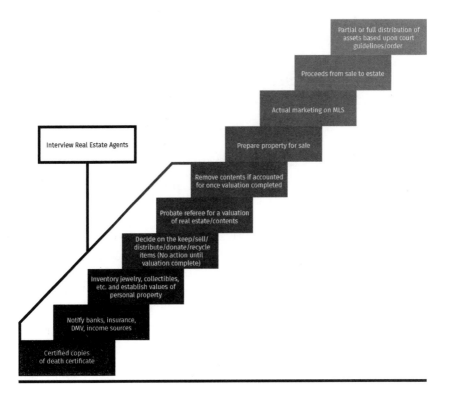

Checking the Property Title

The moment I begin working with an executor on a home sale, I have a title search done to make sure the property is clear of any liens, which can result from unpaid taxes, alimony, or child support, or some other financial or ownership dispute. One time, I was selling a home that had been vacant for many years. I went to see the property, then looked at the lot measurements on the title, and I said, "This lot doesn't feel right. Something's off." The neighbor had moved the fence.

Checking the title before you put a home on the market ensures that you don't have surprises when the sale closes, like having to find a long-lost relative who is on the title or pay off a lawsuit from twenty-five years ago.

Valuing the Assets

Probate law requires an independent valuation of the household contents be included in the total estate value. With some exceptions for property such as expensive art and antiques, a probate referee handles the valuation. In California, each county has at least one probate referee appointed by the comptroller, a statewide elected official, on the recommendations of a panel of lawyers and judges who interview qualified candidates.

Most people imagine someone will be walking through the house with a yellow notepad meticulously jotting down every single item, down to the last teaspoon. The reality couldn't be further from that picture. The referee is an appraiser who takes continuing education courses in the latest valuation methods but usually does not even visit the property. Referees mostly make what's called a desktop assessment, a calculation based on square footage. The referees also get paid a percentage of the valuation, so the higher the price, the more they make. This system might seem to make no sense whatsoever, but this is the way our government works.

The average value placed on all the household furnishings is likely to be around $6,000. That's all of the furniture, artwork, and family heirlooms (like Aunt Sue's china that was stored in the attic for twenty-five years). Furnishings may have originally cost tens of thousands of dollars, but they won't be valued that way unless they are real antiques or masterworks that are appraised privately and sold or auctioned separately from the overall household contents.

Cleaning Out the Assets

There are four steps to cleaning out the household goods and any assets the decedent may have kept in storage or safe-deposit boxes: distribution, sale, donation, and disposal.

1. Distribute to family members and other heirs. Invite beneficiaries to walk through the property together and point out to you any items they would like to have as personal keepsakes or to identify something they feel was promised to them. I usually have blue painter's tape ready, which can be stuck on pieces with the names of the proposed recipient. As mentioned in chapter 4, online video and photos can help those who cannot be present from feeling excluded.

2. Sell whatever else you can. Advertising or auctioning items online can be a lot of work, but you might be surprised how much money you can raise.

3. Donate to charity. Some resale stores will send a truck to pick up major pieces of furniture and appliances.

4. Dump in the trash, or recycle. The local waste-management company can provide bins, and there are services that will pick up items—for a fee. But don't be too hasty spending hundreds of dollars cleaning out a place when someone might do it for free. One man's trash is another's treasure.

Visit our website for a list of our recommended vendors and helpful checklists to guide you. The heirs of a plumbing-company owner spent a lot of money disposing of his huge stash of supplies when they could have had a metal recycler pick it up at no charge. I've worked with people whose homes were jammed floor to ceiling with old electronics. We found an electronics recycler was more than happy to pick it all up for free.

Don't Rush to Clean Out a Home

If you have decided it is in everyone's best interests to quickly sell or rent out a house, you may be in a rush to clean out the contents. Instead, you've got to slow down. Check the pockets of all the clothing. Look underneath the drawers when you pull them out, and look behind for taped envelopes and behind the medicine cabinets. Check the attic. The paint-can story was an extreme example but not that uncommon. It's not just a myth that old people bury cash in pipes in the backyard.

I remember another case involving two brothers who cleaned out stacks of magazines and newspapers from their mom's house in affluent Burlingame, California. It wasn't until they got them all outside and started throwing them into a large trash bin that they noticed the dollar bills flying into the air. By the time they went through all their mother's books, magazines, and newspapers, they had found close to $40,000 in cash tucked away.

I was with clients in San Francisco cleaning out the house of a World War II veteran when something in the basement stopped them dead in their tracks. It was a hand grenade that had probably been sitting there for more than fifty years. We wound up having to call the bomb squad. If they had just picked up that live grenade and thrown it into the trash bin, we could have had a disaster.

Home Seller Disclosures

Home sellers in California must fill out a form called a Transfer Disclosure Statement, or TDS, in which they tell the buyer what they know about defects, disputes, or various other facts that might affect their home's value. In requiring the TDS, current California law exempts the executor, who probably has not been living in the property and might even be from out of state. The executor is not expected to have the same knowledge of the property as an owner. But not having to fill out the form does not completely absolve the executor of any responsibility for disclosures.

An executor who has material knowledge of some defects (the house was built on a potential sinkhole or an ancient Indian burial ground, etc.) must make full disclosure. The executor must also disclose if there has been a death in the home, even from natural causes, within three years of the death.

If there was a violent death, such as a murder or suicide, we make a point of making disclosures going back five years or even longer. I had one property where a neighbor jumped over a fence and hanged himself from my client's trellis. We had to disclose that death, even though it wasn't directly connected with the family that owned the house. Certain cultural groups have more issues than others with someone passing away on a property, which can affect how the property is marketed, depending on the ethnic makeup of the area.

Inspections Are Important

Inherited property is sold during probate in an "as-is" condition. Nevertheless, I recommend my clients order at least a termite inspection and possibly a complete home inspection. Knowing the condition of the home guides us toward the right kind of buyer and helps us set the price. We can proactively tell prospective buyers about any defects and make it clear that they were already factored into the selling price. That strategy stops the buyer from coming back demanding a price reduction or threatening to walk away even though it is an "as-is" sale.

Even if the buyer is in love with the home and doesn't care about an inspection, a bank is often involved in financing the purchase. The bank has no emotional connection to the house and will most definitely want to know what condition it's in. If the property is in a severe state of disrepair, we will be looking for buyers with the means to pull off that kind of purchase—investors or someone making an all-cash offer, or at least a buyer with a large down payment.

Informal Purchase Offers

When a home comes onto the market after someone's death, a neighbor often wants to buy it. An executor I worked with in Palo Alto had already been approached by a neighbor and agreed to a sale. It was not a formal agreement but what I call a "napkin contract"— to convey the idea that no matter how or where you write down the price you would agree to, it can still be a binding contract. The price was way too low because this executor—I'll call him Sal—didn't realize what the real market value was. Sal just wanted to get through with the sale and didn't realize he had a fiduciary duty to the estate and to the other heirs to get the property the highest value.

I had an attorney write a letter to the neighbor explaining that Sal did not have the legal authority to enter into an agreement on behalf of the estate at that time. Sal had been appointed as executor, but the letters testamentary had not arrived yet from the court. If the neighbor had challenged us further, we could have turned the tables and accused him of being predatory and taking advantage of a grief-stricken beneficiary. We would have pushed back pretty hard because that neighbor was about to get the deal of a lifetime.

We've seen some of the dangers of rushing to clear out or sell a home and have given you guidance about how to make a timeline, stay organized, and methodically go through the steps to value and dispose of assets and prepare a home for the market. As we begin transitioning from the planning and preparation stage to the marketing stage of settling the estate, the next chapter will explain how the right real estate agent can make a difference in selling an inherited home.

PART III
The Marketing Phase

CHAPTER 7

Finding the Right Real Estate Agent

I recently handled an estate involving four adult children whose parents owned two homes in San Mateo, California, in the heart of Silicon Valley, south of San Francisco. These postwar tract homes had been used to raise the family and then to provide income as rental properties.

In many families, one of the kids is just a little different from the rest, which can be a good or bad thing. In this family, one of the daughters had become heavily involved with drugs and had many run-ins with the law. When the father passed away, this estranged daughter reacquainted herself with the family and somehow worked her way back into what was once the family home, along with her husband and one or two of their teenage children. Over the next nine or so months, the home fell into disrepair, and there were people coming and going at all hours of the night. Anyone could guess that what was going on was drug related.

Not many months later, the mother (who was in her late sixties and had been living with the daughter in question) passed away, and the cause of death was determined to be an overdose of methamphetamine. I cannot say for sure what happened, but I think a reasonable guess is that every morning Mom's coffee contained more than sugar—and most likely she became addicted to meth without knowing it.

The night the mother died, the other siblings had come to the house, and—wouldn't you know it—all the jewelry and money were gone. An argument broke out; it got heated and turned into a physical fight, neighbors called the police, two of the brothers almost got arrested, and all family communication broke down.

The family was then referred to me because of my experience with difficult estate settlements. The oldest brother had been named as the executor. But the sister with the drug issues hired an attorney and brought legal action to be appointed as the executor instead. That legal fight took a few months before the brother eventually won the appointment. Time is always an issue in settling an estate, and delays are always bad. But, just to add another wrinkle, the home had a reverse mortgage. A reverse mortgage allows an older homeowner to borrow against the equity of the home. That income stream eventually has to be repaid, which can be accomplished by having the estate sell the home after the older person's death. Under the terms of the mother's reverse mortgage, the estate had six months after her death to provide the lender a sales-listing agreement or show escrow information if the home was already sold. But the daughter living in the house wouldn't leave, and time was beginning to run out.

I suggested the eldest brother hire an eviction attorney to deal with his sister squatting in the home. The sister, claiming to be a tenant, obtained free legal aid and pushed the stay as long as possible. It didn't really make sense for her to put the assets of the estate in jeopardy since she was one of the beneficiaries, but drugs can make people do odd things. In this case, the daughter could only focus on how she needed the house, and she saw herself as a victim while she was thwarting her family's best interests. She also was squandering her share of the inheritance by borrowing against it from one of those companies that provide such loans at an extremely high interest rate, typically almost fifty percent.

The eldest brother, as executor, was in a tough spot, dealing not only with the probate and eviction attorneys but also having to comply with the strict requirements of the bonding company that was ensuring the performance of his duties. In an estate deal, if all the heirs are harmonious and they trust the executor, they can waive what's called the bonding requirement. In other words, they do not require the executor to be insured against stealing from the estate. In this case, the executor was required to get that insurance because of his sister's legal challenge—costing the estate additional money.

The executor not only had his hands full making sure he was not liable for any missteps as executor, but he also was going through a divorce at the time. His life had many moving parts. Other issues kept coming up. The sister failed to pay utility bills, so the power was cut off, and the family had to pay thousands of dollars to the gas and electric companies. She left lots of stuff behind, requiring nearly $5,000 worth of hauling and disposal charges. She let the dishwasher damage the flooring, which caused additional rot, and so on.

Adding to the pressure was a foreclosure threat from the holder of the reverse mortgage. The mother originally obtained the reverse mortgage from a well-known national bank, but the loan was sold, as often happens, to investors. The people running the Florida company that held the note could not be deterred from pushing ahead with the foreclosure. I was regularly keeping them informed of our progress toward selling the home, but their response was, "We're going to take it all away through foreclosure, and if your sale is ready to close, we'll see what we can do then." There was no spirit of cooperation. If anything, it was absolute gunpoint pressure, which kept us from spending time making repairs. In a neighborhood where other houses were selling for more than a million dollars, the potential expense of improving the home's condition would be far exceeded by the increase in value, possibly by $100,000.

Ultimately, it became clear we could no longer hold the lender off for more than a few days after we got the sister out. I had to step in and coordinate a marathon salvage job. We had the house cleared out, all debris removed, had it painted, and had new carpeting installed within about seventy-two hours. We had people working through the night but didn't even have time to get the power turned back on. We had to get neighbors to let us run extension cords to power the paint sprayers. We had to move so fast it was like a fire drill, only more chaotic.

In rushing to get the home on the market, I advanced the sellers the money to cover the repairs, along with the landscaping and the final cleaning. So, I had a lot of capital in the deal, but we finally got a premium for the property. We'll never know what price the property *could* have gotten if we had more time, but with the fore-closure date having been set, we knew we had less than five days to accept that offer.

We showed the investors that the property was under contract with a close-of-escrow date that was the soonest for which the buyer could get financing. It turned out that was the same date the investors had chosen to sell the property under the foreclosure. We had pushed everybody to the limit to get this one to close on time. Normally once you're in escrow and the investors can confirm that the property is actually being sold, they'll allow you to go ahead, and they'll postpone their sale date by a week or two, or give you some reprieve, but in this case they wouldn't lift that date whatsoever. So, if the buyer had stumbled for any reason, that property was going to be foreclosed on.

This story was dramatic, but it accurately reflects the fact that any estate can have many moving parts. For this unfortunate family, I didn't just sell a home—I used my thirty-plus years of developing specialized skills to keep those moving parts from colliding or crashing. I knew the probate statute well enough to understand that the brother would ultimately be appointed executor. I met with the family, excluding, obviously, the troublesome sister, to coach them on strategy, timing, and what they could legally do before the formal appointment of the executor. We went over the psychology I would employ to get the sister in the property not to see me as a threat so I could go through the home and see what it needed. I discussed and eventually took action on the eviction proceedings and I did all the formal notices and ultimately was in court to testify at the hearing. Once we had the authority to get into the house, I used my agency's capital and list of vetted contractors and vendors to get the work completed when the estate had assets but no real cash.

Saving the house for the estate required my ability to ferret through lenders and their bureaucratic landscape to find out whom we really needed to talk to at the reverse-mortgage company. My staff and I spent hours just to get through the voice mail maze that banks and investment companies set up, in my opinion, to frustrate people fighting foreclosure and to ultimately just get them to acquiesce or quit. Knowing how to work with government bureaucracy also helped. In this case, I worked with San Mateo city officials involved in code enforcement to make sure they wouldn't file citations or even lien the property, which could have led to additional delays and foreclosure.

Finally, there was the human aspect of getting this sale done. I was helping a family reeling from the deaths of both Mom and Dad within a one-year period, and obviously the grief was compounded by fear, uncertainty, frustration, and anger over the complications. I was constantly coaching them to remain calm so I could help them through a process that ultimately worked out.

To explain how an estate can find the right real estate agent, the pages ahead will address:

- *Why hire a realtor?*
- *Reverse-mortgage time bomb*
- *What to look for in a realtor*
- *Local expertise*
- *Marketing and disclosures*
- *Cultural sensitivities*
- *Having a good match*
- *My sales philosophy*

Why Hire a Realtor?

Since I'm a Realtor, you won't be at all surprised that I recommend everyone hire a real estate professional for a home sale or purchase. If an estate has only one or two heirs and they agree to take on a sale by owner, that method is an option. However, they'll never know whether they could have gotten more for the property or sold it faster through the broader exposure that comes with a professional real estate listing. If an estate has multiple heirs, particularly in different parts of the country, I strongly urge using the Realtor's multiple-listing service, because then if anybody ever questions whether they did their best to get the highest value for the property, they stay above reproach. An heir unfamiliar with the local market's property values may suspect that a sale-by-owner left money on the table.

Having a local Realtor check in on the property regularly is crucial, especially if the executor doesn't live nearby. I had a case recently where I discovered that a roof, which had never before leaked, suddenly started letting rain pour in. I was able to catch that damage before it developed into a costly mold-abatement issue. Once the property is in the estate, the executor must disclose to buyers any new damage. Property owners in their declining years, ones who grew up in the Depression Era, and ones whose finances have suffered may have failed to maintain a house in a way that prevents last-minute surprises that could come to light during a sale.

Reverse-Mortgage Time Bomb

Thinking back to the mom-on-meth story at the beginning of this chapter, while the cause of death was unusual, it was not uncommon that I had to help the heirs deal with a foreclosure threat from the holder of a reverse mortgage. As Baby Boomers have aged and retired, they have all too often begun using their houses for economic shelter. They have turned to reverse mortgages to tap their houses like a bank account.

Let's say they paid off their home loan long ago, and now it is worth a million dollars. The bank appraises the property and offers them fifty percent of the value, or $500,000, through a reverse mortgage. If they take the $500,000 all at once, they have to start paying interest on that loan from the day it starts. But, if the bank sends them a check every month, it's like a retirement-account withdrawal, and they only pay interest on the growing portion of the reverse mortgage they have taken. That approach keeps interest costs under control and guards against the retiree or family members overspending. The reverse mortgage becomes a supplement to their Social Security, pension, or other income, and enables them to cover expenses, including maintenance of the house.

The downside to the reverse mortgage is that when the loan signer dies, the estate must repay the lender while also keeping up with property taxes, insurance, and other ongoing expenses (such as homeowner-association fees). The lenders have little (if any) sympathy for survivors who cannot pay promptly. The banks or investors that hold the loans know where the wealth in our society resides—mostly in the population over age sixty. Younger heirs often lack the financial capacity to keep the estate's properties. If the estate is going to be distributed among multiple children, even if one is wealthy enough to make payments, others may not be, and the property has to be sold quickly. The reverse-mortgage holders are not taking any chances with waiting many months for an estate to be settled—for a house to be sold and the mortgage paid off. So, a reverse mortgage has become a real time bomb for executors, forcing them to rush through probate. It's good for executors to feel *some* motivation to keep moving forward—but if other issues (such as a problematic tenant) are causing delays, the foreclosure threat is a real headache.

I worked with an estate that inherited a row house in San Francisco where a man of modest means had a friend living in the basement and helping with chores. With the reverse-mortgage company beginning the foreclosure process, the executor had to sell the house quickly. But, under the city's rent-control guidelines, the man in the basement was considered a tenant, and his eviction would have been time-consuming. Selling the house with a tenant in place would have cut the property value substantially. We calculated that the price difference would more than cover the cost of buying the tenant out for $30,000. Since the estate didn't have the money, an agreement had to be set up that the tenant would be paid from the sales proceeds. But then the tenant didn't have money to move, so one of the heirs had to come up with enough money to cover the move and security deposit on a new apartment.

A person who had been a helping hand to the decedent wound up costing way more than anybody ever expected as a result of the rent-control laws. My understanding of local guidelines helped the family come up with the best plan to get possession of the property and the best value for it.

What to Look for in a Realtor

This next section will help you choose an agent who is up to the complex task of handling a probate real estate sale.

Choosing the right Realtor should be done as early as possible in the estate-settlement process so the agent can step in and help with potential complications like the ones recounted throughout this book. So, how do you find an agent who understands the logistics of the process, won't just be a bystander, and will roll up his or her sleeves and get involved in the sale?

🏠 Choosing the right Realtor should be done as early as possible in the estate-settlement process, so the agent can step in and help with potential complications like the ones recounted throughout this book.

You really need to vet your prospective agents by asking critical questions to find out how much knowledge and experience they have in whatever issues pertain to your estate. An estate might have federal, state, or local tax liens; legal issues arising from divorce, alimony, and child support; and other lawsuits that result in liens. If someone is living in the house, whether a tenant or a relative, knowledge of landlord-tenant law will be crucial. If the house has significant contents, which can range from garbage to valuable collectibles, does the agent have resources to help get those items where they need to go, whether it's the dump or an auction house?

Do they know how, when, and where to help the estate generate the best value for its property? Do they know about getting a home cleaned, painted, and fixed up, and how much flooring, carpentry, landscaping, and other work is the right amount for the marketplace where the property is located?

How do the agents dovetail their efforts with the estate attorney, executor, and beneficiaries? How will they handle potential conflict? Or—even if there is harmony in the estate and everybody wants to pitch in and help—how will they find and resolve any gaps in the effort without seeming overly controlling or aggressive?

A Realtor doesn't just put a "For Sale" sign in front of the property and then hope that it sells.

QUESTIONS TO ASK WHEN HIRING AN AGENT

- Can you tell me about your experience in dealing with situations involving (the specific issues the estate is facing)?

- How do you recommend we get the best value from this property?

- What resources can you provide for getting the property in the best shape to go to market?

- What will you do to make sure the estate attorney, executor, and beneficiaries communicate well with each other and work together?

Local Expertise

I learn through my local public records about the appointment of executors and then contact them wherever they are located. That's how I came to be talking by phone to a man on the East Coast who told me his family would probably need to sell some inherited properties in San Francisco. "Oh, that's great!" I thought. He admitted to not knowing much about the properties and asked me to find out for him.

I realized that their grandfather had bought property along the Bayshore Highway, which was constructed on land created by filling in a section of the San Francisco Bay. The land was in a subdivision that someone probably intended or hoped to develop by filling in a lagoon, but ultimately it was left to be a natural wetland and wildlife sanctuary. So, I explained to them that, unfortunately, those lots had no value but, "Congratulations, you own a piece of San Francisco."

The serious point behind this story is that the right agent understands local market value and knows the best way to prepare and present a property for the likely buyers.

Marketing and Disclosures

I had an estate that had to sell a house where the roof was falling in and was covered with blue tarps. We photographed the house using angles that did not show the tarps. We were not going to be cagey about the condition of the roof but didn't see any point in promoting a property by showing its blemishes. That's dumping a bucket of cold water on the buyer and then trying to warm him up. We wanted to tell the best story about the property first, and then disclose the negative aspects, which would then seem smaller in relationship to the buyer's original impression.

Chapter 6 mentioned that an executor of an estate does not have to fill out the standard disclosure form that California law requires sellers provide to buyers. That exception is logical because executors generally have not lived in the house they are selling and might not know all of the potential defects. Agents with some large real estate companies require the executor to fill out the form anyway as a company policy. The companies have teams of attorneys looking out for themselves, making sure they don't get sued, but as a result, the executor might be making unnecessary disclosures. For that reason, I advise people involved with an estate to ask agents before hiring them to provide the disclosures that the real estate company will require. In most probate real estate sales, the property is offered "as-is."

Cultural Sensitivity

You need a real estate agent who knows how to tell bad news about a property in a way that potential buyers can understand and accept. For example, different cultures have superstitions or strong feelings about a death having happened in the property.

We sold a home in Hillsborough, an extremely affluent town in Silicon Valley, where there had been a highly publicized murder. An attorney contacted us to handle the sale because it was going to be challenging. After a contentious divorce, the wife was killed in the house. The husband, who was still battling his ex-wife over financial interests and child custody, was away and denied involvement. He had the alibi of being photographed at a gala benefit while two gunmen came into the house, fatally bludgeoned his wife in the bedroom, and beat and stabbed her new boyfriend. The daughter from a previous marriage, who became executor of her mother's estate, believed the assailants were hired hit men from Asia who were back on an airplane out of the United States before the murder was discovered.

Needless to say, working with the executor involved extensive cleanup of the crime scene, removing all of the bedroom's contents, replacing carpet, painting, and so on. But just as important, I had to be able to discuss with potential buyers how an unsolved home-invasion murder happened in such a safe neighborhood. Potential buyers in this ethnically diverse area were clearly deterred by superstitions about living in a home where there had been a violent death.

Some segment of buyers stayed away because they believed the home was cursed, but I was able to tell others a bad story in a way that was not alarming, and we wound up getting a phenomenal price for the property. I could tell that my skill won the day for the estate.

Having a Good Match

I feel so strongly that an estate needs to find the right agent that I will pass up a listing if I don't think I'm the best person for the job. One case involved a man who needed to sell an inherited property by a certain deadline, wanted to make extensive repairs, yet also wanted to stay in the house the whole time. What's more, he wanted my agency to hire the contractors from our vetted list—but he wanted to be there supervising them daily because he had some background in construction. I couldn't put the contractors into that kind of precarious position where they might not be sure who was in charge. That uncertainty and having the house occupied could produce delays, and my capital would be at risk. So, I said, "Look, I'm not the right man for you. I've got to pass."

In other cases, I'm the perfect match, because I *will* put up my own capital, which most agents won't or can't do. If the estate has the equity but not the liquid cash, I may be able to assist in getting a property fixed up to a much higher value. Typically, this scenario involves homes that were bought many years ago in neighborhoods that are now phenomenal. The house has fallen into a state of disrepair, but some cosmetic or even structural and functional improvements will make it sell for much more than the cost of the renovation. Giving the estate a secured cash advance to pay for the work is not only profitable for us, but it makes our job of selling the property much easier. So, whether or not to invest some capital is a business decision that I make on a case-by-case basis.

My Sales Philosophy

The last thing an executor needs is a real estate agent who is thinking, "It's an estate sale. We're just going to unload this thing." What I am thinking is, "How do we really help this estate get the highest price?" I go into a probate real estate sale knowing that it may be complicated, but confident that I have built up the necessary skills over more than thirty years to handle any complexities.

When your health is on the line, going to a specialist, and not just any doctor, may help you get a better outcome. Real estate is similar in that some agents specialize in commercial properties, houses, or apartment complexes, and others act like general practitioners. The necessary skills overlap, but a specialized skill set can be crucial in many circumstances. In my niche, for example, the agent has to interact with probate court. Do you want to have an agent who has to have someone explain what the court is asking for—or do you want someone like me, who is comfortable explaining the process to others?

In this book, you have seen how a real estate agent can help an estate take a property in significant disrepair and get the best price, and you've also seen all the complexities that occur with family dynamics, legal struggles, and all the other potential issues we've illustrated through cases I have experienced.

Probate covers every type of property, whether it is commercial or residential, tenant-occupied, or vacant land. Having an agent who really understands probate and how the rules apply to the specific types of properties is a real benefit. I think my expertise in this subject area is in the top 1 percent among all real estate agents nationally. The variation in expertise is not always noticeable in simple estates but makes a huge difference when heirs are vying for multiple properties of different types. The agent must have the capacity to deal with landlord-tenant law, lien processes, trust attorneys, forensic accountants, and all the other players and systems that can show up in probate.

Vetting for the right agent—someone with the experience and confidence to guide you through the various scenarios we have discussed—will put the estate in a much better position to get the best outcome. The next chapter goes into the details of the probate process that an executor must understand as part of planning the marketing of estate properties.

CHAPTER 8

The Probate Process

You can find entire books explaining the probate process, but the simple overview is that when somebody dies, a representative of that person petitions the court to appoint an executor of the estate. That executor is empowered to settle everything, unless the court decides it has to get further involved. People often hire a probate attorney to start the process, but some take it on themselves in the expectation that their estate is not too complicated.

I had a client whom I'll call Mei, whose friends convinced her she could easily handle her probate filing. An earnest and sensible retired kindergarten teacher, Mei read a book about probate "for dummies" and filed the petition with the court to get herself appointed as executor. As the process went along, Mei started feeling lost because it can be confusing and daunting to anyone who's not used to it. She started to second-guess herself at every turn, fearing she was not doing the steps in the right order or was making wrong decisions. I tried to help her, but her fear just started to compound to the point where it immobilized her. In the end, I helped her find an attorney who walked her through the remaining parts of the process at no charge. Ultimately, her initiative at handling her own probate saved the estate some money, but it gave her some gray hairs and heartache because she wasn't constitutionally prepared to take on the whole task.

Some of my clients have successfully filed their own probate and saved the standard 10 percent attorney fee. That course is easier to take if it is a simple, clear-cut estate, and even then, some clients still hire an experienced probate paralegal to help with handling the paperwork.

The court's job is to vet the person who has come forward to be the executor, to be sure that the written wishes of the decedent are being carried out or the heirs have agreed on that person. The estate's representative goes to the county court and files a petition asking the court to appoint the chosen person. Unless there is an objection, the appointment happens without ceremony. Eventually a court clerk provides the executor the letters testamentary—the official, ink-stamped document that empowers the executor to access bank accounts, sell a home, and so on. If the estate owns properties in multiple states, then the executor needs authority from each jurisdiction—because, again, probate laws vary by state.

To help you understand how executors interact with the probate process, the pages ahead will address:

- *Family dynamics*
- *Sale through court confirmation*
- *Avoiding probate-court hassles*

- *Stigma around probate sales*

- *The distribution process*

Family Dynamics

An executor might be clearly named in a will or be a sole heir, such as an only child. If there is no will, usually one family member rises to the task, or sometimes all are reluctant but one draws the short straw and gets the job. Alternatively, busy or distant family members can hire a professional fiduciary. The big retail banks have trust departments offering that service, but it's a pretty sterile process. Family members may be disappointed by the strict deadlines and lack of caring when a fiduciary says, "Pick up your stuff, or it will be sold or donated" on a specific date.

When there's no will, a large estate, and a lot of heirs, choosing an executor is not so easy. The scale of difficulty grows in proportion with the size and complexity of the asset classes and the existence of any factions within the family. Some examples of asset classes that might add complexity are commercial property, land that can be developed, apartments, vacation homes, and time-shares. The decedent may have bought some of these properties as investments with business partners or friends.

> 🏠 The scale of difficulty grows in proportion with the size and complexity of the asset classes and the existence of any factions within the family.

Now, overlay on that complexity of holdings three siblings inheriting what their parents owned—or, to make it more complicated, if one of the siblings died earlier, it could be two siblings and the three adult children of the third. Now, five heirs are on the same level of authority in deciding what to do about that investment property. Maybe the grandkids want to hold on to the property because they need a long-term income stream, and the two children of the decedent want to sell it to enjoy the money in their remaining retirement years. That kind of friction is natural and understandable. The family is not dysfunctional, and the people are not disagreeable, but they are approaching the decision from different stages of life. Family members in the spring, summer, or winter of their investment life often have different goals and ideas about real estate.

All this background is to explain why the court does not always take the simple route of giving the executor unfettered independent powers. Courts don't want to micromanage estates, but there are other ways they can accommodate heirs who distrust the executor for any reason. Unless the heirs waive the requirement, the executor must be bonded or insured to act in fidelity with the financial interests of the estate.

With the bond waived, the executor can sell assets such as a house almost as though it's a conventional sale. With the bond in effect, the executor must follow bonding-company guidelines. But even less desirable for an executor is to be under a court-confirmation requirement.

Sale through Court Confirmation

The court-confirmation process makes a real estate sale more arduous. The property must be advertised and shown for set periods of time that the estate's probate attorney feels comfortable will satisfy the court. The time frame must indicate the property was adequately promoted prior to the specific dates set for bids to be called for and accepted. During the bidding period, potential buyers submit offers to the executor in sealed envelopes. A cashier's check for 10 percent of the bid price must accompany the purchase offer, which is submitted on a simple, non-conditioned offer form. In other words, the sale can have no preconditions, such as being contingent on the buyer getting financing or inspections.

Some buyers will be deterred by the 10 percent requirement—that's a cashier's check for $100,000 on a $1 million bid. Even coming up with a check for $50,000 on a house worth $500,000 will cut out a segment of buyers. They also may be deterred by the "as-is" sale, but they can obtain their own inspections in the weeks prior to the bidding deadline. As a result, a buyer may show up at the court with the clean, non-conditioned offer that the seller finds acceptable. At that point, the seller has to make public the amount and acceptance date, which can be done through the multiple-listing service or a classified legal advertisement. The attorney for the estate then petitions the court to set a confirmation date, normally about thirty days out. The publication of the accepted offer alerts any other prospective buyers that would like to show up in court on that confirmation date to submit a higher bid.

That part of the process is worrisome for the winning bidder, so a property being sold with court confirmation often gets less than it would have on the open market. The bidding process especially hurts the estate in a really hot market because most buyers cannot afford to tie up substantial capital for thirty days earning no interest and with a lot of uncertainty about getting overbid. So, buyers are less likely to bid on this type of property, which in turn minimizes the amounts offered.

When the estate makes public the court-confirmation date, it also must publish what's called the overbid amount, which is based on a formula. For example, if the accepted offer was $1 million, someone can't just come in and bid $1,000 more. To protect the initial bidder, the courts require the amount of the overbid be the sum of 10 percent of the first $10,000 of the original bid and 5 percent of the balance of the original bid. So, if the initial bid is $1 million, 10 percent of the first $10,000 is $1,000, then 5 percent of the balance would be $49,500. So, showing up in court to reopen the bidding would require a minimum of $1,050,500. The judge would call for any additional bids at that minimum level. At that point, the person who would like to overbid would typically stand up, be acknowledged, identify himself or herself, and present a cashier's check for 10 percent of the new, higher bid. If there are other bidders present, the judge could continue to take bids and set an increment from $1,000 to $5,000 for bid amounts. Once the bidding has stopped, the judge signs a court order confirming the sale at the final bid price.

The original bidder gets a refund of the 10 percent deposit if outbid but still has lost time and earned no interest on the money deposited. Whoever wins the bidding generally is given thirty days to close the deal. So, the buyer is not required to have all the cash ready the moment the gavel falls. Buyers who have lined up financing in advance must take the court order to the lender to complete their financing.

The court confirmation process is complicated, and as I said, buyers are reluctant to get involved in it. Yet, if beneficiaries tried to come back and claim that the property didn't get fully exposed and receive its highest value, the courts would say the estate offered its property to the marketplace with adequate advertising, promotion, and time for bids and counteroffers. That illusion of fairness doesn't reflect the reality of the market, especially if home prices are rapidly rising or if interest rates are moving quickly.

You might be wondering who is doing the overbidding and on what kinds of properties. In many cases, investors are buying properties that need extensive work. They may have been under the control of the public guardian for someone who didn't have family members, was in long-term care, and had left a home sitting vacant. Since investors don't get emotional in their bidding like some homebuyers do, the process tends to also keep a lid on the pricing.

Avoiding Probate Court Hassles

Every jurisdiction has some kind of probate court. In a rural area, the same judges may handle all kinds of civil and criminal cases, so probate court is really just a part of their calendar. In big cities, the schedules get reshuffled, sometimes at the last moment, to the point where I have had trouble finding the right courtroom. At one court confirmation, we ran through the doors right as the judge was dropping the gavel and successfully entreated the judge to reopen the overbidding process, benefitting the estate by an extra $50,000.

What's even better than a good day in probate court is proper estate planning. It begins with conversations elderly parents have with their children, or anyone has with expected survivors, about how to get their affairs in order. For the person who may be leaving an estate, having at least two family members and an attorney involved in the conversation about a will or trust alleviates concern that any one person exercised undue influence.

Death is an uncomfortable topic, but it has to be addressed. There's no need to walk on egg shells. The topic does not need to be treated with a special, highly spiritual sensitivity, because all of us, the moment we're born, are on our way to passing. We just never know when. The point of the conversation is to get a clear and workable plan in the will or trust that the beneficiaries can accept without disharmony. That acceptance increases the chance that nobody will challenge the executor's right to administer the estate independently.

A California law, the Independent Administration of Estates Act, waives bonding and court confirmation when there is no challenge to the executor's authority. But when executors acting independently accept offers for real estate sales, they have to send out what's called the Notice of Proposed Action, notifying all the heirs about the sale terms and asking if there are any objections. The heirs have fifteen days to file an objection, at which point an executor's moving ahead with those sale terms triggers the court-confirmation process. That possibility is one of the disclosures required in sale agreements of properties being sold by an independently administered estate.

So far in this chapter, we have been discussing real estate sales. But if the estate also includes prized artworks, antiques, or other items that have been appraised for the probate as having substantial value, the court may become involved in approving how those collections are sold. Courts are not likely to get involved when there's just one piece that might be worth sending to an auction house. Courts don't want itemized lists of everyone's possessions, but they do have ways to get involved when it's the estate of an art dealer or a diamond broker, for example. The probate referee, an officer of the court, asks the executor whether the estate contains items of significant value, at which point the referee can require independent appraisals by specialists.

People collect stamps, guns, figurines, and everything else under the sun. Valuable collections can become bargaining chips among the heirs if somebody wants to maintain that collection intact or wants to break it up for sale. Deals can be made to keep the beneficiaries harmonious. The biggest issue I have encountered with collections is when family members begin removing, distributing, or disposing of the contents before the executor has gotten authority to do so. That action puts those people in a precarious position legally, especially if the estate has creditors who might accuse them of hiding assets.

The takeaway here is to get legal authority first before you take away items from the estate or begin acting in any way as an executor. Digital technology provides tools for date-stamping photos and videos and showing when an item was listed for sale. An old reliable way to show how recently something was photographed is to put a newspaper in the picture. If there is an atmosphere of distrust surrounding an estate, video recordings that include a newspaper are proof that action taken on a property occurred after the date the executor got authority.

Stigma around Probate Sales

Some buyers are reluctant to even look at a property being sold in probate. As explained in chapter 6, sellers in probate have limited disclosure requirements because an executor cannot be assumed to know everything about the property. The probate court shields the seller from some liability and makes the sale "as-is"—so "buyer beware." Then there's the stigma of a death having prompted the sale, possibly a death inside the home being sold, and the possible complications of a court being involved. To avoid keeping some potential buyers from considering the property, I never openly advertise a home as a probate sale. We're going to disclose that fact once we have buyers interested, and they can choose whether they want the property or not. If they already have become emotionally connected to the home, we've got a higher probability of getting a better price.

The Distribution Process

Heirs may be surprised to learn that when the property is sold, the proceeds are not immediately distributed to the beneficiaries of the estate. Instead, the money goes into the bank account the executor set up on behalf of the decedent. The executor will be paying the estate's bills and filing a final tax return using a taxpayer identification number set up for the estate, so all money must be collected into the estate account and distributed from there. The distribution of probate real estate sales proceeds and agent fees can take up to six months from the time of a home sale.

🏠

You've seen the complexity of the probate process and how family dynamics and the need for court confirmation can make a property sale more difficult. Settling an estate efficiently requires good estate planning, expert assistance, and patience. The next chapter covers unnecessary delays, what causes them, and how to prevent them.

CHAPTER 9

Stall in the Family

An attorney whom I work with on many estate sales asked me to assist a family that had inherited the mother's property in affluent Palo Alto, a city best known as the home of Stanford University. The executor had a prominent position at the elite university, but no matter how smart, accomplished, or economically comfortable people are, family dynamics can tie up the settling of estates. Emotional ties, old feuds, and power and control issues are some of the factors at work.

I'll call the executor Rose. She was a middle-aged woman, direct and businesslike, as you would expect a university department head to be, but with a sweet, caring tone of voice. Her sister had been living in the mother's house and wanted to buy it, but they could not agree on the price. It's not unusual for family members who occupy a house to give it a lower value, because they know everything that's wrong with it. They think the house is falling apart and the price needs to be deeply discounted. Relatives who haven't lived in the house focus on broader market trends and ask, "How much could it cost to fix up the property?"

In this case, the sister in the house was seeking a price she said she got from "a Realtor friend," and the executor was seeing a higher value on websites like Zillow and Trulia. This was a nondescript house that might sell for a few hundred thousand dollars in much of the country, but in Palo Alto we were deciding whether it was worth $2.2 million or $2.6 million. The two sisters started by having very civil back-and-forth negotiations by telephone, but the tension escalated to the point where they would only discuss the matter in writing, first by e-mail and then in more formal letters. After months of delay, Rose and her sister finally had attorneys negotiating for them. Meanwhile, Palo Alto's superheated housing market had begun to cool down a bit, which was good for the sister buying the home but meant the rest of the heirs would lose money because of the delay. Keep in mind that until the sale closed, although there was no mortgage on the house, the estate had to pay other costs associated with carrying the property, including insurance, taxes, and maintenance.

The lesson—a recurring one I see in all types of properties from primary residences to rental houses to vacation homes—is to keep the process moving for everybody's sake. People think every negotiation has a possible "win-win" outcome, but this was a case in which a fair settlement was going to leave neither sister exactly happy. The way they eventually agreed on a price was methodical: The purchaser listed all the issues she saw with the home and got estimates from contractors and a handyman for all the repairs. The estate got an appraisal and had me do a market valuation, and they worked from all those real numbers.

The sister in the home had started with a number that overestimated the deficiencies and underestimated the market value. She had consulted a Realtor friend to get that market value, but because there had been no home sales in the past two or three years in that same, exclusive enclave, he was using accurate but outdated comparable sales data. We were able to establish that there were higher comps, and we were supported by the appraisal. So, once they established the value, they were able to deduct the cost of repairs and get the transaction done without having to put the house on the market. Keeping the house in the family made everybody feel better, and the rest of the estate was able to close out.

To help you understand how to expedite a sale to an heir and avoid delays, the pages ahead address:

- *Sales within the family*

- *Procrastination and market cycles*

- *Occupants with nowhere to go*

Sales within the Family

When an estate contains a property and enough cash, one of the heirs can buy the property using his or her share of the cash inheritance, in effect passing that amount of cash back to the estate and the other heirs. If there is not enough cash for that arrangement to work, the executor has to take control of the sale process to protect the interests of the estate and the heirs who are not getting the house. The buyer may be a close relative but still has to prove he or she has the cash or can get a loan to close out the sale on time and make sure the estate can pay its taxes and other bills, and ensure the other heirs are not shortchanged. The executor must make sure certain actions are performed in a timely way, including these four main steps:

🏠 The buyer may be a close relative but still has to prove he or she has the cash or can get a loan to close out the sale on time and make sure the estate can pay its taxes and other bills, and ensure the other heirs are not shortchanged.

1. **Preapproval**: I strongly recommend executors make sure that the potential buyer is preapproved for a mortgage, if needed. The potential buyer and any cosigners or others involved in the purchase should go through the full preapproval process in which the lender looks at their credit, savings, and financial history. Sometimes potential buyers will say they have been "prequalified," but that's just a lender saying they could get a certain size mortgage based on the finances they claim to have. In a preapproval, the lender is ready to write a mortgage on condition they present an acceptable property appraisal and purchase contract.

2. **Down payment**: Lenders require a down payment, for example 20 percent of the purchase price. So, even before the appraisal and purchase contract, the executor must establish the approximate value of the property to make sure the potential purchaser has enough cash to put down. If that cash can't be produced from the buyer's share of the estate, the executor must ask where the cash is coming

from. I recommend the executor see a bank statement for proof of funds. I tell them, "People don't do what's expected. They do what's inspected." The better the executor establishes the buyer's capacity early, the smoother the sale will go. It's too easy for someone to say they want to buy a property and then not admit until too late that they don't have the capacity to do so.

An executor can run into trouble by waiting to push the potential buyer to come through until it's too close to the deadline for settling the estate. If the family member gives up on the purchase, the property may have to go on the market at a bad time. But if the preapproval and down payment have checked out, the next step is to get the actual valuation.

3. Two Forms of Valuation: If you have looked up home prices on the internet, you know how easy it is to find data that will at least provide a good starting point. I always recommend that the executor get two forms of valuation. One should come from a certified appraiser, hired by the estate or by the bank making the loan. I also recommend asking two Realtors to provide a market assessment, which takes into account whether the market is trending upward or downward. The appraiser is looking at the condition of the property and comparable sales numbers. But those comps may be a few months old, and if the market is heating up, the Realtors might project that the upward trend should give the property a higher value by the time the sale closes. Equally important, if the market's headed downward, that trend shows the executor must move quickly to get the greatest value for the estate.

4. Purchase Contract: If a family member is buying directly from the estate, the 6 percent commission that would have been paid to real estate agents can be deducted from the sales price. But the estate should still hire a Realtor or an attorney for a flat fee to make the purchase contract. That fee needs to be added back into the sale price, or split between buyer and estate, whichever the people involved prefer.

Earlier in the book, we discussed how the executor should keep a journal documenting every conversation and action. When making a sale within the family, the executor's journal should note the dates that every task above was started or assigned and when it should be completed. Without deadlines, these sales tend to stretch on. If the sale falls through and the buyer complains, "You didn't give me enough time," the executor can point to the dates in the journal and the notations of when the conversation started and when tasks were to have been completed.

Procrastination and Market Cycles

A market slowdown affected the home sale in Palo Alto that we discussed at the beginning of this chapter, and other market factors are important to look at for other estates. Consulting local Realtors and looking up trends online is important because markets have different peak-activity cycles depending on their locations. For instance, markets with snowy winters may not kick into gear until spring, while some vacation-destination markets are strongest in the summer. Those cycles must be seen as a context in looking at comparable sale prices.

Timing is crucial because of the tendency for family disagreements to result in procrastination. Delays are especially costly to estates when the market trend is downward. But, knowing that's the case, an executor can set tighter deadlines for potential buyers in the family or for taking the property to the open market. If potential buyers can't produce proof of funds or a loan preapproval quickly, it's rare that they can do so by delaying. So, the sooner guidelines for action are established, the better the outcome will be for everyone.

One way to deal with a dispute within the family over the market value is to put the house on the market with the disclosure that there is a first right of refusal. In other words, the family member who was a potential buyer has the right to match or exceed the highest offer we get on the open market. That's a gamble for me as a Realtor because I spend time and money marketing the house without getting the usual fee if somebody from the estate ends up buying it. But in most cases, there wouldn't be a dispute if the buyer in the family were willing to pay the fair market value. So, once the family member sees how much people on the open market are willing to pay, he or she tends to back off from wanting to buy the property.

Occupants with Nowhere to Go

Another cause of delays occurs when occupants of the property who were living with the decedent have no place to go. They'll typically do anything in their power to delay the sale process. Their procrastination can take many forms:

- They may appear to be immobilized by grief.

- They are suddenly ill and need "a little more time" before they can leave the house.

- They plead hardship because someone in the family lost a job.

- They explain that a breakup, divorce, or some other emotional issue has come up and made this a really bad time for them to move.

- They say they can't leave because they're taking care of the decedent's pets and can't find a place to move to that will accept the animals.

In each case, they get some sympathy from the other people involved in the estate. The excuse involving pets is quite common and likely to prompt other family members to want to give them more time. Some of the occupants with nowhere to go have substance-abuse problems, but family members can still be sympathetic when they say their grief has restarted or worsened their addiction.

These occupants may be a son, daughter, or grandchild of the decedent, a new spouse or some other relatives, friends, or even tenants. What they often have in common is a propensity to feel they had been doing the decedent a favor and that the executor is just after the money and was never there to take care of the decedent. As an attorney who works with executors once told me, "If you've got a male over forty still living with mom, you're screwed," because that is the most common profile of the occupant with nowhere to go who feels most entitled to stay.

Sometimes executors have to set hard deadlines and start eviction proceedings if it's time to move forward and put the property on the market for the best interests of the estate. Allowances must be made for grief, but beware the drama dungeon. It's easy to get locked in there.

———

We've seen how family dynamics can delay and complicate the settling of estates, especially when a family member wants to buy the house or won't vacate it to make way for a sale. The executor's job is to establish the rules, outline actions that potential buyers must take, set a schedule, and follow up with all the participants, including potential buyers and their lenders and attorneys. Executors must be mindful of real estate market trends and avoid stall tactics that could undermine the value of the estate. Success comes from setting clear expectations, writing them down, and holding people to them. They may not like the process, but they'll love the fact that it does get done at the end. But sometimes getting it done takes professional help, which we'll cover in the next chapter.

AN EXPERT NEGOTIATING TIP

I was in a mastermind group in which sales professionals were sharing their experiences. We had invited a speaker, Bill Mitchell, one of the nation's top sales consultants, who told a story that might help readers encountering some of the problems described in this chapter.

When Bill and his twin brother were growing up during the Depression, their mother had only enough money to make one peanut butter and jelly sandwich for the two of them to take to school each day. She would let them cut the sandwich in half but would say, "Whoever cuts the sandwich gets the smaller piece." What they learned was to get very good at cutting it right down the middle.

Here's how I apply that story. If two brothers inherit a house they know is worth $2 million and one of them says, "I want to buy it for $1.5 million," what should the other brother say? "All right, then, I want a right to buy it from the estate at that same price, because if you're going to cut the sandwich that far off of center, I want the bigger piece." When family members are stuck on negotiating a price for a direct sale within the estate, I have to tell the one who has made a lowball offer, "Just remember, if that's your offer, you are saying that's what it is worth, and everybody should be able to buy it at that price."

CHAPTER 10

The Unexpected Sale Requires Experience and Skill

I have been involved in well over two thousand property sales, including more than five hundred estates and trusts, but one in particular represents a lesson I hope you will take away from this book. The house was a health hazard—totally uninhabitable. The man who lived and committed suicide there was the estranged brother of the siblings who inherited the property. The Robinsons, as I'll call them, just wanted to get rid of the house. They lived in another part of the country and didn't think it was worth any more than the mortgage on it. They really didn't care if it just went into foreclosure.

I explained to them that there are always better options. No matter what condition a property is in, the executor of an estate has the duty to try to create a profitable sale. I laid out a plan to get the property back into market condition and a work schedule timed to produce the greatest value. I then brought together the team of vendors that we've worked with for many years. We disposed of all the contents, got the house cleaned, and got estimates for some light renovations. Once we could see the home without the distraction of dirt and clutter, we set a sale price.

The end result was that we not only were able to prevent the home from going into foreclosure, but we also managed to sell it at a nice profit. Beyond the money, the heirs received the emotional benefit of feeling that they had done something for their late brother.

To help you understand how an experienced agent can help an estate get through probate as methodically and peacefully as possible, the pages ahead cover:

- *Probate, pressure, and practice*
- *Recap of My three-part system*
- *Expertise, creativity, and comfort*

Probate, Pressure, and Practice

Being an executor is a highly responsible, time-consuming, and largely thankless job that people often must handle at an emotionally charged time in their lives because of the death of a loved one. If the estate includes a house that has to be sold in probate, the executor is sent into a bureaucratic maze with a deadline clock ticking. Even if the estate is under no time pressure to sell a house, it's advisable for the executor to do so during probate. The process provides the legal protections, requires fewer disclosures, and makes it easier for the executor to act, even if all of the beneficiaries are not in agreement on a sale.

People often think that because probate is a legal process, they'll get clear guidelines from the courts. If only it were that simple—like painting by the numbers! A better analogy is that probate is like a shoe. Every shoe has a heel, sole, and upper with the same functions, but they are hardly one-size-fits-all. Shoes come in countless combinations of sizes, shapes, styles, and colors. Estates likewise have common characteristics, yet each one is different.

A popular concept holds that it takes ten thousand hours of deliberate practice in any field to become a world-class master. I've spent a lot more than ten thousand hours selling real estate in probate, developing effective checklists and processes over the past thirty years. Watching people unfamiliar with the process sweat through it alone made no sense to me, so I wrote this book to share what I have learned. But even sharing a whole book's worth of knowledge can't match the skills I can bring by being personally involved in settling the estate.

RECAP OF MY THREE-PART SYSTEM

This book has used a three-part system to walk you through the handling of an inherited property from beginning to end. The three parts are:

1. The ASSESSMENT Phase
2. The PLANNING and PREPARATION Phase
3. The MARKETING Phase

From the moment I meet the sellers or executors, I focus on helping them assess their situation: What is the physical condition of the property? What is the desired outcome they're trying to accomplish? What people, emotions, and family dynamics are they dealing with? What is their best strategy, taking into account my knowledge of the local sales market? What's the timeline they can expect? What deadlines and legal requirements must they meet? What resources do they have or could I help them find to best complete this process?

Once we have completed this *assessment phase* and have a handle on what will be happening, my next step is to break out the planning tools. We move from discussing a possible timeline to making actual checklists and a calendar. We bring in family members or other resources to assist the executor in completing an action plan. What work does the property need to enhance its value? Who will do that work? When will it get done, and how will it get paid for?

The next step for the executor is to execute the action plan, making sure the property is prepared for the market in a timely way. The *planning and preparation phase* should have taken into account the best windows of time for getting work done and getting value from the money spent. The execution then has to be timed to maximize that value so that the money spent on repairs and landscaping is not wasted by putting the home on the market in the slowest sale season.

The final step is the *marketing phase*, best accomplished by a real estate agent with the skills to properly promote a probate sale. Some estates are selling showplace homes, and others have something more like a haunted house—so the agent must have the capacity to adapt without any hesitation or reservations. Someone with experience is not going to be shaken by difficult sale conditions, whether the property is in dire physical condition, someone died in the home, or even if there are complicating family dynamics. The agent has to be the lightning rod that keeps prospective buyers from feeling any shock.

Expertise, Creativity, and Comfort

I strongly urge executors to thoroughly vet agents before hiring a Realtor and not simply make sure that they understand the process, the legal requirements, and the forms required. It takes more than knowing the proper paperwork to handle a real estate sale in probate. If you have read this far, you know that my approach involves using practical psychology to bring peace to the process and be the calming force in a highly stressed situation. My goal has been to become the best agent who could show up when family dynamics have resulted in a struggle or uncertainty about the real estate transaction. And, when dealing with the necessary disclosures, my goal has been to tell the truth without alarming and to give bad news in a good way.

Over the past few decades, it has become more common for families to be scattered across the country or around the world. Executors sometimes live long distances from an inherited property, so I have developed skills to help them with all of the logistics involved, from routine maintenance to major renovations. No matter who handles projects, however, I urge executors to recognize that they are the responsible decision-makers and need to double-check every estimate and make sure they have any necessary government approvals.

Your best friend or your sister could be a real estate agent, but neither may be the right choice for handling an estate. The agent must truly understand the probate process and, more importantly, understand the psychological aspects for both sellers and buyers to move the process forward without creating more drama within it. All too often I find that agents get caught up in the family's emotions. That's no more appropriate for a real estate agent than it would be for a surgeon, whom you'd expect to be able to calmly explain a process and respond to anxious relatives' concerns. Like a surgeon, the agent should also be thoroughly familiar with the desired outcome and all the steps necessary to get there.

Executors shouldn't make the mistake of thinking their situation is too simple to require an agent who specializes in probate sales. Even if the estate has an attorney, the Realtor is the one working hand in hand with the executor, coming up with creative ideas to get around any delays or setbacks. Returning to my operating room analogy, when I had knee surgery, I found it comforting to know that my surgeon had worked with professional sports teams. I'm no high-performance athlete, but I liked having a surgeon who had performed at a high level of expertise.

As you have seen in this chapter and throughout the book, it is crucial to vet your Realtor for skills and experience dealing with probate and the ability to put the executor and family members at ease. In the conclusion, I'll provide resources to help.

INTRODUCING MY TEAM

I've told you several stories in this book about how I personally interacted with clients and how "we" helped them get things done. I lead a team of specialists in my agency:

- The *listing coordinator* handles the marketing. She also coordinates any inspection reports and the steps necessary to bring a property to market, which can include cleaning, staging, and photographing a home. In the case of an estate, she has the title company prescreen the trust or estate documents to ensure no surprises at closing.

- The *transaction coordinator*, once we have an offer, supplies attorneys, title companies, lenders, buyers, and sellers with all the documentation necessary to make sure the closing of escrow goes smoothly. She makes sure everything in the sales agreement is carried out completely and accurately.

- The *project coordinator* works with the property before it is listed, which is especially helpful to executors who live in another area. This coordinator gets estimates for work such as content removal and debris hauling, lets people in to pick up items, and when the property is all ready to be marketed, hands the keys to the listing coordinator.

- The *prospectors* assist our marketing efforts by knocking on doors in the neighborhood. We have two full-time prospectors, riding Segways, who each knock on over twenty thousand doors a year. Depending on whether it's a conventional sale or estate, they have different approaches when promoting the property.

CONCLUSION

Go for the Best Outcome

Selling an inherited property through probate requires the assistance of someone with experience and specific skills. An executor has legal responsibilities that cannot be overlooked and needs a real estate agent who understands the probate process. The truth is that most do not.

An executor needs an agent who's experienced in coping with family dynamics and is able to stay calm and soothe people when infighting flares. The ability to sell a property is important, but so is the ability to make sure that all of the parties involved are comfortable.

The executor needs an agent who will make sure the property title is thoroughly investigated, taxes have been taken into account, and there is a clear and locally appropriate strategy to get the maximum value from a sale. Nearly everyone has a friend or relative in real estate, and it is tempting to want to give them business, but handling a house going through probate is too full of pitfalls to be left to someone who will be learning on the job.

I have shown you my methodical approach of assessment, planning and preparation, and marketing that my team and I use to sell properties throughout the Silicon Valley-San Francisco Bay Area. What I have seen over the years is that when someone skips steps in that process, a mess results.

It is never too soon to think about how an estate can be handled with minimal tension and frustration for everybody involved. If you have read this far, maybe you know you will be an executor and like to plan ahead, or perhaps you're in the middle of an estate process and experiencing some of the friction points we just discussed. Either way, feel free to reach out to me right away while the issue is on your mind. I can't give legal advice, but we can discuss how to get the best outcome for the estate or trust that you're handling.

E-mail me at Alex@LehrRealEstate.com or visit my website at www.lehrrealestate.com.
